The Classical Style

THE CLASSICAL STYLE

Haydn, Mozart, Beethoven

Charles Rosen

NEW YORK THE VIKING PRESS

For Helen and Elliott Carter

Preface and Acknowledgements

I have not attempted a survey of the music of the classical period, but a description of its language. In music, as in painting and architecture, the principles of 'classical' art were codified (or, if you like, classicized) when the impulse which created it was already dead: I have tried to restore a sense of the freedom and the vitality of the style. I have restricted myself to the three major figures of the time as I hold to the old-fashioned position that it is in terms of their achievements that the musical vernacular can best be defined. It is possible to distinguish between the English language around 1770 and the literary style of, say, Dr. Johnson, but it is more difficult to draw a line between the musical language of the late eighteenth century and the style of Haydn—it is even doubtful whether it would be worth the trouble to try to do so.

There is a belief, which I do not share, that the greatest artists make their effect only when seen against a background of the mediocrity that surrounded them: in other words, the dramatic qualities of Haydn, Mozart, and Beethoven are due to their violation of the patterns to which the public was conditioned by their contemporaries. If this were true, the dramatic surprises in Haydn, for example, should become less effective as we grow familiar with them. But any music-lover has found exactly the contrary. Haydn's jokes are wittier each time they are played. We can, of course, grow so familiar with a work that we can no longer bear to listen to it. Nevertheless, to choose only the most banal examples, the opening movement of the *Eroica* Symphony will always seem immense, the trumpet call of *Leonore No. III* will always be a shock to anyone who listens once again to these works. This is because our expectations do not come from outside the work but are implicit in it: a work of music sets its own terms. How these terms are set, how the context in which the drama is to be played out is created for each work, is the main subject of this book. I am concerned, therefore, not only with the meaning or the significance of the music (always so difficult to put into words) but also with what made it possible to possess and to convey that significance.

In order to give some idea of the scope and variety of the period I have followed the development of different genres for each composer. The concerto, the string quintet, and comic opera were obvious choices for Mozart, as were the symphony and the string quartet for Haydn. A discussion of Haydn's piano trios will convey the idiosyncratic nature of the chamber music with piano of that time. *Opera seria* demanded separate treatment, and Haydn's oratorios and masses provided an occasion to discuss the general question of Church music. The relation of Beethoven to Mozart and Haydn clearly needed to be defined by a more general essay, but the major part of the examples could be drawn easily from the piano sonatas. By such subterfuge I have hoped to represent all the important aspects of the classical style.

There is a glaring inconsistency in the pages that follow: 'classical' has always a small 'c,' while 'Baroque,' 'Romantic,' etc., are proclaimed by their initial capitals. The reason for this is partly aesthetic: I have had to use the word 'classical' very often, and the capital letter—turning it into a proper name as if it denoted something that really existed—was too much to face on every page. Although I believe the concept of a style is necessary for an understanding of the history of music, I should not wish to dignify it with the status of solid fact. In any case, I am willing to accept the inadvertent consequences of this whimsical typography. The word 'classical' with a small 'c' implies a style that is exemplary and normative. The music of the classical period, like the painting of the High Renaissance, still provides today a standard by which the rest of our musical experience is judged.

*   *   *

It would be impossible to acknowledge the contribution of ideas that have come from so many conversations with friends, each one in turn bringing forward a new example to illustrate the other's observation. Many of the ideas in this book are the common currency of musical thought, derived from the experience of all musicians who have played and listened to the music involved. In most instances I could no longer distinguish, even if I wanted to, which ideas are my own and which I have read, or learned from my teachers, or simply heard in discussion.

Much easier to acknowledge is the invaluable help I received in writing this book. I am deeply indebted to—indeed, still marveling at—the patience and kindness of Sir William Glock, who read the entire manuscript and made hundreds of suggestions which strengthened both the style and the ideas. Henri Zerner of Brown University helped at every stage, and made considerable improvements and corrections; without his excisions, as well, the book would have been slightly longer and much more dubious. I am also grateful to Kenneth Levy, of Princeton University, who read the first half of the manuscript and improved several points. (No one but myself, of course, is to blame for the faults that remain.) I should like to thank Charles Mackerras, David Hamilton, Marvin Tartak, Sidney Charles of the University of California at Davis, and Lewis Lockwood of Princeton University, who gave me material I did not have or did not know, and Mischa Donat, who prepared the index.

My gratitude goes to Donald Mitchell of Faber Music, for his encouragement when only two chapters of this book had been written, and for his invaluable help afterward; to Piers Hembry, who did the reduction of the musical examples; and to Paul Courtenay, who so beautifully copied them.

8

Preface and Acknowledgements

I owe more than I can express to the continued encouragement and editing of Aaron Asher, both while he was at Viking and after he left, and to the intelligence and tact of Elisabeth Sifton, who helped with the final revisions and made the last stages of producing the book so much more agreeable than any author has a right to expect.

New York, 1970   Charles Rosen

Bibliographical Note

A proper bibliography of the Viennese classical style would be considerably longer than this book. As for my own reading, there must be many essential articles and books that I missed in spite of all my efforts. It seems prudent to draw a veil of silence over these matters and confound in one decent obscurity those secondary sources which I have not read, those which I read but which taught me nothing, and, finally, those which taught me a good deal and which I am ungratefully not listing. I am not, however, totally without conscience, and some of the greatest debts are acknowledged immediately below and a few others in the course of the book. If the list were longer, the injustice to those inevitably left out would be only the more flagrant.

There is no satisfactory book on the late eighteenth and early nineteenth centuries, but Manfred Bukofzer's *Music in the Baroque Era* is, with all its limitations, a magnificent work, and in returning to it recently, I realize how much I owe to many of its general concepts for an understanding of the earlier period.

Heinrich Abert's *W. A. Mozart* (1923) has not yet been equalled for its discussion of Mozart's style. In English, Alfred Einstein's *Mozart* (1945) is less satisfactory, but it has the inestimable merit of having been written by a man who loved Mozart and knew his music thoroughly, and it discusses almost everything that Mozart wrote. The greatest of Tovey's numerous articles on Mozart is his essay on the C major Concerto K. 503, and the best of recent articles on Mozart's style seems to me Edward Lowinsky's 'On Mozart's Rhythm,' reprinted in *The Creative World of Mozart* (1963). Heinrich Schenker's analysis of the G minor Symphony is perhaps the most stimulating of his discussions of the classical style.

On Haydn, we are all grateful for the work of Jens Peter Larsen and of H. C. Robbins Landon, particularly the latter's recently completed edition of all the symphonies. No general book on Haydn has the stature of Abert's *Mozart*, but Rosemary Hughes's short study, *Haydn*, is the best introduction to this composer I know. Emily Anderson's translation of the Mozart and the Beethoven correspondences, Robbins Landon's edition of Haydn's letters and diaries, and O. E. Deutsch's documentary biographies of Mozart and Schubert have made much of the material available in English.

Thayer's *Life of Beethoven* remains fundamental to all study of this composer; the best edition is that of Elliot Forbes (1964), cited hereafter simply as Thayer. Tovey's unfinished *Beethoven* is underestimated today. The most interesting studies of the Beethoven sketches since Nottebohm are certainly those of Erich Herzmann and, more recently, Lewis Lockwood.

11

Note on the Music Examples

I am grateful to the generosity of the publishers in agreeing that almost everything of importance discussed would be illustrated, sometimes at great length. We have hoped to make it possible to read the book without regret for the absence of scores. I have not tried specifically to quote my favorite passages, but many of them have slipped in nevertheless. I have, however, tried to balance the familiar with the less known.

In reducing the orchestral and chamber scores by grouping several instruments on one stave, the object has been to combine ease of reading with the possibility of seeing all details of the full score. It should be possible to reconstruct the original score in almost all cases: those examples where not everything has been indicated are marked by an asterisk (*). The examples of orchestral or quartet writing on two staves are, therefore, in no sense transcriptions for piano but transliterations of the originals—although of course I welcome the idea of reading these examples at the piano, which is what I have often done with them myself, faking what my hands cannot reach.

I have used the best texts I could find without normalizing, although I have sometimes found it reasonable not to repeat dynamic markings when successive instruments entered at the same dynamic level. One abbreviation, the plus sign (+), needs a word of explanation: it has been used to indicate doubling (at the unison, unless otherwise indicated). That is, 'Fl.' means the flute takes over the line at the point indicated; '+Fl.' means that the previously indicated instrument continues to play and is now doubled by the flute. Ease of reading took precedence over uniformity, and I hope that the inconsistencies will puzzle no one and give no offense.

Contents

Part I

INTRODUCTION

1

The Musical Language of the
Late Eighteenth Century

When Beethoven left Bonn in 1792, he had with him an album in which his patron, Count Waldstein, had written: 'You are going to Vienna in fulfillment of your long frustrated wishes . . . You will receive the spirit of Mozart from the hands of Haydn.' It was, indeed, with Mozart that Beethoven wished to study; he had traveled to Vienna some years earlier and, it seems, impressed Mozart with his playing. But Mozart had recently died, and the twenty-one-year-old Beethoven turned to Haydn, who had already encouraged him during a visit to Bonn.

It would appear as if our modern conception of the great triumvirate had been planned in advance by history. The idea was, in fact, already sanctioned by Beethoven's contemporaries. Years after the death of Haydn, but long before that of Beethoven, when music-lovers complained of the frivolity of Viennese musical life, they compared the infrequent performances of Haydn, Mozart, and Beethoven with the popularity of the new and more modern Italian opera. Even those who believed that music had stopped with Mozart thought of Beethoven not as a revolutionary but as an eccentric betrayer of a great tradition. The more perceptive placed him quite simply on a level with Haydn and Mozart. As early as 1812, in the writings of the finest contemporary music critic, E. T. A. Hoffmann (who loved Mozart so much that he changed one of his names from Friedrich to Amadeus), these were the three great figures, and there was no other to set by their side except Gluck, who stood out for the seriousness and the integrity of his conception of opera. 'Haydn, Mozart, and Beethoven,' Hoffmann wrote in 1814, 'developed a new art, whose origins first appear in the middle of the eighteenth century. Thoughtlessness and lack of understanding husbanded the acquired treasure badly, and, in the end, counterfeiters tried to give the impression of the real thing with their tinsel, but this was not the fault of these masters in whom the spirit was so nobly manifest.'

This new art is, partly by convention, called the classical style. It was not E. T. A. Hoffmann's name for it: Haydn and Mozart were, for him, the first 'romantic' composers. Whatever the name, the originality of this new style and its integrity were felt very early.

Nevertheless, the concept of a style does not correspond to an historical fact but answers a need: it creates a mode of understanding. That this need was felt almost at once belongs not to the history of music but to the history of musical taste and appreciation. The concept of a style can only have a purely pragmatic definition, and it can at times be so fluid and imprecise as to be useless. Confusion of levels is the greatest danger. For example, to compare High Renaissance painting, envisaged as the work of a small group of artists in Rome and Florence and an even smaller group of Venetians, with Baroque painting, conceived as international and as stretching over more than a century and a half, could only lead to methodological chaos, however fruitful the individual observations it may suggest. The scope of the context is not arbitrary, and it is essential to distinguish between the style of a small group (French Impressionism, Ockeghem and his disciples, the Lake Poets) and the more 'anonymous' style of an era (nineteenth-century French painting, late fifteenth-century Flemish music, English Romantic poetry).

This distinction, however, is harder to make in fact than in theory: the style of what is sometimes called the High Baroque in music (from 1700 to 1750) is international, and has no group that corresponds in importance and cohesion to the three classical Viennese composers (none of whom was from Vienna). Yet the High Baroque provided a coherent and systematic musical language which could be used by the three classical figures and against which they could measure their own language. Mozart could produce a good, if not perfect, facsimile of High Baroque style when it was needed, and the combination of his own manner with that of a High Baroque composer (as in his reinstrumentation of *Messiah*) is an example of a clash not so much between two musical personalities as between two isolatable and definable systems of expression. It should be remarked, however, that the High Baroque style for Mozart and for Beethoven meant Handel and Bach above all,[1] and that both Handel and Bach effected a synthesis, a very different and personal one in each case, of the disparate national styles—German, French, and Italian— of their time. The opposing character of the personal styles of Bach and Handel gives them a complementary relation which paradoxically allows them to be considered as a unity.

The reason why the style of a group and the style of an age may sometimes be legitimately confused is that a group-style often appears to realize the imperfectly formed aspirations of the age. A style may be described figuratively as a way of exploiting and focusing a language, which then becomes a dialect or language in its own right, and it is this focus which makes possible what might be called the personal style or manner of the artist, as Mozart worked against the background of the general style of his age, yet with a more specific relation to Haydn and to Johann Christian Bach. But analogies with language break down because a style is finally itself treated

---

[1] In spite of Mozart's acquaintance with later composers who tried to continue the contrapuntal tradition, a remarkable development comes over his work from the moment he begins to know the music of Johann Sebastian Bach.

as a work of art, and judged as an individual work is judged and by much the same standards: coherence, power, and richness of allusion. In current changes of fashion and revivals of interest in one past style after another—Pre-Raphaelite painting, Baroque music—each successive style is almost a solid object, a piece of period furniture to be possessed and enjoyed. Yet such treatment of a period style as itself an *objet d'art* suggests one possible elucidation of the style of a group. More convincingly than the 'anonymous' style of an age, the style of a group represents a synthesis like a work of art, a reconciliation of the conflicting forces of the period into one harmony. It is almost as much an expression itself as a system of expression.

'Expression' is a word that tends to corrupt thought. Applied to art, it is only a necessary metaphor. Accepted as legal tender, it often gives aid and comfort to those who are more interested in the artist's personality than in his work. Nonetheless, the concept of expression, even in its most naïve form, is essential to an understanding of late eighteenth-century art. In any period, of course, the formal qualities of the smallest detail of a work of music cannot be divorced from its affective and sentimental, as well as its intellectual, significance within the work and, consequently, more generally within the stylistic language, and I shall be concerned throughout with the meaning of the elements that make up the classical synthesis. But it is a gross and common error to define a style by specifically expressive characteristics, isolating the 'elegant' painting of the sixteenth century as Mannerist, calling the classical style Apollonian, the Romantic enthusiastic or morbid. Just in so far as a style is a way of using a language, musical, pictorial, or literary, is it capable of the widest range of expression, and a work by Mozart may be as morbid, as elegant, or as turbulent in its own terms as one by Chopin or Wagner. It is true that the means of expression have an influence on what is expressed, and it is the ease or the tension with which the language is used—the grace of expression—that counts so heavily in art. Yet at the point that grace begins to take on such importance, a style ceases to be strictly a system of expression or of communication.

The history of an artistic 'language,' therefore, cannot be understood in the same way as the history of a language used for everyday communication. In the history of English, for example, one man's speech is as good as another's. It is the picture as a whole that counts, and not the interest, grace, or profundity of the individual example. In the history of literary style or of music, on the other hand, evaluation becomes a necessary preliminary: even if Haydn and Mozart improbably differed in all essentials from their contemporaries, their work and their conception of expression would have to remain the center of the history. This stands the history of a language on its head: it is now the mass of speakers that are judged by their relation to the single one, and the individual statement that provides the norm and takes precedence over general usage.

What makes the history of music, or of any art, particularly troublesome is that what is most exceptional, not what is most usual, has often the greatest claim on our interest. Even within the work of one artist, it is not his usual procedure that characterizes his personal 'style,' but his greatest and most individual success. This, however, seems to deny even the possibility of the history of art: there are only individual works, each self-sufficient, each setting its own standards. It is a contradiction essential to a work of art that it resists paraphrase and translation, and yet that it can only exist within a language, which implies the possibility of paraphrase and translation as a necessary condition.

The idea of the style of a group is a compromise that avoids this impossible fragmentation without falling into the difficulties of the 'anonymous' period style, which fails to distinguish between painting and wall paper or between music and commercial background noises for dinner. The style of a group, so conceived, is therefore not necessarily what is called a 'school'—a tightly knit sect of artists and their disciples—although it may sometimes be that in fact. It is a fiction, an attempt to create order, a construction that enables us to interpret the change in the musical language without being totally bewildered by the mass of minor composers, many of them very fine, who understood only imperfectly the direction in which they were going, holding on to habits of the past which no longer made complete sense in the new context, experimenting with ideas they had not quite the power to render coherent.

The relation of the classical style to the 'anonymous' style or musical vernacular of the late eighteenth century is that it represents not only a synthesis of the artistic possibilities of the age, but also a purification of the irrelevant residue of past traditions. It is only in the works of Haydn, Mozart, and Beethoven that all the contemporary elements of musical style—rhythmic, harmonic, and melodic—work coherently together, or that the ideals of the period are realized on a level of any complexity. The music of the elder Stamitz, for example, combines a primitive classical phrasing with the most old-fashioned Baroque sequential harmony, so that one element rarely reinforces the other, but instead diffuses its effect. Later in the century, the works of Dittersdorf, the operas above all, have melodic charm and a certain jolly good humor, but anything more than the simplest tonic-dominant relationship is beyond them. Even in respect to historical importance and influence, but above all as regards the significance of the musical development of the eighteenth century, the work of Haydn and Mozart cannot be understood against the background of their contemporaries: it is rather the lesser man who must be seen in the framework of the principles inherent in Haydn's and Mozart's music—or, at times, as standing outside these principles in an interesting or original way. Clementi, for example, stands somewhat apart, both in his fusion of Italian and French tradition and in his development of the virtuoso passagework so essential to the post-classical style of Hummel and Weber. It is significant that this kind of passagework, which was to be given artistic importance by Liszt and Chopin, was emphatically rejected by Beethoven in most of his piano music; in his remarks on fingering and the position of the hand, he opposes the style of playing most suited to it. Although he recommended Clementi's music for the use of piano students, he disliked a piano technique of the 'pearly' manner, and criticized even Mozart's playing as too choppy.

What unites Haydn, Mozart, and Beethoven is not personal contact or even mutual influence and interaction (although there was much of both), but their common understanding of the musical language which they did so much to formulate and to change. These three composers of completely different character and often directly opposed ideals of expression arrived at analogous solutions in most of their work. The unity of style is therefore indeed a fiction, but one which the composers themselves helped to create. A considerable change is evident in the music of both Haydn and Mozart at about 1775, the date of Mozart's E flat Piano Concerto K. 271, perhaps the first large work in which Mozart's mature style is in complete command throughout; around this time Haydn became more fully acquainted with the Italian comic opera tradition to which the classical style owed so much. The date is not arbitrary; one five or ten years earlier could have been chosen for different reasons, but the discontinuities here seem to me of greater importance than the continuities. It is only from this point on that the new sense of rhythm which displaces that of the High Baroque becomes completely consistent. It is also evident that I take seriously Haydn's claim that the *Scherzi* or *Russian* Quartets, op. 33, of 1781, were written according to entirely new principles.

The musical language which made the classical style possible is that of tonality, which was not a massive, immobile system but a living, gradually changing language from its beginning. It had reached a new and important turning point just before the style of Haydn and Mozart took shape.

There are so many conflicting accounts of tonality that it will be useful to restate its premises, axiomatically rather than historically for brevity's sake. Tonality is a hierarchical arrangement of the triads based on the natural harmonics or overtones of a note. The most powerful of these harmonics are the octave, the twelfth, the fifteenth, and the seventeenth; the octave and the fifteenth may be omitted as being the same note at higher pitches (I shall evade a discussion of the reasons, psychological or conventional, for this); the twelfth and the seventeenth transposed nearer to the original note or tonic produce the fifth and the third, or the dominant and the mediant.

In this triad of tonic, mediant, and dominant, the dominant is the more powerful harmonic and naturally the second most powerful tone. The tonic, however, may be considered as itself the dominant of the fifth below it, called the subdominant. By building successive triads in both ascending and descending directions, we arrive at a structure which is symmetrical, and yet unbalanced:

23

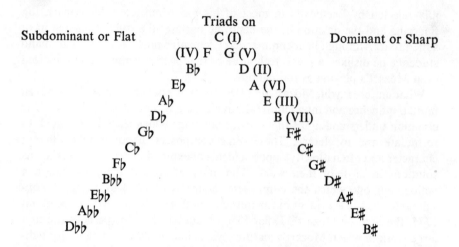

The structure is unbalanced, because harmonics all rise from a note, and the dominant or sharp direction, based on the successive second overtones of the previous note, outweighs the subdominant direction, which descends. The subdominant weakens the tonic by turning it into a dominant (that is, by using the tonic note not as the root of the central triad, but as an overtone). This imbalance is essential to an understanding of almost all tonal music, and from it is derived the possibility of tension and resolution on which the art of music depended for centuries. The imbalance can be perceived immediately in the formation of the diatonic scale (the notes marked with roman numerals above) which uses the root of only one triad in the subdominant direction, but of the first five triads on the sharp or dominant side.

The two directions in just or natural intonation do not lead back to the beginning: following the natural harmonics of the tones, D♭♭ is not the same note as B♯, and neither coincides with C. None of the triads produced on the dominant side is consequently the same as those of the subdominant, but some of them are very close. Almost from the inception of tonality, and even from the very beginning of musical theory itself with the Greeks, musicians and theorists have tried to identify the triads that are significantly close, producing a system which is not only symmetrical but circular, called the circle of fifths:

$$
\begin{array}{ccc}
 & \text{C (I)} & \\
\text{(IV) F} = \text{E}\sharp & & \text{G (V)} = \text{A}\flat\flat \\
\text{B}\flat = \text{A}\sharp & & \text{D (II)} = \text{E}\flat\flat \\
\text{E}\flat = \text{D}\sharp & & \text{A (VI)} = \text{B}\flat\flat \\
\text{A}\flat = \text{G}\sharp & & \text{E (III)} = \text{F}\flat \\
\text{D}\flat = \text{C}\sharp & & \text{B (VII)} = \text{C}\flat \\
 & (\text{G}\flat = \text{F}\sharp) &
\end{array}
$$

24

This entails enforcing an equal distance between the twelve notes arranged in stepwise or scale progression (which produces the chromatic scale), and it distorts their relation to the natural overtones: the system is called equal temperament. Modulating around the circle of fifths in either direction will now bring one back to the original starting point. There were considerable attempts to establish the system of equal temperament in the sixteenth century, where it is essential to much of the chromatic music written then, but it did not become the theoretical basis for music until the eighteenth (and some tuners of keyboard instruments used compromises between equal temperament and just or natural intonation until the nineteenth century).

Equal temperament absolves us from considering at length whether or not tonality is a 'natural' or a 'conventional' language. It is quite evidently based on the physical properties of a tone, and it equally evidently deforms and even 'denatures' these properties in the interests of creating a regular language of more complex and richer expressive capacities. The ear or mind had already learned to make a semi-identification of major and minor thirds, although if the lower third of a triad is major and the upper third minor, this makes for a much closer approximation of the natural overtones; a major chord is therefore more stable than a minor one, which is also—like the relative weakness of the subdominant direction—an essential fact in comprehending the expressive significance of tonal music.

The basis of all Western musical form starting with Gregorian chant is the cadence, which implies that the forms are 'closed,' set within a frame and isolated. (Not until the nineteenth century is the final cadence attacked, although the improvisatory introduction attempts to open up the front end as early as the sixteenth century.)

The greatest change in eighteenth-century tonality, partly influenced by the establishment of equal temperament, is a new emphatic polarity between tonic and dominant, previously much weaker. Cadences had still been formed in the seventeenth century with either dominant or subdominant triads, but as the significant advantages of emphasizing the built-in imbalance of the system (the strength of the sharp over the flat direction) began to be realized, the subdominant or plagal cadence was dropped. The dominant cadence became the only one, and was reinforced by the increased importance of the dominant-seventh chord: if the notes of the diatonic scale alone are used in forming triads, then there can be no true fifth or stable triad on VII, which has only a diminished fifth or tritone. VII is the next tone or leading-tone to the tonic, and putting V under its triad produces the dominant seventh (V^7), at once a dominant chord and the most unstable dissonance demanding immediate resolution into the tonic chord. The pre-eminence of the dominant seventh was reinforced as the medieval distaste for using diminished fifths disappeared from music with the less inhibited use of all dissonances, now integrated and resolved within a more complex arrangement.

25

Introduction

The polarity of tonic and dominant was affirmed by modulation, which is the transformation of the dominant (or another triad) temporarily into a second tonic. Modulation in the eighteenth century must be conceived as essentially a dissonance raised to a higher plane, that of the total structure. A passage in a tonal work that is outside the tonic is dissonant in relation to the whole piece, and demands resolution if the form is to be completely closed and the integrity of the cadence respected. It is not until the eighteenth century, with the full establishment of equal temperament, that the possibilities of modulation could be completely articulated, and the consequences of this articulation were only realized in the latter half of the century.

The chromatic modulations of the sixteenth century, for example, do not distinguish clearly between the flat and the sharp directions: the chromaticism is therefore much more what its name implies—a coloring. Even in the early eighteenth century, modulation is more often a drifting movement than the genuine if temporary establishment of a new tonic: in this passage from the *Art of Fugue*, there is a kaleidoscopic shift through several keys with no firm hold on the way:

(Triple Fugue à 4)

But in Mozart and Haydn, the full implications of the hierarchical arrangement of triads are drawn: the various tonalities possible can be contrasted articulately and even dramatically with the central one so that the range of significance is considerably expanded.

The hierarchy is more complex than the place of each triad on the circle of fifths, and depends on many factors, not all of which need be brought into play by the composer at the same time. The tonality on II, for example, although apparently close to I, is actually one of the most remote, or most contradictory in its relation to the tonic, simply because the tonic I creates a dominant seventh chord out of the major triad on II (supertonic) by adding its fundamental note, or root, to it. As a brief summary of the classical use: the keys of III and VI (mediant and submediant) are sharp keys close to the dominant and imply an increase in tension (or dissonance on the level of structure) and to some extent they can substitute for a dominant; the flat mediant and submediant are largely subdominant keys, and are used like the subdominant to weaken the tonic, and lower tension; the other tonalities must be more precisely defined by the context of the music, although the tonalities at a distance of the tritone (diminished fifth) and the minor seventh

26

are most remote or, in other words, most dissonant in their large-scale effects.[1]

All of Haydn, Mozart, and Beethoven is written with the system of equal temperament in mind, even music for string quartet. When Beethoven, in the following passage from the Quartet, op. 130:

writes D♭ for the first violin and C♯ for the second, he obviously does not intend a different pitch. It is true that Beethoven distinguishes the direction a note is going in a modulation; in the opening measures of the same movement:

the ambiguity of B flat minor–D flat major is reflected in the B♭♭–A♮. I once heard a quartet play this passage in just intonation with horrible effect. This is not to say that string players play, or should play, in strict equal temperament: pitch is always subtly altered, but for expressive reasons which have little to do with just intonation. Most violinists find it in practice more natural to adjust the pitch in the least 'natural' way. In actual physical terms, here B♭♭ is higher than A♮, but since the A♮ is part of an uncompleted B flat minor cadence, it sounds more expressive and more logical when it is very slightly sharpened, and a leading-tone is more often sharpened than flattened. The theory that string players should play in just intonation seems to be a late nineteenth-century one, mainly due to Brahms's friend Joachim; and Bernard Shaw claimed savagely that Joachim did not play in just intonation, but quite simply out of tune. Such are the dangers of theory applied to performance.

---

[1] The important pathetic role of the flat supertonic (or Neapolitan) will be discussed later on p. 88.

Introduction

Beethoven did say that he could distinguish between music in D flat and C sharp, but his remark applies even to music played on the piano, and has nothing at all to do with intonation or temperament. What Beethoven was talking about was the 'character' of the different tonalities, a subject that is more relevant to the psychology of the composer than to actual musical language. Donald Francis Tovey ascribed the idea that keys have definite characteristics to their relation to C major, unconsciously treated as basic since that is the first one every musician learns as a child. F major is, therefore, by 'nature' a tonality with a subdominant quality or a release of tension relative to C major, and most pastorals are, indeed, written in F. The traditional use of certain instruments in certain keys, horns in E flat, for example, also influenced the connotations of the tonalities. The dominant character of C sharp and the subdominant character of D flat are bound to have affected any composer's sensibility. Within a classical work, the character of a subordinate tonality (that is, not the main key of a piece) is dependent on the manner of arriving at it—either from the subdominant or the dominant direction—but this does not interfere with the absolute supremacy in theory of equal temperament; in practice the modifications of equal temperament, by vibrato or actual distortion, are expressive and not structural.

The second half of the eighteenth century represents an important stage in the centuries-long process of the destruction of the linear aspect of music. The linearity of music is not only horizontal, as it is most often conceived, with only the independent and continuous voices of a contrapuntal texture recognized as lines. There is a vertical aspect as well. The figured bass of the Baroque from 1600 to beyond 1750, in which the music is structured by a series of chords, is a conception of the flow of music in terms of a series of vertical lines; in fact, the notation yields this vertical linearity easily to the eye. (Even in solo music without any actual continuo instrument there is rarely any doubt, in spite of the independent movement of the voices, where one chord ends and the next begins.) These vertical 'lines' were carried by a strong horizontal bass line throughout the entire Baroque period, and both aspects were heavily attacked by the new style of the later eighteenth century.

The significance of this change appears in the pervasive influence of the many accompaniment figures already developed earlier in the century. The best known of these is the Alberti bass:

This accompaniment blurs the independence both of the three contrapuntal voices which it theoretically contains and of the chordal or homophonic harmony which it supposedly illustrates. It breaks down the isolation of the voices by integrating them into one line, and of the chords by integrating them into a continuous movement. Linear form is essentially the isolation of

28

the elements of music, and the history of music, until our day, may be seen as a gradual breakdown of all the various isolating forces of the art—contrapuntal independence of voices, homophonic progression, closed and framed forms, and diatonic clarity.

The attack upon the tendency to isolate comes paradoxically from within by means of the isolating forces themselves—just as, in painting, Impressionism went beyond Delacroix in its attempt to avoid isolating the larger forms, and yet its method was a doctrinaire isolation and equalization of each brush stroke. In music, the classical style attacked the horizontal independence of the voices and the vertical independence of the harmony by isolating the phrase and articulating the structure. Late eighteenth-century phrasing is emphatically periodic, and comes in clearly defined groups of three, four, or five measures, generally four. Imposing this new periodic system upon the musical flow and blurring the inner progression of that flow by the new accompaniment figures meant that the linear sense of the classical style was transferred to a higher level, and had to be perceived as the continuity of the whole work, and not as the linear continuity of the individual elements.

The vehicle of the new style was a texture called the sonata.

2

Theories of Form

Sonata form could not be defined until it was dead. Czerny claimed with pride around 1840 that he was the first to describe it, but by then it was already part of history. The original meaning of 'sonata' was 'played' as opposed to 'sung,' and it only gradually acquired a more specific, but always flexible, sense. The definitions generally given are far too limited even for the latter part of the eighteenth century, and apply only to the romantic sonata. In any case, the 'sonata' is not a definite form like a minuet, a da capo aria, or a French overture: it is, like the fugue, a way of writing, a feeling for proportion, direction, and texture rather than a pattern.

It is often difficult to distinguish the defining characteristics from the acquired characteristics of a form, partly because as time goes on the latter tend to become the former. That is, we must distinguish between what an eighteenth-century composer would have called a sonata (how far he would have stretched the term and at what point he would have said, 'This is not a sonata, but a fantasia') and the way sonatas were generally written (the patterns they gradually fell into and which were later unhappily considered as rules). The line between the two is often blurred, and it is doubtful if even the composers of the period would have been able to draw it with any certainty. It was not only that the meaning changed, but that the word was intended to cover a large range and even to foresee the possibility of change.

Since Czerny, the sonata has been most often defined as a melodic structure. The account (misleading in a number of ways) generally goes somewhat as follows: the exposition starts with a theme or group of themes in the tonic, followed by a modulation to the dominant and a second group of themes; after a repetition of the exposition comes the development, in which the themes are fragmented and combined in various keys ending with a return to the tonic and a recapitulation of the exposition, this time with the second group of themes in the tonic, and an optional coda. In this presentation of the traditional account, I have avoided the academic analysis of the exposition as first theme, bridge passage, second theme, and concluding theme, all this even more unsatisfactory than the above. Nor have I mentioned the 'rule' that one new theme is 'allowed' in the development. The fact is that while the placing, number, and character of the themes, at least from Scarlatti to Beethoven, have an importance which ought not to be underestimated, they are in no sense the determining factors of the form.

The destruction of the nineteenth-century account of 'sonata form' is a

30

game too easy and too often played. The description's insufficiency is manifest when we consider that Haydn often used only one theme for his sonatas and, in particular, generally marked the modulation to the dominant by repeating the opening measures in their new place even when he used several themes; that Mozart preferred to mark the change to the dominant by an entirely new theme (although he followed Haydn's practice on occasion); and that Beethoven often favored a compromise in which the new theme marking the change is clearly a variant of the opening theme of the work. The presence of a new theme at this point, far from being indispensable as is often thought, is not even remotely a decisive element of the form.

Nor did the presence of a second theme seem even desirable to Haydn's contemporaries. When the great Symphonies 92–94 were first played in Paris, for which city they were written, the critic of the *Mercure de France* wrote admiringly that while less gifted composers needed many themes to sustain a movement, Haydn needed only one. A good tune was always welcome, and it was often used to reinforce and clarify the outlines of a sonata, but a sonata was not built with a succession of themes as its structure.

Although the nineteenth-century description of sonata form is grandly deceptive, it is important to try and understand how and why such a formulation became possible. Inevitably the first generation of Romantics, which thought of structure essentially in melodic terms, tried to arrive at a thematic scheme for the sonata. What is interesting is their apparent success. 'Sonata form' as conceived after 1840 may not work for a great many classical sonatas, but it fits an even larger number. It does so in spite of elevating the purely melodic aspect of music to a position it never held in the eighteenth century, and it satisfies only in so far as there is no tension between this aspect and other determinants of the form. When it fits, it is as misleading, perhaps even more so, than when it does not, but it cannot be easily dismissed. We are allowed one new theme in the development, and it often appears; the 'bridge passages' are most often where they are supposed to be, and sometimes they even sound connective rather than expository; the development not infrequently starts according to rule with the main theme in the dominant.

The trouble with this account of sonata form—unhappily still taught today in most schools and music appreciation courses—is not its inaccuracy but its being couched in the form of a recipe (and for a dish that could no longer be prepared). It admits that a large number of sonatas have heretical characteristics, but ascribes that to licence on the part of the composers, and implies that sonatas ought to be written in the 'orthodox' manner. In fact, except for those of Chopin, most nineteenth-century sonatas *were* written according to the orthodox recipe, and mostly for the worse. The recipe was not only inflexible; it also did not take account of the fact that by 1840 the proper ingredients were no longer being produced. Nineteenth-century tonality had become too fluid for the system of strictly defined modulations, bridge passages, and the like set up by the theorists (indeed, eighteenth-century harmony was itself already too subtle and complex, but it fitted the Procrustean bed later prepared for it more easily). A description of the sonata in fundamentally melodic terms was as unsuited to the eighteenth century's more dramatic structures as the long-breathed melodies of the nineteenth century were inapt for the late eighteenth-century forms. The sonata was as archaic in 1840 as the Baroque fugue in Haydn's day: unfortunately the prestige of Beethoven and, to some extent, of Mozart was so great as to prevent a free adaptation of the form to entirely different purposes comparable to the classical composers' adaptation of the fugue. There was no Baroque composer who weighed upon Haydn as Beethoven did upon Schumann.

The most dangerous aspect of the traditional theory of 'sonata form' is the normative one. Basically the account is most comfortable with the works that Beethoven wrote when he was closely following Mozart's lead. The assumption that divergences from the pattern are irregularities is made as often as the inference that earlier eighteenth-century versions of the form represent an inferior stage from which a higher type evolved.

This is implied, too, but in a more specious way, in a good deal of twentieth-century musical thought. Now the attitude is statistical rather than hortative: the pattern for 'sonata form' is no longer an idealized one but is based on the common practice of eighteenth-century composers. 'Sonata form' is taken to mean the form generally used by a majority of composers at a given time. This is a more attractive procedure, taking better notice of the historical development of the 'sonata,' and it is more scientific in terms of description and classification. The primacy of the tonal over the thematic structure is accepted, along with the importance of periodic phrasing in eighteenth-century form. The defect of this treatment is that it is too democratic. Composers are not equal in the sight of posterity or even in the eyes of their own contemporaries. (We reach here the delicate problem of the relation between the 'anonymous' classical vernacular and the style of Haydn, Mozart, and Beethoven.) The style of any age is determined not only by what is done but by the prestige and influence of what is done, although the prestige of a composer among the public and among his fellow musicians may differ considerably. The importance of a work of music is at least partly contingent upon its success—its immediate attraction for the contemporary public and, in the end, its coherence and depth. But to understand the success of a work, either in the long or the short run, we are not given much help by a theory of style constructed with an eye toward the most conventional and standard procedures. We need to know what may seem impossible to know if music is treated as a conventional language: not what was done, but what artistic purpose these standard procedures were expected, generally in vain, to serve. In keyboard works of Carl Philipp Emanuel Bach, for example, published as late as the 1780s, all kinds of 'sonata' patterns exist, with and without complete development sections, with partial and complete recapitulations, etc.

32

What should be crucial is the relation of these various forms to the harmonic and thematic material: if they could co-exist, why did the composer choose one in preference to another?

An account of the sonata in purely tonal terms does not falsify the way a classical sonata moves, but it obscures the significance of the form, which must ultimately be considered inseparable from the form itself. There is no question that every sonata-exposition goes from the tonic to the dominant (or to a substitute for the dominant, relative major or mediant and submediant being the only possible ones), but I cannot believe that a contemporary audience listened for the change to the dominant and experienced a pleasant feeling of satisfaction when it came. The movement to the dominant was part of musical grammar, not an element of form. Almost all music in the eighteenth century went to the dominant: before 1750 it was not something to be emphasized; afterward, it was something that the composer could take advantage of. This means that every eighteenth-century listener expected the movement to the dominant in the sense that he would have been puzzled if he did not get it; it was a necessary condition of intelligibility.

The isolation of the harmonic structure, while an advance over a basically thematic definition of 'sonata form,' is therefore generally unsatisfactory; rhythm is given short shrift, and themes are absurdly seen as subsidiary— decorations added to emphasize, or even to hide, a more basic structure. Above all, we are given no hint of the relation of the structure to the material: the terms of the description are either so rigid that the material is only there to fill a pre-existing mold, or so loose that the form is left entirely but vaguely dependent on the material—as if a composer wrote without the example of previous works, his own as well as those of others, to act upon his inspiration, as if an audience expected an ordering of chaos with each new work, as if, in fact, their expectations on hearing a new symphony were not to some extent rhythmic, melodic, and even emotional.

Two more sophisticated rivals in the description of form must be mentioned briefly here. They may be called respectively linear and motivic. Analysis of a work in linear terms is due chiefly to Heinrich Schenker. The complexity of his theory is only partly responsible for the fact that knowledge of his ideas is confined to a small group of professional musicians and historians: some of the blame must be given to a literary style that is often offensive and an arrogance that is easy to confound with fatuity. Music which did not fit his theory was beyond his range, and Brahms is the last composer for whom he had a good word to say. Schenker's theories, as he formulated them, work only for tonal music, and they fit Bach, Handel, Chopin, and Brahms better than the three great classical figures. But there is no question of the relevance and the importance of his ideas (divested of the mystique which has surrounded them) for the period with which we are dealing.

Composers undeniably can think in linear terms in a larger sense than the detailed working-out of polyphony. Nothing is more typical of a fine work than the feeling that the music has moved toward one note which represents and clarifies a point of definition, and the working-out of which has been conceived (and is heard) in larger terms than its most localized and immediate preparation and resolution. (The greater the composer, the larger the terms of his control over the significance of his ideas, even when the range of his conception is deliberately narrowed: that is why Chopin must be considered in the company of the greatest in spite of the limitations of genre and medium that he imposed upon himself.) Both the preparation and the consequent movement are linear before 1900, as linear resolution is the only acceptable form in tonal music, and the search for other resolutions in the twentieth century has had a tangible and yet (so far) only partial success.

In other words, the notes of a tonal composition have a significance beyond the immediate context in which they are found, a significance that can be understood only within the total scheme of the whole work; beyond their meaning in the 'foreground,' there is a 'background' meaning, based principally on the tonic triad, which is the harmonic center of any tonal work. In Schenker's theory, the structure of every tonal work is a linear descent toward the tonic note, and the piece as a whole is the flesh that is put on this skeleton. One might rephrase this by saying that underlying every piece, and mirrored on all levels of its facture, is a simple cadential formula. On historical grounds alone (although Schenker's ideas are fundamentally anti-historical), this conception is justifiable: the cadence is the basic structural element in all Western music from the twelfth century until the first quarter of the twentieth —it is the determining element in all styles; from the cadence grow the conceptions of the modes, tonality, the periodic phrase, and the sequence (which is largely the repetition of cadential patterns). All of this, of course, seems obvious when we reflect that Western music has capitalized more than any other on the passage of time and has rarely tried, like the music of other cultures, to overcome or to disregard this sense of direction toward the final cadence, just as the sense of the frame governs Western painting of the same period.

The psychological accuracy of many of Schenker's observations is unchallengeable: a number of his analyses go further than any others toward explaining the sense of a unity that transcends the apparently sectional exterior form which we find in so many works. It is also true that our sensitivity as listeners to many of these long-range effects is often greater than we consciously realize, and that this sensitivity grows with successive hearings of a work. A small but striking example of this long-range linear sense, overriding the immediate voice-leading and demanding a clear feeling for the separation of different registers, is this passage from the slow movement of Beethoven's *Hammerklavier* Sonata:

where the rising scale progression is broken, or, rather, transposed downward in the middle, leaving a note (G) hanging in the air, unresolved and un-connected. Yet two measures later the melody curves upward with a move-ment of exquisite grace, resolving the note to an F♯ and, in so doing, connects and resolves audibly, even at first hearing, a part of its own past. This technique—or, better, this sense of line and register, only slightly magnified and transposed to the level of the whole structure—gives us the linear skeleton moving toward the cadence that can be heard in so many works.

An adequate consideration of what we may call linear analysis cannot be undertaken here. Most discussion of it is violently partisan. There are two questions which have never been answered, or even satisfactorily raised. The first is whether, even at its most audible, the linear skeleton that Schenker abstracts and prints in large notes in his diagrams is in all cases the main principle of unity: in other words, the relation of 'background' to 'foreground' does not always seem happily defined. There are other structural principles of unity besides the long-range horizontal one, and in certain works they are not only more striking but even more fundamental. 'Where are my favorite passages?' Schoenberg is said to have exclaimed on seeing Schenker's diagram of the *Eroica*; 'Ah, there they are, in those tiny notes.' Proponents of linear analysis would never claim that the basic line is directly heard in the fore-ground of our consciousness, but it is disquieting when an analysis, no matter how cogent, minimizes the most salient features of a work. This is a failure of critical decorum.

Introduction

The most signal result of Schenker's frequent disregard of the audible facts is his almost total neglect of rhythm, even in its most obvious manifestations. It makes no difference to one of his analyses if a piece is fast or slow; nor is there any significant difference in his diagrams between the forms of first and last movements, so widely contrasted in their rhythmic organizations. This omission is not easy to repair, unless one holds that the harmonic and linear structures remain unaffected by the rhythmic development, and it should be emphasized that harmony and rhythm in the late eighteenth century are everywhere interdependent. The rhythmic terminology available to us, which is either primitive or rebarbative, does not encourage analysis, and it is difficult with the present vocabulary even to distinguish pulse from tempo, and rate of harmonic change from the actual duration of notes; but a refusal to face these questions leads to a viewpoint so partial as to be radically false even when useful or stimulating.

The second problem concerning linear analysis is whether it is adequate to the whole range of tonal music. It is remarkable that Schenker's methods of analysis do not differ significantly for Bach, Mozart, Chopin, and Reger. They do not work without considerable revision for non-tonal music or, indeed, for composers like the pre-serial Stravinsky, but even within the tonal field alone, the similarity of approach is *prima facie* suspect. Tonality was not for two centuries a frozen and unchanging institution, nor is it possible to believe that the gulf between Beethoven and Chopin was one only of sensibility, not of method. Schenker naturally does not concern himself with the historical development of styles: all forms—fugue, *Lied*, sonata, rondo—from 1650 to 1900 are merely differently adapted versions of the long-range linear structure, and a composer's choice of the 'apparent' form takes on an arbitrary coloring. Linear analysis has undoubtedly considerable validity for late eighteenth-century music, but the rate of progression from one point of the basic line to another and the proportions of the form, in particular the length of the final tonic section, are completely irrelevant to the theory. Proportions and dramatic movement are, nevertheless, central to late eighteenth-century style, and they cannot be so dismissed without our feeling that an important aspect of the general intention has been evaded.

Is the unity that we sense in a work of art an illusion? only a critical hypothesis? If it has any reality at all, then a description of its form will not merely name the parts but try to tell us why it seems one whole. The attempt to derive a work of music from one short basic motif uses a method of analysis called 'diminution technique' by Schenker, in whose theory it plays a role less overwhelming than in the work of many of his followers. It is based on a considerable amount of nineteenth-century analytic theory, principally that of Hugo Riemann.

The unity of thematic material in Beethoven, however, was already appreciated during his lifetime. As early as 1810, E. T. A. Hoffmann wrote a review of the C minor Symphony in which he remarked:

The inner arrangement of the movements, their development, instrumentation, the manner in which they are ordered, all this works toward a single point: but most of all it is the intimate relationship among the themes which creates this unity, which alone is able to keep the listener held in *one* sentiment (*Stimmung*). Often this relationship becomes clear to the listener if he hears it in the combination of two phrases, or discovers a common ground-bass in two different phrases, but a more profound relationship which does not manifest itself in this manner often speaks only from spirit to spirit, and it is this which reigns in the two allegros and the minuet and magnificently proclaims the controlled genius of the master.

Hoffmann adds elsewhere that this unity of motif is already present in the music of Haydn and Mozart. Anyone who has played the works of the Viennese classics has sensed over and over again the weight of these thematic relationships. What distinguishes more recent critics from earlier ones is their insistence on motivic development as the fundamental principle of structure, taking precedence over harmonic, melodic, or any other more 'exterior' forces.

This motivic development is sometimes presented as a mysterious process, something within the power only of the greatest composers. Nothing could be further from the truth. A really incompetent composer may throw together the most disparate material without any regard for its fitting together, but much the same thematic unity that we find in Mozart can be found in a lesser composer like Johann Christian Bach. In addition, obvious manifestations of thematic unity are not only frequent but traditional. The Baroque suite in which each successive dance begins with the same notes is not an uncommon form; examples may be found easily in Handel. The early Romantics revived this technique with greater power along with their interest in cyclic form, and there are many works in which each section is derived from the same motif: Schumann's *Carnaval*[1] and Berlioz's *Symphonie Fantastique* are only the most celebrated examples.

If the use of a central motif seems less evident, less a part of the work's candid intention, between 1750 and 1825 than before and after, this does not mean that it had become less cogent, let alone disappeared. To some extent it only went underground. Quite often, particularly in Beethoven from the beginning of his career on, it becomes explicit; if we do not feel the 'second' theme of the *Appassionata* Sonata as a variant of the opening, we have missed an important part of the discourse. The less explicit examples of thematic unity, however, arouse the greatest controversy, some of it surprisingly acrimonious. Much of the bitterness is based on misunderstanding.

---

[1] *Carnaval* is derived from *two* short motifs, but they are harmonically very similar and are used in a way that brings them even closer to each other.

Musicians become indignant at the idea that there are thematic relationships in a work of Beethoven, for example, which they think they are unable to hear. Tovey, with a lack of sympathy rare for him, denied the importance of thematic relations if the actual mechanism was not directly audible as an effect: that is, if one could not hear one theme being derived from the other step-by-step during the course of the piece. But a composer does not always want his developments, however carefully he may have worked them out, to take the form of a logical demonstration; he wants his intentions made audible, not his calculations. A newly introduced theme may not be intended to sound logically derived from what precedes it, yet one may reasonably feel that it grows naturally out of the music, fitting in an intimate and characteristic way with the rest of the work. The final melody of the slow movement of Beethoven's *Tempest* Sonata, op. 31 no. 2, is just such a new theme:

and Tovey has claimed that it is vain to try to derive it from anything else in the movement. Yet its harmony is clearly allied to measures 81–89, as is the most poignant part of its melodic curve:

as well as to the diminished chords that are such an insistent feature of the whole movement. Tovey is right to draw attention to the character of this melody as something new, but he leaves as unanalyzable our feeling that it fits in so well with all that comes before. Yet our sense of its organic relation to the rest is not inexplicable. If a composer wishes two themes to sound as if they belong together, it is natural to base both of them on similar musical relationships: to maintain that the effect of these relationships is of little importance unless we can identify them while listening, or give them a name, is like saying that we cannot be either moved or persuaded by an orator unless we are able to identify the rhetorical devices of synecdoche, chiasm, syzygy, and apostrophe with which he works upon our feelings.

Not only the themes but also many of the accompanying details, and even, indeed, the large structure are often derived from a central idea. The coherence of a work of art is, after all, not a modern ideal anachronistic in the late eighteenth century, but the oldest commonplace of aesthetics, handed down from Aristotle through Aquinas. Motivic relationship has been one of the principal means of integration in Western music since the fifteenth century. Direct contrapuntal imitation is its most common form, but motivic development or diminution technique takes on even greater importance in the classical period, although by then it already has a long history behind it. A short motif may not only generate the melody to some extent, but also determine its coloring and the course of what will follow. An example of this kind of expression, on a scale small enough to quote, is the opening of the finale of Beethoven's Sonata in B flat major op. 22:

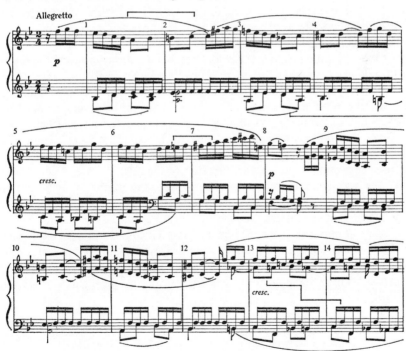

Here the four-note motif ♩♩♩♩ in the first two measures is echoed in the bass twice from measures 3 to 6 with the rhythm changed and the accent displaced. A short repeated motif, particularly a rising chromatic one, always gains in intensity, and this generates the accelerated echoes of the melody's graceful swell: ♩♩♩ becomes transposed to the dominant with ♩♩♩ and then to the dominant of the dominant ♩♩♩ in the seventh measure, and each of these transpositions has been suggested and prepared in measures 2 and 4. We hear this not as thematic echo, but as harmonic correspondence: a less intellectual effect, but one more directly affecting our sensibilities. In this way, the motif calls up the harmonic movement to C (or the dominant of the dominant) towards which note the first part of the phrase rises, as well as all the chromatic echoes. When the A♭ is introduced in the twelfth measure to harmonize with the B♮, all twelve notes of the chromatic scale have entered as a specific response to the motif: it is for this reason that the final chromatic scale in measures 16 and 17 appears not simply decorative but convincingly logical, almost thematic. The short motif has been used to increase the speed and heighten the color; it is, in fact, the prime agent of tension and transformation, changing its meaning at each successive appearance.

It is easy to neglect this changing significance. To point out the recurrence of one short motif, and even to remark on its role in the development of the work, while ignoring its dynamic qualities—its use for musical action—is to forget that music takes place in time. In too much writing on music, a work appears like a large system of inter-relationships in which the order, the intensity, and, above all, the direction of the relations are of secondary, and even negligible, consideration. Too often, the music could be played backward without affecting the analysis in any significant way. This is to treat music as a spatial art. Yet the movement from past to future is more significant in music than the movement from left to right in a picture.[1] That is why so many analyses of motivic structure are difficult to relate, not only to what is heard, but also to the *act* of listening; there is a difference between what one *can* hear, and how one listens. In this respect Schenker is far superior,

---

[1] Not that the movement from left to right is without significance in painting, as Wölfflin has shown in a famous essay. But the direction of a picture can be reversed (as in an engraving) and still leave many of the significant formal values unchanged.

for his theory rests firmly on the direction of time—the movement towards the tonic, the tendency of resolution to go downward. There must be a coherent interaction between the individual motif and the direction of the piece—the intensity and the proportions of its gradual unfolding.

Above all we must avoid the ludicrous suggestion of a secret art, the idea that composers (only the great ones, naturally) wrote their music by an esoteric process like motivic development, but arranged it into easily understandable forms like sonatas and rondos so that the dim-witted public could grasp it without too much difficulty. This notion, advanced by Schenker and lesser critics like Réti, of an exterior and basically trivial form imposed for the sake of clarity upon a more fundamental process, will not bear even passing scrutiny: it does not correspond to the psychology of any composer—surely not of Haydn, who had not a trace of the conspirator in his nature and whose compositional technique is never *sub rosa*, or of Beethoven, whose disregard for the listening comfort of his public is sufficiently evident in many works; nor, above all, does it bear any relation to even the most perceptive musician's experience of listening to music. It is not true that themes, modulations, and changes of texture are superficial phenomena, less fundamental than diminution technique. This absurdity can be avoided only if a truly intimate relation—not just a marriage of convenience—can be shown between the motivic development and the larger elements of form.

The priorities of hearing must be respected. When relations between themes exist (and they are indeed crucial in the classical period), we ought to know whether they are clarified by the connecting material—that is, if they are part of the discursive logic of the music—or if they are only part of the texture, in which case they are not necessarily less important, but their effect is more an indirect appeal to the sensibility through the total sound of the piece as well as a unifying device. Most important of all, when there is a relation between the details of a work and the larger structure, how is this relation made audible? When there is a correspondence between the detail and the structure, merely to uncover it in the score is insufficient: we must be able to claim that it has always been heard, without being put into words perhaps, but with an effect upon our experience of the musical work.

The cause of our disquiet is above all the rigid linear dogmatism of so much contemporary theory: the insistence that the generating or central idea of composition be conceived only in linear terms, mostly, indeed, as a pure arrangement of pitches without regard to rhythm, intensity, and texture. Much of the malaise in relating this view of the form to the actual music as played arises because our hearing is not exclusively linear—nor is it desirable that it should be. The conception of form as generated by a linear series is no doubt congenial to an age which has seen the development of dodecaphonic music, but it is less natural to the eighteenth century, particularly the second half. (And though a great deal of Baroque music is composed by the elaboration of a short motif, this linear concept is not even very satisfactory for the

41

early eighteenth century.) There is no question that a central idea, a musical idea, often binds together and unifies a late eighteenth-century work, but this cannot be so simply reduced to linear form—either as the working-out of a short linear series or as Schenker's long basic line; both views are too partial to be satisfactory. Nor can 'sonata form' be described simply but ungracefully as only a superficial frame for far weightier processes; both logic and the historical development of the eighteenth century will urge us to a conception that accounts for the profound contemporary feeling for proportions and dramatic movement satisfied by the style.

3

The Origins of the Style

The creation of a classical style was not so much the achievement of an ideal as the reconciliation of conflicting ideals—the striking of an optimum balance between them. Dramatic expression, limited to the rendering of a sentiment or of a significant theatrical moment of crisis—in other words, to a dance movement full of individual character—had already found musical form in the High Baroque. But the later eighteenth century made further demands: the mere rendering of sentiment was not dramatic enough; Orestes must be shown going mad *without his being aware of it*, Fiordiligi must desire to yield while trying to resist, Cherubino fall in love without knowing what it is that he feels, and, some years later, Florestan's despair give way and merge with his delirium and his apparently hopeless vision of Leonora. Dramatic sentiment was replaced by dramatic action. Handel was already capable, in the famous quartet from *Jephtha*, of representing four different emotions: the daughter's courage, the father's tragic sternness, the mother's despair, and the lover's defiance. But the lovers in the second-act finale of *Die Entführung aus dem Serail* move from joy through suspicion and outrage to final reconciliation: nothing shows better than the succession of these four emotions the relation of the sonata style to operatic action in the classical period, and it is tempting to assign to the sequence of emotions the relation of first group, second group, development, and recapitulation.

This requirement of action applies equally well to non-operatic music: a minuet with a character of its own will no longer suffice. No two of J. S. Bach's minuets are alike in character, while there are a number of Haydn's that resemble each other almost to the point of confusion. Yet every one of Bach's has a seamless, almost uniform flow, which in Haydn becomes a series of articulated events—at times even surprising and shockingly dramatic events. The first significant examples of this new dramatic style are to be found not in Italian works for the stage but in the harpsichord sonatas of Domenico Scarlatti, written in Spain during the second quarter of the eighteenth century. Although there is little sign in his works of the classical technique of transition from one kind of rhythm to another, there is already an attempt to make a real dramatic clash in the changes of key, and a sense of periodic phrasing, still small-scale. Above all, the changes of texture in his sonatas are the dramatic events, clearly set off and outlined, that were to become central to the style of the generations that came after him. It was, in fact, under the weight of this dramatic articulation that the High Baroque aesthetic collapsed.

43

Introduction

What took its place at first was nothing coherent: that is why, although every period is one of transition, the years 1755–1775 may be given this title with particular relevance. Briefly and, indeed, over-simply, during these years a composer had to choose between dramatic surprise and formal perfection, between expressivity and elegance: he could rarely have both at once. Not until Haydn and Mozart, separately and together, created a style in which a dramatic effect seemed at once surprising and logically motivated, in which the expressive and the elegant could join hands, did the classical style come into being.

Before this synthesis, the children of Bach had divided up the principal stylistic possibilities of Europe among themselves: Rococo (or *style galant*), *Empfindsamkeit*, and late Baroque. Johann Christian's music was formal, sensitive, charming, undramatic, and a little empty; Carl Philipp Emanuel's was violent, expressive, brilliant, continuously surprising, and often incoherent; Wilhelm Friedemann continued the Baroque tradition in a very personal, indeed eccentric, fashion. Most of their contemporaries were indebted to them in one way or another. There were, however, many other complex influences in music at that time: a weakened form of the High Baroque style still held sway in most religious music, the serious operatic traditions of Italy and France still had vitality, and the Neapolitan and Viennese symphonic styles were full of experiment, as was the relatively new form of *opera buffa*.

The invention of the orchestral *crescendo* by the orchestra at Mannheim is often credited with a seminal importance, but if ever a development was inevitable, it was this. The dynamic transition is a logical and even necessary corollary to a style that starts with articulated phrasing and develops methods of rhythmic transition from one kind of texture to another. The gradual fitting of Venetian swell shutters to harpsichords is only another and less fruitful aspect of the same stylistic movement. The *crescendo* would have been invented even if Mannheim had never existed, and the music of the Mannheim symphonists is less interesting and less influential than the Italian *buffa* overture.

The greatest contribution of the early Viennese symphonists was their recognition of the need for continuity, quite literally the overlapping of phrases, in holding the attention of audiences. The chamber works of the middle of the century are full of holes, moments where the tension ceases to exist, where the music stops and picks up again with no inner necessity: even in the earlier works of Haydn and Mozart we can see this occurring with sad frequency. The Viennese symphonists had no way of overcoming this defect beyond an occasional injection of the Baroque fugal style and its consequent impression of continuous movement (imitative effects are, for example, used to cover the joins between phrases); but at least they recognized the existence of a problem (or created a problem, which has its own historical merit) that was to be solved quite differently.

The early Viennese symphonists represent the first appearance of a pattern that was to become a regular part of the development of Haydn and Mozart, the return to Baroque complexity to recapture some of the richness lost with the original simplification and destruction that attend any revolution. The articulated Italian manner was essentially thinner than the learned Baroque technique, and each advance entailed a loss that had later to be made good.

The distinction between orchestral style and chamber style, or music for the general public and music for amateurs to play privately, was never absolutely clear-cut, but it is still important for an understanding of the music of the 1750s and '60s. Except in the use of dynamic contrast, the distinction was less clear earlier in the century: at least two of the Brandenburg concertos are intended for one instrument to a part—the sixth, for example, is almost certainly a sextet—while others require a small chamber orchestra with a contrast between solo and ripieno, but the musical style of both kinds is very similar. Toward the middle of the century, however, the symphonies and overtures written for public performance, and the sonatas, duos, and trios written for amateurs are noticeably different in style. The chamber music is more relaxed, diffuse, and simple, in both outline and detail; the finale is often a minuet, the opening movement a set of variations. Public works began to be more formal. The string quartet, for connoisseurs, bridged the gap between the two styles, more formal than music predominantly for keyboard with or without string accompaniment, less richly worked out (until Haydn) than the symphony. This distinction prevails with Haydn even through the last works: long after the quartet, sonata, and piano trio had benefited from symphonic style, the symphonies were more tightly organized, less free, with more massive finales, and with opening movements rarely in the moderate tempi we often find in the chamber works. It remains true, however, that Haydn brought all the weight of his symphonic experience to bear on his chamber music, as Mozart assimilated operatic and concerto style in his sonatas and quartets. The blending of the genres in their music from 1780 on is striking: the finale of Haydn's C major Sonata (H. 48) is a symphonic rondo, and the finale of Mozart's Sonata in B flat major K. 333 is a concerto movement complete with cadenza. The influence went the other way as well: the last movement of Mozart's F major Concerto K. 459 is a symphonic finale in the fugal style that Haydn had done so much to develop, and the slow movements of many of the later Haydn symphonies have the improvised intimacy of much of his chamber music. (Whichever version came first, symphony or piano trio, the slow movement of Symphony no. 102 is closer to traditional keyboard style than to orchestral—which is not to say that it sounds better in the version with piano.)

This development is, of course, related to the history of public concerts in the eighteenth century, as well as to the rise of the amateur musician. Since most public performances in the early part of the century were almost entirely religious or operatic in character, any strong contrast between orchestral and chamber styles would have been unlikely: the real contrasts of the High Baroque are between religious and secular music—although a good deal of music hovers between the two (even if it is understood that panegyric cantatas for royal and ducal houses must be classed as religious music); between vocal and instrumental styles—although here again only the extremes are clear and the dividing-line impossible to draw; between strictly contrapuntal textures and the more popular styles based on the dance and the concerto—although the fugal gigue is by no means uncommon, and Handel wrote fugues on melodies in English hornpipe style; and finally between French and Italian styles, the one decorative and based principally on the old dance forms, and the latter more progressive, dramatic, and relying on the new concerted textures. In the great German masters Bach and Handel, the contrasts are of little importance, the styles fused. They pick and choose where they please; it is perhaps one of their advantages over Rameau and Domenico Scarlatti.

As public orchestral performances grew in frequency, and as at the same time music became more and more a social grace, the difference between public and private music became more distinct. Is the amateur nature of most keyboard music of the latter half of the eighteenth century due to the fact that the pianoforte became the particular province of the female musician? Most of Haydn's piano sonatas and piano trios, many of Mozart's concertos and Beethoven's sonatas were especially written for ladies. One of Mozart's publishers objected to the technical difficulty of his piano quartets, and it should be emphasized that violin-and-piano sonatas and piano trios, quartets, and even quintets were considered basically piano music until well into the nineteenth century, and as such were expected to be simple enough in style and technical difficulty to appeal to amateurs. That Beethoven with his usual ruthlessness made no distinction between amateur and professional, and that Haydn late in life found an English widow equal to the technical demands of his imagination at the keyboard should not blind us to the fact that these are the exceptions. Even the late B flat Sonata K. 570 of Mozart represents a deliberate attempt to accommodate the pianist with a limited technical (and even musical) equipment; and we misunderstand the Haydn sonatas written before 1780 if we interpret them as examples of a still undeveloped style—it was the pianists who were not yet developed, as the far richer and more complex symphonies Haydn wrote during the same period demonstrate.

A newly forged style is a formidable weapon in the conquest of new territory. The temptation to make keyboard and chamber music symphonic (and even operatic) must have been strong: few composers can resist applying the ideas worked out in one genre to another. No doubt the greater frequency of public, or at least semi-public, performance of chamber works helped, and the continuous mechanical changes (improvements?) of the piano were a challenge as well as an answer to changes in style. But that the impetus of the style itself was a major factor in the increasing seriousness of chamber works is without question. The last area to be completely taken over by the classical style was religious music, where the Baroque retained its dominance even in Mozart and Haydn. Here, too, the last defenses fell with the two Beethoven masses—ironically, at the last minute, just as a new interest in the Baroque was beginning to reach the public as well as the professional musician. But a style of such power of integration did not exist before the work of Mozart and Haydn in the late 1770s. Before then the scene was more chaotic with many seemingly equal rival forces; for this reason the period from the death of Handel to Haydn's *Scherzi* (or *Russian*) Quartets, op. 33, is difficult to describe. This is, of course, all hindsight: to a musician of the 1780s there were as many rivals as before, and their claims as difficult to assess. Nevertheless, to appreciate the music of the 1760s, we need all our historical sympathy, we have constantly to keep in mind the difficulties, inward as well as outward, that the composers had to face. On the other hand, from 1780 onward we have only to sit back and watch two friends and their disciple sweep almost every kind of music, from the bagatelle to the mass, into their orbit, mastering the forms of the sonata, concerto, opera, symphony, quartet, serenade, folk-song arrangement with a style so powerful that it can apply almost equally well to any genre. We do not have to call upon any historical sympathy to appreciate the work of Mozart and Beethoven, and the late works of Haydn: they are still in the blood of most musicians today.

It is the lack of any integrated style, equally valid in all fields, between 1755 and 1775 that makes it tempting to call this period 'mannerist.' The word has been so abused that I advance it only with hesitation. In order to surmount the problem of style that faced them, the composers of that time were reduced to cultivating a highly individual manner. The neoclassicism of Gluck, with its wilful refusal of so much traditional technique, the arbitrarily impassioned and dramatic modulations and the syncopated rhythms of Carl Philipp Emanuel Bach, the violence of many of the Haydn symphonies of the 1760s— much of this is the 'manner' that tries to fill the vacuum left by the absence of an integrated style. But so is the sophisticatedly smooth and flat courtly style of Johann Christian, the 'London' Bach; the effect is often chic rather than expressive, and the elegance is chiefly one of surface, as we are always conscious of what is being deliberately renounced for the sake of this grace— what is omitted disturbs the listener as it never does with Mozart even at his most *faux-naïf*. The conscious rejection of his father's style seems to haunt the music of Johann Christian Bach. It is paradoxical that a period which owed so much to Christian and Emanuel Bach, which was so dependent on their craftsmanship and their innovations, could not produce a major style of its own until it had reabsorbed (partly transformed and partly misunderstood) the work of Handel and Sebastian Bach. Nevertheless, this kind of disorganized environment may be stimulating to minor composers: the violin sonatas that Boccherini wrote in the 1760s experiment in much the way Haydn did at that time, and if Boccherini has less crude force and more elegance, this was a disadvantage only when seen in the light of later develop-ments. At any rate, these early sonatas are more estimable than the bland, and even anodyne, music that he was to turn out with such facility in the more ordered classical atmosphere of the latter part of the century.

I have called the period between the death of Handel and the first mature works of Mozart 'mannerist,' with the hope of avoiding both a tone of moral indignation and the fashionable connotation of the term. To strike a strong moral attitude toward an entire historical period inevitably leads to ludicrous misunderstanding—pardonable, perhaps, only when we are dealing with con-temporary phenomena: when we have, so to speak, a stake in the next choice that will be made, when our attitude is a hope or an anxiety, and not self-indulgence masking as principle.

But while every age may demand equal consideration it cannot claim equal eminence. From the death of Handel to 1775 no composer had suffi-cient command over all the elements of music for his personal style to bear the weight of a large series of works, a genuine *oeuvre*. We disapprove nowa-days of the idea of progress in the arts, but the deficiency of technique of even the finest talents of the period is a hard fact. It is for this reason that the experiments of the time, rich and interesting as they are, lack direction: the successes are all partial. Even in Haydn's finest works of the 1760s, the rhyth-mic insecurity is too often impossible to overlook. The relations between regular and irregular phrase-lengths are still unconvincing, and the typical Haydn use of dramatic silence is effective, but illogical within a larger context. The same can be said of Carl Philipp Emanuel Bach's most striking passages: they exist in and for themselves, with little relation to any conception of the whole work. The personal style, or 'manner,' of composers then was defined almost in a void, or, better, against a chaotic background of Baroque work-manship and tradition and half-understood classic and *galant* aspirations. Neither the imperturbable facility of the Romantic and Baroque composer nor the controlled dynamic transformation of the three great classical com-posers was as yet within reach. For experimentation to succeed, except by accident, one must be able to foresee the result and the import even if only half-consciously.

Perhaps the most glaring weakness of this period is the lack of co-ordina-tion between phrase rhythm, accent, and harmonic rhythm. This is partly due to a contradiction between classical and Baroque impulsion. The motor force of the new style is the periodic phrase, that of the Baroque is the harmonic sequence. When the strongly articulated periodic phrase is combined with a sequence, particularly a descending one as most sequences then were,[1] the result is not an increase of energy, but a loss. The articulation of the phrase, and the powerful new accentuation demanded a corresponding or analogous movement from the harmony: an accented change that comes close

---

[1] Tovey has stressed the originality of the rising bass in Beethoven.

to modulation. Both the accent and contour, which derive energy from their clarity, are weakened by the continuity inherent in the sequence, above all the cherished circle of fifths, which in the middle of a classical work can give the impression of treading water. It is unhappily used by Philipp Emanuel Bach in many expository passages for an illusion of motion. In the great classical works, however, it is mostly used precisely for this quality of *suspended* motion: in a number of Beethoven developments (as in the first movement of the *Waldstein* Sonata), when a point of extreme tension is reached, a sequence, often of considerable length, holds the music poised, immovable, in spite of a violence of dynamic accent. Mozart's most breathtaking uses of the sequence are at the ends of his developments: we sense that the tonic is about to reappear, and with the conviction that Mozart's sense of proportion conveys, we often know in just how many measures, and yet we are led to it by a sequence richly worked out with a felicity of detail that makes us half forget the inevitability of the larger action, or sense it in our pulse while we are dazzled by what appears to be ornament and is really a heightening of the dramatic form.

In this intermediate and confused period between the High Baroque and the development of a mature classical style, certain general conceptions of structure and proportion outline themselves with increasing clarity. The tonal pattern of most pre-classical sonatas is little more than the dance-form of the High Baroque. The first part goes from the tonic to the dominant, the second part from the dominant to the tonic. The return to the tonic in the pre-classical styles is, however, rarely marked by a significant cadence—the strong cadence on the tonic is reserved for the very end. The second part contains a certain amount of what must be called development, and a great deal of recapitulation in the tonic, but the lack of a clear separating tonic chord blurs the distinction between the development and the recapitulation, a distinction that was to be made by the later eighteenth century. In the High Baroque, too strong a tonic cadence long before the end had its dangers: given the fluid, continuous, and self-generating rhythm of Baroque music the only way to stop a piece was a forceful tonic cadence. This was an effect which could be used only with caution before the final page. In order to make a long section after a tonic cadence possible, the classical period had to develop a new and powerful system of rhythm and phrasing.

The composer of a sonata (or of anything else) was concerned with reconciling the demands of expression and proportion. Symmetry withheld and then finally granted is one of the basic satisfactions of eighteenth-century art. By the first third of the century, dramatic expression was beginning to reveal itself not only in detail (the melodic line, its ornaments, the individual harmonic effects) and in texture, harmonic as well as rhythmic, but also in the large structure of the work. A syntactic art of dramatic movement was becoming possible, leaving behind it the more static art of dramatic situation

49

and sentiment.[1] Several of the old Baroque symmetries had to be relinquished: the *ABA* form of the da capo aria, in particular, was too static for the newly developing style, although it was never completely forgotten and had its influence on what was to come. The symmetries of the classical period had to be used for the resolution of dramatic tension, and there were many possibilities. None of them was prescribed or proscribed, although choice was not an arbitrary matter. The most obvious symmetry was originally the most common: the second part repeats the material of the first part, but instead of going from tonic to dominant it goes from dominant to tonic. Thus we have a double symmetry of $A \to B: A \to B$ melodically and $A \to B: B \to A$ tonally. This does not mean that there is no development; there is plenty of development in Domenico Scarlatti and even in J. S. Bach and Rameau, but it is woven seamlessly into the recapitulation.

Development, in the classical and pre-classical styles, is basically nothing more than intensification. The earliest classical way of developing a theme, and one that was never lost, was to play it with more dramatic harmonies or in a remote key. At times, the more dramatic harmonies all by themselves even without the melodies would serve as development, and we find 'development sections' in many sonatas which make no direct allusion to the themes of the 'expositions.' The most common Baroque means of intensification, the extension of a theme and the avoidance of cadence, never disappeared, and its effect was only enhanced by the classical expectation of periodic cadence. Indeed, the avoidance of periodicity (the breakdown of symmetrical organization) is the fundamental classical means of rhythmic 'development,' and the fragmentation of the melodic material together with the use of contrapuntal imitation is only the thematic aspect of 'development,' corresponding to the rhythmic and harmonic aspects and uniting with them. The move from tonic to dominant in the 'exposition' is already in the direction of greater intensity, and the 'development' in the second part of the sonata form only serves to increase this long-range effect, to make the work dramatic in detail as well as in tonal structure, before it is resolved at the end.

There is a general tendency among historians to judge a pre-classical symphony or sonata as 'progressive' to the extent that it has a separate and lengthy development section. This is to ignore how much of the so-called 'recapitulation' is often given over to development, to an intensification of feeling and direction by the use of all the possible techniques—fragmentation, contrapuntal imitation, the use of remote harmonies or tonalities, the extension of melodies, avoidance of cadence. It also obscures the fact that exposition, development, and recapitulation are not watertight compartments. The addition of one or more new themes in the second half of a sonata means that the 'development section' has taken up the role of exposition. When the

---

[1] How far we find ourselves from the meaning of the terms 'classical' and 'Baroque' in the visual arts!

second half starts, as it so often does, with a complete replaying of the first subject in the dominant, then the 'development' has the role of a thematic recapitulation, just as the recapitulation (and even the exposition) often 'develop.'

Historically, in fact, this frequent appearance in the late eighteenth century of the opening melody at the beginning of the development is a heritage from the pre-classical form of the first years of the century. As the style developed, a purely symmetrical second half became less and less desirable; there always had been a tendency to heighten the feeling and the harmony after the appearance of the first melody played in the dominant at the opening of the second half. This tendency was to increase, and ultimately to create a radical change in the feeling for proportion. The greater dramatic tension that became common soon after the beginning of the second part of a 'sonata allegro' disrupted the simple melodic *AB/AB* symmetry of the Baroque dance-form, and required a more decisive resolution. An emphatic and marked return to the tonic at a point *no more than three-quarters of the way through a movement* is basic in late eighteenth-century style. Its placing is almost always an *event*, and it is never glossed over as the earlier eighteenth century tended to do. It is this dramatization of the return to the tonic that provokes the discussion whether the sonata is binary or ternary, a debate which treats musical proportions as if they were spatial rather than temporal.

Tovey has justly remarked that Mozart's piano concertos are not really in 'sonata form,' but in a variant of 'aria form'; nevertheless, the fact that he needed to make the point is instructive. The concerto at the time of Mozart is an aria that has been affected (or contaminated) by 'sonata form' to the point of resembling it closely. For a while, most major forms began to resemble sonatas: the rondo became a sonata rondo with a full-fledged development and recapitulation. The slow movement absorbed all of 'sonata form,' at first with rudimentary, and then with complete, developments. Minuets and scherzos also took on lengthy developments after their first double bar, and then even marked their opening halves, now become expositions, with a clear section in the dominant, which would be repeated in the tonic at the end. Finally the trios of the scherzos, always simpler and less developed, gradually took on some of the more complex characteristics of the sonata, so that now there was a sonata framed by another sonata. Even the magnificent finales of Mozart's operas, it has been pointed out, have the symmetrical tonal structure of a sonata.

We need a view of eighteenth-century musical style that allows us to distinguish what is abnormal only in a statistical sense from what was genuinely astonishing. For example, the development section of Mozart's Sonata in C major K. 330 makes no overt thematic allusion to the exposition, and this happens relatively rarely in works written during the last quarter of the century, although more often before. But it does not sound at all here as if this were an unusual procedure, either radical or reactionary: it sounds, as do many works of Mozart at this period, normally and normatively beautiful, unpretentious and finely ordered. It would be a mistake to find anything extraordinary in this movement except its balance and the wonderfully expressive detail: its large structure cannot have been intended to surprise. The opening of Beethoven's *Moonlight* Sonata, however, satisfies a definition of 'sonata form' on most counts, but it does not sound like what we expect of a sonata, and even Beethoven called it *quasi una fantasia*. The first movement was obviously intended to sound extraordinary. The principles of 'sonata form' for Haydn, Mozart, and Beethoven did not necessarily include a *thematic* development-section, nor did they require contrasting subjects, a complete recapitulation of the exposition or even a recapitulation that begins in the tonic. These are the patterns most commonly used, the easiest and most effective ways of meeting the demands the public made of the composer or, rather, that he made upon himself. But these patterns were not the form, and they only became so when the creative impulse and the style that generated the form had almost completely died away.

I should not like to set up a mysterious, unverifiable metaphysical entity, a Form, independent of the individual works, and revealed rather than invented by the composer. But a concept of style based mainly on the statistical frequency of certain patterns will never help us to understand irregularities of form or to appreciate the fact that most of these 'irregularities' were not thought to be irregular at all. Nor will it account for historical change—it can only register it. We must comprehend the imaginative significance of these patterns to understand why a recapitulation beginning in the dominant as in Domenico Scarlatti and Johann Christian Bach, gradually became unacceptable, while one that began in the subdominant (at a later point of the work) as in Mozart and Schubert became a reasonable possibility. Three examples may clarify the nature of the problem: the recapitulation of the first movement of Mozart's D major Sonata K. 311 begins with the 'second subjects,' returns to the opening theme only at the end and sounds witty, surprising, and satisfying when the opening finally reappears; the recapitulation of Beethoven's F major Sonata, op. 10 no. 2, which begins in the submediant, sounds witty and thoroughly unsatisfactory, and Beethoven promptly tells us that it was all a joke by going right back to the tonic; the recapitulation of Mozart's C major Sonata K. 545, which begins in the subdominant, sounds neither witty nor surprising but conventionally satisfactory, although it was as rare a form as any of the others at the time it was written.

The idea of a Form striving to define itself, to become flesh in all these different ways, is attractive, but even as a metaphor it sets a trap. It leads one to assume that there was such a thing as 'sonata form' in the late eighteenth century, and that the composers knew what it was, whereas nothing we know about the situation would lead us to suppose anything of the kind. The feeling for any form, even the minuet, was much more fluid. But 'complete liberty' describes the situation no better than 'occasional licence.' In a long-range way, it is no doubt true, or at least fruitful as an hypothesis, that art can do anything it wants; societies and artists call forth the styles they need to express what they wish—or, better, to fulfil the aesthetic needs they themselves have created. It is also true, particularly since the Renaissance, that artists are not so confined by their era as has sometimes been imagined. Not only have some styles offered extraordinary range and freedom, but even the possibility of pastiche exists: Michelangelo and Houdon produced fake antiques and Mozart wrote a suite in the style of Handel. An artist is in many ways free to decide what will influence him: Masaccio turned back a hundred years to Giotto as did Manet to Velásquez, and Beethoven's use of Gregorian chant in the D major Mass and the Quartet op. 132 is a measure of what the classical style could absorb. Nevertheless, for a composer, music is basically what was written last year, or last month (generally by himself, once he has developed his manner). His own work is not determined by it in any rigid sense, but it is what he must work with or against. The 'anonymous style' of an age, the buildings whose architects are without distinction, the books that have only a period interest, the painting that is only decorative—all this comes about by accretion, and it takes a generation to make a really noticeable change. An 'anonymous style' has little tenacity, but a tremendous inertia. If 'style' is used to mean an integrated form of expression—which only the finest artists can muster—there is still a limitation on development: the sustaining of a style in this sense is as heroic an act as its invention and an artist rarely creates his own possibilities, he only perceives them in the work he has just done.

An understanding of the sense of continuity and the proportions of classical style would enable us largely to dispense with a further discussion of 'sonata form.' For the late eighteenth century, a sonata was any *organized* series of movements, and the proportions of the music changed according to whether it was the opening movement, a middle movement, or a finale. Old forms, like the fugue and the theme and variations, were still used, thoroughly transformed; some forms, like the concerto, the overture, the aria, and the rondo, contain vestiges of older forms buried within them; and there are dances, mostly minuets, Ländler, and polonaises. Everything else is sonata: that is to say, plain music. In this case, we cannot be content with the description of a form: we need to know first how the sense of music in general differed from that of the previous age; above all, we need to grasp this in specifically musical terms. The possibilities of art are infinite but not unlimited. Even a stylistic revolution is controlled by the nature of the language in which it is to take place, and which it will transform.

Part II

THE CLASSICAL STYLE

1

The Coherence of the Musical Language

The classical style appears inevitable only after the event. Looking back today we can see its creation as a natural one, not an outgrowth of the preceding style (in relation to which it seems more like a leap, or a revolutionary break), but a step in the progressive realization of the musical language as it had existed and developed since the fifteenth century. At the time, nothing would have seemed less logical; the period from 1750 to 1775 was penetrated by eccentricity, hit-or-miss experimentation, resulting in works which are still difficult to accept today because of their oddities. Yet each experiment that succeeded, each stylistic development that became an integral part of music for the next half-century or more was characterized by its aptness for a dramatic style based on tonality.

It is a useful hypothesis to think of one element of a new style as a germinal force, appearing in an older style at a moment of crisis, and gradually transforming all the other elements over the years, into an aesthetic harmony until the new style becomes an integral whole, as the rib-vault is said to have been the creative, or precipitating element in the formation of the Gothic style. In this way the historical development of a style seems to follow a perfectly logical pattern. In practice, things are rarely so simple. Most of the characteristic features of the classical style did not appear one by one in an orderly fashion, but sporadically, sometimes together and sometimes apart, and with a progress despairingly irregular to those who prefer a hard-edged result. The final product does, however, have a logical coherence, as even the irregularities of a language, once investigated, become consistent. So the procedure of isolating the elements and considering how one leads to the other, implying the other elements and completing them, is unhistorical but helpful.

The clearest of these elements in the formation of the early classical style (or proto-classical, if we reserve the term classical for Haydn, Mozart, and Beethoven) is the short, periodic, articulated phrase. When it first appears, it is a disruptive element in the Baroque style, which relied generally on an encompassing and sweeping continuity. The paradigm is, of course, the four-measure phrase, but historically this is not the model, but only, at the end, the most common. Two-measure phrases are almost a trademark with Domenico Scarlatti, becoming four-measure phrases when they are, in turn, grouped by twos. Haydn's Quartet op. 20 no. 4 starts with seven completely independent six-measure phrases, and this is only one example among thousands. Three- and five-measure phrases appear frequently from the very beginning, and 'real' seven-measure phrases become possible in the latter part of the century ('real' as opposed to eight-measure phrases where the last measure disappears by overlapping with the beginning of a new phrase). Not until about 1820 did the four-measure phrase gain its stranglehold on rhythmic structure. Before then, its supremacy was purely practical—it was neither too short nor too long, and it was easily divisible into balanced and symmetrical halves as three- and five-measure phrases were not. But there is no magic in the number four, and what is important is the periodic breaking of continuity.

Naturally, the periodicity makes this possible by providing a continuity of its own. The periodic phrase is related to the dance, with its need for a phrase pattern that corresponds to the steps and to groupings. In Italian instrumental music of the early eighteenth century, this phrase grouping is reinforced by the harmonic sequence, and it is amusing to see the most basic device of High Baroque rhythm contribute to the effectiveness of an element that was eventually to lead to the fall of the Baroque system. Not that the sequence was ever abandoned; it has remained an important part of music until our own day. In the classical style, however, it loses its primacy as a force for movement (some of which it regained during the nineteenth century). A Baroque fugue is kept moving largely by sequence: a classical sonata has other means of locomotion as well. In a classical work, in fact, a sequence is often a means of decreasing tension: after a series of surprising modulations, it is a way of calling a halt, and is often used for this purpose, placed over a pedal point, particularly toward the end of a development section. All large-scale movement has ceased, and the sequence is only a kind of pulsation. In this way the basic impulsive element of the Baroque is employed but down-graded in the classical system.

Articulated, periodic phrasing brought about two fundamental alterations in the nature of eighteenth-century music: one was a heightened, indeed overwhelming, sensitivity to symmetry, and the second was a rhythmic texture of great variety, with the different rhythms not contrasted or super-imposed, but passing logically and easily into each other. The dominance of symmetry came from the periodic nature of the classical phrase: a period imposes a larger, slower pulse upon the rhythm, and just as two similar measures are almost always necessary for us to understand the rhythm of the music and to identify the downbeat, so now a comparable symmetry of phrase structure was necessary to hear and to feel the larger pulse. The preference for articulation also increased the aesthetic need for symmetry. When the main consideration was rhythmical flow, as in the High Baroque, the balancing of one half of a phrase by another was not of predominant concern; it was more important for the end of each phrase to lead imper-ceptibly and urgently to the next. As each phrase assumed a more independent existence, the question of balance asserted itself with greater clarity. One example, the opening measures of perhaps the first unequivocal masterpiece in a classical style purified of all mannerist traces, Mozart's Concerto for Piano and Orchestra K. 271, will show how this balance was achieved, and also illuminate the variety and integration of rhythmic textures:

Measures 1–3 and 4–6 are the extreme form of balance, absolute identity. Yet it would be a mistake to think that the identical halves are identical in meaning. The repetition has greater urgency (a third would be exasperating), and gives the phrase greater definition, a clearer existence as an element of

the work we are about to hear. This is an astonishing and delightful opening, surprising not only for its use of the soloist at the very outset, but also for the wit with which he enters, as he replies to the orchestral fanfare. For this wit, the exquisite balance of the phrase is essential: the orchestra falls an octave and rises a fifth, the piano then rises an octave and falls a fifth within an equal length of time. We are not by any means intended to hear this as an inversion, as would be the case with a theme inverted in a fugue. That is the last thing the style requires, and the most ruinous of effect. The symmetry is concealed, delicate, and full of charm.

The concealment and, above all, the charm depend on the rhythmic variety: in effect the orchestra is in *alla breve*, with two long beats to the bar, while the piano is in a clear four (₵ and C). The stately is opposed to the impertinent, and balanced perfectly by it. The High Baroque is capable of such contrast, but rarely aimed at this kind of balance. The extent of the classical achievement is not, however, seen in the first half-dozen measures but in the ones that follow, where a convincing fusion of the two kinds of pulse is heard. The phrasing in measure 8 is a synthesis; it beautifully combines the pulse of *alla breve* and common time, while the melody in the first violins in measures 7–11 combines the opening motives of both the piano and the orchestra. It is this that makes the transition from measures 6 to 7 masterly: the urgency of the repeated phrase justifies the increased movement in eighth notes of the accompaniment in measure 7, while the first violins, who play the repeated B♭'s of the first measure half as fast, keep the change from being obtrusive and draw the two phrases together. With this seventh measure, the animation begins to increase, but the transition is imperceptible, a natural growth of what comes before. This kind of rhythmic transition is the touchstone of the classical style; never before in the history of music had it been possible to move from one kind of pulse to another so naturally and with such grace.

The High Baroque preferred music with a homogeneous rhythmic texture, using different kinds of rhythmic movement only under certain conditions. Contrast of rhythm could occur in two ways: by the superimposition of one rhythm over another, in which case the dominant rhythm of the piece inevitably becomes the faster one; and by the placing of large blocks of one kind of rhythm next to another (as in the plague of flies from *Israel in Egypt*), in which case the two or even three sorts of rhythm are superimposed before the end, generally at the climax, thus being reduced to the first case. In both cases, the rhythms remain essentially distinct; no transition is envisaged or attempted. A sudden and violent change in the rhythmic texture is sometimes attempted by Bach and other composers for dramatic reasons, as in the organ chorale-prelude *O Lamm Gottes* and in the last movement of the Fourth Brandenburg Concerto. Here the effect is one of wilful rhythmic eccentricity, always giving a moment of shock to the listener, deeply emotional in the one piece, dramatic but amiable in the other. But even these works are exceptions:[1] the most common Baroque form is one of simple and unified rhythmic texture. When a rhythm has been established, it is generally continued relentlessly until the end, or at least until the pause before the final cadence (at which point a change of rhythm is possible without giving the impression that something very out-of-the-way is happening). A fugue theme, for example, may open with long notes and finish with ones of smaller value (rarely the other way round), and it is the faster notes that become the basic texture of the whole: the longer notes of the theme are invariably accompanied by the faster rhythm in the other voices. Once the piece is under way an impression of *perpetuum mobile* is not uncommon.

The *perpetuum mobile* is occasionally found in classical works, and it is interesting to compare the difference in treatment. The chief rhythmic interest of the classical *perpetuum mobile* is focused on the irregular aspects: that is, the rhythmic variety is as great as in any other classical work. In the finale of Haydn's *Lark* Quartet op. 64 no. 5, the phrases are clearly articulated and never overlap, in spite of the continuous movement; the strong off-beat accents of the middle section in the minor provide still greater assurance of variety. The syncopated accents of the finale of Beethoven's F major Sonata op. 54 are even more surprising: they occur alternately on the second and third sixteenth notes of groups of four as follows:

This provides two contradictory forces that challenge the weight of the downbeat. The *sforzando* on the tonic in the bass reinforces the second sixteenth note, which is the weakest in the measure, making the accent most destructive to a sense of unvaried flow. For a classical composer the *perpetuum mobile* is only an added challenge to his desire to break up the rhythmic texture, and the tension adds dramatic force. It is, however, typically a device for finales, where the greater rhythmic stability of a continuous

---

[1] The one real exception that I know in the High Baroque, where a form of rhythmic transition, as opposed to contrast, is attempted, is the 'Confiteor' of the *B minor Mass*. In this profound work, the means used are, however, almost anti-classical, and a gradual change of tempo is meant, not a fusion of different pulses.

movement can serve as an alternative to a squarely articulated melody. The *perpetuum mobile* of the last movement of the *Appassionata*, a piece more stable than the first movement, has its dynamic share of rhythmic violence, and finally breaks down just before the return to the tonic in an access of passion followed by a moment of complete exhaustion. Indeed, the rhythmic violence of this movement often makes us forget its ceaseless flow. The Baroque *perpetuum mobile*, on the other hand, is not a dramatic form, or one that generates any particular tension. It is the normal procedure, and there are so many examples that citation is unnecessary—any work in which the thematic material moves evenly (almost any Allemande, for example) will do.

Baroque dynamics provide a perfect analogy with Baroque rhythm, perhaps because dynamic inflection is as much a part of rhythm as it is of melodic expression. Just as the rhythmic motion may be constant throughout the work, or different rhythms may be either superimposed horizontally or juxtaposed vertically without mediation, in the same way a Baroque work may be played at a fairly constant level of sound, or two levels may be superimposed or juxtaposed without any use (at least structurally) of *crescendo* and *diminuendo*.[1] A great deal has been written about 'terraced dynamics,' but the typical performance, except when a solo or several soloists were to be contrasted with a larger group, was probably at a constant level: 'terraced dynamics' were not a necessity but a luxury of Baroque music. Most harpsichords were built with only one keyboard, so that two levels of sound were impossible at the same time, and sometimes even the quick juxtaposition of two levels was made more than difficult by the inconvenient placing of the stops at the side of the instrument. Changes in registration on the organ during the middle of a piece generally required the presence of an assistant with a plan of operations: only an important virtuoso work would have been performed in this way, and then only when practicable. It should be remembered, too, that the use of two keyboards does not imply two dynamic levels, but rather two kinds of sonority. In reality, this contrast of sonority is more fundamental to High Baroque music than the contrast of dynamic levels, which is only a special form of it. The division between tutti and soli in the concerto grosso is less an opposition of loud and soft than of two different qualities of sound, which clarify the structure as the two keyboards clarify the voice-leading in those of the *Goldberg* Variations where the voices cross each other. Equally matched levels are, however, normal in the Baroque, though we are sometimes prevented from realizing it by nineteenth-century habits that have led us to demand greater dynamic variety from music. Often we badly distort the music even when we do not exceed what was possible on an early eighteenth-century instrument. Much of Domenico Scarlatti's

---

[1] *Crescendo* and *diminuendo* as ornamental and expressive nuances were, of course, important to the Baroque period, particularly in vocal music.

music, for example, is made up of short passages played twice or even three times in a row; to play these repetitions as loud-soft echoes is to betray the music, for much of the effect should come from its insistence. The belief that everything that appears twice should be differentiated is an unconscious and sometimes noxious principle in the mind of almost every performer today. The High Baroque looked for variety mainly through ornamentation and not through dynamic contrast, 'terraced' or not.

Even here circumspection is necessary. Some music (a great deal of Handel's) needs heavy ornamentation even the first time round; other music (most of Scarlatti's and almost all of Bach's) needs very little or absolutely none. Scarlatti had worked out an early form of the more articulated classical style, and an indiscriminate application of ornament would cause his phrases to overlap. And it was already a contemporary complaint against Bach that he wrote everything out and left no space for the performer to add his ornaments; the answer, quite rightly made at the time, was that this is one of the great beauties of his music. It is sometimes held that the repeats of all the *Goldberg* Variations should be decorated. This is what comes of reading eighteenth-century theorists (or about them) and paying no attention to the music. A few of the variations could indeed be ornamented, but most of them resist any attempt beyond the addition of a mordent or two, and this would only make the performance sound fussy. The problem is that performance has become largely a public affair since the eighteenth century: and with the formality has come a need for variety of effect and dramatization. The purpose of ornamentation (except in opera) was not to capture and retain the attention of a large audience: one ornamented to please oneself and one's patron and friends. The *Well-Tempered Keyboard* and the *Art of Fugue*, for example, were indeed intended to be performed, but only in private, as many fugues at a time as one wanted, on any keyboard instrument that was handy. It is obvious from suites and partitas that the early eighteenth century could bear longer stretches of the same tonality than any succeeding period, along with lengthier works in the same rhythm and at the same dynamic level.[1] The chamber music of the High Baroque was certainly played with subtle dynamic inflections, and required, what is most difficult to recapture, a *rubato* proper to the style and a decorative system for emphasizing these inflections, for its expression, in fact. But it was not an art that relied heavily upon large dynamic contrasts, or in any way at all upon transition between dynamic levels. What dynamic contrasts there were can be found mainly in the public genres: opera, oratorio, and concerto. This distinction between genres developed greater importance in the middle of the eighteenth century, becoming blurred only at the end. The symphony, for example, demanded a greater overlapping of phrases—i.e., less articulation and more directional movement—than the solo sonata, but by the time the late eighteenth-century

---

[1] Even if these suites were treated to some extent as anthologies, a work like the Handel Chaconne, which *was* played in its entirety, makes a modern ear impatient.

theorists had pointed this out, Haydn and Mozart were already writing their solo works in a more symphonic style.

The articulated phrase required its individual elements to be discrete and set off from each other in order that its shape and symmetry might be clearly audible, and this in turn brought about a greater variety of rhythmic texture and a much larger range of dynamic accent. In the opening phrase of the Mozart Concerto K. 271, cited above (p. 59), the Baroque contrast between a section of music for orchestra and a new section for solo has been concentrated into a single phrase. When the most emphatic extremes are forced into one detail, then a style must be found that can mediate between them: a work made up of such contrasts so dramatically juxtaposed at close range with no possibility of long-range transition between them would either be very short or intolerable. It is this style of transition or mediation that the later eighteenth century created. The development of the *crescendo* in orchestral music, particularly at Mannheim, is well known, but also the possibility of mediating between different kinds of rhythms now appeared for the first time. One of the most common practices of the classical period was to introduce a faster rhythm first into the accompaniment and only some measures later into the main voices, thus smoothing over the join until no break is felt. Beethoven's Fourth Piano Concerto opens with a feeling of two slow beats to a measure:

and by the end of the exposition we hear eight quick beats per measure:

where the *sforzandi* on the weak eighth notes double the pulse from the previous four. As the movement proceeds, the transition from two to eight is imperceptible.

Rhythmic transition in the late eighteenth century is achieved with discrete, well-defined elements, generally related to one another by each in turn being twice as fast, or half as fast, as the preceding, so that all the rates of speed tend to come from the series 2, 4, 8, 16, etc. But the movement from one rhythm to another is felt as a transition and not as a contrast. This sense of unbroken continuity is achieved not only by starting the faster rhythm in a subsidiary or accompanying voice so that its entrance is less noticeable, or by subtle nuances of phrasing, as in the above example from Mozart, but also by the placing of accents and by harmonic means as well. Mozart and Haydn were the first composers to understand the new demands on harmonic movement made by the periodic phrase, and it is in their works that a convincing relation is first heard. Much of their success hangs on a comprehension of dissonance and harmonic tension: it is often an exceptionally dissonant chord that introduces a new and faster rhythm,[1] and both composers made full use of the added animation that is so natural at the end of a musical paragraph in its drive toward a cadence and resolution. Both also succeeded after 1775 in handling the introduction of triplets into duple time convincingly—always a difficult matter in a style so heavily concerned with symmetry and with the clear independence of the individual elements.

With the classical style, a means of transition can even become a thematic element. In Haydn's Quartet in C major op. 33 no. 3 of 1781, the *crescendo* is perhaps the most important element of the main theme:

Here is the classical style during its first years of perfection; not only is there symmetry from phrase to phrase, but even within the phrase itself. The *crescendo* of the first three measures (to which the grace notes and turn in the violin are a contribution) is balanced by the descent of the first violin in measures 4 to 6, itself counterbalanced by the rising figure of the cello, so

---

[1] See the new triplet rhythm introduced at the end of the example from Mozart's D major Quintet K. 593 on p. 283.

that the general effect is still one of ascending. More important, the opening measures are not only a *crescendo* but also a gradual acceleration little by little from the uninflected pulsation of the opening measure to the sixteenth-note rhythm of measures 4 to 6. The first four bars represent an increase of pulse (0, 1, 2, and 4 in each successive measure) within the same tempo. The *sforzando* that accompanies the entrance of the cello strengthens the sense of four beats in that bar, and also foreshadows the violin line of the next bar. Even the transition back to the feeling of zero beats per measure is beautifully handled. Bar 4 has a *sforzando* on the second beat, bar 5 has only the accent that comes from the sustained notes, and bar 6 withholds all accent from the second beat and follows it with a surprising silence; all this prepares the return to the uninflected pulsation of the opening. The silence is as much a part of the theme as the *crescendo*; it is even developed afterwards, first by being filled up with the violin's decorated notes from bar 3 played twice as fast:

and later by being doubled in length:

These examples introduce another kind of transition, thematic transition, which is sometimes used for development. In this movement, a closing theme of the exposition is derived from the same violin motif of bars 2 and 3, played at double tempo, and its connection with the opening is made through measures 31–32 and the surrounding section. In this way, each theme appears to grow from the preceding one, gaining an independent identity and still keeping its relationship to the whole. This delightful five-measure theme (or four-measure theme with an echo in the middle) demonstrates a kind of thematic relationship in which the logical steps are successively spelled out in the music itself:

It should be noted here that the quartet's opening six-measure phrase (quoted p. 65) can be looked at either as a four-measure phrase with a one-bar introduction and an echo at the end, or (since a new figure is introduced at the climax at the opening of bar 4) as two three-measure phrases. Both interpretations, of course, are right; or, rather, we hear the rhythmic tension between these two patterns as part of the phrase. The harmony of this opening phrase is more subtle than it appears at first: nothing but tonic with a little dominant thrown in at the end to define the key, it sounds grandly simple, but tension is introduced by withholding the root position of the tonic, so necessary to this style, until the end of the *crescendo* and then by bringing it in on an off-beat. The spaciousness is tempered with wit: no chamber music before this had ever achieved such a combination.

The capacity of the classical style to go imperceptibly from one dynamic level to another, from one kind of rhythm to another, was limited only in the direction of how slowly it could be done: how fast was unimportant, since, at a very fast rate of change, a transition disappears and becomes a contrast. A slow transition, however, was always more difficult, and the immensely long and very gradual changes that Wagner was to perfect were impossible within a classical scheme. The stability of the tonal sense and the need for balance were there as a barrier; not until nineteenth-century tonality became less stable could the pace at which things happened (as opposed to the tempo) be slowed down. The third act of *Parsifal* is, in a formal sense, an enormous modulation from B major back to the A flat major of the Prelude to the first act, and Wagner can make it last so long because he is able to take so much time defining his first key: the third act prelude is in a vague region floating between B flat minor and B major, and this lack of tonal definition allows Wagner's rhythm to proceed in a series of waves and the tension to be increased at a very slow pace. The dynamic level can then be raised at a similarly slow rate, and the range can be greatly enlarged.

For Haydn, Mozart, and Beethoven, no such technique was available or even conceivable, although Beethoven extends the power of the style and slows the rate of change almost miraculously in such places as the slow *crescendo* and *accelerando* ('poi a poi di nuovo vivente') in the finale of the A flat Sonata, op. 110, from the inversion of the fugue to the end. Here all the discrete thematic units of the classical style are used so that they appear to blend with each other, and to achieve this continuum Beethoven uses an abnormal harmonic movement, modulating from the key of the leading tone to the tonic (G minor–major to A flat). The distance of the relationship, although classically lucid, blurs the force of the tonic and allows for a great expanse of time so that its eventual return and re-establishment may carry the full weight demanded by the triumph of the last pages. Beethoven's method, with the relationships sharply defined, has nothing to do with the Romantic procedure of withholding the tonic. In general, for an event to happen in slow motion we must wait for the middle of the nineteenth century: the classical style is capable of very slow tempi, but the music is always eventful, and a single continuous movement longer than twenty minutes is beyond its reach.

There is, however, a sense in which the classical style moves more slowly than is sometimes thought. The modulation to the dominant is not always an affair of a few measures; sometimes it starts with the opening phrase, and the whole first page of a movement may be a series of successively stronger approaches and withdrawals. In Haydn's E flat major Quartet op. 20 no. 1, bars 7–10 are already in the dominant and there is a return to the dominant in bars 14 and 15; the tonic reappears after each of these places, and the final move to the dominant is not made until bars 21–24. All this must, of course, be changed in the recapitulation, which is completely re-written. We can speak here of a long dominant preparation, but it is more accurate to describe it as a general drift to the dominant made articulate at a given moment. The extent of the drift is often obscured by the terminology of 'sonata form,' which concentrates on the moment of articulation: what are called 'bridge passages' between tonic and dominant are common enough in classical expositions (how could they not be?), but there are innumerable cases where the movement to the dominant begins right at the opening, with the establishment of the tonic. This is often found in Haydn and is even more frequent with Beethoven. The drift away from the tonic starts at the opening of the *Eroica* Symphony, and the *Waldstein* Sonata establishes the tonic only after the movement away from it has apparently started. The Sonata in A major op. 101 marks the extreme development of this technique as Beethoven here starts directly with the movement to the dominant. The tonic is established by implication with an extraordinarily poetic effect of beginning in the middle, and only a firmness that is taken for granted without being emphasized could make possible the emotion that is built on it.

Sometimes the change of key is startling and abrupt, and the new tonality is introduced without modulation. When this happens, something in the opening section has made it possible. The first of Haydn's op. 33 Quartets, in B minor, restates the main theme in D, the relative major (the 'normal' secondary key for a movement in the minor after 1770), after a fermata and without any modulation at all:[1] this is possible because the main theme was originally announced, at the very opening of the work, in what appeared to

---

[1] Quoted on page 116.

be the relative major, the B minor becoming clear only in the third bar. The movement to the new key is therefore accomplished simply by reharmonizing the melody in the way already implied by the first two measures. The preparation of the new key is not explicit, but implicit in the material itself.

We can see from this example both how free classical form was, and how closely it was tied to tonal relationships. At this point Haydn is drawing the logical conclusion of his opening. He is bound less by the practices of his contemporaries than by a sensitivity to harmonic implication; the suggestion of D major placed at a point as critical as the opening measure makes Haydn realize that he can dispense with a modulation. The same sensitivity will lead Mozart, after *La Finta Giardiniera*, to write each opera in a definite tonality, beginning and ending with it, and organizing the sequence of numbers around it.

An articulate movement to the dominant (or its substitute) is all that is required harmonically of a sonata exposition: how it is done is completely free, or, rather, bound only by the nature and material of each individual work. There is a movement toward the dominant in most Baroque music, too, even in the early Baroque, but it is rarely made either articulate—that is, decisive—or dramatic. What the late eighteenth century did was to intensify this movement toward the dominant and give it a stronger feeling of direction.

A clear hierarchy of tonal strength was demanded by the classical style. Tovey and others have commented on the difference between being *on* a tonality and being *in* it. In reality, a subtle series of degrees is set up by the classical composers: stronger than being *in* a key, is its establishment as a secondary key, a weaker pole of force reacting against the tonic. Still stronger, of course, is the tonic itself. This hierarchy (a continuous one, with each stage blending into the next) explains how Mozart's G minor Symphony K. 550, for example, can have a development section which goes through a kaleidoscopic succession of keys, without ever reaching the stability achieved by the relative major at the end of the exposition. As an example of even greater resourcefulness, the first tutti of Beethoven's Fourth Piano Concerto also goes through a series of tonalities but without once really leaving the tonic. It is a mistake to speak of classical modulation without specifying an order of magnitude; unfortunately, we lack a concise technical language. A Baroque *composition* moves to another tonality in much the same way that a late eighteenth-century *phrase* goes normally from tonic to dominant or back. In the classical style, modulation is given a power commensurate with its role.

In short, the larger harmonic structure was transformed in order to make it fit the proportions as well as the nature of the classical phrase. It had, indeed, already been remarked in the eighteenth century that a sonata exposition was an expanded dance-phrase. This expansion was accomplished not merely in the Baroque fashion of extending and repeating the motion of individual motifs, but by dramatization as well.

The Baroque and classical styles are sometimes contrasted as decorative and dramatic respectively. This leads to misunderstanding only if taken to refer to expressive character rather than to the technical procedures of the two styles. A Baroque work is undramatic in that its tension remains fairly constant until the final cadence, and only rarely rises above the level set at the beginning. Nothing can be more dramatic in character than the opening chorus in E minor of Bach's *St. Matthew Passion,* yet it achieves its dramatic affect by transcending the variation (chorale prelude), a decorative form, and the concerto grosso form (which, like the Baroque rondo, works by alternation and generally does not build to a specific area of climax). This chorus moves like a sonata from the minor to the relative major, but the cadence on G major actually lowers the dramatic energy, which is recaptured only with the entrance of the third chorus singing the chorale. Through its throbbing rhythm, anguished harmonies, and the cumulative effect of its three choruses, the music acts as a dramatic image, not as a scenario. On the other hand, in a classical sonata in a minor key the apparent relaxation of the relative major is always compensated for by Haydn, Mozart, and Beethoven, who make certain that the tension is raised, not lowered, at this point. The second subject of Beethoven's *Appassionata* is both more lyrical and more nervous than the opening; it moves faster and the bass steadily mounts. There were, of course, no rules about second subjects in the late eighteenth century, nor were second subjects even necessary, but when they occur in Haydn, Mozart, and Beethoven, they are usually more intense than the first subject. The dramatic character of the sonata calls for contrast, and when the main theme is vigorous, some of the succeeding themes generally take on a softer character. But then their harmonic movement tends to be faster (as in Beethoven's opp. 53, 57), more agitated (Mozart K. 310, Beethoven op. 31 no. 2) or more chromatic and passionate (Beethoven op. 109). Haydn prefers themes of equal intensity and relies on harmonic movement for the necessary dramatic effect. It is true that in Schumann and Chopin, the second themes are generally more relaxed in every way than the first, but by that time the sonata was an archaic form, fundamentally unsuited to contemporary style, with the initial tonic section so unstable emotionally that a decrease in tension was inevitable.

The stability and clarity of the opening and closing pages of a classical sonata are essential to its form, and they make the increased tension of the middle sections possible. The difference between the Baroque movement toward the dominant and the classical modulation is not only one of degree: the classical style dramatizes this movement—in other words, it becomes an event as well as a directional force. The simplest way to mark this event, to articulate it, in fact, is by a pause on the dominant of the dominant before continuing, and sophisticated versions of this device can be found even in the latest works of Beethoven.

This event can be further articulated in two ways: it can be emphasized by the introduction of a new theme (the practice of Mozart and the majority of his contemporaries), or by the repetition of the opening theme, preferably in such a way that its new significance at the dominant is clear (the device preferred by Haydn). Beethoven and Haydn often combine both methods, first restating the main theme with changes and new details that show how it is reinterpreted by being transposed from the tonic, and then adding a new theme. The presence or absence of a new melody is of less moment than the extent to which the new key is dramatized, and how continuity is achieved to offset the articulated structure.

This moment of dramatization and where it occurs make an essential contrast with the Baroque style. Modulation already exists in all dance-forms of the early eighteenth century; but in High Baroque style a pause to mark the arrival at the dominant is hardly ever placed in the middle of the first half but at the end of it; the music is a gradual flow to the dominant with a resolution at the end of the section. Early in a sonata, however, there must be a moment, more or less dramatic, of awareness of the new tonality: it may be a pause, a strong cadence, an explosion, a new theme, or anything else that the composer wishes. This moment of dramatization is more fundamental than any compositional device.

For this reason, the classical style needed more forcible means of emphasizing new keys than the Baroque, and it used for this purpose a quantity of 'filling' almost unparalleled until then in the history of music except in pieces of an improvisatory character. By 'filling' I mean purely conventional material, superficially unrelated to the content of the piece, and apparently (and in some cases, actually) transferable bodily from one work to another. Every musical style, naturally, relies on conventional material, principally at cadences, which almost always follow traditional formulas. The classical style, however, further magnified and elongated the cadence in order to strengthen the modulation. A Baroque composer worked mostly with vertical filling (the figured bass), and the classical composer with horizontal: long phrases of conventional passagework. Aside from accompaniment figures and cadential ornaments, the two basic forms of conventional material are scales and arpeggios, and they fill classical works to a degree that would only have been possible for a Baroque composer in a toccata, or in a form that tried to sound improvised rather than composed. The means employed by an early eighteenth-century composer to give the impression of freedom were needed by Mozart to organize the form; he used whole phrases of scales and arpeggios the way Handel used sequences—to tie sections of the work together. But in the finest Baroque work the sequence is generally clothed and covered by thematic material, while even in the greatest works of Haydn and Mozart the 'filling' is displayed nakedly, and appears to have been prefabricated in large pieces.

Another reason for the use of large conventional phrases and their deployment in block-form was the increase of instrumental virtuosity, although it is moot whether the instrumentalist inspired the composer or vice versa: probably both. In any case, the following passage from one of Mozart's finest works, the Sonata for Piano K. 333, is absolutely conventional:

It could be transferred to any work in common time which needs an F major cadence. The passage has a certain amount of brilliance and is obviously derived from concerto style. It also provides a climax by sounding the first high F in the piece, the top note of Mozart's piano. But that is not its only *raison d'être*; it is placed where it is because Mozart needs four bars of emphatic cadence. In fact, less conventional, more thematic material will not do; thematic interest would distract from the essential—which is exactly what it appears to be: four bars of cadence. We have reached a style in which proportion has become a major interest. Starting with conventional passages, such as the one in K. 333, we shall end with the unbelievably long final cadence of Beethoven's Fifth Symphony, where fifty-four measures of pure C major are needed to ground the extreme tension of that immense work. But already in Mozart, the length of this conventional material is sometimes astounding.

It should be remarked that this passage in Mozart is not arbitrary but grows logically out of the phrase that precedes it. The block use of conventional material often goes, however, much further in this style. The opening movement of Mozart's C major Symphony K. 338 has no melody at all in the first forty measures. There is nothing but completely conventional march-like flourishes and a harmonic pattern that eventually moves to the dominant, and only at this point are we finally given a melody. Yet it is one of Mozart's most brilliantly laid-out pages, serving not only to define tonality as a Baroque opening would do, but also to set up an area of great stability: much of the power of this opening comes from its avoidance of any thematic expressivity. (This is also why a good part of this first page is reserved for the end and not the beginning of the recapitulation: the classical style demands a resolution midway through the second half of a movement but a resolution of such magnitude would make the remainder of the recapitulation an anticlimax.)

It is the classical sense for large areas of stability, impossible before and lost since, that establishes what might seem to be the one fixed rule of sonata recapitulation: material originally exposed in the dominant must be represented in the tonic fairly completely, even if rewritten and reordered, and only material exposed in the tonic may be omitted. This is, of course, not a rule at all but a sensitivity to tonal relationships. (It is amusing to recall that

Chopin was censured by contemporary academic critics—and called unorthodox even by some in the twentieth century—for omitting the recapitulation of much of the first subject in his sonatas, a well-worn eighteenth-century device.) Material presented outside the tonic must have created, in the eighteenth century, a feeling of instability which demanded to be resolved. When the tonic was reaffirmed in the second half of the piece, the material already presented in the tonic could be, and often was, drastically cut, but the rest of the exposition cried out for resolution in the tonic. Today, our harmonic sensibilities have become coarsened by the tonal instability of music after the death of Beethoven, and the strength of this feeling is perhaps difficult to recapture.

It is worth examining this in some detail, at least briefly. First for an exception to prove a rule. There is one Haydn quartet, op. 64 no. 3 in B flat, in which one of the second subjects appears nowhere in the recapitulation. It is a strange quartet with an eccentric and comic opening. The first melody in the dominant, F major, is also the first regular-sounding melody in the quartet (mm. 33–42). A four-measure phrase, it is played first in the major and immediately repeated in the minor, and it clearly functions in the exposition to reaffirm the dominant. (It is not the only theme so used: the opening theme is replayed in the new tonality, and yet another new theme is then introduced, also in F major.) The repeated four-measure phrase does not, as I said, reappear in the recapitulation, but it does, however, reappear *in its full form* in the development section, *and on the tonic*. This time the phrase is played twice in the minor. In this way the theme is satisfactorily recapitulated, as one half of it was already in minor to begin with; in addition, the tonic major is avoided in the development. All the various classical demands for balance and tonal resolution have thus been reconciled.

A use of the tonic minor after the recapitulation has been reached invariably means a reduction in stability, and this explains Haydn's reluctance to employ it.[1] In another quartet, op. 50 no. 6 in D major, four measures of the exposition (26–29) are in the dominant minor, and again they are not in the recapitulation; again, however, they appear in the *tonic* minor in the development section. In this way, Haydn manages to avert a difficult situation: the tonic minor may be used towards the end of a recapitulation in major only if its effect is successfully countered. In the first movement of the *Waldstein* Sonata, for example, Beethoven has a phrase in the exposition that is played twice in the minor; it is played twice in the recapitulation, but the second time in the major (mm. 235–243).

The danger of using the tonic major in the development is obvious, as it weakens the dramatic effect of its return. Unless it occurs briefly in passing, it, too, needs to be offset, generally by following it with the tonic minor. The

---

[1] In Symphony no. 85 (*La Reine*), a section of the exposition in the dominant minor is also avoided in the recapitulation, and there are other examples.

most important use of it in a development is naturally the false reprise, or false recapitulation. But this dramatic effect of incongruity cannot be used with impunity if it lasts beyond a few measures; when it does, Haydn makes it do an important part of the work of the main reprise. In the Quartet, op. 77 no. 1 in G major the opening subject is repeated in the exposition at the dominant with the theme in the cello; this is the way it appears in the tonic in the false reprise, and accordingly it does not have to be recapitulated in this form later. In this same movement there is a further example of the absence of a theme in the 'second group' from the recapitulation: again it is played in the tonic (major) in the development, but only at the end of the development, as it is used to re-establish the tonic and reintroduce the main theme.

These are the rare cases in the Haydn quartets of material exposed in the dominant and missing from the recapitulation, and at each point we have seen that some form of tonic recapitulation has been provided. This is not a rule of form but a rule of the classical aesthetic—a part of the age's, or of Haydn's, musical sensibility. The amount of material exposed in the *tonic* and omitted from the recapitulation could be as much or as little as the composer wished. In one earlier form of the sonata, of course, current around 1750, the recapitulation normally began with the second subject (did Chopin use this form because Warsaw, provincial by comparison with Vienna and Paris, preserved the older version?), and Haydn, Mozart, and Beethoven generally shortened the tonic material in the recapitulation, or omitted part of it and intensified what remained.

Remarkably, the quartets of Haydn mentioned in the past few pages are almost the only ones in which the recapitulations[1] are noticeably shorter than the developments. In most of the others (and there are more than eighty in all), the two sections are approximately equal in length, or else the recapitulations are longer, sometimes very much so. In the examples just given, we have seen that the development has taken over, even tonally, part of the role of the recapitulation. That is, we are dealing here not only with the rare exceptions of thematic material remaining unresolved after the return to the tonic, but also with the infrequent cases where the final area of stability is somewhat shorter than the area of dramatic tension called development with which the second part of a sonata begins. This firm area of final stability is an essential part of the classical style, as vital to it as the dramatic tension that precedes it; its proportions are vital, too, and they are demanded by the articulated nature of the form and required for the balance and symmetry central to the expression.

The emotional force of the classical style is clearly bound up with this contrast between dramatic tension and stability. In this respect, a fundamental

---

[1] I use 'recapitulation' here to mean everything that follows the final reintroduction of the tonic, including what is generally called a coda, if there is one.

change took place towards the middle of the century. In most Baroque music, a relatively low level of tension is created and sustained, with certain fluctuations, only to be resolved at the end of the piece: the music works cumulatively—it is rare that one moment is notably more dramatic than another. The middle section of a da capo aria, however, unlike the center of a sonata movement, is almost always less brilliant and intense, if more expressive, than the outside sections: it is often in a more relaxed key (the relative minor, for example) and scored for a reduced orchestra, sometimes for continuo alone. This lessening of tension and weight towards the center is characteristic of the High Baroque sectional work: Bach's Chaconne for unaccompanied violin, for example, or the great A minor Fugue for organ, where the central section omits the pedal—when the pedal re-enters in the tonic to accompany the return of the main subject, the effect of the recapitulation is not the classical one of resolution, but of a fresh injection of energy. The climax of a Baroque work is to be found in the increase of motion towards the final cadence: a stretto is one of its typical manifestations.

The climax of a classical work is closer to its center, and that is why the proportions of the final area of stability are so important. Temporal proportions are not like spatial ones: we cannot refer back and forth at a performance, and we must rely on memory, emotional and sensuous as well as intellectual, for comparison. The sense of balance in music is not arithmetical; a set of factors larger and more complex than a mere count of measures come into play. As we have seen, if a phrase is played twice, the effect is not like that of the repetition of an architectural motif on a façade; each playing has a different weight. In addition, the resolution of harmonic tension, and the symmetry of material (and of phrase) were not the only questions affecting classical proportions: the variety of large-scale rhythmic elements within a dramatic pattern demanded the resolution of rhythmic tension, a resolution that had to be combined with the need for keeping the piece moving until the end. With all of these forces interacting, the proportions of each classical work are individual, torn in every case between drama and symmetry. One requirement remains fixed: a long, firm, and unequivocally resolved section in the tonic at the end, dramatic if need be, but clearly reducing all the harmonic tensions of the work.

Common technical terms are often exasperating in their inappropriateness to particular cases, and none more so than 'recapitulation.' If we use it to mean a simple repeat of the exposition with the secondary material put into the tonic, then the whole idea must be thrown out as unclassical: this type of recapitulation is the exception rather than the rule in the mature works of Haydn, Mozart, and Beethoven. There is always a reinterpretation of the exposition after the return to the tonic. Even Mozart, who uses polythematic expositions with long melodies, and who can therefore afford a more literal repeat, often reinterprets considerably. An added short development section following the reappearance of the first theme is a common feature in his works, and by no means is it always used as a replacement for the exposition's modulation to the dominant. Haydn, who tends to the monothematic and whose motifs are shorter, needs even greater reinterpretation: the whole exposition has generally been conceived as a dramatic move to the dominant so that a literal repetition at the tonic would be nonsensical. It is understandable that Tovey, irritated by the academic use of 'recapitulation,' should write that 'the very idea utterly breaks down' in late Haydn, and that he 'used fully developed codas instead of recapitulations.' This is only to substitute one injudicious term for another in the hope of correcting an abuse: if 'coda' is to have any meaning for audible experience, then it is not possible to use the word for everything that comes in Haydn after the return to the tonic. Although Haydn's music is too dramatic in conception for an exact repeat transposed to the tonic, he never neglected the function of 'recapitulation' as 'resolution.' By this I mean not merely a firm re-establishment and concluding reassertion of the tonic—a 'coda' could indeed do that, as in Chopin's G minor Ballade—but a 'resolution' of material, that is, of the 'exposition' as well as of the 'development.' There is a moment in the exposition when the dominant appears established as a secondary pole, and everything that occurs after that moment invariably has its counterpart in a Haydn 'recapitulation,' rewritten, reinterpreted, rearranged in another order, perhaps. Haydn had understood that there are more complex forms of symmetry than naïve repetition. 'Recapitulation' may be a poor term, but we still need it to describe the resolution of the exposition, of which a literal repeat at the tonic is only a limiting form.

This insistence on stability at the beginning and, above all, at the end of each work allowed the classical style to create and integrate forms with a dramatic violence that the preceding Baroque style never attempted and that the Romantic style that followed preferred to leave unresolved, the musical tensions unreconciled. For this reason, a classical composer did not always need themes of any particular harmonic or melodic energy for a dramatic work: the drama is in the structure. A Baroque composition reveals its dramatic character in its first measure by the nature and shape of its melody, but nothing except the pianissimo of the opening two measures of the *Appassionata* would allow us to suspect the storm to be unleashed, and even the dissonance in the third measure adds only another hint. In particular, the most placid Baroque melody becomes more urgent as it proceeds; even when it rises and falls as in the first fugue of the *Well-Tempered Keyboard*:

the effect of its fall is annulled by the second voice's appearing to grow from the first and to continue its rise. Classical melodies for the most part are rounded off, resolved as they end—and the fact that they end at all sets them apart so clearly from many themes of the Baroque. The Baroque melody (like Baroque structure) is extensible, almost indefinitely so; none of the three great classical composers could have written a melody anywhere near as long as the one in the slow movement of Bach's *Italian Concerto*; such a melody seems to end only when compelled to, when a tonic cadence is at last unavoidable, while the climax is left largely undefined, the tension diffused rather than concentrated—this diffusion making it possible to sustain the melody at such length. Both the energy and the tension of a classical theme (often uniting a variety of rhythmic elements) are much more clearly concentrated, and this climax logically demanded a symmetrical resolution of the melody.[1] Historically, symmetry preceded drama. It was the symmetrical organization of the Rococo style[2] from the early eighteenth century on that made the dramatic concentration of the later classical style a reality. The balance and the stability provided a framework for the drama.

The classical recapitulation does not differ from the exposition for the sake of variety; the changes made are rarely ornamental, except in slow movements and in some rondos. Even variation form begins to be conceived dramatically. This is not to say that ornamentation did not exist, or that it was not occasionally added by performers (a subject best considered in relation to concertos and the operas, where a long virtuoso tradition was still influential). But the music itself implies that at no time in history had musicians less objection to hearing the same thing twice the same way. Beethoven, for example, insisted upon the repeat of the exposition of the *Eroica* Symphony (still often omitted in performance today) in spite of the abnormal length of the movement. The Baroque tradition of improvised ornamentation was certainly moribund, if not actually dead, except in opera; even there it is sometimes difficult to say whether the composers wanted the ornaments that the singers were certain to add, or whether they merely tolerated them because they were forced to. (About the appoggiaturas in recitatives, there is no question; the composers expected them, but recitatives are a special case, and have little to do with the other forms of the late eighteenth century.)

Haydn's symphonies before 1790 generally have recapitulations that follow the expositions more closely than do those of the quartets, although much of the tonic section or 'first group' is likely to be cut, and a good deal of development added. The melodies themselves reappear with less change than in the quartets, but this is not because Haydn was less concerned with variety and interest in his more public compositions, which would be astonishing. It is because the symphonies, written for larger audiences, are composed with

---

[1] The concentration of tension without clear resolution could be achieved only at the cost of weakening the firm tonal foundations of the style. It took many years for this to happen (with Schumann and Liszt), and much else in music had to change as well, the large rhythmic conceptions in particular.

[2] The Rococo in the other arts (painting and architectural decoration) tends to the asymmetrical, and no comparison is intended.

broader strokes, while the expositions of the quartets imply a degree of complex harmonic tension that cannot simply be transferred to the tonic at the end of the movement. The themes of the symphonies, less fluid than those of the quartets, neither need nor support so much alteration, and it is the structures of the symphonic recapitulations which tend to differ from the expositions, and in ways that are dramatic and rarely ornamental. Even these dramatic changes are generally implied by the preceding development. It is the nature of these changes that allowed Tovey to claim that, given a page of an unknown work by Haydn, Mozart, or Beethoven, one could tell whether it was from the beginning, middle, or end of a movement, something which could not be done with a page of Bach or Handel.

The classical style is a style of reinterpretation. One of its glories is its ability to give an entirely new significance to a phrase by placing it in another context. This can be done without rewriting, without reharmonizing, and without transposition: the simplest, wittiest, and most superficial form of this is an opening phrase which becomes a closing phrase as (one example from so many) in Haydn's Quartet op. 33 no. 5:

A more refined case of reinterpretation is a phrase in Mozart's Piano Sonata K. 283:

which in the exposition is a modulation to the dominant, and in the recapitulation is a return to the tonic. In the exposition it is preceded by

where the strong tonic cadence makes what follows sound like a movement away from the tonic. The second time, in the recapitulation, it is preceded by

where the indecisive feminine cadence and the strong subdominant coloring now imply a return to the tonic. With this feeling for tonal coloring, we have arrived at one of the most important distinctions between the style of the three great classical masters and the preceding generations.

Mozart is the first composer consistently to use the subdominant with a full sense of its relaxation of long-range harmonic tension; he generally introduces it as a regular feature of the recapitulation immediately after the re-entry of the tonic. Haydn's practice was similar, but less consistent, and Mozart's sensitivity to large tonal areas remained unequalled until Beethoven.[1] Johann Christian Bach and the other composers Mozart followed show none of his feeling for the balanced relations between the main and subordinate tonalities in a work, and have generally nothing more than a sense of the tonic-dominant effect. C. P. E. Bach's horizon is wider harmonically, but his practice is incoherent: he is more interested in local effects—he delights in harmonic shock, as did Haydn; but Haydn knew how to weld his effects together, and his most disparate harmonies are not only reconciled but even explained by what follows as well as implied by what precedes. (The first composer with a fine ear for the more complex relationships is probably Scarlatti; the logic of his movement from one tonal area to another is generally impeccable, but the style remains unclassical in that the areas follow one by one and neither blend nor interact.)

The classical sensitivity to the secondary tonalities and their relation to the

---

[1] Beethoven often uses the subdominant at the opening of the development section (*Waldstein* Sonata, Quartet op. 18 no. 1); the dimensions of his developments are considerably larger than those of Mozart or Haydn, and he needs the momentary retreat before starting to build the climax.

tonic can produce moments of astonishing poetry. The opening theme of the *Eroica* Symphony is essentially a horn-call, but the horn is never allowed to play it solo until the recapitulation is under way: at this point the orchestra modulates from the tonic (E flat) to the supertonic (F) and the horn enters *dolce* with the theme, followed by the flute playing it in D flat major. Much of the sweetness and delicacy, and the air of stillness, come from the new keys as well as from the orchestration: D flat major, the key of the flat leading-tone, is heard as a remote and exotic subdominant, and Beethoven, in an extension of Mozart's practice, is using it exactly where Mozart always uses the subdominant. Most remarkable is that the F major is also heard as a subdominant: it not only leads to D flat major but is introduced itself by a D♭, the unexplained dissonance in the main theme already played at the opening of the movement. Beethoven's practice here is different in range from Mozart's, but not different in kind, and Mozart was capable of effects of the same complexity. The emotional power is dependent on our hearing these phrases a few moments after the tonic has been re-established following the unprecedentedly long development section; as substitutes for the sub-dominant, the supertonic and the flatted leading-tone have a feeling of tran-quillity, while as remote keys coming at such a crucial moment they bring a tension to the heart of the stillness.

This complex, almost contradictory, emotion is another achievement of the style: it is not the kind of emotion that had changed since the early eighteenth century—Bach's sentiments were surely as complex as Beethoven's—but the expressive language. The affective character of a Baroque composition is much less complex; the emotion is sometimes deeply poignant, and it can attain an expansiveness that the classical style reaches with much greater difficulty, but it is generally more direct, and always more unified. The emotional complexity of the classical language is what makes the operas of Mozart possible. Even irony was possible in music now, as E. T. A. Hoffmann remarked of *Così fan tutte*. This complexity depends in large part on the classical harmonic relationships. The proto-classical composers—Rococo, mannerist, or early classical—increased the tension between tonic and domi-nant, and, for most of them, large-scale harmonic effects began and ended with that. It was Haydn and Mozart who took this tension, understood its implications throughout the entire area of harmony, the circle of fifths, and created a new language of the emotions.

The new emotional complexity entailed the use of contrasting themes and of themes in which a contrast was already built-in. The use of contrasting themes, however, has often been overemphasized: in a style essentially dramatic, and in which the different sections of a work are marked clearly enough for their proportions to be audible, it is only natural for melodies of differing character to occur. But the contrast of themes is not an end in itself, nor is the contrast of different sections of the movement. A fusion of dramatic effect with a profound sense of symmetry and proportion demands an evident sense of the degree of tension and stability in each part of the work and a clear articulation of these parts, but this can be, and sometimes is, achieved without any contrast of character, either in the various themes or in the different sections of a movement. The first movement of Haydn's *Military* Symphony has two themes of much the same character, both jolly, and both fairly square in rhythm (the second has only a more popular style, and rounds off the form). Nor do the tonic and dominant sections of the exposition of this movement differ much in character, as the dominant section begins with the first theme played exactly as it was at the beginning (enabling Haydn, in the recapitulation, to omit the entire section in the tonic). The sections are articulated by orchestration and not by contrasting themes, as each begins with woodwinds alone, then continues with strings alone (or, in the dominant section, antiphonal strings and winds), and finally allows the full orchestra with timpani to be heard—a pattern that has a remarkable clarity. (In the recapitulation the pattern is reordered both for dramatic surprise and increased stability, as the opening woodwind section is followed immediately by the theme in the full orchestra, and only then by the antiphonal strings and winds.) Contrasting themes are, of course, an aid in articulating a structure; but it is the clarity of outline that is essential, and not the contrast. As for the dramatic effect of contrasting themes, the power of the same theme played in different ways is as great, if not greater, and it is through the transformation of themes and not their contrast that the classical composer affects us most.

It is for this reason that we can dismiss as merely quaint the observation that in sonatas the first subject tends to be masculine and the second subject feminine. The very terminology of first and second subjects is already distressing enough, although it has become so ingrained that it is now difficult to excise it altogether; calling them 'first' and 'second groups,' however, does not help much in identifying themes, when the same melody may appear in both groups. (I should prefer to speak of tonic and dominant areas in an exposition, always remembering that the composer has often created a no-man's land between the two.) In any case, the masculine–feminine distinction amounts to nothing more than the fact that the very opening of a sonata is most often more direct and more forthright than the later material—reasonably and naturally so, as the opening must define the tonality and the tempo, and create the energy to move to the dominant. This can be done with a non-'masculine' sounding theme: there are numerous examples from all three classical composers, especially Mozart. It has even been said that Mozart's F major Piano Sonata K. 332 starts with what would be a second subject in another composer's hands: I should like to see a sonata with a second subject that so firmly and irrevocably, although gracefully, defines a tonality. In Beethoven's op. 31 no. 1, both subjects seem to me equally masculine; op. 31 no. 2 has hermaphrodite subjects; and as for op. 31 no. 3, the first subject is decidedly the more feminine. So much for the sex of themes.

Contrasting themes are, however, an inevitable, if not an invariable, part of the classical style. Perhaps even more significant are the themes of internal contrast, both rhythmic and dynamic. Before 1750, such contrast is almost always external—between voices, between different phrases, between separate orchestral choirs—and rarely internal, rarely within a melodic line. In classical melodies, however, internal contrast is not only frequent, but essential to the style, which relies so heavily upon dynamic inflection.

The need to reconcile dynamic contrast is as important and as typical as the contrast itself. This reconciliation, or mediation, takes many forms. One of the simpler ways to resolve a contrast of loud and soft is to follow it with a phrase that goes gradually from one to the other. In the opening phrases of the minuet from Mozart's Sonata K. 331:

the *crescendo* in measures 7 and 8 bridges the gap between the *forte* and the *piano* of the first four bars. It also prepares the more expansive and dissonantly expressive form of the downward scale motif; the *crescendo* is as much an element of continuity as of mediation. This reconciling of dynamic opposites is at the heart of the classical style, and is analogous to the mediation between two kinds of rhythm cited from Mozart's K. 271 on page 59. An entirely different way of resolving a dynamic contrast is shown in the *Jupiter* Symphony; the opening phrase

is played twenty measures later with a counterpoint

that binds the two halves together; even though both parts of the phrase are now played *piano*, their appearance in this form so soon after the opening is to turn opposition into unity.

This synthesis is, in small, the basic classical form. I do not want to turn Haydn, Mozart, and Beethoven into Hegelians, but the simplest way to summarize classical form is as the symmetrical resolution of opposing forces. If this seems so broad as to be a definition of artistic form in general, that is because the classical style has largely become the standard by which we judge the rest of music—hence its name. It is, indeed, clearly a style that is normative in aspiration as well as achievement. In the High Baroque, on the other hand, there is resolution indeed, but rarely symmetrical, and the opposing forces, rhythmic, dynamic, or tonal, are not very sharply defined. In the music of the generation of 1830, the symmetry is less marked or even evaded (except in academic forms, like the Romantic sonata), and a refusal of complete resolution is often part of the poetic effect. Not only, however, does the description fit the large classical form, but, as we have seen, the classical phrase as well: in no other style of music do the parts and the whole mirror each other with such clarity.

It is interesting to be able to document a composer's consciousness of this relation of large-scale form to phrase. Around 1793, Haydn wrote a Piano Trio in G minor for Prince Anton Esterházy which begins with a set of double variations. The second theme, in G major, is derived from the last phrase of the first theme, a procedure that Haydn often employs in sectional movements (particularly minuets with trios) to tie them together, and which Brahms copied faithfully. The second variation of this second theme is a complete sonata movement, and it is amusing to see how Haydn expands a 20-measure theme into a larger work[1].

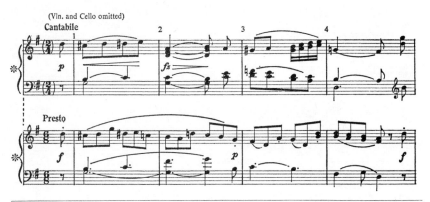

---

[1] I omit the violin and cello parts where they merely double the piano.

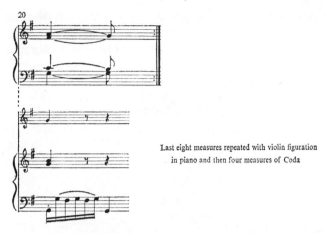

Last eight measures repeated with violin figuration
in piano and then four measures of Coda

From this witty expansion it can be seen that sonata form is an immense melody, an expanded classical phrase, articulated, with its harmonic climax three-quarters of the way through and a symmetrical resolution that rounds it off in careful balance with the opening.[1] Haydn not only elongates and repeats elements of the phrase, he also amusingly magnifies four little thirty-second notes in measure 6 into eight full measures of virtuoso passagework to become a full new closing theme. The *sforzando* in measure 18 of the melody, the loudest chord of the unexpanded form, becomes a pedal point over the dominant in the sonata, replacing the alternative movement of the bass of the exposition; the accented A♯ in measure 6 of the theme becomes a little two-measure sequence.

The points of his theme that Haydn expands most significantly are the central modulation and the end. This corresponds to the historical development of the sonata, and explains the gradual increase of importance during the century of the 'development section' and the 'coda.' An expansion of the end of a phrase is the articulated form of an older technique, and the foundation of the cadenza; it is essentially the High Baroque method of expansion, which works by extending and developing the last few notes of the phrase. But the expansion of the *center* of the phrase is peculiar to the classical style, and is the key to its sense of proportion.

Most revealing of all in this central expansion is the elaboration of the initial subdominant harmony at the beginning of measure 11 of the theme into a full-scale modulation to the subdominant in the sonata. Haydn does this simply by sitting on the fundamental note of the chord for two measures. No more delightful audible and visible proof could be offered that a modula-

---

[1] In about the same year that Haydn wrote this trio, the most impenetrable, although most acute, of contemporary theorists, H. C. Koch, published a method for expanding an 8-measure bourrée-phrase into a sonata exposition (see L. Ratner, 'Eighteenth-Century Theories of Musical Period Structure,' *Musical Quarterly*, October, 1956). His methods are more pedestrian than Haydn's and less up to date. There is no reason to think that Koch knew Haydn's trio, or that Haydn had read Koch's book.

tion is only the expansion of a chord, its transference to a higher level of the structure.

On this new level, the modulation naturally requires more elaborate resolution than a chord, and the succeeding measures of the little sonata form lead by way of a series of sequences back to the tonic area with a half-cadence on the dominant. The status of a subordinate tonality within any classical work is exactly the relation of its chord to the tonic triad.

No composer was a greater master of the expansion of the center of a phrase than Mozart, and in this lies part of the secret of his breadth in dramatic writing. The string quintets offer perhaps the most impressive examples of this central expansion:

The first measure offers a simple cadence, and the next five measures repeat it but expand the center into one of Mozart's most passionate and intense ideas. The intensity depends in part on the original cadence's presence as model: not only a resolution but a symmetry is implied, withheld, and then granted.

This passage from the slow movement of the G minor Quintet shows that the Neapolitan harmony (a minor second above the tonic) draws its pathos from being conceived as an expressive appoggiatura, again on the more powerful level of large structure. The B♮ of the cello in measure 62 appears in the place of an expected B♭, and it demands resolution (like the first violin's F♭): the anguish and the intensity come not only from withholding the resolution of the minor second, but from raising the cello astonishingly through B♯, C♯, and D♮ to E♭ before letting it sink back into the cadence. The relations of note to chord to modulation are preserved at separate and articulated levels throughout the classical style. It is not until the nineteenth century that these levels are confounded, and one arrives with Wagner at the possibility of phrases which are tonally dissonant, but at the level of the chord and not only of the larger form.

This relation of modulation, chord, and note appears with great simplicity on the first page of Beethoven's *Appassionata* Sonata (the tonalities are again a minor second apart, and the work makes the most striking use of the Neapolitan throughout):

The alternation of the keys of D flat major and C major is followed by the laconic motto of the single notes D♭-C in the left hand in measure 10, in which the appoggiatura which is the basis of the harmonic effect is presented thematically, its significance isolated and detached. The relation of individual note to modulation is further exemplified by the duration. The alternation of D flat major and C major takes almost four bars, the rhythmic motto based on the alternation of notes only two beats. The weight of harmonic significance is reflected in the length of the rhythmic units, and it would not be fanciful to consider the whole passage as an expression of the motto stated at its end.

This correspondence among the elements is, of course, characteristic of every style at its maturity: the extensible Baroque form is intimately related to the Baroque melody, which seems to generate itself, spin itself out to exhaustion; the rigid eight-measure phrase pattern of a good deal of Romantic music corresponds to the frequently obsessive use of one rhythm within the phrase. What is unique in the classical style is the clarity of the audible and symmetrical pattern given to the phrase and reflected in the structure as a whole. The audibility of the pattern depends on the way in which the motifs which make up the classical phrase are isolated and set in relief. The little four-note motto at the end of the example from the *Appassionata* Sonata is typical, and the thematic treatment of the four opening drum beats of Beethoven's Violin Concerto is perhaps the most spectacular instance of such high relief. It is fundamental to the compositional technique of Haydn and Mozart as well. The clarity of definition in their works requires just this separate and isolatable nature of the different parts of the phrase. What we call 'thematic development' today is generally the detaching of these separable parts and their arrangement into new groupings. This detachability, indeed, makes possible the high degree of characterization and contrast within the phrase itself.

The clarity of the phrase is not only reflected in the total structure but at the lowest level of detail as well. The most striking rhythmic consequence is the characterization and inflection of the individual beat. In the first half of the eighteenth century the beats are much more nearly equal in weight; the first, or downbeat, is somewhat heavier, and the last, or upbeat, is given importance by a slight lift; but the inequalities are never underscored. In a classical work, each beat in a measure has a distinctive weight of its own: in 4/4 time the upbeat has now a much greater weight than the second beat. It is understood that this new differentiation is not used relentlessly throughout a work of Haydn or Mozart but is present as a latent force, to be called upon as needed. A comparison of a minuet by Bach with one by Haydn will show what had happened in half a century:

In the Bach the beats are almost exactly equal in weight: even the downbeat is given only slightly greater importance by the melodic pattern. But the sequence of strong, weak, and moderately strong is evident in every measure of the Haydn. The examples are tendentiously chosen to prove a point, of course, but they are not atypical. No minuet of Bach attains the strong characterization of the beat so clear in Haydn, while no minuet of Haydn reduces the beats to something so close to undifferentiated pulsation.

The life and energy of classical rhythm depends on this distinctive character—the possible isolation, in fact—of each beat. The hierarchy of weight resulting from this individualization is given dynamic form in these dramatic and witty measures from the slow movement of Haydn's Quartet in E flat op. 33 no. 2:

The succession in measures 22 and 24 of *f*, *pp*, *p* is the classical gradation, and the brilliance of Haydn's dynamic conception comes from the fact that each successive stage is an echo of a beat and not a beat itself, so that the weight of the beat is felt in the silence and reflected in the sound.

The articulated movement between detail and total structure made possible that intimate relation between the material and the large-scale proportions of the 'sonata' style. For this reason, along with the ideal shape of the sonata, we must abandon any idea of second subjects, bridge passages, closing themes, and so on as determinants of the form. Not that they do not exist; they mostly do. But it is not abnormal or eccentric when Haydn dispenses with a bridge passage between the tonic and dominant in op. 33 no. 1; it would be eccentric only if the material demanded one.[1] The symmetry of sonata form which the nineteenth century tried to codify was in the eighteenth a free response to symmetrically ordered material, and the symmetry could take many forms, some of them surprisingly complex. That some form of symmetrical resolution was felt as essential to the sonata (and to almost everything else) is unquestionable: in the rare cases where the material implied either a markedly asymmetrical resolution, or a form (like that of the *Moonlight* Sonata) that is relatively unarticulated, the result was a Fantasy. But the structure of a Fantasy was no less strict than that of a sonata, equally bound by sensibility and not by formalities.

The kind of material impossible for the ordered resolution of the sonata may be seen in the opening of Mozart's C minor Fantasy K. 475:

It is wrong to think only of the opening theme as the material of a work, and this Fantasy is created out of a much larger conception, but even in these

---

[1] See discussion of this point on page 116.

few bars we can see the direction the music is taking. The phrases are as symmetrical as one could wish, but the abrupt, poignant changes of harmony destroy all the stability of the tonic, creating instead a mysteriously expressive atmosphere. With the stability of the tonic disappears any possibility of clear harmonic tension and thus any chance of clear resolution. We do indeed reach the dominant (G major) a dozen measures later

but it has become a remote foreign key. This music offers, within the classical style, no way of continuing without the introduction of new material, new tonalities, and new tempi. Even in this work, the final pages have a firm symmetry, with the tonic re-established dramatically and all the opening material repeated, but it is not possible to speak of symmetrical resolution of the first section. When the tension between tonic and dominant has been so weakened with no substitute offered, resolution loses its meaning. What the 'recapitulation' resolves is not the harmonic tensions of the opening, but the tensions set up by all the different tonalities in the course of the piece (which has six clearly distinct sections). The resolution is less like that of a sonata (except in its use of the same material) than of the final section of an operatic finale— although in no opera does Mozart ever weaken the tonic as he does at the opening of this work. This is not to say that the Fantasy is in any way unsuccessful; it is a magnificent piece, but for once we have a work that is truly abnormal by classical standards.

The unusual form of this work is explained by its purpose: it is not a separate piece but an introduction to a sonata and, brilliantly and tightly constructed as it is, it is intended to have something of the quality of an improvisation.[1] In K. 475, to give the effect of improvisation, the opening tonal

---

[1] The other C minor Fantasy by Mozart, K. 396, is quite different; it is not a Fantasy at all, but a slow sonata movement, unfinished, for piano with violin obbligato, although the idea of the obbligato was perhaps only introduced in the course of composition.

firmness so characteristic of the period is deliberately weakened, and only gradually returns as the piece continues, finishing with a massive establishment of the tonic just before the final section. The form has a very subtle balance:

    I Tonic: C minor with the tonic weakened by immediate modulation, going finally to B minor

    II Dominant of the dominant: D major (since G major has been weakened, its dominant is used in its place)

    III Continuous modulation

    IV Subdominant of the subdominant: B flat major (used as subdominant in place of F major, by analogy with section II)

    V Continuous modulation, affirmation of C minor

    VI Tonic: C minor throughout

The symmetry is clear, as is the relation of the form to the use of tonic, dominant, and subdominant in the sonata. The music has the sound of improvisation and all the advantages of organized form: only in this way could it give such an impression of unity while sounding so rhapsodic.

This relation of the individual detail to the large form even in apparently improvisational works, and the way the form is shaped freely in response to the smallest parts, give us the first style in musical history where the organization is completely audible and where the form is never externally imposed. In the Baroque period, the form of the chorale prelude is decidedly imposed from without; it is not just that the counterpoint that accompanies the *cantus firmus* is generally inspired by the first phrase of the chorale, but that even in some of the greatest works of Bach we have, not a total conception, but a successive modification to respond to the changing phrases of the chorale. This is a way of writing that suits the additive nature of Baroque style: a building that has been conceived little by little, modified as it proceeds, may give an impression of unity in the end, but it is a different kind of unity from one designed as a whole and as a single form, although the former may be no less beautiful. The order of the canons in Bach's *Goldberg* Variations is not an audible one; that is, the idea of arranging them as canon on the unison, on the second, third, fourth, and so on, is mathematical rather than musical: this order, too, has its own beauty and gives pleasure, but not a specifically musical pleasure. Much has been written about Bach's musical symbolism, perhaps too much, but there is no doubt that a number of details in his work—the startling rhythmic and harmonic change in the chorale-prelude *O Lamm Gottes*, for example—demand a knowledge of their symbolism, and cannot be understood strictly musically. This is never true of Mozart, except in the operas, and even there musical considerations predominate: Figaro's chromatic moan about his twisted ankle is both a final cadence in C for one section and a modulation to F for a new beginning; the chromaticism has a musical function completely independent of the words. But the distinction between *legato* and *staccato* in 'Et in unum Deum' from Bach's *B minor Mass* is there to illustrate the difference in identity of the Father and the Son: it sounds charming in itself but it has no further musical consequence in the piece. Even the Baroque fugue, the freest and most organic of the forms of that period, sometimes has a structure that is not determined in a fully audible fashion: the form of a *ricercar* fugue, for example, is not dependent on the sound of its theme but on its capacity for stretti. Each stretto can, of course, be heard, but it is only latent when the theme is first played; the *possibility* of stretto is a fact, but not an audible one. It has been pointed out that the opening theme of the slow movement of Beethoven's F minor Quartet op. 95 can be combined with the fugato that forms the middle section of the movement, but that Beethoven does not take advantage of this. A Baroque composer writing a fugue would probably have been unable to resist the temptation.

The structure of a classical composition is related to the way its themes *sound*, not to what might be done with them. This principle of audibility even extends to the cancrizans, or backward version of a melody: in the finale of the *Jupiter* Symphony, the cancrizans may not be immediately clear as such, but at first hearing it sounds evidently derived from the main theme; and the fugue theme of the *Hammerklavier* Sonata finale has a shape so individual that one is always aware, when a performance reaches the cancrizans, which part of the melody is being played backwards—perhaps with the minuet of Haydn's Symphony no. 47[1] the only cancrizans of which this is so. In the late eighteenth century all extramusical considerations, mathematical or symbolic, have become completely subordinate, and the whole effect, sensuous, intellectual, and passionate, arises from the music alone.

This is not to say that extramusical considerations play no role in the classical style, but they do not play a determining role. Even politics can enter into music. When Don Giovanni welcomes his masked guests with 'Viva la libertà,' the context does not specifically imply political liberty (or the opera would certainly have been banned at once). Coming after 'È aperto a tutti quanti' ('anyone is welcome'), the words have a meaning much closer to 'freedom from convention' than to 'political freedom.' However, this is to reckon without the music. Starting with a surprising C major (the last chord was E flat major), Mozart brings out the full orchestra with trumpets and drums *maestoso* in an exhilarating passage full of martial rhythm. In 1787, during the ferment that followed the American Revolution and preceded the French, an audience could hardly have failed to read a subversive meaning into a passage that may look fairly innocuous in the libretto, particularly

---

[1] Quoted on p. 152.

after hearing 'Viva la libertà' repeated a dozen times with full force by all the soloists, accompanied by fanfares from the orchestra. Even here, however, there is a purely musical reason for this passage. It is the central moment of the first act finale, and Mozart's finales are conceived as complete movements in spite of their separate numbers, and begin and end in the same tonality, in this case C major. Just a few minutes before the entrance of the masked guests, there is a change of scene, and the C major needs a massive restatement to hold the finale together.[1] The section can be interpreted in purely musical terms (which again is not to deny the importance of the extramusical significance).

This musical independence illuminates the originality of classical comedy. Even humor becomes possible in music without outside help; the music of the classical style could be genuinely funny, not merely jolly or good-natured. Truly musical jokes could be written. There are jokes in music previously, but they are based on non-musical allusions: the Quodlibet of the *Goldberg* Variations is only amusing if one knows the words of the combined folksongs; some of the popular atmosphere comes through, but without the words the effect is only one of grandiose good humor. The contrasts of dynamics and register in the 13th of the *Diabelli* Variations of Beethoven, however, are grotesquely funny by themselves with no outside reference:

[1] The finale then proceeds, in Mozart's usual fashion, to an intensification (for the attempted rape of Zerlina) by the dominant G major and a series of modulations, which is resolved by the subdominant and a final tonic section, a pattern harmonically close to sonata form.

as is the following passage at the end of Haydn's Quartet op. 33 no. 3; the tempo is *Presto*:

It was, indeed, for passages like this that Haydn was attacked as a 'buffoon' by his contemporaries.

The buffoonery of Haydn, Beethoven, and Mozart is only an exaggeration of an essential quality of the classical style. This style was, in its origins, basically a comic one. I do not mean that sentiments of the deepest and most tragic emotion could not be expressed by it, but the pacing of classical rhythm is the pacing of comic opera, its phrasing is the phrasing of dance music, and its large structures are these phrases dramatized. This relation between the classical and comic styles was remarked by Carl Philipp Emanuel Bach, who at the end of his life deplored the loss of the contrapuntal Baroque style, and added: 'I believe, with many intelligent men, that the present love for the comic accounts for this more than does anything else.'

If the taste for the comic in music grew in the second half of the eighteenth century, this was at least in part because the development of style had at last made a genuinely autonomous musical wit possible. The incongruous seen as exactly right, the out-of-place suddenly turning out to be just where it ought to be—this is an essential part of wit. The classical style, with its emphasis on reinterpretation, made a wealth of double meaning a part of every composition. Finally, the highest form of wit, the musical pun, came into being. In the finale of the D major Trio H. 7 by Haydn, the E♭ as a dominant of A flat major is turned as a joke into the D♯ which is the third of B major:[1]

---

[1] I do not wish to suggest that any distinction between D♯ and E♭ was made by the late eighteenth-century composers. The joke would still be there if the note remained E♭ and the key changed to C flat.

The sharp distinction between tonalities in the classical style gives this passage its wit, along with the pause and the insistent repetition. Clarity of articulation is essential to this kind of comedy. The contrast between the melodic and accompanying parts in classical style (replacing the Baroque autonomy of the individual parts and the use of figured bass) allows us the delicious moment in Haydn's *Clock* Symphony when the accompaniment is transposed into the upper register:

where the double meaning is made even more evident by giving the figure to the solo flute and bassoon.

The comic becomes not only the characteristic mood of a work but often, particularly with Haydn, an essential technique. In the delightful B flat major Quartet op. 33 no. 4, the modulation to the dominant is a joke:

If wit can take the form of a surprising change of nonsense into sense, a classical modulation gives a splendid formula: all we need, as here, is one moment when we are not sure what the meaning of a note is. Haydn sets up his joke by having the three little notes at the end of the phrase in bars 8–9 and 10–11 played in unison with no harmonies, and *piano*. Then the cadence, symmetrically repeated, seems to finish a section at the middle of bar 12—but the three notes occur inexplicably once more, still *piano*, still unharmonized, and played by the cello alone in its low register. It is not until the next chord that we understand why the little motif was left without harmonies: because the low D was to become the dominant of G minor, and thus to start the modulation to the dominant. Playing the three notes softly each time sets them apart, hides their true significance, and so contributes to the joke; indispensable, of course, is the irregularity of the phrase rhythm, particularly the last repetition of the little motif in the cello, and the tone of witty conversation that characterizes the thematic material. For a quick shift of context or a witty reinterpretation of a note, a dramatic and forceful modulation is also indispensable. In the Baroque style, the preference for continuity over articulation and the lack of clear-cut modulation leave wit little place except as a general tone or atmosphere in some very few works; the Romantic modulation, on the other hand, at times so heavily chromatic that the two keys blend into each other, and often much slower and more gradual, nullifies the effect of wit altogether, and we return, with Schumann, to something resembling the Baroque good humor and air of jollity. The civilized gaiety of the classical period, perhaps already somewhat coarsened, makes its last appearances in the Allegretto of Beethoven's Eighth Symphony, and in some of the movements of the last quartets. After that, wit was swamped by sentiment.

2

Structure and Ornament

The feeling for a closed, symmetrical structure, the central position of the most extreme tension, and the insistence upon an extended and complete resolution, together with a newly articulated and systematized tonality, produced a variety of forms, all with a right to be called 'sonata.' To distinguish them does not imply that they existed as norms or even as molds. They were only the result of musical forces and not to be identified with these forces themselves. For this reason, they should not be described too closely in the abstract, much less defined, or one would miss seeing how each of them could blend into the other, and how much freedom remained latent in these forms throughout the latter half of the eighteenth century.

1) FIRST-MOVEMENT[1] SONATA FORM falls into two sections, either of which may be repeated[2]: some symmetry between the two is essential but it is not very strictly defined. The movement begins by establishing a strict tempo and a tonic as frames of reference. The first section, or *exposition*, has two *events*, a movement or modulation to the dominant, and a final cadence on the dominant. Each of these events is characterized by an increase in rhythmic animation. Because of the harmonic tension, the music ʾn the dominant (or second group) generally moves harmonically faster than that in the tonic. These events are articulated by as many melodies as the composer sees fit to use. The second section also has two events, a return to the tonic, and a final cadence. Some form of symmetrical resolution (called *recapitulation*) of the harmonic tension is necessary: an important musical idea played anywhere except at the tonic is unresolved until it is so played. The return to the tonic is generally (but not always) clarified by playing the opening measures again, as they are most closely identified with the tonic. If the return to the tonic is long delayed to heighten its dramatic effect (by modulating to other keys or by sequential progressions at the dominant), then the work has an extensive *development section*. The breaking of periodic rhythm and the fragmentation of the melody serve to reinforce the harmonic movement of this development. The harmonic proportions are preserved by placing the return to the tonic or beginning of the recapitulation no later than three-quarters of the way through the movement. The most dramatic point is generally just before (or, more rarely, just after) the return.

---

[1] This form may, of course, be used for second movements or finales, but it is most commonly associated with the more complex first movement.
[2] The second half was scarcely ever repeated alone, although the finale of the *Appassionata* is an exception, and similar forms may be found in the Mozart operas.

2) If the return to the tonic is not delayed at all, so that there is a symmetrical resolution but no 'development,' then the form may be called SLOW-MOVEMENT SONATA FORM.

3) MINUET SONATA FORM is in two parts, but always in three phrases: phrases two and three belong together. The two parts are always repeated. The three-phrase shape may be expanded, but the proportions and the essential outline are always in evidence. The first phrase may end on the tonic or on the dominant. (Tovey sees a profound difference between these two possibilities, but Haydn, Mozart, and even Beethoven use both, and the two forms often produce minuets of exactly the same shape, size, and dramatic effect. The second form is naturally easier to expand, and became more frequent; it merges with first-movement form.) The second phrase often plays the double role of a development section and of a second group of an exposition, and the third phrase resolves or recapitulates. The minuet is generally part of a larger ternary *ABA* form, with a trio usually more relaxed in character.

4) FINALE SONATA FORM is more loosely organized and is conceived as resolving the tensions of the entire work. This looseness gives rise to a greater range of patterns than in any other movement. If a first-movement form returns to the opening theme in the tonic before the development section, then it is called a sonata-rondo. There is often a new theme at the subdominant towards the center of the movement, sometimes placed in the 'development section,' sometimes as a substitute for it. This new subdominant theme may be found in finales which are not rondos, like the last movement of Mozart's A major String Quartet. Both the return to the tonic before the development and the theme in the subdominant are reductions of tension and a loosening of formal structure. What is essential in this movement is a relative squareness and clarity of rhythm and phrasing.

These forms are arranged here in a progressively relaxed order, and the order itself parallels the interior pattern of tension and resolution within the individual forms. From this we can see that they are less to be viewed as pre-existent shapes to be followed than as the habitual working-out of unifying principles. The main principle is one of recapitulation through the resolution of previous tensions, harmonic and rhythmic, and the return of the thematic material is always in an aspect significantly different from its first appearance in the exposition.

There is a radical distinction between all these forms and the ternary form of the Baroque in any one of its guises—da capo aria, dance-form with trio—or its extensions—the early rondo, and the concerto grosso form. In all these variants of *ABA*, the initial *A* returns unaltered at the end—unaltered on paper, that is, as in practice the return was often considerably decorated by the performers.

The idea of the recapitulation as a dramatic reinterpretation of the exposition attacks the practice of decoration at its root: the structure itself now does the work of the improvised ornaments. The ornamentation of the repeat of the exposition becomes an actual embarrassment: it implies either that the material heard in a dramatically different form in the recapitulation will be less ornamented and inevitably less elaborate than the repeat of the exposition, or that the recapitulation must also be ornamented, which can only obscure and minimize the structural changes with their radically different expressive significance. This is why the three great classical composers added almost nothing to the art of ornamentation, whatever their interest in it may have been. Only with Rossini, Chopin, Paganini, Liszt, and Bellini did a skill and originality in decoration comparable to that of Bach and Couperin reappear at last. The practice of improvised ornamentation, however, did not die, although it was largely superfluous in the classical style. Performance always lags behind composition in its adaptation to new conditions. By the last quarter of the century, the most famous of the guides to performance, Türk's book on keyboard-playing, advises against any ornamentation in a piece 'where the reigning character is sad, serious, nobly simple, solemnly and exaltedly grand, proud, and the like.' This seems to leave only the merely pretty to be ornamented. Hardly a slow movement of Mozart's would not fall into one of the categories where ornament is to be shunned. We must wait for the Italian opera of the early nineteenth century for ornamentation to gain new vitality and to be more than a dead weight from an earlier style.

Nevertheless, several problems remain. They arise not from the music itself but from the complex relation of contemporary performance to a changing style. For example, there is no doubt that ornamentation can, and even should, be added to some passages in Mozart's concertos and arias. But how much, and where? Our guides are most unreliable. The ornamented versions published by well-meaning admirers of Mozart some years after his death are mostly vile. Hummel's versions are, of course, better than most—he was a pupil of Mozart as well as a fine musician—but they are impossibly rich. To use them would be to forget how musical taste can change in twenty-five years. Hummel belongs, in his musical outlook, to the age of Rossini, not to the age of Haydn and Mozart; the development of Beethoven who carried on the classical tradition against the current of his time must have been incomprehensible to him. Indeed, the whole tendency of the classical style is against the heavy ornamentation of the Baroque and mannerist styles, and it considerably purifies the lighter ornamentation of the Rococo. The music of Haydn after 1775 cannot be ornamented, and as for Beethoven, we know what he thought of musicians who added anything to his music from his explosion when Czerny did so, and his subsequent apology: 'You must pardon . . . a composer who would have preferred to hear his work exactly as he wrote it, no matter how beautifully you played in general.'

The principal document in favor of heavy ornamentation in Mozart's concertos is by no means as straightforward as is sometimes thought. In answer to a letter from his sister complaining of the bareness of a certain passage in the slow movement of the D major Concerto K. 451, Mozart sent her an ornamented variant. This is generally taken to imply that the custom of the time was to ornament all such passages whenever they occur. Nevertheless, the exchange of letters cuts both ways: it may also be interpreted as meaning that one never added ornamentation without asking the composer first, even if one were a close relative as well as an accomplished musician. The most cogent evidence we have for Mozart's attitude to improvised ornament unfortunately describes only the position he took on the matter when he was seven years old. In 1780, when he was twenty-five, his father wrote to him about a certain 'Herr Esser, whom we met in Mainz eighteen years ago, and whose playing you criticized by telling him that he played well, but that he added too many notes and that he ought to play music as it was written.' There is, moreover, no reason to think that Mozart changed his mind about this in later years.

Mozart stands apart from Haydn and Beethoven, however, because of his closeness to the operatic style, and the tradition of ornamentation in opera was very powerful. It is known that arias in Mozart's operas were sung with added ornaments during his lifetime. How much of this did he plan for, how much did he merely tolerate, and how much did he deplore? We do not know. The existence of two versions of some concert arias, unornamented and ornamented, both by Mozart himself, proves the relevance of ornamentation to Mozart's vocal style. But it may also indicate that if an aria was to be ornamented, Mozart preferred to write out the ornaments himself. It does not prove the unornamented version to have been inacceptable.

That Mozart was not averse to ornamentation, we know, too, from several other authentic variants. The slow movement of the Piano Sonata in F K. 332, and the eleventh variation of the finale of the Sonata in D K. 284 were both published in 1784 (by different publishers) with extra ornaments certainly added by Mozart himself. It is significant that both these pieces are marked Adagio. Mozart's Allegros can absorb ornamentation no better than Haydn's; the style had transformed them to a point where the technique of improvised ornament was irrelevant. It was still possible in a slow movement, however (although by no means as essential as in a work of the 1740s), while at certain points of a decorative form like a set of variations, it was indispensable. When, as in the A major Sonata for Piano K. 331, Mozart has not written out the repeats of the penultimate variation (traditionally an Adagio in a set of variations, and so marked here), one should add ornaments during performance, using the analogous place in K. 284 as a model; even here, discretion is necessary, as the melody of this variation is more complex than the one in K. 284, and less well adapted to a generous addition of ornaments.

It should be noted that the original manuscript of K. 284 already contains rich ornamentation and that the principal additions to the published version are directions for dynamics and phrasing. The following measures give a good idea of the additions:

from all of which we may safely conclude that dynamic contrast was beginning to replace decoration, and that Mozart added ornaments to those of his compositions which were already in an ornamental style. The operatic manner of the concerto, however, demanded a more decorative style from the soloist than from the orchestra. In the variation sets in the concertos, the heavier decoration for the piano has already been written out by the composer: this is even true of movements like the variation finale of the C minor Concerto K. 491, where the left hand was sketchily indicated and filled in later, while the decorated form of the melody for the soloist was written out from the very first.

Slow movements present a touchier problem than variation sets; tradition is less of a guide here, as Mozart was changing tradition more radically in this instance. It is even difficult to use the added ornaments of the slow movement of K. 332 as a model for later works: the original form of its melody is already full of decoration, and in the last years of his life Mozart was developing and refining melodic lines of deliberate simplicity. It is possible to add ornaments to 'Dove sono' in *Figaro* (although questionable whether there is any musical gain in doing so), but the music for the three boys in *Die Zauberflöte* cannot be ornamented at all without becoming nonsense. Nor can the duet between Pamina and Papageno, 'Bei Männern,' be decorated: Mozart has himself added the most sparing decoration for the second verse, making the melodic line more expressive in the most economical way; any further addition would only mean a loss. The music of Haydn and Mozart killed Rococo decoration, and how dead it was in Vienna can be seen in the music of Hummel, where it appears swollen and unsupported by the structure, insubstantial as a ghost. As for Beethoven's music, decoration is unthinkable: in all the vagaries of operatic production has anyone anywhere ever tried to decorate the canon in *Fidelio*?

Our knowledge of contemporary performance from descriptions, memoirs, and treatises can help here, but we must beware of letting it lead us blindly. I have never read a didactic book on contemporary performance which could be trusted very far: most so-called piano methods will appear wrong or irrelevant to any pianist. We all know how misleading almost all descriptions of performances are: the few that are relatively accurate will be almost indistinguishable in twenty years from the others. There is no reason to think that writing about music was any better in the eighteenth century than it is today. Almost any rule about eighteenth-century performance-practice will find its contemporary contradiction somewhere or other. Above all, when we remember how fast musical fashions change, we must beware of applying the ideas of 1750 to 1775 or to 1800.

At once the best and the worst evidence for improvised ornamentation are the written-out versions contemporary with the composer, or prepared shortly after his death. The best evidence, because they were actually performed; the worst, because they are, in most cases, abominably crude, and even when they are not, there is no reason to think the composer would have approved. Most performance is already bad enough without our being hamstrung by the habits of inferior eighteenth-century musicians and the aesthetic of the worst eighteenth-century taste. I sometimes wonder about the response, a century from now, to tapes or recordings of the music of today in which the tempi are misjudged, the ensemble is sloppy, and the rhythms have come out all wrong. Will this be taken as the true style of our time? Will the fact that a 5/8 section of one of the best-known works of a famous composer was generally omitted by an equally famous conductor because he had trouble beating it be understood in a hundred years as evidence of the composer's approval (his protest was, of course, private and unavailing)? Is there any reason to think that performance has deteriorated since the eighteenth century? One needs merely to remember how Mozart was forced to spoil *Don Giovanni* for the Vienna production or recall the première of Beethoven's Violin Concerto, at which the soloist fiddled a sonata of his own composition for one-stringed violin held upside down between Beethoven's first and second movements.

This leaves us, for the most part, basically with the musical text, but this in turn does not imply that literal treatment is desirable. Nothing disconcerts a composer more than an exact but lifeless performance of the notes. In the end, it is painful to think what little good erudition alone can do us. From Mozart's own description of *rubato*, for example, it is certain that he sometimes played with his hands rhythmically apart like Paderewski and Harold Bauer, but in the where, the how often, and the how far apart lies all the difference between music and nonsense. How tricky the problem is may be seen if we recall that Chopin is reported (correctly?) to have played with great freedom, taught his students with a metronome, and made a public scene when he heard Liszt play one of his mazurkas with too much liberty.

On the whole, if anything is to be added to a work of Mozart, we should consider in each case whether or not the manuscript is completely written-out and for whom. The E flat Concerto K. 271, written for Mlle. Jeunehomme, for example, is obviously complete down to the last notes of the cadenzas; the C minor K. 491, written for the composer himself, was hastily set down.

Cadenzas must *almost* always be provided at fermatas, and if other ornamentation is added at all, it should mostly be in the slow movements.

One rule often given today as in the eighteenth century is always to preserve the original shape of the melody. This admirable rule, however, brings the besetting problem of added ornamentation into clearer focus. In spite of contemporary theory, it is not a rule that anyone at the time would have subscribed to in practice. Not even Mozart. Throughout the eighteenth century, the preservation of the original melody's outline was a relatively minor consideration when ornaments were to be added. Much more important were the interest, grace, and expressive quality of the additions: if the original idea was buried or transformed, so much the worse for it. The ornamentation that Handel, Bach, and even Mozart wrote out often changed the original shape considerably. A few examples should suffice; here is a phrase of Handel, in its original, simple form and then as ornamented by the composer:

here is the first measure of the adagio variation of the Sonata K. 284, and Mozart's own writing-out of the repeat:

and here, finally, are the first and last appearances of the slow movement's melody in the Sonata in C minor K. 457:

Handel buries his melody; Mozart reshapes his for expressive effect.

When we listen to Mozart, are we interested in the music or in an authentic eighteenth-century performance? The two interests coincide only up to a certain point. The Caravaggios of San Luigi dei Francesi cannot be seen easily in the place where they are hung and for which they were painted; taken down and placed on exhibition recently they became really visible for the first time in centuries. The original ambiance is not always the most helpful one for seeing a work of art. Similarly, eighteenth-century practice, no matter how authentic, is of no use to us when it distracts from, and even renders inaudible, those qualities of Mozart's music that were most revolutionary and most personal; and it becomes intolerable when we are offered the worst traditions of the past as a model, as we often are.

Ornament must be related to style, and it is necessary to decorate only when the musical sense requires it. For this, each composer and each work must be reconsidered individually. A very brief cadenza must be inserted at fermatas like this one in the slow movement of the Concerto in C minor K. 491:

because the melodic outline makes no sense in the context of Mozart's style without a bridge. The appoggiaturas must be added to recitatives in operas because a cadence like the following:

fa - rà buo-na fi - gu–ra in que-sto lo -co

is (or should seem to be) ugly when we consider the nature of Mozart's melody and harmony (or that of any other eighteenth-century composer) outside the recitative, and also because we know that recitatives were written in a kind of shorthand conventionally filled out by the singer—melodic originality had no place in a *secco* recitative. Handel's solo melodies should be ornamented because they make more sense and sound better that way—

they are structures built for decoration, unlike his choruses—but if we find the original outlines beautiful, we should allow them to be audible through the decoration. The early sonatas of Haydn cry out for ornament, particularly when they are played on a harpsichord: it would be folly to add a note to the last ones, even in the repeats. A performance is not an archaeological dig. Paradoxically, in so far as the purpose of a performance of a Mozart concerto is reconstruction of eighteenth-century practice rather than pleasure or dramatic effect, just so far does it differ from an actual performance by Mozart.

There is, furthermore, little reason to provide what we imagine to be completely 'authentic' ornamentation on instruments which are radically 'inauthentic.' The sound of the modern piano, the modern bows of string instruments, the increased power of the woodwinds—all this changes the significance of ornamentation, which largely provided the possibility of expressive and dynamic emphasis. In the modern context it makes for a fussy effect. An entire string section attacking a trill in a Handel oratorio with an explosive vigor unimaginable on eighteenth-century instruments does not add to our better understanding of the music. Ornamentation in an opera or a concerto against the heavier sound and, above all, the more intense sonority of the modern orchestra has nothing like the significance it had in the late eighteenth century. The reproduction of eighteenth-century sonorities with modern instruments is, however, a disastrous solution. Music is as much idea and gesture as sonority. If a fortissimo on an eighteenth-century instrument produces mezzo piano by our standards, it is the violence and the drama that are important and not the actual volume of sound.

In all the arts, the taste for ornamentation changed radically in the last quarter of the eighteenth century. To take only one example, the infinitely repeating designs for fabrics used in the upholstery of chairs and sofas were gradually replaced by centralized compositions. For mural decoration the simple folds of hanging draperies were preferred to more elaborate systems. These tendencies are obviously reflected within the musical style of the period, with its centrally placed point of tension and its clarity of form.

Most important of all, the function of decoration became the exact contrary of what it had been. In Rococo interiors, the decoration was used to hide the structure, to cover over the joints, to enforce a supreme continuity. Neoclassical decoration, however, always much more sparing, was used to emphasize structure, to articulate it, and to sharpen the spectator's sense of it. The analogous change in the function of musical ornaments does not need a mystical correspondence of the arts to explain it. The solid body of aesthetic doctrine which condemned ornament as immoral dominated the second half of the century, and there were few pockets of resistance. To equate the practice of Mozart (and Haydn after 1780) with that of J. S. Bach or even C. P. E. Bach is to ignore one of the most sweeping revolutions of taste in history.

The musical ornamentation of the first half of the eighteenth century was an essential element in the achievement of continuity: the decoration not only covered the underlying musical structure but kept it always flowing. The High Baroque in music had a horror of the void, and the *agréments* fill what empty space there was.

The decoration of the classical style, on the other hand, articulates structure. The chief ornament retained from the Baroque is, significantly, the final cadential trill. Other ornaments are used more rarely, and they are almost always fully written out—necessarily so, as they have become *thematic*.[1] This development was carried by Beethoven as far as it could go. In his later music, the trill lost its decorative status: it is no longer an ornament but either an essential motif—as in the *Archduke* Trio or the fugal finale of the *Hammerklavier*—or a suspension of rhythm, a way of turning a long sustained note into an indistinct vibration which creates an intense and inward stillness. In the last works of Beethoven the notion of ornament often completely disappears, drowned in the substance of the work.

---

[1] See the purely thematic use of an *acciacatura* in Haydn's Quartet op. 33 no. 3 in C major, quoted on pp. 65–67.

Part III

HAYDN FROM 1770 TO THE DEATH OF MOZART

1

String Quartet

The musical scene in Europe during the third quarter of the eighteenth century, with its many conflicting national traditions, makes a cluttered impression today. In Italy, indeed, there was barely even a national style but rather several municipal ones, each with its own claims. The greater unity of the end of the century is not an illusion, or an historical scheme imposed by our own evaluation. Although some of the independent national styles—French grand opera, for instance—continued to exist and to develop in a direction not much affected by Viennese classicism, the supremacy of the Viennese style, or rather of Haydn and Mozart, is not just a modern judgment, but an historical fact, internationally acknowledged by 1790. As for Beethoven, in spite of difficulties in winning acceptance for his larger works, by 1815 even most of those musicians who did not like his music would have admitted that he was the greatest living composer: some of the admiration he won may have been unwilling, but it was uncontested (except of course, by the lunatic fringe that is the normal burden of the taste and criticism of any age).

It would be romantic to think of Haydn as arriving like Malherbe to bring order and logic into a 'mannerist' chaos and irrationality. To begin with, Haydn was as interested as anyone else in the disruptive and shocking effects of the music of the 1760s: he retained a taste for such effects to the end of his life, remaining a master of the surprise modulation, the dramatic silence, the asymmetrical phrase; and he added to this an aptitude for the facetious that no other composer enjoyed. The proportions of his works became 'classical,' the harmonic vision more logical, but he never abandoned his earlier 'manner': his latest works, in fact, are at times even more shocking than the earlier ones. His eccentricity lost none of its power, but it was integrated into a conception of musical form larger and more coherent than any other composer of the 1760s had imagined.

The qualities of Haydn's music that we often find most astonishing today are oddly his least personal: daring juxtaposition of remote keys, abrupt use of silence, irregular phrasing—all this was a legacy from the music of the 1750s and 1760s. Every one of these traits can be paralleled, often more startlingly if less coherently, in the work of other composers, Carl Philipp Emanuel Bach in particular. In Haydn's last Piano Sonata in E flat major, the slow movement is in E major, and the surprise of the distant new tonality is much admired; Tovey has pointed out that C. P. E. Bach in his D major

111

Symphony also wrote a slow movement in the flat supertonic, but, for once more timid than Haydn, conciliatingly placed a modulating coda after the first movement by way of explanation. But a B minor Sonata by C. P. E. Bach, published in 1779, has a slow movement in G minor, an even more startling relationship than the Neapolitan tonic-supertonic, and this time there is no transition to mitigate the effect, although the end of the movement modulates back to B minor. (The strange sound of the G minor second movement is enhanced by Bach's use of F sharp minor, and not D major, as the secondary key, or 'dominant,' of the first movement.)

Next to Carl Philipp Emanuel Bach, Haydn appears like a cautious, sober composer: his irregularities of phrase and modulation are almost tame compared to those of the elder man. What is unprecedented, however, is the synthesis that Haydn gradually developed, in the late 1760s and the early 70s, out of dramatic irregularity and large-scale symmetry. Until then, the symmetry of his forms had been exterior, and sometimes even perfunctory: the dramatic effects either broke the structures, or depended upon a very loose organization for their existence. Haydn developed a style in which the most dramatic effects were essential to the form—that is, justified the form and were justified (prepared and resolved) by it. Haydn's classicism tempered his ferocity, but in no way curbed or tamed his irregularities. It was the tradition of eccentricity that protected him against the insipidity of the 'Rococo' or 'galant' mode. Mozart, of a generation younger than Haydn's, was raised in the latter style at a time when the late Baroque manner of C. P. E. Bach was itself already somewhat out of fashion. He therefore had to develop his own taste for dramatic discontinuity and asymmetry, mostly from within himself but partly inspired by his contact with the music of Johann Sebastian Bach.

The greatness of Haydn's synthesis may perhaps be estimated if we compare the way he and C. P. E. Bach treated an effect deliberately outrageous to an eighteenth-century ear: beginning a piece in the wrong key. It would be fairest to take works written close to each other in time. Of the sonatas published in 1779 by C. P. E. Bach, no. 5 in F major begins:

in which the strange C minor opening and the sequence it initiates continue to disturb the tonal stability as far as their echoes in the sixth and seventh measures. The last movement of Haydn's Symphony no. 62 in D major, written around the same time, opens in a fashion at once more troubling and more stable:

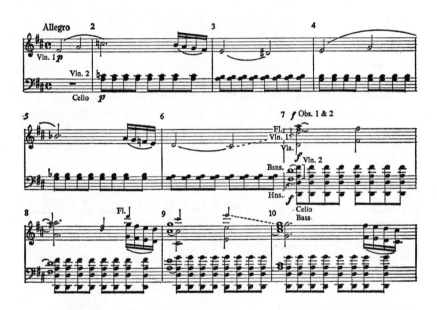

more troubling because the first two measures mysteriously define no definite tonality at all—the 'wrong' key, E minor, is implied clearly only in measure 3, while C. P. E. Bach defines his false key at once; more stable because Haydn's sequence moves simply and logically into the D major tonic, so that the real tonality is a consequence of the false opening, and is established merely by continuing the sequence thematically. Haydn's opening is, of course, additionally stable in that it begins a finale, and we have the D major still in our ears from the previous movements (all, unusually, in the tonic): this means that the surprise is greater in C. P. E. Bach when the real tonality appears, but it also enhances the mystery of Haydn's opening. C. P. E. Bach certainly comprehends the larger harmonic consequences of his ideas (as we have seen, his 'false' opening continues to color the movement after the tonic is established), but Haydn's scheme is on a wider scale to begin with. It is also capable of greater elaboration, as at the recapitulation:

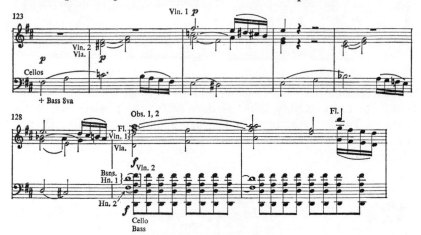

where the added contrapuntal voices enrich the effect.

One further comparison of 'false' tonal openings will show Haydn's logic even more clearly, the two examples coming again from the same period as those previously quoted. The 1779 Sonata no. 3 in B minor of C. P. E. Bach, the one with the slow movement in the remote key of G minor, has an opening which implies D major for two measures:

The end of the first measure, with its G♯, suggests that something is wrong, and B minor soon arrives. The following modulation to F sharp minor also has several surprises, the most conspicuous being the sudden turn to G major, emphasized by the *forte* and the startlingly heavy chord. Thus the 'false' opening is once again not without its consequences, and perhaps it even makes the G minor slow movement more plausible, just as Haydn prepares the E major movement of the E flat major Sonata by an emphasis in the first movement on the remote key to come. C. P. E. Bach's most subtle touch here is that the opening, while apparently in D major, hides the B minor triad of the real tonic in its first three notes. By Haydn's standards, or even by J. S. Bach's, this work is not completely coherent; yet it is a pity not to accept the standards that it lays down for itself. Even so, resistance is almost inevitable, because the style implied by these standards is a little thin even at its most dramatic, and small-scale even when it achieves an effect of brilliance. C. P. E. Bach's grandeur lacks breadth just as his passion lacked wit.

Two years after this sonata was published, Haydn wrote the Quartets op. 33, of which the first also pretends to begin in D major and quickly turns to B minor.[1] But the logic is more rigorous, the dramatic force far more compelling:

---

[1] Tovey thought that Haydn got the idea of the quartet from the Bach sonata, but this seems unlikely: the works are too different in procedure, and the idea of a false beginning was not uncommon.

A♮, the one note in D major to clash with B minor, appears innocently in the melody in the second measure, but the accompaniment, which had already introduced the A♮, now contradicts with an A♯ two beats later. Then Haydn seizes on this as a pivot to establish B minor, the expressive detail and the fundamental harmonic structure becoming identical here: in measures 3, 4, 7, and 8 he plays the A♯ and the A♮ together again and again, along with a *crescendo* and the rising line in the first violin. Although we are now fully in B minor, resolution is withheld until the eleventh measure, with the appearance of a new but related theme. The effect is at once broader and more concise than in C. P. E. Bach, more logical and yet no less strange: the only way in which Haydn's new 'classicism' could be said to temper oddity, to rein in eccentricity, was by avoiding the root position of the D major chord in the first two measures. The change to B minor seems, therefore, not a modulation, as in Bach, but a reinterpretation, a new clarity. In return, he can dispense with a modulation when he goes to the relative major as a dominant; he merely reharmonizes the opening with a D major chord, in root position for the first time:

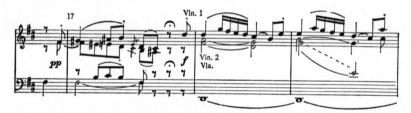

sweeping away all unnecessary transitions.

This opening page just cited is a manifesto. Haydn's claim that the Quartets op. 33 were written 'in an entirely new and special style' has sometimes been discounted as mere sales talk, but his last series of Quartets, op. 20, written almost ten years before, had circulated widely and was well known: he must therefore have thought that his claim had some chance of seeming plausible. In point of fact, this page—the beginning of the first quartet of the series, the first thing a contemporary quartet player would have seen when he bought his copy—represents a revolution in style. The relation between principal voice and accompanying voices is transformed before our eyes. In measure 3, the melody is given to the cello and the other instruments take up the little accompanying figure. In measure 4, this accompanying figure has become the principal voice—it now carries the melody. No one can say just at what point in measures 3 and 4 the violin must be judged the principal melodic voice, and where the cello shifts to a subordinate position, as the passage is not divisible. All that one knows is that the violin starts measure 3 as accompaniment and ends measure 4 as melody.

This is the true invention of classical counterpoint. It does not in any way represent a revival of Baroque technique, where the ideal (never, of course, the reality) was equality and independence of the voices. (J. S. Bach's admirers boasted that he could print keyboard works like the six-voice ricercar from the *Musical Offering* in full score.) Classical counterpoint generally abandons even the pretense of equality. The opening page of this quartet, for example, affirms the distinction between melody and accompaniment. But it then transforms one into the other.

No doubt there are precedents for any revolution, and it would not be surprising if one turned up for this. But I do not yet know an earlier instance of an accompaniment figure changing imperceptibly and without a break into the principal melodic voice.[1] If one should be found, the Quartets op. 33 would remain the first application of this principle—i.e., the accompaniment conceived at once as thematic and as subordinate—on any scale and with any consistency. In this way the texture of the string quartet is incomparably enriched without disturbing the late eighteenth-century hierarchical scheme of melody and accompaniment. It meant, of course, that the thematic elements in Haydn often became very short since they were to be used as accompanying figures. In compensation the new-found power was considerable, as can be seen in this B minor Quartet from what happens to measures 5 and 6 when they reappear in the recapitulation:

---

[1] In Haydn's Quartet op. 20 no. 2 in C major, an accompanying cello figure in measures 16 and 17 becomes melodic in measure 19, but only on being transferred to the violin. There are, of course, many previous examples, generally witty, of accompanying figures

where the little two-note accompaniment now has the force of an explosion. This is one example of Haydn's placing the true climax of the work not just before, but just after the beginning of the recapitulation.

There are other changes of equal importance in the style of op. 33. Transitional figures and phrases are almost completely eliminated. Earlier, in op. 20, to get from one phrase to another, Haydn had had to write:

where the cello figure in measure 4 has a purely transitional function, and is never needed except in this place. Ten years later, Haydn is more economical. The end of each phrase implies what is coming, generates it. New themes (or new versions of old ones) enter without transition: they do not need to be introduced, they are already implicit. This is partly because the phrasing has become more systematic. For those who love the passionate irregularity of the phrasing in earlier Haydn, no doubt this means a loss. There is, however, a gain: the more intimate relation between the larger structure and the small detail that starts with op. 33 makes the slightest irregularity more telling —its consequences are more considerable, and less localized. The most insignificant elements achieve a sudden power, as with the expressive meaning given to the distinction between the staccato and legato in the twelfth measure of the opening of op. 33 no. 1 quoted above. Some of this new power comes

used melodically, but then they make no pretense at any point of being accompaniments; and many Baroque accompaniments are thematically derived but lack classical subordination.

from the thematic relationships, but most important and original is the sense of pace that comes from the greater concision and regularity of the phrase.

Where did this new feeling for pace come from, and what had Haydn been doing for a decade since his last set of quartets? The nickname of the Quartets op. 33, *Gli Scherzi*, hints at Haydn's source of new strength. Between 1772, when the *Sun* Quartets op. 20 were published, and 1781, most of Haydn's output consisted of comic operas written for the court at Esterházy. Even a considerable part of his symphonic works then consisted of arrangements from his comic operas.[1] The Quartets op. 33 are called *Gli Scherzi* because they replace the traditional minuet with a scherzo; the change is largely one of name, Haydn's minuets having frequently had a jocose enough character in the past, but the new title is significant. The quarters are informed throughout by the pacing of comic opera. They are informed, too, by the comic spirit, but that is nothing new for Haydn. The Quartets op. 20 have moments of pure fun that equal anything Haydn was to compose later. The *Scherzi* Quartets are, indeed, generally comic in style, but this has, I think, been exaggerated. The fugal finale is absent here, but Haydn for the moment feels no need to buttress the originality of his thought with the complexities of an older style. Many of the movements are as serious as any in the previous set of quartets. (Tovey finds only wit in the false tonal opening of op. 33 no. 1, and feels that it is a device that Brahms elevated into the pathetic with the Clarinet Quintet; on the contrary, it seems to me that if the procedure in Haydn is wit, the intent is deadly earnest, the effect as pathetic as in Brahms, and more powerful if less nostalgic.) But the *Scherzi* Quartets have the rhythmic technique that comes from the experience of writing comic opera: a rapid action demanded a regularity of phrasing in order to be intelligible, and the music needed a tight continuity articulated logically to keep time with what happened on the stage. What Haydn had learned in ten years, what these new quartets show, is, above all, dramatic clarity. Expressive intensity had previously caused Haydn's rhythm to clot, and rich, intricate phrases had been followed all too often by a disappointingly loose cadence. With the *Scherzi* Quartets, he was able to construct a framework in which the intensity and the significance of the material could expand and contract freely and still be supported by the basic movement. They are, above all, lucid.

Haydn was not a successful writer of opera, comic or serious; his musical thought was too small-scale—or, if one prefers a gentler word, too concentrated. But he learned from comic opera, not freedom of form—he had never needed to be taught that—but freedom in the service of dramatic significance. When the words in a libretto denied his musical ideas their implied development and balance, he invented new ways to restore both. In his operas, too, we can see the strengthening of his sense of the dynamic force of his material.

---

[1] Starting in 1776, the number of operatic productions at Esterházy considerably increased.

Haydn from 1770 to the Death of Mozart

This sense that the movement, the development, and the dramatic course of a work all can be found latent in the material, that the material can be made to release its charged force so that the music no longer unfolds, as in the Baroque, but is literally impelled from within—this sense was Haydn's greatest contribution to the history of music. We may love him for many other things, but this new conception of musical art changed all that followed it. It was for this reason that Haydn did not tame his eccentricity or his coarse humor, but used them, no longer self-indulgently, but with respect for the integrity of each individual work. He understood the possibilities of conflict in musical material within the tonal system, and the way it could be used to generate energy and to create drama. This accounts for the extraordinary variety of his forms: his methods changed with the material.

By 'material,' I mean largely the relationships implied at the opening of each piece; Haydn had not yet arrived at Beethoven's conception of a musical idea unfolding gradually, let alone at Mozart's larger vision of tonal mass which in some ways surpassed even Beethoven's. Haydn's fundamental ideas are terse, and stated almost at once, and they give an immediate impression of latent energy that Mozart rarely looked for. They express an immediate conflict, and the full play and resolution of the conflict is the work: it is Haydn's view of 'sonata form.' The freedom of this form is no longer just the exercise of a whimsical imagination in a loosely organized scheme, as in some of the great works of the 1760s, but the free play of an imaginative logic.

The two principal sources of musical energy are dissonance and sequence— the first because it demands resolution, the second because it implies continuation. The classical style immeasurably increased the power of dissonance, raising it from an unresolved interval to an unresolved chord and then to an unresolved key. The 'false' tonal opening of Haydn's B minor Quartet op. 33 no. 1 is a dissonant *tonality*, for example, and the movement resolves it in two ways, first by treating it as the dominant or secondary key (temporarily making a tonic of it, which is a half-resolution), and then by expanding this in the 'development' and resolving everything in a recapitulation which—except for two measures at the opening—insists dramatically on the tonic. One important aspect of Haydn's genius lay in his sense of the energy latent in his material (or, to put it another way, in his invention of material that gave him the requisite energy): so, in the B minor Quartet, he at once plays over and over (six times in measures 3 to 8) the painful dissonance of A♮–A♯ (quoted above, page 115).

Haydn's invention cannot be given full justice without going into most of what he wrote, but some idea can be given of the variety and logic with which he treated the sonata style. The first movement of the Quartet in B flat major op. 50 no. 1 is built from almost nothing at all: a repeated note in the cello and a six-note figure in the violin. Everything in the exposition is restricted to these two small elements:

There are two measures of one note softly repeated by the cello (motif *a*), a tonic pedal. This is a charming joke: op. 50 no. 1 is the first of the quartets written for the King of Prussia, who was a cellist. Accordingly the set opens with the cello all by itself, playing a motif hardly taxing to the royal virtuosity—a solo on one note. The six-note figure, which I call (*b*), is used in sequence in measures 3–8, with its rhythm and accent delightfully transformed halfway up. The sequence, rising by thirds, is then balanced by a vigorous descent, which starts with (*b*) in measure 9 and continues in a scale, stopping on the way to emphasize the E♭–D which are the outer shape of (*b*) in its first appearance, harmonized, at the *sforzando* climax in measure 10, on G minor, a harmony that prepares the later movement away from the tonic. (The F♯ in measure 9 is the first chromatic alteration in the movement and it will be emphasized and finally used in measure 28 to begin the modulation to the dominant.) In measures 12–27, (*b*) is used with expressively altered harmonies to form a cadence, the final cadential figure four times repeated (measures 20, 24, 25, 26), while the pedal (*a*) is gradually transferred upward with amusing effect: it is a pun, as an ostinato that is typically bass in character is raised to the alto and then to the soprano voice.

The gradual increase in harmonic intensity can be seen by comparing measures 3–4, 9–10, 14–16, and 28. At measure 28, the F♯ that has appeared so prominently is made more striking by being presented as the bass of an augmented triad. Its new form starts a downward sequence, ending on a C major triad (the supertonic, or dominant of the dominant). The motif (*b*) has still the same shape at measure 35, but develops a unified triplet rhythm as at measure 7: the sequences now all move downward and the rhythm has naturally become more animated. In measures 33–40 (and 45–46 and 51–53), (*a*) is no longer a tonic, but a dominant pedal (at the dominant), which gives it, of course, greater energy. The first cadence at measures 47–50 again recalls measures 9–10, and is an augmentation of (*b*). New forms are found for (*b*) (measures 50–54), its shape twisted but still audibly derived from its original statement, until a second cadence at measures 55–56. At 56, (*a*) becomes a tonic pedal again (at the dominant), and still another form is found for (*b*); the final F major cadence at measures 59–60 is a more decisive version of the B flat cadence at measures 11 and 12.

One could say that in this exposition Haydn treats the six-note figure (*b*) as a row, except that his procedure has absolutely nothing to do with serial technique. The way its shape is twisted, while remaining always recognizable, shows us that Haydn may be said to work topologically—his central idea remaining invariant even when its shape is deformed—while a serialist works geometrically. More to the point, however, is that (*b*) alone is not the source of the piece, but rather the tension between (*b*) and the calm one-note ostinato (*a*). The fixed, unmoving sound of that one repeated note allows (*b*) to be set up against it as a series of sequences, from which all the rhythmic animation of the work comes. In fact, the ostinato (*a*) by itself largely explains much of the shape of the piece—in particular, why Haydn does not, as he generally does, leave the tonic as soon as he can, but stays without moving from it for a considerable space, even closing strongly on the tonic in measure 27. Neither (*a*) nor (*b*) alone, however, is sufficient, but from the opposition between them and from their shape Haydn derives his larger structure. There are no tunes, few rhythmic surprises, fewer dramatic harmonies. Yet it is fascinating and witty music, in which Haydn, intent on dazzling us with his technique, makes splendid bricks with hardly any straw at all.

Haydn reserves all his harmonic surprises for the development, which begins by reinterpreting the outer shape of (*b*) (E♭–D):

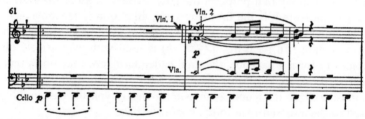

and this falling second unifies the movement, marking (as it did in the exposition) the points of structural importance.[1] The recapitulation enters without warning in the middle of a phrase:

so that the precise moment of the return to the tonic is almost unnoticed. The recapitulation rephrases the exposition, moving to the stabilizing subdominant, but with greater rhythmic animation and an exhilarating brilliance. One final stroke is reserved for the very end of the movement where, along with the final appearance of the falling second (E♭–D), the rhythm of (*a*) is quietly tripled:

---

[1] It insistently appears to shape each climax of the recapitulation (mm. 114–115, 121, 133–138, 145) as well as at the beginning and end of this section. The development section from measures 87 to 102 is a large-scale movement from E♭ to D.

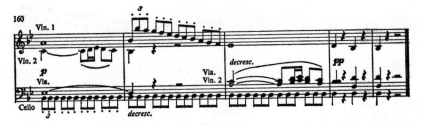

If we ask why the two notes E♭–D play such a large role, we must look back to their first appearance at the beginning where the E♭ enters softly and magically after the mysterious one-note ostinato in the cello: it is the melodic note of the first chord, a sweetly dissonant harmony and an unforgettable opening. The E♭ is also present in every dissonant chord for the first fifteen measures. The entrance, marked *dolce*, and the repetition of the pattern make this not a hidden relationship—a recondite compositional element—but an immediate audible experience, far easier to hear than to see on a page. The most important musical relationships in Haydn are never theoretical, but those which immediately strike the unprejudiced ear as significant, as the extraordinary hushed chord at the opening of this quartet does. 'Unprejudiced ear' is perhaps a misleading expression; we not only need to recapture an innocence of nineteenth- and twentieth-century developments, but we also need the prejudices of the eighteenth century. The opening ostinato pedal, the strange, soft chord, and the little six-note figure—the significance of these in the language of eighteenth-century tonality give Haydn all he needs: his imaginative understanding of the dynamic impulse they contain shapes the form the material itself seems to create.

This movement, with its obsessive use of one six-note figure, may seem atypical (although there are many such pieces in Haydn, whose material could be even more laconic). When the material is more complex, however, Haydn's procedure remains the same; an entirely different shape results, of course, as the relation to the material is central to his method. The tensions implied at the opening determine the course of the work. The exposition of the D major Quartet op. 50 no. 6 only appears so different a way of writing a sonata from op. 50 no. 1 because the musical material is so radically different:

Here, wit is omnipotent. The opening phrase is a final cadence. No tonic is defined by the first measure; we start on an unexplained, unharmonized, and therefore ambiguous E. If a dissonance is a note that requires resolution, then the E, standing by itself, is dissonant although we are only aware of its dissonance after it has disappeared; surprise will, however, keep it ringing in our ears long enough to realize that we have been fooled. The line then descends to the E below, and we resolve it with the cadence II–V–I. The *diminuendo* is the wittiest stroke of all and the tonic chord, when it arrives, does so unassumingly. The good humor of this opening is boundless.

In the most straightforward terms, we have been given an E in place of a D (or at least in place of an A or an F♯: almost all the pieces written at that time start with a note of the tonic triad, and the few exceptions at least do not puzzle us for a full measure with a mysteriously unexplained note). With the imaginative logic that he had both invented and tempered with experience, Haydn proceeds to exploit this contradiction between the D we ought to have had and the E that we were given instead. From measures 5 to 15, he continually sounds the E dissonantly against a D, more and more insistently. Meanwhile, the rhythm of the opening measure ♩ ♫♫, which we may call (*a*), appears in varied guises throughout. The tonic cadence at measure 16 closes the first period.

This dissonant E is, of course, the dominant of the dominant: its very nature implies the traditional first modulation almost by definition. Accordingly in measure 18, E is established as the climax of a stretto using (*a*); and then in measure 23, after decorated forms of (*a*), it is established as the bass. It is interesting to note the octave transpositions, and to see at how many levels the E is made prominent. The note now has such force that it no longer demands resolution, but can itself be used to resolve. To bring out this force, an F♮ is set up against it with a *sforzando* repeated four times under (*a*) in measures 26–29, an F♮ that also serves to prepare the splendid surprise cadence on an F major chord *subito piano* at measure 38. This F is now prolonged for six measures (measures 39–44) with all the orchestral power Haydn's string quartet can manage, using the opening phrase (*a*): measures 38 to 47 are essentially an inner expansion—a withholding of the cadence at measure 37. A new theme, square and decisive, is finally introduced in measure 48 to round off the form. To appreciate the full mastery of this exposition, we must play it with the repeat. When the opening phrase returns it has an entirely different sense: it is now a modulation from the dominant back to the tonic.

The difference between the expositions of these two quartets does not imply freedom or variety in the usual sense, but comes from a new conception of the demands of the material, the central idea. A long and completely separate tonic section in the B flat Quartet above arises from the opening tonic pedal, while the uninterrupted flow of the D major Quartet's exposition is in answer to the tension at the beginning which immediately directs the music towards the dominant of the dominant. It should be noted that, because of this impulsion, there is no cadence on the dominant until almost the end of the exposition: again, this is not a whimsical evasion of normal practice, but a sensitivity to musical forces. That is why the F major section (measures 38–45) is both so astonishing and so logical. (It is, naturally, not really in F major; these ten measures act on the E as an appoggiatura raised to a higher power.) In both these works, as in almost all of Haydn from 1780 on, the most eccentric musical ideas (and both works are astonishing) are purged of mannerism by an understanding and a display of their full musical significance. There are no plums or (to mix a metaphor) purple passages in this style, as there are in the great works of the 1760s.

To speak of any of Haydn's structures without reference to their material is nonsense. Any discussion of second themes, bridge passages, concluding themes, range of modulation, relations between themes—all this is empty if it does not refer back to the particular piece, to its character, its typical sound, its motifs. Haydn was the most playful of composers, but his frivolity and his whimsicality never consisted of empty structural variants. After 1770 or so, his recapitulations are only 'irregular' when the expositions demanded an irregular resolution, his modulations surprising when the logic of their surprise was already implicit in what preceded them.

Briefly, Haydn is interested in the directional power of his material, or, what is much the same thing, its dramatic possibilities. He found ways of making us hear the dynamic force implicit in a musical idea. The primary directional element is generally a dissonance which, strengthened and properly reinforced, leads to a modulation. Before Haydn, the modulation of any sonata exposition was imposed almost always from without: the structure and the material were not strangers to each other, and the material could, indeed, demand a certain kind of structure (a movement away from the tonic) but without itself providing the full impulse necessary for its form. With all of Haydn's works of the 1780s, as well as some of those before, it becomes more difficult to disentangle the central musical ideas from the total structures in which they work themselves out. Secondary directional forces implicit in the material were its capacity to form sequences (a way of fixing interest and enforcing continuity already part of High Baroque technique, which created its material with that possibility in view) and its aptness for reinterpretation—development, fragmentation, and, above all, for creating new significance when transposed. This aptness was certainly recognized and appreciated before Haydn, but with nothing like his acuteness and his largeness of vision.

129

Haydn from 1770 to the Death of Mozart

As to the primary element, dissonance, Haydn developed a remarkable sensitivity to its most delicate implications, an imaginative ear that caught each expressive accent. In the Quartet in B flat major op. 55 no. 3, the most dramatic effects follow from a clash between E♭ and E♮ in the opening measures; the emphasis given to this opposition is swift and controlled:

The E♭ is made prominent as early as its first appearance in the second measure by the hint of a tritone with the preceding A, and this sets into relief the surprise of an E♮ (m. 4)—which is at once contradicted, *forte* (m. 5), and then the bass (m. 6) plays both E♭ and E♮, resolving one into the other. (The other chromatic alterations—B♮ and then A♭—are called up harmonically by the E♮ and help to sustain its significance.) The impulsive power of this relation is first realized in measure 20, where the two notes together (in the viola) start the modulation to the dominant, a passage immediately reiterated (m. 22). The most sensitive detail is the playing of the main theme at its original position, but reharmonized with an E♮ in the bass (m. 27), so that the opening melody is now itself the bridge passage to its own appearance in the cello at the dominant (m. 31).

There is no end to the subtleties of Haydn's ear at this time; the second theme depends on the same opposition of E♭ to E♮:

but it is now the E♭ which is the dissonant note, an inversion of harmonic function that complements the inversion of rhythm, emphasized by *sforzandi* which substitutes (♩ ♪) for (♩ ♩). In the recapitulation, where the second theme is transposed to the tonic, Haydn now inverts the theme:

in order not to relinquish the E♭–E♮ relation (which would otherwise have become A♭–A♮ here). The delicacy of Haydn's procedure and the large range of effects it reached is unprecedented: no composer before him had depended so exquisitely on the facts of hearing to form his larger structures.

Haydn's close interest in the *immediate* audible effect may best be seen in his understanding of the implications of his openings. The first striking dissonance we hear is generally used later as the means of launching the first large harmonic movement. The F major Quartet op. 50 no. 5 begins:

131

and the witty C♯ in measure 5 makes its effect at once. It is both charming and logical when, twenty measures later, the same note is superimposed on the first measure to begin the modulation to the dominant:

This is not a prepared modulation, in the academic sense, but a comprehension of the drama that could be played out in tonality.

It is not only that Haydn's 'irregularities' of form must be seen in the light of his interest in working out the possibilities of his material; in addition, his infractions of the academic rules of harmony must be interpreted as a desire for dramatic emphasis. At the opening of the beautiful E flat major Quartet op. 64 no. 6, there are surprisingly exposed parallel unisons between in-dependent voices in measures 9 and 10:

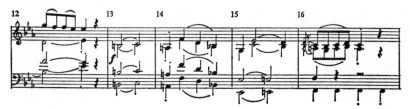

The little two-note motif, the rising second in the second violin, which is thus called to our attention, appears throughout the opening measures (m. 1: 1st violin; m. 2: viola; m. 4: cello, etc.), but it is not just passively the principal element in the melody: it is about to take on an active role, to become the agent of movement in measure 13. The parallel unisons are a hint, an apparently decorative way of bringing it to the listener's attention. This dynamic change, perhaps the most essential creation of the classical style, affects the rhythm significantly: the difference in phrasing of the same figure in measures 2 and 14 is the result of a new significance; the later form moves towards a new tonality as the earlier affirms the tonic. This conception of phrasing is original, transforming a decorative and an expressive element into a dramatic one.

More daring are the parallel fifths in measures 147–149 of the recapitulation of the opening movement of the C major Quartet op. 64 no. 1:

but here the more brutal emphasis in measures 147 and 149 is not a fore-warning of changed significance, but the height of an accumulation of force, as this phrase, in its various forms, has been the agent of much harmonic movement.[1] Most important, however, is that it is a way of resolving the surprising change of harmony in measure 133, a dominant-seventh chord on Ab which has remained suspended so long that its resolution demands this painful intensity. The whole passage from measures 133 to 147 is an expansion of this chord, one of the most remarkable in Haydn, and an example of the physical excitement this kind of expansion can generate. The dramatic intensity is curiously appropriate, as Haydn works out at this place a climax that rivals the end of the development section in power. A secondary climax of such importance in the recapitulation was only occasionally used by Haydn and Mozart, but it was to become almost second nature to Beethoven after the *Waldstein* Sonata.

What I have called the secondary directional forces—sequence and re-interpretation by transposition—are most important only when the material does not provide a dissonance sufficiently dynamic for Haydn's purpose. The opening of the finale of the quartet just cited, op. 64 no. 1, obviously implies the formation of sequences based on its sharply defined rhythm:

---

[1] It is used dramatically at most of its appearances before, particularly throughout the development section, and the expansion of this passage is prepared by what has preceded. It is the climax of the movement.

but nothing in these first two measures prepares us for the spectacular crescendo of sequences that makes up its development:

This *tour de force* transforms Baroque sequential technique beyond all recognition, even if it would be difficult to conceive without the rediscovery of Handel and Sebastian Bach in the early 1780s. The gradual reconquest of contrapuntal mastery was necessary, but the energy of this passage is a classical one, arising from the brilliant articulation of phrase which makes the opening of the sequential phrases on weak beats so forceful, the one-and-a-half measure phrases in the violin at measures 49–52 so striking.

Reinterpretation by transposition as a directional force also exists in the Baroque, but the greatly enhanced force and clarity of modulation in the late eighteenth century give it a new power. Its most common form (in Haydn as in earlier composers) is the replaying of the main theme at the dominant, where a new place and a new meaning give thematic shape to the harmonic form. There are, however, subtler uses, the most interesting, perhaps, being to reinterpret the material by transposing the harmony while leaving the melody at the same place. At the beginning of the F sharp minor Quartet op. 50 no. 4, the melodic line of measures 5 to 8 is played three times, changing only instrument and register, but at the end we have reached A major:

The same melodic shape has a new harmonic meaning; only the last note has to be altered at the end. Haydn was particularly given to this kind of wit in movements in a minor key, treating the minor mode as a whole as an unresolved dissonance. Transposition within the sonata implies, in general, a dissonance on a higher plane, or, better, a tension with the original or potential tonic form of the transposed phrase.

Most of the examples I have given come from opening movements because these are almost always the most dynamically conceived of the four, and such dynamism was Haydn's most original achievement. The first movement and the finale were evidently the difficult ones for him to write: in his old age, he only had the strength to finish the middle movements of his last quartet. But his new conception of musical energy makes itself felt throughout the quartets, transforming even the relaxed middle sections of those slow movements that are in ternary form into a kind of development, and much the same thing happens in many of the trios of the minuets. The finales are as daring as the opening movements, looser in structure, yet more concise in their use of fundamentally less concentrated ideas.

By the early 1770s, in the dozen quartets of op. 17 and op. 20, Haydn had affirmed the seriousness and richness of the string quartet. With the application, in the *Scherzi* Quartets op. 33, of thematic transformation to the entire texture including the accompaniment, so that a linear vitality now present in every instrumental part does not entail a return to the Baroque ideal of largely unbroken and always unarticulated linear continuity, Haydn established the string quartet as the supreme form of chamber music.

For most people, the string quartet is almost synonymous with chamber music, yet its prestige comes entirely from its pre-eminence in the classical period, from 1770 to the death of Schubert. Outside these limits, it is not the normal form of expression, nor even an entirely natural one. In the first half of the eighteenth century, the use of continuo for all concerted music makes at least one of the four instruments redundant: the trio sonata (three instruments and a harpsichord) was then a more efficient combination. After Schubert, music generally seeks to avoid the kind of linear definition implied by the string quartet, and it becomes an archaic and an academic form—a proof of mastery, and a nostalgic recall of the great classicists. Fine works were still written in this form, of course, but they all bear the mark either of strain or of the composer's increasingly special adaptation of his style to the medium (or the medium to his style, as with Bartók's imaginative use of percussive string effects).

Nevertheless, the leading role of the string quartet is not the accidental result of a handful of masterpieces: it is directly related to the nature of tonality, particularly to its development throughout the eighteenth century. A hundred years earlier, music had not yet shaken off the last traces of its dependence on the interval: in spite of the central importance of the chord— the triad in particular—dissonance was still conceived in intervallic terms, and the resolution of dissonance, consequently, even in late seventeenth-century music, very often satisfies the aesthetic of two-part counterpoint and ignores the tonal implications. By the eighteenth century, dissonance is always dissonance to a triad, stated or implied, although music theory naturally lagged far behind practice. Rameau's heroic and awkward attempt at reformulating harmonic theory must be seen against this background of changing practice and of the new but absolute harmonic supremacy of the triad. It is rare in later eighteenth-century music that the full triadic form of every chord except brief passing ones is not explicitly played, either by three voices or by the outline of one voice's motion (just as, in the first half of the century, when a note was missing from a triad, it was supplied by the continuo). The few exceptions are always for special effect, as in Haydn's Trio in B flat major H. 20 where the piano plays a melody for left hand alone (and the dissonances are *without exception* resolved in terms of the previously implied triad), or where a single note is used in such a way that it could imply one of several triads—an ambiguity which is always dramatic when it is not merely incompetent.

The string quartet—four-voice polyphony in its clearest non-vocal state—

is the natural consequence of a musical language in which expression is entirely based on dissonance to a triad. When there are fewer than four voices, one of the non-dissonant voices simply must play two notes of the triad, either by a double stop or by moving quickly from one note to the other: the richness of the sonority of Mozart's Divertimento for string trio, which mainly uses the latter method and is sparing of double stops, is a *tour de force* almost miraculous in its ease and variety. (The resolution of certain dissonances will, of course, itself create a triad and therefore demand no more than three-part writing, but some of the basic dissonances of late eighteenth-century harmony, like the dominant seventh, require four voices.) More than four voices gave rise to questions of doubling and spacing, and the woodwind quartet created problems of the blending of tone-color (and, in the eighteenth century, of intonation as well). Therefore only the string quartet and the keyboard instrument allowed the composer to speak the language of classical tonality with ease and freedom, and the keyboard had the disadvantage (and the advantage!) of less striking linear clarity than the string quartet.

After the Quartets op. 33 of 1781, Haydn waited for almost five years before returning to the form, except for the masterly single Quartet op. 42, simple to the point of austerity. From 1786 until his first trip to England in 1791, he produced no less than eighteen works in this form. All these quartets follow the six that Mozart dedicated to him, and many historians find an influence of Mozart in the works of this period. That there was an influence is easy to believe, but isolating it is not without its risks: the beautiful A flat Piano Sonata H. 46 was once dated about twenty years too late because of a supposed influence of Mozart in the slow movement. It is perhaps more practical to assume that by 1785 Mozart and Haydn were working on parallel lines that occasionally converged. Tender and graceful 'second themes,' in particular, generally ascribed to Mozart's ascendancy, are found often enough in earlier works by Haydn for their slightly greater frequency after 1782 to be attributed to the increasing complexity of Haydn's technique, which now enabled him to encompass very different moods within one movement without sacrificing any of the nervous muscularity of his style. Nevertheless, Haydn was certainly strongly affected by Mozart's harmonic range and ease of phrasing.

Written for the King of Prussia, the six quartets op. 50 of 1786 are grander than those of op. 33. The solo cello passages placed as a tactful homage to the royal amateur call forth complementary solo displays from the other instruments, the long solo for second violin at the opening of the slow movement of op. 50 no. 2 being perhaps the most remarkable. The F sharp minor Quartet op. 50 no. 4 contains Haydn's greatest fugal finale, in which the element of academic display present in almost all classical fugues loses itself completely in pathos. In this work, too, Haydn's sense of the unity of a whole quartet has grown immensely; the F sharp major minuet seems only to be an interlude in the major: its key is unstable, continually drawn back to the minor of the first movement. The third quartet of the set, in E flat major, starts with a logically refined, subtle version of the famous joke in the last movement of op. 33 no. 2, which pretends to be finished before the end; in op. 50 no. 3 the recapitulation begins in the middle of the opening theme and continues for considerable length until the cadence on the tonic, one which just lacks that last degree of firmness which would make it absolutely conclusive. Then after a silence of two measures the beginning of the opening theme appears at last, and starts a short but brilliant coda. In all these quartets, the independent solo writing entails an emphatic and complex contrapuntal display, even in the slow movements, which consequently attain a lyrical breadth and a tranquil gravity rare in Haydn until now. The opus as a whole represents a solidification and an expansion of the light-hearted revolutionary procedures of op. 33.

The greater contrapuntal richness of op. 50 may also have a more significant purpose. With the change in style of op. 33 came a considerable simplification: the music was leaner than the great quartets of ten years previously. It is not so much that every advance involves a loss, but rather that Haydn was forced to simplify his textures in order to deal with a new and more complex system of phrasing (the co-ordination of asymmetry within a larger periodic movement) and a new conception of thematic relationships. The partial return to the rich and more 'learned' technique of the High Baroque is an attempt to compensate for this consequent thinness. A simplification to try out a new technique and then a swing back to an elaborate, and sometimes even old-fashioned, counterpoint, was a strategy common to both Mozart and Haydn at various stages of their careers. (The pattern had, in fact, already appeared in Haydn's life before the 1780s. The Quartets op. 17 are sparer and, in most ways, less extravagant than those of op. 9: that was the price of their more advanced technique, and to recapture a former richness, Haydn turned to strict counterpoint in the great Quartets op. 20 of 1772.) For both Haydn and Mozart, as well as for Beethoven, there was an attempt to reconquer the past once the present had been won.

The six quartets, op. 54 and 55, published two years later in 1789, are more experimental: the slow movements, in particular, take on a character even more dramatic than Haydn had ventured before. The swifter pacing of the Allegretto slow movement of op. 54 no. 1 may derive as much from the slow movement of Mozart's F major Concerto K. 459 of 1784 (also an Allegretto) as from previous essays of Haydn in a flowing 6/8 time (op. 33 no. 1, for example). Not only the continuity and the apparently artless and melancholy simplicity, but the chromatically sensuous harmonic movement are more often found in Mozart than in Haydn. The second movement of op. 54 no. 2 is far stranger, with a rhapsodic solo violin part in a written-out rubato that delays melodic notes so as to produce painful cross-harmonic effects. The rubato of the classical period (as we can see from those passages where

Mozart, Haydn, and Beethoven wrote it out) was used to create the most affecting dissonances: unlike the romantic *rubato* (and the one most in use today), it was not just a delaying of the melody, but a forced overlapping of the harmony as well. I should imagine that as a kind of suspension it was originally related to the appoggiatura, the most expressive of ornaments and almost always a dissonant note. (The dramatic middle section of the slow movement of op. 54 no. 3 also shows a brief use of the same *rubato* in a strangely violent passage, and this movement has a nervous rhythmic power characteristic of Haydn, but unusually and even astonishingly effective here.) Even more curious is the presence, in op. 54 no. 2, of a second slow movement, as the finale is an extended Adagio, with a Presto middle section which is actually a concealed variation, a rare example of an enigmatic form in this period. The ear is oddly satisfied, but the mind can only grasp the relation with difficulty in performance. The harmonies in the trio of the minuet that just precedes sound equally enigmatic and equally right as they derive from the strange harmonic effects arising in the solo violin's *rubato* in the first slow movement.

The second movement of op. 55 no. 1 is monothematic and in 'slow-movement sonata form' (i.e., without a central development section), but the customary secondary development after the recapitulation is so impressive that Tovey has held up the piece as a rare example of rondo form in a slow tempo. The last movement is almost a sketch for the great finale of the *Clock* Symphony: it starts in rondo style, squarely cheerful, but the first return of the main theme becomes an extended triple fugue. At the end the theme returns amiably, in all its original simplicity, and the triple fugue has served as a development section. Op. 55 no. 2 in F minor starts with its slow movement, a double variation form of great depth: the stormy Allegro in first-movement form takes second place.

The mature power and variety of the six quartets op. 64, which followed a year later, were never surpassed by Haydn. The B minor Quartet no. 2 looks back to op. 33 no. 1 not only in its ambiguous opening in D major, but even in the shape of its thematic material in the first movement. The exquisite Adagio uses a slow four-note scale figure, transposing it to the dominant, inverting it, and ornamenting it: for all its presence everywhere in the melody, the figure is not used as a series, but as a *cantus firmus* on which a florid and expressive decoration is draped. Op. 64 no. 3 in B flat major is one of the great comic masterpieces: the listener who can hear the last movement without laughing aloud knows nothing of Haydn. Both op. 64 no. 4 in G major and no. 5 in D (the *Lark*) have a double recapitulation of the main theme, but for entirely different reasons: the *Lark*, because its principal melody is a violin solo high on the E string, which cannot be developed, only played simply in all its glory—it appears untouched in the development at the subdominant and is then abandoned until the recapitulation; the G major, partly because the main theme appears briefly a second time in the exposition, but mainly because the first recapitulation goes almost at once to the tonic minor, and appears to be a false reprise—it is nothing of the sort, however, as it stays at the tonic to recapitulate essential material of the second group (much of which was in the dominant minor). A false false-reprise is an exceptionally sophisticated irony even for Haydn, and a second beginning of the main theme at the tonic after an emphatic pause restores equanimity. Most original in the *Lark* is the wide spacing of the registers, with a new range and openness of sonority.

I have hesitated to mention perhaps the most striking innovation of Haydn's string-quartet writing: its air of conversation. Subjective impressions are awkward to analyze, but this is too important a characteristic of Haydn's to leave without trying to isolate it. The combination of independence of voice-leading with a retention of the early classical emphasis on hierarchy of melody and accompaniment, the conception of the phrase as an articulated member with a clearly marked cadence or half-cadence at the end which gives it the air of a lucid proposition—all this will only go part of the way to an explanation. The opening of the Quartet in E major op. 54 no. 3 may help us further:

The second violin and viola begin a melody, and are literally interrupted at once by the violin, which takes immediate precedence. In the fourth and fifth measures the two middle voices try once more, and are again interrupted. The sociable comedy of Haydn's art becomes radiant at the end of the eighth measure: the second violin and viola, resigned, give up their phrase and accept the first violin's melody; begin it—and are again comically interrupted. Perhaps the wittiest point is that now (m. 9–10) the first violin retorts this time with the emphatic *end* of his opening phrase (m. 3–4) transposed up a ninth, and telescoping the original periodic movement. All the dramatic asymmetries melt into the regular phrasing, and what seems at one moment to be pure musical pattern appears suddenly as dramatic wit.

This passage is like a model for a dramatic and yet conversational dialogue in a comedy, in which the content of the words has become irrelevant to the wit of the form (although I should not wish to imply that the harmonic significance of this opening does not contribute to its vitality). The isolated character of the classical phrase and the imitation of speech rhythms in all of Haydn's chamber music only enhance the air of conversation. Eighteenth-century prose in England, Germany, and France had become, in comparison with the previous age, much more syntactic, relying more exclusively on balance, proportion, shape, and the order of the words than did the heavier cumulative technique of the Renaissance. The eighteenth century was cultivatedly self-conscious about the art of conversation: among its greatest triumphs are the quartets of Haydn.

2

Symphony

Our time has blurred the line between public and private forms of art, but Haydn's symphonies speak primarily to the listener, not to the players, as the quartets do. This distinction between symphonic and chamber music was, if anything, accentuated during Haydn's lifetime. Many solo passages in the earlier symphonies seem to exist as much for the performers' enjoyment as for the audience's, and in the small musical world at Esterházy, where Haydn worked for so many years, it may have been politic to keep the important musicians happy with frequent opportunities to display their virtuosity. Orchestral music in the 1760s at Esterházy and elsewhere was still in conception a relatively intimate affair, in spite of the existence of several famous orchestras, but in the last quarter of the century composers began to take more and more notice of the possibilities of very large ensembles, and their music reflects this new fact of concert life. In 1768, Haydn was still able to write: 'I prefer a band with three bass instruments—cello, bassoon and double bass—to one with six double basses and three celli, because certain passages stand out better that way.'[1] By the 1780s, Haydn's orchestration had certainly progressed beyond this stage, which represents a taste midway between chamber and orchestral styles. Ten years later, the Viotti orchestra he used in London for his last concerts there was a large one, and by this time the different orchestral colors are less contrasted and opposed than blended to form a new kind of mass sonority. The orchestra that Mozart preferred is surprisingly large, but he is quite clear about what he wanted: 40 violins, 10 violas, 6 celli, 10 double-basses (!) and double wind on each part.[2] Even remembering that all the instruments of the time were a little softer than those of the present day, this is still a force almost twice that which any conductor dares to use now for a Mozart symphony. Of course Mozart did not often get an orchestra of such size, but there is no reason today to perpetuate those conditions of eighteenth-century performance which obtained only when there was not enough money to do the thing properly.

Most interesting is the exceptional weight given, towards the end of the century, to the bass instruments. It is evident that as the Baroque contrapuntal style was superseded, and as the figured bass disappeared, the massive

---

[1] *Collected Correspondence & London Notebooks of Joseph Haydn*, ed. H. C. Robbins Landon, London, 1959, page 9.
[2] Mozart, *Letters*, ed. Emily Anderson, London, 1966, Vol. II, page 724.

sound of the bass became as important as the clarity of line. From the letter cited above, it is also apparent that this development was proceeding too fast for Haydn's taste in the 1760s, and it was more than ten years before his own writing took full account of the new sonority. But today's performances of all the later symphonies of Haydn and of Mozart suffer from an insufficient reinforcement of the bass line as well as from a belief that the small orchestras that were so common in the late eighteenth century represent the sonority that Haydn and Mozart had in mind as ideal, and not merely the one they were forced to accept for lack of anything better. From 1780 on, composers wrote their symphonic works with large, heavy-sounding ensembles in mind; performance by smaller groups was only a makeshift, like the performance of some of the Mozart piano concertos with string quintet in place of full orchestra.

The distinction between public and private music implied a distinction in style of performance, too. The virtuoso conductor did not exist until he was invented during the lifetime of Beethoven. When Beethoven explained to individual members of the orchestra how he wanted certain passages played and demanded slight, expressive variations of tempo, it was an orchestral innovation for the time and noticed as an eccentricity. The solo music of the late eighteenth century allowed, of course, for a good deal of freedom and flexibility in performance, but even a quick comparison of one of Haydn's symphonies with a solo sonata will show that the symphony avoids all those effects which require the individual nuances and refinements of *rubato*, even slight, that the sonata demands throughout. The symphonic music is always more coarsely organized, and more tightly written as well: the relative looseness of the solo sonatas of the 1770s, with their clearly marked cadences, which can be given so much individuality by the performer, and their more elaborate detail intended to be interpreted and expressively shaped, gives way in the symphonies to overlapping phrases which enforce continuity and to the broader strokes implied by the heavier sonority. To play a symphony of Mozart or Haydn as if it were a sonata, interpreted and molded in an individual way by a conductor, is to betray its nature, to obscure rather than to reveal. It is not that music in general should be allowed to speak for itself— an impossible principle and doubly mistaken as regards any work written with a solo interpreter in mind—but rather that it should be performed without distorting its character, and the freedom of the virtuoso conductor does not add a new grace to Mozart but only obscures an old one. Above all, the elaborate but firm rhythmic organization of a Mozart symphony requires a steady tempo in order for it to speak to us clearly.

The music of the nineteenth century, on the other hand, demands the services of the virtuoso conductor, and Brahms, Tchaikovsky, and Strauss are unthinkable without him. With Beethoven, however, some prudence is still required. Even the late orchestral works like the Ninth Symphony clearly imply a performance with few of the individual refinements of tone, accent, and tempo of the sonatas and quartets: the music stands alone without these embellishments, which are, in the more intimate works, not embellishments but necessities of style. Here, some variation of tempo as well as other nuances are essential: Beethoven himself, in sending a metronome mark for a song to the publisher, said that the indication was only valid for the opening measures because no metronomic restriction could be put upon sentiment. In late Beethoven, in particular, *espressivo* certainly means a *ritenuto* as can be seen in the markings of the Sonatas, op. 109 (*un poco espressivo* followed by *a tempo*) and 111 (where every *espressivo* is accompanied by *ritenente*). Changes of tempo, however, must always be understood as coming under a large and controlling idea of the rhythm. I have no wish further to impugn the testimony of Beethoven's friend Schindler—who wrote many years after Beethoven and under the influence of a much later aesthetic, and who has been sufficiently attacked for his romantic overinterpretations—but even he is quite firm that when Beethoven said that the pace of the Largo of the D major Sonata op. 10 no. 3 must be changed ten times, the composer himself added, 'but only so as to be heard by the most sensitive ear.' It is evident from this that Beethoven wished a movement, whatever the variations in pace motivated by the expression, to sound throughout *as if it were in one tempo*, and in this he remains firmly within the bounds of the tradition of Mozart and Haydn. The solo music of the period just before Mozart, from 1750 to 1770, however, does not by any means require this kind of rhythmic unity. It is even inappropriate to much of the work of Gluck and Philipp Emanuel Bach, although it should be added that in the latter's work the rhapsodic freedom of the solo music can never be transferred to the orchestral works.

This need, not only for rhythmic strictness but also for a much simpler and even more literal interpretation of late eighteenth-century symphonic music, is more easily grasped when we read Haydn's letter of October 17, 1789, about the advanced and difficult Symphonies 90–92:

> 'Now I would humbly ask you to tell the Princely *Kapellmeister* there that these 3 symphonies [90–92] because of their many particular effects, should be rehearsed at least once, carefully and with special concentration, before they are performed.'[1]

This represents, again, the worst traditions of the eighteenth century, and it would be ridiculous to take it as a standard or guide for the present. But it explains the existence of a special symphonic style in which even the greatest complexity of musical idea was conceived in terms of a straightforward execution, and which can only be marred by the imposition of later standards of orchestral virtuosity. A straightforward execution, of course, is by no means a straightforward affair any longer, and every musician, orchestral or otherwise, when playing the music of the classical period, has irrelevant and ingrained habits of performance derived from later styles.

---

[1] Haydn, *Correspondence*, page 89.

The development of Haydn as a symphonist raises one of the great pseudo-problems of history: the question of progress in the arts. The achievements of 1768 to 1772 are very great ones in a style that Haydn almost at once abandoned. In these years he wrote a series of impressive symphonies in minor keys—dramatic, highly personal, and mannered. The most important, in roughly chronological order, are the G minor no. 39, the *Passione* no. 49, the *Trauer Symphonie* no. 44, the C minor no. 52, and the *Farewell* no. 45. To these symphonies, more significant than all but a few of those in the major mode of the same years, must be joined the great Piano Sonata in C minor of 1770, H. 20.[1] The Quartets opp. 17 and 20, written in 1771 and 1772, are all—in major or minor—on a level that no other composer of Haydn's time could equal or even approach, and in assessing the level he had reached, one must also add the beautiful slow movement of the Piano Sonata in A flat H. 46. None of these works gives a clear indication of the direction that Haydn was to take, and one might imagine the history of music to be very different if only he had explored the paths suggested in some of them. They seem to presage not the sociable and lyrical wit of his later work (and of Mozart's), but a style harshly dramatic and fiercely emotional without a trace of sentimentality. Taken on their own terms the works of the late 60s and early 70s inspire admiration: they are defective only when measured by the standards of Haydn's later works. Why then do we impose these standards? Why do we refuse the same tolerance to the early work of an artist that we grant—indeed, insist upon granting—to an earlier style? No one, for example, would reproach Chaucer with a failure to shape his verse in the dramatic speech rhythms of the Elizabethans, Masaccio with a lack of the atmospheric integration of High Renaissance painting, or Bach with a refusal to seek the rhythmic variety of the classical style.

The analogies are, however, less pertinent than we who love so many of the early works of Haydn would like them to be. A style is a way of exploiting and controlling the resources of a language. J. S. Bach's mastery of the contemporary language of tonality was as complete as could be imagined, but in the twenty years between his death and the *Sturm und Drang* symphonies that Haydn wrote in the early 70s, this language had changed significantly: the syntax was less fluid, the relation between tonic and dominant more highly polarized. Haydn's style of 1770, while it had taken account of the development, was not yet able to embrace its full implications. The higher degree of articulation of phrase and polarity of harmony raised problems for continuity that were difficult to solve: the shapes and rhythms move without

---

[1] The G minor Sonata H. 44 may belong here as well, but I think it is now being dated too early as it used to be dated too late. Its co-ordination of harmony, accent, and regular cadence would place it later than 1770, and perhaps after 1774. Its publication with works of the late 60s does not give so cogent a reason for dating it with them when it is recalled that one of the other sonatas in the group is not by Haydn at all as the publisher claimed. A batch as mixed as that could have been heterogeneous in other ways as well.

transition from the squarely regular to the unsystematic, relying in the latter case almost entirely upon repetition or upon Baroque sequences to justify the sense of motion. This dichotomy can be felt most strongly in pages like the opening of the *Farewell* Symphony, where all the phrases are not only of the same length but of exactly the same shape, and where a later departure from this regularity (mm. 33 on) is almost entirely sequential in nature. The classical ideal of balanced asymmetrical variation within a large period is only dimly foreshadowed.

It should be clear, in fact, that if today we judge the fine symphonies of 1772 by a standard of coherence that the works themselves do not impose (and which were only arrived at by Haydn years after), this standard is met not only by the later work of Haydn but also, within an earlier state of the tonal language, by Bach and Handel. It is not therefore paradoxical that we should refuse the criteria of excellence implicit in the *Sturm und Drang* works, while granting those of the early eighteenth century. There is no 'progress' between Bach and late Haydn, only a change in the musical 'vernacular.' There is, however, a genuine progress in style between early and late Haydn: the younger Haydn is a great master of a style that only imperfectly realizes what the language of his time had to offer, the later is the creator of a style that is an almost perfect instrument for exploiting the resources of that language. (In all this, I am, I hope, begging the question of the extent to which changes in style themselves precipitate changes in the common language.)

It is a delicate point, and an idle one, whether Haydn could have arrived at so richly complex and so controlled a style by continuing in the direction that may have seemed so finely promising in 1770. Hindsight is cruel to unrealized possibilities. Yet it is worth remarking that the greatest success of Haydn's early style, its fierce dramatic power, was inseparable there from a harsh simplicity, a refusal of complex control, and a willingness at times to break almost any rhythmic pattern for the sake of a single effect. It is difficult to see how a richer art could have arisen from this often brutal contrast between a coarse but urgent regularity and a dazzling eccentricity, except by abandoning the very virtues which made the style of the early 1770s so compelling—which is, indeed, what Haydn did. It is, perhaps, a pity that with the attainment of a more disciplined style, some of the fierce energy that was so admirable had gone out of his art. His later style could support such fierceness (as Beethoven was able to show almost at once), but the discipline of comedy which transformed and enriched Haydn's style left an ineradicable impression on his musical personality.

I do not wish to give the impression that his art around 1770 was all emotion, drama, and effect: it had already a formidable intellectual power. A fine example of this musical logic is the Symphony no. 46 in B major, of 1772, with the surprising return of the minuet in the middle of the finale, an anticipation of the return of the scherzo in the last movement of Beethoven's Fifth Symphony. As in Beethoven, it is not the opening of the minuet that returns: Haydn has chosen to begin at exactly the moment that the minuet resembles the main theme of the finale. The opening measures of the last movement are:

and here even the phrasing, emphasized by the omission of the accompanying voice on the third beat, is related to the return of the minuet:

But these measures are themselves, for the ear if not on paper, a backward version of the original opening of the minuet:

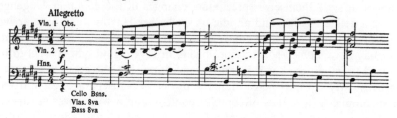

(Haydn was concerned with cancrizans or back-to-front effects at that time, and it is interesting to see how it takes a freely audible, rather than theoretically strict, form here.) All these shapes come directly from the third and fourth measures of the first movement:

thus demonstrating the logic of Haydn's imagination. It should be clear, however, that these are striking effects with little power to range beyond their immediate context.

Thematic relationships of this sort, while the easiest to write about and in some ways the easiest to perceive, are actually the least persuasive and the least compelling. They work less directly on the nerves, communicate less physical excitement than harmonic movements and relationships of pulse and rhythm. (Of course, any hard-and-fast separation of these elements of music is nonsense, and even a theoretical division can be abused.) The kind of thematic relationships that Haydn employs to such effect in Symphony no. 46 are, in fact, common enough throughout the early eighteenth century; what is interesting here is that they are used with dramatic point as never before. They have, in short, become events. But these events arrive unsupported by the rhythmic and harmonic conceptions, which allow them to take place but in no way reinforce them. The thematic logic remains isolated.

The weakness of Haydn's early style, in fact, viewed from the heights of his later work, is not in its logical relations, nor in its moments of drama and poetry, but in the passages of necessary prose. Haydn could manage tragedy or farce, and even magnificent strokes of high comedy. His middle style was awkward. It was at times difficult for him to impart urgency or energy to material of a more sober cast. Even in the opening of as fine a symphony as the *Mercury*, no. 43 in E flat major, his struggles are apparent:

The series of weak endings on the tonic is viable only if one does not expect anything from the phrase which will imply an articulate shape and a necessary continuation. The relaxed beauty of this beginning is evident, but a style which will accept it at the price of such a flaccid co-ordination between cadential harmonies and large-scale rhythm can reach a dramatic effect only through the extraordinary. The later Haydn is dramatic without effort, as a matter of course and with the most everyday material. In this passage, we can see Haydn beginning to struggle: not only the opening *forte* chords for each phrase but also the successive elongation of the phrase-length attempt to enforce a sense of growing energy. We must not ask for more success as we listen further, but the faster rhythm of measure 27 is not persuasive because it is not what it would like to be: it is not faster at all, but only an extra excitement in the violins.

This kind of writing is not rare in Haydn around 1770; the opening of the Quartet in D major op. 20 no. 5 almost duplicates the above:

The beginning of the A flat Sonata H. 46 for piano shows the same limping tonic cadences, which enforce nothing beyond themselves:

and the same unprepared animation, convincing only if one does not put too high a price upon one's convictions.

To characterize Haydn's symphonic development after 1772 is not easy, partly because of its continuity. The break in quartet-writing made the difference between the new achievement of op. 33 of 1781 and the earlier op. 20 of 1772 much simpler to grasp; the change in symphonic style appears more tentative because it was more gradual. Many of the symphonies of the 1770s, too, are arrangements of music originally intended for the stage. The composition of operas, mainly comic, was evidently occupying too much of Haydn's time now for him to devote so much concentration to either chamber music or pure symphonic works. But there are still twenty symphonies written between 1773 and 1781, a large, varied, and uneven production. The broad outlines of Haydn's progress are clear enough, starting with the restraint put upon his most characteristically violent inspirations, and the new smoothness of surface. Most significant, however, in the late 70s is the synthesis of continuity and articulation, a beautiful understanding of the ways that accent and cadence could be combined to form an impelling sense of movement without falling back on the unvaried rhythmic textures of the Baroque.

Sometime during the 1780s, Mozart jotted down the opening themes of three of Haydn's symphonies, nos. 47, 62, and 75, undoubtedly with an eye to conducting them at his concerts. Symphony no. 47 in G major is a typical work of 1772, one of Haydn's most brilliant and satisfying. The second parts of the minuet and trio, which are their first parts played backward note for note, are only the least subtle of the surprises in this work. Most agreeable about these cancrizans, however, is Haydn's device for ensuring our awareness of what he has done:

The *forte* accents on the first beat, reappearing on the third, turn an academic exercise into a witty and intellectual effect. Mozart evidently found the melody of the slow movement particularly successful, as he recalled it in the B flat major serenade for winds, K. 361, but thickened its two-part counterpoint. Haydn's melody has, indeed, an almost Mozartean grace:

and the later inverting of these two voices displays a skill in double counterpoint that rivals the minuet's *al rovescio*. As with every composer except Schubert, Haydn's real education took place in public; however, the use of contrapuntal technique was not experiment but the necessary reinforcement of a style too thin as yet to be commensurate with Haydn's ideals. Even in the slow movement, these devices remain somewhat extraneous to the music's inner tensions and to its essential feeling for harmonic conflict. Still more of an alien intrusion upon a blandly formed scheme is the opening of the recapitulation of the first movement, which uses an effect derived from the Neapolitan symphonists: beginning in the minor without any previous warning or preparation.[1] It is a measure of Haydn's art of the period that any

---

[1] The tonic minor can be used in a recapitulation as a substitute for the subdominant, but its startling appearance here in place of the tonic major precludes any such interpretation: the key does not resolve tensions but adds a new one.

attempt to integrate his most dramatic ideas into a coherent scheme would only ruin them. Nevertheless, that Haydn became a significantly greater composer ten years later is no reason for not admiring this splendid symphony as Mozart evidently did.

The influence of operatic style is evident in the second of the symphonies that interested Mozart, no. 62 in D major, recently dated around 1780, but perhaps composed a few years earlier—the manuscript of the first movement, in any case, which existed separately as an overture, is dated 1777. A brilliant, lively piece, this movement was also used as an alternate finale to the *Imperial* Symphony, no. 53, a function for which its operatic style clearly fits it: it is lightweight for a first movement. In other symphonies of this time made up of music originally meant for the theater, Haydn's concern for unity is as minimal as it is here; *Il Distratto*, no. 60, 'that old pancake' as Haydn later called it, is particularly heterogeneous. In no. 62 the air of potpourri is increased by the fact that all the movements are in the same key, as in a Baroque suite; the contrasts of key had by then become almost taken for granted in a symphony. The slow movement, an Allegretto, is a most curious work: the opening measures

and, indeed, most of the piece, are not only derived from the least possible material—two notes and a banal accompaniment *con sordini*—but impudently display it in a way unusual for Haydn. The ostentatiously naïve sound of the accompaniment, in spite of the poetry that is drawn from it, seems to imply some exterior motivation, as if derived from music written for the stage, like so many of Haydn's works at that time. The last movement has been cited above (p. 113) for its ambiguous opening and for the smoothly efficient logic of Haydn's growing technique.

Haydn's operatic experience as both conductor and composer gave him an invaluable lesson in the relation of musical form to action. The eternal problem in opera is not of expressing or reinforcing action and sentiment—

this would leave us with background music for poetry readings or the films—but of finding a musical equivalent for action which will stand alone as music. It is an insoluble problem: Mozart and Wagner came closest of all composers to solving it, and none of their operas would entirely hold up as a work of absolute music without the words or the actions. Moreover, the problem is meant to be insoluble: when the music achieves absolute intelligibility without the drama, it detaches itself, lives on as independently as the Overture to *Leonore* no. 3, and ceases to exist as opera. The attainment of the ideal would kill the species almost by definition, but it remains as the goal, the point of infinity towards which each work tends: a state in which every word, every feeling, every action on the stage has not only its musical parallel, but its musical justification as well. For this, one needs a style in which violent disruptions of texture—harmonic, rhythmic, and purely sonorous—can be integrated and given a purely musical coherence.

Haydn found this style at about the same time as Mozart, and, although he never arrived at Mozart's sense of long-range movement or his handling of harmonic areas on a very large scale, he applied this new coherence magnificently to the field of purely instrumental music. The relation of music to action in opera has its analogue in absolute music as well. In a style as articulated as that of the late eighteenth century, where the music had become a series of clear events and not merely a cumulative flow, a powerful emotion or a dramatic intensity could no longer rely on High Baroque continuity and would have ended—did, indeed, so end in many works—by smashing the frame of the piece and by dissipating its force. Haydn learned from opera a style that could concentrate that force as he had never been able to do in the 1760s, and with it he effected a synthesis between the tuneful Rococo *Gemütlichkeit* of Austria and North German expressive mannerism, both of which he had already mastered, but rarely been able to combine.

Mozart, brought up in the more comfortable style and already the composer of music whose prettiness alone amounted almost to genius, arrived at the same point from the opposite direction. *Opera buffa* was his school, as well. It stimulated and developed his talent for dramatic expression; Haydn's needed no stimulating, but a chance to be organized and to achieve balance. Operatic experience serves to curb and tame as well as to inspire the feeling for drama. In opera a composer has a certain freedom that purely instrumental music does not grant: the public will forgive coarseness of conception and lapses from musical decorum for the sake of drama, and, in general, the logic of the music and of the book can be considered loosely as intertwined strands, only at rare moments becoming completely unified. But the composer must pay for his freedom by the constraint of bending his imagination to a form not originally musical. The cleverest librettists of the century, like Metastasio, prided themselves on supplying books that gave the musician all he needed and left him full play, but all they actually did at their best was to provide words which fitted the operatic forms that had served in the past—the cavatina, the da capo aria—and to construct scenes in which the singers could give vent to the static display of sentiment that was so ingrained in the style of the High Baroque. Until Mozart forced the hand of his librettists,[1] even comic opera, hidebound by habit, cliché, and a limited repertory of forms, was a strait-jacket as confining as a crab canon, and could have been satisfactory only to a composer like Piccinni, whose urge to dramatic gesture was minimal in spite of all his spirited tunefulness. *Opera buffa* could be a discipline as rigorous as the most academic forms, and it was of the highest importance for two crucial and related aspects of the classical style: the integration of dramatic events within symmetrically resolved closed forms, expanding these forms without changing their essential nature; and the development of a rapidly moving and clearly articulated large rhythmic system that unified the smaller phrase articulations, and gave a cumulative force to the animating impulses sufficient to override the inner cadences. With the sense of the event or individual action and the new technique of an almost systematized intensity, the classical style became at last capable of drama even in non-theatrical contexts.

The application of dramatic technique and structure to 'absolute' music was more than an intellectual experiment. It was the natural outcome of an age which saw the development of the symphonic concert as a public event. The symphony was forced to become a dramatic performance, and it accordingly developed not only something like a plot, with a climax and a dénouement, but a unity of tone, character, and action it had only partially reached before. Unity of action was, of course, one of the classical requirements of tragedy, and the symphony as drama gradually abandoned every trace of the looseness of the suite. By 1770 Haydn needed no lessons in dramatic character or expression: what he added to his equipment by 1780 is something of the economy of the stage. His music becomes, not more concise, but less: true dramatic economy is not concision, but clarity of action. His most striking inspirations now unfold with less of the old laconic harshness, and with more reference to their place in a total conception.

This new efficiency is already evident in the third of Haydn's symphonies that Mozart noted, no. 75 in D major, which dates from around 1780 or a little later. It attains grandeur at once in the slow, grave introduction, without the nervous, sinewy brilliance that had generally served Haydn before as a substitute for weight: the musical line is everywhere deeply expressive and unforced. When the introduction turns into a somber minor for more than half its length, and is then followed by a Presto which opens quietly:

---

[1] It is possible that da Ponte understood the dramatic necessities of Mozart's style without prompting; but before his association with da Ponte, Mozart had already bullied several librettists into giving him the dramatically shaped ensembles he so clearly loved.

it is impossible not to think of the overture to *Don Giovanni*, which was to be written only a few years later.

An instructive part of operatic writing is the achievement of symmetrical balance when the words or the action will not admit of a literal repetition of the music: one of the few great strengths of Haydn as an opera composer was his ingenuity at finding splendid formal subterfuges and hidden solutions for problems of this kind, and he transferred to the symphonies of the 1780s some of this new technique. An example of his skill may be found later in the same movement from Symphony no. 75. One part of the 'second group' of the exposition never reappears in the recapitulation:

replacing it is a canonic passage based on the opening theme:

Significantly the two passages, otherwise so unlike, have the same harmonic elements, their shapes emphasizing the same dissonances. They have also the same harmonic function in the larger design, while the later, canonic passage has, in addition, the more typically cadential effect of a *stretto* in a fugue, and its more explicit reference to the opening theme rounds off the form more strikingly. The slow movement, too, must have been exceptionally interesting to Mozart, as the soft hymn-like theme, a type of melody that Haydn appears to have been the first to write, is a model for much of the music that Mozart was later to develop in the *Magic Flute*.

Haydn's witty play with the elements of form is now controlled within the structure of the whole work: his effects are far-reaching as well as immediately astonishing. His orchestration, too, now uses color to emphasize and underline form as well as to charm. Solo instruments no longer give the effect of an independent *concertino* (except, of course, in the *Sinfonia Concertante* of the London period), but are integrated within a truly orchestral conception; they play from within the larger body of sound, and rarely in contrast or opposition to it. As a consequence, they play less often alone, but are now given remarkable chances to double each other, as at the opening of the beautiful slow movement of the Symphony no. 88, where the melody is played by the solo oboe and violoncello an octave apart. In the earlier symphonies, the solo passages often stand out as the most exceptional and striking moments, but they are only loosely related to the rest of the piece.

The clarity of definition in Haydn's works of the 1780s together with his new sense of proportion makes possible the greatest play of imagination without disturbing the equilibrium of the whole work. In the first movement of the Symphony no. 89 in F major of 1787, for example, the development and recapitulation delightfully exchange roles. The development section, with all its wide and continuous modulations, contains an almost complete and orderly recapitulation of the melodic outline of the exposition, while the recapitulation fragments the themes and regroups them, resolving everything harmonically at the same time into the tonic of F major. The displacement of function does not disturb the large symmetry of this movement, but only adds to it, as Haydn is now empowered, by the regrouping, to form a mirror symmetry by placing the opening theme's full appearance *after* the second theme, with an enchanting reorchestration for violas and bassoon accompanied by horns, flute, and strings. No work shows better the gap between the academic *post facto* rules of sonata form and the living rules of proportion, balance, and dramatic interest which really governed Haydn's art.

Haydn's new-won classical sobriety was easily mated with his fantasy and his wit. It is now rare when the odd and the eccentric (still as frequent as ever in his work) are not transfigured by poetry. In the little-appreciated Symphony no. 81 of 1783, the opening measures are conceived so as to admit of a subtle and blurred return to the tonic at the recapitulation. The opening is mysterious after the straightforward first chord:

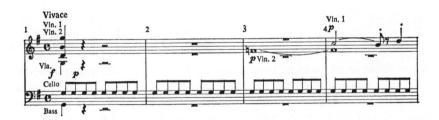

but the recapitulation is far more evasive:

Where is the exact point of return? Somewhere between measures 105 and 110, but it steals in upon us. The pivot upon which this fine and deeply felt ambiguity turns is the mysterious F natural at the opening of the movement above (at measure 3), which inspires the two soft poignant long-held notes at the return (B♭ in measure 96, E♭ at 103). The means of development are the three suspensions at the opening (measures 4–6) which turn into a much longer sequence of suspensions (measures 104–109), ever more expressive as all the winds enter softly one by one. The rapid eighth-note motion is stilled: the tonic does not appear but makes its presence felt gradually, like a light whose distant glow precedes its brilliance. In spite of the blurred contour, the arrival of this recapitulation is a true classical 'event.' The sudden stillness of the rhythm with only the pulsations of the violas and cellos (at measure 94) is a sign that something is about to happen, and the disappearance of this animation (at measure 104) with the tranquil entrances of the winds into the serene harmonic movement tells us that it is happening now. The absence of articulation is not a coquettish reference to traditional ways of beginning a recapitulation, a withholding of the habitual and the expected for the sake of an effect: to refuse to articulate by means of such an extraordinary and moving transition is itself a form of articulation and a decided setting into relief of the moment of resolution.

During the 1780s Haydn wrote more than twenty symphonies, among them the two great sets of six and three symphonies for the Comte d'Ogny (82–87 and 90–92). Haydn's success in Paris was only part of his general European triumph, which had proclaimed him the greatest living composer even before his first trip to England in 1791. There is not a measure, even the most serious, of these great works which is not marked by Haydn's wit; and his wit has now grown so powerful and so efficient that it has become a sort of passion, a force at once omnivorous and creative. True civilized wit, the sudden fusion of heterogeneous ideas with an air paradoxically both ingenuous and amiably shrewd, characterizes everything that Haydn wrote after 1780.

The finest of the symphonies written for Paris is the last, no. 92 in G major, called the *Oxford* because Haydn played it when he received a degree there, having no new one ready in time. The trio of the minuet is high farce: it is impossible for a listener not already in the know to guess where the first beat is at the beginning:

The orchestration is part of the joke, as the winds and strings seem to have different downbeats. Later, by the time the listener has caught on, Haydn shifts the accent, and introduces pauses long enough to throw him off again. This minuet is the greatest of all practical jokes in music. The deeply felt slow movement may be cited for the economy of adding expressive color to a little motif and building a climax:

The chromatic motif in measure 15 reappears in measures 17, 19, and 21, and each time it is less detached, more expansive, and harmonically warmer until the full rich legato at the end. The method is still that of wit, but at the point where it is indistinguishable from fantasy.

The first movement of the *Oxford* is Haydn's most massive expansion of sonata form until then. The material is stripped down to a bare minimum to offer the greatest ease of construction, and every possible event of the re-capitulation—the return to the tonic, the move to the subdominant (here the tonic minor is used as a normal substitute), the playing of each of the themes—is a cue for a new development. In one respect, Haydn's technique of expansion in the recapitulation is less sophisticated than Mozart's, as it consists of a periodic return to the first theme, largely unaltered, as a springboard for quasi-sequential developments, while Mozart is able to expand the phrase, or the individual member of the larger form, as he expands the whole. But this distinction cannot be made a reproach to Haydn, as he has deliberately contracted the phrases of the exposition in preparation for the great expansion of the second half of the movement: the recapitulation seems to be made up of separate small bits of the exposition, like a mosaic, but the spirit that put the pieces together had a tough, dynamic conception of the total controlling rhythm that even Mozart could rarely attain outside opera. The following passage from the recapitulation is, indeed, based wholly on one tiny motif, a two-note upward leap:

but this leap—although it is the only *thematic* element that counts here—is not the center of interest, which is now entirely directed to the larger movement, the downward chromatic progression in the bass answered by the swifter and more powerful diatonic rising motion. The sense of detail is still sharp, but everything is commanded by a musical sense that hears far beyond the individual motif. With this work and with Mozart's *Prague*, the classical symphony finally attained the same seriousness and grandeur as the great public genres of the Baroque, oratorio and opera, although without ever aspiring to their enormous dimensions. Haydn equalled but never surpassed the *Oxford* Symphony.

E. T. A. Hoffmann once wrote that listening to Haydn was like taking a walk in the country, a sentiment destined to make anyone smile today. Yet it seizes on an essential aspect of Haydn; the symphonies of Haydn are heroic pastoral, and they are the greatest examples of their kind. I am alluding not only to the deliberately 'rustic' sections of the symphonies—the bagpipe effects, the Ländler rhythms in the trios of the minuets, the imitation of peasant tunes and dances, the melodies based on yodeling. Even more characteristic is the pastoral tone, that combination of sophisticated irony and surface innocence that is so much a part of the pastoral genre. The rustics in pastoral speak words whose profundity is apparently beyond their grasp; the shepherds are not aware that their joys and sorrows are those of all men. It is easy to call the simplicity of the pastoral artificial, but it is this simplicity which is most moving, the country simplicity that speaks with a sharp nostalgia to the urban reader. The symphonies of Haydn have that artful simplicity, and, like the pastoral, their direct reference to rustic nature is accompanied by an art learned almost to the point of pedantry. Haydn's most 'rustic' finales generally contain his greatest display of counterpoint. Nevertheless, the apparent naïveté is at the heart of Haydn's manner. His melodies, like the shepherds of the classical pastoral, seem detached from all that they portend, unaware of how much they signify. Their initial appearance is almost always without the air of mystery and unexplained tension that introduces the themes of Beethoven. The importance of this polished surface for Haydn cannot be exaggerated: his seriousness would be nothing without his air of amiability. His genial tone is the triumph of his new sense of phrase and of the dancing, energetic pulse that unifies so many of his longest works.

Sophisticated simplicity of surface is typical of most seventeenth- and eighteenth-century pastorals, as well as a pretence of opacity, a claim that the surface was everything—with the understanding that if the claim were granted, the whole traditional structure would collapse. This is the irony that underlies the poetry of Marvell, and even the poignance that flows from the landscapes of Claude and Poussin. The pretence that Nature is as we have imagined her to be, and that Philis and Strephon herd sheep, gives us a form of art more direct than the realistic novel in that its unabashed artificiality openly calls for an act of faith. Pastoral is perhaps the most important literary genre of the eighteenth century: it infected all other forms—the comedies of Marivaux and Goldoni; the philosophical novels of Goldsmith and Johnson; the erotic novels of Prévost, Restif de la Bretonne, and the Marquis de Sade; and the satirical novels and stories of Wieland. Even Voltaire's Candide is basically the shepherd who speaks innocently of truths more universal than he suspects—it is only his world that has turned Nature upside down. In most of these works, the dominant stylistic pattern is a naïveté or simplicity that demands absolutely and without appeal to be taken at face value, even though it is belied by everything else in the work.

The pretension of Haydn's symphonies to a simplicity that appears to come from Nature itself is no mask but the true claim of a style whose command over the whole range of technique is so great that it can ingenuously afford to disdain the outward appearance of high art. Pastoral is generally ironic, with the irony of one who aspires to less than he deserves, hoping he will be granted more. But Haydn's pastoral style is more generous, with all its irony: it is the true heroic pastoral that cheerfully lays claim to the sublime, without yielding any of the innocence and simplicity won by art.

Part IV

SERIOUS OPERA

Serious Opera

The problem of eighteenth-century tragedy can only be considered with the limitations of the artistic language in mind—rather, the problem of the failure (or, if you like, the non-existence) of eighteenth-century tragedy. Not only in literature, but in music as well, secular tragedy was the unattainable ideal. *Opera seria* is today a curiosity on the stage; the finest examples have a sort of twilight existence, not as whole works of art, but only by virtue of the fineness of their parts. If we limit, perhaps unwisely, the meaning of 'form' to a way of integrating details within a larger conception, then *opera seria* is not a form at all: it is only a method of construction. The total form was never made to live; the sub-forms are sometimes very much alive indeed—arias from the operas of Cavalli, Alessandro Scarlatti, and Handel, ensembles from Rameau's, almost any page of Mozart's *Idomeneo*. The composer who came closest to real success with the form was Gluck, during the period of experimentation when the classical style had not yet been really fixed and the High Baroque seemed no longer capable of inspiration. At least three of Gluck's operas reached dramatic heights unknown in secular music in the hundred years since Monteverdi (and religious drama in music posed entirely different problems). Yet even here there are pages of such incoherence, harmonically and in particular rhythmically, that Gluck's musical supremacy can be granted only with misgiving.

The failure of Mozart is the most striking. The harmonic and rhythmic coherence that Gluck arrives at only by an effort which leaves the signs of his struggle still perceptible seems to have come to Mozart with an ease granted to no other composer. Yet sometimes in *Idomeneo*, the mastery of large rhythmic movement over a long stretch of time inexplicably seems to have deserted him. The musical action is unconvincing, and yet the inspiration is consistently high. More puzzling still, in an entirely different way, is the case of *La Clemenza di Tito*, Mozart's last opera. Written (in haste, it is true) at a time when Mozart was composing some of his greatest music, it is a work of exquisite grace and rarely redeemed dullness. I have heard it performed, but have never seen it and cannot believe that even the greatest of stagings could save it. *La Clemenza di Tito* has all the finish of Mozart's finest works— Mozart's music is never less than beautiful—but it is difficult to convey how unmemorable it is. Mozart was, indeed, capable of tragedy in his dramatic works, but in comic opera—*opera buffa* and *Singspiel*.

The inability of even the greatest composer to breathe life into *opera seria* has been blamed on the restricting conventions of the genre. There is, indeed, a certain comic side to a convention that forces the hero, just so that he may be able to return and take a bow, to leave the stage without waiting for an answer immediately after a proposal of marriage couched in the form of an aria. But Mozart himself, in his comic operas, dealt with situations equally destructive of illusion. Constanze, in *Die Entführung aus dem Serail*, when informed by the Pasha of the tortures that await her if she does not yield to his demands, must stand and listen to an introduction at least two minutes long in full concertante style before replying. In present-day performances, the stage director's problems with this aria are almost greater than the singer's, difficult as the coloratura may be with its full-blown written-out cadenza accompanied by solo winds. The director's conscientious realism invariably distracts our attention from the ritornello—how to explain the long wait before the reply? Is Constanze thinking it over? Speechless with rage? Trembling with fear before she can screw up her courage to say that torture will be unavailing? Should she pace? Sit down? Strike one attitude and hold it for the full two minutes? None of this, of course, was a problem during Mozart's time; no such psychological questions were asked. Mozart realized the aria was unconscionably long, and said apologetically that he could not stop, but the problem of holding an audience's interest was not, in the *Singspiel*, more than partially coincident with the question of preserving naturalistic illusion. The soprano waited because a concertante aria of that size and dramatic importance required a long ritornello.

It may be objected that the aria concertante is one of the conventions of *opera seria* rather than of the *Singspiel*, and that the ridiculousness of the situation is a reflection on that already unfortunate genre. But the situation need not seem ridiculous if it is accepted without qualms by the stage director; the aria is dramatically necessary as well as a fine piece of music. The trouble arises partly because directors continue to work in a tradition of naturalistic psychology entirely foreign to eighteenth-century opera, and partly because they cannot conceive of music going on with the curtain up without inventing business to fill what seems to them so much empty time. Today, if Constanze did nothing during the ritornello, this, too, would be felt as an obtrusive effect. What is clear even in a misguided production, however, is the dramatic rightness and force of the aria, and of its place in the opera as a whole, giving the needed weight to the first act, and bringing back the brilliance (and the tonality) of the overture (and therefore of the opera as a whole). There seems to be nothing wrong with the conventions of *opera seria*, provided that they appear within the framework of comic opera.

Even characteristic *buffa* conventions can seem ridiculous enough to any-one who refuses to suspend his disbelief. At the beginning of *Le Nozze di Figaro*, the floor must be measured twice by Figaro only so that his music may be combined with Susanna's. Wagner rejected the convention of repeating everything four or five times mainly because the musical forms which required repetition were obsolete by his time; of course, he gave more philosophical reasons for his decision. But Wagner's own conventions are, in other ways, no less formal and unrealistic: in a Mozart aria, passages are repeated four times mostly at a pace approximating normal speech; in Wagner, everything is sung once but generally four times as slowly. In any case, *opera buffa* has conventions as artificial as those of any other art form: one must accept the idea that it gets dark enough outdoors for a valet to disguise himself as his master by the mere exchange of cloaks; that a young man can go unrecognized by his fiancée if he puts on a false mustache; and that if someone is to get a box on the ear, it is almost always somebody else standing nearby who receives it by mistake. As for the *Singspiel*, its preposterousness is grandiose even when compared to *opera seria*. The failure of eighteenth-century heroic and tragic opera to create enduring works which could still seem artistically relevant to us today cannot be explained by its conventions. Handel and Mozart, at least, succeeded with everything else they put their hands to, and they came near to succeeding with *opera seria*.

A popular explanation of the weakness of *opera seria* is the general failure of tragedy throughout the eighteenth century. The ideal of poetic tragedy was as important in literature as in music, and its failure there was even more disastrous. Individual arias from Handel's operas have lost none of their effect, isolated revivals of *Idomeneo* reveal magnificent sections of great beauty, and Gluck came close to creating a viable style for musical tragedy. Yet the tragedies of Voltaire and Crébillon can only be read today for their historical interest, and Metastasio is intolerable except in the smallest of doses. Even lovers of Addison and Johnson cannot get through more than one act at a time of *Cato* and *Irene*. Undeniably, respect for the high art of tragedy and a failure to produce anything above mediocre examples of it are both characteristic of the period. The evidence for the century's incapacity for tragic art appears to be overwhelming. Why should we expect more from the musicians than from the poets?

The arts often show roughly parallel developments (sometimes by mis-understanding each other), but we cannot assume that success in one is relevant throughout a culture. Elizabethan music has none of the large-scale dramatic qualities to be found in the plays; French painting of the sixteenth century produced nothing to set beside Rabelais; Verdi's operas have no peers in the Italian theater of their day. Even within the confines of one art, two genres may show a striking inequality: eighteenth-century French poetry is a wretched affair compared with the magnificent prose of the time. Yet it is only primitive taxonomy to say that the century of reason and light was a prosaic age. The English eighteenth century, too, we are told, was a prosaic age, but there are Pope, Johnson, and Smart: in France, we must settle for Parny and Jean-Baptiste Rousseau, and it is not much consolation to invoke the spirit of rationalism. It is a mistake to hold the *Zeitgeist* responsible for a crime when one cannot be sure of the *modus operandi*. The eighteenth century may not have been able to produce tragedy, but it was not for lack of aspiration, appreciation nor popular interest. Neither talent nor effort could create an enduring tragic form, while pastoral, a genre equally antique and sclerotic, could be made to live again.

It may be that our understanding is parochially blind to the ideals of another age. The heroic operas of Rameau and Handel, the tragedies of Voltaire and Addison had their admirers, even passionate ones, in their time. It is not, however, the success of eighteenth-century tragedy on its own terms that is being challenged, but its claims to transcend those terms and to break out of its localization in historical time. The exercise of taste is often a definite act of will: Stravinsky was counseled by Rimsky-Korsakov not to listen to Debussy as he might come to like that sort of music. The effort to like *opera seria* has been made. Handel's operas have been brought out of oblivion, and no one can deny that they contain scores of beautiful pages; his invention and imagination were as great in *Giulio Cesare* as in *Israel in Egypt*, but the result is far less satisfactory in the former. Nothing can redeem the weaknesses in every one of Gluck's finest scores, and it is sad to think that a staging of his works is generally an act of archaeological piety. To resuscitate Rameau's operas, even performances with perfume and a Wagnerian orchestra have been tried. As for *Idomeneo*, if it could have been saved for the repertory, it would have happened by now. In this century, opera managers have been delighted to find that *Cosi fan Tutte* and *Die Entführung* could be produced with a success almost equal to that of the already popular *Don Giovanni*, *Figaro*, and *Die Zauberflöte*, and they would be even happier to add a grand tragic opera to the pentalogy. Performances are, indeed, no longer rare. Yet every one, riddled with cuts and rearrangements born of desperation, has the air of a revival.

Neither the High Baroque style of Bach, Handel, and Rameau nor the classical style of Haydn and Mozart was apt for the rendering of secular tragedy, not even of contemporary works like the tragedies of Voltaire. With little possibility of transition, High Baroque rhythm was almost unmanageable for dramatic purposes, and the constant reliance upon falling sequences for harmonic motion only added to the heaviness. Dramatic movement was impossible: two phases of the same action could only be statically represented, with a clear division between them. Even a change of sentiment could not take place gradually: there had to be a definite moment where one sentiment stopped and another suddenly took over. This reduced the heroic opera of the Baroque to a succession of static scenes, with all the rigid nobility of Racine and little of his extraordinary and supple inner movement. The monotony of Baroque opera has been blamed on the massive use of the da capo aria; but the da capo aria is the form best suited to this rhythmic conception, and, in fact, offers the greatest chance of variety and relief in its contrasting middle section. No doubt Handel and Rameau transcended this style and worked miracles with it at moments, but it was not one which lent itself with any ease to dramatic action.

I have spoken above of 'secular' tragedy in order to avoid a quibble about the Passions of Bach and the oratorios of Handel, but the quibble is worth discussing. There can be no question of the dramatic intensity of these works, and it is interesting to see how this is achieved. The dramatic parts of the Bach Passions are concentrated entirely in the recitatives and in some of the choruses; these are set within a framework of personal meditations in the form of arias, and of public meditations in the form of hymns. The whole of the *Passion according to St. Matthew* is framed by two great tableaux: the first, superbly visual, is the road to Golgotha, and the final chorus is the burial of Christ. In this way the static nature of High Baroque style is both accepted and magnificently overcome. Just as Mozart could realize his most heroic and tragic effects only in the setting of *opera buffa*, so Bach arrives at his dramatic effects only in what must be called an elegiac setting. Even the recitatives are not strictly drama but narrative epic, and recitative all by itself is not a musical form that can sustain much interest for any length of time. The dramatic power of Bach's works depends upon the juxtaposition of the recitative with the elegiac arias, the chorales, and the descriptive choruses. High tragedy is achieved only through means that remain largely narrative or pictorial.

Dramatic development being impossible within Baroque style, dramatic juxtaposition must act as a substitute, and this, too, is Handel's solution in the oratorios. In Handel as in Bach, it is the contrast of chorus and solo voice that makes possible the development of a dramatic logic. No oratorio of Handel is organized with the intensity of the two great Bach Passions, with their tight relationship between each part and its neighbors, and the significance of the movement from recitative to commentary in the chorales and the arias. But within the choruses, Handel often shows a dramatic, if not an emotional, force that Bach rarely attempts: where Bach's choruses are generally built from one homogeneous rhythmic texture, Handel can deploy two or more rhythmic blocks, and without making any attempt at transition between them, place them side by side with the most vigorous contrast, and then pile them one on top of another, all of this with a motor energy that has never been surpassed for excitement.[1] This is accomplished with a texture that is considerably thinner than Bach's, and a consequent loss of intensity is compensated by a gain in clarity. Unlike the Bach Passions, the oratorios of Handel are truly public, meant for a concert performance or with simple staging, almost out of place in a church. Handel went bankrupt twice as an operatic impresario and made a good deal of money from his oratorios; the

---

[1] The supremacy of Handel's choruses was recognized throughout the eighteenth century: when Wieland preferred them (and those of Lully) to the arias, he claimed to be expressing a common judgment.

contemporary public may only have reacted with the same kind of enthusiasm to Handel's subjects that an audience today shows for Biblical epics at the movies, but their judgment has endured.

It is therefore not the dramatic or tragic instinct which was lacking in the first half of the eighteenth century, or even the capacity and the genius to achieve it. Missing was a style that could encompass a sustained theatrical effort with the use only of recitative, aria, and solo ensemble; even the latter is rare in Handel's operas and of much greater interest in the oratorios, and the solo ensembles of *Jephtha* and *Susanna* have no parallels of equivalent dramatic force and characterization in the operas. Concentration on the aria, given a style in which interior dramatic development was close to impossible, made Baroque opera a series of display pieces for the singers. There was nothing to set off or enliven the static nature of the individual numbers as convincing as the use of narrative form in the Passions and the oratorios, together with the use of choruses for description and of arias for religious meditation and commentary.

Rameau's avoidance of narrative and elegiac forms—the one so natural for recitative and the other so well adapted to the normal musical structures of the High Baroque—may partly account for his failure to create a large musical work that is completely satisfactory. He makes magnificent use of the chorus, and many of the ensembles are highly developed, but with the unyielding rhythm of the period and a magnetic attraction to the tonic more typical of contemporary French music than of the German school, his scenes tend to separate into marble reliefs, noble, graceful, and oppressively immobile. If heroic tragedy was to be possible in French music, a chorus providing a background and philosophical commentary was necessary, and the possibility of rendering in one musical form a progressively developing conflict rather than a clearly defined opposition would have to be evolved. In other words, French Baroque opera had to become more like Greek drama, if it was not to start all over again on an entirely new basis. This, of course, is exactly what Gluck tried to achieve, with a neoclassic dogmatism and a daring originality typical of the period. If the success was only partial, the effort was heroic.

Gluck is generally described as a composer of genius with astonishingly defective technique. About the genius there is no question at all, and there is little question, if much misunderstanding, of the 'imperfections' that can be found in any of his works. It would be interesting to ask if these 'defects' arose, not from lacunae in Gluck's equipment, but from what he was trying within his historical moment.

The history of music is encumbered by half-exploded theories about the deficiencies of the greatest composers: Beethoven's lack of ease in contrapuntal writing, Chopin's difficulties with large forms, Brahms' awkward orchestrations. These dead horses rise like ghosts, and still require occasional beating. But with Gluck's operas, the faults are, at times, too glaring to be denied or to be turned into virtues by any aesthetic and historical reconsiderations. Nevertheless the faults, to a large extent, derive from the nature of the contemporary style applied to the task that Gluck set for it. To say that the style of the 1760s and 1770s was unequal to the problems of creating a tragic work for the stage may seem only a less specific way of saying that it was Gluck who failed to bend his art to the demands of tragedy. But the first way of putting it has a certain advantage, as it draws our attention to the nature of the style and the demands made upon it by *opera seria* and the renewed interest in Greek tragedy. We may then find some idea of the problems facing Gluck, the purpose of many of his innovations, and the reason for some of his failure. To talk of Gluck's defective technique explains little, and is only an excuse for dismissing that part of the music which we dislike. Not that the criticism is irrelevant or even untrue, and it is in any case sanctioned by tradition. It was Handel who said that Gluck 'knows no more counterpoint than my cook,' and although Tovey has pointed out that Handel's cook, who was also a singer in Handel's opera company, probably knew a good bit of counterpoint, it was surely obstinate of Gluck not to have remedied a defect which would have needed no more than a year's study to bring him up to snuff. It would be more reasonable to assume that Gluck no longer had a need for Handel's counterpoint. When we miss contrapuntal mastery in Gluck, we should recall that he had broken with Handel's style and his kind of mastery, and created something that had not yet arrived at Mozart's ease or at Beethoven's range but which was moving towards them. This kind of historical hindsight is cheap, as Gluck was not in any conscious or unconscious way working towards the same goals as Mozart and Beethoven; but a small dose of teleology may be useful in approaching an historical figure as irritating and as admirable as Gluck.

Motives are generally mixed, and the most variegated of all are the unconscious and unconfessed ones that we of necessity conjecture and read into the past in order to explain historical change. The most evident of Gluck's operatic innovations is his drastic simplification—of action, of form, and of texture. What were the reasons for this reform? The official answer, and Gluck's own, is greater dramatic naturalness. The return to Nature is the reason for almost every dramatic reform, and it is even, of course, true in each case, but it is not always easy to fix what was natural as opposed to artificial, particularly as regards eighteenth-century tragedy: to some extent it meant getting rid of the crippling conventions of the previous generations. The more interesting puzzle, why these conventions just at that time suddenly seemed crippling, is complicated by a further consideration, the rising interest in Greek art and the development of neoclassicism. The Renaissance, largely Roman in the fifteenth and sixteenth centuries (except in France), became predominantly Greek by the eighteenth. This growing enthusiasm for Greek culture, however, was colored by a curious kind of primitivism. The eighteenth-century belief in progress was offset by a nostalgia for a utopian past, which gave an easy outlet to the old belief that the world was continually degenerating, not improving. If the Greeks had achieved an ideal civilization, it was because they were less complicated and sophisticated than the moderns. The eighteenth century tried not so much to imitate the Greeks as to improve on them by attempting a drastic simplicity which had little to do with the Greeks. Writers and architects went back not so much to Greek art as to what they considered the theoretical source of Greek art, to Nature, in short. Greek architecture is not as ostentatiously 'natural' as neoclassic eighteenth-century style could become when it deliberately tried to recall or reconstruct the primitive origin of architectural elements. The derivation of columns from tree trunks so evident to the rationalist mind implied that the use of bases for columns was over-sophisticated, unnatural: the columns in many neo-classic buildings grow straight out of the ground. Neoclassic painting is distinguished not so much by the use of classical subjects—they were common enough since the Renaissance, and even before—but by the moral earnestness with which they were treated; in addition, classical mythology became less important than subjects drawn from history illustrating the civic virtues. Above all, neoclassic painting pretends to none of the emotional complexity of Poussin or Raphael in their treatment of classical subjects: it makes a direct appeal to simple and basic emotions, or such, at least, was the claim.

Neoclassicism is aggressively doctrinaire: it is art with a thesis. This makes the relation of practice to theory a peculiarly sensitive one. Normally, in most styles, the relation is loose and somewhat muddled: artistic theories— that is, those accepted by the artists themselves—may be nothing more than pious sentiments which are justified by tradition or appear to sound well; they may be rationalizations, *post facto* attempts to justify the works already finished by principles which had little to do with their creation (while foreshadowing, perhaps, the direction in which the artist hopes to go); they may, finally, reflect in an oblique or even a direct way the actual practice of the artist. If these different kinds of principles are most often confused (so that artists are either reproached or commended for not practicing what they preach), the excuse for historians—a lame one—is that they are difficult enough to disentangle. In the case of a style like neoclassicism, the problem becomes the more complex as there is a conscious attempt on the part of the artist to make practice follow theory, even when this theory, professed and expounded, collides head on with artistic habits and with less conscious principles which only practice can gradually bring to light. In most neoclassic works, a considerable tension results from this conflict, a desire for theoretical coherence which leads paradoxically at moments to an incoherence within the artistic language, forced into contradiction with itself in order to conform to something exterior. The deliberate cult of the natural leads in neoclassicism to an effort of self-denial and repression which becomes indistinguishable from the 'perverse': it gives the greatest neoclassic works—the operas of

Gluck, the architecture of Ledoux, the paintings of David—an explosive force that is in excess of the works' own pretensions.[1]

What this comes to, in fact, is that the greatness of so much of neoclassicism arises from the incomplete repression of instinct by doctrine (instinct being here nothing more mystical than unformulated doctrine). It has, therefore, the curious result that the theory of neoclassicism is in a special sense built into the works themselves. In Gluck's operas, the examples of classical virtue on which they are based—Alceste, Iphigenia, Orpheus—are not only expressed, but literally illustrated by the chastity of the music itself: the refusal to permit vocal display, the absence of ornament, the endings of arias which leave no possibility for applause, the simplicity of the musical texture with contrapuntal enrichment reduced to the barest essentials. The austerity is not only a form of stoicism, a holding back from pleasure, but one of the main sources of pleasure in itself. There is, of course, no virtue in refusing to yield to what does not tempt; Gluck's reduction in the number of roulades he would write for singers and his attempt to escape the da capo form which would allow them the chance to improvise are no longer artistically impressive. What is far more significant are the moments of strained simplicity, where Gluck is obviously denying himself something he loved. The severity of much of his finest work is analogous to the box-like space and metallic colors of David, and the pure geometrical forms of Ledoux, all of which have a significance as much ethical as aesthetic.

The theory of art as an imitation of Nature is an ancient piety: neoclassicism gave it a new force by a simplistic and even primitivist view of Nature. The doctrine of the imitation of Nature gave rise to such difficulty in music (in painting the application was so self-evident as to retard aesthetics for centuries) that it had to be completely rephrased: music imitated—or, better, represented and expressed—the purest and most natural feelings, and was to be judged by its success or failure at this task. Along with neoclassic doctrine, eighteenth-century psychological ethics implied a considerable reduction of sophistication of feeling; coloratura virtuosity did, surely, express feeling, but of an 'unnatural' and unacceptable kind. In any art so closely involved with its own theory, the influence of political and educational thought was inevitable: Gluck's music is as much affected by the ideas for which Rousseau was the greatest spokesman as by the revived interest in classical virtue. This restressed relationship between music and feeling tied operatic music emphatically to the words almost at the very moment that Mozart was about to achieve its emancipation by making the music not so much an expression of

---

[1] I have used 'neoclassicism' in a narrow sense of a return to the assumed simplicity of Nature through the imitation of the ancients. The body of doctrine in the eighteenth century was coherent, cohesive, and supranational. Gluck claimed that the accent of Nature in music would abolish the absurdity of national styles. The aesthetics of neoclassicism may be summed up in Winckelmann's belief that the thinnest line was the most apt for the portrayal of a beautiful form.

175

the text (although still partially that) but an equivalent for the dramatic action. Mozart's achievement was revolutionary: for the first time on the operatic stage, the music could follow the dramatic movement while still arriving at a form that could justify itself, at least in its essentials, on purely internal grounds.

Before Mozart (or before the development of the Italian comic opera for which Mozart was to find a definitive form), a musical drama had always been so arranged that the more formally organized music was reserved for the expression of feeling—generally only one sentiment at a time—in an aria or duet, while the action was left to be conveyed in recitative. This meant that except in so far as the music had values of its own unrelated to the drama, it remained essentially an illustration and expression of the words; it could only be combined with the action in the most primitive way and in the least interesting fashion. This primacy of the text reigns from the start, even in Monteverdi, where the difference between aria and recitative, between more and less formally organized structure, is not always clear-cut. This does not at all imply that the music took a servile position, but it does impose a hierarchy in the transmission of meaning: the music interprets the text, and the text interprets the action—the words standing in almost every case between the music and the drama. An aesthetic of music as the expression of feeling was ideal for Baroque opera: it fitted the da capo aria like a glove, with its homogeneous rhythmic texture, its principle of additive extension of a central motif, and its relatively equal distribution of tension throughout—even the contrast provided by the middle section was so static as to raise no contradiction. The difficulty—leaving aside for the moment the rupture between music and the essential scenic movement—is that in so far as music is an expressive art, it is pre-verbal, not post-verbal. Its effects are at the level of the nerves and not of the sentiments. For this reason, in music like the Baroque da capo aria, devoted to the depiction of one sentiment or *Affekt*, the words come to seem like a commentary, generalized and denatured, on the music. The musical line speaks directly to the listener, and the singer adds, as a bonus, the words which can act only as a sort of dampening program notes. Opera cannot exist without an aesthetics of expression, but a complete subservience to it destroys the possibility of drama. It is from this fundamentally static aesthetic that arise all the problems, all the malaise encountered in the production of Baroque opera today, and it is significant that the Mozart comic operas, which partially broke with the aesthetic of expression, have held the stage continuously and successfully since their composition. *Figaro, Don Giovanni*, and *Die Zauberflöte* are the first operas that have never had to be revived.

If Gluck appeared to accept an aesthetic of expression and, indeed, to give it a new force by an exquisite and unparalleled concentration on details of declamation, there are signs in his work that its static implications caused him a certain uneasiness. There are a number of experiments of arias in continually changing tempi, the most remarkable being Alceste's 'Non, ce n'est point un sacrifice.' For the most part, these different tempi are treated as separate blocks; in all of Gluck's music there are only a few hints that a rhythmic transition is even attempted. The aria from *Alceste* is one of Gluck's most successful works, and without calling either its greatness or its beauty into question, it must be said that the scheme of so many different tempi is a measure of desperation. Within the frame of one piece, Gluck seems almost always to experience grave difficulties in changing the rhythmic movement. The following measures from the Overture of *Iphigénie en Tauride* have an effect of clashing gears when the change arrives:

and such passages are not infrequent.

Seen from the viewpoint of the classical style, Gluck's rhythmic system contains an important contradiction. The phrasing is classically articulated, while the pulse-beats are only very weakly differentiated in a manner better suited to Baroque continuity. In Paris' aria 'Di te scordarmi,' from *Paride ed Elena*, one phrase appears in two forms:

The second form in the minor takes half a measure less, and surely gains in concentrated force. Comparing the two forms, it is difficult, however, to see whether much distinction has been made between the force of a first and of a third beat: the phrase in the minor begins with a more dramatic accent, but after this the rhythmic impulse is oddly more fluid than the phrasing. In the music of Haydn and Mozart, such shifts in 4/4 time occur frequently, but (at least after 1775) it is always clear exactly what has happened: either there is a phrase of unusually irregular length, so that the downbeat has now shifted temporarily to the third beat (later composers would write a single 2/4 measure and move all the bar-lines), or the downbeat retains its force and we are to hear the phrase-articulation as a syncopated accent against the beat. The choice is not so clear-cut in Gluck, and there are many such ambiguous passages throughout the operas.

Because of this rhythmic looseness, Gluck's greatest achievements resolve into a series of tableaux, some of them magnificently conceived. In one important respect, there is an astonishing advance upon earlier *opera seria:* that is, in the idea of psychological contradiction and tension within the frame of a single movement. The most famous of such moments is Orestes' pathetic belief that he has found peace while his inner turmoil is so evident in the music, but the anguished hesitation of Helen in *Paride ed Elena* is as striking:

the syncopations, the cross-rhythms, and the half-parlando declamation are combined with great originality.

Still more original is Gluck's conception of dynamic accent. It is true that the rhythmic texture retains the almost total homogeneity of the High Baroque, but the dynamics thrust in an entirely new element. Most of the greatest passages in Gluck rely in one way or another upon a rhythmic ostinato, which is given shape by accent and by an irregularity of super-imposed articulation: the conception of the static tableau is being destroyed by pressure from within. The most remarkable and largest construction of this kind is Iphigenia's aria with chorus from *Iphigénie en Tauride*, Act II, scene VI, but it must be quoted at great length before any of its power can be understood. An almost equally moving ostinato is found in the trio of the last act of *Paride ed Elena*:[1]

---

[1] Gluck was sufficiently pleased with this trio to use it in *Orphée* as well.

The free-flowing declamation against the syncopated ostinato, the tension imposed on the texture by the *sforzandi*—all this has no parallel within the classical style. It appears in opera again with the Italian romantic style, above all with the ostinati of Verdi (an example close to the above is Otello's exhausted monologue in Act III). However, the true inheritor of Gluck is, to no one's surprise, Berlioz, for whom the conception of a syncopated ostinato reinforced by accent is central: the 'Lacrimosa' from the *Requiem* could never have come into being without Gluck.

Mozart owes an important artistic debt to Gluck, above all in the dramatic power of his accompanied recitatives. There are even occasional clear references to Gluck's personal style, as in the Chaconne from *Idomeneo*. Nevertheless, it is surprising how many of Gluck's most successful and suggestive innovations seem not even to have existed for Mozart. He owed almost nothing to Gluck's declamation in the arias, or to his conception of accent; he never tried Gluck's experiment of multiple tempi within an aria; and only once, in *Die Zauberflöte*, written at the end of his life, did he use an operatic chorus with Gluck's majesty (and even then he did not aim at Gluck's dramatic force, except in the off-stage pianissimo phrase for the chorus at the end of Tamino's scene with the priest). Beethoven owes perhaps even less to Gluck, in spite of his attempt to write a thoroughly 'serious' opera, although Florestan's hallucinatory vision of Leonora at the opening of Act II of *Fidelio* has both Gluck's fluidity of rhythm and phrase and even something of his orchestral sonority in the lone oboe high above the pulsating strings.

Mozart destroyed neoclassicism in opera. This was quite clearly understood by his contemporaries, and it accounts, at least in part, for the opposition to his style. Already in 1787 in his *Italian Journey*, Goethe wrote: 'All our endeavor . . . to confine ourselves to what is simple and limited was lost when Mozart appeared. *Die Entführung aus dem Serail* conquered all, and our own carefully written piece has never been so much as mentioned in theatrical circles.'[1] Goethe's ideals were much the same as Wieland's: the latter (one of the few authors Mozart is known to have admired) wrote in his essay on the German *Singspiel* that 'the greatest possible simplicity of plan is proper and essential to the *Singspiel*. Action cannot be sung.' It was, of course, just this point that Mozart was so triumphantly to prove wrong.[2]

It was not, however, in *opera seria* that Mozart succeeded in setting action to music. Perhaps the most disastrous weakness of *Idomeneo* viewed purely as a work for the stage is that the dénouement takes place almost entirely in recitative and this in the teeth of the richness and formal complexity of so much else in the work.[3] It is hardly to the point that every detail of the score is masterly. Mozart nevertheless had no style able to deal with the dramatic climax of a tragedy, and it should be stressed that this is by no means the same thing as saying that he had no style with which to express tragic sentiment. Beethoven later struggled similarly to write a serious opera, and subjected his work to even more stringent revision; if parts of *Fidelio* are more effective as sheer stagecraft than *Idomeneo*, the considerable expansion of the classical style in Beethoven's hands is a partial explanation.

The style that Mozart had inherited and developed was only applicable to the tragic stage with difficulty, and the sense of strain is inevitable. The classical style was, indeed, one which dealt clearly with events, and its forms were anything but static, but its pace was too rapid for *opera seria*. Tovey has remarked that Beethoven was not insufficiently dramatic but rather *too* dramatic for the stage: his music compresses into ten minutes the complexity of a three-act opera. Although the principal modulation within late eighteenth-century style is conceived as an event, there is no way that this event can be evaded for any length of time without the delaying action of a considerable amount of chromaticism, and Mozart's language was essentially diatonic, at least in its long-range aspects. He could write a love-duet with as much passion (on his own terms) as Wagner, but the prospect of making it last more than an hour, or, indeed, more than a few minutes would have seemed absurd to him. The slow, dignified pace of a tragic opera broke into small pieces in his hands, as it did in everyone else's at that time: *Idomeneo* remains a beautifully conceived mosaic, and if its limitations are those of the contemporary language, it is not true that every language is

---

[1] Cited by Abert, and by Deutsch, *Mozart*, Black, London, 1965.

[2] Mozart's practice was less opposed to Wieland's other views on *Singspiel*. Wieland had complained of overtures that had nothing to do with the operas and no one, not even Gluck, linked his overtures so intimately with what followed as Mozart. With Wieland's complaint of overlong ritornelli Mozart cannot have been much impressed, and the writer's distaste for overdecorated display arias, unnatural da capos, and perfunctory recitatives would have been shared in the late 1770s by any musician of taste.

[3] It should be emphasized that Mozart himself was very uneasy about this section, with the voice from heaven, and he rewrote it several times. The shortest version is naturally the least unsatisfactory.

equally apt for every form. On the other hand, the pacing of the classical style worked supremely well for the comic theater, with its quick changes of situation and the numerous possibilities of accelerated action.

It is, however, a pity that standards of dramatic and even musical cogency, no matter how justified, should militate against frequent performances of *Idomeneo*, at least in concert form. The opera's great quartet was never surpassed by Mozart, and he was justifiably proud of it. If the problem of the total dramatic rhythm is not completely solved, there are detailed touches of the greatest subtlety, and Mozart never moved with such sensitivity from recitative into the more formal aria as he did in many places here.

Since classical rhythm could not, as we have seen, easily manage long-range non-comic dramatic pacing, Beethoven, in writing *Fidelio*, went to the much more loosely organized traditions of French grand opera, of Cherubini and Méhul, mostly in an attempt to slow the movement to a pace commensurate with his subject's moral dignity. This is even more evident in the original version of the opera, where there is a continuous and heavy repetition of small phrases and parts of phrases: this repetition, much of it cut in the final version, gave both clarity and a kind of loose dignity to French opera, and also diluted its dramatic force. Beethoven's rewriting reflects a decision to return largely to the much tighter *opera buffa* organization, and this is particularly evident in the substitution of the *Fidelio* overture for the earlier ones; in spite of romantic horn calls, its lighter movement is far closer to comic style. Except for the inspired revision of Florestan's air, this return to classical concision accounts for the largest part of the rewriting (although the unfortunate change in the opening melodic line of the final duet in G major of the dungeon scene must have been motivated by singers' difficulties with the original form, which is musically more spontaneous).[1]

The mixture of traditions is most noticeable in the first act, where the opening duet is almost pure *opera buffa*, while the Mozartean models are only too evident behind the exquisite canon 'Es ist mir wunderbar' (the canon of *Così fan tutte*) and Rocco's aria (which has parallels with many Mozart arias, especially 'Batti, batti, bel Masetto'). The melodramatic scenes that follow are more diffuse in character except for Leonora's aria, heavily influenced again by Mozart, and the prisoners' chorus. Pizzarro's aria, effective as it is, is more musical gesture than substance. The dungeon scene, however, is pure Beethoven, and it is the weight of his symphonic style that makes the digging of the grave and the giving of the crust of bread so moving. The

---

[1] Beethoven's difficulties with *Fidelio* have been overemphasized: much of the failure of the first version of the opera can be ascribed to the bad luck of a production in time of war. Nevertheless, Beethoven was not ordinarily willing to rewrite a piece merely because it had failed to find favor with the public, and his successive revisions (in large part a tightening of the rhythmic structure) showed that he acknowledged a problem. If even the final version cannot be accounted completely satisfactory, it stands easily by the side of Mozart's successes.

almost intolerable excitement of the quartet, 'Er sterbe,' is something entirely new and original on the musical stage, and was made possible by Beethoven's expansion of sonata form: the double climax of Leonora's 'First kill his wife' and the off-stage trumpet (both symmetrically centered on an electrifying B♭ within a D major sonata form) is an example of extreme harmonic tension both just before and after the beginning of the recapitulation—such as we already find in Haydn and Mozart, but which Beethoven was to carry far beyond its original form.

With all its greatness, *Fidelio*, in comparison with the ease of style of Mozart's comic operas, is a triumph of personal will. It is a work which shows its strains. Like a language, a style has unlimited expressive capacities, but ease of expression—which carries more weight in art than in communication, and can even overpower content in importance both for artist and public—is very severely tied to the structure of the style. Even the innovatory nature of a style is bound by its own rules, and only those stylistic changes which fit most comfortably into the already established system are acceptable in the long run. Like most of Beethoven's work, *Fidelio* is not a beginning but the end of a tradition, and in this case it is an almost completely isolated effort within that tradition.

Part V
MOZART

———

1

The Concerto

Mozart's most signal triumphs took place where Haydn had failed: in the dramatic forms of the opera and the concerto, which pit the individual voice against the sonority of the mass. At first glance, the disparity of achievement may seem inexplicable. The surface of Haydn's music is, if anything, more, not less, dramatic than that of Mozart's. It is the elder composer who is inclined to the *coup de théatre*, the surprise modulation, the sudden farcical deflation of pomposity, the scandalously excessive dynamic accent. It may even be argued that Mozart's melodies are not only more conventional than Haydn's, but in general less 'characteristic,' less immediately descriptive of a specific sentiment or action. Mozart's musical references rarely descend to the particularity of Haydn's tone-painting and sentiment-painting in his two great oratorios. The 'characteristic' moments that we find throughout Haydn's symphonies differ from the tone-painting in the *Seasons* only in their lack of explicit reference, and they are no less marked and individual. The personages of an opera by Mozart live with a physical presence never found in Haydn's operatic work, but their music is neither more dramatic nor more 'expressive.' And while Mozart's psychological penetration may seem to give a satisfying explanation of his success in opera, it cannot account for his equal success in the closely related form of the concerto.

Mozart's early career as an international virtuoso performing concertos and his first-hand acquaintance with opera in all the capitals of Europe are experiences that Haydn missed. Nevertheless, Haydn's knowledge of opera should not be underestimated, and his interest in spectacular instrumental virtuosity in some ways surpassed Mozart's. Haydn was neither indifferent to virtuosity nor unable to handle it, and his relative insecurity with concerto form must have other roots. How evident this is may be seen by comparing the tame display of his only piano concerto, a good but unremarkable work, with the extravagant virtuosity of his piano trios and late sonatas, and the surprisingly complex demands he made upon the solo orchestral players in the symphonies, both early and late. Haydn's interest in virtuosity evidently flowered best in chamber music and in the symphony. The reasons for Mozart's superiority to Haydn in opera and concerto are more specifically musical than wider experience, or a taste for virtuosity and dramatic expression: they must be sought both in his handling of long-range movement and in the direct physical impact of his music.

The unsurpassed stability of Mozart's handling of tonal relations paradoxically contributes to his greatness as a dramatic composer. It enabled him to treat a tonality as a mass, a large area of energy which can encompass and resolve the most contradictory opposing forces. It also allowed him to slow down the purely formal harmonic scheme of his music so that it would not outstrip the action on the stage. The tonal stability provided a frame of reference which allowed a much wider range of dramatic possibilities. The firmness of this frame of reference may be heard even in Mozart's most daring harmonic experiments. If we stop the famous chromatic introduction to the String Quartet in C major K. 465 at any point and play the chord of C major, we find that not only have Mozart's complex and weirdly disquieting progressions established the key from the outset without once actually sounding the tonic chord, but they never leave that key: the chord of C major will appear always as the stable point around which every other chord in these measures revolves. The opening of a work by Mozart is always solidly based, no matter how ambiguous and disturbing its expressive significance, while the most unassuming first measures of a quartet by Haydn are far more unstable, more immediately charged with a dynamic movement away from the tonic.

The balance of harmonic relations needed to achieve this stability is a delicate one, but even the most dissonant material was dealt with by Mozart with an ease which is itself the outward sign of the harmonic equilibrium. The opening of the E flat Quartet K. 428 shows how widely Mozart could range without losing the larger harmonic sense:

The opening measure is an example of Mozart's sublime economy. It sets the tonality by a single octave leap (the most tonal of intervals), framing the three chromatic measures that follow. The two E♮'s are lower and higher than any of the other notes, and by setting these limits they imply the resolution of all dissonance within an E flat context. They define the tonal space:

and the resolutions trace the fundamental tonic triad of E flat major. The melodic line is unaccompanied, but not unharmonized: it is given complete harmonic meaning by the opening octave. We hear all these chromatic alterations so resolved into a completely diatonic significance because of the resonance of that opening measure: the fact of the octave leap is as important as everything that comes after. The 'unharmonized' chromatic progression is not only resolved, and harmonized by the first measure, but itself implies the harmonies that follow:

The fifth measure, which outlines the chord of II against the tonic note, has already been defined by the melodic line. The dramatic effect of full harmony after a unison passage is in no way minimized by the impeccable logic.[1]

This extraordinary power of Mozart's allows him to use a range of subsidiary modulation, of remote tonalities, in his expositions which Haydn generally had to reserve for the development sections. Haydn's more energetic conception of his material implies, too, a recapitulation that is very different from the exposition, as the nervous energy of the exposition must be completely reconceived when it is used at the end of the movement to affirm stability. Mozart's more massive treatment of the tonal areas of the exposition often results in recapitulations that are symmetrically equivalent, in which the musical discourse that resolves is almost a literal transposition of the pattern that established the initial tension. The large-scale symmetry is mirrored in the rich symmetry of the details, so that the music seems to achieve a state of constant balance, untroubled by the expressive violence that nevertheless so frequently characterizes Mozart's work. The symmetry is a condition of grace.

The complexity of the equilibrium in Mozart has sometimes been contrasted with the bland, mechanical symmetry in the music of his contemporaries, notably Johann Christian Bach and Dittersdorf, whose details echo themselves tamely and monotonously. Mozart's avoidance of strict repetition is not primarily for variety's sake: symmetry is not the same thing as literal reproduction, above all not in music, where the cumulative force of repetition is directly opposed to the feeling for balance. Music is, of course, asymmetrical with respect to time, which moves in only one direction, and a style that depends on proportion must seek in some way to redress the inequality. The

---

[1] The symmetry is always expressive. The second violin in measures 5 to 8 resolves its own motif ♪♪♪♪ by playing it backwards ♪♪♪♪

'sonata' is itself a form based on a partial compensation of the one-way movement of time, as the pattern of the exposition is not literally repeated at the end but rewritten so as to suggest that the music is drawing to a close. The inner symmetry of a Mozart phrase takes similar account of the direction of time, and its apparent variety is a subtle adjustment of balance, a more perfect symmetry.

The combination of power and delight that Mozart gained by adjusting his sense of symmetry to an irreversible forward movement is difficult to illustrate only because one would like to quote everything. The following eight-measure phrase from the finale of the *Hunt* Quartet must suffice:

The last four measures are a hidden repetition of the first four (as one can see at once by playing the first violin parts of both halves together, and noting the parallel octaves). In addition, there is also a mirror symmetry, as the second part of the phrase descends almost exactly as the first part rises; that is why the second half sounds so much like a resolution of the first half, in spite of their closely parallel structure. Along with these symmetries, however, there is another force at work, revealed most directly in the faster note-values of the second half of the phrase. This sense of forward movement is already apparent in the first half, which not only doubles the tempo of the initial motif as it transposes it upward, but plays it at the faster speed in the bass, so that the motif generates the harmonic movement as well as the melody. Controlled within the framework of symmetries are the elements reflecting the flow of time: the increased animation and the cumulative repetition of the motif reinforce each other. Both the symmetrical control and urgent sense of motion are essential to Mozart's dramatic genius.

This profound understanding of the relation of symmetry to movement in time appears as the sign of Mozart's mature style with *La Finta Giardiniera*, written at the age of nineteen. This new dramatic power can be felt throughout, most strikingly at the opening of the finale of Act I, with Sandrina's sensuous and despairing cry:

The symmetry of this seven-measure phrase is concealed, but it is nevertheless absolute. The last three measures not only balance the first three, with the fourth measure standing as a pivot, but also outline essentially the same melodic shape. In repeating and decorating this shape, however, they give it a new and more agitated rhythm and a harmonic movement of greater tension. The symmetrical balance is caught up in the dramatic movement, but gives it a stability that allows the drama to unfold as if impelled from within.

A sense of drama had become more important to the age in general. We can see this in one detail in the development of the keyboard concerto during the period that preceded Mozart's maturity. From 1750 to 1775 a figured-bass or continuo accompaniment on the keyboard was sometimes still harmonically necessary in all the purely orchestral sections, or ritornelli. Accompaniment by the soloist, however, was already felt as injurious to the dramatic effect of his entrances as a soloist, and to reinforce the contrast between the orchestral and solo passages, the continuo was generally suppressed for a few measures before each solo entrance. The following solo entrance from a concerto by Johann Christian Bach represents the common practice of the time:

Here the *unisono* implies the disappearance of the figured bass so as not to spoil the solo that is about to begin. It is a device obviously derived from a special form of the Baroque aria and concerto in which the entire ritornello is *unisono*, but by the middle of the century it is generally used only at the close of the opening orchestral tutti: this is the norm rather than the exception.

Mozart, however, never bothers to set off his solo entrances in this way. If we were to believe, as some would now have us do, that he continued to use the solo instrument in the tutti, it would imply that the minor composers of the preceding age were more interested than Mozart in the dramatic effect of the solo. This conclusion is plainly not easy to accept. In every way, Mozart made the soloist of his concertos even more like a character from an opera than before, and emphasized the dramatic qualities of the concerto. The derivation of concerto form from the aria was more than an historical fact for Mozart, it was a living influence.

Nevertheless, the evidence for the piano's role as continuo-instrument in Mozart's concertos after 1775 is attractive. It consists of the following: (1) the manuscripts of the concertos clearly show that Mozart has almost always written *col basso* in the piano part (or actually copied out the bass into the piano part) wherever the piano is not playing solo; (2) every one of the editions of the concertos published in the eighteenth century, most of them not during Mozart's lifetime, give a figured bass for the piano during the tutti sections; (3) there is a realization in Mozart's handwriting of a continuo for the Concerto in D major K. 238, of 1776, and some of the manuscripts of the early and lightly scored concertos contain continuo figures written in Leopold Mozart's hand; (4) the Artaria edition of K. 415, one of the few printed before Mozart's death, has a figured bass for the tutti which is not only very richly indicated, but carefully distinguishes sections of mere doubling of the bass from full chordal accompaniment: it has been conjectured[1] that the figured bass, generally added by the publishers, is in this case by Mozart himself, as it is so carefully worked out.

This last piece of evidence may be dismissed almost out-of-hand: the figured bass of the 1785 edition of K. 415 may be richly indicated, but it cannot be by Mozart. It is full of the kind of mistakes that Mozart cannot have made and which cannot be ascribed to printer's errors. The figured bass is the work of a publisher's hack.[2]

We must remember the conditions of public performance during the late eighteenth century. No one played from memory, and a full score at the

---

[1] H. F. Redlich; introduction to Eulenburg edition of the score, 1954.

[2] For example: in measure 51, the F in the bass is figured $\frac{6}{5}$. Yet at that point the full orchestra *forte* (trumpets, drums, horns, oboes, bassoons, and strings) plays only the notes F, A, and C—if Mozart had wanted the D required by the figured bass, he would not have asked the piano alone to play it against so much opposition. The figuring, of course, makes a perfectly sensible cadence at that place from the point of view of the bass alone, and it is a way of harmonizing that the hack evidently preferred; when the same cadence occurs for full orchestra in measure 156 as the end of quite a different phrase, he again harmonizes a note with 6, while the other instruments play a triad in root position. In similar fashion in measures 56, 57, and 58 he puts a 7 to a chord accompanying a simple triad: the dominant seventh *would* make harmonic sense in this place, except that Mozart did not write it, and if it were played, even on a modern nine-foot concert grand, nobody would hear it—a consoling thought. There are many more mistakes in the figuring of K. 415 as given in the Eulenburg score. In the second movement, bars 15–16 make no sense, and the natural is not indicated in bars 5 and 6; in the third movement the second 6 in bar 21 should be a $\frac{6}{4}$, the 6 of bar 46 should be $\frac{6}{\sharp}$, and there is something wrong in bars 138–139 (where $5\frac{6}{3}$ are written for $7\frac{5}{3}$). How many of these mistakes are due to misprints, and where they come from (Artaria or Eulenburg), I do not propose to find out. If Mozart did not write it, I do not care how they print it.

keyboard would have been too cumbersome. Not even the conductor always used a full score at that time; it was common to use only a first violin part. The pianist used the violoncello part for cues, a tradition that dates back to a time when he actually had to play continuo. Even Chopin's concertos were published with a continuo part; this persistence of an old-fashioned notation has, indeed, created some textual problems; there are notes at the beginnings and ends of phrases in concertos by Beethoven and by Chopin about which there remains some uncertainty as to whether they belong to the solo part, and are therefore to be played, or to the continuo part, in which case they are only cues, or an aid to performance. In the concertos of Mozart there is absolutely no place where an extra note is needed to fill in the harmony, or where the texture of the music requires the kind of continuity that the steady use of figured bass can give. Continuo playing in secular music died out in the second half of the eighteenth century, although only gradually, and everything about the music of Haydn and Mozart tells us that it was *musically*, if not practically, dead by 1775. An analogue to the purely notational aspect of the continuo as a mnemonic aid in performance is the score of Mozart's Clarinet Concerto, where, in flat contradiction to all that we know of Mozart's delicacy and tact in doubling the string parts with wind instruments, we would have to believe that whenever the clarinet is not playing solo, it incessantly doubles the first violin part throughout; this doubling is, of course, nothing but a system of cueing.[1]

Eighteenth-century performance was, in general, a less formal affair than it is today, and the attitude to the musical text was decidedly more cavalier. (Haydn's letter about the *Paris* Symphonies, suggesting that at least one rehearsal would be advisable before a performance, gives an idea of what went on.) Did a pianist ever play some part of the continuo, if not all of it? When the pianist conducted from the keyboard, he did play chords to keep the orchestra together, and perhaps even to add a little extra sonority to the louder sections. The tradition among soloists of playing the final chords of a concerto with the orchestra dates back a long way, but whether to the time of Mozart I do not know. A tradition may be as mistaken as an innovation, but it undoubtedly looks better if the pianist does not relax measures before everybody else. Eighteenth-century piano sound was so weak that even if the pianist played some of the continuo, he would have been inaudible most of the time except to members of the orchestra unless he tried to play very loud, and there is no reason, musical or musicological, to suppose that anyone in the late eighteenth century ever tried to play a continuo part other than discreetly. As the size of the orchestra for concertos increased, the

---

[1] In Haydn's *Mass in Time of War*, when the organ is silent (and Haydn writes '*Senza Org.*'), the continuo figures together with the bass line are still put into the organist's part. These figures have no meaning except as cues, either for the organist or—if the work was conducted from a bass part instead of full score—for the conductor.

continuo became not only unnecessary but absurd as well. From the point of view of modern performance, it would be acceptable if the pianist played the figured bass provided that no one could hear him.

There was, however, a way of playing the more lightly scored concertos, and that was at home with a string quintet. Mozart himself apologized for not sending his father the manuscripts of some new concertos, but 'the music would not be of much use to you . . . [they] all have wind-instrument accompaniment and you very rarely have wind-instrument players at home.'[1] The continuo figures in Leopold Mozart's hand could have been used only for performance in private of the concertos which did not need winds, and the keyboard then surely filled out the string sonorities. Mozart, after all, would not have needed the figures—and Leopold could only have used them at home.

The continuo part of K. 238 in Mozart's handwriting adds much more cogent evidence that this was the case. The piano accompanies the orchestra solely during the passages marked *forte*, and (most striking characteristic of all) it doubles the melody at only one point—significantly at the only place in the entire concerto where the melody is played by the winds alone without help from the strings (Andante, measures 9–12). This realization, then, must have been for a performance without winds, almost certainly with string quintet alone. This unique piece of evidence in Mozart's own hand has, therefore, no bearing on public performances of the concertos.

The indication of continuo in the Mozart concertos should be considered together with the evidence for piano parts in the later Haydn symphonies. Haydn himself conducted the first performances of the *London* Symphonies from the keyboard; there is even a little eleven-measure piano solo that has come down to us for the end of Symphony no. 98. Yet in all of the half-dozen editions of this symphony published during Haydn's lifetime, the solo is omitted: it is found only in an edition published after his death, and in arrangements for piano quintet and piano trio—and in one of these arrangements it is assigned to the violin. Against the background of the immense amount of solo writing for all other instruments in the Haydn symphonies, eleven optional measures for piano exist only as an example of Haydn's wit. The responsibility for keeping the orchestra together at the first performance was divided between the concert-master, Salomon, and the composer at the keyboard; it must have been delightful at the end of a symphony to hear an instrument suddenly begin to play a solo when, until then, it had had only the musical significance of a prompter at an opera. The charm of this passage is not that the piano was used for symphonic works, but that, except for these eleven measures, it was seen but not heard. (It would be impossible to appreciate the joke at a modern performance, although the sonority of the little piano solo is so enchanting that it is a pity to leave it out.) The keyboard had,

---

[1] Mozart, *Letters*, ed. Emily Anderson, p. 877, letter of May 15, 1784.

by then, long since lost its function of filling in the harmonies,[1] and it was already losing that of keeping an ensemble together.

One might add that Mozart's indication *col basso* in the manuscripts of the concertos is absolutely mechanical: proponents of the theory that the figured bass was meant to be heard as well as seen make a great deal of the fact that Mozart sometimes writes rests into the piano part during the tutti. But these rests have no musical significance whatever: in almost every case they are added only when the cello is not playing. They were an aid to the copyist, not a direction to the performer. The cello part (and nothing else) was printed in the piano part when the piano was silent as automatically and traditionally as it is printed in the organ part of Beethoven's *Missa Solemnis* along with the direction *senza organo*. Why bother printing it, then? Simply because the keyboard performer had had the cello part in front of him for at least 150 years and it helped him to keep his place.[2]

Now, in all this discussion, there has been one important absence, an empty chair for the guest of honor who never turned up. It is a question absent from all the literature on the subject, as far as I know. We have asked whether the continuo was used and whether it was necessary, but never what the musical significance of the continuo is. There should, after all, be a difference between a performance of any work with a keyboard instrument adding harmonies and a performance without one—a *specifically musical* difference. If a continuo was a practical aid to performance, a help with the ensemble, why was it abandoned? The disappearance of its harmonic function is an answer that begs the question. Why did composers cease to use the keyboard instrument to fill in the harmonies when it was so much easier than distributing notes elsewhere over other instruments, and also such an advantage in keeping an orchestra together? Why, for example, would the addition of even a discreet continuo to a Brahms quartet or a Tchaikovsky symphony seem so ludicrous?

A continuo (or any form of figured bass) is a way of outlining and isolating the harmonic rhythm. That is why it can be indicated generally by figures under the bass rather than by writing out the exact notes. The emphasis on

---

[1] Even in the early symphonies of Haydn, the stylistic evidence for continuo-playing is only a thinness of texture typical of Haydn and which continued to delight him to the end of his life, as a glance at the late quartets will show.

[2] It is amusing to note to what extremes those in favor of the continuo function of the soloists are sometimes driven to save their theory. In bars 88–89 of the D minor Concerto K. 466, Mozart wrote four low notes into the left hand (doubling the timpani) along with some chords two octaves above while the right hand plays some rapid passage-work. Obviously since no one hand can stretch three octaves, these bars have elicited some fancy explanation. A second piano to play continuo on the low notes has been suggested, along with the use of a piano with pedal keyboard (which it seems Mozart actually owned at some time). It now appears most probable that Mozart originally wrote the low notes and then changed his mind and added the chords without crossing out the first version. What this passage shows, if anything, is that when Mozart wanted the soloist to fill in the harmony, he wrote down the notes for it.

the change of harmony is the only important thing—the doubling and the spacing of the harmony are secondary considerations. This isolation—this setting in relief of the rate of change of the harmony—is essential to the Baroque style, particularly the so-called High Baroque of the early eighteenth century. This is a style whose motor impulse and energy comes from the harmonic sequence, and which depends upon this to give life and vitality to a relatively undifferentiated texture.

But the energy of late eighteenth-century music is based not on the sequence but on the articulation of periodic phrasing and on modulation (or what we may call large-scale dissonance). The emphasis of the harmonic rhythm is therefore not only unnecessary but positively distracting. The tinkle of a harpsichord or a late eighteenth-century piano is a very pretty sound when it is heard in a Haydn symphony, but its prettiness has no relevance to the music and no significance beyond its agreeable noise-value. The fact that Haydn and Mozart were unable to conceive of a more efficient way of conducting an orchestra puts them along with all the other *performers* of their day, whose idea of performance had not yet caught up with the radical change of style which had occurred since 1770 and for which Haydn and Mozart themselves were so largely responsible. This raises the question—does the composer know how his piece is to sound?

The problem is a delicate one, and it lies at the heart of our conception of music. If music is not a mere notation on paper, then its realization in sound is crucial. We assume generally that the ideal performance is the one the composer imagined as he wrote the piece, and that this imagined ideal performance is the real piece, not the notes on paper or the wrong notes of an actual performance. But this assumption is flimsy and fails to stand up under examination. And none of these—not the imagined or the actual performance or the schematic representation on paper—can be simply equated with a work of music.

Let us put this in the simplest possible terms. When a conductor in 1790 conducted from the keyboard, we know from contemporary testimony that he often stopped playing to wave his hands. There is no way of knowing when he did this, but he did not play throughout. When Haydn imagined the sound of one of his symphonies, he must indeed have expected a certain amount of piano or harpsichord sonority as being likely here or there, but there is no place in the music where he implied this as necessary or even desirable except for the little joke in the Symphony no. 98.

This means that a composer's idea of his work is both precise and slightly fuzzy: this is as it should be. There is nothing more exactly defined than a Haydn symphony, its contours well outlined, its details clear and all audible. Yet when Haydn wrote a note for the clarinet, that does not indicate a specific sound—there are lots of clarinets and clarinettists, and they all sound very different—but a large range of sound within very well-defined limits. The act of composing is the act of fixing those limits within which the performer may move freely. But the performer's freedom is bound—or should be—in another way. The limits set by the composer belong to a system which is in many respects like a language: it has an order, a syntax, and a meaning. The performer brings out that meaning, makes its significance not only clear but almost palpable. And there is no reason to assume that the composer or his contemporaries always knew with any certainty how best to make the listener aware of that significance.

New ways of composing precede new ways of playing and singing, and it often takes as long as ten to twenty years for performers to learn how to change their own styles and to adapt themselves. The use of the continuo in the piano concerto was, by 1775, a vestige of the past that was to be completely abolished by the music itself, and we have every reason to believe that the figured bass was already nothing more than a conventional notation which provided the soloist and the conductor with a substitute for a score during performance, or, at most, a way of keeping an orchestra together which had no longer any musical significance. The occasional indignation about its omission either from performance or edition is historically unwarranted and musically unjustifiable.

In 1767, Rousseau complained that the conductor at the Paris opera made so much noise beating a rolled-up sheet of music paper on the desk to keep the orchestra in time that one's pleasure in the music was spoilt. The audible use of a keyboard instrument during a symphony or the orchestral section of a concerto written after 1775 is no doubt less irritating, but its authenticity and its musical value are the same.

The most important fact about concerto form is that the audience waits for the soloist to enter, and when he stops playing they wait for him to begin again. In so far as the concerto may be said to have a form after 1775, that is the basis of it. This is why the concerto has so strong and so close a relationship to the operatic aria; in fact, an aria like 'Martern aller Arten' from *Die Entführung* is nothing less than a concerto for several solo instruments, the soprano being only the principal soloist of a concertante group. The relationship is perhaps closer at the end of the eighteenth century than at any other time: essentially what the classical period did was to dramatize the concerto, and this in the most literally scenic way—the soloist was seen to be different.

In the Baroque concerto, the soloist or soloists were part of the orchestra, playing with them throughout; the contrast of sound was achieved by having the ripieno, or the non-solo elements of the orchestra, stop playing while the soloists continued. There is scarcely ever any effect of dramatic entrance in the early eighteenth century, except from the full orchestra; even when the famous cadenza in the Fifth Brandenburg Concerto begins, there is a sense of the soloist continuing without a break from the previous texture, as the orchestra has gradually effaced itself by a beautifully timed series of gradations in which Bach for once overcomes the contemporary style's resistance to dynamic transition. (The slight pause with which many harpsichordists mark the opening of the cadenza is an anachronism, an intrusion of our modern theatrical idea of the concerto.) With the classical concerto, things are on a different footing: in every concerto by Mozart from 1776 on, the entrance of the soloist is an event, like the arrival of a new character on the stage, and it is set off, emphasized, and colored by a bewildering variety of devices. It should be noted here that this detachment of the soloist from the ripieno was not an invention of Mozart's but a gradual development during the century, a part of the general evolution of the articulated form and a consequence of the taste for clarity and dramatization; but only Mozart, of all the composers before Beethoven, understood the implications of this dynamic contrast between soloist and orchestra, and its formal and coloristic possibilities. Even Haydn remained tied largely to the conception of the soloist as a detachable part of the orchestra.

The Baroque concerto is a loose alternation of ripieno and solo sections, with a strong tonic cadence avoided except at the end of the first and last orchestral passages, and with the solo sections derived from the tutti, almost always generated by the opening motifs. This account overlooks the sources of energy within the Baroque style, which make the great concertos of Bach and Handel more than a loose succession of contrasts, but these sources, in any case, had long since dried up by Mozart's time. The development of the concerto after 1750 has often been described as a fusion of the new sonata form and the older concerto form, but this way of looking at it, even if not positively misleading, has the disadvantage of leaving it as a puzzle why anybody should have wanted arbitrarily to fuse such opposed conceptions. Why not drop the old form and write a completely modern work, a sonata for soloist and orchestra? It will be easier to look at the subject from a viewpoint at once simpler and less mechanical. Treating the sonata not as a form but as a style—a feeling for a new kind of dramatic expression and proportions —we may see how the functions of a concerto (the contrast of two kinds of sound, the display of virtuosity) are adapted to the new style. There is not much point in listing the variety of Mozart's formal devices in concerto form unless we understand their expressive and dramatic purpose.

To return to the opening orchestral pages, or the first ritornello: once it is accepted that the soloist's role is to be a dramatic one, the ritornello poses a problem, simply (as I said) that the audience is waiting for the soloist to enter. In other words, to a certain extent the opening tutti always conveys an introductory atmosphere: something is about to happen. If it is very short, as in most arias, the problem disappears, but in a work of larger dimensions, this introductory character trivializes the opening, and the material first heard in it tends to lose its importance and its urgency. To turn it completely into an introduction—to give it harmonically the character of a dominant rather than a tonic chord—and to have the soloist expose the principal material alone or only accompanied would be an outrage to the classical sense of decorum, given the comparative weight of the orchestral and solo sonorities (this was possible only more than a century later as a joke, in a work like Dohnanyi's *Variations on a Nursery Theme*, although Beethoven's *Kakadu* Variations adumbrate the effect). To drop the opening ritornello altogether and to have the material presented by soloist and orchestra as almost equal partners (as in the concertos by Schumann, Liszt, Grieg, and Tchaikovsky) is to renounce the classical delight in large-scale effects, to make the contrast between solo and orchestra one of short alternations, losing the breadth of the long sections. On the other hand, to make the opening ritornello overdramatic in an attempt to raise its importance and seize the audience's attention would be to undercut the dramatic effect of the soloist's role and to destroy one of the principal advantages of the concerto form.

At the age of twenty, with what may be considered his first large-scale masterpiece in any form, Mozart solved this problem in a manner as brutal and as simple as breaking the neck of a bottle to open it. At the opening of the Concerto in E flat K. 271 (quoted above, p. 59), the piano participates —as a soloist—in the first six measures, and is then silent for the rest of the orchestral exposition. It was a solution so striking that Mozart never used it again (although it was developed by Beethoven in two famous examples, and by Brahms in an expansion of Beethoven's conception). With one stroke, the opening presentation is made more dramatic and the orchestral exposition is given the weight it might have lacked. For this purpose, the most striking entrance of the soloist—the first one—is thrown away at the second measure, before we have heard enough of the orchestral sonority to deepen the contrast. And this, in turn, creates a problem for the next entrance of the solo instrument, solved with equal daring and brilliance. The piano enters before the orchestral exposition has had time to close, in the middle of what is evidently a long final cadence[1]; coming in with a trill, which serves doubly and ambiguously as a signal of solo virtuosity and as a coloristic accompaniment to the orchestral phrase, the piano continues with a witty insouciance apparently in the middle of a phrase of its own, as if continuing a conversation.

The orchestral exposition of K. 271 remains in the tonic throughout without modulating: it is, in fact, exactly like the orchestral opening of an operatic aria. The dramatic modulation is left to the soloist; in so far as there are two real expositions in a concerto, one is necessarily passive and the other active, and the nineteenth century, which did not understand this, was often forced to do away with the orchestral exposition as tautological. In Mozart's E flat Concerto, however, not only is the harmonic direction different, but also the thematic pattern is not the same in the two expositions. The ritornello fixes the nature of the work, providing the tonal and motivic foundation; the piano's exposition gives the concerto its dramatic movement, dropping some of the thematic material and adding new material for the purpose. Almost

---

[1] See themes (9) and (10) cited below, p. 202.

all this material, various and rich as it is, holds together by a logic that is immediately convincing: much of it is audibly derived from the opening phrase.

The two expositions, different as they are, have a relationship that is by no means arbitrary, and, still leaving aside for the most part all ideas of concerto form and sonata form, it is interesting to see how Mozart molds his material and how he dramatizes it. The motto of the work is its opening measures, a theme (1) from whose two opposing parts much of the rest of the movement follows. The orchestral fanfare I label (*a*), and the concealed symmetry of the piano's witty answer (*b*):

After being repeated, this is immediately followed by a theme (2) which ingeniously combines both the rhythms and the shapes of (*a*) and (*b*) together in a dancing movement:

which brings a faster rhythm in the accompaniment, and a fanfare (3) that clearly resembles (*a*) while the oboes continue the phrasing of (2):

Then a transitional four measures, made up of two completely conventional elements, which I call (3A) and (3B), although it is an idle question to decide whether the phrase belongs more with what precedes or with what follows. I cite it not only for its mastery of transition, but because of its importance in later sections, as Mozart will use it like a pivot to make the listener associate in his mind two sections of different material but similar function:

(3A–B) slows the movement down: the whole phrase functions, of course, as a pedal-point on the dominant, and the music is poised before continuing with a new kind of motion. Then follows a melody of the most ravishing grace (4), apparently new, and so derived from (*b*) that it fits everything that precedes: it is an augmentation of the basic thematic pattern, and has an effect of breadth, of giving greater space to the original terse motif:

A new theme follows immediately (I call (5) a separate theme although it is never presented apart from (4) except in the cadenza: for any other composer, without Mozart's richness of invention, it would have done service as an independent melody); it is derived from (4) through the graceful movement upwards at the opening of each measure:

and the derivation is intended to be heard as part of the music's conversational logic. But it is a rhythmic and an expressive intensification, with one out of two leaps made twice as fast with a *sforzando* on a weak beat: even the accompaniment becomes contrapuntally richer and more chromatic. There is a heightening of the expression and of the pace which accelerates towards the end and breaks immediately into (6):

derived directly from (*a*), echoing the trill heard a few seconds before at the end of (5), and coming to an expressive climax and to a sudden stop. Until this point of the work, every note of the chromatic scale has been played except one, D♮. It is now sounded, syncopated and fortissimo.

This is not only the first fortissimo in the movement, but, in a sense, the only one, as the others are all literal repetitions. The D♮ is also the longest melodic note so far, and the silence that follows its immediate resolution into an F minor chord is the longest silence we have heard until now. A study of the phrase patterns reveals an even more interesting aspect of this climax: all the phrases until this point except one have fallen into a symmetrical and regular rhythm. The opening measures are no exception: they are clearly a four-measure phrase played twice, with the first playing interrupted at the opening of the fourth measure. The slight assymmetry is compensated by the symmetrically literal repetition. Other phrases are not only squarely regular, but have symmetrical echoes: bars 8–9 mirror 10–11, 18–21 exactly repeat 14–17, as 43–44 repeat 41–42. The only interruption of this regularity before the climax we have just reached is in measures 12 and 13, which stand out as an exception in the procession of four-measure groups and which outline an F minor sixth chord:

the same chord which resolves the fortissimo diminished seventh under the D♮ in measures 45–46—a resolution which itself needs to be resolved in turn. In this way, the climax at measures 45–46 is prepared; and it, too, is an interruption of the regular four-measure pattern, but a much more violent and dramatic one.

If the climax is beautifully prepared, it is also itself a preparation and a foreshadowing of what is to come. The phrase that follows, indeed, insists on the importance of what has just happened. So far, the large rhythmic pattern has come in two waves, the increase of intensity from (1) to (3), and the even greater one from (4) to (6). At this point the rhythmic motion breaks down completely, and the climax of (6), its last two notes, is turned into a recitative (7) which again outlines an F minor chord:

This recitative acts as a fermata (or, in broader terms, as a cadenza), an expressive wait before the closing phrase, a refusal to resolve the tension. Here is a mastery of rhythm that Mozart derived from opera, and that no other composer has ever employed with such ease. A closing phrase, a fanfare (8) based on (*a*), follows:

and there is a splendidly witty effect when it appears that it is not a closing phrase at all; a second cadence (9) follows, which is nothing but (*a*) inverted:

interrupted by the piano (10), with its second dramatic entrance.[1] Two closing phrases are by no means a luxury: Mozart needs both of them later in the work.

The role of the piano is to dramatize this pattern with such force as to make its resolution urgent and demanding enough to support the weight of the symmetrical patterns that so delighted Mozart even in his operas. In terms of Mozart's style, dramatization means development (thematic fragmentation and extension) and modulation (large-scale harmonic opposition or dissonance), and we find both kinds in the piano's presentation of the form already outlined by the orchestra. Even the orchestration of the same material is more dramatic and more colorful in the second exposition than in the first. This double exposition has very little to do with the repeat in the exposition of a sonata: the solo exposition is an expansion and a transformation as much rhythmic as harmonic. It is the most crucial misunderstanding of Mozart to think, in this concerto, of his repeating a pattern and adding color, drama, and variety to the individual elements: the entire pattern is what Mozart is dramatizing—the real material is not the individual themes but their succession—and the second exposition is not a repeat but a transformation. Only when the creative impulse had died out of the concerto form, as from the sonata, did the double exposition become like the repeat of the first half of a sonata allegro (as in the concertos of Chopin, for all their poetry). But no one who listens to a Mozart concerto without formal preconceptions has any doubt that the soloist's exposition is not a repeat with variations and an added modulation, but a radically different presentation of ideas heard first in the orchestra, with the significance of the pattern completely altered by new ideas and a new approach.

The transformation starts at the beginning. The opening theme (1) interrupts the piano's new entrance (10) and is played twice as at the opening. But we do not go on with (2) as before; instead, the piano, accompanied by two oboes, begins to develop (*a*) along with a cadential trill (found in so many of the themes, above all in (6) and (10B)):

---

[1] Details are wearisome, so I reserve this for a note: the entrance of the piano returns in measure 60 to the F minor sixth chord, and its opening trill and the whole phrase that follows serve once again to resolve the top C of this chord into a B♭.

The accompaniment speeds up its motion and the music modulates immediately to the dominant, B flat major, and reinforces the modulation with a passage of mechanical and conventional brilliance:

The brilliance is used to set the modulation into relief, and less conventional material would not do: the inexpressive nature of the music here, its banality serves as a contrast to the more complex logic of a development which fragments the opening theme and forces it into another key. The virtuosity stabilizes the new tonality.[1]

To re-establish the pattern, themes (4) and (5) are now played, but first preceded by the transitional passage (3A–B), which appears to grow logically out of the end of (12):

However, it is now divided dramatically between the piano and the orchestra, and the rhythm of its third measure is vigorously different. The use of this transitional phrase (and a part of the logic we unconsciously accept while listening) tells us that (11) and (12) have a role analogous to (2) and (3): that

---

[1] As part of the more expansive art of the second exposition, it should be remarked that measures 78–81 are harmonically a magnified version of measures 12 and 13.

is, (2) and (11) are both developments of (*a*), and (3) and (12) both close a section by adding brilliance and increasing the sense of movement. But the new version of (3A–B) responds to the greater intensity of the piano's exposition by its more dramatic orchestration and rhythm.

The graceful melodies (4) and (5) are also not merely repeated by the piano, but (5) is played twice, the second time by the piano supporting the oboe with an accompaniment that moves twice as fast as before, and the theme is then further lengthened by a deeply expressive phrase (13) that is like a fermata over measure 115, a refusal to accept the inevitable descent:

We hold our breath here, waiting for the phrase to finish, and we are kept suspended by the surprise cadence in the middle (m. 114); the end of the phrase, however (m. 117), leaves us harmonically at exactly the same unresolved point as the opening. This tension is immediately relieved by a final and lengthy burst of virtuosity, played twice (14):

This closes and by measure 135 completely grounds the modulation started in measure 70; once again the conventionality of the material is necessary for the feeling of a stable cadence. This is also the perfect point for an extensive display of pianistic brilliance, which is, after all, the essence of the concerto form.

It is natural (as well as traditional) to re-establish the symmetry by having the orchestra return here and end this exposition with the closing phrases of its own ritornello; (6), (7), and (8) accordingly follow in order and in the dominant. But the recitative of (7) is given to the soloist after the orchestral climax, an operatic gesture so natural and yet so effective that it is hard to know whether to ascribe it to imagination or logic. Mozart's most fantastic strokes are always his most reasonable. The climax at the opening of (7), now transposed to the dominant, is less imposing than on its first appearance, because it has followed a very long display of virtuosity from the soloist which rises several times to the highest note on Mozart's piano. The virtuosity is part of the dramatization. The piano's exposition is, as we have seen, a free adaptation of the orchestral ritornello, which is only a concise introductory statement: both expositions are, however, a development and an expansion of the motto with which the work opens, and both are shaped towards a climax, but a different one in each case. The orchestral climax leading from a high D♭ to a sustained F minor chord[1] is not so much transposed by the piano's exposition as replaced by the greater dramatic power of the modulation to the dominant and by the brilliance of the solo writing. But it is, in the end, the original orchestral climax which will play the more important role in the total form of the movement.

Only two phrases of the orchestral exposition—here labelled (2) and (3)—do not appear in the piano's exposition, and both are played by the piano in the section that follows (which we may call the 'development,' an intensification of the exposition's modulation to the dominant and an increased dramatization of its material); but the two phrases are no longer continuous, being widely separated to frame the 'development.' The piano begins to play (2), now at the dominant, in a way that cuts off the orchestra's cadential phrase before its finality has a chance to make its effect, and blurs the distinction between the exposition and the development; certainly, since we have not heard (2) either in the piano or at the dominant, it would be hard to decide whether this passage does not have as much right to be called 'exposition' as 'development,' and our doubt is strengthened by the new and graceful arc with which the piano rounds off the phrase and which leads directly to the opening fanfare of (1). The motto theme (1) is played, complete with its repeat, and seems as much as ever to be a beginning, and to mark once again an initiation of the pattern twice presented.

This section does, indeed, follow the sequence already described, but with greater intensity. As in the piano's exposition, (1) is followed by (11), which is a development of (1a), and as if to emphasize its parallelism with the exposition, it is again scored as before with the piano accompanied only by the two oboes. But the development is more extensive, and modulates immediately to F minor, the key that played so important a role in the orchestral exposition. It leaves this key to touch briefly and inconclusively on the tonic, and then returns with this dramatic passage, where the orchestral climax of

---

[1] Sustained by the phrase that follows, which dwells on the notes of the F minor triad even while the harmony changes beneath it.

the ritornello in (6) (with the D♭ resolved as before into a sixth chord of F minor) is here reiterated four times[1]:

This hammering of D♮ is the extreme point of tension, the center of the work.

This moment is a synthesis as well as a culmination, a fusion of the aims of the two expositions. Using the developmental material initiated in the second exposition, and starting from the modulation to the dominant effected there, Mozart arrives at the dissonant climax of the first exposition, now more urgent and more expressive, and with much greater rhythmic energy. The symmetry is not the mechanical symmetry of textbook form, but implies a new dramatic level. It is the understanding of symmetry as a dramatic force that gave Mozart his supremacy in opera and the concerto, an understanding that extended to the most insignificant detail. Even the resolution of the climax just quoted has its parallel: it is resolved by (3) in the orchestra, and repeated, at long last, by the piano. At its first appearance (3) was preceded, exactly as it is here, by an F minor sixth chord, in a passage singled out by its irregular phrase-length. In other words, the conventional little phrase (3)—the most ordinary stock-in-trade of the contemporary composer—is the resolution both of the initial moment of tension and of the central climax of the movement, binding the two together.

---

[1] It has already been played just eleven measures before, so that the repetition is even more striking.

After the playing of the short phrase (3A) and a transitional passage[1] which replaces (3B), the original pattern begins again ('recapitulation') with (1) played, as always, twice—or almost twice. This time, however, the scoring is symmetrical mirror-fashion: the piano, not the orchestra, begins and is answered by the orchestra and then the order is reversed. In the second playing of (1), the piano answers with a difference—it accompanies the melody with the rhythm of the development section, and, indeed, starts a new development on its own. This second development section is, of course, one of the most characteristic features of classical sonata style from Haydn's *Russian* Quartets to the *Hammerklavier* Sonata, and it is almost always harmonically a reference to the larger development, as if the energy of the latter had not yet been dissipated, and was spilling over into what follows. The first of Mozart's mature concertos is no exception, and the passage opens with an unmistakable return to the climax of the previous development:

which is resolved after four measures of modulation with a return to the tonic quoted here to show how even the orchestration with the entrance of the oboe emphasizes the resolution of the F minor chord that has had such importance:

---

[1] For those ill-at-ease with perfection, I should add here that this short transitional phrase seems to me awkwardly contrived. There is nothing wrong with its thematic logic—it is derived both melodically and rhythmically from (3A) which immediately precedes it. But it is harmonically awkward in that its shape emphasizes the tonic while its function is to sustain a dominant, and I think the alternation of *p* and *f* is not convincingly motivated. But I advance this with a certain timidity, as the phrase is not ineffective, nor does it alter the dramatic force of what follows.

All of the transitions to the recapitulation in Mozart's piano concertos before K. 450 seem to me below the level of ease and power he was consistently to attain later. K. 414 in A major works best only by cutting the Gordian knot—it is dramatically abrupt, and there is no transition at all. K. 413 in F major merely repeats the entrance of the soloist without change, as it entered before on a dominant, and K. 415 in C major tries to gloss over this place with a little Adagio cadenza. K. 449 in E flat major has a sequential passage so weak that it makes pianists uncomfortable to play—one tries in vain to add dramatic interest by a *crescendo*, and the phrase will not bear the weight. But the analagous place in K. 450 (B flat major) is enchanting, logical, and completely natural. After this work, the return to the tonic is generally one of the most gracefully accomplished, and often one of the most memorable moments in Mozart's forms. The phrase that is so weak in K. 449 has a fairly close analogue in K. 456, for example; but there it is prepared harmonically and so strengthened by the orchestration that no awkwardness is left.

It may be said that the final resolution of the climax at measure 176 has been postponed until this point. Even though this passage is a new departure, it stands as a foil to the exactly analogous place in the solo exposition: there (1) is followed by (11), a development of (1*a*), and here (1) is followed by a development of (1*b*). This relation is underlined, as both (11) and (15) lead directly into (12).

In the recapitulation, along with some enchanting reorchestration, Mozart again contrives to make his most logical strokes seem surprising. The section of the soloist's exposition that was in the dominant is transposed almost exactly, although the brilliant passagework of (14) is largely rewritten with, naturally, a much heavier emphasis on the tonic chord; but the virtuosity is interrupted this time. The delightful phrase (2) cuts in, to be played this time twice, once by the orchestra and again by the soloist. Its surprising appearance here in the tonic is, nevertheless, a consequence and a resolution of its equally surprising appearance in the dominant between the solo exposition and the beginning of the development.

The extraordinary form of the end of the movement has the same rightness. After the piano has finished with the closing trill of (14), and the orchestra with (6) and (7) returns to the climax on the D♭, it is the piano, as before, that resolves it with the recitative-like phrase. Then the orchestra astonishingly enters with the fanfare of (1)—played yet again twice with its answer in the piano—and with one more climax in which the high D♮ is again prominent, there comes the traditional pause before the cadenza. In this way, like every other development section in the movement, the cadenza is preceded by the opening phrase played twice.

The last surprise is that the piano interrupts and accompanies the traditional orchestral conclusion with solo passagework, but the interruption is performed with a reasonableness that makes the humor only the more delightful. The cadenza is followed by the concluding phrases of the orchestral exposition (8) and (9), and the piano begins to play (10) in the middle of (9) exactly as it did before: this final licence is not licence at all, but strict re-capitulation. Nothing is more logical with reference to the form of this individual movement, and nothing more eccentric with regard to the supposed traditional form of the concerto.[1]

What shall we term this manner of creation, freedom or submission to rules? Eccentricity or classical restraint? Licence or decorum? With a sense of proportion and dramatic fitness unsurpassed by any other composer, Mozart bound himself only by the rules he reset and reformulated anew for each work. His concertos are not ingenious combinations of traditional concerto-form with the more modern sonata allegro, but independent creations based on traditional expectations of the contrast between solo and orchestra reshaped with an eye to the dramatic possibilities of the genre, and governed by the proportions and tensions—not the patterns—of sonata style. We shall arrive only at a misunderstanding, more or less serious depending on the work, if we try to impose the form of a Mozart concerto from outside the work without considering the dramatic intention and the directional thrust of the material. Above all, we must remember that it is not the themes of the work—or the motifs—that form the material, but their ordering and their relation: a 'development' is not merely a development of themes, but takes into account, intensifies—'develops,' in short—the order and the sense of what has gone before. It is the exposition as a whole that is developed, not the individual motifs.

---

[1] The following diagram of one aspect of the form—the succession of themes—may make this fundamental logic perhaps more visible (the numerical labels are as above):

Orchestral exposition	Solo exposition	Develop-ment	Recapitu-lation	Coda
1(*a–b*)	1(*a–b*)	1(*a–b*)	1(*a–b*)	1(*a–b*)
2	11	11	15	Cadenza
3	12*a–b*	3	12*b*	[3]*
3A–B	3A–B	3A	3A–B	
4–5	4–5		4–5	[5]*
	13		13	
	14		14	
			⎡2⎤	
			14	
6	6		6	
7	7		7	
8	8			8
9	⎡2⎤			9
10				10
				Conclusion

* [Order from Mozart's own cadenza]

The equilibrium is even clearer if we remember that (2) is sequential and a combination of (1*a*) and (1*b*), (11) is a sequential development of (1*b*), (15) a sequential development of (1*a*), and the cadenza a development of whatever the soloist chooses.

How important this is for K. 271 may be seen not only in the recurrence of points of climax and resolution, but also in the way development already begins within the exposition at measure 69 (called (11)), a passage which returns and is extended within the development proper at measure 162, and in the way the tension of the development spills over into the recapitulation, starting a new development (15)—a few seconds after the opening of the recapitulation—harmonically related to the central one. This second development at the beginning of the recapitulation is the rule rather than the exception—in the works of Haydn, Mozart, and Beethoven—but it can only be understood as related to dramatic intent, not as part of a thematic order; it comes from a powerful sense of long-range harmonic dissonance, a conception not of the dissonant note in a chord, but of the long dissonant section in a tonally resolved work.

Heard with the same freedom from formal preconceptions, the other movements of K. 271 are no more problematic than the first. The slow movement is built very like the first, but more simply. As an expression of grief and despair, this movement stands, with the slow movements of the *Sinfonia Concertante* and of K. 488, almost alone among Mozart's concerto movements; not until the Andante con moto of Beethoven's G major Concerto is the same tragic power recaptured. The opening phrase of the orchestra is the introductory exposition: it is 16 measures long, but irregularly divided into 7 and 9 measures—a beautiful example of Mozart's irregular variation of a fundamental regularity. The piano enters and expands this phrase, decorating the 7-measure opening and modulating to the relative major with new but related material. It then enlarges the first measures of the 9-measure half into 16 measures (mm. 32–48), and closes with the last 6 measures, the whole oscillating between E flat major and minor, retaining the minor effect of the original even in transposition, but heightened by the dissonant major-minor clash.[1]

Both in the first and second movements, the solo exposition is essentially an expansion of the introductory exposition, or first ritornello; but in the first movement, the ritornello is itself the expansion of a short, initial motto. The opening phrase of the slow movement is both more complex and more complete, more self-sufficient—above all, less concise—than the opening of the first movement. As everything in the slow movement is derived from this long phrase, I give the first violin part, with fragments of the accompaniment:

---

[1] The expansion of this one orchestral phrase into the entire solo exposition that follows is shown in the following parallel measures:

1–7		7–10		11–16
17–23	{ 24–31 modulation and new form of theme	{ 31–34 in E flat major	35–47 extension	48–53

The relation of this to the other themes is too evident at first hearing to require analysis or comment:

as well as the relation to the first movement[1]:

What is most striking, however, about the opening phrase of the Andantino is its masterly architecture: the accents on the low A♭ (repeated in canon by the second violin) prepare the climax on an A♭ an octave higher in measure 4, and a second climax still another octave higher in measure 6; the level is sustained until the A♭ once again breaks out despairingly in measure 11 (harmonized by a D♭ chord to bring out its full power, and reinforced by the winds accompanying the muted strings) and is concluded (exactly as the exposition of the first movement) by a recitative (mm. 12–15). The whole phrase is like a great arch,[2] its classical rise and fall controlling and mastering the span of tragic grief from the canonic beginning to the climax and then to the halting, almost stammering end.

---

[1] The main theme of the finale is derived from the same mold.
[2] Measures 11–16 are a free mirror version of 1–4, and 7–11 clearly reflect 4–7.

The opening phrase's triple climax on an A♭ dominates the recapitulation within a framework analogous to the first movement's reiterated parallel moments of harmonic tension. Everything moves towards this moment and prepares for it, as the opening itself prepares for it on a smaller scale; after the cadenza it reappears again at the very end, and for the only time in the movement the strings take off their mutes and on the same climactic chord of measure 11 the full sound of the orchestra, *forte*, is heard at last.

The interplay between dramatic expression and abstract form that relates concerto to opera is strikingly shown by the return before the cadenza of the recitative that closed the first ritornello (mm. 12–15). This time it is heard in canon between the piano and the first violin (mm. 111–114), so that Mozart both makes a dialogue of great sadness between solo and orchestra in which the speech rhythms inescapably evoke the sound of words, and at the same time gives us the end of the ritornello in canon as a pendant to the canonic opening. It is rare for the demands of both symmetry and drama to be served so strikingly and in a way so true to the nature of a concerto.

The last movement is, in true classical style, the most relaxed in form. The main theme, ostensibly a brilliant but square rondo opening, is in reality very subtle in phrase structure. The most common way of beginning the finale of a concerto is for the main theme to be played first by the soloist (accompanied or unaccompanied) and then *forte* by the orchestra; all of Beethoven's concerto finales except that in the G major Concerto begin this way, and most of Mozart's. This is not so much tradition, as a necessity of style (although by the time of Brahms the weight of tradition was probably greater than the stylistic rationale). As the finale is itself a resolution of the entire work, and demands melodic material that will resist, rather than imply, development—in other words, a theme that gives the impression of squareness, regularity, and completeness—antiphonal treatment both brings out this character most clearly and colors it most effectively. In the few concerto finales where Mozart does not employ this effect at the opening he either reserves it for a later point in the movement (as in K. 451 and K. 503) or he writes a set of variations (K. 453, K. 491), in which the piano first appears more fittingly to decorate the first variation. The finale of K. 467 is a special case: the main theme, which begins in the orchestra, ends with a repetition of its first phrase, and this phrase, which now rounds off the melody, is surprisingly played, not by the orchestra, but by the piano; so the soloist both finishes what the orchestra began, and also begins exactly as the orchestra did. This is a pun based on the nature of concerto form: nothing could better illuminate the double-faced character of this phrase. In all of this, however, the principle of the alternation of orchestra and solo presenting a squarely cut theme is in no way vitiated.

The Presto finale of K. 271 is full of brio and an unflagging motor energy. The new subdominant theme that Mozart loves to place in the developments of his sonata rondos (or even in any finale in sonata form) here turns into a full-scale minuet with rich, florid ornamentation enchantingly orchestrated; there is a chromatic, almost improvisatory coda leading to a transitional cadenza before the return of the Presto. The later E flat Concerto, K. 482, also has a similar minuet in the subdominant in the middle of its finale, less luxuriant this time, perhaps; it was evidently a device that Mozart judged a success.

In the end, very little of earlier concerto form was considered indispensable by Mozart. He always retained some kind of introductory orchestral exposition, part of which would recur to set off the solo divisions clearly and symmetrically, and he never abandoned the cadenza as a reinforcement of the final cadence. Brilliant passagework to close each solo section is not so much a tradition as a self-evident necessity of the genre: no composer gave this up until virtuoso display itself became distasteful to twentieth-century preciosity. Nor did Mozart invent the opening of the second solo section (the 'development') as a completely unaccompanied and extended solo: this device he did not, however, always employ. Methods of sonata form that had been worked out in chamber music and symphonic style were never applied for their own sake, but only in so far as they were the groundwork for the dramatic contrast of soloist and orchestra. This is the reason for the variety of forms in Mozart's concertos, and for their resistance to codification. Each one sets its own problems, and resolves them without using a pre-established pattern, although always with a classical feeling for proportion and drama.

Half a dozen years went by before Mozart wrote another solo piano concerto. Before K. 271, his concertos had naturally shown his melodic genius and his grace of expression, but they had not broken, except in small details, with the common sociable style of his contemporaries. The violin concertos, with all their charm, have none of the dramatic force of K. 271 and the later piano concertos. Soon after K. 271 came the two-piano Concerto K. 365, an amiable, brilliant, and unimportant piece, and the Concerto for Flute and Harp K. 299, which is hackwork: it is true that Mozart's hackwork is a lesser composer's inspiration, and his craftsmanship is significant even here, but it would be doing Mozart less than justice to discuss this work along with the great concertos. The horn concertos deserve more attention: slight and often perfunctory, they are full of splendid details, lacking only seriousness— which is not to say that the serious works lack humor. For a number of years the concerto form seems not to have interested Mozart greatly, with one remarkable exception, the *Sinfonia Concertante* in E flat major K. 364 for violin and viola.

In the same key as K. 271 and written two years later, this masterpiece is in some ways a companion to it; in particular the principal themes of the slow movements are similar in outline and have the same sorrowful, almost tragic quality. But the sonority of the *Sinfonia Concertante*, inspired by the solo viola part which Mozart probably wrote for himself to play, is unique. The very first chord—the divided violas playing double-stops as high as the first and second violins, the oboes and violins in their lowest register, the horns doubling the cellos and oboes—gives the characteristic sound, which is like the sonority of the viola translated into the language of the full orchestra. This first chord alone is a milestone in Mozart's career: for the first time he had created a sonority at once completely individual and logically related to the nature of the work.

The slow movement and finale of the *Sinfonia Concertante* are less ambitious in form than the corresponding movements of K. 271, if equally beautiful. As in that piano concerto, the slow movement makes important use of canonic imitation, but only for its closing theme; until then, the two soloists play antiphonally, each phrase seeming to outdo the previous one in depth of expression, and the successive phrases becoming shorter and more intense, but forming one long unbroken line. The form is the archaic sonata form, where the second part repeats the material of the first closely, modulating now from the dominant (here the relative major) to the tonic: a feeling of development is achieved as in the sonatas of Scarlatti through the detailed intensity of the modulation. The Presto finale has a form both simple and surprising: we might call it a sonata rondo without a development, which may seem paradoxical. The orchestra presents the main theme, and the soloists continue the exposition with a new series of related themes starting in the tonic and going to the dominant; then both soloists and orchestra return to the tonic and the main theme. If there is a development it is only four measures long, for after a surprise modulation, an exact note-for-note recapitulation starts as a second surprise with the soloists' opening theme in the subdominant (one of Schubert's favorite devices, but rare in Mozart). Everything exposed in the dominant is of course now neatly transformed into the tonic; and the only change is the insertion of a splendid tune for the horn from the opening ritornello. An exhilarating movement, full of invention, it manages to be almost absolutely symmetrical and astonishing at the same time.

The opening movement is perhaps the most significant of the three. The eloquent pathos of the semi-recitatives which open the development is only the most obvious of its unusual features. The material is as tightly linked as in K. 271, by the sonority as well as the melodic outline and the rhythm. The following succession of themes, all from the opening tutti, speaks for itself:

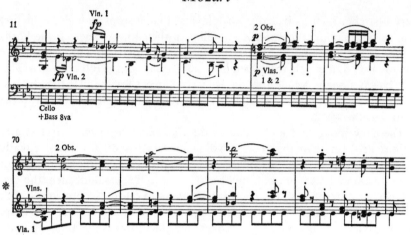

The last-quoted passage, perhaps the least obviously derived from the preceding one, is, however, felt by Mozart as being so close that it is used as a substitute for it in the recapitulation.

The logic of the discourse in this movement represents a great step forward in both maturity and subtlety. The sound of the viola, an instrument Mozart loved, gave him an opportunity to indulge in a richness of inner-part-writing that can only be called luscious. The discourse has a corresponding richness of movement; one passage must suffice here as an example, the extensive preparation for the first solo entry:

With their first two notes the soloists play all the main octave overtones of the E♭'s of the horns and orchestral violas: almost drowned in their sonority at first, the solo instruments—in part because they are doubling the octave overtones of the bass—vibrate intensely after the initial attack. The entrance of the soloists is defined only gradually as they sustain their first notes: the initial grace note—an upward swoop of an octave—blurs the sense of the beat, which has already been disrupted by the syncopations of the preceding measures. The harmonies of the two measures where the soloists hold the high E♭'s are dissonant to the bass that the soloists are doubling, and they continue to affirm their consonance with the bass until the dissonances melt away.

Equally extraordinary is the urgency given by the thematic relationship: the almost painfully expressive orchestral climax at measures 62–63, with the sudden drop to piano, is picked up again by the solo instruments. The relation between measures 62–63 and measure 74, for those with no auditory memory, is elucidated by the repetition of the scale motifs (a_1) and (a_2) four times by the oboes and violins. The miracle of Mozart's style was to make a clearly marked event, an action defined and set apart like the entrance of a character in an opera or the soloist in a concerto, seem to rise almost organically from the music, an integral part of the whole without losing a particle of its individuality or even its separateness. This conception of articulated continuity was a radical departure in the history of music.

By the beginning of 1783, Mozart had three new piano concertos for himself to play, all, however, less imposing than K. 271, and written for a small orchestra in such a way that the wind parts could be omitted and the works performed as piano quintets: this was an attempt to increase their attraction to amateurs, as even before publication manuscript copies of these works were sold to subscribers to Mozart's concerts. K. 413 in F major and K. 415 in C major remain somewhat slight in a style less advanced than that of K. 271 (the last movement of K. 413 even being a minuet, a finale better suited to contemporary chamber music with piano than concerto style), although both have a concision that Mozart could not have achieved easily before. The last movement of K. 415 is in a form that remains odd and complicated in spite of its logic and its workmanship: a sonata-rondo with a double exposition, the first entirely in the tonic (Mozart's normal practice with sonata expositions in concerto form), and a recapitulation that reverses the first and second themes (again not unusual in a Mozart rondo), the whole piece interrupted twice by a plaintive, florid, half-humorous Adagio in the tonic minor. The first interruption is between the two expositions (and justifies the pretension of the double exposition in so loose a form), and the second, quite naturally, as part of the recapitulation before the final appearance of the opening theme. Even in a light work in the popular style of a divertissement, Mozart's feeling for large symmetrical balance remains paramount.

The A major Concerto K. 414, however, is not only more lyric but more broadly conceived than its companions (in spite of K. 415's more brilliant orchestration and military character). The breadth of K. 414 comes from its wealth of melodic material in the first movement: without taking short motifs or transitional material into account, there are four long tunes in the ritornello alone (one of which is never heard again) along with a closing theme, and the piano adds two new ones. The entire development section as well is based on completely new material, and never refers at all to the exposition. This is not lavishness: Mozart uses melodies at once so complex and so complete that they do not bear the weight of development. All the tunes (for that is what they are) turn out to be completely regular: the eight-measure phrase is preserved intact in each one of them and the second phrase of all the melodies begins exactly like the first. Yet there is no feeling of squareness or monotony, and no lack of continuity: the transitions are masterly, and the sense of the weight of each melody and its place in the succession cannot be faulted. What gives this movement its dignity and keeps it from being light-weight is the richness and the continuously expressive quality of the melodies: in no other concerto first movement did Mozart so renounce the advantages of dramatic surprise or the tensions of resolved irregularity. It is, in its way, a *tour de force*, but it stands closer to the violin concertos than to the other more dramatically conceived piano concertos.

A year after these three works, Mozart returned to the grander conception of the concerto he had already shown with K. 271. In 1784 he began to experiment heavily with the form and wrote no less than six concertos, three of them specifically for himself to play at the subscription concerts he was giving in Vienna. The series of six, however, begins apparently somewhat timidly with the Concerto in E flat major K. 449, written for a pupil, Babette Ployer. Like the three concertos that preceded it, K. 449 may be played as a piano quintet, omitting the winds. But it is a more vivid work than any of these, even if written for accompaniment by a small orchestra as Mozart himself affirmed. The slow movement in B flat tries an interesting experiment of repeating the entire solo exposition with its modulation to the dominant in the key of the flatted leading tone or A flat: because of its remote key, this has the effect of a development, and yet the parallel modulation brings us reasonably to the more comfortable subdominant, to which Mozart adds a brief but very startling modulation to B minor before resolving the entire movement with the recapitulation.

The last movement of K. 449 recalls an earlier try at writing a contrapuntal finale to a concerto, K. 175; this time, however, the success is undeniable in a work of great complexity and subtlety with an outward appearance of witty ease. This success is due to the combination of contrapuntal art with *opera buffa* style, the one balancing the other so happily that the lightness and brilliance of a concerto finale are only enhanced by the weight of the more learned technique. The sonata-rondo form is used with great delicacy, and the possibility of an influence of Haydn (in the use of part of the second group in the tonic to effect the return to the main theme after the 'development,' so that the recapitulation actually has already started in the 'development') only emphasizes the originality of the work. Not one of the entrances of the main theme is the same, the comic-opera style and rhythm enabling Mozart not so much to decorate it as to transform and enliven it each time. The recapitulation, in particular, is marvelously subtle: a new theme introduced in C minor in the development is resolved in it, and after a long, electrifying modulation to D flat minor (the extension of a chromatic hint in the exposi-tion), there is a fermata, and the first theme reappears in a new tempo and a new rhythm. We could safely label everything that follows a coda, except that it is used to recapitulate a theme from the 'second group' that had so far appeared only in the dominant. Every detail of this piece has been lovingly worked out, and, in spite of its modest appearance, K. 449 is a bold, even revolutionary concerto.

The two concertos that follow, K. 450 and 451, were written by Mozart for himself. K. 450 in B flat major is, as Mozart himself thought, technically the most difficult of his concertos up till then, and indeed, of those he wrote later. It is also the first to employ the winds with a complete sense of their color and their dramatic possibilities. The winds, in fact, boldly open the concerto on their own, as if to proclaim this new venture from the beginning:

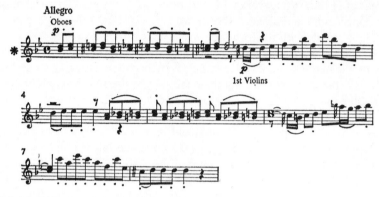

This initial theme, which falls into the form

is the model for all the principal themes of this movement:

and for much of the episodic material as well. The use of winds for solo effects solves one problem for Mozart, that of giving interest to an extended ritornello entirely in the tonic so that the modulation can be reserved for the soloist. K. 449 with only accompanying winds had tried a ritornello which went to the dominant, and the result was a weakened interest in the second exposition. The two expositions of K. 450 are much more strongly differentiated; not only does the ritornello remain in the tonic, but one of its themes, perhaps its most striking one, is never replayed until the recapitulation. All three movements are equally masterly, and the enlarged orchestra that Mozart used is deployed at the opening of the last movement in genuine symphonic style. The cadenzas that Mozart himself composed for this concerto are elaborate, and certainly the most brilliant and powerful he ever wrote out.

The Concerto in D major K. 451, written at the same time, is difficult for many listeners to appreciate today. All three movements, and the first in particular, are built with extremely conventional, impersonal material: an imposing, even brilliant, architecture is created, using this material in the form of blocks. What counts is the ordering, the brilliance, and, above all, the proportions: the significance, the resonance of the individual phrase has much less interest. This is not the Mozart we love, but he himself was proud of this work. We must be grateful for it, in any case: it was Mozart's experience in the handling of such harmonically conventional material that taught him the rhythmic control which he was able to apply in more expressive works. In K. 451 the relation of pure diatonic phrases to heavily (although still conventionally) chromatic ones is perfectly gauged, as is the outlining of large areas of both range of sound (the two-octave ascent from measure 1 to 10) and of rhythm (the introduction of syncopation along with the first chromatic phrase at measure 43). The Concerto in B flat major K. 456, written a little later in 1784, has something of the same quality: less brilliant and grandiose than K. 451, its charm and its melancholy also seem impersonal. But the handling of chromatics is even more far-reaching, and an experiment in combining chromaticism with syncopation is carried as far as Mozart's audacity would go, when a section in the distant key of B minor brings with it a clash of $\frac{2}{4}$ against $\frac{6}{8}$.

Written just before K. 456, the G major Concerto K. 453 (intended like K. 449 for Babette Ployer) contains innovations of much greater significance. In the first movement, perhaps the most graceful and colorful of all Mozart's military allegros, the ritornello stays in the tonic, but has a second theme so restless and so unstable harmonically that the monotony of a long stretch of the home key is forgotten:

(This device of a modulating second theme was shamelessly appropriated by Beethoven for his piano concerto in the same key.) The harmonic plan of K. 453 is also remarkable—a surprise descent to the flat submediant marks the climax of the ritornello:

the opening of the development (now descending from the dominant):

and the end of the recapitulation:

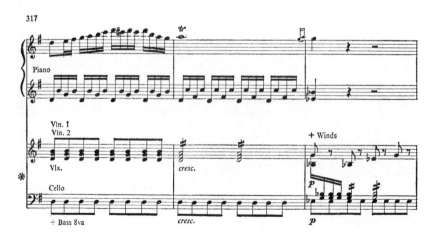

The first of these passages prepares the role that the minor mode is to play in the movement, and the others justify it. (Brahms was evidently so impressed by this effect that he absentmindedly put it in at the end of his cadenza for this concerto, where it makes harmonic nonsense.) It should be clear that these surprise cadences are not an intricate system of cross-references but a means of emphasizing and clarifying the inner proportions of the movement.

The C major slow movement is even bolder. In a number of his works in sonata form, Haydn makes no modulation proper to the dominant, only a pause and a bold leap. But there is no record of his trying this when the material before the leap lasts only a few seconds. This, however, is what Mozart does here. The first exposition, or ritornello, in the tonic is what makes the dramatic concision of the second exposition possible without smashing the tonal aesthetic on which Mozart depends. Even in the ritornello, the effect is already impressive and moving, without the use of modulation: a quiet, expressive, opening five-measure phrase in the strings, followed by a silence; then the orchestra softly begins an accompanied and unrelated oboe solo, as if the first phrase had never existed. The piano starts with the same opening phrase, with a *ritenuto*[1] before an even longer pause, and then plunges brutally into the dominant minor with a passionate new melody. No slow movement of Mozart had ever before attempted a dramatic stroke of such magnitude; even the turbulent development section in the second movement of the A minor Sonata K. 310 is arrived at gradually. In K. 453, however, this effect is used as a frame as well, so that its significance is as much formal as emotional: the development section starts with the same five-measure phrase followed by a silence, but this time in the dominant, and scored for solo winds alone. After the silence, the piano, again with an abrupt change, begins a series of chromatic modulations that reaches sequentially to C sharp minor. The return to the tonic is the boldest stroke yet and the logical outcome of all that has gone before. This return and the first seven measures of the recapitulation show how much dramatic movement can be compressed into a few measures:

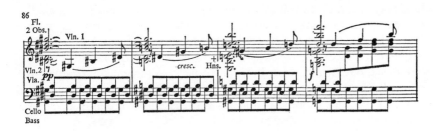

---

[1] The added fermata may indicate not only a *ritenuto* but a very short expressive cadenza: to play a cadenza in the fermata over the rest is unthinkable. (See mm. 93–94, p. 224.)

In these eleven measures, the first four cut directly and powerfully from G sharp major and minor to C major, and from *pp* to *f*; the beautiful opening phrase returns and is played, this time with the barest minimum of added ornamentation.[1] Then after the silence, a new brusque attack, which will resolve the dominant minor of the first one (in the analogous place of the exposition at measure 35) into the tonic minor. The recapitulation reserves the closing theme of the exposition for a coda, after the soloist's cadenza. But before this closing theme, the initial phrase is used once more with magnificent effect. The woodwinds play it immediately following the cadenza; until now, each time it appeared it was left unresolved on the dominant—not only unresolved, but almost isolated, with a silence that separated it from all that followed. This last time, it melts into the succeeding phrase and is resolved in one of the most expressive, and yet perhaps most conventional, phrases that Mozart could have written:

---

[1] Here is the question of ornamentation in Mozart at its most problematic: if we have added anything to the phrase in its previous appearance, we must add still more here. Yet the music requires a marked simplicity for its full effect.

moving chromatically through the subdominant into the piano's cadence. This withholding of the resolution of the main theme until the very end of the movement, together with the silence that sets off each one of its appearances except the last, are only the most salient points of a work that is an important step in Mozart's transformation of a genre, making it capable of bearing the greatest musical weight.

The last movement of K. 453 also represents a new departure. Here Mozart first tries the variation form as a concerto finale. The relaxed looseness of this form is not an unmitigated advantage in a finale. While it provides a resolution for the more dramatic and less decorative forms of the previous movements, it is hard to hold it together, or to give the repetitive pattern a clear architecture. The simplest and most common variation scheme throughout the whole eighteenth century is to arrive at a climax by decreasing the note-values (i.e., increasing the speed) with each successive variation. In the latter part of the century, brilliance was achieved by making the last two variations a florid Adagio with coloratura effects followed by a brilliant Allegro, a scheme that could be both loose and mechanical to the point of superficiality. Another scheme was to enforce unity by a return to the opening tempo after the acceleration: for the return to have its full effect, a basically slow tempo was needed, and while this could be used for the finales of intimate chamber works like Beethoven's Sonatas op. 109 and op. 111, it was unthinkable for the ending of the more sociable classical concerto.[1] A variation-finale in a quick tempo is much more difficult to write: the strain can be sensed in the last movement of the *Eroica* and even in the more impressive choral variations

---

[1] An attempt to combine both the return to the opening and a more brilliant finale can be found in Mozart's Violin Sonata in G major K. 379, where the original theme returns but at a faster tempo.

of the Ninth Symphony, and in the latter, the success of the form is due to Beethoven's widening of the frame.

Mozart's solution is a coda, Presto, in comic opera style. The theme of the variations is a bourrée of great popular charm. While the tempo remains the same, the note-values of the accompanying figures and decoration in the first three variations decrease from eighth-notes to triplets to sixteenth-notes. The fourth variation is in minor and so heavily chromatic that it has the modulatory effect of a 'development' section (the conception of variation-form being guided in Mozart's hands by the ideals of the sonata style); in this variation, too, we find Mozart's most remarkable use of wind doubling so far in any concerto:

where the first violin is doubled two octaves below, and the second violin an octave above; later in the variation, the piano is dramatically accompanied by an interjection of triple octaves in the wind. The last variation, half in military style and half like a cadenza from the piano—a remarkable conception—leads to the *opera buffa* coda, in which the main theme of the variations only reappears impertinently after almost half the Presto is over. Today, these variations are generally played too fast for Mozart's plan of gradual acceleration in the first four variations and the contrast with the Presto to be appreciated; most Allegrettos of the period were meant to be played more slowly than those written after the turn of the century.

The greatest of all Mozart's concerto finales is that of K. 459 in F major. The first two movements of this work are already heavy with Baroque sequences and contrapuntal imitation, as if to prepare for the final Allegro assai, for the last movement is a complex synthesis of fugue, sonata-rondo-finale, and *opera buffa* style. The weightiest and the lightest forms of music are fused here in a work of unimaginable brilliance and gaiety, going far beyond the finale of K. 449, with all its contrapuntal ingenuity. The light rondo theme is stated by the piano solo and each of its two phrases repeated by the wood-wind alone. The full orchestra, *forte*, immediately starts a fugue on an entirely new theme which leads to a long symphonic development and cadence in the manner of an opera overture. Then the soloist begins his exposition which quickly modulates with a variant of the main theme, a new second theme, and the orchestral fugue theme for a dominant cadence. After a full return of the main theme, a second tutti starts without a break in D minor: this time it is a double fugue, with the original fugue-theme combined with the main rondo-theme. The piano does not enter until more than thirty measures of symphonic fugal development have gone by, and when it does come in, the writing remains still largely contrapuntal. The recapitulation is in mirror form, with the first theme last—held back, in fact, until after the cadenza. The movement finishes in a witty burst of *opera buffa* echo effects. The long contrapuntal tuttis give this movement the most symphonic sonority of any of the finales: even if the trumpet and drum parts, now lost, were replaced, the impression could not be any greater.[1] The form of this movement, at once concise and expansive, is the synthesis of Mozart's experience and of his ideals of form. Everything plays a role here—operatic style, pianistic virtuosity, Mozart's increasing knowledge of Baroque counterpoint and of Bach in particular, and the symmetrical balance and dramatic tensions of sonata style. The first movement, military but tranquilly dominated by its calm sequences, and the lyrical, restless, and poignant Allegretto 'slow' movement are equally sensitive. The whole concerto is one of Mozart's most original.

The principal lines of the classical piano concerto were laid down in 1776 by K. 271, but until the six great concertos of 1784, Mozart had never explored the technical range of the form. From this point on, there was no advance in skill; everything that follows is, in a sense, merely an expansion of what he had found out with these six concertos. What remained to be tried, however, was the emotional weight that the genre would bear. Mozart had not yet written a concerto in the minor mode. Nor had full symphonic grandeur been essayed: the brilliance of K. 451 (like that of K. 415) is the brilliance of the operatic overture compounded with virtuosity. In 1785, the year following, the range and the depth of Mozart's achievement were extended by two works written within a month of each other, the concertos K. 466 and 467.

With the D minor Concerto K. 466, in particular, we leave the history of

---

[1] Unless Mozart's memory failed him when he wrote his catalogue, and there never were any such parts.

the concerto as a specific form. It is not superior to the concertos that preceded it—the level reached earlier makes any such preference arbitrary, even though it was historically a more influential work. But the D minor Concerto cannot be considered only as a concerto, even as a supreme example of the form. With both K. 466 and K. 467, Mozart created works that belong as much to the history of the symphony and even the opera as the concerto, just as with *Figaro* we enter a world where opera and chamber music meet.

The D minor Concerto is almost as much myth as work of art: when listening to it, as to Beethoven's Fifth Symphony, it is difficult at times to say whether we are hearing the work or its reputation, our collective image of it. It is probably not the most played of Mozart concertos. But even at a time when Mozart's reputation was low—when his grace obscured his power—the estimation of this work remained high. It is not a work, of course, that is much discussed (it excites no controversy) or much imitated; nor is it the favorite Mozart concerto of many musicians, just as no one's favorite Leonardo is the *Mona Lisa*. Like the G minor Symphony and *Don Giovanni*, the D minor Concerto may be said to transcend its own excellences.

The historical importance of K. 466 is that it belongs to the series of works which made Mozart the supreme composer in most musicians' minds within ten years of his death. It represents the Mozart who was considered the greatest of 'romantic' composers, and it was the character of this work and a few others like it that pushed Haydn into the background for more than a century. It was the concerto that Beethoven played and wrote cadenzas for. It is one of the fullest realizations of that aspect of Mozart which the nineteenth century quite rightly named 'daemonic,' and which, for so long, made a balanced assessment of the rest of his work so difficult.

There is room here only for a brief discussion, and it is best to approach the work obliquely in order to get somewhere near its center. There is, as I have said, in the D minor concerto no progress in concerto technique proper, but it manifests an important advance in purely musical skill—the art of sustaining an increase in rhythmic motion, that is, the creation of excitement. In the classical style, this can only be done by discrete steps, but there are many such steps possible, and the art of controlling their relations—i.e. sustaining and intensifying a climax—is very complex. Let us look at the first important climax that concerns both the soloist and the orchestra:

The increase of motion in this passage is induced in a great variety of ways:

1. In measure 93, the melody, which has been pulsating on one note, begins to move.

2. The piano, silent until measure 95, adds sixteenth-note motion to the syncopated quarters of the orchestra. The pattern of the right hand begins again every half-note.

3. Measure 97: the right-hand pattern now begins again every quarter note.

4. Measure 98: the horn entrance in the middle of the measure doubles the basic accent of the measure.[1]

5. Measure 99: the harmony, which has been changing every measure, now begins to change three times every two measures. There is an increase in a subordinate melodic rhythm, as the piano's sixteenth-notes all begin to have melodic significance, not merely harmonic. The syncopated quarter-note rhythm in the violins begins to change into eighth-notes every two beats.

6. Measure 100: the upper melodic voice in the piano moves every quarter-note, instead of every half-note.

7. Measure 102: The second wind entrance (bassoons, measure 101) was two and a half measures later than the first; the third entrance, here in the oboe, is only one measure and a half later.

8. Measure 104: The harmony changes four times a measure instead of twice a measure.

9. Measure 106: The motion of the violins and violas is doubled.

10. Measure 107: The upper melodic voice in the piano is quadrupled in motion, as by the end of the measure it has clearly taken over the sixteenth-note motion.

11. Measure 108: The melodic line of the bass begins to move twice as fast, and its rhythmic animation four times as fast.

12. Measure 110: The motion of the accompanying voices is increased by the entrance of the winds.

13. Measure 112: The speed of the melodic pattern is doubled and the harmony changes twice a measure instead of once. (Even the dotted figure in the winds now occurs twice a measure.)

This new range of sustained acceleration accounts in part for what might be called the 'romantic' excitement generated by this concerto.[2] The juggling with rhythmic counters—note-values proper, harmonic motion, melodic pattern—is done in so accomplished a way that when one of them disappears

---

[1] These measures are a repetition of the opening of the ritornello; at the corresponding place there, the horn enters on the *first* beat, while here the accent is put on the weaker beat.

[2] This excitement is reflected even in the orchestral color. There is an astonishing passage at measure 88 where the timpani alone (without the cellos) softly double the bass two octaves below the rest of the orchestra and the piano.

or slows down, another doubles or quadruples its speed, and it is always the accelerating part on which the weight of interest lies. Even the introduction of a faster rhythm, generally accomplished with such tact and, indeed, given here as so often in an accompanying part, is signalled by its being the entrance of the soloist. Everything concurs in this drive towards the climax: the whole shape of the passage is a gradual and passionate ascent (even the bass ascends with the upper voices for the first half) followed by an orchestrated crescendo. One aspect of the classical aesthetic can be seen here with particular lucidity: the dramatic manipulation of discrete and well-defined shapes to achieve an impression of continuity by finely graded transitions.

In addition, one of the limits of the classical style is reached: the first four measures of the example cited above (which are an exact repeat of the concerto's opening) go as far as the style will allow in the direction of rhythmic instability.[1] There is a similar figure at the opening of the *Prague* Symphony, but the syncopations cease once the voice takes on a melodic character: in K. 466 the syncopations continue and carry the burden of the initial theme. Combined with the menacing bass motif, these syncopations give a powerful impression of foreboding. When these measures are played *forte*, they have to be radically transformed (mm. 16 ff.) into something very like Don Giovanni's duet with the Commendatore; for the concerto starts (like K. 459, K. 467, and K. 491, along with so many sonatas of the period) with the complete theme played *piano* and then *forte*, but breaks the bonds of this symmetry. The energy of the music is such that it is difficult to hold it within the tonic for the entire opening ritornello: this recurrent formal problem is resolved here by a brilliant compromise. The modulation to the relative major begins, and goes too far—so far, in fact, that it turns back into the tonic in just the way it will later in the recapitulation. This reserves the larger action (the establishment of a secondary tonality) for the solo piano, but gives the opening tutti its share of dramatic movement. It also makes the recapitulation at this point both a faithful reflection of the first exposition and a resolution of the second.

No concerto before K. 466 exploits so well the latent pathetic nature of the form—the contrast and struggle of one individual voice against many. The most characteristic phrases of the solo and the orchestra are never interchanged without being rewritten and reshaped: the piano never plays the menacing opening in its syncopated form, but transforms it into something rhythmically more defined and more agitated; the orchestra never plays the recitative-like phrase with which the piano opens, and which it repeats throughout the development section. Yet the material of the concerto is remarkably homogeneous; so much of it is related with striking effect to the opening piano phrase, and always accompanied by the same parallel thirds:

---

[1] Except, of course, in a recitative, or an improvisatory cadenza-like style, where definition is not expected.

opening of first solo

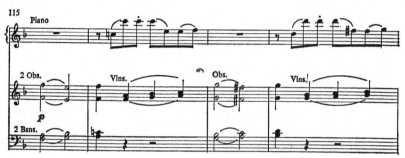

opening of the "second group"

theme of "second group"

opening of finale

Finale: second theme of tonic group

The relations are almost too obvious; together with the chromatic phrase cited above (mm. 99–102) and all its derivations,[1] the motif on which they are based and the continuous appearance of the parallel thirds dominate the sound of the concerto. For the first time the first and last movements of a concerto are so strikingly and openly related, although the *Sinfonia Concertante* K. 364 had already made a first gesture in that direction. This new openness of thematic relations, this parade of unity, arises from an inward dramatic necessity, the sustaining of a unified tone demanded by the tragic style. The power of this tragic character is such that it even spills over into the slow movement; if we isolated this movement, the Romanza, from the others, its dramatic middle section would be inexplicable. There is a similar eruption of violence in the slow movement of the great A minor Sonata K. 310, the first of Mozart's essays in the tragic vein. Although the exposition of that movement has already a pronouncedly dramatic character, the force of the development is there, too, almost unmotivated unless it is seen in relation to the opening movement. The even greater contrast of the D minor concerto is a mark of Mozart's greater ease of control. The most remarkable sign of this ease, however, is the supple phrase structure of the first movement as well as the expressive transformations of its recapitulation.

In spite of its looser structure and the resolution in major of the coda, this tragic atmosphere permeates the finale to the point of turning the relative major into minor—the F minor theme at measure 93 is striking—and transforming the recapitulation of one of the secondary themes into an oscillation between major and minor that is a foreshadowing of Schubert's pathos. Almost all the modulations are brusque to the point of brutality, and the first orchestral tutti has a brilliant violence that Mozart had never employed in a symphony until then, much less in a concerto. The resemblances of this movement to the finale of the G minor Symphony K. 550 are more than thematic, but in the latter work Mozart was able to be even more uncompromising. However, I should not like this last remark to be taken as an expression of the usual disapproval, which I do not share, of the brilliance and gaiety of the coda of K. 466.

The pendant to the D minor Concerto, the Concerto in C major K. 467, is a work of symphonic majesty, and follows it as the *Jupiter* Symphony K. 551 does the G minor. The *Jupiter*, however, has a surface conventionality which is deceptive—it will not condescend to material which is too clearly

---

[1] The phrase first appears in measures 9–12, and from it come the themes at measures 44–47, 58–60; the relation to 28–30 is also obvious, and to all further appearances of these passages. The relations between the first movement and finale are also wider and deeper than I have exposed here.

striking. The C major Concerto makes no such pretense, although its main theme is similar to the opening of the *Jupiter*. This concerto is Mozart's first true essay in orchestral grandeur. Before this, the symphonies, even the *Linz*, K. 425, had striven more for brilliance than for majesty: with the rhythmic structure of the classical style it was a more easily attainable goal. It is the tranquil breadth of K. 467 that leads to the achievements of the *Prague* and the *Jupiter*. More than in any other previous work is Mozart's ability to work with large masses—to think in blocks and areas of sound—so in evidence.

The opening tutti masses the winds as a group against the strings with no solo wind effects except briefly at measure 28. The rhythmic breadth is particularly remarkable: while the excitement of K. 466 brought in a large number of short phrases in the opening ritornello, and several dramatic pauses, the beginning of K. 467 is continuous and massive, the tonic key laid out as a wide and firm base. The phrases are all a regular four measures in length (with one overlapping at measure 12) and, towards the end of the tutti, broader five-measure phrases (at measures 48, 60, and 64—the latter overlapping to preserve a four-measure rhythm and acting in the end like a *ritenuto* that holds back the final beat). Only just before the entrance of the soloist, as a preparation, does the rhythm become fragmented.

The piano part is particularly rich and inventive in new kinds of keyboard figuration, sometimes of a remarkable density. Most striking in this movement, too, is the long-range feeling for tonal areas and their stability. The modulation to the dominant is heavily reinforced by quickly turning to the dominant minor,[1] which I quote because of its extraordinary repercussions later in the piece:

---

[1] A dominant minor at this point of the exposition is both disruptive and stabilizing: it stabilizes the dominant major, and in so doing increases the tension with the tonic.

This passage never actually appears again except for measures 121–123; what happens in the recapitulation is the reappearance of the opening theme in the subdominant—a means of resolution that Mozart uses so frequently—and proceeds as follows:

It is not the *melodic* material of measures 110–120 that appears in the recapitulation, but its *harmonic* structure, which is there resolved by the turn to the subdominant minor, as can be seen from the identical ending of both passages. The primacy of harmony over melody in the recapitulation considered as resolution is clear: harmonic resolution is more important to the classical style than melodic symmetry.

The development section also is affected by the grandeur of style: it is entirely based on subsidiary material,[1] and it is not intended deliberately to recall the exposition, which has already given considerable development to the main theme. The tranquil introduction of what sounds like new material only adds to the breadth, and the richly passionate climax is in the tonic minor, so that the return of the main theme in the major brightens and clarifies with the greatest economy of motion. The tutti that follows is twice as long as the orchestral section opening the recapitulation of any other Mozart concerto; moreover, for nineteen of its twenty-two measures it is an unvaried replaying of the opening measures. This kind of expansive gesture is of a peculiarly symphonic nature: the concerto generally requires more embroidery, but the largeness and the freedom of Mozart's central conception here enable him to forego variation.

The same simplicity reigns in the Andante, an aria with muted strings and a pizzicato bass. Over a continuously throbbing accompaniment that never ceases except for one breathtaking moment, the soloist traces a series of long-breathed cantilenas of the greatest poignance: the only hint of virtuosity is exclusively vocal, an imitation of the long expressive leaps from one register to another in the operatic cavatina. If the form appears complicated to describe, it is only because it is so individual that we have no words with which to categorize it. The description is worth attempting: nowhere else are Mozart's freedom and his sensitivity to the emotional power of a structure more in evidence.

The opening twenty-two measures in the orchestra seem like one unbroken melody, but they are split by Mozart into three parts for the rest of the movement: *A* (mm. 2–7), *B* (8–11), and *C* (12–22) will make convenient labels. After the ritornello the piano plays *A* and *B* in the tonic; ten measures later, *B* and *C* are played in the dominant (mm. 45–55). Since there is clearly developmental material at measures 55–61 and 65–72, and a recapitulation from 75 to the end, we could describe the form logically as a sonata—but that is not the way it sounds. For a new melody in the relative minor appears after a modulation at measure 38, and this is preceded by a strong tonic cadence and a long trill from the piano. The tonic close followed by the relaxed harmonic relationship of the relative minor and the strongly sectional phrasing are those of the da capo aria or the rondo, like the Romanza of the D minor Concerto. And in the middle of the development—again after

---

[1] Mainly that exposed in measures 170, 28, and 160.

a cadential trill from the piano—yet another new melody is introduced (m. 62), this time in the subdominant, an even more relaxed key equally typical of the rondo. Still more characteristic of the rondo form (C.P.E. Bach's, in particular) is the recapitulation which begins in the flat mediant A flat major, after a modulation that is set apart—as if to emphasize how extraordinary it is—by its being the only moment in the entire movement when the accompanying triplets cease, and we can hear the slow melody of the winds alone (mm. 71–72). This modulation, the single moment of stillness, has the magical quality of some of Schubert's, and it is all the more unexpected as the passage just before has prepared an obvious return to the tonic. What we expect, in short, is to hear the original melody once again all the way through in the tonic. Mozart never completely fails to gratify a wish that he has himself aroused: after *A* in the flat mediant, *B* appears highly decorated in the tonic minor as a transition to *C* in its original tonic position; for a coda, *B* appears once more in the tonic major, and a new theme, only four measures long, concludes the work.

If a description is to correspond to what is actually heard, this is not a sonata movement at all, in spite of our being able to fit it neatly into that category. What we hear is almost like an improvisation, a series of melodies freely extended, softly floating over a pulsating accompaniment. Like a continuous flow of song, it seems the simplest, most naïve of forms: the simplicity is underlined by each new melody's being introduced by a straightforward change of key, as if there were no tight tonal pattern, and as if the continuity came only from the throbbing rhythm that passes from the strings to the winds to the piano, steadily and quietly supporting a stream of melody. Yet all of this is subtly guided—influenced rather than molded—by the ideals of the sonata style, nothing is arbitrary, and only when it is over does one realize with what a delicate balance everything has been weighed. The phrase structure seems as irregular, too, as an improvisation, yet the total shape has a regularity that defies belief. The principal melody, the opening ritornello, has the following shape: $3 + 3, 2 + 2, (1 + 1 + 1 + 1 + 1)$ or $5, 3 + 3$; the climax is dead center, at the beginning of the five-measure phrase, and the symmetry of $3 + 3$ at the beginning and the end is achieved without the last phrases being in any way a repetition of the first ones:

The quickening of the large rhythmic pattern comes in the change from 3-measure phrases to 2-measure phrases: the 5-measure phrase falls into units of single measures, thus continuing the increase of animation, and yet its greater length counters and balances this with a holding-back that is a transition to the final symmetry which resolves. The apparent irregularity gives us—as does the entire movement—that deeply moving impression of improvised song and formal design.

These two concertos, K. 466 and K. 467, written in 1785, cannot, in any sense, be called 'better' than many others Mozart had written and was to write. Nevertheless, they represent a liberation of the genre, a demonstration that the concerto could stand with equal dignity beside any other musical form, capable of expressing the same depth of feeling and of working out the most complex musical idea. What could follow these works might seem to be only further refinement, yet some great works were still to come, and they contain surprises.

In the winter of 1785–86, while working on *Figaro*, Mozart wrote three piano concertos for his subscription concerts. They are the first such works he had written with clarinets, his favorite wind instrument, in the orchestra. (At the end of this period, he also wrote the great Clarinet Trio K. 498.) The clarinets dominate the first of the three concertos, K. 482 in E flat major. The woodwinds altogether play a larger role than in any other concerto; even the bassoon has a considerable share of solo melodic work. Perhaps for this reason, this concerto places the greatest musical reliance on tone-color, which is, indeed, almost always ravishing. One lovely example of its sonorties comes near the beginning:

(Full score)

A few measures before, this same passage was scored an octave lower for horns and bassoons, and here we have the unusual sound of the violins' providing the bass for the solo clarinets. The simplicity of the sequence concentrates all our interest on tone-color, and what follows—a series of woodwind solos—keeps it there. The orchestration throughout, in fact, has a greater variety than Mozart had wished or needed to use before, and fits the brilliance, charm, and the somewhat superficial grace of the first movement and the finale. The slow movement in C minor is of a much deeper cast, but its pathos is elegant and even theatrical, above all accessible, and it does not abandon this new interest in pure color. Its form is close to Haydn's beloved double-variation scheme, being a rondo-variation set: the use of muted strings, long sections for woodwind alone, a duet for flute and bassoon, and menacing trills in unison strings all contribute to the orchestral palette; the movement was a great success at its first performance, being encored. Like K. 271, also in E flat major, the rondo-finale is interrupted by a minuet in A flat major, with the orchestration here, too, making a striking but less lavish use of pizzicato. If this minuet is not as impressive as the earlier one, that is in part because the high spirits of the last movement occasion much purely mechanical brilliance; the movement as a whole is an imitation of the finale of K. 450 without the latter's invention and freshness. The simplicity of the minuet is perhaps an advance on the heavily ornate style of K. 271, where expression still depends largely on luxuriance of detail. This new spareness does not come from Mozart's failure to fill out ornamentation, even though the concerto shows a few places incompletely written out (he composed it, after all, only for his own use). The melody appears equally unadorned in the orchestral parts, which double the solo, and while the solo part may need the addition of a few ornaments, most of the simplicity must be ascribed not to carelessness but largely to the development of Mozart's style.

One great suppleness of the concerto form—a freedom that it shares with no other—is illustrated in the happiest way by the Concerto in A major K. 488; that is, the placing of the end of the exposition, or—to give it a description that does not convey such a strong impression of a label—the placing of the last firm cadence on the dominant. There is naturally always a tutti or ritornello following the solo exposition, and the last cadence on the dominant may occur in one of three places: with the last solo phrase before the tutti, so that the orchestra begins the series of modulations called the development (as in K. 459 and K. 467); at the end of the tutti, so that the solo part begins in the dominant and initiates the new sense of movement (as in K. 456, K. 466, etc.); or in the middle of the tutti (K. 451, K. 482, among others). Mozart's first mature work in this form, K. 271, already played with this freedom by having the piano interrupt the tutti and so emphasize this ambiguity. Whatever is done, the opening of the tutti is always an affirmation of the dominant—a declaration, in short, of where we are and a reinforcement of the polarity of the exposition.

K. 488 takes advantage of this situation in a new way: after the pianist's closing trill on the dominant, the ritornello begins its cadential theme only to cut it off sharply and surprisingly after a brief six measures. Then, as we naturally expect a strong dominant cadence to resolve this, we are given something else, an entirely new theme (mm. 143–148):

The new theme has a cadential flavor, but a relatively weak one. The following development is entirely based on this theme (and another new one, much shorter, introduced by the piano). It was not unusual to begin a development section with new material; Mozart did it frequently in the sonatas, and a minor composer like Schroeter, whose work Mozart liked, frequently did it in concertos. What is rare and striking is that this beautiful theme is both an end and a beginning: a final cadence for the tutti, and the opening of the development—it acts as a kind of pun within the structure. Its double nature may be sufficiently indicated by the fact that Mozart evidently also considers it a part of the expository function of the movement, and replays it in the tonic in the middle of the recapitulation.

This is not a formal gesture for an effect of novelty, or a surprise for its own sake. Mozart returns in this work to the melancholy lyricism of the earlier A major Concerto K. 414; by withholding part of the exposition until the development, and by making this final theme as much a resolution of the transitional ritornello as the opening of a new section, he attains the uninterrupted melodic flow of the earlier work without its looseness of structure. The classical period worked almost entirely with separate, articulated units: vanquishing the overarticulate and sectional tendency of the style was the real mastery of Haydn and Mozart. Paradoxically, the clarity of function of the stylistic units made possible such effects of ambiguity as we have just seen: if the passage cited were not so clearly both a cadential resolution (and therefore the end of a section) and a new theme, Mozart would not be able to glide with such lyrical ease over what would ordinarily be a break of continuity.

Mozart's ability to draw the utmost poignance of expression from the simplest means is seen at its most striking in the Adagio that follows, and, above all, in the opening melody. The skeleton of the theme is a simple descending scale, accompanied by a parallel longer movement above it. Like so many of Bach's melodies, Mozart's single voice traces two polyphonic lines. In schematic form:

arranged so that every detail comes forth with the greatest possible pathos:

The harmonic suspension at the opening of measure 2 brings out the full expressive quality of the drop of the seventh in the melody: the displaced resolution of the suspension into the low E♯ of the bass only serves to make the second B in the right hand an expressive dissonance. The structure of the melody may be two regular parallels, but its beauty and its passionate melancholy lie in the irregularity of rhythm and variety of phrasing which reveal every possible expressive facet of the two simple descending lines. The difference in the outline of the sixth in each of the first three measures is an example of the richness of invention. Most remarkable, perhaps, is the with-holding of the resolution of the D in the third measure of the melody until the sixth measure, and most expressive is the almost tragic retracing of the whole line in the seventh measure. I must content myself with those details, but this wonderful theme would repay more study than I have room for, particularly in its spacing of voices.

Before there is a misunderstanding, I hasten to add that I do not suppose that Mozart started with any such skeleton as I have given, and then em-bellished it. Reading a composer's mind, retracing the steps by which he worked, is not a viable critical method even when the composer is alive and one can ask him how he did it—he generally does not know. A composer's sketches are not as much help as is sometimes believed; Beethoven, the most prodigious sketcher of all time, expressly said that the sketches were only a kind of shorthand to remind him of the more complete ideas he carried in his head. How Mozart wrote the opening of the slow movement of K. 488—whether he started with the beginning or the middle, or whether it came forth from his brain as a fully-armed *Gestalt*—we shall never know. Although Mozart, too, made many sketches (more and more as he grew older), he could certainly carry in his head as much or more than any other composer in history.

The skeleton of the melody I have indicated is then, emphatically, not the 'musical idea.' Nor is it (although it is not irrelevant) what makes this theme so beautiful: when we admire the bone structure of a beautiful face, we are not really interested in osteology. But the tendency to think in terms of diatonic scale progressions is basic to late eighteenth-century composers, above all in the use of expressive dissonances and their resolution downwards. Mozart's genius lay in the understanding of how the expressive possibilities of such a simple progression could be used, and how it could give unity to a phrase, and to the movement between phrases, while the melodic line that traced and decorated the progression was as varied in rhythm and phrasing as the character of the music demanded.

Another device of unity—this time between larger sections—may be seen if we compare the opening phrase of the piano, the opening of the first tutti, and the opening of the next solo section:

in the third example, the piano begins its melody again, but combines it with the shape of the orchestra's phrase, so that the two are fused into one. This synthesis of musical elements which later extends to the second theme in A major enables Mozart to give the second theme the character both of a second subject and of the central section of an A B A form,[1] using certain elements of sonata style to dramatize an essentially looser structure.

The last of the three concertos is the greatest, the Concerto in C minor K. 491. Like K. 466, it is in the tragic vein: more intimate, it evades the theatricality of the earlier work. It is less operatic and closer to chamber music. What it loses in grandeur it makes up in refinement, and it achieves an equivalent breadth in a very different way. This concerto gave Mozart considerable trouble, not just in details, but in its proportions. There is a great deal of rewriting in the manuscript, and—what is uncommon for Mozart, who rarely made such large changes—there is an insertion of a new long section in the opening ritornello. The reason for this considerable change lies in the solo exposition. A full hundred measures after the piano has entered, we have:

---

[1] There is a direct expository movement from first to second theme, but no recapitulation of the second theme: however, the themes are closely related, and a recapitulation of the first ritornello is used as a substitute.

and yet, sixty measures later, we find the same cadence in the relative major, more expansively:

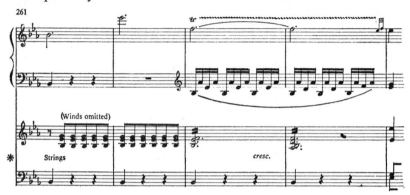

In other words, the exposition formally closes twice—the passage preceding the first cadence has, in fact, most of the signs of being the end of the exposition, with all the virtuosity and—almost—all the finality. If the opening ritornello were as short as it originally was before Mozart extended it, the relative proportions of solo exposition and ritornello would already be perfect at the first of these cadences—the solo exposition in all the concertos being the more expansive of the two.

What follows the first cadence, however, is not a cadential tutti but a new secondary theme and a new closing theme, both presented at length. Between them occurs a passage at first consideration even more extraordinary: the opening theme is replayed, beginning in the relative major—the normal practice of Haydn during the second half of an exposition, and not uncommon in Mozart—but quickly modulating within one measure to E flat minor and sustaining a series of modulations before returning to E flat major. Harmonically this has the character of a development section, and in this place it has a force and a passion that are unforgettable.

Mozart is experimenting once again, and this time more daringly, with the placing of the final dominant cadence of the exposition. There are, in a sense, two solo expositions after the orchestral exposition, which therefore had to be enlarged to fit the wider proportions. None of this is experimentation for its own sake, or even for the sake of novelty and surprise: it comes from the character of the music and from the material.

The main theme has a terse, concentrated outline that is not often found in Mozart, and is much more typical of Haydn. The first movement of the C minor Concerto is, in fact, closely related to Haydn's Symphony no. 78 in the same key, written only four years before. The opening of the Haydn:

is recognizably like the beginning of the concerto, although Mozart's conception of phrase and period is much broader and less constrained:

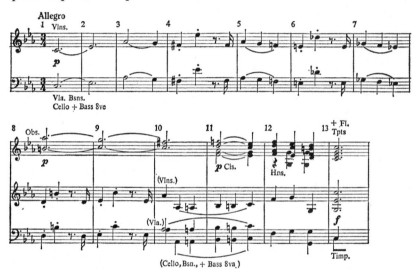

The entrance of the oboes in measure 8 is that of an accompanying harmonic voice, but by measure 11 they have imperceptibly become the melodic part. This shift from accompanying to principal role is done with even greater smoothness than Haydn's similar procedure at the beginning of op. 33 no. 1.[1] Mozart needs all his subtlety to arrive at the high seriousness of tragedy with material essentially so shortwinded—in comparison with K. 466 and 467— and so angularly characterized. The irregularity of the phrase-structure sets the details in relief.

More than the opening of any previous concerto, these measures make us concentrate on their linear aspect, and not only because the first few bars are all played in unison. Above all, the nature of the melody, its angular

---

[1] Quoted and discussed on pages 115–117.

chromaticism, the phrasing, the sequences with rising sixths that follow each other staccato, give unusual importance to the intervallic relations. (On the first page of K. 466, for example, we are far more aware of the texture—the menacing rumble in the bass, the syncopated pulsations.) The beginning of K. 491 is almost oddly neutral for a few measures until its implications make themselves realized; there is a reserve, a restraint about this work that is absent in K. 466. In the earlier work, breadth is achieved easily by the regularity of the opening paragraph, all in four- and two-measure groups: the rise to the first climax is achieved smoothly. In the C minor Concerto, the material seems to have shrunk: the opening phrase stakes everything on a series of rising sixths and descending seconds. The first page of K. 466 is not really built out of much more, but there the regularity both of phrasing and of the opening ascent gives the listener a sense of paragraph and not of separate clauses; the irregularity of the opening of K. 491 sets the details rather than the larger movement in focus and we are inevitably more conscious of the individual units.

The 'double' solo exposition (making a triple exposition with the first ritornello) is a natural consequence of this—the fragmentation of the larger form corresponding to the inner divisions of the opening statement. This is not a mystical or holistic doctrine of correspondence between totality and part. When a classical composer wanted to use material that was melodically fragmented (as Beethoven, for example, did most of the time), where each detail appears *immediately* to have a significance that can only be understood beyond the phrase, he combined such material with extreme regularity of phrasing in the opening statement in order to overcome the divisive effect: the opening of a sonata may be a motto but not an epigram. It should be recalled that regularity of phrasing implies the imposition of a longer and slower beat over the main pulse, and the consciousness of a larger time scale. There are many works of Mozart with irregular phrase-lengths which enforce breadth by a largeness of statement and a symmetrical balance of the irregular elements as in the slow movement of K. 467 (the slow movement of the G minor Quintet is a more momentous example). But in the C minor Concerto, Mozart is dealing with a fragmentary melodic line that requires an irregularity of phrase. That is why there is a great variety of clearly defined although related themes in this movement, and yet each insistently repeats a fragment of itself, as if they were all constructed as a kind of mosaic:

These are the main secondary themes, and the insistent repetition of the smaller units is unusual for Mozart (although typical of Haydn). They are not themes that can be developed into long paragraphs at leisure, as the balanced opening statement of K. 467 can; yet to draw out the tragic implications of the material which can be so clearly sensed by the end of the first phrase, Mozart needs far grander proportions than the material will easily yield. This is why a new page was inserted into the opening tutti, and why, too, there is a 'double' solo exposition. If we half expect a development section instead of the second solo exposition, we are also half granted one within it by the far-reaching modulations of the main theme in E flat minor (from measure 220 on). Here the fragmentation of the harmonic movement of the exposition corresponds to the fragmentation of the structure (as well as to the melodic and rhythmic fragmentation of the material). The series of diminished chords in the opening statement of the main theme clearly presage and justify such a large-scale chromatic instability, and the exposition-as-development, subsequently brings a passion, even a kind of terror, that is central to the work. Although here Mozart works technically with the smaller units of Haydn, he still demands the much greater range of emotion that was always his own.

The recapitulation must sum up the three expositions. The two secondary themes (*b*) and (*c*) of the piano's expositions are played now one right after the other but with (*c*) before (*b*), and (*a*), the passage inserted in the opening tutti, is combined with (*d*) as a closing theme:

The piano interrupts the coda with a beautiful symmetry: a reworking of the last measures of the development. The end of the movement unites all the disparities.

The orchestration has a refinement and a fragmentation comparable to the structure: the inner part-writing is so detailed that the violas are often divided into two sections, and there are oboes as well as clarinets. The orchestral sound is not, however, colorful as in K. 482, but rich and somber. The use of the timpani and trumpets in soft passages is comparable in its strange, veiled quality to parts of K. 466 and *Don Giovanni*. With all its dramatic power, this concerto comes closer to the late chamber-music style of Mozart than any other, except for the last of all. The 'chamber' style of three earlier concertos—K. 413, K. 414, and K. 449—is only that of the serenades: with K. 491 we reach the inward-looking detail of the string quartets. Not only the despair of the music but its energy is introverted, turned away from all that was theatrical even in Mozart himself.

The other movements are less original in conception, although equally fine. The Larghetto is like the Romanza of K. 466 without its violent central section. The finale, Allegretto, is a set of variations in march-tempo. It is generally taken too fast under the delusion that a quick tempo will give it a power commensurate with the opening movement. Mozart, however, is not a composer whose defects have to be made good by his interpreters: if he had wanted that kind of power, he would have written it. The part-writing is as rich here as Mozart could make it, but the clarity of the theme is never obscured: it is always intended to be heard, and even the two transformations into major, while free on paper, sound strict to the ear. A classical finale, even when it can be categorized as a sonata, is always a looser form than a first movement, inevitably easier to grasp. With all its sobriety, nevertheless, this movement has enough of the passionate despair of the first movement for Beethoven to recall part of the coda in the finale of the *Appassionata*.

The Concerto in C major K. 503 has never been a favorite with the public. Completed at the end of 1786, eight months after the last of the group of three piano concertos with clarinets, it is a magnificent and—to many ears—a cold work. Yet it is the one that many musicians (historians and pianists alike) single out with special affection. The unattractiveness for the public comes from the almost neutral character of the material: in the first movement in particular this material is not even sufficiently characterized to be called banal. An opening phrase built as a series of blocks from an arpeggio:

cannot be called even a cliché. It is conventional, highly so, but in no pejorative sense: it is merely the basic material of late eighteenth-century tonality, the bedrock of the style. Even a later, more attractive theme in a military spirit is equally conventional in this sense: like bread, it cannot cloy.

The splendor of the work and the delight it can inspire come entirely from the handling of the material. There are other concertos of Mozart in which the material is almost wholly conventional—K. 451, for instance, of which Mozart was so proud, and K. 415—but none of them reveals the powers of K. 503. The different ideas in the first movement are treated in block fashion: in spite of the masterly transitions, we are conscious of the juxtaposition of large elements, and above all we are aware of their weight. Indeed, throughout this concerto, we are made to feel how much pressure the form itself can bring to bear even while using almost completely inexpressive ideas. To see this mastery, any join of the form will suffice. Here is the first entrance of the piano, nothing but a continuously repeated dominant seventh-tonic cadence:

I have been obliged to cite extensively, because the sense of mass is important, and, above all, because so much depends on sheer repetition—and repetition of the most conventional harmonic sound in eighteenth-century music. The acceleration of measures 83–89 is handled with the technique that Mozart displayed at its most striking in K. 466, although he had the essentials within his grasp years before. The harmony of measure 88 moves four times as fast as before, and the last two beats of measure 89 double this once again. All this is now routine to Mozart (and only his ease in handling it was exceptional in the classical period). What is striking is that measure 90 is exactly enough of an end without being quite final: it is about two chords away from an absolutely final cadence. With the addition of only one measure, in fact, it does later serve as the last phrase of the movement: it is marvellous to see how Mozart is able to stop at the very edge here. It is, paradoxically, the pause that both provides a transition and extends the tension—a tension engendered rhythmically by a tonic cadence! This is the beginning of Beethoven's understanding of the exciting rhythmic power of pure repetition. We have, however, not yet done with the dominant seventh–tonic cadence: the orchestra starts it again, more slowly, like a resolution of the previous excitement, and the soloist enters. The cadence is played three times. We can identify the exact moment when the section we have been hearing ends: on the first beat of measure 96, which has the sound of a conclusion withheld before. Yet at this point the piano has already started a series of phrases which it continues—echoing the very same cadence three times more. In this way, the first beat of measure 96 is both the end of a section, and the middle of a statement from the piano; the overlapping device is the insistent repetition of one simple cadence. The conciliation of continuity with articulation—movement and clarity of shape— was never accomplished with more efficiency.

This economy of means is one of the first signs of the final development of Mozart's style. It is not, however, until the year of his death that the full significance of this tendency extends to all the elements of his music. In the

C major Concerto K. 503, the renunciation of harmonic color is already a marked characteristic: almost all the shadings arise from a simple alternation of major and minor. This can, of course, lead far: the use of C minor against C major brings up E flat major early in the work (m. 148), and, at its reappearance in the recapitulation, it calls up E flat minor; the dominant, G major, is introduced by G minor. But these are all major–minor and major–relative minor relations: that is, they are modulations that do not move, that leave the tonality unchanged.

It is not that in Mozart's late style the more dynamic modulations do not exist: on the contrary, there are no more brutal modulations than the ones in the finale of the G minor Symphony or the last piano concerto. But their very brutality is a sign of the economy with which they are used, and of their dramatic purpose: they are not harmonic exoticisms, like the B minor in the last movement of the B flat major Piano Concerto K. 456. Nor does Mozart renounce the use of color, orchestral or harmonic, but each effect becomes more telling and more penetrating. *Die Zauberflöte* has the greatest variety of orchestral color that the eighteenth century was to know; the very lavishness, however, is paradoxically also an economy, as each effect is a concentrated one, each one—Papageno's whistle, the Queen of the Night's coloratura, the bells, Sarastro's trombones, even the farewell in Scene I for clarinets and pizzicato strings[1]—a single dramatic stroke.

The alternation of tonic major and minor is the dominant color of K. 503, and a prime element of the structure as well. We find it first hinted in measure 6 (quoted above, page 251) and more openly displayed a few measures later:

This alternation is more than consistent; it is almost obsessive. The fundamental rhythmic element of the piece is first introduced by the violins in measures 18–19 (cited above); at measure 26 it appears in the bass:

---

[1] Quoted on page 320.

A principal theme based on this rhythm

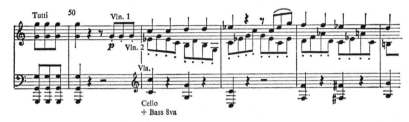

is immediately played in the tonic major a few measures after this appearance in minor. Another 'second' theme is first played in major and repeated half in minor[1] as its own second phrase:

---

[1] It should be noted that this is also a *tonic* major–minor, as G major is by now firmly established as the tonality of this part of the exposition (the use of a major and minor contrast within a subordinate chord would have the more purely coloristic effect of a chromatic harmony). In measure 175, all editions suggest a high A in the piano, as it is evident that Mozart used the lower one only because his keyboard stopped at F; the parallel place in the recapitulation shows that he would have kept the upward form of the melody both times as in measure 170. Unfortunately we cannot stop there; a comparison with the parallel place (measure 345) will show that if we change measure 175, we must also rewrite the next measure as follows:

as the high A would otherwise be left hanging. It is not as easy as editors think to rewrite even a detail of Mozart, which is why it is best as a general rule to print (and play) exactly what he wrote.

And finally, most Mozartean and most classical of all, after further alternation, the cadence ending the exposition is *both in major and minor at once:*

It is a summary, an example of classical resolution as synthesis.

The central and insistent opposition and synthesis of major and minor is
remarkable for its long-range conception. It means that the bass generally
remains absolutely stable against the continuous tensions of the harmony,
often with the immobility of a pedal-point. Since the major–minor contrast
occurs immediately within the opening phrases of the movement, its use in
the structure on a larger scale follows naturally.[1] This grandiose ambiguity
of stability and tension—a characteristic sound, massive and yet disquieting
—is the key to this work's tranquil power.

All the elements of the piece contribute to this effect of mass. The use of
obstinate repetition, as we have seen above, is marked throughout: this work
not only recalls Beethoven to us, it is probable that Beethoven remembered
it himself when he wrote his Fourth Piano Concerto. The beginning of the
development section has the piano make a surprising shift of tonality by
softly taking over the orchestra's rhythm:

---

[1] For example, the opening ritornello goes directly to the dominant G major (mm. 30–
50) but immediately returns to the tonic *minor*: the solo exposition uses this gravitation
towards C minor to make the move to the dominant more expressive, as the music goes
by way of E flat major (established by now with ease) and G minor (mm. 140–165). The
profoundly expressive quality of the music here comes almost entirely from the structure
and not from the material. The parallel place in the recapitulation (mm. 320–340) is harmonically more startling, although equally logical within the framework (the E flat major
turns into E flat minor and chromatically back to a C minor–major) and even more deeply
expressive.

and Beethoven uses exactly the same rhythm with the same dynamic contrast at the same place of the G major Concerto; even the function of the phrase is the same—a surprising modulation. (Beethoven, however, strengthens the effect by having the modulation appear a more remote one, and by having the piano interrupt the orchestra.)[1] The rhythm is thrown into relief in both cases by being a repetition of one note; in both the repetition is thematic. Beethoven's version is more dramatic and more striking but it is perhaps Mozart who achieves the greater impression of ease and power. The final triumph of the massive power of K. 503 is the second half of the development section which—in addition to the piano's figuration—is in full six-part polyphony, with imitative writing almost strict enough to be called canonic, a *tour de force* of classical counterpoint comparable to the finale of the *Jupiter* Symphony or the ball scene in *Don Giovanni*.

In general, the lyricism of Mozart's works lies in the details, and the larger structure is an organizing force; in K. 503, the details are largely conventional, and the most striking expressive force comes from the larger formal elements, even to the point of pervading a heavily symphonic style with melancholy and tenderness. For the most part, too, this melancholy arises miraculously from the simplest of changes from major to minor, often leaving a tonic chord in root position: the resulting impression of tranquil

---

[1] Quoted on pages 391–2.

power and lyricism is unique in music before Beethoven.[1] The emotion is less poignant than in some of the other concertos, but it is the combination of breadth and subtlety that has made this work so admired.

The slow movement is a beautiful combination of simplicity and lavish decoration (with a great variety and contrast of rhythms), which it would be a pity to spoil by decorating the leaner phrases. I have myself added ornaments to a few measures when playing this work, and am sorry for it now. The finale is also colored, like the first movement, by frequent changes from the major to the minor mode, and has Mozart's favorite rondo devices of a recapitulation in reverse order (main theme last). Written at the same time as the *Prague* Symphony and the String Quintets in C major and G minor, K. 503 stands well in this company of the grandest works.

After this, Mozart's interest in the concerto almost ceased completely. From 1784 to 1786 he had written a dozen works in this form; during the last five years of his life he was to write only three. All three works stand somewhat apart in character as well. Perhaps the strangest of them is the so-called *Coronation* Concerto in D major K. 537. Musicians and historians alike have been very hard on it. The most popular of all Mozart's concertos throughout the nineteenth and much of the twentieth centuries, the music deserves more respect: it is historically the most 'progressive' of all Mozart's works, the closest to the early or proto-Romantic style of Hummel and Weber. It is even the closest in its style of virtuosity to the early concertos of Beethoven. We have only to compare

with Beethoven's first piano concerto

to see one detail among many. One might say that this is the concerto that Hummel would have written if he had had not only a remarkable talent but genius.

---

[1] Beethoven's violin concerto, in its first movement, uses a similar emphasis on the root of the tonic triad and a series of changes from major to minor, for its expansive effect of power and tenderness.

The Concerto

In one important respect, this concerto is a revolutionary work, as it shifts the balance between the harmonic and melodic aspects so that the structure now depends largely on melodic succession. This is already evident in the opening ritornello, which has long transitional athematic passages, setting off one section from another:

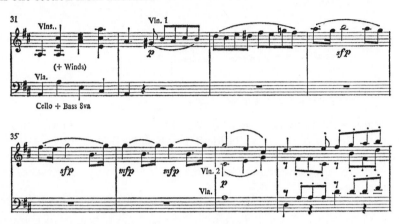

or, even more remarkably:

where the beginning of the melody in the next-to-last measure cited (m. 59) is itself like an up-beat, and therefore like a continuation of the transition as well as a beginning. These transitional phrases, generally reserved for the solo exposition as expansions and here already in the initial orchestral statement, serve to loosen the structure. The melodic aspect of the themes is emphasized over their harmonic function, and over their place in the directional flow. It should be noted that neither of these transitional phrases is a resolution; they come after a resolving cadence, and they are, therefore, pure suspensions of movement, filled silences. Their only purpose is beautifully to make us wait for a melody to begin.

This loosening of the harmonic and rhythmic structure requires that the resultant weakening of tension be compensated from somewhere else. There is a consequent luxuriance of virtuoso figuration. At the end of an exposition, the use of such figuration had been, in Mozart's previous concertos, only the enhancement of already established tension; now it is used actually to create excitement. The increase of brilliance and intricacy is natural:

259

This is not weighty or majestic as in K. 467 or dramatic as in K. 466 (the two concertos with the most brilliant piano figuration before this), but complicatedly rich and a little more difficult for the ear to follow: it has an interest of its own almost out of relation to the other material of the movement.

Both the loose melodic structure and the reliance on figuration for tension are characteristics of the early Romantic style, as in the concertos of Hummel and Chopin. It was not Beethoven but Mozart who showed how the classical style might be destroyed. To appreciate K. 537 we cannot listen to it with the same expectations that we have for the other works. It demands to be judged by later standards: viewed in this light, it can be seen as the greatest of early Romantic piano concertos. The brilliant rondo has the same character as the opening movement, but the Larghetto is a foretaste of Mozart's last development. It is so simple in character that if it were not a masterpiece, it would be merely pretty. Already it is an example of that popular, lean, almost *faux-naïf* grace that is the glory of *Die Zauberflöte*.

In the last of his life, Mozart wrote two concertos which depend more upon the delicate interplay of chamber music than upon the dramatic interplay of concerto style. The Clarinet Concerto in A major K. 622 is very close in its lyricism and even in the shape of its themes and their harmonic content to the A major Piano Concertos, K. 414 and K. 488. The last Piano Concerto, K. 595 in B flat major, written six months before, also has the same freely lyrical quality, here gradually permeated by an expressive, even painful chromaticism that dominates everything by the beginning of the development section. Both concertos give the sensation of an inexhaustible and continuous melodic line, somehow both seamless and yet clearly articulated. The structure, nevertheless, is neither a loose succession of melodies (as in K. 537) nor an unvaried flow.

Mozart uses a system of overlapping phrase-rhythms in these two late works, and puts it unobtrusively at the service of a lyrical invention which pours forth unimpeded, yet without losing either tension or poignance. In the Clarinet Concerto, for example:

a new phrase starts somewhere between measures 102 and 105 without—at the moment of hearing—its being clear just at what point. Hindsight tells us (by the time we hear measure 106) that the new phrase began at the first beat of measure 104, yet when we had heard that measure we were aware only of the continuity of movement. In this way, Mozart has both the clear articulation and the uninterrupted flow at the same time. This example may be called the articulation of continuity: the complementary process—the integration of an interrupted movement—may be seen a few pages before:

measures 76–77 are both an end to the cadence at measure 75 and the beginning of a new phrase; 78–79 repeat the harmonies of 76–77 changed into minor, and the exact parallelism of the orchestral accompaniment makes them an answer to 76–77 and the end of a four-measure phrase; yet at the same time measure 78 is the beginning of a new phrase in the clarinet which goes to measure 80 and even beyond. Similar examples could be multiplied indefinitely. Neither the dovetailed articulation nor the double significance of a phrase facing both ways—a completion and a fresh start—are new in Mozart, but I do not think he had ever developed them with the subtlety and the constant invention he displays in his last two concertos. This balance between clarity of shape and continuity makes the first movement of the clarinet concerto seem like an endless song—not a spinning-out of one idea, but a series of melodies that flow one into the other without a break.

The opening Allegro of the last piano concerto, K. 595, is more complex, but leaves the same impression of continuous melody. The means of attaining lyrical continuity are even more delicate here. It is a temptation to quote one of the loveliest passages in the work:

The beginning of the phrase that starts at measure 29 is given the most subtle urgency by our having to wait a split second for the resolution of the viola and second violin line coming out of measure 28: the harmony overlaps across the eighth-note rest, an added link between two phrases already tied together by the first violin line of measures 28–29. The phrase is repeated at measure 33, and the unity with what precedes is now far more emphatic, as the beautiful bass line in the cellos and basses starts in measure 32 and goes uninterruptedly until measure 35.

In this same passage, the sweetness of Mozart's dissonance is at its most powerful: the clash in measure 33 between a D♮ in the first violins and a D♭ three and four octaves below in the cellos and basses is one of the most painful in tonal music. The brutality of this clash is neatly sidestepped in the shortest possible time, and a more acceptable dissonance is substituted, yet our ear and our memory supply all the expressive force, above all because the first violins rise so suddenly to the D♮ (doubling the D in the bass just before it moves to D♭). In this way, on the third beat of the measure there is the unplayed but audibly imagined harshness of a minor ninth (D–D♭) along with the major seventh (D♭–C), which gives the effect of the most dissonant and most expressive harmony without the harshness of actually playing it. Throughout the work the most painful dissonances are evoked and yet softened. This passage is an important moment in the concerto, the first appearance of the minor mode and of the chromaticism that plays such a crucial role, the first sign of the work's limitless melancholy. The development section, where the key changes almost every two measures, carries classical tonality as far as it can go; the chromaticism becomes iridescent, and the orchestration and spacing transparent: the emotion, with all its anguish, never disturbs the grace of the melodic line.

Both the last piano concerto and the Clarinet Concerto are private statements: the form is never exploited for exterior effect, the tone is always one of intimacy. The slow movements aspire and attain to a condition of absolute simplicity: the slightest irregularity in the phrase structure of their themes would have appeared like an intrusion. The melodies accept the reduction to an almost perfect symmetry and triumph over all its dangers. It is fitting that Mozart, who perfected as he created the form of the classical concerto, should have made his last use of it so completely personal.

2

String Quintet

By general consent, Mozart's greatest achievement in chamber music is the group of string quintets with two violas. The viola was his favorite string instrument, the one he habitually chose when playing quartets; in the *Sinfonia Concertante* K. 364 it was probably the viola solo he played and not the violin. His partiality may have come not only from the instrument's sonority but from his love for rich inner part-writing: in his music there was a fulness of sound and a complexity in the inner voices that had disappeared from music since the death of Bach. 'Too many notes' was the reproach cast at Mozart as it had been at Bach: it was not a sonority fashionable after about 1730, and the later eighteenth century preferred a drier and leaner sound. In spite of this taste, the string quintet was already a popular form when Mozart took it up, as the enormous number of insipid but agreeable works in this form by Boccherini attest. Before Mozart, however, the heavier sonority was avoided largely by treating the form as a duet between two soloists—first violin and first viola—with accompaniment. This concertante element is not entirely absent from Mozart, particularly in his immature first essay, K. 174 in B flat major, but this approach translates the form into a kind of divertimento, taking away all serious possibilities: it allows neither the dramatic contrast of the concerto between a large force and a soloist, nor the complex intimacy of chamber music. Only with the eccentric and rhapsodic style of the late Haydn trios was a kind of concertante chamber music to reach real profundity, and then the full resources of the keyboard were needed as well. The concertante string quintet is a lazy extension of the habit of treating the string quartet superficially as an accompanied solo for the first violin: if this kind of quintet has greater variety, it is not essentially more interesting.

At three different times in his life, Mozart turned to the string quintet, and always directly after having written a series of quartets, as if the experience of composing for only four instruments prompted him to take up the richer medium. His first quintet was composed when he was only seventeen years old. In 1772, having recently come into contact with Haydn's Quartets op. 20, and inspired by the new conception of chamber music he found there, he wrote six quartets in which his struggle to assimilate Haydn's language results in a constant alternation of awkwardness with his more natural grace. The Quintet K. 174 followed a year later, a less constrained and more conventionally ambitious work. It is, of course, filled with remarkable things, most of them Haydnesque: a witty play on a two-note figure in the minuet that is almost worthy of the older master, a genuine false reprise in the finale, and an unusually dramatic use of silence in the exterior movements. More typically Mozartean is the exploitation of the special sonority of the medium, with the echo effects in the trio of the minuet, and the constant use of doubling (at the octave or the third) and antiphonal exchanges between the higher and lower instruments. The most original moment is perhaps the beginning of the slow movement, with its use, muted, of an accompanying figure *unisono* for its expressive quality as a melody:

In a passage like this, a witty ambiguity—a grammatical pun, in fact—is so much a part of the style that it cannot disturb the intensity, but remains only as a trace of good manners in the expression of sentiment.

What is most astonishing about this early work is the breadth of conception, which goes far beyond any of the string quartets he had written just previously. The classical feeling for balance demanded that the fuller and richer sonority of the quintet be given a larger framework—within the context of Mozart's own style of the moment—than was fitting for the string quartet. The concertante element may have been instrumental in creating this added breadth, but, in fact, the new grandeur is most striking in K. 174 when the concertante style is completely absent. The finale is the most complex contrapuntal work that Mozart was to write for many years to come, far more intricate than the fugal movements of the early string quartets; the opening movement, along with its solo passages and antiphonal effects, has moments of an expansively dramatic character unattempted by Mozart as yet in the string quartet. The immediate model for this work is not at all Michael Haydn, as has been thought, much less Boccherini, but the *Sun* Quartets of Joseph Haydn. The experiment of adapting Haydn's technique to the richer sound and more relaxed pace demanded by the string quintet is, however, only partially successful; the changes of texture are often more startling than convincing. Still, Mozart's instinctive understanding at the age of seventeen of the fundamental difference between quintet and quartet is remarkable. Beethoven, too, reached the same conclusion in his first and only work in this form: the Quintet op. 29 was written in 1801, the same year that he finished the six quartets op. 18, and it has a breadth and a tranquil expansiveness possessed by none of them; but then he had Mozart's great series of quintets to point the way.

It was fourteen years before Mozart came back to the string quintet. After 1773 he abandoned the string quartet as well for almost a decade; his return to chamber music was again inspired by Haydn: the appearance of the revolutionary *Scherzi* Quartets op. 33. Mozart's six quartets of the years 1782–85 were once more in emulation of the elder composer, and in tribute to him, though now with a full mastery and a new originality; and a year after they were finished, he wrote the beautiful and completely personal *Hoff-meister* Quartet. He then returned to the string quintet in 1787, and wrote two works grander in scope than anything that Haydn had ever conceived even for the orchestra. Nevertheless, he had still the memory of Haydn's op. 33 echoing in his ears. The opening of the C major Quintet K. 515:

inevitably recalls the first measures of Haydn's op. 33 no. 3, the *Bird* (cited on p. 65): there is the same mounting phrase in the cello, the same inner accompanying motion, the same placing of the first violin. Yet Haydn's nervous rhythm is avoided; in place of his independent six-measure phrases —the motion broken abruptly between them—Mozart has a linked series of five-measure phrases with absolutely uninterrupted continuity. In other words, a larger period is imposed on Haydn's system of phrasing: the twenty measures of the first paragraph are divided into 5, 5, 5, 4 plus 1 (the last being a measure of rest—even Haydn's remarkable use of silence in op. 33 no. 3 is turned to account here, but in a grander sense in the context of the larger period). The irregular phrase-length helps to assure the feeling of continuity, and the symmetrical arrangement gives it balance. The transition from the third to the fourth phrase of the paragraph is imperceptible; it is almost impossible to say where the new phrase begins as the violin and cello overlap: while the violin finishes the echo of the first phrases, the cello enters (m. 15) —without waiting the expected two measures—on a new harmony, a dissonance that is given poignance and even sweetness in a spacing that covers four octaves. The symmetrical articulation dissolves at the end, and the measure of rest is all the more dramatic. The second large paragraph begins with a symmetrical repetition, reversing the violin and cello roles, and starting brutally in the tonic minor, a surprise that is all the more effective for being at once so solid as well as so unexpected.

This tonal solidity is the principal source of the breadth and majesty of this work. For a longer time than in any work he had written until then, Mozart avoids a real movement away from the tonic: he transforms it into minor, he alters it chromatically, but he returns to it decisively again and again before moving to the dominant. His powers of expansion—the delay of cadence, the widening of the center of the phrase—are called into play on a scale he had never before known. When the movement to the dominant finally comes, it, too, like the tonic, is established with tranquil firmness: there are three complete themes in the 'second group,' and each one is played twice. This 'second group' has a majestic symmetry of its own: its first theme begins with an emphatic pedal on G, now become the tonic, and an expressively serpentine phrase above it:

and is repeated with a counter-subject. The second theme has a syncopated rhythm in the first violin, and its diminution in the other instruments:

After the expressive instability of this cadence, the pedal-point returns:

with a phrase above it that gradually alludes more and more to the winding chromatic phrase quoted before. The expressive syncopations are thus framed by two similar pedal points; and the immobility of the bass for such long sections of the 'second group' is the balance to the concentration on the tonic and the length of the 'first group.' I have emphasized these proportions because, although the C major Quintet is accepted as one of Mozart's greatest works, it is not generally recognized as perhaps the most daring of all.

The first movement of the C major Quintet is the largest 'sonata allegro' before Beethoven, longer than any other Mozart ever wrote, or any that Haydn had written or was to write. Even the Allegro of the *Prague* Symphony is shorter, and the whole first movement of that work attains the dimensions of the C major Quintet only by virtue of its Adagio introduction. In the quintet, Mozart's principal expansion of the form takes place in the exposition, which is, astonishingly, longer than any first-movement exposition of Beethoven, I believe, except that of the Ninth Symphony, which it equals. Even the exposition of the *Eroica* is shorter.

Size, by itself, of course, means little; pacing and proportion are everything. What is extraordinary in this exposition is that Mozart has discovered the secret of Beethoven's dimensions. First, there is the marked hierarchy of periodic movement—phrase, paragraph, and section. It is for this reason that Mozart does not begin the movement with a clearly defined melody, but with motivic fragments, following Haydn's more usual practice, and anticipating Beethoven's use of these motifs in a continuous unbroken motion within the paragraph. Not only does Mozart abandon melody, he also renounces much of the seductive harmonic color that appears in the first measures of almost all his other works which reach the expressive intensity of this quintet.[1] He postpones, as he so rarely did, the use of the supertonic, the submediant, and the subdominant: for fourteen measures he defines nothing but pure tonic and dominant. In this, too, he anticipates Beethoven, the openings of whose grandest works more often than not outline only the tonic chord. The tonal areas of Mozart's expositions generally have a tranquil solidity absent from Haydn's more nervous and more openly dynamic forms: when this solidity was combined, as it is here, with Haydn's motivic technique of exposition and expansion integrated within a subtle and clearly marked feeling for a large periodic structure, the majestic proportions of this movement became possible, without weakening the lyric intensity that diffuses itself throughout the work.

In expanding that small but resilient symmetrical structure derived from the dance that was later called 'sonata form,' the problem was always how and where to add weight without undoing the proportions and wrecking the unity. The simplest solution was the addition of a long, slow introduction, as in the *Prague* and the E flat symphonies, or in the splendid G major Sonata for Piano and Violin K. 379: but this always remained an exterior device—an additive concept, rather than a synthetic one, until Mozart's D major Quintet and the Haydn symphonies of the 1790s, which reveal new relationships between the introductions and the following allegros. In expanding the form itself, Haydn generally enlarged the second half—not only widening the 'development' but often continuing it throughout the recapitulation. To increase the length of the first half is both difficult and dangerous: the exposition of a sonata is based on only one action, the establishment of one polarity; to delay its arrival too long is to diffuse all the energy, to risk chaos; once it has arrived, everything remaining in the first half tends to have a purely cadential function. In a concerto, the with-

---

[1] There is a similar concentration on simple tonic and dominant at the opening of works, like the first movement of the *Jupiter* and the earlier C major Symphony K. 338, but they have none of this intensity and intend only grandeur or brilliance.

holding of this cadence is the simplest and most justifiable procedure, the occasion for virtuoso passagework from the soloist: cadential virtuosity is, after all, the origin of the 'improvised' cadenza at the end of the movement. This kind of brilliance, which would be empty in a piano sonata,[1] is a dramatic necessity in a concerto: it gives the solo instrument an equivalent for the weight of the full orchestra, and allows a satisfactory equilibrium to be reached. (Only when, as in some works of the nineteenth and twentieth centuries, the virtuosity reaches such proportions that the orchestra is itself overwhelmed, does the brilliance become tasteless.) In any case, this recourse is not open to the 'sonata form' outside the special case of the concerto.

In the C major Quintet, Mozart chose the most difficult and most satisfactory way of increasing the range of the first half of the sonata—the expansion of the opening tonic section, or 'first group.' This meant the dramatization not of an action, but of a refusal to act, the creation of tension while remaining at the extreme point of resolution. To achieve this dramatization, Mozart uses a beautiful variety of means. He withholds all chromatic color from the opening, introducing it more and more as the section proceeds. He employs what was a traditional means of going to the dominant, the counterstatement (i.e., repeating the opening phrases of the movement and beginning the modulation before the repetition has been completed), but radically alters its aspect and its function: the opening phrases are repeated, but in the tonic minor—giving the illusion of harmonic motion while staying essentially in the same place, making the tonic unstable without actually denying it.

This is followed by one of the most extraordinary expansions of a progression; a simple plagal phrase IV–I

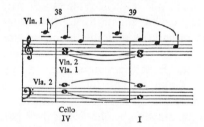

is decorated:

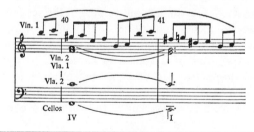

---

[1] The finale of the B flat Sonata K. 333 achieves it only by a witty and frank imitation of a concerto rondo.

The F major starts once again and then is turned into F minor, and the cadence is lengthened, and made deceptive:

and finally and most magnificently this phrase is repeated with the A♭ of the F minor chord made the basis of an extraordinary inner expansion, still outlining essentially the same cadence:

in which the five previous measures have become ten, and the harmonic resonance is immensely widened without really leaving the tonic. (In the recapitulation, this phrase is even longer, and goes as far as C sharp minor, without otherwise changing its fundamental shape or purpose.) Following this, and for the first time, the chromatic movement becomes at last truly directional:

although still returning to the tonic once more with the same IV–I cadence before the movement to the dominant begins. The unprecedented majesty of this work comes from the long immobility and the firm tonic harmony, its lyric poignance from the chromatic alterations that made the proportions conceivable.

It should be remarked in passing that Beethoven expands the 'first group' in quite different ways when he elected—infrequently—to do so. In a number of works (op. 10 no. 3 and op. 2 no. 3, for example), he goes to another secondary key with a new theme before establishing the dominant, which has occasionally given rise to foolish discussions as to which was the 'real' second theme: musicology sometimes considers odd metaphysical questions. In the Sonata op. 111, following the finale of the *Jupiter* Symphony, he expands the tonic area with a fugal development before modulating to the submediant, which serves him as a dominant. The Ninth Symphony has an exceptionally subtle device: Beethoven replays the main theme on B flat major, the submediant (which he will again use as a dominant), but in such a way that it still sounds as if the tonality had not left the tonic D minor: in this way he lengthens the first group, strikingly and dramatically widens the significance of the tonic, and prepares his modulation—all with one stroke. It is typical of Beethoven that his largest works should be also the most economical.

If listeners measured their experiences by the clock, the development section of the C major Quintet would seem too short; but complexity and intensity are a more than adequate substitute for length. The development is one of Mozart's richest: the climax is a double canon in four voices with a free counterpoint in the fifth (second viola):

and almost the whole development is in minor, making the return to C major grand and luminous. (This minor coloring also entails the elimination in the return of the first group of the counter-statement in the tonic minor, which would be pleonastic here.) The coda, demanded by the dimensions of what precedes, is masterly: the closing theme, which in the exposition was a tonic pedal on G,[1] starts once again as a pedal on G, becoming thereby a dominant pedal instead of a tonic:

the beginning of a gigantic cadence of 47 measures, essentially the simplest of all cadences in its outline, although brilliantly enlivened in its detail:

The simplicity of the structure is a proof of the life of the style: when the 'sonata' became academic, it had to be expanded by the continuous injection of new material and sequential development, but Mozart is still able to heap on the form all the weight—in terms of both expression and mass—that he wishes it to bear.

The same spaciousness is found in the other movements of the quintet. Both the slow movement and the finale are sonata movements without development sections, with the expositions laid out on a grand scale: both begin leisurely with a succession of two clearly separate themes in the tonic. The slow movement is an operatic duet for the first violin and first viola: there is even a written-out but well-defined cadenza for them towards the end. The finale, though organized like the slow movement, has, appropriately, some characteristics of the rondo: the squarely articulated themes, the loose transitions, the sectional structure. The 'secondary development' of the sonata (between the first and second groups of the recapitulation) is expanded, and emphasizes the subdominant, as it traditionally does; but this is also exactly the place that the 'development' of the 'sonata rondo' occurs, and we often find there, too, a new theme in the subdominant. In this movement we can see, as it were, the sonata rondo latent in the sonata finale, and we can understand the reasons—not historical but aesthetic—for its existence. The necessary looseness of a finale and its less dramatic character allow for

---

[1] Quoted on page 268.

Mozart's great melodic abundance: in the 'second group' there are three complete new melodies, a fourth clearly derived from one of them, and a fifth developed from the opening theme, the last being perhaps the most striking, if not the most gracious of them:

The first violin plays the opening theme here in its original form, but the first viola has already inverted part of it with a shift of rhythm. With an exposition as rich and complex as this in a finale, it is easy to understand why Mozart chose to dispense with a principal development section, or a new theme after the return of the opening—thus avoiding both the full sonata and the full rondo form. The finale of the G minor Quintet K. 516 is cast in much the same mold, including two generous themes in the tonic at the beginning, but it takes two steps further towards the rondo: a new theme in the subdominant after the recapitulation of the first theme, and a fragmentary reappearance of both opening themes at the end as a coda.

The finale of the G minor Quintet raises the problem of the classical finale in all its complexity, real and imagined. It is a movement that has often disappointed. It is, indeed, almost always played with less understanding than the other movements but this only challenges us to explain why it inspires such heartless performances. The role of a finale in the late eighteenth century needs to be disentangled from a later age's conception of an effective ending. The G minor Quintet is one of the great tragic works, but it is not Mozart's fault if, for that very reason, many listeners today would openly or secretly prefer an ending with the frank pathos of Tchaikovsky's *Symphonie Pathétique*. Things change very little with Beethoven: the coda to the finale of the Quartet op. 95 has often seemed irrelevant, if not positively frivolous, and objections to the finale of the Ninth Symphony are common enough to cause no surprise, even when they come from those who should know better.

The problem of the finale is naturally one of weight, of sufficient seriousness and dignity to balance the opening movement, but there would be no problem at all if it were not for the classical conception of the finale as a resolution of the entire work. There was, after all, nothing except his sensibility to prevent Mozart from writing a last movement as complex and closely knit as a first movement, like the finale of Brahms's Third Symphony, for example. Beethoven was capable of a choral work as tightly organized as the *Gloria* from the Mass in D, and he must have felt that the looser shape of the choral finale to the Ninth Symphony was necessary in its place. A finale demanded a simpler and less complex form than an opening movement: that is why it is generally a rondo, or a set of variations (as in Mozart's G major Concerto, or the *Eroica* and Ninth Symphonies of Beethoven). If it is a 'sonata,' then it is necessarily a squarer and simpler version of that form; sometimes the structure is loosened as in Beethoven's Fifth Symphony by a change of tempo in the development (the return of the Scherzo), or a new theme at the same place in the subdominant as in Mozart's F major Sonata K. 332. But, in any case, the thematic material of a finale is always rhythmically squarer than that of a first movement,[1] the cadences heavily emphasized, the phrases well-defined, and the first theme completely rounded off before any harmonic movement can take place. (In the finale of Beethoven's Eighth Symphony, for example, the cadences are hammered brutally, and there is even a brief pause when the theme is over (at the tonic cadence in measure 28), while, on the other hand, the opening theme of the first movement, simple as it appears, moves directly into what follows.) If the finale was to be a slow movement, a complex form (as in Mahler's Ninth) was out of the question: in this case the only formal possibility was a set of variations[2] or a slow minuet.

The limit of dramatic complexity in a classical finale is reached with Mozart's G minor Symphony: despairing and impassioned, it is also rhythmically one of the simplest and squarest pieces that Mozart ever wrote. The main theme is absolutely regular, in two equal halves, each half rounded off with the same tonic cadence and each played twice. Except for an electrifying second at the opening of the development (even there integrated within two four-measure phrases, followed by a regular two-measure transition), the rhythm impels gloriously but does not surprise. All the harmonic daring is concentrated in the development section, while the exposition, although it has a few chromatic passages, has nothing to parallel the harmonic ambiguity

---

[1] The only exception to this squareness is the contrapuntal finale, as in many of the Haydn quartets, the Mozart G major Quartet K. 387, the *Jupiter* Symphony, and the equally famous essays of Beethoven. These form a special case, first because they are all to some extent revivals of an earlier style—the composers themselves felt these works an anachronism, or better, a modernizing of the past; second, because they are all to some extent displays of technique—they were to the eighteenth-century composer what the virtuoso finale is to the soloist. The emotional complexity is, therefore, always less than that of the other movements: even the Great Fugue of Beethoven is structurally looser and simpler than the opening of op. 130, in spite of its complex texture.

[2] The Adagio last movement of Haydn's Quartet op. 54 no. 2, a strange work in every way, while appearing to be a loose ternary form, is set of free variations.

of such a passage in the first movement's exposition as the one at measures 58–62. The phrasing, too, is absolutely straightforward: all the dove-tailing, all the syncopations and suspensions of the opening movement have disappeared. This is not to deny the dramatic tensions within this finale, but essentially it resolves, grounds, and settles. This is perhaps only a hidden tautology, a way of saying that a finale ends and completes, but the classical composer took the idea of finale literally, and had no inkling of the 'open' effects, the attempts to break down the feeling for a frame that were to come with the first Romantic generation.

A finale in major to a work in minor was naturally nothing more than a *tierce de Picardie* in larger terms; in eighteenth-century tonality a major chord still had less tension than a minor one, and gave a more satisfactory resolution. Haydn's abandonment of minor endings in his later work is not an outbreak of cheerfulness in middle age, but a development of the classical taste for resolution. In the late trios, where he can use the minuet form as a finale, he allows himself the deeply moving last movement in minor of the F sharp minor trio. The turn to major at the end was anything but a concession to the public: the second, Viennese version of *Don Giovanni* makes more concessions to outside pressure than the original production in Prague, and it is this version which deletes a great part of the original D major ending. On the rare occasions when Mozart chose to end in minor—that is, with some of the harmonic tension still echoing in the mind when the music is over—he always compensated for this by an added simplicity of phrasing and articulation, as in the E minor Sonata for Piano and Violin K. 304 and the A minor and C minor Sonatas for piano, K. 310 and K. 457, or by the sectional variation-form as in the D minor Quartet K. 421 and the C minor Piano Concerto K. 491. And none of these immediately follows music as complex and as anguished as the first three movements and the introduction to the finale of the G minor Quintet.

Not that the problem of weight in a finale was not a real one for Mozart, as we can see from the manuscript of the A major Sonata for Piano and Violin, K. 526. Like those of the C major and G minor Quintets, the last movement opens with two successive and distinct melodies in the tonic. Mozart could not at first decide whether to round off the second theme in the tonic before modulating, as in the G minor Quintet, or to use it as a springboard to the dominant before it seemed complete, as in the C major Quintet. The problem here was essentially how much looseness of form and squareness of periodic rhythm would be desirable. He eventually decided on the less sectional form, and then proceeded with a 'sonata rondo' in which the development section combines two resolving harmonic forces: a new theme in the relative minor, and a recapitulation that starts in the subdominant. The loose structure of the finale admitted as much variety of mood and technique as the more 'organically' conceived opening movement. (It must be admitted that these relaxed forms could sometimes produce finales that seem inadequate even when judged by classical standards, as in Beethoven's *Kreutzer* Sonata or the G major Sonata for Piano and Violin K. 379 of Mozart, where the variations, lovely as they are, substitute an ornamental stylishness and brilliance for the raging power that preceded them.)

It is evident from the G minor Quintet that the greatly increased dimensions of its companion C major Quintet are not an isolated and eccentric experiment in Mozart's development. The enlargement remains part of his conception of the genre. The increase of space demanded by the sonority entails an increase not so much in the span of time as in tonal mass. The first movement of the G minor Quintet, like that of the C major, concentrates on the tonic area far beyond the limits that Mozart allowed himself in any quartet. This makes possible an opening page of a chromatic bitterness and insistence that can still shock by the naked force of its anguish. It is an opening that was unique for the last quarter of the eighteenth century in presenting directly so deeply troubled an emotion, reaching a point of tension by the twentieth measure that all other works hold in reserve until much later.

Yet the mastery and the control are as serene as ever: a new theme is brought forward in the tonic, used as a bridge to the relative major, and then played again, profoundly intensified. Its two forms are:

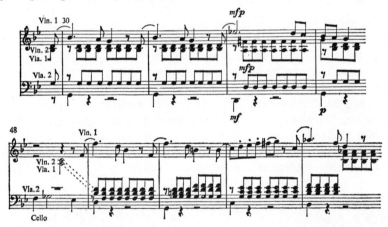

In this way, any feeling of anti-climax and of slackening after the storm of the opening is evaded by the later more complex and agitated form of this new theme, and, at the same time, the 'first group' is enlarged as in the C major Quintet so that the dimensions correspond to the intensity. The tragedy is allowed to expand freely, which is why this work, like the G minor Symphony, has an emotional force as objective as it is personal. (Later composers need procedures almost diametrically opposed: Chopin, Liszt, and Schumann constrict the expressive elements so that they can be cut off at the moment of their greatest intensity, a technique that Wagner attempted to diffuse through a longer time-span, and that Brahms tried to reconcile with classical form; this constriction is particularly evident in works of neo-Romantic composers like Mahler and Berg.) The essence of Mozart's 'classicism' is the equilibrium between the intensity of the expression and the tonal stability which fixes the dimensions of each work. That is why the larger implications of the sonority of five instruments allow him, as the quartet did not, both the massive, tranquil grandeur of the C major and the limitless anguish of the G minor quintets. There is a freedom to resolve dissonance in the widest sense, not only the immediate clashes, but the far-reaching tensions. The form is always a closed one, and we are left with the memory of a struggle resolved and not with its contradictions alone.

The other movements reach towards the same expressive limits. It is difficult to go further than the opening of the minuet without destroying the contemporary musical language:

the syncopated contrasts of texture and accent in measures 4 and 6 are surely extreme for the time. As the quintet proceeds, it moves as a complete whole within the framework—in terms of intensity and phrasing—of the sonata aesthetic, as if the entire work were conceived as one sonata movement. In spite of its violence, the minuet in second place, right after the first movement, has the decisive simplicity and concision of the closing theme of an exposition. The slow movement, like a development[1] rhythmically the most complex point of the entire quintet, breaks up its material more strikingly than any other movement. Already at measure 5, we find the kind of fragmentation characteristic of a development section:

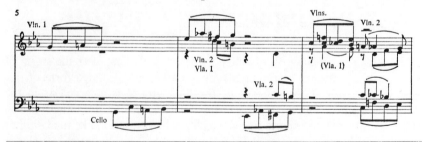

---

[1] It is interesting to note that in Mozart's works in a minor key, if the slow movement has a marked expressive complexity, it tends to be in the submediant major (i.e. Sonata for Piano in A minor K. 310, G minor Symphony, Concerto in D minor K. 466), while the simpler movements are in the less remote relative major (Concerto in C minor K. 491, D minor Quartet, K. 421, C minor Sonata K. 457).

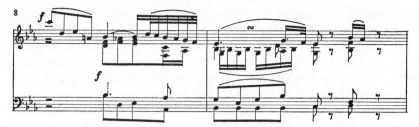

And the four-note motif developed here is used a few measures later in a remarkable disruption of the rhythm and phrase:

The motif, expanded, is already implied in measure 14 by the first violin, but in measures 16 and 17 it is simply inverted with an astonishing shift of accent. The phrase lengths, which change throughout (here they are a measure and a half long), indicate the continuous alteration of the pulse which moves from *alla breve* as in the first quotation to common time in the second, and becomes eight in the measure at a later point. The harmony is correspondingly intricate.

The finale acts as a recapitulation; its Adagio introduction gives it the weight to meet the rest of the quintet on equal terms, and divides the functions of recollection and resolution. The introduction even surpasses the other movements in its open use of direct expressive symbolism: the sobbing rhythm in the inner strings, the sighing appoggiaturas, the harsh expressive dissonances, the aria at once sustained without end and continuously broken, the *parlando* insistence on one note, the unceasing chromatic movement. Nothing closer to an ultimate despair has ever been imagined: recalling the first movement in tonality and in mood, it exceeds it in emotional turbulence. To have followed this movement with an Allegro of any dramatic complexity would have been an outrage: the final Allegro is a necessary reconciliation as well as a resolution. The device of breaking off the separate clauses of the main themes at their final appearance in the coda, soon to become so familiar in Beethoven and Schubert, and already used, generally with comic effect, by Haydn, has here an air of sadness and resignation. Like the last movement of the B flat Concerto K. 595, it cannot be played for brilliance without trivializing it. It makes its effect by the spaciousness and breadth of its structure, and by its alternation of passages of great simplicity with others contrapuntally richer and more openly expressive.

Placing the minuet second instead of third in the order of the movements throws the expressive weight of a quartet or quintet towards its latter half. It is an order that Haydn used frequently in his quartets until 1785, after which he almost entirely abandoned it[1] (except for op. 64 nos. 1 and 4, and op. 77 no. 2). Mozart used it in chamber music almost as often as the more usual order. When the slow movement in third place is followed, as in the G minor Quintet, by a long Adagio introduction to the finale, the shift of the center of gravity within the work is even more perceptible. Not that the place of the minuet was so clearly fixed: the divertimento often had two—one before and one after the slow movement. But it seems clear that both Mozart and Haydn, working towards a more unified concept of the whole work, were experimenting with the possibility of shifting the proportions and the order of the movements. With Mozart, the principal reason for placing the minuet in second place may have been the desire to separate an exceptionally complex slow movement from the traditionally dramatic opening movement. (He does this not only in the two Quintets, K. 515 and 516, but in three of the *Haydn* Quartets and in the *Hoffmeister*, all works with slow movements of unusually serious character or, as in the variations of the A major Quartet K. 464, of great length.) This gives a more equal balance to the first and second halves of the work. Beethoven, who generally followed the more traditional order, at the end of his life rediscovered or reinvented Mozart's proportions and put the scherzo before the slow movement in his two most massive works,[2] the *Hammerklavier* Sonata and the Ninth Symphony; in both, the scherzo is conceived partly as a parody of the first movement, but the order serves again as a more equal distribution of the expressive weight. The late works of Beethoven in many respects show a marked return to the ideals of Mozart and Haydn within a very different emotional context.

In 1788, the year after completing the two great quintets, Mozart wrote no chamber music for strings except the Divertimento K. 563 for string trio. An essay in contrapuntal and harmonic richness, with a surface ease of man-

---

[1] Considerably greater importance was given to the scherzo after that, however.

[2] In the quartets, Beethoven also chose this order for his first attempt in a new broad style: op. 59 no. 1. The A major Quartet op. 18 no. 5 is a movement-for-movement imitation of the Mozart A major Quartet, and this order prevails there, too, with the slow variation movement in third place. The slow variations of op. 135 are similarly placed after the scherzo. The order of the movements of the last quartets cannot be described in summary fashion, but the B flat Quartet op. 130 clearly belongs with the *Hammerklavier* and the Ninth Symphony in this respect.

ner that makes light of its ingenuity, this work is a distillation of Mozart's technique and experience. The mastery of the normative technique of writing for four instruments in the seven quartets of the years 1782 to 1786, and the immense expansion of scope in the two quintets of 1787 are now concentrated within the limits of the string trio. No other composer of the eighteenth and nineteenth centuries ever understood the demands of writing for three voices as Mozart did, except for Bach in his six trio-sonatas for double manual and pedal keyboard. As a string trio, this one of Mozart's stands alone, far above all other works in that form. It is also an interesting precursor of the last quartets of Beethoven, in its transference of the divertimento form, with two dance movements and two slow movements (one a set of variations), into the realm of serious chamber music, making purely intimate what had been public, and, as Beethoven was to do in so many of the short, interior movements of his late chamber works, transfiguring the 'popular' element without losing sight of its provenance. In Mozart's Divertimento the synthesis of a learned display of three-part writing and a popular genre is accomplished without ambiguity or constraint.

In 1789 he began the series of three quartets, which were to be his last; they were composed for the King of Prussia, who carried on the musical tradition of his family as an amateur cellist. The great increase of solo writing in these quartets is generally ascribed to Mozart's wish to please the king; balancing the solo passages for the cello with solos for the other instruments saved the integrity of the style. The assumption is that brilliance for its own sake was offensive to the classical mind. Nevertheless, every great composer has loved brilliance for itself, and a high value was put upon it by Mozart. It is a way of increasing emphasis without thickening mass, or a way of expanding the frame when the stylistic concentration is so intense (as it was with Mozart in the *Haydn* Quartets and the two great quintets that followed) that further development would have endangered the equilibrium of tension and resolution. Throughout Mozart's career, the oscillation between soloistic elements and ensemble technique is a rising spiral: the solo style stimulating a richer ensemble form, and then the new synthesis in chamber or symphonic style becoming still further expanded by virtuosity.

A few months after finishing the *Prussian* Quartets, Mozart wrote two more string quintets: his recent experiments with solo writing in chamber style are evident in the first and greater of the two. The brilliance of the individual instruments is more remarkable here than in the previous quintets, and each is often pitted against the other four; there are fewer duets and less antiphonal writing (except in the alternation of solo and ensemble). There are passages which demand an exceptionally bright sound of virtuosity: the trio of the minuet displays both the first and second violins (and the cello) as soloists in the most striking way. The famous correction of the main theme of the finale is not by Mozart at all, but probably the emendation of a fiddle-player who found the original and more characteristic chromatic form

281

too difficult to play. The recent discovery that the change in the manuscript is not in Mozart's hand is particularly gratifying as there are several passages —above all one starting twenty-five measures before the end—which are only odd in the 'corrected' version, but directly and intimately derived from the main theme in the original.

The opening movement essays a remarkable integration of introduction and Allegro in a way that looks forward to Haydn's *Drum-Roll* Symphony, and Beethoven's *Pathétique* Sonata and E flat Piano Trio op. 70 no. 2. The themes of both the Larghetto introduction and Allegro

outline a shape similar enough for the listener to sense their closeness at once. The Larghetto reappears as a coda, but not as part of a static frame; the Allegro comes back once more at the very end. Indeed, the opening eight measures of the Allegro are wittily tailored so that they are both a beginning and a final cadence: their return at the end is absolutely unaltered. The return of the Larghetto is also a resolution of its more dynamic first appearance: it is a true recapitulation in sonata style, not a variant of da capo form.

The conception of an opening slow section rewritten as a resolution at the end (i.e., with the original closing dominant cadence replaced by a tonic, all that precedes taking on a new form) is not an original idea. One finds it as far back as the Baroque overture, Bach's French Overture in B minor being only one example. But we are dealing here with two kinds of cadence on the dominant: the French Overture's opening slow section has the cadence of the regular dance form, and therefore of the sonata exposition—a movement to the dominant in a pattern which implies symmetrical resolution. The cadence of the opening Larghetto of the D major Quintet is *on* the dominant but without leaving the tonic: it is a true introduction, it accomplishes no action, it only presages, foreshadows, hints at what is to come. That is the reason the Larghetto turns immediately to the tonic minor, troubling the tonality with a darker color without weakening it (an introduction acts as an extended dominant chord within a tonic area—the latter sometimes, as in the C major Quartet K. 465 but not in the Quintet, defined only gradually and clarified little by little). To treat this as a more than local event, as a tension to be resolved not only by the following Allegro but much later at the end of the movement—as if it were part of the exposition—is original, even radical for its time. The concept of exposition is widened, and we are forced to hear the tensions in a larger temporal sense than we are accustomed to.

Even more radical is the relation between the coda and the Allegro: not the thematic similarity, a common enough device (a way of ensuring the unity of separate pieces at least as old as the late medieval *chanson* mass), but the interaction of texture and harmony. The end of the Allegro takes on more and more the minor coloring of the introduction, the texture so thinning out that the quiet sound of the cello alone, as at the opening of the work, seems too natural and inevitable to surprise.[1] In this way, the Allegro blends into the return of the introduction, and the contrast of tempi is not only rhythmic, but inheres in the harmonic development as well. The most masterly stroke of all is the return of the first phrase of the Allegro at the very end, not only bringing a witty symmetry, but retaining for the slow coda its still essential quality of introduction, and weaving the two tempi together in an even more intricate unity.

The D major Quintet exploits a scheme of descending thirds throughout. The harmonic pattern of the main theme of the first movement is:

---

[1] The very last measures of the recapitulation are the same as those at the end of the exposition, since the second part of the Allegro is also meant to be repeated, and the thin texture is common to them both, but the gradually increased minor coloring is largely new in the closing section of the recapitulation.

the descending thirds forming one of the simplest of all tonal progressions. This shape also inspires the large outline for the thirty-six-measure long principal theme of the finale. The pattern is not essentially melodic, however, but a way of constructing sequences, a motor impulse, in short. How it is used can be seen from the first violin part that follows the principal theme of the first movement. The harmonic sequence of the opening theme is used here to construct the modulation to A major:

In the minuet the descent in thirds takes over all aspects of the work, and everything is derived from it:

At the end of the minuet the capacity of such a progression to render the writing of a canon childishly simple is fully demonstrated. When a melody descends in regular thirds, a canon is almost automatic:

The minuet here only exposes and simplifies what was latent and complex in the other movements.

The most exceptional use of descending thirds is in the slow movement from the climax of the development through the return to the tonic:

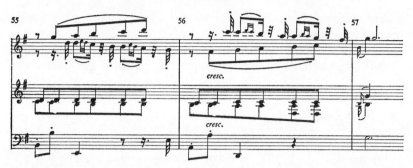

In the sequence at the opening of this passage, each new phrase takes up the descending thirds where the previous one left off, even where there is a half-cadential pause between. The climax is the sudden creation of a void: a cadence, built up powerfully and with the fierce energy that the cumulated descent can arouse, is, in measure 52, *not* played—not only postponed but permanently withheld. Instead of the cadence, all motion ceases, and with a sudden *piano* only the soft throbbing of the two violas is left. As the other instruments enter with a new sequence that leads directly back to the main theme, we find four completely different kinds of rhythm superimposed in a contrapuntal texture at once complex and deeply touching. The exchange of lines in measure 56 between first and second violins is a last refinement and prepares the entrance of the main theme after a *crescendo*. The sequence and the superimposition of rhythmic textures achieve a condition of stillness after the vigorous descent of thirds: everything is resolved quietly and inevitably, suspended motionless almost without breath after the arrest of impulse by the daring non-cadence.

The Quintet in E flat major K. 614 is a tribute to Haydn: it is Mozart's last work of chamber music. Along with the previous one in D major, it is said to have been written for Johann Tost: the imitation of Haydn may have been due at least partly to Tost's friendship with the elder composer, who had only recently written twelve quartets for him. Did Mozart's commission perhaps come through Haydn? The musical debt to Haydn, in any case, is as considerable in this work as in the first String Quintet K. 174. The finale of K. 614, written in 1791, is derived from the finale of one of the quartets that Haydn dedicated to Tost in 1790, op. 64 no. 6:

The slow movement is very close to the slow movement of Haydn's Symphony no. 85, *La Reine*, written in 1786; while the rustic drone bass trio of the minuet is surely influenced by the similarly conceived trio in Haydn's Symphony no. 88 of 1787. The imitation of technique is more relevant than melodic reference. The finale is Haydnesque throughout, even to the point of a comic inversion of the theme at the end. This work, which—in its outer movements—combines a detailed treatment in Haydn's fashion of the dynamic qualities of the tiniest motifs with a typically Mozartean sonorous and complex inner part-writing, makes a few musicians uncomfortable, perhaps because it lacks the expansive freedom of the other quintets, and seems to concentrate its richness. In the first movement, only the leisurely opening of the 'second group' has Mozart's typical generosity. The contrapuntal complexity of the finale, too, seems antagonistic to its asserted jollity. But these are only defects if we expect, not more, but something else than this splendidly conceived work is prepared to give. It is only fitting, after all, that, in his last chamber work, Mozart should once again appear to submit to Haydn's instruction. It was Haydn who created this chamber style, made it viable, and endowed it with the power to bear dramatic and expressive weight without flying apart. In the quintets Mozart expanded the range of the form beyond Haydn's range, and attained a massiveness that Beethoven himself never surpassed. The fundamental and imaginative vision, of chamber music as dramatic action, however, was Haydn's; and his conception and his innovations were a living presence in every work of this kind that Mozart wrote.

3

Comic Opera

On November 12, 1778, Mozart wrote to his father from Mannheim about a new kind of drama with music that was being produced there, and about the invitation extended to him by the producer to compose one: 'I have always wanted to write a drama of this kind. I cannot remember whether I told you anything about this type of drama the first time I was here? On that occasion I saw a piece of this sort performed twice and was absolutely delighted. Indeed, nothing has ever surprised me so much, for I had always imagined that such a piece would be quite ineffective. You know, of course, that there is no singing in it, only recitation, to which the music is like a sort of obbligato accompaniment to a recitative. Now and then words are spoken while the music goes on, and this produces the finest effect. . . . Do you know what I think? I think that most operative recitatives should be treated in this way—and only sung occasionally, when the words *can be perfectly expressed by the music*.'[1] The letter ought not, perhaps, to be taken at face value: Mozart's attempt to conquer the musical world of Paris had failed miserably, and he now faced what he most hated and dreaded, a return to Salzburg and the Archbishop's service once again. How much of his enthusiasm is genuine, and how much only an effort at persuading his father, who was waiting impatiently in Salzburg, that it was practical to put off the return for the moment, and that there were other prospects in view? Nevertheless, Mozart's attitude, his experimental approach, is revealing. He is delighted with the possibilities of what is called 'melodrama' (spoken dialogue accompanied by music), and his feeling for theatrical effect is by no means centered upon vocal music. On the contrary, he assumes a clear distinction between music that is an equivalent for dramatic action and music that is the perfect expression of the words.[2] It is the first concept that has priority, and he is willing to abandon sung words for spoken ones when the action can be made more telling this way.

Zaïde has some splendid effects of melodrama which look forward to the second act of *Fidelio*, but we have lost everything else that Mozart wrote in

---

[1] Mozart's own emphasis, cited from the *Letters of Mozart and his family*, ed. Emily Anderson, London, 1966.
[2] In a letter of November 8, 1780, he objected to the idea of an aside in an aria: 'In a dialogue all these things are quite natural, for a few words can be spoken aside hurriedly; but in an aria where the words have to be repeated, it has a bad effect, *and even if this were not the case I should prefer an uninterrupted aria*' [my emphasis, C. R.], *ibid.*, p. 659.

this form that so interested him for a moment, unless one counts the interruptions of Pedrillo's serenade and Osmin's song by spoken dialogue in *Die Entführung*, or the moment in *Die Zauberflöte* when Papageno counts three before preparing to commit suicide. Yet Mozart never lost his desire to experiment or his sense that, in opera, music as dramatic action takes precedence over music as expression. This is not to deny Mozart's skill at writing for the voice, or his love for elaborate vocal coloratura. Nevertheless he was not always tender with the vanity of singers who wished to show off the beauty of their voices. Particularly in ensembles, like the great quartet in *Idomeneo*, he insisted that the words should be more spoken than sung.[1] Mozart's brief interest in 'melodrama' while in Mannheim is the enthusiasm of a young composer who has just discovered that music on the stage can do more than meet the requirements of singers or express sentiment, but can become one with plot and intrigue as well. This was an idea that he had only half understood when writing the beautiful and little-known *La Finta Giardiniera*.

The style of the early eighteenth century had been equal to any demands that words alone could make. The operatic music of Handel and Rameau could transfigure the sentiment and the situation at each moment, but it left untouched the action and the movement—anything that was not static, in short. To say that the sonata style provided an ideal framework for the rendering of what was most dynamic on the stage is to oversimplify only insofar as it does not take account of the important role that opera itself played in the development of the sonata style. *Opera buffa*, in particular, was influential, and the classical style moves with the least strain in its depiction of comic intrigue and comic gesture.

The three points that made the new style so apt for dramatic action were: first, the articulation of phrase and form which give a work the character of a series of distinct events; second, the greater polarization of tonic and dominant, which allowed for a much clearer rise in tension in the center of each work (as well as more specifically characterizing the significance of related harmonies, which could then also serve a dramatic meaning); and third, by no means the least important, the use of rhythmic transition, which permitted the texture to change with the action on the stage without endangering the purely musical unity in any way. All these stylistic characteristics belong to the 'anonymous' style of the period; they were the common currency of music by 1775. There is no question, however, that Mozart was the first composer to comprehend, in any systematic way, their implications for opera. In one sense, Gluck was a more original composer than Mozart, his style was much more personally forged by a stubborn act of will rather than by an acceptance of the traditions of his age. But this very originality barred the way to that ease and facility with which Mozart mastered the relation of music to drama.

[1] Letter of December 27, 1780, *ibid.*, p. 699.

The adaptability of the sonata style to opera can be seen in its least complex and most perfect form in Mozart's own favorite among the individual numbers of *Figaro*, the great sextet of recognition in the third act, which is in slow-movement sonata form (i.e., without a development section, but with a recapitulation starting in the tonic—although the 'second group' of the exposition is sufficiently heightened and intensified here as to provide some of the effect of a development). The sextet begins with Marcellina's expression of joy at finding that Figaro is her long-lost son (*a*):

The tonic section has three main themes, of which this is the first. The second (*b*) appears after Doctor Bartolo has sung a variant of (*a*); Don Curzio and the Count express their irritation:

the third (*c*), an ecstatic one based on a diminished fifth, is divided between Marcellina, Figaro, and Doctor Bartolo:

The painful dissonance outlined by this melody gives it its passionate character. The section ends on a semi-conclusive dominant cadence as Susanna enters with the money, no longer necessary, to buy Figaro out of his contract of marriage with Marcellina:

This is the beginning of what is respectably called the 'bridge passage' in a sonata exposition, and the added tension that comes with the change to the dominant is admirably calculated to parallel Susanna's ignorance of what has been happening and her inevitable misunderstanding. As at the beginning of the second group of most of Haydn's sonatas and many of Mozart's, part of the first group reappears:

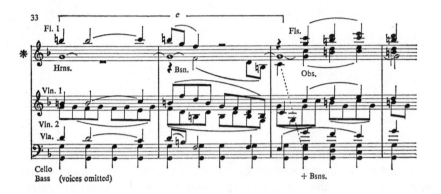

It is (*c*) that is repeated, as Marcellina, Figaro, and Bartolo are still lost in their discovery. A dissonant sonority appears with a turn to the dominant minor and Susanna's rage at seeing Figaro kissing Marcellina (*d*):

While Figaro tries to appease her, a new caressing motif appears in the violins:

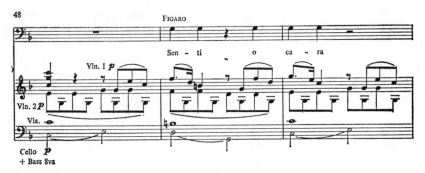

but it is derived from the violin part in (*a*), and has the same sensuous swell as (*c*). The exposition continues with a motif (*e*) derived from it and combining with it—which expresses Susanna's indignation:

and closes with a firm cadence on the dominant, as every exposition did then.

Only the recapitulation of a sonata requires any ingenuity in being adapted to the stage; an exposition is, as it stands, a model for an intrigue that becomes more complex and more tense with the introduction of new elements and new events. For a recapitulation, on the other hand, the classical composer had to find the elements of symmetry and resolution in the situation and in the very words of the libretto. It need hardly be emphasized that this is not a playful or pedantic adaptation of a fixed form to a dramatic genre; the symmetry and resolution of the sonata were permanent needs of the classical composer, not dispensable elements of form.

The resolution in the sextet begins when the situation is carefully explained to the furious Susanna; accordingly the tonic returns, and the recapitulation begins with (*a*) once more:

The words, of course, will no longer fit the opening melody, so it is the winds of the orchestra that play the melody (*a*) here, and Marcellina who decorates it.

Susanna is bewildered, and her confusion is expressed by a variant of (*b*), used in the exposition for the consternation of the Count and Don Curzio, quoted above:

Finally, there is a concluding section in which all express their joy, except, of course, the Count and Don Curzio:

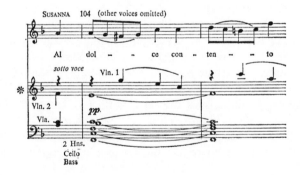

which recalls, above all, the deeply expressive character of (*c*). There is even a move towards F minor (mm. 110–117) which parallels the C minor of (*d*). We are given a fine example of the priorities of classical form: the harmonic structure and the proportions outweigh the letter of the melodic pattern here, just as they do in so many of Haydn's and Mozart's abstract works.

In fact, no description of sonata form can be given that will fit the Haydn quartets but not the majority of forms in a Mozart opera. This coincidence between abstract and dramatic pattern is significant in many ways, particularly in the insight it provides into the nature of late eighteenth-century form. There are no fixed 'rules,' although there are successful patterns imitated and even aped, and unconscious habits. The abstract forms, no more than the theatrical ones, do not make their effects by breaking 'rules,' as is so often thought: the element of surprise in the string quartets and the operas does not depend upon a deviation from some imagined musical norm outside the individual work. It is the work itself (once its language is understood) that provides its own expectations, disappoints and finally fulfils them: the tensions are implied more by the music and very little by the specific experience and prejudices of the listener, although he must have an educated ear to know what to listen for, educated in the stylistic language and not just in its superficial formalities. One must accept the essentially innovatory nature of the style, like that of any language, its built-in possibility of creating original combinations. In other words, such rules as the classical style genuinely developed—the need for resolution, the sense of proportion and of a closed and framed pattern—are never broken at all. They are its means of communication, and it could say astonishing things without violating its own grammar. As for the conventional patterns that so many composers used unthinkingly, they were not rules of grammar but clichés: they were turned into rules when the musical language changed, and the pressures and the forces that had produced the classical style (along with its idioms and formulas) were exhausted and died.

When the dramatic situation will not lend itself easily to a symmetrical resolution and recapitulation, the sonata aesthetic still remains valid in Mozart's operas. Its use is only superficially more complex: there is the same need for resolution, the same sense of proportion. The second act sextet of *Don Giovanni* has a form as clear but far less openly symmetrical than the sextet of *Figaro*, yet it satisfies the same aesthetic demands. The dramatic complexity—the gradual introduction of new characters, the surprising changes of situation—requires an immense expansion of the 'development section,' and much new material: the resolution is equally immense and emphatic. The opening in E flat major, a small sonata exposition, is short and succinct: like the exposition of Haydn's *Oxford* Symphony, it gives no hint of the enormous consequences that await. At the beginning, Donna Elvira and Leporello (whom she believes to be Don Giovanni) are lost in the dark. Donna Elvira is frightened at being abandoned and her shudder of fear is rendered by the orchestra with a motif (*a*) which will appear later:

The music moves to the dominant as Leporello gropes for the door; as he finds it, he sings the typically regular closing theme and cadence of a sonata exposition. Then there is a most extraordinary moment, as Donna Anna and Don Ottavio appear dressed in mourning. The oboes hold their final notes of the dominant cadence, then with a soft drum-roll the music luminously moves to the remote key of D, and as Don Ottavio begins to sing, the transitional phrase is wonderfully repeated as a counterpoint. The overlapping enforces both continuity and articulation:

The tonal relations here entail an important paradox. D is a remote key in a work in E flat, but it is the basic key of the whole opera. The significance of this moment of modulation is therefore an ambiguous one, and it is· no wonder that every listener senses its mysterious quality. The trumpets and drums, appearing in the sextet for the first time here, set the moment into sharp relief. The connection with the opening of the opera and the conviction that we have reached the central key are made strikingly evident in two ways. First Don Ottavio even recalls the main theme of the overture in the measures that follow:

This is by no means a thematic allusion: it only comes because the conception of the key of D is so emphatically a unity throughout the opera and calls up the same associations. Then, when Donna Anna replies to Don Ottavio, the music shifts to the D minor mode of the opening of the overture and the Commendatore's murder. The change is once again marked by mysterious soft drum-rolls:

Until this point of the opera, whenever Donna Anna appeared, it was always with the fundamental key of D, except in the large ensemble numbers. Her first duet with Don Ottavio after the death of her father is in D, and the opening recalls her phrase in the sextet:

Fug - - gi, cru-de - le, fug- gi

Her great aria 'Or sai chi l'onore' is also in D.[1] Moreover, when Donna Anna and her masked companions, Don Ottavio and Donna Elvira, appear for the first time in the finale of Act I, they bring the key of D minor with them:

The opening motif (given to Donna Elvira) is again close to the one in the sextet. These are not thematic references, but the result of a total conception of the opera in which everything is related to a central tonality, which itself has, not only a symbolic reference, but an individual sonority that it seems to evoke. The fact alone of having one singer so closely associated with the tonality lends it an immediately recognizable sound. Whatever key the individual section may be in, the appearance of D minor unequivocally calls up the death of the Commendatore.[2]

One does not, therefore, need perfect pitch to hear a reference to the tonic of the entire opera at this point in the sextet. Nevertheless, even in a non-operatic work an eighteenth-century composer's sensitivity to such long-range relations may have been greater than some critics, Tovey in particular, have been willing to admit. No composer, of course, has ever made his crucial effects depend on such perception: even if he expects his most subtle points to be appreciated only by connoisseurs, he does not write the entire work calculatedly above the head of the average listener. But there is at least one person who is sure to recognize the reappearance of a tonic even without thematic reference: the performer. It is for this reason that subtle effects based on tonal relations are much more likely to occur in a string quartet or a sonata, written as much for the performers as for the listeners, than in an opera or a symphony, more coarsely if more elaborately designed. The

---

[1] Her later aria, 'Non mi dir,' is in the relative major of D minor, F major, and it is preceded by an accompanied recitative largely dominated by D minor.
[2] Even the ghostly voice of the statue in the cemetery starts his first phrase with a D minor chord, while his final appearance in the last act is the signal, not only for the most emphatic return to D minor, but for an explicit recapitulation of much of the overture.

last sonatas of Haydn play with distant tonal relations, for example, in a way that he never attempts in the *London* Symphonies. Mozart, however, as we have seen, has dramatic ways of making these relations clearly felt in the operas.

The entrance of Don Ottavio and Donna Anna in the E flat major sextet, and the strange modulation that heralds it, make D into a second dominant in some ways more powerful than B flat major. (The search for a substitute dominant became very important later with Beethoven, but only once, at the end of his life, with the Sonata op. 110, did he attempt anything as harmonically daring as the key of the leading-tone. Mozart's success, however, depends as much on dramatic considerations that receive their harmonic justification outside the sextet as on the inner logic.) The D major and minor, in spite of the breadth with which they are established and drawn out, are therefore unstable and lead to a modulation to C minor, which by its immediate relation to E flat major reduces the highly charged atmosphere, but still moves as within a 'development section.' An important new theme for Donna Elvira (*b*) is introduced, built of sobs:

and Leporello, trying to leave, repeats his concluding theme and is stopped by the entrance of Zerlina and Masetto.

The discovery of Leporello brings back the little motif (*a*) that previously represented Donna Elvira's terror:

300

and then a long development of the sobbing phrase (*b*) begins, as Donna Elvira begs mercy for the man she believes to be Don Giovanni, and the music stays for many measures in G minor, which serves both to resolve the D major partially and to bring us closer to the tonic E flat major. Leporello, almost weeping, begins his plea, followed and seconded by a whining chromatic scale from all the winds: there is a marvelously witty passage at measures 108–109, where his phrase grows more impassioned and desperate, and the winds cannot wait to let him finish and impose their phrase contrapuntally over his. The development ends on a chord of G major, made doubly unstable by the sequences that have just preceded it. The signal for these sequences is the discovery that the terrified captive is Leporello, not Don Giovanni; they begin with a surprise cadence, and could be called a 'bridge' to the recapitulation, except that they do not lead directly to E flat major, but only serve to weaken the firm G minor of Leporello's plaint and to make it evident that the dissonant tonality is about to be resolved.

At this point, dramatic exigency has required that an 'exposition' of twenty-seven measures be succeeded by a 'development' of 113 measures: the resolution that will follow is properly grandiose. Everything that happens in the final section (mm. 131–277) is nothing more than a series of (V-I) tonic cadences on E flat, dramatized, decorated, expanded, and fantastically enlivened. The fundamental harmony does not really move: no matter how remote the chords or how complicated the harmony, there is no true modulation. The rhythmic motion, precipitate and furious, is all on the surface. This whole section, marked 'Molto allegro,' sticks even closer to the tonic than any abstract sonata recapitulation would dare to do; there is an E flat major triad in almost half the measures. The Molto allegro resolves as a recapitulation does, and its relative proportions are those of a sonata, given the greatly enlarged 'development' that preceded: the 140-odd measures of the Molto allegro go about twice as fast as the rest of the sextet, so that its length is equivalent to seventy of the preceding measures and its heavy concentration on the tonic make an adequate classical balance and resolution for all the harmonic tensions of the sextet. The climactic points of the sextet are, too, at the same places and have the same character as in a sonata: the startling change at the opening of the development when Donna Anna and Don Ottavio enter, and the long drawn-out tension at the end of it when Leporello reveals who he is. The last section Molto allegro may be said to follow the sonata aesthetic almost in spite of the words, as 'Mille torbidi pensieri' hardly implies so rigid an attachment to the tonic.

The sextet should not be considered as an abstract musical form; it is responsive to other than purely musical pressures. Nevertheless, the proportions and ideals that help to shape it are the same as those which created the sonata form. Mozart explicitly said that the words must be the servant of the music, but he also emphasized the parity of the dramatic and musical conceptions. In his operas, the intrigue and the musical forms are indissoluble. The capacity of the sonata style to fuse with a dramatic conception as no other previous style had done was Mozart's historical opportunity. Without this complementary relation between musical style and dramatic conception, the greatest music cannot make an opera viable; with it, the most foolish libretto can barely undo one.

This sextet is conceived fundamentally as an *opera buffa* 'finale,' and for the development of this form Mozart owed little to his predecessors: he may be considered as at once the creator and the only master of it. Formally defined, the finale consists of all the music between the last *secco* recitative and the end of the act, and it may have as many as ten numbers or as little as one. Mozart appears to have been the first composer to conceive of the more complex finale as a tonal unity. It cannot have been a theoretical principle of the age; the finales of his earlier operas (*La Finta Giardiniera*, for example) begin and end in different keys. From *Die Entführung* on, however, the finale of every act of every opera ends in the key it started with, and the tonal relationships within them (and they are often very complex) are so conceived as to produce a harmonic equilibrium in terms of sonata style. Contemporaries of Mozart are either so inconsistent that we may consider the occasional finale that appears to be shaped around a tonic as an accident, or else (like those by Piccinni) they venture so little from their original key that the tonal relationships are unified only by remaining unvaried.

For the more complex finales, Mozart needed a libretto that provided him with a series of events so arranged that the music could both clarify and dramatize the order. He was prepared to insist upon transferring the beginning of one act to the end of the previous one if it would give him the situation and the order he wanted, even if it also entailed a less reasonably distributed action and forced the librettist to invent unnecessary complications to fill the gap. The supreme example of a librettist's achievement in constructing a finale is generally considered the reworking of Beaumarchais by da Ponte in the second act of *Figaro*, where the successive addition of new characters constantly enriches the sonority, and the growing complication of the plot is the ideal foil to the increased brilliance and animation of the music: it is a finale worked out with the musical style in mind.

Unity in late eighteenth-century music is imposed chiefly by framing devices, and the more strongly the outer frame is defined as part of the work, the greater will be the tendency to set off individual sections within a larger whole by analogous framing. The opening scene of *Don Giovanni* starts in F major with Leporello alone on the stage, and the music ends before the first *secco* recitative (after the death of the Commendatore) in F minor. This long scene, however, is contained within a larger grouping, a fact emphasized by a slight dissolution or blurring of the inner frame at both ends: the orchestra modulates from the overture directly into Leporello's F major, and there is no full close at the end of the F minor, but rather a terrifyingly effective shading into the whispered recitative. The larger grouping is framed by the overture and the scene between Donna Anna and Don Ottavio, both of them in D, a tonality emphasized by its return in the central section of the group for the duel. This handling of the half-frame within a frame serves to establish D as the fundamental tonality of the opera, a function rigorously demonstrated when the next scene also ends in D major with Leporello's brilliant and comic catalogue aria, so that the D minor of the larger group (as well as of the smaller one of the overture alone) has a traditional D major resolution.[1]

The Mozart finale is made up of separate numbers, but many of them run directly one into another, and they are intended to be heard as a unit. Those large groupings represent the closest that Mozart came to the conception of large-scale continuity. The separate large divisions correspond to the inner articulation of the classical phrase; Beethoven, who tried (in the *Missa Solemnis*, in particular) for continuity on a greater scale than Mozart ever attempted, still relies on this kind of sectional form as the basis for a longer one (and there are even clear traces of it in Wagner). The importance of the Mozart finale within the operas as a whole cannot be placed too high: they gather together the disparate threads of both the drama and the musical form and give them a continuity that the opera had never before known. The arias, beautiful as they are, serve in part only as a preparation for the finale of the act, which is the set piece of the occasion.

It is not surprising that the development of the finale as a unified conception had, as one effect, the reduction of the musical importance of the *secco* recitative. Not that there is any less of it quantitatively in the later operas, but they are both less daring and less expressive. There is little *secco* recitative in Mozart after *La Finta Giardiniera* that can parallel the chromaticism of this passage from that early work:

---

[1] I have remarked above (pp. 94–5) on the similar framing of part of a larger whole in the finale to Act I of *Don Giovanni*.

Starting with *Idomeneo*, the *secco* recitatives are more workaday in their harmonic conception, although there are several interesting dramatic interruptions, particularly in *Figaro*. The *secco* recitatives now provide a truly dry contrast to the more expressively conceived large structures.

The sense of form in the finales is very similar to that in the symphonies and chamber music; the dramatic exigencies of eighteenth-century comedy and musical style have no difficulty walking in step. In the penultimate number of the second act finale of *Figaro*, the Countess reveals herself with the most gracious of transitions back to the tonic major: a sudden turn to the tonic minor represents the Count's shamed surprise as a secondary development section, and he turns back to the tonic major to ask forgiveness in a long resolving passage. The recapitulation of a string quartet has a dramatic shape that is not very different, and it would be a misunderstanding of Mozart's chamber music style to miss this point. Within the larger context of the whole finale, this penultimate number as a whole has a significance as ordered and as direct: it is in the subdominant (G major) of the basic D major tonality of the whole opera, and serves, as within an even larger recapitulation, to reinforce the final symmetry and resolution.

A finale is an opera in miniature: the same tonal unity that reigns there may be found—more loosely understood as is appropriate to its greater length—within the opera as a whole. Once again Mozart appears to stand alone among his contemporaries in his insistence on this integrity. It is also a mature development: only after the age of twenty did Mozart invariably finish an opera in the key of the overture. Was this theory or developing instinct? This is not a question that can be fruitfully pursued, but in any case it would be absurd to consider Mozart's working habits as a form of somnambulism.

Where instinct surely played a role is in the constitution of classical proportions within the harmonic structure of the opera as a whole. The most highly organized and the most brilliant of the finales is never the last (or second of the two large ones) but the first: it is, like a development section, the extreme point of tension within the work. It is also placed harmonically as far away from the tonic of the whole opera as Mozart could go. The first finale of *Figaro* (actually in the second act of four) is in E flat major against the entire opera's tonic of D, and the other works follow the same pattern: D to C major for *Così fan tutte*, C to E flat major for *Die Zauberflöte*, C major to D minor/major for *Don Giovanni*. These central finales are indeed the heart of each work, and they are worked out with an elaboration and a complexity that Mozart reaches nowhere else. To many people, this has made the second finales of the operas, particularly those of *Figaro* and *Così*, disappointing.

The classical sense of an ending is the element of the style most antipathetic to modern taste, yet it is as essential to the style as the more organized textures of the opening and central sections of a work. In every one of the opera finales, without exception, the last number does not modulate, but remains firmly fixed on the tonic. It serves as a cadence to the finale as a whole, an expanded dominant-tonic (V–I), just as the last finale serves as a cadence to the entire opera. The last number of a finale is a harmonic resolution of all the preceding dissonance like the recapitulation of a sonata.

The looseness and even squareness, inseparable from the classical rondo-form so often used for the last movement of a sonata or symphony, is rendered in a striking way by the second act finale of *Don Giovanni*, which begins with an orchestra on the stage playing a medley of popular operatic tunes of the day. There is here a determined attempt to break down the dramatic concentration of the opera, and even to weaken the continuity. A similar looseness is evident in the fourth and last act of *Figaro* when it is performed uncut, with the arias of Basilio and Marcellina included. Even if these numbers were only provided because the singers had a right to at least one aria apiece, it is evident that both composer and librettist felt that the disruption of dramatic continuity would be most suitable in the last act. The finale of the second and last act of *Così fan tutte* has a modulatory structure that is bewilderingly rapid and sectional with none of the intensity and concentration of the first one; the inspiration and the mastery are, however, fully as consistent.

305

The solidity and clarity of the classical ending, above all the harmonic resolution of all the long-range dissonance, gave a new form to the operatic aria. With the finales and the sextet from *Don Giovanni* in mind as a model, we can understand the role of the final short allegros of arias like 'Non mi dir' and 'Battì, battì, bel Masetto.' An aria in moderate tempo with a faster concluding section is often found in operas of the last quarter of the eighteenth century, and the final section is not a coda or an independent movement, like the second part of Bellini's 'Casta diva,' but a harmonic resolution of the previous tensions. The slower first part of almost all these arias is outwardly an *ABA* form which has nothing to do with the da capo aria, or with normal ternary form: the *B* goes always to the dominant, and has the character of a 'second group' in a sonata (followed sometimes by a development). The faster concluding section that follows the return of the opening theme substitutes harmonically for the recapitulation of *B*, or the 'second group': like the end of the sextet in *Don Giovanni*, this section never leaves the tonic, except for a glance at the subdominant, even in such long examples as the final Allegro moderato of ' Per pietà, ben mio' from *Così fan tutte*.[1] The Countess's aria 'Dove sono' in *Figaro* acknowledges this incomplete form of the first slow section by breaking off the return of the opening melody in the middle of a phrase: the Allegro that follows both resolves the phrase and the whole piece. This form of aria (Andante (tonic—dominant—tonic)—Allegro (tonic)) conforms to the harmonic ideal of the sonata by moving first towards the dominant, and by devoting at least the entire last quarter of its length to a firm tonic resolution; the harmonic climax is placed at the center, and the resolution is sustained by virtuosity as in the concerto.[2]

With the growth of his experience as a composer of operas, however, Mozart's conception of the aria became more imaginative. The sonata patterns of most of the arias in the earlier operas—*La Finta Giardiniera, Zaïde, Idomeneo*—are relatively simple and straightforward, the melodic symmetries clearly and literally marked. Many of them could be used as ideal textbook examples for the most rigid and most narrow definitions of sonata allegro. Even those arias with the most surprising innovations are relatively direct. Several times in *Idomeneo*, Mozart attempted a fusion of sonata and da capo forms (nos. 19, 27, and 31). The arias begin with a regular tonic-dominant sonata exposition, and they all have recapitulations which resolve

---

[1] Like his feeling for the tonal unity of an opera, this feeling for tonal proportion is a later development of Mozart's style, starting in this case with the *Entführung*. It is not true, for example, of the E major trio 'O selige Wonne' in *Zaïde*, which follows an unresolved sonata exposition with a complete sonata form.

[2] The duet 'Là, ci darem la mano' from *Don Giovanni* begins with a clear slow-movement sonata form (without a development section) with a full recapitulation; the faster section (in 6/8) that follows is an extended cadence, and it never leaves the tonic. It may be called a genuine coda, as its emphasis on the tonic has none of the urgency of the final section of the arias previously cited. With no formal need for resolution, the luxury of such an indulgence in the most consonant of harmonies, developed with the lilting dance rhythm of a siciliana, is a reflection of Zerlina's delighted surrender.

the 'second group' in the tonic (no. 27, 'Nò, la morte,' even shows the older dominant-tonic form of recapitulation). The middle section is in a different and contrasting tempo, which sometimes begins with the relaxed air of the trio of a minuet and then begins to show the more dramatic character of a 'development' section leading directly back to the opening. These examples are experiments in Mozart's career, and ideally none of them should be considered apart from their dramatic function, the words, and their place in the opera as a whole. One example of an unusual formal device must suffice for all, Electra's 'Tutto nel cor' (*Idomeneo*, no. 4), where a D minor exposition has a recapitulation that begins for 12 measures in C minor, the key of the flat leading tone—as far removed from resolution as one could imagine. It is, of course, a departure that Mozart justifies dramatically and formally, as a perfect equivalent for the violence and rage of Electra's character; the same harmonic instability is revealed in her other arias. But it is equally noteworthy that this D minor aria is followed without interruption by a stormy chorus in C minor, describing the shipwreck: the abnormal opening in C minor of the recapitulation of the aria prepares this without lessening its dramatic effect. This recapitulation, in turn, is itself prepared by the exposition, which goes from D minor to F minor as much as to F major. The C minor seems natural when it appears as it arises from the F minor; only the realization that it is the true beginning of a complete recapitulation, and not a development, is a surprise. The return of the *tonic* paradoxically provides the real shock, an effect typically concise and powerful.

To some readers these considerations may appear unnecessarily finicky: still others may find such large-scale tonal significances simplistic. Yet there is no question that Mozart himself thought in exactly such terms, as is shown by the often-quoted letter to his father about *Die Entführung*, where he explains the choice of A minor to finish an aria of Osmin that begins in F major. There is, one must add, an element of self-justification in the letter: he is explaining one of his more surprising harmonic effects—indeed, almost explaining it away: 'as music, even in the most terrible situations, must never offend the ear, but must please the listener, or in other words must never cease to be *music*, so I have not chosen a key remote from F (in which the aria is written) but one related to it—not the nearest, D minor, but the more remote A minor.' This is, no doubt, the expression of a deeply classical taste, one which had repudiated the mannerism of the previous generation; but it is also an attempt to reassure a father always afraid his son will write clever, *avant-garde* music unintelligible to the general public, and not make any money—which is, of course, more or less what happened. The change of key in the aria of Osmin in question (no. 3 of the *Entführung*)[1] does not in any way invalidate Mozart's insistence on unity of key, as the different sections

---

[1] It is a relationship that symmetrically reappears (once again to illustrate Osmin's rage) in the *vaudeville* at the end of the opera, but is there resolved within a larger frame.

are clearly, if briefly, separated by spoken dialogue; a naïve device, perhaps, but the tonal patterns of the *Entführung* are not yet as sophisticated as those of the later operas. The whole of the letter to his father, however, makes it clear that a definite symbolic meaning was to be attached to a change of key.

The arias in the later operas are much more subtle and infinitely more varied. The more common symmetries of sonata form, as manifold as they were, are no longer used so directly and simply, although they remain the guiding principles: the harmonic and rhythmic energies of the sonata style are combined with the dramatic situation in ever more imaginative ways. Susanna's 'Deh vieni, non tardar' seems, at first hearing, to be pure song, untrammeled by any strict conception of form. It is, however, in what I have called sonata-minuet form, in which a more animated combined 'second-group'-and-'development' starts in the dominant after the first double-bar. In 'Deh vieni' the recapitulation is a half-disguised variation of the opening:

The final form interchanges and expands both halves of the opening, and in this way the first measure of the melody is turned into the lyrical expansion of a cadence. There are many sketches for this exquisite and subtle aria, and its perfection was not easily arrived at.

Figaro's cavatina 'Se vuol ballare' is an even more remarkable example of a freedom supported by a strict sense of proportion and balance. It begins as a monothematic sonata, the opening melody reappearing at the dominant, and a modulation to D minor acting as a clear development section. The Presto that follows is a variation of the opening theme; it stays entirely in the tonic and functions as a resolution and recapitulation, but it admirably represents Figaro's menacing sense of triumph as he contemplates the future ruin of the Count's plans. The opening must be compared with the Presto, to see how powerful the transformation is in its change of rhythm and speed, and yet how the original outline remains unaltered:

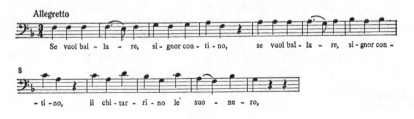

The wittiest stroke is to have the basic melodic elements move twice as fast in a phrase which sums up the whole aria at top speed:

The original tempo is brought back at the end before a very short final burst of Presto to make the relation more telling and the balance more dramatic. Mozart's recapitulations in all the operas after the *Entführung* became less and less literal, but his sense of harmonic proportion and symmetry never wavered.

The economy of a Mozart aria is exactly that of a Haydn quartet. The little phrase 'signor contino'

becomes a triumphant assertion of victory with 'le suonerò sì,'

merely by transposing the final note up an octave, and the motif that makes this change possible runs through all the transformations of the melodic outline in the cavatina. This kind of dynamically conceived motivic development derives, as a technique, from Haydn, but its dramatic propriety is incontestable. The changing forms of a motif not only give a logical coherence to the music, but allow it to express not a fixed sentiment, but an emotion that changes before our eyes from menace to triumph. Here, as elsewhere, the classical style achieves unity and continuity with the use of discrete, separable elements.

The coincidence of musical and dramatic events is the glory of Mozart's operatic style. In an essay defending the complexity of Mozart's operatic music, E. T. A. Hoffmann describes a moment from *Don Giovanni*:

> When in *Don Giovanni* the statue of the Commendatore sounds his terrible 'Si' on the tonic E, but the composer now takes this E as the third

of C and thus modulates to C major, which tonality is seized upon by Leporello, no layman in musical matters will be able to understand the technical structure of this transition, but in the depths of his being he will tremble with Leporello; similarly the musician who has attained the highest level of culture will, in the moment of this most profound emotion, give as little thought to this structure, because the construction has long since occurred to him and so he has come round again to the layman's position.

The descent admired by Hoffmann is only one of a series in this E major duet, and forms part of a 'sonata' symmetry. There are four such descents, two from the dominant (B major) to a G♮, and then two—as a recapitulation —from the tonic to C♮. The first occurs when Don Giovanni threatens to kill Leporello if he refuses to approach the statue:

the second when the statue terrifyingly nods its head:

obviously recalling the first. The two descents from the tonic to C♮ are more elaborate,[1] first when Don Giovanni steps forward to command the statue to speak:

---

[1] The descent to C♮ in measure 49 has a different harmonic sense, as it is immediately preceded by the drop to G♮ just cited, and it is in the context of the dominant key of B major.

(again clearly recalling the earlier examples), and immediately following this, with the most dramatic sudden accents as the statue sings his one word of acceptance:

There is no better example of the ease with which Mozart's style offers a true equivalent for stage action and not only an expression of it: the symmetries he needed were not a hindrance but an inspiration.

Not only the new classical style made this equivalence of drama and music possible. There was also a corresponding revolution of dramatic technique in the eighteenth century, most significantly in the development of the rhythm of comic intrigue. The comedy of character was dethroned, and the comedy of situation took its place. The comedy of situation had, of course, always existed: *Twelfth Night* and the *Comedy of Errors* are only the most famous English examples of a genre that goes back to Menander. But comedy based on character was the dominant mode, and it was considered the higher form by most critics, Lessing being the most authoritative German dramatist to proclaim its superiority. By the end of the eighteenth century, however, Herder was to insist that the comedy of character was dead, and that the only plays of Molière which could still hold the stage were those based on situation, like the *Médecin malgré lui*. In an article, 'Das Lustspiel,' Herder reversed the usual critical commonplace and insisted that characters (like Tartuffe and Harpagon) dated and changed from era to era, while situations—comic intrigue and the dramatic upsets and reversals of comic plots—remained eternally valid and ever fresh.

Character, of course, is as eternal—and no more so—than situation, but the eighteenth-century preference went very deep. The pre-eminence of the comedy of situation did not come from its novelty, as it was hardly new, but from the development of dramatic rhythm. The eighteenth century created a new kind of art from the sheer mechanism of stage management; what was new was not the awkward discovery, the inopportune arrival, the disguise unconsciously revealed, but the speed, controlled and accelerated, with which these events occurred. Already at the end of the seventeenth century, the successors of Molière (Dancourt and Le Sage, in particular) had begun to develop this art of rhythm, and to neglect the powerful psychological typology of Molière. The greatest masters by the middle of the eighteenth century were Beaumarchais and Goldoni; in spite of the latter's continuation of the comedy of picturesque characters and of local manners, he wrote several masterpieces of pure comedy of situation like *Il Ventaglio*, where the interest centers almost exclusively upon the rhythm of the intrigue.

By the end of the nineteenth century, the genre finally attained an almost abstract form, the comedy of adultery, in which there is no sensuality at all, and illicit sexual relations are only strings that pull the puppets and make them run. The comedies of Feydeau are the greatest examples: character has disappeared, and there is a mathematical poetry drawn from the manipulation of a formidable number of adulterous liaisons and cross-liaisons in and out of the doors of several hotel rooms. But this is the old age of the form, and in the eighteenth century we have only its first moment of maturity. The origin is the improvised theater—the *commedia dell'arte*, the *Théâtre de la Foire*, for which many of the greatest writers of the eighteenth century wrote scenarios. Mozart came along at the exact moment when the improvisation had been replaced by a fixed and literary art, when the sketched scenarios of a series of comic situations became plays and librettos, developing the new rhythm of intrigue learnt from the popular, improvising troupes. It was an opportune time for Mozart, and we must be grateful that it coincided so neatly with the new dramatic possibilities of the sonata style. The arts do not always run so smoothly in harness, but eighteenth-century theater had developed the same feeling as music for an articulated series of events and for controlled rhythmic transitions. This conjunction made it possible for Mozart's genius to be deployed with such ease in his operas: he had the feeling lacking in Haydn for large-scale dramatic movement, and he had a control of the sonata style that only Haydn, of all his contemporaries, could equal. From the point of view of large-scale rhythmic movement, *Figaro* is his masterpiece, and for this Beaumarchais and da Ponte must share in the credit. It is the supreme musical example of the comedy of intrigue.

The development of the rhythm of comic intrigue was facilitated by a changing conception of personality in the eighteenth century, based on a new, although still primitive interest in experimental psychology. Earlier centuries produced a more striking and more individual conception of personality: Molière's Harpagon, to take only one example from so many in his plays, is neither an average miser nor an allegorical personification of avarice but a man possessed by avarice as if by a demon; Alceste, in *Le Misanthrope*, struggles against the misanthropy which controls him, and ends by yielding to it with delight. This conception of personality is reflected throughout the seventeenth century in the interest of the animal in man, the fables of La Fontaine, the studies by Della Porta and Le Brun of facial resemblances between animals and men, and it is closely related to the idea of human personality dominated by the humors. All men are different, each can be set off from his fellows, characterized by the abstract forces that govern his individual nature. The eighteenth-century view, by contrast, was a more leveling one: all men are the same, all dominated by the same motifs; *così fan tutti:* they all behave the same way; the differences between Fiordiligi and Dorabella are only superficial, the one like the other will end in the arms of a new suitor. One of the most revealing moments in *Le Nozze di Figaro* is when the valet, misled by Susanna, becomes as blind with jealousy as his master. Eighteenth-century comedy springs from the tradition of masked players, but it made the mimes drop the masks as the century went on, as if the fixed grimace were irrelevant to the blander, more mobile, real face underneath.

The relation of eighteenth-century comedy to the popular improvised theater cannot be overestimated, but it can be misunderstood. All the great comedies of the time are in some way related to this tradition, yet none of them allow for improvisation—in fact, they destroyed it. The *opéra-comique* arose from a scenario where only the songs were written out, but it was not long before the dialogue was set down as well. Even Gozzi, who promoted the improvised, masked theater in opposition to Goldoni, wrote out all the dialogue after the success of his first scenario, *The Love for Three Oranges*. The stylization of the masked troupes fitted in very well with eighteenth-century psychology: the outward personality is a mask, what is real is the *tabula rasa* underneath upon which experience writes. For the seventeenth century, beneath the mask lie features even more strikingly characterized, more individual; beneath the eighteenth-century mask is only human nature. In comparison to the individualized characters of the sixteenth- and seventeenth-century stages, the personages of the eighteenth century are almost blanks; their reactions can be controlled and manipulated by the intelligent rascal and the clever valet—except that they, too, can be caught in their own plot when the complexity escapes them. The reliance of the popular theater upon stylized characters and upon the comedy of situation—the development of intrigue—was an inspiration to the eighteenth-century playwright, but the theater did not remain popular for long under his hands. It was for the masked troupe of the Italian Comedians that Marivaux developed his highly sophisticated plays and created a genre that may be called the comedy of experimental psychology, a kind of play that was quickly taken up in Italy and Germany. These are not 'thesis' plays but 'demonstration' plays: there is never anything controversial about their ideas. They demonstrate—prove by acting out—psychological ideas and 'laws' that everyone accepted, and they are almost scientific in the way they show precisely how these laws work in practice.

Così fan tutte belongs in the center of this tradition: if the book is less profoundly conceived than the finest of Marivaux, it is still, because of its music, the greatest example of its kind. The interest in such a play lies chiefly in the psychological steps by which the characters move to an end known in advance: as in Marivaux' *Le Jeu de l'Amour et du Hasard*, how a young girl disguised as a maid and a young man disguised as a valet will overcome their feelings of class and, first, become aware that they are in love and, then, openly admit it. There must be a disguise, or the play would be not a psychological comedy, but a social drama about marrying outside one's class; and it must be a double disguise, so that both lovers may be guinea-pigs. In plays where only the man is disguised, the valet-scientist must fool him so that he, too, will become a part of the experiment, and weep real tears. In *Così fan tutte*, we know in advance that the girls will be unfaithful, but we expect a demonstration of how they will yield: step by step, it must be true to the eighteenth-century laws of psychology. It is necessary that the new lovers be the old ones disguised, or we would have a *comédie larmoyante* of the returning soldier who finds the girl he left behind in the arms of another; but it is necessary, too, that the disguised lovers each take the other's former girl, or the girls would be unconsciously faithful, and the play would prove quite a different psychological theorem.

In short, what is essential is a closed system. No outside influences may be allowed to enter: the atmosphere of the rest of life is sealed off. There are only victims and scientists; and the two young men, who start by thinking they are among the scientists, learn, to their rage, that they are numbered among the victims. That is why in *Così fan tutte* Guglielmo cannot join in the beautiful A flat major canon at the wedding but mutters that he hopes they are drinking poison. In order to isolate the experiment, the scientists play all the necessary roles: the notary and the doctor are both Despina disguised. The libretto has been condemned as absurd and cynically immoral, and oddly defended as realistic (by W. J. Turner): it is none of these. It constructs an artificial and completely traditional world in which a psychological demonstration may be acted out, and it is true, not to life, which never intrudes here, but to the eighteenth-century view of human nature. The psychological viewpoint was one that the nineteenth century found outdated, and yet so recently overthrown as to be distasteful: the opera was, in fact, the very end of a tradition and had to deal with a changed atmosphere from the start. Soon after its first performance it was already being censured as immoral and trivial, and for the next hundred years only exceptional critics, like E. T. A. Hoffmann, understood the warmth and irony that the libretto enabled Mozart to achieve.

The music follows the psychological progression with great sensitivity. Fiordiligi's two famous arias strikingly reflect the individual psychological moment: the first, proclaiming her fidelity 'like a rock,' is magnificently comic, with her display of virtue accompanied by two trumpets, and with vocal leaps as enormous and as ludicrous as the words. At moments, pride is mocked by the gaiety of the music as it forces the singer into an ungrateful register:

que - sto e - sem - pio di. co - stan-za,

In the second aria 'Per pietà, ben mio,' however, Fiordiligi is deeply troubled by the realization that her fidelity was, not a sham, but the most fragile of constructions. The two trumpets are replaced by two horns, the long leaps are no longer ridiculous but deeply expressive, the phrasing more complex.

From the point of view of the opera, when Fiordiligi yields to Ferrando (in the great A major duet 'Per gli amplessi') she becomes more herself as she becomes more like every woman: after the mock grandeur of her first aria and the real grandeur of the second, the music of the duet is correspondingly more human. The relation of musical style to operatic psychology is ambiguous at best, and always indirect, but in this duet Mozart abandons the immediately perceptible formal clarity that he commanded so readily, although the final resolution and the proportions are as satisfying as ever. The normal movement to the dominant E major has only begun when it is cut short by the entrance of Ferrando, and a surprising modulation to C major establishes this key (the flat mediant) as a new 'dominant' or secondary key. This is another anticipation of Beethoven's use of a substitute dominant, that is, a chord sufficiently akin to the dominant to be reasonably set against the tonic, and yet remote enough to give a chromatically expressive, large-scale dissonance to the structure: its purpose here is symbolic, but dramatically and not only expressively so. Fiordiligi's music expresses real anguish, but her most despairing cry, 'Ah non son, non son più forte':

is the conventional operatic representation of tears, nonetheless deeply touching: she is at her most desperate as the music obviously moves (from C major to A minor) towards a return of the tonic. We know how near Fiordiligi is to admitting her love, as we become aware how close the sound of A major is. When it finally comes, we sense that Ferrando has won, and he begins his final plea in a new tempo (Andante), full of confidence. Fiordiligi's answer—her defeat—is the most exquisite of cadences:

in which it is no longer the vocal line that carries the dramatic meaning, but the long-drawn-out and finally resolved phrase of the oboe. The classical realization of the cadence as an articulate dramatic event finds its triumph here.

It should not be concluded that the music becomes more sincere as the characters drop their pretenses. Mozart is as direct—and as pretentious—in the one instance as in the other. The irony of the opera depends on its tact; it is a masterpiece of 'tone,' this most civilized of all aesthetic qualities. There is no way of knowing in what proportions mockery and sympathy are blended in Mozart's music and how seriously he took his puppets, just as we cannot know how seriously Ariosto took his tales of ancient chivalry or La Fontaine the morals of the fables he versified. Even to ask is to miss the point: the art in these matters is to tell one's story without being foolishly taken in by it and yet without a trace of disdain for its apparent simplicity. It is an art which can become profound only when the attitude of superiority never implies withdrawal, when objectivity and acceptance are indistinguishable. Those who think that Mozart wrote profound music for a trivial libretto misunderstand his achievement almost as radically as those who, like Wagner, felt that with *Così fan tutte* he had put empty music to a foolish book.

The farewell quintet in the first act ('Write to me every day,'—'Twice a day') is a touchstone of Mozart's success: heartbreaking without ever for a moment approaching tragedy, and delightful without a trace of explicit mockery in the music, it seems to hold laughter and sympathy in a beautiful equilibrium. Even the parody of the operatic sob is done with great delicacy (as it is in Stravinsky's parody of, and homage to, this quintet, the chorus of sentimental prostitutes in *The Rake's Progress*).

This virtuosity of tone is everywhere visible in the score. One of its most remarkable manifestations is in the finale of the first act: as the two men, supposedly dying of poison, lie stretched out on the ground, and the ladies examine them with more tenderness than before ('What an interesting face!'), the orchestra plays what would be a long double fugue—except that there is only one voice at a time, and almost no accompaniment. The music becomes genuinely and richly polyphonic after this long passage, but the surprising combination of baroque contrapuntal movement and the thinnest of *opera buffa* textures once again holds the finest of balances between seriousness and comedy.

The operas of Mozart are international in style, and borrow eclectically from all the important contemporary dramatic traditions of Europe. Even the *Singspiel* has not much more specific local character for Mozart than the Italian operas. The background of French culture, for example, is perceptible throughout *Die Entführung*, not least in its vaudeville ending. The 'seraglio' comedy, in fact, was developed with more grace and wit in France by Favart than by any of the Italian playwrights. The only dramatic form in eighteenth-century Europe not to have affected Mozart's work at all is the serious German comedy that found its first great exponents in Lessing and Lenz and its masterpiece later in *Der zerbrochene Krug* of Kleist. This tradition, the most original of all the German contributions to comedy, seems not to have existed for Mozart. Otherwise he took his material wherever he found it: Beaumarchais, Wieland, Favart, Metastasio, Molière, Goldoni. The essentially Viennese transformation of the Italian clown into the Hans Wurst figure is, of course, important for *Die Zauberflöte*, but even in this supposedly most Viennese of Viennese operas, the model and the inspiration for the form comes essentially from Italy through the work of a Venetian, Carlo Gozzi, and his influence on the Viennese comedy of magic.

Turandot and *The Love for Three Oranges* still keep Gozzi's name alive today. Enormously popular in Germany during the last quarter of the eighteenth century, he provided a challenge and an alternative to the rational, bourgeois comedy of his arch-enemy Goldoni, who was influenced heavily by the French tradition. Gozzi called his own works dramatic fables, and what he says about them (in his *Memoirs of a Useless Man*) reads like a hand-tailored description of *Die Zauberflöte*:

> 'the dramatic genre of the fable . . . is the most difficult of all . . . it should have an imposing grandeur, a fascinating and majestic mystery, arresting novelty of spectacle, intoxicating eloquence, sentiments of moral philosophy, the sophisticated wit (*sali urbani*) of nourishing criticism, dialogue that springs from the heart, and above all the great magic of seduction that creates an enchanting illusion of making the impossible appear as truth to the mind and spirit of the spectators.'[1]

The impossible fabulous fairy-tale plot made to seem real, the spectacle, the mystery, the didacticism, the critical approach, the heartfelt sentiments—all this strangely mixed together can be found in *Die Zauberflöte*. In addition, the incongruous juxtaposition of vulgar traditional clowning and political and religious allegory so characteristic of *Die Zauberflöte* was already at the heart of Gozzi's first play.

The theater that Gozzi partly invented, partly revived, was both aristocratic and popular, fiercely reactionary in philosophy and brilliantly innovatory in its mixing of previous genres. Essentially it was based on a combination of fairy-tale adventure of great nobility with the farcical tradition of the *commedia dell'arte*; originally an attempt to revive the inspired improvisatory style of the discredited *commedia dell'arte* troupes, it quickly turned into something new, fully written out and heavily charged with ideological content. Perhaps only through the Viennese *Singspiel* could this hybrid inspiration—this monstrous child of farce, philosophy, dialect comedy, fairy-tale and Spanish tragedy—be transformed into musical theater. The *opera buffa* was too well-defined a tradition to tolerate such a metamorphosis, but the *Singspiel* remained as yet undeveloped and malleable.

Mozart's correspondence testifies to his interest in Gozzi's work, and Schikaneder, the librettist of *Die Zauberflöte*, was producing plays of Gozzi with his troupe in Salzburg at a time when Mozart was still there. What Gozzi provided was a structure—a systematic conception of drama and even stage-craft—that enabled Mozart to unite and to fuse the most popular and the most complex and learned forms of art. The action of *Die Zauberflöte* ranges (as in Gozzi's dramatic fables) from the popular farce of Papageno (partly

---

[1] Bari, 1910, vol. I, p. 267.

improvised by Schikaneder at the first performances, it appears) to fairy-tale illusionism and spectacle and even to religious ritual. Sensitive people are sometimes made uncomfortable by the vulgar diction of *Die Zauberflöte*, but the conception, flawed as it is by inconsistencies, is among the noblest on the operatic stage. The music correspondingly goes from the simplest of tunes and the most farcical of patter-effects to the fugue and even the chorale-prelude (a revival of this very special Baroque form that was to remain unique in the classical style until Beethoven's Quartet op. 132 with its working of *Veni Creator, Spiritus*). In *Die Zauberflöte*, too, Mozart was able to create the first genuinely classical religious style that could be placed with honor beside his imitations of the Baroque religious forms and textures.

With the role of Sarastro and the chorus of priests, the classical hymn makes its first appearance; it is a texture rather than a specific form, and one that was to be of central importance in Beethoven's development. It attains gravity while deliberately avoiding the rich and complicated movement of inner voices of the Baroque. Above all, it avoids the Baroque harmonic dissonance, and replaces the continuously expressive suspensions almost entirely by pure triadic sonority. Harmonically, therefore, it is partly a return to sixteenth-century sound, above all that of Palestrina, whose music remained alive and performed throughout the eighteenth century. The melodic line, however, is the classical one, expressively shaped, symmetrical, and with a sharply marked climax; the articulation is equally sharp and the phrases lack not only the rich continuity of the Baroque, but the delicacy of the sixteenth-century divisions as well. The appearance of this texture in the classical style was not unprecedented in *Die Zauberflöte*; it affects the same harmonic simplicity as one finds in many passages of Gluck. The neo-classical ideal finds in passages of *Die Zauberflöte* a most remarkable in-carnation. The immediate origin of the classical 'hymn,' however, is to be found in some of the symphonic slow movements of Haydn: the idea of applying it within a religious context belongs to Mozart. The renunciation of his favorite appoggiaturas, which invariably emphasize dissonance, and the reliance on the undecorated shape of the melodic line alone are managed by Mozart with exquisite virtuosity.

Die Zauberflöte develops, as a corollary to the hymn, a conception of music as a vehicle for simple moral truths: in this work, the expressive range of music is decisively enlarged in an intellectual direction. There is no question, of course, of music as a substitute for verbal expression, but of the creation of a viable setting for the exposition of ideas. 'What shall we say to Sarastro?' Papageno whimpers, and as Pamina cries 'The truth,' the music takes on an heroic radiance unheard in opera before then. The morality of *Die Zauberflöte* is sentitious, and the music often assumes a squareness rare in Mozart, along with a narrowness of range and an emphasis on a few notes very close together that beautifully illuminate the middle-class philo-sophy of the text:

Nur der Freundschaft Har – mo – nie mil – dert die Be – schwer – den; oh – ne die – se

Sym – pa – thie ist kein Glück auf Er – den

Mozart's *Gemütlichkeit* here is as much intellectual as sensuous, and it is characteristic that in responding to the bourgeois, sentimental world of *Die Zauberflöte*, with its self-satisfied farcical comedy and its easy Masonic mysticism, his sonorities become purer, less chromatic in detail than in any other work. Sometimes this purity is clearly symbolic, as in the march of the trial by fire, where the majestic dwelling on the tonic, varied only by a dominant-seventh chord, is the musical equivalent for the steadfastness of the Masonic initiate:

The bare, strange sonority, entirely of flute, brass, and timpani, reflects and enhances the absolute simplicity here. The transparency, however, is often its own justification:

This is Mozart's late style developed as far as he carried it: the purity and the bareness are almost exotic, so extreme have they become, and this almost wilful leanness is only emphasized by the exquisite orchestration. Each of the mature operas of Mozart has its characteristic sonority, but in none is this sonority so much to the fore, so direct in its action and so fundamental, as in *Die Zauberflöte*.

Gozzi's 'fable' was a two-edged weapon: with its reliance upon old-fashioned popular farce and tales of magical enchantment for the conveyance of philosophical and political ideas, he hoped to combat the nefarious influence of the French Enlightenment and to reinforce the waning prestige of the aristocracy. In the hands of Mozart and Schikaneder, it became an arm of middle-class liberalism, a covert attack on the government, and a splendid work of propaganda for the Freemasons. Gozzi's aristocratic bias remains implicit in the form, however, in the contrast between the princely, idealistic Tamino and the materialistic Papageno, a figure made complex only by the venerable farcical tradition in which he exists, and which he implicitly recalls. Gozzi's work was, in the most profound way, an attack on contemporary rationalism, and his mixed forms released new springs of imagination. His influence on Mozart cannot be confined to *Die Zauberflöte*: the dramatic current that he set in motion had its effect on *Don Giovanni* as well. To some extent the text of da Ponte follows, not Molière, but the version of Gozzi's arch-enemy Goldoni, who had, however, sensibly removed from the story the childish devices of the stone statue that walked and talked, and the descent into hell—in his play, Don Giovanni was more reasonably struck by lightning. Childish popular traditions of this kind were, however, the very stuff of Gozzi's conception of drama—they gave the chance for elaborate spectacle, and most of all they represented the old order, the old way of things, they preserved the traditions by which the aristocratic life could survive. Gozzi's was not the first, nor the last, romantic alliance of the aristocracy and the lower-class against the bourgeoisie. With all da Ponte's and Mozart's dependance on Goldoni, their conception of the Don Juan story was essentially Gozzian in taste and outlook: the statue and the descent into hell are restored, and it is these Punch-and-Judy elements and the clowning of Leporello that have the greatest share in the imaginative and philosophical depth of the opera.

The comic side of *Don Giovanni* has given rise to the kind of controversy that, by its very nature, does not admit of a straightforward solution. Is *Don Giovanni* tragic or comic? Phrased this way, the question makes any answer right, but this would be to mistake the importance of the genre in eighteenth-century operatic practice. Is *Don Giovanni opera seria* or *buffa*? In the passion of the argument, intelligent men have lost their heads over even this innocuous technical point. Dent claimed that none of the characters of the opera had anything to do with *opera seria*, which is patently extravagant.

The structure and pacing of *Don Giovanni* are those of *opera buffa*, but it is evident that at least one of the characters, Donna Anna, comes directly from the world of *seria*, and Donna Elvira and Don Ottavio and even Don Giovanni himself mediate in varying degrees between the two worlds. This is not to imply that Donna Anna, too, is not contaminated at some points by the more fundamental *buffa* atmosphere, particularly in the ensembles. Nevertheless, the range of style of *opera buffa* is considerably broadened: Donna Elvira's aria 'Ah fuggil traditor' is a parody of old-fashioned *seria*, while Donna Anna's 'Or sai chi l'onore' is pure *seria* in its noblest form. The pathos of *Don Giovanni* is no greater than that of *Idomeneo*, but it is at moments as elevated and far more concentrated. The speed of the *opera buffa*'s large-scale rhythm and its emphasis on action in place of the dignified expression of *opera seria* enable the work to move at a dazzling pace from aria to ensemble: the moments of terror and pity are all the sharper in such surroundings. The first minutes of the opera set the tone, and establish the contrast, as the comic complaint of Leporello leads swiftly to the duel, and the pianissimo trio of horror as the Commendatore dies. No *opera seria* moves with this velocity. The comic pacing is essential to the effect, yet the result is anything but comic. This range of tone is, of course, not confined to *Don Giovanni*; the nobility of Fiordiligi or the Countess equally depends on the surrounding *opera buffa* structure for its full significance. The fusion is so perfect in *Don Giovanni* that the mixture of genres is no longer noticed today, but it was decidedly remarked upon and often condemned at the end of the eighteenth century.

The mixed genre in the eighteenth century is a sign of indecorum, and *Don Giovanni*, in more ways than one, is decidedly indecorous. In acknowledgement of this, da Ponte and Mozart called it not an *opera buffa*, but a *dramma giocoso*. Like *Così fan tutte* it was attacked from the beginning: it was immoral, shocking, out-of-date, and childish. The artistry of the music was naturally recognized, if its complexity was often bitterly resented. (The first Italian production had to be given up in despair after many rehearsals because of the difficulty of the score.) It was a frequent complaint of the time that Mozart's style was too learned to speak directly to the heart, but his enormous skill was never questioned. The dramatic conception, however, by no means always found favor. A critic of the first Berlin production wrote that the ear was enchanted while virtue was trampled underfoot.

The scandalous side of *Don Giovanni* had political, as well as artistic, overtones. It will not do to overstate this, but an element of liberal revolutionary aspiration is decidedly, if unsystematically, present in the work. No one in 1787 (the year when the meeting of the Estates-General echoed over all of Europe) could have missed the significance of Mozart's triumphantly overemphatic setting of 'Viva la libertà'[1], or of the wicked exploitation of

---

[1] See above, pp. 94–5, for the structural role of this passage in the first act finale.

peasant innocence for dissolute aristocratic vice. The novels and political pamphlets of the time were filled with references to such matters. Mozart's ideological bias is clear in all the late operas, except for *La Clemenza di Tito* and *Così fan tutte*, which exist in abstract worlds of their own. The cartoon-like attack on the Catholic Establishment of Austria is not a negligible part of *Die Zauberflöte*; it has been denied that the identification of Maria Theresa with the Queen of the Night was intended, but it was made from the beginning, and Schikaneder and Mozart would have had to be astonishingly obtuse not to have foreseen this in a work so heavily charged with Masonic doctrine and ritual (Freemasonry was the principal outlet in Austria at that time for bourgeois revolutionary ideals). In *Figaro*, too, the omission of the more overtly political passages of Beaumarchais' play can have made little difference to a public which, for the most part, knew quite clearly what was being left out; and in any case the call for the renunciation of unjust aristocratic privilege is sufficiently underlined in the opera as it stands. *Don Giovanni*, however, goes beyond all of this in its deliberate picture of a complete world disrupted by aristocratic immorality. The great ball scene in the first act is not mere musical virtuosity with all its three separate orchestras on the stage, and the complicated cross-rhythms of the dances. Each of the social classes—peasantry, bourgeoisie, and aristocracy—has its own dance, and the total independence of every rhythm is a reflection of the social hierarchy; it is this order and harmony that is destroyed by the attempted rape of Zerlina off-stage.[1]

The political ambiance of *Don Giovanni* is given greater weight by the close relation in the eighteenth century between revolutionary thought and eroticism. I have no wish to draw a consistent doctrine from the work, but only to set in relief the significance of some of its aspects. Political and sexual liberalism were intimately connected in the 1780s; even for the most respectable citizens the idea took the shape of a governing fear that republicanism implied complete sexual license. The Marquis de Sade, in his pamphlet *One More Step* did, indeed, claim the most extravagant sexual freedom as a logical corollary of political liberty; his ideas were current everywhere in a milder form, and were the end of an already considerable amount of eighteenth-century speculation. Mozart's early and devoutly Catholic horror at French liberal thought must surely have abated considerably when he became a Freemason, but in any case his personal beliefs have little importance in this connection. The political connotations of sexual liberty were very much alive at the première of *Don Giovanni*, and they would have been inescapable. Part of the outrage and the attraction that this work inspired for years to come must be understood in this context. After 1790, the repudiation of sexual liberty and the extreme puritanism of the revolutionary government

---

[1] Don Giovanni lowers himself and raises Zerlina as he dances with her to the music for the bourgeoisie, meeting her halfway, as it were.

of France (and of the counter-revolutionary governments elsewhere as well) are a reaction to the intellectual climate that produced *Don Giovanni*, and are reflected in Beethoven's rejection of Mozart's libretti as unworthy of being set to music.

This sense of outrage connected with the opera—and it is implicit in Kierkegaard's view of *Don Giovanni* as the only work that perfectly embodies the essentially erotic nature of music, and in E. T. A. Hoffmann's stressing of what he called its 'romanticism'—this sense of *Don Giovanni* as an attack, at once frontal and oblique, upon aesthetic and moral values is more useful for understanding the opera, and Mozart's music in general, than the common-sense view which shrugs off this aspect impatiently. Music is the most abstract of all the arts only in the sense that it is the least representational: it is, however, the least abstract in its direct physical assault on the listeners' nerves, in the immediacy of effect that its patterns gain from the apparently almost total reduction of mediating symbolism, of all ideas that seem to call for decoding and interpretation, and so to stand between music and listener. (If, as a matter of fact, the reduction is very far from total, and the listener must expend considerable labor decoding the symbolic relationships set before him, his activity is less conscious, less verbalized, than in any other art.) When this physical immediacy of music is stressed, then its erotic aspect stands well to the fore. Perhaps no composer used the seductive physical power of music with the intensity and the range of Mozart. The flesh is corrupt and corrupting. Behind Kierkegaard's essay on *Don Giovanni* stands the idea that music is a sin: it seems fundamentally sound that he should have chosen Mozart as the most sinful composer of all. What is most extraordinary about Mozart's style is the combination of physical delight—a sensuous play of sonority, an indulgence in the most luscious harmonic sequences—with a purity and economy of line and form that render the seduction all the more efficient.

A more prosaic and more conventionally respectable view of Mozart comes not from the sober perspective of the twentieth century but from the height of Romantic enthusiasm: in the G minor Symphony, a work of passion, violence, and grief for those who love Mozart most, Schumann saw nothing but lightness, grace, and charm. It should be said at once that to reduce a work to the expression of sentiments, however powerful, is to trivialize it in any case: the G minor Symphony is not much more profound conceived as a tragic cry from the heart than as a work of exquisite charm. Nevertheless, Schumann's attitude to Mozart ends by destroying his vitality as it canonizes him. It is only through recognizing the violence and the sensuality at the center of Mozart's work that we can make a start towards a comprehension of his structures and an insight into his magnificence. In a paradoxical way, however, Schumann's superficial characterization of the G minor Symphony can help us to see Mozart's daemon more steadily. In all of Mozart's supreme expressions of suffering and terror—the G minor Symphony, *Don Giovanni*, the G minor Quintet, Pamina's aria in *Die Zauberflöte*—there is something shockingly voluptuous. Nor does this detract from its power or effectiveness: the grief and the sensuality strengthen each other, and end by becoming indivisible, indistinguishable one from the other. (Tchaikovsky's grief, for example, has an equal lubricity, but his diffuse and wasteful technique of composition makes him far less dangerous.) In his corruption of sentimental values, Mozart is a subversive artist.

Almost all art is subversive: it attacks established values, and replaces them with those of its own creation; it substitutes its own order for that of society. The disconcertingly suggestive aspects—moral and political—of Mozart's operas are only a surface appearance of this aggression. His works are in many ways an assault upon the musical language that he helped to create: the powerful chromaticism that he could employ with such ease comes near at moments to destroying the tonal clarity that was essential to the significance of his own forms, and it was this chromaticism that had a real influence upon the Romantic style, on Chopin and Wagner in particular. The artistic personality that Haydn created for himself (related to, but not to be confused with, the face he wore for everyday purposes) prevented, by its assumption of an easy-going geniality, the full development of the subversive and revolutionary aspect of his art: his music, as E. T. A. Hoffmann wrote, appears to have been composed before original sin. Beethoven's attack was naked, no art was less accommodating in its refusal to accept any other conditions than its own. Mozart was as unaccommodating as Beethoven, and the sheer physical beauty, prettiness, even, of so much of what he composed masks the uncompromising character of his art. It cannot be fully appreciated without recalling the uneasiness and even dismay that it so often evoked in its time, and without recreating in our own minds the conditions in which it could still seem dangerous.

Part VI

HAYDN AFTER THE
DEATH OF MOZART

———

1

The Popular Style

By 1790, Haydn had created and mastered a deliberately popular style. The immensity of his success is reflected in the volume of his production in the next ten years, the decade after the death of Mozart: fourteen string quartets, three piano sonatas, fourteen piano trios, six masses, the *Sinfonia Concertante*, the *Creation*, the *Seasons*, twelve symphonies, and a great number of minor works. Today, when Haydn is almost a connoisseur's composer whose music cannot compete at the box office with that of Mozart or Beethoven, this atmosphere of enormous popular success must be borne in mind in order to understand the late works, above all the symphonies and the oratorios. There have been composers who were as much admired and others whose tunes were as much whistled and sung during their lifetimes, but none who so completely won at the same time the unquestioned and generous respect of the musical community and the ungrudging acclaim of the public.

A relationship between Haydn's late style and folk music is evident, but the nature of that relationship questionable and even slippery. There is a story, surely apocryphal but worth telling in this context, about the professor who went to do field research on Haydn among the peasants of that ethnically indecisive section of the Austro-Hungarian Empire where Haydn spent part of his childhood. The professor's method of investigation was to sing some of the better tunes of Haydn to the peasants, and ask if they recognized them. The peasants, with an earthy shrewdness even older and more traditional than folk music, quickly discovered that they were given a bigger tip when they recognized a melody than when they failed to do so, and their memories accordingly became richly accommodating. And to this day, the story ends, the peasants of that little Danubian region sing the songs that the professor taught them.

The folk songs that Haydn actually used on occasion are largely indistinguishable from many of the undoubtedly original melodies of his late years. To discuss the influence of folk music on Haydn's style is to set the matter on its head. The use of folk music or the invention of folk-like material becomes increasingly important in Haydn's works from 1785 on: there had always been some allusions to popular tunes, hunting-calls, yodels, and dance-rhythms in his music as in the music of most composers from Machaut to Schoenberg, but before the *Paris* and *London* Symphonies these had remained in the margin of his style. It will not do to sentimentalize over the elderly composer turning more and more to the songs he heard as a child. Mozart similarly developed a style close to folk music with *Die Zauberflöte* at the same time as Haydn, and the age of thirty-five is hardly advanced enough for Mozart to have been impelled by a similar nostalgia. The movement towards a 'popular' style must certainly be related to the republican enthusiasm of the latter part of the eighteenth century, as well as to the growth of national sentiment and the consciousness of particular national cultures. Nevertheless, an autonomous development of the musical language must be admitted to a role at least partially decisive here, as the interest in folk music had a long history already by the time it took on such significance for Haydn and Mozart, but it is only in the late 1780s that the classical style was able thoroughly to assimilate and to create elements of folk style at will.

The assimilation is the crux of the matter, and it is entirely new in eighteenth-century music. When Bach uses folk songs, as he does on rare occasions, either they lose their folk characteristics, or appear as quotations from a foreign language: both processes can be seen in the Quodlibet from the *Goldberg* Variations and in the *Peasant* Cantata. In Haydn, however, the opening of the finale of the Symphony no. 104.

is at once a folk song (and sounds it), and a perfectly normal Haydn rondo subject; even its rusticity is not unusual.

Even more illuminating is a comparison with the Baroque treatment of chorale-tunes, which, if not folk music, had become folk property long before Bach. The chorales are, indeed, completely assimilable into the Baroque style, but only because their original rhythms had, in time, been thoroughly flattened into an almost totally uniform movement. Not only the original dance rhythms have been destroyed in the early eighteenth-century chorale, but even the inflections of speech have largely disappeared. The opening phrase of *Ein feste Burg* in its original and its eighteenth-century forms[1] show this progressive regimentation:

It was only at this price that the tunes could be received by the homogeneous rhythmic structures of the High Baroque. In the process their popular character is almost entirely lost.

Haydn, too, rarely accepts a melody without altering it, but often the

---

[1] Cited from Schweitzer, *J. S. Bach*, London, 1945, vol. I, pp. 23–24.

alteration only serves to reinforce the popular character. The slow movement of the *Drum-Roll* Symphony no. 103 is a double variation set in which both themes are based on folk melodies. The two themes resemble each other closely:

The F♯ in the second theme is not in the original folk song, however, which goes:[1]

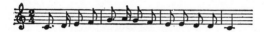

Rosemary Hughes remarks that the added F♯ makes the major melody recall the minor one. The addition of the trill and its downward close also brings the second theme in closer relation to the first, as they now outline the same shape (Haydn's double variation sets are almost never intended to sound as if they contain two distinct themes; the second melody appears as a free variation of the first, and the form is that of a monothematic rondo). But the F♯ also strengthens the popular character of the theme, which, in its original form, was evidently not folk-like enough for Haydn. The rustic, modal dissonance that is Haydn's invention belongs of course, to a world of pseudo-folklore, a world like that in Perrault's tales: it is the world of eighteenth-century pastoral.

For this reason it makes not the slightest difference whether Haydn invented his folk tunes or remembered them. The melody in the major of the *Drum-Roll* Symphony's slow movement, for example, is very like several dozen other folk tunes, among them the mock serenade that Bach used in the *Goldberg* Variations:

and it was as easy to invent variants as to find them. We know that Haydn was interested in collecting folk tunes, and that, as a young man, he gained experience in the popular music of street serenading. Nevertheless, the technique of thematic elaboration and the balanced and articulated symmetry of his style were worked out and perfected before the folk themes were used in

---

[1] Cited from Rosemary Hughes, *Haydn*, London, 1950, p. 131.

his music in any way except that of incidental quotation and external humor. In any collision between his style and the folk tune, it was always the tune that had to give way, and for this reason if for no other it would be difficult to allow the folk melodies a formative influence. Both melodies cited from the *Drum-Roll* Symphony are radically altered before the end of the first phrase, so that they each form miniature sonata patterns, with developments and recapitulations all in place.

There are composers (Bartók is perhaps the most famous of them) who have used research into folk music for the specific purpose of forming a style. Even in such cases, the development is a little mysterious and by no means straightforward. Bartók treats the folk music of entirely different cultures very much alike: his arrangement of Rumanian, Hungarian, and Czecho-slovakian folk songs do not differ from each other in any way that can be easily related to the original qualities of the songs. They provided him with non-diatonic modes, which was what he was looking for in the first place. The composer who employs folk material for patriotic reasons is also a familiar figure, and, as the Negro spirituals in Dvořák's music can testify, it does not seem to matter which folk material he chooses. But none of this has any relation to the folk material in the works of Haydn and Mozart, who used it only when needed within an already formed style, and who were perfectly ready to invent it when they found it necessary.

The procedures of Haydn and Mozart must be understood in a larger context, that of the creation of a popular style which abandons none of the pretensions of high art. Their achievement is perhaps unique in Western music: Beethoven attempted a similar synthesis with the last movement of the Ninth Symphony, and his triumph, which seems to me incontestable, has nevertheless been contested. This solitary success in the history of musical style should make us wary of critics who reproach the *avant-garde* composer for an uncompromisingly hermetic style, or the popular composer (like Offenbach or Gershwin) for low ideals; that is like blaming a man for not having blue eyes or for not having been born in Vienna. The most esoteric composer would welcome the popularity of Mozart in Prague, where people whistled 'Non più andrai' in the streets, if he could achieve it as Mozart did without sacrificing a jot of his refinement or even his 'difficulty.' Only for one brief historical period in the operas of Mozart, the late symphonies of Haydn, and some of the Schubert songs, has the utmost sophistication and com-plexity of musical technique existed alongside—or better, fused with—the virtues of the street song.

It is, of course, not the mere use of popular elements of style that achieves this fusion. The *chanson* masses of the Renaissance used popular as well as art songs, but the melodies were subjected to a treatment which removed their most characteristic qualities. The folk elements in Mahler—Ländler rhythms and turns of phrase now even more urban than pastoral—are deliberately left unassimilated, unfused with the strikingly advanced orchestral style in which they are embedded. It is their unmitigated banality—vulgarity, even—upon which so much of the tragic irony in Mahler depends. The fusion of popular and high art depends on a delicate equilibrium: Verdi's popular style goes hand in hand with a technique that proclaims its naïveté, for all his genius, and greater sophistication is gained at the end of his life only with a progressive abandonment of the most characteristically popular effects. The style of Mozart in *Die Zauberflöte* and Haydn in the *Paris* and *London* Symphonies, however, became not less, but more learned, as it became more popular.

For this achievement of the classical style, comparable to the brief glory of late Elizabethan drama, a new social situation had to coincide with a powerful stylistic development. The situation is easy enough to identify: it is the rising aspirations of the commercial class throughout the eighteenth century and their growing interest in music as an element of aristocratic culture and a proof of social distinction; the increase in amateur musicians (and the increase in population) provided a new and affluent public. In short, secular high art became public. The unexpected discovery of the existence in the 1730s of a commercial public for religious music gave Handel his immense success, but he had only a limited use for specifically popular stylistic elements in winning it. Public symphonic concerts and comic opera became the new forces behind the historical development of style in the later part of the century.

The freshness of this new mass appeal of high art has never been re-captured. It was, at least socially, bound to disappoint: the snob value of music has never been taken off the market but it has also rarely paid the dividends hoped for. There was also an inevitable conflict of interest among music as science, music as expression, and music as public spectacle: it was not to be expected that the synthesis of the Mozart piano concerto could occur again. Beethoven's Fourth and Fifth Concertos are something of a miracle; one should not underrate the difficulty of calculating the relation of social forces to individual genius.

What made this achievement possible, the process by which learned and popular elements were wedded, must be looked for within the musical language itself. The melodies with a marked popular flavor are most striking in three places of Haydn's symphonies and quartets (and, to a lesser extent, of Mozart's): towards the close of the expositions of the first movements, the openings of the finales, and the trios of the minuets. The first movement is generally the most complex and the most dramatic, and the problem of integrating a 'folk' melody (whether borrowed or invented need not concern us here) is at its most delicate. The use of an obviously popular tune at the beginning had its dangers, as any opening theme that seemed to exist for its own sake would have failed to provide the dynamic impulse for the whole movement. Mozart could overcome the danger of opening his expositions with a long and well-rounded melody by disturbing the surface from the outset by a restless motion and a gradually increasing harmonic intensity (as in the G minor Symphony) or by the more subtle disturbance of an ambiguity of accent, as in the Symphony in E flat K. 543:

where the feminine endings and the imitation in the horn throw the accent onto the third and fifth measures, while, on the other hand, the pause and the syncopation in the melodic line turn it towards the second and fourth measures. Haydn's most complex ideas are initially more straightforward and he rarely tries for this shadowy interplay between resonance and significance.

The themes near the end of the expositions of the Symphonies nos. 99 and 100 are less complex than the opening themes, and they both serve a similar purpose:

that is, they ground the tension previously generated. The full measures of
introductory accompaniment common to both is revealing: nothing else
would bring out so well the atmosphere of a popular band while anchoring
the music so firmly in place. The squareness of the tune that follows, and
which gives it the air of unbuttoned, unsophisticated relaxation, does the
rest. These 'popular' tunes are used as cadential forces, to round off and to
articulate the form.

They have consequently the same function as the virtuosity in a Mozart
concerto, which is, as we have seen, always most in evidence towards the
end of the exposition. Mozart uses tunes of the same character at the same
place in his symphonies, as the end of the exposition of the *Jupiter* shows:

and the accompaniment also starts before the melody after a pause as in the
examples from Haydn. This sort of melody is rarely used in the opening
movements of the piano concertos, as it is displaced there by brilliance in the
solo part. In short, the 'popular' tune is used for its squareness and symmetry
as a substitute for the banal cadence formulas, for the 'filling' that would
otherwise have been needed in its place.

In Haydn's brilliant D major Quartet op. 71 no. 2, the main theme is a
rich and complex contrapuntal elaboration of an octave leap:

while the closing melody of the exposition has the popular squareness of the
closing themes of the symphonies:

and further examples of this contrast could be added with ease. It should be noted that when the opening theme has a markedly regular character, the closing theme is generally made even more decisively popular in style. The first theme of the Quartet in G major op. 76 no. 1 is, on the surface, as jolly and square as one could wish:

but the end of the exposition outdoes it with ease:

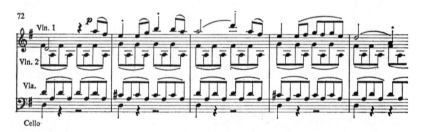

and the stable bass and introductory accompaniment figure appear here once more. The main theme of the *Drum-Roll* Symphony has a dance-like character:

but it is nothing to the Ländler rhythm and frankly popular dance accompaniment of the later theme:

In sum, the popular tune could be integrated into high art as a means of clarifying the form (I need hardly add that this was only the method of integration and not the reason for it).

The opening themes of the finales have almost always the same symmetrical regularity of rhythm that indicates the popular style. The argument may seem circular: the identification of 'folk' music with regularity and squareness of rhythm is neither evident nor, indeed, true. However, most people expect of a tune exactly the regularity of phrase-length always divisible by four and partial symmetry of outline which the classical composer took from the dance and from folk music. It was their recurrent symmetries that interested him, and he conditioned most listeners to expect them for more than a century. What is meant when Beethoven and Stravinsky are denied the title of great melodists is not that the linear patterns in their music are not beautiful, a contention only too clearly ridiculous, but that these patterns do not often fall into the symmetrical forms and four-measure lengths of Schubert and Prokofiev, for example. A great deal of folk music, some of it surely known to Haydn, is strongly asymmetrical and rhythmically irregular, but that is not what interested Haydn. He could provide all the rhythmic irregularity one needed (although it has perhaps not been sufficiently emphasized in the literature about him to what an extent his irregular and unexpected rhythmic effects are tightly controlled after 1780 within a large-scale system of symmetries, with an eight-measure phrase pattern dominating, and the odd-numbered phrase lengths balanced by appearing in pairs). The folk style has significance in Haydn's music mainly as an element of popular style in general and this, as it appears in Haydn's music, is used largely for its stabilizing effect. That is why it so often comes in the form of a drone bass as in the finales of the Symphonies no. 82 (the *Bear*) and 104 and the D major Quartet op. 76 no. 5.

The clear, well-defined, eminently detachable shape of the finale-theme is the basis for one of Haydn's best-loved and most dramatic effects: the surprise return. A great deal of ingenuity is expended upon the return of the theme, almost always with rollicking effect: the trick is to keep suggesting the return but to delay it until the listener no longer knows when to expect it— although if he keeps his sense of long-range symmetry he can generally make a good guess. A theme with an upbeat is most useful, as the upbeat can be played over and over, as in the finale of the *Surprise*:

Consequently most of the finales of the late symphonies start with an upbeat. Those with two upbeats work even better, and the result in Symphony no. 88 is incomparably funny:

while the same witty effect is raised to the point of comic magnificence in Symphony no. 93:

with its powerful contrast between the full orchestra with timpani and one solitary cello. The most subtle returns are, however, those in the rare finales where the theme has no upbeat, and Haydn must seek other inspiration for his humor. The return in the finale of the *Clock* is a pianissimo fugato, and the return of the last movement of Symphony no. 104 is an effect of such delicacy that it would have to be quoted at great length for its radiant poetry and wit to be appreciated.

Haydn needed *three* upbeats to write the finale with the most outrageous rhythmic effects, that of the Quartet in E flat major, op. 76 no. 6, which surpasses even the duplicity of the minuet of the *Oxford* Symphony in fooling the listener as to the place of the downbeat. The opening, indeed, sounds clearly not like three upbeats, but like *five*:

and the development section disrupts what rhythmic equilibrium the listener has retained by an apparently random distribution of accents:

although the entire development (from measures 66 to 118) is controlled by a completely rational system of four-measure phrases reinforced by a regular harmonic movement. The beginning of the recapitulation is calculated to throw off even the quartet-players:

The *sforzando* in measure 118 is Haydn's charity, otherwise we should never recognize the first note of the theme at all. The brief double canon at measures 111 to 114 was not hard to write (anyone can make a canon out of a descending scale), but the comic rhythmic complexity is a true display of virtuoso invention.

The melodies of marked popular character in the trios of the minuets (and sometimes in the minuets themselves, which became more boisterous as Haydn grew older) are the most striking examples of Haydn's pastoral style. It is above all at these moments that the traditionally aristocratic form is made democratic—or at least available to the new audience. They make an unabashed appeal to popular taste (although we must remember that in London it was most often the slow movements of Haydn's symphonies that were encored at their first performance). The minuets, however, do not patronize the folk style as Rousseau's *Devin du Village* or Gay's *Beggar's Opera* did, or present it as exotic; they transfigure it musically and integrate it with the whole work. No doubt the ostentatious presence of the rhythms and turns of phrase of the popular dance-forms are heard as a frank extra-musical reference—the irruption of the ideals of the non-aristocratic classes into the world of high art; but the style that Haydn had elaborated was, by 1790, one of such power that it could accommodate these ideals without loss of its own integrity. Haydn's technique of thematic development was able to accept almost any material, and absorb it: the simplest yodel phrase is transformed by the instrumentation, and a subtle alteration of its rhythm allows it to bear the weight of a modulation, as in the minuet of the *Drumroll Symphony*:

Sometimes the element transformed is even less elaborate, being nothing but a rhythmic scrap.

The popular material retains its character exactly because Haydn's technique isolates what it intends to develop. The identity of each element had to be clarified before it could enter into the larger continuity of the work. This enabled Haydn to exploit the most characteristically popular side of his material while using it as the basis for the most sophisticated structures, provided only that the material had a strong tonal orientation. (Yodelling is so obsessively triadic that it might easily have been invented by the classical style if it had not already existed, and it is difficult to take seriously the formative stylistic influence of something structurally so inevitable and so logical.) This isolating tendency of the classical style preserved the integrity of both the style and the material.

Haydn after the Death of Mozart

The orchestration of Haydn's minuets is often enchanting: Mozart was rarely so ingenious. The most memorable passages are those where the combination of different orchestral colors remains deliberately heterogeneous, totally unlike the more solidified textures of Beethoven and Mozart even when these contrast woodwinds and strings. In the following passage from the minuet of Symphony no. 97:

we can see why Rimsky-Korsakov declared Haydn to be the greatest of all masters of orchestration. The oom-pah-pah of a German dance band is rendered with the utmost refinement, amazingly by kettledrums and trumpets pianissimo, and the rustic *glissando* (a sort of glottal stop on the first beats) is given a finicky elegance by the grace notes in the horns as well as by the doubling of the melody an octave higher with the solo violin. These details are not intended to blend, but to be set in relief: they are individually exquisite.

This minuet is admittedly extraordinary with all of its repeats written out to allow for changes of instrumentation and dynamics, but the preciosity of orchestration is by no means exceptional in Haydn. The extensive writing for the strings on the bridge of their instruments in the slow movement of the same work is only another example. In the following passage near the beginning of the exposition of the first movement of Symphony no. 93, the instrumental color is used to reinforce a rhythmic tension:

343

The three measures 40 to 42 expand by repetition, sustaining like a fermata not over the preceding note but over the whole of the preceding measure: the change of wind doubling from flute to bassoon to oboe is not intended to blend with the violins but to stand out sharply from it. (These measures are a beautiful model both of the classical isolation of a motif, and of the charging of a tonic chord with tension almost by rhythm alone.) In his conception of orchestration Haydn is often far closer than either Beethoven or Mozart to the coloristic ideals of much twentieth-century music; the use of solo instruments isolated within the mass of the orchestra, and the employment of trumpets and timpani in many of the slow movements as pure tone-color recall the orchestration of Mahler more than anything else in the eighteenth or nineteenth centuries.

What would once have been called the high seriousness of this deliberately popular style needs to be seen clearly: the artistic personality of 'Papa Haydn' that the composer created—surely as much in response to his own needs as to those of his public—had more than its jocular, genial side. The moments of sentimental poetry are far more frequent than the grossly humorous effects, although both are tempered by wit, and the care for dramatic line is constant. The increased weight of Haydn's style can be felt in his transformation of two formal structures, the introduction, and the traditional ternary *ABA* form. The metamorphosis of the ternary form is part of the logical development of the classical style: the middle section becomes, not a relaxation of tension, but a move towards a climax, and the return of the first part is consequently a genuine harmonic resolution. The opening movement of the D major Quartet op. 76 no. 5, for example, begins with a long symmetrical melody that resolves firmly on the tonic, and the second section opens, like many trios, in the minor mode: however, it quickly takes on the sequential modulations and the melodic fragmentation of a development section. After the return of the first section in a decorated form like a da capo aria, a long coda provides an astonishing second development. The loose da capo or ternary form could no longer satisfy Haydn, and he now often conceived the middle section so far as possible as a true classical development. The most significant result of his new approach are the dramatic dance-finales (minuets and German peasant dances) of the late piano trios.

Haydn turned the introduction into a dramatic gesture. Before his late works it had been largely a way for him to indicate a solemn mood while fixing the tonality; basically it did nothing but add importance.[1] An introduction implies a sense of expectancy: in more technical language, it is rhythmically an expansion of an upbeat, and if it extends to any length, it must end as an unresolved dominant chord without having modulated. Examples from the early part of the century include accompanied recitatives before an air, as in the Bach cantatas, and of a certain number of preludes, but the means used are always more diffuse than in the classical period, which concentrated the harmonic sense and gave the rhythmic beat greater definition. (The slow opening section of a Baroque work like a French overture is not introductory at all, but modulates to the dominant and is a beginning in its own right.)

The new dramatic role of the introduction can be seen at its most laconic in the opening of Haydn's Quartet op. 71 no. 3:

---

[1] For the difference between the classical introduction and the opening section of a Baroque work like a French overture see page 282.

The introduction has here become a single, brusque chord. As before, this creates expectancy (the lengthened, unmeasured silence in the second bar would see to that); it adds importance to the light comic theme that follows; and it defines E flat major with a rare economy. But it also has a new dramatic interest of its own. After the pause in the second bar, we are aware that the first chord was not a true beginning of the discourse. It was only a gesture, in the literal sense of a physical movement that conveys a meaning.

Beethoven may have remembered this opening when he wrote the *Eroica*, which begins with a similarly spaced E flat chord played twice, but Haydn did something like this often enough for the procedure, rather than a particular instance of it, to have been the influence. All six of Haydn's Quartets op. 71 and op. 74 play with this idea, which goes from one or two chords (there are three in op. 76 no. 1) to a fanfare (op. 74 no. 2), and finally, in op. 74 no. 3, to a first theme that is made to sound like an introduction:

The two-measure pause gives the opening phrase the air of an introductory motto, and this phrase is not replayed in the recapitulation; nevertheless it is an integral part of the exposition, to be repeated with it, and dominates the development section; the second theme is directly derived from it. Haydn was not a good opera composer, but his sense of a dramatic musical gesture intimately linked with the general action was exceedingly sharp.

The slow introductions of the *London* Symphonies (eleven out of the twelve begin with one[1]) are more elaborate, but none of them overstep the limits of being only a stepping-stone to a movement of more pronounced character. These opening symphonic Adagios have a longer history in Haydn's work than his experiments with brief introductions to the quartets of 1793. Slow introductions appear very early in his orchestral works; the finest examples

---

[1] The Symphony no. 95 is the only exception, and it is also the only one in the minor mode, which guarantees its seriousness even without the added weight of an introduction.

before 1787 are all in D major: no. 57 of 1774, nos. 73 (*La Chasse*) and 75 of 1781, and no. 86 of 1786. Some of the dramatic character of the later works appears as early as 1774.

In 1786, Mozart wrote the *Prague* Symphony (also in D major, a key that inspired brilliance perhaps because it provided a full sonority for both brass and string instruments), a work with perhaps the richest and most complex introduction before Beethoven's Seventh Symphony. It has a breadth of movement that none of Haydn's ever attains, and a wealth of contrapuntal and chromatic detail that Haydn rarely attempted. Yet Mozart, in the *Prague*, makes no attempt to emulate Haydn's system of thematic transition between the introduction and the Allegro (and his later use of it in the E flat Symphony K. 543 of 1788, while subtle and lovely, does not carry the conviction it almost always has in Haydn).[1]

These thematic relationships in Haydn always respect the character of the introduction, and are based upon a profound psychological understanding of its nature. When we hear the related theme in the Allegro, we recognize immediately (and generally with delight at the witty presentation) the kinship with the introduction. But when it had appeared first in the introduction itself, it did not sound like a theme. The essential character of an introduction (Mozart's as well as Haydn's) is a lack of precise definition; if it does not retain enough of this nebulous quality, it risks sounding like the true opening in itself.[2] That is why these close thematic relationships can be dangerous within the scheme of the classical introduction. Haydn's handling of the problem is one of his greatest triumphs. The theme which is to reappear in the Allegro generally makes its first entrance unobtrusively in the introduction, sometimes as part of the accompaniment (in *La Chasse*) and sometimes almost unnoticed as part of a conventional formula for a cadence. When it has a shape that cannot be so hidden, it is played so slowly that it seems, not a melody, but the majestic outline of a harmony, as in Symphony no. 98. The *Military* Symphony opens with a theme

that is a half-formed premonition of the main theme of the Allegro

and the Symphony no. 102 presents the same effect of the melody taking shape out of the not quite fully formed material of the introduction.

---

[1] To these two introductions of Mozart, one should add the openings of the *Linz* Symphony, of the magnificent four-hand Sonata in F major (for *one* piano) K. 497, completely symphonic in style, and above all, the Quartet in C major K. 465.
[2] The introduction of the Symphony no. 104 has more clarity than most, but the melodic cells (and they are very small here) remain fragments.

Perhaps most remarkable in this respect are the Symphonies nos. 97. and 103. In the former the introduction both opens and closes with a simple but expressive cadence, which appears later as the cadence of the Allegro exposition itself, there written out in longer note-values so that the tempo is approximately the same as the opening Adagio. This way of recalling an introduction was vivid enough to inspire Beethoven to employ it in the E flat Trio for Piano and Strings op. 70 no. 2. In Symphony no. 103, the *Drum-Roll*, the rhythm of the opening phrase is completely uniform:

the very slow tempo makes it seem to have no rhythmic definition. The opening theme of the Vivace (cited above p. 336) is clearly but very freely drawn from it (as in the *Military* Symphony), but it also returns with its sequence of pitches intact, and a new and highly characteristic rhythm:

and further makes a startling reappearance at its original very slow tempo near the end of the movement.

When this slow, rhythmically almost shapeless, theme rises in the bass out of the long opening drum-roll (and if the new edition is surely unwise to accept the *fortissimo* attack suggested by the piano quintet arrangement of 1797, it is certain that the timpanist should make this a very long and effective roll), we have the impression of the gradual molding of form from indeterminate matter itself. The technique behind the writing of these slow introductions made it possible for Haydn to conceive the famous depiction of chaos in the *Creation*.

Harmonically these symphonic introductions have little directional force. The most frequent pattern is a simple one: a fixing of the tonic major, and a move to the minor so the major can begin again with the Allegro. There are a few which start, like Mozart's C major Quartet K. 465, directly with the minor mode. The extensive chromaticism that appears in almost all of them serves the same purpose as the minor mode: a disturbance of the sense of harmonic stability that, nevertheless, lies only on the surface of the fundamental harmonic structure. These introductions are, of course, delaying actions.

The significance of any work of late eighteenth-century music depends on the establishment of the tonic: to delay this process is essentially to widen the proportions and the range of possible action. The expansion is one not merely of the time-scale, but of the scale of dramatic and expressive significance as well, as the brusque introductions to the quartets of 1793 have shown.

The classical introduction also enlarged the thematic possibilities of the style, in two complementary ways. First, they enabled the composer to use as a principal theme of the following Allegro a melody too light to serve as the opening of the entire work. The *Drum-Roll* Symphony is one of Haydn's largest achievements, but the beginning of the Vivace would be too trivial by itself to initiate a work of such magnitude: it gains weight by being at once a contrast to the slow introduction and a clearly recognizable derivation from its material. In the same way, the massive introduction to Beethoven's Seventh Symphony frees the dance-like theme that opens the Vivace from the responsibility of establishing the dimensions of the whole movement. The introduction opened up a new range of themes that could otherwise have been used only in far more modest frameworks.

The second and perhaps more interesting expansion of the thematic possibilities is the radical change of significance of the first theme enforced by the preceding introduction. The opening theme of the Allegro becomes an answer to the resolved tension of the introduction. In Mozart's Symphony in E flat major K. 543, the melody of the Allegro literally extends the unfinished cadence of the Adagio:

as the violin moves to take up the line left suspended by the flute. The opening phrase is therefore an end as well as a beginning. Haydn made extensive use of this effect and never neglected its importance, but the most subtle example is probably in Beethoven. The two brusque chords with which the *Eroica* Symphony begins change the rhythmic sense of the theme that follows. If we play the theme alone, it begins on a bar which carries the strong accent of the pulse. The two opening bars of concise introduction shift the accent away from the first note of the theme and place it two bars further on, and so add a rhythmic impulse that moves forward with an energy the theme could not achieve by itself.

Once again, it was Beethoven who carried these possibilities to the outer limits beyond which the language itself would have had to change. How little the actual duration in measured time has to do with the range of expression is shown in the beautiful opening of his F sharp major Sonata op. 78:

One step beyond this lies the Romantic introduction, with a melody so well-rounded, so complete that it can be attached only with difficulty to the movement that follows (as in Schumann's F sharp minor Sonata or the famous opening section of Tchaikovsky's B flat minor Concerto). Beethoven stops just in time: his melody remains only a fragment. The immovable F♯ in the bass defines the tonic with the clarity of Haydn and denies real harmonic movement to the melodic line; the fermata in the fourth measure ensures the same feeling of expectancy as the introductions of the *London* Symphonies. For the hesitant phrasing and carefully undefined movement of Haydn's symphonic introductions, or the brusque, dramatic opening chords of Haydn's quartets, Beethoven substitutes a simple phrase that finishes on the tonic, but seems not to end. The fragmentary character is indispensable: the classical introduction is an 'open' effect in a system which demanded a closed form, and which exacted a price for each expansion of the language.

2

Piano Trio

Haydn's piano trios are a third great series of works to set beside the symphonies and the quartets, but they are the least known of the three groups for reasons which have nothing to do with their musical worth. They are not chamber music in the usual sense, but works for solo piano, solo violin, and accompanying cello. For the most part the cello serves only to double the piano's bass, although in a very few places it is briefly independent. Under Haydn's influence, the string quartet developed from a work for solo violin and accompanying instruments to one in which all instruments have independent importance (although the first violin remained dominant until the twentieth century, and still retains much of its former prestige). Haydn's failure to develop a similar independence for the cello in the piano trio, and to balance the roles of the piano and the violin is generally a heavy charge laid against these trios. They may be splendid pieces, but they are unprogressive, backward in style, and should have been written differently. Even Tovey, who admired them, rewrote one to give greater prominence to the cello. Part of the prejudice against the trios comes from a snobbish preference of many musicians (mostly amateur) for chamber music over other forms (opera, for example, is sometimes considered a particularly degrading form of art). Some of this snobbery is a reaction, a righteous and rightful one, against the mass public for its lack of interest in chamber music. (Logically, why should the public take an interest, when chamber music is by definition not public? It was never intended to be a success, as Monteux has said of Debussy's *Pelléas*.) Another cause for neglect is a purely practical one: if Haydn's trios are essentially solo piano works with added solo violin passages, then the proper place for them is at piano recitals, where the hiring of extra musicians is not economically attractive.

No doubt Haydn was working against history when he wrote these trios, but there is no reason to judge them any the worse for that. Almost all of them were written late in Haydn's life when he knew perfectly well what he was about. Before many of them were written, Mozart had already produced several piano trios in which greater independence is given to the cello, works which Haydn surely knew; but, with the exception of the great E major and B flat major Trios, all of Mozart's are thinner in style and less interesting than the best dozen or sixteen of Haydn's. The brilliance of Haydn's piano writing in these works is surprising to one who knows only the sonatas; there are even some wrist-breaking octave passages (those in the C major Trio H. 27 were certainly intended as *glissandi*). They are, in fact, along with the Mozart concertos the most brilliant piano works before Beethoven. Nor does virtuosity imply a loss of profundity: it has harmed these works no more than the Mozart concertos or the Beethoven sonatas. A string quartet written with an overdominating first violin part does, indeed, lose in musical value, but that is because of the nature of the medium, which in this case would entail a loss of contrapuntal richness and thematic significance in the other parts. No such corresponding loss is implied by the dominance of a piano—the only instrument, after all, capable of both complex polyphony and dynamic inflection.

The fact that these trios are essentially solo works makes possible their greatest quality, a feeling of improvisation almost unique in Haydn's work, and, indeed, rarely found in any of the three great classic composers. Haydn was a composer who needed the piano in order to write music; these trios seem to give us Haydn at work. They have a spontaneous quality that the composer rarely sought elsewhere; their inspiration seems relaxed and unforced, at times almost disorganized, when compared with the quartets and symphonies. The forms are also more relaxed: a great many of the trios have dance finales—minuets or German peasant dances—and some of the first movements are among Haydn's finest double-variation sets.

Piano trios in the eighteenth century were written for the best amateurs, although the gap between amateur and professional at that time appears to have been very small. They were not serious pieces, like quartets, written chiefly for connoisseurs, and a display of compositional virtuosity would have been out of place: a fugue, for example, was possible in a string quartet, but unthinkable in a piano trio. The performer's virtuosity, on the other hand, was very much in place. We should do wrong to despise the inspiration of virtuosity in late eighteenth-century composition. Without it we should not have Mozart's operas or piano concertos or even the finale of Haydn's *Lark* Quartet. In Beethoven's piano music, the virtuosity has become so integral an element of the style that it is impossible to detach it for analysis: it is taken for granted in every one of the great sonatas. However, the virtuosity demanded by Haydn's trios is of a special nature: if they are not chamber music in the sense of compositions for several instruments of more or less equal importance, they are chamber music in the most literal sense, that of not being public. To the extent that they are display pieces, they are for private display. The violin also takes part in the display, and is not used only as a doubling instrument like the cello. Even when a modern concert piano is used, the cello is still necessary in these pieces, although it plays few notes that the piano does not also play. I have found that cellists, when they are persuaded to play one of the trios, are surprised to discover their part a fascinating one, more interesting, in fact, than in the Mozart trios, where relative independence is bought at the price of a great many patches of silence.

If the trios needed any justification, it would be found in a consideration of the pianoforte of Haydn's day. The bass was thin and weak, the sustaining power was poor. The piano trio was the solution to all the mechanical difficulties, with the cello reinforcing the bass and the melodies that most needed singing power given to the violin. In this way, Haydn's fantasy was set free, and the performer, too, had the chance at virtuoso effects impossible for a piano alone; the orchestra did the same thing for Mozart in his concertos that the violin and cello did for Haydn.

The contemporary piano was incapable alone of the powerful effects that Haydn and Mozart needed for their most imaginative works. By the beginning of the nineteenth century, pianos were being built that were more adequate to the demands made by composers. For this reason, the most congenial instruments for many works are not the ones for which they were written but those that were built twenty years later in response to the music. The piano was still in an experimental stage at the end of the eighteenth century, and its development was stimulated by the music of the period, which demanded greater possibilities of dynamic inflection. Both Haydn and Mozart sought instruments of greater power and response, and with a few magnificent exceptions their works for piano alone tend to be more inhibited and less rich than the compositions for piano with accompanying instruments. The use of one or more stringed instruments released their imaginations through the combination of an instrument that could sustain and sing together with the contrapuntal resources of the piano.

Instrumental changes since the eighteenth century have made a problem out of the balance of sound in Haydn's piano trios, and, in fact, in all chamber music with piano. Violin necks (including, of course, even those of all the Stradivariuses and Guarneris) have been lengthened, making the strings tauter: the bows are used today with hairs considerably more tight as well. The sound is a good deal more brilliant, fatter, and more penetrating. A less selective use of vibrato has added to the contrast. The piano, in turn, has become louder, richer, even mushier in sound, and, above all, less wiry and metallic. This change makes nonsense out of all those passages in eighteenth-century music where the violin and the piano play the same melody in thirds, with the violin *below* the piano. Both the piano and the violin are now louder, but the piano is less piercing, the violin more. Violinists today have to make an effort of self-sacrifice to allow the piano to sing out softly; to do so is as much an exercise in virtue as in musicianship. The thinner sound of the violin in Haydn's day blended more easily with the metallic sonority of the contemporary piano and made it possible for each to accompany the other without strain.

All this applies to violin sonatas as well as to trios. It is sometimes claimed that Mozart and Beethoven did not fully understand the problem of balancing a piano and a violin, and that we can congratulate ourselves on the progress in composition since then. It is true that they did not grasp the nature of the future piano and violin as well as might be hoped, but they more than adequately understood the instruments of their own time. Changes in sonority, it should be added, call for a different phrasing, and it is impossible on modern instruments completely to achieve the kind of inflections and the dynamics these pieces call for. (But this does not imply that it is not, after all, better to play them on instruments of our own day than to turn a performance into an historical reconstruction.)

The use of the cello essentially to double the piano bass has been called a hangover from an earlier style; it comes, in short, from the *basso continuo*, and in this specific sense Haydn's trios may be called stylistically regressive. This is historically correct, but trivial: the doubling of keyboard basses by a cello does, indeed, come from an earlier period, but it would only be stylistic-ally reactionary if it were unnecessary. No one who had heard the sound of the cello doubling in the slow movement of Haydn's great E flat major Trio, the last one he wrote, would doubt the necessity; that magnificent line (quoted below, p. 364) spanning almost two octaves in two measures has its full poignancy only with the cello. The piano alone will not do—nor will the cello alone, as the piano is needed to tie the music together and give it a unified texture. Like Haydn's quartets this is music that rarely makes use of a contrast of instruments: or, rather, it makes use of the individual qualities of the different instruments without seeming to exploit them. The piano plays what suits it best, and the violin takes over what the piano cannot properly make effective—the long sustained melodies. Much of the time the two instruments double each other.

It is odd to have to defend some of the greatest music ever written. In any case, the Haydn trios are doomed. Only pianists will ever want to play them, and the modern piano recital is no place for them. The following pages are a brief guide written for the pleasure of music-lovers who will read the trios at their pianos, while imagining the violin and cello parts.

Haydn's imagination is particularly luxuriant in these trios. Unconstrained by considerations of public effect, as in the symphonies, or by impressive refinements of style as in the quartets, Haydn wrote them for the sheer pleasure of the solo instrumentalists. There are twenty-six such trios; the thirty-one usually published under his name include two by other composers (one by Michael Haydn, which Joseph Haydn evidently thought he had com-posed himself as he put it into a catalogue of his own works); and three for flute, piano, and cello, pleasant works of no great interest. (One of these, too, is probably by brother Michael.) Two trios are very early (before 1769), one before 1780, nine between 1784 and 1790, and fourteen masterpieces written between 1793 and 1796—six of them right after the first *London* symphonies, and eight after the second set. To say with Tovey that 'the works cover Haydn's whole career' is to obscure the concentration at the end of his life, twenty-three of the twenty-six being written after Haydn was fifty years old, fourteen of them after he was sixty. It would be best to speak of them largely as products of his latest and most mature style.

The first Trio in G minor H. 1, however, is already a lovely piece, with a first movement almost completely in the French Baroque style in harmony, melody, ornamentation and rhythm—in everything, in fact, except its more fully articulated phrasing. Of the nine written in the 1780s, three should be singled out as among Haydn's greatest achievements. The Trio in C minor H. 13 has a double-variation first movement, where the main theme in minor is transformed into major for the second theme with such glorious effect that Haydn hardly varies the third appearance of the version in major. It is one of the finest examples of Haydn's ability to create an emotion that was completely his own and that no other composer, not even Mozart, could duplicate—a feeling of ecstasy that is completely unsensual, almost amiable. There is no recipe for producing this effect, but it depends in part on a preference for melodies that reach their climax (not necessarily their highest note) on the upper tonic as in the Austrian national anthem, rather than on the sixth, ninth, or fourth as Mozart's most often do; and, above all, from the use of harmonies in root position under very expressive melodies and an avoidance of complex past-writing. How this harmonic effect is employed can be seen in the opening of the slow movement of another trio, H. 14, from the late 1780s:

A melody of such uncomplicated beauty, it could be used at a funeral to be absolutely certain of a few tears. Part of the direct intensity of the chromatic progression in the last four measures comes from the fact that every chord is in root position, while the inner parts are as simple as possible.

In the finale of this trio, the recapitulation is introduced by this extraordinary passage:

where Haydn disrupts the sense of tonality—only as a joke, of course—partly by the octave displacement, partly by the chromatic alteration. For a moment the B♮ sounds like nonsense, and only when the melody starts do we understand it. The last trio of the 1780s that cries out for special mention is the great E minor H. 12, where the first movement, one of Haydn's most dramatic, ends still in minor instead of turning to the major as he generally did by then. The slow movement is in fully developed sonata style, and the finale is a brilliant symphonic rondo, full of surprises.

The trios of the 1790s fall into four triads (each dedicated to a different lady) with two separate trios at the end. The two sets of 1793 are dedicated to the Esterházy princesses. The three for Princess Nicholas Esterházy (for whom Haydn had already written three sonatas), are powerful, imaginative works (H. 21–23), the one in D minor having the most brilliant finale full of rhythmic ingenuity (including a passage in the recapitulation where Haydn goes into 4/4 without changing the 3/4 time signature), and the one in E flat the most imposing first movement. The opening measures of the latter are immediately transformed in a way that is worth quoting not only for its own sake, but also because it shows what Haydn could do more easily in the piano trio than in any other form. The first four measures:

become

This feeling of spacious, relaxed, almost improvised expansion is almost never found in the symphonies, and rarely in the quartets. This is why the tempo mark for the majority of opening sonata movements in the trios is Allegro moderato, occurring almost twice as often as Allegro. Not only is the organization looser than that of the quartets, but also the effects are broader, with a brilliance and a massiveness that the sonatas for piano solo never reach and only approach in the early C minor H. 20 of 1770 and the two very late ones in E flat major.

The three works for the wife of the elder Prince, Princess Anton Esterházy, are even more interesting than those dedicated to her daughter-in-law. The Trio in B flat major H. 20 follows a first movement in brilliant virtuoso style with a set of variations in which the theme is played by the piano as a solo for the left hand alone, an example of the bare two-part counterpoint beloved by Haydn. The unusual first movement of H. 19 in G minor is discussed above (pp. 83–7). The finale of the A major Trio H. 18 shows Haydn's rondo form at its most original: it is a dance movement which begins with a two-part theme, both parts repeated, with the light air which generally implies the old-fashioned *ABA* form. What succeeds, however, is in the dominant, a second group of a sonata using (as Haydn mostly does) material based on the opening theme. A development does not follow, but rather a reprise of the opening in the tonic, giving us what appears to be an *ABA* form, after all—except that this, too, is followed by a recapitulation of the second group in the tonic, with large interpolations of development. To call this last part a coda would be a misnomer: it does not sound like a coda, but like a recapitulation and development combined, satisfying all our instincts for adventure and for resolution. Nothing shows better the fluidity of forms of the period: it has affinities with the sonata rondo, and if there were a few more examples we should have a name for it. It is a comic, high-spirited piece, full of syncopations.

Almost three years later, after his second and last visit to London, Haydn wrote two more sets of three Trios. One set was dedicated to Theresa Jansen, the wife of the engraver Bartolozzi; at about the same time, he wrote for her his last three piano sonatas. These Trios H. 27–29 are the most difficult Haydn ever wrote, and are a formidable musical and intellectual achievement. Mrs. Bartolozzi must have been a more than ordinary pianist: the C major Trio in particular is a compliment to her technique. The first movement, at once brilliant and leisurely, has a profusion of motifs unusual for Haydn, and a wealth of rhythmic contrast that would have made a work of the 1770s fall to pieces. The faster rhythms are gradually introduced one by one with the ease of apparent improvisation (real improvisation is much more lumpy), and the movement never loses its flow except for a dramatic silence in the contrapuntal development. The slow movements of these trios are all surprising: here, after a lyric opening section that is at once ingenuous and intricate, the minor section starts as a shock with a *forte* in the middle of a measure and continues with a dramatic power that is close to brutality. The finale, Presto, is a symphonic rondo, possibly the most humorous piece that Haydn wrote. Everything about the movement is unexpected: the opening theme is an enchanting joke, with the harmony changing to make accents on off-beats, an angular melody that appears at times in the wrong register, and a scherzando rhythm that allows the melody to start when one is least ready for it. The style of writing for the piano in this movement is, at times, close to the Beethoven of op. 31 no. 1.

The E major Trio is even more extraordinary, in some ways the strangest of all Haydn's late works. In part, many of the eccentricities of the compositions of this period may be considered a return to an earlier style, and affinities with the mannerist qualities of 1750 to 1775 can be found above all in the late trios. In this sense they could be said to be reactionary works if it were not for the transformation that the mannerism undergoes here. The control of the classical style is everywhere apparent: not for a moment does the large rhythmic movement fall to pieces or develop the effect of nervous indecision that occurs at least once in any work of Haydn's before 1775. It is true that Haydn does not often try for the impression of perfect regularity that Mozart preferred: Haydn's irregularity is more overt; dramatic silence and the fermata play a greater role in his music than in Mozart's, even including the operas. But in Haydn's later works, the silence is in every case a preparation for something crucial. The E major Trio, for example, has a close relationship with an earlier E major Piano Sonata H. 31 written probably in 1776; there are resemblances between all three movements of each work, particularly the two second movements. The first movement of the sonata comes to rest for a full measure in the development: the effect is one of exhaustion, and it starts up again only to resume its previous motion. There is a parallel moment in the development section of the trio where the music dies away: what follows is electrifying—the main theme, played *forte* for the first and only time, in the remote key of A flat major, in full rich harmony, and *arco* instead of pizzicato as it is elsewhere. This is, in fact, the climax of the whole movement: everything before leads up to it, everything afterwards resolves it. Pianistically this is one of Haydn's most imaginative works: the opening theme is scored for piano in such a way that it, too, sounds as if it were playing everything pizzicato except the sustained melody notes, even without the pizzicato accompaniment of the two stringed instruments.

The sonority of the second movement, an Allegretto in E minor, is peculiar to Haydn, written for the most part in a bare, harsh two-part counterpoint with the voices often three to four octaves apart. The relationship of the classical style to the preceding Baroque and to the Romantic that was to come is posed by this piece; one of the most startling creations of Haydn, it is a passacaglia like no other. It is Baroque in formal character, in the unchanging, relentless rhythm of the bass maintained until the final cadence, in its 'terraced' dynamics, in its superimposition of one rhythm on another with each remaining absolutely distinct, and in its use of a sequential pattern as a generating force within the main theme itself and not only in its development. The music is classical, however, in its firmly established movement to the relative major, articulated by the introduction of new melodic material, and in its wealth of dynamic accents serving to vary the pulse. Finally, it is Romantic in its tension, keyed to a steadily higher pitch than most eighteenth-century works could bear, in its dynamics which give the impression not only of a step-by-step ascent but of continuous *crescendo*, and, above all, in the fact that the final cadence after a fermata serves, not to resolve the excitement as a Baroque ending generally does, but to increase it through a series of brusque but elaborate flourishes that offer a resolution only with the violent final chord. To the extent that Romantic style meant the reintroduction of Baroque procedures and textures modified by a classical sense of climax, the movement may be said to be already Romantic. This work is a warning against too unified and dogmatic a view of style, and reminds us how elements may remain dormant ready to reappear at any moment as an artist goes back to the day before yesterday to find something newer and more progressive.

In the third and last trio for Mrs. Jansen, in E flat major, the opening movement shows what a personal turn Haydn gave at the end of his life to a simple *ABA* form. *B* is a dramatic development in the minor of *A*'s thematic material. The second appearance of *A* becomes a variation, and there is a further dramatization of the material in a lengthy coda. In this way the decorative form of the variation is given a dramatic framework more in keeping with the whole tendency of Haydn's style. The slow movement (*innocentamente*) is a slow-moving modulation from B major to E flat major by means of a plain two-part melody, another way of dramatizing a less complex form: here a simplicity of melody and a dramatic form combine to produce a sweetness rare in Haydn (or in any music, indeed). The last movement, Allemande Presto assai, is a German dance in rustic style with a grossly comic evocation of a village band; it is a difficult virtuoso piece for the piano as well as a form of low comedy for which the trio, more intimate than the symphony and less highfalutin than the string quartet, is particularly suited.

The three trios for Rebecca Schroeter are musically as distinguished but technically less demanding. She was a young widow in London who copied Haydn's music for him, and whose letters to Haydn express an affection which the sixty-year-old composer apparently returned. The Trio in G major H. 25 ends with the famous *Rondo all'Ongarese*, a real work of love for a pianist—brilliant, exciting, and sounding harder to play than it really is.

The Trios in D major H. 24 and F sharp minor H. 26 are both lyric works. The latter is the more exceptional, and not only in its somber tone which it keeps to the end. The full form of one of the closing themes in the exposition is not heard (or exposed) until the recapitulation, where it is also played much nearer the opening material. The development is short, but its harmonic range is unusually wide. The other movements intensify the seriousness of the first. The slow movement derives from that of Symphony no. 102 (unless the trio is the original). Without Haydn's varied orchestral sonority, the melody seems more personal and unrolls like an improvisation:

The skeleton is very simple, with the melody defining an ornamental and expressive arabesque and a descent down the notes of the scale from D♯ back to the tonic note. Yet it not only sounds eccentric but appears to accelerate. The acceleration is real: the first beat of the second measure plays the arabesque twice as fast. The irregularity is part of the acceleration: the high note of each measure is successively closer to the first beat, and the arabesque occurs twice in the third measure, where the movement is slowed by making the last appearance almost a written-out *ritenuto*. Even with a melody of such personal emotion, there are all the signs of a controlled energy. The minuet-finale has the same intimate gravity, and it has, too, the dramatic power of the minuet from Mozart's G minor Symphony without departing so far from the character of the dance. It is this movement better than any other, perhaps, that shows the superiority of the piano trio to the solo sonata for Haydn: of all the dance movements with which so many of the sonatas end, none even tries to attain the power and the depth of feeling of this work. What Haydn has done is to dramatize the minuet (that is, make it more like a sonata) while never losing the elegance of its rhythm. The trio, like the piano sonata, was for

Haydn a form light enough for the dance-finale to be possible as it was not for the symphony and only rarely for the quartet: with the finale of the F sharp minor Trio, the genre is transformed by a melancholy so intense it is indistinguishable from the tragic.

After these four great sets, Haydn wrote only two individual trios. One in E flat minor in two movements H. 31 is the only piece of Haydn's I can think of in that key. The first movement is a deeply expressive slow rondo-variation-set; the second theme, in the major, begins as an inversion of the first, and a third is surprisingly added—a long high soaring melody for the violin, one of Haydn's finest solos. The finale is Allegro ben moderato, a German dance in elaborate and sophisticated style, where the accompaniment is so important it becomes a counter-theme. The whole movement appears to be built out of fragments, almost without melody of any kind, yet the continuity and the lilt of the dance are always there. This is the kind of work that can only come at the end of a long career. The return of the main section is fantastically varied—the original form of the following five measures:

is changed into:

In this difficult movement, the violin collaborates on an equal, if less brilliant, footing, although the cello still remains principally a reinforcing instrument.

The last Trio in E flat major H. 30 is a work on a larger scale. One of the most massive of all Haydn's movements, its opening Allegro moderato is expansive, almost leisurely, and has a Mozartean wealth of themes. The succession of melodies comes in a continuous flow with little development in the exposition proper, which is unified, however, by passing allusions to the opening measures; the melodies grow one from the other, each continuing an aspect of the previous one, and their interdependence is such that they seem to well from one source in a fusion of power, lyricism, and logic. The slow movement alone would make this the most unjustly neglected masterpiece in all of Haydn's works. The opening bass line immediately brings forward a deeply expressive wide chromatic space:

and continues in a way that anticipates passages of *Tristan*:

and

The return of the opening melody is combined in decorated form with the rhythmic pattern of a middle section, at once a trio which does service both as the central part of a large ternary form (or *B* of an *ABA* form) and as an extension of the opening section. Haydn then makes the return into a sonata recapitulation by resolving in the tonic a theme of the middle section that had appeared in the dominant. As grand and as complete as the form of this movement feels, it does not actually end, but after a surprise cadence modulates mysteriously to prepare for the last movement. This is another German dance, Presto, Beethoven-like in its boisterous humor and in the dramatic development that acts as a bridge between the middle section in minor and the return of the opening. The coda is brilliant and difficult. In this last work, Haydn's achievement in the field of the piano trio is resumed: accepting the virtuosity of a light and informal genre, and without greatly altering its character, he made it the vehicle of some of his most imaginative and inspired conceptions.

3

Church Music

The classical style is at its most problematic in religious music. This was a genre beset with difficulties that could not trouble the secular field. Each composer met with a special and different kind of ill luck. Mozart's two greatest religious works remained only half-finished: the C minor Mass of 1783, K. 427, and the Requiem that he was working on when he died. Joseph Haydn's masses were already under attack for their unsuitable character during the composer's lifetime. He himself thought his brother Michael's church music superior to his own. Beethoven's first Mass in C major was responsible for his most humiliating public failure, the contemptuous reception given it by the Prince Esterházy for whom it was written. His *Missa Solemnis* in D major can still seem a difficult work today. As for the oratorio, *The Mount of Olives*, it is unique in Beethoven's entire output for its total lack of interest: it almost never rises above the merely competent, or falls below it.

The hostility of the Catholic Church to instrumental music throughout the eighteenth century was a factor in these difficulties. The use of instruments in church was even restricted by order of the Austrian government during the 1780s, a time of great creative activity for both Haydn and Mozart. In most periods the Church has not encouraged stylistic innovation: it disliked the heavily chromatic music of many Renaissance composers just as it refused to accept the centralized church preferred by most Renaissance architects. There are many works even of Palestrina that would not pass the church's test for orthodoxy in music style. A conservative taste is not illogical in an institution that relies so fundamentally on continuity of tradition. Nevertheless, the dislike of instrumental music is more deeply motivated: vocal music has always been considered more apt for a religious service, and the reputation for purity that is attached to *a capella* writing has symbolic value. At least with purely vocal music the words of the service make their presence felt. The classical style, however, was in all essentials an instrumental one.

In addition, there was an important conflict of musical ideology. Was the music there to glorify the mass or to illustrate its words? Is the function of music expressive or celebrative? Art has other uses but they were only obscurely formulated in the eighteenth century. Since the Renaissance the concept of music as an expressive art has dominated, and this was the principal source of much of the discomfort. The problems were, naturally, greater within a Catholic context: the Protestant sense of religion as personal and even individual expression made a happier partner with eighteenth-century aesthetics.

An uneasy relation between art and religion is not confined to the eighteenth century. In music, the contradiction is felt at its most acute in the opening and closing sections of the mass: if music is essentially celebrative, these sections should be brilliant and imposing; if expressive, then quiet and pleading in character. The celebrative tradition is the older one, but while it remained a powerful force in practice, it had long ceased to influence aesthetic theory by the 1700s; the eighteenth century is filled with complaints of unnaturally brilliant and inaptly jolly settings of the *Kyrie* and the *Agnus Dei*. If music is to express the sentiment implied by the words 'Kyrie eleison' ('Lord have mercy upon us'), most of the masses of the century would have to be judged as defective by this standard. Composers were largely obstinate in their refusal to yield to the expressive aesthetic, and Bach stands out in his achievement of a *Kyrie* at once grandiose and supplicatory.

Things were not improved after 1770 by a style firmly rooted in the rhythmic techniques of Italian comic opera. This produced settings of the mass which appear strikingly irrelevant to the text—not only to us today but to contemporaries as well and even, it appears, to the composers themselves. Some of the coloratura passages of a Mozart mass are as intrinsically absurd as the nineteenth-century adaptations of Donizetti arias to Latin texts— although the absurdity only shows its head if a demand for relevance is made, a demand which was itself irrelevant if the music was there only to glorify and to decorate. Nevertheless, given the nature of classical texture and rhythm, it was more difficult than in the early part of the century to encompass an imposing and lengthy opening movement of an emotional neutrality—avoiding the twin traps of the amiable gaiety or, more rarely, the dramatic ferocity of the classical Allegro. Not until the *Creation* of Haydn does classical rhythm have enough weight for a long slow opening movement that pretends to more than introductory status. The style of the High Baroque, with a heavy contrapuntal texture and the almost indefinitely extensible phrase, can provide some of this weight. One avenue open to the classical composer of religious music is, therefore, archaism. An imitation of High Baroque style, a moribund but not buried tradition by the 1780s, had the advantage that a reference to the past always has in religion: using the contrapuntal style was like continuing to address God as 'Thou,' and brought by itself a satisfaction that a more modern style could never have provided.

Mozart was the greatest of parodists. His works in Baroque style are not, it is true, quite perfect as period-style: Lowinsky has pointed out a squareness and clarity of phrasing in the fugues that is most un-Baroque in spirit. It is difficult, as well, to imagine Bach agreeing with Mozart's dictum that fugues must be played slowly so that the entrances of the theme are always heard: many of the entrances of Bach's fugues are securely hidden, tied to the previous notes, and the listener can only be gradually and belatedly aware of the theme. Nevertheless, Mozart's mastery of the older style is unquestionable. It would take a sharp ear and a considerable amount of hindsight to distinguish stylistically between the great double fugue in the *Requiem* and one of Handel's, and if some of the chromaticism is not Handelian, it was not beyond the reach of Bach. Mozart's knowledge of both composers and of Hasse was profound if not extensive: he certainly knew *Israel in Egypt* and the *Messiah*, and he studied the *Art of Fugue* and the *Well-Tempered Keyboard*. The 'Qui tollis' of the unfinished Mass in C minor comes almost directly from *Israel in Egypt*, but with a more personal use of both chromaticism and syncopation. The opening *Kyrie* of this mass, unrelievedly Baroque in its harmonic sequences and its homogeneous rhythmic texture, has an austerity of feeling that contrasts surprisingly with the beautiful Rococo decoration of the solo soprano 'Christe,' which is its middle section.

These successes of parody are personal victories, triumphs of virtuosity: they do not belong to the history of style, except as the *Requiem* influenced the revival of Baroque technique that became so important after the death of Beethoven. To some extent Mozart preserved what life still remained in the heritage of Bach and Handel until it became so important to Chopin and Schumann. But most of his church music remains perfunctory, less profound and even less carefully written than the great secular works. The arias in the masses, fine as some few of them are, are almost indistinguishable from their operatic counterparts except by their slightly more sedate motion, and not even that decorum was always considered. Only in the Masonic works, transfigured in *Die Zauberflöte*, does an original spirit become apparent. One other exception is the ensemble for solo voices (the greatest example being the 'Quoniam' from the C minor Mass), where Mozart combines a continuously rich and expressive contrapuntal motion with a sweetness of line and a large-scale pacing that he derived directly from his operatic experience. On the other hand, Mozart's use of the chorus differs from Handel's only in being less imaginative. Nevertheless, the most impressive part of Mozart's achievement in the composition of religious music remains a deliberate exercise in an old-fashioned style.

Haydn had little of Mozart's talent for mimicry, and his music, although influenced by Handel, remained almost unmarked by that of Johann Sebastian Bach. Haydn could write an old-fashioned fugue, but it always retained much of the modern instrumental style. The discomfort that his religious style caused his contemporaries was ruefully acknowledged by Haydn with the magnificently disingenuous remark that whenever he thought about God it made him feel cheerful. Disingenuous but surely true: Haydn's religious faith was, from all evidence, simple, direct, and popular in character. I emphasize this only because of the naïve notion that stylistic development is directly related to the strength and sincerity of the artist's beliefs. Haydn's comparative failure as a composer of liturgical music cannot be related to his own faith, and only very indirectly and tenuously to the general tenor of eighteenth-century religious development. In addition, it cannot be set down to lack of interest, as Haydn's concentration on church music was considerable at the end of his life: after the *London* Symphonies he virtually abandoned pure instrumental music except for the string quartet, and the principal works of his old age are six masses and two oratorios.

The masses are, of course, full of admirable details and contain much writing of great power. They remain, however, uncomfortable compromises. The *Kyrie* of the *Mass in Time of War* opens with an expressive Largo introduction, but the Allegro moderato that follows has passages that can only have sounded as trivial to Haydn's contemporaries as they do to us today:

Haydn's symphonic style transfigures scraps like these: in ecclesiastical music, however, he cannot do without them, but he does not dare to do much with them.

Parts of the text of the mass are handled very easily within the classical style. The opening section of the *Gloria* can be accommodated by a symphonic Allegro of normal character. The more dramatic sections also present no problems, and there are passages in Haydn's masses, particularly the magnificent *Kyrie* of the *Windband* Mass and the 'Crucifixus' of the *Theresa* Mass, which are among the most affecting that Haydn ever wrote. Yet even at such places the incoherence of the late eighteenth-century's tradition of religious music and the lack of a stable and acceptable framework for liturgical settings can lead to effects of peculiar irrelevancy: the long sentimental cello solo of the *Mass in Time of War* has great sweetness, but to be accepted as an adequate setting of *Qui tollis peccata mundi* it requires more tolerance than the most emotional religiosity of eighteenth-century painting, which had at least a coherent symbolic organization and a visual harmony with the architecture that surrounded it.

The most immediate weakness of Haydn's religious style appears naturally enough in the settings of the Athanasian Creed. A naïve aesthetics of expression was of little help in facing a text of pure doctrine except in its single moments of narrative drama: the Incarnation, Crucifixion, and Resurrection. These represented opportunities that every composer seized, but how was the rest to be turned into music? Expressive relevance could be abandoned, as it so often was, but even then decorum prevented a style that relied so heavily on irony and wit from creating works of much character. As a result, when Haydn and Mozart are not attempting the grandeur of the Handelian style as a stop-gap, their religious music, while never falling below the competent, is graceful (in Mozart's case often enough) or brilliant, but rarely compelling or, indeed, interesting. The setting of the first part of the *Credo* in the *Theresa* Mass of Haydn, for example, has vigor and some power, but one would have to look far in Haydn's music to find another rhythmic structure equally turgid and unimaginative.

Haydn's escape was through his beloved pastoral. In neither the *Creation* nor the *Seasons* is the high level of writing always as successfully and as continuously sustained as in the great symphonies and quartets (although the less admired *Seasons* seems to me more successful in this respect), but they are among the greatest works of the century, and music of specifically religious character settles with ease in a framework that allows it to escape from liturgical constraints. Above all, the pastoral tradition provided unequivocal solutions to the problem of setting a text which the late eighteenth-century religious style, corrupted by logical contradictions, was no longer capable of giving. In particular, the pastoral accommodated itself without misgivings to the shape of the 'sonata,' which it had, after all, helped to create.

The famous depiction of chaos at the opening of the *Creation* is in 'slow-movement sonata form,': nothing could show better how, for Haydn, the 'sonata' is not a form at all, but an integral part of the musical language, and even a necessary minimum for any large statement that can be made within that language. The themes are here reduced to very small fragments, as are the musical paragraphs, but the proportions of a sonata movement without an isolated development section but with articulated exposition and symmetrical recapitulation (both with two regular groups of themes) is as present as ever in Haydn's slow movements. The opening theme:

is as much dynamic marking as a series of pitches, and it is later enriched by a staccato arpeggio as the movement becomes more complex. The second theme, in the relative major:

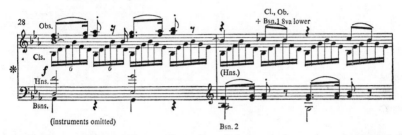

(actually an inversion of an earlier phrase) has an even more characteristic outline. The beginning of the recapitulation could not be more easily identifiable:

and the most unusual formal device is only that the second theme is recapitulated and resolved at the tonic with the first theme in counterpoint:

where the clarinet's ascending motif is a decorative form of the opening notes in the first violins quoted above.

By what, then, is chaos represented, and how can Haydn's musical language express this and still remain language? Simply by the absence of clear articulation in the large phrase-groups, which merge and blend with each other, and by the withholding of clear and definite cadences. The progression to the relative major is at first as clear as in any sonata movement in a minor tonality, but there is a sudden evasion to a surprisingly remote VIIb:

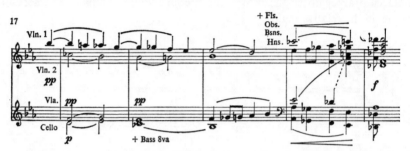

and the return to the more normal E flat major, while effected almost immediately, is never granted an ending in root position:

so that the second theme begins without the firmness of the usual cadence. The extremely slow tempo, the syncopated string chords and the irregular phrase-lengths do the rest; in spite of the breadth of feeling, the facture is concentrated on movement in the miniature, and everything depends on detail.

With the two oratorio texts, the pastoral tradition at last allowed Haydn a structure which enabled him to sum up his technique and his life's work: they were to him what the *Art of Fugue* was to Bach, and the *Diabelli* Variations to Beethoven. The *Seasons* and the *Creation* are descriptions of the entire universe as Haydn knew it. The imposed simplicity of the pastoral style was the condition which made it possible to grasp subjects of such immensity: without the pretense of naïveté in the deepest sense of the spontaneous and unaffected response of the child's eye to the world, these works could not exist at all. The subject of pastoral is not Nature itself, but man's relation to nature and to what is 'natural': this is the reason for the extreme stylization of Haydn's descriptive writing in the oratorios. He did not like the purely programmatic parts of his texts, and called them 'French trash,' but they were an essential part of the tradition, which had, indeed, become largely French during the eighteenth century.

The greatness of the two oratorios lies in their range of expression, and for once Haydn equalled Mozart's breadth if not his control. The *Seasons* makes an unabashed appeal for popular favor; as early as the fourth number, Haydn shrewdly quotes the tune from the *Surprise* Symphony that had become so popular. But this is not the only allusion to Haydn's previous works[1]: the *Seasons* contains references to Haydn's music from years back. When he finished it, he was written out. The last years of Haydn's life, with all his success, comfort, and celebrity, are among the saddest in music. More moving than the false pathos of a pauper's grave for Mozart (who was only buried there because Baron Van Swieten advised the economy to Constanza) is the figure of Haydn filled with musical ideas which were struggling to escape, as he himself said; he was too old and weak to go to the piano and submit to the discipline of working them out.

It was left to Beethoven to reconcile the liturgical tradition with the classical style, and paradoxically by evading the problem altogether; both his masses are frankly concert pieces, and more effective outside than inside a church. Yet the evasion is compensated by an evocation of ecclesiastical atmosphere attempted in no work of Haydn or Mozart. The care taken to that end is heard at once in the opening measures of the C major Mass op. 86 of 1807:

[1] The closeness of 'Sei nun gnädig' (no. 6) to the slow movement of Symphony no. 98 is almost as candid as the quotation from the *Surprise*.

The first two notes are for the basses of the chorus alone without orchestral accompaniment, a deliberate and brief allusion to the ancient *a capella* style which becomes even more marked a few pages later:

The sixteenth-century Italian liturgical style, theoretically *a capella* if not practically so, had never died out: Palestrina was still performed, if seldom. Michael Haydn already made heavy use of the style. In writing his masses, Beethoven made a deliberate study of the older forms of religious music, and with many of his contemporaries he believed that they were more suitable for religious texts than the more modern style. His assimilation of the older style never takes the form of pastiche, still less that of quotation, even in the famous 'Et incarnatus est' of the D major Mass. There are also more than a few Handelian references in the C major Mass, but in general the texture is as symphonic and as personal as ever. The *Kyrie* of the C major Mass integrates its references to the older contrapuntal style within a sonata form with a short development section, and, like the *Waldstein* Sonata, uses the mediant E major as a dominant.

This opening solves the problem of pacing as if it had never existed, but nevertheless Beethoven was more than usually preoccupied with the tempo-mark; the manuscript has no tempo indication and a later copy has *Andante con moto*, but when Beethoven came to publish the work, it had become *Andante con moto assai vivace quasi allegretto ma non troppo*, where concern has become almost comic. Nevertheless, as the magnificent breadth and steady, unfolding line of the opening measures rises to a *forte* in the ninth measure, the conciliation of the contradictory stylistic forces in the setting of the mass is accomplished for the first time in European music since Bach.

The *Missa Solemnis* in D is perhaps Beethoven's most considerable single achievement. With it he developed a manner so intellectually powerful as to be completely adequate even for the purely doctrinal sections of the mass. The Mass in D provides a musical equivalent for almost every word of the Creed: the music is no longer just a framework, a setting, against which the words are to be understood. Not even the greatest difficulties are shirked. The magnificent and seemingly endless series of crossing scales at the end of the *Credo*, which seem to go ever higher and lower like a Jacob's ladder as the complexity of sound hides the new beginnings, must be accepted as Beethoven's audible image of eternity, and they are the equivalent of the words, 'I believe in the life to come, world without end, amen.'

The two masses of Beethoven present each of the five great parts of the Mass as almost completely unified movements, in place of the undisguisedly sectional treatment of earlier composers. In this respect the *Gloria* of the D major Mass is perhaps most remarkable by its use of a recurrent texture to organize the form, and by the reappearance of the opening words, now Presto, at the end. Even the relations between the large sections are closely knit: the *Credo* opens with a brilliant and rapid modulation to the new key, a modulation which becomes itself a thematic element. The unification of each of the separate parts of the Mass derives from Beethoven's tendency, at the end of his life, to combine a four-movement work within the frame of a first-movement sonata. Basically, however, he relies on the technique of Mozart's operatic finales both for the unity and the sense of pace, and the greatest achievements of the classical style in liturgical music are related as closely as ever to the *opera buffa* which helped to shape the style.

Part VII

BEETHOVEN

———

Beethoven

In 1822, five years before his death, Beethoven felt himself almost completely isolated from the musical life in Vienna. 'You will hear nothing of me here,' he said to a visitor from Leipzig. 'What should you hear? *Fidelio?* They cannot give it, nor do they want to listen to it. The symphonies? They have no time for them. My concertos? Everyone grinds out only the stuff he himself has made. The solo pieces? They went out of fashion long ago, and here fashion is everything. At most Schuppanzigh occasionally digs up a quartet.'[1] The ageing artist, unappreciated and half-forgotten, is a familiar figure, and the neglect is as often imagined as real, yet Beethoven's visitor, the editor of Leipzig's musical journal, if he felt that Beethoven exaggerated, did not remain unconvinced. At the end of his life, Beethoven was most decidedly out of fashion.

That he was, at the same time, universally accepted as the greatest living composer, did not in any way alter his increasing isolation. Not only musical fashion but musical history had turned away from Beethoven. In the music of his younger contemporaries (with the exception of Schubert) and of the generation that followed his death, his work, while admired and loved, is hardly a vital force; not until Brahms and the later operas of Wagner will it play a significant role. The prestige of his music blinds us to this fact, in the same way, indeed, that it blinded the musicians of the first half of the nineteenth century. Only *An die ferne Geliebte*, a sport among his forms, played an important part in the musical development of the 1830s and 40s. The rest of his achievement was not an inspiration but a dead weight in the style of those who immediately followed him.

The prestige, however, was immense. Perhaps only Chopin, coming from a provincial musical culture, succeeded in being completely free from its spell.[2] For the other composers, Beethoven's achievement provoked an emulation which led, and could have led, only to disaster. Both Mendelssohn and Brahms imitated the *Hammerklavier* with singularly awkward results. The sonatas and symphonies of Schumann are constantly embarrassed by the example of Beethoven: their splendor breaks through his influence, but never starts from it. All that is most interesting in the next generation is a reaction against Beethoven, or an attempt to ignore him, a turning away into new directions: all that is weakest submits to his power and pays him the emptiest and most sincere of homages.

---

[1] Thayer, vol. II, p. 801.
[2] It is not astonishing to find the most Philistine of all comments on Beethoven's music on Chopin's lips. In Delacroix' Diary, he is reported as saying, 'Beethoven turned his back on eternal principles.'

Beethoven

The antagonism between generations, and the swing of fashion between one generation and the next are well-known phenomena in the history of styles. Too much weight is sometimes placed on them. The changes effected by reaction alone are rarely profound. With all Beethoven's declared independence from preceding influences, and his evident resentment of Haydn, there was in his career no radical movement away from the style of Mozart and Haydn comparable to the break with the past made by the generation of Schumann and Chopin. As for Mozart and Haydn, the antagonism between succeeding generations hardly existed even on a personal level. The changes of fashion between generations are really only pretexts, at worst, and, at best, reinforcements in the strategy of revolutionaries. Beethoven transformed the musical tradition he was born into, but he never challenged its validity. If he resented Haydn's patronage and even his help and support, he never abandoned Haydn's forms and the greater part of his technique, nor, musically, did he ever express anything but veneration for Mozart even when he condemned the frivolous moral outlook of the opera libretti.

In fact, with age, Beethoven drew closer to the forms and proportions of Haydn and Mozart. In his youthful works, the imitation of his two great precursors is largely exterior: in technique and even in spirit, he is at the beginning of his career often closer to Hummel, Weber, and to the later works of Clementi than to Haydn and Mozart.[1] The first movement of the Piano Sonata, op. 2 no. 3, has a rigid sectional structure and, above all, a wealth of connecting material that is never found in the opening movement of a work of Haydn or Mozart, with the exception of the latter's *Coronation* Concerto. The equilibrium between harmonic and thematic development so characteristic of Haydn and Mozart is often lost in early Beethoven, where thematic contrast and transformation seem to outweigh all other interests. Beethoven, indeed, started as a true member of his generation, writing now in a proto-Romantic style and now in a late and somewhat attenuated version of the classical style, with an insistence on the kind of broad, square melodic structure that was to find its true justification later in the Romantic period of the 1830s. The early song *Adelaïde* is as much Italian Romantic opera as anything else: its long, winding melody, symmetrical and passionate, its colorful modulations and aggressively simple accompaniment could come easily from an early work of Bellini. Many of the slow movements of the early sonatas, too, foreshadow the easy-going, sprawling long-range rhythmic sense of Weber's piano music and of much of Schubert. (Later both Schubert and Weber were to start by disapproving of what they considered Beethoven's wilful eccentricity, and Weber became for a time one of his most vicious

---

[1] The earliest of his works (the sonatas published when he was only thirteen, in 1783) start clearly from Haydn's work of the late sixties: we tend to forget that Beethoven's early musical education antedated any knowledge (in Bonn, at least) of the works of Haydn and Mozart in the fully developed classical style—the works by which they are best known. Bonn was less advanced than Vienna.

critics. Schubert made amends by a respect that amounted almost to idolatry, and by a consistent use of Beethoven's forms as models.) The Septet, the work that became so embarrassingly popular that Beethoven in later years winced when it was mentioned, and the Quintet for Piano and Winds may be called 'classicizing' rather than 'classic' in style, like the works of Hummel: they are reproductions of classical forms—Mozart's in particular—based upon the exterior models, the results of the classical impulse, and not upon the impulse itself. 'Classicizing' works have a beauty that is often unappreciated: these early pieces of Beethoven have an easy freshness and serenity that redeem their awkward lack of unity. His technical mastery of the 'reproductive' style has often been underestimated; as a young man he was already the greatest of its practitioners. In his A major Quartet op. 18 no. 5, modeled faithfully on Mozart's quartet in the same key, he produces a fine and yet original example of one of Mozart's most refined effects, difficult to achieve in a manner that is neither tasteless nor perfunctory: the phrase that can turn either to the tonic or the dominant depending upon what has preceded it. It cannot have been easy for Beethoven to abandon such facility for a more experimental approach. Only gradually did he return to more definitely classical conceptions: but with the *Appassionata* he set himself firmly against the squarely organized and yet loose and apparently improvisatory structures of late classicism and early Romanticism, and returned decisively to the closed, concise, and dramatic forms of Haydn and Mozart, expanding these forms and heightening their power without betraying their proportions.

The question of Beethoven's position as a 'classical' or 'Romantic' composer is generally ill-defined, additionally complicated by the fact that Haydn and Mozart in the early nineteenth century were called 'Romantic' composers as often as anything else. It is not a question that would have had any meaning during Beethoven's own lifetime, and it is difficult to give it a precise significance today. Nor is it a helpful tautology that a man belongs to his own time: historical time in this sense is not bounded by dates. Every period of time is traversed by forces both reactionary and progressive: Beethoven's music is filled with memories and predictions. Instead of affixing a label, it would be better to consider in what context and against what background Beethoven may be most richly understood.

To begin with what may appear the larger issues—the spiritual content, the emotional ambiance of the music—would be to lame discussion from the start. It would be to risk confounding personal expression with general stylistic changes, and inevitably to muddle the different significance of similar expressive devices within disparate systems. That Haydn and Beethoven, or Schumann and Beethoven, used the same details or worked within forms that resemble each other, implies no sort of musical kinship if the details have entirely different meanings or if the forms function in different ways and for different ends. Meaningless resemblances between composers can be found wherever sought for. Until we know how the details work and to what purpose, comprehension can only be, not simply provisional (for that is what it is at best), but illusory. It is, of course, difficult to avoid assuming a knowledge of the larger context in advance, regimenting the details accordingly: Beethoven often appears to speak too directly for us to admit the possibility that we have misunderstood him. A little methodological false humility in criticism, however, may go a long way towards revealing a genuine ignorance.

For example, in his frequent evasion of strict dominant-tonic relations within a single movement, Beethoven may seem to be closer to Schumann, Chopin, and Liszt in their most successful, least academic forms than to Haydn and Mozart. In almost any work of Haydn and Mozart, the twin poles of tonic and dominant are firmly maintained: an increase of tension at the opening almost always implies the imminent establishment of the dominant as a secondary tonality; the more remote harmonies are played, not only against the tonic, but against the polarity of tonic-dominant as a continual area of reference; resolution always goes to the tonic through the dominant. This polarity has a much less fundamental role in the work of the first generation of Romantic composers, and sometimes disappears completely: the A flat Ballade of Chopin never employs E flat major, and the F minor Ballade has little to do with either C major (or minor) or A flat major; only an already reactionary and high-principled view of sonata form imprisoned Schumann at times within a tonic-dominant relationship which was evidently largely uncongenial to him, if one is to judge by the more imaginative works: *Davidsbündlertänze*, the *Carnaval*, the C major Fantasy, and the great song cycles.

Almost from the beginning of his career as a composer, Beethoven attempted to find substitutes for the dominant in the classical tonic-dominant polar relation. His first efforts were prudent, not to say timid: he does, indeed, go to the dominant by the end of the exposition of his early sonatas, but often before doing so, he establishes a more remote key first: in op. 2 no. 3, the dominant minor; in op. 10 no. 3, the submediant minor. The establishment of a succession of tonalities is typical of the early style of Beethoven, and illustrates its closeness to the loose, additive forms of his contemporaries. He turned back later from this coloristic use of keys towards a more cohesive scheme. By op. 31 no. 1 he ventures to dispense with the dominant as a secondary tonality altogether: from G major he goes to the mediant B, and oscillates between its major and minor forms. A short time before this work, he had experimented in a similar way with a largely minor submediant in the String Quintet with two violas, op. 29. Here the continual swing back and forth between the major and minor is even more essential as the submediant minor is the relative minor of the tonic and implies a relaxation of tension, a subdominant relation, in fact; the submediant major, however, counteracts this by its orientation towards the dominant. It was not a relationship that Beethoven ever attempted in a sonata movement again, even with an alternation of major and minor to safeguard the dramatic character.

After the *Waldstein* Sonata, Beethoven is almost as likely to use the more remote mediant and submediant keys as to employ a straightforward dominant. The logical possibilities of these keys within a diatonically conceived aesthetic may be said to be exhausted in his works: only chromaticism could further enlarge the field. More astonishing than their frequency are the imaginative resources which Beethoven calls upon in the use of these substitute dominants and the variety of ways of arriving at them. Their effects cannot be easily subsumed in any simple formula: sonata movements like those of the *Waldstein*, the *Hammerklavier*, the op. 111, the Ninth Symphony, and the Quartets op. 127 and op. 130 all use a mediant or submediant key for very different expressive purposes.

It is tempting to think of Beethoven's substitute dominants as having something in common with the harmonic structures of the Romantic period, but his harmonic freedom is of a different order and nature. When the Romantic composer is not following an academic theory of form—that is, when he is not writing what he felt should be called a 'sonata'—his secondary tonalities are not dominants at all, but subdominants: they represent a diminishing tension and a less complex state of feeling, and not the greater tension and imperative need for resolution implied by all of Beethoven's secondary tonalities. Each of the three movements of Schumann's C major Fantasy goes clearly to the subdominant, and all its material is directed towards this modulation. For much of the F minor Ballade, Chopin avoids establishing a secondary key with any degree of clarity: when one arrives, it is astonishingly B flat major. These are two of the most remarkable works of the period, and they are only two instances out of many.

No comparable subdominant relationship can be found in any work of Beethoven (except, of course, those based on a ternary *ABA*, or minuet and trio form, which has no relation to the unified dramatic forms of Schumann and Chopin cited in this context). His expansion of the large-scale harmonic range took place within the limits of the classical language, and never infringed on the tonic-dominant polarity or the classical movement towards a greater tension away from the tonic. These secondary tonalities to his work, mediants and submediants, function within the large structure as true dominants. They create a long-range dissonance against the tonic and so provide the necessary tension for a move towards a central climax. In addition, Beethoven always prepares their appearance so that they seem almost as closely related to the tonic as the dominant is, so that the modulation creates a dissonance of greater power and excitement than the more usual dominant without disturbing the harmonic unity and tearing the structure apart. Within a tonal system this naturally imposes an inner contradiction, but a secondary tonality already exists as such a contradiction in its own right. Beethoven's harmonic practice only serves to heighten the effect of a style which depends for its dramatic expressiveness upon exactly this contradiction and its harmonious resolution. Beethoven, indeed, here enlarged the limits of the classical style beyond all previous conceptions,[1] but he never changed its essential structure or abandoned it, as did the composers who followed him. In the other fundamental aspects of his musical language, as well as in the key relations within a single movement, Beethoven may be said to have remained within the classical framework, even while using it in startlingly radical and original ways.

The foregoing naturally does not imply that the tonic-dominant relationship disappeared during the Romantic period—it is still with us to some extent today. But to Schumann and his contemporaries it was no longer the exclusive central principle of long-range harmonic movement. It is significant, however, that they used it, as far as I can remember, in all their movements in 'sonata-allegro' form. In other words, with all their harmonic daring and exploration in other forms, when it came to the 'sonata' they were far more conservative than Beethoven. Their greatest harmonic conceptions could not be applied to the sonata without making nonsense of it, whereas all of Beethoven's most startling innovations took place easily and comfortably within the sonata style.

We cannot even claim that Beethoven's harmonic licence within the classical style was a step towards the greater freedom of the Romantic generation, or that his magnificent stretching of the tonic-dominant polarity made it possible for those who followed to supersede it, or at least to bypass it. If Beethoven's daring had provided an example of such consequence, the Romantics would hardly have produced such uniformly conservative 'sonata' forms. The great harmonic innovations of the Romantics do not come from Beethoven at all, and have nothing to do either with his technique or his spirit. They arise from Hummel, Weber, Field, and Schubert (without taking into account Schubert's acquisition and mastery of classical procedure in the last years of his life), and, too, from Italian opera. They are made possible, in other words, not by an aesthetic in which the tonic-dominant polarity has been expounded to the limits of its effective power, but by one in which it has been loosened and weakened, where the orientation towards a powerful tonic area at the beginning and end has been threatened by a new and pervasive chromaticism, and by a more lyric and less dramatic conception of form. It was, for example, Schubert—in the last movement of the *Trout Quintet*—who first wrote an exposition which went to the subdominant. In the early works of Schubert, as in the music of Weber and Hummel, there is the first large development of a truly melodic form, one in which the classical harmonic tension is replaced by a relaxed and expansive succession of melodies. A new conception of harmonic tension was later developed by

---

[1] The use of the mediant or submediant as a dominant is, however, only an extension of Haydn's emphasis on them within the sonata exposition in his late works.

Schumann, Mendelssohn, and, above all, by Chopin, but they could not start from the classical style at its most highly organized, and Beethoven was of no use to them. The Romantic style did not come from Beethoven, in spite of the great admiration that was felt for him, but from his lesser contemporaries and from Bach.

It is worth noting, in this respect, the extremely limited influence of the music of Bach in Beethoven's works, in spite of the fact that his knowledge of Bach was considerable. He had been brought up on the *Well-Tempered Keyboard*, made his reputation as a child prodigy by playing it in its entirety, and continued to play it all his life. He copied out passages of Bach while making sketches for the last movement of the *Hammerklavier* as well as for the Fugue for String Quintet in D major. He had a copy of the Inventions, and two copies of the *Art of Fugue*, and he certainly knew the *Goldberg* Variations. Yet, except for an obvious and touching reference to the *Goldberg* in the conception of the final variations of the *Diabelli* set, the use he made of all his familiarity is very small, almost negligible in comparison to the continuous reference to Bach in the music of Mendelssohn, Chopin, and Schumann. The classical style had already absorbed all that it could of Bach as seen through the eyes of Mozart in the early 1780s, and as Beethoven continued to work within these limits, his love for Bach remained always in the margin of his creative activity.

That Beethoven's musical language remained essentially classical—or, better, that he started with a late and diluted version of classicism and gradually returned to the stricter and more concise form of Haydn and Mozart—does not mean that he stood outside his time, or that his conception of classical form was the expression of an outlook identical to the late eighteenth century's. To cite only one trait, his music often has a sententious moral earnestness that many people have found repellent, and which is presented with an enthusiasm far more typical of Europe after the French Revolution than of the *douceur de vivre* that preceded it. Much of his music, too, is autobiographical, sometimes openly so, in a way that is unthinkable before 1790 if not presented playfully; it is embarrassing when historians read into the music of Haydn and Mozart[1] the kind of directly personal significance appropriate to Beethoven and other nineteenth-century composers. Yet it is certain that Beethoven assumed a position not only contrary to the fashion of his time, but also in many ways against the direction that musical history was to take. He was perhaps the first composer in history to write deliberately difficult music for a great part of his life. Not that he ever set his face against popular success, or lost hope of achieving it despite the uncompromising difficulty of his work. The fame and the love that his music inspired during his lifetime were, in any case, considerable; but the ovations

---

[1] Even Chopin resented this approach to his music, but it is deliberately provoked by certain aspects of Schumann's.

he received at the premieres of the Ninth Symphony and *Missa Solemnis*—works apparently difficult enough to understand even today and which must have been almost disastrously executed when first played, to judge by the reports—are more a testimony to the respect in which the elderly composer was held than to a genuine acceptance of the music itself. No composer before Beethoven ever disregarded the capacities of both his performers and his audience with such ruthlessness. The first of his truly 'difficult' works, his stumbling blocks for critics, were written soon after the first signs of deafness, while the earliest works—even when they were found startlingly original or eccentric—won an almost immediate acceptance. He was already known throughout Europe as one of the greatest living composers by 1803, before he had written the *Eroica*, *Fidelio*, or the *Waldstein* Sonata. Whether the solitary path that he chose in music and his increasing physical isolation from the world are connected can remain a matter only for speculation.

Once having turned back to the language of Haydn and Mozart, Beethoven showed an almost wilfully tepid appreciation of most of his contemporaries: Handel appears to have interested him more than any of them. His special contempt was reserved for Rossini: one can easily see why. To have written even the greatest of Rossini's masterpieces before the *Comte d'Ory* only genius was necessary: intellect or hard work hardly entered into it. Rossini's reputation as the laziest of composers was not undeserved. (There should be no mystery about the reasons for his virtual retirement from music at the age of thirty-five: it is the age when the most fluent composer begins to lose the ease of inspiration he once possessed, when even Mozart had to make sketches and to revise.) For Beethoven, whose own compositions were the result of a meditation and a labor almost unparalleled elsewhere in music, the magnificent thoughtlessness of Rossini's work must have been as exasperating to him as Rossini's public triumph in Vienna with a genuine popular success that Beethoven could never equal. 'He needs only as many weeks as the Germans need years to write an opera,' he remarked, with what must have been envy as well as scorn.[1]

Of all his contemporaries Beethoven seems to have preferred one of the most conservative and classicizing of all, Cherubini. When asked who was the greatest living composer after himself, he is said to have replied Cherubini, but not too much weight should be placed on this judgment, as he appears to have had some difficulty in thinking of any name. However, he is known to have greatly admired Cherubini's (and Méhul's) success in writing serious opera: his own struggles and revisions of *Fidelio* made him set a high price upon this achievement. He also respected both Weber and Schubert, the former somewhat unwillingly: at least, he is known to have spoken disdainfully of Weber, and his more admiring comments are reported chiefly by Weber's son. Beethoven's enthusiasm for Schubert is also not well

---

[1] Thayer, vol. II, p. 804.

attested, as the evidence comes chiefly from Schindler in a polemical article defending his own admiration, and Schindler was not only inaccurate but prone to invention when his passions were roused.

None of this need surprise: few composers past a certain age are genuinely interested in anybody's music except their own, unless they find an invention, an idea, or even only a texture that they can use themselves, as Beethoven could use Handel, and Mozart learn from Bach. The most revealing remark of Beethoven's, however, about another composer—revealing about himself, that is—is his crushing verdict on Spohr: 'He is too rich in dissonances, pleasure in his music is marred by his chromatic melody.'[1] If this is exactly what Beethoven said—it was reported in memoirs published only many years later—it shows how deep was his lack of sympathy with the newly arising Romantic style. No one today could find Spohr more dissonant than Beethoven if by dissonance is meant harshness, or even if the more technical sense of an unresolved interval or chord is taken: Beethoven is as rich as any composer in emphatic dissonance of both kinds. What was 'dissonant' in Spohr to Beethoven's ear was evidently a new chromaticism, left insufficiently integrated within a diatonic framework; and it was just this kind of chromaticism which became so essential a part of the music of the 1830s. There are moments when Beethoven is as chromatic as any composer before late Wagner, including Chopin, but the chromaticism is always resolved and blended into a background which ends by leaving the tonic triad absolute master.

It is, in fact, with this fundamental triad that Beethoven attains his most remarkable and characteristic effects. At one point in the G major Piano Concerto, he achieves the seemingly impossible with it and turns this most consonant of chords (into which all dissonance must be, by definition, resolved by the end of the piece) itself into a dissonance. In the following measures, almost by rhythmic means alone and without modulating from G major, the tonic chord of G major *in root position* clearly requires a resolution into the dominant:

---

[1] Thayer, II, p. 956.

The majesty and the excitement combined in measure 27 come from the fact that it is the fundamental chord of the piece that is being held for a full measure after being rendered unstable by the steadily repeated (and increasingly animated) movement into a D major chord.

Withholding the D major chord in measure 27, however, is the source of its power: not only does the G major tonic chord sound unresolved, but reining in its resolution for so long even forces the beautiful resolution in the next measure beyond the D major chord to an A minor triad. The grandeur of the sonority comes from the use only of root positions for all the chords in measures 26 to 28 and the consequent purity and stability of sound[1] in a phrase of extreme instability.

The sudden and complete halt in measure 27 is an act of will. It implies an almost muscular effort that justifies the relaxation of what follows. To encompass this, the animation of the previous measures is essential. The acceleration and the *ritenuto* are completely articulated: the movement of the pattern:

occurs once per measure in 23, twice in 24 and 25, and four times in 26; but in 27 and 28, it is now spread over two measures. The classical conception of increased animation in discrete units of 1, 2, 4, 8, etc., is given its most exemplary form. It is hard to see how the system could have been carried further than Beethoven does here. The Romantic composer rejected it, with some malaise, in favor of a more fluid conception, but Beethoven was absolute master over the classical articulation of rhythmic forces. The occasions when he, too, attempted to go beyond it were very rare.

---

[1] The spacing of the chord and its instrumentation (to discuss one is inevitably to consider the other) serve to reinforce what is said here.

It should be remarked that if, in this passage, the integration of melodic, rhythmic, and harmonic forces is such that they seem indissoluble, the material is not only simple but could not possibly be simpler. The two alternating tonic and dominant chords are the basic chords of any tonal work. The passage quoted is, of course, a transitional one, and serves to introduce the new theme that begins in measure 29. It is also, however, not only the first climactic moment of the work but has thematic significance as well. The two chords are the opening chords of the movement:

heard very shortly before. In short, the climax—the written-out and measured fermata of measure 27—is the opening chord of the work now rendered unstable, or, in other words, transformed into a dynamic element. This is very close to Haydn's practice of charging the openings of his movements with directional force, but no one before Beethoven was able to do this so powerfully with the simple tonic chord in its most fundamental position. And no one since Beethoven could repeat this dramatic effect without weakening the tonic; the fact that the tonic is as powerful as ever—in short, that it remains within the classical language—is proved by the majestic breadth of this whole section.

The use of the simplest elements of the tonal system as themes lay at the heart of Beethoven's personal style from the beginning. It was only little by little, however, that he realized its implications. The traditional division of his music into three periods is not untenable, but it can be as misleading as it is useful. There is no line that can be drawn between the first and second periods, and if there is a clear break in the continuity of his work around the beginning of what is called the third period, the works that contain many of the characteristic new developments belong just before the break as well as after it. When the division into three periods is retained, it should be clear that it is a fiction for the purposes of analysis, a convenience for understanding, and not a biographical reality. The steady development discernible in Beethoven's career is as important as its discontinuities even if these are easier to describe. It is only in comparing works several years apart that the discontinuities assume a demonstrable and persuasive sense.

Beethoven's return to classical principles may be measured by such a discontinuity if one compares the Third Piano Concerto in C minor of 1800 with the Fourth in G major of 1808. Both works rely heavily on Mozart but in entirely different ways. The C minor is full of Mozartean reminiscences, in particular of the concerto in the same key, K. 491, which Beethoven is known to have admired. Most striking is the imitation of the coda of K. 491, with its exceptional use of the solo instrument playing arpeggios at the end of the first movement. Beethoven omits a final ritornello after the cadenza and leaps directly to the coda; the Mozartean arpeggios are made almost melo-dramatic with timpani playing part of the main theme. In this superbly effective coda, only the arpeggios are not thematic, and this makes their borrowed character all the more apparent. In the development section, a curiously beautiful non-thematic passage also turns out to be inspired by Mozart, this time the B flat Piano Concerto K. 450. But it is the C minor K. 491 again which dominates many of the thematic details, at least of the first movement.

There is, however, nothing genuinely Mozartean about this movement except for the borrowings and the perhaps unconscious reminders. The orchestral tutti which opens the movement is set off from what follows by a full halt and a dramatic fermata; it is almost a complete work by itself, appearing thoroughly self-sufficient. This exaggerated separation, which makes for a relaxed looseness of structure, tends to make the solo exposition a decorated form of the tutti instead of a new and more dramatic conception of the material as in Mozart.[1] It is, in fact, the form of the first two piano concertos as well, and of the concertos of Hummel and the other post-classic composers (including the two concertos of Chopin both composed before he was twenty). The completely separate introductory orchestral exposition is a characteristic of all these works, and this became an embarrassment when the loose and rambling manner was no longer acceptable to the task of the early Romantic composers. The response of Schumann and others was to fuse both these expositions into one.

The diffuse forms of the early nineteenth century had clearly become un-acceptable to Beethoven as well by 1808, but his solution was a resurrection of Mozart's practice. The Fourth Piano Concerto in G major contains few direct imitations of Mozart in the classicizing, almost academic manner of the earlier works, but the principles of large-scale construction have now become Mozart's, transformed and rendered more fluid. The double sonata exposi-tion of the first three concertos is renounced in favor of the Mozartean ideal of a double presentation, static and dynamic, of the material—the orchestral one introductory and stable, the soloist's in a more dramatic sonata exposi-tion. As in many of Mozart's first movements, the two presentations are welded together, the second interrupting the first with a cadenza-like version of the opening thematic elements. The orchestral exposition remains in the tonic throughout: its only secondary theme has a series of surface modulations

---

[1] Mozart has many opening tutti in the concertos which round themselves off with a cadence, but these tutti have only the completeness of the introduction to an aria, and never of a full sonata exposition.

so rapid that it is difficult to realize that we have never really left G major. As Mozart does in the G major Concerto K. 453, Beethoven obscures what might be too monotonous a unity of key for several pages and then lets the soloist make the decisive move.

Most important of all, Beethoven takes up the conception of the dramatic entrances of the soloist where Mozart had left it, and so realizes some of his own most imaginative ideas. Two of the most original effects in the Fourth Piano Concerto are paradoxically occasions for the only direct references in the work to Mozart. The entrance of the piano in the first measure of the work immediately brings to mind the opening of K. 271, where Mozart has the piano enter in the second measure in direct answer to the opening orchestral motif. Beethoven's opening, at once poetically resonant and reticent, recalls Mozart's only conceptually, but they both result from a similar logic or way of thought. The *Emperor* Concerto also brings in the piano at the opening, but with very different effect, as does the unfinished sketch for a sixth piano concerto in D major: in both these works the soloist enters with a cadenza, postponed in the unfinished concerto until after the first statement in the orchestra of the main theme—an interesting foreshadowing of Brahms. The device obviously interested Beethoven but he never permitted it to alter the classical relation between orchestral and solo expositions.

The second reference to Mozart amounts almost to a quotation: the entrance of the piano at the beginning of the development is directly modeled on the same moment in Mozart's C major Concerto K. 503, quoted on page 257, except that Beethoven closes the slight gap between orchestra and soloist and makes the entrance the occasion for an abrupt change of key, so sudden that it is not immediately intelligible and becomes so only some measures later:

The difference between Beethoven and a classicizing composer like Hummel is that Beethoven, particularly after 1804, is inspired by Mozart's most imaginative and most radical conceptions, while Hummel starts from the most normative ones.

The finale of the G major Concerto makes masterful use of the Haydn-esque device of appearing to start in the wrong key, and with all its virtuosity it is closer to Haydn's symphonic finales than to any of the concerto finales of the early 1800s. The episodic rondo form has been tightened and unified, rather than loosened, as it was by other composers of that time. Even the slow movement, perhaps the most dramatically conceived ever written, has its roots in the late eighteenth century: only some of Haydn's slow movements in the quartets and the trios and the slow introduction to the last movement of Mozart's G minor Quintet are so uncompromisingly theatrical. (The second movement of Beethoven's first Concerto in C major is a far more typical example of the common style of the first quarter of the nineteenth century.) The slow movement of the G major Concerto is, in another respect, comparable to the Adagio introduction to the finale of the G minor Quintet: it stays so close to the tonic E minor that it is to be conceived almost as an expanded E minor chord, and is not an independent piece but must be played, by Beethoven's own direction, without a pause before the last movement. Its only short modulation is not to its own dominant but to VII, D major, which is the dominant of the finale. The beginning of the finale *pp* on a chord of C major transcends the Haydnesque idea of a 'false' opening, makes it far more cogent, as it is now a modulation directly out of the E minor of the previous movement back to the G major of the concerto as a whole. Much of the poetry of this slow movement derives from its incomplete nature: it defines and establishes, not itself, but something to come.

The first of Beethoven's immense expansions of classical form is the *Eroica* Symphony, finished in 1804, the same year that produced the *Waldstein* Sonata. The symphony, much longer than any work in that form that preceded it, provoked some displeasure at its first public performance. The critics complained of its inordinate length, and protested against the lack of unity in this most unified of works. This unity is so intense that a cello–oboe duet which is almost always called a new theme in the development is directly derived from the main theme. It is the oboe line that is later dropped, and the cello's motif remains and is transferred to the winds. The relation between the cello line and the main theme is very close:

This is not merely a relationship on paper, but one that is clearly audible if the conductor observes the *sforzandi* as genuine accents and not, as is so often the case, as expressive swells. This small detail is significant here because, while there is an unusual richness of motifs in the first movement, almost every one with a specific melodic character is directly linked to the opening measures. Everyone is immediately aware of the relation to the first theme of the following motifs:

along with many other similar motifs too numerous to cite; but these relationships are far less remarkable than the extraordinary continuity into which they are woven. Partly because of the variety and number of episodes, the exposition does not fall into as simple a sectional form as in the two symphonies that preceded it, and this helped to make the music more painful to grasp at first.

The public, indeed, seems to have been ill-natured at the first performance and the work immediately divided its hearers into two furiously opposed factions. Not only the bitterness of the criticism, but its nature remind one of more recent attacks on what is thought to be the *avant garde*: one critic wrote that Beethoven's 'music could soon reach the point where one would derive no pleasure from it unless well trained in the rules and difficulties of the art, but rather would leave the concert hall . . . crushed by a mass of unconnected and overloaded ideas and a continuing tumult by all the instruments.' It is understandable that the symphony was found so difficult, as the extension of the range of hearing in time is remarkable: the dissonant C♯ in the seventh measure finds its full meaning only much later at the opening of the recapitulation, when it becomes a D♭ and leads to an F major horn solo; yet the unprecedented scope of modulation in the development is carried out without the slightest diffusion of the sense of tonal unity; above all, the proportions are firmly defined.

It is clear that such an increase in size without altering the fundamental classical proportions (the placing of the climax, the ratio of harmonic tension to resolution) could not start from the long, regular and complete melodies of Mozart, but had to base itself on Haydn's treatment of tiny motifs.[1] The short motifs could easily form a tissue of periods essentially much larger than Haydn's with a correspondingly slower harmonic motion, while complete melodies—in order to keep the proportions of period to the whole—would have to be made much longer. This presents a problem for any symphonic style that is to move at a faster pace than Bruckner. For this reason Beethoven is sometimes called a weak melodist, although it is difficult to see how that could ever have been said about the composer of the second movement of the Piano Sonata op. 90, or the minuet of op. 31 no. 3, to mention only two of Beethoven's many long and beautifully regular melodies. Musical ideas that form a complete whole in themselves—tunes, in short—were rarely of any use to Beethoven in his dramatic expansions of Mozart's forms, although Mozart's proportions were most relevant. In the relation of development to recapitulation he more often follows Mozart than Haydn, and his large codas are less an imitation of Haydn, as Tovey thought, than the restoration of a Mozartean balance.

Haydn's codas, at least in his later years, are inextricably fused, even tangled with his recapitulations: Beethoven's, like Mozart's, are often separate, articulated entities. They are generally preceded by tonic cadences, and their most immediate analogues are the last numbers of a Mozart opera finale: like them, they saturate the ear with the tonic chord. The astonishingly long coda to the first movement of the *Eroica* (astonishing by previous standards, although completely logical and expected by its own) serves to ground the extreme tension of the development, which was not only long but far-ranging harmonically; the coda, in fact, balances the development. Starting with the initial tension of juxtaposing powerfully spaced and orchestrated chords of D flat major and C major, without any explanatory modulation, he soon goes briefly through a series of keys of basically subdominant character, the relative minor in particular. From there we arrive at one of the longest tonic cadences ever written, pages of nothing but V–I repeated over and over. It is certain that the lyrical alterations at the opening of the recapitulation along with its traditional move to the tonic were not sufficient to counteract the climax of the development, and that this enormous tonic cadence in the coda is necessary to give the movement a satisfactorily closed form.

---

[1] Except for the songs, the early works of Schubert (like all the piano music of Weber and Hummel) start from the long Mozartean melody while greatly expanding the size of Mozart's forms, with the result of a breakdown in rhythmic tension never found in Beethoven.

The length of the movement being so unusual, Beethoven briefly thought of omitting the repeat of the exposition: he finally decided the repeat was essential. Without it, as we still sometimes hear the symphony played, the exposition is dwarfed by what follows. The question of repeats is often grasped by the wrong end of the stick: that of contemporary practice. Unfortunately no distinction is generally made between what was approved and what one could get away with—the distinction between morality and law, in fact, and it is a pity in such matters to decide legalistically. It might be said that there is almost no possible desecration of a classical work that is not sanctified by a tradition dating back to the composer's lifetime. Beethoven's friends indignantly reported to him a performance of the Fifth Symphony which went from the C major Trio of the scherzo directly into the pedal point of the transition to the finale.

A better basis for decision would be the question of significance (and in the classical style, proportions are an essential part of meaning); even if it becomes longer, a work can only gain in interest if it makes more sense. There is no rule: some repeats are dispensable, others absolutely necessary; some succeed in clarifying what is only half-intelligible without them. The development sections of the Sonatas op. 31 nos. 1 and 2 both begin with the opening measures of the exposition: if the repeat of the exposition is carried out, and the circular form heard in its entirety, the new turning of the development after a few measures becomes only more effective. The use of repeats is, in fact, transformed during the classical period, and is carried by Beethoven far beyond the point to which Mozart and Haydn had brought it.

The repeat during the Baroque period is a way of accenting the regularity of a dance-form; repeating an entire piece as a unit only serves to continue the dance, but repeating each half separately emphasizes its symmetry. In Bach, particularly in the *Goldberg* Variations, the end of each section—moving back to the beginning or forward to the second (or concluding) half—is the occasion of much subtlety. In the third quarter of the eighteenth century, the repeat was above all the opportunity for expressive ornamentation, for the display of sentiment or virtuosity (they are more closely related than is sometimes thought, and both of them were realized through traditional decorative figures). It is largely in the music of Haydn and Mozart after 1775 that structure replaced ornamentation as the principal vehicle of expression. The repeats (particularly in the first movements, the slow movements always retaining some of their ornamental character) then became above all an essential part of the proportions, the balance of tonal areas, and of the interplay of harmonic tensions. It makes a great deal of difference to the effect of the first movement of Mozart's G minor Symphony if the second and more dramatic half is repeated (as it so rarely is in performance today) as well as the expository first half. In Haydn, where the direction of tonal movement is perhaps even more important than its weight, a repeat will entirely change the significance of a section: many of Haydn's opening phrases have a new sound, a different force when they are heard returning from a dominant cadence. Beethoven, who after 1804 dispensed with the traditional repeats as often as not, used them when he did in such a way that they add significance and weight (as in Haydn and Mozart), and yet concentrated and extended their effect so that their omission either falsifies the sense of what follows, as in the Sonatas op. 31 nos. 1 and 3, or even, as in the *Hammerklavier*, makes the transition to the development illogical.

A similar concentration and, at the same time, expansion of Haydn's way of letting the music grow dynamically from a small kernel, or central idea, is found increasingly in Beethoven's music. It is even more tempting in Beethoven's case to think of this central idea in exclusively linear terms and even more dangerous: this often works magnificently on paper and strays far from what can actually be heard. For example, all the themes of the first movement of the *Waldstein* Sonata without exception can be related easily in linear terms, as they all move in stepwise fashion, are all based on scale progressions. Some of these linear relationships are indeed audible because they have been made so by Beethoven, and are a part of the discursive logic of the surface. Nevertheless, the music hardly ever moves in a purely linear fashion, and listening with a totally innocent ear is no worse than accepting a theory which obscures more than it enlightens.

The first movement of the *Waldstein* Sonata has a characteristic sound, not only unlike the music of other composers, but unlike any other work of Beethoven, an energetic hardness, dissonant and yet curiously plain, expressive without richness. It is the consistent harmonic interpretations of the stepwise progressions that give this movement its specific character. In each phrase of the themes, every second chord is a dominant seventh:

a)

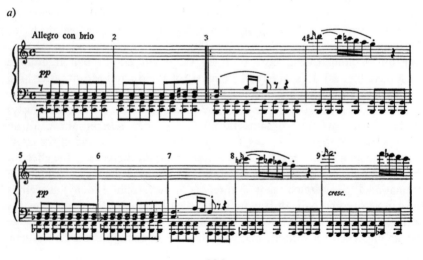

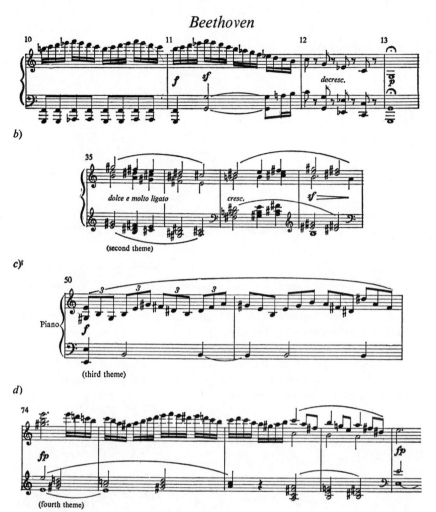

(second theme)

(third theme)

(fourth theme)

The dominant seventh is the plainest, the most neutral of dissonances; its relentless alternation in scale progression with pure triads invests this movement with its particular sonority and invades every phrase. It immediately provides the first climax from measure 9 on, with a spacing of the hands that brutally emphasizes its character. (A work of Mozart or Haydn has a sonority as characteristic as one of Beethoven's, but rarely so concisely and so concentratedly individual.) I do not mean that the central idea of the *Waldstein* can be entirely reduced to this simple but pervasive alternation of triads and dominant sevenths, but it is enough to show that the idea cannot be described in purely linear terms.

The *Waldstein* also establishes its themes in a genetic order; that is, they appear to be born one from another even more than in Haydn's technique of thematic derivation, although the method is not very different. The descending fifth outlined in the fourth measure (itself an expanded echo of the third measure) produces the right hand of what will become the fourth or closing theme[1] quoted above:

It is only on paper, however, that we can identify this with the descending fifth outlined more slowly by the opening of the 'second group' (mm. 35–36): they are only distantly related, as the descent of the second theme is more directly presented as an inversion of the rising motion of the first three measures of the movement. This relationship is forced on our attention by the transition to the second theme:

where the rising third of the opening theme is used as the beginning of an ascending scale in the bass, of which the new theme, *dolce e molto ligato*, is an inversion and a clear balancing movement. (The descending fifth in the first theme (measure 4) is also an answer and a balance to the rising motion of the first three measures, so the indirect relationship is nevertheless one that contributes to the unity of conception in this movement.)

The pulsating energy in this work is perhaps its most remarkable innovation. Description in purely rhythmic terms, however, will not do. Part of the energy comes from the immediate recourse to modulation in the second measure. There is not the slightest obscurity about key and the effect has nothing in common with Haydn's 'false' starts. What the widening of the

---

[1] The left hand of this fourth theme comes directly and obviously from the second theme.

harmonic range at the outset enables Beethoven to do is to expand the time-scale of his music as well. To establish a key in almost all music from 1700 to 1800 is to present the tonic and dominant in their proper relationship to each other, that is, by at least an implied or passing resolution on the tonic. In spite of the fact that there is no tonal ambiguity, it takes the entire first thirteen measures of the *Waldstein* Sonata to define the key of C major. Except in cases where a deliberate mystification is intended (as in Haydn's pun at the opening of op. 33 no. 1) or where there is an introduction (which often retards a decisive resolution on the tonic by resolving towards the dominant as an harmonic up-beat), no work of Haydn or Mozart can delay tonic stability for so long. The greater breadth of Beethoven's harmonic movement and the larger scale on which he worked provides the steady energy and excitement of the opening rhythm with a controlling framework. What this entails is combining Haydn's technique of dynamic growth from the smallest details with Mozart's feeling for large harmonic masses and for tonal areas. This is why Beethoven can so often appear at once more dramatic and more stable than Haydn.

The development by Beethoven of a unity of conception, rhythmic and harmonic as well as thematic, very close to the concepts of Haydn and Mozart although on a larger scale takes shape during the years 1804–6. In 1803, the *Kreutzer* Sonata has a first movement unequalled in formal clarity, grandeur, and dramatic force by anything that Beethoven had yet written; the beautiful slow movement, however, a set of variations in F major, belongs to a totally different style, elegant, brilliant, ornamental, and a little precious, the style of the F major Variations for Piano, op. 34, without the latter's original harmonic scheme and dramatic contrasts, but with a more artistic care for detail; the finale, a light and brilliant tarantella, was written for another sonata altogether. Beethoven never again presented such a hybrid as one work. For the slow movement of the *Waldstein*, in 1804, he had originally written a rondo in a style very similar to the variations of the *Kreutzer*, but replaced it with the far more suitable half-slow-movement half-introduction-to-the-finale that now stands there. The next year, 1805, with the *Appassionata*, he finally arrived at a conception of a sonata where all three movements have been formulated as one. (The tradition of playing a Beethoven sonata without pausing between the movements is an old one, at least as old as von Bülow, and whether it is correct or not,[1] it is a response to an important element in Beethoven's style.) The years 1804–6 represent a growth in artistic conscience for Beethoven. They were years of consolidation in all fields: the first version of *Fidelio* and the Quartets op. 59 were written then, as well as the *Eroica*, the Fourth Piano Concerto, the *Waldstein* and the *Appassionata*.

It might be said that the *Appassionata*, the most concise of all these, is a

---

[1] I am not, of course, discussing the cases where Beethoven expressly directs that no pause be made.

cautious work in one important respect: the opening movement is almost rigidly symmetrical in spite of its violence, as if only the simplest and most unyielding of frames could contain such power. This kind of prudence is typical of the most revolutionary works: suppleness comes only when experiment has succeeded. The first movement of the *Appassionata* falls into four clear sections: all of them (exposition, development, recapitulation, and coda) begin with the main theme; the recapitulation follows the thematic pattern of the exposition with the minimum of alteration necessary to return the second group in the tonic; both the development and the coda conform to this pattern by playing the thematic material they select in the order set forth in the exposition; in addition, the development and the coda have very similar structures, except for the final Più allegro at the end.

The violence is achieved simply and efficiently. The most original and remarkable moment is another of Beethoven's uses of the tonic chord: the harmony at the beginning of the recapitulation is naturally a tonic chord, but in six-four position—that is, with a dominant pedal pulsating continuously, which turns an important moment of resolution into a long-sustained, menacing dissonance. The pathetic harmonies of the Neapolitan chord are used with great fierceness throughout, pervading all the thematic material, and culminating in the harsh pedal blurring of the minor second D♭–C at the climax just before the Più allegro. The rising bass of the development, as Tovey pointed out, creates an excitement unknown in music before then. The control of complex rhythmic effect is more impressive than ever before. The exposition moves from the disjunctive phrases of the opening, balancing rhythmic and harmonic tension as the movement grows more animated until the harsh and turbulent closing theme, which is not in the relative major but decisively in the minor of the relative major. Almost all of Mozart's and Haydn's works in minor color the relative major of the second group with this minor mode, but neither of them had gone so far as to close an exposition with it: once again, in this work, Beethoven extended classical harmonic language without violating its spirit. It is evident that, in 1805, the classical style was not yet exhausted, and that its framework was still serviceable. Only in this sense do styles appear to develop according to a logic of their own, but it is useless to ask if the conclusions waiting to be developed would have been so without Beethoven. It would also be a mistake to ignore other pressures on Beethoven's development, in spite of their lesser importance.

Three examples of these different pressures of musical style and taste may be mentioned: the Thirty-two Variations in C minor, *Wellington's Victory*, and *An die ferne Geliebte*. The C minor Variations for Piano, written in 1806, quickly became popular. As the only set to take up the Baroque form again, it stands apart from all Beethoven's other variations. It is, stylistically, a remarkably prescient work as well, a forecast of the revival of Baroque rhythmic development and harmonic movement that was to produce

Romanticism, or its musical form. The piece was to become the basis for Mendelssohn's *Variations Sérieuses*. Beethoven's set follows Handel's passacaglia form closely, imposing only a classically articulated sense of climax within the phrase and over the series of variations, as the first generation of Romantic composers were to do. Its immediate popularity testifies to the direction in which music and taste was moving. Beethoven was not happy about this essay in early Romanticism, professing later to be ashamed of it.

Wellington's Victory of 1813 is so frankly a potboiler that shame would have been of little comfort, and Beethoven, reproached for it during his lifetime, indignantly put the best possible face on it. It is in large part not by him at all, but by Mälzel, who was responsible for the structure, many of the ideas, and even, it seems, some of the actual writing. It was, in fact, originally written for Mälzel's mechanical organ and only later, again at Mälzel's suggestion, orchestrated and performed. Descriptive pieces of this kind were not new; their history goes back several centuries, at least to Jannequin. Yet the combination of descriptive realism in music with the stimulation of enthusiasm and excitement (in this case, of the patriotic variety) begins to be important in music after the French Revolution. The persuasive excitement envisaged by Beethoven's potpourri is, perhaps, more progressive than its realism, and leads in the direction of what was to become one of the most important Romantic genres, the programmatic symphony. Beethoven's contribution lacks the serious pretentiousness or the incorporation of ideology of Mendelssohn's *Reformation Symphony*, or of Berlioz' *Symphonie Funèbre et Triomphale*, but it is only the less interesting for its modesty. It was, ironically, the composer's greatest popular success.

The kind of evocative and nervous realism in *Wellington's Victory* should not be equated with the descriptive effects of the Sixth Symphony, which, as Beethoven himself wrote, is 'a matter more of feeling than of painting in sounds.' The *Pastoral* is, for the most part, a true classical symphony strongly influenced by the then fashionable doctrine of art as the painting of feelings or sentiments, a philosophy better suited to the music of the 1760s (and before) than to the dramatic style that succeeded it. An aesthetic doctrine is more often unconsciously a codification or even a rear-guard action than a reflection of current practice: the works precede the doctrine. Beethoven's *Pastoral*, however, has not only a certain ambiguity, but a decided split in its expressive position: the moments of outspoken realism are naïve rather than evocative (the birds and the thunder and lightning, for example, go far beyond anything Haydn had ever written in his descriptive effects), and they intrude rather than blend with the mood-painting. It cannot be said that this contradiction affects the beauty of the work: the mood-painting is contained easily within a classical symphonic structure organized as dramatically as ever; even the realistic bird-calls are presented as a solo cadenza, almost a final trill, so that their heterogeneous relation to the rest of the movement passes as easily as the 'improvised' cadenza of a concerto. Nevertheless, there is a loss of unity of tone; if one compares Beethoven's Sixth with the more obviously 'pastoral' works of Haydn (the symphony *The Bear*, for instance, or *The Seasons*), one sees that the less stylized realism, the substitution of nature for rusticity, and the more obvious mood-painting in Beethoven have both coarsened and sentimentalized a genre, and that the loss of a delicate balance is only compensated for by Beethoven's magnificently lyric energy. The five-movement structure is sometimes noted as a forecast of later Romantic experiments (like Berlioz' *Symphonie Fantastique*), but this is an illusion; Beethoven's fourth movement has no independent existence, but is treated as an expanded introduction to the finale as in Mozart's G minor Quintet. Nothing in the language or the structure of the *Pastoral* can be related in any meaningful way to the later programmatic works concerning outdoor life of Raff, Goldmark, and Richard Strauss,

An die ferne Geliebte, however, is a work which not only steps outside the classical aesthetic, but which also had a deep and genuine influence upon the music of the generation immediately after Beethoven's death. In this cycle of songs, it is astonishing that Beethoven goes even beyond Schubert to the open and circular form of Schumann. The last phrase of the cycle is the only ending in Beethoven so inconclusive, so obviously implying a continuation. Since this last phrase is also the opening phrase of the cycle, the effect of open, unending form is only the more compelling:

There are many lengthy songs by Schubert which are more a string of separate *Lieder* than one single work, but the problems of continuity and articulation among the different sections are very loosely handled; and Schubert's large cycles are sets of independent songs each one of which makes sense by itself and can stand alone, even if it gains in depth from being placed in context. The individual songs of *An die ferne Geliebte*, however, like many of those in Schumann's cycles, cannot stand by themselves; at several points Beethoven has tried to blend the rhythms of one with those of the next song and make the transition almost imperceptible. Schumann's conception is at once simpler and more subtle; although each song of his cycles appears to be complete in itself, many are impossible to conceive outside their setting, and cannot be heard as significantly independent pieces. In this way, Schumann arrives at a series of genuinely open forms, and by seeming to accept the divisions annuls them, as Beethoven never succeeds in doing. Nevertheless, Beethoven's set stands as the first example of what was the most original and perhaps the most important of Romantic forms.

An die ferne Geliebte was written in 1816, towards the end of a crisis in Beethoven's musical development; since 1812 he had composed nothing of importance except the sonatas for cello op. 102 nos. 1 and 2, and for piano op. 90 and op. 101. The revision of *Fidelio* and the composition of a fine *pièce d'occasion*, the Overture *Zur Namensfeier*, also took place during this time, but the rest amounts to a handful of canons and other short pieces. This is not a poor harvest, but it seems meager compared to that of the years both before and after this period. The slim production of this time cannot be ascribed to the usual slowing-down due to age, as the prodigality of the years from 1818 on would then be difficult to explain. It is possible that this crisis was accompanied by one in Beethoven's personal life (the famous letter to the unknown Immortal Beloved can be dated 1812), but a biographical explanation of this kind does nothing to elucidate the rare musical experiments that broke the silence of the period. Not only *An die ferne Geliebte*, but also the cello sonatas and the Sonata for Piano op. 101, show a development towards openly cyclic form, a tendency that was abandoned later.[1] In addition, the Piano Sonata op. 101 begins as if in the middle of a musical paragraph; in other words, here is an essay in, or at least a movement towards, the open forms of the Romantic period, even if the harmonic language retains the firmly closed nature of the classical style. The harmonic structure of the finale of op. 101 has an unclassical looseness that brings it close to many works of Mendelssohn. The exposition is as classical as any other of Beethoven's, but the development consists entirely of a fugue, its opening is completely detached from what precedes, and it remains in the tonic minor throughout. This is a way of evading classical tension (harmonically here) and reaching the relaxed expansion of large Romantic forms. This is also true of the Sonata op. 90, where, after a despairing and impassioned first movement, laconic almost to the point of reticence, a moderately slow, *cantabile* rondo follows, symmetrical, relaxed, and with an exquisitely beautiful, squarely regular theme that is repeated many times without the slightest abridgement and is varied only at the end by placing the melody in another register. This loose, melodically centered structure was to become a standard Schubertian form,[2] and it is, indeed, typical of the post-classical style from

---

[1] The passages which return from earlier movements in the finale of the Ninth Symphony are not only presented as quotations, but completely isolated within a new context, while the return of the opening in op. 101 and the song cycle are much more integrated into the discourse. (The reference to the first movement in the finale of the Quartet op. 131, is neither a return in cyclic form nor a quotation, but a result of a new conception of the unity of the musical material in a work in several movements.)

[2] This is not the only foreshadowing of Schubert in Beethoven, the Minuet of the Trio op. 70 no. 2 in E flat major being even more remarkable, but the rondo of op. 90 is the only work of Beethoven after 1804 to use this loose and melodically based large form.

1800 on, but such a degree of squareness is very rare in Beethoven, and in no other piece does he rely on the unaltered repetition of a long melody to bear so much of the expressive weight.

During this time when it was so difficult for him to complete a work, it was as if the classical sense of form appeared bankrupt to him, spurring him to search for a new system of expression. In the preceding years from 1807 to 1813, he had written four symphonies (5 through 8), the Mass in C, the Piano Trios op. 70 nos. 1 and 2, and op. 97, the Cello Sonata op. 69, the Quartets op. 74 and 95, and the *Emperor* Concerto. These works are a formidable series which may well have seemed to exhaust beyond renewal the style and the tradition he worked in; it may be only an accident that this musical crisis coincided with a personal one, or we may even surmise that it was artistic exhaustion and despair that provoked the turmoil in his personal life. 'Art demands always something new from us,' he once said to an admirer of an early work. Except for *An die ferne Geliebte*, the Romantic experiments are only tentative: neither classical tonality nor classical proportions are really abandoned except in details. Yet it is in the rare works of this period that Beethoven is closest to the generation that followed his death.

The decision to continue with the more purely classical forms was, in its way, heroic. The act of will was marked by the composition of the *Hammerklavier* Sonata, which took him the two years of 1817 and 1818. He declared that it was to be his greatest. It is not, however, a work that sums up a lifetime of experience, a compendium of art, like the late works of Bach, but a demonstration of power, a gesture. By contemporary standards, it was monstrously long and scandalously difficult: Czerny wrote in Beethoven's conversational scrapbook that a lady in Vienna who had been practicing for months complained that she still could not play the beginning of the sonata. With this work, the emancipation of piano music from the demands of the amateur musician was made official, with a consequent loss of responsibility and a greater freedom for the imagination. Even so, Beethoven said later that he felt constricted by the limitations of the piano, although there is no reason for the claim (now happily out of fashion) that he ever calculated without those limits when writing for the keyboard. The opening of the *Hammerklavier*, which sounds so feeble and ineffective in any orchestral transcription, is gigantic on the piano.

The new, almost obsessive, clarity of this work released the fertility of imagination which had been held back for so long; if no important new work followed immediately, that was only because Beethoven had begun work on the *Missa Solemnis*, which he hoped, vainly, to finish in time for Archduke Rudolph's installation as cardinal-archbishop. Between 1819 and 1824, he completed three immense works (the D major Mass, the *Diabelli* Variations, and the Ninth Symphony) along with the three last piano sonatas; in the remaining two years of his life he composed five string quartets. The *Hammer-*

klavier had pointed the way to this renewed activity, and in the severity of its treatment it put an end to experiments with more loosely constructed, open patterns. The apparently freely expanded forms of the late quartets are closely tied to the severity of the *Hammerklavier* and to its clarity of definition. They start from its principles, transforming and reworking them, rather than from the experimental works of 1813–16, although it would be a mistake to set these completely apart from what followed (the D major Cello Sonata, for example, adumbrates many ideas that reach maturity only in the op. 106). The last works are most precisely related to the *Hammerklavier* above all in their extreme concentration of material.

The sets of bagatelles that Beethoven wrote in the early 1820s are sometimes considered as rejected sketches for larger works, ideas too simple to be developed. In reality, the fundamental material of many of the bagatelles is more complex, even at times richly so, than the material of the larger works. It may almost be stated as a rule in Beethoven that the longer the work the simpler the material that goes into it. Both the range and the length of the *Diabelli* Variations were made possible by the existence of a theme with primitive virtues (which is not to say that they are not indeed virtues). The forms of late Beethoven descend clearly and directly from Haydn's technique of allowing the music to grow out of a small kernel, the simplest, most condensed of musical thoughts announced, generally, at the very opening. During what is called his 'third period,' Beethoven extended this technique far beyond any limits that could previously have been imagined.

To what an extent a composer can describe his working habits is more dependent on chance, the right interviewer, or an irrelevant talent with words than upon any distinction between reason and instinct. On at least one occasion, nevertheless, Beethoven put into words something about the interplay between the central musical idea and the total form of his works. Speaking to a young musician from Darmstadt, Louis Schlösser, he is supposed to have said: 'The working-out in breadth, length, height and depth begins in my head, and since I am conscious of what I want, the basic idea never leaves me. It rises, grows upward, and I hear and see the picture as a whole take shape and stand forth before me as though cast in a single piece, so that all that is left is the work of writing it down.'[1] These words were published more than fifty years after they may have been spoken; it is perhaps unwise to put too much faith in the exactitude of the reporting. The suggestion that a work was finished in his head before he began to write certainly does not tally with what we know of Beethoven's voluminous sketches through all stages of a piece, but it is by no means certain that he would not so have represented his methods of composing to a young visitor. In any case, the phrase about conceiving the work in several dimensions, working it out 'in

---

[1] Thayer, vol. II, p. 851. (The conversation took place during the period when Beethoven was working on the Ninth Symphony.)

breadth, length, height and depth,' is striking enough to make it likely that this was really a phrase of Beethoven's that would remain in the memory.

The conception of a work as a whole, and in a way that brought the details and the larger structure together more intimately than in the music of any other composer, is reflected in Beethoven's working procedures. He not only sketched extensively and exhaustively, but (as Lewis Lockwood has shown[1]) he began to make a sketch in full score of an orchestral piece— laying out all the measures, writing out the subsidiary details as well—even before the thematic material had reached its final state. This was a manner of working that he used at least by 1815, if not consistently. In Beethoven's music, one can literally speak of the basic material and the final shape being worked out together, in constant interdependence.

This growth from a central idea had been used by Beethoven before 1817 to determine, not only the entire thematic development of a movement, but also (to a much greater extent than in Haydn or Mozart) the texture of a work, its rhythm, spacing, thickness—as the *Waldstein* is dominated by the constant dominant seventh chords, the pulsating rhythms, and the descending scale a fifth long, the *Appassionata* by its insistent rhythms, its Neapolitan harmonies, and its repeated climaxes on a D♭.

Beethoven's power of thematic transformation, his ability to make much of little, was already astonishing. For example, both halves of the second theme of the Fifth Symphony are constructed out of the same small pattern:

so that the second half is a decorated form of the first, with the appoggiaturas making a contrast out of a unity. The four-note pattern that lies at the basis of this theme is already itself only an augmentation (in intervalic range, not in time) of the four-note pattern of the opening

so that what originally covers a fourth is stretched out over an octave. (Every composer before serialism played with the shapes of his themes, abstracting them from the exact pitches; only during the first three decades of twelve-tone music did pitch exert so absolute a tyranny that it deprived shape of its importance.)

---

[1] 'On Beethoven's Sketches and Autographs: Some Problems of Definition and Interpretation,' *Acta Musicologica* Vol. XLII, 1970, Fasc. II-I, Januar–Juni, Basel.

Starting with the *Hammerklavier*, Beethoven extended Haydn's technique to large-scale harmonic structure. Not only the development of the tensions implicit in the musical ideas, but also the actual course of their resolution is now more fully determined by the material itself. Put less teleologically, not only the discursive melodic shape but the large harmonic forms as well have become thematic, and derive from a central and unifying idea.

In the *Hammerklavier*, the use of descending thirds is almost obsessive, ultimately affecting every detail in the work. Chains of descending thirds (and their twins, ascending sixths) are, of course, common throughout tonal music: Brahms' Fourth Symphony is based on such a chain, and I have given examples above (pp. 283–5) of the importance of similar sequences in Mozart's D major Quintet. There is a relentless succession of descending thirds and rising sixths near the end of the first movement of Mozart's *Hunt* Quartet K. 458:

and the chain continues for some measures in ever greater contrapuntal complexity. Examples could be multiplied indefinitely. It is interesting to note that the opening of Beethoven's Fifth Symphony was originally sketched as such a chain of descending thirds.[1]

---

[1] Cited in Thayer, vol. I, p. 431.

The use of these chains in the language of tonality is many-sided. They are central in that they start by defining a triad.[1] In addition, as the example from Mozart shows, they provide the easiest way of writing a canon, and of thickening the contrapuntal texture, as every note in such a group forms a consonance with the two preceding, and the two following, notes. Haydn uses a very long chain of them at the climax of the finale of the Symphony no. 88. The counterpoint is child's play, but the energy is masterly:

---

[1] A triad is made up of a major and a minor third, and this asymmetry of classical harmony considerably enlarges the possibilities of a string of descending thirds. Our ear accepts, as part of the conventions of the language, a semi-identification of a major and a minor third in such a series, but also accepts a descent of minor thirds alone, which outline a dissonance and can be used to initiate a modulation.

and this example also reveals another useful characteristic of descending thirds, the possibility of forming a variety of harmonic sequences.

The kind of sequence achieved depends upon the placing of the rising sixth within the series of descending thirds: in the example above, Haydn gets magnificent rhythmic surprises by varying the grouping—a rhythmic device which has no name in musical terminology, and which we may call the rhythm of melodic pattern. The beginning of the excerpt from Haydn, however, groups the descending thirds in threes and creates a rising sequence, since the lowest note of each group continues to rise. To group them by fours, as Mozart begins above, is a way of producing a descending harmonic sequence of a common Baroque character: Verdi, in the 'Libera Me' from the *Requiem*, has a fugue which starts with descending thirds,

and the soprano soloist enters with a derived, falling sequence of thirds almost exactly the same as Mozart's Baroque progression:

Both the rising and falling sequences based on descending thirds are important in the *Hammerklavier*, and with them Beethoven realizes opposed kinds of motion with almost identical material.[1]

The development section[2] of the *Hammerklavier* uses sequences of descending thirds as almost its only method of construction, and concentrates on them with a determination and a fury previously unheard in music:

[1] Chains of rising thirds are much less frequent than descending thirds in tonal music. They would seem to be useful since they also define triads, but grouping them in threes sounds like parallel fifths and in fours like parallel sevenths: this is because the first note of a rising series continues to function as a bass for what follows it, and influences the fundamental harmony even after its release.

[2] The structure of the first movement may be summarized as follows:

Establishment of B flat major by the single rising and falling thirds of the opening theme and by definition of the octave space B♭–B♭.

G major (second group): chain of descending thirds in thematic form, and opposition of B♭–B♮ affirmed.

E flat major (development): complete exposition of sequence of falling thirds and modulation to B major.

Resolution by modulating through the subdominant direction (G flat major as flat submediant) to B minor, and reduction of B♭–B♮ and F♯–F♮ oppositions to the murmur of a trill.

The development has taken over the major task of exposition, which is why I begin this analysis with it. The progressive revelation of the material is the basis for the musical drama. (The second movement also follows this form.) The structure was a major innovation for Beethoven: when he had finished the *Hammerklavier* he said about it, 'Now I know how to write music.'

What determines the energy is not only the melodic rhythm or the changes of harmonic rhythm (with the enormous harmonic *ritenuto* towards the end of the passage), but also the rate of speed at which the thirds descend, and the change in their movement at cadences. The sequence of thirds starts as an interacting double sequence; that is why the answer of the fugato opening is at the subdominant, so that one sequence of descending thirds makes a descending sequence in canon with the other, while both retain their integrity. The double chain of thirds becomes a more complex and more exciting quadruple chain in measure 156 and even more emphatically in measure 167. The movement of thirds becomes very slow in measure 177, as does the harmonic rhythm, and comes to a dead halt at measure 191 with a pedal point on D that lasts a full ten measures.

The last descent of a third from D to B at measures 200–201 is the most important of all; after the long pause on D, this descent changes the key, and modulates—enharmonically, without warning and with a magical sonority—to B major. This is perhaps Beethoven's greatest innovation in structure; the large modulations are built from the same material as the smallest detail, and set off in such a way that their kinship is immediately audible. After the endless sequences of thirds, the slower movement and the pause, this modulation appears only as the last and inevitable step of the process; the pause before it only sets it in relief, and signifies that it is a descending third of a different nature, one which changes the tonal framework. We can see why one seems to *hear* structure in the late works of Beethoven as in the music of no other composer.

This modulation is only one step of the large structure of the first movement, and every major structural event is a descent of a third. The changes of key signature correspond exactly to the successive events:

B flat major	Opening themes	} Exposition
G major	'Second group'	
E flat major	Opening of development	
B major	End of development	

which is a triple descent by thirds to a point tonally remote from the tonic. The opposition between B♭ and B♮ arrived at in such a way creates an immense tension that can be resolved in the recapitulation only by extraordinary means.

The return to B flat major at the beginning of the recapitulation is so brutally abrupt as to resolve none of the tension at all. There is an almost immediate descent of another third to G flat major, which is related to B flat major as a key of subdominant character, and balances and resolves the G major of the exposition. But G flat (F sharp) major is also the dominant of B major, which is the heart of the unresolved tension. After a page in G flat major, the magnetic force of the still unresolved tension of B♮ on G♭ (F♯) is finally realized by an explosion:

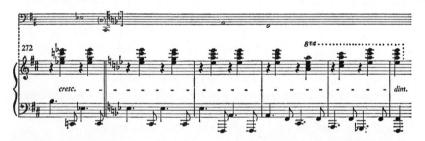

and this time it is *B minor* (!), even more remote from B flat major than the B major of the development, which had at least the relation of a pathetic Neapolitan chromaticism. After this climax, there is an exhausted descent (by thirds) to F, the dominant of B flat, and the rest of the movement continues firmly in the tonic. This is the greatest example of a climax placed after, instead of just before, the beginning of the recapitulation; it is only in a work of considerable dramatic ambition that it can be so effective.

This large structure is derived from the thematic material (or the themes are derived from the structure—Beethoven's method of composition makes both formulations equally valid). The descending thirds and the resultant clash between B♭ and B♮ are the governing factors. The beginning of the 'second group' is derived from the falling thirds:

The continuity of the series of descending thirds is emphasized here by Beethoven: the ascending sixths are always doubled at the octave below by the descending third, so that the equivalence is stressed and the movement uninterrupted. (This form of doubling produces an ascending harmonic sequence that rises much faster than the grouping by threes cited above.) The harmonic movement here is once again obsessive, except for the interruption of a cadence after which the melody starts again. The thirds shift from the melody to the bass; at the moment of the shift the direction of the harmonic sequence changes from a rising to a falling motion as the familiar Baroque progression appears. The ascending sequence balanced by the succeeding downward harmonic movement gives this melody its familiar classical symmetry. The two indications of *rubato* (*poco ritard.*) mark the articulation of the structure (the first at the interruption of the chain of thirds, and the second at the shift from the melody to the bass line) and show the expressive sensitivity of the sequence. The sudden doubling of the speed of the thirds at the end carries the line over into what follows.

The most important of the themes at the end of the exposition derives from the clash between B♭ and B♮:[1]

---

[1] When this theme appears in the recapitulation, the B♭–B♮ becomes D♭–D♮, but Beethoven is less interested in the major–minor sound than the B♭–B♮ clash, and he accordingly changes the inner voice here to bring it out:

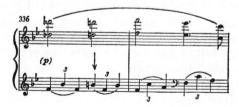

and the clash here inspires an analogous one between E♭ and E♮ in the two phrases. This contrast has already been prepared a few bars before in a magnificent arabesque at the end of the theme quoted above:

and Beethoven's accents make certain we hear this clash. In these two passages, the major–minor (or flat–natural) opposition engenders a true pathos that appears rarely elsewhere in the movement.

The main theme, with a dynamic opposition of *forte* and *piano* that is a standard classical opening, defines the interval of a third in both a rising and then descending form over the whole range of the piano:

so that all the principal themes of the movement are related closely to the larger plan. Measures 5 to 8, indeed, outline exactly the same thematic shape as the two heroic fanfares of the first four measures, but this shape is now softened, conciliated, and united in a gradual swell. The rhythmic unity of the movement appears in this softer version, which already announces the rhythm ♪♪ | ♩♩♩ of the first G major theme cited above, page 415. A significant element in these measures is the gradual introduction of the accidentals of the B major to come (B♮, F♯, and E♮) into the tonic B flat major. The long-range clash of B♭–B♮ is prepared from the beginning.

To reinforce the framework of this opposition and hold it firmly, the next phrase melodically defines an octave from B♭ to B♭, and ranges from the highest to the lowest B♭ on Beethoven's keyboard:

while the long, sinuous bass line still insists on the F♯ (or G♭). It is the powerful and insistently diatonic sound of B flat major against the harsh, chromatic and non-pathetic alterations of B major that gives this movement a sonority unlike any other, and it dominates every page. The following phrase shows how far the ordinary progressions of a normally diatonic B flat major are already contaminated by the B major which still lies in the future:

This is less a preparation than an overflow from the later tension into every corner of the work.

The modulation down a third to G major is as abrupt and rapid as possible:

and is tempered only by graceful strings of descending thirds:

where the left hand now develops the opening third of the main theme rhythmically.

G major already has the B♮ that clashes with the B♭, and the ending of the exposition exploits this to the full:

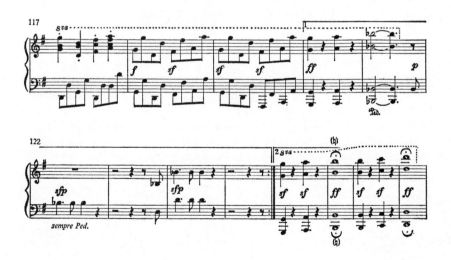

To hear this ambiguity, the repeat of the exposition is essential. When the
B♭ is heard in the first ending's context of G major (measure 121), it is a
shock. The B♮ of the second ending is an equal, or even greater shock, but
only if the first ending has already made its mark. Not only does this effect
incomparably clarify the structure, but it has a dramatic force that no
pianist should wish to miss.

This harsh opposition dominates the coda, from the dissonant inner trill
of its opening:

(where the B♮ is written as C♭) to the later and even harsher written-out bass
trills of F♯/G♭–F♮, which combines with fragments of the opening theme:

and which continue till the end of the movement. The sonority created is
dissonant but without pathos, and that is why many people, even musicians,
have found the *Hammerklavier* disagreeable. Nevertheless, the characteristic
sound is charged with an immense vitality.

The pervasive sonority and the structure that creates it can remove two
stumbling blocks in discussions of the movement; the metronome marking,
and the famous A♯/A♮ of the transition to the recapitulation:

I used to believe that the A♯ of measure 225 was correct, but I now think that Beethoven probably forgot to add a natural. Tovey also believed that it should be A♮, but that the misprint was a stroke of genius! He was surely right; the A♯ would fit the sound of the movement better, and I suspect that Beethoven's musical subconscious caused the error. Critics are always going on about the importance of instinct in composition, and a slip of the pen would be the most convincing proof of its operation and guidance.

The textual evidence for the A♮ is not, however, as strong as some writers would have us believe; the sketch by Beethoven proves nothing, as he made far more radical changes between sketch and final version. I have heard it asserted by a fine pianist that the A♮ is necessary for the climax, as its sonority provides the brightness of a bare fifth with the E rather than the tritone given by the A♯. But it is neither necessary nor possible to make much noise; the real climax does not occur here but pages later with the sonorous return to B minor, marked by a fermata. The unmeasured pauses in this movement are beautifully placed, and they mark the most significant steps in the tonal structure, the modulations to G major, E flat major and B minor; they should be held with a full sense of their necessary breadth, as they are the successive end points of each energetic onslaught of the music.

The metronome mark is ♩ = 138, which is very fast. There is nothing sacred about any metronome mark, and Beethoven was, after all, deaf and unable to test the justice of his suggestions. What can be heard clearly by the imagination may often be blurred and muddy in actual performance. Tempo indications, however, must be taken very seriously indeed, because they reveal the character of the work, and Beethoven was very careful about his markings. The tempo of the first movement of the *Hammerklavier* is Allegro, which for Beethoven was always a fast tempo. He never wrote a simple 'Allegro' when he meant 'Allegro maestoso' or 'Allegro ma non troppo.' It does not matter what metronome marking a pianist chooses for this movement providing it *sounds* Allegro; there is no excuse, textual or musical, for making it sound majestic, like Allegro maestoso, and such an effect is a betrayal of the music. It is often done, because it mitigates the harshness of the work, but this harshness is clearly essential to it. A majestic tempo also saps the rhythmic vitality on which the movement depends.[1] As we have seen,

---

[1] A metronome mark of from 126 to 132 to the half-note seems to me the most reasonable, but one must reckon with the sound of different pianos and different halls. It should also be emphasized that passages marked *espressivo* are meant to be played with a slight *ritenuto* in late Beethoven, as, for example, the theme cited above, page 416, marked *cantabile dolce ed espressivo*. As Beethoven himself said, you cannot put a metronome mark to sentiment.

the actual material of the work is neither rich nor particularly expressive; it only lives up to its reputation for greatness if its rhythmic power is concentrated. And it is meant to be difficult to listen to.

Insofar as a musical idea can be circumscribed by words, it should be obvious that even in a purely formal description, the central idea of the opening movement of the *Hammerklavier* is not merely a series of descending thirds, but the relation of the large tonal structure (with its powerfully dissonant long-range clash of B flat major and B major) to the rhythmic and harmonic energy of the sequences formed by the falling thirds. From this relation between far-flung dissonance and the impetuous force of the details comes not only the sonority peculiar to the work but also the combination of stern brilliance and transitory pathos.

The change in Beethoven's methods of composition can be measured by comparing the *Hammerklavier* with the early B flat major Piano Sonata, op. 22. There are interesting coincidences, as certain tonalities seem to develop different and individual qualities for almost every composer, and Beethoven's treatment of B flat major throughout his life is almost as characteristic as his emphasis on Neapolitan harmonies whenever he wrote in F minor. The Sonata op. 22 begins as if the *Hammerklavier*'s first theme were on a miniature scale:

and has a second theme that is also basically our series of descending thirds:

but nothing in the large-scale structure is derived from this material, which is used concisely, but with a less urgent logic than Haydn or Mozart brought to the form in their last years.

The other movements of the *Hammerklavier* follow the pattern of the first very closely, but, as always in a classical sonata, with a gradual loosening of the formal tensions. The scherzo is a parody of the first movement; even its main theme is like a humorous form of the main theme of the first:

and the structure of descending thirds is even more in evidence. The main theme of the trio (in B flat minor) begins like the major theme, and throughout the scherzo there is the same detailed insistence on B♮ that we found in the first movement:

At the end the B♮ finally explodes again, in a mocking parallel to the climax of the first movement, a brutal joke that is as much sinister and dramatic as good-humored:

The elaborate structure of the first movement is missing here, but reflections of its dramatic shape and its sonority are heard as if in a distorted echo.

The slow movement is in F sharp minor, a key which is a third down from the B flat major of the first two movements. Its opening theme has the series of descending thirds, and Beethoven added in proof an opening measure which gives the rising third with which the first two movements and the theme of the last begin, and which serves as a transition from the scherzo:

The structure of descending thirds is not audibly prominent here in its shift from treble to bass, but it is set very much in relief when the theme is repeated at the opening of the development (which, *like the development of the first movement*, continues the sequence of thirds remorselessly to the end of the section):

A quotation from Brahms' Fourth Symphony would seem to be inevitable in a work built out of similar material.

There are both literal, untransposed echoes throughout this movement of the earlier B♭–B♮ ambiguity, and an analogous opposition of F sharp minor and G major. The major–minor opposition here, although again that of tonic and flatted supertonic, is intended for pathos, and the deep expression of grief is one of Beethoven's most moving achievements. Much of the writing (marked *con grand'espressione*, a rare indication in Beethoven) is in arabesques of a Chopinesque grace and chromatic poignance. The rich decoration of the return of the main theme has few parallels in the rest of Beethoven's music.

Although in 'first-movement sonata form,' the exposition of this Adagio goes, not to the relative major, but down a third to D major; as in the two preceding movements, the principal climax is withheld until after the recapitulation. It is again a climax on the supertonic, but the symmetry of the relations does not prevent a less formal emotional ambiance of an entirely different order. It is obvious that the sequence of descending thirds and all it implied, almost identifiable with the actual content of the music in the first movement, have here been relegated to the formal structure; the expressive interest of the slow movement is now centered above all on the almost operatically expressive and decorative line of the melody, and on a chromatic texture which has little in common with the dissonant and harshly diatonic sonority of the other movements.

What follows is less an introduction to the fugal finale than a transition from the slow movement, and to be understood it must be played without pause after the Adagio.[1] The transition begins with the drop of a minor second from the last measures of the slow movement: the long series of soft F sharp major chords is followed by a soft arpeggio, *dolce*, of every F♮ on Beethoven's keyboard:

---

[1] Beethoven's letter to Ries for the English edition suggesting cuts and rearrangements of the movements if Ries felt the work was too difficult for English taste has no value as evidence of his artistic intentions. He was concerned only with a good sale in England, and the sonata was being correctly printed in Vienna.

Beethoven

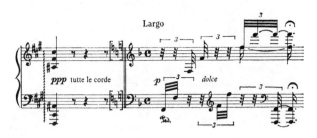

This mysterious, unharmonized and therefore unexplained F♮ is the dominant of B flat major, and into the soft ending in F sharp major a hint is given of what is to come, without a complete resolution into the new tonality. This is a device almost exactly repeated in the Ninth Symphony, there with a terrifying dissonance, as Beethoven takes the last B flat chord of the slow movement and places under it the dominant A♮ of the next movement.

In the *Hammerklavier*, however, the music first returns immediately to the F sharp major of the Adagio. The transition sets up an improvisatory motion, partly without barlines, and is the most interesting of all the concentrations of descending thirds. It is the bass that outlines the thirds, moving down them and supporting a succession of soft, hesitant chords: the series of thirds is interrupted every so often by an interlude, each one a little more brilliant in character. The first interlude is based on falling thirds as well, so that there is a small set within the large one:

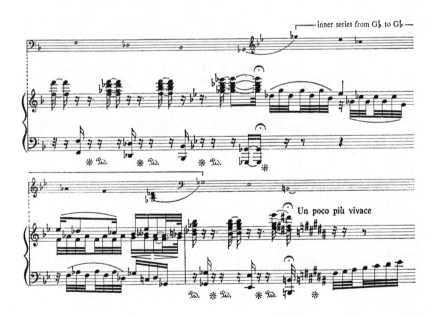

When the falling bass has reached G♯, the third interlude is a pastiche of Baroque counterpoint, and the sketches for this movement show that Beethoven copied out little phrases of Bach's *Well-Tempered Keyboard* along with his work on the themes. It is evident that he wished here for an effect of the gradual creation of a new contrapuntal style, arising from the improvisatory structure of the transition.

After the interlude in Baroque style, the thirds begin again, and reach an organ point on A♮, to which the opening arpeggio on F♮ is now transposed:

This long-range succession of F and A is the first hint of the theme of the fugue. The thirds in the bass begin to descend again faster and faster until at *Prestissimo* they return to A once more, at which Beethoven hammers away. Slowing down, there is a final descent of a third, *pianissimo*, to F♮:

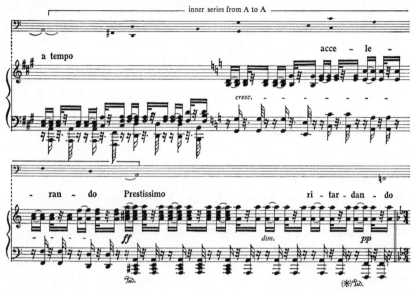

so that we have now returned to the F with which these pages began, yet with a new significance and with a new firmness.[1] This transitional page is one of the most astonishing in the history of music. No other work until then, to my knowledge, combined the effect of almost uncontrolled improvisatory movement with such a totally systematic structure. Even the notation is revolutionary, as the syncopated spacing of the chords serves to enforce less a hesitant rhythm than a delicate, uninsistent tone-quality. We have the sense of a contrapuntal texture taking shape, and growing organically out of unformed material.

When the bass reaches F♮, we have arrived at the tonic key of B flat major, and the left hand hints again at the opening F–A of the fugue theme:

---

[1] The last descent before the A at *Prestissimo* is not a third but a fourth (D to A): in Beethoven's sketches the series was originally to continue on in thirds (D, B, G, E, C, A) back to A, but this entailed harmonic and rhythmic problems; consistency was abandoned without much loss as the descent in this passage is only an interior set from A to A, and not part of the larger movement.

and in its leap of a tenth from the bass, we can hear its relation to the opening of the first movement.

Where the first movement makes little distinction between thirds and transpositions of a third to a tenth and even to a seventeenth, using them almost interchangeably, the finale insists upon keeping the integrity of the tenth as fundamental and thematic. The fugue theme states its opening tenth leap followed by a trill, and then goes at once through the series of descending thirds that dominates the work:

The last two measures bring up the dissonant B♮ that plays such an important role throughout. Arranged in a new pattern and with a radically different character, the elements of the fugue-theme are exactly the same as those of the first movement.[1]

The plan of the fugue is also a descent in thirds similar to that of the first movement, but leaning more heavily upon the subdominant and minor keys, and so retaining one of the traditional features of the classical finale. This movement resolves not only by its harmonic character but also by its looser organization, a decided articulation into sections midway between a rondo and a set of continuous variations, both forms typical of the finale as conceived in the late eighteenth century.

The fugue-theme is transformed by its context throughout the movement. At each entirely new form or treatment of the theme, there is a modulation which is, as one might expect, always the descent of a third. (The return of the theme in a previously heard form provides subsidiary modulations.) The first half of the form falls into the following sections:

1. B flat major   Exposition; re-exposition with a shift of accent (D flat major)
2. G flat major   Episode (variant of the theme)[2]
3. E flat minor   Theme in augmentation; return of episode (A flat major)
4. B minor   Theme in contrary motion with new counter-theme; return of original form of theme (D major)
5. G major   Theme in the inversion

[1] Even the trill is derived from the figure of a descending second at the end of the first measure of the opening movement.

[2] The episode is based only on a decorated form of the opening leap of a tenth of the fugue theme ♪ which appears as ♪

At this point a descent by thirds back to the tonic would entail five more sections, and Beethoven uses instead a descent of a minor second that is found at so many crucial points of the work: B major to B flat major at the beginning of the recapitulation of the first movement, and once again in the middle of the recapitulation; B major–minor to B flat major at the end of the scherzo, G major to F sharp minor at the end of the slow movement, and F sharp to F at the opening of the transition to the last movement. The modulation by minor second is neither makeshift nor short-cut. All of these descents of a minor second are the larger counterpart of the B♭–B♮ clash from which the most pathetic and lyrical moments of the work derive. Ultimately, they must be related to the complex harmonic situation entailed by the modulations of descending thirds, which substitutes tonic-mediant relations for tonic-dominant. This is, in fact, the principal reason for the 'difficult' sound of the *Hammerklavier*, as the ear is traditionally used to the dominant-tonic resolution implied by the language, and Beethoven withholds such resolutions fairly consistently throughout the work. Almost all the large resolutions are uncompromising juxtapositions of minor seconds (which arise directly from the descent by thirds of B♭, G, E♭, B♮ and the return from B♮ to B♭), and they sound and even echo long after as 'enharmonic.' But they are the main source of the work's expressive and dramatic tension.

The fugue therefore continues from the G major inversion of the theme without a break by a descent of a third to:

6. E flat major   Short development and stretto ending with a brilliant cascade built from the opening tenth leap and descending harmonically by thirds:

which modulate down a minor second to:

7. D major   Second episode (variant of the theme)

This new and delicately lyrical episode (which begins with the ubiquitous descent by thirds) is formed freely from the main theme:

and, as the end of the section can show, it is constructed with the harmonic sequences that characterize the rest of the work:

The modulation at the end of this passage (mm. 277–8), one of the most moving in all music, and in which the chromatic detail has a purity of sound within the diatonic frame that it would never find again in the nineteenth century, is the last inner change of tonality in the work: it returns (by a drop of a third) to the tonic B flat major.

8. Establishment of B flat major   Transition: combination of second episode with fragments of the main theme.

The establishment of the tonic here is once more by a sequence of thirds:

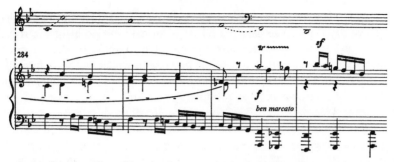

and the final section, like the last number of a Mozart operatic finale, stays close to the tonic for all of its very considerable length.

> 9. B. flat major Theme inverted and in original form simultaneously, followed by stretto and coda.

In this final section, Beethoven unleashes a demonic energy and a torrent of dissonance that make the harmonic progressions, basically simple, very difficult to hear.

In passing, it may be mentioned that the descent in thirds was so important to Beethoven that in his sketches he tried to turn the opening of the *inversion* of the fugue into a descent by thirds. However, this made for an uninteresting melodic form, and he quickly dropped it. There was a compensation, however. The counter-subject of the theme in its original form descends by thirds:

In the inversion, it should, of course, ascend. Instead, while the main theme is inverted (and rises by thirds), the counter-subject continues to descend:

so that the basic character of the harmonic movement is retained.

The fugue of the *Hammerklavier* is essentially a dramatic set of variations; each new form of the theme is an event, emphasized and set in relief. With this movement, the fugue is at last transformed into a classical shape. The analogies of its structure with that of the preceding movements are obvious; like the first, it descends by thirds from B flat major to the remote B minor, and the harmonic detail is largely identical. What is new in the movement (and indeed in the history of music) is the treatment of the trill on the second note of the theme, employed with a violence that deprives it of any decorative character: Beethoven's trill is not an ornament, but plays a role as thematic as the opening measures of the Fifth Symphony.

The *Hammerklavier* is not typical of Beethoven, and does not sound it; it is not even typical of his last period. It is an extreme point of his style. He never again wrote so obsessively concentrated a work. In part, it must have been an attempt to break out of the impasse in which he found himself. Much longer than any piano sonata he (or anyone else, I believe) had written until then, it was an attempt to produce a new and original work of un-compromising greatness, and Beethoven himself talked of it in those terms. It is just this extreme character which makes it a statement of such clarity, and allows us to see, as almost no other piece does, the principles by which he worked, particularly at the end of his life; through it we can understand how the total structure as well as the details of a work of Beethoven have such an audible power.

It is also a work which extends (and even, to some extent, strains) the relation of musical form and content in a specific way. The content—the subject-matter—of the *Hammerklavier* is the nature of the contemporary musical language. The work of art which is literally about its own technique is almost too familiar by now: the poem about poetry itself (like most of those by Mallarmé), the film in which the principal subject-matter is cinematic technique and the cross-references to other films, the painting which actually attempts to depict the process of projecting space upon a flat surface or which refers, not outside itself, but directly to the medium of paint. This paradoxical interchange of form and content is a normal process of any art, which naturally tends to displace the weight of significance away from that which is signified towards the sign. But music, where denotation is at once precise and totally unspecific, presents a special problem. If we omit the occasional imitative effects (from bird-song in Jannequin to insect noises in Bartók) and the direct conventions of pathos, we can deny neither that music has significance nor that it signifies most clearly and most often itself.

Beethoven sharpens the focus of this self-reference, as the introduction to the fugue of the *Hammerklavier* makes peculiarly explicit. Out of an undefined rhythm and a harmony which evades a fixed context, there are a series of gestures towards a polyphonic form. The third of these gestures is an exercise in Baroque style, which is not only left unfinished like the first two, but broken off abruptly in the middle as if emphatically cut off and rejected. The search is resumed, the arpeggio on A echoes the opening one on F, and out of this succession F–A is born the theme of the fugue after the whirlwind descent of thirds which attains prestissimo. A more open and direct statement about classical counterpoint and its historical relations to the preceding style could not be made within a strictly musical language. Yet the language of the other movements is no less immediate for being implicit. The subject-matter of the *Hammerklavier*, the first movement in particular, is the nature of one aspect of tonality, but it makes no statement which can be given purely verbal form, and Beethoven's art is here as sensuous as a Schubert song.

Beethoven

Throughout his life, Beethoven increasingly relied directly upon the fundamental tonal relationships for material. His continuous attempt to strip away, at some point in each large work, all decorative and even expressive elements from the musical material—so that part of the structure of tonality is made to appear for a moment naked and immediate, and its presence in the rest of the work as a dynamic and temporal force suddenly becomes radiant—this ever greater use of the simplest blocks and elements of the tonal language gives his development, seen as a whole, an undeniable consistency. It is interesting that the harshness of much of his music, his ruthless disregard of the desires and even of the needs of both public and performer, and the loneliness of the stand he took were proof for most of his contemporaries of his wilfulness, and his eccentricity. For us, as for E. T. A. Hoffmann, they are a sign of his selflessness and his 'sobriety'—his logic, in short. This logic is most manifest in his transformation of the only two forms which had, in the hands of Mozart and Haydn, still managed to retain part of their Baroque nature: the fugue and the variation. By the end of his life Beethoven had succeeded in turning these last survivals of an earlier style into fully classical forms, with a dramatic shape and an articulation of the larger proportions analogous to the sonata, and that are, in fact, based on sonata style.

Haydn had already attempted a new approach to variation-form in his double variation-sets with contrasting themes. It was, however, a static contrast that he reached; in addition, his approach to the actual writing of variations remained always decorative, except in his essentially personal disinclination to allow decorative patterns to continue and develop with any regularity. Beethoven's patterns are (like Mozart's) more regular, but the structure of his variation sets undergoes radical change: what takes place is a drastic simplification.

How much of any given melody must be immanent in a variation, how much of the shape is essential, is largely a matter of stylistic definition. The whole of the theme is almost always completely recognizable in any of Mozart's or Haydn's variations. Beethoven, however, made the requirements absolutely minimal—only the barest skeleton of the melodic and harmonic shape is necessary, after which, of course, the superfluous elements of the theme can be used both dramatically and decoratively. What Beethoven did to *Rule, Britannia* is as good an illustration of the extremity of his methods as anything in the larger and more famous sets. The first four measures of the theme

Tempo moderato

435

are, in Beethoven's first variation, reduced to:

The only part left of the theme is the barest minimum of its shape:

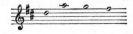

and this shape is then broken up by being transposed into different registers.

The wide difference between this kind of simplification and that of, say, Bach's *Goldberg* Variations cannot be overemphasized. Bach's method is to isolate one element of the original theme, the bass, and to build upon that. Beethoven's system is to make an abstract of the total shape of the theme; the form implied by his first variation, a form which supports the variation and relates it to what follows, is not the melodic shape alone (as is shown by the use of the first measure entirely as a bass) nor the bass alone, but a representation of the theme as a whole. The classical attack on the independence of voices made the linear approach of the Baroque variation-form no longer satisfactory, or even feasible except as pastiche. Beethoven's conception of the action in a sonata as arising from material as concentrated as Haydn's but even simpler in nature enabled him to effect a comparable simplification of material within the variation-form, and this, in turn, released an imagination that would otherwise have been bound to the decoration of an already complex line.

This sense of a supporting non-linear musical scaffold informs all of Beethoven's large variation sets (even the oddly Baroque C minor Variations, although this stands naturally somewhat apart). For this reason, although no two themes sound superficially more disparate than Diabelli's waltz and the Arietta of the Sonata op. 111, the last page of one appears to quote the last page of the other textually at one point: a descending fourth underlies the otherwise so different openings of both themes, and the coincidence of the later development is an almost inevitable result of Beethoven's way of looking at a musical idea.

In many of the late variation sets (opp. 109, 111, 127, etc.) there is a progressive simplification as the variations proceed—not of the texture but of the conception of the underlying theme. That part of its shape to which the variations allude becomes gradually more and more skeletal in nature. There is also a progressive isolation of different aspects of the theme, as if they were being illuminated one by one. It is true that we need less to be reminded of what is gradually becoming more familiar by repetition, but in any case Beethoven tends to simplify as the texture becomes more complex. For this reason, his late variations give the impression that they are not so much decorating the theme as discovering its essence.

The development of the large structure made for changes that are still more profound. Essentially static and decorative, almost always in one key so that the interplay between harmonic tension and general texture could only be on the level of small details, variations presented a problem to the dramatically conceived classical style. Even the rigidly fixed proportions of the form were alien to it. Relatively early in his career, Beethoven made a striking attempt to overcome the harmonically static nature of the form: in the Variations on an Original Theme in F Major, op. 34, he set up a sequence of descending thirds, each variation starting a third lower than the preceding. The sequence is, however, resolved with unusual prudence: the penultimate variation is in C, and the finale's immediate return to F restores a dominant-tonic relation. The succession of tonalities in this work, moreover, is basically coloristic, not structural. There is nothing in the theme, or, for the most part, in the variations themselves that implies such treatment. The florid writing, operatic in its decoration, corresponds in texture to the coloristic harmonic structure: in no other work is Beethoven closer to the ornamental style of Hummel, a style in which Chopin was to find his beginning and which he never entirely renounced. These F major Variations, therefore, in spite of their great charm and an unusual lyric fullness, represent a purely exterior attempt to break out of the decorative formula imposed by the variation form. Yet at the end of his life in the choral finale of the Ninth Symphony, Beethoven returned to the scheme of changing the key by descending thirds for successive variations, now modified and justified both formally and dramatically.

The *Eroica* Variations, in both the orchestral and the piano versions, are also an exterior solution, but of a different kind, in which the form is dramatized by the separation of the bass and treble elements of the theme, and by the delayed introduction of the latter. The theme is, as it were, anatomized at the opening, and reconstituted. The bass alone makes a theme that is bare to the point of being grossly humorous, and nothing is more typical of Beethoven's comedy than his insistence on it. The emphatic awkwardness of the bass and its violent dynamic and rhythmic contrasts prevent the appearance of any suggestion of the Baroque passacaglia. Nevertheless, such a split conception of bass and melody as independent fits less well with the later work of Beethoven than with the first generation of Romantic composers, who tended to combine a melodically centered structure with a Baroque sequential bass. The opening of the *Eroica* Variations was, indeed, directly imitated by Schumann in the early *Impromptus on a Theme of Clara Wieck*, a work whose high inspiration is almost matched by its maladresse, and which Schumann marred without pity in rewriting it for a second edition.

The *Eroica* Variations (particularly the version for piano) also take the first step towards a classical dramatization of the variation-finale. The typical late eighteenth-century set of variations generally followed a French scheme, in which the penultimate variation, a very slow one filled with brilliantly florid coloratura, was followed by a fast and extended virtuoso finale like a fantasy on the theme. In the *Eroica* set, the Largo, florid enough for any taste, is introduced by a minor variation, remarkably restrained and delicate in its chromatic expression; these two form a clear slow movement, set off all the more by the harsh virtuosity of the preceding variation, which provides a clear close to all that has gone before. The finale itself is a brilliant fugue which leads directly to a replaying of the theme—a written out da capo, decorated and transformed by trills. Once again at this time we find Beethoven trying to enlarge the forms of the late eighteenth century by referring to earlier eighteenth-century models—the fugal finale to a set of variations (as in Bach's Passacaglia and Fugue in C minor) and the da capo return of the theme—and once again the form attained was one even more suitable for a later period, as in Brahms' later imitation of many of its features in the *Handel* Variations.

We tend to consider a composer's development as if it were the most gradual of approaches towards a satisfactory form, a completely integrated ideal; yet when this form actually appears, it is often with a surprising discontinuity, with a novelty and simplicity of conception that is difficult to relate to what has preceded. The slow-movement variations of the *Appassionata* are a classical solution in the most inward sense: without any attempt at significant innovation of form, they reach the proportions of the sonata style, the dramatic shape and the placing of tension and resolution. Moreover, they attain this with the minimal use of harmonic tension, without modulation, and almost by rhythm and melodic texture alone. The complete stillness of the hymn which is its theme makes the slightest increase of motion deeply telling: its static harmony—almost an unmoving upper pedal on A flat— gives the least chromatic alteration the larger significance of a modulation. Most important, perhaps, is the restriction of register within each variation: the successive rise step by step from the low bass to the treble is the clearest articulation of the form. The acceleration of note-values and the increased syncopations are the main vehicle of expression and build the most powerful of climaxes, so that the return of the theme in the low register comes to seem not like a da capo but like a true sonata recapitulation[1] (it is even rewritten to include a reminiscence of the obbligato bass line of the second variation). The most extraordinary part of the achievement is the feeling of release that comes with the return of the theme in its original form, and the resolving force of this 'recapitulation.' Through this, the variation form loses

---

[1] This effect of resolution upon the return to the original shape of the theme in variation sets was already attempted by Haydn (the *Surprise* Symphony is as good an example as any), but with far less cogency. Nevertheless, Beethoven is, in effect, returning here to Haydn's principles after the more 'advanced' experiments of a few years before.

its additive character, and conforms to the dramatic and almost spatially conceived figures of sonata style.

With this movement it is possible at last to say that the variation set has become a classical form: the forces that created the sonata, the same feeling for event and for proportion, move here unrestricted within a form that they have themselves shaped. It is from this model that the slow movements in variation form of the later works are taken. The most subtle is the set in the last quartet, op. 135, where the change to minor which brings a strong move to the mediant major has the effect of a genuine modulation without actually moving, and the return to the tonic major, like a decorated recapitulation, is all the more touching. The resolving character of the last variation is essential to this conception: by means as delicate as they are powerful, Beethoven succeeds in giving harmonic tension to a work that does not move from the tonic. Only in this way can the essential classical preference for recapitulation over da capo be satisfied, and the symmetry of the return be conceived not as a frame but as a dramatic resolution.

The idea of the finale of the *Eroica* Variations reappears transfigured in the *Diabelli*. Here the traditionally florid slow penultimate variation has become a series of three in the minor mode: Rococo decoration has completely disappeared, to be replaced in the last and most profoundly beautiful of the trio by a homage to J. S. Bach, with an imitation of the famous ornamented minor variation of the *Goldberg*. The powerful double fugue that follows is frankly Handelian; at the end, again as in the *Goldberg*, the dance returns—not Diabelli's simple waltz any longer, but the most delicate and complex of minuets, with a lavish play of sonorities that Beethoven rarely permitted himself. It is an ending conceived in the comic spirit (even the last chord is a surprise). In the *Diabelli*, as in the Quartet in F major op. 135 and, above all, the magnificent scherzando movement in D flat major from the Quartet in B flat major op. 130, Beethoven attained the witty combination of lyricism and irony that was part of Mozart's natural grace, and that Haydn was too good-humored to imitate.

In the structure of the *Diabelli*, there is a clear attempt to consider the variations in large groups, as if to find a unifying equivalent for the several movements of a sonata or symphony. The same grouping is even clearer in the choral finale of the Ninth Symphony, in which Beethoven has used the variation form to combine at once the symmetry of the sonata-allegro form and the larger conception of the four-movement symphony. Here, too, there is a return to an earlier experiment, the series of descending thirds of the F major Variations op. 34. In the choral finale, the successive modulations are no longer isolated events, but are comprehended within a larger scheme, the modulations justified in the same way as those of a sonata. More precisely, it is not the 'sonata' itself which provides the background against which the finale must be understood, but the classical concerto form. The choral variations begin, in fact, with the double exposition of a concerto (even the opening solo recitative is astonishingly included in more elaborate form in the orchestral tutti); as in Mozart's concertos, the striking modulation is reserved for the solo exposition. Once the sonata is conceived as a set of proportions regulating tensions (or large-scale dissonances) and their resolution, it is easy to see that the purely orchestral fugue in the last movement of the Ninth Symphony plays the role of a development section (as well as standing in the place of the traditional second tutti of a concerto). The recapitulation (or resolution), with its return of the tonic, is equally set into relief.

Over this enormous sonata concerto form, a four-movement grouping which has equal weight is superimposed.[1] The opening expository movement leads to a B flat major scherzo in military style with Turkish music; a slow movement in G major introduces a new theme; and a finale begins with the triumphant combination of the two themes in double counterpoint. These groupings are not to be conceived as emphasized articulations, but as the result of pressures which give a more specifically classical shape to the variation form. About the shape itself there is no question: the proportions and the feeling for climax and expansion are solely those of the classical symphony, and even the use of the variation form itself fulfils the classical demand for a finale looser and more relaxed than a first movement. The ideals of the sonata style enabled Beethoven to endow a set of variations with the grandeur of a symphonic finale; until the *Eroica*, this form had been reserved for the lesser genres of the concerto and chamber music (lesser only on a scale of magnificence). The new principle can be felt already in the *Eroica* finale, but it is only in the Fantasy for Piano, Chorus, and Orchestra of 1808 that it became the principal shaping element.[2] With the Ninth Symphony, the variation set is completely transformed into the most massive of finales, one that is itself a four-movement work in miniature.

Beethoven's development of the fugue is best comprehended within the context of the transformation of the variation. The two fugal finales—the *Great Fugue* op. 133 (the last movement of the String Quartet op. 130) and the fugue of the *Hammerklavier*—are both conceived as a series of variations, each new treatment of the theme being given a new character. Like the last movement of the Ninth Symphony, they both have the harmonic tensions characteristic of sonata-allegro form, along with its sense of a return and extensive resolution. They both, too, impose upon this another structural idea of several movements: this is particularly evident in the *Great Fugue*, which

---

[1] This superposition of sonata-allegro and four-movement form is one of the rare experiments of the last years of Beethoven's life to have a genuine repercussion in the more original work of the first Romantic generation. The Liszt sonata is an attempt to repeat this conception. In spite of the frequent vulgarity of both his taste and his inspiration, Liszt was surely the composer of his generation who best understood Beethoven.

[2] The relation of the 'Choral Fantasy' to 'sonata-allegro' form was pointed out by Hans Keller in an article in *Score* (January, 1961).

has an introduction, Allegro, slow movement (in a new key), and Scherzo finale as almost completely separate divisions; but the D major section of the *Hammerklavier* Fugue also provides a perceptible sense of a slow movement before the stretto-finale.

No one model, however, can exhaust the variety of ways in which Beethoven was able to integrate the fugue into a classical structure. The simplest and most Haydnesque device is the use of a fugue for a development section, as in the last movement of the Piano Sonata op. 101, and the first movement of the *Hammerklavier*. The Sonata op. 110 uses the inversion of the fugue and a stretto of augmentation and diminution as both development section and preparation of the return of the original theme and tonality; the fugal texture is dropped once the tonic is reached. Perhaps the most remarkable integrations of the fugue within a larger plan are in the Quartet in C sharp minor op. 131, and the Piano Sonata in C minor op. 111.

Both Haydn's E flat major Sonata H. 52 and Beethoven's C sharp minor Quartet op. 131 have second movements in the Neapolitan major—that is, a half step above the first movement. Both are prepared, but on different levels of power and effectiveness. Haydn's E major slow movement is prepared by an emphasis on that tonality in the development section of the E flat major first movement, and by allusions to E major harmonies in the narrative thread of the recapitulation. In Beethoven's quartet, however, the D major movement is prepared at once by the opening theme of the initial fugue with its *sforzando* on A♮: this dominant of the next movement is dramatized throughout the fugue, and, played over and over with the theme transposed so that the *sforzando* falls on a D♮, it is the fulcrum which bears all of the expressive weight, and the pivot upon which everything else turns. The texture is given a directional force in the classical sense, totally alien to Baroque fugal style. The change to D major at the beginning of the second movement, therefore, seems at once as inevitable as it is astonishing; where Haydn's relationship is only prepared by the working-out of the previous movement, Beethoven's is implied by the main theme of the opening fugue, and is already potentially in the stuff out of which the form is created.

In the C minor Piano Sonata op. 111, the combination of fugue and sonata form takes a form almost the opposite of Mozart's brilliant solution in his G major Quartet finale, which Beethoven imitated in the last movement of the Quartet op. 59 no. 3. In the two quartet finales, the fugal texture of the opening measures gradually turns into the more normal *obbligato* writing of the late eighteenth century, in which accompaniments have only a shadowy independence given by their thematic significance. The Allegro con brio ed appassionata of the Sonata op. 111 starts with what is evidently a fugue theme, but withholds fugal texture until a good part of the statement has already taken place. When it comes at last the actual sonority of fugal writing provides the increased animation demanded by sonata style.

The development is largely a double fugue in which the second theme is an augmentation of the first. The first four notes of the theme

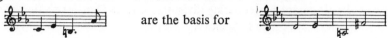 are the basis for

in which, as so often, Beethoven is more interested in the shape of his theme than in the exact pitch relationship of the notes.

The first movement as a whole springs from the initial series of diminished seventh chords. The introduction has the following simple skeleton of three phrases:

The third diminished seventh is prolonged by a chromatic expansion over several measures before finding its resolution on an F minor chord (it is the length of this expansion and the consequent delay of the resolution that make the phrase spill over at once into the dominant of C minor). The main theme of the Allegro that follows is derived from these diminished sevenths and their resolutions:

although the melodic form is nowhere clarified in the introduction, which presents only the harmonic aspect (as the *Eroica* Variations begin with the bass alone). However, to make the derivation doubly clear, at the end of the movement Beethoven harmonizes the theme with the chords

where the diminished sevenths occur in the same order as in the introduction.

This order of the chords also fixes the harmonic structure of the development section almost in its entirety:

The three chords and their resolutions provide a basis for this development, and the order of the chords is once again always that of the introduction. The expressive significance of these chords needs no comment; they color most of the piece, appear with extreme violence at every important climax, and supply the dynamic impulse for most of the harmonic transformations.

Most of Beethoven's works in C minor from the *Sonate Pathétique* on rely heavily upon diminished sevenths at climactic movements. Yet none before the Sonata op. 111 fixes an order for these chords so firmly throughout a movement (the three chords and their inversions exhaust the range of possible diminished sevenths), derives the principal melodic material so directly from their sonority, and makes such a consistent attempt to integrate the whole movement by their means. It is this concentration upon the simplest and most fundamental relationships of tonality that characterizes Beethoven's late style most profoundly. His art, with all its dramatic force and its conception in terms of dramatic action, became more and more an essentially meditative one.

The aspect of many of these late works is not ingratiating; to many, the *Great Fugue* is disagreeably harsh. But when it is played, as it should be, as the finale of the B flat Quartet op. 130, there is nothing eccentric in this harshness, or in the broken sobs (marked 'strangled') of the *Cavatina* that precedes it. What makes some of these works appear wilful is that they are uncompromising. This was understood during Beethoven's lifetime by E. T. A. Hoffmann. Against those who granted Beethoven only genius without control, imagination without order, he wrote:

> But what if it were only *your* weak sight which misses the profound unity of inner relation [*innere tiefe Zusammenhang*] in each composition? If it were only *your* fault that the language of the master, understood by the consecrated, is incomprehensible, if the door to the holy of holies remains closed to you? In truth, the master, who is the peer of Haydn and Mozart in self-possession [*Besonnenheit*], carves his essential being [*sein Ich*] from the inner kingdom of tones, and reigns over it as its absolute ruler.

Since the Renaissance at least, the arts have been conceived as ways of exploring the universe, as complementary to the sciences. To a certain extent, they create their own fields of research; their universe is the language they have shaped, whose nature and limits they explore, and in exploring, transform. Beethoven is perhaps the first composer for whom this exploratory function of music took precedence over every other: pleasure, instruction, and, even, at times, expression. A work like the *Diabelli* Variations is above all a discovery of the nature of the simplest musical elements, an investigation of the language of classical tonality with all its implications for rhythm and texture as well as melody and harmony. There was no doubt an element of good fortune in his arriving on the scene to find a universe, a language already so rich in possibilities and resonances as the one formed by Haydn and Mozart. His singlemindedness, however, is unparalleled in the history of music, and it is this unrelenting high seriousness which can still create resentment.

Beethoven was the greatest master of musical time. In no other composer is the relation between intensity and duration so keenly observed; no one else understood so well, not even Handel or Stravinsky, the effect of simple reiteration, the power that can be drawn from repetition, the tension that can arise from delay. There are many works (the finale of the Eighth Symphony is only the most famous) in which an often-repeated detail becomes fully comprehensible only near the end of the piece, in which case we may quite literally speak of a logical tension that has been added to the familiar harmonic and rhythmic tensions of sonata form. Stravinsky once wrote that 'one misses in all so-called post-Webern music the tremendous leverage which Beethoven makes of time.' This mastery of time was dependent on a comprehension of the nature of musical action, or, rather, musical actions. A musical event takes place on different levels; the fastest *perpetuum mobile* can appear immobile, and a long silence can be heard *prestissimo*. Beethoven never miscalculated the intensity of his musical actions, and the technique carried so far by Haydn and Mozart of endowing the proportions themselves with a weight both expressive and structural reaches the height of its development in Beethoven. The dissolution of classical articulation made its revival impossible.

The weight given within a work to duration alone (both of the whole and the parts) is by no means purely, or even principally, rhythmic in nature. Harmonic mass, the weight and scope of a line or of a phrase, thickness of texture—all these play roles equally influential. The fusion of these elements in Beethoven with a synthesis that not even Mozart knew[1] allowed him a command previously unknown over the largest forms. The slow movement of the op. 111 succeeds as almost no other work in suspending the passage of time at its climax. After almost a quarter of an hour of the purest C major, we reach what appears to be the cadential trill, and we must remember the temporal weight and mass of the preceding C major to understand the following:

---

[1] Tovey has remarked that Mozart is a more enchanting orchestrator than Beethoven because his greatest strokes stand out as such, whereas those in Beethoven's mature works seem inconceivable for any other instrumental pattern (nonsensical attempts to orchestrate the *Hammerklavier*, and the composer's financially motivated piano transcription of the Violin Concerto notwithstanding).

The only place in this movement where there is any harmonic motion is here, where the larger rhythmic motion is completely suspended: there is not the slightest directional force in these trills or in the modulation, and they are only a means of hovering before returning to C major and resolving the cadence. In the sense that a cadenza is a glorified cadence, this is a cadenza, and that is, in fact, its structural point. The mastery lies in Beethoven's understanding that a sequence does not move, that a diatonic circle of descending fifths within classical tonality does not exist on a plane of real action, so that the long series of tiny harmonic movements that prolong this immense inner expansion serve only as an harmonic pulse and in no sense as a gesture.

This power to suspend motion, seeming to stop the movement of time, which is measured only by action, is closely related to Mozart's exquisite feeling for a pause in harmonic movement before his recapitulations, but it became one of Beethoven's most personal traits. The development section of the first movement of the Quartet op. 130, with the continuous soft pulsation, the tiny ostinato theme, the long repeated lyrical phrase all combined into one, suspends motion in the same way as the quiet beginning of the development of the Ninth Symphony, with its syncopated and unaccented shifts of harmony that defer all sense of action: both build an intensity more terrifying and moving than any less inward motion could induce. With all their tension, these effects are essentially meditative in character, and they make one aware to what an extent the exploration of the tonal universe was an act of introspection.

EPILOGUE

Epilogue

Robert Schumann's homage to Beethoven, the Fantasy in C major, op. 17, is the monument that commemorates the death of the classical style. The beginning of the last song of Beethoven's cycle *An die ferne Geliebte* (a setting of the words 'Take these songs then, my love, that I sang')

Nimm sie hin denn, die - se Lie-der

is clearly quoted at the very end of the first movement of Schumann's work:

but also hinted at throughout the movement[1] in such phrases as

Nevertheless, in all significant respects of structure and detail the Schumann Fantasy is totally unclassical: even the appearance of Beethoven's melody is itself unclassical by its reference to a personal and completely private significance exterior to the work—the words of the Beethoven phrase are surely

---

[1] The motto of the Fantasy—four lines from Schlegel placed at the head—tells us that a hidden tone runs secretly through the whole. The homage to Beethoven is also suggested by the canceled titles to the movements: 'Ruins—Triumphal Arch—Starry Crown.'

present for Schumann as an autobiographical reference—and by its exposition of the definitive and basic form of the main thematic material only at the last moment.

Most important of all, this moment is the only stable one; the full reference to Beethoven on the last page of the movement is the first appearance in the work of the tonic chord of C major in root position. In other words, unlike every classical work, Schumann's Fantasy neither starts from a point of stability, nor reaches one until the last possible moment. (This was probably an instinctive procedure with Schumann; as a matter of strict truth there is a tonic chord in root position just a few measures before the final and complete reference to the secret motto, although it sounds there, indeed, not like a tonic but as a dominant of the subdominant, and makes only a minimal difference to the proportions and effect.) In spite of the thematic recapitulation in this movement, there is therefore no harmonic resolution until the very end. Most of the long symmetrical recapitulation is not even remotely in C major, but in E flat major, and the long, stable tonic section of the classical sonata is of no interest to Schumann.

The opening instability, as well, annuls the classical canon of a closed framework. The excitement of Schumann's first measures

is unparalleled in a classical work, and its emotional turbulence is conveyed by the accompaniment's shapeless version of the theme above it. In performance it is not easy to define even the rhythm of this accompaniment clearly, and there is no reason to suppose that Schumann expected a clear definition. The defining rhythmic framework of the classical style is rejected in favor of a more open sonority out of which the theme gradually assumes a shape. This shape is one which implies a direction, not to a classical dominant, but to the subdominant F major, and the movement does indeed go to F. The classical pattern of a rise in tension towards the center is consequently destroyed, and it would be difficult, after all, to imagine such a form starting from the violence of this opening. Most Romantic works of the 1830s imply a lowering of tension after the opening, and the succeeding fluctuations of tension evade the clear outline of the classical dramatic form.

In harmony and rhythm, as well as in formal outline, there is a return to the principles of the Baroque. The first movement of the Fantasy has a long middle section in the tonic minor and in a slower tempo, which gives it a shape closer to the Baroque ternary form, the da capo aria, than any opening movement of the classical period. The second movement of the Fantasy exhibits a similar form, and has also a relentless and obsessive use of a dotted rhythm that was almost unknown in the latter half of the eighteenth century, and which begins to reappear in music only with the post-classical style in the works of Schubert and Rossini. Like the homogeneous rhythmic texture of the Baroque, the rhythmic forms of the first generation of the Romantics are not syntactical (i.e., they do not depend on balance and ordering) but cumulative in their effect. Schumann set down only the literal truth when he wrote that his music (and that of Chopin, Mendelssohn, and Hiller) was closer to the music of Bach than to the music of Mozart. The impulsive energy of the Romantic work is no longer a polarized dissonance and an articulated rhythm, but the familiar Baroque sequence, and the structures are no longer synthetic but additive. The music of Schumann in particular (Chopin retains some of the classical clarity) comes in a series of waves, and the climax is generally reserved for the moment before exhaustion.

Romantic style is by no means a reactionary movement, in spite of the great influence of Bach. The 'revival' of the greatest of Baroque figures was not a cause but a symptom of the stylistic change; the homogeneous rhythmic structures of Schubert, for example, can have had nothing to do with Bach. Over a unified texture, the Romantic composer imposed a rigid periodicity derived from late classical music: this very slow beat of the fixed eight-measure phrase gives Romantic music a basic movement much less rapid than the classical style and yet retains the ideal of the symmetrical melody. One might say that the typical form of the Romantic style is Gounod's *Ave Maria*: that is, a Baroque movement of harmony and rhythm (in this case Bach's C major Prelude from the *Well-Tempered Keyboard*, Book I) with a post-classical melody superimposed.

With the change in style came a change in the tonal language itself. The chromaticism of Chopin, Liszt, and Spohr is only a surface manifestation of this change. Schumann's music is not exceptionally chromatic, and yet there is an ambiguity of tonal relations in his work that has no precedent in the half-century from 1775 to 1825. The opening piece of the *Davidsbündlertänze* shifts so rapidly and so frequently from G major to E minor as to destroy any clear feeling for a tonal center. The *Kreisleriana*, like the great song-cycles, is written around a set of related keys, none of which is felt as more important than the others. This lack of a central reference arises, like Chopin's chromaticism, from a weakening of the tonic-dominant polarity. There are phrases by Beethoven, particularly in the *Diabelli* Variations and in the late quartets, which display a chromaticism as radical as anything outside Gesualdo, but they all imply a firm diatonic structure as a background. With Chopin it is the background that shifts chromatically as well. In such a fashion, even the classical harmonic pun—the violent fusion of two different harmonic contexts—is no longer possible, as the context no longer has sufficient clarity of definition.

The sources of the new style—if sources are understood not as causes but as inspirations freely chosen from the past—are easy enough to identify. They are, above all, Bach and Rossini, and a host of greater and smaller figures from the late classical period: Hummel, Field, Cherubini, Weber, Paganini, and others. Clementi, a figure from an earlier generation, remained a force in his development of loose, basically melodic structures; and by his importance for keyboard pedagogy, he transmitted a part of the heritage of Scarlatti. Haydn was almost completely ignored, Mozart admired but misunderstood, and the reverence for Beethoven can be accounted only a pernicious influence for at least a generation after his death, producing with few exceptions only the most lifeless and academic imitations of forms no longer either comprehensible or acceptable.

The disappearance of an old style is perhaps more mysterious than the birth of a new one. Is it abandoned because it is logically exhausted, written out? Have the needs and ideals of a new generation forced an old system into the shadow? Or is it merely a desire for novelty, and must we revive the threadbare historical mechanics of a change of fashion every twenty years? The figure of Schubert stands before us as a warning against generalization.

Except for a handful of works from his last years when he unexpectedly returns to a more thoroughly classical spirit, Schubert is in part the most significant originator of the new Romantic style and in part the greatest example of the post-classical composer. After the first tentative experiments, the principles on which most of his songs are written are almost entirely new; they are related to the *Lieder* of the past only by negation: they annihilate all that precedes. The classical idea of dramatic opposition and resolution is completely superseded: the dramatic movement is simple and indivisible. In those exceptional songs with a strong contrast, the opposition is not the source of the energy: on the contrary, in 'Die Post' from *Die Winterreise*, for example, the contrasting section brings only a deadening of the energy, a deadening which is not a resolution of tension but only a withdrawal before the final climax. The unvaried, anticlassical texture of the Schubert song reflects the singleness of its emotional vision.

Like the finest and most original works of the other Romantic composers, the songs of Schubert are largely cumulative rather than syntactical in effect. The extreme example is 'Der Leiermann' from *Die Winterreise*, in which there is a slight increase in intensity in the shape of some of the later phrases, but in which the heartbreaking effect depends largely on sheer repetition, and—which is only a reinforcement of the same principle—on the place of the song as the last of a long cycle. If this is an extreme instance, the weight of even an early song such as 'Gretchen am Spinnrade' is achieved by a similar iterative technique. Schubert's rhythm is unyielding by classical standards, but it is evident that these standards do not apply and are irrelevant.

On the other hand, in most of the chamber and symphonic pieces, Schubert works within the late and loosely organized post-classical style, in which the melodic flow is essentially more important than the dramatic structure. This is a degenerate style, judged solely as a style: the very looseness of organization prevented the dramatic concision, the close correspondence of part to whole and the consequent richness of allusion of the classical style. In this case, the classical standards can be considered relevant, but to apply them rigorously entails a failure to appreciate many works that, while never quite making virtues of their deficiencies, have virtues of their own that more efficiently organized music can rarely achieve.

Unfortunately, the classical standards cannot be set aside in the last analysis because Schubert is a classicizing composer, like Hummel, Weber, and the young Beethoven: that is, he constantly chooses specific classical works as models and thus admits their standards as he imitates them. Sometimes the thematic relationship with the model is so candid that one feels as if a deliberate allusion were intended. The minuet of Schubert's Symphony no. 5 in B flat major combines the third and fourth movements of the Mozart G minor Symphony:

so that one hears a blurred echo of the past in its outline. Even more disconcerting is the relation of the late Introduction and Rondo in B minor for violin and piano to the first movement of Beethoven's *Kreutzer* Sonata: here what is borrowed is trivialized, and every dramatic detail becomes petty and even decorative.

Schubert was not the first nor the last composer to write with specific models in mind, and Beethoven, for example, was older than Schubert ever was to become before his references to the past became allusive rather than direct. Brahms and Stravinsky, to name only two, continued the imitation of models into their old age. But Schubert's imitations are too often more timid, less disturbing than the originals. For this reason, the structures of most of his large forms are mechanical in a way that is absolutely foreign to his models. They are used by Schubert as molds, almost without reference to the material that was to be poured into them. It is this post-classical practice, of course, which finally produced the idea of a 'sonata' as a fixed form like a sonnet.

The nature of Schubert's dependence on classical models can be seen most clearly in the last movement of the late A major Sonata which is based on the rondo finale of Beethoven's G major Sonata op. 31, no. 1. The two movements have themes that are alike in nothing but their firmly articulated rondo character:

Beethoven

Schubert

The borrowing is not of thematic shape but strictly of formal structure. The process starts the moment the theme has been played once: in both works it is immediately replayed with the melody in the left hand and a new triplet rhythm in the right:

Beethoven

456

Schubert

This new triplet motion continues for the second theme, and is transferred to the left hand for the return of the theme:

Beethoven

Schubert

and the development section begins, heavily contrapuntal, stormy in character, and largely in minor in both cases. For the second return of the theme, the accompaniment is reduced to pure pulsation and the harmony to a point of complete immobility:

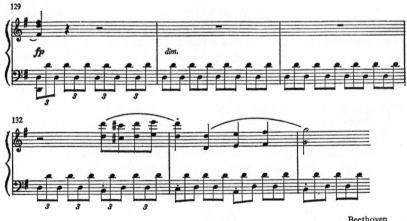

Beethoven

Schubert

The most magical effect here in Schubert, the placing of this return not in the tonic but in the submediant, has no parallel in Beethoven's rondo. Schubert's coda, however, is once more subservient; nowhere is the presence of the model felt so strongly. Beethoven slows down his theme, breaks it into fragments, returns to the original tempo and slows down once more, separating the fragments by long pauses, and at the end follows the whole section by a brilliant and extended Presto. Schubert imitates him point for point, adding of his own invention mainly the extraordinary idea of a final phrase which is like a mirror version of the opening phrase of his own *first* movement.

What is most remarkable in this close imitation is its lack of constraint: Schubert moves with great ease within the form which Beethoven created. He has, however, considerably loosened what held it together, and stretched its ligaments unmercifully. Schubert's movement is very much longer than Beethoven's, although the opening themes of both are exactly the same length. This means that the correspondence of part to whole has been considerably altered by Schubert, and explains why his large movements often seem so long, since they are being produced with forms originally intended for shorter pieces. Some of the excitement naturally goes out of these forms when they are so extended, but this is even a condition of the unforced melodic flow of Schubert's music. It must be added that with the finale of this A major Sonata Schubert produced a work that is unquestionably greater than its model.

The relaxation of form typical of the post-classical style inspired Schubert's conception of the long-range sequence, particularly in development sections, a conception only partially based on Beethoven's practice. This device by which whole sections of a development are exactly repeated, only being transposed an interval up or down (almost always up to meet the rising tension), makes it possible to conceive developments in a form as symmetrical as an exposition and recapitulation.[1] It is one of the last stages in the

---

[1] This use of the sequence on the large scale reveals the extent to which the sequence in general had become the animating impulse.

complete systematization of the sonata, and no device was more abused by nineteenth-century symphonists, for whom it became almost a substitute for composition. The relaxed form, however, made it possible for Schubert to indulge in a play of sonority which not even Mozart in *Die Zauberflöte* could equal. The effects are so delicious as to be almost self-indulgent, and they are at their most remarkable in Schubert's extensive production of music for one piano four hands.

At the end of his life with the G major Quartet, the C major Symphony, and the C major String Quintet, Schubert returns to classical principles in a manner almost as striking if not as complete as Beethoven. The G major Quartet opens with a simple opposition of major and minor, and the whole first movement springs from the energy of the material:

This is not the normal major–minor coloring of Schubert, and the sense of pathos is almost completely absent. What is remarkable is the rebirth of the classical conviction that the simplest tonal relationships can alone provide the subject-matter of music. The investigation of these relationships is more diffuse than Beethoven's, but not essentially different. The C major Quintet, perhaps even more successful, is only apparently more complex. The C major Symphony, however, starts with a true Romantic introduction, a complete well-rounded tune, but the mastery of classical rhythm in the Allegro gives the movement a concision greater than that of any other symphonic work of Schubert (far more than the *Unfinished* Symphony, which works with a lavishness of material that the C major does not emulate). The shift of accent from

to

is a perfect recreation of Beethoven's rhythmic procedure. In all these works, the technique is more leisurely than Beethoven's, and even than Mozart's at his most relaxed, but the classical forms are no longer imposed from without, but rather implied by the material.

Epilogue

The synthesis of the means of expression we call the classical style was by no means exhausted when it was abandoned, but submission to its discipline was not an easy matter. A discontinuity of style between Beethoven and the generation that followed is an inescapable hypothesis for understanding the musical language of the nineteenth century. Schubert, however, cannot be easily placed into any one category—Romantic, post-classical, or classical—and he stands as an example of the resistance of the material of history to the most necessary generalizations, and as a reminder of the irreducibly personal facts that underlie the history of style.

A style, when it is no longer the natural mode of expression, gains a new life—a shadowy life-in-death—as a prolongation of the past. We imagine ourselves able to revive the past through its art, to perpetuate it by continuing to work within its conventions. For this illusion of reliving history, the style must be prevented from becoming truly alive once again. The conventions must remain conventional, the forms lose their original significance in order to take on their new responsibility of evoking the past. This process of ossification is a guarantee of respectability. The classical style could originally bring no such assurance: *Don Giovanni* and the *Eroica* were scandalous, the *London* Symphonies sublimely impertinent. But just as the Handelian fugue in Mozart served to match the high seriousness of a sacred ritual, the sonata-forms in the symphonies and chamber music of Mendelssohn and Schumann are essays in decorum and respect. In these works, sadly out of favor today, the evocation of the past is only incidental: the intent was to attain the prestige of the style imitated. The sense of the irrecoverable past, however, is omnipresent in the music of Brahms, resignedly eclectic, ambiguous without irony. The depth of his feeling of loss gave an intensity to Brahms's work that no other imitator of the classical tradition ever reached: he may be said to have made music out of his openly expressed regret that he was born too late. For the rest, the classical tradition could be used with originality only through irony—the irony of Mahler, for example, who employed sonata-forms with the same mock respect that he gave to his shopworn scraps of dance-tunes. The true inheritors of the classical style were not those who maintained its traditions, but those, from Chopin to Debussy, who preserved its freedom as they gradually altered and finally destroyed the musical language which had made the creation of the style possible.

Index of Names and Works

References to Haydn, Mozart, and Beethoven other than these relating to specific works are not indexed.

Abert, Hermann, 13, 180n.
Addison, Joseph, 169, 170
Alberti, Domenico, 28
Anderson, Emily, 13, 143n., 193n., 288n.
Aquinas, St. Thomas, 39
Ariosto, Lodovico, 317
Aristotle, 39

Bach, Carl Philipp Emanuel, 32, 44, 47, 48, 49, 79, 96, 107, 111, 112, 115, 116, 145, 239
  Keyboard Sonata in B minor (1779), 112, 114–15, 115n.
  Keyboard, Sonata in F major (1779), 112–14
  Symphony in D major, Wq. 183/1, 111–12
Bach, Johann Christian, 20, 37, 44, 47, 52, 79, 187
  Piano Concerto in E♭ major (1770), 189–90
Bach, Johann Sebastian, 20, 20n., 33, 36, 43, 46, 47, 50, 60, 63, 78, 80, 93, 101, 105, 107, 112, 115, 135, 146, 147, 170, 197, 227, 243, 264, 330, 345, 367–8, 375, 387, 404, 453, 454
  Art of Fugue, BWV 1080, 26, 63, 368, 372, 385
  Brandenburg Concertos, 45
    No. 4, in G major, 60–1
    No. 5, in D major, 196–7
    No. 6, in B♭ major, 45
  Cantata BWV 212 ('Peasant Cantata'), 330
  Chaconne—see Partita for violin in D minor
  Chorale Prelude, 'O Lamm Gottes,' BWV 618, 60–1, 93
  French Overture, in B minor, 282
  Fugue for Organ in A minor, BWV 543, 75
  'Goldberg' Variations, 62, 63, 93, 95, 330, 331, 385, 395, 436, 439
  Inventions for keyboard, 385
  Italian Concerto, BWV 971, 77
  Mass in B minor, BWV 232, 61n., 94, 367
  Partita for keyboard No. 1 in B♭ major, 89–90
  Partita for violin No. 2 in D minor, 75
  Passacaglia and Fugue for organ in C minor, BWV 582, 438
  Passions, 171
    Passion According to St. Matthew, 70, 171

Peasant Cantata—see Cantata BWV 212
Trio-Sonatas for keyboard, 281
Well-Tempered Keyboard, 63, 76, 368, 385 426, 453
Bach, Wilhelm Friedemann, 44
Bartók, Béla, 137, 332, 434
Bartolozzi, Theresa, 358, 360
Bauer, Harold, 104
Beaumarchais, Pierre-Augustin Caron de 302, 312, 313, 317, 323
BEETHOVEN
  Adelaide, Op. 46, 380
  An die ferne Geliebte, Op. 98, 379, 400, **402–3,** 403n., 404, 451–2
  Bagatelles, Opp. 119 & 126, 405
  Choral Fantasy—see Fantasy for Piano, Chorus and Orchestra
  Concertos for Piano and Orchestra
    No. 1 in C major, Op. 15, 258, 392
    No. 3 in C minor, Op. 37, **389–90**
    No. 4 in G major, Op. 58, **64,** 69, 198, 211, 213, 222, 256–7, 333, **387–92,** 399
    No. 5 in E♭ major, Op. 73 ('Emperor'), 198, 333, 391, 404
    In D major (sketch), 391
  Concerto for Violin and Orchestra in D major, Op. 61, 89, 104, 258n., 446n.
  Fantasy for Piano, Chorus and Orchestra, Op. 80, 440
  Fidelio, 43, 103, 179, 180, **181–2,** 181n., 288, 379, 386, 399, 403 (*See also* Overtures)
  Fugue for String Quintet, Op. 137—*see* Quintets
  Great Fugue, Op. 133—see Quartets
  'Kakadu' Variations, Op. 121a—see Trios
  Masses, 47, 373–4
    Op. 86, in C major, 366, **373–5,** 404
    Op. 123 in D major ('Missa Solemnis'), 53, 194, 275, 303, 366, 374, **375** 386, 404
  The Mount of Olives, Op. 85, 366
  Overtures
    Leonore No. 3, Op. 72a, 9, 154
    Zur Namensfeier, Op. 115, 403
  Quartets (String), 98, 145, 281
    Op. 18, 265
    Op. 18 no. 1 in F major, 79n.

461

Index of Names and Works

Index of Names and Works

Rimsky-Korsakov, Nicolai Andreyevich, 170, 344

Robbins Landon, H. C., 13, 143n.

Rossini, Giacomo, 101, 386, 453, 454
Le Comte d'Ory, 386

Rousseau, Jean-Baptiste, 169

Rousseau, Jean-Jacques, 175, 196
Le Devin du village, 341

Rudolph, Archduke Johann Joseph Rainer, 404

Sade, Donatien Alphonse François ('Marquis') de, 163, 323
One More Step, 323

Salomon, Johann Peter, 193

Scarlatti, Alessandro, 167

Scarlatti, Domenico, 30, 43, 46, 50, 52, 57, 62-3, 79, 215, 454

Schenker, Heinrich, 13, 33, 34, 35-6, 40-1, 42

Schikaneder, Emanuel, 318, 319, 321, 323

Schindler, Anton, 145, 387

Schlegel, August Wilhelm von, 451n.

Schlösser, Louis, 405

Schoenberg, Arnold, 35, 329

Schroeter, Johann Samuel, 243

Schroeter, Rebecca, 360

Schubert, Franz, 52, 137, 152, 215, 235, 239, 280, 332, 337, 379, 380-1, 384, 386-7, 394n., 402, 403, 434, 453, **454-60**
Gretchen am Spinnrade, D. 118, 455
Introduction and Rondo for Violin and Piano in B minor, D. 895, 455
Der Leiermann—*see* 'Die Winterreise'
Die Post—*see* 'Die Winterreise'
Quartet (String) in G major, D. 887, **459**
Quintet for Piano and Strings in A major, D. 667 ('Trout'), 384
Quintet for Strings in C major, D. 956, **459**
Sonata for Piano in A major, D. 959, **456-8**
Symphony No. 5 in B♭ major, D. 485, 455
Symphony No. 8 in B minor, D. 759 ('Unfinished'), 459
Symphony No. 9 in C major, D. 944, **459**
Die Winterreise, D. 911, 454-5

Schumann, Robert, 32, 70, 77n., 98, 198, 277, 324, 368, 379, 380, 381, 382, 383, 384, 385, 385n., 390, 402-3, 453-4, 460
Carnaval, Op. 9, 37, 37n., 382
Davidsbündlertänze, Op. 6, 382, 454
Fantasy in C major, Op. 17, 382, 383, **451-3**

Impromptus (Variations) on a Theme of Clara Wieck, Op. 5, 437

Kreisleriana, Op. 16, 454

Sonata, in F♯ minor, Op. 11, 350

Schuppanzigh, Ignaz, 379

Schweitzer, Albert, 330n.

Shakespeare, William
Comedy of Errors, 312
Twelfth Night, 312

Shaw, George Bernard, 27

Smart, Christopher, 169

Spohr, Ludwig, 387, 453

Stamitz, Johann, 22

Strauss, Richard, 144, 402

Stravinsky, Igor, 36, 170, 317, 337, 445, 455-6
The Rake's Progress, 317

Swieten, Baron Gottfried von, 373

Tchaikovsky, Peter Ilyich, 144, 194, 198, 325
Concerto for Piano and Orchestra No. 1 in B♭ minor, Op. 23, 350
Symphony No. 6 in B minor, Op. 74 ('Pathétique'), 274

Thayer, Alexander, 13, 379n., 386n., 387n., 405n., 407n.

Tost, Johann, 286

Tovey, Donald Francis, 13, 28, 38-9, 49n., 51, 69, 76, 100, 111, 115, 119, 140, 173, 180, 299, 351, 354, 390, 394, 400, 421, 446n.

Türk, Daniel Gottlob, 101

Turner, W. J., 315

Velasquez, 53

Verdi, Giuseppe, 169, 179, 333
Otello, 179
Requiem, 409

Viotti, Giovanni Battista, 143

Voltaire, Francois Marie Arouet de, 169, 170
Candide, 163

Wagner, Richard 21, 67, 88, 154, 168-9, 180, 277, 303, 317, 325, 379, 387,
Parsifal, 67

Waldstein, Count Ferdinand, 19

Weber, Carl Maria von, 22, 258, 380-1, 384, 386, 394n., 454, 455

Webern, Anton, 445

Wieland, Christoph Martin, 163, 171n., 180, 317

Winckelmann, Johann Joachim, 175n.

Wölfflin, Heinrich, 40

467

THE COLONIZATION OF NORTH AMERICA

THE COLONIZATION OF NORTH AMERICA

THE MACMILLAN COMPANY
NEW YORK · BOSTON · CHICAGO · DALLAS
ATLANTA · SAN FRANCISCO

MACMILLAN AND CO., Limited
LONDON · BOMBAY · CALCUTTA · MADRAS
MELBOURNE

THE MACMILLAN COMPANY
OF CANADA, Limited
TORONTO

THE COLONIZATION OF
NORTH AMERICA

1492–1783

BY

HERBERT EUGENE BOLTON, Ph. D.

PROFESSOR OF AMERICAN HISTORY IN THE UNIVERSITY OF CALIFORNIA

AND

THOMAS MAITLAND MARSHALL, Ph. D.

PROFESSOR OF HISTORY IN WASHINGTON UNIVERSITY

New York
THE MACMILLAN COMPANY

12261

PREFACE

This book represents an attempt to bring into one account the story of European expansion in North America down to 1783. Text-books written in this country as a rule treat the colonization of the New World as the history, almost solely, of the thirteen English colonies which formed the nucleus of the United States. The authors have essayed to write a book from a different point of view. It has been prepared in response to a clear demand for a text written from the standpoint of North America as a whole, and giving a more adequate treatment of the colonies of nations other than England and of the English colonies other than the thirteen which revolted. This demand is the inevitable result of the growing importance of our American neighbors and of our rapidly growing interest in the affairs of the whole continent, past as well as present.

The book is divided into three main parts: I. The Founding of the Colonies; II. Expansion and International Conflict; III. The Revolt of the English Colonies. The keynote is expansion. The spread of civilization in America has been presented against a broad European background. Not only colonial beginnings but colonial growth has been traced. This method accounts for the development of all geographical sections, and shows the relation of each section to the history of the continent as a whole. When thus presented the early history of Massachusetts, of Georgia, of Arkansas, of Illinois, or of California is no longer merely local history, but is an integral part of the general story. The colonies of the different nations are treated, in so far as practicable, in the chronological order of their development, the desire being to give a correct view of the time sequence in the development of the different regions.

A principal aim of the authors has been to make the book comprehensive. The activities of the Dutch and Swedes on the Atlantic mainland are given a large setting in both Europe and the New World. The account of French expansion in North America has been extended beyond the conventional presentation to embrace the West Indies, the founding of Louisiana, and the advance of the French pioneers across the Mississippi and up its tributaries, and up the Saskatchewan to the Rocky Mountains. The story of English expansion embraces not only the thirteen colonies which revolted, but also the Bermudas, the West Indies, Hudson Bay, Canada, and the Floridas. The treatment of the new British possessions between 1763 and 1783 aims to present in one view the story of the expansion of the whole English frontier, from Florida to Hudson Bay.

The Spanish colonies of North America, in particular, have been accorded a more adequate treatment than is usual in text-books. To writers of United States history the Spaniards have appeared to be mere explorers. Students of American history in a larger sense, however, know that Spain transplanted Spanish civilization and founded vast and populous colonies, represented to-day by some twenty republics and many millions of people. The notion, so widely current in this country, that Spain "failed" as a colonizer, arises from a faulty method. In treating Spain's part in the New World it has been customary, after recounting the discovery of America, to proceed at once to territory now within the United States—Florida, New Mexico, Texas—forgetting that these regions were to Spain only northern outposts, and omitting the wonderful story of Spanish achievement farther south. This book being a history of the colonization of North America, Spain's great colonies in South America, now powerful nations, fall beyond our geographical limits.

When approached from a new viewpoint many familiar things appear in a new light. Hitherto, for example, the inter-colonial wars in North America have been regarded mainly as a struggle between France and England, and as confined chiefly to the Canadian border. By following the larger story of European expansion, however, it becomes plain that there was an Anglo-Spanish and a Franco-Spanish, as well as a Franco-English struggle for the continent, not to mention the ambitions and efforts of Dutch, Swedes, Russians, and Danes. In nearly all the general inter-colonial wars the Caribbean area and the Carolina-Florida frontier were scenes of frequent conflicts quite as important as those waged on the Canadian border. Between France and Spain a border contest endured for more than a century and extended all the way from the Lesser Antilles to the Platte River. The Anglo-French contest ended in 1763; but the Anglo-Spanish conflict, which began in the sixteenth century, endured to the end of the eighteenth and, in the hands of the American offspring of Spain and England, to the middle of the nineteenth century.

Some teachers may for special reasons wish to treat the development of the colonies of a single nation as a continuous movement, or in longer periods, less frequently broken by happenings in the colonies of other nations. This can be done conveniently by grouping the chapters in the desired order. A continuous account of Spanish expansion is given in Chapters II, III, XIII, XVI, and XXI. A connected story of French America is told in Chapters IV, XIV, XV, XX. By omitting these and Chapter IX a continuous narrative of English expansion is obtained.

August, 1920.

TABLE OF CONTENTS

THE FOUNDING OF THE COLONIES

PAGES

CHAPTER

XI. EXPANSION UNDER THE LATER STUARTS (1660–1689) 196–215
New York 196
The Jerseys 198
Pennsylvania 202
The Insular Colonies 206
The Carolinas 207
Western Trade and Exploration 211
Hudson's Bay Company 212

XII. THE ENGLISH MAINLAND COLONIES AT THE CLOSE OF THE
SEVENTEENTH CENTURY 216–231
New England 216
New York and East New Jersey 221
Colonies along Delaware River and Bay 224
The Chesapeake Bay Region 227
South Carolina 230

EXPANSION AND INTERNATIONAL CONFLICT

XIII. THE SPANISH ADVANCE IN THE SEVENTEENTH CENTURY . 233–256
Spain and the Colonies in the Seventeenth Century 233
Frontier Administration 234
The Missions 235
The Jesuits in Sinaloa and Sonora 237
Efforts to Occupy Lower California 240
The Settlement of Chihuahua 242
New Mexico in the Seventeenth Century 243
Coahuila Occupied 247
First Attempts in Eastern Texas 249
The Struggle with Rivals in the West Indies 251
The Struggle with the English on the Carolina Border . . . 253

XIV. THE WARS OF THE ENGLISH AND SPANISH SUCCESSIONS (1684–
1713) 257–274
The Preliminary Struggle for the Northern Fur Country . 257
The War of the English Succession 261
The War of the Spanish Succession 267
The Peace of Utrecht 273

XV. THE FRENCH IN LOUISIANA AND THE FAR NORTHWEST (1699–
1762) 275–298
The Founding of Louisiana 275
Louisiana under the Company of the Indies 278
Louisiana under the Royal Governors 280
The Trans-Mississippi West 282
The Advance Toward New Mexico 284
The Far Northwest 287

TABLE OF CONTENTS

LIST OF MAPS

THE COLONIZATION OF NORTH AMERICA

THE COLONIZATION OF NORTH AMERICA

THE FOUNDING OF THE COLONIES

1900-1500   CHAPTER I

THE BACKGROUND AND THE DISCOVERY

The fifteenth century witnessed the culmination of the Renaissance, the rise of the Turkish Empire, the shifting of the commercial center from the Mediterranean to the Atlantic, the discovery of America and the opening of the Cape route to India. Portugal and Spain started on their careers as great commercial and colonizing nations, the former destined for a time to control the commerce of the Far East, the other to possess more than half of the Americas and to dominate the Pacific.

GROWTH OF GEOGRAPHICAL KNOWLEDGE

Classical ideas of the world.—The discoveries of the century completely transformed the conceptions of geography. Greek and Roman scholars had agreed that there were three continents, Europe, Asia, and Africa, encircled by the ocean. Aristotle, Strabo, and others accepted the theory that the earth was a sphere, but they usually underestimated its size. Ptolemy, the greatest of the ancient geographers, made two fundamental errors, which most of the Arab and Christian scholars accepted. He depicted the Indian Ocean as an inland sea, and greatly extended Africa until it filled the entire southern hemisphere, China and Africa being connected.

Arab theories and Christian scholars.—The Arabs believed that the earth was a disc or ball, which was the center of the universe. The center of the earth's surface they called Arim, meaning the cupola of the earth. At the eastern extremity stood the pillars of Alexander, at the western the pillars of Hercules, while the north and south poles were equally distant from Arim. The Ptolemaic idea of Africa was accepted by most of the Arabs, but many of their later map makers decreased its size, cutting it off in the neighborhood of Cape Bojador on the African coast, and calling the region beyond the "Green Sea of Darkness." Others sketched in a great southern continent below Africa. The "Green Sea of Darkness" was filled with terrors, whirlpools ready to destroy the adventurous mariner, a sea of mist, fog, and vapor, peopled by monsters. If he escaped these as he ventured southward, he would come to a zone of torrid heat where no man could survive. Roger Bacon, the great Christian scientist, accepted the Arabian theories but supplemented them by a study of the classics. He believed that the habitable world was more than half of the whole circuit, an idea which was repeated in the *Imago Mundi* of Pierre d'Ailly, a work which may have influenced Columbus.

Early Asiatic contact with America.—Some scholars believe that the western coast of North America was visited by Asiatics long before the eastern shores were reached by Europeans. In 499 a Buddhist priest returned from a voyage claiming to have been to a country called Fusang, lying far to the east. The location of Fusang has interested numerous students, whose conjectures have been marshalled by Vining to prove that it was Mexico. Some have attributed the remarkable sporadic growth of cypress trees below Monterey, California, to this episode. The trend of opinion accepts ethnographic and linguistic similarities as of greater conclusiveness than recorded Chinese history. Belief in early Japanese contact with America rests on a similar basis.

The Northmen.—The first Europeans to venture far out on the Atlantic were the Northmen, a people but little touched by classical, Arabic, or Christian culture before their great period of expansion. The western sea to them had no terrors. Near the close of the eighth century they appeared in England; in 860 they sighted Iceland and in 874 commenced its colonization. Three years later they discovered Greenland, but it was not until 986 that Eric the Red colonized it. In the year 1000, Lief, the son of Eric, went in quest of a land to the west, of which he had

heard report. The result of the voyage was the discovery of Vin-
land, the exact whereabouts of which has been one of the puzzles
of history, some scholars claiming it to have been Nova Scotia,
others New England. Wherever it may have been, it probably
played no part in the Columbian discovery of America, for though
the settlements in Greenland continued until early in the fifteenth
century, scientists and mariners remained in almost complete
ignorance of the far-off activities of the Northmen.

Mediæval travelers.—During the period of the Crusades,
travel became more and more extensive. Returning crusaders
told of their adventures and of the lands which they had visited.
Pilgrims returning from the East increased the store of geographical knowledge and repeated marvelous tales of Russia, China,
and India, although none of them had first-hand knowledge. But
during the thirteenth century accurate information was obtained.
John de Plano Carpini, a Neapolitan Franciscan, went as a legate
of Pope Innocent IV to the Great Khan in Tartary. His *Book
of the Tartars* is the first reliable account of the empire of the
Great Mogul. A few years later William de Rubruquis was sent
by St. Louis of France to the same court, and returned to tell a
tale of wonders.

Between 1255 and 1265 two Venetians, Nicolo and Matteo
Polo, were trading in southern Russia, and eventually they
visited the court of Kublai Khan in Mongolia, later returning
to Europe. In 1271 they again visited the Far East, this time
accompanied by their nephew, Marco, whose account of their
journeyings is the most famous book of travel. Marco became
an official at the Mongol court and was sent on various missions
which carried him over a large part of China. He also learned
of the wonders of Cipango or Japan. In 1292 the Polos left
China, visited Java, India, and Ceylon, and eventually returned
to Europe. Their travels made known a vast region which had
previously lain almost outside the reckoning of geographers, and
gave to Europeans a fairly accurate as well as a fascinating account of the Far East.

Early maritime activities on the African coast.—While the Polos
were in Asia, mariners were beginning to explore outside the
Pillars of Hercules. In 1270 the Canaries were discovered by
Malocello and a few years later Genoese galleys reached Cape

Nun. In 1341 the Canaries were again visited, this time by an expedition from Lisbon, and in 1370 an Englishman, Robert Machin, who had eloped from Bristol with Anne d'Arfet, was driven from the French coast in a storm and came to Madeira where they both died from exposure. Some of the crew, however, returned to tell the tale. In 1402 a Norman, De Béthencourt, reached the Canaries and several of the islands were soon colonized.

Advance of maritime science.—As sea voyaging progressed, maritime science was also advancing. A large number of coast charts called Portolani were made, which plotted with remarkable accuracy the coast lines of Europe and northern Africa. Over four hundred of these charts are still in existence. Their accuracy was largely due to the use of the compass and astrolabe, which are known to have been invented before 1400.

PORTUGUESE DISCOVERIES

The rise of Portugal.—In the work of geographical and commercial expansion Portugal now took the lead. The little kingdom, from a small territory to the north of the Douro, had gradually extended its domain to the southward by driving out the Moors. Its commercial importance began by the opening of a trade with England. From 1383 to 1433 Portugal was ruled by John the Great, and during his reign the oversea expansion of the country began.

Henry the Navigator.—The greatness of Portugal was largely due to one of King John's sons, Prince Henry. He was born in 1394 and at an early age became interested in furthering trade with the interior of Africa. In 1410 or 1412 he is said to have sent caravels down the coast. In 1415 he assisted in the capture of the Moorish stronghold of Ceuta, where he gained great military renown. In 1419 he was made governor of Algarve, the southern province of Portugal. He established himself at Sagres, on Cape St. Vincent, where he enlarged the old naval arsenal, built a palace, chapel, study, and observatory, and here it was that he spent the greater portion of his life.

Henry had three main objects: first, to open trade with the

interior of Africa; second, to found a colonial empire; third, to spread the Christian faith. A tale was current that somewhere in Africa lived a Christian king called Prester John, who was cut off from the world by Islam. To find his kingdom and unite with him in the overthrow of the Mohammedans was a natural ambition in a prince who had already assisted in the capture of Ceuta.

Henry gathered about him a group of trained mariners, some of whom were Italians, made a study of geography and navigation, instructed his captains, and sent them out from Lagos to find new markets. Between 1420 and 1430 Cape Blanco was discovered and the first slaves were brought back, this being the beginning of an extensive traffic. Four years later Cape Verde was reached, and in 1455 the Cape Verde Islands were discovered and the coast of Senegal explored. The results of the Portuguese explorations under Prince Henry were incorporated in a map of the world, made by Fra Mauro in the convent of Murano, near Venice.

Discovery of a route to India.—During the sixty years which followed the death of Prince Henry, 1460–1520, the Portuguese completed the exploration of the west coast of Africa, discovered a route to India, explored a considerable part of the eastern coast of North and South America, and founded a colonial empire. In 1486 Bartholomew Diaz passed the Cape of Good Hope and in 1498 Vasco da Gama, spurred on by the discoveries of Columbus, crossed the Indian Ocean to Calicut.

It has been customary to ascribe the diversion of trade from the eastern Mediterranean to the Cape of Good Hope route to the rise of the Turkish Empire, which was supposed to have cut the old lines of communication to the Far East. Recent investigation has shown that such is not the case. As Professor Lybyer says, "They [the Turks] were not active agents in deliberately obstructing the routes. . . . Nor did they make the discovery of new routes imperative. On the contrary they lost by the discovery of a new and superior route." This superiority was due to the fact that the Cape route was an all-water route which did not require the rehandling of goods and expensive caravan transportation. Not the Turk, but cheap freight rates, diverted trade from the Mediterranean to the Cape route.

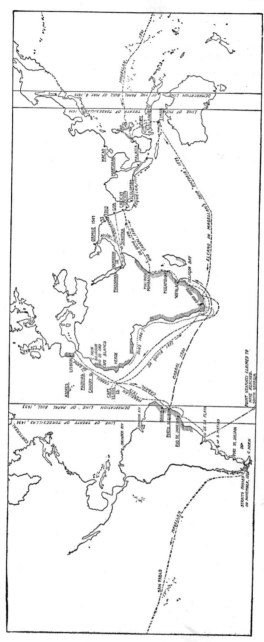

Portuguese Expansion and Magellan's Voyage

COLUMBUS AND THE DISCOVERY OF AMERICA

Early life of Columbus.—Meanwhile America had been discovered by Christopher Columbus, in the service of Spain. Much that was formerly believed to be true concerning the early life of Columbus recent research has proved to be false or to rest upon doubtful evidence. He was born at or near Genoa, probably in 1452, and was the son of a woolen weaver. Little is known of his education, but in some manner he acquired a knowledge of Latin, read the principal geographical works then accessible, and acquired a wide knowledge of navigation. Three books which he studied with care were the *General History and Geography* by Æneas Sylvius, the *Imago Mundi* of Pierre d'Ailly, and the *Travels* of Marco Polo.

He entered the marine service of Portugal, probably lived for a time on the island of Porto Santo, one of the Madeiras, visited the coast of Guinea, and sailed as far north as England. He married Felipa Moniz, a niece of Isabel Moniz, whose husband was Bartholomew Perestrello, who served under Prince Henry. It is probable that a correspondence occurred between Columbus and the Florentine geographer, Toscanelli, who is said to have suggested to the navigator the possibility of reaching the Indies by sailing west and to have sent him a copy of a chart which he had prepared. The Toscanelli map has not come down to us, the so-called reproduction of it being an adaptation of Behaim's globe of 1492. Through these various influences Columbus conceived the plan of seeking new lands in the Atlantic and became convinced of the feasibility of opening a western route to the Indies.

His sojourn in Spain.—After unsuccessfully urging his views in Portugal, in 1484 Columbus went to Spain, where he presented himself at the court and made the acquaintance of many influential persons. He also sent his brother Bartholomew to obtain assistance in western exploration from Henry VII of England. Columbus met with slight encouragement in Spain, and decided to seek French aid, but just as he was making his departure he was recalled, Queen Isabella having been brought to a favorable decision by Fray Juan Pérez, a former confessor, by Luis de Santangel, the treasurer of Aragon, by the Count of Medina-Celi, and by the Marquesa de Moya.

His commission.—Columbus was given a commission author-izing him to explore and trade. It said nothing of a route to the Indies. The enterprise of discovery was essentially a new one, and it was natural that the first patent should contain only general provisions. Indeed, the document was so brief and incomplete that many supplementary orders had to be issued before the expedition was ready. In return for services and to provide a representative of Spanish authority in anticipated discoveries, Columbus was ennobled and made admiral, viceroy, and governor-general in such lands as he might add to the Castilian realm. These offices were patterned after well-known institutions then in use in Spain. The titles were to be hereditary in Columbus's family. The admiral was to have a tenth of the net profits of trade and precious metals within his discoveries. By contributing an eighth of the expense of commercial ventures, he was entitled to an additional eighth of the profits from trade. To encourage the expedition all duties on exports were remitted.

Outfitting the expedition.—The story that Isabella pawned her jewels to equip the expedition is now disproved, the royal share of the money apparently being loaned to the Castilian treasury by Luis de Santangel. The total cost of outfitting was probably somewhat less than $100,000, of which Columbus or his friends furnished an eighth. Three vessels, the *Santa María*, the *Pinta*, and the *Niña*, were provided. The number who sailed is variously estimated at from ninety to one hundred and twenty men.

The discovery.—In August, 1492, the three vessels sailed from Palos to the Canaries, those islands then being a possession of Spain which she had acquired from Portugal in 1479. During the entire colonial period they were an important factor in navigation, being a place for refitting before the long trans-Atlantic voyage. The vessels left the Canaries on September 6 and sailed almost due west. They met with fair weather, but the length of the voyage caused much complaint, which resulted in a plot to get rid of Columbus. The Admiral succeeded in quelling the mutiny, however, and shortly afterward land was sighted.

On the evening of October 11 a light in the distance was twice seen by the commander, and before morning the moonlight disclosed to the lookout of the *Pinta* a sandy beach. The landfall

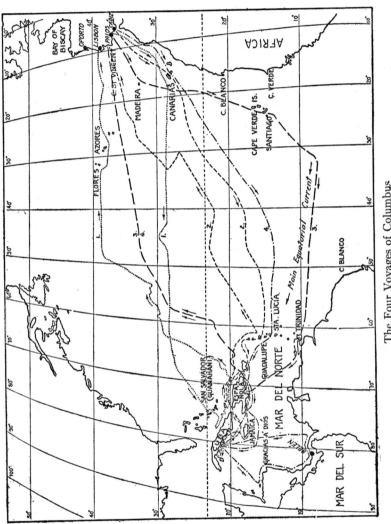

The Four Voyages of Columbus

was a small coral island of the Bahamas, which Columbus named San Salvador and which was probably the one now called Watling's Island. Believing that he had reached the Indies, he called the inhabitants Indians, a name which has clung ever since to American aborigines.

Sojourn in the West Indies.—Through all of his sojourn in the West Indies, Columbus was filled with the idea that he had found the Indies. Hearing of Cuba and believing that it was Cipango, he planned to visit the mainland and go to the city of Guisay, the Quinsai of Marco Polo. From the Bahamas he proceeded to Cuba and explored the eastern third of its northern coast. He despatched an interpreter to the Grand Khan, but instead of a mighty city, an Indian village was discovered. There Europeans first saw the smoking of tobacco. From Cuba the expedition went to Haiti, which Columbus named Española (Little Spain), corrupted in English to Hispaniola, and there the *Santa Maria* was wrecked.

The return voyage.—Having built a fort on the northern shore of Española not far from its westernmost point, which he named La Navidad (the Nativity) because the neighboring harbor was entered on Christmas day, Columbus left forty-four of the crew with ample provisions, implements, and arms, and began the return voyage on January 4, 1493. Two violent storms were encountered, but both were weathered, and on March 4 the vessels came to anchor in the mouth of the Tagus.

His reception.—In Lisbon the news of the discovery created great excitement. The King of Portugal invited Columbus to court and entertained him royally. On March 13 he sailed for Spain, arriving at Palos two days later. The citizens adjourned business for the day; bells were rung, and at night the streets were illumined with torches. From there he proceeded to Seville and then to the court at Barcelona, where the greatest honors were bestowed upon him. He was allowed to be seated in the presence of the sovereigns, who showed the keenest interest in his specimens of flora and fauna, pearls and golden trinkets, but especially in the Indians whom he had brought from Española. The theory that he had reached the outlying parts of the Indies was readily accepted, and the sovereigns at once prepared to take possession of the newly discovered lands.

The line of Demarcation.—The king of Portugal, jealous of Spain's triumph, is said to have planned to send a fleet across the Atlantic to dispute the Spanish claims. Ferdinand and Isabella hurried a messenger to Rome asking the pope to confirm their rights to the new discoveries. Accordingly, on May 4, 1493, Pope Alexander VI assigned to Spain all lands west of a meridian one hundred leagues west of the Azores and Cape Verde Islands. King John was not satisfied, and a year later, by the treaty of Tordesillas, a division line was fixed at 370 leagues west of Cape Verde Islands. This change gave Portugal title to her later discoveries on the Brazilian coast, though it lessened her possessions in the Orient.

READINGS

GROWTH OF GEOGRAPHICAL KNOWLEDGE

Beazley, C. R., *The Dawn of Modern Geography; Prince Henry the Navigator*, 1–105; Fischer, J., *The Discoveries of the Northmen in America;* Fiske, John, *The Discovery of America*, I, 151–255, 363–381; Hovgaard, W., *The Voyages of the Norsemen to America*, 221–255; Marco Polo, *The Book of Ser Marco Polo the Venetian*, Yule ed.; Olson, J. E., and Bourne, E. G., eds., *The Northmen, Columbus, and Cabot (Original Narratives of Early American History)*, 3–84; Vining, E. J., *An Inglorious Columbus; or evidence that Hwi Shan . . . discovered America in the Fifth Century*; Winsor, Justin, *Narrative and Critical History of America*, I, 1–58; Fossum, A., *The Norse Discovery of America;* Steensby, H. P., *The Norsemen's Route to Wineland;* Larson, L. M., "The Church in North America (Greenland) in the Middle Ages," in *The Catholic Historical Review*, V, 175–194.

PORTUGUESE DISCOVERIES

Beazley, C. R., *Prince Henry the Navigator*, 123–307; Bourne, E. G., "Prince Henry the Navigator," in *Essays in Historical Criticism*, 173–189; Cheyney, E. P., *European Background of American History*, 60–70; Helps, Arthur, *The Spanish Conquest in America*, I, 1–54; Jayne, K. G., *Vasco da Gama and his Successors*, 7–240; Lybyer, A. H., "The Ottoman Turks and the Routes of Oriental Trade," in *The English Historical Review*, XXX, 577–588; Major, R. H., *The Discoveries of Prince Henry the Navigator;* Martins, J. P. O., *The Golden Age of Prince Henry the Navigator*, 66–84, 205–231; Stephens, H. M., *Portugal*, 115–248; Vander Linden, H., "Alexander VI., and the Demarcation of the Maritime and Colonial Dominions of Spain and Portugal," in *American Historical Review*, XXII, 1–20.

COLUMBUS

Biggar, H. P., "The New Columbus," in Am. Hist. Assoc., *Ann. Rpt.*, *1912*, pp. 97–104; Bourne, E. G., *Spain in America*, 8–32; Channing, Edward,

History of the United States, I, 14–25; Hart, A. B., *American History told by Contemporaries*, I, 28–48; Helps, Arthur, *The Spanish Conquest in America*, I, 55–88; Herrera, Antonio, *Historia General;* Las Casas, Bartholomew, *Historia de las Indias;* Major, R. H., *Select Letters of Columbus;* Markham, Clements, *Life of Columbus;* Navarrete, M. F., *Colección de los Viages y Descubrimientos;* Olson, J. E., and Bourne, E. G., eds., *The Northmen, Columbus, and Cabot* (*Original Narratives*), 89–383; Peter Martyr, *De Orbe Novo* (F. A. McNutt, trans.); Richman, I. B., *The Spanish Conquerors*, 1–63; Thacher, J. B., *Columbus;* Vignaud, Henry, *Toscanelli and Columbus:* Winsor, Justin, *Columbus.*

CHAPTER II

THE FOUNDING OF NEW SPAIN (1492-1543)

SPAIN DURING THE CONQUEST

The discoveries of Columbus opened to Spain the opportunity to found a great colonial empire in the new world. For this work Spain had been prepared by the welding of the nation which was perfected during the reign of Ferdinand and Isabella.

The Christian reconquest.—In the eighth century the Mohammedan Berbers had overthrown the Visigothic kingdom, the unconquered Christian princes retiring to the mountain regions of the north. Gradually they reconquered the country. By 910 they had established the kingdoms of León and Navarre, and the county of Barcelona. By 1037 León and Castile had united and conquered a wide tract south of the Douro River. Aragon, originally a Frankish country, had also become an independent kingdom. By 1150 almost two-thirds of the peninsula had been conquered; Portugal now extended from the Minho River to the Tagus; Castile occupied the central region, and Aragon had incorporated Barcelona and Catalonia. During the next two centuries the rest of the peninsula, except the small kingdom of Granada, was conquered, and Aragon established her power in the Balearic Isles, Sardinia, and southern Italy. In 1469 Isabella of Castile married Ferdinand of Aragon, thus uniting the two great states. In 1481 they made war upon Granada, completing its conquest in the year of the discovery of America. All of these changes had been chiefly of rulers, the great body of the people remaining of the original Iberian stock.

Lack of unity.—But there was neither unity of speech, customs, nor institutions. There were three main religious groups, Christians, Mohammedans, and Jews. The people were also divided into social classes, nobility, clergy, common people, and slaves. The ranks and privileges of the nobility varied greatly, some having immense estates and almost sovereign powers, others

being landless soldiers of fortune. Castile was the land of castles.
The nobles were turbulent and warlike. They delighted in chivalry, which probably attained a higher development in Spain
than in any other country. Furthermore, there were three great
military orders, which had grown in strength during the Moorish
wars; these were the Knights of Santiago, of Calatrava, and of
Alcántara, at the head of each of which was a grand master. The
orders, the landed nobility, and the church owned about one-
third of the land and controlled large military forces. The cities
were also powerful; they were strongly fortified, regulated their
own affairs, and many of them had great fleets and extensive commerce. Life outside of the cities was largely pastoral, wool
growing being the principal industry. Both Castile and Aragon
contained governing bodies called *Cortes*, to which some of the
larger cities sent representatives, but they were of little importance, most of the work of lawmaking being done by the sovereign acting with his Council of State.

Establishment of unity.—To bring the entire country into
religious and political unity was the great task of Ferdinand and
Isabella. This was accomplished partly through the *Hermandad*
and the organization of several royal councils. The *Hermandad*,
originally a local police, was organized as a state police; captured
offenders were punished before local officers of the crown called
alcaldes. Turbulent nobles and brigands were made to feel the
long arm of the royal power. The nobles were also curbed by
transferring the grand masterships of the military orders to the
crown and the sovereigns resumed control of many estates which
had been granted to churches and nobles. The royal council of
twelve had been the principal governing body. Under Ferdinand
and Isabella it was divided into three councils, justice, state, and
finance. Other councils were added from time to time; among
these was the Council of the Inquisition, whose business it was
to stamp out heresy. By its efforts unbaptized Jews and Moors
were expelled. The rulers also sent royal officers called *corregidores* into the local communities, who gradually extended the
powers of the crown at the expense of local government. Thus
were laid the foundations of an absolute monarchy, which, in the
sixteenth century, became the most influential in Europe.

Charles V.—The prestige of Spain was greatly enhanced in the

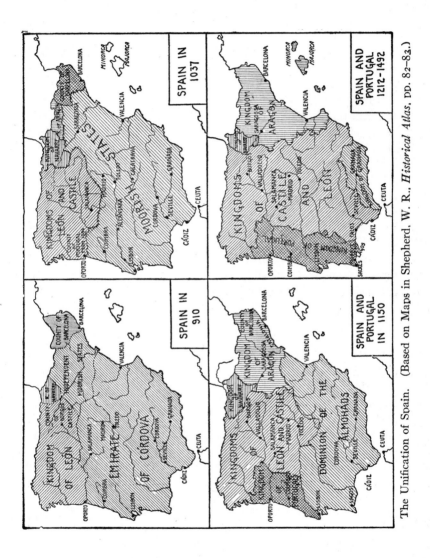

The Unification of Spain.   (Based on Maps in Shepherd. W. R. *Historical Atlas*, pp. 82–83.)

sixteenth century by the Emperor Charles V, the grandson of
Ferdinand and Isabella. From his mother he inherited Spain,
Naples, and Sicily, and possessions in the new world and the Far
East; from his father the Netherlands; from his grandfather,
Maximilian I, the Hapsburg inheritance in Germany. By election he became Holy Roman Emperor. The larger part of the
reign was occupied by three great European contests; a series
of struggles with Francis I of France for the control of Italy, the
Reformation in Germany, and the curbing of the westward advance of the Turks. The almost constant wars of the Emperor
kept him away from Spain nearly his entire time, but he used the
centralized system of Ferdinand and Isabella to supply him with
soldiers and money. The constant drain of treasure overtaxed
the resources of Spain, but the rich mines of the new world furnished the surplus for his vast undertakings. The fact that
Charles was successful in retaining his power in Italy, coupled
with his struggle against the Protestants and the Turks, made
him the recognized protector of the Catholic church. His reign,
marked by many sad failures in Europe, witnessed a phenomenal
expansion of Spain's colonies.

THE OCCUPATION OF THE WEST INDIES

The rule of Columbus in the Indies.—When Columbus discovered a new world for Spain, that country was placed in a new
situation, and a settled colonial policy was developed only with
experience. A department of Indian affairs was created at once
and put in charge of Fonseca, a member of the royal council.
A combined interest in commerce, religion, and colonization was
shown in all the arrangements for a second voyage by Columbus,
but commerce was the primary object. At first it was planned
to send a thousand colonists, but so eager were the applicants
that fifteen hundred embarked. The expedition was equipped
at the queen's expense, and most of the colonists were in her pay.

Reaching Española in November, 1493, Columbus found
Navidad destroyed by Indians; he accordingly established a new
settlement, named Isabella, at a point farther east. Leaving his
brother Diego in charge, Columbus explored the southern coast
of Cuba, discovered Jamaica, and circumnavigated Española.

Complaints being made against his administration, in 1495 Columbus returned to Spain to defend himself. Shortly after his departure, gold being found in the southern part of Española, the new town of Santo Domingo was founded there and became the capital. Other men were eager for commercial adventure, and, in response to their demands, in 1495 trade in the Indies was opened to all Spaniards, at their own expense. Columbus regarded this an infringement upon his rights, and on his return to Spain he protested, but to little purpose.

In 1498 Columbus sailed on a third voyage, taking some two hundred colonists. On the way he discovered the mainland of South America near the Orinoco River, and, farther west, valuable pearl fisheries. During his absence a civil war had occurred in Española, and, at the end of two years of trouble with the contending factions, Columbus was sent to Spain in chains by Bobadilla, a royal commissioner, who remained to govern in his place. The charges against Columbus were dismissed, but he was not restored to his rule in the Indies. In 1502 Nicolás de Ovando was sent to replace Bobadilla, taking with him 2500 new colonists.

Spread of settlement in the West Indies.—After 1496 Santo Domingo became the chief town of Española and the seat of Spanish rule in America. In rapid succession posts and mining camps were established in various parts of the island, and by 1513 there were seventeen chartered towns in Española alone. Santo Domingo at that time had a population of fifteen hundred persons. It was some fifteen years after the settlement of Española before the other islands began to be occupied, attention being first given to making cruises along the southern mainland. Ovando began the conquest of the other islands, however, and Diego Columbus, his successor, prosecuted the work with more vigor. In 1508 Ponce de León was sent to conquer Porto Rico, and in 1511 the present city of San Juan was founded. The settlement of Jamaica was begun in 1509 by Esquivel, under orders of Diego Columbus. Several towns were soon established, and a shipyard opened. In 1537 Jamaica became a possession of the family of Columbus, with the title of Marquis till 1557, then of Duke of La Vega. In 1508 Ocampo circumnavigated Cuba and in 1511 Velasquez began the conquest of the island. Santiago

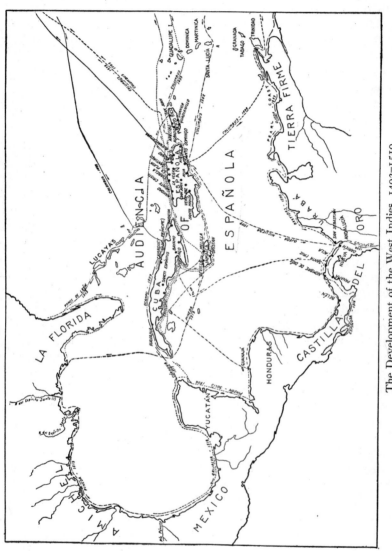

The Development of the West Indies, 1492–1519

was founded in 1514 and Havana a year later. Thus the West Indies became the nursery of Spanish culture and institutions in America.

Gold mining was important in Española for a time, but the mines were soon exhausted. In all the islands cotton, sugar, and cattle raising soon acquired some proportions, but the native population rapidly decreased, negro slaves were expensive, and rich profits attracted the settlers to the mainland; consequently, after the first quarter century the islands declined in prosperity and Porto Rico was for a time actually abandoned.

BEGINNINGS OF COLONIAL ADMINISTRATION AND POLICY

The Casa de Contratación.—For ten years Fonseca remained at the head of American affairs, being in effect colonial minister. In 1503 the Casa de Contratación or House of Trade was established at Seville, to direct commerce, navigation, and all related matters of the Indies. In charge of the Casa was a board of officials, including factors, treasurer, auditor, and notary. They maintained a warehouse for receiving all goods and treasure going to or from the islands. They were required to keep informed of the needs of the Indies, assemble and forward supplies, organize trading expeditions, and instruct and license pilots. Later on a professorship of cosmography was established for the purpose of instructing pilots, who were required to keep diaries of their voyages. This provision resulted in the accumulation of a vast amount of historical and geographical information in the government archives, much of which is still extant.

The Council of the Indies.—Spanish America was a possession of the sovereigns of Castile, as heirs of Queen Isabella, under whose patronage America had been discovered. At first, legislative and political matters relating to the Indies had been considered by the sovereigns in consultation with Fonseca and other personal advisors, but to supervise these matters a new board was gradually formed. In 1517 it was formally organized, among the members being Fonseca and Peter Martyr, the historian. In 1524 the board was reorganized as the Council of the Indies. This body was the supreme legislative and judicial authority, under the king, of Spanish-America. The Casa de Contratación was subordinate to the Council, which likewise supervised all civil and ecclesiastical appointments in the colonies. Usually some of the members of the Council had served in the Indies.

The governors-general and the audiencia.—Ovando ruled in Española until 1509, when Diego Columbus, son of Christopher, after a struggle for his hereditary rights, was made admiral and governor-general of the Indies. Complaint against Diego's administration led to the establishment at Santo Domingo of a superior court with appeals from the decisions of the governor-general. This was the germ of the Audiencia of Santo Domingo, which, for a time, was the administrative head of the greater part of the Indies. By decree of September 14, 1524, the Audiencia was formally established, with a president, four judges, a fiscal, a deputy grand-chancellor, and other officers.

The towns.—In the early sixteenth century the colonial towns showed some political activity. In 1507 the municipalities of Española sent delegates to Spain to petition for the rights enjoyed by Spanish towns. The request was granted, and, among other privileges, fourteen towns were granted coats-of-arms. Conventions of delegates from the towns were often held in these early days, to consider common needs and to draw up memorials to the home government. In 1530 Charles V decreed that such conventions should not be held without his consent, and the tendency thereafter was toward stronger absolutism and away from local political life. But there never was a time when the right of petition was not freely exercised, and with great effect on actual administration. In the sixteenth century the towns sometimes elected proctors to represent them before the Council of the Indies. In the seventeenth century they sometimes employed residents of Spain for this purpose.

In the colonial towns, both Spanish and native, there was some degree of self-government. Each Spanish town had its *cabildo* composed of *regidores*. In 1523 the *regidores* were made elective, but the tendency was to secure the office by purchase or inheritance, as was the case in Spain. The functions of the *cabildos* were similar to those of a New England town council, embracing legislation, police matters, care of highways, sanitation, and analogous functions.

Emigration.—The notion sometimes voiced that Spain did not
·"colonize" America is unfounded. Emigration to America was
encouraged by subsidies and other means, and in early days large
colonies were sent by government authority. It has been seen,
for example, that on his first three voyages Columbus took over
about 100, 1500, and 200 colonists respectively, and that Ovando
took 2500. During the entire sixteenth century the emigration
to America averaged from 1000 to 2000 persons per year. In
general, emigration was restricted to Spaniards of undoubted
orthodoxy, hence Jews, Moors, and recent converts were excluded. Naturalization was relatively easy, however, and by
means of it many foreigners were admitted. Portuguese, for
example, were numerous in the Indies, especially among the
seamen. Charles V adopted the liberal policy of opening the
Indies to subjects of all parts of his empire, but Philip II returned to the more exclusive practice. Later on, as the trade
monopoly broke down, it became necessary to admit foreign
traders to American ports, but they were required to return
within specified periods.

Married Spaniards emigrating from Spain were urged or even
required to take their families, but the emigration of unmarried
Spanish women was discouraged. Intermarriage of Spaniards
with native women was favored by the authorities, and, as a large
majority of the immigrants were single men, the practice was
common, either with or without formal sanction. An effort to
supply the lack of women by sending white slaves to the islands
failed, and in 1514 marriage with Indian women was approved
by royal order. With the opening of Mexico and Peru the island
colonies were in danger of depopulation. To prevent this from
happening, migration to the mainland was forbidden under heavy
penalties (1525-1526), and the recruiting of new conquering
expeditions in the islands was prohibited. To secure settlers for
Española, in 1529 attractive feudal lordships were offered to
founders of colonies.

Agriculture.—Agriculture in the West Indies was encouraged
by all means available. Duties on imports were remitted for a
term of years. In 1497 the sovereigns ordered a public farm established to provide loans of stock and seed, to be paid back by
colonists within a term of years. Free lands were granted to

settlers, with a reservation of the precious metals to the crown.
Special orders were given for mulberry and silkworm culture.
These efforts to promote agriculture in the West Indies, however,
were made largely nugatory by commercial restrictions and the
superior attractions of the mainland.

Indian policy.—Columbus found Española inhabited, it was
estimated, by a quarter of a million of Indians, and the other
islands similarly populated. He was instructed to treat the
natives well and to do all in his power to convert them. The
sovereigns frequently repeated these orders, and commanded
that the natives be treated as free men and paid for their work.
But the shortage of a labor-supply and the relative position of the
two races led quickly and almost inevitably to the practical enslavement of the weaker.

Encomiendas.—Following the rebellion of 1495, the subdued
natives were put under tribute in the form of specified amounts
of products, commutable to labor. In 1497 a practice was begun
of allotting lands to Spaniards, the forced labor of the natives
going with the land. Complaint being made by priests and
seculars that the Indians could neither be made to work, nor be
taught or converted without restraint, in 1503 it was ordered
that they should be congregated (*congregados*) in permanent
villages and put under protectors (*encomenderos*), who were
obliged to teach and protect them, and were empowered to exact
their labor, though for pay and as free men. This provision contained the essence of the encomienda system, which was designed
to protect and civilize the native, as well as to exploit him. But
there was always danger that the former aim would yield to the
latter, and, contrary to royal will, the condition of the natives
fast became one of practical slavery.

Depopulation of the islands.—Moreover, in a very short time
the islands became nearly depopulated of natives. Many were
slain in the wars of conquest and during rebellions, or died of
starvation while in hiding. Perhaps a greater number died of
smallpox, measles, and other diseases brought from Europe.
The result was that by 1514 the native population of Española
was reduced to 14,000. A similar reduction of native population
occurred in the other islands as they were successively occupied.

Indian slavery.—Indian slavery was not generally allowed in theory. But the Lesser Antilles, the Bahamas, and Florida were found to be inhabited by hostile cannibals, who were regarded as fair prize for enslavement. As early as 1494 Columbus suggested that permission be given to sell Caribs. In 1498 he took a cargo of six hundred of them to Spain. Soon it became an accepted legal principle that cannibals and rebellious Indians could be enslaved. The idea was encouraged by the lack of Spanish laborers, and by the disappearance of the native population of Española. Slave-hunting was soon extended, therefore, to the coasts of Florida, Pánuco, and other parts of the mainland. The practice was continued, as the frontier advanced, to the eighteenth century when, for example, Apaches of Texas and Pawnees of Kansas were often sold to work on plantations in Louisiana or Cuba.

Las Casas.—Numerous prominent Spaniards in the Indies early opposed encomiendas on moral grounds. Among them the most aggressive was Father Bartolomé de las Casas. He had come to the Indies as a layman, had held an encomienda after becoming a priest, but in 1514 had renounced it. In the following year he went to Spain, secured the appointment of a commission of Geronymite friars to enforce the laws regarding Indians in the islands, and was himself made Protector of the Indians. In 1516 he returned to Española, but, being dissatisfied with the work of the commission, he returned to Spain, where he favored negro slavery as a means of sparing the natives. In 1521 he tried to found a Utopian colony on Tierra Firme, to furnish an humane example, but through unfortunate circumstances it failed completely.

EXPLORATION OF THE MAINLAND COASTS AND THE SEARCH FOR A STRAIT

Voyages toward the South.—The discovery by Columbus (1498) of pearls on the southern mainland, combined with the Portuguese successes in India, gave new incentive to voyages, and within the next few years many thousands of miles of coastline of South and Central America were explored in the interest of trade, discovery, and international rivalry. In 1499 Ojeda explored from near Paramaribo to the Gulf of Maracaibo. In 1500

Pinzón and DeLepe sailed north to the Pearl Coast from points near 8° and 10° south, respectively, and Bastidas made known the coast from the Gulf of Maracaibo to Nombre de Diós, on the Isthmus of Panama.   The chain of discoveries was carried in 1502 from the north shore of Honduras to Nombre de Diós by the fourth voyage of Columbus, made primarily in search of a strait through the troublesome lands which he had discovered.   In 1504 La Cosa and Vespucius, during a trading voyage on the Gulf of Urabá, ascended the Atrato River two hundred miles by a route which has since been proposed as an interoceanic canal.   Meanwhile numerous other voyages were made to the Pearl Coast for commercial purposes.   They added little more to geographical knowledge, but led to colonization on the southern mainland.

Portuguese competition.—Spanish efforts to find a passage to the Indian Ocean by going to the southward were stimulated by the Portuguese voyages in the same direction.   In 1500 Cabral, on his way to India, took possession for Portugal at a point near 18° south latitude on the Brazilian coast.   In the following year a Portuguese expedition, in which Americus Vespucius was pilot, explored the coast from 5° to 32° south latitude, discovering the La Plata River on the way.   It was to this voyage of Vespucius, made in the interest of Portugal, that America owes its name.   First applied to South America, it was soon extended to the northern continent.   A Portuguese voyage made in 1503 by Jaques, in search of a passage to the East, is said to have reached 52° south.

Establishment of the Portuguese Empire in the East.—Gama's voyage was promptly followed by the founding of Portuguese colonies in the East.   The chief actor in this work was Alburquerque, who accompanied an expedition to India in 1503 and became viceroy in 1509, an office which he held until his death in 1515.   During his rule the Portuguese established themselves at Goa, which gave them control of the Malabar coast, and at Malacca, from which point they were able to control the trade of the Malay Peninsula and the Spice Islands.   Ormuz was captured, making them supreme in the commerce of the Persian Gulf.   In succeeding years they acquired Ceylon and established trading settlements in Burma, China, and Japan.

Continued quest for a strait.—These Portuguese successes were an incentive to further Spanish efforts to find the strait. In 1506 Vicente Yâñez Pinzón, accompanied by Juan de Solís, in search of a passage explored the Gulf of Honduras and eastern Yucatan from Guanajâ Islands, the western limit of Columbus's voyage, to the Island of Caría. In 1509 Solís, in the service of Spain, reached 42° south, while in search of the desired route. The discovery of the Pacific Ocean by Balboa in 1513 aroused Spain to renewed efforts to find the strait. Exploration was at once undertaken on the southern shores of Panama, and in 1515 Solís again was sent down the Brazilian coast. Reaching the La Plata River, he was killed and eaten by the savages.

Magellan and Elcano.—The solution of the problem of the southern strait was left for Ferdinand Magellan, a Portuguese who had seen service in the Far East. Returning to Portugal, he proposed to the king the opening of a route to the East by going west. His offer being refused, like Columbus he turned to Spain, where his plan found favor. Sailing with five vessels in 1519, he discovered the Straits of Magellan and crossed the Pacific Ocean to the Philippines, where he was killed in 1521. Part of the crew, led by Elcano, continued round the world and reached Spain in September, 1522, after one of the most remarkable voyages in all history.

The mapping of the Gulf coast.—Meanwhile the outlines of the Gulf of Mexico had been made known, and by 1525 the continued search for the strait and efforts to settle on the mainland had carried Spanish explorers nearly the whole length of the North Atlantic coast. In 1508 Ocampo had circumnavigated Cuba. Sailing from Porto Rico in 1513 Juan Ponce de León, who was interested in slave-hunting and exploration, discovered and coasted the Peninsula of Florida.

Four years later Córdova, under a license from Velásquez, governor of Cuba, explored Yucatan, finding signs of large cities and of wealth. The reports aroused new interest in the mainland, and Velásquez sent out Grijalva, who coasted the shore from Yucatan to Pánuco River, securing on the way twenty thousand dollars' worth of gold. To take advantage of Grijalva's discoveries, Velásquez organized another expedition and put it in charge of Hernando Cortés. Garay, governor of Jamaica, also sent out an expedition, under Pineda, with instructions to seek new lands and look for a strait. Sailing north to the mainland in 1519, Pineda completed the mapping of the Gulf by coasting from Florida to Vera Cruz and back. On the way west he discovered the Mississippi River, which he called Río del Espíritu Santo. On the strength of Pineda's discoveries, Garay now secured a patent to the northern Gulf shore, and undertook to colonize the province of Amichel.

The North Atlantic coast.—The exploration of the North Atlantic coast soon followed. In 1513 De León had rounded the Peninsula of Florida. Eight years later Gordillo, sailing from Española in the employ of Ayllón, and Quexos, a slave hunter whom Gordillo met on the way, reached the mainland at 33° 30', near Cape Fear in a region called Chicora. Ayllón in 1523 secured a patent authorizing him to seek a strait in the north and found a colony. In Ayllón's employ, Quexos in 1525 coasted north perhaps to 40°. In the same year Stephen Gómez, under contract to seek a northern strait, descended the coast from Nova Scotia to Florida. Over the northern part of his route he had been preceded by the English explorer John Cabot (1497). With the return of Gómez the entire Atlantic shore from the Straits of Magellan to Nova Scotia had been explored by expeditions made in the name of Spain.

THE MAYAS AND THE NAHUAS

A Double Movement.—Having subdued the islands and run the eastern coastline, the Spaniards proceeded to take possession of the mainland. To the southward they were attracted by trade, rumors of gold, and the hope of finding a strait leading to the East. To the westward they were drawn by the semicivilized Nahuas and Mayas, who lived in substantial towns, possessed accumulated wealth, had a stable population used to hard labor, and were worth exploiting. The advance into the interior was a double movement, one proceeding north from a base on the Isthmus of Panama, the other radiating in all directions from the Valley of Mexico.

Two Civilizations.—The Nahuas occupied Mexico south of a line drawn roughly from Tampico through Guadalajara to the Pacific Ocean. The Mayas lived principally in Yucatán and

Guatemala. The Nahuas had acquired much of their culture from the Mayas, and the cultural areas overlapped. These peoples had several features in common. They lived in substantial pueblos, or towns, and practiced agriculture by means of irrigation, raising extensively maize, beans, potatoes, and tobacco. Maguey was a staple crop in the Valley of Mexico and henequén in Yucatán. Mayas and Nahuas both lacked important domestic animals. They were dominated by a powerful priesthood and practiced slavery and human sacrifice.

Maya Characteristics.—Certain features distinguished the two civilizations. The Mayas had imposing architectural structures devoted to religion, notably at Palenque, Uxmal, and Chichén Itza. They had made considerable advance toward written records in the form of ideograms. More than 1500 Maya manuscripts, written on henequén, have been preserved but are as yet in the main undeciphered.

The Nahuas.—The Nahuas had made remarkable progress in astronomical calculations, and their worship was closely connected with the planetary system. The most notable religious monuments were the pyramids which are widely scattered over the country. Some of these, it is believed, are of Maya origin. Calendars of great perfection had been devised, the famous Calendar Stone now preserved in the National Museum at Mexico being one of the rare treasures of archæology. The Nahuas had achieved a more highly developed agriculture than the Mayas, had a stronger military and political organization, and larger and better constructed towns. Of these the most notable was Mexico (Tenochtitlán). It was built in a lake in the center of the great valley of Anáhuac, and had a population of perhaps 60,000 when the Spaniards came.

Nahua History.—The Nahuas had come from the north about the time when the Germanic tribes were overrunning southern Europe. According to their own traditions the first Nahua tribe, the Toltecs, entered the Valley of Mexico in 596 A. D., and were overpowered by the barbarians whom they found there, but civilized them. In succeeding centuries they were followed by other Nahua tribes, whose names are now borne by numerous cities in the Valley of Mexico. Among the late comers were the Aztecs, who, according to tradition, founded their lake-city in 1325 A. D. Their military stronghold was the crag of Chapultepec, where the presidential mansion of Mexico now stands.

The Triple Alliance.—Among the numerous cities or pueblos built by these struggling tribes four emerged into prominence. First Atzcapotzalco, then Tezcuco, then Mexico acquired supremacy. Placing itself at the head of a triple alliance (Mexico, Tezcuco, and Tacuba), Mexico in the fifteenth century engaged in a series of conquests which carried the Aztec power to the Gulf of Mexico, to the Pacific Ocean, and well into the Maya regions of Central America. War became a national impulse, closely identified with the religion of which human sacrifice was a central feature. The "empire" was but a military overlordship, however, and had for its chief objects tribute and human beings for sacrifice.

The hegemony was not secure, nor did it embrace all of the semi-civilized peoples. The Tarascans and other tribes to the west had resisted its power, and shortly before the advent of the Spaniards the Tlascalans to the east had defeated the Aztecs in battle. At the coming of the Europeans the "empire" was losing its hold. The subject peoples were becoming more restless under the burden of tribute; and the ruler, Montezuma II, was a superstitious fatalist. The Spanish conquerors arrived at the opportune moment for success.

THE CONQUEST OF CENTRAL AMERICA

Castilla del Oro.—At the same time that the islands other than Española were being occupied, beginnings of settlement were made in Central America. In 1503 Christopher Columbus had attempted to establish a colony on the Veragua coast, but had failed. After several successful trading voyages had been made, however, two colonies were planned for the southern mainland. Ojeda received a grant called Urabá, east of the Gulf of Darién, and Nicuesa obtained a grant called Veragua, lying west of that Gulf. Ojeda founded a colony at San Sebastián (1509), which was shortly afterward moved to Darién, where Vasco Nuñez de Balboa soon became the leading figure and governor *ad interim* (1511). Nicuesa's colony was founded at Nombre de Diós (1510), but it did not flourish. The Darién region became known as

Nueva Andalucía, and in 1513 the whole southern mainland, excepting Veragua, Honduras and Yucatán, to the west and Paria, to the east, was reorganized into one grand jurisdiction called Castilla del Oro, and made independent of Española.

Balboa.—Hearing of gold and a sea toward the south, Balboa led a band of men in 1513 across the Isthmus of Panamá and discovered the Pacific Ocean. The discovery was an important factor in leading to Magellan's great voyage, already recounted, and it set in motion a wave of explorations both up and down the Pacific coast, and led to the conquest of Peru. Balboa had made enemies, and he fell under the suspicion of the new governor of Castilla del Oro, Pedrarias de Ávila, who arrived at Darién in 1514 with a colony of fifteen hundred persons; but a conciliation occurred, and in 1515 Balboa was made Adelantado of the Island of Coiba, in the South Sea. To explore that water he built vessels on the north coast and had them transported across the Isthmus on the backs of Indians. The vessels proved unseaworthy, and while Balboa was building two more at the Isle of Pearls, he was summoned by Pedrárias, charged with treason, and beheaded (1519).

Exploration on the South Sea.—Balboa was succeeded by Espinosa in charge of the southern coast. He at once began plundering raids westward by land, seeking gold and slaves. The South Sea now became the chief center of interest, and, to provide a better base, in 1519 Pedrárias founded Panamá, moved his capital thither, refounded Nombre de Diós, and opened a road across the Isthmus between the two places.

Rapidly now the conquerors and explorers, under Pedrárias, pushed their way westward, by water and by land. With two of the vessels built by Balboa, in 1519 Espinosa sent an expedition under Castañeda which reached the Gulf of Nicoya, some five hundred miles from Panamá. In 1522 Andrés Niño and Gil González Dâvila fitted out a joint expedition, planning to sail west one thousand leagues, to seek spices, gold, and silver. After sailing one hundred leagues westward, González proceeded west by land, while Niño continued with the fleet. González reached and conquered the country bordering on the Gulf of Nicoya and Lake Nicaragua, places so named from local chieftains. Niño sailed west to Fonseca Bay, thus coasting the entire length of

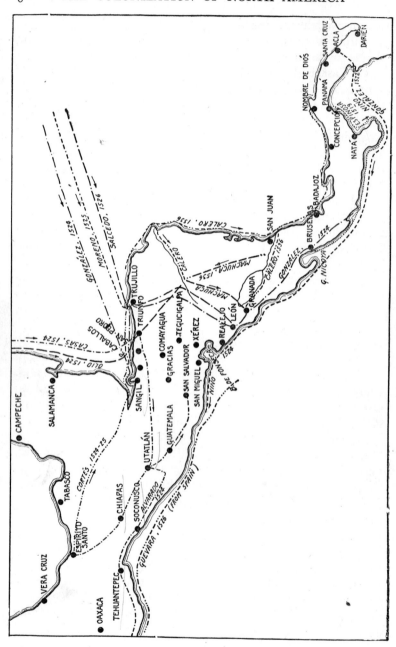

The Development of Central America, 1509–1543

Nicaragua. When the commanders returned to Panamá they reported thirty-two thousand baptisms, and presents in gold and pearls worth more than $112,000.

The Conquest of Costa Rica and Nicaragua.—These profitable explorations stimulated renewed interest, and were followed by conquest and settlement in Costa Rica and Nicaragua. González desired to return at once to occupy the country which he had explored, and, meeting hindrance from Pedrarias, he went to Española to organize another expedition, while awaiting royal consent. Meanwhile Pedrarias set about conquering Nicaragua for himself. With funds borrowed from Francisco Pizarro and others, he equipped a small expedition and sent it under Francisco Hernández de Córdova. One of the commanders was Hernando de Soto, who later became famous in Peru and Florida. Proceeding westward, in 1524 Córdova founded Bruselas, on the Gulf of Nicoya, and parceled out the natives among the settlers. Continuing into Nicaragua, he founded the cities of León and Granada. In the struggle which followed, Bruselas was abandoned and the settlement of Costa Rica proceeded slowly.

González in 1524, having secured royal permission, entered Honduras from the northeast, with an expedition destined for Nicaragua. De Soto, sent against him by Córdova, was easily subdued, but González was defeated by the agents of Cortés, who was now engaged in the conquest of Mexico. In Nicaragua Córdova revolted against Pedrárias and was executed. In 1527 Pedrárias became governor of Nicaragua, where he ruled till 1531. During all these wranglings the Indians were the chief sufferers. They were granted in encomienda, employed as beasts of burden, or branded and sold as slaves in Panamá, Peru, or the West Indies.

Guatemala, San Salvador, and Honduras.—Meanwhile the north-moving conquerors who went out from Panamá had met and struggled in Guatemala, San Salvador, and Honduras with the companions of Cortés, moving southward from Mexico. The history of the conquest of these disputed regions, therefore, becomes a part of the story of the exploits of Cortés and his lieutenants, recounted below.

Exploration of San Juan River.—One of the acts which relieve the bloody story of the career of Pedrarias was the sending in

1529 of an expedition under Estete to find the outlet to Lake Nicaragua. Estete descended the San Juan River until a glimpse was had of the sea, but hostile Indians prevented him from reaching it. It was believed that the lake and river drained a country rich with gold, and explorations continued. In 1536 the San Juan, with tributary branches, was explored by Alonso Carrero and Diego Machuco, under orders from the new governor of Nicaragua. Soon the lake and river became the principal highway from Nicaragua to the Atlantic Ocean, and to the Porto Bello fairs.

The Dukedom of Veragua.—It was a long time after Nicuesa's failure in 1510 before another attempt was made to settle Veragua, one reason being that the region was tenaciously claimed by the heirs of Columbus. In 1535 Alonso Gutiérrez was made governor of Veragua, as agent of the widow of Diego Columbus, but misfortune attended his efforts to found a colony. Shortly afterward (1537) the discoverer's grandson, Luís, was made Duke of Veragua; several attempts to colonize it failed, however, and in 1556 the region was surrendered for a small pension.

Continued struggle in Central America.—These conquests were but the beginning of a long struggle of the Spaniards with the natives in Central America. The first stages of the conquest were over by the middle of the sixteenth century, but many parts of the country were still unconquered at the end of the seventeenth. Some tribes, indeed, are unsubdued and uncivilized to this day.

THE CONQUEST OF THE VALLEY OF MEXICO

The revolt of Cortés.—In the very year of the founding of Panamá Hernando Cortés entered Mexico. The return of the expeditions of Córdova and Grijalva to the Mexican coast had caused excitement in Cuba. Governor Velásquez prepared an expedition to follow them up, and appointed Cortés to lead it. Becoming distrustful of his lieutenant, Velásquez sent messengers to recall him, but Cortés set forth, nevertheless. In defiance of the governor, on February 18, 1519, he left Cuba, a rebel, with eleven vessels, some six hundred men, and sixteen horses. Proceeding to Tabasco and up the coast, he founded Vera Cruz, by whose *cabildo* he was chosen captain-general and *justicia mayor*, and his position was thus given the color of legality. By this act Cortés placed himself under the immediate protection of the king.

The march to Mexico.—On the way and while at Vera Cruz Cortés had learned that the Aztec "empire" was honeycombed with dissension, and that the subject peoples were burdened with tribute and filled with hatred for Montezuma, the native ruler at the city of Mexico. He therefore assumed the rôle of deliverer, and the Indians rallied to his standard. At Cempoalla he connived at a revolt against Montezuma's tax gatherers. Scuttling his ships and thus cutting off all chance for retreat, in August he set out for Mexico. His march was a succession of audacious deeds. At Cempoalla he threw down heathen idols and imprisoned the chiefs. At Tlascala he was attacked by several thousand warriors, but his genius changed them into allies in his train. At Cholula, discovering a conspiracy, he raked the streets with cannon shot and burned the leaders at the stake. In triumph he entered the great pueblo of Tenochtitlan or Mexico. While lodged as a guest of Montezuma in the center of the city, he seized the Aztec ruler and held him prisoner.

The loss and recapture of the city.—In the spring of 1520 Cortés learned that Pánfilo de Narváez had arrived at Vera Cruz with nearly a thousand men, under orders from Velásquez to arrest him. Leaving Pedro de Alvarado in charge, he hastened to the coast, won over most of Narváez's men, and then hurried back to Mexico. During his absence the Aztecs had revolted, through the rashness of Alvarado. Soon after the return of Cortés the natives rose again, killed Montezuma, and replaced him by Cuautehmoc, a more vigorous leader. Cortés now sought safety in flight, but during the night retreat he lost more than half his men. This "unfortunate night" became known as "Noche Triste." But the defeat was only temporary. Raising new allies, Cortés conquered the towns round about Mexico, built a fleet at Tlascala, launched it on Lake Tezcuco, besieged the city, and by a combined attack, by land and water, on August 13, 1521, he recaptured Mexico, the most important native town in all America.

Cortés's contest with Velásquez.—Knowing that Velásquez would oppose him, Cortés, while at Vera Cruz in 1519, had at once sent agents, bearing rich presents, to represent him at the court of Charles V. Then began a three-year contest with the agents of the Cuban governor. The delay was fortunate for Cortés, for in the course of it he won favor by his remarkable feats of conquest. Through the influence of Fonseca, Velásquez secured the appointment of Cristóbal de Tápia, an official of Española, as governor of New Spain, to take charge of the government and investigate Cortés. But Cortés got rid of him as he had disposed of Narváez. Arriving at Vera Cruz in December, 1521, Tápia was met by a council of delegates from the conqueror and practically driven from the country, on the ground that new orders were expected from the king.

Cortés made Governor and Captain-General.—Before this Cortés had sent Avila to the Audiencia of Santo Domingo to obtain its favor. Scarcely had Tapia been ejected when Avila returned with tentative authority for Cortés, subject to royal approval, to continue his conquests and to grant encomiendas. This greatly strengthened Cortés's position. Having succeeded so well in Española, Avila was now sent to Spain. Here he triumphed also, for on October 15, 1522, the emperor approved the acts of Cortés and made him governor and captain-general of New Spain. The victory of Cortés was as complete as the discomfiture of Velásquez and Fonseca.

Mexico rebuilt. Encomiendas granted.—The work of conquest on the mainland was accompanied by the evolution of government and the establishment of Spanish civilization, just as had been the case in the West Indies during the earlier stages of the struggle. Wherever the Spaniards settled, they planted their political, religious, economic, and social institutions. Mexico was rebuilt in 1522 as a Spanish municipality, Pedro de Alvarado, the most notable of Cortés's lieutenants, being made first *alcalde mayor*. In the regions subdued the principal provinces were assigned to the conquerors as encomiendas. Much of the actual work of control was accomplished through native chiefs, who were assigned Spanish offices and held responsible for good order and the collection of tribute. This method was later adopted by the British in India.

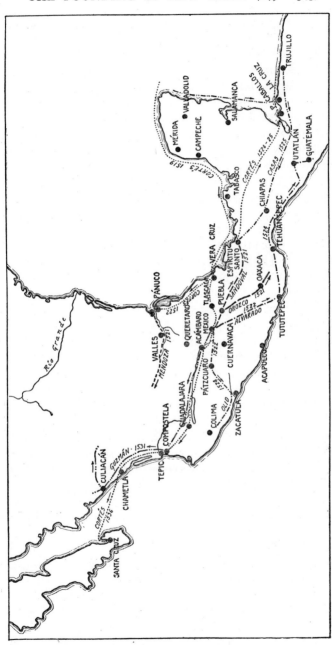

The Development of Southern Mexico, 1519–1543

THE SPREAD OF THE CONQUEST

The semi-civilized tribes.—With the fall of the city the first stage of the conquest had ended. Within the following decade most of the semi-civilized tribes of southern Mexico and Central America were brought under the dominion of Spain. During this period Spanish activities were directed from the Valley of Mexico to the eastward, southward and westward. From the south came rumors of gold and reports of the South Sea, while to the north, among the barbarian tribes, there was little, at this stage of the conquest, to attract the conquerors.

Factors in the conquest.—Several factors explain the marvelous rapidity with which Spanish rule was extended. The conquerors were looking for gold and accumulated treasure; not finding it in one place they hastened to another, led off by any wild tale of riches. The fame of the Spaniards preceded them and paralyzed resistance. They were everywhere aided by great armies of allies, eager to help destroy their hated enemies. Finally, Cortés, himself a genius, was assisted by an able body of lieutenants; in the spread of the conquest Cortés remained the central figure, but the actual work fell mainly to Orozco, Alvarado, Olid, Sandoval, Chico, Avalos, Montejo and other subordinates.

Vera Cruz, Oaxaca, and Tehuantepec.—In the fall of 1520 Sandoval, in search of gold and to punish rebellious Indians, invaded southern Vera Cruz with a handful of soldiers, aided by thirty thousand Indian allies. To hold the district he founded the towns of Medellín and Espíritu Santo. Before the expulsion of Cortés from the city, goldseekers had been sent to Oaxaca and Tehuantepec and were well received, but the "Noche Triste" was followed by a reaction. Orozco was sent, therefore, to subdue Oaxaca, which he reported to be rich in gold. In 1522 an attack by hostile neighbors called Alvarado to Tehuantepec. Gold was found, and as the district bordered on the South Sea, settlements were formed to hold it.

Olid in Michoacán.—The same year, 1522, marks the extension of Spanish rule into Michoacán, the territory of the hitherto independent Tarascans. The cacique Tangaxoan visited Cortés and made submission, and in return Olid was sent to found a settlement at Patzcuaro on Lake Chapala. Before the end of the year part of the settlers moved to the seacoast and settled at Zacatula, in the modern state of Guerrero, where a post had been established.

Colima and Jalisco.—From Michoacán the conquest at once spread north into Colima and Jalisco. Gold being reported in Colima, Avalos and Chico, lieutenants of Olid, entered the country, but were defeated by the natives. Thereupon Olid followed, subdued the mountain region by force, and founded the town of Colima (1524), which became a base for new advances. On his return to Mexico, Olid brought samples of pearls from Colima, and reports of an Amazon Island ten days up the coast, where there were said to be great riches. To investigate these reports, in 1524 Francisco Cortés was sent north. He reached Río de Tololotlán, and secured the allegiance of the "queen" of Jalisco, but found little gold and no Amazon Island.

Amichel and Pánuco.—In 1522 the Huasteca country, to the northeast, came under the control of Cortés. It was three years before this that Pineda, as representative of Garay, governor of Jamaica, had visited the region. Garay applied for a grant of a province called Amichel, extending from Florida to Mexico, and set about colonizing it. In 1520, before the patent was secured, a party of his men met disaster near Pánuco River. Hearing of Garay's operations, in 1522 Cortés led forty thousand allies into the country, subdued it, and founded San Estéban, on Pánuco River. In 1523 Garay led a colony to the same region, but found himself forestalled by Cortés, by whom he was sent to Mexico, where he soon died. The rivalry of the Spaniards encouraged an Indian revolt, but Sandoval, as agent of Cortés, put down the disturbance with extreme cruelty. In 1527 the Pánuco district, under the name of Victoria Garayana was separated from Mexico, Nuño de Guzmán being made governor, while the region called Florida, further north, was assigned to Pánfilo de Narváez. Guzmán's rule of six months was characterized by attempts to extend conquests northward into Narváez's territory, by wars with the Huasteca chieftains, and by constant slave-hunting raids, through which the country was nearly depopulated.

Alvarado in Guatemala and San Salvador.—By this time the conquests of Cortés and his lieutenants had extended into Central America, where they encountered the agents of Pedrarias.

In 1522 embassies from the large cities of Utatlan and Guatemala had visited Cortés and made submission. In the following year Alvarado, with four hundred Spaniards and twenty thousand allies, entered the region and conquered the Quichés and Cakchiquels. This task partially completed, he continued south and extended his conquests into San Salvador (1524).

Olid and Casas in Honduras.—Cortés believed that Honduras was rich, and that a strait lay between it and Guatemala. Moreover, Gil González and the agents of Pedrarias had begun to operate there. Consequently, at the same time that Alvarado went to Guatemala, Olid was despatched to Honduras. Reaching there in 1524 he tried to imitate his master's example by making a conquest for himself. He succeeded in defeating González, as has been seen, but was in turn beheaded by Francisco de las Casas, who was sent by Cortés to overthrow him. During this struggle the city of Trujillo was founded.

The march of Cortés to Honduras.—In doubt as to the wisdom of sending Las Casas after Olid, in October, 1524, Cortés set out for Honduras in person, with about one hundred and forty Spaniards and three hundred Indians in his train, the latter led by three famous Aztec chiefs. In his rear was driven a herd of swine. The route lay through southern Vera Cruz, Tabasco, and Chiapas, to Golfo Dulce, his way being obstructed by vast morasses, swollen streams, and flint-strewn mountains. In a single province fifty bridges had to be constructed in a journey of as many miles. In Chiapas it became necessary to bridge with trees a channel five hundred paces wide. On the way the Aztec chieftains, including the noble Cuauhtemoc, being charged with conspiracy, were hanged, an act which is variously characterized as a "necessary punishment" and a "foul murder." Leaving his cousin, Hernando Saavedra, in command as captain-general in Trujillo, Cortés sent his men home by way of Guatemala and returned by sea to Mexico in May, 1526. After attempting for two years to explore on the South Sea, in 1528 he went to Spain to refute his enemies, chief of whom was Nuño de Guzmán, now president of the recently established Audiencia of Mexico. He returned two years later.

Yucatán.—The conquest of Yucatán was begun in 1527 by Francisco de Montejo, an agent of Cortés. Initial success was

followed by native revolts, and it was 1541 before the conquest
was made secure. There were frequent rebellions thereafter,
but never again united resistance.

Las Casas in Guatemala.—Thus far the conquest had been
one of force. But now an example of the power of gentleness
was furnished by Father Las Casas, the Dominican friar who
had opposed encomiendas so vigorously in Española. About
1532 he entered Nicaragua as a missionary, where he attacked the
ill-treatment of the Indians. Being opposed by the governor, in
1536 he went to Guatemala. Shortly before this he had written
a treatise to prove that conversion by force was wrong, and that
only persuasion should be used. To test his views he was granted
sole control for five years of a hostile region known as "the Land
of War," and by mild means he and his companions soon converted the district into a land of True Peace (Vera Paz), as it is
still called.

Guzmán in Sinaloa.—While Cortés was in Spain Guzmán,
fearing his own downfall, and hoping to save himself by offering
new provinces to the king, undertook the conquest of northern
Jalisco and of Sinaloa. Leaving Mexico in December, 1529,
with ten thousand allies, he marched through Michoacán and
Jalisco, leaving behind a trail of fire and blood, for which he has
ever since been execrated. Part of Sinaloa was explored, and
Culiacán was founded as an outpost in 1531. The region subdued
by Guzmán was named Nueva Galicia, of which the conqueror
became governor and Compostela the capital.

Buffer province of Querétaro.—At the coming of the Spaniards
the country north of the valley of Mexico had never been conquered by the Aztecs. The Spaniards, in turn, adopted the
policy of entrusting its subjugation to native caciques, treating
the region as a buffer Indian state. The leading figure in the
conquest was a Christianized Otomí chief, named Nicolás de San
Luis. By Charles V he was made a knight of the Order of Santiago and a captain-general in the army. Another Otomí cacique
who played a similar though less conspicuous part was Fernando de Tapia. The most notable event in the conquest
was the reduction of Querétaro in 1531. For thirty years
San Luís served the Spaniards in the control of the Querétaro
border.

The Mixton War.—The first half century of expansion toward the north was closed by a widespread native uprising in Nueva Galicia which for a time checked advance in that direction and even caused a contraction of the frontier. Guzmán had left Nueva Galicia in a deplorable condition. After several minor uprisings, the rebellious natives broke forth in 1541, during the absence of Governor Coronado and his army in New Mexico. The Indians refused to pay tribute, killed their encomenderos and the missionaries, destroyed the crops, and took refuge in the *peñoles* or cliffs of Mixton, Nochistlân, Acatic, and other places near Guadalajara. The defence fell to Cristóbal de Oñate, lieutenant governor of Nueva Galicia. Pedro de Alvarado, who chanced to arrive from Guatemala at Navidad with a force of men, led them against Nochistlân and lost his life in the encounter. Viceroy Mendoza at last took the field with four hundred and fifty Spaniards and thirty thousand allies, and crushed the revolt.

EXPLORATIONS IN THE NORTHERN INTERIOR AND ON THE PACIFIC

FLORIDA

De León.—While some conquerors were struggling in Central America, Mexico, and Peru, others were trying to subdue the vast northern region called Florida. In 1514 Juan Ponce de León secured a patent to colonize Florida and Bimini, which he had explored in the previous year. Instead of proceeding to the task, however, he engaged in a war against the Caribs, and it was not until 1521 that he attempted to carry out his project. In that year he led a colony of two hundred men to the Peninsula, landed on the west coast, and tried to establish a settlement. But he was attacked by natives, and driven back to Cuba, mortally wounded.

Ayllón's colony on the Carolina coast.—To carry out his contract to colonize Chicora, in July, 1526, Ayllón sailed from Española with six vessels and a colony of five hundred men and women, Dominican friars, and supplies, prepared to find a new home in Carolina. But the experiment was doomed to be another failure. Landing was first made on the river called the Jordan, perhaps

Cape Fear River. On another stream, perhaps the Peedee, the settlement of San Miguel de Gualdape was begun. But supplies gave out, and at the end of two years Ayllón died (October, 1528). Quarrels ensued, and in midwinter the survivors, only about one hundred and fifty now, returned to Santo Domingo.

Narváez.—At the same time the conquest of Florida was attempted by Panfilo de Narváez, the man who had been sent to Vera Cruz to arrest Cortés. In 1526 he secured a patent to the lands of Ponce de León and Garay. Raising a colony of six hundred persons in Spain, in 1528 he reached Florida, landing near Tampa Bay. Hearing of a rich province called Apalachen (Apalache), he sent his vessels along the coast and himself marched up the peninsula at the head of three hundred men to find the Promised Land. He found the place sought near modern Tallahassee, but it proved to be a squalid Indian village of forty huts. A few weeks having been spent in exploration and warfare, Narváez went to the coast near St. Marks Bay, built a fleet of horse-hide boats, and set out for Pánuco. After passing the mouth of the Mississippi a storm arose, and all were wrecked on the coast of Texas.

Cabeza de Vaca.—In a short time most of the survivors of Narváez's party died of disease, starvation, and exposure, or at the hands of the savages. Having passed nearly six years of slavery among the Indians, Alvar Núñez Cabeza de Vaca, the treasurer of the colony of Florida, with three companions, escaped westward, crossed Texas, Coahuila, Chihuahua, and Sonora, and in 1536 reached Culiacán, the northern outpost of Sinaloa, after a most remarkable journey.

De Soto.—Vaca went to Spain (1537) to apply for the governorship of Florida, but it had already been conferred on Hernando de Soto, who had taken a prominent part in the conquest of both Central America and Peru. In 1539 De Soto reached Florida with a colony of six hundred persons. Landing at Tampa Bay, as Narváez had done, he soon set out to look for a rich province called Cale. This was the beginning of an expedition lasting nearly four years, during which the Spaniards were led on by tales of gold and treasure from one district to another, hoping to repeat the exploits of Cortés and Pizarro. As he passed through the country De Soto imitated those captains by capturing the chiefs, holding them as hostages, and compelling them to provide food and men to carry the baggage. Going to Apalachen he wintered there, meanwhile discovering Pensacola Bay. From Apalachen he went to the Savannah River, thence northwest to the North Carolina Piedmont, south toward Mobile Bay, northwest to the Mississippi near modern Memphis, westward across Arkansas into Oklahoma, thence down the Arkansas River to its mouth, where he died, in May, 1542, being buried in the Mississippi.

Moscoso in Arkansas and Texas.—De Soto's followers, led by Luís de Moscoso, now set out for Pánuco, crossing Arkansas to the Red River, then turning southwest through eastern Texas, perhaps reaching the Brazos River. Giving up the attempt by land, they returned to the Mississippi, built a fleet of boats, descended the river, and skirted the Texas coast, reaching Pánuco in 1543. Thus ended the fourth attempt to colonize Florida.

CÍBOLA AND QUIVIRA

Cortés on the South Sea and in California.—Another line of advance toward the northern interior had been made by way of the Pacific slope. The discovery of the South Sea was followed immediately by exploration along the western coast. Balboa himself had begun that work, before his death in 1519. Espinosa had reached Nicaragua in 1519, and three years later Niño had reached Guatemala. By this time Cortés had also begun operations on the South Sea by building a shipyard at Zacatula, hoping to discover a strait, find rich islands and mainland, reach India by way of the coast, and open communication with the Moluccas. In 1527 he sent three vessels under Saavedra across the Pacific. The operations of a new fleet built by him were hindered by the Audiencia of Mexico, but in 1532 he sent an expedition north under Hurtado de Mendoza, which reached Río Fuerte in northern Sinaloa. In the following year another expedition sent by Cortés under Jiménez discovered Lower California, which was thought to be an island and where pearls were found. The discovery of an island with pearls confirmed the geographical ideas of Cortés, and in 1535 he himself led a colony to La Paz, but within a few months it was abandoned. This was the first of a long series of efforts to colonize California.

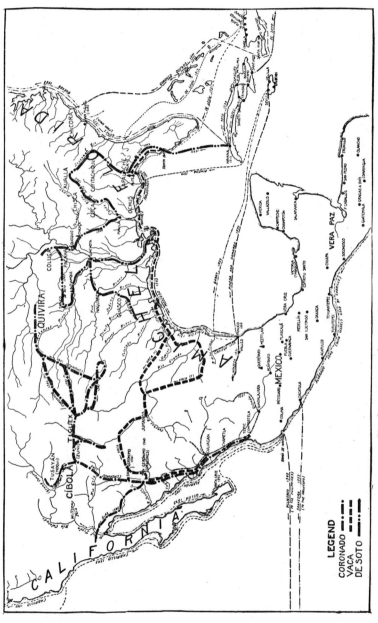

Explorations in the Northern Interior, 1513–1543

LEGEND

CORONADO
VACA
DE SOTO

Friar Marcos discovers Cíbola.—Interest in the north country, both in Spain and America, was greatly quickened by the arrival of Cabeza de Vaca in Mexico after his journey across the continent. He had seen no great wonders, but he had heard of large cities to the north of his path, and it was thought that they might be the famed Seven Cities. The viceroy took into his service the negro Stephen, one of Vaca's companions, and sent him with Friar Marcos, a Franciscan missionary, to reconnoitre. In March, 1539, they set out with guides from Culiacán. Going ahead, Stephen soon sent back reports of Seven Cities, called Cíbola, farther on. Friar Marcos hastened after him, and reached the border of the Zuñi pueblos in western New Mexico, where he learned that Stephen had been killed. Returning to the settlement, he reported that Cíbola was larger and finer than Mexico. This story, of course, was the signal for another "rush," like that to Peru a few years before.

Ulloa rounds the peninsula of California.—Rivalry between Cortés and the viceroy regarding exploration was now keen, and about the time of the return of Fray Marcos, Cortés, hoping to forestall his competitor, sent three vessels north to explore under Francisco de Ulloa. One of the vessels was lost, but with two of them Ulloa succeeded in reaching the head of the Gulf of California, and learned that California was a peninsula. Descending the Gulf he proceeded up the outer coast of California to Cabo del Engaño.

The contest for leadership.—While Ulloa's voyage was still in progress, Cortés hurried to Spain to present his claim of exclusive right to conquer the country discovered by Fray Marcos and Ulloa. He never returned to Mexico. Other contestants arose. The agents of De Soto, who at the time was in Florida, claimed Cíbola as a part of the adelantado's grant. Guzmán claimed it on the basis of explorations in Sinaloa. Pedro de Alvarado claimed it on the ground of a license to explore north and west, for which purpose he had prepared a fleet.

The Coronado expedition.—But the royal council decided that the exploration should be made on behalf of the crown, in whose name the viceroy had already sent out an expedition under Francisco Vásquez Coronado, governor of Nueva Galicia. To coöperate with Coronado by water, Alarcón was sent up the coast from Acapulco with two vessels.

In February, 1540, Coronado left Compostela with some two hundred horsemen, seventy foot soldiers, and nearly one thousand Indian allies and servants. So eager were the volunteers that it was complained that the country would be depopulated. The expedition was equipped at royal expense with a thousand horses, fine trappings, pack-mules, several cannon, and with droves of cattle, sheep, goats, and swine for food. From Culiacán Coronado went ahead with about one hundred picked men and four friars. Following behind their leader, the main army moved up to Corazones, in the Yaqui River valley, where the town of San Gerónimo was founded and left in charge of Melchor Díaz.

Zuñi, Moqui, the Colorado, and the Rio Grande.—In July Coronado reached the Zuñi pueblos, which he conquered with little difficulty. But the country was disappointing and the expedition resulted only in explorations. These, however, were of great importance. At Culiacán Alarcón procured a third vessel, then continued to the head of the Gulf, and ascended the Colorado (1540) eighty-five leagues, perhaps passing the Gila River. Shortly afterward Melchor Díaz went by land from San Gerónimo to the Colorado to communicate with Alarcón, but failed and lost his life. During the journey, however, he crossed the Colorado and went some distance down the Peninsula of California.

Hearing of the Moqui pueblos, to the north of Zuñi, in July Coronado sent Tobar to find them, which he succeeded in doing. Shortly afterward Cárdenas went farther northwest and reached the Grand Canyon of the Colorado. Moving to the Rio Grande, Coronado visited the pueblos in its valley and camped at Tiguex above Isleta. In the course of the winter the Indians revolted and were put down with great severity.

Gran Quivira.—Meanwhile Coronado heard of a rich country northeastward called Gran Quivira, and in April, 1541, he set out to find it. Crossing the mountains and descending the Pecos, he marched out into the limitless buffalo-covered plains, the "Llanos del Cíbola," inhabited by roving Apaches. Near the upper Brazos he turned north, crossed the Texas Panhandle and Oklahoma, and reached Quivira in eastern Kansas. It was probably a settlement of Wichita Indians. Disappointed, and urged by his men, Coronado now returned to Mexico. Three fearless missionaries remained to preach the gospel, and soon achieved the crown of martyrdom. Coronado had made one of the epochal explorations of all history.

The Pueblo Indians of New Mexico.—Coronado found large parts of New Mexico and adjacent regions inhabited by Indians who dwelt in substantial towns (pueblos) and possessed a civilization similar to that of the Aztecs. Their terraced dwellings, which were also fortifications, were built of stone or adobe, and were several stories high. The inhabitants lived a settled life, practiced agriculture by means of irrigation, and raised cotton for clothing. They were constantly beset by the more warlike tribes all about them, and were already declining under their incursions. At the time of the conquest there were some seventy inhabited pueblos, whose population may have been from 30,000 to 60,000. The principal pueblo regions were the upper Rio Grande, the upper Pecos, Ácoma, and the Zuñi and Moqui towns. Remains of prehistoric pueblos occupy a much wider range in the Southwest, and are now the scene of important archæological research.

CALIFORNIA AND THE PHILIPPINES

Alvarado's fleet.—Shortly after Coronado left New Mexico, two important expeditions were despatched by Viceroy Mendoza to explore in the Pacific. Magellan's voyage had been a signal for a bitter conflict between Spain and Portugal in the East, in which Portugal long had the upper hand. After the failures of Loaisa (1525) and Saavedra (1527) Charles V sold Spain's claims on the Moluccas to Portugal, but continued to claim the Philippines. In spite of former disasters to eastern expeditions, both Cortés and Pedro de Alvarado planned discoveries in the South Sea. In 1532 Alvarado made a contract for the purpose, but was led off by the gold "rush" to Peru. In 1538 he obtained a new grant, authorizing him to explore "in the west toward China or the Spice Islands," or toward the north at the "turn of the land to New Spain." Early in 1539 he left Spain with equipment for a fleet, which he transported across Honduras and Guatemala on the backs of natives. On hearing of the discoveries of

Fray Marcos, he hastened north with his fleet, but stopped in Mexico, where he and Mendoza, who had already sent out Coronado, made an agreement, as mutual insurance, to divide the profits of their respective explorations. Before continuing his expedition Alvarado was killed in the Mixton War (1541). This left the fleet in Mendoza's hands, and with it he carried out Alvarado's plans by despatching two expeditions, one up the California coast, the other across the Pacific.

Cabrillo and Ferrelo.—The coast voyage was conducted by Juan Rodríguez Cabrillo, and was especially designed to look for a northern strait. Leaving Navidad in June, 1542, Cabrillo explored the outer coast of the Peninsula, discovered San Diego Bay, reached Northwest Cape (latitude 38°31′), descended to Drake's Bay, and then returned to the Santa Barbara Channel, where he died. Sailing north again in 1543, his pilot, Ferrelo, reached the Oregon coast (42½°), returning thence to Navidad. Cabrillo and Ferrelo had explored the coast for more than twenty-three degrees, but had missed both San Francisco and Monterey bays.

Villalobos.—The other expedition was led by López de Villalobos, who was instructed to explore the Philippines and to reach China, but not to touch at the Moluccas. Sailing in November, 1542, he took possession of the Philippines, but, being forced to leave on account of native hostility, he was captured by the Portuguese. Villalobos died in the Moluccas, where the enterprise went to pieces. The expeditions of Coronado, De Soto, Cabrillo, and Villalobos brought to an end a remarkable half century of Spanish expansion in North America and in the Pacific Ocean.

THE ESTABLISHMENT OF THE VICEROYALTY OF NEW SPAIN

Cortés as administrator.—Cortés was not a mere conqueror. He appointed officers, and issued general ordinances affecting nearly all lines of activity. Encomenderos were required to equip themselves for defense and to promote agriculture. Cortés himself became a great planter, notably at Oaxaca. He introduced agricultural implements, opened a port at Vera Cruz, and established markets in Mexico City. In 1523 the king had forbidden encomiendas, but Cortés made so strong a protest on the grounds of policy and royal interest that the order was withdrawn.

Royal officials arrive.—In 1524 a corps of royal officials arrived to take the places of those appointed by Cortés. Estrada came as treasurer, Salazar as factor, Albórnoz, as contador, and Chirinos as veedor. They came empowered to interfere in the government of Cortés, especially in matters of finance, a policy quite in keeping with the general Spanish practice of setting one officer to watch another.

The powers of Cortés curtailed.—The new officials were not slow to make trouble for Cortés. While he was in Honduras his enemies set about undermining him, both in Mexico and Spain. Salazar and Chirinos usurped authority, persecuted the conqueror's partisans, confiscated his property, and spread reports that he was dead. At last the friends of Cortés rebelled, overthrew the usurpers, Salazar and Chirinos, and sent for Cortés to return from Honduras. In May, 1526, he reached Vera Cruz. Two years of investigation and persecution by other crown officials followed.

In response to complaints in Spain, Luís Ponce de León was sent early in the same year as governor and to hold a *residencia* of Cortés, while the latter's jurisdiction as captain-general was lessened by the appointment of Nuño de Guzmán as governor of Pánuco. Ponce de León died in July, leaving Aguilar as governor. Aguilar died early in 1527 and Estrada became governor. He interfered with Cortés's explorations in the South Sea, and banished him from Mexico City as dangerous, but the breach was soon healed when both were threatened by the usurpations of Guzmán. It was at this time that Cortés, finding his position unbearable, went to Spain for redress and to answer charges.

The first Audiencia of New Spain.—In view of the disturbed conditions in New Spain, in 1528 Charles V created an Audiencia or supreme court for Mexico, and empowered it to investigate the disorders and hold the *residencia* of Cortés. It was composed of four *oidores* and a president. To the latter office was appointed Nuño de Guzmán. He proved to be an extreme partisan against Cortés, and so avaricious that he soon won the hatred of almost everyone except a few favorites. The old friends of Cortés stood by him and he secured the support of Bishop Zumárraga.

Cortés made Marquis of the Valley.—The arrival of Cortés in Spain caused his detractors to slink from sight, and he was conducted to court with almost royal honors. In consideration of his brilliant services, in 1529 he was granted twenty-two towns, with twenty-three thousand vassals, with full civil and criminal jurisdiction and rentals for himself and his heirs. With these honors he was given the titles of Marquis of the Valley of Oaxaca, captain-general of New Spain, and governor of such islands as he might still discover in the South Sea. In 1530 he returned to New Spain, where he was acclaimed by the people, though opposed by the Audiencia.

The second Audiencia.—The abuses of the first Audiencia led to its replacement in 1530 by a new corps of judges, of whom the president was Sebastián Ramírez de Fuenleal. The oidores appointed were Salmerón, Maldonado, Ceynos, and Quiroga. They were especially instructed to hold the *residencias* of their predecessors, restore the estates of Cortés, and consider the abolition of encomiendas. To replace control by encomenderos, local magistrates called *corregidores* were introduced. A few of these functionaries were appointed, but the colonists raised such a cry that little change was accomplished, and the Audiencia confined itself, in this particular, to checking abuses of the encomienda system. Quiroga later became bishop and civilizer of Michoacán, where he is still gratefully remembered.

The viceroyalty established.—The difficulties of government and the spread of conquests made closer centralization necessary, and New Spain was now made a viceroyalty. The first incumbent of the office of viceroy was Antonio de Mendoza, a nobleman of fine character and ability. He arrived in 1535. As viceroy he was president of the Audiencia, governor, and captain-general, personally representing the king in all branches of government.

The Audiencias of Panamá and Guatemala.—Alvarado served as governor and captain-general of Guatemala through appointment by Cortés till 1528, when he was commissioned directly by the emperor. Though frequently absent, he continued in office till his death in 1541. In 1537 Panamá and Veragua were erected into the Audiencia of Panamá, which was later attached to the viceroyalty of Peru, because the commerce of Peru crossed the

Isthmus. Six years later the Audiencia of the Confines of
Panamá and Nicaragua was established. After various changes,
by 1570 Guatemala became the seat of an Audiencia embracing all of Central America except Panamá, Veragua, and
Yucatán.

The New Laws.—Las Casas and others continued to oppose
the encomienda system. In 1539 the great missionary returned to
Spain to conduct the fight. While there he wrote his celebrated
works called *The Destruction of the Indies* and the *Twenty Reasons*
why Indians should not be enslaved. His pleadings were not
in vain, for in 1542 the Council issued a new Indian code called
the *New Laws*, which provided that encomiendas should be
abolished on the death of the present holders. But so great was
the opposition that in 1545 the vital clauses of the ordinance were
repealed. In Peru the attempt to enforce the laws even led to
bloodshed.

Mendoza sent to Peru.—Viceroy Mendoza continued to rule
for fifteen years. He proved to be a wise, able, and honest administrator, who tried to improve the condition of both the colonists
and the helpless natives. He prohibited the use of the Indians
as beasts of burden. In 1536 he established the printing press in
Mexico, the first book published on the continent appearing in
1537. In that year he founded the college of Santa Cruz de
Tlatelalco for the education of noble Indians. He opened roads
from Mexico to Oaxaca, Tehuantepec, Acapulco, Michoacán,
Colima, Jalisco, and other distant points. In 1550 he was sent to
rule in troubled Peru, where the Spaniards were duplicating the
brilliant exploits of Cortés and his followers.

READINGS

SPAIN DURING THE CONQUEST

Armstrong, E., *The Emperor Charles V.;* Bourne, E. G., *Spain in America,*
Ch. I; Chapman, Charles E., *A History of Spain,* 1–246, especially Chapters X–XXII; Cheyney, E. P., *European Background of American History,*
Ch. V; Hume, M. A. S., *Spain, its Greatness and Decay;* Hume, M. A. S.,
The Spanish People; Lane-Poole, S., *The Moors in Spain;* Lowery, W.,
Spanish Settlements within the present limits of the United States, 1513–
1565, pp. 79–101; Merriman, R. B., *The Rise of the Spanish Empire;* Prescott, W. H., *Ferdinand and Isabella;* Haring, C. H., *Trade and Navigation
between Spain and the Indies in the Time of the Hapsburgs.*

THE WEST INDIES, CENTRAL AMERICA, AND MAGELLAN

Altolaguirre y Davale, D. Angel de, *D. Pedro de Alvarado, Conquistador de Guatemala y Honduras; Vasco Nuñez de Balboa;* Bancroft, H. H., *Central America*, I, 183–247, 321–412, 478–511; Bourne, E. G., *Spain in America*, 20–53; 115–132; Fiske, John, *The Discovery of America*, I, 465–512, II, 184–212; Fortier, A., and Ficklen, J. R., *Mexico and Central America*, 1–102; Guardia, R. F., *History of the Discovery and Conquest of Costa Rica;* Guillemand, F. H. H., *Life of Magellan;* Helps, Arthur, *The Spanish Conquest*, I, 89–142, 193–320; Lowery, Woodbury, *Spanish Settlements within the present Limits of the United States*, 102–122; Richman, I. B., *The Spanish Conquerors*, 64–91, 139–154; Wright, I. A., *The early History of Cuba, 1492–1586.*

CORTES AND HIS FOLLOWERS

Bancroft, H. H., *Central America*, I, 522–643; Diaz del Castillo, Bernal, *True History of the Conquest of New Spain;* Fortier and Ficklen, *Mexico and Central America*, 181–238; Helps, Arthur, *Life of Cortés; Life of Las Casas; The Spanish Conquest*, III, 23–67, 164–289; McNutt, F. A., *Cortés and the Conquest of Mexico*, 43–67; *The Letters of Cortés to Charles V;* Prescott, W. H., *The Conquest of Mexico*, Bks. II–IV; Bolton, H. E., *The Spanish Borderlands;* Means, P. A., *History of the Spanish Conquest of Yucatán and of the Itzas.*

EXPLORATIONS TO THE NORTH AND IN THE PACIFIC

Bancroft, H. H., *History of California*, I, 64–81; Bandelier, A. D. F., *The Gilded Man; Journey of Cabeza de Vaca (Trail Makers' Series);* Blair and Robertson, *The Philippine Islands*, I–II; Bolton, H. E., *Spanish Exploration in the Southwest, 1542–1706 (Original Narratives Series)*, 1–39; Bourne, E. G., *Spain in America*, 158–174; *Narratives of the Career of Hernando de Soto (Trail Makers' Series);* Brittain, Alfred, *Discovery and Exploration*, 343–361; Hodge, F. W., and Lewis, T. H., *The Spanish Explorers in the Southern United States, 1528–1543 (Original Narratives Series);* Irving, Theodore, *The Conquest of Florida;* Lowery, Woodbury, *Spanish Settlements within the present Limits of the United States*, 130–350; Richman, I. B., *California under Spain and Mexico*, 3–11; Schafer, Joseph, *Pacific Coast and Alaska*, 3–23; Winship, G. P., *The Coronado Expedition* (Bureau of American Ethnology, *14th Report*, Part I.); *The Journey of Coronado (Trail Makers' Series);* Richman, I. B., *The Spanish Conquerors*, 91–139.

CHAPTER III

THE EXPANSION OF NEW SPAIN (1543-1609)

OLD AND NEW SPAIN UNDER PHILIP II

Philip's inheritance.—Charles V's stormy reign came to a close in 1556, when he abdicated in favor of his son, Philip II, who inherited Spain with its colonies, Naples, Milan, Franche Comté, and the Netherlands. The imperial office and the Hapsburg possessions went to Charles's brother, Ferdinand I.

The Protestant movement.—The Protestant movement, which began in Germany and Switzerland, spread into France, England, Scotland, the Netherlands, and the Scandinavian countries. The Catholic church saw itself in danger of losing the religious supremacy in Europe, and put forth all its power to check it. Its three great agencies in the Counter-Reformation were the Council of Trent, the Jesuits, and Philip II.

The Revolt of the Netherlands.—The Spanish king devoted all his resources to stamping out Protestantism in the Netherlands, France, and England. To the wealthy Dutch burghers Philip was a foreigner; they resented the quartering of his soldiers and they objected to his regent, the duchess of Parma, the king's half sister. The Inquisition had been introduced into the Netherlands by Charles V, and it became more active under his son. In 1566 the Dutch nobles headed a revolt, which was furthered by the Protestant preachers. The Duke of Alva was sent with an army to suppress it. William of Orange and other leaders fled the country, as did many Flemish weavers. Alva established a special court which became known as the Council of Blood; a reign of terror followed, thousands being executed. William of Orange, known as the Silent, in 1568 collected a small army and began the struggle for independence. After many years of warfare the Protestant provinces in the north gained their autonomy.

The Defeat of the Armada.—In France the Protestant leader, Coligny, attempted to unite both Catholics and Protestants in a national war against Spain. This was frustrated by the Guises. Later, when they intrigued to place Mary Queen of Scots upon the English throne, Philip entered into their designs, but was prevented from giving much assistance by the revolt in the Netherlands. The English retaliated by raiding the Spanish Main. The culmination of the struggle was the defeat of the Spanish Armada, in 1588, which freed England from the danger of invasion. In Spain Philip carried out his policy of expelling the rest of the Moors, the most industrious and enlightened of his subjects, and by rigorously pushing the work of the Inquisition.

Spanish weakness.—The reign of Philip II had witnessed a vast change in Europe. England had become a Protestant country. In France the wars of religion had culminated by Henry IV ascending the throne. In the Netherlands the northern half had risen into an independent state. Portugal had become a Spanish province. In Spain the expulsion of the Moors, the constant drain upon the country to carry on Philip's foreign enterprises, and the commercial losses inflicted by the English, had weakened the country to such an extent that it could no longer be looked upon as preëminent in Europe. Nevertheless, the Spanish colonies continued to develop and expand. The story of that expansion is the subject of this chapter.

Luís de Velasco, second viceroy (1551-1564).—Viceroy Mendoza was succeeded by Luís de Velasco, a member of a noble Castilian family, who took possession in Mexico in 1551 and ruled till 1564. Velasco installed his rule by releasing 160,000 natives from forced labor in the mines. To put down disorder and protect the natives in 1552 he established in Mexico the Tribunal de la Santa Hermandad. A year later the royal University of Mexico was founded, the first in North America. During Velasco's rule the great canal of Huehuetoca for draining the City of Mexico was begun, 6000 Indians being employed in the work. Velasco was an expansionist, and vigorously promoted the colonization of Florida, the Philippines, and Nueva Vizcaya.

Martin Cortés, second Marquis of the Valley.—At the same time with Velasco came Martin Cortés, son of the conqueror, and second Marquis of the Valley of Oaxaca. He possessed city property in Mexico, Oaxaca, Toluca, and Cuernavaca, and his estates were the richest in New Spain. Other encomenderos looked to him as their protector against the royal officials and induced him to conspire for an independent crown. He yielded, but with six others was arrested in 1568. Two of the conspirators were executed, Cortés and the rest being sent to Spain.

Expansion of the frontiers.—Having exploded for the time being some of the notions of great wonders in the far distant interior, the Spanish pioneers fell back on the established frontiers, and by a more gradual and rational process extended them northward, much as the English a century later slowly pushed their settlements from the Atlantic shoreline across the Tidewater and up into the Piedmont.

On the Atlantic seaboard Spanish outposts were advanced from the West Indies into what are now Florida, Georgia, South Carolina, and, momentarily, into Virginia. In Mexico, missions, mines, farms, and stock ranches advanced northward in regular succession or side by side. Between the return of Coronado and the end of the century the frontiers of actual occupation moved forward, roughly speaking, from Guadalajara, Querétaro, and Pánuco, to a line drawn irregularly through the mouth of the Rio Grande westward to the Pacific, with many large spaces, of course, left vacant to be filled in by subsequent advances. The Spanish pioneers, like those of England and France, recorded their home attachments by the place names given their new abodes, and thus the whole northern district of Mexico was comprised within the three provinces of New Galicia, New Vizcaya, and New León. During the same period the Philippine Islands had been occupied as an outpost of Mexico.

The Adelantados.—The latter sixteenth century was still within the age of the *adelantados*, when the development of the Spanish frontiers was left largely to men of means, obligated to bear most of the expense of conquering and peopling the wilderness, in return for wide powers, extravagant titles, and extensive economic privileges. As types of these proprietary conquerors of the period there stand out Ibarra in Nueva Vizcaya, Menéndez in Florida, Legazpi in the Philippines, Carabajal in Nuevo León, and Oñate in New Mexico. The period likewise was still within the age of the *encomienda*, when the right to parcel out the natives was inherent in the privilege of conquest. With the turn of the century the custom practically ceased, a fact which sharply distinguishes Florida and New Mexico from the later frontier Spanish provinces of Texas, California, and Louisiana.

A new spirit.—The age of wanton bloodshed, too, had largely passed. The New Laws, promulgated in 1543, stood for a new spirit, and royal authority had by now become somewhat established on the frontiers. In proportion as the *encomenderos* were discredited for their abuses and as their power over the Indians was checked, a larger and larger place was found on the frontier for the missionaries, to whom passed much of the actual work of subduing and controlling the natives.

THE MINES OF NORTHERN MEXICO

Audiencia and diocese of Nueva Galicia.—In 1544 Compostela became the seat of the new diocese of Nueva Galicia. Four years later the new Audiencia of Nueva Galicia was established there. About 1550 Guadalajara became the seat of both jurisdictions, and the judicial and ecclesiastical capital of all the country to the north and northeast, a position which it long occupied. The Audiencia district was subdivided into *corregimientos*, each under an alcalde, subject to the Audiencia. Within the *corregimientos* were Indian *partidos*, each under a native alcalde, subject to the encomenderos or the missionaries.

The Zacatecas mines.—In spite of the check caused by the Mixton War, northward expansion in Mexico was soon stimulated by the discovery of rich mines, and by the ambitions of the new viceroy. Mines developed in southern Nueva Galicia were soon eclipsed by those of Zacatecas, which were opened in 1548 by Juan de Tolosa, Cristóbal de Oñate, Diego de Ibarra, and Baltasar Treviño. These men soon became the richest in America, and Zacatecas the first mining town in New Spain. The fame of the "diggins" spread, and other parts of the country were for a time nearly depopulated by the rush of miners.

Francisco de Ibarra.—Inspired by the "boom" at Zacatecas, the Audiencia of Nueva Galicia planned to subdue the districts of Sinaloa and Durango. Ginés Vázquez de Mercado, sent for this purpose in 1552, wasted his energies in a fruitless search for a fabled mountain of pure silver, and was defeated by the Indians near Sombrerete. Martin Pérez, sent by the Audiencia to the same district in 1558, came into conflict with Francisco de Ibarra, agent of the viceroy. In 1554 Ibarra began a series of explorations by means of which, in the course of eight years, he and his men opened in northern Zacatecas the mines of San Martín, San Lucas, Sombrerete, Chalchuites, Aviño, Fresnillo, and other places. To make these expeditions, he equipped himself at his own or his uncle's expense with soldiers, horses, Negro slaves, Indian servants, and droves of stock for food. He attracted miners and settlers by furnishing them with outfits and by giving them free use of mineral deposits.

Nueva Vizcaya founded.—In 1558 Velasco planned to send Ibarra northward to pacify a region called Copala, but his departure was delayed by the sending of the De Luna expedition to Florida. In 1562 Ibarra was made governor and captain-general of a new province called Nueva Vizcaya, comprising the unconquered districts beyond Nueva Galicia, to which Zacatecas remained attached. In the following year he founded Nombre de Diós and Durango, the latter of which became and long remained the military capital of all the northern country. In the same year Rodrigo del Río de Losa was sent with soldiers and miners to open the mines of Indé, and of Santa Bárbara and San Juan in southern Chihuahua. The shortage of Indian labor in the mines there resulted by 1580 in slave hunting raids down the Conchos River and across the Rio Grande into modern Texas.

Ibarra on the Pacific slope.—Amid extreme hardships in 1564 Ibarra crossed the mountains to the westward, and conquered Topia, which he had hoped would prove to be "another Mexico." Disappointed in this, he spent two or three years in developing Sinaloa. Beyond Culiacán, on the Río Fuerte (then called Río Sinaloa) he founded the Villa of San Juan. From here with new recruits from Mexico and Guadalajara, in June, 1567, he set out northward. Ascending the Yaqui valley, at Zaguaripa he defeated the very Indians who had destroyed Coronado's town of San Gerónimo. Crossing the sierra eastward, he emerged on the plains at the river and ruined pueblo of Paquimé (Casas Grandes) in northern Chihuahua. Turning back along the eastern slope of the Sierras, he recrossed them, with terrible hardship, into the lower Yaqui valley. Returning to Chiametla, he died about

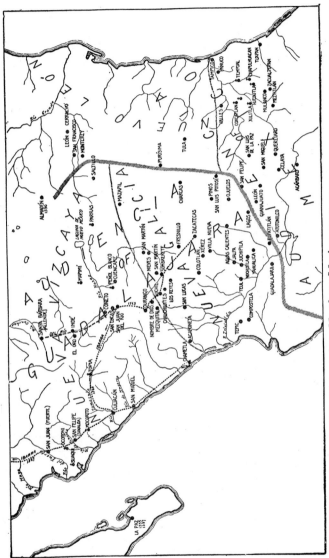

The Advance into Northern Mexico, 1543-1590

1570, after twenty years of exploring, mining, colonizing, and administration. He was one of the ablest of the second generation of colonizers in New Spain.

Development of Nueva Vizcaya.—Shortly after Ibarra left Sinaloa the Indians of San Juan revolted, drove out the encomenderos, and murdered the friars; the settlement was therefore moved to the Petatlán (Sinaloa) River, and named San Felipe. In the last decade of the century a presidio and an Aztec-Tlascaltec colony were founded at San Felipe, and Jesuit missions were planted in the vicinity. East of the mountains, in Durango and southern Chihuahua, mining, stock raising, and agriculture developed side by side. In 1586, for example, Diego de Ibarra branded 33,000 head of cattle, and Rodrigo del Rio, then governor, 42,000 head. Several new mining districts were opened before the end of the century. In 1574 Nueva Galicia and Nueva Vizcaya (including Zacatecas and Sinaloa) had a population of 1500 Spanish families, perhaps 10,000 persons living in some thirty settlements, about half of which were mining camps. Guadalajara had a population of one hundred and fifty families and Culiacán about thirty. The Franciscan missionaries had played an important part in the founding of Nueva Vizcaya. They accompanied or went before the explorers and established themselves at the principal mining camps and towns. In 1590 the custodia of San Francisco de Zacatecas embraced ten monasteries east of the Sierras. In 1591 the Jesuits entered the province.

Querétaro, Guanajuato, and Aguas Calientes.—For twenty years after the battle at Querétaro (1531) the Chichimec border was left practically unsettled, under the control of native leaders. But the need of communication with the Zacatecas veins made its complete subjugation necessary, and Viceroy Velasco undertook the task. In or about 1550 the town of Querétaro was founded, and Silao three years later. The marvelous Guanajuato mines were now opened; in 1554 the city of Santa Fé de Guanajuato was founded; and shortly afterward rich veins were opened at Aguas Calientes. These "strikes" caused "rushes," just as those in Zacatecas had done, but they were offset by others in Durango, where Ibarra was operating. To secure further the roads to the mines, new towns and presidios were established along the way, and thus San Miguel el Grande (Allende), San Felipe, Santa María de Lagos, Aguas Calientes, Ojuelos, Portezuelos, Jérez, and Celaya came into being. To supplement the presidios, strong houses (*casas fuertes*) were provided as camping stations for travelers and silver trains, and parties were equipped with fortified wagons or movable strong houses.

San Luis Potosí and Southern Coahuila.—For some time the region of Charcas, now called San Luis Potosí, was a sort of No-man's-land between the westward, eastward, and northward moving columns of frontiersmen. It was the home of the powerful but savage Guachichiles. The definite conquest of the region, already known to explorers and missionaries, was begun about 1550 by Francisco de Urdiñola, who operated under Velasco's orders, and who is said to have reached the vicinity of Saltillo and Monterey. The settlement of the district soon followed. Matehuala was founded in 1550, San Gerónimo in 1552, Charcas in 1564, and the San Pedro mines about 1568. By 1576 San Luis Potosí, the site of rich ores, had become a villa, and before long was the seat of an *alcaldía mayor*.

Mining developments spread northeastward from Zacatecas to Mazapil and Saltillo. By 1568 Mazapil was the seat of an *alcaldía mayor*, under the Audiencia of Nueva Galicia. In that year Francisco del Cano, sent by the "very magificent alcalde mayor," went north and discovered the "Lake of New Mexico," perhaps Laguna de Parras. In 1575 Francisco de Urdiñola, son of the former conqueror, is said to have settled sixty families at Saltillo, within the jurisdiction of Nueva Vizcaya. As early as 1582 a Franciscan monastery was established there, and in 1592 Saltillo was created a villa.

The Tlascaltecan colonies.—Querétaro had been the scene of one interesting experiment in utilizing the natives as agents of control; in San Luis Potosí another was now tried. As a means of reducing the great central region, the plan was devised of planting in it colonies of Tlascaltecan Indians, to defend the settlers and to teach the rude tribes the elements of civilization. The Tlascaltecans had proved their loyalty in the days of Cortés, and this loyalty was insured by their exemption from tribute and by other privileges. The practice of using them as colonists in San Luis Potosí seems to have been begun as early as 1580.

In 1591 four hundred families were sent northward, most of them being distributed at various places in modern San Luis Potosí, but eighty families were established at Saltillo in a separate pueblo called San Estéban. Thence in later days little colonies were detached to all parts of Coahuila, Nuevo León, and Texas.

Parras; Urdiñola the Younger.—In 1594 Jesuits from Durango founded the mission of Santa Maria de Parras, and shortly afterward a colony of Spaniards and Tlascaltecans was established there. Of this district Urdiñola the Younger, lieutenant-governor of Nueva Vizcaya, became the magnate. He opened mines, subdued Indians, established immense ranches, and was veritable feudal lord. His principal hacienda was at Patos, but he had others, as at Parras and Bonanza. In 1594 he secured a commission to conquer New Mexico which was subsequently rescinded. A female descendant of his became the wife of the first Marquis of San Miguel de Aguayo, a title created in 1682 and long held by the leading men of the northeastern frontier.

Nuevo León.—A new jurisdiction was now carved out on the Gulf coast. In 1579 Luis de Carabajal, a Portuguese of Jewish extraction, secured a patent naming him governor and captain-general of the Kingdom of Nuevo León, a region extending two hundred leagues north and west from Pánuco, and delimiting Nueva Vizcaya and Nueva Galicia on the north and east. Carabajal's was the first conquistador's patent issued for New Spain based on the general ordinance of 1573 regulating new conquests. He was made governor and alguacil-mayor "for two lives," with a salary of 20,000 pesos and two encomiendas for himself. He had authority to grant encomiendas, and was obligated to make new conquests and settlements. Raising two hundred men in Spain and Mexico, he established headquarters for a time at Pánuco, whence he made exploring, gold hunting, and slave hunting expeditions.

León and Monterey.—Discovering minerals in the Sierra de San Gregorio, near the Rio Grande, in (or by) 1583, Carabajal founded there the city of León (now Cerralvo). Securing other families from Saltillo, in 1584 he founded San Luís, near the later Monterey, and appointed Castaño de Sosa alcalde mayor. Slave hunting expeditions from León proved so profitable that soon two hundred or more adventurers were attracted to the place, for the slaves found ready market at the mines of the interior. When the viceroy checked the abuse, León was gradually abandoned. With another colony from Saltillo, Carabajal founded Nuevo Almadén, near the present Monclova. While thus engaged he was charged with heresy, arrested, and condemned by the Inquisition together with almost his entire family. In 1596 Luis de Montemayor, lieutenant-governor of the province, founded Monterey with families from León and Saltillo. Three years later Montemayor was made governor, directly under the viceroy. In 1603 a Franciscan monastery was founded at Monterey, and became a new missionary center. Conflicts of jurisdiction between Nuevo León and Nueva Vizcaya became chronic and a serious hindrance to prosperity.

THE SETTLEMENT OF THE ATLANTIC SEABOARD

Fray Luís Cancer.—Meanwhile Florida and the Philippines had been conquered and colonized. Shortly after Coronado returned from New Mexico, the Moscoso party reached Pánuco. Viceroy Mendoza, in spite of previous failures, was willing to try his hand in ill-fated Florida, and he offered to equip Moscoso and his men for another attempt, but they declined. Florida had been "running with the blood of Indians," but Fray Luís Cancer, a disciple of Las Casas, offered to try to subdue it by peaceful methods. With a royal license he equipped a vessel at Vera Cruz, and with a few companions went in 1549 to Florida to convert the natives. He was murdered by them, however, and his companions returned.

De Luna and Villafañe.—But Florida was thought to be rich, especially at Coça, in northern Alabama, and new attempts at settlement were made. In 1558 the new viceroy was ordered to colonize Santa Elena, the scene of Ayllón's failure on the Carolina coast, and some other point not specified, the missionary work to be entrusted to the Dominicans. In the following year, therefore, Velasco sent Tristán de Luna, Coronado's second in command, from Vera Cruz with thirteen vessels and 1500 soldiers and colonists. Of the six captains three had been with De Soto, a fact which indicates the continuity of frontier interests.

The expedition landed at Pensacola Bay. Three vessels sent

on to Santa Elena were storm-driven and returned to Vera Cruz. Establishing a garrison at Pensacola (Ichuse), De Luna moved about a thousand colonists inland to Nanipacna on the Alabama River, whence an expedition was sent north to Coça. In 1560 the colony returned to Pensacola, where De Luna was replaced by Villafañe, who had been sent with supplies from Mexico. In the following year Villafañe went with most of his colony to Santa Elena, but failed to make a settlement, and the Pensacola garrison was soon withdrawn. In view of these repeated disasters, in 1561 Philip II declared that for the present no further attempt should be made to colonize Florida.

The French in Florida.—Notwithstanding this decision, there were reasons why Florida should be occupied. The route of the treasure and merchant ships lay through the Bahama channel, and French and English pirates had begun to attack them. To lessen the danger, vessels were ordered to go in company, and as early as 1552 a fleet of war vessels was sent to escort them to Havana. But a port was needed to give aid against the pirates, as well as to provide refuge from the violent storms on the Florida coast. Moreover, the French were operating on the northern Atlantic, and it was feared that they would occupy this region.

This fear was realized in 1562 when Jean Ribaut led a French Huguenot colony to Port Royal, South Carolina. The colony miserably failed, but in 1564 another, led by Laudonnière, settled on St. John's River and built Fort Caroline. Just as Laudonnière was about to abandon the place, Ribaut arrived with a third colony, bearing instructions to fortify a position that would enable him to command the route of the Spanish treasure fleets.

Menéndez de Avilés, and the expulsion of the French.—Philip decided now to eject the French and colonize Florida, and entrusted the task to Menéndez de Avilés, a great naval officer. He was made adelantado of Florida, and promised a private estate twenty-five leagues square, or some 300,000 acres. In return he agreed to take a colony of five hundred persons to Florida, build at least two fortified towns, and expel foreign "settlers and corsairs." In September, 1565, Menéndez reached Florida and founded St. Augustine. Ten days later he marched overland against Fort Caroline, surprised and captured it, and mercilessly

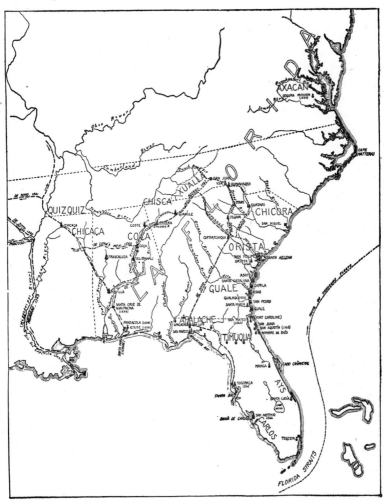

Spanish Florida

slew most of its defenders. On the spot the garrison of San Mateo was established.

Menéndez's relentless deed caused an outburst of indignation in France, and perhaps only Catherine's reliance on Philip in her troubles with the Huguenots prevented war. Vengeance was left to a private individual, Dominique de Gourgues. Getting up an expedition ostensibly to trade, in 1567 he went to Florida, and slew the garrison at San Mateo. The prisoners taken were hanged "not as Spaniards" but "as traitors, robbers, and murderers."

New settlements in Florida.—Menéndez planned great things. He would fortify the Bahama Channel, occupy Santa Elena and Chesapeake Bay, and in the latter seek the northern strait. As a base for expanding toward Pánuco, he would occupy the Bay of Juan Ponce, and he had great hopes of agricultural prosperity.

To carry out these plans, active steps were taken. Before Menéndez returned to Spain in 1567, several new Spanish posts were founded between the point of the peninsula and South Carolina. San Mateo was reoccupied. At Charlotte Bay Menéndez made an alliance with the much-feared Chief Carlos by marrying his sister, and founded there the presidio of San Antonio. Other garrisons were established on the peninsula at Ays, Santa Lucía, Tocobaga, and Tegesta. At Santa Elena, in South Carolina, Menéndez founded the colony of San Felipe, and in Guale (northern Georgia) he founded a presidio.

Explorations in the Alleghanies.—In November, 1566, Menéndez sent Juan Pardo from Santa Elena "to discover and conquer the interior country from there to Mexico," to join the two frontiers. Going northwest, he reached the snow covered Alleghanies in western North Carolina, established two garrisons on the way, and returned. Boyano, left at one of the garrisons, made expeditions into the mountains, and in 1567 marched southwest to Chiaha near Rome, Georgia. Being joined there by Pardo, they set out "in the direction of Zacatecas and the mines of San Martin," in Mexico, but were turned back by Indian hostility. On his way to San Felipe Pardo left two garrisons, which were soon massacred by Indians.

The Jesuit missions in Florida.—In 1566 Menéndez secured three Jesuit missionaries for Florida. Another band arrived in 1568, and went to Santa Elena, Orista, and Guale, where they founded missions. At first they were successful, but in 1570 they were driven out by native opposition. By this time the garrison at Tocobaga had been massacred and those at San Antonio and Tegesta withdrawn on account of Indian hostility.

The Virginia mission.—Father Segura, the Jesuit superior, now transferred his efforts to Chesapeake Bay, whither he went in 1570 with six missionaries. They founded a mission, perhaps on the Rappahannock, but soon all were slain. In 1571 Menéndez went in person to avenge the outrage. Two years later his nephew explored the entire coast from the Florida Keys to Chesapeake Bay. In 1573, the year before his death, Menéndez's grant was extended west to Pánuco.

Franciscans on the Georgia coast.—The martyrdom of Father Segura and his band caused the Jesuits to abandon the field for Mexico, but in 1573 Franciscans began work in the province. Twenty years later (1593) twelve more arrived under Father Juan de Silva. From the central monastery at St. Augustine they set forth and founded island missions all up the Florida and Georgia coast, on Amelia, Cumberland, St. Simon, San Pedro and Ossabua islands. Fray Pedro Chozas made inland explorations, and Father Pareja began his famous work on the Indian languages. Owing to an Indian uprising in 1597 the missions were abandoned for a time, but were soon restored as a check against the English, who now entered Virginia.

FOREIGN INTRUSIONS IN THE ATLANTIC

The Spanish trade monopoly.—The French had been expelled from Florida, and the coast occupied up to Port Royal Sound, but freebooters continued to prey on treasure and merchant vessels. Spain undertook to preserve the trade and wealth of the Indies as an absolute monopoly. All trade must be conducted by Spaniards in Spanish vessels, from specified Spanish ports to specified American ports. This monopoly was objectionable not only to the traders of other nations but to the Spanish colonists as well. To this economic grievance was added the bitter hatred felt by Protestant Frenchmen, Englishmen and Dutchmen for Catholic Spain, whose subjects were regarded as lawful prey.

The merchant fleets.—To prevent the plundering of commerce in the Indies, by French, English, and Dutch, Spain was forced to adopt a system of fleets sailing periodically and protected by convoys of armed galleons. After 1561 it became unlawful for vessels to sail alone to the Indies, except under special circumstances. Two fleets left Spain each year, one for Tierra Firme and Nombre de Diós (later Porto Bello) and the other for Vera Cruz. In the later sixteenth century the Nombre de Diós fleet comprised as many as forty armed galleons, but thereafter the number was much smaller, as foreigners cut into Spanish trade. The Vera Cruz fleet comprised fifteen or twenty merchantmen convoyed by two galleons. At Nombre de Diós goods and treasure from Peru and Chile were taken on. At Vera Cruz were gathered the exports from New Spain, the cargo from the Manila galleon brought overland from Acapulco, and the ten or twelve million dollars of royal revenues from the mines and taxes.

The freebooters.—This arrangement was an improvement, but French, Dutch, and English freebooters hung in the wake of the fleets to plunder any vessel which fell behind the galleons, while smuggling and town-sacking grew in frequency with the growing jealousy and hatred of Spain. The prototype of the English freebooters was John Hawkins, whose fleet was destroyed by the Spaniards at Vera Cruz in 1567. More famous was Francis Drake, who in 1585, during his third marauding expedition, went to the West Indies with twenty-five vessels, captured Santo Domingo, held Cartagena for ransom, and in May, 1586, sacked and burned St. Augustine, Florida. Hawkins and Drake were only two of a score of English freebooters who in the later sixteenth century harried Spanish commerce and plundered the coast towns. In the list are the names of Oxenham, Raleigh, Grenville, Clifford, Knollys, Winter, and Barker. The last exploit of the century was Clifford's capture of San Juan, Porto Rico, in 1598.

The English in the north Atlantic.—The voyages of Frobisher, Davis, and Gilbert in the northern Atlantic between 1576 and 1587, in search of the northwest passage, caused uneasiness for the security of Florida and of the northern strait. Equally disturbing were the efforts of Raleigh and his associates to colonize Roanoke Island and Guiana.

Decline of the West Indies.— The raids of the freebooters, the restrictions placed on commerce, the decline of mining and of the native population, and the superior attractions of Peru, Central America, and Mexico, had greatly reduced the prosperity of the West Indies. In 1574 Española had ten towns with 1000 Spanish families, and 12,000 negro slaves. The native population had dwindled to two villages. Santo Domingo, seat of the Audiencia and of the archdiocese, had seven hundred families. Cuba was less prosperous than Española, and population was still declining. The island had eight Spanish towns with a total population of some three hundred families and about an equal number of Indians. Santiago, once with a population of one thousand families, now had thirty. Havana, somewhat larger, was the residence of governor and bishop. Jamaica had three Spanish settlements and no Indians. Porto Rico, with three Spanish towns, had a population of some two hundred and eighty families, of whom two hundred lived at San Juan. The principal industries in all of the islands were sugar and cattle raising. There being no Indians in the West Indies now, there were no encomiendas.

THE PHILIPPINES AND CALIFORNIA

A new attempt in the East.—At the same time that Menéndez was establishing the province of Florida, the right wing of the Indies, Legazpi was conquering the Philippines, the left wing. The principal result of the Villalobos expedition (1542) had been to give the name of the Philippines to the Lazarus, or Western Islands. For nearly two decades thereafter nothing was done to advance the interests of Spain in the Far East, but Portuguese profits in the spice trade were tempting to both sovereign and subject, and the king set about making a new effort to share in these advantages.

The obvious base for such a trade was Mexico, and in 1559 Philip ordered Velasco to equip two vessels for discovery in the western islands, to test the chance for profits and the possibility of a return voyage across the Pacific. This order was issued just at the time when Spain was attempting to occupy the Carolina coasts, with a view, in part, to finding a northern strait leading to the Spice Islands. Thus were all these widely separated enterprises unified.

The Legazpi expedition.—To lead the expedition, Miguel López de Legazpi was chosen, with Fray Andrés de Urdaneta as chief navigator. The spiritual work was entrusted to Urdaneta and a band of Augustinians. Owing to many delays it was November, 1564, when the fleet left Navidad. In February, 1565, seven months before Menéndez reached Florida, Legazpi reached the Philippines. Three of the vessels were sent back with Urdaneta on board to discover a return route to New Spain. Instead of sailing east against wind and current, he turned northward beyond the trade belt, and entered that of the westerly winds. After a long and hard voyage he reached the American continent off the northern California coast, which he descended to Mexico. At last the Spaniards had discovered a way to return from the East safe from the Portuguese attacks.

Meanwhile Legazpi had occupied Cebú. Portuguese resistance caused a removal to Panay, but in 1571 Cebú was reoccupied and Manila founded. In the previous year Legazpi had received a commission as adelantado of the Islands, subject to the viceroy of Mexico. When Legazpi died in 1572 the conquest of the principal islands had been effected and with little bloodshed. In 1583 the Audiencia of Manila was established, subordinate to Mexico.

The Manila galleon.—In 1580 Portugal was united with Spain, and, until 1640, when Portugal regained her independence, Manila was an important center for the commerce of the combined Spanish and Portuguese colonies. A regular trade was established from Manila to Mexico and Spain, but was restricted to one or two annual galleons each way between Manila and Acapulco.

New interest in the California coast.—The development of the Philippine trade, the necessity of protecting it from other nations, continued interest in the Northern Mystery, and the opening of pearl fisheries in the Gulf of California, led to renewed exploration of the northern Pacific coasts and to renewed attempts to settle and develop California.

The regular course of the east-bound Manila galleon lay along the path marked out by Urdaneta northeastward from Manila to about latitude 42,° thence across the Pacific to the American

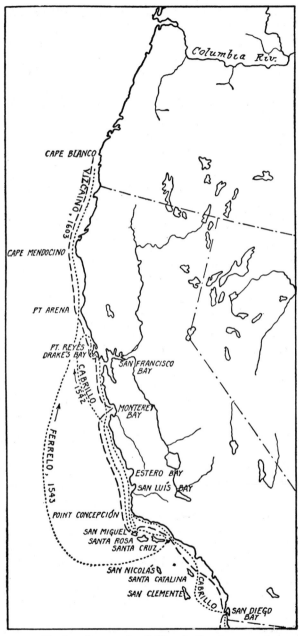

Explorations on the California Coast, 1542–1603

continent off Cape Mendocino, and down the coast to Acapulco. The voyage was arduous. By the time the vessels reached the American coast half of the scurvy-afflicted crew and passengers were dead, and the vessels needed repairs. Hence a port of call was gravely needed for the Manila galleons.

The Strait of Anian.—Moreover, Spanish interests in the Pacific were insecure. The Portuguese were no longer rivals, but French and English freebooters were active on the Atlantic and might venture upon the Pacific. Besides, there was the fear that the French, English, or Dutch, operating in the northern Atlantic, would discover the Strait of Anian and secure control of the direct route to the Spice Islands, just as Portugal had monopolized the African route.

Drake and Cavendish.—These fears were made realities in 1579 when Drake appeared on the California coast. In 1577 he had passed through the Straits of Magellan. Reaching the Pacific with only one vessel of the five with which he had started, he proceeded up the coast of South America, plundering as he went. In the harbour now known as Drake's Bay, just north of San Francisco, he refitted, claiming the country for England, and calling it New Albion. Drake then sailed to the East Indies, obtained a cargo of spices, crossed the Indian Ocean, rounded the Cape of Good Hope, and reached Plymouth in November, 1580. He claimed to have discovered the Strait of Anian, and this further disturbed the minds of the Spaniards. For his daring voyage he was knighted by Queen Elizabeth.

In 1586 Thomas Cavendish followed Drake's course. Reaching the point of California, he plundered the Manila galleon, the *Santa Ana*, and burned it to the water's edge. The voyages of Drake and Cavendish were soon followed by the formation of the British East India Company (1600) and by conflicts with the Spanish merchants in the Orient. In the wake of the English came the Dutch, who had passed the Straits of Magellan before the end of the sixteenth century.

Gali and Cermeño.—With the needs of the Pacific coast in view, Viceroy Moya Contreras (1584–1585) instructed Francisco de Gali to explore the northwestern coasts of America on his return from Manila in the galleon. Nothing came of Gali's orders, and Moya's successor discouraged further exploration. The second Viceroy Velasco (1590-1595), however, took up Moya's plan, and in 1595 Sebastián Rodríguez Cermeño undertook to carry out the project on his return from Manila. He was wrecked at Drake's Bay, however, and his crew made their way to Mexico in an improvised craft. The plan of reconnoitering the coast with laden Manila galleons was now given up for one of exploring in light vessels sent out from the ports of Mexico.

Vizcaíno's colony.—Royal interest in the protection of California was now combined with private interest in the pearl fisheries of the Gulf of California. Occasional expeditions had been made for this purpose since the days of Cortés and Alarcón. In 1595 Sebastián Vizcaíno, who had been engaged in the Manila trade, and, indeed, had been on the *Santa Ana* when it was captured by Cavendish, secured a contract authorizing him to gather pearls, in return for subduing and colonizing California. Leaving Acapulco late in 1596 with three vessels and a good-sized company, he established a colony at La Paz and explored some distance up the Gulf. But disaster soon followed, and early in 1597 the survivors returned to Mexico.

Vizcaíno's exploring expedition.—Vizcaíno attributed his failure to ignorance of the seasons, and proposed making another attempt at settlement and pearl fishing. While this question was being discussed, the king in 1599 ordered the outer coast of California explored again, with a view to finding a port for the Manila galleons. To conduct the expedition Vizcaíno was chosen. Leaving Acapulco in May, 1602, with three vessels, he ran all the coasts covered by Cabrillo and Ferrelo sixty years before. At Magdalena Bay, Cerros Island, San Diego Bay, and Santa Catalina Island extensive explorations were made. The capital event of the expedition, however, was the exploration of the Bay of Monterey (probably entered by Cermeño) and its designation as the desired port. One of the vessels reached Cape Blanco, but San Francisco Bay was missed, as before.

Plans to Occupy Monterey Bay.—Plans were now made for occupying the port of Monterey, but delays ensued and a new viceroy concluded that a port in the mid-Pacific was more needed than one on the California coast. Accordingly, in 1611 Vizcaíno was sent to explore certain islands called Rica de Oro and Rica de Plata, but the expedition failed.

THE FOUNDING OF NEW MEXICO

Renewed exploration of New Mexico.—The expansion of Nueva Vizcaya and renewed activities on the Pacific coast in the later sixteenth century stimulated a new advance into New Mexico. Coronado's expedition had proved disappointing, and for four decades no further explorations had been made in the region. Nevertheless, the tales of great cities had not been forgotten, and in the meantime a new line of approach to New Mexico had been opened by way of the central plateau. By 1580 mines and missions had reached Santa Bárbara, while slave hunting expeditions had descended the Conchos to the Rio Grande. Through reports given by the outlying tribes, a new interest in the Pueblo region was aroused.

Rodríguez and Espejo.—To follow up these reports, with a view to missionary work, trade, and exploration, an expedition was organized at Santa Bárbara in 1580 by Fray Augustín Rodríguez, a Franciscan lay brother, and Francisco Sánchez Chamuscado. In the next year the party of three friars and nine soldiers and traders descended the Conchos River, ascended the Rio Grande to the Pueblo region, visited the buffalo plains, Ácoma, and Zuñi, and returned, leaving two friars at Puaray, one having been killed. In the following year a rescue and trading party was led to New Mexico over the same trail by Fray Bernaldino Beltrán and Antonio de Espejo. The friars had already been slain by the natives, but before returning Espejo went to Zuñi, Moqui, and western Arizona, where he discovered mines, returning to Santa Bárbara by way of the Pecos River.

Plans to colonize New Mexico.—The expeditions of Rodríguez and Espejo aroused new zeal for northern exploration and settlement, and there were dreams now, not only of conquering New Mexico, but of going beyond to colonize Quivira and the shores of the Strait of Anian. The king ordered a contract made for the purpose, and soon there was a crowd of applicants for the honor. While these men were competing for the desired contract, Castaño de Sosa in 1590 led a colony from Nuevo León up the Pecos to the Pueblos and began their conquest, but was soon arrested and taken back. Some three years later two men named Leyva and Gutiérrez de Humaña led an unlicensed expedition from Nueva Vizcaya to New Mexico, whence Gutiérrez went to northeastern Kansas, and apparently reached the Platte River.

Oñate and the founding of New Mexico.—The contract to colonize New Mexico was finally assigned in 1595 to Juan de Oñate, son of Cristóbal, one of the founders of Zacatecas. In accordance with the ordinances of 1573 he was made governor, adelantado, and captain-general, granted extensive privileges, lands, and encomiendas, while his colonists were given the usual privileges of first settlers (*primeros pobladores*). It was February, 1598, when Oñate left northern Nueva Vizcaya with his colony. It included one hundred and thirty soldiers, some with their families, a band of Franciscans under Father Martinez, and more than seven thousand head of stock. Previous expeditions had followed the Conchos, but Oñate opened a more direct route through El Paso. Without difficulty he secured the submission of the tribes, settled his colony at San Juan, and distributed the friars among the pueblos.

Oñate's explorations.—Having established his colony, Oñate turned to exploration in the east and the west. In the fall of 1598 Vicente Zaldívar was sent to the Buffalo Plains, while the governor set out for the South Sea. At Moqui he turned back, but Marcos Farfán continued west with a party, and staked out mining claims on Bill Williams Fork. Ácoma rebelled at this time and as a punishment was razed. In 1599 Zaldívar was sent to the South Sea and seems to have reached the lower Colorado. Early in 1601 Oñate, with seventy men, descended the Canadian River and crossed the Arkansas to an Indian settlement called Quivira, apparently at Wichita, Kansas. During Oñate's absence most of the colonists deserted, but they were brought back, with reinforcements. Still bent on reaching the South Sea, in 1604 Oñate descended Bill Williams Fork and the Colorado to the Gulf of California, where he got the idea that California was an island. He had reëxplored most of the ground covered by Coronado and had opened new trails. But he had lost the confidence and support of the authorities, and in 1608 resigned and was displaced by a royal governor.

Santa Fé Founded.—In 1609 Santa Fé was founded and became the new capital. This event, which occurred just a hun-

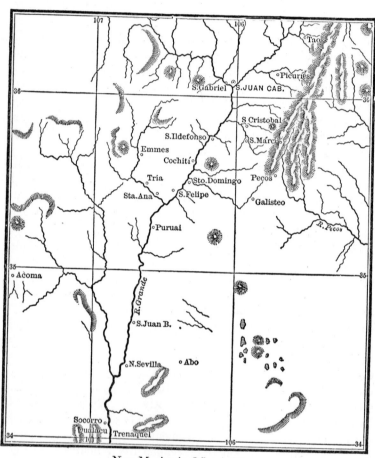

New Mexico in Oñate's Time
(From Bancroft, *Arizona and New Mexico*, p. 137)

dred years after the occupation of Darién, may be regarded as
the culmination of a century of northward expansion.

SPANISH ACHIEVEMENTS IN THE SIXTEENTH CENTURY

Population and industries.—The heroic age of Spanish colonization had now passed. The surprising results achieved in the
New World during the first eighty years, not counting the work
of exploration, are set forth in a description of the colonies in
1574 written by López de Velasco, official geographer. At that
time there were in North and South America about two hundred
Spanish towns and cities, besides numerous mining camps,
haciendas, and stock ranches. The Spanish population was
32,000 families, or perhaps from 160,000 to 200,000 persons. Of
these about five-eighths lived in North America. In the two
Americas there were 4000 encomenderos, the rest being mainly
miners, merchants, ranchers, and soldiers, with their families.
The population included 40,000 negro slaves, and a large element of mulattoes and mestizoes. About 1,500,000 male Indians
paid tribute, representing a population of 5,000,000. In many
parts occupied by Spaniards there were no encomiendas, for the
Indians had died out. Mining, commerce, cattle ranching, grain
and sugar raising had been established on a considerable scale.

Cities and towns.—Before the end of the sixteenth century most
of the present-day state capitals and other large cities in Spanish
North America had been founded. Mexico City had a population of over 2000 Spanish families (perhaps 15,000 persons),
Santo Domingo, Puebla, and Guatemala 500 families each,
Trinidad (in Guatemala) and Panamá 400 each, Oaxaca 350,
Zacatecas 300, Toluca, Zultepec, Vera Cruz, Granada, Chiapas,
and Nombre de Diós 200 each, Guadalajara and San Salvador 150
each, and many others lesser numbers.

Administrative divisions.—Spanish America was now divided
into two viceroyalties, New Spain and Peru. New Spain included
all of the American mainland north of Panamá, the West Indies,
part of the northern coast of South America, the Islas del Pon-
iente, and the Philippines. It comprised the four audiencias of
Española, Mexico, Guatemala, and Nueva Galicia, the Audiencia
of Panamá being a part of the viceroyalty of Peru. The four

northern audiencia districts were subdivided into seventeen or eighteen gobiernos or provinces, corresponding closely to the modern states. The provinces were divided into *corregimientos* embracing Indian *partidos*. North America embraced twelve dioceses and the two archdioceses of Santo Domingo and Mexico.

Churches and monasteries.—Many fine churches, some of them still standing, had been built in the larger towns. The Franciscans, Dominicans, and Augustinians were well established in New Spain, and the Jesuits had just begun their work. The friars were subject to their chapters and the Jesuits to their general in Spain. The Franciscans already had four provinces in New Spain, the Dominicans and Augustinians only one each. Hundreds of monasteries had been established, especially wherever there were Indians in encomienda. The expense of erecting them was borne jointly by king, encomenderos, and Indians.

The Universities.—"Enthusiasm for education characterizes the earliest establishment of the Spanish colonies in America. Wherever the priests went, a school was soon established for the instruction of the natives or a college for its clericals who were already at work as well as for those who were soon to take holy orders. From the colleges sprang the universities which, in all the Spanish dominions, were founded at a very early date for the pursuit of the 'general studies' which were at that time taught in the great peninsular universities of Alcala and Salamanca. Half a century before Jamestown was founded by the English, the University of Mexico was conferring degrees upon graduates in law and theology. Before the seventeenth century closed, no less that seven universities had been erected in Spanish America, and their graduates were accepted on an equality with those of Spanish institutions of like grade." (Priestley.)

READINGS

THE REIGN OF PHILIP II

Chapman, Charles E., *A History of Spain*, Chapter XXXIII; Gayarré, C. E. A., *Philip II of Spain;* Hume, M. A. S., *Philip II of Spain;* Hume, M. A. S., *Spain, Its Greatness and Decay;* Hume, M. A. S., *The Spanish People;* Lea, H. C., *A History of the Inquisition of Spain;* Merriman, R. B., *The Rise of the Spanish Empire;* Prescott, W. H., *History of the Reign of*

Philip the Second; Cheyney, E. P., *European Background of American History*, Chapter X.

ADVANCE INTO NORTHERN MEXICO

Bancroft, H. H., *History of Mexico*, II, chs. 22, 24, 34; *North Mexican States and Texas*, I, ch. 5; Cavo, Andrés, *Tres Siglos de Mexico;* Coroléu, José, *America, Historia de su Colonización;* Frejes, Fr. F., *Conquista de los Estados;* Gonzáles, J. E., *Collección de Noticias; Historia de Nuevo León;* León, A., *Historia de Nuevo León;* Mota Padilla, M., *Historia de Nueva Galicia*, ch. 23; Ortega, Fr. Joseph, *Apostólica Afanes.*

SETTLEMENT OF FLORIDA

Hamilton, P. J., *The Colonization of the South*, chs. 1-2; Lowery, Woodbury, *Spanish Settlements*, I, ch. 8, II; Shea, J. G., *The Catholic Church in Colonial Days*, pp. 100-183.

SETTLEMENT OF NEW MEXICO

Bancroft, H. H., *Arizona and New Mexico*, 74-146; Bandelier, A. D. F., *Final Report of Investigations among the Indians of the Southwestern United States* (Papers of the Archæological Institute of America, III-IV); Benavides, *Memorial on New Mexico* (Mrs. E. E. Ayer, trans.); Bolton, H. E., ed., *Spanish Exploration in the Southwest*, 135-278; Davis, W. H. H., *Spanish Conquest in New Mexico*, 234-407; Farrand, Livingston, *The Basis of American History*, 176-187; Lummis, C. F., *Spanish Pioneers in the Southwest*, 125-143; Prince, L. B., *Historical Sketches of New Mexico*, 149-166; Twitchell, R. E., *Leading Facts of New Mexican History*, I, 7-45, 252-333; Villagrá, Gaspar de, *Historia de Nuevo Mexico.*

THE PHILIPPINES AND CALIFORNIA

Barrows, D. P., *A History of the Philippines;* Blair and Robertson, *Philippine Islands*, II, 23-330; Bolton, H. E., *Spanish Exploration in the Southwest*, 41-133; Carrasco y Guisasola, Francisco, *Documentos Referentes al Reconocimiento de las Costas de las Californias;* Hittell, T. H., *History of California*, I, 79-111; Richman, I. B., *California under Spain and Mexico*, 12-24; Robertson, J. A., "Legaspi and Philippine Island Colonization," in American Historical Association, *Rpt., 1907*, I, 145-165; Zárate, Salmerón, "Relation," in *Land of Sunshine*, XI, 336-346, XII, 39-48, 104-114, 180-187.

CHAPTER IV

THE ESTABLISHMENT OF THE FRENCH COLONIES

THE FRENCH BACKGROUND

Mediæval France and the Italian wars.—The history of Mediæval France is largely the story of the struggle of the French kings to overthrow the feudal nobility and to perfect the governmental machinery of absolutism. The process which began with the accession of Hugh Capet in 987 was practically completed by the end of the reign of Louis XI, in 1483. During the reigns of Charles VIII, Louis XII, and Francis I, the great ambition of the French monarchs was to get control of Italy, a policy which brought them into conflict with Spain. The wars were barren of results as far as conquests in Italy were concerned, but the dangers to which France was exposed united the French people into a great nation, which was destined to be the leading continental power.

The religious wars.—The Reformation spread into France, Calvinism being the form of Protestantism which there took root. Calvin's religious system had three distinguishing features: (1) the church was to be independent of any temporal power, (2) laymen and ministers were to join in the government of the church, and (3) a strict moral discipline was to be enforced. This program was distinctly democratic, and was certain to come into conflict with the absolutism of the crown. France became divided into two great parties. The Huguenots, as the French Protestants were called, were found mainly among the rich burghers of the towns and the nobles of the country districts, their chief power being in southwestern France. They were also strong in Dauphiné and Normandy. Their great leaders were Coligny and the Bourbon princes, the most distinguished of whom was Henry of Navarre. The Catholic party was headed by the Guises and Catherine de Medici. The kings during this period were mere puppets, who were used by the leaders to further their political ends.

78

War broke out in 1562 and continued with occasional inter-missions until 1596. The most important events were the assassin-ation of Francis of Guise in 1563, the ascendency of Coligny, dur-ing which he tried to unite the nation in a war against Spain, the massacre of St. Bartholomew's in 1572, the organization of the Catholic League headed by Henry of Guise, his assassina-tion in 1588, and the murder of Henry III the following year, which made the way clear for Henry of Navarre to ascend the throne. In 1593 he accepted Catholicism. The last resistance in France was overcome in 1596, but war with Philip II continued two years longer. In 1598 Henry issued the Edict of Nantes, which secured toleration to the Huguenots.

Reforms of Henry IV.—During the religious wars, the nobles had regained some of their former power, and the ravages of war had almost ruined the industries of the country. Henry set to work to repair these conditions. The lesser nobles were forced to submit and the privileges of the more powerful were purchased. The king's great minister, Sully, carried out many of the economic reforms. The land tax called the *taille*, which rested most heavily upon the peasants, was more equitably distributed, and the hunt-ing privileges of the nobles were decreased. New lines of agricul-ture were introduced, marshes were reclaimed, and restrictions on the marketing of grain were removed. The king encouraged manufactures, especially of the more expensive fabrics, glass, and metal work. Commerce was stimulated by securing safe transportation along the post roads, by a system of canals con-necting the Seine and the Loire, and by commercial treaties with foreign states. Attempts were also made to stimulate commerce and colonization by the formation of mercantile companies, and from this period date the first successful French colonies in America.

Richelieu.—Henry IV was assassinated in 1610, and his son, who ascended the throne as Louis XIII, was a child of nine years. During the regency of his mother, Mary de Medici, the nobles again became turbulent, the Huguenots revolted, and the policy of hostility toward Spain was reversed. The regent was under the influence of favorites who looted the treasury. Under such conditions a strong leader was greatly needed; the man of the hour was Richelieu. In 1624 he was placed in control of public affairs, and for the next twenty years practically ruled France. His policy aimed to make France the first power in Europe. To accomplish this he worked at home to strengthen the power of the crown. Abroad he aimed to weaken the power of the Hapsburgs, to extend the boundaries of France, and to build up a colonial empire.

The chief steps by which his policy was carried out were as follows: La Rochelle, the great Huguenot stronghold, was captured and the power of the Protestants was curbed effectually; the intrigues of Mary de Medici were thwarted; an alliance was made with Sweden, and to weaken the Hapsburgs the power of France was used to assist the Protestants in Germany in the Thirty Years' War; a navy was built and important ports were fortified; to extend commerce and colonies, colonial enterprises were entrusted to exclusive corporations. During the administration of Richelieu the French hold upon eastern Canada was strengthened, settlements were made in Guiana and the West Indies, and an attempt was made to occupy Madagascar.

The Council of State.—The work of strengthening the crown at the expense of the nobility was continued. The power of the nobles was maintained by their fortified castles and by their position as governors of provinces. An edict was issued for the destruction of all but the frontier fortifications. Most of the work of administration was centered in the *conseil d'etat*, or council of state, which was the highest judicial tribunal. It also issued edicts, made peace or war, determined the amount and method of taxation, and acted as a high court of justice. In appearance this body was supreme, but in reality the power centered in the king and the chief minister, the other ministers being merely advisers. Local administration was taken from the nobles and was placed almost wholly in the hands of *intendants*, who were officers of justice, police, and finance.

Mazarin.—Richelieu died in November, 1642, and Louis XIII a few months later. Louis XIV was a child of five years and his mother, Anne of Austria, became regent. Mazarin, who was probably secretly married to her, was to rule France during the troubled minority of the king. It was a period of civil and foreign war, in which the minister found no time to devote to the development of colonies. The importance of the period lies in the fact that the great nobles were effectually quelled, that the absolutism of the crown was completely established, and that France proved herself superior to the power of Spain and the Hapsburgs. When Louis XIV took the reins of power in 1661 he was the most absolute and most powerful monarch in Europe.

Colbert.—Colonial development during the reign of Louis XIV was due mainly to Colbert, who was given charge of the finances, of the navy, and of the colonies. The finances had become deranged under Mazarin, and Colbert attacked the abuses. To stimulate commerce and manufactures, he established a protective system, furnished governmental aid to companies, and granted monopolies. The royal navy and mercantile marine were greatly increased. To develop foreign trade, corporations were granted monopolies of the commerce of the West Indies, the East Indies, Senegal, and Madagascar. Colonies were fostered by paternalistic regulations. The system of Colbert, as time proved, was founded on mistaken principles, for monopoly and overregulation stifled the growth of trade and of the colonies. Although a vast area was brought under control, the colonies never attracted a large population, or were allowed a free growth of institutions.

EARLY EXPLORATIONS AND COLONIZING EFFORTS

First French voyages.—The first Frenchmen who visited America appear to have been Norman and Breton fishermen, who engaged in fishing off the Newfoundland coast perhaps as early as 1500. Sailors from Dieppe also visited the coasts of North and South America. Vague accounts have come down to us of attempts to explore the Gulf of St. Lawrence in 1506 and 1508, and of an unsuccessful colony on Sable Island in 1518. The first expedition under the government sanction was that of the Florentine, Verrazano, sent out by Francis I in 1524. The details of the voyage are somewhat obscure. He probably explored the coast from Cape Fear to Newfoundland.

Cartier and Roberval.—The wars between Francis I and Charles V prevented the French king from giving further attention to exploration until 1534, when Cartier was sent out with two ships from St. Malo. He sighted land on the Labrador coast, passed through the straits of Belle Isle, and explored the Gulf of St. Lawrence, locating the Bay of Chaleurs, Cape Gaspé, and Anticosti Island, thence returning to France.

In 1535 he again visited America in search of a passage to China. He sailed along the northern shore of the Gulf of St. Lawrence and entered the mouth of the river, soon becoming convinced that the passage did not lead to the Far East. He stopped at the site of Quebec and later proceeded to the La Chine rapids, and to a hill which he named Montreal. He wintered at Quebec where twenty-five persons died of scurvy. The return to France was made the following summer.

Exploration was again interrupted by the wars, and it was not until 1541 that Cartier's third expedition sailed. Francis I had granted a commission to Roberval, a Picardy nobleman, as viceroy and lieutenant-general in Canada, Newfoundland, Labrador, and neighboring lands, this being the first time that the name Canada was officially used. In the king's proclamation Canada was mentioned as the extremity of Asia. The objects of the expedition were discovery, settlement, and conversion of the Indians. Cartier was appointed captain-general. He sailed in 1541, but Roberval remained in France to collect supplies and materials for defence. Cartier wasted six weeks in Newfoundland and then proceeded to Quebec, where the winter was spent in great hardship.

The colonists started to return to France, but at St. Johns, Newfoundland, they met Roberval, who ordered them to return to Quebec. Cartier, however, disobeyed, and returned to France. Roberval proceeded to Quebec, where habitations were erected and the forts of Cartier repaired. Supplies, however, ran short, and during the following winter a third of the settlers died. A mutiny threatened and Roberval checked it with great harshness. After lingering a little longer, the unfortunate remnant returned to France. In 1543 Francis I declared the Western Sea to be open to his subjects, but advantage of it was not taken, and it was over a half century before another attempt was made to colonize in the St. Lawrence Valley.

Ribaut and Laudonnière.—The next colonizing efforts were of Huguenot origin, and were made at the suggestion of Coligny.

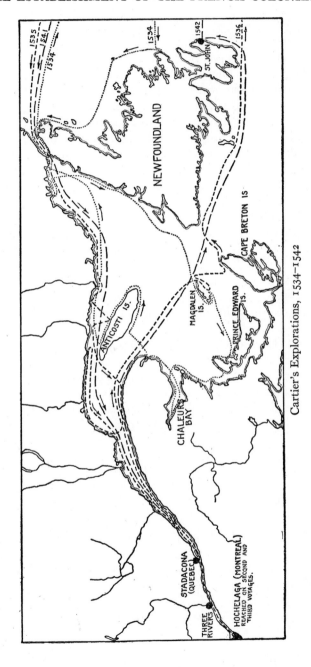

Cartier's Explorations, 1534–1542

In 1555 an attempt was made to found a colony in Brazil, but it was destroyed by the Portuguese. When Coligny developed his plan for an attack upon Spain, he determined to found a colony in the region then known as Florida. A Huguenot from Dieppe named Jean Ribaut was placed in command of the expedition, which set sail from Havre in 1562. Land was seen not far from the site of St. Augustine; they sailed northward and planted a settlement on Port Royal Sound, where thirty men were left. Ribaut explored the coast as far as the fortieth degree and returned to France. Misfortune beset the colonists, and after great suffering they built a rude vessel and succeeded in getting back to Europe.

In 1564 a large expedition was sent out under Laudonnière, which erected Fort Caroline on St. John's River. Dissensions and starvation played havoc with the colony, and when the English Captain John Hawkins offered to sell them a ship and provisions, they eagerly embraced the opportunity. When they were about to depart, Ribaut with seven vessels and six hundred soldiers hove in sight, and the idea of returning to France was abandoned.

Philip II learned of the French colony, probably from Catherine de Medici, and in 1565 sent an expedition of nineteen vessels and fifteen hundred men under Menéndez to destroy it. Ribaut's fleet was found near the mouth of the river but the larger craft escaped and Menéndez, finding the rest in a secure position, proceeded southward about fifty miles and founded St. Augustine.

Ribaut followed but failed to attack, and shortly afterwards a hurricane dispersed the fleet. Taking advantage of the misfortune, Menéndez marched overland and surprised and captured Fort Caroline, putting most of the prisoners to the sword. A little later Ribaut and his followers fell into the hands of Menéndez, and most of them were put to death. To avenge the butchery, the Chevalier de Gourgues, at his own expense, fitted out three small ships in 1567 and attacked the Spanish forts on the St. John's. They were captured and the garrisons slain. His force being too small to risk an attack on St. Augustine, De Gourgues returned to France, and Florida ceased to be a scene of French activity.

ACADIA

Colonization renewed.—The scene of the next colonization by the French was the region about the Bay of Fundy. After the religious wars, in 1598, the Marquis de la Roche landed two shiploads of colonists on Sable Island. Going in search of a site on the mainland, he encountered severe storms and returned to France. Five years later the survivors were rescued.

The fur monopoly.—In 1600 a partnership was formed between Pontgravé, a St. Malo mariner, and two Huguenot friends of Henry IV, Chauvin, a merchant of Harfleur, and Sieur de Monts, the associates being granted a fur-trading monopoly. A settlement was made at Tadoussac, on the lower St. Lawrence, but it did not prosper; two trading voyages, however, proved profitable. Shortly afterward the company was reorganized, the king making De Chastes, the governor of Dieppe, his representative. An expedition commanded by Pontgravé was sent out in 1603. Associated with him was Samuel de Champlain, who had already gained fame by a voyage to Spanish America and by his writings. A profitable trade in furs was carried on, and the St. Lawrence was explored as far as the La Chine rapids. Champlain also examined the Acadian coast as far as the Bay of Chaleurs.

Port Royal.—Upon the return of the traders, De Chastes having died, the king issued a patent to De Monts granting him viceregal powers and a trade monopoly between the fortieth and forty-sixth degrees. Settlements were to be founded and the savages were to be instructed in Christianity. In 1604 De Monts and Champlain sailed for Acadia. An unsuccessful attempt at settlement was made at St. Croix Island and later the survivors moved to Port Royal. De Monts then returned to France to defend his rights against those who objected to his patent, and Champlain busied himself with the exploration of the New England coast, on one expedition rounding Cape Cod. In 1607 it became known that De Monts's patent had been revoked, and Champlain returned to France.

Acadia, 1610–1632.—In 1610 Poutrincourt reëstablished Port Royal and soon afterward his son, Biencourt, was placed in command. The coast was surveyed as far as the Kennebec. Pontgravé had a trading post at St. John, and this Biencourt captured. In 1613 Port Royal was taken and burned by a Virginia expedition under Argall, but was soon rebuilt. In 1623 or 1624 Biencourt died and his lieutenant, Charles de la Tour, succeeded him. Before his powers could be confirmed, Acadia, in 1628, fell into English hands, but was restored in 1632.

Charnisay and La Tour.—Isaac de Rezilly was sent to receive the submission of the English, being shortly afterward succeeded by Charnisay. La Tour soon afterward received from the company of New France a grant at the mouth of the St. John's River, where he built Fort St. Jean. A civil war broke out in which La Tour finally secured aid from Boston. For a time he was successful, but Charnisay obtained help from France and La Tour was defeated. From 1645 to 1650 Charnisay was supreme in Acadia. Upon his death La Tour was made governor and lieutenant-general, and the animosities of the past were dissipated by his marriage to Charnisay's widow.

English Rivalry.—In 1654 an English fleet captured the French forts, and Acadia remained under English rule until 1667, when it was restored to France by the treaty of Breda.

THE ST. LAWRENCE VALLEY

The founding of Quebec.—In 1608 De Monts obtained a renewal of his patent for one year, and, after consulting Champlain, he decided to found a settlement at Quebec. Champlain was appointed his lieutenant with full powers, and with two vessels he arrived at Quebec on July 3. A storehouse and dwelling were built surrounded by a palisade and ditch. Of the twenty-eight men who began the settlement, only eight survived the first winter, but considerable reinforcements arrived in the spring. In the summer of 1609 Champlain accompanied a war party of Algonquins and Hurons up the Richelieu River to the lake which bears his name, where a successful attack was made upon the Iroquois. The consequences of this act were far reaching, for from that time the Iroquois confederation was hostile to the French, crippling the colony for many years.

A new company formed.—De Monts's exclusive privileges were not renewed, but he was allowed to retain his position of king's representative. Seeing no chance for profit, he withdrew from further activities in the New World. Another company was at once formed, composed of traders of Rouen and St. Malo. Champlain was retained by the new company.

Champlain's explorations.—In 1613 Champlain explored the Ottawa River to a point about one hundred miles above the modern capital of Canada. In 1615 four Recollet friars were induced to come to Quebec, this being the beginning of missionary activities in New France. The same year Champlain joined a Huron war party, passed up the Ottawa to Lake Nipissing, thence by the French River to Georgian Bay, being the first white man to find the way which eventually became the regular fur trader's route to the interior. Lake Ontario was also seen and crossed for the first time on this expedition. Fur trading was actively carried on, but because of dishonest dealings the company gradually lost influence with the Indians, a condition which also hampered the missionaries. As the Recollets met with little success, in 1625 the Jesuits were induced to send out five representatives, thus beginning the activities of that order in New France.

The Company of the Hundred Associates.—In spite of all the efforts which had been made, the financial results were trifling. So badly were affairs going that Richelieu determined to change the organization; in 1627 he established the Company of the Hundred Associates, who were to send out annually from two to three hundred settlers and a sufficient number of clergy to meet the needs. The company was to possess all lands between Florida and the Arctic Circle, and from Newfoundland as far west as it was able to take possession. With the exception of the cod and whale fisheries, the company was granted a complete monopoly of trade.

The English occupation.—Before the company could land colonists, difficulties arose between France and England, and a fleet of privateers under Captain David Kirke raided the French possessions off Gaspé, capturing eighteen vessels which were carrying colonists and supplies to Quebec; after destroying the settlements in Acadia, Kirke sailed for England. The following year he landed at Tadoussac and sent three vessels to Quebec to demand its surrender. The place capitulated and over a hundred of the inhabitants were sent to England. Upon their arrival, it was found that peace had been made. Negotiations were terminated in 1632, Canada and Acadia being restored to France.

Last years of Champlain. Nicolet.—Upon his return Champlain immediately repaired the buildings at Quebec, and established a fort at Three Rivers to protect the Hurons against the Iroquois. From time to time Champlain had heard of a great waterway in the west. Believing that it might be a route to China, in 1634 he sent Nicolet on an exploring expedition. Nicolet passed up the Ottawa, traversed Georgian Bay, and reached Sault Ste. Marie. He then explored the south shore of the upper peninsula of Michigan, and reached the southern extremity of Green Bay. From the Winnebagoes he learned of a "great water" three days' journey toward the south. After visiting the Illinois country, he returned without having reached the Mississippi. In 1635 Champlain died; there was no master mind to direct operations, and the colony languished.

The Jesuits.—The first Jesuit superior was Father Le Jeune, who in 1632 was stationed at Quebec in the residence of Notre Dame des Anges, the parent establishment of the missions of New France. Le Jeune ministered to the Algonquins of the neighborhood. In 1633 Bréboeuf headed a group of missionaries to the Huron villages at the southern end of Georgian Bay, and in 1641 a mission was founded at Sault Ste. Marie, but it was not permanent. Pestilence and the war parties of the Iroquois gradually destroyed the Hurons; the Jesuits toiled amid scenes of famine, disease, and death, several succumbing to the hardships, others suffering martyrdom. So constant were the attacks of the Iroquois, that in 1649 it was determined to establish a more sheltered mission on the Island of St. Joseph in Georgian Bay. The missions on the mainland being destroyed by the Iroquois, and the Hurons having been greatly reduced in numbers, in 1650 the Jesuits abandoned that region. Attempts to establish missions among the Iroquois also failed completely at this time. In the settlements the Jesuits were the most important social factor, until 1665 practically controlling the life of the people. At Quebec they established schools for Huron and French boys, and at their suggestion the Ursulines opened a convent. Private endowments made possible a school for girls near Quebec and a hospital at Montreal.

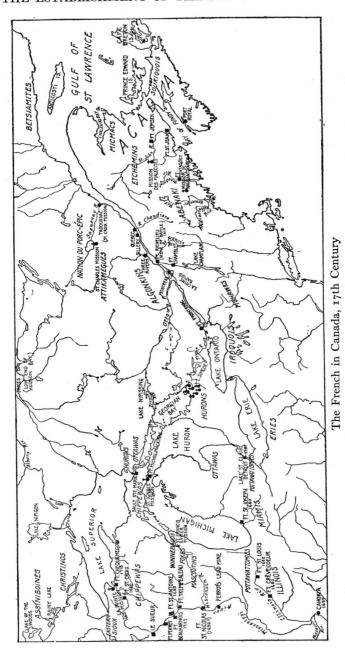

The French in Canada, 17th Century

The founding of Montreal.—For the purpose of founding an evangelical colony, a group of religious persons at Paris formed an association called the Association of Montreal. The island on which the city now stands was purchased, and in 1641 De Maisonneuve, with a Jesuit priest and thirty-seven laymen, sailed from La Rochelle. After taking formal possession of the island, the party wintered at Quebec, and the following spring founded the town of Montreal.

The New Company.—The Hundred Associates not having fulfilled their agreement regarding settlers, and the colony having proved a financial failure, an arrangement was made in 1645 between the company and the inhabitants acting as a corporation, henceforth known as the New Company. The old company retained its governmental rights, but the fur trade was thrown open to the New Company on condition that it would assume the expenses of civil administration, defence, and religion, that it would bring in twenty settlers annually, and would pay to the old company a thousand pounds of beaver skins every year.

Coureurs de bois.—Up to this time the fur trade had been carried on mainly at the settlements, but after the New Company was formed a larger number of men began to frequent the forests, giving rise to the type known as *coureurs de bois*. These were of two classes, those who merely traded with the Indians for peltries, and those who attached themselves to native tribes. This latter class lapsed into barbarism and became a lawless element which gave great annoyance to the officials. Later a third class of traders appeared when the governors were allowed to grant licenses to frequent the forests. Great abuses crept into the fur trade, large quantities of spirits being sold to the Indians, who were roundly cheated when intoxicated. It was the intention of the French government to restrict the trade to the settlements, but the officials usually winked at violations of the law, and some of them shared in the illicit trading. The most famous of the fur traders of this period were Radisson and Groseilliers, who, in 1658–1659 and possibly earlier, traded and explored in the country at the western end of Lake Superior.

REORGANIZATION AND THE IROQUOIS WARS

A centralist system established.—As complaints arose regarding the last governmental arrangements, the king changed the form of control, creating a council to consist of the governor, any ex-governor who might be in the country, and the superior of the Jesuits, who was later to give way to a bishop when one was appointed; these were to select for membership two inhabitants, or three if no ex-governor was in the colony. Quebec, Montreal, and Three Rivers were each to select a syndic, who could hold office for three years and could deliberate with but could not vote in the council. The centralist system, which Mazarin was perfecting in France, was thus established in Canada.

Laval.—New France had been attached to the archbishopric of Rouen, and De Queylus, a Sulpician priest at Montreal, had acted as vicar-general for the whole colony. His followers hoped that he would be created bishop, but instead, in 1659 a Jesuit, the Abbé Laval, was appointed vicar-apostolic and Bishop of Petraea *in partibus*. After a spirited contest with De Queylus, Laval was successful in establishing his supremacy, the power of the Jesuits thus being assured.

War with the Iroquois.—The following year witnessed a serious Iroquois outbreak. News arrived that twelve hundred warriors had gathered to wipe out the settlements. A young nobleman, popularly known as Dollard, conceived the quixotic scheme of intercepting a large force of Iroquois who had wintered on the Ottawa. With sixteen enlisted men and a few Hurons and Algonquins he proceeded to a palisade at the great rapids of the Ottawa, and there met the Indians. Dollard and his followers were slain to a man, but so stubborn had been their resistance that the Iroquois retired to the forests and New France was saved. A regiment was sent out to protect the colony, forts were established along the Richelieu, and two expeditions were sent into the Iroquois country, the result being that a peace was made with the Indians which lasted for several years. Later an expedition was sent to the outlet of Lake Ontario to impress the savages with the power of France.

The West India Company.—In 1663 the company of New France surrendered its rights to the king, who created a council to consist of the governor, bishop, and five councillors chosen by them jointly. The following year, at the suggestion of Colbert, he chartered a new corporation known as the West India Company, to which was given a monopoly of all the trade of New France and the west coast of Africa, with the privilege of nominating the governor of Canada. The office of intendant was also created to act as a check upon the governor. This official was to act as a legal and financial officer who was to report directly to the crown. The first intendant was Talon, who was a prominent figure for several years. The governor who was the military, political, and administrative agent of the king, the intendant, and the bishop were the real rulers of New France. Their divided authority and jealousies later led to frequent disputes, which greatly retarded the development of the colonies.

Talon.—It was Talon who first realized the possibilities of New France. To promote commerce he built a vessel which he despatched to the West Indies with a cargo of fish, staves, and lumber. He planned an overland road to Acadia and urged the occupation of the Hudson River Valley, projects, however, which were not realized. At Quebec he erected a brewery and tannery. Young women were brought from France as wives for the colonists and soldiers, and bounties were offered for the birth of children. In 1666 the total population was 3418; five years later it had increased to 6000.

Seignorial grants.—To aid in colonization and protection Talon established a type of feudalism. Along the Richelieu River as high up as Chambly and along the St. Lawrence from the neighborhood of Montreal to a point several miles below Quebec, most of the lands were portioned out. The majority of these seignorial grants were made to officers of the regiment of Carrigan, which had been stationed in Canada. Discharged soldiers were settled on the grants as tenant farmers. The seignorial holdings varied in size from half a league to six leagues on the river and extended back from half a league to two leagues. The buildings of the seigniory were the "mansion," which was usually a log house, a fort, chapel, and mill. The poverty of the proprietor, however, frequently prevented the erection of some of the buildings, the mill sometimes being lacking or serving the double duty of fort and mill; on other grants chapel, mill, and fort were never built. In the more exposed localities the houses of the tenants were built together in palisaded villages. On other grants the dwellings lined the shore, forming what were called *cotes*. Near Quebec Talon laid out a model seigniory and three model villages, each village being provided with a carpenter, mason, blacksmith, and shoemaker. But the settlers did not profit by the example and continued to build near the rivers. With the exception of Talon's villages, one could have seen nearly every house in Canada by paddling a canoe up the St. Lawrence and the Richelieu. One of the most famous seigniories in Canada was that of the Le Moyne family.

THE WEST INDIES

The Company of St. Christopher.—In 1625 a small brigantine commanded by Pierre d'Esnambuc and Urbain de Roissey, "the pirate of Dieppe," sailed to the West Indies. After escaping from a Spanish galleon near Jamaica, they proceeded to St. Christopher, where a settlement was begun. The following year the Company of St. Christopher was formed, and three vessels with over five hundred men set sail from France in 1627, but only half of them survived the voyage. Two settlements were formed, one at each end of the island, the English having already occupied the middle. In 1628 and 1629 about five hundred more were sent out, and in the latter year ten vessels were despatched to defend the colonists. In spite of this a Spanish fleet broke up the settlements; the fugitives fled to St. Martin, and after a vain attempt to settle Antigua and Montserrat, most of them returned to St. Christopher, which had been abandoned by the Spanish. Only three hundred and fifty survived.

Santo Domingo.—A few of them went to the northern coast of Santo Domingo, whence they carried on buccaneering enterprises against the Spaniards. After the Spanish attack the company did little to assist, and the colony was left to its own devices. Trade with the Dutch immediately sprang up and the settlers began to make a profit from tobacco.

Guadeloupe, Martinique, and Tortuga.—In 1634 the Company of St. Christopher was bankrupt, and the following year it was reorganized as the Company of the Isles of America. Guadeloupe and Martinique were immediately occupied. In 1640 the

English were expelled from Tortuga, and the island was occupied by Levasseur, who soon broke loose from the control of the company and conducted a pirate haven. Several of the smaller islands were also occupied. The French West Indies soon attracted a considerable immigration, in 1642 the population being estimated at more than seven thousand. The tobacco business not continuing profitable, sugar began to take its place as the staple product. Due mainly to the clash of authority among officials, a condition which led to anarchy, by 1648 the company was bankrupt.

Other Islands occupied.—Between 1649 and 1651 the various islands were sold to proprietors who ruled them until 1664. Between 1648 and 1656 settlements were made on St. Martin, St. Bartholomew, St. Croix, The Saints, Marie Galante, St. Lucia, and Granada, and by 1664 the French flag floated over fourteen of the Antilles. The sugar business proved to be exceedingly profitable and cultivation of the cane made slave-labor desirable. Population increased rapidly, in 1655 the whites numbering about fifteen thousand and slaves being almost as numerous. During the period of the proprietors there was little restriction on commerce, most of the carrying trade passing into the hands of the Dutch.

The Crown assumes control.—Colbert became controller-general of the finances in 1662, one of his functions being the control of the colonies. He determined to send a representative to assert the king's authority; in 1663 De Tracy was made lieutenant-general in all the French colonies and was given supreme executive and judicial powers. The following year he sailed with De La Barre who was about to establish a colony at Cayenne. De Tracy soon established the king's authority and corrected abuses in the West Indies, and then proceeded to Quebec, where he remained until 1667.

The West India Company.—In 1664 Louis chartered the great company which was granted the mainland of South America from the Orinoco to the Amazon, the island of Cayenne, the French West Indies, Newfoundland, Acadia, Canada, the rest of the mainland of North America as far south as Florida, and the African coast from Cape Verde to the Cape of Good Hope. Former proprietors were to be compensated, and with the excep-

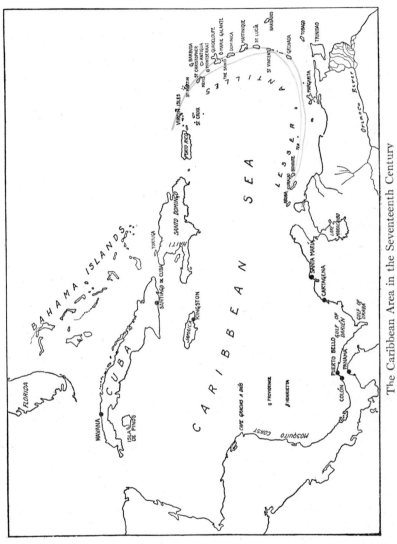

The Caribbean Area in the Seventeenth Century

tion of the fisheries of Newfoundland, the company was to have a monopoly of trade and colonization for forty years. After considerable opposition the company succeeded in establishing its authority in the islands, but the war which broke out in 1666 between France, and England and Holland proved disastrous, a French fleet which was sent to protect the Antilles being destroyed by the English. Colbert assisted the company financially, but it failed to become a profitable undertaking and in 1674 was dissolved. The inhabitants, however, continued to prosper, mainly because of the increasing number of independent merchants who traded with the islands and the growing importance of the sugar industry.

OPENING THE UPPER LAKE REGION AND THE MISSISSIPPI VALLEY

Two Lines of Approach.—The French had now established themselves firmly in the lower St. Lawrence basin and in the Caribbean area. From these two bases they now proceeded to the Mississippi Valley and the northern Gulf littoral. From the St. Lawrence they made their way over the portages to the tributaries of the Father of Waters. From the West Indies the Gulf of Mexico served as a highway.

Occupation of the upper lakes.—After the failure of the Huron missions, the Jesuits extended their field of operations to the shores of Lake Superior and Lake Michigan. The mission at Sault Ste. Marie was revived; in 1665 La Pointe mission near the western end of Lake Superior was established by Father Allouez, who was succeeded by Marquette four years later. Between 1670 and 1672 St. Ignace, at Michillimackinac, and St. Xavier on Green Bay (at De Pere) were established. In 1670 Talon despatched Saint Lusson to take possession of the Northwest; at a meeting of the tribes at Sault Ste. Marie the following year the sovereignty of the king over that region was proclaimed. Albanel was also sent to open communication between the St. Lawrence and Hudson Bay.

Marquette and Joliet.—In 1672 Count Frontenac became governor and lieutenant-general of New France. Shortly after his arrival at Quebec, at the suggestion of Talon, he sent the fur trader Joliet to find the Mississippi. At Michillimackinac he met the missionary Marquette, who decided to accompany him. On May 17, 1673, they started westward; after reaching Green Bay, they followed the Fox and Wisconsin rivers to the Mississippi, which they descended to the mouth of the Arkansas, just at the time when Father Larios was founding Spanish missions near the Rio Grande. Being convinced that the Mississippi emptied into the Gulf of Mexico, and fearing that they might fall into the hands of the Spaniards, they determined to turn back. The return was by the Mississippi, the Illinois, and Chicago rivers and the western shores of Lake Michigan. Father Marquette returned to work among the Illinois, but was soon forced by illness to abandon the field. On his way north he died at the site of Ludington. His work among the Illinois was taken up by others, among them being Fathers Allouez and Hennepin.

Fort Frontenac.—While Joliet and Marquette were exploring the Mississippi, the governor was engaged in founding Fort Frontenac, on the northern shore of the outlet of Lake Ontario, near modern Kingston, his purpose being to overawe the Iroquois, and to divert their trade and allegiance from the English. With the governor was La Salle, who later became commandant of the new fort.

Frontenac's quarrels.—Shortly after Frontenac became governor the king again changed the form of government. The council was increased to seven members who held office directly from the king. Its chief function was judicial. A minor court called the *prévôté*, having original jurisdiction in civil and criminal cases, was reëstablished, appeals being taken from the *prévôté* to the council. Frontenac, who was of an imperious nature and exceedingly jealous of his authority, quarreled with the officials and clergy of Montreal, with Laval who had recently been made Bishop of Quebec, with the new intendant Duchesneau, and with the council. Regulation of the fur trade and questions of authority were the fruitful sources of disagreement. Under such conditions the colony did not advance rapidly. As Le Sueur says in his life of Frontenac, "The great trouble in Canada was that it was an overgoverned country. . . . What these people needed in the first place was freedom to seek their living in their own way, and secondly, an extremely simple form of government." The constant bickering finally exhausted the patience of the home government, and in 1682 both Frontenac and Duchesneau were recalled.

La Salle's fur trade monopoly.—During Frontenac's admin-istration La Salle was engaged in the exploration of the Illinois country and the Mississippi. Having secured a royal patent to build forts and engage in the fur trade in the interior, La Salle, with a party which included Tonty, an Italian soldier of fortune, and the Recollet Hennepin, erected a fort at Niagara Falls and built a vessel called the *Griffon*, on which in 1679 they sailed up the lakes to Green Bay. The boat was sent back with a cargo of furs, but never reached its destination. The shores of Lake Michigan and the Illinois country were explored and Fort Crêvecœur was erected near the site of Peoria. From there Accau and Hennepin were sent to explore the upper Mississippi. La Salle then returned to Fort Frontenac, crossing lower Michigan and following Lake Erie and Lake Ontario.

Exploration of the Mississippi.—While La Salle was gone, Tonty occupied Starved Rock, later known as Fort St. Louis, but a mutiny and an Iroquois invasion forced the French to return to Green Bay, so that when La Salle returned he found the country abandoned. After a fruitless search, he heard from the Indians of Tonty's whereabouts and hastened north to meet him. Together they returned to Fort Frontenac. Nothing daunted, they again sought the Mississippi. On December 21, 1681, they were again at Fort Miami, at the mouth of the St. Joseph River. On February 6, 1682, they reached the Mississippi, and arrived at its mouth in April, when they took formal possession of the great valley, naming it Louisiana in honor of the king. By the end of September they were back at Fort Miami, and in 1683 the leader returned to Quebec.

La Salle's Colony on the Gulf.—La Salle now planned a colony at the mouth of the Mississippi River, as a means of developing the fur trade, controlling the Mississippi Valley, providing a base for commanding the Gulf, and, in case of war, for attack on the coveted mines of New Spain. France and Spain were on the verge of war, and in 1683 French buccaneers three times sacked the Spanish settlement of Apalache. La Salle's pro-posals were favored, therefore, by Louis XIV. In the summer of 1684 La Salle left France with a colony of some four hundred people. In the autumn he reached the West Indies, the ketch *St. François* having been captured by the Spaniards on the way. Continuing the voyage in November, La Salle missed the mouth

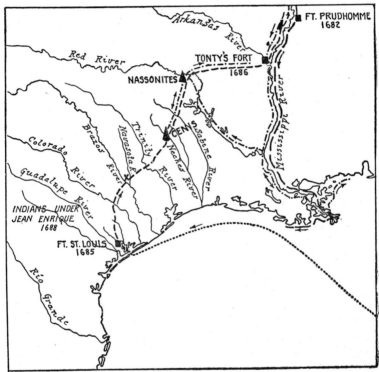

La Salle's Colony on the Texas Coast, 1684–1689

of the Mississippi and landed on the Texas coast at Matagorda Bay. Tonty descended the Mississippi to coöperate (1686), but did not find his chief. On the way he built a small post on the Arkansas.

Failure.—The expedition rapidly went to pieces. One vessel was wrecked in landing, and Beaujeu, the naval commander, returned to France with a second, and part of the men and supplies. La Salle moved his colony inland to the Garcitas River, near the head of the Lavaca Bay, where he founded Fort St. Louis, and then began a series of expeditions northeastward in the hope of finding the Mississippi River. While engaged in exploring, the last of his vessels was wrecked. Through desertion and sickness the colony rapidly dwindled. On his third expedition northeastward, in 1687, La Salle reached the Hasinai (Cenis) Indians, east of the Trinity River. On his fourth expedition he was murdered by his companions near the Brazos River. The remainder of his party, led by Joutel, made their way to the Arkansas post and to Canada. In the fall of 1689 Tonty, in an effort to rescue La Salle's colonists, descended the Mississippi River, and made his way to the Cadodacho and Hasinai villages. Meanwhile the colony on the Gulf had been completely wiped out by an Indian massacre which occurred early in 1689. La Salle's occupation of Matagorda Bay later became a basis of the claim of the United States to Texas.

Explorers in the Southwest.—The failure of La Salle's colony did not put an end to exploration in the Southwest. Interest in a passage to the South Sea was perennial, and no tale of Spanish treasure was too glittering to find credence on the French frontier. Mathieu Sagean told of a golden country of the Accanibas, and Baron La Hontan of a Long River. The *coureurs de bois* were ever led west and southwest in their fur trading operations. The result was that in this western country traders from Canada roamed far and wide at an early date. A Canadian is known to have reached the Rio Grande overland before 1688 and by 1694 Canadian traders were among the Missouri and Osage tribes.

The upper Mississippi—Duluth.—While La Salle was operating in the Illinois country, others were at work in northern Wisconsin and Minnesota. In 1678 Duluth, a cousin of Tonty, left Montreal for the west. For several years he traded among the tribes west of Lake Superior. Hearing in 1680 that Frenchmen were near, he went in search of them, and found Accau and Hennepin, who had explored the upper Mississippi. Duluth went to France, where he secured a license to trade with the Sioux. In 1683 he returned to Wisconsin with thirty men, proceeded to the north shore of Lake Superior, and built forts near Lake Nipigon and Pigeon River. The highway from Brulé River to the St. Croix became known as Duluth's Portage. In 1686 he erected a temporary fort near Detroit to bar the English traders.

Le Sueur.—Between 1683 and 1700 Le Sueur, a prominent fur trader, operated in Minnesota and Wisconsin. In 1683 he was at St. Anthony's Falls. The Fox Indians of Wisconsin opposed the passage of the French to the Sioux and practically cut off their trade route. For this reason Le Sueur protected the Brulé-St. Croix highway. To effect this, in 1693 he built a fort at Chequamegon Bay, on the south shore of Lake Superior, and another on the Mississippi near the mouth of the St. Croix. This post became a center of commerce for the western posts. In 1697 Le Sueur was in France, where he secured permission to work copper mines near Lake Superior. In 1699 he went from France to Louisiana with Iberville. Thence, with twenty-nine men, he ascended the Mississippi to Blue River, Minnesota, and built Fort L'Huiller (1700) at Mankato, where he traded with the Sioux.

Perrot.—In 1685 Nicholas Perrot, who had been in Wisconsin as early as 1665, and had acquired great influence over the western tribes, was made "commander of the west" and sent among the Sioux. In 1686 he built Fort St. Antoine on the Mississippi near Trempealeau, Wisconsin. Other posts established by him were Fort Perrot on the west side of Lake Pepin, Fort Nicholas at Prairie du Chien, and one farther down the Mississippi near the Galena lead mines, which he discovered and worked.

The Illinois and Detroit.—In the Illinois country the French Jesuits labored from the time of Marquette, among his successors being Fathers Allouez and Hennepin. In 1699 a Sulpician mission was established at Cahokia and in 1700 the Jesuits moved down the Illinois River to Kaskaskia. A year later Detroit was founded to protect the route from Lake Erie to Lake Huron, cut off English trade with the Indians, and afford a base for the Illinois trade. Missionaries entered the region of the lower Mississippi and the lower Ohio, where Tonty and other Frenchmen maintained a considerable trade.

Traders on the Tennessee.—Because of Iroquois control of the country south of the Great Lakes and as far as the Tennessee River, the French in La Salle's time had little knowledge of the Ohio and its tributaries. At that period the Shawnee of the Tennessee and Cumberland Rivers were declining under Iroquois attacks. On the upper Tennessee lived the Cherokees. In spite of the Iroquois, however, by the end of the century several *coureurs de bois* of Canada had ascended the Ohio and Tennessee Rivers, crossed the divide, and descended the Savannah River into South Carolina, in defiance of the government, which tried to maintain a trade monopoly. Their activities brought them into rivalry with the English on the Carolina frontier.

Couture and Bellefeuille.—Among these pathfinders was Jean Couture, who had been left by Tonty at the Arkansas post. As early as 1693 he deserted the French colony and made his way overland to the English. In 1699 he was on the Savannah, where he proposed to lead the English to certain mines in the west. Returning, he led a party of English traders, sent by Governor Blake of South Carolina, up the Savannah, and down the Tennessee and Ohio, in an attempt to divert the western trade from Canada to the English. In February, 1700, they reached the Arkansas River, where they were met by Le Sueur on his way up the river to Minnesota. At the request of Iberville, the new governor of Louisiana, the government now permitted Illinois traders to sell their peltry in Louisiana, to prevent them from carrying it over the mountains to the English. In 1701 a party of Frenchmen under Bellefeuille and Soton crossed the mountains to South Carolina, and attempted to open up trade. Returning they descended the Mississippi and visited Biloxi. It was now proposed, in order to stop the road to Carolina, that posts be established on the Miami and the lower Ohio. For this purpose Juchereau de St. Denis established a post at Cairo in 1702. Through the establishment of Louisiana and the opening of trade with Canada, this danger was largely averted.

READINGS

EARLY EXPLORATIONS AND COLONIZING EFFORTS

Baird, C. W., *Huguenot Emigration;* Brevoort, J. C., *Verrazano the Navigator;* Channing, Edward, *History of the United States,* I, 90–112; De Costa, B. F., *Verrazano the Explorer;* French, B. F., *Historical Collections of Louisiana and Florida,* 117–362; Hamilton, P. J., *The Colonization of the South,* 27–41; Hart, A. B., *Contemporaries,* I, 102–112; Leacock, Stephen, *The Mariner of St. Malo;* Lescarbot, Marc, *History of New France;* Munro, W. B., *Crusaders of New France,* 11–32; Murphy, H. C., *Voyage of Verrazano;* Parkman, Francis, *The Pioneers of France in the New World,* 1–228; Shea, J. G., in

Winsor, *Narrative and Critical History*, II, 260–283; Tracy, F. B., *Tercentenary History of Canada*, I, 20–37; Winsor, Justin, *Cartier to Frontenac*, 1–47; Biggar, H. P., *The Precursors of Jacques Cartier.*

ACADIA AND THE ST. LAWRENCE VALLEY

Biggar, H. P., *Early Trading Companies of New France;* Bourne, E. G., *Voyages and Explorations of Champlain (Trail Makers' Series);* Champlain, Samuel, *Œuvres* (Laverdière, ed.); Colby, C. W., *The Founder of New France;* Dionne, N. E., *Champlain;* Grant, W. L., *Voyages of Champlain (Original Narratives Series);* Kingsford, William, *The History of Canada*, I, 147–294; Le Sueur, W. D., *Frontenac*, 1–60; Marquis, T. G., *The Jesuit Missions;* Parkman, Francis, *Old Régime in Canada*, 3–168; *Pioneers of New France*, 324–454; *The Jesuits in North America;* Thwaites, R. G., *France in America*, 10–48; Tracy, F. B., *Tercentenary History of Canada*, I, 41–279; Winsor, Justin, *From Cartier to Frontenac*, 77–183; Munro, W. B., *Crusaders of New France.*

REORGANIZATION AND THE WEST INDIES

Chapais, Thomas, *The Great Intendant;* Haring, C. H., *The Buccaneers in the West Indies in the XVII Century;* Mims, S. L., *Colbert's West India Policy;* Munro, W. B., *The Seigneurs of Old Canada;* Parkman, Francis, *The Old Régime*, 169–330.

THE UPPER LAKES AND THE MISSISSIPPI VALLEY

Bolton, H. E., "The Location of La Salle's Colony on the Gulf of Mexico," in *Mississippi Valley Historical Review*, II, 165–182; Charlevoix, P. F. X., *Histoire Générale de la Nouvelle France* (J. G. Shea, trans.): Cox, I. J., *Journeys of La Salle (Trail Makers' Series);* Folwell, W. W., *Minnesota*, 59–65; Hamilton, P. J., *The Colonization of the South*, 187–196; Kellogg, L. P., ed., *Early Narratives of the Northwest (Original Narratives Series)*: Le Sueur, W. D., *Frontenac*, 61–169; Ogg, F. A., *The Opening of the Mississippi*, 59–163; Parish, J. C., *The Man with the Iron Hand;* Parkman, Francis, *La Salle and the Discovery of the Great West;* Phelps, Albert, *Louisiana*, 6–20; Shea, J. G., *Exploration of the Mississippi Valley;* Thwaites, R. G., *France in America*, 48–71; *Wisconsin*, 40–71; Winsor, Justin, *Cartier to Frontenac*, 183–295.

CHAPTER V

THE BEGINNINGS OF ENGLISH EXPANSION (1485–1603)

THE TUDOR PERIOD

Periods of English activities.—While the French were colonizing Canada and the West Indies, and the Spaniards were opening mines and ranches in northern Mexico, the English were founding still more vigorous settlements on the Atlantic seaboard, in the islands, and in the region of Hudson Bay.

The history of English activities in America before 1783 may be divided into four periods: (1) The Tudor epoch (1485–1603), which was a period of commercial expansion, exploration, and attempted colonization; (2) the Stuart and Cromwellian era (1603–1689), the period of colony planting; (3) the international struggle for territory (1689-1763); and (4) the struggle of a part of the English colonists for independence (1763-1783).

Henry VII.—When Henry Tudor ascended the throne of England a new era was ushered in. The continental possessions except Calais had been swept away in the Hundred Years' War. The Wars of the Roses had broken the power of the feudal barony, and the middle class Englishman had become the most important political element in the nation. The general form of the constitution had become fixed, the functions of the three branches of the government, the king and his council, parliament, and the courts, having become fairly well defined. The work of Henry Tudor was to restore the finances, to build up commerce and industry, to keep England at peace, and at the same time, by a series of marriage alliances and by adroit diplomacy to raise England to her former position as a great European power. He also built up the kingship at the expense of a subservient parliament.

The English Reformation.—During the three succeeding reigns, England played little part in exploration. While Spain was founding her vast colonial empire, the attention of Englishmen was centered on the European situation created by Charles V and on the great religious controversy, which resulted in the break with Rome and the establishment of the Anglican church.

Queen Elizabeth.—With the accession of Queen Elizabeth a new situation arose. To the Catholic powers, Elizabeth had no right to the throne of England. Philip II of Spain hoped to restore the country to the Catholic fold; his first wife was Queen Mary of England, and under his influence a short-lived Catholic reaction had been produced; if Elizabeth could now be induced to turn Catholic and marry Philip, England might be won back to the Roman church. Elizabeth, however, followed an independent course, dangling before the eyes of the Spanish ambassador the possibility of a marriage with Philip, while perfecting the organization of the Anglican church, increasing her hold upon the affections of her subjects, strengthening her treasury, army, navy, and defences, and stimulating industry and commerce. Her path was beset with additional difficulties, for the powerful Catholic party in France was intriguing to place Mary Stuart, the queen of Scotland, on the English throne. To weaken her foes, Elizabeth aided the Huguenots, assisted the Dutch in their war against Spain, and connived with English mariners to raid the Spanish Main. In 1588 the patience of Philip was exhausted, and he sought to humble the haughty queen by sending the Invincible Armada against England. A running fight occurred in the Channel and several of the galleons were sunk or driven on shore. The Armada entered the roads of Calais but a great storm shattered the fleet. Of the original one hundred and thirty vessels only one-third returned to Spain. The defeat of the Armada marks a turning point in Spanish and English history. From that time Spain was thrown on the defensive and her power on the continent gradually declined, though her colonies continued to expand. England followed up her success by taking the offensive; an era of greater commercial activity followed, and she soon entered upon her rôle of a colonizing nation.

COMMERCIAL EXPANSION

John Cabot.—The discovery of new lands in the west soon became known in England, and when the Venetian citizen, John Cabot, applied for letters patent to go on a western voyage,

Henry VII readily complied. In May, 1497, his single ship
with eighteen men set sail from Bristol and crossed the north Atlantic.   It is impossible to state with certainty what part of
the coast was visited, but it appears to have been in the neighborhood of Cape Breton Island.   The idea that Sebastian Cabot
accompanied his father is generally rejected by the best authorities.   The importance of the voyage lies in the fact that it was
used at a later date to strengthen the English claim to a large
part of North America.   The following year John Cabot sailed
for the new found land but never returned.

The Newfoundland fisheries.—Cabot's voyage had another
important result. He had discovered a convenient trade route
to the fisheries of Newfoundland, and English, French, Spanish,
and Portuguese fishing vessels soon swarmed the region.   English
ships are thought to have traded there regularly after 1502.
Expeditions are known to have been made thither in 1527 and
1536, and before 1550 fishing fleets went from southern England
to Newfoundland every spring and autumn.

The Muscovy Company.—The latter half of the Tudor period
witnessed the formation of great companies which reached out
for foreign trade.   In 1553 a group of London merchants decided to make an attempt to reach China and the East Indies
by a northern route.   Under the command of Willoughby and
Chancellor, three ships sailed along the Norway coast and
rounded the North Cape. Willoughby and the crews of two of the
ships perished on the coast of Lapland, but Chancellor entered
the White Sea and penetrated to Moscow, where he was promised
trading privileges by Ivan the Terrible.   In 1555 the merchants
who were interested in the expedition were granted a royal
charter, the company being familiarly known as the Muscovy
Company.   Annual fleets were despatched to the White and
Baltic seas, warehouses were established at various points in
Russia, and the agents of the company extended their activities
to the Caspian Sea, to Bokhara, and to Persia.   In 1580 the
Turks cut them off from the region outside of European Russia.
Occasional unsuccessful attempts were also made by the company to reach China by the northern route.   In 1579 the East-
land Company, a rival organization, was chartered to trade in
the Baltic, and developed an extensive trade in Poland.

The Levant Company.—English merchants also turned their attention to the Mediterranean to renew a trade which had formerly been of some importance. In 1581 a charter was issued to the Levant Company, which engaged in trading with the Turkish ports along the southern and eastern shores of the Mediterranean. The same year a charter was granted to the Venetian Company and in 1592 the two were combined as the Levant Company. Among those interested in the Mediterranean commerce were Sir Thomas Smythe and Sir Walter Raleigh, both of whom were important figures in the colonization of Virginia. Other groups of merchants opened trade with Morocco, and the Senegambia and Guinea coasts. In all of these enterprises Englishmen were reaching out for the trade with the East Indies, which had long been monopolized by the Portuguese. In 1581, the year in which the Levant Company was chartered, Portugal was incorporated with Spain, and hostility to that power added another incentive to reach the East.

THE ELIZABETHAN SEA–DOGS

John Hawkins.—Among those interested in the African trade was William Hawkins, who filled the important positions of mayor of Plymouth and member of parliament. He made three voyages to Guiana and Brazil. His son, John Hawkins, became one of the most famous mariners of his time. In 1562 he sailed for Africa to obtain slaves, which he disposed of in Española. In 1564–1565 he engaged in a second voyage which resulted in great profit. A third voyage in 1567–1568 ended disastrously. The Spanish government had sent a fleet to stop the traffic; but in spite of it he forced an entrance to the West Indian ports and disposed of his cargo. Being driven by a storm into the harbor of Vera Cruz, he was attacked by a Spanish fleet and but two of the English vessels escaped.

Drake and Cavendish.—Francis Drake, a nephew of John Hawkins, had accompanied him on his third expedition and had suffered the loss of his investment. He soon began a series of reprisals. In 1572 he made an unsuccessful attack on Nombre de Diós and ascended the Chagres River where he waylaid a train of mules laden with bullion. The example set by him was frequently followed by raids of English mariners in the following decade. In 1577 another fleet sailed under Drake's command. After capturing several Spanish and Portuguese vessels on the African coast, the fleet crossed the Atlantic and attempted to pass through the Straits of Magellan. Only one vessel reached the Pacific. Drake proceeded up the western coast, plundering as he went. In a harbor known as Drake's Bay, north of San Francisco Bay, he refitted, and claimed the California region for the queen, calling it New Albion. He then sailed to the East Indies where a cargo of spice was obtained. From Java, Drake crossed the Indian Ocean, rounded the Cape of Good Hope, and proceeded to England, entering the harbor of Plymouth in November, 1580, having completed the first English circumnavigation of the globe. In 1586 Thomas Cavendish followed almost the same course, plundered the Spanish commerce in the Pacific, and in 1588 completed the circumnavigation of the world. Besides Hawkins, Drake, and Cavendish a score of English mariners engaged in raiding the Spanish Main. They were assisted financially by the queen and by many of her councillors who considered the raiding of Spanish commerce good business as well as good state policy.

East Indian trade.—A party of English merchants had also succeeded in penetrating from the Syrian coast to India. The report of their journey and the voyages of Drake and Cavendish stimulated the desire to open trade with the Far East. The result was that in 1591 an expedition was fitted out which rounded the Cape of Good Hope and reached Ceylon, India, and the Malay Peninsula. Reports of the successes of the Dutch in the East Indies increased the interest of the English merchants, and in 1600 the East India Company was formed.

SEARCH FOR A NORTHWEST PASSAGE

Frobisher.—The unsuccessful attempts of the Muscovy Company to reach the East by a northeast passage led to the search for a northwestern route. The great exponent of the idea was Martin Frobisher. After vainly seeking many years for a patron who would furnish funds, in 1574 he received the support of Michael Lock, a member of the Muscovy Company, and the following year a royal license was granted to undertake the work.

In June, 1576, Frobisher sailed from England in command of three small vessels, only one of which reached America. The vessel passed along the Labrador coast, crossed the entrance of Hudson Strait, and coasted Baffin Land, entering the inlet now known as Frobisher's Bay. Upon his return to England, Frobisher took back a large stone, which an assayer claimed contained gold. In consequence the queen and many influential men subscribed liberally for another voyage. The Company of Cathay was formed which was to have a monopoly in all lands to the westward where Englishmen had not traded before. Expeditions in search of gold were sent out under Frobisher in 1577 and 1578, but the rocks which were brought back proved to be worthless.

Gilbert.—Among those interested in the search for a northwest passage was Raleigh's half-brother, Sir Humphrey Gilbert, who believed that a colony might be established on the American coast. In 1578 he obtained a six-year monopoly of discovery and settlement in America. A fleet was equipped, but being twice scattered by storms, the attempt was abandoned. In 1583 Gilbert made a second venture. Arriving at St. Johns, Newfoundland, Gilbert informed the crews of the fishing fleet of his commission, and took possession in the name of Elizabeth. On the return voyage the *Squirrel* with Gilbert and all on board was lost in a storm just north of the Azores.

Davis.—In 1584 John Davis, Walter Raleigh, and others were granted a charter to explore a route to China and to trade in lands which might be discovered. Command of an expedition was given to Davis, who sailed from Dartmouth in 1585. The southern coast of Greenland was explored and Davis Strait was crossed, but the illusive opening was not found. In 1586 and 1587 Davis sought the passage but without success.

ATTEMPTS AT COLONIZATION

Raleigh and the attempted colonization of Virginia.—England's struggle with Spain for empire did not end with an attack on her fleets and her colonies. Men soon arose who dared to dispute Spain's monopoly by planting colonies in the lands claimed by His Catholic Majesty. The leader in the enterprise was Sir

Walter Raleigh.   In 1584 he received a patent similar to that of
Gilbert.   Two vessels were soon despatched under Amadas and
Barlowe.   They followed the southern route by the Canaries and
the West Indies, and finally landed on Roanoke Island, taking
possession of that region, which was named Virginia in honor of
Elizabeth, a name which was soon applied to the country from
the Spanish settlements to Newfoundland.   In April of the
following year Grenville commanded a second expedition
which took out the first colonists, who made a settlement on
Roanoke Island.   In 1586 supply ships were sent out, but they
found the settlement deserted.   Wearied by the hard winter,
the settlers had accepted an offer from Sir Francis Drake,
who had been raiding in the Caribbean, to carry them back to
England.

In 1587 another group of colonists including almost a hundred
men, seventeen women, and several children, was sent out under
Governor John White and landed at Roanoke.   White returned
to England, but owing to the naval war with Spain and other
difficulties he was unable to go to Virginia again until 1591,
when he found only deserted ruins.   News of the English intrusion
caused alarm on the Spanish frontier, and the governor of Florida
in person led a counter expedition up the coast as far as Chesapeake Bay.   To this day the fate of the Roanoke colony is a
mystery, but light on the matter may yet be shed by the Spanish
archives.

Raleigh's Orinoco expedition.—The discoveries of the Spaniards in Mexico and Peru spurred the Englishman to attempt
to find similar lands of treasure.   A story became current that
in the interior of South America on the upper waters of the
Amazon and the Orinoco was a great kingdom, which contained
a powerful city called Manoa.   It was also believed that in the
interior there was a mountain of sapphire and a land ruled by
female warriors called Amazons.   After the failure of the Roanoke
enterprise, Raleigh became interested in this land of wonders,
and in 1594 sent a vessel to the Guiana coast to obtain information.   The following year Raleigh himself made an exploration
of the delta of the Orinoco and ascended the main stream a considerable distance.   But the city of Manoa proved elusive, supplies ran short, and the expedition returned to England.

READINGS

CABOT

Bourne, E. G., *Spain in America*, 54–61; Channing, Edward, *History of the United States*, I, 33–42; Fiske, John, *Discovery of America*, II, 2–15; Markham, C. R., *Columbus*, 226–233; Olson, J. E., ed., *The Northmen, Columbus and Cabot.*

COMMERCIAL COMPANIES

Cheyney, E. P., *A History of England from the Defeat of the Armada to the Death of Elizabeth*, I, 309–348, 375–422, 433–459; Cunningham, William, *The Growth of English Industry and Commerce in Modern Times—The Mercantile System*, 214–279; Scott, W. R., *The Constitution and Finance of English, Scottish and Irish Joint-Stock Companies to 1720*, II, 3–11, 36–52, 83–89; Tilby, A. W., *The English People Overseas*, I, 38–43.

SEA ROVERS, THE NORTHWEST PASSAGE, AND RALEIGH

Buchan, J., *Sir Walter Ralegh;* Channing, Edward, *History of the United States*, I, 115–140; Cheyney, E. P., *A History of England from the Defeat of the Armada to the Death of Elizabeth*, I, 349–374, 423–459; Corbett, J. S., *Drake and the Tudor Navy; Sir Francis Drake;* Hume, M. A. S., *Sir Walter Ralegh;* Nuttall, Zelia, *New Light on Drake;* Payne, E. J., *Elizabethan Seamen;* Scott, W. R., *The Constitution and Finance of English, Scottish and Irish Joint-Stock Companies to 1720*, II, 76–82, 241–245; Tilby, A. W., *The English People Overseas*, I, 24–38; Woodward, W. H., *A Short History of the Expansion of the British Empire*, 17–63; Wood, W., *Elizabethan Sea-Dogs.*

CHAPTER VI

THE CHESAPEAKE BAY AND INSULAR COLONIES

ENGLAND UNDER THE EARLY STUARTS, 1603–1640

James I.—When James Stuart came to the throne, he had an exalted idea of the kingship, believing that he ruled by divine right. The Tudors had wielded almost absolute power, the privy council overshadowing parliament. James naturally intended to rule in a similar manner, and resented any legislative action which tended to decrease his prerogative. He also stood as a staunch supporter of the English church. His foreign policy was based upon a sincere desire for peace. With this in view he ended the war with Spain and projected a marriage between his son and a Spanish princess. In the latter part of James' reign, when the Thirty Years' War broke out, the king hoped to become the arbiter of Europe. Though he failed in this, he at least had the satisfaction of keeping his country out of war.

Charles I.—The Parliamentarians who had nursed their wrath during the reign of James, soon clashed with his successor. Charles I was a man of staunch self-righteousness, who had little of pliability and much of stubbornness in his nature. His idea of the royal prerogative was fully as exalted as that of his father. From the beginning of the reign, king and parliament clashed. When a war, which broke out with France and Spain, went badly, the unpopularity of the king increased. When he summoned parliament in 1628 to ask for supplies, he found that body unwilling to comply with his demands until he had signed the Petition of Right.

The experience which the king had with parliament determined him to rule without it, and from 1629 to 1640 he carried on a personal government. Acting through his privy council, the king ruled England. His chief difficulty was to secure sufficient revenue to carry on the government. Ancient feudal laws were resurrected and put into force. So long as no extraordinary emergency arose the king was able to carry on the government. During this period the religious controversy was also becoming acute, the tyranny of Laud, the Archbishop of Canterbury, constantly adding fuel to the fire. Puritans and Parliamentarians found a common ground of opposition. When the king attempted to force the English prayer book and church organization on the Scotch Prebysterians, war broke out. Charles found it necessary to summon parliament, whereupon he found religious and political opponents united against him.

THE COLONIAL ADMINISTRATIVE SYSTEM OF THE EARLY STUARTS

Early experiments.—During the reigns of the first two Stuarts a colonial administrative policy was developed. With James I permanent settlements began. They were regarded as dependent upon the crown rather than as an integral part of the state. The king created a Council of Virginia which was to have general control over settlements between 34° and 45° north latitude. But the council was short lived and the privy council soon became the center of the colonial system. The connecting links between the settlers and the crown were the corporations which were granted jurisdiction over more or less definite areas. Both king and parliament claimed to have jurisdiction over the colonies, but the first two Stuarts were able to keep control in their hands.

The privy council in charge.—The charters of the commercial companies could be annulled by the courts in suits brought by the crown. Such was the method followed when the charter of the Virginia Company was revoked; the work of administration then passed into the hands of the privy council. As this council was large and its duties numerous, the actual work was usually done by committees, such a committee being appointed to look after Virginia. Late in the reign of James I the crown also appointed commissioners to examine the state of the colony, and report on a form of government.

Policy of Charles I.—Under Charles I, though the commissioners continued to attend to some business, most of the work of administration devolved upon the privy council. In 1631 the commission was revived, but in 1634 it was superseded by another at whose head was Archbishop Laud. This was made up of the highest officers of church and state, and it was given jurisdiction over all dependencies. Its chief acts required the approval of the crown, and as this could only be obtained through the privy council, it was responsible to that body. A standing committee of the privy council for foreign plantations was also appointed, the membership of this committee and the commission headed by Laud being identical. Sub-committees composed of men of lower rank but who had expert knowledge of colonial affairs were also appointed to assist the higher bodies.

Special administrative bodies.—From time to time special bodies were created for aiding the development of commerce and industry. In 1622 James constituted a council of trade for investigating commerce, shipping, and industry. Charles I, in 1625, created a similar council, but it did not become very active, and soon its duties devolved upon a committee of the privy council, which investigated all phases of economic activity, the regulation of the tobacco industry of Virginia being one of the important subjects which occupied its attention.

THE FOUNDING OF VIRGINIA

Opposition of the Early Stuarts to Spain.—The settled policy of Spain was to maintain a territorial and commercial monopoly in all the lands west of the line of the treaty of Tordesillas. During the reign of Elizabeth, the mariners of England had struck at Spanish commerce and had made unsuccessful attempts at colonization; in the reigns of the first two Stuarts, serious attempts were made by Englishmen to wrest from the Spanish colossus some of his island possessions, and to occupy Guiana and portions of North America. The attitude of James I toward these enterprises depended upon the state of his negotiations with Spain. In 1604 a treaty was signed which brought the long war between the countries to an end. By the treaty the English crown surrendered the right of trade to the Indies. The English mariners snapped their fingers at the treaty and continued to visit the Indies, either running the chance of being taken as pirates, or registering their vessels under the flags of Holland or Savoy. The difficulties besetting this trade led some of the merchants to invest their capital in enterprises of colonization.

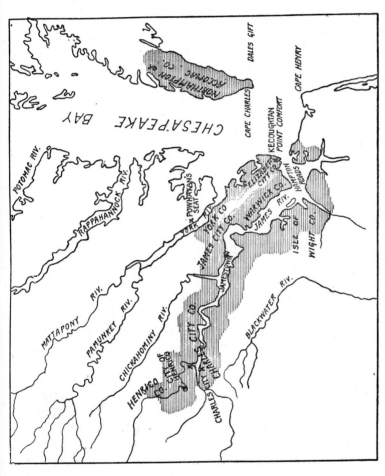

Settlements in Virginia, 1634

The charter of 1606.—Between 1602 and 1606 several voyages were made to America, the most important being that of George Weymouth, who visited the New England coast in 1604; his favorable report greatly stimulated the desire to plant colonies. In April, 1606, a charter was drawn up which provided for two companies; one composed of men from London, familiarly known as the London Company, which was to operate between the thirty-fourth and forty-first degrees of latitude; the other made up of men from Plymouth, Bristol, and Exeter, known as the Plymouth Company, which was to plant colonies between the thirty-eighth and forty-fifth degrees.   Each company was to have control of fifty miles both north and south of its first settlement, a hundred miles out to sea, and a hundred miles inland. Neither was to settle within one hundred miles of the other. Each company was to have a council of thirteen persons, and each was to have the right to mine gold, silver, and copper; the king was to receive one-fifth of all the precious metals and one-fifteenth of the copper.   No import duties were to be levied for seven years.   The charter also provided that the Christian religion was to be spread among the natives.   Colonists who went to the New World were guaranteed all the privileges of Englishmen.

Founding of Jamestown.—In August, 1606, Henry Challons was sent ahead in the *Richard* to select a site for the London Company, but was captured off Florida by a Spanish fleet and taken a prisoner to Seville.   In December, three vessels, which belonged to the Muscovy Company, the *Susan Constant*, the *Godspeed*, and the *Discovery*, sailed for Virginia under the command of Sir Christopher Newport.   They followed the southern route by the Canaries and the West Indies, arriving in Chesapeake Bay in May, 1607.   Of the hundred and twenty colonists who had embarked, sixteen died during the voyage.   Sealed instructions had been sent for the government and management of Virginia.   When opened, they disclosed the names of the members of the council, a body possessed of executive, legislative, and judicial powers, presided over by a president.   A site was to be selected on an island in a navigable river, marshy or heavily wooded ground to be avoided.   Contrary to instructions, the site selected was on a swampy peninsula, located near the mouth of the James River. Near the western end of the peninsula a triangular log fort was laid out. The settlement was in the district known to the Spaniards as Axacan, and not far from the site of the Jesuit mission founded in 1570. While the fortification was being built, Newport explored the James River as far as the site of Richmond. While he was gone, the Indians attacked the fort but were driven off. Besides the fortification, a church and storehouse were erected. In July Newport sailed for England, taking with him worthless specimens of rock which were believed to contain gold.

Early difficulties.—Shortly after the departure of Newport the colonists began to suffer from famine, malaria, and Indian attacks. President Wingfield husbanded the stores left by Newport, an action which angered the settlers, and he was soon deposed. John Smith was sent to secure food from the Indians, and succeeded in obtaining a considerable supply. When Newport returned in January, 1608, he found only forty survivors. During 1608 and 1609 the little settlement was barely able to hold its own. The few additional settlers who came merely offset the ravages of disease and starvation. During this period John Smith appears to have been the chief factor in keeping the colony alive. So precarious had conditions become by May, 1609, that he dispersed the colonists in groups, one being sent to live among the Indians, another to fish at Point Comfort, and a third to obtain oysters. In July a vessel commanded by Samuel Argall arrived with supplies, bringing the news that the first charter had been repealed and a new one granted.

Charter of 1609.—The lack of success in the original venture had caused those interested to make an effort to enlarge the company. The incorporators of the charter of 1609 were fifty-six of the guilds and companies of London, and six hundred and fifty-nine persons, among whom were included twenty-one peers, ninety-six knights, eleven professional men, and fifty-three captains. The new company was to have the land two hundred miles north and two hundred miles south of Point Comfort and stretching from sea to sea west and northwest, and the islands within one hundred miles of the coast. The government was vested in a council, which was given power to appoint its own officers, to make laws for the government of the colony, and to take in new stockholders. The English church was established as the religion of the colony.

The starving time.—In June, 1609, nine vessels commanded by Newport sailed from England with the new governor, Sir Thomas Gates, and about five hundred emigrants. Beset by pestilence and storms, many died on the voyage, about four hundred being landed at Jamestown in August. The vessel carrying the governor was stranded in the Bermudas, and he did not arrive at Jamestown until May, 1610. There he found the colonists in a frightful condition, dissensions among the officers, Indian attacks, disease, and starvation having brought the colony to the brink of destruction. Gates decided to give up the ill-fated attempt, and taking all the settlers on board, sailed down the James River, but met a vessel bearing the news that a new governor, Lord Delaware, had arrived at Point Comfort with supplies and a hundred and fifty emigrants. Gates immediately returned to Jamestown. Of the nine hundred persons who had been landed in Virginia during the first three years, only one hundred and fifty were alive upon the arrival of Delaware.

Spanish resistance.—Spain regarded the Jamestown colony as an intruder, and both Spaniards and Englishmen considered it as a menace to Spain's northern outposts, and to her merchant fleets, which passed close by on their homeward voyage. Dale remarked that the settlement "wyll put such a byt in our ainchent enemyes mouth as wyll curb his hautynes of monarchie." Zúñiga, Spanish ambassador to England, urged that "such a bad project should be uprooted now, while it can be done so easily."

At Jamestown fear of a Spanish attack was almost constant, and Newport sought aid in England lest the "all devouring Spaniard lay his ravenous hands" upon the infant colony. Spanish resistance had already been felt by way of vigorous diplomatic protest and through the capture of the *Richard* in 1606. In 1609 a Spanish expedition was sent to Jamestown under Captain Ecija, commander of the garrison at St. Augustine. On July 24 Ecija entered Chesapeake Bay. Concluding that the settlement was too strong to capture with one small vessel, he withdrew, but on his way down the coast he conferred with the Indian tribes, and sent a delegation of natives overland to spy upon the

English. On Ecija's return to St. Augustine another native delegation was sent to Virginia from Florida by Governor Ybarra. The success of these embassies has been inferred from the Indian massacres at Jamestown in the following winter. Two years later another Spanish expedition was sent to Jamestown. Captures were made on both sides and the episode was followed by a demand at the English settlement for reinforcements.

Zúñiga continued to urge the destruction of the colony, but Philip III temporized, allured by the hope of an English alliance and encouraged by his informants to believe that the struggling colony would fail through misery. Instead of dying out, however, as time went on Virginia waxed stronger, and soon became a base for attacks on Spanish commerce, as had been predicted. The founding of Jamestown in Axacan was the first English nibble at the Spanish mainland possessions, a process which continued for a century and a half.

Delaware's governorship.—Delaware remained in Virginia less than a year, during which period new colonists arrived, the settlement at Jamestown was rebuilt, the Indians were driven from Kecoughtan, and forts Charles and Henry were established at the mouth of the James River. An expedition was also sent to the falls in search of a gold mine, but it found none. Delaware was unable to check the ravages of disease, and during the summer a hundred and fifty died. The governor left the colony in March, 1611, but remained in office until his death in 1618, during which period the government was administered by deputy governors.

Dale's strong hand.—Sir Thomas Dale was left in charge. He was a brusque old soldier who had seen service in the Netherlands, and during his administration, the colony was governed by military law. The men were forced to work like slaves, and those who rebelled were punished with the greatest severity, several captured runaways being burned at the stake. The Indians along the James and York rivers were attacked; Pocahontas, the daughter of Powhatan, was captured, and the hostage was used to force that powerful chief to make peace. Hearing of the French occupation of Acadia, Dale sent Captain Argall to destroy the settlements.

Charter of 1612.—During the administration of Dale, a change was made in the charter, the powers of the council being considerably enlarged. The Bermudas were also placed under its jurisdiction. The rights in the islands, however, were subsequently sold to some of the members of the London Company, who obtained a charter in 1614 under the name of the Somers Island Company.

Change in the management of the company.—Sir Thomas Smythe had been the moving spirit of the company, but in spite of his efforts, the colony had proved a financial failure, and he was willing to let others carry on the enterprise. The central figure in the company after 1618 was Sir Edwin Sandys. Smythe had realized that it was necessary to change the communal form of ownership to one of landed proprietorship, and had issued instructions that fifty acres of land be assigned to every person who would transport one person to the colony. This policy was carried out by Sandys, and the "old colonists" were allowed to obtain larger tracts of land.

House of Burgesses.—In April, 1619, Sir George Yeardley assumed control as governor of Virginia. He brought out instructions by which the inhabitants of each place and plantation were to elect two burgesses, who were to meet at Jamestown in a general assembly. This first representative assembly in America met in the church at Jamestown on July 30. It was composed of the governor, councilors, and twenty-two burgesses. At the first session, the assembly sat in the two-fold capacity of law makers and court of law.

Agricultural development.—The original instructions had provided that the products of labor should belong to the community instead of to the individual, an arrangement by which the slothful profited at the expense of the industrious. During the first season, only four acres were cleared and planted. The insufficiency of the supply of grain made it necessary to depend upon the Indians for maize. In 1608 John Smith succeeded in getting forty acres of land broken, and the following year this was planted to maize. Just before the arrival of Delaware, the attempts at agriculture were abandoned, the colonists relying for subsistence on roots, herbs, nuts, berries, and fish. Delaware immediately set to work to right conditions, the hours of labor being set from six to ten in the morning, and from two to four in the afternoon.

When Dale took charge he forced the men to plant seed and assigned to each a garden. Livestock had been imported, and were allowed to roam at large in the woods. Dale erected a blockhouse on the mainland to protect them, and warned the settlers against letting stock wander. Henrico was selected as the site for another settlement and the town site of seven acres he caused to be fenced in. Other palings back of the settlement were erected and within the fenced areas corn was planted. On the south side of the river fences were built which protected a circuit of twelve miles, the enclosed land being used for a hog range. The lands of the Indians near the mouth of the Appamatox River were seized, fenced, and planted with maize.

In 1612 the cultivation of tobacco began, the first tobacco planter being John Rolfe, who had married Pocahontas. Tobacco soon became the only export, its cultivation absorbing the economic life of the colony. To make certain of the food supply, Dale commanded that no one should be permitted to plant tobacco until he had planted two acres of grain. To encourage industry, Dale allowed some of the "old colonists" to lease three acres. He also put in force a rule that every man with a family who arrived in the colony should be provided with a house free of rent, tools, and livestock, and with subsistence for himself and family for the first year. If he confined himself to the planting of grain and vegetables, he was given twelve acres of fenced land. At the time of Dale's departure in 1616 there were three hundred and fifty inhabitants settled at Henrico, Bermuda, West and Shirley Hundreds, Jamestown, Kecoughtan, and Dale's Gift.

Immigration.—In 1619 twenty negroes were brought into Virginia, the first blacks to be introduced. Up to this time there were few women in the colony, but the company succeeded in sending over several ship-loads of unmarried women. Upon arrival there was a speedy courtship, and the lucky swain gladly paid a hundred and twenty pounds of the best tobacco for the cost of transportation. In general the type of settler was excellent, but in the later years of the company convicted felons and a large number of waifs and vagabonds from the streets of London were sent. The emigrants who had no capital were usually indented servants, the terms of indenture varying from two to seven years.

Growth of large estates.—In this early period began the formation of great estates. The company retained twelve thousand acres for itself. As new officers were created lands were set aside to support them. The treasurer, marshal, and cape merchant were each granted fifteen hundred acres, the physician and secretary five hundred acres each. The large estates were worked by tenants, the number on each estate being fixed by the company. Grants of large tracts were also made to groups of capitalists who agreed to bring out settlers.

The Indian massacre of 1622.—The reaching out for new lands for tobacco culture resulted in encroachment upon the fields of the Indians. Angered by this the Indians suddenly attacked the outlying plantations, killing between three and four hundred persons, nearly one-fourth of the entire population. The planting of the crops was interrupted and a winter of hardship followed. When the Indian maize crop was nearly ripe, the settlers retaliated, almost exterminating the natives along the lower courses of the James and York rivers.

Crown regulation of the tobacco industry.—To free himself from parliamentary control and to regulate industry, James I granted monopolies to private individuals. Royal commissioners were appointed to inspect the tobacco and to prevent smuggling, and planting in England was prohibited. In 1620 the London Company petitioned the king to do away with the tobacco monopoly and as a result the London and Bermuda companies were allowed to import fifty-five thousand pounds annually. The companies immediately attempted to ship Virginia tobacco to Holland; this led to a dispute with the privy council and the matter was discussed in parliament, where Sandys defended the right of free shipment. The dispute was settled by a compromise, by which the companies agreed to ship the entire product to England, and no restriction was placed upon the amount which they might import.

Neither side was entirely pleased with the arrangement and in November, 1622, an agreement was reached by the Lord Treasurer and the companies. The companies were given the sole right for seven years to import tobacco into England and Ireland; they were to pay into the royal exchequer the net proceeds of one-third of all tobacco imported; no tobacco was to be planted in England and Ireland, and a small amount of Spanish tobacco was to be imported for three years. Like previous arrangements, this did not meet with the approval of all, and it was annulled in 1623, the companies being allowed the exclusive right to import tobacco into England and Ireland, except a small amount of Spanish tobacco, and to pay a duty of nine pence a pound.

End of the London Company.—The king had looked with scant favor upon the administration of Sandys, for popular government was not to the liking of James. Friction between the king and the company also added to the royal displeasure. James, who was personally opposed to the use of tobacco, was also trying to please the Spanish court, which made frequent protests against the Virginia enterprise. Internal dissensions also disturbed the company, a group headed by Sir Thomas Smythe being opposed to the Sandys faction. Royal commissioners were appointed to examine the condition of affairs, and as a result of their report, in 1624 the charter of the London Company was annulled, the colony passing under the direct control of the crown.

Increase of population by 1625.—When Charles I came to the throne Virginia contained about twelve hundred inhabitants, of whom nearly five hundred were servants, and about a hundred were children. They were scattered through nineteen settlements, the largest being Elizabeth City, which contained two hundred and fifty-seven inhabitants. Jamestown had thirty-three houses and a population of one hundred and seventy-five.

Population in 1635.—By 1635 the population had increased to five thousand. The country had been divided into shires, which later were called counties. The six counties along the James River contained about four thousand inhabitants; Charles River County on the York River five hundred, and Accomac County on the opposite side of the bay four hundred. By 1640 the population had increased to seven thousand five hundred.

Tobacco lands.—The most desirable lands for tobacco were the bottoms along the streams. Tobacco exhausted the soil rapidly, three years being the usual life of a field. This made it necessary for the planter to take up new lands and increased his desire for larger holdings. Land patents were issued for large tracts, usually of from one hundred to three hundred acres, although many obtained patents for a thousand acres.

Charles I and the tobacco business.—Charles was opposed to the tobacco business, but he realized that it was necessary to the colony. The king favored Virginia by reducing the duty on tobacco and excluding the Spanish leaf from England and Ireland. But in 1627, when parliament had not granted adequate supplies to the crown, he renewed the monopoly. To put it in force, a proclamation was issued which forbade the annual importation of more than fifty thousand pounds of Spanish tobacco, prohibited the growing of the plant in England and Ireland, and made London the only port of entry. As the colonists objected to the monopoly, the king issued another proclamation, which provided that no colonial tobacco should be imported without special license and should be delivered to tobacco commissioners, who were to have the sole right of disposing of the product. The price was to be fixed by agreement between the shippers and commissioners. Efforts were made to have the colony engage in the production of more substantial commodities, the planters being commanded to produce pitch, tar, potash, timber, iron, and salt, to plant vines and grain, and to search for minerals. The efforts of the king, however, were but partially successful, and tobacco remained the great staple. It had also become the medium of exchange, and though attempts were made to introduce a metallic currency, they did not succeed, in spite of the fact that the fluctuating price of the staple made financial transactions difficult.

Harvey's tobacco policy.—In 1630 Governor Harvey commenced his administration. He immediately began to encourage the planting of grain and the raising of stock. The low price of tobacco at this time assisted him, and in 1631 the colony was able to export a large quantity of grain. Efforts were also made to improve the quality of tobacco. A law of the colonial legislature of 1632 provided for five points of inspection. Storehouses were built where inspectors examined the stock and condemned the poorer qualities. The number of plants to be raised by each family was limited to two thousand, and not more than nine

leaves were allowed to be taken from a plant. In 1633 the number
of plants per family was reduced to fifteen hundred. English
merchants trading to the colonies purchased a considerable
amount of tobacco, which they took in exchange for other commodities, for which they charged abnormally high prices. To
right this and to increase the royal revenues, in 1634 the king
again renewed the monopoly. When Governor Harvey attempted
to contract for the crop, an acrimonious debate ensued. This,
coupled with the fact that the governor attempted to assist
Lord Baltimore's colonists, caused the council illegally to depose
the governor.

Continued efforts to enforce the monopoly.—The king continued to make efforts to enforce the monopoly. In 1638 he issued
another proclamation, stating that it was necessary to regulate
tobacco planting, to decide how much was to be imported, and
to handle the product. The colony as usual objected. Owing
to the troublous times in England, the proclamation was not
strictly enforced and much tobacco was sold to other than government agents.

THE FOUNDING OF MARYLAND

Calvert's attempted settlement in Newfoundland.—The northern end of Chesapeake Bay was soon occupied by a rival tobacco
colony, the proprietary province of Lord Baltimore. In 1609
George Calvert became a stockholder of the Virginia Company,
and ten years later was made secretary of state by James I.
His new office gave him an opportunity to begin an independent
colony. In 1620 he bought the southeastern peninsula of Newfoundland from Sir William Vaughan, to whom it had previously
been granted, and the following year sent out a few colonists.
In 1623 the king granted him a charter for his colony, which was
called Avalon. Two years later Calvert resigned the secretary-
ship. In spite of the fact that he had recently become a Catholic,
he was raised to the Irish peerage with the title of Baron of Baltimore. In 1627 he visited Newfoundland with his family, but the
inclemency of the climate convinced him of the undesirability of
Avalon.

Application for land in Virginia.—In 1629 Baltimore applied
for a grant in Virginia, to which colony he immediately proceeded.

There he met with a cold reception and shortly departed for England, where he made every effort to obtain a charter. The Virginians opposed him strongly, but in April, 1632, his suit was successful and the grant was made. George Calvert died

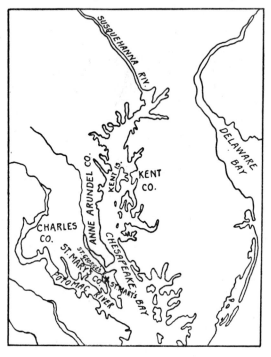

Settlements in Maryland, 1634

the same month and the charter was drawn in the name of his son Cecilius.

The charter.—The province was named Maryland in honor of Henrietta Maria, the wife of Charles I. In general it extended from the fortieth parallel to the southern bank of the Potomac River, and from the meridian which crossed the source of that river to the Atlantic; but the description of boundaries was so indefinite, because of the lack of precise geographical knowledge, that many disputes soon arose over ownership of territory.

The government of Maryland was modeled upon that of the Palatinate of Durham, a feudatory on the border of Scotland in which the bishop had almost absolute powers; but the lord proprietor of Maryland was restricted by several clauses in the charter. He was given the right to ordain, make, and enact laws, provided they were approved by the freemen of the province, or by a majority of them, or by their delegates, and were not contrary to the laws of England. Baltimore was given very large judicial powers, such as the creation of courts and the pardoning of criminals. He was also given the right to make ordinances, provided they did not deprive any person of life, limb, or property. The proprietor could collect taxes, make grants of lands, and create manors, over which the lord of the manor would have the rights of a feudal baron. The proprietor was also given control of ecclesiastical matters such as the power of appointing ministers and founding churches, which were "to be dedicated and consecrated according to the Ecclesiastical Laws of our Kingdom of England." The charter did not prohibit him from permitting the establishment of other churches, an omission which Baltimore used to assist the Catholics. The proprietor's motives, however, were not entirely religious; he no doubt desired to found an asylum for people of his own faith, but he was also a keen business man and desired to increase his worldly goods.

The first settlers.—In October, 1633, Baltimore sent two small vessels, the *Ark* and the *Dove*, to Maryland. On board there were about twenty gentlemen, most of whom were Catholics, and probably two hundred laborers, the majority of whom were Protestants. Among the influential members were the governor, Leonard Calvert, the brother of Lord Baltimore, and the two councilors who were to assist him in the government. Three Jesuit priests accompanied the expedition, which arrived at the mouth of the Potomac in March, 1634. The site for a settlement was selected nine miles up St. George's River, a small stream which flows into the north side of the Potomac near its mouth, the place being named St. Mary's. The location was favorable, for it was surrounded by fields cleared by the Indians. The tribes in the neighborhood had been at war with the Susquehannas, and were glad to sell their lands and move across the Potomac.

Trouble with Virginia.—William Claiborne had been the principal opponent of George Calvert, when he attempted to obtain the charter for Maryland. In 1631 Claiborne had established a settlement on Kent Island in Chesapeake Bay, which fell within the bounds of Maryland. In 1634 Governor Calvert informed Claiborne that he would not molest the settlement, but that the owner of Kent Island must be considered as a tenant of the proprietor. Claiborne laid the matter before the Virginia council, which decided that the Maryland charter infringed upon the rights of Virginia. A miniature war followed which was ended by a decision of the king, who ruled that the Virginia charter of 1609 had become null when the crown took over the colony in 1624, and that Kent Island belonged to Maryland.

Religious, economic, and social life.—The religious life of the colony was greatly influenced by the presence of the Jesuits. Father White and his colleagues labored incessantly to convert the Protestant colonists and to establish missions among the Indians. In 1641 the Catholics made up about one-fourth of the population but included most of the influential families. The economic life of the colony developed much like that of Virginia, although unaccompanied by the great hardships of the James River settlements. Nor did the Indians prove as troublesome, although from 1639 to 1644 an expedition was sent against them each year. Tobacco cultivation became the principal occupation. The plantations developed along the rivers and the shore of the bay, for many years extending but a few miles inland. The manors usually contained from one thousand to two thousand acres, although a few contained five thousand acres or more, the lords of the manors being granted lands in proportion to the number of colonists they provided. Many of the large grants were later divided, and small proprietors increased in number. There was practically no town life, the seat of government containing only a few houses. There were few mills and no factories. Few roads were built, the water courses and the bay affording the principal means of communication.

The government.—Cecilius Calvert never visited the colony, but he appointed all the important officers, who resided in the province. The chief of these was the governor, to whom the proprietor delegated most of his powers. He was at the head of military affairs. As chancellor he was the keeper of the seal and issued patents for land, commissions for office, and other legal documents. As chief magistrate he appointed officers for the preservation of peace and the administration of justice, and had power to issue and enforce ordinances, to establish ports, fairs and markets, to remit fines, and pardon all offenses except high treason. He could summon the legislative assembly, prepare bills for its consideration, assent to the laws, and dissolve the assembly. He also acted as chief justice. Leonard Calvert occupied the position until 1647. Assisting the governor was a council. In 1636 it contained three members, but was gradually increased in size in later years. Before this body the governor brought matters of importance, such as the creation of offices, establishment of courts, granting of pardons, levying of taxes, issuing of ordinances, and military expeditions.

The legislative assembly at first was made up of all the freemen, but as the colonists took up more distant lands, a custom of giving proxies grew up. The first assembly met in 1635, but about all that is known of it is that it attempted to initiate legislation, to which the proprietor objected. The second assembly, which met in 1638, consisted of the governor and council, freemen especially summoned by the governor, freemen present of their own will, and proxies. The governor presented a code approved by the proprietor, but it was rejected by the assembly. The same year the proprietor temporarily yielded the right of initiating legislation, authorizing the governor to consent to laws enacted by the assembly until the proprietor could examine them. In 1639 the local divisions, which were called hundreds, sent representatives. This assembly fixed its own membership, which was to be composed of councilors, persons especially summoned, and burgesses elected in hundreds. The assembly sat at times as a law court, but most of the cases were brought before the governor and his councilors, who acted as associate justices, or before the local courts.

THE BERMUDAS

The Somers Islands Company.—Almost simultaneously with the occupation of the Atlantic seaboard, the English had been establishing vigorous colonies in the islands adjacent to North America. In 1609 a Virginia supply ship commanded by Sir George Somers was wrecked on one of the Bermuda Islands.

Upon his return to England, he interested people in the islands and in 1612 the Somers Islands Company was formed, most of the stockholders being members of the Virginia Company.

Settlement and economic development of the Bermudas.—Settlers were immediately sent out and the colony prospered from the first. In 1614 it contained six hundred persons. Fortifications were built, some tobacco was shipped, and a land survey begun which was completed in 1617. By 1625 the population had increased to between two and three thousand and a larger supply of tobacco was being produced than in Virginia. As in the James River settlements, there was considerable opposition to the government monopoly of tobacco, and in 1628 a petition against it was addressed to the crown. In 1631 the privy council decreed that only a moderate amount of tobacco should be planted, and the company succeeded in getting a complete monopoly of the trade. The low price of tobacco at that time caused the colonists to devote themselves less exclusively to that business, and corn, potatoes, hogs, fowls, and fruit were produced in such quantities that the islands were able to export large amounts to the colonies on the mainland. The cedar forests also began to be utilized for ship-building. With the growth of the mainland colonies, the Bermudas became of relatively less economic importance, but they continued to be considered an important naval base.

Representative government.—The Bermudas were the second English colony to receive representative government. Besides the governor and council there was a general assembly, the first being held but a year after the establishment of the Virginia house of burgesses.

GUIANA

For a hundred years the Caribbean had been a Spanish sea. Hardy English mariners had frequently penetrated it, but always at their peril, and they had never seriously injured the Spanish colossus. To gain a foothold on its shores and to appropriate a portion of the commerce of tropical America became powerful forces in English activities.

Expeditions.—During the closing years of the reign of Elizabeth, many English ships visited the coast of Venezuela to procure salt, and after the treaty of 1604 with Spain, to obtain

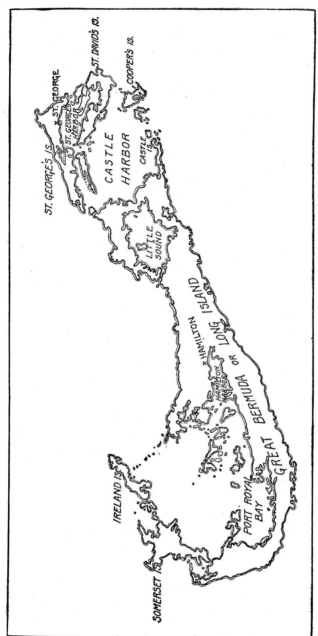

The Bermudas

131

tobacco. Several attempts were also made to explore and colonize Guiana. In 1604 Captain Charles Lea planted a colony on the Wyapoco, but in two years abandoned the enterprise. During 1606–1607 Sir Thomas Roe traded along the Guiana coast and explored the swamps of the Cuyuni and Wyapoco. In 1608 Robert Harcourt and two associates received a patent to lands between the Amazon and Essequibo rivers. Harcourt with ninety-seven men landed in Guiana, but after a sojourn of three years he returned to England. Part of the settlers remained and scattered among the Indians. Harcourt attempted to obtain more capital, and in 1616 another expedition was sent out but without success.

Raleigh's last attempt.—Since the first year of the reign of James I, Raleigh had been imprisoned on a charge of conspiring against the king. But in 1616 he was released, and having obtained a commission as admiral, sailed for Guiana the following year with a fleet of fourteen vessels. Attacked by the Spaniards, he lost several vessels and returned to England, where, upon complaint of the Spanish ambassador, Gondomar, he was again imprisoned and soon after executed.

North's expedition.—In 1620 an attempt was made to reorganize Raleigh's company, and Captain Roger North was sent with one hundred and twenty men to Guiana, where they joined the remnant of Harcourt's colonists. But the attempt again failed because of opposition of the Spanish ambassador.

THE LESSER ANTILLES

The English occupation.—In a great half circle at the eastern end of the Caribbean are the Lesser Antilles. After the failures on the South American coast, the English grasped these outposts of the tropics and, side by side with the French, were soon firmly established across one of the principal highways of Spanish commerce. In 1623 St. Christopher was temporarily occupied and was actually settled in 1625. The same year (1625) Sir William Courten started the first colony in Barbados. In 1627 Lord Carlisle received a grant which covered the Caribbees, and the following year the Earl of Pembroke and Montgomery also obtained rights to Trinidad, Tobago, and Barbados. In the contest between the claimants Carlisle won. He ejected Courten's settlers and established his own colonists. In 1628 Nevis was occupied. The following year the settlers on St. Christopher and Nevis were evicted by the Spaniards, but upon the retirement of the fleet the colonists returned to their plantations. In 1632 settlements were made on Antigua and Montserrat. As in the Bermudas, tobacco became the leading crop, but later the production of sugar cane superseded it. Barbados soon contained 6,000 inhabitants and in 1639, when Virginia had a total population of about 7000, there were 20,000 planters in the islands governed by Carlisle. In the Lesser Antilles the proprietary form of government prevailed for half a century.

THE PROVIDENCE ISLAND COMPANY

The Puritan leaders.—During the great struggle between king and parliament, several of the merchant princes were on the Puritan side. One of the most powerful of these was Robert Rich, Lord Warwick. He had been an active member of the Virginia and Somers Islands companies, of the Guinea and Guiana companies, and of the Council of New England. Closely associated with Warwick were Lord Saye and Sele, Lord Brooke, Sir Nathaniel Rich, and John Pym. As the parliamentary contest increased in intensity, these leaders decided to plant a Puritan colony in the Caribbean.

The Providence Island Company.—The site selected was on one of the Mosquito Islands off the coast of Nicaragua. In 1629 a company was formed which was granted the greater part of the Caribbean Sea, from Haiti to the coast of Venezuela and to the mainland of Central America. Besides Jamaica, then in the possession of Spain, the Caymán Islands fell within these limits. The English fleet which was sent out in 1630 temporarily occupied Tortuga, where colonists from Nevis had recently arrived, and the company asked that this island be included in the patent. The request was granted, but the English were able to hold the island only until 1635 when they were driven out by the Spaniards. The islands along the Mosquito coast were occupied by the company, and a project was formed to colonize the mainland. In 1635 Providence Island was unsuccessfully attacked by a Spanish fleet, but in 1641 the Spaniards succeeded in overcoming the colony, thus for the time ending English operations on the Central American coast.

READINGS

VIRGINIA

Becker, Carl, *The Beginnings of the American People*, pp. 65–80; Beer, G. L., *The Origins of the British Colonial System*, 78–175; Brown, Alexander, *Genesis of the United States; The First Republic in America;* Bruce, P. A., *Economic History of Virginia in the Seventeenth Century*, I, 189–330; *Institutional History of Virginia in the Seventeenth Century*, II, 229–262; Channing, Edward, *History of the United States*, I, 143–224; Doyle, J. A., *English Colonies in America*, I, 101–184; Eggleston, Edward, *The Beginners of a Nation*, 25–97; Fiske, John, *Old Virginia and her Neighbors*, I, 40–222; Hamilton, P. J., *Colonization of the South*, 55–119; MacDonald, William, *Select Charters Illustrative of American History*, 1–23; Osgood, H. L., *The American Colonies in the Seventeenth Century*, I, 23–97; Scott, W. R., *The Constitution and Finance of English, Scottish, and Irish Joint-Stock Companies to 1720*, II, 246–289; Tyler, L. G., *England in America*, 34–103; Tyler, L. G., ed., *Narratives of Early Virginia;* Wertenbaker, T. J., *Virginia under the Stuarts*, 1–84; Johnston, Mary, *Pioneers of the Old South;* Flippin, P. S., *The Royal Government in Virginia, 1624–1775.*

MARYLAND

Brown, W. H., *Maryland*, 1–50; Channing, Edward, *History of the United States*, I, 241–268; Doyle, J. A., *English Colonies in America*, I, 275–296; Eggleston, Edward, *Beginners of a Nation*, 220–257; Fiske, John, *Old Virginia and her Neighbors*, I, 255–275; Hall, C. C., ed., *Narratives of Early Maryland;* MacDonald, William, *Select Charters*, 53–59; Mereness, N. D., *Maryland as a Proprietary Province;* Osgood, H. L., *The American Colonies in the Seventeenth Century*, II, 58–79; Tyler, L. G., *England in America*, 118–132.

THE BERMUDAS AND THE CARIBBEAN

Beer, G. L., *The Origins of the British Colonial System*, 12–20; Cunningham, William, *The Growth of English Industry and Commerce in Modern Times*, I, 331–339; Lucas, C. P., *A Historical Geography of the British Colonies*, II, 5–14, 43–50; Newton, A. P., *The Colonizing Activities of the English Puritans*, 13–282; Scott, W. R., *The Constitution and Finance of English, Scottish, and Irish Joint-Stock Companies to 1720*, II, 259–299, 327–337; Tilby, A. W., *Britain in the Tropics*, 44–50.

CHAPTER VII

THE BEGINNINGS OF NEW ENGLAND

THE PURITAN MOVEMENT IN ENGLAND

The Puritans.—While the planting of colonies on the shores of Chesapeake Bay and on the Caribbean islands was in progress, other settlements were being formed in New England by English Separatists and Puritans. By the beginning of the reign of Elizabeth the Anglican church was firmly established, but it was not long before groups within the church began to show dissatisfaction. At first protests were made against some of the ceremonies and formulas of the service. After 1570 the Puritans, as they were derisively called, began to object to the episcopal form of government and to advocate the Presbyterian or Calvinistic system, which was based upon the idea of a representative form of church government. During the later years of the reign the Puritans laid more and more stress on morals. They believed that life should be sternly ascetic, that the Sabbath should be kept strictly, and that pleasures and extravagance should be suppressed.

The Independents.—Most of the Puritans had no wish to withdraw from the church, but desired to reform it. A more radical group, however, who became known as Independents, looked upon the national church as an unholy institution contrary to scripture. They wished to reëstablish the church as it was believed to be in the days of the Apostles. There were several groups of Independents or Separatists, the various groups being named after their leaders, the followers of Robert Brown being known as Brownists, those of Henry Barrow as Barrowists. They met in small groups which were called conventicles. The English church, through the Court of High Commission, proceeded with considerable severity against the Puritans, whom they attempted to make conform, but against the Separatists they showed no mercy, breaking up the conventicles, imprisoning many, and hanging some of the leaders.

James I and the Non-Conformists.—Soon after James I became king, the Puritans presented a petition asking for changes in the church. The king called the Hampton Court Conference that he might hear the views of the various parties. James soon found that many of the Puritans believed in presbyteries, a form of government with which he had had unpleasant experiences in Scotland, and he angrily ended the conference. Shortly afterward, because of the so-called "Gunpowder Plot," the king became convinced that he was personally in danger. From this time on he supported the Anglican church. Severe laws were passed against the Catholics, and the laws against Non-Conformists were enforced with greater vigor.

PLYMOUTH COLONY

Failures of the Plymouth Company.—The Plymouth Company, which received its charter in 1606, took immediate measures to occupy its territories. In that year two unsuccessful attempts were made to found colonies. The information brought back, however, so interested the company that another expedition was fitted out the following year. Colonists were landed at the mouth of the Kennebec River; but great hardships were experienced during the winter, and in the spring the discouraged settlers abandoned the enterprise.

Activity on the New England Coast, 1607-1619.—No successful settlement in New England was made until 1620, but in the meantime the coast was frequently visited. In 1613 Captain Argall attacked the French settlements at Mount Desert, Port Royal, and St. Croix. The following year John Smith explored and mapped the New England coast. In 1615 he was made Admiral of New England by the Plymouth Company and he attempted to found a colony, but it proved a failure. Several fishing and trading voyages were also made under the direction of Sir Ferdinando Gorges, an influential member of the Plymouth Company.

The Council for New England.—The failure of the company to plant a colony led Gorges and others who were still interested to petition for a new charter; on November 13, 1620, the document passed the seals incorporating the Council for New England, which was given jurisdiction over the territory from 40° to 48° north latitude.

Origin of the Pilgrims.—The first permanent settlement in New England was not the work of the Council, but of a group of Independents. Separatist congregations were located at Scrooby, Gainsborough, and Austerfield, villages in Nottinghamshire, Lincolnshire, and Yorkshire. In the Scrooby congregation were three men of unusual ability, Pastor John Robinson, Elder William Brewster, and William Bradford. To avoid persecution many Separatists had migrated to Amsterdam, and there in 1608 Robinson and his followers gathered, removing later to Leyden. From time to time a few others joined them, among the late comers being John Carver and Miles Standish. Most of the congregation found the making of a livelihood among the Dutch extremely difficult. In spite of this, some of them enrolled in the University of Leyden and Brewster set up a printing press from which appeared several theological works.

Reasons for removal from Holland.—By 1617 the leaders determined to seek new lands. Bradford in his *History of Plymouth Plantation* gives the following reasons for removal: (1) Daily life was so hard in Holland that few cared to emigrate there and in consequence the congregation did not grow; (2) many were growing old, and there was fear that the congregation would soon break up; (3) life was too hard for the children, and in addition many were slipping away, some becoming soldiers and sailors; it was also found that the morals of the young were endangered in the gay city of Leyden; (4) it was hoped to spread the gospel in remote lands. In addition, intermarriage with the Dutch had begun and it was evident that the little community would soon lose its English identity.

Removal to America.—Guiana, New Netherlands, and Virginia were discussed as possible places for settlement, the last named being the final choice. A patent was obtained from the Virginia Company, and John Carver was made governor. Seven thousand pounds were raised by Thomas Weston and other merchant adventurers to back the enterprise. A portion of the Leyden congregation sailed for England, and at Southampton met with others from London, who had determined to join them. The company, including Carver, Brewster, Bradford, and Standish, left England in the *Mayflower* and the *Speedwell*, but the latter proving unseaworthy, about twenty abandoned the enterprise. The *Mayflower* arrived at Cape Cod in November, 1620.

The Mayflower Compact.—As the region was outside of the jurisdiction of the Virginia Company, the colonists on their own initiative drew up what is known as the Mayflower Compact, by which they combined into a civil body politic, and agreed to enact such just and equitable laws as were for the general welfare of the colony. After the signing of the compact, Governor Carver was confirmed in his office. The Mayflower Compact marks the origin of the English colony based upon a social compact the basis of which was the will of the colonists rather than that of the sovereign. Of a similar nature were Rhode Island, Connecticut, New Haven, and New Hampshire in their inception, and in the latter half of the eighteenth century, when the frontiersman had crossed the mountains and freed himself from the restraints of the tidewater governments, the social compact became the basis of western state making.

Settlement at Plymouth.—Exploring parties were sent along the shores of Massachusetts Bay, and Plymouth was selected as the site for the colony, but the classic story of the landing on Plymouth Rock is now known to be only a romance. From the first settlers suffered exceedingly. Bradford describes the situation as follows: "But that which was most sadd and lamentable was, that in 2. or 3. moneths time halfe of their company dyed, espetialy in Jan: and February, being the depth of winter, and wanting houses and other comforts; being infected with the scurvie and other diseases . . . ; so as ther dyed some times 2. or 3. of a day, in the foresaid time; that of 100 and odd persons, scarce 50. remained. And of these in the time of most distres, ther was but 6. or 7. sound persons."

Indians, fur trade and maize.—The region which the Pilgrims had selected for their first settlement was almost deserted by the Indians, many of them having been swept away by a plague. At some distance to the southward lived the Wampanoags, whose chief was Massasoit. Shortly after the arrival of the Pilgrims an Indian named Squanto, who previously had been carried to Europe by one of Smith's captains, appeared in the settlement. Squanto prevailed upon Massasoit to come to Plymouth, where a treaty of peace was made which lasted for fifty years. This led to the opening of a fur trade, which became the chief source of wealth for the colony. Squanto proved to be of great service, teaching the settlers the planting of maize and instructing them in hunting and fishing. Carver died in the spring of 1621, and William Bradford was elected governor, a position which he held almost continually until 1657. In the fall the *Fortune*, poorly provisioned, arrived with thirty-five settlers, an influx which led to another winter of hardship. The boat also brought a patent from the Council for New England.

" Weston's rude fellows."—In May, 1622, sixty-seven persons arrived, having been sent out by Thomas Weston, who had obtained a grant from the Council for New England. Later they moved to Wessagusset, where they lived a turbulent life. In 1623 the Indians to the northward planned to exterminate the Wessagusset settlers, who appealed to Plymouth for aid. Captain Miles Standish led a force against the Indians, who were so severely punished that peace was established.

Expansion of Plymouth.—At first the wealth of the colony was held in a common stock. Bradford determined to assign a tract of land to each family, an experiment which greatly stimulated industry. From this time the colonists were never in danger of starvation, and in a few years they were able to pay off their debts to the English merchants. To increase the fur trade, posts were established on Buzzard's Bay, on the Kennebec River, at Penobscot, and at Machias Bay, the two latter posts, however, being soon broken up by the French. A group of traders who established themselves at Merry Mount under Thomas Morton shocked the austere people of Plymouth, who in 1628 broke up Morton's establishment. A trade was opened with the Dutch, and in 1636 a fur trading post was established on the Connecticut River. In 1624 there were one hundred and eighty settlers in the Plymouth colony, and in 1630 only three hundred; but after that the number increased rapidly, by 1642 the population being three thousand.

Government of the colony.—The first governor exercised executive and judicial powers, and the same powers were vested in Bradford and an assistant. The number of assistants was increased in 1624 to five and in 1633 to seven. The freemen composed the legislative body, which was called the General Court, one of its sessions being devoted annually to the election of officers. In 1638 a representative system was introduced, Plymouth being allowed four delegates and other towns two each. Legally every freeman could vote, but in practice the suffrage was restricted to church members. Pastors and elders were elected by the adult males of each congregation, and attendance at church meetings was vigorously enforced.

COLONIZING ACTIVITIES ON THE NEW ENGLAND COAST

Land grants and settlements.—While Plymouth was developing, the Council for New England was attempting to settle the New England coast. The region from the Bay of Fundy to Narragansett Bay was divided among twenty patentees. Captain John Mason and Sir Ferdinando Gorges procured a patent to lands between the Kennebec and Merrimac rivers; Mason received lands between Salem and the Merrimac; Sir Robert Gorges ten miles of coast lands along "the north east side of Boston Bay," and Lord Sheffield and Lord Edward Gorges extensive tracts to the south of Sir Robert Gorges's lands. Lord Warwick also received lands on Massachusetts Bay. The grantees obtained the assistance of English merchants, who, in 1623 established small settlements at Portsmouth and Dover, within the present state of New Hampshire, and at Saco Bay, Monhegan Island, and Casco Bay, within the modern state of Maine. Sir Robert Gorges made an unsuccessful attempt to plant a settlement at Weymouth, and a group of Dorchester merchants planted a settlement on Cape Ann.

Lyford, Oldham, and Morton.—In 1624 a group of colonists, including a minister named John Lyford, arrived at Plymouth. There he joined with John Oldham to get control of the government. They were banished from the colony and went to Weymouth, where they joined with Roger Conant and others, and moved to Nantasket. The following year, on the invitation of the Dorchester men, Lyford, Conant, and Oldham moved to Cape Ann. This angered the Plymouth people, who had obtained a tract on Cape Ann from Lord Sheffield. Difficulties over fishing rights soon developed, and Miles Standish was sent to the cape with a troop of soldiers. A compromise was effected, but the Plymouth men soon abandoned the enterprise. The Dorchester men found little profit in the business and in 1626 most of them departed. Oldham returned to Plymouth. Conant and three others remained, but shortly afterward removed to Naumkeag, the modern Salem. In 1625 a settlement was established a little north of Weymouth, where Thomas Morton became the leader. He established the Episcopalian service, set up a May-pole which became the scene of gaiety, and engaged in the fur trade, but Plymouth men soon broke up the settlement.

The Canada and Laconia companies.—When war broke out between England and France in 1628, Sir Ferdinando Gorges and Captain John Mason organized the Canada Company to conquer the French fur-trading colonies of Acadia and Canada, and in 1629 a fleet under Captain Kirke captured the French colonies, but in 1632 they were restored to France. The Maine proprietors also attempted to tap the fur trade of the Lake Champlain region and accordingly, in 1629, obtained a grant embracing the lake country and a thousand acres of sea coast land, the territory being known as Laconia. A governor was appointed and attempts made to penetrate the fur country in the interior, but the efforts proved abortive.

THE MASSACHUSETTS BAY COLONY

Rev. John White's association.—The Reverend John White of Dorchester interested people in Lincolnshire and London, and formed an association, which, through the assistance of Warwick, in 1628 procured a patent for lands between the parallel which passed three miles north of the source of the Merrimac to that which passed three miles south of the head of the Charles River, and from the Atlantic to the Pacific. In September, 1628, John Endicott with about fifty followers arrived at Salem.

The Massachusetts Bay Company.—Trouble for the new association was brewing in England. Members of the Gorges family attempted to interfere with the new settlement, and Morton and Oldham joined with them. The new association, however, succeeded in defeating the former patentees, and in March, 1629, a royal charter was obtained which confirmed the grant made to Endicott and his partners. The new corporation was called the

"Governor and Company of Massachusetts Bay in New England." The administration was placed in the hands of a governor, deputy governor, and eighteen assistants, who were to be elected annually by the freemen or members of the corporation. Four times a year the officers and freemen were to meet in a general court at which new freemen might be admitted to membership, subordinate officers might be appointed, and laws and ordinances enacted. On June 27, 1629, five ships with about four hundred settlers arrived at Salem.

The Cambridge agreement.—At this time Laud had begun his persecution of the Puritans and the king had started on his career of personal government. Under these circumstances the Puritan leaders looked to the New World for an asylum. John Winthrop, a wealthy gentleman of Groton in Suffolk, who had been a follower of Warwick in parliament, now became interested in the Massachusetts enterprise. Winthrop and several prominent men of Cambridge met and agreed to emigrate to New England provided the charter and government might be legally transferred to America. The company decided to transfer the government. Winthrop was made governor, and Thomas Dudley deputy governor.

The " Great Migration."—In June, 1630, eleven ships anchored at Salem and before the winter six more arrived, bringing in all over a thousand people. They found Endicott's followers in a deplorable condition. About one-fourth had died during the previous winter; many of the survivors were sick and there was a shortage of provisions. The new arrivals had brought only a limited supply and for the first year famine stalked in the land. The dreary prospect caused about a hundred of the newcomers to return immediately to England. Winthrop and most of his followers removed to Charlestown. By December two hundred had died. Believing that the inadequate water supply at Charlestown was the main cause of sickness, the settlers began to scatter, and before the new year settlements had been started at Dorchester, Boston, Watertown, Roxbury, Mystic, and Lynn.

The hardships endured by the followers of Endicott and Winthrop prevented many from coming during 1631 and 1632, but in 1633 a new wave of migration set in. Laud became archbishop in that year and began a rigorous enforcement of the laws against nonconformists. Many ministers with their congregations in consequence migrated. By the end of 1634 there were nearly four thousand settlers in Massachusetts. The migration continued until the outbreak of war in 1642, by which time the population had increased to about sixteen thousand.

The form of government.—The charter vested the government in the governor, deputy governor, assistants, and freemen of the company but not more than twelve of the colonists were legally eligible to membership in the general court. Before disembarking this little group decided that each of the assistants should exercise the same powers as an English justice of the peace. The colony was to be governed by the common law of England, which was to be supplemented by biblical law. At the first general court, held at Boston, October 19, 1630, one hundred and nine men applied for admission as freemen of the corporation. This Winthrop and his associates hesitated to grant, but finally they agreed to admit them, allowing them to elect assistants, but not to hold office. It was also provided that in future no person should be admitted as a freeman unless a member of some church within the colony. Though Winthrop and his followers at first claimed to be members of the Church of England, the necessities of the frontier soon asserted themselves, and each community became a political, economic, and a religious unit.

The New England towns.—The New England towns were based upon the idea of group settlement and wherever New Englanders migrated the local organization was reproduced. As Professor Osgood says, "The settlement of a town normally began with the laying out of a village plot and the assignment of home lots. This to an extent determined the location of highways, of the village common, and of some of the outlying fields. On or near the common the church was built, and in not a few cases the site that was chosen for this building went far toward determining the entire lay-out of the town. The idea of a home lot was a plot of ground for a dwelling-house and outbuildings, for a dooryard and garden, and usually also an enclosure for feeding cattle and raising corn."

The first settlers located wherever they pleased, but the Massachusetts general court soon took over the superintendence of town founding and prescribed more or less definitely the bound-

aries of each town. The grants were made in tracts of thirty-six
square miles or more. Within a town were many common fields

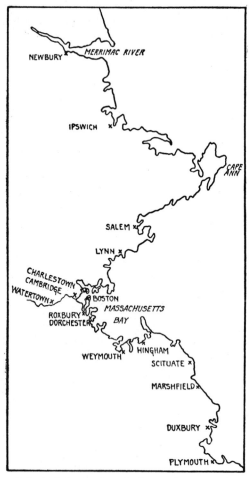

Principal Settlements in Massachusetts, 1630

which were handled by associated proprietors. The fields were
surrounded by common fences and were cultivated by a joint system. The herds were also held in common. The original grantees and their legal heirs or successors made up the commoners
or proprietors. Originally the town and the proprietors were

approximately the same. An important function of the town
meeting was in allotting land. Soon each community began to
receive newcomers who were freemen but not proprietors. At
first the proprietors were in control, but as the freemen increased
in number frequent struggles occurred over the arrangement of
town lands.

The meeting house was the center of local life. There the town
meeting was held and there the people repaired on the Sabbath.
In early days the military stores and equipment were usually
kept in the edifice and the men attended service with arms in
hand. The town constructed and took care of the meeting
house and the minister was supported by taxation. One of the
early acts of each town was to establish a school, the meeting
house frequently being used as a school-house.

A representative system introduced.—The governor and assistants soon found their power challenged. In 1632 a tax was
voted for fortifying Newtown, the modern Cambridge. The tax
caused considerable grumbling, and the general court decided
that, in future, the governor and assistants should be advised
in matters of taxation by two delegates from each town, and
that all magistrates should be elected by the entire body of freemen. In 1634 a committee of two freemen from each town demanded larger rights. The result was a representative system,
each town sending representatives according to its size to meet
with the general court. This system was in no sense a popular
government, the franchise continuing to be restricted to a limited number of church members, the leaders of whom were distinctly aristocratic.

The struggle with Laud.—The patentees who had been deprived of their rights found a ready listener in Archbishop Laud,
who disliked the Puritan commonwealth growing so lustily on
the shores of Massachusetts Bay. Grounds for accusation were
found in the fact that the Massachusetts magistrates expelled
those who disagreed with their religious ideas. Complaints were
filed with the privy council by Gorges and Mason, but a committee of the council in 1633 made a report which was favorable
to the colony. In 1634 the attack was renewed, and this time
with better success, for the king appointed the Commission for
Foreign Plantations, headed by Laud, to take over the general

supervision of all the colonies.   Immediately a demand was made
for the charter of the Massachusetts Bay Colony.   Governor
Dudley and the assistants replied that the charter could not be
returned except by order of the general court, which was not in
session.   They immediately fortified Castle Island, Dorchester,
and Charlestown.

In 1635 the coast of New England was reapportioned, Sir
Ferdinando Gorges receiving the lands in Maine between the
Penobscot and the Piscataqua, Mason receiving New Hampshire
and northern Massachusetts as far as Cape Ann, and Lord Edward
Gorges from Cape Ann to Narragansett Bay.   The same year the
Council for New England resigned its charter, and the king decided to seize the charter of the Massachusetts Bay Company.
The pecuniary difficulties of the king, the destruction of a boat
which was built by Mason and Gorges, and the death of Mason
combined to help the colony.   Though the charter was again
demanded in 1638 by the lord commissioners, the general court
refused to recognize the order, and the increasing difficulties of
the king made it possible for the Massachusetts authorities to
continue their independent course.

EXPANSION OF THE MASSACHUSETTS BAY COLONY

RHODE ISLAND

Roger Williams.—The power of the Massachusetts magistrates
was exercised to maintain the ideal of a biblical commonwealth,
whose principles were expounded by John Cotton of the Boston
church.   Those who did not agree were in danger.   Among the
dissenters was Roger Williams, a brilliant young student from
Cambridge, who arrived at Boston in 1631, where he was invited
to become one of the ministers.   He refused to commune with
those who had not broken with the English church and repaired
to Salem where he was invited to become the minister, but the
general court prevented his ordination.   Williams soon departed
for Plymouth, where he devoted much time to the study of the
Indians.   He concluded that the title to land belonged to the
natives and that the king had no right to grant it away, a view
which somewhat disturbed Brewster and Bradford.

He returned to Salem where, during the illness of Skelton, the pastor, he occasionally preached; when Skelton died, **Williams** became the teacher of the organization. In his sermons he argued that church and state should be separate, and denied the right of the magistrates to regulate churches. He also considered it a sin to follow the forms of the established church. When the colony was attacked by Laud, the general court ordered that a new oath of fidelity be taken. Williams objected to enforced oaths, as he thought that they obliged wicked men to perform a religious act, thus invading the freedom of the soul.

Providence plantation.—To punish Salem for harboring Williams, title to its lands on Marble Neck was refused by the general court and the town was denied the right of representation. Endicott yielded but Williams remained obdurate. In a letter to the churches he protested against the arbitrary act. Williams was summoned before the magistrates and in October, 1635, was sentenced to banishment. The sentence was not immediately enforced and at Salem he continued to be the center of a group of Separatists, who proposed to remove in the spring to the shores of Narragansett Bay. This again alarmed the magistrates, and they decided to send Williams to England. Hearing of the project, he fled from his persecutors and found refuge among the Narragansett Indians. He was warned away from the territory of Plymouth, and in June, 1636, settled at Providence, where he soon had a considerable following, this being the first settlement in Rhode Island.

Title to the land was obtained from the Indians. As the Providence people were outside of any special jurisdiction, they established a government on democratic lines. Church and state were kept separate, no one being forced to support religion. In 1640 an agreement was drawn up which served as a form of government for several years. The governing body was composed of five men called disposers, who were chosen four times in each year. They disposed of the land and managed the common stock. The freeholders retained the right to ratify or disavow, in general meetings, the acts of the disposers. There was a lack of a strong executive and judiciary. Disputes were usually settled by arbitration, but as there was no authority to enforce the settlement, disorders frequently occurred.

Anne Hutchinson.—No sooner had Williams been driven from Massachusetts Bay Colony than a second controversy shook the commonwealth. In the congregation of John Cotton was Mrs. Anne Hutchinson. She became popular by ministering to the sick, and began to hold meetings for women, where the sermons were discussed. Mrs. Hutchinson assumed the roll of teacher, discussing the questions of "a covenant of works" and "a covenant of grace." By the covenant of works she referred to the practice of the Catholic church, which considered penance, confession, and pilgrimages as means of salvation. By a covenant of grace she meant that condition of mind of Protestant Christians which found peace in the thought of the holiness of Christ. She believed that the divine spirit existed in every true Christian. John Cotton and her brother-in-law, John Wheelwright, were held up as examples of those who lived in the covenant of grace. To many of the Boston leaders it seemed as if Mrs. Hutchinson claimed to be inspired, and they feared that her teachings would endanger the authority of the church.

The Boston congregation split into two factions. In Mrs. Hutchinson's party was Governor Harry Vane. On the other side were John Winthrop and the pastor, John Wilson. Cotton attempted to remain neutral but favored the Hutchinsonian party. The question soon became a bitter political quarrel between Winthrop and Vane. At the election in 1637 Vane was defeated. Without the support of the chief executive the followers of Mrs. Hutchinson soon lost power. A synod of ministers was held at Cambridge to root out the heresies. Cotton succeeded in making his peace with the magistrates, but Wheelwright was banished, as was Mrs. Hutchinson. She was allowed to remain in the colony during the winter, but early in the spring of 1638 Winthrop ordered her to depart.

Settlements on Rhode Island.—She found a temporary asylum at Providence, but soon went to the island of Aquidneck, afterward called Rhode Island, where she joined her husband and some of her friends. The little group of nineteen settlers constituted themselves a body politic, electing William Coddington chief magistrate. Many emigrants joined the people of Portsmouth and in 1639 a new settlement was founded at Newport.

SETTLEMENTS IN THE CONNECTICUT VALLEY

Early claimants.—One of the patentees who had received lands from the Council of New England was the Earl of Warwick, whose grant covered a large part of the Connecticut Valley. In 1631 he transferred his rights to Lord Saye and Sele, Lord Brooke and others, who contemplated founding a Puritan colony, but for several years they did nothing to settle their domain. In 1633 the Dutch erected a fort where Hartford now stands, and shortly afterward men from Plymouth built a trading post ten miles farther up the river. In 1635 the English patentees, wearied with the Providence Island project, sent out settlers under John Winthrop, Jr., who erected Fort Saybrook at the mouth of the river. Scarcely were the cannon in place when a Dutch vessel appeared, but finding the English strongly posted, the Dutch made no attempt to take possession.

The migration of 1635-36.—A more important movement came from Massachusetts. Congregations from Watertown, Dorchester, and Cambridge, desiring better lands, migrated to the rich Connecticut Valley. The first Dorchester men arrived at Windsor in the summer of 1635. In June, 1636, the Rev. Thomas Hooker led the Cambridge people to Hartford, the rest of the Dorchester congregation joined those already at Windsor, and the people of Watertown settled at Wethersfield. By the end of 1636 eight hundred people were living in the three towns. Another congregation from Roxbury settled at Springfield.

The Pequot War.—The Pequot Indians saw with chagrin the increasing numbers of the whites. The settlers also angered them by purchasing lands from the Mohegans, and ignoring the Pequot chiefs. In 1633 the Pequots had murdered a Virginia sea-captain named Stone, and Governor Winthrop had inquired concerning the homicide. In 1634, fearing the Dutch and the Narragansetts, the Pequots had sought an alliance with Massachusetts Bay Colony. As a price of forgiveness for Stone's murder and for protection, Winthrop demanded heavy tribute. In 1636 John Oldham, who had come to collect the tribute, was murdered at Block Island. Though the Pequots were probably not guilty, Endicott led a force against them, destroying several wigwams and seizing considerable maize. Angered by the raid,

the Pequots attempted to form an alliance with the Narragansetts, but Williams prevented it, and in the ensuing war Mohegans
and Narragansetts fought on the white man's side. In the spring
of 1637 Pequots attacked Wethersfield. A general court was
immediately convened at Hartford to take measures for protection, and an expedition was sent against the Pequot fort on the
Mystic River, where the defenders were exterminated. Another
stronghold to the westward was also destroyed. A remnant of
the tribe was wiped out near New Haven by Connecticut and
Massachusetts troops and the captives were made slaves, some
being retained in New England, others being shipped to the West
Indies. The Indian menace was thus removed and the settlers
were free to push farther into the wilderness.

" The Fundamental Orders."—In 1639 Hartford, Windsor,
and Wethersfield formed a constitution, which provided that the
freemen were to hold two general meetings each year. At one
of these meetings the governor and assistants were elected, who,
with four representatives from each town, were to make up a general court with legislative and judicial powers.

New Haven.—The successful issue of the Pequot War opened
the Connecticut Valley to another important migration. This
was led by Rev. John Davenport and Theophilus Eaton, who
had come to New England to plant a colony on purely theocratic
lines. In 1638 they founded New Haven, and the following year
drew up a form of government. Citizenship was restricted to
church membership and an annual general court of freemen was
to elect a governor and assistants, who were to conduct all
governmental affairs, the only restriction on their authority being the law of Moses. Guilford, Milford, and Stamford sprang
up in the neighborhood, and each adopted a similar form of
government.

Settlement of Long Island.—English settlements also appeared
on Long Island. In 1632 Sir Edmund Plowden obtained a grant
from Charles I of Long Island and a portion of the adjoining
coasts. Three years later the Council for New England assigned
Long Island to Sir William Alexander. In 1640 settlers from
New Haven obtained a title to Long Island from Alexander's
representative and settled at Southold. Others from Massachusetts attempted a settlement opposite Manhattan, but, being

driven away by the Dutch, moved to Southampton at the eastern end of the island.

READINGS

GENERAL

Andrews, C. M., *The Fathers of New England, passim;* Becker, Carl, *The Beginnings of the American People,* 80–124.

THE PURITAN MOVEMENT AND THE PLYMOUTH COLONY

Adams, C. F., *Three Episodes of Massachusetts History,* I, 1–182; Arber, Edward, *The Story of the Pilgrim Fathers;* Bradford, William, *History of Plymouth Plantation;* Channing, Edward, *History of the United States,* I, 271–321; Cheyney, E. P., *European Background of American History,* 216–239; Dexter, Morton, *The England and Holland of the Pilgrims; The Story of the Pilgrims;* Doyle, J. A., *The Puritan Colonies,* I, 11–81; Eggleston, Edward, *The Beginners of a Nation,* 98–181; Fiske, John, *The Beginnings of New England,* 60–87; Griffis, W. E., *The Pilgrims in their Three Homes;* Neal, D., *History of the Pilgrims;* Osgood, H. L., *The American Colonies in the Seventeenth Century,* I, 98–137; Palfrey, J. G., *History of New England,* I, 101–238; Tyler, L. G., *England in America,* 148–182; Weeden, W. B., *Economic and Social History of New England,* I, 8–45; Young, Alexander, *Chronicles of the Pilgrim Fathers;* Usher, R. G., *The Pilgrims and Their History.*

MASSACHUSETTS BAY COLONY

Buffington, A. H., "New England and the Western Fur Trade, 1629–1675," in Colonial Society of Massachusetts, *Publications,* XXVIII, 160–192; Channing, Edward, *History of the United States,* I, 322–351; Doyle, J. A., *The Puritan Colonies,* I, 83–112; Eggleston, Edward, *Beginners of a Nation,* 188–215; Ellis, G. E., *The Puritan Age and Rule;* Fiske, John, *The Beginnings of New England,* 88–111; Johnson, Edward, *Wonder-Working Providence;* Newton, A. P., *The Colonizing Activities of the English Puritans;* Osgood, H. L., *The American Colonies in the Seventeenth Century,* I, 141–199, 424–467; Palfrey, J. G., *History of New England,* I, 283–405; *A Compendious History of New England,* I, 91–133; Tyler, L. G., *England in America,* 183–209; Weeden, W. B., *Economic and Social History of New England,* I, 47–164; Winthrop, John, *Journal.*

RHODE ISLAND AND THE CONNECTICUT VALLEY

Channing, Edward, *History of the United States,* I, 362–411; Doyle, J. A., *The Puritan Colonies,* I, 113–199; Eggleston, Edward, *Beginners of a Nation,* 266–346; Osgood, H. L., *The American Colonies in the Seventeenth Century,* I, 224–254, 301–370; Richman, I. B., *Rhode Island, a Study in Separatism,* 13–61; *Rhode Island, its Making and its Meaning,* 3–62; Tyler, L. G., *England in America,* 210–264; Weeden, W. B., *Early Rhode Island.*

CHAPTER VIII

THE ENGLISH COLONIES DURING THE REVOLUTIONARY PERIOD, 1640-1660

POLITICS, ADMINISTRATION, AND EXPANSION

Attitude of the colonies during the Puritan Revolution.—The personal rule of Charles I came to an end in 1641 and for eight years England was convulsed with civil war. During the struggle both Royalists and Parliamentarians claimed jurisdiction over the colonies, but neither was able to exert authority, and each colony followed its own course. The New England settlements were largely Puritan and naturally sided with parliament. In Maryland two factions formed, one Protestant, the other in favor of the Catholic proprietor. Virginia and the West Indies were almost entirely on the king's side. Incapable of rendering assistance, they attempted to maintain neutrality until the contest in England was decided.

The Bermudas and expansion in the West Indies.—In the Bermudas the colonists were divided, but the company leaders were Puritans. In 1643 the Independents seceded from the established Church, and two years later parliament granted freedom of worship in the islands. Religious feeling in the Bermudas led to a migration to a new asylum. In 1646 Captain William Sayle, who had been governor, led a colony to Segatoo, one of the Bahamas, which he now called Eleutheria, in allusion to the aim of the project. Later on Bermudans conducted extensive salt works in the Turks Islands in spite of frequent attacks by the Spaniards.

The Commonwealth, 1649-1653.—The military party, dominated by Cromwell, drove from parliament all those who hesitated to execute the king, the remnant being known as the Rump Parliament. It named a Council of State which was to carry on the executive work. The Commonwealth proceeded at once to overthrow its enemies outside of England. Rebellions in Ireland and Scotland were ruthlessly put down; the navy was greatly strengthened, and Admiral Sir George Ayscue was sent to the West Indies and Virginia to overthrow the Royalists. Friction with the Dutch had been growing for some time, due mainly to rivalry for the commerce of the East and West Indies and the growing trade of the Dutch along the Atlantic seaboard. Navigation laws were passed in 1650 and 1651 which were intended to deprive the Dutch of the trade of England and her possessions. War followed in 1652 and lasted for two years with varying success.

Colonial administration during the Commonwealth.—Colonial administration was carried on by various committees of parliament or of the Council of State. On March 2, 1650, the Council of State ordered that the entire council or any five of the members, should be a Committee for Trade and Plantations. In 1652 the Council of State appointed a standing committee of Trade, Plantations, and Foreign Affairs of which Cromwell and Vane were members. Special committees were also appointed from time to time to handle special colonial business or committees already in existence discussed matters referred to them.

Acquisition of Jamaica.—In December, 1653, Cromwell was made Lord Protector for life and in 1654 the war with the Dutch was brought to a close. To divert attention from home affairs Cromwell desired a foreign war. West Indian expansion had brought England into close contact with Spain. The aggressive acts of the latter against the Providence Island Company and the intercepting of English ships, gave a ready excuse for reprisals. Admiral Penn sailed from England on Christmas Day, 1654, in command of a large fleet to attack the Spanish. An attempt to gain a footing in Española was a complete failure, but Jamaica proved to be an easy prize and became a permanent English possession.

Colonial administration during the Protectorate.—The Council of State lost most of its powers and became simply the advisory council of Cromwell. The committee system of the council was continued. In 1655 a special committee for Jamaica was appointed, and about the same time a Committee for Foreign Plantations. The Protector also obtained the assistance of a body of officers and merchants to advise regarding colonial affairs.

NEW ENGLAND DEVELOPMENT, 1640–1660

The period from 1640 to 1660 was one of practical independence for the New England colonies. This neglect and freedom from

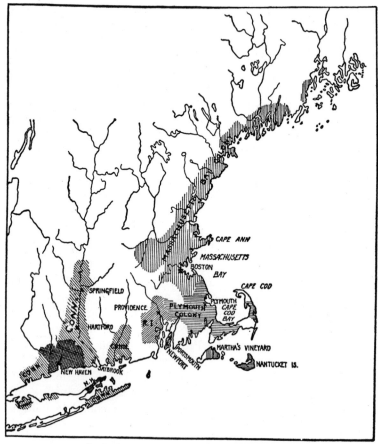

Settled areas in New England, about 1660

interference gave rise to three distinct developments: the formulation of provincial codes of law, the confederation of the colonies and of settlements within colonies, and territorial expansion.

The Massachusetts Body of Liberties.—The first of the colonial codes to be formulated was the Massachusetts Body of Liberties adopted by the general court in 1641. It provided for the protection of the private and political rights of the individual, methods of judicial procedure, rights of women, children, servants, foreigners, and strangers, the protection of animals, and the rights of the churches. Death penalties were specified, the capital crimes being the worshiping of false gods, witchcraft, blasphemy, murder, manslaughter, kidnaping, bearing false witness, and treason. Provision was also made for trial by jury. The code was amended from time to time, arson, cursing or smiting of parents, burglary, and highway robbery being added to the list of capital crimes. The Massachusetts code became the basis of the Connecticut code of 1650 and the New Haven code of 1656.

Causes of federation.—The development of self-government was fostered not only by neglect on the part of England, but also by the necessity of protection. Being hedged in on the north by the French and on the west by the Dutch, and with hostile Indian tribes encircling the English frontiers, the various groups of settlements were in danger. Massachusetts was strong enough to protect herself, but the settlements in the Connecticut Valley and on Long Island were menaced by the Dutch and Indians.

One of the fruitful causes of dispute between New England and the Dutch was the fur-trade. The choicest hunting grounds to the west were possessed by the Dutch and Swedes. To obtain a foothold on the Delaware, the upper Connecticut, and the Hudson became a settled economic policy of several of the New England colonies and was a potent factor in the formation of the New England Confederation. To exploit the Delaware River trade a company was formed at New Haven and in 1641 a settlement was made at Varkens Kill on the site of modern Salem, New Jersey, and later another post was established at the mouth of the Schuylkill, above the Dutch and Swedish forts. The Dutch, probably assisted by the Swedes, destroyed the Schuylkill fort, and the settlement at Varkens Kill did not prosper, most of the settlers dying or removing to New Haven. Massachusetts also attempted to obtain a share in the Delaware trade. In 1644 prominent merchants of Boston formed a company, but when their pinnace appeared in the Delaware, it was turned back by the Dutch, and shortly afterwards a small group of Boston traders were severely handled by the Indians.

The New England Confederation.—For several years plans for a confederation had been discussed, but the Dutch war against the Indians in 1642 and the struggle between De la Tour and D'Aulnay in Acadia brought matters to a head. At the general court which met at Boston on May 10, 1643, commissioners from Massachusetts, Plymouth, Connecticut, and New Haven signed a compact, Rhode Island and the settlements in Maine being excluded. The government of the confederation was placed in the hands of two commissioners from each of the four colonies. Internal affairs were not to be interfered with, but the confederation was to determine matters of war and foreign relations. Expenses were to be assessed on the colonies according to population. A vote of six commissioners was necessary to determine matters, the three small colonies thus being able to override Massachusetts. The confederation contained two serious defects which eventually led to its abandonment. The central government had no authority over individuals, and the equal vote of each colony violated the principle of representative government, Massachusetts having no more power then her weaker neighbors.

Work of the Confederation.—No incident occurred to require action on the part of the confederation until 1645, when the Narragansetts attacked the Mohegans. A force of three hundred men was raised by the confederation, an action which brought the Narragansetts to terms without hostilities. When a society for the propagation of the faith was incorporated in England to assist the missionary efforts of John Eliot and Thomas Mayhew, the commissioners handled the funds. When questions of boundaries and customs arose, they were settled by the commissioners. When Massachusetts assisted De la Tour against D'Aulnay, the commissioners exerted their influence to keep the colony from interfering in French affairs. In 1650 a treaty was made between Stuyvesant, the Dutch governor, and the commissioners, with the result that the Dutch retained their fort at Hartford, but were otherwise excluded from the Connecticut Valley and the eastern part of Long Island. The English were granted the right of colonization on the Delaware, but when New Haven men attempted to found a settlement, they were turned back by the Dutch and the confederation failed to take action. When hostilities broke out between the Dutch and English in 1651, the three smaller colonies desired war, but the Massachusetts general court refused, and when Cromwell's fleet appeared at Boston in 1654 on its way to attack the Dutch settlements, Massachusetts continued her opposition. Possible complications were averted by the treaty of peace. The action of Massachusetts in the relations with the Dutch so weakened the confederation that it soon ceased to be an important factor in New England history.

The Puritan movement into New Hampshire.—Massachusetts took advantage of the disturbed conditions in England to absorb the territory to the northward. In 1629 Mason had obtained a second patent for a tract extending sixty miles inland and lying between the Merrimac and Piscataqua rivers, which he named New Hampshire, and Mason and Gorges obtained title to lands between the Merrimac and Kennebec. In 1631 the two patentees and others obtained a tract of twenty thousand acres which included the Portsmouth settlement. In 1633 the English merchants who had founded Dover sold their shares in the settlement to Lord Saye and Sele, Lord Brooke, and others, a transaction which was followed by a Puritan migration. The same noblemen also obtained title to the Portsmouth settlement. During the Hutchinsonian controversy, Wheelwright and others found refuge at Dover, but shortly afterward established themselves at Exeter. Massachusetts claimed that the New Hampshire settlements fell within her boundaries, and in 1641, upon the suggestion of Lord Saye and Sele and Lord Brooke, extended her jurisdiction over Portsmouth and Dover. In 1643 Exeter also came under the protection of Massachusetts.

The incorporation of Maine with Massachusetts.—Several conflicting patents to lands in Maine were issued between 1630 and 1645. Few settlers came, the only new group of importance being the three towns of Georgiana (York), Welles, and Kittery on the Piscataqua. Massachusetts claimed that her charter entitled her to the Maine region, and in 1639 took the first step toward ownership by purchasing a tract on the Androscoggin River. When the region about Saco and Casco bays became a matter of dispute between rival patentees in 1644, the case was referred to the Massachusetts general court, but no decision was reached. When referred to the English commissioners for plantations, the Gorges estate lost most of its property, being left only the settled region near the Piscataqua. In 1647 Gorges died and the settlers were left without guidance. Two years later the three towns declared themselves a body politic. In 1651 Massachusetts asserted her claim to the Maine region, and the Royalists there found themselves powerless. The following year the Massachusetts authorities ordered the survey of the Merrimac and established civil government at York. In 1653 all the settlements in southern Maine accepted the jurisdiction of Massachusetts. The settlements about Casco Bay refused to submit until 1658, when they also acknowledged the authority of Massachusetts.

Massachusetts hopes to obtain the trade on the Hudson.—In 1657 the general court of Massachusetts declared that the fur-trade ought to be controlled by the commonwealth and in the following year a report was made which showed that fur-trading privileges at Springfield, Concord, Sudbury, Lancaster, Groton, Marlborough, and Cambridge were farmed out to various individuals. In 1659 a company was formed whose main purpose was to obtain access to the fur-trade of the upper Hudson, but it failed to carry out the project.

Connecticut.—In the Connecticut colony the period from 1640 to 1660 was one of expansion and consolidation. Southampton and East Hampton on Long Island, and on the mainland Farmington, Saybrook, New London, and Norwalk were brought under the jurisdiction of the colony.

New Haven.—In the New Haven colony the danger from the Dutch and Indians in 1643 brought about a union of the isolated units. A constitution was adopted which restricted the suffrage to church membership. Minor cases were to be judged in each town, and a governor, deputy-governor, and three associates were to judge the more important cases. No provision for trial by jury was made. The general court, consisting of the magistrates and two deputies from each of the towns, was to meet at New Haven twice a year to enact laws. In 1649 Southold on Long Island, in 1651 Bradford, and in 1656 Greenwich were added to the New Haven confederation.

Rhode Island.—Admission to the New England Confederation was denied to the Narragansett Bay settlements. Providence,

Portsmouth, and Newport had all been founded by outcasts from Massachusetts, and a fourth settlement of a similar nature was founded at Shawomet, now Warwick, in 1643 by Samuel Gorton. The danger from powerful and grasping neighbors caused Williams to seek a patent to the lands about Narragansett Bay, and on March 14, 1644, a patent was granted which allowed the inhabitants of Providence, Portsmouth, and Newport to form their own government. The Warwick settlers were asked to join the others.

In 1647 a code remarkable for its mildness was adopted, and by 1650 the government had been formed. The legislative powers were vested in a general court composed of six representatives from each town, the presiding officer of which was called a president. In executive matters he was to be aided by an assistant from each town. Provision was also made for a treasurer, sergeant, general recorder, attorney-general, and solicitor-general. The president and assistants acted as a court for important cases, which were to be tried by jury. The legislative body and the court made the circuit of the towns. The initiative and referendum were introduced, each settlement having the right to propose legislation, and acts of the general court were referred to the towns for ratification or rejection. Membership in a particular church was not made the basis of citizenship as in the other New England colonies. The disturbing element in Rhode Island at this time was Coddington. In 1651 he obtained from the Council of State a commission as governor of the islands in Narragansett Bay, but his power was short-lived, for the following year Williams obtained a revocation of the Coddington patent and in 1654 was elected president of the confederation.

VIRGINIA AND MARYLAND, 1640–1660

Virginia loyalists.—During the civil war Virginia remained loyal to the king. The large plantation owners, who were almost all members of the Established Church, were in control of the house of burgesses. The small landowners made up the minority. In this class were a few Puritans and many freemen who had formerly been indented servants. Their sympathies were on the side of parliament. Sir William Berkeley, who was appointed in 1642, was a staunch supporter of the king. His administration seems to have been tempered with justice, and he showed little of the arbitrary attitude which appeared in his later career.

Opechancanough's War.—The chief event in Berkeley's administration was the Indian war of 1644. The plantations had gradually spread up the James and Rappahannock, encroaching upon the Indian lands. The chief Opechancanough planned to massacre the whites. On April 18 the outlying settlements were attacked and five hundred people were massacred. The governor led several expeditions against the Indians, their crops and villages were destroyed, and their chief became a captive. While in captivity he was foully murdered. The Indians sued for peace, and in a treaty acknowledged the rights of the white man to all the lands between the York and the James as far as the falls.

Berkeley's struggle with the Commonwealth.—When the news of the death of Charles I reached Virginia, Berkeley proclaimed Charles II as king and the assembly declared it high treason to question his right to Virginia. Parliament decided to punish the colony by blockading it. Berkeley, nowise daunted, delivered a defiant address to the assembly, which warmly supported him. The blockade proved a failure, for Dutch traders sailed unmolested into Chesapeake Bay. A group of Virginia parliamentarians visited England and demanded that Berkeley be overthrown. The Council of State responded by sending out a fleet to subdue both Barbados and Virginia. Commissioners were also sent to Virginia to persuade the colony to submit peaceably. In the spring of 1652 when the fleet appeared in the James River, it found the governor prepared for resistance. The commissioners intervened, and by offering lenient terms, bloodshed was avoided. It was agreed that the colony should "voluntarily" acknowledge the authority of the Commonwealth, that the Virginians should have as free trade as the people of England, and that taxation was to be in the hands of the house of burgesses. Neither Berkeley nor his councilors were to be compelled to take the oath of allegiance for a year, and the use of the Book of Common Prayer was permitted for a similar length of time. Berkeley retired from the governorship but remained in the colony.

Government under the commonwealth.—The burgesses and commissioners proceeded to remodel the government. The house

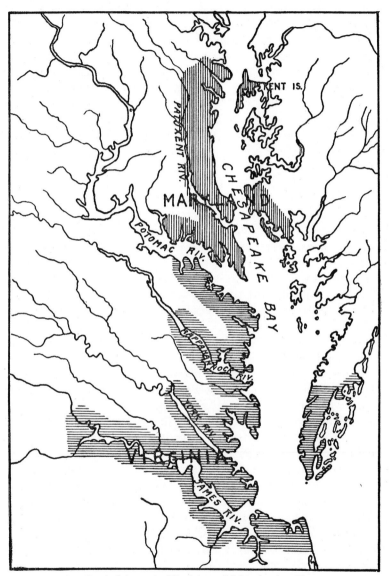

Settled Areas in Virginia and Maryland, 1660

of burgesses was made the chief governing body, with unlimited powers except the veto of the English government. It was to elect the governor and council, specify their duties and remove them if they proved unsatisfactory. All officials were also appointed by the burgesses.

A period of prosperity.—The kingless period was one of prosperity for Virginia. In 1649 the colony contained about 15,000 people; in 1666 the population was estimated at 40,000. This great migration was recruited from various classes: Cavaliers who sought refuge after the death of the king, people who fled from the horrors of civil war, prisoners who were sent as indented servants, gentlemen, tradesmen, and laborers, all found room in the abundant lands of tide-water Virginia.

Maryland during the civil war.—During the first part of the civil war, Lord Baltimore leaned toward the royalist side, but in the colony there was a strong Protestant element, augmented by this time by Puritans from Virginia. In 1645 they got control and expelled the Jesuits. The following year Governor Calvert, who had been in England, returned and reëstablished his authority, but his rule was shortlived, for he died in 1647.

Puritan rule in Maryland.—Fearing that he would be deprived of Maryland, Baltimore veered to the parliamentary side and appointed as governor William Stone, a prominent Virginia planter, and invited Virginia Puritans to settle in his territory. This was followed by a religious toleration act passed by the Maryland assembly in 1649. Baltimore's trimming, however, did not save him from trouble, for in 1650, when the Commonwealth expedition was sent out, the commissioners were instructed to reduce all the Chesapeake Bay plantations. For a time Stone was left in authority, but in 1654 he was deposed and the government was placed in the hands of a council, at the head of which was a Puritan, William Fuller. In the ensuing assembly the Royalists and Catholics were barred. Baltimore ordered Stone to recover his authority by force, but he was defeated and imprisoned by the forces of Fuller, and four of his followers executed. Baltimore appears to have ingratiated himself with Cromwell, for in 1657 he was restored to power.

READINGS

NEW ENGLAND

Channing, Edward, *History of the United States*, I, 414–420; Doyle, J. A., *The Puritan Colonies*, I, 220–319; Frothingham, Richard, *The Rise of the Republic*, 33–71; James, B. B., *The Colonization of New England*, 119–157; Mathews, L. K., *The Expansion of New England*, 31–34; Osgood, H. L., *The American Colonies in the Seventeenth Century*, I, 392–423; Palfrey, J. G., *A Compendious History of New England*, I, 247–268; Tyler, L. G., *England in America*, 266–281, 297–317.

VIRGINIA AND MARYLAND

Beer, G. L., *The Origins of the British Colonial System*, 340–424; Browne, W. H., *Maryland*, 72–104; Channing, Edward, *History of the United States*, I, 485–507; Doyle, J. A., *Virginia, Maryland, and the Carolinas*, 207–228, 314–327; Hamilton, P. J., *The Colonization of the South*, 118–122; Mereness, M. D., *Maryland as a Proprietary Province;* Osgood, H. L., *The American Colonies in the Seventeenth Century*, II, 58–87; Tyler, L. G., *England in America*, 105–117, 140–148; Wertenbaker, T. J., *Virginia under the Stuarts*, 85–114.

CHAPTER IX

THE DUTCH AND SWEDISH COLONIES

DUTCH EXPANSION

Commercial expansion of the Netherlands.—During the reign of Philip II occurred the revolt in the Netherlands. Spanish political and commercial restrictions, and the establishment of the Inquisition, united the great commercial cities, the nobles, and the common people of the northeastern provinces in a rebellion which did not cease until the Hollanders had secured virtual independence by the truce of 1609. During the struggle Dutch ships raided the Spanish and Portuguese trade routes. As early as 1577 a trade to the White Sea was begun. Soon Dutch ships were trading to Italy and the Baltic, and by 1598 they had extended their commerce to Alexandria, Tripoli on the Syrian coast, and Constantinople, to the Cape Verde Islands and the Guinea coast. The desire to reach India influenced Dutch statesmen to attempt to find a northeast passage. Between 1594 and 1597 four expeditions were sent out; they failed to find the passage but gained considerable knowledge of Nova Zembla and Spitzbergen.

East Indian trade.—For years Dutch sailors had been employed by the Portuguese and were well acquainted with the routes to India and America. In 1596 a company was organized to open a trade with the Far East; their fleet sailed around the Cape of Good Hope, stopped at Madagascar, and then proceeded to Java and the Moluccas, returning home the next year. Several companies were immediately formed, and in 1598 twenty-two vessels sailed by the Cape of Good Hope route for the East, and Olivier van Noort passed through the Straits of Magellan and circumnavigated the earth. In 1602 the States General chartered the United East India Company. Several fleets were despatched and succeeded in gaining a foothold in Ceylon and along the coasts of India, in Java, the Moluccas, and various other places. The traders met with great opposition from the Portuguese and Spaniards, but when peace was made in 1609 the Dutch were given the right of trading to Spanish ports outside of Europe, and they soon firmly established their power in the Far East where they absorbed much of Portugal's commerce.

Henry Hudson.—The East India Company hoped to find a shorter route to India and in 1609 employed an English mariner, Henry Hudson, to search for a northwest passage. Meeting with ice and storms, he headed his ship, the *Half Moon*, toward the west. Sighting land at Newfoundland, he examined the New England coast, rounded Cape Cod, and sailed to Virginia and southward. Turning north, he probably ran into Chesapeake Bay, certainly entered Delaware Bay, and then sailed northward to what is now New York harbor. The Hudson River was explored to a point above Albany and friendly relations with the Iroquois were established. The East India Company, however, was making such handsome profits in the East that the furs of New Netherlands failed to attract it.

The Cape Horn route discovered.—The Dutch were still hopeful of finding another route to India, and when Jacques le Maire quarreled with the directors of the East India Company, he planned to form a separate corporation and seek a route south of the Straits of Magellan. The people of Hoorn assisted him in fitting out two vessels which were placed under the command of William Corneliaz Schouten. On the long voyage the smaller vessel was destroyed, but Schouten with the larger one in 1616 discovered Cape Horn.

Dutch activities in the Hudson River region, 1610-1621.—The Hudson River region was visited by traders in 1610-1611, and in 1612 Dutch merchants sent Christianson and Block to Manhattan Island to engage in the fur trade. In 1613 Cornelius May was also sent over. The next year Fort Nassau, later named Fort Orange, was built near the present site of Albany. An extensive exploration of the coast was also made, Block sailing along the northern shore of Long Island, examining the lower waters of the Connecticut River, and exploring Narragansett Bay and Cape Cod. The result of these activities was the formation, in 1614, of the New Netherlands Company, which was given the monopoly of the trade between the fortieth and forty-fifth parallels. An important fur trade was rapidly developed in the Hudson Valley and exploration of the coast was continued. In 1616 Hendrickson examined Delaware Bay, and in 1620 the same region and Chesapeake Bay were visited by May. The southern extremity of New Jersey still bears the name of the Dutch explorer.

The West India Company.—One of the most enterprising Dutch merchants was William Usselincx, who had long hoped to profit by the opening of West Indian trade. The idea was opposed by the East India Company and by some of the Dutch statesmen, especially Olden Barnevelt, who feared that it would bring about new difficulties with Spain. In spite of this, Dutch vessels appeared in Guiana and the Antilles, and in 1613 settlements were attempted in Guiana at Essequibo and Berbice. In 1618 Olden Barnevelt fell from power and Usselincx immediately became active in the formation of a company. In 1621 the West India Company was chartered, receiving a monopoly of Dutch trade for twenty-four years on the coast of Africa as far as the Cape, and for America and the islands east of New Guinea. Usselincx, believing that the directors had too much power and the shareholders too little, and desiring a colonizing rather than a trading corporation, severed his connection with the company and departed for Sweden, where he interested Gustavus Adolphus in commercial enterprises.

Dutch settlements in Brazil, Guiana, and the Antilles.—Settlements were now established by the "Beggars of the Sea" all the way from Brazil to Hudson River, and there were prospects that the Caribbean Sea would become a Dutch instead of a Spanish lake. Brazil was the most important base. Bahía, taken in 1624, lost in 1625, and recaptured in 1627 by the celebrated Piet Heyn, was again lost, but by 1637 Olinda, Recife and Pernambuco had been captured in spite of determined resistance. Prince Maurice of Nassau now took possession of Brazil from Bahía to the Amazon River, and established there a Dutch state, with its capital at Mauritiópolis. In spite of liberal Dutch rule, however, and of an alliance now with Holland against Spain (1641), the Brazilians arose, and after years of heroic fighting expelled the intruders (1661). Meanwhile the Dutch had established colonies in Guiana at Berbice, Aprouage, and Pomeroon, as well as at Essequibo. In the Antilles they had settlements at Curaçao, Buen Aire, Aruba (1634), St. Eustatius, Saba (1635), and St. Martin (1638). During the same period the West India Company had established a flourishing colony on the northern mainland and called it New Netherlands.

NEW NETHERLANDS

Activities of the company.—Licenses were at once granted to several traders, who in 1622 visited the Hudson, Delaware, and Connecticut rivers and trafficked with the Indians as far east as Buzzard's Bay. Thirty families of Walloons, Protestants from Flanders, were sent over in 1623, these being the first colonists. Most of them settled on Manhattan Island, at Brooklyn, and on Staten Island. A few migrated to the vicinity of Fort Orange near Albany, and others settled near the present site of Gloucester on the Delaware, where a new fort named Nassau was erected. Other settlers soon followed; the fur trade was developed; and by 1625 the success of the colony seemed assured.

Government of the colony.—The West India Company was governed by a board of directors called the College of Nineteen; of these eight were from Amsterdam, and to them was given the control of New Netherlands. In the colony the chief officer was the director-general. To assist him was a council invested with local legislative, executive, and judicial powers, subject to the supervision and appellate jurisdiction of the Amsterdam directors. There were two minor officials, the "koopman" acting as commissary, bookkeeper, and secretary, and the "schout-fiscal" as an attorney and sheriff.

Administration of Peter Minuit.—In 1626 Peter Minuit became the director-general. One of his first acts was to secure a title to Manhattan Island by purchasing it from the Indians at the nominal price of twenty-four dollars' worth of goods. A fort, the location of which is known to-day as The Battery, was immediately constructed. Near by was built the stone counting house with a thatched roof, and thirty bark houses straggled along the east side of the river, the meager beginnings of a great metropolis. Fearing for the safety of the little groups of settle-

Van Der Donck's Map of New Netherland, 1656

at Fort Orange and Fort Nassau, Minuit brought them to New Amsterdam, leaving only a few soldiers and traders at Fort Orange.

Minuit's preparations for defence were not confined to fortifying the land. Conscious of foreign danger, inspired perhaps by the victories which Heyn was just now winning over Spaniards and Portuguese in the southern waters, and aided by two Belgian shipbuilders, the governor built and launched the *New Netherland*, a vessel of eight hundred tons and carrying thirty guns. The ship cost more than had been expected, and the bills were severely criticized by the West India Company.

The patroon system.—The returns from the southern raids made the small income from New Netherlands appear paltry, and the company decided to attempt an extensive colonization with a view to larger profit. A type of feudalism known as the patroon system was decided upon. The company reserved Manhattan Island, but other regions were opened to settlement. Each patroon was to receive lands four leagues along one side of a navigable river or two leagues on both sides and extending "so far into the country as the situation of the occupiers will permit," provided that within four years he settled fifty people over fifteen years of age upon his lands. Patroons were forever to "possess and enjoy all the lands lying within the aforesaid limits, together with the fruits, rights, minerals, rivers, and fountains thereof," and were to have complete control over "fishing, fowling, and grinding."

The fur trade was reserved by the company, but the patroons were allowed to trade on the coast from Newfoundland to Florida and to ship goods to neutral powers; they could also engage in fishing and the making of salt. They were to satisfy the Indians regarding land titles and were given the right to establish their own courts, from which appeal might be made to the director-general and his council. The colonists were exempt from taxation for ten years, but they could not leave the service of the patroon without his consent. The system was not intended to exclude other colonists who might come over and take up as much land as they could improve, but no colonists were to "be permitted to make any woolen, linen or cotton cloth, nor weave any other stuffs there." Patroons and colonists were "to find out ways and

means whereby they may support a Minister and Schoolmaster."
The company promised to defend the colonists and to endeavor
to supply them "with as many Blacks as they conveniently
can."

The patroons.—While the details of the charter were being
discussed, several directors took advantage of the intended system to secure large grants.   Samuel Godyn and Samuel Blommaert and several associates secured practically all of what is now
Delaware and that part of the Jersey shore extending twelve
miles north from Cape May and twelve miles inland.   Kiliaen van
Rensselaer obtained the lands about Fort Orange, comprising
what is now a large part of Albany and Rensselaer counties.
Michael Pauw received title to Staten Island and the region where
Jersey City is now situated.   Godyn and Blommaert sent colonists to Swannendael on the present site of Lewiston, but they
were massacred by the Indians, the colonization of the grant was
abandoned, and in 1635 the company purchased the lands of the
patroons on the Delaware.   In 1637 Pauw sold his holdings to the
company.   The Van Rensselaer tract remained in the possession
of that family until after the American Revolution.   Jealousies in
the company, due to the securing of patroonships by some of the
directors, and to the fact that the patroons attempted to obtain a
share in the fur trade, and that Minuit appeared to be working
in the interest of the great land holders, led to the recall of the
director-general.

Attempts to secure the frontiers.—The new director-general
was Wouter van Twiller.   He had been a clerk in the West India
Company's warehouse at Amsterdam, and probably owed his
appointment to the fact that he was married to a niece of Van
Rensselaer.   One of his first acts was to secure possession of the
Delaware.   In 1633 a tract along the Schuylkill was purchased
from the Indians and a trading house was erected, the first in the
present state of Pennsylvania.   In 1635 a party of Virginians
attempted to gain a foothold on the Delaware, but were expelled.
On the Connecticut the Dutch had profited by the fur trade, but
had never sent colonists to that region.   In 1633 lands were purchased from the Indians, and Fort Good Hope was built at modern Hartford, but the Puritan migration soon secured the Connecticut Valley for the English.

Reforms.—Van Twiller and other officials appear to have profited by securing extensive land holdings on the islands at the mouth of the Hudson, Governor's Island deriving its name from the fact that Van Twiller owned it. Complaints began to be heard in the Amsterdam chamber and in 1637 Van Twiller was removed from office, his successor being William Kieft, who arrived in 1638. The new director-general immediately set about correcting abuses. Illicit fur trading and the sale of firearms to the Indians were prohibited. The Amsterdam chamber removed some of the trade restrictions and made easier the acquisition of land. The result was a considerable increase in the number of settlers, who came not only from the Netherlands, but from New England and Virginia as well. Restrictions on manufactures were abolished and the Dutch Reformed Church was established.

Difficulties.—Kieft's administration was beset by difficulties. In the Connecticut Valley and on Long Island the English settlements were increasing, and on the Delaware the Swedes had gained a footing. In the colony a disastrous Indian war brought devastation and ruin. The Indians on the lower Hudson and on Long Island had watched the growing settlements with alarm, an alarm which turned to resentment when they found the Iroquois supplied with firearms from Fort Orange, a privilege which was denied to them at New Amsterdam. Kieft increased the ill-feeling by demanding a contribution of corn, fur, and wampum. He also accused the Raritans of attacking fur trading vessels, and sent an expedition to punish them. In 1641 the Indians retaliated by killing several settlers.

Kieft and the twelve men.—Kieft promptly called together the settlers, who chose a committee of twelve to advise the director-general. Much to his disappointment, they counseled delay. In January, 1642, he again summoned the twelve, who consented to send an expedition against the Indians, provided Kieft should command it. At the same time they demanded that the council should contain at least five members and that the inhabitants should be allowed greater freedom of trade. To these demands Kieft assented grudgingly, and to save further embarrassment, dissolved the committee. An expedition was sent against the Indians, but it accomplished nothing.

Indian hostilities, 1643-1645.—Early in 1643 the Mohawks attacked the river Indians who sought refuge near New Amsterdam. Kieft determined to attack the fugitives, and eighty of them were massacred. The Long Island Indians were also plundered. Aroused by these acts, the Indians united and attacked the settlers. The colonists who escaped fled to Fort Amsterdam. A lull occurred in the fighting while the Indians planted their crops, but hostilities were soon renewed. Kieft again summoned the people and a committee of eight was chosen who counseled war. Settlers and servants of the company were drilled, and fifty English also enlisted. A series of expeditions were despatched against the Indians, whose villages were ruthlessly destroyed. In 1645 treaties were made with the various tribes, and the long war came to an end. One of the incidents of the war was the building of a wall across the lower end of Manhattan Island. It is from this that Wall Street takes its name.

Stuyvesant, 1647.—Both in New Amsterdam and the Netherlands Kieft was blamed for the war. The West India Company decided to remove him, and Peter Stuyvesant, the director of Curaçao, was appointed to succeed him. The first important act of Stuyvesant was to organize the council. Police regulations were made to control Sabbath-breakers, brawlers, and the sale of liquors. The court of justice was also organized, but the director-general required that his opinion be asked in all important cases, and reserved the right to preside in person when he saw fit.

Popular representation.—While Kieft was director-general, he had appealed to the people on several occasions. In answer to the public demand for representation, the council recommended to Stuyvesant that it be granted. Accordingly, the director-general ordered an election at which eighteen were chosen, from whom Stuyvesant and the council selected nine. The nine were to advise and assist, when called upon, in promoting the welfare of the province, and were to nominate their successors. The director-general retained the right to preside at meetings.

Struggle for municipal rights.—The trade restrictions of the West India Company were irksome to the people of New Amsterdam, who hoped to right conditions by obtaining a larger share

in the government.   After considerable trouble with Stuyvesant,
the nine men submitted to the States General a remonstrance setting forth their grievances and a memorial suggesting remedies.
They asked that the States General establish a citizens' government, that colonists be sent over, and that the boundaries of New
Netherlands be definitely established.   The Amsterdam chamber
opposed the petitioners, but in 1652 it decided to make concessions.   The export duty on tobacco was removed, the cost of
passage to New Netherlands was reduced, and the colonists were
allowed to procure negroes from Africa.   A "burgher" government was allowed for New Amsterdam, the citizens being allowed
a schout, two burgomasters, and five schepens, who were to form
a municipal court of justice.   They were not to be popularly
elected, however, Stuyvesant being allowed to appoint the members.   No sooner were municipal rights granted to New Amsterdam than the settlements at the western end of Long Island
demanded a larger share in government.   A convention was held
at the capital to formulate grievances.   This was brought to an
end by Stuyvesant, but a little later municipal rights were granted
to several of the towns.

A provincial assembly.—In 1664, during the war between England and the Dutch, so great was the alarm at New Amsterdam,
that a provisional assembly was elected, composed of two delegates from each of the Dutch settlements, twenty-four representatives in all.   Little was accomplished by this body, however,
for shortly afterward the colony passed into English hands.

Economic development.—During the administration of Stuyvesant the material prosperity of New Netherlands steadily
increased.   He found New Amsterdam a town with straggling
fences and crooked streets, and containing about five hundred
people.   Under his supervision it took on the appearance of a
well-kept Dutch town.   In 1656 it contained a hundred and
twenty houses and a thousand people.   By 1660 it had three
hundred and fifty houses.   By 1664 the population increased to
fifteen hundred.   The area of settlement in New Netherlands had
gradually expanded, covering Manhattan and Staten islands,
the opposite Jersey shore, the western end of Long Island, both
banks of the lower Hudson, a considerable district about Ft.
Orange, and scattering settlements on the Delaware.   The chief

source of wealth was the fur trade which was carried on largely with the Iroquois who were friendly to the Dutch and hostile to the French. In 1656 Ft. Orange alone exported thirty-five thousand beaver and otter skins, but soon afterward the trade began to decline and agriculture increased in importance. When the province passed into English hands, the population had reached ten thousand.

THE DUTCH AND THE SWEDES ON THE DELAWARE

Swedish territorial and commercial expansion.—In the first half of the seventeenth century Sweden rose to the position of a first class power. When Gustavus Adolphus ascended the throne in 1611, Sweden was at war with Denmark, Russia, and Poland. After defeating each power, the king entered the Thirty Years' War as the champion of Protestantism, his victorious career coming to an untimely end at Lützen. Until 1654 Christina was queen but the real ruler was Oxenstierna, who piloted Sweden through the closing years of the war and secured advantageous terms in the treaty of peace. From 1648 until 1654, Sweden enjoyed peace, but the frivolities of the court ruined the possibilities of greatness and the decline began. Charles X became king in 1654, and his brilliant but disastrous military ventures reduced his country to a third-rate power. At the beginning of the period of Swedish greatness, her commerce was confined to the Baltic, but when nearly all the lands on its shores had been acquired, Swedish statesmen looked forward to a wider commerce, a policy which brought them into rivalry with Holland and England. Numerous trading companies were formed, among the most important being the African and Russian companies, and the various organizations which operated on the Delaware River and in the West Indies.

Usselincx.—The attention of Sweden was drawn to the Delaware by Usselincx, the promoter of the Dutch West India Company, who had left Holland in disgust and who hoped to interest the Swedes. In 1624 he laid his plans before Gustavus Adolphus; this resulted in the granting of a charter to The South Company to establish trade "for Asia, Africa, America and Magellanica." Usselincx experienced great difficulty in raising money, and the directors ruined his schemes by diverting the capital to commer-

cial enterprises in Sweden. In 1629 the company was reorganized
and an attempt was made to trade with Spain, but this ended in
disaster. Usselincx continued his endeavors, and in 1633 The
New South Company was organized, but this like its predecessors came to naught.

The New Sweden Company.—The settling of the Swedes on
the Delaware was directly due to the Dutchmen, Samuel Blommaert and Peter Minuit. Blommaert held out the idea that the
West Indies would be a market for Swedish copper; Minuit that
the Delaware region offered a place for the fur trade and colonization. Several other Dutch merchants were interested, and
half of the capital of the Swedish company was furnished by
Hollanders. By 1637 the company was organized and the first
expedition set sail.

Fort Christina.—The two vessels arrived in the spring of 1638,
lands were purchased from the Indians, fur trade opened, and a
fort established on Christina Creek two miles from the Delaware.
The Dutch at Ft. Nassau protested, but were too weak to oust
the newcomers. In 1640 two boats arrived with settlers and
goods, large tracts of land at various points on both sides of the
bay and river as far as Trenton were purchased, and farms and
tobacco plantations were started.

Governor Printz.—In 1642 the company was reorganized, the
Swedish government taking part of the stock, the Dutch being
eliminated. At the request of the Swedish council of state
Johan Printz, a prominent officer in the army, became governor,
a post which he filled until 1653. He erected Ft. Elfsborg and
established his capital at New Gothenborg, where a fort was built.
A blockhouse was also erected on the Schuylkill, other vantage
points were occupied, and the Swedes soon secured the fur trade
of the Delaware. From the first the weakness of the Swedish
project was the lack of colonists, a few hundred being the total
migration in the first ten years. In 1644 there were only one
hundred and twenty men and a few women and children in the
colony. During the next five years not a vessel arrived, and when
Printz retired in 1653 there were only two hundred people in the
colony.

End of Swedish power on the Delaware.—Stuyvesant determined to get control of the river trade. In 1651 he went to

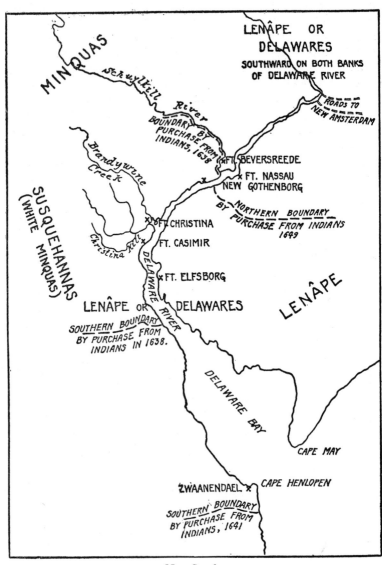

New Sweden

the Delaware with a considerable force.   In spite of protests from Printz, lands were purchased from the Indians, and Ft. Casimir was built near the present site of New Castle, the other Dutch forts being abandoned.   In 1653 the Swedish crown planned to help New Sweden.   In the spring of 1654 about three hundred and fifty colonists were sent over under John Rising. He immediately seized Ft. Casimir.   At Ft. Christina a town was laid out, new tracts were purchased from the Indians, and lands were assigned to the colonists.   The action of the Swedes in seizing Ft. Casimir angered Stuyvesant, and he urged the West India Company to occupy New Sweden.   In September, 1655, a Dutch fleet appeared in the Delaware, and the forts surrendered, thus ending the colony of New Sweden.

ABSORPTION OF NEW NETHERLANDS BY THE ENGLISH

Boundary treaty with New England—On the eastern frontier Stuyvesant had another difficult problem.   English settlers were crowding into the Connecticut Valley and onto Long Island. In 1647 Stuyvesant informed the New England officials that the Dutch claimed all lands between the Connecticut and Delaware rivers, but the New Englanders ignored the claim.   In 1650 Stuyvesant visited Hartford, where commissioners were appointed who agreed that Long Island should be divided by a line running along the western part of Oyster Bay; that on the mainland the line was "to begin at the west side of Greenwich Bay, being four miles from Stamford and so to run a northerly line twenty miles up into the country, and after as it shall be agreed by the two governments of the Dutch and New Haven; provided the said line come not within ten miles of Hudson's River;" and that the Dutch were to keep their holdings at Hartford.

The end of Dutch rule.—In 1659 Massachusetts asserted her claim to a sea to sea grant, and in 1662 the charter of Connecticut extended the bounds of the colony to the Pacific.   In 1663 Stuyvesant visited Boston to attempt a settlement of existing difficulties, but to no avail, and upon his return he found that some of the Long Island settlements west of the line claimed to be under the jurisdiction of Connecticut.   Dutch commissioners were sent to Hartford, but without result, and the following year Connecticut asserted her rights to the whole of Long

Island.   In 1664 Charles II granted to his brother, James, the Duke of York, the whole of Long Island and all the lands from the Connecticut River to Delaware Bay.   A fleet was despatched to New Amsterdam, which surrendered without bloodshed, and Dutch rule in North America came to an end three years after it had failed in Brazil.

READINGS

THE DUTCH

Blok, P. J., *History of the People of the Netherlands*, III, 267–303; Brodhead, J. R., *History of the State of New York*, I; Channing, Edward, *History of the United States*, I, 438–484; Fiske, John, *The Dutch and Quaker Colonies in America*, I; Goodwin, M. W., *Dutch and English on the Hudson;* Innes, J. H., *New Amsterdam and its People;* Jameson, J. F., ed., *Narratives of New Netherlands;* Janvier, T. A., *Dutch Founding of New York;* MacDonald, William, *Select Charters*, 43–50; O'Callaghan, E. B., *History of New Netherlands;* Roberts, E. H., *New York*, I, 19–119; Van Loon, H. W., *The Golden Book of the Dutch Navigators*.

THE SWEDES

Acrelius, Israel, *History of New Sweden* (Pennsylvania Historical Society, *Memoirs*, XI); Holm, T. C., *Description of the Province of New Sweden* (Pennsylvania Historical Society, *Memoirs*, VII); Johnson, Amandus, *The Swedish Settlements on the Delaware;* Keen, G. B., in Winsor, *Narrative and Critical History*, III, 469–495.

CHAPTER X

THE OLD ENGLISH COLONIES UNDER THE LATER STUARTS

COLONIAL POLICY AND ADMINISTRATION

The Restoration.—In 1660 Charles II was restored to the English throne and ruled until 1685, when his brother, James, the Duke of York, became king, ruling until deposed in 1688. In England the period was characterized by a reaction against Puritanism and the firm establishment of the English church. Abroad the Restoration was an era of commercial and colonial expansion. On the coasts of Asia, Africa, and America, the great trading companies were active, and powerful English nobles strove for possessions beyond the seas. To this era belong the occupation of New Netherlands, the founding of the Carolinas, the Jerseys, and Pennsylvania, and the establishment of the Hudson's Bay Fur Company. The activities of Englishmen led to clashes with rival commercial peoples, especially the Dutch, with whom two naval wars were fought in which England maintained her supremacy upon the seas. In the handling of her colonies previous to the Restoration, her efforts had been largely experimental. Under the later Stuarts colonial management was molded into a system. In private life Charles II was a man of pleasure. In his dealings with parliament he was tenacious, but when pushed to extremities, he preferred to yield rather than to "go again on his travels." In matters which affected the material prosperity of his country the king was a hard-headed man of business, warmly supporting commercial and colonial enterprises.

The Mercantilist system.—The economic theory of the time was expressed in the Mercantilist system. The welfare of the state was the main object of statesmen; this they believed required a full treasury, a large population, and extensive shipping. Specie was looked upon as the principal form of wealth; therefore exports must exceed imports so that coin would flow into the realm. In order that it might have a large amount of goods to sell, the state desired to import raw materials, which could be manufactured and exported. The ideal colony was to be a source of supply of raw materials, and was to be a market for goods of the mother country, but was not to be a manufacturing competitor. The state policy was shaped to shut out the foreigner and to build up the productivity of the colonies.

Attitude toward emigration.—The desire for a larger population in England caused statesmen to view emigration with disfavor. During the period the number going to the colonies was relatively small. The government, however, encouraged the emigration of Scotch, Irish, and Huguenots, and sent over many political prisoners, nonconformists, and criminals. Many of those who emigrated were too poor to pay for their passage and bound themselves for a period of years, a form of temporary bondage known as indenture. Many servants and children were also kidnaped and sent to the colonies. Because the colonies in the West Indies and the South mainly produced raw materials and used slave labor, thus drawing relatively less population from England, they were looked upon with the greater favor by the home government. The northern colonies produced little except fish, furs, and naval stores, which could be of use to England. The free labor system of the North was likely to drain the population of England. For these reasons the northern colonies were looked upon with scant favor.

Navigation Act of 1660.—During the Cromwellian period, parliament had asserted the right to legislate for the colonies and the restored Stuarts accepted the principle. In 1660 a new navigation act was passed which was intended to give English shipping an advantage over competitors, especially the Dutch. The act provided that goods carried to or from English possessions in America, Africa, or Asia, must be carried in English, Irish, or colonial vessels. Under penalty of forfeiture, cargoes of sugar, tobacco, indigo, and several other products could not be shipped to any ports except in England, Ireland, or some English colony.

Staple Act of 1663.—Under the navigation act of 1660 alien merchants could send foreign goods to the colonies in English ships. To obviate this the Staple Act was passed, which, with a few exceptions, such as Portuguese wines, salt, and horses, prohibited the importation into the colonies of goods which had not been loaded in England.

Plantation Duties Act of 1673.—Under the previous acts goods shipped from colony to colony escaped paying duties. In 1673 an act was passed which imposed duties on sugar, tobacco, and many other products of intercolonial trade.

Imperial defence.—The burden of defence of the empire against foreign powers fell upon England. Ships of the navy were stationed in the West Indies, Chesapeake Bay, and at Boston to protect the colonies, and suppress piracy and illegal trade. The buccaneers of the West Indies were brought under control. The Barbary pirates also were frequently attacked, and convoys for merchant vessels and fishing fleets were often furnished. Garrisons were usually stationed in Barbados, Jamaica, and St. Kitts, but on the mainland soldiers were not regularly maintained.

The fiscal system.—By the civil war parliament made good its contention that it alone had the right to levy taxes. In 1660 a general taxation act was passed by which Charles II was granted for life the income from tonnage and poundage; the former being a duty on imported wines, the latter a five per cent duty on imports and exports, whose valuation was fixed in a book of rates. To compensate the colonies somewhat for the resulting higher prices, a preferential system was introduced. By this system the valuation of the principal products of the colonies was made lower than on the same products coming from foreign countries.

MACHINERY OF GOVERNMENT

Council for Foreign Plantations.—The work of enforcing the laws devolved upon the crown and privy council. The accumulation of business and the specialized knowledge required in colonial matters made it desirable to have a body created which might handle the business in a more efficient manner. Accordingly in December, 1660, a Council for Foreign Plantations was commissioned. Members of the council were to inform themselves regarding the colonies, were to introduce a more uniform system of government, and were to see that the navigation acts were enforced.

Council of Trade.—From the English standpoint the colonies were mainly commercial enterprises. To foster commerce a Council of Trade was created. The work of the two bodies was to sift the mass of business so that matters of first importance only might come before the privy council. Lack of authority interfered with the interest of the members of the minor councils; the sessions became less and less frequent, and by 1665 both had ceased.

Council for Trade and Plantations.—Supervision of the colonies again devolved upon a committee of the privy council. In 1667 Clarendon fell and the small group known as the Cabal came into power. The following year the privy council was reorganized, four standing committees being constituted, one of which had charge of trade and plantations. The need of experts, however, continued to be felt, and in 1668 a new Council of Trade was appointed. In 1670 the Council for Plantations was also revived, and in 1672 the two councils were consolidated as the Council for Trade and Plantations. The council prepared preliminary drafts of instructions to governors, examined colonial legislation, and investigated questions which arose.

Lords of Trade.—Executive powers remained in the privy council, and this necessarily curbed the Council for Trade and Plantations, which was purely an advisory body. In 1674 the latter council was abolished, and the following year the king again committed its work to the Committee for Trade and Plantations of the privy council. This committee, known henceforth as the Lords of Trade, was a permanent body with its own clerks. William Blathwayt soon became the secretary and for twenty years he held the position. The efficiency of the body and the development of the colonial policy was due more to him than to any other person. The Lords of Trade prepared the instructions to governors, supervised the development of the colonies, examined colonial questions, and enforced the navigation laws.

The Admiralty.—After the Restoration the Duke of York was appointed Lord High Admiral of England and in 1662 his powers were extended to the colonies. Cases concerning vessels seized for violating some of the clauses of the commercial laws were tried in admiralty courts which were established in the crown colonies, deputies were appointed by the admiral to attend to the business, and ships were stationed in the colonies to seize illegal traders.

Governors and customs officials.—In the colony the chief executive officer was the governor. He was expected to enforce the trade laws, but outside of the crown colonies there was great laxity in this regard. The work of enforcing the navigation laws was usually entrusted by the governor to a clerk called the naval officer but at a later period these officials were appointed by the crown. The right of collection of the English customs was leased to certain individuals who were known as farmers of the customs. They frequently complained that the governors were remiss in enforcing the navigation laws. Accordingly, the farmers of the customs were allowed to send, at their own expense, officers who would attend to the collection of duties. The farming system was soon abandoned and commissioners of customs were appointed, who sent out collectors, usually one to each colony. To examine the collector's accounts and act as a check upon him, officials called comptrollers were placed in most of the colonies, and in 1683 a superintendent for all the colonies, called the surveyor-general of the customs, was appointed. The activities of these officials led to considerable friction with colonial governors and proprietors, who resented the interference of the customs officials.

MISRULE AND REBELLION IN VIRGINIA

Effect of the trade laws.—In 1660 Sir William Berkeley began his second administration, which proved to be as unsuccessful as his first administration had been successful. Economic distress and arbitrary misrule beset Virginia for sixteen years, culminating in a popular outbreak known as Bacon's rebellion. The navigation acts fell heavily upon the tobacco planters, who were deprived of the Dutch trade. The population at the same time rapidly increased. In 1671 the inhabitants numbered about forty thousand and nearly doubled in the next decade. The increasing population meant an increasing acreage of tobacco. The price of tobacco fell, while freight rates increased and imported goods went up in price. To alleviate the situation the assembly passed several acts to encourage new industries, but the planters held to their one great staple. Several attempts were made to limit the production of tobacco, a policy in which the Virginians asked the people of Maryland and the Albemarle district to the south to coöperate, but the efforts failed. The act of 1673 worked an added injury, for it deprived the planters of the New England market.

Wars and other misfortunes.—The wars with Holland increased the economic distress. In 1667 a Dutch fleet entered the James River, captured an English frigate, and destroyed several trading vessels. Soon afterward a hurricane destroyed hundreds of houses and ruined the crops. In the winter of 1672–1673 a disease carried off fifty thousand cattle, more than half of all the stock in Virginia. A second Dutch raid in 1673 destroyed a large part of the tobacco fleet.

Governmental abuses.—Berkeley was a firm believer in the divine right of kings, and looked with disfavor upon any interference from the people. To him it seemed fitting that, as the king's representative, he should control every branch of governmental activity. His council was entirely subservient and he gained control of the house of burgesses by controlling the county elections through dishonest officials. In 1670 the assembly limited the franchise to freeholders, thus depriving the poor of voting. In the counties the justices of the peace were appointed by the governor. They exercised judicial, executive, and legislative functions. The county courts settled the more important suits and the individual justices determined minor cases. The courts also levied the direct taxes, which were very heavy. In addition, the local church divisions were governed by vestries which were selected by the governor. These bodies levied the taxes to pay the church expenses. The whole machinery of government was thus controlled by the governor. The form of taxation aggravated the situation. Instead of a property tax, which would throw the burden upon the great landholders, the poll-tax was the usual method of raising money, the poor man thus having to pay as much as the wealthy. There was also much bad judgment displayed in the use of public funds. In a period of low prices and overproduction, the heavy expenditures proved a serious burden, and discontent gradually developed into rebellion.

Proprietary grants.—The action of the English government also alarmed the colonists. In 1660 an attempt was made to renew the old Virginia Company. Berkeley visited England to prevent it and his mission proved successful. In 1649 the king had granted the region between the Potomac and the Rappahannock rivers to several of his supporters, and after the Restoration they leased their rights to Sir Humphrey Hooke and two others. In 1669 the grant was renewed. The Virginia assembly immediately sent agents to England to obtain the annulment of the patent or to allow the colony to purchase the tract. Before a settlement was made the king in 1673 granted the whole of Virginia to the Earl of Arlington and Lord Culpeper with full proprietory rights for thirty-one years. The assembly was greatly alarmed and directed its agents to seek the annulment of this patent also. The matter was finally settled by an arrangement with the proprietors by which they agreed to relinquish the patent provided the colony paid them the quit-rents and assured them the escheated property. The agents then asked the government that they be assured that no portion of the colony would be granted in future to any proprietors and that taxation would not be imposed without the consent of the house of burgesses. Before a settlement was reached Bacon's rebellion occurred.

Indian war.—The spark that kindled the rebellion was an Indian war. The Senecas, pressing upon the Susquehannas, forced them into Maryland and Virginia, where they committed depredations in the summer of 1675. The settlers retaliated by killing several Indians. The Susquehannas joined with the native tribes and harried the frontiers. Berkeley sent Colonel John Washington in command of several hundred men to join the Marylanders against an Indian fort on the Potomac, but after several weeks of fighting the red men escaped. This was followed by renewed depredations. Early in 1676 the governor prepared a second expedition but suddenly abandoned the project. In March the assembly met and decided to wage a defensive war. Forts were to be built upon the upper waters of the rivers and heavy taxes were demanded to pay for them.

Bacon's rebellion.—The people were greatly incensed at the policy, and demanded that the assembly be dissolved and a free election held. The frontiersmen also demanded that they be allowed to go against the Indians. Both of these demands the governor stubbornly refused. A rebellion immediately broke out in Charles City County, and Nathaniel Bacon, of Henrico, a member of Berkeley's council, was induced to lead it. The governor was asked to grant Bacon a commission to proceed against the Indians. Without waiting for the governor's decision, Bacon led his men against the Pamunkeys. Bacon's act angered Berkeley, who refused the commission and ordered Bacon and his men to lay down their arms. This they refused to do and retired beyond the frontier, where they destroyed an Indian stronghold on an island in the Roanoke River. Berkeley issued a proclamation declaring Bacon's acts disloyal and rebellious. To obtain popular support he dismantled the forts, dissolved the assembly, and called an election.

Bacon was elected in Henrico County and an armed guard accompanied him to the capital. Berkeley's troops fired upon Bacon's sloop, but that night Bacon entered the town to consult with friends. He was discovered, and eventually captured and brought before the governor, who, in view of the popular clamor, became lenient, granting him a pardon and promising him a commission as general. As the commission was not forthcoming, Bacon collected several hundred men and marched upon Jamestown, which he entered without opposition, and forced Berkeley to sign the commission and to write a letter to the king justifying Bacon's acts. The assembly now passed several bills which struck at the governor's power, and repealed the act which restricted the franchise to freeholders.

The burgesses had just completed their work when news came that the Indians were again on the war-path, and Bacon hastened with his volunteers to the frontier. No sooner was he gone than the governor began to enlist troops to proceed against the popular leader. Hearing of this Bacon returned and Berkeley fled to the eastern shore of Chesapeake Bay. Bacon was now in full control of the larger part of the colony. To justify his acts he took the oath of allegiance, imposed it upon his followers, and called an election. He then organized two expeditions, one against the governor, the other against the Indians. An English ship was seized and two hundred men were sent to capture Berkeley, but the governor's followers surprised the crew and captured the leaders. Berkeley then returned to Jamestown. While these events were occurring, Bacon marched against the Indians and captured a stronghold of the Pamunkeys. He then captured Jamestown and burned it, soon afterward retiring into Gloucester County, where he was taken sick and died. In a few months the people wearied of anarchy, many of the leaders surrendered, and Berkeley was again in control.

Berkeley's revenge.—In June, 1676, Berkeley had tendered his resignation to the king. Charles decided to allow him to retain the title of governor, but to have him return to England, leaving the government to a lieutenant-governor, Colonel Jeffreys being appointed. He was assisted by two commissioners, Berry and Moryson. A general pardon for the rebels was also drawn up. Berry and Moryson arrived in the colony and found the governor intractable. Jeffreys, with about a thousand troops, arrived soon afterward, but instead of asserting his authority, he allowed Berkeley to ignore the pardon proclamation and many were hung. Knowledge of Berkeley's disobedience reached the king, who ordered him to return to England at once, but before the order arrived Berkeley had embarked. He died soon after reaching England, and Lord Culpeper was appointed governor, but he did not reach Virginia until 1680.

Culpeper and Howard.—In the meantime the commissioners investigated the causes of the rebellion, and in July, 1677, Berry and Moryson took their report to England where it was laid before the privy council. Jeffreys, who was left in control, had little authority, and the government again fell into the hands of Berkeley's friends. Culpeper arrived in 1680, but he proved to be a weak individual who spent most of his time in England and did little when in the colony. In 1684 a new governor, Lord Howard of Effingham, proceeded at once to curb the powers of the house of burgesses. The right of appealing cases from the lower courts to the assembly was denied, henceforth the governor and council being the final court of appeal. The right of the king to annul laws passed by the assembly was also asserted in spite of violent opposition. The session of 1685 proved a stormy one. An attempt was made to take the power of taxation away

from the assembly. The king, who had taken over the proprietory rights of Arlington and Culpeper, demanded that the
quit-rents be paid in specie instead of tobacco. This the burgesses violently opposed, but they finally compromised by agreeing to pay somewhat less than the governor had demanded.
A "bill of ports" was introduced which was intended to fix the
points at which ships might load and unload. Another violent
struggle occurred. Finally, on recommendation of the governor,
the king dissolved the assembly. Lord Howard unseated several
members and appointed the clerk of the assembly. The governor
also collected certain fees, an act which the burgesses claimed
was an encroachment upon the power of taxation. The colony
was nearing another rebellion. In 1688 the assembly drew up
a statement of grievances, which they sent to the king, but by
the time it reached England James II had been driven from the
throne and Effingham was soon recalled.

DISCONTENT IN MARYLAND

Conditions in Maryland.—Economic conditions in Maryland
were similar to those in Virginia, the navigation laws affecting
the colony in a similar manner, the price of tobacco falling continually after 1660 for many years. Political discontent also
manifested itself, but the religious element played a larger part
in Maryland than in Virginia. No widespread rebellion occurred,
however, for Baltimore's government was more temperate than
that of Berkeley, the settlements were more compact, frontier
dangers were less acute, and no popular leader of great ability
arose to lead the malcontents.

Charles Calvert's administration.—After the turmoil of the
Cromwellian period, the Restoration brought comparative security to the proprietor of Maryland, who succeeded in ingratiating
himself with Charles II. In 1675 Charles Calvert succeeded to
the proprietorship. Previously for several years he had personally directed the governorship and had worked conscientiously
to bring about prosperity in the colony. He was less tactful
than his father and was exceedingly strong-willed. He placed
his relatives in the important positions, restricted the suffrage,
and frequently summoned to the assembly only half of the
elected delegates, thus keeping out influential opponents. In

1676, while Baltimore was in England, a few malcontents attempted an uprising, but Notley, the acting governor, overthrew and hanged two of the leaders, nipping the rebellion in the bud. The proprietor and assembly continued to have difficulties, but in the main Baltimore succeeded in maintaining his power. He also had trouble with William Penn over the northern boundary, and with the Lords of Trade over the right of collecting the customs. Baltimore's Catholic leanings naturally made him support James II. When that monarch was driven from the throne, a miniature bloodless revolution occurred in Maryland. An Association for the Defense of the Protestant Religion was formed. In July, 1689, the leaders seized St. Mary's and held a representative assembly. But to their chagrin, William and Mary restored the old colonial system, and Baltimore was soon back in power.

ROYAL INTERFERENCE IN NEW ENGLAND

Massachusetts and the king.—During the Cromwellian period the New England colonies had followed their own devices, but when Charles II came to the throne, they could not expect to pursue their independent course. To forestall trouble, Massachusetts hastened to acknowledge the king's authority, and none too soon, for numerous complaints had been lodged against her. The most forceful of these came from the Quakers. In 1655 Mary Fisher and Ann Austin, two Quaker missionaries, had landed in Barbados, the first of that sect to come to the colonies. The following year they went to Boston from which they were promptly expelled. Rhode Island proved hospitable. Those who had believed in Anne Hutchinson's "covenant of grace" found the Quaker idea of the "inner light" an acceptable doctrine. From Rhode Island Quakers frequently penetrated the neighboring colonies which took violent means to expel them. The Massachusetts persecution reached its height in 1660 when three Quakers were hanged, one of them being Mary Dyer, a former friend of Anne Hutchinson. This high-handed proceeding reached the ear of the king, who was in no amiable frame of mind toward the Puritan colonists, who were believed to be sheltering two of the regicides. He accordingly ordered the Boston authorities to send Quakers to England for trial, but

Massachusetts sent representatives to England, who succeeded in getting the king to grant the colony free hand in dealing with Quakers. Charles also confirmed the Massachusetts charter, but changed the basis of voting from church membership to a property qualification.

The Connecticut charter.—Connecticut fared well with Charles II. When the king's messengers visited the colony in search of the regicides, they were given assistance, while New Haven aided the fugitives in escaping. The results of this were soon apparent. In 1661 when Connecticut sent Governor John Winthrop to England to obtain a charter, he was graciously received and the following year the document was issued. It provided for a popularly elected governor, a deputy-governor, council, and assembly. The boundaries were described as "All that part of our Dominions . . . bounded on the East by the Narrogancett River, comonly called Narrogancett Bay . . . , and on the North by the lyne of the Massachusetts Plantation, and on the South by the Sea, and . . . from the said Narrogancett Bay on the East to the South Sea on the West parte, with the Islands thereunto adjoyneinge." The boundaries included a part of the territory of Rhode Island and the whole of New Haven, and entirely ignored the Dutch possessions in the Hudson Valley. New Haven protested violently, but in 1664, when the king granted the lands between the Connecticut and Delaware rivers to the Duke of York, the New Haven towns submitted to Connecticut rather than be annexed to New York.

The Rhode Island charter.—Fearful that Charles II might divide her territory among her neighbors, Rhode Island hastened to proclaim the king and petitioned that she be granted a charter. The Rhode Island representative protested against the inclusion of Narragansett Bay territory in Connecticut and the difficulty was adjusted by fixing the boundary at the Pawtucket River, which was renamed the Narragansett. The form of government was similar to that of Connecticut, but in Rhode Island religious freedom was established.

The royal commissioners.—In 1664, when the English government had determined upon the seizure of New Netherlands, commissioners were sent to America. Respecting New England, their duties were to settle boundary questions, to consider local disputes, and to see how the colonies might be made more profitable.   The commissioners visited Boston in July, 1664, where they obtained troops and demanded the repeal of the law which restricted the franchise to church membership.   After the conquest of New Netherlands, three of them returned to New England.   They were well received in Connecticut and Rhode Island. Plymouth at this time was attempting to obtain a charter, and the commissioners suggested that the colony might have its lands confirmed without cost if it would receive a royal governor, an offer which was declined.   In Boston their reception was stormy, the Massachusetts authorities denying that the commission had any right of jurisdiction.   Nicolls, the fourth commissioner, soon arrived and the debates continued, but without result.   The king rebuked Massachusetts for its lack of respect, but took no immediate steps to coerce the colony.

The frontier on the eve of King Philip's War.—In 1675 the Penobscot marked the most northern settlement.   Along the coasts and in the lower valleys of the short New England streams settlements had been planted.   Eastern Massachusetts and Plymouth contained numerous towns.   In Rhode Island the island was fairly well-settled, but with the exception of Providence and Warwick, the mainland had attracted few.   Other settlements were located near the mouth of the Thames, and in the valley of the Connecticut as far up as Northfield.   The coast lands of western Connecticut had also been occupied. The total population of New England did not exceed fifty thousand.   The lands beyond the fringe of settlement were occupied by powerful Indian tribes, which could muster about thirty-five hundred fighting men.

Causes of the war.—The encroachment of the frontiers on the Indian hunting ground was the primary cause of the war, but other events were contributory.   By 1660 the fur trade had declined, fish and lumber having become the important exports. This trade brought in silver, and wampum ceased to be the medium of exchange.   With the passing of furs and wampum, the Indian became less and less useful to the white man, who looked upon him with contempt.   The christianizing of the Cape Cod Indians by the Reverend John Eliot and other missionaries was viewed sullenly by the Wampanoags, who saw in it an attempt to weaken their power. Massasoit, Sachem of the Wampanoags, died in 1662, leaving two sons, called by the whites Alexander and Philip. The sudden death of Alexander gave rise to a belief among the Indians that he had been poisoned.

The war.—In the summer of 1675, outbreaks occurred in Rhode Island, and a settler was killed. An expedition was immediately sent against the Wampanoags, but Philip succeeded in escaping with his followers. The Nipmucks attacked Deerfield, Northfield, Springfield, and Hatfield, spreading terror in the Connecticut Valley. Believing that the Narragansetts were about to enter the war, Massachusetts, Plymouth, and Connecticut joined forces, and in December attacked their stronghold. After a bloody battle they captured it and dispersed the tribe. The survivors joined the other hostiles and harried the frontiers as far north as the Maine settlements. In April, 1676, Chief Canonchet, of the Narragansetts, was captured and shot, and the following month the Indians were decisively defeated near the falls of the Connecticut. After that the Indian confederation broke up and effective resistance came to an end in August with the death of Philip. The power of the tribes was broken and the way cleared for the advancement of the frontier.

Complaints against Massachusetts.—The independent course which Massachusetts had followed in her dealings with the home government had irritated Charles and the privy council, but the fall of Clarendon and the Dutch war of 1673 had kept the king from taking action against the headstrong colony. Complaints continued to be made. The heirs of Mason and Gorges claimed that Massachusetts had usurped their rights; London merchants complained that the colony was evading the navigation acts by carrying tobacco and sugar directly to Europe from other colonies; lack of respect for the king's authority, the exercising of powers not warranted by her charter, and numerous other complaints were lodged against her.

Edward Randolph.—In 1676 the king sent Edward Randolph to Massachusetts with an order that the colony send agents to England within six months to answer the Mason and Gorges claims, an order which was tardily fulfilled. He was also empowered to collect information which might be useful to the Lords of Trade. Randolph was not well received, being looked upon as an agent of the Mason and Gorges heirs. When he complained to Governor Leverett of the violation of the navigation laws, the governor boldly asserted that parliament had no power to legislate for Massachusetts, and denied that appeals might be made to the king. Randolph returned to England convinced that a change of government was necessary.

In 1678 Randolph was appointed collector of the customs, but he did not arrive in Boston until the following year. In the meantime the Massachusetts title to New Hampshire had been examined. Randolph bore a letter from the king which commanded the colony to give up its jurisdiction over both New Hampshire and Maine. The former command Massachusetts immediately obeyed, but the latter was ignored as the agents of Massachusetts had recently purchased the Gorges title.

Annulment of the charter.—As collector of the customs Randolph's course was beset with difficulties, and his reports were filled with complaints of frequent violations of the navigation acts. In 1681 he returned to England and advised that the charter of Massachusetts be abrogated and that all the New England colonies be united under one administrative head. Randolph soon returned to the colony, but the friction continued and his complaints became more and more violent. The king and the Lords of Trade finally wearied of the strong-willed colony, legal action was taken, and in 1684 the charter was annulled.

Temporary government.—The annulment of the charter did not bring about an insurrection in Massachusetts, for the colonial leaders realized that the protection of the mother country was necessary to preserve them from being conquered by the French. While the Lords of Trade were considering a form of government, a temporary plan was put in operation. Joseph Dudley was made president, Randolph secretary, and a council was appointed, but no provision was made for a legislative assembly. To enforce the laws of trade, in 1686 an admiralty court was established.

Affairs in New Hampshire.—Since New Hampshire was separated from Massachusetts, affairs in the northern colony had been going badly. A president and council had been established, but when Randolph attempted to enforce the trade laws, he had met with difficulties. The colonists also objected to paying quit-rents to the Mason heirs. In 1682 Edward Cranfield was appointed governor and was soon at loggerheads with the people over the Mason right, and in 1685 he left the colony in disgust.

Dominion of New England.—The Lords of Trade for some time had been considering the advisability of consolidating the New England colonies in order to cut down expense, to make the enforcement of the navigation acts more effective, and to bring the colonies into a closer dependence on the crown. When James became king, the plan was put into operation. In the new form of government the central figure was a governor-general who was to be assisted by a council, but no provision was made for a popular assembly.

Edmund Andros.—Andros, the former governor of New York, was appointed governor-general and arrived at Boston in December, 1686. In a businesslike manner he organized his government. Boston was made the seat of power. Andros acted as commander of the army and vice-admiral, and exercised the pardoning power. With the advice and consent of the council he made laws, levied taxes, and administered justice. He also made land grants and collected quit-rents. He demanded that Plymouth, Rhode Island, and Connecticut surrender their charters. Plymouth and Rhode Island complied and their representatives were admitted to the council, but Connecticut temporized. Finally Andros visited the obdurate colony, dissolved the government, and admitted representatives to his council. The charter, however, according to Connecticut tradition, was hidden in an oak tree and never left the colony. In 1688 the Lords of Trade determined to bring all the territory from the St. Croix and the St. Lawrence to the Delaware under the supervision of Andros.

Overthrow of Andros.—The system aroused the anger of the colonists, who looked upon the governor-general as a tyrant. Mutterings of discontent grew louder and louder, and when news reached Massachusetts that James II had fled from England, the people of Boston rose in revolt, seized the fortifications and royal frigate, and imprisoned Andros and Randolph. A council was established, a convention was summoned, and the old charter government was reëstablished.   Connecticut and Rhode Island also restored the charter governments.

READINGS

COLONIAL POLICY AND ADMINISTRATION

Andrews, C. M., *Colonial Self-Government*, 1–40; Beer, G. L., *The Old Colonial System*, I, 1–315; "The Commercial Policy of England toward the American Colonies," in Columbia University, *Studies in History, Economics, and Public Law*, III, Pt. 2, pp. 29–54; Channing, Edward, *History of the United States*, II, 1–13; Egerton, H. E., *A Short History of British Colonial Policy*, 66–80; MacDonald, William, *Select Charters*, 106–115, 119–120, 133– 136; Osgood, H. L., *The American Colonies in the Seventeenth Century*, III, 143–241.

VIRGINIA AND MARYLAND

Andrews, C. M., *Colonial Self-Government*, 202–251; Andrews, C. M., ed., *Narratives of the Insurrections*, 11–141, 299–314; Channing, Edward, *History of the United States*, II, 80–91, 209–213; Fiske, John, *Old Virginia and her Neighbors*, II, 45–107, 131–173; Osgood, H. L., *The American Colonies in the Seventeenth Century*, III, 242–308; Wertenbaker, T. J., *Virginia under the Stuarts*, 115–259.

NEW ENGLAND

Andrews, C. M., *Colonial Self-Government*, 41–73, 252–287; Andrews, C. M., ed., *Narratives of the Insurrections*, 165–297; Andrews, C. M., *The Fathers of New England;* Channing, Edward, *History of the United States*, II, 65–79, 155–203; Doyle, J. A., *The Puritan Colonies*, II, 190–276; Ellis, G. W., and Morris, J. E., *King Philip's War;* Fiske, John, *The Beginnings of New England*, 199–278; James, B. B., *The Colonization of New England*, 213–295; Osgood, H. L., *The English Colonies in the Seventeenth Century*, III, 309–335, 378–443; Palfrey, J. G., *Compendious History of New England*, II, 1–20; *History of New England*, III, chs. 3, 7–9, 12–14.

CHAPTER XI

EXPANSION UNDER THE LATER STUARTS

NEW YORK

The period of the later Stuarts was remarkable for colonial expansion. New Netherlands was acquired, the Jerseys, Pennsylvania, and the Carolinas were founded, the Hudson's Bay Fur Company was formed, and new settlements were made in the West Indies.

Causes of the attack upon the Dutch.—In 1664 New Netherlands was seized. This was not an isolated event but was a part of a general plan to weaken Dutch power. England had three main objects: to cripple the Dutch carrying trade, to get control of the slave trade, and to obtain New Netherlands, an acquisition which would give geographical unity to the colonies on the Atlantic seaboard. The navigation acts were weapons against the carrying trade. The African Company was organized to strike at the slave trade.

The African Company.—During the first half of the seventeenth century, the Dutch had obtained a monopoly of the trade in slaves to the Spanish and Portuguese colonies in America. To break this monopoly the African Company was formed in 1660, headed by the Duke of York. During the next two years the Dutch vigorously opposed the English Company, soon convincing its officers that it must be organized on a larger scale if it would succeed. In 1663 the Company of Royal Adventurers trading to Africa was organized, being granted the coast from Sallee to the Cape of Good Hope. Vessels sent to the African coast encountered such opposition that in 1664 a squadron was sent to protect them and succeeded in capturing several Dutch forts, but Admiral DeRuyter soon recaptured them.

Seizure of New Netherlands, 1664.—At the same time England prepared to seize New Netherlands, a territory which she had always claimed. The king granted to the Duke of York the northern part of Maine, Long Island, Martha's Vineyard, Nantucket, and New Netherlands. The Duke in turn granted the Jerseys to Carteret and Lord Berkeley. A royal commission was despatched to America with three war vessels and several hundred men. At Boston the expedition was reinforced and then proceeded to New Amsterdam, which surrendered without a struggle. One member of the commission went to the Delaware and took possession. In the Treaty of Breda (1667) the English were given important slave trading privileges, their conquests between the Hudson and the Delaware were confirmed, and Lord Willoughby's colony of Surinam was ceded to the Dutch, who had captured it in the course of the recent war.

Administration of Nicolls.—Nicolls was made governor and his administration was conducted with tact and firmness. In dealing with Connecticut he insisted upon the Duke's right to Long Island. In New Netherlands several Dutch place names were changed, New Amsterdam becoming New York, and Ft. Orange, Albany. The right of property was not disturbed; judicial districts were organized; and to New York City he granted a charter which provided for a mayor, aldermen, and sheriff, whom he appointed. Nicolls drew up a code, known as the Duke's Laws, which was a combination of portions of the codes of Massachusetts and New Haven, Dutch customs, and original ideas. Religious toleration was allowed, and landholding was made the basis for voting. The lack of a representative assembly was a noticeable feature, which led to discord when taxes were demanded.

Representative government demanded.—Lovelace became governor in 1668, and during his administration of five years friction increased, but he managed to maintain his authority. In 1673 when war broke out between England and Holland, New York was captured by the Dutch, but the following year it was restored to the English. Edmund Andros was then appointed governor. He informed the proprietor of the desire for a representative assembly, but James stubbornly refused. In 1681, when James neglected to renew the customs duties, the merchants refused to pay them. Because of the resulting loss of revenue Andros was ordered to England, and during his absence the disaffection greatly increased. Thomas Dongan was appointed governor in 1682. He was instructed to call a representative assembly to advise the governor and council regarding taxation and law making. In October, 1683, seventeen representatives met at New York and drew up a Charter of Franchises and Liberties. This was sent to the Duke, who signed it, but when he became king he rejected it.

Dongan's administration.—Dongan administered the province of New York with marked ability. He granted a new charter to New York City by which the mayor, recorder, and sheriff were appointed by the governor, and the aldermen were popularly elected. He maintained the boundaries of the province against the claims of Penn on the west and Connecticut on the east. In 1684 he made a treaty with the Iroquois, and henceforth they sided with the English in the great international struggle for trade and territory.

Leisler's rebellion.—When James II attempted to consolidate all of the northern provinces under one head New York was included. But when the king was overthrown, Jacob Leisler led a rebellion and drove out Nicholson, the royal representative. Leisler summoned a convention which gave him dictatorial powers. He maintained authority until 1691, when Henry Sloughter arrived as governor. Leisler surrendered, but was tried and hanged.

THE JERSEYS

Settlements in the Jerseys.—When the Jerseys passed into the hands of Carteret and Berkeley, there were two settled areas, one of Dutch origin about Bergen, Hoboken, and Wiehawken, the other of Dutch, Swedish, and Finnish settlements on the Delaware. When Nicolls came to New York he was not aware that part of the province had been granted to others. He immediately sought to bring in settlers; about two hundred people, descendants of New Englanders, moved from Long Island to the neighborhood of what was later known as Elizabethtown. Others, most of whom were Quakers, settled at Middletown and Shrewsbury under a special grant from Nicolls.

Government in East New Jersey.—In 1665 Philip Carteret, probably a brother of the proprietor, arrived with a governor's commission. With him were about thirty persons, most of whom were French people from the Island of Jersey. Elizabethtown was made the capital. Carteret brought with him a plan of government, which provided that the governor was to choose a council of not less than six, nor more than twelve members. The freemen were to choose twelve representatives, who were to join with the governor and council in law-making. When local divisions were established each division was to elect a representative to an assembly, which would then take the place of the twelve. The assembly could pass laws subject to certain restrictions, create local divisions, incorporate towns, erect forts, provide for a militia, wage war, naturalize foreigners, and perform many other acts. Religious liberty and property rights were carefully protected. The enforcement of laws, appointment of officers, and pardoning power were left in the hands of the governor and council.

Difficulties with New Englanders.—During 1666 many families from the Connecticut Valley migrated to East New Jersey, most of them settling on the Passaic River, Bradford and Guilford being founded. Newark was also settled. The settlers drew up a form of government copied from New Haven, which restricted the franchise to membership in the Congregational church. In April, 1668, the first assembly was called by Carteret, but the people from Middletown and Shrewsbury did not send delegates. To a session held in October these towns sent representatives, but they were not allowed to sit in the meeting. A quarrel ensued between the governor and assembly, which soon adjourned and did not convene again for seven years. In 1670, when Carteret attempted to collect quit-rents, the settlers refused to pay, and for two years the colony was in turmoil. Middletown and Shrewsbury, acting under their original patent from Nicolls, set up an independent government, but the governor refused to recognize it and was sustained by the proprietors, who, however, granted some concessions, whereupon the difficulties subsided.

The Quakers in West New Jersey.—In 1672 George Fox, the founder of the Quaker sect, crossed New Jersey and visited the Quakers in the eastern part. To this visit Penn's interest in the region may be traced. In 1674 Berkeley disposed of his share of

(From Fisher, *The Quaker Colonies*, in the Series, "The Chronicles of America," Yale University Press)

the colony to two Quakers, Edward Byllynge and John Fenwick, this transaction being due to a desire on the part of the Society of Friends to establish an independent colony. Byllynge and Fenwick became involved in a dispute over property rights, and William Penn was made arbiter. Penn awarded one-tenth to Fenwick, who, after considerable litigation, accepted it. Byllynge shortly afterward conveyed his holdings to Penn, Lawrie, and Lucas, who soon acquired Fenwick's interests. In 1676 Carteret and the Quaker proprietors fixed the line of demarcation between East and West New Jersey. It was to run from the "most southwardly point of the east side of Little Egg Harbor" to the point where the Delaware River crossed the forty-first parallel. The Quaker migration to West New Jersey began in 1675, when Fenwick led a group to Salem. In 1677 two hundred and thirty more settled at Burlington. During the next two years eight hundred arrived, and by 1681 nearly fourteen hundred had come to the colony. In every case title to the soil was obtained by purchase from the Indians.

Government of West New Jersey.—The original Burlington colonists brought with them a body of laws which have been described as "the broadest, sanest, and most equitable charter draughted for any body of colonists up to that time." No doubt Penn played the principal rôle in the draughting. It provided for a board of commissioners to be appointed by the proprietors and an assembly chosen by the people, which was to have full rights of making laws if they were not contrary to the charter or the laws of England. The charter provided for public trials by jury and assured the right of petition. Capital punishment was prohibited.

Trouble with the Duke of York.—After the expulsion of the Dutch in 1674, the Duke of York attempted to regain control of the Jerseys and refused to recognize the validity of Berkeley's sale to Byllynge. When Andros became governor of New York he attempted to assert the authority of James over the Jerseys, but the courts refused to uphold the claims of the Duke, and in 1680 he finally gave up the struggle.

Later history of West New Jersey.—In 1680 Byllynge obtained a title to West New Jersey from the Duke of York and the charter of 1677 was put into effect, with the exception that the executive was vested in a single person instead of in commissioners. In 1687 Byllynge died and Daniel Coxe, a London merchant, acquired his properties. Burlington was made the capital, and Coxe bent his efforts to make it a commercial center. In 1688 the colony was placed under the jurisdiction of Andros as a part of the northern administrative unit which included New York and New England, but Coxe was restored to his rights after the dethronement of James, though he soon sold out to the West New Jersey Society.

Later history of East New Jersey.—In 1682 Philip Carteret resigned, and the board of trustees who controlled the estate of Sir George Carteret sold East New Jersey to William Penn and eleven other Quakers. Shortly afterwards twelve others were taken into the company, several of whom were Scotch Presbyterians. In 1683 the twenty-four men received a deed from the Duke of York. Under these proprietors the colony prospered, and population increased rapidly. In 1688 the province came under royal jurisdiction and it was annexed to New York, but after the revolution it was restored to the proprietors.

PENNSYLVANIA

The Quaker faith.—The Reformation produced many religious sects. With the breaking down of one authoritative church and the substitution of the idea that any one might read and interpret the Bible, religious groups began forming. Among the numerous sects were the Quakers, the followers of George Fox. Seventeenth century religion was based upon the fundamental idea that the universe was dualistic, natural and supernatural. The question on which men split was how the chasm was to be bridged. Most of the Protestant sects believed that the crossing was made by a definite revelation of the word of God. Fox believed "that it was bridged by the communication of a supernatural Light given to each soul."

The coming of the Quakers.—Most of the seventeenth century religious sects, once in power, were as intolerant as the Catholics had been. The Quaker was looked upon with disfavor and persecution was his lot. In America he hoped to find an abiding place. Between 1655 and 1680 Quakers appeared in nearly all the colonies. Fox came to America in 1671 and in the course of the following year visited the Quaker communities from Barbados to Rhode Island.

Penn obtains lands on the Delaware.—The desire to obtain lands where they would be in complete control was long in the minds of the Quaker leaders. In 1680 William Penn petitioned for lands along the Delaware north of Maryland, in payment of a debt of 16,000 pounds. In spite of his faith Penn stood well at court, and on March 4, 1681, the charter of Pennsylvania was signed. The extent of the grant was defined as follows: "All that Tract or parte of land in America, with all the Islands therein conteyned, as the same is bounded on the East by Delaware River, from twelve miles distance, Northwarde of New Castle Towne unto the three and fortieth degree of Northerne Latitude if the said River doeth extend soe farre Northwards; But if the said River shall not extend soe farre Northward, then by the said River soe farr as it doth extend, and from the head of the said River the Easterne Bounds are to bee determined by a Meridian Line, to bee drawne from the head of the said River unto the said three and fortieth degree, The said lands to extend westwards, five degrees in longitude, to bee computed from the said Eastern Bounds, and the said lands to bee bounded on the North, by the beginning of the three and fortieth degree of Northern latitude, and on the South, by a Circle drawne at twelve miles, distance from New Castle Northwards, and Westwards unto the beginning of the fortieth degree of Northerne Latitude; and then by a streight Line westwards, to the Limitt of Longitude above menconed."

Both the northern and southern boundaries caused future disputes. Penn claimed as far north as the forty-third parallel, while New York insisted on the forty-second, a difference which was settled a century later in favor of New York. On the south the boundaries conflicted with the claims of Baltimore. In 1682 the question was further complicated by a grant to Penn from the Duke of York of the territory on the western shore of Delaware Bay. The difficulty was finally settled in 1760, and seven years later two surveyors, Mason and Dixon, ran the present line between Maryland and Pennsylvania at 39° 44′, and erected the present boundaries of the state of Delaware.

Powers of the proprietor.—By the charter Penn was made a proprietor, having the right to make laws with the advice and consent of the freemen. The proprietor was given power to execute the laws, issue ordinances, appoint judges and magistrates, pardon criminals except in cases of treason and willful murder, erect municipalities, and grant manors. The form of government in the colony was left to the proprietor. Laws had to be sent to the privy council for approval, but if action were not taken within six months, they were valid. The king reserved the right of hearing appeals. The navigation laws were to be enforced, and if damages accrued from non-enforcement and were not settled within a year, the king had the right to take over the government of the colony until payment was made.

The founding of Philadelphia.—Penn published a prospectus of his colony which was widely circulated, and drew up a body of conditions and concessions which dealt with the division and settlement of the province and with Indian relations. In 1681 he sent to America as deputy-governor his cousin, William Markham, who received the allegiance of the settlers already within the colony. Shortly afterward the first body of colonists arrived bearing instructions to lay out a town. The site of Philadelphia was surveyed the following year, a symmetrical plan being adopted which made Penn's capital the best-arranged city in colonial America.

The " frame of government."—The government devised by Penn consisted of "the Governor and freemen of the said province, in form of a Provincial Council and General Assembly, by whom all laws shall be made, officers chosen, and publick affairs transacted." An elective council was to consist of seventy-two persons "of most note for their wisdom, virtue and ability." This body, with the governor, was to prepare and propose all bills, and together they were to share executive powers. They were to erect courts of justice, elect county officers, provide schools, and perform numerous other duties. The assembly, which was to consist at first of not more than two hundred members, was to be elected annually. Its chief business was to consider and pass upon bills prepared by the governor and council.

Penn's first sojourn in the province.—Penn arrived on the ship *Welcome* in the fall of 1682, and immediately called an election for an assembly, in this case ignoring the details of the frame of government. The first assembly annexed the territory on the western shore of Delaware Bay, naturalized foreigners, and adopted a set of laws proposed by the proprietor, which provided for liberty of conscience, a strict code of morals, and for capital punishment for treason and murder only. Penn inspected his province, watched the building of Philadelphia, and visited New York, Maryland, and West New Jersey. He also held several meetings with the Indians, entering in June, 1683, into a treaty with them which had the salutary effect of keeping Pennsylvania free from Indian war. The number of representatives provided for in the frame of government proving too large, a new frame was drawn up by which the council was reduced to eighteen and the lower house to thirty-six members.

Penn's activities in England.—In August, 1684, Penn went to England to obtain a settlement of his disputes with Baltimore and to aid the persecuted Quakers. His claim to the Delaware tract was confirmed and he secured the release from English jails of more than twelve hundred Quakers. In 1688 he also succeeded in keeping his province from being incorporated within the jurisdiction of Andros.

Friction in the colony.—The political peace for which Penn had hoped was soon disturbed. Friction over the right to initiate legislation broke out between the council and assembly. Trouble with one of the justices also occurred. Hoping to quiet affairs, Penn took away the executive powers of the council and appointed a commission of five councillors who were to compel all to do their duty. As trouble continued, he did away with the commission and appointed Captain Blackwell, a Puritan, to act for him. This choice proved unfortunate, for the Puritan could not get along with the Quakers. In despair, Penn recalled Blackwell and allowed the council to select its own executive. The council again assumed the governorship, and chose Thomas Lloyd president. Friction also existed between the settlers along the shore of Delaware Bay and those in the river settlements, a difficulty which eventually led to the separation of Delaware from Pennsylvania.

Growth of the colony.—In spite of frictions the colony prospered. When Penn acquired his province, it contained about a thousand Swedes, Finns, and Dutch, and a few Quakers. By 1685 the population had increased to more than eight thousand, made up of diverse elements; Quakers, mostly from central and southwestern England and from Wales, Mennonites from the Rhineland, Swedes, Scotch, Irish, and French. Philadelphia soon boasted a tannery, sawmill, and kiln; linen manufacture began; and the colony entered upon a prosperous intercolonial trade in flour, staves, and horses. A weekly post and a school were established, and a printing press installed. It was evident that Penn's "holy experiment" had justified itself.

THE INSULAR COLONIES

Reorganization in the Bermudas.—Complaints by the settlers against the rule of the Somers Islands Company in the Bermudas had been common since its foundation. As time went on it became composed of men who had little interest in the colony. The settlers, on the other hand, grew in numbers and independence. Under the circumstances, in the general reorganization by the later Stuarts, the company was dissolved, and in 1679 the Bermudas became a crown colony.

Reorganization in the West Indies.—Down to 1671 the English Caribbean island possessions were all included in one government within the Carlisle grant. In that year they were separated into two governments, St. Kitts, Nevis, Montserrat, Antigua, Barbuda, Anguilla and "all other the Leeward islands" to the north of French Guadeloupe were separated from Barbados and the Windward Islands, and erected into the government of the Leeward Islands, the islands to the south of Guadeloupe being formed into the government of the Windward Islands. The Leeward Islands were put under one governor-in-chief, each island being given a deputy governor, council, assembly, and courts. In 1689 the islands together were granted a general assembly, which first met in 1690.

New settlements in the West Indies.—During the period of the later Stuarts the Leeward Islands extended their influence among the smaller islands to the northwest. In 1665 a buccaneering expedition from Jamaica captured St. Eustatius and Saba. In 1666 settlers from the Bermudas settled on New Providence, one of the Bahamas, and elected a governor. Four years later six of the

Carolina proprietors secured a patent to the island but did little toward colonizing it.   In 1672 Tortola was taken from the Dutch and added to the Leeward Islands.

Unrest in Barbados.—The first important movement to settle Carolina came from Barbados, the most populous of the English colonies.   A spirit of unrest pervaded the island.   During the Commonwealth it had been a refuge for both Cavaliers and Roundheads, and the newcomers had taken up lands without securing titles.   When the Stuarts were restored, the former proprietors attempted to regain their possessions.   A lively controversy ensued.   The king settled it by establishing his authority in the island, but levied a tax of four and one-half per cent. on its products to be applied to satisfy in part the claims of the proprietors, an arrangement which pleased no one.   The navigation acts also considerably interfered with the trade of the island which had previously been carried on largely with the Dutch.   As a result many settlers were anxious to leave. Between 1643 and 1667 at least twelve hundred Barbadians went to fight or settle in Jamaica, Tobago, St. Lucia, Trinidad, Surinam, New England, Virginia, or Carolina.

THE CAROLINAS

The Carolina coast.—From the James River region to the Spanish settlements in Florida, stretched a vast territory, which, with the single exception of a settlement on the Chowan River, was unoccupied by white men when Charles II came to the throne.   After Raleigh's ill-starred venture it had received little attention until 1629, when Sir Robert Heath obtained a patent to lands between 31° and 36° north latitude, but he did nothing to improve the territory.   The coasts were occasionally visited by mariners, but there is no definite knowledge of any settlement until 1653, when colonists from Virginia appear to have started a settlement at Albemarle on the Chowan River.   About 1660 some New Englanders inspected the Cape Fear River mouth but departed soon afterward.

The charters.—In 1660 Sir John Colleton, a prominent resident of Barbados, went to England where he became a member of the Council for Foreign Plantations.   He soon interested Anthony Ashley Cooper, later known as Lord Ashley, in the Carolinas.

In 1663 a charter was granted to eight proprietors, Cooper, Clarendon, Craven, Albemarle, Carteret, Lord Berkeley, Colleton, and Sir William Berkeley. The territory granted extended from the thirty-sixth to the thirty-first parallel and from sea to sea. Over this region the proprietors were given practically the same rights as Baltimore possessed in Maryland. In 1665 a second patent was granted to the proprietors, extending the boundaries to 36° 30' on the north and to 29° on the south.

The fundamental constitutions.—The philosopher, John Locke, drew up a constitution for the province. It provided for a high official called the palatine, and minor officials designated as admiral, chamberlain, chancellor, constable, chief justice, steward, and treasurer. The province was to be divided into counties, and each county into seigniories, baronies, and precincts. On these divisions were to be based the ranks of the nobility to be designated as land-graves, caciques, and lords of manors. An elaborate system of courts was provided; also a grand council and a parliament. This archaic feudal document is of interest mainly as a study in the political philosophy of the time, but it was of little real importance as it was totally unsuited to the needs of a frontier community. It was never put in force except in certain minor particulars, the settlers themselves soon solving their problems of government in their own way.

Beginnings of settlement.—In 1663–1664 an expedition from Barbados examined the Carolina coast, and in 1665 Sir John Yeamans conducted a group of settlers to the mouth of Cape Fear River. Yeamans soon returned to Barbados and the settlers, left to their own devices, in 1667 abandoned the settlement, most of them going to Albemarle, Virginia, and Boston. In 1669 vessels carrying ninety-two colonists sailed from England to Barbados, where Sir John Yeamans, who had been appointed governor, joined them. They then proceeded to the Bermudas, where Yeamans handed over the authority to William Sayle and abandoned the expedition. The colonists under Sayle then went to Port Royal, but finally settled on the Ashley River, where they laid out old Charles Town (1670). Political strife soon developed, owing mainly to the incompetence of the aged executive. In 1671 he died and Joseph West was chosen governor by the people.

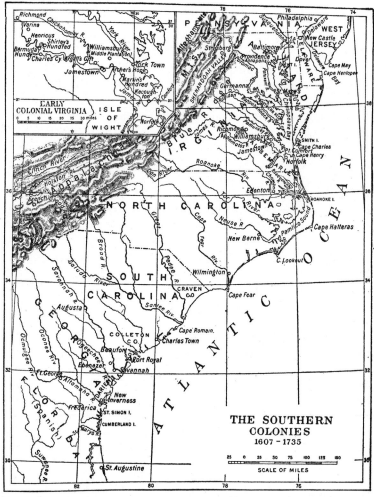

THE SOUTHERN
COLONIES
1607 - 1735

SCALE OF MILES

(From Johnston, *Pioneers of the Old South,* in the Series, "The Chronicles of America," Yale University Press)

Plans of the proprietors.—In 1670 the proprietors obtained a grant of the Bahamas and planned to build up trade between the island and mainland settlements. They also planned to improve the Charles Town settlement and in 1671 secured settlers from Barbados. Yeamans came over and claimed the governorship, but West succeeded in keeping the office for several months. In 1672 Yeamans was again appointed governor, but he managed things so badly that in 1674 West was reappointed and remained governor for eight years.

Development of the Charles Town region.—Colonists came in considerable numbers; in 1672 there were about four hundred people in the colony, and by 1685 the population had increased to about twenty-five hundred. Among the immigrants were a hundred French Protestants, and a colony of Scots who settled at Port Royal in 1683. Other colonists came from Barbados and many from western England. In 1680 the seat of government was moved from old Charles Town to the junction of the Ashley and Cooper Rivers. After 1680 settlements began to expand into the back country. This soon brought on the inevitable Indian war, which continued intermittently for three years. In 1685 the Spaniards raided the settlements, burning many houses, and the following year destroyed the Scotch settlement at Port Royal.

Unrest at Charleston.—During West's administration the colony was not greatly disturbed by political difficulties, the proprietors making little attempt to enforce the Locke constitution. The colony was governed by a popularly elected "parliament," which chose a council of five men. The chief executive was the governor commissioned by the proprietors. From 1682 to 1689 proprietary interference increased, bringing the colony to the verge of rebellion. The colonial parliament had steadily refused to confirm the constitution. During 1682 it was revised by the proprietors, more power being placed in the hands of the people, but still the colonists refused to confirm it. This irritated the proprietors, who retaliated by introducing a new form of land tenure, which required the colonists to pay a cash quit-rent. When James II came to the throne, Governor Morton demanded that they swear allegiance to the king and accept the constitution, whereupon twelve members of the parliament refused and were excluded. The colonists also took with ill grace the attempt to collect the customs. In 1688 the governor and council found themselves at complete loggerheads with parliament, and legislation stopped. James Colleton, the governor, proclaimed martial law. This led to an open rebellion, and in 1691 Colleton was expelled, but the proprietary power was soon restored.

The Albemarle colony.—During these troublous times the Albemarle settlement was slowly developing. The colony was mainly recruited from Virginia, but there was also a considerable influx of Quakers. In 1682 the Albemarle settlement contained about twenty-five hundred inhabitants. When an attempt was made in 1677 to collect the customs and to shut off the New England trade, about a hundred colonists led by John Culpeper rebelled and imprisoned Miller, who was the collector of customs and acting governor. They also arrested the president of the assembly and all but one of the deputies. The proprietors removed Miller from office and appointed Seth Sothell governor, but the people soon drove him from the colony. The turbulence did not quiet down until the appointment of Governor Ludwell, who from 1691 resided at Charleston, Albemarle being governed henceforth by a deputy.

WESTERN TRADE AND EXPLORATION

By now English explorers and fur traders had crossed the Alleghanies. As early as 1648 Governor Berkeley was preparing an expedition to the southwest, where red capped Spaniards riding "long eared beasts," came to trade with the natives. Twenty-five years later (1673) two Virginians, James Needham and Gabriel Arthur, reached the Cherokees on the Upper Tennessee. To these mountain dwellers on the "western waters" the Englishmen were a novel sight, but they had long been acquainted with the Spaniards and possessed "some sixty Spanish flint-locks," and among them lived Spanish mulatto women. Before the end of the century South Carolina traders had established the "Chickasaw Trail" through the Creek and Chickasaw country, and had crossed the Mississippi. In 1699–1700 Carolinians ascended the Savannah, descended the Tennessee, Ohio, and Mississippi to the mouth of the Arkansas. Frontiersmen had gone northwest as well as southwest, and before the end of the century had begun to make their way among the Indians on both sides of the upper Ohio River.

HUDSON'S BAY COMPANY

Continued search for the Northwest Passage.—Some of the same men who represented the Carolinas now extended English enterprises to the region of Hudson Bay. The English search for the Northwest Passage had not ended with the sixteenth century. Henry Hudson, who in 1609 had explored Hudson River in an attempt to find the passage, made further attempts in the following year. Finding his way in the *Discovery* through Hudson Strait, he wintered at the southern extremity of James Bay. He paid dearly for his discoveries, for he was cast adrift by mutinous followers and perished. In Hudson's wake went numerous explorers, backed by syndicates of merchants and sometimes with royal support, still seeking the passage. In 1612 Button crossed Hudson Bay and entered the mouth of Nelson River. At the same time a company was formed to seek the passage. In 1616 Bylot and Baffin discovered Baffin Bay, and in 1631 Foxe made new discoveries in Fox Channel. Denmark also entered the field of northwestern discovery and in 1619–1620 Jens Munck explored Hudson Bay, wintering at Churchill Harbor.

Radisson, Groseilliers, and Gillam.—The primary purpose of the foregoing voyages had been to find a passage to the Far East. They were followed, after an interval, by trading enterprises. The operations of the French fur traders, Radisson and Groseilliers, have been mentioned previously. Having been imprisoned and fined for illicit trading, they left Canada, went to New England, and got up an expedition to Hudson Bay to gather furs. Sailing in 1664 with Captain Zachariah Gillam, they reached Hudson Strait but not the bay. After another failure in 1665, they met Sir George Carteret whom they interested in their project. Going to England, through Carteret's influence they organized a company among whose stockholders were the Duke of York, Prince Rupert, Carteret, the Duke of Albemarle, and the Earls of Craven, Arlington, and Shaftesbury, several of whom were already influential in colonial enterprises. In 1668

the company again sent Gillam to Hudson Bay, where he built
Charles Fort on Rupert's River, and traded profitably in furs.
The part played by Radisson and Groseilliers in this enter-
prise became a basis for French claims to the Hudson Bay region.

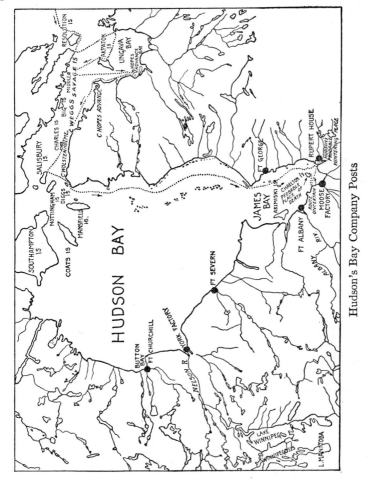

Hudson's Bay Company.—The return of Gillam to London.
in 1669 was followed by the formation of a new Company. On
May 2, 1670, Charles II issued a royal charter to "The Governor
and Company of Adventurers of England trading into Hudson's
Bay." The Company was made absolute proprietor with a com-

plete monopoly of all trade of the Hudson Bay basin. The government was centered in a governor, deputy-governor, and committee of seven, who were empowered to make laws and were given judicial and military authority. They lost no time in establishing posts, and by 1685 there were trading houses at Albany River, Hayes Island, Rupert's River, Port Nelson, Moose River, and New Severn.

Trading Methods.—Ships were fitted out annually in London with merchandise, and brought back rich cargoes of furs. In contrast with the French traders and with the English of the Atlantic seaboard colonies, the Hudson's Bay Company did not penetrate the interior, but depended upon the natives to bring their peltry to the posts on the Bay. In the spring, therefore, after the break-up of the ice, Crees, Chipewyans, and Eskimos came down the rivers in fleets of canoes laden with furs, traded them for merchandise, and returned for another season's hunt. In London the furs were sold at auction at the Company's headquarters, where the annual fair took on the nature of a social function. Gradually the markets widened, agents being sent to establish trade with Holland, Russia, and other parts of Northern Europe. Profits were large, the dividend in 1690 being seventy-five per cent of the original stock.

French Rivalry.—The success of the English aroused the jealousy of the French traders in the St. Lawrence Valley, and there ensued a rivalry which constituted one of the important episodes of the intercolonial wars which now occurred. In the contest Radisson, who had aided in the formation of the Company, played fast and loose between the English and the French. Before the end of the century French rivalry in the interior, beyond Lake Superior, did much to shake the "H. B. C." from its exclusive, seaboard policy. By 1691 Henry Kelsey, an employe of the Company, had made an expedition to the Winnipeg district.

READINGS

NEW YORK

Andrews, C. M., *Colonial Self-Government*, 74–100, 273–287; Andrews, C. M., ed., *Narratives of the Insurrections*, 315–401; Brodhead, J. R., *History of New York*, II; Channing, Edward, *History of the United States*, II, 31–60, 203–209; Doyle, J. A., *The Middle Colonies*, 78–223; Fiske, John, *Dutch and*

Quaker Colonies, II, 1–98, 168–208; New York Historical Society, *Collections*, 1st Series, I, 307–428; Osgood, H. L., *The English Colonies in the Seventeenth Century*, II, 119–168; Winsor, Justin, *Narrative and Critical History*, III, 385–411.

THE JERSEYS AND PENNSYLVANIA

Andrews, C. M., *Colonial Self-Government*, 101–128, 162–201; Channing, Edward, *History of the United States*, II, 31–62, 94–130; Clarkson, Thomas, *Memoirs of Pennsylvania;* Doyle, J. A., *The Middle Colonies*, 287–350, 379–410; Fiske, John, *Dutch and Quaker Colonies*, II, 115–194; Fisher, Sidney, *The Quaker Colonies;* Hodgkin, Thomas, *George Fox;* Holder, C. F., *The Quakers in Great Britain and America*, 169–217; Janney, S. M., *Life of Penn;* Jones, R. M., *The Quakers in the American Colonies*, 357–371, 417–436; MacDonald, William, *Select Charters*, 139–149, 171–204; Osgood, H. L., *The English Colonies in the Seventeenth Century*, II, 169–197, 252–276; Sharpless, Isaac, *A Quaker Experiment in Government; Two Centuries of Pennsylvania History*, 17–77; Smith, Samuel, *The History of the Colony of Nova-Cæsaria or New Jersey*, 35–207; Tanner, E. P., *The Province of New Jersey*, 1–147; Whitehead, W. A., *East Jersey under the Proprietary Governments*.

THE CAROLINAS

Andrews, C. M., *Colonial Self-Government*, 129–161; Andrews, C. M., ed., *Narratives of the Insurrections*, 143–164; Ashe, S. A., *North Carolina*, I; Channing, Edward, *History of the United States*, II, 13–25; Hamilton, P. J., *Colonization of the South*, 133–135; McCrady, Edward, *The History of South Carolina under the Proprietary Government*, I, 1–209; Osgood, H. L., *The American Colonies in the Seventeenth Century*, II, 200–225; Ramsay, David, *South Carolina*.

HUDSON'S BAY COMPANY

Burpee, Laurence J., *The Search for the Western Sea*, 64–95; Bryce, George, *The Remarkable History of the Hudson's Bay Company*, 1–55; Laut, Agnes, *The Conquest of the Great Northwest*, I, 1–255; Laut, Agnes, *The Adventurers of England on Hudson Bay;* Willson, Beckles, *The Great Company*, 1–181; Winsor, J., *Narrative and Critical History*, VIII, 1–34.

WESTERN EXPLORATION

Alvord and Bidgood, *First Explorations of the Trans-Allegheny Region* . . . 1650–1674; Crane, V. W., "The Tennessee River as the Road to Carolina," in *Miss. Valley Hist. Rev.*, III, 3–18.

CHAPTER XII

THE ENGLISH MAINLAND COLONIES AT THE CLOSE OF THE SEVENTEENTH CENTURY

At the close of the Stuart period the English mainland colonies stretched along the Atlantic coast from Pemaquid to Port Royal. The settlements nestled close to the coasts, in the tide-water region, or along the lower waters of the navigable streams. The total population probably did not exceed 225,000, one-half of whom were in Massachusetts and Virginia. At the same period Barbados alone contained over 50,000 white settlers and more than 100,000 slaves.

NEW ENGLAND

Population.—New England contained some 80,000 white inhabitants. About 5,000 were in New Hampshire; Massachusetts, including the Maine and Plymouth settlements, contained about 55,000; Rhode Island probably 5,000, and Connecticut about 17,000. By far the larger part were of English stock, although there were a few Huguenots, Scotch, Irish, and Jews. The settled area extended from the Pemaquid region along the coast in an almost unbroken line to the New York border. In Maine the settled region seldom extended more than ten miles back from the coast, and between Casco and Saco bays there were large unsettled tracts. In New Hampshire the frontier line ran back from the coast fifteen to thirty miles and eastern Massachusetts was settled fifty miles inland. All of Rhode Island except some tracts in the southern part had been occupied. Portions of northeastern and northwestern Connecticut were wilderness, but in the Connecticut Valley the settlers had begun to occupy the valley lands just to the north of the Massachusetts line.

Agriculture.—The mass of the population was agricultural. The clearing of the land and the securing of a food supply were the natural pursuits of the new communities. The small farm was the prevailing type, as neither climate, crops, nor soil were suitable for the large plantation. Corn, wheat, fruits, and vegetables were the principal agricultural products, and cattle, swine, sheep, and poultry were raised for domestic use.

Furs and fish.—The forests and the sea were the principal sources of New England prosperity. In the early part of the century the fur trade was an important factor, but by the end of the century it had considerably decreased. As it declined the fishing business increased. On the Newfoundland banks the boats of the New Englanders were the most numerous. The catch of cod and mackerel was dried and salted, and became a leading export.

Lumbering and ship-building.—The uncleared back country was a continual source of profit. Logging became a regular winter pursuit. From the felled timber were produced lumber, staves, shingles, masts, and spars. The fishing business conducted close to a lumbering region led to ship-building, and almost every seacoast town engaged in the industry. Most of the boats were small, swift-sailing craft, used in the fisheries or in the coasting and West Indian trade. So well-built were they that the New Englander found a ready market in the West Indies for vessel as well as cargo.

Commerce.—Fish, furs, and lumber were the principal products which the New Englanders produced for outside consumption. Most of the carrying business was conducted by Massachusetts men, although Rhode Island also handled a considerable trade. The navigation laws were intended to keep commerce in the hands of English merchants, but in spite of them colonial vessels kept up a coast-wise trade, and shipped fish, lumber, and staves to the West Indies and Madeira. Return vessels brought wine, rum, molasses, sugar, cotton, and wool. The greater part of New England commerce was handled through Boston, although Salem and Newport were rivals. Newport traders carried on a large slave traffic from Guinea and Madagascar, but most of their cargoes were sold in the West Indies.

Manufactures.—In Massachusetts and Connecticut manufacturing for the home market developed at an early date. Grist and saw-mills, tanneries, glass and pottery works, brick yards, and salt works were commonly found in the tide-water region, and at least two iron works were in operation in Massachusetts before 1700. Every village had its cobbler and blacksmith, and the housewives did the spinning and weaving. Most of the people wore homespun, but finer fabrics were also in demand, and at an early date the manufacture of cotton and woolen goods on a more elaborate scale was undertaken in Massachusetts.

Standard of living.—Practically all New Englanders were free settlers, but a limited number of indented servants and a few hundred slaves were intermixed with the population. In the regions near the coast the standard of living had materially improved. In the larger towns the inhabitants enjoyed even a degree of luxury in dress and table, and the log huts of the first settlers had almost disappeared, frame, shingled, and even brick houses having taken their place. Most of the houses of the well-to-do had a second floor, attic, and lean-to. Every community had its meeting house, and in 1670 Boston had three places of worship. As the traveler passed into the back country, he found roads growing poorer and poorer, gradually deteriorating into mere trails. The clearings and log cabins became less and less frequent until he finally reached the wilderness, which was penetrated only by the hunter and trader. When the settlements extended a considerable distance from the coast, they were usually along a navigable stream, the indispensable means of communication in a newly settled community.

Social standards.—Daily life was simple and devoid of ostentation, but in the older communities social lines were rigidly drawn. An austere aristocracy ruled. Admitted to the inner circle were the descendants of the early leaders or of families of rank in England, Oxford and Cambridge men, and those who were selected through natural worth to fill high positions in church and state. Intelligence and piety were more potent factors than wealth in the attainment of position. Of professional men the ministers held an exalted place, exerting a powerful influence socially, religiously, and politically. There were few doctors and lawyers, the latter being looked upon as undesirable trouble makers.

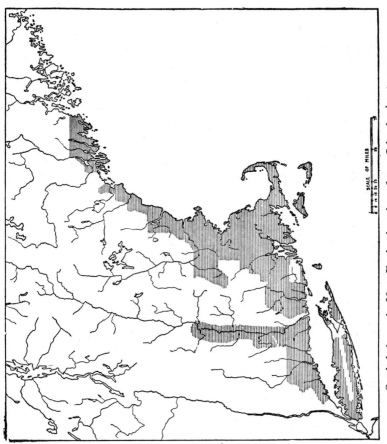

SCALE OF MILES

Settled Areas in New England and on Long Island, about 1700

Religion.—Throughout New England, except in Rhode Island, church and state were united, the Congregational church being in the ascendency. Though in 1660 Charles II commanded that the Anglican church be tolerated in Massachusetts, the authorities resisted its introduction, and not until 1686 was an Episcopalian church established in Boston. In Connecticut there were a few Presbyterians and Quakers. In Rhode Island the Baptists and Quakers were the most important element.

Superstitions.—The seventeenth century Puritan was intolerant and superstitious. Men must conform or be persecuted. Signs and portents were believed in, and strange and often filthy concoctions and ointments were administered at the suggestion of midwives or knowing housewives. Belief in witchcraft was usual both in Europe and America, and such learned men as Increase and Cotton Mather, prominent clergymen of Boston, wrote treatises to prove its truth. The Massachusetts laws recognized it as a capital offense. In 1692 occurred the famous outbreak at Salem in which nineteen innocent persons were executed.

Education.—In the English colonies New England took the lead in provision for popular education. Men who believed that the Bible was the source of authority naturally thought that every man should have sufficient intellectual training to enable him to read the word of God. In 1635 the first Latin grammar school in the English colonies was started at Boston, and several other towns soon followed the example. In 1647 Massachusetts enacted a general education law which required every town of fifty or more freeholders to appoint a teacher to instruct children to read and write. Every town of one hundred or more freeholders was required to support a Latin grammar school which would prepare students for college. Connecticut and New Haven soon followed the lead of Massachusetts. In Rhode Island and Plymouth each community was allowed to follow its own course. In Rhode Island the few schools were usually private enterprises. In Plymouth the first public school was not opened until 1671. Higher education was not neglected, Harvard being founded in 1636. In that year Massachusetts voted £400 toward the support of a college. Two years later John Harvard bequeathed his library and one-half of his estate for the erection of a college, and Harvard College came into existence. For many years it was devoted mainly to the training of religious leaders, and its curriculum reflected the classical viewpoint of the great English universities.

Literature.—The literature of the first century of New England was permeated with a gloomy religious viewpoint, but it was not lacking in dignity or power. It reflected the sternness of standards and purpose of the founders, who saw little of the humor, or of the lighter side of existence. The strongest of the writings were the histories, the best being the *History of Plymouth* by Governor Bradford and *The History of New England* by Governor Winthrop. Of less interest to the present day mind are the controversial religious tracts and sermons of Roger Williams and Cotton Mather, or the crude poetry of Mrs. Anne Bradstreet.

NEW YORK AND EAST NEW JERSEY

Population.—Economically and socially New York and East New Jersey were closely related. At the end of the Andros régime the population of New York was probably 18,000, and that of East New Jersey about 10,000. More than half of the New Yorkers were Dutch. The rest were mainly English, but there were some Huguenots and a few Jews. The settled area covered almost all of Long Island and the Hudson Valley to a point a few miles north of Albany. Most of the population of East New Jersey was along the coast opposite New York harbor. The English predominated, but there was a sprinkling of Dutch, Scotch, and Huguenots.

Industry in New York.—During the first decades of the Dutch occupation of the Hudson Valley the fur trade had been almost the only business, but after 1638 many settlers came who began general farming. Lumbering also developed. The general lines of industry thus begun were carried on after the English occupation. The fur trade was greatly stimulated by Dongan and it was probably the chief source of wealth in the colony. Population increased slowly. The advantageous position of New York attracted shipping, and the merchants developed a commerce with the West Indies and the Dutch possessions in the Caribbean to which were shipped bread stuffs, pease, meat, and horses.

The returning vessels brought wine, rum, molasses, and various tropical products. To England the New Yorkers shipped furs, oil, and naval supplies in return for manufactured goods.

A contemporary description of New York.—Governor Dongan

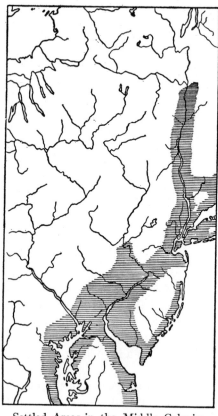

wrote concerning the province in 1687: "The principal towns within the Govermt are New York Albany & Kingston at Esopus. All the rest are country villages. The buildings in New York & Albany are generally of stone & brick. In the country the houses are mostly new built, having two or three rooms on a floor. The Dutch are great improvers of land. New York and Albany live wholly upon trade with the Indians England and the West Indies. . . . I believe for these 7 years last past, there has not come over into this province twenty English Scotch or Irish familys. But on the contrary on Long Island the people encrease soe fast that

Settled Areas in the Middle Colonies about 1700

they complain for want of land and many remove from thence into the neighboring province."

Religion and education in New York.—Regarding religion Dongan wrote, "Every Town ought to have a Minister. New York has first a Chaplain belonging to the Fort of the Church of England; secondly, a Dutch Calvinist, thirdly a French Calvinist, fourthly a Dutch Lutheran—Here bee not many of the

Church of England; few Roman Catholicks; abundance of Quakers preachers men & Women especially; Singing Quakers, Ranting Quakers, Sabbatarians; anti-sabbatarians; Some Anabaptists some Independents; some Jews; in short of all sorts of opinions there are some, and the most part of none at all. . . . The most prevailing opinion is that of the Dutch Calvinists." This description applied to religious conditions in New York City, then as now a cosmopolitan place. On Long Island, where New Englanders were predominant, the Congregational church held sway, while in the Hudson Valley, where most of the settlers were Dutch, the Dutch Reformed church was in the ascendency. The Dutch had maintained elementary schools, but when the English occupied the country, most of the school-masters left, and little was done by the authorities to stimulate education. Such schools as existed were established by the local communities.

Large estates.—During the Dutch régime many large estates had been created, the most important being the patroonship of Van Rensselaer about Albany. Although the other patroons had surrendered their rights, the Dutch governors, officials, and merchants had acquired vast estates, which continued in their families after the English occupation. The English governors followed the example, and several large holdings were created, the most famous of these being the Livingston manor on the east bank of the Hudson below the Van Rensselaer tract.

Conditions in East New Jersey.—The people of East New Jersey came mainly from New England and Long Island, and they built up a miniature New England, each village being an entity surrounded by tributary farm lands. Garden truck, fish, oysters, and fruits were the principal products. The proprietors hoped to develop commerce, but the Duke of York's restrictions throttled it, and East New Jersey was forced into the position of a supply station for New York. Gawen Laurie, the deputy-governor, described conditions as follows in 1684: "There is great plenty of oysters, fish, fowl; pork is two pennies the pound, beef and venison one penny the pound, a whole fat buck for five or six shillings; Indian corn for two shillings and six pence per bushel, oats twenty pence, and barley two shillings per bushel: We have good brick earth, and stones for building at Amboy, and elsewhere: The country farm houses are built very cheap:

A carpenter, with a man's own servants, builds the house; they have all materials for nothing, except nails, their chimnies are of stones; they make their own ploughs and carts for the most part, only the iron work is very dear: The poor sort set up a house of two or three rooms themselves, after this manner; the walls are of cloven timber, about eight or ten inches broad, like planks, set one end to the ground, and the other nailed to the raising, which they plaster within; they build a barn after the same manner, and these cost not above five pounds a piece; and then to work they go: Two or three men in one year will clear fifty acres, in some places sixty, and in some more: They sow corn the first year, and afterwards maintain themselves; and the increase of corn, cows, horses, hogs and sheep comes to the landlord; . . . the servants work not so much by a third as they do in England, and I think feed much better; for they have beef, pork, bacon, pudding, milk, butter and good beer and cyder for drink; when they are out of their time, they have land for themselves, and generally turn farmers for themselves."

Religion and education in East New Jersey.—Another letter of the same date says: "There be people of several sorts of religions, but few very zealous; the people, being mostly New-England men, do mostly incline to their way; and in every town there is a meeting-house, where they worship publickly every week: They have no publick laws in the country for maintaining publick teachers, but the towns that have them, make way within themselves to maintain them; we know none that have a settled preacher, that follows no other employment, save one town, Newark."

COLONIES ALONG DELAWARE RIVER AND BAY

Population.—The settlements along Delaware River and Bay formed an industrial and social group. In 1700 the population numbered less than 20,000, from 12,000 to 15,000 being in Pennsylvania which included Delaware. The interior of West New Jersey was unoccupied, the population remaining close to the coast. From Barnegat to Cape May the settled area was about ten miles wide. Along the eastern shore of the bay and river the population belt widened to twenty-five or thirty miles. In Pennsylvania and Delaware the settled area was continuous from the mouth of the Lehigh River to the southern boundary of Delaware. Back from the river the habitations extended for forty or fifty miles, but on the bay shore none of the settlers were more than ten or fifteen miles inland. The population of the Delaware region was composed of many nationalities. West New Jersey contained many English, but the descendants of the early Swedish and Dutch settlers were there in considerable numbers. Pennsylvania contained about 1,000 Swedes, Dutch, and Finns, the remnant of the early occupations. Penn's advertising and reputation for philanthropy brought to his colony English, Germans, Scotch, and Welsh.

Conditions in West New Jersey.—The following description of West New Jersey, written in 1698, gives an excellent picture of the colony: "In a few Years after [1675] a Ship from *London*, and another from *Hull*, sail'd thither with more People, who went higher up into the Countrey, and built there a Town, and called it *Burlington* which is now the chiefest Town in that Countrey though *Salem* is the ancientest; and a fine *Market-Town* it is, Having several Fairs kept yearly in it; likewise well furnished with good store of most Necessaries for humane Support, as *Bread, Beer, Beef,* and *Pork;* as also *Butter* and *Cheese,* of which they freight several Vessels and send them to *Barbadoes,* and other islands.

"There are very many fine *stately Brick-Houses* built [at Salem], and a *commodious Dock* for *Vessels* to come in at, and they claim equal Privilege with *Burlington* for the sake of Antiquity; tho' that is the principal Place, by reason that the late Governor *Cox,* who bought that Countrey of Edward *Billing,* encouraged and promoted that Town chiefly, in settling his *Agents* and *Deputy-governors* there, (the same Favours are continued by the *New-West-Jersey* Society, who now manage Matters there) which brings their Assemblies and chief Courts to be kept there; and by that means it is become a very famous Town, having a great many stately *Brick-Houses* in it, (as I said before) with a great *Market-House* . . . ; It hath a noble and *spacious Hall* overhead, where their *Sessions* is kept, having the Prison adjoining to it. . . .

"A Ship of Four Hundred Tuns may sail up to this *Town* in the River *Delaware;* for I my self have been on Board a Ship of

that Burthen there: and several fine Ships and Vessels (besides
Governour Cox's own great Ship) have been built there. . . .
There are *Water-Men* who constantly Ply their Wherry Boats
from that Town to the City of *Philadelphia* in *Pensilvania,* and
to other places. Besides there is *Glocester-Town,* which is a very
Fine and Pleasant Place, being well stor'd with Summer Fruits,
as *Cherries, Mulberries,* and Strawberries whither Young People
come from Philadelphia in the Wherries to eat *Strawberries* and
Cream, within sight of which city it is sweetly Situated, being
but about three Miles distant from thence."

Economic conditions in Pennsylvania.—When Penn's colonists arrived they found many farms under cultivation. Many
of the new arrivals took up farming, and the lower counties
became a supply region for Philadelphia. Under Penn's direction, Philadelphia soon became a trading center, and as it grew
Burlington declined. Furs and food-stuffs were exchanged for
manufactured articles from Europe, and for sugar and other
West Indian produce. With the exception of the making of
coarse cloth and cordage, there was little manufacturing. Practically all of the settlers were freemen, although slavery and
indenture gradually crept in. The standard of living was higher
than in most of the colonies, for Indian wars did not disturb
pursuits, the lands were fertile, and the climatic conditions less
rigorous than along the New England coast. Most of the early
accounts tell of well-built houses, and productive gardens and
orchards.

Religion and education.—In church affiliation the Delaware
River country was a mixture. In West New Jersey were found
Presbyterians, Baptists, Quakers, and Lutherans. In Pennsylvania there were the same denominations, but religiously and
politically the Quakers were in the ascendency. In 1695 an
Episcopal church was established at Philadelphia, but the Anglican church made slow progress along the Delaware. The Dutch
and Swedes had established schools under the direction of the
ministers. The Quakers were also keenly interested in education,
and schools were immediately established. In 1682 the West
New Jersey assembly granted three hundred acres for the support of a school at Burlington, and one of the first acts of the
Pennsylvania assembly was intended to begin elementary educa-

tion. In 1689 the Friends' Public School at Philadelphia was founded and was open to all sects. But most of the schools were founded by churches or private individuals.

THE CHESAPEAKE BAY REGION

The settled area.—The Chesapeake Bay country formed another economic unit. By the end of the Stuart régime Maryland contained about 30,000 people, Virginia nearly 60,000, and North Carolina perhaps 3,000, practically all of English extraction. From Cape Charles northward for fifty miles the peninsula was settled. Then came an uninhabited region until opposite Kent Island, where the settlements began again and extended northward to the Pennsylvania line. On the western side of the bay a population belt about twenty-five miles wide extended from the northern boundary of Maryland as far as the Potomac. On the right bank of the Potomac from a point ten miles above Alexandria to the place where the river made its great bend to the eastward the plantations covered a strip about five miles wide. From the great bend the frontier

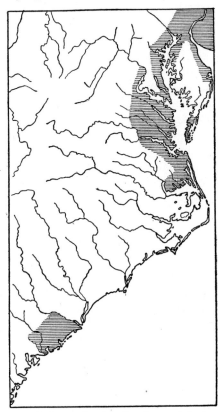

Settled Areas in the Southern Colonies about 1700

ran almost straight south to the neighborhood of Richmond and then gradually curved to the southeast, enclosing a settled area about twenty-five miles wide on the south side of the James River.

The frontier line crossed the North Carolina boundary about forty miles from the coast and ran southwestward to the Chowan River, which with the northern shore of Albemarle Sound formed the limits of the settled region of North Carolina, then politically united but economically and socially separated from the Charleston district.

The plantations.—The Chesapeake Bay country was almost entirely devoted to agriculture. The small land holdings of the early period were rapidly disappearing and great plantations had taken their place. The average land patent in Virginia in the last decades of the century gave title to from six hundred to eight hundred acres, but many of the plantations covered from ten thousand to twenty thousand acres. So plentiful was land and so easily obtained that the planters preferred to take up new acreage rather than resort to fertilization, the result being that the plantations were widely scattered, an important factor in making each estate a social and economic unit.

Tobacco.—The great staple was tobacco. The plantations were usually located near a creek, river, or the bay shore. Each had its wharf or flatboat from which the trader could load his vessel. Most of the crop was shipped to England, and the price obtained determined the year's prosperity or depression. The large plantation owner usually dealt with some London house, which kept an open account with him, crediting his tobacco against orders for the manufactured articles and luxuries which the Virginia and Maryland gentlemen demanded.

Other industrial activity.—Some writers have held that there must have been much poverty in the plantation country because of the uncertain market for tobacco, but such statements do not take into account the fact that the plantations produced an abundance of food products. Wheat, oats, barley, and maize were grown in large quantities, the cereals usually being planted after the third crop of tobacco. At times wheat was exported. Almost every estate had its garden and orchard, and live stock was abundant, horses, cattle, and hogs usually ranging in the woods. So numerous did the hogs become that pork was an item of exportation. New England coasting vessels ran into the rivers and took on wheat, pork, and tobacco, which were exchanged for West Indian slaves, rum, and sugar. There was but little manufacturing. Cotton and woolen cloths were made for home use, and brick-making was carried on to a limited extent, but most of the manufactured articles were brought from England.

The system of labor.—The large plantations were worked either by indented servants or slaves. In 1671 Governor Berkeley estimated that there were 6,000 white servants and 2,000 slaves in Virginia. By 1683 there were about 12,000 indented servants and perhaps 3,000 slaves, and by the end of the century the slaves had probably doubled. In proportion to population the indented servants and slaves in Maryland and North Carolina were in similar ratio to the free white population.

Social position of the planter.—At the top of the social and political structure of society was the planter, his position depending largely upon his acreage. Already in Virginia and Maryland the "great-house" or manor house had made its appearance, a rather unpretentious rambling frame house with a brick chimney at either end, the splendor of which was largely due to comparison with the quarters of the slaves. Articles of luxury such as musical instruments, mirrors, brass fixtures, silverware, table linen, and damask hangings were frequently found in the houses of the wealthier planters. These were by no means typical, for pewter was far more common than silver, and in the home of recently released indented servants or small landholders there was little more than bare necessity demanded.

Religion and education.—In religion there was less uniformity than in industry. In Maryland probably three-fourths of the inhabitants belonged to various dissenting sects. Most of the great landholders were members of the Anglican church, but many were Catholics. Most of the Virginians were Episcopalians, while in North Carolina the Quakers were predominant. Popular education in the South was far below that of the North. Public sentiment was against free schools, and the few secondary educational institutions were conducted through private enterprise. The planters frequently secured educated indented servants who acted as tutors. In 1691 the Virginia legislature sent Dr. William Blair to England to secure a charter for a college and the following year he returned with it, this being the legal beginning of William and Mary College.

SOUTH CAROLINA

Population.—Economically and socially South Carolina was associated with the West Indies rather than with the mainland colonies. At the close of the seventeenth century the white population was about 5,500. Most of the inhabitants came from Barbados, but other Caribbean Islands, England, Ireland, the New England colonies, and France furnished colonists. The settled area extended from the Santee to the mouth of the Edisto, included several of the islands, and reached back from the coast about fifty miles. The social and economic center was Charleston. In the back country there were only two small towns, most of the people being located on plantations along the rivers and on the islands. The Barbadian planters had settled mainly on the Cooper River, Goose Creek, and Ashley River, and on James, John's and Edisto Islands. Four or five hundred Huguenots, most of whom had left their country because of the revocation of the Edict of Nantes, had located on the Santee, where they had received land grants aggregating over 50,000 acres, nearly half of this being the property of two individuals, the other Huguenot estates varying from 100 to 3,000 acres.

The plantations.—At the end of the century rice culture, which was destined to furnish the most important staple, was in its infancy, and a little silk and cotton were produced. The chief business of the planters was the raising of cattle and hogs, corn, and pease. The Barbadians brought in the economic system of the West Indies, which was based upon slavery, and the harsh slave code of Barbados was adopted in the colony. Accurate statistics regarding the number of slaves are inaccessible, but an apparently authentic letter of 1708 states that in that year there were 4,100 negro slaves and 1,400 Indian slaves in the colony, numbers probably in excess of those in 1700, as it was the development of the rice industry which made slaves highly profitable.

Commerce.—Charleston was the great market town. There the trader stocked for the Indian trade, which, at the close of the century was the chief source of wealth of South Carolina. Goods from Charleston are said to have penetrated a thousand miles into the interior. To the West Indies were shipped beef, pork, butter, tallow, and hides, rice and pease, lumber, staves, pitch, and tar; returning vessels brought rum, sugar, molasses, and other West Indian products. To England were shipped furs, rice, silk, and naval stores, in return for manufactured goods.

Religion and education.—The Episcopalian was the established church of the colony, and probably forty-five per cent. of the population belonged to that denomination. An equal per cent. was divided between Congregationalists and Presbyterians, and there were a few Baptists and Quakers. No public school system had been established, but many of the wealthier families employed tutors. A public library was started at Charleston in 1698, but no institution of higher learning had been established.

Society.—Already in South Carolina an aristocratic society was forming which was distinctly different from that of any other mainland colony. When the Barbadians came they brought with them the social viewpoint of the West Indian planter. As soon as the discovery was made that the swampy river bottoms were adapted to rice and indigo, slavery received a great impetus and the Barbadian social system was almost duplicated. In no other colony was such a large part of the population concentrated in a single city. In Charleston lived the merchants, and there the planter built his town house and remained with his family a portion of the year. The gathering of the wealthy classes developed a social atmosphere of gaiety which was in marked contrast to the soberness of Boston or the conservatism of Philadelphia.

READINGS

Andrews, C. M., *Colonial Self-Government*, 288–336; *Colonial Folkways;* Brodhead, J. R., *History of the State of New York*, II; Bruce, P. A., *Economic History of Virginia in the Seventeenth Century;* Burr, G. L., ed., *Narratives of the Witchcraft Cases;* Dexter, E. G., *A History of Education in the United States*, 24–71; Dexter, F. B., "Estimates of Population in the American Colonies," in American Antiquarian Society; *Proceedings*, New Series, V, pt. 1; Eggleston, E., *The Transit of Civilization;* Fiske, J., *Old Virginia and her Neighbors*, II, 174–269; McCrady, E., *South Carolina under the Proprietary Government*, I, 314–363; Mereness, N. D., *Maryland as a Proprietary Province;* Smith, S., *The History of the Colony of Nova Cæsaria, or New Jersey;* Walker, W., *A History of the Congregational Churches in the United States;* Weeden, W. B., *Economic and Social History of New England*, I; Phillips, U. B., *American Negro Slavery*, 67–84, 98–114.

EXPANSION AND INTERNATIONAL CONFLICT

CHAPTER XIII

THE SPANISH ADVANCE IN THE SEVENTEENTH CENTURY

SPAIN AND THE COLONIES IN THE SEVENTEENTH CENTURY

Decline of Spanish power in Europe.—After the reign of Philip II the power of Spain steadily declined. The long period of hostility with the Dutch and the war with Cromwell greatly weakened her power upon the sea. The continental wars sapped her military strength and France superseded her as the first power of Europe. Gradually Spain's continental possessions slipped from her. The first loss was the Protestant Netherlands. Nominally independent from 1609, their complete independence was acknowledged in 1648. By the Treaty of the Pyrenees, Roussillon became French territory, and the Spanish power in the Rhineland and Italy had been practically annulled. In 1640 Portugal threw off the Spanish yoke, and when Philip IV tried to reconquer it (1661–1665), he failed completely. With Portugal, Spain lost Brazil and the Portuguese colonies in the Far East.

Colonial expansion.—Nevertheless, the frontiers of the Spanish colonies slowly expanded, and slowly Spain extended her laws, her language, and her faith over lands and tribes more and more remote from the Mexican capital, the struggle with the natives becoming sterner at each step in advance. In the course of the seventeenth century northern Sinaloa and Sonora were colonized; permanent missionary occupation, after many failures, was effected in Lower California; southern, western, and eastern Chihuahua were settled; the new province of Coahuila was established athwart the Rio Grande, and a new and flourishing missionary district was opened in western Florida. In the course of the century the Spanish colonial frontiers began

233

to clash with those of France and England, on the mainland now as well as in the islands, and there ensued a series of border struggles, all a part of the international conflict for the continent. To restrain the encroaching French and English, Texas was occupied temporarily and Pensacola permanently. The principal setbacks on the borders were the loss of Jamaica to England (1655), the contraction of the Florida frontier through the founding of Virginia and the Carolinas, and the temporary loss of New Mexico through the Pueblo Revolt in 1680. Thus the Spanish frontier line swung round as on a pivot, the gains in the west being partly offset by the losses in the east. Meanwhile the English, French, and Dutch occupied most of the lesser islands of the Caribbean, which had been neglected by Spain. At the same time, Spain's hold on her colonial commerce became more and more precarious through the encroachments of her national enemies.

FRONTIER ADMINISTRATION

The governors.—The old days of the *adelantados*, with un-limited powers, had passed, and the royal arm now reached the farthest outposts. The secular government of the frontier provinces was almost wholly military. A few villas or towns had their elective *cabildos*, or town councils, and a modicum of self government. The official heads of the provinces were the governors, who held office by royal appointment; *ad interim* governors might be appointed by the viceroys. Governors, like other prominent officials, frequently purchased their offices, a practice not confined at that time to Spanish America. The governor was also *capitán general* of his province, and his capital was usually at the principal presidio or garrison. In these capacities he exercised both civil and military authority. Under the governors there were usually lieutenant-governors in the sub-districts, who as a rule commanded the troops of some presidio.

The positions of governor and presidial commander were made attractive largely by the opportunity which they afforded for making money in addition to the fixed salaries. The payment of soldiers was made chiefly in supplies, purchased by the gov-ernor and commanders, and charged to the soldiers at enormous

profits. Thus the post of governor or captain was almost as
much that of merchant as of soldier. Provincial administration
was often corrupt with "graft," as in English and French America. Checks upon the governors were furnished through *visitas* or
inspections, and through the *residencia*, or inquiry at the end of
the governor's term. As a rule the *residencia* was formal, but
sometimes it was a serious matter.

Central control.—All important matters of frontier administration, such as the founding of new colonies, presidios, or missions, or the making of military campaigns, were referred by the
governors to the viceroy of Mexico. He in turn customarily
sought the advice of the fiscal of the *real audiencia*, and of the
auditor de guerra. In case these two functionaries disagreed, or
in matters of unusual moment, a *junta de guerra y hacienda*, composed of the leading officials of the different branches of the
central administration, was called. In all matters of consequence
the decisions of the viceroy were made subject to royal approval,
but it frequently happened that the act for which approval was
asked had already been performed. In ordinary affairs of
provincial administration the fiscal really controlled the government, for the viceroy usually despatched business with a laconic
"as the fiscal says."

Frontier Autonomy.—The government of New Spain was
highly centralized in theory, but the effects of centralization were
greatly lessened by distance. Through the right of petition,
which was freely exercised, the local leaders in the frontier
provinces often exerted a high degree of initiative in government,
and, on the other hand, through protest and delay, they frequently defeated royal orders.

THE MISSIONS

The Missionaries on the frontiers.—In extending the sway
of Spain, as time went on a constantly larger part was played by
the missionaries. During the early days of the conquest the
natives had been largely in the hands of the *encomenderos*. But
abuses arose and the encomienda system was gradually abolished.
Moreover, the wild tribes of the northern frontier, unlike the
Mayas and Aztecs, were considered hardly worth exploiting.
This left an opening for the missionary, and to him was entrusted

not only the work of conversion, but a larger and larger share of responsibility and control. Since they served the State, the missions were largely supported by the royal treasury, which was most liberal when there was some political end to be gained.

The principal missionary orders.—Under these circumstances, in the seventeenth and eighteenth centuries, on the expanding frontiers of Spanish America, missions became well-nigh universal. The work on the northern borders of New Spain was conducted largely by Franciscans, Jesuits, and Dominicans. The northeastern field fell chiefly to the Franciscans, who entered Florida, New Mexico, Nuevo Leon, Coahuila, Nuevo Santander, and Texas. To the northwest went the Jesuits, who, after withdrawing from Florida, worked especially in Sinaloa, Sonora, Chihuahua, Lower California, and Arizona. After the expulsion of the Jesuits the Dominicans and Franciscans took their places.

The missions as civilizing agencies.—The missionaries were a veritable corps of Indian agents, serving both Church and State. Their first duty was to teach the Gospel. In addition they disciplined the savage in the rudiments of civilized life. The central feature of every successful Spanish mission was the Indian pueblo, or village. If he were to be disciplined, the Indian must be kept in a definite spot where discipline could be impressed upon him. The settled Indians, such as the Pueblo Indians of New Mexico, could be instructed in their native towns, but the wandering or scattered tribes must be assembled and established in pueblos, and kept there by force if necessary. To make the Indians self-supporting as soon as possible, and to afford them the means of discipline, the missions were provided with communal lands for gardens, farms, and ranches, and with workshops in which to practice the crafts.

Defence of the frontier.—The missionaries were highly useful likewise as explorers and as diplomatic agents amongst the tribes. As defenders of the frontier they held the allegiance of the neophytes and secured their aid against savages and foreign intruders. Sometimes the mission plants were veritable fortresses.

Missions designedly temporary.—Like the presidios, or garrisons, missions were intended to be temporary. As soon as his

pioneer work was finished on one frontier the missionary was
expected to move on to another, his place being taken by the
secular clergy and the mission lands distributed among the
Indians. The result, almost without fail, was a struggle over
secularization.

THE JESUITS IN SINALOA AND SONORA

The Jesuit advance up the slope.—The advance up the
Pacific coast mainland was led throughout the seventeenth century by the Jesuit missionaries, supported by presidial soldiers
and small citizen colonies. In 1591 the Jesuits entered Sinaloa.
Beginning in the valley of the Petatlan and Mocorito rivers,
their progress was gradual but steady, river by river, tribe by
tribe, to the Fuerte, Mayo, Yaqui, and Sonora valleys, till by
the middle of the century they had nearly reached the head of
the last named stream.

Fathers Tapia and Pérez.—The first missionaries sent were
Fathers Gonzalo de Tapia and Martin Pérez, who began their
work among the tribes of the Petatlan and Mocorito rivers, near
San Felipe, then the northern outpost of Sinaloa. From time to
time they were joined by other small bands of missionaries. The
natives were generally friendly at first, here as elsewhere, and
were assembled in villages, baptized, and taught agriculture and
crafts. Father Tapia was murdered in 1594 and was succeeded
as rector by Father Pérez. By 1604 there had been 10,000 baptisms, the Jesuits had a school for boys at San Felipe, and Father
Velasco had written a grammar in the native tongue. In 1600
regular missionary work was begun in Topia. What was done
there is a good example of the way the Spaniards often uprooted
native society by trying to improve it. Villages were transplanted at will, the chiefs replaced by alcaldes, and native priests
suppressed.

Captain Hurdaide, defender of the Faith.—The year 1600
was marked also by the appointment of Captain Diego Martínez
de Hurdaide, as commander of the presidio of San Felipe. By
the Jesuits he was regarded as the ideal defender of the Faith,
and for a quarter of a century he and his soldiers made
way for and protected the missionaries in their northward
advance

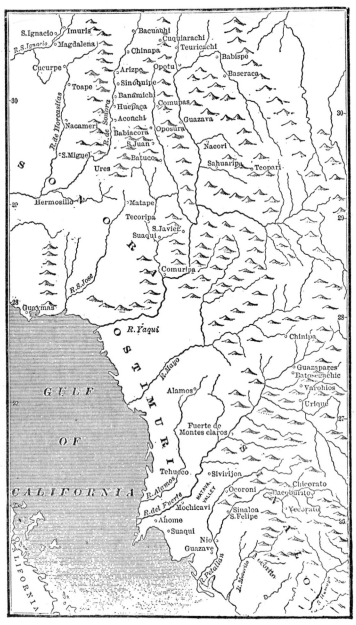

Sinaloa and Sonora in the Seventeenth Century
(From Bancroft, *North Mexican States and Texas*, I, 208)

Missions in the Fuerte valley.—The subjugation of the Suaques and Tehuecos by Hurdaide opened the way for missions in the Fuerte River valley in 1604. Among the founders was Father Pérez de Ribas, later famed as the historian. The initial success of these missions was remarkable, but it was followed by apostasy, revolts, an increase of military forces, and wars of subjugation. This, indeed, was quite the typical succession of events. Apostates fled to the Yaquis, who defeated Hurdaide in three campaigns. Having shown their mettle, in 1610 the Yaquis made peace and asked for missionaries. The Yaqui war was followed by the establishment in 1610 of the new presidio of Montesclaros near the site of the former San Juan. In spite of this new defence, the Tehuecos, led by native priests, revolted. Hurdaide went to the rescue in 1613 with forty soldiers and two thousand allies, restored order, and reëstablished the missions.

In the Mayo and Yaqui valleys.—In the same year Father Méndez and some companions advanced the mission frontier to the Mayo valley, where success was gratifying. Four years later Fathers Pérez and Pérez de Ribas founded missions among the Yaquis, where eight pueblos soon flourished. By 1621 missions had reached the Nevomes and Sahuaripas in the upper Yaqui River valley. A revolt among the Nevomes in 1622 was put down by Hurdaide. The Mayo and Yaqui valleys were now made a separate rectorate.

Several of the pioneers now left the scene. In 1620 Ribas went to Mexico as provincial; in 1625 Father Pérez died, after thirty-five years of service, and in 1626 Hurdaide was succeeded by Captain Pérea. One of the great monuments to the work of these Jesuit pioneers is Father Pérez de Ribas's history, *The Triumph of the Faith*, published in 1644.

In the Sonora valley.—By 1636 Jesuit missions were extended to Ures, in Sonora River valley, a step which was aided by the discovery of mines. Perea was made captain and *justicia mayor* of the Sonora district, called Nueva Andalucía, and established his capital at the mining town of San Juan. By 1650 mission stations had reached Cucurpe and Arispe in the upper Sonora valley. Of the northern district the new rectorate of San Francisco Xavier was now formed. In 1679 thirty missionaries in the Mayo, Yaqui, and Sonora valleys were serving about 40,000 neophytes in seventy-two pueblos.

Spanish settlements.—By the end of the seventeenth century Sinaloa had passed beyond the frontier stage. The population of pure Spanish blood numbered only six hundred families in 1678, but the half-caste Christian population was much larger, there being twelve hundred persons of Spanish or mixed blood at San Felipe alone. In Sonora the people of Spanish or mixed blood numbered about five hundred families. Mining and stock-raising were the principal and by no means inconsiderable industries in both districts.

EFFORTS TO OCCUPY LOWER CALIFORNIA

Pearl fishing and efforts to colonize.—Interest in California did not cease with Vizcaíno's failures. On the contrary, private interest in the pearl fisheries of the Gulf of California continued throughout the seventeenth century, and the government endeavored to utilize it as means of planting colonies. Numerous pearl fishing contracts were granted on condition that the beneficiaries should establish settlements. Other colonizing expeditions were fitted out at royal expense. In nearly every case missionaries were sent with the settlers to help to subdue and teach the Indians.

Iturbi's voyages.—In 1614 Thomas Cardona was granted a monopoly of pearl fishing in both the Caribbean Sea and the Gulf of California. A year later Juan de Iturbi, in Cardona's employ, made a voyage to the head of the Gulf, and like Oñate concluded that California was an island. On his return one of his vessels was captured by the Dutch freebooter Spillberg. In the following year Iturbi made another successful voyage to the Gulf, though he again lost a vessel to freebooters. The pirates in the Gulf in this century were known as the Pichilingues. Iturbi's success inspired numerous unlicensed pearl hunting voyages in the Gulf from the ports of Sinaloa, which were attended by many abuses of the natives. California came now to be commonly regarded as an island.

Later attempts.—In 1633 Francisco de Ortega, another contractor, founded a colony at La Paz, but it was short-lived. Like failures were experienced by Porter y Casante in 1648, by

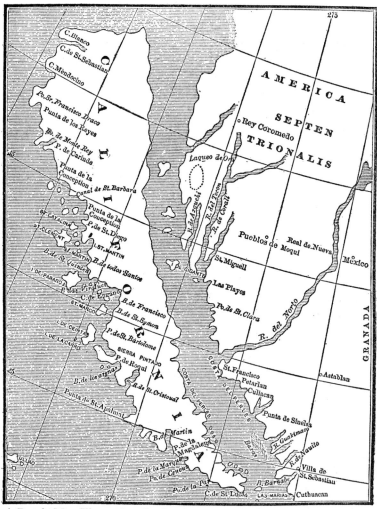

A Dutch Map Illustrating the Insular Theory of California's Geography (1624–1625). (From Bancroft, *North Mexican States and Texas*, I, 169)

Piñadero in 1664 and 1667, and by Lucenilla in 1668. The failures were due to the barrenness of the country and to the fact that colonizing was made secondary to pearl fishing. Somewhat more successful was Admiral Atondo y Antillón, with whom a contract was made in 1679, the superior of the missionaries being the Jesuit Father Kino. For two years (1683-1685) settlements were maintained at La Paz and San Bruno, explorations were made, and Kino achieved some missionary success, but in 1685 Atondo, like his predecessors, abandoned the enterprise. No other serious attempt was made until 1697, when the Jesuits took charge of California.

THE SETTLEMENT OF CHIHUAHUA

New Mexico isolated.—In the central plateau the infant colony of New Mexico, as at first established, had been a detached group of settlements, separated from Nueva Vizcaya by an uninhabited area of five or six hundred miles in breadth. But while the New Mexicans were gradually making their way into the plains of western Texas, missionaries, miners, and settlers were slowly advancing up the plateau into Chihuahua, by way of the Conchos River and by the eastern slope of the Sierra Madre.

Advance of settlement.—The Franciscans, in general, followed the eastern half of the plateau, working among the Conchos tribes; the Jesuits mainly followed the mountain slopes, among the Tarahumares. Advance of settlement was marked by the founding of the town and garrison of Parral, established in 1631–1632. By 1648 missions had been established at San Pablo, Parral, San Gerónimo, San Francisco Borja, Satevó, San Francisco de Conchos, San Pedro, Atotonilco, Mescomaha, and Mapimí. Advance was interrupted by two savage Indian wars, in the decade following 1644, in the course of which most of the missions in Chihuahua were destroyed. As soon as peace was restored, however, both orders reoccupied their abandoned establishments and founded new ones. By 1680 missionaries, miners, and settlers had reached Cusihuiriáchic, Janos, and Casas Grandes, and the last named place had for some time been the seat of an *alcaldía mayor*.

The Diocese of Guadiana.—As the frontier advanced new administrative subdivisions were carved out. The official capital of Nueva Vizcaya was still at Durango, but during the later seventeenth century the governor resided much of the time at Parral, a point near the military frontier. In 1620 the diocese of Guadiana, including Durango, Chihuahua, and New Mexico was formed out of the northern portion of that of Guadalajara.

NEW MEXICO IN THE SEVENTEENTH CENTURY

The missions.—Hopes of finding rich mines and fabulous treasures in New Mexico had failed, and for a long time after Oñate's conquest that province remained chiefly a missionary field, the only Spanish settlement being Santa Fé, founded in 1609. By 1617 eleven churches had been built and 14,000 natives baptized. Four years later the missions were organized into the *custodia* of San Pablo, under the Franciscan province of the Holy Evangel of Mexico, whence came most of the missionaries. The first custodian was Fray Alonso de Benavides, who later became bishop of Goa, in India. Besides Benavides, the best known missionary of this period was Father Gerónimo de Zárate Salmerón, who between 1618 and 1626 labored at Jémez, Cía, Sandía, and Ácoma.

New Mexico in 1630.—In 1630 Benavides made a famous report on New Mexico. The only Spanish settlement was still Santa Fé, where lived two hundred and fifty Spaniards and some seven hundred and fifty half-breeds and Indian servants. The Indians of the province who were not personal servants paid tribute of a yard of cotton cloth and two bushels of maize each year, burdens which they resented and resisted. There were now friars at work in twenty-five missions, which served ninety pueblos comprising 60,000 Indians. At each mission there were schools and workshops where the neophytes were taught reading, writing, singing, instrumental music, and manual arts.

Expeditions to the east.—The subjugation of the pueblos did not exhaust the energies of the conquerors and the friars, and they turned from time to time to exploration. To the east they were interested in Quivira, the "Seven Hills of the Aijados," and the Jumano Indians of the Colorado River. In the pursuit of these objects they heard of the "kingdom of the Texas" farther east. Missionary and trading expeditions were made to the Jumanos in 1629 and 1632. At this time (1630) Benavides proposed opening a direct route from the Gulf coast to New Mexico through the country of the Quiviras and Aijados. In 1634 Alonso de Vaca is said to have led an expedition three hundred leagues eastward to Quivira, apparently on the Arkansas. In 1650 captains Martin and Castillo visited the Jumanos and gathered

pearls in the Nueces (probably the Concho) River. Four years
later the viceroy, interested in the pearls, sent another expedition, under Guadalajara, to the same place. During the next
thirty years small parties of private traders frequently visited

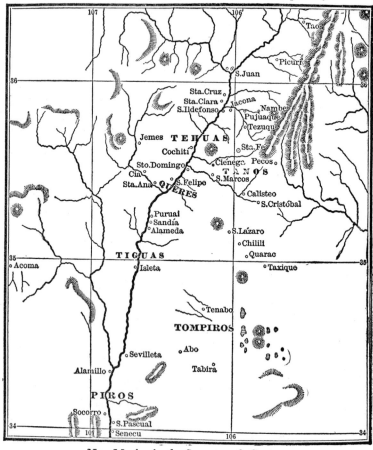

New Mexico in the Seventeenth Century
(From Bancroft, *Arizona and New Mexico*, p. 176)

the Jumanos. In this way western Texas became known to the
Spaniards of New Mexico.

New Mexico in 1680.—Meanwhile the Spanish population
of the province had slowly increased till in 1680 there were over
2500 settlers in the upper Rio Grande valley, mainly between

Isleta and Taos. The upper settlements were known as those of Río Arriba and the lower as those of Río Abajo. The settlers were engaged principally in farming and cattle ranching.

The beginnings of El Paso.—As a result of the northward advance from Nueva Vizcaya and of a counter movement from New Mexico, the intermediate district of El Paso was now colonized. After several unsuccessful attempts, in 1659 missionaries from New Mexico founded the mission of Guadalupe at the ford (El Paso). Before 1680 Mission San Francisco had been founded twelve leagues below, settlers had drifted in, and the place had an *alcalde mayor*. To these small beginnings there was now suddenly added the entire population of New Mexico.

The Pueblo revolt.—The Pueblo Indians, led by their native priests, had long been restless under the burden of tribute and personal service, and the suppression of their native religion. On August 9, 1680, under the leadership of Popé, a medicine man of San Juan, they revolted in unison, slew four hundred Spaniards, including twenty-one missionaries, and drove the remaining 2200 Spaniards from the Pueblo district. Under Governor Otermín and Lieutenant García the settlers retreated to El Paso. In 1681 Otermín made an attempt to reconquer the Pueblos, but it proved futile and the El Paso settlement was made permanent and attached to New Mexico. To hold the outpost a presidio was established there in 1683.

The La Junta missions and the Mendoza expedition to the Jumanos.—From El Paso missions were extended in 1683 to the La Junta district, as the junction of the Conchos and Rio Grande was called. Within a year seven churches had been built for nine tribes, living on both sides of the Rio Grande. At the same time Juan Dominguez de Mendoza and Fray Nicolás López led an expedition from El Paso to the Jumanos of central Texas, where they were to meet Tejas Indians from the east. On their return Mendoza and López went to Mexico to appeal for a new outpost of settlement among the Jumanos. This would probably have been established had not attention been called to eastern Texas through the activities of the French.

Indian uprisings.—The Pueblo revolt was followed by a general wave of Indian resistance, and the late years of the century were marked by raids all along the northern frontier, from Nuevo León to Sonora, in the course of which mines, missions, haciendas, and towns were destroyed, and travelers and merchant caravans raided. To defend the frontier, in 1685 three new presidios were established at Pasage, El Gallo, and Conchos, and two years later one was erected at Monclova. By 1690 two others were added at Casas Grandes and Janos in Chihuahua and shortly afterward (1695) another at Fronteras in Sonora. In 1690 a revolt in the Tarahumara country destroyed settlements in all directions, and was put down only by the efforts of soldiers from all the presidios from El Gallo to Janos.

Vargas and the reconquest of the Pueblos.—After expelling the Spaniards, the Pueblos, under the lead of Popé, returned to their tribal ways, and destroyed most of the signs of the hated Spanish rule. During the next decade and a half several efforts were made to reconquer the Pueblo region. Otermin was succeeded by Cruzate, and he by Reneros, who was in turn followed by Cruzate. In 1688 Cruzate led an expedition against the Queres. At Cía six hundred apostates were killed in battle and seventy captured and shot, or sold into slavery. In 1691 Diego de Vargas Zapata Luján Ponce de León was made governor especially to reconquer the Pueblos. In 1692 he led an expedition against them. As far as Sandia the towns had already been destroyed. Santa Fé he found fortified and occupied by Tanos, but they yielded without a blow, as did all of the pueblos from Pecos to Moqui. Meanwhile the friars with him baptized over two thousand native children.

A new colony.—Submission having been secured, in 1693 Vargas led a colony of eight hundred soldiers and settlers to reoccupy the pueblo region. But submission had been a hollow formality. The Tanos who held Santa Fé were evicted only after a battle, at the conclusion of which seventy warriors were shot and four hundred women and children enslaved. At the mesa of San Ildefonso, Vargas met the combined resistance of nine towns. A second siege in March, 1694, resulted in a repulse. In the course of the summer the pueblos of Cieneguilla and Jémez were defeated, and abandoned Taos was sacked and burned. A third attack on the mesa of San Ildefonso was successful. Resistance now appeared to be over, the pueblos were rebuilt, captives returned, missions reëstablished, and the Spanish régime restored. A number of the pueblos were consolidated and rebuilt on new sites. In 1695 the new Spanish villa of Santa Cruz de la Cañada was founded with seventy families on the lands of San Cristóbal and San Lázaro.

The conquest completed.—In 1696 a new revolt occurred, in which five missionaries and twenty-one other Spaniards were killed, and Vargas conducted another series of bloody campaigns, with partial success. In the following year he was succeeded by Governor Cubero, who secured the formal submission of the rest of the pueblos. The reconquest was now complete and the Spanish rule secured.

COAHUILA OCCUPIED

The Nuevo León frontier.—While there had been definite progress eastward from New Mexico during the first three-fourths of the seventeenth century, and considerable contact between that province and what is now the western half of Texas, from Nuevo León, on the natural line of advance from Mexico to Texas, progress was slow. For nearly a century the northeastern outpost on the lower Rio Grande frontier was León (Cerralvo), founded in the later sixteenth century. Temporarily a more northern outpost had been established in 1590 at Nuevo Almadén (now Monclova), but it was soon abandoned. Again in 1603 and 1644 the place was temporarily reoccupied, but without permanent success.

Zavala's rule, 1626-1664.—Hostile Indians troubled the border, and the intrusions of English, French, and Dutch colonies into the Lesser Antilles awakened fears for the safety of the western Gulf shores. In 1625 Nuevo León, therefore, was again entrusted to a *conquistador*, when a contract similar to that of Carabajal in 1579 was made with Martín de Zavala. At the same time the Florida missions were extended west to the Apalache district. For thirty-eight years Zavala controlled and governed the frontier with exemplary zeal, subduing Indians, granting *encomiendas*, operating mines, founding new towns, and opening highways to Pánuco and the interior. His most able lieutenant after 1636 was Alonso de León, one of the founders and first citizens of Cadereyta.

Looking northward.—By the middle of the seventeenth century, explorations beyond the Nuevo León frontier had been made on a small scale in all directions. That they were not more extensive was due to Indian troubles and the feebleness of the frontier settlements. To the north the Spaniards were led short distances by a desire to establish communication with Florida, by rumors of a silver deposit called Cerro de la Plata (perhaps the later San Sabá mines), and in pursuit of Indians. No doubt the Franciscan missionaries made many unrecorded visits to the outlying tribes. In 1665 Fernando de Azcué led soldiers from Saltillo and Monterey across the Rio Grande against the Cacaxtle Indians. This is the first expedition to cross the lower Rio Grande from the south of which we have any definite record.

The founding of Coahuila.—Another forward step was now taken with the founding of the new province of Coahuila, a step made necessary by Indian depredations. In 1670 Father Juan Larios, a Franciscan from Guadalajara, began missionary work on the troubled frontier. In 1673–1674, aided by other missionaries and by soldiers from Saltillo, he established two missions between the Sabinas River and the Rio Grande.* In the course of this work Fray Manuel de la Cruz visited tribes north of the Rio Grande. In 1674 Coahuila was made an *alcaldía mayor* of Nueva Vizcaya, with Antonio de Valcárcel as first *alcalde mayor*. A colony was now established at thrice abandoned Almadén and later became Monclova.

The Bosque-Lários expedition across the Rio Grande.—In 1675 Valcárcel sent Fernando del Bosque and Father Larios on a tour among the tribes north of the Rio Grande. In the following year (the very year when Bishop Calderón was in Florida) the bishop of Guadalajara visited Coahuila, and urged its further reduction, with a view to passing beyond, to the settled Tejas Indians, across the Trinity River. In 1687 a presidio was established at Monclova, and Coahuila was made a province, with Alonso de León, the younger, as first governor.

The college of the Holy Cross.—The development of Coahuila and Nuevo León was given an impetus by the coming of a new

---

* This was just at the time when Joliet and Marquette descended the Mississippi River.

group of Franciscan friars from the recently founded missionary college of Santa Cruz at Querétaro. Among these friars were Fathers Hidalgo, Massanet, and Olivares, all of whom figured prominently in the later development of the frontier. Beside the Querétaro friars, to the westward worked the friars of the Province of Santiago de Xalisco with its seat at Guadalajara.

FIRST ATTEMPTS IN EASTERN TEXAS

Plans to occupy the mouth of the Mississippi.—The aggressive policy of the French, English, and Dutch in the West Indies, the raids of freebooters on the Spanish settlements, the occupation of Carolina by England, and the advance of the French into the Mississippi Valley caused Spain great uneasiness for the northern Gulf Coast. As a defensive measure missions had been extended to the Apalache district at the same time that Nuevo León had been strengthened. In 1673 Joliet and Marquette descended the Mississippi to the Arkansas, and in 1682 La Salle explored it to its mouth. Four years earlier news had reached the Spanish court that Peñalosa, a discredited ex-governor of New Mexico, had proposed to attack New Spain in the name of France. Spanish officials therefore at once planned to occupy the Bay of Espíritu Santo (Mobile Bay, or perhaps the mouth of the Mississippi) and in 1695 Echagaray, an officer at St. Augustine, was ordered to explore it for the purpose.

The search for La Salle's colony.—A few months later the authorities learned with alarm that in November, 1684, La Salle had left France with a colony to occupy the same spot. Immediately several expeditions were sent out by land and sea to learn where La Salle had landed and, if necessary, to occupy the danger point. In 1686 Marcos Delgado explored west by land from Apalache to the neighborhood of Mobile Bay. In 1686–1688 five coastwise expeditions (under Barroto, Rivas, Iriarte, Pez, and Gamara) explored the Gulf between Vera Cruz and Apalache. They discovered the wrecks of La Salle's vessels at Matagorda Bay, and it was concluded that the French expedition had been destroyed.

Eastern Texas occupied.—While these coastwise voyages were being made, Alonso de León was leading expeditions from Monterey and Monclova by land. In 1686 he descended the

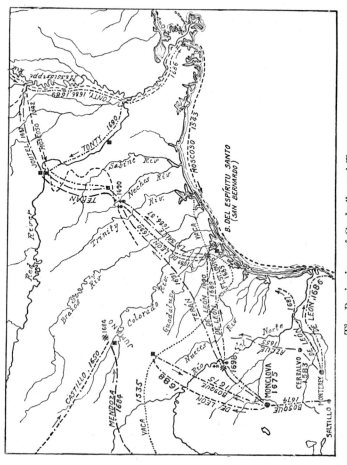

The Beginnings of Coahuila and Texas

Rio Grande to the coast. In 1687 and again in 1688 he crossed the Rio Grande, and in the latter expedition captured a stray Frenchman. Shortly afterward a party of soldiers and Indians from far distant Nueva Vizcaya crossed the Upper Rio Grande to seek out the French intruders. In 1689 De León succeeded in finding the remains of La Salle's settlement near Matagorda Bay, a few weeks after it had been destroyed by Indians. In the following year De León and Father Massanet, one of the Coahuila missionaries, led an expedition across Texas and founded two missions among the Asinai (Tejas) Indians, on Neches River. Texas was now erected into a province and Domingo de Terán made governor.

And then abandoned.—In 1691 Terán led an expedition designed to strengthen the outpost on the Neches, explore and occupy the Cadodacho country (near Texarkana) and, if time permitted, to reëxplore the coast as far as Florida. He reached the Red River but accomplished little else that was new. The Asinai Indians proved hostile, and in 1693 the missionaries withdrew. The Texas project was now abandoned for a time, and attention centered instead on western Florida, which was in danger not only from the French, but also from the English in Carolina, who were visiting the Georgia and Alabama Indians.

THE STRUGGLE IN THE WEST INDIES

Intruding colonies in the West Indies.—In the early years of the conquest Spain had occupied the larger West Indian islands,—Cuba, Española, Porto Rico, and Jamaica—but had neglected the lesser islands. They thus became a field for colonization by Spain's enemies. In the seventeenth century the subjects of Holland, France, and England began to establish settlements in the West Indies, in the heart of the Spanish sea, while England intruded in the northern mainland.

Between 1555 and 1562 the French had made unsuccessful attempts to colonize Brazil, Carolina, and Florida. Between 1585 and 1595 Raleigh had attempted to settle on Roanoke Island and in Guiana. In 1607 Jamestown was founded within Spanish dominions at Chesapeake Bay, and Spain's possessions thus delimited on the north. Between 1609 and 1612 English settlers occupied the Bermudas. Between 1609 and 1619 English, Dutch,

and French all established posts in Guiana. In 1621 the Dutch
West India Company was incorporated for trade and settlement.
Between 1623 and 1625 both English and French settled on St.
Kitts (St. Christopher). During the same period Barbados was
settled by the English, and Santa Cruz by English and Dutch.
By 1632 English settlements had been made at Nevis, Barbuda,
Antigua, Providence Island, and Montserrat. By 1634 the
Dutch had established trading stations on St. Eustatius, Tobago,
and Curaçao, while in 1635 the French West India Company
began the settlement of Guadeloupe, Martinique, and other
Windward Islands.

Privateers.—Meanwhile French, Dutch, and English privateers swarmed the Spanish waters. Early in the century Dutch
ships harassed the coasts of Chile and Peru. In 1628 Peter Heyn
with thirty-one vessels pursued the Vera Cruz fleet into Matanzas
River, Cuba, and captured most of a cargo worth $15,000,000.
"It was an exploit which two generations of English mariners had
attempted in vain." After 1633 the Dutch West India Company
carried on active war against Spanish and Portuguese colonies.
Within two years it sent eighty ships and nine thousand men to
American waters, and its agents captured Bahía (Brazil), Pernambuco, and San Juan (Porto Rico).

English privateers in the early seventeenth century did their
part. In 1642 Captain William Jackson, with a commission from
the Earl of Warwick, made a raid that reminds one of Drake.
With eleven hundred men he cruised the coast from Caracas to
Honduras, plundering Maracaibo and Trujillo on the way. Landing at Jamaica he captured Santiago and held it for ransom.

Spanish retaliation.—The Spaniards often repaid these aggressions with good interest, and frequent raids were made on the
foreign colonies. In 1629 Toledo nearly destroyed the English
and French settlements on St. Kitts. Tortuga was several
times assaulted. In 1635 a Spanish fleet made a five days' attack
on the English colony on Providence Island but was beaten
back. In 1641 Pimienta with two thousand men destroyed the
forts there and captured seven hundred and seventy colonists.
Ten years later a force of eight hundred men from Porto Rico
destroyed the English colony on Santa Cruz Island, killing the
governor and over one hundred settlers.

The English conquest of Jamaica.—Thus far the English settlements had been made chiefly on unoccupied islands. But in 1654 Cromwell sent an expedition under Venables and Penn to gain Spanish territory by conquest. They failed to take Santo Domingo but succeeded at Jamaica (1655). Twice Spain attempted to recover the island but failed (1657–1658), and in 1670 she acknowledged England's right to all her island possessions.

The Danes and Brandenburgers.—Under their absolute monarch, Frederick III, the Danes organized a West India Company, which in 1671 secured the abandoned island of St. Thomas, using it as a planting colony and a distributing center for Guinea slaves. Porto Rico and the Spanish mainland were the principal Danish markets. Even the Brandenburgers, during the latter days of the Great Elector (1685) secured a thirty-year lease of a part of the Danish island of St. Thomas, with a view to using it as a slave-trading station for supplying the Spanish colonies. But the jealousy of other European powers, especially England, prevented their securing a permanent foothold.

THE STRUGGLE WITH THE ENGLISH ON THE CAROLINA BORDER

The Georgia missions restored.—After the massacre of 1597, the Florida missions seem to have been practically abandoned for a time. But new missionaries, requested by the governor in 1601, reoccupied the abandoned sites, pushed farther up the coast, and entered the interior. The settlement of Virginia by the English was followed by remonstrance and a new wave of missionary activity. In 1612 Fray Luis de Oré came with twenty-three friars and Florida was erected into the province of Santa Elena, with the mother house at Havana. In less than two years the new missionaries had established twenty mission residences among the tribes, especially on the Guale (Georgia) coast. In 1612 was published the first of Father Pareja's numerous books in the Timuquanan language. By 1634 some thirty Franciscans were ministering to 30,000 converts in forty-four missions and mission stations. The success was parallel to that of the Franciscans in New Mexico at the same time.

The Apalachee and the Creek missions.—The simultaneous intrusion of the English, French, and Dutch into the Caribbean waters was a new threat at Spain's Gulf possessions, and it was followed by the advance of her outposts into western Florida. Throughout the sixteenth century the warlike Apalachees had resisted Spanish authority, but in 1633 successful missionary work was begun among them by the guardian of the monastery of St. Augustine and one companion. Within two years they had baptized five thousand natives. In 1638 the Apalachees revolted, but they were defeated, and the presidio of San Luís was established among them. This district now became one of the most important missionary centers of Florida, missions being extended to the Creeks of western Georgia.

The missions in 1647.—By 1647 St. Augustine was headquarters for fifty Franciscans, who worked among the neighboring tribes. Northward a line of ten missions extended up the Georgia coast to Chatuache, near the Savannah River. Toward the western interior, within a radius of one hundred and fifty miles there were ten more, and toward the south four. In the Apalachee district there were eight in eight large towns, with three more on the way to St. Augustine. At these thirty-five missions 26,000 converted Indians were served.

The Apalachee revolt.—Just now, however, the prosperous Apalachee missions suffered a severe blow. The chiefs, refusing to render personal service and tribute, headed a rebellion in which several Spaniards were slain. The governor led a campaign against them, several battles were fought, and a number of chiefs hanged. The Indians were subdued, but they were so embittered that the Franciscans abandoned the missions.

The English in the Carolinas.—In 1653 English settlers from Virginia began to establish themselves in North Carolina, and in 1670 the English settlement of South Carolina was begun near Charleston. This intrusion into the old Spanish province of Santa Elena was viewed with alarm by Spain, and, as always in the border Spanish colonies, the foreign danger was followed by renewed missionary activity on the threatened frontiers. Missionary work received an impetus in 1674 by the visitation of Bishop Calderón, of Cuba, who spent eight months in a tour of Florida. In that year and the next, five new missions were founded, and in 1676 Father Moral took to Florida twenty-four additional missionaries. Six or more missions were now in opera-

tion on the northern Georgia coast between Jekyl Island and
the Savannah River, besides those farther south.

English incursions and the Yamassee revolt.—Hostilities with
the English on the border began at once. In 1680 a force of
three hundred Indians and Englishmen invaded Santa Catalina
Island and expelled the garrison and mission Indians. Governor
Marquez Cabrera sent soldiers to build a fort, and asked the
king for Canary Island families to hold the country. The families were ordered sent (1681), but plans were changed and the
Indians of the northernmost missions were moved southward.
The Yamassees refused to move, joined the English, and aided
them in a raid on Mission Santa Catalina (1685). In the following year Spaniards sent by Governor Marquez retaliated by
sacking Carolina plantations and carrying off negro slaves. Another expedition of the same year landed at Edisto Island, burned
the country residence of Governor Morton, and destroyed Stuart
Town (Port Royal).

The English among the Creeks.—The English now threatened
the Spaniards on another frontier. Fur traders from South
Carolina had pushed south and west across Georgia and were
becoming active among the Creeks of western Georgia and
eastern Alabama. In 1685 Governor Marquez sent Lieutenant
Matheos, commander at Apalachee, with twenty soldiers and
four hundred allies to capture traders operating at Kawita,
Kasihta, and Kulumi, Creek towns on the Chatahootchee and
Talapoosa Rivers. The expedition failed but it was repeated,
and Marquez called on the home government for help.

Plans to occupy Pensacola.—It was just at this time that La
Salle formed his establishment in Texas. The combined danger
from the English and the French now made it necessary to protect the northern Gulf coast. La Salle's intrusion was followed
by the temporary Spanish occupation of eastern Texas in 1690,
already described. At the same time (1689) the viceroy sent
Andrés de Pez to Spain to urge the occupation of Pensacola Bay
(Santa María de Galve). The council approved the plan and
authorized the withdrawal from Texas. In 1693 Pez explored
Pensacola and Mobile bays with a view to settlement. Thus,
in a sense, the defence of eastern Texas was given up for the
founding of Pensacola. A new French intrusion was necessary,

however, to bring about the permanent occupation of either Texas or Pensacola.

READINGS

Bancroft, H. H., *Arizona and New Mexico*, 146–224; Bolton, H. E., *Spanish Exploration in the Southwest*, 279–340; "The Spanish Occupation of Texas, 1519–1690," in *Southwestern Historical Quarterly*, XVI, 1–26; Cavo, Andres, *Tres Siglos de Mexico;* Chapman, C. E., *The Founding of Spanish California*, 1–44; Clark, R. C., *The Beginnings of Texas;* Coroléu, José, *America, Historia du Colonización;* Davis, W. H. H., *Spanish Conquest in New Mexico*, 276–407; Dunn, W. E., *Spanish and French Rivalry in the Gulf Region*, 5–215; Frejes, Fr. F., *Conquista de Los Estados;* Garrison, G. P., *Texas*, 10–19; Gonzales, J. E., *Colección de Noticias; Historia de Nuevo León;* Hackett, C. W., "The Pueblo Revolt of 1680," in Texas State Historical Association, *Quarterly*, XV, 93–143; Hughes, Anne, *Beginnings of Spanish Settlement in the El Paso District;* Leon, A., *Historia de Nuevo León;* Ortega, Fr. Joseph, *Apostólicos Afanes;* Portillo, Esteban, *Apuntes para la Historia de Coahuila y Texas;* Prince, L. B., *Historical Sketches of New Mexico*, 176–220; Twitchell, R. E., *Leading Facts of New Mexico History*, I, 333–413; Villagrá, Gaspar de, *Historia de Nuevo Mexico;* Wright, I. A., *The Early History of Cuba*, ch. 17.

CHAPTER XIV

THE WARS OF THE ENGLISH AND SPANISH SUCCESSIONS

The impending conflict.—Before the close of the Stuart period, it was evident that a great international struggle was at hand. Louis XIV of France aspired to overshadow England, Austria, and Spain. The dependence of the later Stuarts upon Louis temporarily delayed the outbreak of hostilities, but when James II was driven from the English throne the contest broke forth and continued intermittently until France was humbled and England had become the foremost commercial and colonial power.

THE PRELIMINARY STRUGGLE FOR THE NORTHERN FUR COUNTRY

Sphere of French influence.—When Frontenac returned to France in 1682, the French were predominant in Acadia, in the St. Lawrence Valley, in the region of the Great Lakes, and in the Illinois country, and were extending their power into the lower valley of the Mississippi. In the West Indies they had secured a foothold. The missionary and the fur-trader had been the instruments of interior expansion, the Indian the source of wealth. To keep control of the natives and to win new tribes to church and trade was the settled policy of France. The Abenaki of Maine were between Acadia and Massachusetts and were friends of the French. To the south of Lake Ontario were the Iroquois, the friends of the English. In the upper lake region the various Algonquin tribes had long been subservient to the French. Their furs were brought to Three Rivers, Montreal, or Quebec, or were traded to the *coureurs de bois*.

The English policy.—To wrest the fur monopoly of the north from the French was one of the mainsprings of Stuart policy. The establishment of the Hudson's Bay Company posts, an alliance with the Iroquois, and the attempt to gain control of the Huron region, thus cutting off the French from the upper lakes

and the Illinois country, were the means adopted to carry out
the policy. To defeat it was the problem of the governors of
New France. A similar conflict was in process in the southwest.

La Barre and the Iroquois, 1684.—The successor of Frontenac
was La Barre. Upon arrival he found conditions deplorable. A
disastrous fire had devastated Quebec and the Iroquois were on
the warpath against the Illinois, Hurons, Ottawas, and other
"children of the French." La Barre at first temporized with the
Iroquois, but their depredations continued, fostered by Dongan,
the governor of New York. La Barre finally realized that his
policy was alienating the interior tribes and he determined upon
war. He gathered a force of Indians and French and entered the
Iroquois country where he was met by a deputation of Iroquois
chiefs. After an extended conference, instead of a war of extermination, peace was ignominiously agreed upon, in spite of
the fact that the Iroquois refused to desist from war on the
Illinois. In the meantime Duluth and other leaders had
brought five hundred warriors to Niagara, who arrived at the
rendezvous only to learn that peace had been made. With sullen
hatred in their hearts, the disappointed warriors returned to
their haunts. French influence in the region of the lakes had
suffered a severe blow.

Denonville and Dongan.—The king had determined upon the
recall of La Barre, and Denonville, "a pious colonel of dragoons,"
assumed the governorship. He at once entered into a correspondence with Dongan. Both governors lacked resources to
carry out an effective campaign; both resorted to Jesuit influence
to obtain control of the Iroquois; and both determined to build
a fort at Niagara. Denonville, in addition, planned to erect
forts at Toronto, on Lake Erie, and at Detroit, and Duluth
actually erected a stockade at the lower end of Lake Huron.
Dongan in 1685 sent eleven canoes to the upper lakes where a
successful trade was carried on. The following year a larger
flotilla was despatched, followed by an expedition which was
intended to make a treaty of trade and alliance with the lake
Indians.

French attack on the Iroquois.—Dongan, however, received
despatches from England which led him to believe that his
policy might not meet with the entire approval of his govern-

ment. He accordingly wrote a conciliatory letter to Denonville, accompanied by a present of oranges. Denonville replied, "Monsieur, I thank you for your oranges. It is a great pity that they were all rotten." His sarcasm was the more effective when it is known that eight hundred French regulars were in the colony, and that as many more were on the way. In the spring of 1687 Denonville was prepared to strike. Leaving eight hundred regulars to protect the settlements, he gathered two thousand men at Ft. Frontenac. In addition Tonty and other post commanders had raised a considerable force in the interior which captured the canoes sent by Dongan. The combined forces of French and Indians, totaling nearly three thousand, penetrated the country of the Senecas, defeated them, and burned their villages. But instead of completing the conquest of the Iroquois country, Denonville led his forces to Niagara where a fort was erected, and then returned to Montreal. The expedition served merely to set the Iroquois hive buzzing, and to increase the influence of the English.

Iroquois reprisals.—The Iroquois soon began a war of reprisal, raid after raid being made on the French settlements. Denonville's courage seemed to be paralyzed. He sent an agent to Albany to make an arrangement with Dongan, who insisted that Forts Niagara and Frontenac be abandoned. Denonville hesitated until the summer of 1688, when Big Mouth, an Onondaga chief, appeared at Montreal. An understanding was reached by which the governor agreed to abandon Niagara and restore captives, no provision being made for protection of the interior tribes. A Huron chief, the Rat, hearing of the treaty, determined that the war should continue. Ascertaining that a party of Onondagas were on their way to the French settlements to complete the peace arrangements, the Rat and his followers ambushed them. The attack had the desired effect, the Iroquois concluding that the treaty was a ruse. An ominous peace prevailed until the French believed that danger had passed. Suddenly in the summer of 1689 a force of fourteen hundred Iroquois attacked the settlements. Instead of retaliating, the frightened governor ordered the abandonment of Ft. Frontenac. This was his last important act, for he was recalled and Count Frontenac was sent to save the colony.

The Hudson Bay posts.—While these events had been taking place, in the far north another conflict was waged.   No attempt

The Intercolonial Wars

was made to impede the English on Hudson Bay until 1682, when Radisson and Groseilliers, now turned French, with two vessels took possession of the English post at the mouth of the

Nelson River, but the Frenchmen soon transferred their allegiance once more to the English. La Barre was instructed to check English encroachments and to propose that neither nation establish new posts. In 1685 a Canadian company was formed to trade in the north. Denonville considered this an excuse for attacking the English. In 1686 a hundred men commanded by De Troyes, one of his lieutenants being Iberville, the future founder of Louisiana, were sent overland to make the attack. Fort Hayes, Ft. Rupert, and Ft. Albany were captured, Fort Nelson being the only post left in English hands. French ascendency for the time being was established on Hudson Bay.

THE WAR OF THE ENGLISH SUCCESSION

William's accession precipitates war.—In spite of these conditions in America, England and France at home had been at peace. It was of more importance to Louis XIV to support a Catholic king of England than to wage open war for the control of the Indian country. But with the overthrow of James II the political situation in Europe was completely changed. William of Orange ascended the throne of England, and Holland, England, several of the German states, Austria, and Spain were welded into a great coalition. Louis XIV championed the Stuart cause and the War of the English Succession was on. In America the struggle is known as King William's War; in Europe it is usually referred to as the War of the Palatinate. In the course of it the Caribbean Sea was the scene of constant conflict. The hostile zones on the mainland had been established in the struggle for the fur trade—the lands of the Abenaki, Iroquois, and upper lake tribes, and the Hudson Bay country.

THE WAR IN THE CARIBBEAN

Four years of war.—In 1689 the French inhabitants of St. Christopher rose against the English inhabitants and expelled them from the island. The French also broke up a Dutch station in Guiana. Early in 1690 England sent Commodore Wright to the West Indies. Convoying a large fleet, his squadron reached Barbados on May 11. Being reinforced by Barbadian troops he reoccupied St. Christopher, the reduction being completed July 16. A few days later St. Eustatius surrendered to the English. In 1690 Trinidad was also attacked by the French. In March, 1691, Wright attacked Guadeloupe but failed to take it or to capture the French squadron under M. Ducasse. Commodore Ralph Wrenn took command of the English fleet in January, 1692, and the following month fought an indecisive battle near Jamaica with a superior French force. In that year a great earthquake destroyed Port Royal, the English capital of Jamaica. The refugees founded Kingston which eventually superseded Port Royal as the seat of government.

Martinique, Santo Domingo, and Jamaica.—In 1693 nine vessels reinforced the West Indian fleet and the combined forces, backed by Barbadian troops, attacked Martinique, but failed to take it. In September of the following year a squadron attacked Léogane, a French town in Santo Domingo, but was repulsed. A French expedition from Santo Domingo also desolated the southeastern coast of Jamaica but at Carlisle Bay was beaten off by the colonial militia. In March, 1695, an English and Spanish fleet attacked the French settlements in Santo Domingo and succeeded in forcing the abandonment of Cape François and Port de Paix.

Cartagena and Petit Gouave.—In April, 1697, a great English fleet under Vice-Admiral John Neville rendezvoused at Barbados to forestall a rumored enterprise of the enemy. M. de Pointis had been sent with large reinforcements to assist M. Ducasse. The combined French fleet attacked Cartagena, took much booty, and eluded Neville. The English commander visited Cartagena, which he found had again been despoiled by buccaneers. He then despatched Captain Mees with nine vessels to burn Petit Gouave, a mission which he accomplished.

THE WAR ON THE CANADIAN FRONTIERS

The Maine frontier.—Andros had sent an expedition against the Abenaki and had fortified the frontier, his most northern fort being at Pemaquid, but with his fall the garrison had been reduced. During the summer of 1689 the Indians destroyed Pemaquid and killed most of the settlers in that region. Casco (Portland) was then attacked but was relieved by a counter expedition.

The French attack.—In August Frontenac was sent to assume the governorship of Canada. In New France he found despair and desolation. He decided to send out three expeditions, one from Montreal into the upper Hudson Valley, the others from Three Rivers and Quebec to raid the New England frontier. The three expeditions started about February 1, 1690. The Montreal party surprised Schenectady, where sixty persons were massacred. A party from Albany started in pursuit and succeeded in killing about twenty of the retreating French and Indians. The Three Rivers expedition attacked Salmon Falls, where thirty persons were killed and about fifty made prisoners. A relief party from Portsmouth caught up with the raiders at Wooster River, but after a spirited fight the French and Indians escaped. Being reinforced by Indians they joined the party from Quebec. The united force of four or five hundred men in May attacked the fort and blockhouses on Casco Bay, killing or capturing the garrison, massacring or carrying into captivity most of the inhabitants, and burning the settlements.

Frontenac's Indian policy.—Frontenac also sent an expedition of one hundred men to Michilimackinac to keep control of the upper lake Indians. On the way an Iroquois war party was defeated at Sand Point on the Ottawa River. The French victory and news of the successful raids on the English frontier had far-reaching effects, for they kept the Hurons and Ottawas in subjection.

The English defence.—The attack upon the English colonies was well-timed, for confusion prevailed in New England and New York. Andros had been overthrown and Leisler's rebellion was in full swing. Little help could be expected from England, for James II, with French and Irish aid, was battling to regain his throne. In May, 1690, the New England colonies sent delegates to a congress at New York to determine on a military policy. A two-fold attack was planned; a land expedition against Montreal and a naval expedition against Quebec.

The Montreal fiasco.—The expedition against Montreal was placed under Fitz-John Winthrop of Connecticut, who led his men as far as the southern end of Lake Champlain. Here small-pox broke out, disagreements with the Indians ensued, and provisions ran short. Winthrop soon discovered that a descent on

Montreal was impossible, and he ingloriously led most of his men back to Albany. Captain John Schuyler, however, with a small detachment proceeded northward and raided the village of Laprairie near Montreal.

The capture of Port Royal.—While New England delegates were at New York a preliminary expedition was sent against Acadia. Sir William Phips, a New Englander who had achieved great renown and wealth by locating a Spanish treasure ship which had been wrecked off the Bahamas, was placed in command of seven vessels. On May 11, 1690, the fleet appeared before Port Royal, which surrendered without a shot being fired. One of the vessels under Captain Alden captured a French post on the Penobscot and seized several settlements on the southern shore of Nova Scotia.

The expedition against Quebec.—In the meantime Massachusetts was preparing for her great attempt on Quebec. Thirty vessels were gathered, but the fleet was short of ammunition, due to the fact that the French had gained temporary control of the sea by defeating the English and Dutch fleets at Beachy Head. The fleet commanded by Phips sailed from Boston on August 9, 1690, but it was not until October 16 that it came in sight of Quebec. The slow progress prevented a surprise and gave Frontenac time to complete his defences. When Phips demanded that Quebec surrender, he received a haughty refusal. Phips then attempted to capture the town, but the plan was poorly executed, ammunition ran short, and reinforcements poured into the city so rapidly that the defenders soon outnumbered the English. A council of war was held, and it was decided to abandon the undertaking. A week of intermittent fighting had brought nothing but failure, which was made the more trying by the loss of several vessels on the return voyage.

Frontenac's policy in 1691.—After the attack on Quebec, the war developed into a desultory frontier conflict in which the French were usually on the offensive. The Iroquois continued to raid the French settlements, but they were soon severely chastised, when forty or fifty warriors were surrounded at Repentigny, near Montreal, and killed or captured. This event and the timely arrival of several French vessels impressed an Ottawa deputation which had come to Quebec, and the French power among the interior tribes was greatly strengthened.

Schuyler's expedition.—The English influence among the Iroquois was waning; to reassert it an expedition under Peter Schuyler was sent from Albany. It traversed Lake Champlain and the Richelieu and proceeded toward Laprairie de la Madeleine where it was attacked by a superior force. After stubborn fighting, Schuyler made an orderly retreat.

Acadia and the Abenaki.—In Acadia Phips had made the blunder of leaving no garrison; the French accordingly reoccupied it. Deeming the location of Port Royal too exposed, M. de Villebon, the lieutenant-governor of Acadia, moved his headquarters to Naxouat on the St. John's River, from which vantage point he was able to direct attacks on New England. In February, 1692, a band of Abenaki wiped out the settlement at York, and later unsuccessfully attacked Wells. Minor raids were also made on the towns of central Massachusetts. To protect the frontier Phips ordered the rebuilding of Fort Pemaquid and the erection of a fort at the falls of the Saco. Scarcely were they completed, when Iberville, in command of two French vessels, attacked Pemaquid but failed to capture it.

The Iroquois frontier.—The Iroquois continued to infest the region between the St. Lawrence and Ottawa rivers, but during 1692 and 1693 they were severely punished, and ceased to be an important factor in the war. Frontenac then determined to reopen the fur trade. He accordingly sent a detachment to Michilimackinac asking that furs be sent to Montreal. In August, 1693, a flotilla of two hundred canoes arrived and shortly afterward Tonty, with a large body of *coureurs de bois* came to discuss matters. Tonty soon returned to the Illinois country well equipped to strengthen his hold on the natives. The fortifications at Quebec were also remodeled. In 1695 Fort Frontenac was reëstablished and the following year an expedition of over two thousand men was sent against the Onondagas and Oneidas. They abandoned their villages and the French destroyed their crops. Though no battle was fought the expedition served its end, for the Iroquois were duly impressed by the power of the French.

The New England frontier.—In 1693 an English fleet from the West Indies arrived at Boston and the idea of an expedition against Quebec was revived, but there was so much sickness among the men that the plan was abandoned. During 1693 and 1694 both English and French sought to control the Abenaki, but in spite of a treaty made by Phips, the French succeeded in holding their allies. In July, 1694, the Indians attacked Durham, massacring over a hundred of the inhabitants, and a few days later killed about forty people at Groton. Two years later Iberville again appeared before Pemaquid and this time succeeded in capturing it. He then sailed to Newfoundland, captured and burned St. Johns, and plundered the settlements on the coast. The English retaliated by burning the French settlement at Beaubassin but were repulsed at Naxouat. In March, 1697, Haverhill was raided by the Indians, and in February, 1698, after the treaty of peace, they attacked Andover. In the last year of the war an attack upon Boston and New York by land and sea was determined upon and a fleet set sail from France, but the treaty of peace ended hostilities.

ACTIVITIES ON HUDSON BAY; PEACE

Operations of Iberville.—When the war opened, the French were in control of the posts about James Bay, while Fort Nelson, commanding the great interior water-ways, was in the hands of the Hudson's Bay Company. In 1689 Fort Albany was captured by the English. The following year Iberville recaptured it, but in 1692 it again passed out of French hands. In 1694 the French government determined to assist the Compagnie du Nord; Iberville, being sent to the bay with two frigates, captured Fort Nelson. Two years later it was retaken by the English. In 1697 Iberville penetrated the bay, this time with five vessels. Becoming separated from the rest of the fleet, Iberville encountered three armed vessels of the Hudson's Bay Company. After a thrilling naval battle the English were worsted, and the French once more took possession of Fort Nelson. At the end of the war the only important post left in English hands was Fort Albany.

The Peace of Ryswick.—In 1697 the war was brought to an end by the peace of Ryswick, by which Louis XIV acknowledged William III as king of England. The results of the fighting in America were ignored, the powers agreeing to restore to each other all places taken in the war. The ownership of the Abenaki and Iroquois lands, and of the Hudson Bay country was left unsettled.

THE WAR OF THE SPANISH SUCCESSION

French expansion.—The peace of Ryswick was only a truce. France took advantage of the peace to begin to establish her power in the Mississippi Valley and to strengthen her hold upon the Northwest. In 1699 Biloxi was founded on the Gulf and in succeeding years France brought under control most of the tribes of the lower Mississippi Valley. In 1701 the French occupied Detroit to cut off the English from one of the routes to the fur country, and strengthened their hold on the Illinois country.*

The Spanish Succession.—Upon the death of Philip IV in 1665 the incompetent Charles II came to the throne of Spain. Court intrigues stimulated by France and Austria, and utter lack of statesmanship at a time when France was reaching out in every direction, brought Spain to the lowest point in her history. Fearing that she would pass under French control, thereby destroying the balance of power in Europe, William III of England sought to check French power by the so-called Second Treaty of Partition, by which the Austrian Archduke Charles was to inherit the crown of Spain upon the death of Charles II, Spanish possessions in Italy were to go to the Dauphin of France, and Spanish and Austrian possessions were never to be united. To this arrangement France, Austria, and England agreed, but the treaty proved to be but a scrap of paper. In 1700 Charles II died and his will designated Philip of Anjou, a grandson of Louis XIV, as his heir.

England determines upon war.—War was not at once declared, for the English people were slow to recognize the danger. But when French troops occupied the border fortresses in the Spanish Netherlands, when French edicts excluded British manufactures, when the English and Dutch trade, especially the slave

* For details see Chapter XV.

trade, was hampered in the Spanish colonies, and when Louis XIV acknowledged the son of James II as king of England, English statesmen were convinced that war was necessary. When Anne ascended the throne in 1702, war was a foregone conclusion.

War zones in America.—The war areas were even more extensive in America than in the War of the English Succession. In the South, the West Indies, and the Carolina, Florida, and Louisiana frontiers, and in the North, the New England border, Acadia, Newfoundland, and Hudson Bay were the scenes of conflict.

THE WAR IN THE WEST INDIES

An indecisive struggle.—When William III became convinced that the war was inevitable, he proposed to strike at Spanish commerce. In furtherance of this policy a squadron was sent in 1701 to the West Indies under Vice-Admiral John Benbow. In July, 1702, Benbow destroyed or captured several vessels near Port-au-Prince, and supported by troops under Major-General Hamilton, he occupied St. Christopher. The fleet in August encountered that of Ducasse off Santa Marta to the northeast of Cartagena and in a running fight which lasted several days the English were worsted. In 1703 General Codrington attacked Guadeloupe but a French reinforcement forced the English to retire. The same year a combined French and Spanish force drove the English inhabitants from New Providence and destroyed Fort Nassau, but it was soon reoccupied by the English Vice-Admiral John Graydon who had been placed in command of the West Indian fleet. Before his arrival several privateers had been destroyed near the island of Santo Domingo and descents had been made on St. Christopher and Guadeloupe. Graydon accomplished nothing and soon sailed to Newfoundland, where his operations were also fruitless.

1705–1708.—During 1705 several prizes were taken and in 1706 the French made a descent on St. Christopher. Their attack on the fort failed, but they burned and plundered several plantations. Hearing that an English fleet was expected, the French repaired to Nevis, which they occupied. The English fleet under Commodore Kerr attacked Petit Gouave but failed to capture it. In 1708 Commodore Charles Wager won an important engagement when he attacked a Spanish fleet near Cartagena. New Providence was a second time attacked by the French and Spanish, which led to the English abandonment of the island.

1711-1712.—In 1710 the Spaniards attacked the salt rakers on Turk's Island but were driven off. In 1711 Commodore James Littleton attempted to find the French fleet, which he located in the harbor of Cartagena. Finding it too strong to attack, he loafed in the neighborhood, picking up an occasional prize. Ducasse, who was convoying a fleet of Spanish galleons, succeeded in getting them out of the harbor without being observed and got them safely to Havana. A French squadron which made an attempt against Antigua was driven into St. Pierre by the English fleet, and a similar expedition against Montserrat was foiled. The following year the French nearly ruined Berbice, a Dutch settlement in Guiana.

THE WAR ON THE FLORIDA BORDER

The southern border.—On the mainland the South Carolina settlements formed the southern English frontier. The Spaniards occupied St. Augustine, contiguous territory up the Georgia coast, Pensacola, and intermediate points. To the west on the Gulf coast were the recently established French settlements. In the interior lived the Apalachees, Creeks, Cherokees, Choctaws, and Chickasaws. To control the trade of the Indians and use them as allies was the policy of English, Spanish, and French alike. The first blow fell on the Apalachee. In 1702 a force of Apalachicolas, allies of the English, destroyed the mission of Santa Fé in the Apalachee district, and a Spanish force was met at the Flint River by Englishmen and Creek allies, and driven back.

Siege of St. Augustine.—The next attack of the English was directed against St. Augustine. Hearing of their plans, Governor Zuñiga sent to Havana for reinforcements, abandoned the town of St. Augustine, and provisioned the castle. The Carolina force of about twelve hundred militia and Indians rendezvoused at Port Royal in September, 1702. Colonel Robert Daniel, conducting the land forces, destroyed the mission settlements on St. Mark's Island, captured the villages of St. Johns and St.

Marys, and plundered St. Augustine. Governor Moore conducted the fleet, and the combined forces besieged the castle.
Governor Zuñiga bravely withstood the siege for fifty days, and
when Spanish vessels arrived, Moore destroyed his ships, burned
St. Augustine, and retreated to Carolina.

Destruction of the Apalachee Missions.—Moore was superseded as governor by Sir Nathaniel Johnson, who immediately
strengthened the fortifications at and near Charleston. Moore,
desiring to build up his waning reputation, persuaded Johnson to
send him against the Apalachee. Setting out with a force of
fifty Carolinians and a thousand Creek allies, in January, 1704,
he captured the Apalachee town of Ayubale, burned the mission,
and then defeated a force of Spaniards and Apalachee. The
Indian villages were next destroyed; of thirteen Apalachee towns,
each with its mission, only one was spared. When Moore
withdrew he carried off fourteen hundred Apalachee prisoners
and slaves.

Spanish expedition against Charleston.—In 1706 the French
and Spaniards at Havana organized an expedition to attack
Carolina. In August a frigate and four sloops, after taking on
men and supplies at St. Augustine, sailed to Charleston and
demanded its surrender. A small landing party was repulsed;
six Carolina vessels sallied out, and after an engagement the
enemy withdrew.

Indian policy of the French.—To use the Indian allies to prevent the spread of English settlement was a fundamental of
French policy. Iberville, the founder of Louisiana, planned to
obtain control of the great interior rivers by establishing forts,
and to weld the Indians into an alliance with the French by
treaties and by trade. He even contemplated moving some of
the tribes to points of greater commercial vantage. He also
believed that he could obtain the aid of several thousand warriors in attacking Maryland, Virginia, and Carolina. Realizing
the danger, the English traders were active among the tribes.
In 1708, probably at the instigation of the English, the Cherokees, Arikas, Catawbas, and Alabamas formed an alliance. Four
thousand warriors descended on the French settlements, but
lack of leadership destroyed the effectiveness of the attack and
but little damage was done.

The Tuscarora War.—In 1711 the Tuscaroras, a North Carolina tribe, went on the warpath and massacred about two hundred settlers. Virginia and South Carolina sent aid, and in 1712 the Indians were defeated. The Tuscaroras continued their depredations and in 1713 they were almost annihilated. The remnant made their way to New York and were incorporated with the Iroquois as a sixth nation.

THE WAR ON THE CANADIAN BORDER

Newfoundland and the New England frontier.—To deprive the French of the profitable Newfoundland fisheries was the first endeavor of England in the north. Captain John Leake arrived at St. Johns in August, 1702. He cruised off Placentia Bay, making several small prizes and destroying fishing craft. Before the end of October he had captured twenty-nine sail, burned two vessels, and destroyed St. Peter's Fort. The New England frontier was harried by the French and Abenaki. In 1699 Massachusetts had made a treaty at Casco Bay with the Maine Indians, but the Jesuits soon brought them back to French allegiance. In 1703 a second peace treaty was made with them, but within two months they were on the warpath, almost wiping out the Maine settlements. In 1704 the French and Indians surprised Deerfield in the Connecticut Valley, killing about fifty and carrying off more than one hundred captives. Almost every frontier settlement was attacked. Even Reading, Sudbury, and Haverhill, within a short distance of Boston, were raided. To add to the distress French privateers did serious damage to commerce and fisheries.

Acadia.—The New Englanders retaliated with small counter raids, but succeeded in inflicting little damage. It was finally determined to strike at Acadia. An expedition was placed under Benjamin Church, a veteran of King Philip's War. French settlements on the Bay of Fundy were ravaged, but he failed to attack Port Royal. In 1707 an expedition, recruited by Massachusetts, New Hampshire, and Rhode Island, was again sent against Port Royal, but the stubborn defense discouraged the attacking force and the siege was abandoned. English vessels under Captain John Underwood raided the Newfoundland coast, destroying many settlements and fishing craft.

Plan to conquer Canada.—The conquest of Canada was urged by many of the colonial leaders, the most active of whom was Colonel Samuel Vetch, a Scotchman who had formerly seen service in the English army.   In 1709 his plan was endorsed by the British government, and preparations were made to send a large force against Quebec by sea and a land expedition against Montreal.   But after great efforts had been made by the New England colonies and New York, the British regulars were diverted to Portugal, and the conquest of Canada had to be abandoned.

Conquest of Acadia.—The following year a force of four thousand colonials, commanded by Francis Nicholson, aided by British men-of-war and a regiment of marines, attacked and captured Port Royal.   Acadia became the British province of Nova Scotia, and the name of its capital was changed to Annapolis Royal.   The following year the English again raided the French fishing stations in Newfoundland.

Failure of Walker's expedition.—In 1710 a Tory ministry came into power, its chief members being the Earl of Oxford and Viscount Bolingbroke.   They were opposed to carrying on the war in Europe, believing that England's best policy lay in colonial undertakings.   The conquest of Canada became the great object.   As before, the attack was to be by land and sea. Under Nicholson the land force, composed mainly of colonials and eight hundred Iroquois, prepared to attack Montreal.   The expedition against Quebec was entrusted to Admiral Sir Hovenden Walker and General Sir John Hill, a court favorite.   Seven of Marlborough's best regiments, veterans of Oudenarde and Ramillies, were placed on transports which were convoyed by a large fleet of war vessels.   The great force gathered at Boston, where it was reinforced by fifteen hundred colonials.   In August, 1711, the fleet entered the St. Lawrence, but there it met disaster.   Sailing too close to the northern shore, ten vessels were wrecked on the reefs and shoals of the Egg Islands. Stunned by the calamity, the faint-hearted commander gave up the enterprise.   News of the disaster reached Nicholson at Lake Champlain.   His force was not strong enough to accomplish the conquest alone, and the attack on Montreal was abandoned.

THE HUDSON BAY COUNTRY

The Hudson's Bay Company had been sadly crippled at the end of the War of the English Succession. Its shares fell in value and most of the original owners sold their holdings. The only post which the company held was Fort Albany, and in 1704 this was unsuccessfully attacked by a party of French and Indians. The same year an English frigate captured the principal ship of the Compagnie du Nord, causing great hardship in the French forts. The Hudson's Bay Company during the war frequently petitioned the Board of Trade for assistance, but, as they received none, they appealed directly to the queen. When the final treaty was made, the Hudson Bay country was taken into account.

THE PEACE OF UTRECHT

At the end of the war a series of agreements was drawn up by the various powers. The treaties involving America dealt both with territory and commerce. England obtained a recognition of her claims in the Hudson Bay country and the possession of Newfoundland and Acadia. The claim of the English to the Iroquois country was also admitted, and they were given St. Christopher. Commercially the agreements dealt with the fisheries and Spanish trade. The French were excluded from fishing on the Acadian coast, but were allowed to keep Cape Breton Island and were given certain fishing privileges on the Newfoundland coasts. An agreement with Spain, known as the *Asiento* or contract, gave the English the exclusive right for thirty years of bringing negroes into the Spanish possessions. The English were also allowed to send an annual merchant ship of five hundred tons burden to trade with Spanish ports.

READINGS
THE STRUGGLE FOR THE FUR COUNTRY

Bryce, George, *The Remarkable History of the Hudson's Bay Company*, 1–46; Kingsford, William, *The History of Canada*, II, 36–107; Laut, Agnes, *The Conquest of the Great Northwest*, I, 97–255; Le Sueur, W. D., *Count Frontenac*, 170–228; Lorin, Henri, *Le Comte de Frontenac*, 275–352; Parkman, Francis, *Count Frontenac and New France under Louis XIV*, 72–183; Thwaites, R. G., ed., *The Jesuit Relations*, LXII–LXIV.

THE WAR OF THE ENGLISH SUCCESSION

Bryce, George, *The Remarkable History of the Hudson's Bay Company*, 47–55; Clowes, W. L., *The Royal Navy*, II, 462–472, 492–495; Kingsford, William, *The History of Canada*, II, 198–386; Laut, A. C., *The Conquest of the Great Northwest*, I, 228–255; Le Sueur, W. D., *Count Frontenac*, 229–362; Lorin, Henri, *Le Comte de Frontenac*, 353–488; Mahan, A. T., *The Influence of Sea Power upon History, 1660–1783*, pp. 173–198; Parkman, Francis, *Count Frontenac and New France under Louis XIV*, 184–427; Willson, Beckles, *The Great Company*, 182–197.

WAR OF THE SPANISH SUCCESSION

Clowes, W. L., *The Royal Navy*, II, chs. 23–24; Greene, E. B., *Provincial America*, 136–165; Kingsford, William, *The History of Canada*, III; Mc-Crady, Edward, *The History of Carolina under the Proprietary Government, 1670–1719*, pp. 364–548; Parkman, Francis, *A Half-Century of Conflict*, I, 1–297; Shea, J. G., *Catholic Church in Colonial Days*, 454–479; Hamilton, P. J., *Colonization of the South*, ch. 15.

CHAPTER XV

THE FRENCH IN LOUISIANA AND THE FAR NORTHWEST
(1699-1762)

THE FOUNDING OF LOUISIANA

Applicants for La Salle's grant.—During the War of the Palatinate Louis XIV showed little desire to develop La Salle's plan for a colony on the Gulf. In the interim, however, a number of individuals proposed taking up La Salle's work. In 1690 his brother, the Abbé Cavelier, strongly urged that it be continued. In 1694 Tonty asked permission to carry out the project. In 1697 De Louvigny, Captain of Marines in Canada, proposed making an expedition against the Spanish mines by way of the Rio Bravo. In the same year Sieur de Argaud, at Paris, sought a grant of the territory between Florida and New Mexico, the Gulf and the Illinois River. The control of the Gulf and the checking of the Spanish advance were prominent among the arguments for all these projects.

Iberville.—But not until the treaty of Ryswick was signed did the king again take up the plan. The founding of the proposed colony was then entrusted to Iberville, a son of Charles Le Moyne, one of the great seigniors of Canada. Iberville and his brother Bienville had already distinguished themselves in their attacks upon the English on Hudson Bay. Activities were hastened by reports that the English were preparing to take possession of the mouth of the Mississippi. To forestall them, Pontchartram, the Minister of Marine, in 1698 sent an expedition to the Gulf of Mexico.

Pensacola founded by Spain.—News of Iberville's preparations reached Madrid early in 1698, and again Spain proved that in an emergency she could act. Assuming that Pensacola was the French objective, the viceroy sent Andrés de Arriola to intercept them, and in November he fortified the place.

Biloxi founded by France.—The movement was timely. Two months behind Arriola Iberville's fleet appeared before the harbor and demanded admission (January, 1699). The request being politely refused, Iberville established himself at Biloxi, after which he returned to France, leaving Bienville in command. During Iberville's absence, the coast and the lower courses of the Mississippi and Red Rivers were thoroughly explored and friendly relations with the Indian tribes promoted. Shortly afterward Iberville returned to the colony, and in 1702 the settlement was moved to Mobile Bay where the Spaniards at Pensacola could be more effectually checked, the new settlement being called St. Louis.

Alliance with the tribes.—An Indian policy was also developed. Tonty, who had found it to his advantage to divert his fur trade to Louisiana, was sent on a peace mission to the Chickasaws. This resulted in a conference of Chickasaws and Choctaws at Mobile Bay, at which the friendship and trade of those powerful tribes were assured. By alliances with the interior tribes, Iberville hoped to be able eventually to check and, if possible, annihilate the English settlements of Maryland, Virginia, and Carolina. After the conference at Mobile Bay, Iberville left the colony, and Bienville became the central figure in Louisiana.

Bienville's first administration.—The government of the colony was of a military type. At the head was the governor, who was assisted by a *commissaire* who had charge of the stores. A council with judicial powers was also established. Like Frontenac, Bienville was beset by many difficulties, quarrels with officials and clergy being frequent. The colony was threatened by an alliance of Cherokees, Choctaws, and other tribes who were instigated to hostility by the English. In 1710 a new site for St. Louis was selected, the settlement being located on the present site of Mobile, and by that name it became known.

Crozat.—The colony had not prospered, and the government desired to rid itself of the expense of the establishment. In 1712 the king therefore granted to Antoine Crozat, a wealthy merchant, a fifteen-year monopoly of trade in the vast territory from Illinois to the Gulf and from the Carolinas to New Mexico. He was also permitted to send a ship annually to the Guinea coast for negro slaves. On the other hand, Crozat agreed to

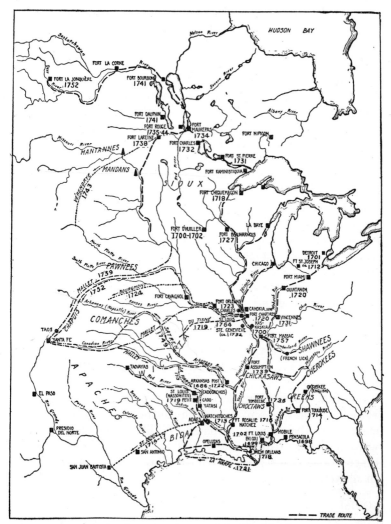

The French in Louisiana and the Far Northwest

send out two shiploads of settlers yearly. The executive powers were vested in a council appointed by the king from nominations made by Crozat; it consisted of a governor, intendant, and two agents of the proprietor. The first governor was Lamothe Cadillac, the founder of Detroit. At first a considerable number of colonists were sent over, but the French commercial laws, the monopoly of Crozat, and the low prices offered for peltries crippled the colony.

Natchitoches.—Cadillac attempted to open a trade with the Spanish colonies. With this in view in 1713 St. Denis, the younger, was sent to take possession of the Natchitoches country on the Red River and to open an overland trade route across Texas into Mexico. A trading post was established at Natchitoches, but the commercial results of the expedition to Mexico were slight. St. Denis was arrested and the Spaniards, alarmed at the French encroachments, began the permanent occupation of Texas.

Fort Toulouse.—In 1714 Bienville built Fort Toulouse, on the Alabama River, near the junction of the Coosa and Talapoosa Rivers, in the country of the upper Creeks, Mandeville being made first commander. Fort Toulouse was a depot where furs were bought from the Indians and floated down the river to Mobile. Round about it the Jesuit missionaries worked among the Creeks. The fort became the base for the control of these tribes, and an outpost against the English of the Carolinas. When the latter settled Georgia, feeling the menace of the French outposts, they built Fort Okfuskee, on the Talapoosa River, forty miles away, and induced the Creeks to destroy the Jesuit missions.

Natchez.—Difficulties arose with the Natchez Indians; in 1716 Bienville was sent to subdue them, and Fort Rosalie was erected on the site of Natchez. Cadillac was shortly afterward recalled. Crozat had found his colony merely a bill of expense and in 1717 he surrendered his patent. At that time there were about seven hundred Frenchmen in Louisiana.

LOUISIANA UNDER THE COMPANY OF THE INDIES (1717–1731)

The Mississippi Bubble.—When Crozat surrendered his patent John Law was ushering in his era of speculation. Louisiana was taken over by the Compagnie d'Occident, which was granted complete political and commercial powers. The capital of the Company, amounting to one hundred million livres, was divided into two hundred thousand shares. In 1719 the company received, in addition, a monopoly of the trade of Africa and the Orient, and increased its capital by fifty thousand shares, thenceforth being known as the Compagnie des Indies. Law made Louisiana the center of his system, and represented the country as an earthly paradise, fabulous in mines.

New Orleans founded.—Bienville was made governor and the capital was established at New Biloxi. In 1718 New Orleans was laid out and named in honor of the regent. A garrison was established at the Natchitoches trading post, and Fort Chartres was built in the Illinois country. Feudal seignories were not extended as in Canada, but extensive tracts were granted to *concessionaires*, who agreed to bring out settlers. In a short time many tracts had been granted on Red River, on the Mississippi, and on the Yazoo. As colonists did not volunteer in sufficient numbers, emigrants were secured from hospitals and jails, or were spirited away from France. A few negro slaves had been previously introduced, but Law's company brought large numbers; the first cargo, landed in 1719, contained two hundred and fifty. With this introduction of slavery, agriculture developed rapidly.

War with Spain.—At this time a brief period of war ensued between Spain and France, due to the ambitions of Elizabeth Farnese and her advisor Alberoni. An expedition from Mobile captured Pensacola, but it was soon after retaken by the Spanish, who also attacked Mobile. Shortly afterward the French again captured Pensacola, but at the end of the war it was restored to Spain. At the same time the Spaniards were driven out of eastern Texas and an expedition under Villazur was defeated by French allies on the Platte River.

Growth of population.—In 1720 the Mississippi Bubble burst, stock in Law's numerous enterprises fell rapidly, and the great financier left France a ruined man. Though Louisiana ceased to be the center of the financial system of France, the Company continued operations with considerable success. The white population had increased to about five thousand. New Orleans had a considerable population, and in 1722 it was made the capital.

The government.—In order that the country might be better governed, it was divided into the nine judicial departments of Biloxi, Mobile, Alibamon, New Orleans, Yazoo, Natchez, Natchi-

toches, Arkansas, and Illinois. The negro population increased so
rapidly that there was considerable fear of an uprising. To
govern them, in 1724 a set of laws known as the Black Code was
promulgated by the governor. The legal religion of the colony
was decreed to be Catholic, and masters were to give religious
instruction to slaves. Intermarriage of whites and blacks was
prohibited. The slaves were forbidden to carry weapons or to
gather in assemblies. Masters were bound to clothe, protect,
and give subsistence to slaves, and negro families were not to
be broken up by sales. Masters were also responsible for acts
of their slaves. The crimes of those in bondage were punished
by whipping, branding, or, in extreme cases, by death. This
code was the last important act of Bienville, who shortly afterward returned to France. The central government under the
company was practically the same as that of Canada in the time
of Frontenac, and similar quarrels between governor and intendant ensued. Ecclesiastically Louisiana was divided roughly
into three districts; the Mobile region was under the Carmelites,
the Jesuits ministered to those in the Illinois country and along
the lower Ohio, and the rest was under the Capuchins.

The Natchez War.—Owing to the French occupation of Natchez lands, the tribe in 1729 formed a conspiracy, which embraced
the Choctaws and other tribes, for the purpose of exterminating
the whites. In the first attack two hundred and fifty French at
Fort Rosalie were killed, and many women and children taken
into captivity. The Choctaws turned against the Natchez. An
army of French and Choctaws was collected, and finally succeeded in dispersing the hostile tribe. A second expedition pursued the fugitives, and the Natchez were so severely chastised
that they ceased to exist as a unit.

LOUISIANA UNDER THE ROYAL GOVERNORS

Bienville again governor.—The expense of the Natchez War
convinced the directors of the company that the Louisiana project could not be made a paying investment, and in 1731 the
king released them from their charter. In 1731 the Company
of the Indies withdrew from Louisiana and it became a royal
province. A council was organized to replace the company and
Bienville was again made governor.

The Chickasaw War: Fort Tombecbé.—After the Natchez War the remnant of the tribe had fled to the Chickasaws. In 1736 Bienville made war on the latter tribe, who had not only harbored the Natchez, but were in alliance with the English and had formed a league to cut off French activities along the Mississippi, Mobile, and Tombigbee Rivers. Bienville led troops from Natchitoches, Natchez, Mobile, and New Orleans, while D'Artaguette from the Illinois coöperated. As a base of attack Fort Tombecbé was built on the Tombigbee River in the Choctaw country. The expedition against the Chickasaws ended in disaster, but Fort Tombecbé continued to be important as a base for the control of the Choctaws, who were kept hostile toward Chickasaws and English. In 1740 a second attempt was made. At Fort Assumption, on the site of Memphis, a force of thirty-six hundred was gathered. The size of the army frightened the Chickasaws, who sued for peace. The French, however, failed to secure their friendship, and they remained allies of the English.

End of Bienville's rule.—In 1743 Bienville retired from the governorship without having succeeded in making the colony a success. The white population near the Gulf had declined to thirty-two hundred and there were about two thousand slaves in the colony, while the Illinois country contained about fifteen hundred people. During the remaining twenty years of French rule in Louisiana the New Orleans region showed but slight development.

The Illinois.—The Illinois district throve especially under the Company of the Indies. At first the settlements had been governed from Canada, but because of the Fox wars and difficulties of transportation, there was little connection with Canada, and after 1717 the Illinois district was attached to Louisiana. The settlement profited by the John Law "boom" in 1719, eight hundred new colonists coming, chiefly from Canada and New Orleans. In 1720 Fort Chartres, in 1723 St. Philippe, and ten years later Prairie du Rocher, were established. Across the river St. Genevieve and St. Charles were founded. Further east, the Wabash was fortified to keep out the advancing English traders. In 1720 Ouiatanon post was established at Lafayette. This post and Fort Miami, at Fort Wayne, were attached to

Canada, while Vincennes, founded in 1731, belonged to Louisiana, as did Fort Massac founded later on the Ohio. The dividing line between the districts was Terre Haute, or the highlands. Ouiatanon was at the head of navigation on the Wabash for larger pirogues. Here peltries for Canada were reshipped in canoes. Twenty thousand skins a year were sent from Ouiatanon in the decade after 1720.

The Garden of New France.—The Illinois district became an important agricultural center, whence large shipments of grain were made to Detroit, the Ohio River posts, New Orleans, Mobile, and Europe. Negro slaves were introduced and tobacco-raising was begun. At Kaskaskia there was a Jesuit academy for white boys, and at Cahokia a Sulpician Indian school.

The Missouri lead mines.—During the rule of the Company of the Indies lead mines were opened in Missouri, where lead had been early discovered, especially on Maramec River. While governor, Cadillac had made a personal visit to inspect them. Mining was begun on an important scale by Renault, who received grants on the Missouri in 1723. He is said to have taken to these mines two hundred miners from France, and five hundred negroes from Santo Domingo. He was actively engaged in mining until 1746.

THE TRANS–MISSISSIPPI WEST

French advance into the Far West.—Meanwhile the French explorers had reached the Rocky Mountains. In or before 1703 twenty Canadians went from the Illinois country toward New Mexico to trade and learn about the mines. By 1705 Laurain had been on the Missouri and in 1708 Canadians are said to have explored that stream for three hundred or four hundred leagues. By 1712 salines were being worked in Missouri and settlers were living about them. Under the Company of the Indies exploration and trade were pushed for a time with vigor in the trans-Mississippi West, all along the border from the Gulf of Mexico to Nebraska. From Natchitoches French traders made their way among the tribes of eastern and northern Texas, and sometimes reached the Spanish settlements. In 1717 St. Denis the younger and several partners made a second trading expedition overland from Mobile via Natchitoches to San Juan Bautista on the Rio Grande. His goods being seized, he went to Mexico, where he was imprisoned, though his goods were sold with profit. His associates, who reached the border somewhat after him, made their way to Presidio del Norte, disposed of their goods, and returned to Louisiana.

La Harpe on the Red River.—While St. Denis was in Mexico, Bénard de la Harpe was sent to establish a post on the Red River above Natchitoches. He was urged to inform himself concerning the source of the Red River and the tribes near New Mexico, and to open commerce with the Spanish provinces. In 1719 he established his post among the Cadodachos. Du Rivage was sent up the Red River, and La Harpe made an expedition to the Touacaras near the mouth of the Canadian River, where he proposed to found a post as a base for trade with New Mexico, the Padoucas, and the Aricaras.

Du Tisné on the Osage and the Arkansas.—At the same time (1719) Du Tisné was on the Missouri, Osage, and Arkansas rivers. He ascended the Missouri River to the Missouri Indian village, on his way to the Pawnees, but was unable to proceed. He returned to the Illinois, and went to the Osage tribe on the Osage River. From there he continued southwest to the Pawnees on the Arkansas. He made an alliance with the Pawnees, bought Spanish horses from them, and established a French flag in their villages. He was prevented by his hosts from going to the Padouca, but he inquired about New Mexico.

La Harpe on the Gulf Coast.—In 1718 the company was ordered to occupy the Bay of St. Bernard, discovered by La Salle. In 1719 and 1720 preliminary expeditions were made, and in 1721 La Harpe himself led an expedition to a bay on the Texas coast, but he was expelled by the Indians. The bay reached by him was the Bay of the Bidayes (Galveston Bay) and not the St. Bernard of La Salle. La Harpe urged a new attempt, to keep out the Spaniards, but the company abandoned the project.

La Harpe on the Arkansas.—After returning from the Gulf coast expedition, La Harpe was sent from Mobile in December, 1721, to explore the Arkansas River, with the idea of developing Indian trade, preventing Spanish encroachment, and opening commerce with New Mexico. He ascended the Arkansas about halfway to the mouth of the Canadian River, and on his return recommended establishing posts at Little Rock, the mouth of the Canadian, and the Touacara villages.

Bourgmont on the Missouri and Kansas Rivers.—In the years immediately following the Spanish expedition under Villazur (1720), the French made active efforts to communicate with New Mexico on the one hand, and to forestall any hostile movement of the Spaniards on the other. Having heard that Spaniards were preparing to return to avenge their defeat and to occupy the Kansas River country, Bienville in 1722 ordered Boisbriant, commander at the Illinois, to anticipate the Spaniards and build a fort. The person sent was Bourgmont, who had lived among the Missouris fifteen or more years, and had been made commander on the Missouri. Late in 1723 he established Fort Orleans above the mouth of the Grand River, in modern Carroll County, Missouri. From there in 1724 he went up the river among the Otos and Iowas, and then southwest to the Padoucas in Western Kansas, taking with him Missouris, Osages, Kansas, Otos, and Iowas. He made peace between these tribes and the Padoucas, and arranged to send traders to the last named. A primary object was to open a way to New Mexico. Shortly afterward Fort Orleans was destroyed by an Indian massacre, and wars of the Foxes for several years practically closed the lower Missouri.

ADVANCE TOWARD NEW MEXICO

The western fur trade.—For a decade and a half after the Bourgmont expedition the French made no noteworthy western exploration. Meanwhile, however, the traders quietly carried on their trade among the western tribes. Important items in this trade were Indian captives, and mules stolen from the Spaniards. French traders sometimes found a ready market for goods smuggled into Spanish settlements on the northern frontier of New Spain. From New Orleans, Opeluzas, Natchitoches, Yatasi, Petit Caddo, and Cadadocho posts they worked among the tribes of eastern and northern Texas. By 1730 they had reached the lower Trinity to trade among the Orcoquiza and Bidai tribes. Further north they traded with the Asinai and Cadadochos, in the very face of the Spanish posts. By the middle of the century they were well established among the Wichita tribes of the Red River Valley, and northeastern Texas was virtually under French control. The way to western Texas and the upper Red River was barred by the hostile Apaches, but in 1753 Governor Kerlérec proposed breaking through this strong barrier.

From the Arkansas post traders worked among the Quapaws and Jumanos, and other tribes adjacent to the Arkansas River, From the Illinois, and from lesser posts among the Osages, Missouris, and Kansas, traders worked among these tribes, the Iowas, Otos, Pawnees of the Platte, and other more northern bands of Indians.

Interest in New Mexico.—French voyageurs, *chasseurs*, and traders of Louisiana and Canada continued to look with covetous eyes toward New Mexico. To the adventurer it was a land promising gold and silver and a path to the South Sea; to the merchant it offered rich profits in trade. The natural avenues of approach to this Promised Land were the Red, Arkansas, and Missouri Rivers. But there were obstacles to expeditions bound for New Mexico. One was the jealous and exclusive policy of Spain, which made the reception of such Frenchmen as might reach Santa Fé a matter of uncertainty; another was the Indian barrier which stood in the way. The Red River highway was effectually blocked by the Apaches, mortal enemies of all the tribes along the lower valley; the Arkansas and Missouri avenues were impeded by the Comanches for analogous reasons. The Apaches and Comanches opposed the passage of the trader to their foes with supplies of weapons. As the fur traders and official explorers pushed rapidly west, one of their constant aims was to open the way to New Mexico by effecting peace between the Comanche and the tribes further east, an attempt at which had been made by Du Tisné and Bourgmont at an earlier day.

The Mallet brothers.—After the cessation of the Fox wars, which had closed the lower Missouri, traders again frequented the Pawnees and Aricaras, and in 1734 one is known to have ascended the Missouri to the Mandans, from whose villages a trade route was soon opened to western Canada. In 1739 a party led by the Mallet brothers made their way, by the Missouri and Platte Rivers, across Nebraska, Kansas, and Colorado to Santa Fé. After a nine months' stay they returned, part going northeastward to the Illinois and part down the Canadian and Arkansas to New Orleans.

Fabry's attempt: Fort Cavagnolle.—The Mallet party had succeeded in getting through the Comanche country to New Mexico and had returned safely and with good prospects for trade. Immediately there was renewed interest in the Spanish border on the part of both government officials and private adventurers. At once, in 1741 Governor Bienville sent Fabry de la Bruyère with members of the Mallet party to open a trade route to New Mexico up the Canadian River, and to explore the Far West. He failed to reach New Mexico. Fort Cavagnolle was established among the Kansas, and the Arkansas route was made safe by effecting a much-desired treaty (1746 or 1747) between the Comanches and their eastern enemies.

New expeditions to New Mexico.—The effect of this treaty was immediate, and at once there were new expeditions to New Mexico by deserters, traders, and official agents. In 1748 thirty-three Frenchmen were reported among the Xicarillas. Early in 1749 a party led by Pierre Satren reached Santa Fé by way of the Arkansas River, conducted by Jumano and Comanche Indians. They were kept in New Mexico to work at their trades. Early in 1750 another party arrived by way of the Arkansas. They were ordered sent to Sonora to prevent their return to Illinois. In the meantime peace had been made between the Comanches and Pawnees, and in 1751 traders reached New Mexico by way of the Missouri. In the same year Jean Chapuis led a party of nine from Illinois with a commission from St. Clair, the commander of Fort Chartres. Arriving at Santa Fé in 1752, via Platte River, he proposed a regular caravan trade with military escort. The intruders were arrested and sent to Mexico, where they languished in prison for many months, and were finally sent to Spain.

The French advance through the Comanche country gives significance to the proposal of Governor Kerlérec in 1753 to break through the Apache barrier and open up a trade with Nuevo Leon, Coahuila, and New Mexico. As a means of doing so he proposed securing an alliance between the Apaches and their eastern enemies. These intrusions of Frenchmen into New Mexico were closely bound up in their effect on Spanish policy, with similar infringements upon the Texas border.

THE FAR NORTHWEST

The Fox wars.—By the end of the seventeenth century Fox hostilities had practically closed the Fox-Wisconsin trade route to the Mississippi. Hostility was increased by the massacre of many Fox Indians at Detroit in 1712. In 1715 De Lignery led a futile expedition against the tribe at Green Bay. In the following year Louvigny with eight hundred men won a partial victory at Butte des Morts, near Lake Winnebago. The European war had now closed, and the Lake Superior posts—Green Bay, La Pointe, Pigeon River, and Lake Nepigon—were reoccupied. The Fox-Wisconsin route being closed, the western trade was divided between the Lake Superior district and that of the Illinois.

The new Sioux posts.—A new movement into the Sioux country was stimulated by the long standing desire to find a route to the Pacific. In 1723 Father Charlevoix suggested finding it either by means of a line of posts through the Sioux country or by way of the Missouri and over the mountains. The former plan was adopted, and in 1727 Fort Beauharnois was built on the west bank of Lake Pepin, with Perrière in command, and with new missions in the vicinity. But, through another uprising of the Fox Indians, the post was soon abandoned. New expeditions against the Foxes and the Sauks, their allies, broke their resistance, and after 1733 the Fox-Wisconsin trade route to the Iowa and Minnesota country was again open. After 1750 the Foxes were regular allies of the French in their wars with the British.

The Vérendrye and the Post of the Western Sea.—The search for the route to the Western Sea was taken up by Gaultier de Varennes (the elder La Vérendrye), commander at Fort Nepigon, who planned a line of posts through the waterways northwest of Lake Superior. His movements were stimulated by the activities of the Hudson's Bay Company in Canada, and by those of the Spaniards in the Southwest. To pay the expenses of his scheme he was granted a monopoly of the northwestern fur trade. In the course of ten years he founded posts on Rainy Lake (St. Pierre, 1731), Lake of the Woods (St. Charles, 1731), Lake Winnipeg (Maurepas, 1732), Assiniboine River (La Reine), and on the Saskatchewan (Fort Dauphin, 1741). In 1742 La France had penetrated the Hudson's Bay Company territory by crossing from Lake Winnipeg to York Factory.

From this line of posts the elder La Vérendrye turned his attention to the upper Missouri, leading an expedition south-westward to the Mantannes in 1738. Four years later his son, Pierre de Varennes, made another expedition to the Mantannes, where they heard of bearded white men to the west. Setting out southwestward, they visited the Cheyennes, Crows, Little Foxes, and Bows. On January 1, 1743, when in the neighborhood of the North Platte River, they saw the Rocky Mountains.

After Vérendrye died, his successor, Legardeur St. Pierre, extended the line of posts up the Saskatchewan to the foot of the Rockies, where in 1752 he founded Fort La Jonquiere. The French had thus reached the Rockies by way of nearly every important stream between the Red River and the Saskatchewan.

READINGS

Bolton, H. E., *Athanase de Mézières*, I, Introduction; *Texas in the Middle Eighteenth Century*, 1–133; "French Intrusions into New Mexico," in *The Pacific Ocean in History;* Dunn, W. E., *Spanish and French Rivalry in the Gulf Region of the United States, 1678–1702: The Beginnings of Texas and Pensacola;* Fortier, Alcée, *History of Louisiana*, I, 30–140; French, B. F., *Historical Collections of Louisiana and Florida;* Gayarré, Charles, *History of Louisiana, French Domination;* Hamilton, P. J., *Colonial Mobile; The Colonization of the South*, 197–275; Heinrich, Pierre, *La Louisiane sous la compagnie des Indies, 1717–1731;* King, Grace, *New Orleans; Sieur de Bienville;* King, Grace, and Ficklen, John, *History of Louisiana;* LePage du Pratz, *Histoire de la Louisiane;* Martin, F. X., *History of Louisiana;* Ogg, F. A., *The Opening of the Mississippi*, 169–237; Parkman, Francis, *A Half-Century of Conflict*, I, 298–368, II, 3–44; Phelps, Albert, *Louisiana*, 20–105; Shea, J. G., *Exploration of the Mississippi Valley; The Catholic Church in the United States;* Thwaites, R. G., *France in America*, 72–88; Villiers du Ter-rage, Marc de, *Les Dernières Années de la Louisiane Française*, 1–48; Winsor, Justin, *The Mississippi Basin*, 1–217; Burpee, Lawrence, *Pathfinders of the Great Plains.*

CHAPTER XVI

TEXAS, PIMERÍA ALTA AND THE FRANCO-SPANISH BORDER CONFLICT

The advance of the French into Louisiana and the Trans-Mississippi West stimulated a new counter movement north-eastward by the Spaniards from Chihuahua, New Mexico, and Coahuila, and there ensued on the Franco-Spanish border a contest for the control of Texas and all the plains country as far north as the Platte River—a contest much like the better-known "half-century of conflict" between the English and the French on the other border. At the same time, the Spanish frontier forged slowly northwestward into Lower California and southern Arizona. On the other hand, the Florida frontier, which in the seventeenth century had been pushed back by the English colonies of Virginia and the Carolinas, was now still further contracted by the establishment of French Louisiana and English Georgia, while in the West Indies and Honduras Spanish rule suffered a like diminution through the continued advance of the English, French, and Dutch. The *Asiento* of 1713 with Great Britain was a particularly hard blow at Spain's commercial independence, and was made worse by England's gross violation of the compact.

NORTHEASTWARD ADVANCE OF THE SPANISH FRONTIER

The Chihuahua mines.—In Nueva Vizcaya two notable forward steps north were taken in the early eighteenth century. These were the opening of the Chihuahua silver deposits and the advance down the Conchos valley. In 1703–1704 rich ores were discovered near the recently founded mission of Nombre de Diós. The mines proved to be among the best in America, and, it has been estimated, produced silver worth from $50,000,000 to $100,000,000 in the eighteenth century. Two *reales de minas*, Chihuahua and Santa Eulalia, were established near by, and became the most thriving centers on the northern frontier. By

1763 each had a population of 5000, and the church at Chihuahua was one of the finest in the new world.

Advance down the Conchos Valley.—At the same time the frontier advanced down the fertile Conchos River Valley and across the Rio Grande into western Texas. In 1715 the abandoned missions at La Junta were reëstablished. Soon six missions were in operation and serving Indian towns on both sides of the Rio Grande. For ten years they succeeded, and then, in 1725, the Indians revolted and deserted. During the subsequent years the padres made them occasional visits, while settlement pushed down the Conchos Valley. In 1753 the La Junta missions were restored, and in 1760 were protected by the new presidio of Belén.

The New Mexico border. Moqui and Zuñi resistance.— The reconquest of the New Mexico pueblos had been effected by Vargas at the end of the seventeenth century. The Moquis and Zuñis, however, stubbornly resisted Spanish influence and harbored apostates. In 1726 and again in 1741 the Moqui district was assigned to the Jesuits of Sonora, but they accomplished little. Rivalry led to new Franciscan visits, and in 1742 the missionaries recovered more than four hundred Tigua fugitives who had fled during the great revolt of sixty years before. In 1745 the field was restored to the Franciscans, but they were unable to make permanent establishments.

Xicarrilla and Navajo missions.—In 1733 a mission was founded near Taos for the Xicarrilla Apaches who were hard pressed by the Comanches. Between 1744 and 1750 efforts were made to convert the Navajo, but without avail.

New settlements.—The population of New Mexico grew slowly but steadily. In 1706 Governor Cubero founded the new villa of Albuquerque and reëstablished La Cañada. In 1760 there were 7666 Spaniards in fourteen settlements in the upper district and 3588 about El Paso. This was a population larger than that of English Georgia at the same time. The largest towns were Albuquerque (1814), La Cañada (1515), and Santa Fé (1285). At the same time the Christian Indians in the province numbered 10,000.

Indian depredations.—New Mexico was constantly harassed by Navajos on the west, Yutas and Comanches on the north, and Apaches on the east and south. The main object of the savages was to steal stock and other property, but they often shed human blood freely.   On the basis of horses and mules stolen in New Mexico, a regular trade was maintained by Indians across the country to Louisiana.   The exterior tribes attacked the Pueblo Indians even more freely than the Spaniards.   The Spanish soldiery, with Indian allies, often retaliated with telling effect and recovered stolen horses and mules.   Captives taken were sold as slaves to the settlers or in the interior.   Yet there were truces between campaigns, and by the middle of the century the Comanches and Yutas in large numbers attended the annual Taos fair, where they sold skins and captives.

Rumors of the French.—The French advance up the Missouri stimulated a counter movement of the Spaniards of the New Mexico border.   Before the end of the seventeenth century wild rumors of the approaching French had reached Santa Fé.   Other interests, especially Indian relations, furnished motives for northeastward expeditions early in the eighteenth century.   In 1706 Juan de Urribarri was sent by Governor Cubero "to the unknown land of the plains" to ransom Christian captives from the northern tribes.   He crossed the Napestle (Arkansas) River, near the present city of Pueblo, Colorado, and reached the Indian settlement of El Cuartelejo, near the Colorado-Kansas border, where he heard new reports of the French among the Pawnees.

Expeditions to the northeast and north.—The frequent campaigns against the Indians were occasions for new exploration. In 1715 Juan Paez Hurtado, with two hundred and fifty men, pursued Apaches into western Texas.   During the next four years several expeditions were made northeast against Comanches and Yutas, in the course of which new reports were heard of the French, who were now pushing up all the western tributaries of the Mississippi.   In 1719 a campaign against the Yutas and Comanches led Governor Valverde across the Arkansas. In 1720 occurred the disastrous Villazur expedition to the Platte described later.   About 1750 Bustamente y Tagle pursued Comanches down the Arkansas nearly to the Jumanos.

Explorers in Colorado.—Explorers also entered the Utah Basin.   Juan María Rivera, sent out by Governor Cachupín in search of ore, visited and named the La Plata (Silver) Mountains, and continued to the junction of the Uncompahgre River with the Gunnison (1765).   In the following year Nicolás de la Fora, writing in New Mexico, stated that the Spaniards were acquainted with the country along the Cordillera de las Grullas (in western Colorado) for a hundred leagues above Santa Fé.   A decade later (1779) Anza ascended the San Luís Valley, descended the Arkansas River, and returned to Santa Fé over the mountains.

THE FOUNDING OF TEXAS

The Coahuila frontier.—In 1693 eastern Texas, after a temporary occupation, had been abandoned, and the frontier fell back to Coahuila.   In the course of the next decade, however, it was gradually extended until it crossed the Rio Grande.   A most important factor in the work were the Querétaro friars, who ever urged the government forward.   By 1698 Boca de Leones and Lampazos had become the seats of flourishing mines, missions, and ranches.   Between 1699 and 1703 three missions and a presidio had been established on the Rio Grande at San Juan Bautista, below modern Eagle Pass.   The site, being a great rendezvous and trading place for the tribes, was known as the "Cádiz of the interior."   Near most of the missions small colonies of Spaniards and Tlascaltecans settled.   These missions served many Indians from beyond the Rio Grande, and frequent expeditions were made into the outlying country.

Plans to reoccupy Texas.—During all this time the missionaries were desirous of returning to the Asinai or Texas Indians, whom they had left in 1693, and with whom they had since maintained communication.   In 1706 the governor of Coahuila urged the founding of a mission on the Rio Frio as a means of securing the road to the Asinai.   Three years later Fathers Olivares and Espinosa made an expedition to the Colorado River, where they hoped to meet the tribe.   Father Hidalgo long made strenuous efforts to get permission to return to his former charges, and Father Olivares went to Spain to procure it.   Frequent rumors of French incursions from Louisiana were discussed in government circles, but it required an actual danger to cause the government to act.

St. Denis in Mexico.—In 1714, led by two survivors of La Salle's expedition, St. Denis made his expedition across Texas to trade.   At San Juan Bautista he was arrested and taken to

Mexico, where it was realized by the officials that a real menace had arisen. In a council of war held on August 22, 1715, it was decided to reoccupy Texas with missions, a garrison, and a small colony. Domingo Ramón, a frontier officer, was put in charge of the expedition, and the missionary field was assigned to the two Franciscan colleges *de Propaganda Fide* of Querétaro and Zacatecas. Of the missions of the former, Father Espinosa, later known as the historian, was made president; of the latter the president appointed was the still more renowned Father Antonio Margil.

Eastern Texas reoccupied.—In February, 1716, the expedition left Saltillo, and in April it crossed the Rio Grande at San Juan Bautista. In the party were nine friars, twenty-five soldiers, six women, and enough other persons to make a total of sixty-five. They drove with them more than 1000 head of cattle and goats, and an outfit for missions, farms, and a presidio. A direct northeast route was followed, through San Pedro Springs, where the city of San Antonio later grew up. By the Asinai Indians they were given a warm welcome, and four missions were at once founded near the Neches and Angelina Rivers. Near the latter stream the presidio of Dolores was established. At the same time an attempt was made to establish a mission on the Red River among the Cadodachos, but it was frustrated by the Indians, who were under French influence.

A new base needed.—Eastern Texas had been reoccupied, but the outposts there were weak and isolated. The French were trading among the surrounding tribes; St. Denis was known to be planning another commercial expedition to Mexico; and it was rumored that a large French colony was to be established at the mouth of the Mississippi. This prediction was verified by the founding of New Orleans in 1718. On the other hand, Father Olivares urged advancing from the Rio Grande to the San Antonio. These motives to action coincided with a more aggressive Spanish policy toward the French since the death of Louis XIV, a policy exemplified by the new viceroy Linares.

San Antonio founded.—In a *junta de guerra* held December 2, 1716, it was therefore decided to establish posts on the San Antonio and among the Cadodachos, while Ramón was to destroy the French establishments at Natchitoches. The new enterprise

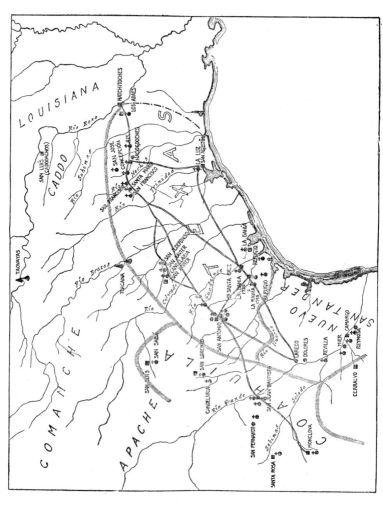

Texas in the Eighteenth Century

was entrusted to Martin de Alarcón, who was made governor of
Texas and, before setting out, of Coahuila. While the expedition
was preparing, St. Denis reached the Rio Grande (April, 1717),
where his goods were confiscated. Going to Mexico, he was
there imprisoned. Meanwhile Ramón had reconnoitered Natchitoches, and on his return early in 1717 two new missions were
founded among the Ays and Adaes, the latter being within seven
leagues of Natchitoches, and thenceforth a vital spot in the
history of international frontiers.

Early in 1718 Alarcón left Coahuila with a colony of sixty-two
persons, besides the neophytes of mission San Francisco Solano,
who were to be transferred to the new site on the San Antonio
River. Arrived there, a mission, presidio, and town were founded,
the beginnings of the modern city of San Antonio. In the east
Alarcón accomplished little more than to displease the missionaries and to protest against La Harpe's new French establishment among the Cadodachos.

WAR WITH FRANCE

Attack on Pensacola and Texas.—In January, 1719, as a result of European complications, France declared war on Spain.
The war extended at once to the colonies, where a border contest
ensued at various points all the way from Pensacola to the Platte
River. In the course of the summer Pensacola was captured
by the French of Mobile, recaptured by the Spaniards, and
again taken by Bienville and Serigney. In June, Blondel, commander at Natchitoches, invaded eastern Texas, whence the Spanish missionaries and garrison retreated to San Antonio without a
struggle. For two years thereafter the region was left unoccupied
by Spain. While waiting at San Antonio Father Margil in 1720
founded there a new mission called San José, which later was
called the finest in New Spain.

Spanish plans to fortify the Platte River.—In the course of
the campaigns against the Indians to the northeast of New
Mexico, constantly more disturbing reports had been heard of
the French, who were now making their way up all the western
tributaries of the Mississippi. In 1719 Governor Valverde pursued Yutas and Comanches across the Napestle (Arkansas) and
heard that the French had settled on the Jesus Maria (North

Platte) River. New significance was attached to these reports because of the outbreak of war between France and Spain a short time before. Valverde warned the viceroy of the danger; wild rumors spread through the northern provinces; and measures for defence were taken. In 1720, while plans were being made to recover Texas, the viceroy ordered counter alliances made with the tribes northeast of New Mexico, a Spanish colony planted at El Cuartelejo, in eastern Colorado, and a presidio established on the Jesus María River, that is, in Nebraska or Wyoming.

Destruction of the Villazur Expedition.—Although a truce had already been declared between France and Spain, Governor Valverde, perhaps in ignorance of this fact, sent Pedro de Villazur in June, 1720, at the head of one hundred and ten men to reconnoiter the French. Passing through El Cuartelejo, in August he reached the Jesus María. Not finding the French, he set out to return, but on the San Lorenzo (South Platte), in northern Colorado, he was killed and his expedition cut to pieces by Indians using French weapons. There are indications that tribes living as far north as Lake Winnebago in Wisconsin took part in the attack, a fact which illustrates the wide-reaching influence of these international contests. The Spaniards charged the massacre to the French, and there was a new panic on the frontier. But peace had been restored between France and Spain, and, in spite of appeals from New Mexico, the plans for advancing to El Cuartelejo and the Platte were dropped.

The Aguayo Expedition.—An offer to assist in the reconquest of Texas was made by the Marquis of Aguayo, governor and the most prominent figure of Coahuila. Abetted by Father Hidalgo, he had been interested in a new attempt to discover Gran Quivira, and the Texas crisis seemed to give him an opening. His offer was accepted, and before the end of 1720 he had raised, partly at his own expense, eight companies of cavalry, comprising over five hundred men and five thousand horses. By his instructions he was expected to reoccupy and strengthen the abandoned posts and occupy Cadadachos, on the Red River, and Bahía del Espíritu Santo on the Gulf.

Eastern Texas reoccupied.—The Marquis left Monclova in November, 1720, shortly after Villazur's defeat on the Platte.

From the Rio Grande in January, 1721, he sent Captain Ramón with forty soldiers to take possession of Bahía del Espíritu Santo, to which a supply ship was sent from Vera Cruz. This was shortly before La Harpe attempted to reoccupy the place for the French. Because of swollen streams, Aguayo made a wide detour to the north, crossing the Brazos near Waco. Peace had been declared in Europe, and at the Neches he was met by St. Denis, who agreed to permit an unresisted reoccupation of the abandoned posts. It was learned here that St. Denis had recently assembled Indian allies with a view to seizing Bahía del Espíritu Santo and San Antonio, in coöperation, no doubt, with La Harpe.

Proceeding east, between August and November Aguayo reestablished the six abandoned missions and the presidio of Dolores, and added a presidio at Los Adaes, facing Natchitoches, and garrisoned it with one hundred men. To this last act Bienville made vigorous protest. On the return to San Antonio the weather was so severe that of five thousand horses only fifty were left when Aguayo arrived in January, 1722. After establishing there another mission and rebuilding the presidio, he took forty additional men to La Bahía, and erected a presidio on the site of La Salle's fort. Having thus completed his work, he returned to Monclova.

Texas won for Spain.—Aguayo's expedition fixed the hold of Spain on Texas. He left ten missions where there had been but seven, two hundred and sixty-eight soldiers instead of sixty or seventy, and four presidios instead of two, two of them being at strategic points. Since 1718 Texas and Coahuila had been under the same governor, but now Texas was made independent, with its capital at Los Adaes (now Robeline, Louisiana) where it remained for half a century. The Medina River now became the western boundary of Texas. In 1726 the La Bahía establishment was moved to the lower Guadalupe River.

THE EXPANSION OF TEXAS

Rivera's inspection of the frontiers.—In the years 1724–1728 a general inspection of the frontier defences of New Spain was made by Pedro de Rivera, ex-governor of the province of Tlascala. His remarkable journey of 3082 leagues began at the City of Mexico on November 21, 1724, and ended there on June 9, 1728. The northern line of military outposts at this time ran from Fronteras through Janos, El Paso, Santa Fé, Conchos, Monclova, San Juan Bautista, Cerralvo, San Antonio, Bahía del Espíritu Santo, Dolores, and Los Adaes. On the whole Rivera found the presidios in fair condition, but encountered many abuses. His reforms in the main were in the direction of retrenchment. This was particularly true regarding Texas, and in 1729 the post on the Angelina was suppressed and the forces of others reduced.

San Antonio strengthened.—Rivera's policy of retrenchment was strongly opposed by the missionaries; among the Indians of eastern Texas they had had little success, and when the garrison of Dolores was withdrawn the Querétaran friars moved their three missions to San Antonio, where they were reëstablished in 1731 and where their ruins still stand. In the same year a colony of Canary Islanders was established beside the presidio and missions, and formed into the Villa of San Fernando. There were now at San Antonio five missions, a presidio, and a municipality. Texas was now definitely formed in outline; Spain had maintained her claim as against France, and had established three centers of occupation, Los Adaes, Bahía del Espíritu Santo, and San Antonio.

The Apache Wars.—For a decade and a half after the founding of the Villa of San Fernando the province of Texas underwent little expansion. From the beginning of San Antonio its inhabitants were subjected to raids by the Eastern Apaches, who also infested the highways. To check their outrages occasional campaigns were made into their country by the soldiery, supported by contingents of mission Indians. Notable among the forays were those of Captain Flores (1723), Governor Bustillo (1732), Captain Jose Urrutia (1739), and his son Captain Thoribio Urrutia (1745). These expeditions served not only to punish the enemy and recover stolen horses and mules, but to capture slaves as well, and to make known the northwestern frontier. In the course of them the Spaniards learned of mineral deposits in the Llano River country.

The work of the missionaries.—In spite of Apache hostilities, the missionaries on the San Antonio and the Guadalupe made some progress. The leading figures of the period were Fathers Santa Ana and Dolores y Viana, presidents. No new missions were founded in the fifteen years' interval, but the friars improved their buildings and farms, and sought new neophytes in regions constantly more remote from the mission centers. At the mission of San Antonio de Valero alone no less than forty bands or tribes were represented by the baptisms between 1731 and 1745.

The Tonkawa missions.—During the next fifteen years the frontiers of Texas were expanded in all directions. Between 1745 and 1749 Fathers Viana and Santa Ana founded three missions on the San Xavier (San Gabriel) River, in the Tonkawa country, and in 1751 a presidio was established there. But quarrels ensued, the location proved unsuitable, and the missions were abandoned, efforts now being transferred to the Apache country.

The Apache missions.—Under pressure from the southward moving Comanches, the Lipan-Apaches had ceased their hostilities and asked for missions. Minerals had been found near the Llano River, and communciation with New Mexico was desired. Accordingly, with the aid of a munificent gift by Don Pedro de Terreros, in 1757 a great plan for reducing the Apaches by means of missions was launched. A presidio and mission had scarcely been founded on the San Sabá, however, when the mission was destroyed by the Comanches and their allies (1758). In the following year Colonel Parrilla, with a force of some six hundred men, raised in various parts of northern New Spain, set out to punish the offenders. At the fortified village of the Taovayas, on the Red River, where French influence was predominant, he was routed and driven back. The Apache mission was now transferred to the Upper Nueces, and for several years the San Sabá post sustained incessant war with the northern tribes.

Nuevo Santander.—Wars with England and Indian hostilities now made imperative the colonization of the Gulf coast between the San Antonio River and Tampico—the eastern portion of Nuevo León—and in 1746 the district was erected into a new colony called Nuevo Santander. Colonel José de Escandón, a distinguished officer of Querétaro, was put in charge of the enterprise, and the missionary work was entrusted to the Zacatecan friars. Within the next three years the entire region was explored by Escandón and his lieutenants and a number of colonies were planned. In 1749 Escandón led a colony of more than three thousand people from Querétaro, and in a short time established them in more than twenty settlements, most of which persist to-day. North of the Rio Grande the principal ones were Laredo and Dolores, but ranching soon spread as far as the Nueces River. The post and mission of La Bahía were now moved to the lower San Antonio River and a new mission for the Karankawa (Rosario) was established near by. Though legally in Nuevo Santander, this district was administered as a part of Texas, and by 1775 the Texas-Nuevo Santander boundary was officially moved west to the Nueces.

THE FRANCO–SPANISH BORDER

The Texas-Louisiana boundary question.—The proximity of Los Adaes and Natchitoches had furnished numerous grounds for irritation between Texas and Louisiana. French traders engaged in contraband trade, and the international boundary was uncertain. In 1735, when Natchitoches was moved from the island in the Red River to the west bank of the stream, a quarrel ensued. After several years of bickering, the Arroyo Hondo was tentatively adopted as the international boundary in that region.

Meanwhile French traders had invaded the coast tribes and monopolized the Indian trade of northern Texas. In 1750 the military strength of Louisiana was considerably augmented, and it was reported in Mexico that the new arrivals were for the western Louisiana frontier. These conditions again brought forward the quiescent boundary question, which was inconclusively discussed in Spanish circles for several years. While the higher authorities debated, residents on the frontier generally agreed on the Arroyo Hondo. In 1754 the King of Spain declared that "boundaries between the Spaniards and the French in that region have never been a subject of treaty nor is it best at present that they should be."

The New Mexico border.—By this time renewed French intrusions into New Mexico were becoming alarming. The return of the Mallet party (1739) and the peace between the Comanches and their eastern enemies (ca. 1746) were followed by the arrival in New Mexico of trading parties from Canada and Louisiana under Fébre, Chapuis, and others. A more vigorous policy was now adopted and the recent comers were arrested and sent to Spain. The intrusion into New Mexico found an echo in far western Sonora, where in 1751 the French advance was given by a prominent official as a reason for Spanish haste to occupy the Colorado of the West.

The lower Trinity fortified.—The more stringent policy toward intruders was extended to Texas, where a new outpost was established to ward off French aggression. In the fall of 1754 traders on the lower Trinity were arrested and sent to Mexico, and in 1756-1757 the region was defended by a presidio (San Agustín) and a mission east of the stream among the Orcoquiza Indians. Thus another point on the Texas-Louisiana frontier was occupied and defended by Spain. The site was disputed by Governor Kérlerec, of Louisiana, who proposed a joint boundary commission. The offer was rejected and the viceroy of Mexico, on the contrary, proposed a Spanish post on the Mississippi "to protect the boundaries." With his proposal he sent to Spain a map showing Texas as extending to the Mississippi. Thus the region in dispute extended from the Trinity to the Mississippi, at least.

PIMERÍA ALTA

The Jesuits.—The occupation of Texas was contemporaneous with the advance into Pimería Alta (northern Sonora and southern Arizona) and Lower California. The work of the indefatigable Jesuits on the northern frontier of New Spain is admirably illustrated by that of Father Kino and his companions in this region.

Kino.—After the failure of Atondo's enterprise in California in 1685, Father Eusebio Kino entered northern Sonora, arriving in March, 1687, just at the time of La Salle's death in Texas. Mission Dolores, founded by him in the upper Sonora Valley, became his headquarters for twenty-four years of exploration, ranching, and missionary work among the upper Pimas, between the Altar and Gila Rivers.

Explorations in Arizona.—In the Altar Valley Kino and his companions founded a number of missions, which were destroyed during the revolt in 1695 and then rebuilt. In 1691, accompanied by Father Salvatierra, who later went to California, Kino descended the Santa Cruz River to the village of Tumacácori. Three years later, by the same route, he reached the Casa Grande on the Gila. In 1697, with a military escort from Fronteras (Corodéguachi), he again went to the Casa Grande, this time by way of the San Pedro River. In the following year he was again on the Gila, whence he returned across the Papaguería (the country of the Pápagos) by way of Sonóita, Caborca, and the Altar Valley. In 1699 he went to the Gila by way of Sonóita and the Gila Range, and then ascended the Gila.

A land route to California.—The current view still was that California was an island, but during the last journey Kino returned to the peninsular theory. If this were true, he reasoned, it would be possible to find a land route over which to send supplies to Salvatierra's struggling missions just established in Lower California. To test his views he made several more journeys, crossing the lower Colorado in 1701 and reaching its mouth in 1702. He was now convinced that California was a peninsula. In 1705 was published his map of Pimería Alta, setting forth this view.

Missions and ranches in Arizona.—Meanwhile Kino and his companions had pushed the missionary frontier to the Gila and the Colorado. Kino's exploring tours were also itinerant missions, in the course of which he baptized and taught in numerous villages. During his career in Pimería Alta he alone baptized 4000 Indians. In 1700 he founded the mission of San Xavier del Bac, and within the next two years those of Guebavi and Tumacácori, all in the valley of the Santa Cruz River, and within the present Arizona. To support his missions, near them he established flourishing stock ranches, thus making the beginnings of stock raising in at least twenty places still existing in northern Sonora and southern Arizona.

Decline of the missions.—The power of Spain was now at its lowest ebb, funds were scarce, and Kino's last days were to him a time of stagnation and disappointment. To a certain ex-

Father Kino's Map of Pimería Alta
(Bancroft, *Arizona and New Mexico*, p. 360)

303

tent royal support was transferred for the time being to the missions in Lower California. After Kino's death in 1711 stagnation became decline, few new missionaries were sent, and northern tours became infrequent or ceased altogether. Officials and frontier leaders often planned to advance the frontier of settlement to the Colorado River, but other interests interfered.

Revival after 1732.—A visit by the bishop of Durango in 1725, the military inspection of that frontier by Rivera in 1726, and a royal decree of 1728 gave new life to the moribund missions. New missionaries arrived in 1732, the northern missions were reoccupied, and journeys to the Gila were renewed after 1736 by Fathers Keller and Sedelmayr.

The Arizonac mines.—Interest in the northern frontier was accentuated at this time by a temporary mining excitement at Arizonac in the upper Altar Valley, where in 1736 silver nuggets of astonishing size were discovered. There was a "rush" to the place, and considerable wealth was found, but in 1741 the surface veins were exhausted and the camp was abandoned. The mining incident furnished an occasion for new plans to advance to the Gila. But Indian troubles in Sinaloa and Sonora interfered. These troubles, on the other hand, served to advance the military frontier by the founding of two presidios at Pitiqui (Hermosillo) and Terrenate in 1741.

Keller and Sedelmayr.—After much discussion, in 1741 the Moqui district was assigned to the Jesuits, who now tried to reach that region. In 1743 Keller crossed the Gila, but was driven back by the Apaches. In 1744 Sedelmayr ascended the Colorado to Bill Williams Fork. In the following year the Moquis were again assigned to the Franciscans.

Plans to occupy the Gila and Colorado.—Sedelmayr now turned his attention to exploring the lower Gila and Colorado Rivers, and his Order, particularly Father Escobar, the provincial, urged the occupation of these valleys, both as a means of support for Lower California, and as a base for advance to Moqui and Alta California. In 1748 Father Consag of California explored the Gulf to its head in the interest of this plan. Royal interest was aroused also by the entry of the French of Louisiana into New Mexico and the need of protecting California. In 1744 and 1747, therefore, the king approved advancing to the

Gila. Five years later, especially because of emphatic reports
of the French advance toward the Pacific Ocean, the king seriously considered occupying the Bay of Monterey.

The Pima Revolt.—The new viceroy, Revillagigedo, was occupied with founding Nuevo Santander and other absorbing tasks,
while new Indian wars in Sonora made advance impossible.
In 1750 a war of extermination, led by Governor Diego Parrilla,
was begun on the Seris and lasted several years. In 1751 a revolt
occurred among the northern Pimas. At Caborca and Sonóita
the missionaries were slain, over one hundred settlers were killed
on the Arizona border, and missions and ranches were abandoned. The uprising was suppressed by Parrilla without great
difficulty; most of the missions were reoccupied; and for greater
security two new presidios were founded, at Altar, near Caborca,
and at Tubac near San Xavier del Bac. Thus, each uprising
helped to advance the military frontier.

Continued obstacles to advance.—For twenty years more the
question of advance to the Colorado was subordinate to that of
good order and settled conditions in Sonora, necessary preliminaries to advance. The Pima War was followed by a bitter
quarrel between Governor Parrilla and the Jesuits. The Seris
made constant trouble, and when attacked retreated safely to
Cerro Prieto. Apache wars on the northern border were even
more severe, and many settlements in Sonora and Nueva Vizcaya
were destroyed by them. Nevertheless, within the protection
of the presidios several small Spanish settlements grew up, as at
Terrenate, Guebavi, Santa Bárbara, Buenavista, Tubac, Saric,
Altar, and San Ignacio. The Jesuits continued to appeal, and
others, pointing out the danger from advancing Russians, English, and French, urged the settlement of Alta California. But
Spain was occupied elsewhere.

The northwestern frontier in 1763.—Sinaloa and Sonora had
been detached from Nueva Vizcaya in 1734, when the province
of Sinaloa was erected. Both were still within the diocese of
Durango. By 1763 Sinaloa and Ostimuri (southern Sonora)
had ceased to be frontier regions. Most of the missions had been
secularized, the Indians had become assimilated, and there was
a considerable white population. In Sinaloa there were six
towns with white and mixed populations ranging from 1000 to

3500 each. In Ostimuri, the part of Sonora south of Yaqui River, there were five towns with populations ranging from 300 to 3400. In the Sonora Valley there was a string of mining towns and small Spanish settlements extending as far north as Fronteras. In Pimería Alta there were eight missions and several Spanish settlements, the latter aggregating, with the garrisons, nearly 1500 persons. In all of the frontier settlements there was a large element of mulattoes and mestizoes.

THE JESUITS IN LOWER CALIFORNIA

California assigned to the Jesuits.—While Kino and his successors were struggling to advance the frontiers of Pimería Alta, another band of Jesuits founded missions and opened trails nearly the whole length of the Peninsula of Lower California, and made explorations northward with a view to meeting the mainland group at the Colorado River. After repeated failures to occupy the Peninsula, the government of Spain turned it over to the Jesuits, with full military and civil authority, as in Paraguay. The missions depended at first mainly on private alms, and in a short time $47,000 were subscribed. This was the beginning of the famous Pious Fund of California.

Salvatierra and his companions.—In 1697 Juan Maria Salvatierra, who had been a missionary in Sinaloa, entered the Peninsula with a handful of soldiers, and began work at Loreto, opposite Guaymas, which became the supply base. Missionary work was attended by unusual difficulties, because of the sterility of the country. More than once the abandonment of California was prevented only by the aid of Father Kino, who drove cattle hundreds of miles to Guaymas and shipped them across the Gulf. Transportation was difficult, and many precious cargoes were wrecked. By the time of Salvatierra's death in 1717 he, Picolo, Juan de Ugarte, and their companions had planted five missions in the middle region of the Peninsula, and had made extensive explorations, north, south, and across California to the Pacific. In 1701 Salvatierra had explored with Kino in quest of a land route from Sonora. In 1721 Father Ugarte in the same interest explored the Gulf to its head.

Development in the South.—Salvatierra's death was followed by more liberal royal aid and private alms, and by more rapid mission extension, particularly in the South. The importance of this step was enhanced by making San Bernabé a stopping place for the Manila galleon. By 1732 Fathers Guillen, Tamaral, and Taraval had explored the west coast as far as Cedros Island. A widespread Indian rebellion in 1734, attended by the martyrdom of Fathers Carranco and Tamaral, caused the founding of the presidio of San José del Cabo, which protected the Cape, but by 1748 Indian disturbances had greatly reduced the southern missions.

The Jesuits, fearful of interference in their work, as a rule opposed Spanish settlements, presidios, and the development of industries in the Peninsula. In 1716, 1719, 1723, and later, the government urged the founding of forts and colonies on the western coast, with a view to protecting and advancing the frontier, but the Jesuits usually objected, and the settlements were not founded. The Indian revolt, war with England in 1739, Anson's raid on the coast in 1742, and the westward advance of the French toward the Pacific Coast, increased the anxiety, and in 1744 new orders were given looking to the defence of the Peninsula, but nothing came of them.

By 1750 the exclusive policy of the Jesuits had given way to some extent, pearl fishing was again permitted, private trading vessels came from time to time, and the Manila galleon stopped regularly at San José. Mines were opened in the South, and around them a small Spanish and mixed breed population grew up, La Paz becoming the principal center.

Missions in the North.—The conditions which had stimulated efforts to advance to the Gila by the mainland after 1744, had a corresponding effect on California development. Sterile California needed overland communication with a mainland base. It was with this need in view that in 1746 the Jesuit provincial, Escobar, sent Father Consag to reëxplore the Gulf, whose head he reached shortly before Sedelmayr descended the Colorado to the same point.

The Colorado-Gila base was not supplied, but with new private gifts and royal aid, the Jesuits on the Peninsula pushed northward. Santa Gertrudis (1752), San Francisco Borja (1762), and Santa María (1767) were the last Jesuit foundations, while Father Link's land journey to the head of the Gulf in 1766 was the final step in Jesuit explorations.

READINGS

TEXAS

Arricivita, *Crónica Serafica y Apostólica*, 321–442; Bancroft, H. H., *North Mexican States and Texas*, I, 391–406, 609–617; Bolton, H. E., *Athanase De Mézières*, I, 1–66; "The Native Tribes about the East Texas Missions," in Tex. State Hist. Assoc., *Quarterly*, XI, 249–276; "The Location of La Salle's Colony on the Gulf of Mexico," in *The Mississippi Valley Historical Review*, II, 165–182; Bolton, H. E., ed., *Spanish Exploration in the Southwest*, 281–422; Bonilla, Antonio, in Tex. State Hist. Assoc., *Quarterly*, VIII, 1–78; Buckley, E., "The Aguayo Expedition into Texas and Louisiana, 1721–1722," in Tex. State Hist. Assoc., *Quarterly*, XV, 1–65; Clark, R. C., *The Beginnings of Texas;* Cox, I. J., "The Early Settlers of San Fernando," in Tex. State Hist. Assoc., *Quarterly*, V, 142–161; "The Louisiana-Texas Frontier," in Tex. State Hist. Assoc., *Quarterly*, X, 1–76; "The Southwestern Boundary of Texas," in Tex. State Hist. Assoc., *Quarterly*, VI, 81–103; DeLeón, A., "Itinerary," in Tex. State Hist. Assoc., *Quarterly*, VIII, 199–224; *Historia de Nuevo León*, 310–348; Dunn, W. E., "Apache Relations in Texas, 1718–1750," in Tex. State Hist. Assoc., *Quarterly*, XIV, 198–274; "The Apache Mission on the San Saba," in *Southwestern Historical Quarterly*, XVIII, 379–415; Espinosa, Isidro, *Chrónica*, 1–10, 41–158, 206–227; Garrison, G. P., *Texas*, 20–96; Manzanet, in Tex. State Hist. Assoc., *Quarterly*, III, 252–312; Parkman, Francis, *La Salle and the Discovery of the Great West*, chs. 20–29.

PIMERÍA ALTA

Alegre, Xavier, *Historia de la Compañía de Jesus*, III; Bancroft, H. H., *Arizona and New Mexico*, 344–407; *History of the North Mexican States*, I, 237–274, 548–580, 660–691; Bolton, H. E., *Kino's Historical Memoir of Pimería Alta*, especially Vol. I, 27–65; Bolton, H. E., ed., *Spanish Exploration in the Southwest*, 425–463; Chapman, C. E., *The Founding of Spanish California*, 1–67; Ortega, José, *Apostólicos Afanes*, libros II–III; Richman, I. B., *California under Spain and Mexico*, 42–61.

LOWER CALIFORNIA

Alegre, Xavier, *Historia de la Compañía de Jesus*, III, 91–309; Bancroft, H. H., *History of the North Mexican States*, I, 276–304, 407–466, 476–491; Bolton, H. E., *Kino's Historical Memoir*, consult Index under "California," "Picolo," and "Salvatierra"; Engelhardt, Fr. Zephyrin, *Missions and Missionaries of California*, I, 61–600; Hittell, T. H., *History of California*, I, 148–308; North, A. W., *Mother of California*, 1–78; Richman, I. B., *California under Spain and Mexico*, 1–41; Venegas, Migual, *Natural and Civil History of California*, I, 215–455, II, 1–213.

CHAPTER XVII

THE ENGLISH ADVANCE INTO THE PIEDMONT, 1715–1750

THE WESTWARD MOVEMENT

The colonization of North America by the English was not complete with the founding of the seaboard settlements, but continued in a series of steps westward. At each step American society has returned to simple frontier conditions, under which it has been free to try out new experiments in democracy. Each stage of advance has made its special contribution to our institutions.

In a broad way these steps in the westward movement have corresponded with great physiographic areas. The seventeenth century had witnessed the occupation of the Tidewater region, between the coast and the Fall Line. Within that area there had been established two types of society which now projected themselves westward. The New England type was democratic, corporate, theocratic, and industrial, and here the township became the unit of local government. The Southern type, based on a plantation system, staple crops, and dependent labor, was aristocratic, individualistic, and expansive. Here the county became the unit of local government. Intermediate between these types was the society of the middle Tidewater. In spite of these special characteristics, due chiefly to American environment, Tidewater society at the end of the century was still largely European in thought and feeling.

The first half of the eighteenth century witnessed the movement of settlement into the next great physiographic region, the Piedmont, or the area lying between the Fall Line and the Appalachian Mountains. Here, under frontier conditions, was formed a society farther removed from that of Europe, and further modified by American conditions.

This westward movement was the resultant of numerous factors. To the frontier people were attracted by cheap land and unlimited opportunity. From the Tidewater settlements emigrants were driven by increase of population, scarcity of good land, and class conflicts. The less prosperous everywhere, and in the South indented servants who had served their time, were glad to begin life anew on the frontier. Prosperous planters whose estates had been exhausted by tobacco sought the Piedmont, and left their former lands to become "old fields." Speculation in frontier lands became a passion, and while John Law floated his Mississippi Bubble in Louisiana, New England deacons and Virginia aristocrats alike built hopes of fortune on tracts purchased for a song on the border. The movement to the frontier was stimulated in some cases by intercolonial and international rivalry; thus the settlement of Georgia was at once a philanthropic experiment and a defensive movement against Spain. Of larger consequence than the emigrants from the Tidewater settlements were the new arrivals from Europe, who came in tens of thousands, attracted by cheap land and opportunity or driven by economic, political, or religious unrest.

Trails to the Piedmont had been opened by furtraders, who, even in the seventeenth century, had made their way into the wilderness in all directions; by official explorers, like Governor Spotswood; and by the Southern cattlemen who had established "cowpens" at long distances beyond the frontiers of settlement. The Indian barrier was removed at the turn of the century by a series of frontier wars, which either evicted the natives or broke their resistance. Of these the chief examples are King Philip's War in New England, the Susquehannah War in Virginia, the Tuscarora War in North Carolina, and the Yamassee War in South Carolina. The process of expansion, however, involved further struggles with the Indians, and border conflicts with French neighbors on the north and Spanish neighbors on the south.

Under these influences the migration took place and by the middle of the century a continuous back-country settlement had been formed, all the way from Maine to Georgia. New England industries were coastwise, the Piedmont was rough and stony, and expansion was consequently slow. But the open spaces were nearly all filled in, to the northern boundary of Massachusetts, while long spurs of settlement were pushed up the rivers into Vermont, New Hampshire, and Maine, where French rivalry

Mainland Regions occupied by the English, 1700–1760

was encountered. In New York settlement was retarded by the practice of land leasing instead of sales, a relic of the patroon system. Nevertheless a narrow ribbon of settlement pushed up the Mohawk from Albany nearly to Oneida Lake, while the lower Hudson River settlements widened out toward Pennsylvania and into New Jersey.

Into the Southern Piedmont the movement was a double one. Some newcomers and many old settlers crossed the Tidewater and pushed over the Fall Line. But for the Germans, Swiss, and Scotch-Irish, Philadelphia was the chief port of entry and the main distributing point. Thence some pushed up the Delaware into New Jersey and northeastern Pennsylvania; others west into the valleys east of the Kittatiny Range. Those who followed, finding the lands occupied, and meeting here the mountain barrier to the westward march, moved south across the Susquehannah and up the Shenandoah Valley, whence they turned eastward into the Piedmont of Virginia, North Carolina, South Carolina, and even of Georgia. The Scotch-Irish in general kept nearest the outward frontier and became *par excellence* the Indian fighters.

DEFENSE OF THE NORTHERN FRONTIER

English policy.—After the War of the Spanish Succession the English government was keenly alive to the necessity of defending the colonial frontiers. Although the period has been characterized as one of "salutary neglect" on the part of the home government, nevertheless the frontier defences were greatly strengthened. Soon after the signing of the Treaty of Utrecht, the English government became aware of French activities in Louisiana, and advice was sought from several colonial governors as to the best means of checking French and Spanish advance. A policy of defence was soon developed. It included the erection of forts, exploration of the mountain passes, alliances with Indian tribes, development of trade, reorganization of the incompetent proprietary government of the Carolinas, the establishment of the buffer colony of Georgia, and the encouragement of the settlement of the back country by the Germans and Scotch-Irish.

Acadia and the Maine border.—A strange apathy regarding

Acadia was shown by the English government. A small garrison was maintained at Annapolis, but the Acadians continued loyal to the French, and French priests and officials from Cape Breton Island and Canada continued to exert influence over them. The Maine border was strongly held. English settlers again appeared on the lower Kennebec and forts were erected at Augusta and at the falls of the Androscoggin. Somewhat later Ft. Richmond was built on the Kennebec. English activity alarmed the Abenaki and the French soon influenced them to go on the warpath. From 1720 to 1725 a border war continued, but after much bloodshed on both sides the Indians sought peace.

The New York border.—On the New York border, efforts of the French to bring the Iroquois into alliance aroused the English and in 1727 Governor Burnet erected a fort at Oswego. Owing to petty strife between New Hampshire and Massachusetts, and between New York and New Jersey, funds were not provided for a fortification on Lake Champlain, an oversight which gave the French an opportunity to erect a fort at Crown Point.

Pennsylvania and Virginia.—In 1716 Governor Spotswood of Virginia led an expedition to the Blue Ridge and entered the Shenandoah Valley. In his subsequent report he advised the making of settlements on Lake Erie and the securing of the mountain passes. The proposals were not carried out, but soon the back country was settled by Germans and Scotch-Irish, who formed a stronger barrier of defence than walls and palisades.

REORGANIZATION OF THE CAROLINAS

Separation of the Carolinas.—Economically the Carolinas had been drifting apart. Between the Albemarle and Cape Fear districts lay a primeval wilderness two hundred miles in width. The northern district was devoted to the production of naval stores and tobacco, the southern more to rice culture. Politically the governments had been practically separate almost from the beginning, the governor being located at Charleston and a deputy governor being appointed for the north. In 1713 the proprietors appointed Charles Eden as governor of North Carolina, and from this time the two provinces were practically separate.

The Yamassee War.—Between the South Carolina and Span-ish settlements lived the Yamassee Indians. In the War of the Spanish Succession they had remained faithful to the English, but by 1715 they were won over by the St. Augustine officials. The French at Mobile were also working on the Creeks and Cherokees, and a confederation was formed whose object was the destruction of the South Carolina settlements. The war began on April 15, 1715, the Yamassee beginning the attack without the assistance of their allies, and the plantations and settlements were assailed all along the border. Martial law was immediately proclaimed in the province, volunteers were organized, and calls for assistance were sent to North Carolina, Virginia, New England, and England, the two former respond-ing with men and ammunition. Several bloody engagements were fought which turned in favor of the Carolinians. The Yamassees received reinforcements and renewed their incursions, but Governor Craven showed such a superior force that the Indians fled beyond the Edisto and were subsequently driven far back into the interior.

Overthrow of the proprietors.—The responsibility of defence against Indians and pirates who infested the coast devolved upon the settlers, the proprietors showing little ability to assist. The assembly now took matters in its own hands and changed the method of elections, so that many large landholders were prac-tically disfranchised. The acts were not approved by the pro-prietors and the slumbering discontent in the province soon approached rebellion. The situation was made worse by the refusal of the proprietors to allow the distribution of the Yamas-see lands, and by an order that tracts be set aside for themselves. Rumors spread that another Spanish invasion threatened and Governor Johnson sought means of meeting it, but when he asked advice as to how funds might be raised, he was informed that the duty which had been imposed after the Yamassee War was still in force and that other legislation was unnecessary. The colonists answered the governor's call to arms but soon showed that they were against him. When Johnson refused to act in the name of the king instead of the proprietors, he was set aside. The proprietary government had been in ill favor with the Eng-lish government for some time. Its incompetence in the Yamassee War had convinced the Board of Trade that a change was necessary, and it upheld the popular movement. In 1729 an act of parliament established royal governments in both North and South Carolina.

THE FOUNDING OF GEORGIA

The debatable land.—In the great triangle formed by the Carolinas, Florida, and southeastern Louisiana, English, Spanish, and French came into close proximity. The international boundaries had never been satisfactorily defined and each power strove to acquire control of the powerful Indian tribes of the interior, thereby gaining territory and trade. To protect the border and to aid the Charleston traders, in 1716 the Carolinians established a fort on the Savannah River, and from 1721 to 1727 maintained Ft. King George on the Altamaha. In 1730 Sir Alexander Cuming was sent on a mission to the Cherokees, on which he succeeded in obtaining an acknowledgment of English supremacy, considerably strengthening the English position.

Azilia.—The need of a buffer colony on the southern border was long realized by English statesmen. In 1717 a project was launched which gave promise of fulfillment. Sir Robert Montgomery secured from the Carolina proprietors a grant of the lands between the Savannah and Altamaha Rivers which was called the Margravate of Azilia. Plans for its settlement were drawn up and an attempt made to obtain colonists, but Sir Robert failed to attract settlers and the grant lapsed.

Oglethorpe.—It remained for James Oglethorpe to carry out the project. Oglethorpe had seen considerable military service, and for thirty years was a member of the House of Commons, in the latter capacity advocating an aggressive policy against Spain. Possessed of broadly humanitarian sympathies, he became interested in ameliorating the conditions of imprisoned debtors. He conceived the idea of planting a barrier colony on the southern frontier, which would serve the two-fold purpose of protecting Carolina against Spanish and Indian attacks, and of offering a place of refuge for the debtor class. In 1732 he secured a charter conveying to himself and a group of interested persons the land between the Savannah and Altamaha Rivers and extending westward from their head waters to the sea.

The government.—The government was of the proprietary type, but the proprietors were not to receive any profits individually; financial reports and legislation were to be submitted to the crown for approval. The proprietorship was limited to twenty-one years, after which the province was to become a royal colony. Religious liberty was guaranteed to all but Catholics; provision was made to prevent large land holdings; slavery was prohibited, a restriction which was subsequently removed; the importation of rum was forbidden, as was trade with the Indians without a license.

Savannah.—In the autumn of 1732 about one hundred men, women, and children were sent to America, arriving at Charleston in January, 1733. A treaty was made with the Creeks who surrendered most of their coast lands and the town of Savannah was immediately laid out. The colony was soon strengthened by German and Scotch immigration. In 1737 a fort was established at Augusta and a town grew up which soon developed an important trade with the Cherokees.

Measures of defence.—The Scotch were settled near the mouth of the Altamaha. In 1736 Ft. Frederica was established on St. Simon's Island at the mouth of the river, and military posts were built between the Altamaha and the St. John's Rivers. This encroachment aroused the ire of the Spanish government, which demanded Oglethorpe's recall, but instead, while in Europe, he was given permission to raise a regiment of troops for the protection of Georgia, and upon his return he visited the Creeks, with whom he renewed the former alliance.

THE GERMAN AND SWISS MIGRATION

In 1690 the population of the English colonies on the continent of North America was only two hundred thousand; fifty years later it had increased to a million, and by 1760 another half million had been added. In part this was due to natural increase, but a large population came from the influx of Europeans other than English, the two principal immigrant peoples being the Germans and the Scotch-Irish.

The German migration.—The causes of the German migration are to be found in the disturbed condition of Germany. Religious persecution, political oppression, and economic distress caused

by wars and bad seasons, each played its part in the movement.
Most of the immigrants came from southwestern Germany,
especially from the Palatinate, Württemberg, and Baden, and
from Switzerland. The first period of migration, dating from
1683 to 1710, was characterized by a small movement of per-

Principal Areas of German Settlement before 1763

secuted sects; but after 1710 an ever-increasing migration took
place in which the religious, political, and economic causes
blended.

The early migration to Pennsylvania.—The first German
settlement in the English colonies may be traced directly to
William Penn's visit to the Rhineland in 1677. A group of

pietists from Frankfort-on-the-Main purchased fifteen thousand acres of Penn's land and in 1683 sent over a young lawyer, Francis Daniel Pastorius, as advance agent, who became the recognized leader of the Pennsylvania Germans. He was soon followed by a considerable number of emigrants. More land was purchased and the settlement of Germantown begun. In 1684 a group of Labadists settled on the Bohemian River in the present state of Delaware. Every year a few people joined the original group at Germantown. The most important addition was in 1694 when forty Rosicrucians under John Kelpius settled on the banks of the Wissahickon.

The migration to New York.—Not until 1710 did the great flood of migration begin. In 1707 a portion of the Palatinate was devastated. The following year sixty-one homeless people led by Joshua von Kockerthal made their way to London. The Board of Trade sent them to New York, where Governor Lovelace gave them lands on the Hudson, where they began the town of Newburg. Religious persecution, political oppression, the devastation of Württemberg and a part of the Palatinate, and a hard winter caused a great exodus in 1709. In May of that year the Germans began to arrive in London, and by October the numbers had swelled to thirteen thousand. About thirty-five hundred were sent to the colonies. Six hundred and fifty were settled at Newbern near the mouth of the Neuse River in North Carolina, and about three thousand were sent to New York, where Governor Hunter hoped to settle them on lands where tar and pitch could be produced. The story goes that in London the Palatines had met a delegation of Indian chiefs who had promised them lands on the Schoharie, a branch of the Mohawk. Instead of being sent there, however, many were placed on lands along both sides of the Hudson near Saugerties. The colony on the west side was called West Camp, and contained about six hundred people. The East Camp, which was located on the manor of Robert Livingston, received nearly twelve hundred; it was here that difficulties occurred. The attempts to produce tar and pitch failed, and the colonists demanded that they be moved to the Schoharie. After much bickering with the governor, in 1712 and 1713 many of the people from East Camp moved to the Schoharie; but their troubles did not end, for the question of land title brought them into disputes with certain landowners from Albany. Some of the Palatines moved again, many taking up lands in the Mohawk Valley between Ft. Hunter and Frankfort, while others in 1723 and 1727 migrated to Pennsylvania, settling in Berks County.

The later Pennsylvania migration.—The harsh treatment in New York and the kind reception of Germans in Pennsylvania made the Quaker colony a favorite place for their coming. Between 1710 and 1727 from fifteen to twenty thousand entered Pennsylvania and settled in Lancaster, Berks, and Montgomery counties. Between 1727 and 1740 the arrivals numbered about fifty-seven thousand, and between 1741 and 1756 about twenty thousand. Many of the newcomers settled in Philadelphia, and neighboring counties, but the desire for cheap land carried a large number into the fertile valleys of the Susquehanna, Lehigh, and Shenandoah. In the words of Professor Faust, "They . . . pushed northward and westward to Lehigh, Northampton, and Monroe counties, and to Lebanon and Dauphin; reaching the Susquehanna they crossed and settled the counties of York, Cumberland, and Adams, then following the slopes of the mountains they went southward through Maryland into Virginia, ascending the Shenandoah Valley and settling it from Harpers Ferry to Lexington, Virginia. Using this main avenue for their progress, they settled in North Carolina and Virginia and later in Kentucky and Tennessee. Pennsylvania, therefore, was the distributing center for the German immigrations, whence German settlers spread over all the neighboring provinces."

New Jersey.—As early as 1707 several members of the German Reformed Church appear to have settled in Morris County, and later spread into Somerset, Bergen, and Essex counties. Later groups, mainly of Lutherans or German Reformed, settled in Hunterdon, Somerset, Morris, Sussex, and Warren counties, and there were scattered settlements elsewhere.

Maryland.—A few Germans came to Maryland before 1730, but with the founding of Baltimore in that year a considerable German migration began, enterprising Germans from Pennsylvania finding the new town a place for their capital and energy. At about the same time the Germans were settling in western Maryland. In 1729 Germans from Pennsylvania settled about ten miles north of the modern town of Frederick, and soon many German settlements dotted Frederick and neighboring counties.

Virginia.—The first Germans in Virginia were skilled ironworkers from Westphalia, brought in by Governor Spotswood to operate his iron works which were located on the Piedmont Plateau at Germanna, in modern Orange County. The settlers at Germanna afterward migrated to Germantown near the Rappahannock and to Madison County. A far more important movement was the migration into the Shenandoah Valley. The northern part was settled almost entirely by Germans, but in the southern part they formed only a small part of the population. The first of the settlers came from Lancaster County, Pennsylvania, in 1726 or 1727, settling near Elkton. They were soon followed by others, among them Joist Hite at the head of sixteen families from York, Pennsylvania, who settled at the site of Winchester. In 1734 Robert Harper founded Harper's Ferry. The most remote settlements were located in the Alleghanies within the present state of West Virginia; one on Patterson's Creek, another on the south branch of the Potomac, and a third on the New River, which with the Greenbrier forms the Great Kanawha. Thus the frontier had already reached the "Western Waters."

North Carolina.—As already noted, the first migration of Germans into North Carolina was connected with the Palatine movement of 1710; the lands of Baron Graffenried on which they settled being at the confluence of the Neuse and Trent Rivers. In the following year the Tuscaroras went on the warpath; about sixty of the newcomers were slain and their settlement destroyed. The Tuscaroras eventually were incorporated with the Iroquois Confederation and the settlers took advantage of the removal to occupy their lands, soon spreading over a large part of what is now Craven County. About 1745, Germans from Pennsylvania began to arrive in the western part of North Carolina, taking up lands along the Yadkin River. Not until 1750 did the immigrants become numerous. By the time of the Revolution there were important German settlements in Stokes, Forsyth, Guilford, Davidson, Rowan, and Cabarrus counties.

South Carolina.—In South Carolina the first German colonists settled in or near Charleston. In 1732 a settlement was made in Beaufort County and German villages soon dotted both sides of the Edisto and Congaree Rivers in Orangeburg and Lexington counties and spread out toward the Georgia boundary, Baden, Württemberg, Switzerland, and discontents from Maine furnishing most of the South Carolina Germans.

Swiss migration to Carolina and Pennsylvania.—With the exception of Graffenried's project, no large enterprise for bringing Swiss settlers to America was launched until 1725, when Jean Purry of Neufchatel began to advertise for Swiss Protestants to found a colony in Carolina. In 1732 Purry succeeded in establishing Purrysburgh, which soon had several hundred inhabitants. Crop failures in Switzerland coupled with heavy taxation and a dislike for foreign military service caused a large number to migrate between 1730 and 1750. Although accurate statistics are lacking, recent investigation shows that during the eighteenth century probably twenty-five thousand Swiss emigrated to Pennsylvania and the Carolinas.

Georgia.—In 1731 thirty thousand Protestants of Salzburg were exiled. Some of them made their way to England and eventually became settlers in the newly-constituted colony of Georgia. The first ones arrived at Savannah in 1734 and moved to lands on the Savannah River about forty miles from its mouth, naming their settlement Ebenezer. Others soon followed. Oglethorpe wished some of them to settle about the fort on St. Simon Island, but they objected to bearing arms and were allowed to go to Ebenezer. Others, who had no religious scruples regarding war, were settled at Frederica. The settlers from Ebenezer soon moved down the river eight miles to New Ebenezer, across the river from Purrysburgh. By 1741 over twelve hundred Germans had come to Georgia.

New England and Nova Scotia.—A small number of Germans made their way to New England. The head of the movement was Samuel Waldo, who became interested in lands on the shores of Broad Bay in Maine. In 1740 forty families from Brunswick and Saxony founded Waldoborough. In 1749–1750 Massachusetts made an effort to increase German immigration by setting aside lands for their use. One of these districts was near Fort

Massachusetts in modern Franklin County and extended beyond into what is now Vermont. Three years later the first German settlers entered the region. In 1751 Joseph Crellius brought over twenty or thirty families who founded Frankfort, subsequently called Dresden, on the Kennebec River. It has been estimated that fifteen hundred Germans entered New England in 1752–1753, but many of them moved subsequently to South Carolina. Another group settled at Braintree near Boston, but by 1760 they had all moved to the Maine settlements. During 1750–1753 occurred a considerable German migration to Nova Scotia, sixteen hundred settling in Lunenburg County. In the latter year the English Government checked the movement, which was deflected to New England, and the settlements at Broad Bay and on the Kennebec were considerably enlarged.

THE SCOTCH–IRISH

Causes of the Scotch-Irish migration.—Of equal importance with the German migration was that of the Scotch-Irish from Ulster. The causes of the migration to America were both religious and economic. The Presbyterianism of the Scotch found scant favor with the English authorities. The efforts to enforce uniformity, and the various religious laws of the reign of Charles II and Anne were especially obnoxious to Presbyterians. Though few migrated because of them, they left a feeling of injury, which, coupled with industrial hardships, brought about the great migration to America. English restrictive legislation was also an important factor. Laws prohibiting the importation into England of Irish stock and dairy products, acts excluding Irish vessels from American trade and prohibiting direct importation to Ireland from the colonies, and the act of 1699 prohibiting the exportation of Irish wool worked great hardships on the people of Ulster. The enforced payment of tithes to support the Episcopalian clergy touched both the purse and the conscience of the Scotch-Irish. But more important than any of these was the tenant system. In 1714–1718 many of the original leases expired and the landlords doubled or trebled the rents. This is the chief explanation of the great acceleration of the movement to America which began in 1714. No doubt the natural business instinct of the Scotch

The Areas Largely Populated by Scotch-Irish before 1763

people, and occasional crop failures, such as the potato famine in 1725, 1740–1741, also hastened many who otherwise might have lingered in Ulster.

Seventeenth century migration.—In 1612 the Rev. George Keith, a Scotchman, went to Bermuda, the first dissenting minister in the English colonies. In 1652 Cromwell sent about two hundred and fifty Scotch prisoners to New England. Before 1669 a considerable number of Scotch and Scotch-Irish settled on the eastern shore of Chesapeake Bay and by 1680 some Scotch Presbyterians were located near Norfolk. In 1683 Scottish colonists landed at Port Royal and Charleston, and others founded Stuartstown. In 1684 and 1685, many Scotch dissenters sought refuge in East New Jersey, the beginning of a movement which eventually made New Jersey one of the strongholds of Presbyterianism.

The great migration.—During the early years of the eighteenth century a few Scotch-Irish made their way to America, but not until after the close of the War of the Spanish Succession did the movement assume large proportions. The tide of immigration which set in brought the Scotch-Irish to every colony. Many of them found homes in the tide-water lands among the older settlements, where vast areas were still thinly settled, but a larger number sought the frontier.

New England.—Between 1714 and 1720 fifty-four vessels brought Scotch-Irish immigrants to Boston. The large influx of foreigners began to alarm the authorities. When over five hundred arrived at Boston in the summer of 1718, a shortage of provisions threatened. To place the immigrants on a self-supporting basis was highly desirable. In addition the more remote settlements needed protection. The plan was accordingly adopted of sending the Scotch-Irish to the frontier. About fifty miles from Boston was the post of Worcester containing about two hundred people. Soon its population was doubled by Scotch-Irish. Others came and Worcester became the distributing point for interior settlement. In 1731 Pelham was started thirty miles to the westward, and two years later Colerain, twenty miles farther in the wilderness, was formed. In 1741 Warren and Blandford were incorporated. From western Massachusetts the settlers turned northward, following the Connecticut Valley,

forming settlements in Windsor, Orange, and Caledonia counties
in Vermont and in Grafton County in New Hampshire.

While Worcester was being settled, other immigrants sought
lands in Maine. Thirty families were landed at Falmouth on
Casco Bay, another group settled on the Kennebec near its
mouth, and by 1720 several hundred families had settled on
the Kennebec or the Androscoggin, but soon afterward Indian
troubles caused a large part of them to move to New Hampshire
or Pennsylvania. In 1719 Nutfield on the site of modern Manchester was founded. When the town was incorporated in 1722
its name was changed to Londonderry. It became the distributing point for Scotch-Irish in that region; from there Rockingham, Hillsboro, and Merrimack counties in New Hampshire
were settled. Emigration spread over into Vermont, joining
that from Worcester, and pushed on to the north and west.
Still other Scotch-Irish settlements were formed later in Maine.
A hundred and fifty families from Nova Scotia in 1729 settled
at Pemaquid and Samuel Waldo induced a few to settle on the
St. George at Warren. Connecticut and Rhode Island also
received an infusion of Scotch-Irish blood but in a much less
degree than the northern frontier.

New York.—About 1718 large numbers of Scotch-Irish came
to New York, most of them settling in Orange and Ulster counties. In 1738 John Lindesay and three associates obtained an
extensive land grant in Cherry Valley in modern Otsego County.
Many settlers were induced to come from Londonderry, New
Hampshire, and from Scotland and Ulster, but the exposed position prevented a great influx in succeeding years.

Pennsylvania.—As in the German movement, in the Scotch-
Irish migration the largest number came to Pennsylvania. The
earliest comers appear to have settled on either side of the
Pennsylvania-Maryland line in the Susquehanna Valley. The
exact date of their arrival is uncertain, but a church had been
organized as early as 1708. About 1720 the immigrants began
working up the Delaware River, settling in Bucks County and
spreading over into Northampton County. Another stream of
immigrants passed up the Susquehanna Valley, settling along
the creek bottoms on the east side of the river, their chief centers
being in Chester, Lancaster, and Dauphin counties in Penn-

sylvania, and in Cecil County, Maryland. Before 1730 the settlers pushed over into Cumberland County, Pennsylvania, which gave them access to the valleys of the interior. They spread into Franklin, Adams, and York counties and the later movement carried them southward into the great valleys.

The Southern Piedmont.—By 1735 or earlier, the Scotch-Irish began moving into the Shenandoah Valley. Some of them remained in Maryland and the most eastern counties of what is now West Virginia, but most of them moved into Virginia, taking up the lands west of the Blue Ridge Mountains. Many went through the passes and made their homes in the Piedmont region to the east of the Blue Ridge. The movement was greatly stimulated by the fact that several large land grants were made to various Pennsylvanians and Virginians, who encouraged the settlement of their lands. The early records of the Scotch-Irish in the southern Piedmont give us little exact data, but between 1740 and 1760 scattered settlements were made along the frontier from Virginia to Florida. In North Carolina the lands between the Yadkin and Catawba Rivers were settled. By 1750 the vanguard appeared in the western part of South Carolina, and a few years later in the upland country of Georgia.

SIGNIFICANCE OF THE SETTLEMENT OF THE PIEDMONT

By the middle of the century results of great significance had come about. All the way from New England to Georgia a back country society had been formed, with characteristics in many ways distinct from that of the Tidewater settlements. A large portion of the settlers, particularly south of New York, were of non-English stock, and had brought with them diverse notions; but, under the influence of frontier environment, they had been moulded, together with the English stock, into a more or less homogeneous mass. In the main the settlers were persons of slender means, and lived hard, frontier lives. They tilled small farms with their own hands, and indentured servitude and slave-holding were consequently unimportant. Society, on the whole, was democratic, individualistic, tolerant, and self-reliant. In spite of this homogeneity of the frontier, the original traits of the settlers persisted, and can still be found in the Pennsylvania

"Dutch" or in the Scotch Presbyterians of the Southern Piedmont.

Being distinct in character and interests, the Piedmont and Tidewater clashed at many points, and thus arose "sectional" contests between the East and the West, a feature which has marked American development down to the present. The simple back country constituted a debtor society, in need of an expanding credit; the coast was more aristocratic and more capitalistic. The East attempted to dominate politics, legislation, and administration. The West resisted, and before the Revolution contests arose in nearly every colony. In many instances the back country won; its victories are reflected in the provisions for religious toleration and in the democratic tendencies of the new state constitutions formed during and after the Revolution.

There were other important consequences from the settlement of the back country. In spite of divergent interests, there were bonds of union between the East and the West. The new settlements furnished a market for eastern goods and provided commodities in exchange, and thus lessened the dependence of the coast upon Europe. Attended by Indian wars and border hostilities with French and Spanish neighbors, the westward movement had created a fighting frontier. At the same time, by bringing the international frontiers into conflict, it had prepared the way for the final struggle between France and England in America.

It was the southern Piedmont which furnished leaders for the southwestward movement in the succeeding generations. Says Turner: "Among this moving mass, as it passed along the Valley into the Piedmont, in the middle of the eighteenth century, were Daniel Boone, John Sevier, James Robertson, and the ancestors of John C. Calhoun, Abraham Lincoln, Jefferson Davis, Stonewall Jackson, James K. Polk, Sam Houston, and Davy Crockett; while the father of Andrew Jackson came to the Piedmont at the same time from the coast. Recalling that Thomas Jefferson's home was in this frontier, at the edge of the Blue Ridge, we perceive that these names represent the militant expansive movement in American life. They foretell the settlement across the Alleghanies in Kentucky and Tennessee; the Louisiana Purchase, the Lewis and Clark's transcontinental exploration; the conquest of the Gulf Plains in the War of 1812–15; the annexation of Texas; the acquisition of California and the Spanish Southwest. They represent, too, frontier democracy in its two aspects personified in Andrew Jackson and Abraham Lincoln. It was a democracy responsive to leadership, susceptible to waves of emotion, of a 'high religious voltage'—quick and direct in action."

READINGS

DEFENCE OF THE FRONTIERS

Channing, Edward, *History of the United States*, II, 341–365; Dickerson, O. M., *American Colonial Government*, 326–332; Fiske, John, *Old Virginia and her Neighbors*, II, 383–389; Greene, E. B., *Provincial America*, 181–184, 249–262; Hamilton, P. J., *The Colonization of the South*, 291–308; Jones, C. C., *The History of Georgia*, I, 67–313; Kingsford, William, *The History of Canada*, III, 121–201; McCrady, Edward, *A History of South Carolina*, I, 531–680; Parkman, Francis, *A Half-Century of Conflict*, I, 183–271, II, 53–56; McCain, J. R., *Georgia as a Proprietary Province*.

THE GERMAN AND SWISS MIGRATION

Bernheim, G. D., *German Settlements in North and South Carolina;* Bittinger, L. F., *The Germans in Colonial Times*, 11–183; Cobb, S. H., *The Story of the Palatines;* Faust, A. B., *The German Element in the United States*, I, 30–262; "Swiss Emigration to the American Colonies in the Eighteenth Century," in *The American Historical Review*, XXII, 21–44; Jones, C. C., *The History of Georgia*, I, 163–173, 208–214; Kuhns, O., *The German and Swiss Settlements of Colonial Pennsylvania*, 1–192; Wayland, J. W., *The German Element of the Shenandoah Valley of Virginia*.

THE SCOTCH-IRISH

Campbell, Douglas, *The Puritan in Holland, England, and America*, II, 469–485; Ford, H. J., *The Scotch-Irish in America*, 1–290; Hanna, C. A., *The Scotch-Irish*, II, 6–126; Turner, F. J., "The Old West," in Wis. Hist. Soc., *Proceedings, 1908*.

CHAPTER XVIII

ENGLISH COLONIAL SOCIETY IN THE MIDDLE EIGHTEENTH CENTURY

GENERAL FEATURES

Population and settled area.—By 1760 the population of the English continental colonies was probably 1,650,000; of these the New England colonies contained about a half-million, the middle group about four hundred and fifty thousand, and south of the Mason-Dixon line there were about seven hundred thousand. Nearly half of the inhabitants were in Massachusetts, Pennsylvania and Virginia. The bulk of the population still clung to the coastal regions, but the rivers had pointed the way to the interior; many of the valleys were occupied for a considerable distance, and the Germans and Scotch-Irish had penetrated the great valleys of the central and southern Appalachians. Practically the whole of Massachusetts, Rhode Island, and Connecticut had been occupied; to the northward extended three narrow lines of settlement, one along the New Hampshire and Maine coast as far as the Penobscot and extending fifty miles up the Kennebec, another reaching up the Merrimac for sixty miles into central New Hampshire, and a third following the Connecticut for fifty miles above the northern Massachusetts line. Long Island was almost entirely settled, as was the Hudson Valley to a point a little above Albany, and the lower Mohawk Valley had been settled. New Jersey, except in the central part and a small section of the eastern coast, was occupied. Eastern Pennsylvania, the lower valley of the Susquehanna, and adjacent valleys were peopled, as was the western shore of Delaware Bay. Maryland and Virginia were settled up to the mountains and had overflowed into the valleys of the Blue Ridge. In North Carolina the settlements extended back for a hundred and fifty miles or more from the coast and as far south as the valley of the Cape Fear River. In the back country of North and South Carolina and Georgia the valleys were occupied and the population had flowed over onto the eastern slopes of the Appalachians. The coast lands of South Carolina and Georgia as far as the Altamaha, and the lowlands along the Pedee, Santee, and Savannah Rivers were occupied for a hundred miles from the coast.

The older settled areas were below the Fall Line. There the industrial and social life was less in a state of flux than along the ever-advancing frontier. The economic tendencies in the coast country were already fixed and showed little change until machinery and transporation worked an industrial revolution early in the nineteenth century. The social life was also comparatively stable and was so to remain until the Revolutionary War.

Manufacturing and mining.—During the colonial period manufacturing made little progress, due mainly to the abundance of cheap land and English restrictions. The colonists depended mainly upon England for manufactured goods. Nevertheless, manufacturing made some headway, especially in the North, where agricultural pursuits brought less profit than in the South. The coarser fabrics, linen, hats, and shoes were produced for the local markets. Mining was also beginning, iron mines having been developed in New England, Pennsylvania, Maryland, and Virginia, and at least one copper mine was worked in New Jersey. Ironworks were established in the neighborhood of the mines and supplied many of the local needs. In 1750 an act was passed by parliament which allowed colonial pig-iron to be imported into England and bar-iron to enter the port of London. The manufacture of rum was an important northern industry.

NEW ENGLAND INDUSTRY

Farming.—During the colonial period the great mass of the people were engaged in agriculture. In New England, where soil and climate were less favorable than in the South, the small farm with diversified crops was the prevailing type. The supply of labor was limited and wages relatively high. Under such conditions, the farmer, his sons, and the "hired man" worked the place, and by dint of industry made a living. The New England farmer was more nearly self-sufficient than any other class, a condition which no doubt increased his feeling of independence. The products of the farm were usually adequate for local needs but furnished practically nothing for exportation.

Lumbering and ship-building.—The New England forests continued to be a source of wealth. Lumber was produced in large quantities and ship-building was carried on extensively in the coast and river towns, the craft being of a somewhat larger type than formerly, vessels of five hundred tons burden frequently leaving the ways. The English navy and merchant marine obtained large quantities of masts and spars from New England.

The fisheries.—The importance of the fisheries increased greatly after the War of the Spanish Succession. From the Newfoundland banks were derived the chief products for foreign trade. Almost every coast town had its fishing fleet, Gloucester alone boasting nearly a hundred vessels. The cod was the most important catch, but as the century progressed whaling became a more and more important industry.

Commerce.—With the West Indies the New Englanders carried on an extensive trade, lumber, fish, and rum being exchanged for sugar, molasses, and other tropical products. Rum was also an important factor in the slave trade, which was carried on mainly by the Rhode Islanders, who exchanged the products of the distilleries for negroes on the Guinea Coast and in the West Indies. These in turn were traded to the southern colonies for tobacco, rice, indigo, and naval stores. From the profits of southern commerce and from fish, lumber, and naval stores, the New Englanders were able to puchase English textiles, hardware, glass, and other manufactured articles. The chief port was Boston which contained about twenty thousand inhabitants.

THE MIDDLE COLONIES

Intensive farming was at its best in the middle colonies, which were the great producers of provisions. Live stock, cereals, fruit, and vegetables were raised in large quantities, the animal products and grain furnishing the chief products for exportation. Lumber and furs were also important items of commerce.

New York.—An observant English traveler who visited New York in 1760, gives the following excellent description of the colony: "The province in its cultivated state affords grain of

all sorts, cattle, hogs, and great variety of English fruits. . . .
The people . . . export chiefly grain, flour, pork, skins, furs,
pig-iron, lumber, and staves. . . . They make a small quantity
of cloth, some linen, hats, shoes, and other articles of wearing
apparel. They make glass also, and wampum; refine sugars,
which they import from the West Indies; and distil considerable
quantities of rum." He also noted that the New Yorkers were
engaged in ship-building. The Indian traffic was mainly carried
on through Albany. The foreign and coastwise trade was concentrated at New York, a city with a population of sixteen
or seventeen thousand.

New Jersey.—New Jersey was fortunate in having an historian who has left us an excellent account of the province.
Samuel Smith's history gives the following description: "Almost
the whole extent of the province adjoining on the atlantick, is
barrens, or nearly approaching it; yet there are scattering settlements all along the coast, the people subsisting in great part by
raising cattle in the bog undrained meadows and marshes, and
selling them to graziers, and cutting down the cedars. . . . Another means of subsistence along the coast, is the plenty of fish
and oysters, these are carried to New-York and Philadelphia
markets. . . . The lands in general, (perhaps something better
than two thirds of the whole) are good, and bear wheat, barley,
or anything else suitable to the climate, to perfection. As the
province has very little foreign trade on bottoms of its own, the
produce of all kinds for sale, goes chiefly to New-York and
Philadelphia; much of it is there purchased for markets abroad;
but some consumed among themselves."

Pennsylvania and Delaware.—Agriculture was the mainstay
of the people of Pennsylvania and Delaware. The thrifty
Quakers, Germans, Scotch-Irish, and Swedes who formed the
bulk of the population, produced large quantities of grain and
live-stock. The surplus was brought to Philadelphia, a well-
built city of nearly twenty thousand inhabitants. Peter Kalm
has left the following picture of its industrial life: "Several
ships are annually built of American oak in the docks. . . . The
town carries on a great trade both with the inhabitants of the
country and to other parts of the world, especially to the West
Indies, South America, and the Antilles; to England, Ireland,

Portugal, and to several English colonies in North America. Yet none but English ships are allowed to come into this port. Philadelphia reaps the greatest profits from its trade to the West Indies: for thither the inhabitants ship almost every day a quantity of flour, butter, flesh, and other victuals, timber, plank, and the like.   In return they receive either sugar, molasses, rum, indigo, mahogany, and other goods, or ready money. . . .   They send both West India goods and their own products to England; the latter are all sorts of woods, especially walnut, and oak planks for ships; ships ready built, iron, hides, and tar. . . .   Ready money is likewise sent over to England; from whence in return they get all sorts of goods there manufactured, viz: fine and coarse cloth, linen, iron ware, and other wrought metals, and East India goods; for it is to be observed, that England supplies Philadelphia with almost all stuffs and manufactured goods which are wanted here.   A great quantity of linseed goes annually to Ireland, together with many of the ships which are built here. Portugal gets wheat, flour, and maize which is not ground.   Spain sometimes takes some corn.   But all the money which is got in these several countries, must immediately be sent to England, in payment for the goods which are got from thence, and yet those sums are not sufficient to pay all the debts."

THE SOUTHERN COLONIES

The tobacco colonies.—Maryland, Virginia, and the northeastern part of North Carolina continued to be devoted largely to the raising of tobacco.   Except on the frontiers the small farms had disappeared, having been absorbed by great landholdings.   Many of the plantations covered thousands of acres, but probably not more than a tenth of the land was under cultivation.   The tobacco crop was extremely exhaustive to the soil, and when the land had been cropped until its productivity decreased, wheat or corn were usually planted, or it was turned into pasturage.   The tangled thicket soon sprang up and in the wilderness ranged cattle and hogs.   The breeding of horses was attended to with care, for horse-racing and fox-hunting were favorite diversions among the planters, but the cattle and hogs were of inferior quality.   The great article of commerce was tobacco, but grain, pork, and lumber were also exported.   From the Madeiras the planters received wines and from the West Indies rum, sugar, molasses, and slaves. Most of the manufactured articles came directly from England. In spite of the considerable trade, no large towns had sprung up, the plantation continuing to be the economic and social unit of the tobacco colonies.

The industries of North Carolina were more diversified than those of the other southern colonies as is shown by the following statement from Edmund Burke's *Account of the European Settlements in America:* "Exported from all the ports of North Carolina in 1753:

Tar.........................	61,528 barrels
Pitch........................	12,055 ditto
Turpentine...................	10,429 ditto
Staves.......................	762,330 no.
Shingles.....................	2,500,000 no.
Lumber......................	2,000,647 feet
Corn........................	61,580 bushels
Peas, about..................	10,000 ditto.
Pork & Beef.................	3,300 barrels
Tobacco, about...............	100 hogsheads
Tanned lea[ther] about..........	1,000 hundred weight
Deer skins, in all ways, about.....	30,000

"Besides a very considerable quantity of wheat, rice, bread, potatoes, bees-wax, tallow, candles, bacon, hog's lard, some cotton, and a vast deal of squared timber of walnut and cedar, and hoops and headings of all sorts. Of late they raise indigo, but in what quantity I cannot determine, for it is all exported from South Carolina. They raise likewise much more tobacco than I have mentioned, but this, as it is produced on the frontiers of Virginia, so it is exported from thence. They export too no inconsiderable quantity of beaver, racoon, otter, fox, minx, and wild cat skins, and in every ship a good deal of live cattle, besides what they vend in Virginia."

The rice country.—The great staple of South Carolina was rice, which was grown upon the marshy lands. A limited amount was also produced in North Carolina and Georgia. The unhealthfulness of the rice fields, coupled with the large profits from the business, were factors which made negro slavery seem desirable. In 1733 the whites in South Carolina numbered about seven thousand, in 1748 about twenty-five thousand, and in 1765 about forty thousand, but this increase was due largely to the great migration to the back country. Between 1753 and 1773 it is estimated that about forty-three thousand slaves were brought into the province.

Indigo.—In 1741 or 1742 Miss Elizabeth Lucas, the daughter of the governor of Antigua, planted some indigo seed on the Lucas plantation near Charleston. From this beginning the indigo business rapidly developed. In 1747 the colony produced 134,118 pounds; in 1754 over 200,000 pounds were exported, and shortly before the Revolution over 1,000,000 pounds were shipped annually.

Commerce.—Charleston was the commercial center. Its white population was about five thousand in 1760 and it contained about an equal number of negroes. In the summer and autumn the population increased, as the planters' families stayed in the metropolis to escape the unhealthfulness of the back country. Hundreds of vessels were engaged in the South Carolina trade, the products being shipped to the northern colonies and to the West Indies, to Holland, Portugal, the Mediterranean, and England. From the profits the planters purchased the necessities and luxuries of English manufacture, the wines of Portugal and Madeira, and the rum, sugar, molasses, and slaves of the West Indies.

Georgia.—In 1760 Georgia contained about six thousand whites and thirty-five hundred negroes. Industry was diversified, as is shown by a report of Governor Wright of 1766 which says: "Our whole time and strength . . . is applied in planting rice, corn, peas, and a small quantity of wheat and rye, and in making pitch, tar, and turpentine, and in making shingles and staves, and sawing lumber and scantling, and boards of every kind, and in raising stocks of cattle, mules and hogs. . . ." In addition there was considerable fur trade, for which Augusta was the center.

LABOR SYSTEMS

Free labor.—The preponderance of agriculture and the abundance of cheap land made a continual demand for laborers. The climatic and soil conditions determined the labor system of each area. In the north the small farm was usually tilled by the owner and his sons, aided by hired help especially during harvest time. The men of a neighborhood frequently combined to do important pieces of work, such as clearing land, house-building, haying, harvesting, and corn-husking.

Indented servants.—The great plantations of the south demanded large forces of laborers, and there the bond servants and slaves formed the important elements of the laboring classes. The indented servants were of two classes, voluntary and·involuntary. The voluntary servants were those who, for transportation and maintenance, willingly bound themselves to a master for a term of years. In the seventeenth century the usual term had been seven years, but in the eighteenth the demand for labor was so strong that the limit was usually four years. At the end of the term of service the servant either worked for hire or "took up" land. Many moved to the frontier where they soon became prosperous farmers.

The involuntary bond servants were paupers, disorderly persons, and criminals. The harsh penal laws of England at that time recognized three hundred capital crimes. Imprisonment for debt and for political offenses swelled the numbers in confinement. To relieve the situation parliamentary acts were passed which allowed the commutation of the death penalty to a service of fourteen years in the colonies, and seven years in place of branding and whipping. We have no data for exact numbers of indented servants, but a careful student of industrial life in the colonies has estimated that they probably constituted one-half of all English immigrants, the middle colonies, Maryland, and Virginia, receiving the larger numbers.

Slavery.—In the seventeenth century negro slavery was of minor importance in the mainland colonies, but as the plantation system developed slaves became an ever-increasing element. In the New England colonies and Pennsylvania they were used principally as house servants. In New York and New Jersey they formed from eight to ten per cent. of the population. It has been estimated that in 1760 there were four hundred thousand slaves south of Pennsylvania. In Maryland they constituted about thirty per cent. of the population, probably forty per cent. in Virginia, and sixty per cent. in South Carolina.

FEATURES OF SOCIETY

Near the coast.—Colonial society in the older settled regions was aristocratic rather than democratic. This was due mainly to English customs and traditions, to an increasing wealth and corresponding raising of the standard of living, to the strength of the religious institutions, and to the colonial system, which provided for a considerable body of officials. In New England the ruling classes were the clergy and the selectmen, who occupied the important places both in the church and in political life; the official class, at the head of whom was the governor; and a third group, the merchants, who usually were not admitted to the governor's circle, and who were apt to voice their social disapprobation in their influence upon legislation. In New York and eastern New Jersey the great landholders and the official group controlled politics and society. In western New Jersey and Pennsylvania the Quakers were politically, socially, and commercially the preponderant element. In the South the plantation owners formed an aristocracy whose social lines were drawn with distinctness.

The frontier.—In contrast to the tide-water country, frontier society was distinctly individualistic and democratic. The Scotch-Irish and Germans had flocked to the mountain country. There they had built their cabins, made their clearings in the forest, and lived a life free from the conventions of the longer settled communities. Hunting, fur-trading, lumbering, and cattle raising were their chief pursuits. The danger from Indian attack was a constant menace, and personal bravery and resourcefulness were strongly marked characteristics. With it all they were a religious people, the Presbyterians and Pietists being predominant.

The Anglican church.—The religious lines marked out in the seventeenth century were followed in the eighteenth with one notable exception, namely, the growth of the Anglican church. This was due mainly in the first instance to the efforts of the Bishop of London who sent commissaries to America, the first being James Blair who was sent to Virginia in 1689, and the second Thomas Bray, who in 1695 was sent to inquire into the state of the colonial church. The result of Bray's inquiry was the founding in 1701 of the Society for Propagating the Gospel. At the time of its foundation nearly all of the Episcopal churches were in Virginia and Maryland. In 1759 Thomas Sherlock, the Bishop of London, reported that, "at least one half of the Plantations are of the established Church. . . . This is the case of S° Carolina, N° Carolina, Virginia, Maryland, Jamaica, Barbadoes, Antegoa, Nevis, and the rest of the Caribbee Islands. On the other side—Pennsylvania is in the hands and under the governmt of the Quakers, and New England and the adjoining Colonies are in the hands of the Independents. But in some of them are great numbers of Churchmen."

The Great Awakening.—The eighteenth century witnessed a great change in the New England churches. After a hundred years the early enthusiasm of the Puritan church had subsided, and though its doctrine had changed but slightly, a marked change in emphasis had taken place. Conversion was still considered a divine work, but the belief had become current that the soul could be put in touch with the spirit of God by prayer, scriptural study, regular church attendance, participation in the Lord's Supper, a moral life, and having been born of parents who belonged to the church, by "owning the covenant." Against these views Jonathan Edwards rebelled. In 1734 at Northampton, Edwards preached a series of sermons in which he defended the doctrine of justification by faith alone. He pleaded for immediate repentance and denied that good deeds would lead to salvation. The religious revival, started at Northampton, soon spread throughout Connecticut, and reverberated in Boston. At the height of the movement George Whitefield, the friend of the Wesleys, after preaching in Georgia and South Carolina, in 1740 visited New England where thousands were converted. By 1744 the movement had somewhat spent itself, and when Whitefield arrived at Boston for a second preaching tour he found that a reaction had set in. The followers of Edwards and Whitefield had come to be known as the "New Light" party, while the reactionaries formed the "Old Light" party. Two generations later this led to the separation of the Congregational body into the "Orthodox" and "Unitarian" groups.

Colleges.—Religion played a large part in eighteenth century education. William and Mary College, founded in Virginia in

1691 under Anglican influence, was the only institution of advanced learning in the South. Yale, founded in 1701 under strong clerical influence, became the seat of orthodox Calvinism. Harvard also came on apace, in 1721 and 1727 establishing professorships in divinity and natural philosophy. Through the influence of Presbyterian ministers, in 1746 the College of New Jersey was granted a charter. King's College, now Columbia University, founded in New York in 1754, was made possible by the efforts of Dean Berkeley. In 1755, largely through the instrumentality of Benjamin Franklin, the first college was founded in Pennsylvania, the institution being freer from religious influence than any other colonial college.

BARBADOS, THE LEEWARD ISLES, AND JAMAICA

West Indian planters.—In the British West Indies, the production of sugar profoundly influenced social and economic conditions. The West Indian planter with his vast estate worked by slaves had crowded out the small landholder. He represented the capitalistic class, belonged to the Anglican church, and held views similar to those of the rural aristocracy of the mother country. It has been customary for historians to paint a roseate picture of life on the West India plantations, and no doubt there were many pretentious homes and many of the planters were possessed of great wealth. But it is a striking fact that a large percentage of the owners spent much of their time in England where their reckless living gave a false impression of West Indian prosperity. Slavery fostered industrial waste, and coupled with a tropical climate, produced a manner of life which undermined character; drinking, gambling, immorality, and sloth were common vices. Earthquakes and hurricanes frequently devastated the islands, the numerous wars destroyed shipping and cargoes, and slave insurrections were a constant terror. Churches, schools, and newspapers were sadly inadequate. Codrington College in Barbados, the only notable school in the islands, had but fifty students. Children of the planters were frequently sent to England to be educated, but they there acquired a point of view which made plantation life distasteful and tended to swell the large group of absentee landlords.

Barbados and the Leeward Isles.—During the seventeenth century most of the British sugar came from Barbados and the Leeward Isles, but lack of fertilization and slave labor had brought about deterioration on the estates, and during the eighteenth century both population and productivity were on the decline. In 1762 the white population of Barbados was about 18,000 and the blacks numbered 70,000. In 1736 the island produced 22,769 hogsheads of sugar, while during 1740–1748 the average annual production was 13,948 hogsheads. In 1744, Antigua, St. Christopher, Nevis, and Montserrat contained a total of about 11,000 whites and 60,000 slaves. As the lands became less productive, the planters attempted to make up the loss by increasing the number of slaves, a method which probably aggravated the condition.

Jamaica.—In the eighteenth century, Jamaica was the West Indian frontier. There could be found large tracts of unoccupied land suitable for sugar culture. In spite of this the population increased slowly; this was mainly due to slave insurrections which were frequent until 1739, to the fact that there was a constant migration of small landholders from the British West Indies, and to a depressed sugar market. The Island of Jamaica contained 3,840,000 acres; in 1754, 1620 planters had under cultivation 1,671,569 acres. The demand for slaves was keener than in any other British sugar island. During 1702–1775 it has been estimated that the planters purchased about 5,000 negroes a year from the slave traders.

A contemporary description of Jamaica.—Leslie described the island customs in 1740 as follows: "The Gentlemens Houses are generally built low, of one Story, consisting of five or six handsome Apartments, beautifully lined and floored with mahogany, which looks exceeding gay; they have generally a Piazza to which you ascend by several Steps, and serves for a Screen against the Heat. . . . The Negroes have nothing but a Parcel of poor miserable Huts built of Reeds, any of which can scarce contain upwards of two or three.

"The common Dress here is none of the most becoming, the Heat makes many clothes intolerable, and therefore the Men generally wear only Thread Stockings, Linen Drawers, and Vest, a Handkerchief tied around their Head, and a hat above.

. . . The negroes go mostly naked, except those who attend Gentlemen. . . . The Laidies are as gay as any in *Europe*, dress as richly, and appear with as good a Grace. . . . Learning is here at the lowest Ebb; there is no publick School in the whole Island, neither do they seem fond of the Thing. . . . The Office of a Teacher is looked upon as contemptible, and no Gentlemen keeps Company with one of that Character; to read, write, and cast up Accounts is all the Education they desire, and even these are but scurvily taught. . . . The Gentlemen, whose Fortunes can allow, send their children to *Great Britain*. . . . The Laidies read some, dance a great deal, coquet much, dress for Admirers, and at last, for the most Part, run away with the most insignificant of their humble Servants. Their Education consists entirely in acquiring these little Arts."

Emigration.—There was a constant migration of small land-holders from the British West Indies to the French and Dutch islands, to Guiana and to the North American colonies. Several acts were passed whose object was to increase the number of colonists, but they had little effect, for the small landowners could not compete with the great slave proprietors. The colonists with small capital preferred to start where lands were cheaper and where social lines were not so tightly drawn.

Illicit trade.—The largest market for northern goods was found in the West Indies. Here was a field which required the products of the temperate zone. As Pitman observes, "Its demands upon Northern lumbermen, stock-raisers, and farmers, furnish a powerful incentive for the clearing and settlement of the continent." In spite of legal restrictions the Yankee skipper plied his trade. The planters of the sugar islands believed that the Molasses Act would restore their prosperity, but they soon found that natural economic laws were stronger than parliamentary enactments and that the northern sea-captain smuggled as of old. A considerable inter-island trade which ignored nationality was also carried on. St. Eustatius and the Virgin Isles became important smuggler havens, and even when war was in progress, the British Americans did not hesitate to supply their enemies with provisions and lumber in exchange for sugar, rum, and molasses.

READINGS

THE CONTINENTAL COLONIES

Bassett, J. S., *ed.*, *The Writings of Colonel William Byrd of Westover in Virginia, Esqr.;* Bogart, E. L., *The Economic History of the United States,* 53–104; Burke, Edmund, *An Account of the European Settlements in America,* II, 145–273; Burnaby, Andrew, *Travels through the Middle Settlements in North America;* Callender, G. S., *Selections from the Economic History of the United States,* 6–84; Clark, V. S., *History of Manufactures in the United States, 1607–1860,* 73–214; Cross, A. L., *The Anglican Episcopate and the American Colonies;* Dexter, F. B , "Estimates of Population," in Am. Antiquarian Society, *Proceedings, 1887;* Fiske, John, *Old Virginia and her Neighbors,* II, 174–369; Greene, E. B., *Provincial America,* 270–342; Hart, A. B., *Contemporaries,* II, 224–311; Johnson, E. R., and others, *History of Domestic and Foreign Commerce of the United States,* I, 84–121; Kalm, Peter, *Travels in North America,* in Pinkerton, *Travels,* XIII, 374–700; McCrady, Edward, *The History of South Carolina under the Royal Government, 1719–1776,* pp. 376–540; Smith, Samuel, *The History of the Colony of Nova Caesaria, or New Jersey,* 419–509; Weeden, W. B., *Economic and Social History of New England,* II, 449–713; Andrews, C. M., *Colonial Folkways;* Phillips, U. B., *American Negro Slavery,* 67–114.

THE WEST INDIES

Edwards, Bryan, *History of the West Indies;* Gardner, W. J., *History of Jamaica;* Long, Edward, *History of Jamaica;* Pitman, Frank W., *The Development of the British West Indies, 1700–1763;* Phillips, U. B., *American Negro Slavery,* 46–66.

CHAPTER XIX

THE ENGLISH COLONIAL SYSTEM (1689–1763)

Before 1689 English colonial administration had been largely a personal matter with the king. Royal control had been exercised through the Privy Council assisted by advisory committees, boards and commissioners, after 1674 the most important of these bodies being the Lords of Trade. Between 1689 and 1714 colonial administration underwent fundamental changes both in theory and organization. By the end of the reign of Anne it had become largely departmental and official rather than personal, and Parliament had begun to take a somewhat larger hand in running affairs than during the former period. The Board of Trade, a body independent of the Privy Council, replaced the Lords of Trade in 1696 and for a time was the chief agency in the direction of colonial affairs. It lacked executive authority but conducted routine business and gathered information on which the Privy Council, Parliament, and the departments of the treasury, admiralty, and war acted. Under the Hanoverians the Secretary of State for the Southern Department became the colonial minister and the Board of Trade lost much of its importance. In America the principal agents of imperial control were the royal governors, judges, customs officials, and naval and military officers.

THE FIRST REORGANIZATION OF WILLIAM III

The system as William found it.—When William III ascended the throne, the later Stuart colonial system had not been perfected. It had been characterized by the principles that the authority of the crown should be strengthened at the expense of the colonial legislatures, that commerce should be regulated by the imperial administration, and that larger governmental units should take the place of the multiplicity of colonies. The colonial governments had gradually evolved toward a common type composed of governor and council representing the crown or proprietor, and a legislature in which the council acted as an upper house while the lower elective house represented the interests of the colony.

Committee on trade and plantations.—William III at first adopted the machinery of colonial administration as he found it, continuing the committee of the privy council on trade and plantations, but he appointed new members, including leading ministers from both the Whig and Tory parties. The navigation laws were continued in force, and Edward Randolph was retained as surveyor general of the customs.

Governmental changes in New England.—In the colonies several changes were introduced, the most striking being in New England. The idea of a consolidated New England was abandoned. The charters of Rhode Island and Connecticut were restored, and New Hampshire was established as a royal province. In 1691 Massachusetts, Plymouth, Maine, and Acadia were consolidated into the Province of Massachusetts Bay, but the immediate reconquest of Acadia by the French made the new charter inoperative in that region.

Massachusetts charter of 1691.—The form of government established in the Province of Massachusetts Bay was a compromise between the old independent form of earlier days and the type of the royal colony. The charter provided for a governor, deputy-governor, and secretary, to be appointed by the crown; a council of twenty-eight; and a lower house composed of freeholders, elected by the people. The general court composed of the governor, council, and lower house, was given the power, after the last Wednesday in May, 1693, of selecting annually the members of the council, at least eighteen of whom were to be from the old colony of Massachusetts, four from New Plymouth, and three from Maine. Legislation which met the approval of the governor was sent to the king in council, who within three years of the passage of the act, could disallow or nullify the colonial legislation. Laws not disallowed within three years remained in force.

New York.—The Leisler rebellion in New York complicated the problem of reorganization. Instead of Leisler being countenanced, New York, shorn of New Jersey, was again made a royal colony, with a government composed of governor, council, and elected assembly. Governor Henry Sloughter arrived on March 19, 1691, and the first assembly met on April 9. It promptly repealed the Duke's Laws, and voted that the revenues be made payable to the receiver-general, a crown appointee, and that issuance of funds be made by the governor's warrant, an action which made the governor for the time being independent and paved the way for future disputes. Sloughter died in July, 1691, and in August, 1692, Colonel Benjamin Fletcher arrived to assume the governorship, Richard Ingoldesby, an appointee of the council, having acted as governor in the interim.

Virginia.—In Virginia the revolution was effected without violence. Lord Howard of Effingham continued in the governorship but remained in England, Sir Francis Nicholson, who had been deposed in New York, being sent out as governor in 1690. Though he resisted the calling of an assembly, popular clamor forced his hand. A new capital city called Williamsburg was immediately laid out.

The Jerseys.—No settled policy regarding the proprietary governments was followed by William. Instead of attempting to readjust them after some formulated plan, each colony was dealt with as an individual unit with its own problem. In the Jerseys William restored the proprietors. Little authority was exercised by them, however, until 1692, when Andrew Hamilton was sent out as governor of both East and West New Jersey, a distinct step toward consolidation into a single province.

Pennsylvania.—The marked favor with which James II looked upon Penn placed the Pennsylvania proprietor under William's suspicion. Charges of misgovernment on the part of Penn's appointees, bickerings in the colony between the upper and lower counties, controversies among the Quakers, claims of religious intolerance, and the set attitude of the Quakers against war, made an accumulation of troubles for the proprietor. In 1692 he was deprived of his government, Benjamin Fletcher being sent over as governor. Fletcher introduced the royal colony type of government, selecting a council and summoning an elective assembly from both the upper and lower counties. When Fletcher demanded appropriations to assist in the war, the assembly proved factious, claiming that the governor was violating the chartered rights of the colony. Fletcher was unable to overcome the constitutional objections and withdrew to New York, sending a deputy to the colony to represent him. Penn in the meantime had been pressing his claims, and having succeeded in convincing the king of his loyalty, in 1694 was restored to his rights.

Maryland.—The Catholicism of Baltimore placed him under the ban of the government, in spite of the fact that he hastened to proclaim the new sovereigns. A rebellion against the proprietor gave ample excuse for the crown to take over the government of the colony. Baltimore was left in possession of his territorial rights, retaining the quit-rents, ownership of vacant lands, and his share of the customs, but the government was taken from him. In 1692 Sir Lionel Copley came over as royal governor, a council was selected from the anti-Baltimore party, and an assembly was convened. The assembly established the Episcopal church and divided the counties into parishes. Copley died in 1693, and for a brief period Sir Edmund Andros was governor, but Francis Nicholson soon succeeded him, and transferred the capital from St. Mary's to Annapolis.

The Carolinas.—The proprietors of the Carolinas fared better. Though there was much opposition to them in the colonies, they succeeded in ingratiating themselves with William and were left in undisturbed possession. In 1691 the Charleston and Albermarle districts were united under a single government, Philip Ludwell, who in 1689 had been appointed governor of the district north and east of Cape Fear, being made governor of the whole of Carolina.

WILLIAM'S SECOND REORGANIZATION

The Board of Trade.—As the war progressed, the enforcement of the navigation laws became more and more difficult; piracy and smuggling increased, and the Dutch obtained a larger part of the carrying trade than formerly. The complaints of English merchants were voiced in the House of Commons, where an insistent minority demanded a reorganization of the machinery of colonial administration and a revision of the navigation laws. William was opposed to the creation of a new board by parliament, considering that such action would be an encroachment upon the prerogative of the crown. The parliamentary bill was dropped, and in May, 1696, the king organized the Board of Commissioners for Trade and Plantations. Instead of being a committee of the privy council, the new board was an independent organization. It was composed of nominal and real members. The nominal members were the chief officers of state who seldom attended meetings. The working members of the board were eight non-ministerial paid officials, among those first commissioned being John Locke and William Blathwayt, the efficient secretary of the old committee.

The board had general supervision of colonial trade and government, gathered information, and reported on colonial affairs to the king or to parliament. Instructions to royal governors were draughted by them and they made nominations in cases of vacancy in the colonial service. They examined colonial legislation with a view to its confirmation or disallowance, listened to complaints, examined the accounts of the colonial treasuries, and attended to many minor matters. The board was in reality a clearing house for colonial administration; it examined, reported, and recommended, but it could not execute. During the reigns of William and Anne, its recommendations carried great weight, but its importance gradually declined as the cabinet system developed.

The secretaries of state.—Of William's ministers, those to whom colonial affairs were usually entrusted were the two secretaries of state, one or the other attending to the work. Governors usually corresponded directly with the secretaries. Questions which involved foreign countries, questions of defence, Indian outbreaks, and violations of the navigation acts were usually handled by the secretaries without being referred to the Board of Trade.

The privy council.—The privy council continued to be the executive center of the system. Recommendations which were read before it were usually referred to a committee of the whole, and upon the decision of this committee the council acted. As Dickerson says, "The whole machinery . . . for colonial administration included a Board of Trade to investigate, gather facts, and make recommendations; a committee of the Privy Council to act as a board of review and a court of appeals, both administrative and legal; and the privy council, meeting with the king, before which all final actions of importance were registered."

The Board of Trade and other departments of government.—The commissioners of the customs worked in close touch with the Board of Trade. The bodies were mutually helpful in collecting information. The admiralty and the treasury were also necessarily in close touch with the Board of Trade as was the Bishop of London. Many members of the Board of Trade occupied seats in parliament and prepared bills which affected the colonies. The board members also furnished information to parliament concerning trade and colonial matters.

Evasion of the trade laws.—The earlier navigation laws had not been thoroughly enforced. Most of the customs officials and some of the governors exerted themselves to enforce the laws, and several ships were fitted out to stop illicit traffic, but many of the officials were negligent, and several of them no doubt profited by non-enforcement of the laws. When arrests were made convictions proved difficult, for the juries were in sympathy with the law-breakers. In 1693 a Scotch commercial company was organized with the object of trading to India and Africa. This alarmed the English East India and the Royal African companies. The complaints of the customs officials and individual merchants, when reinforced by these powerful corporations, resulted in the passage of "An Act for preventing Frauds and regulating abuses in the Plantation Trade," a law familiarly known as the Navigation Act of 1696.

Navigation Act of 1696.—The act provided that after March 25, 1698, no goods should be imported into or exported from any English colony in Asia, Africa, or America, or be carried from or to any colony, or England, Wales, or Berwick-upon-Tweed, except in ships built by English subjects and navigated by English masters, with three-fourths of the crews English subjects. Exception was made of prizes condemned in the admiralty courts, and, for three years, of ships which were under contract to deliver supplies to the English navy. All ships engaged in colonial trade were made subject to the same rules of search and the same penalties for violations as prevailed in England. No vessel was allowed to engage in colonial trade until one or more of the owners had registered the vessel and taken a prescribed oath.

The Lord Treasurer, Commissioners of the Navy, and Commissioners of the Customs were allowed to appoint customs officers for any place which they saw fit. Forfeiture of vessel and cargo was the penalty for breach of the law, one-third of the proceeds to go to the crown, one-third to the governor of the colony, and one-third to the informant who brought the suit. Governors or commanders-in-chief of the colonies were required to take oath to enforce the acts of trade, under penalty of a fine of a thousand pounds and removal from office. Naval officers in the customs service were required to give ample security to the Commissioners of the Customs in England. In order to secure convictions, the act provided that in cases arising under the navigation laws, only natives of England, Ireland, or persons born in the English colonies could serve on juries. Those having land grants were forbidden to dispose of any lands to foreigners without an order in council, and the crown reserved the right to approve the nomination of governors in the proprietary colonies. Any colonial act at variance with the navigation laws was declared null and void.

Woolen Act of 1698.—The frequent interruptions of trade during the War of the English Succession caused the New Englanders to manufacture many woolen goods. In order to retain a monopoly for English manufacturers, in 1698 an act was passed forbidding the colonists to ship wool or woolen products from one colony to another.

Admiralty courts.—The Navigation Act of 1696 presupposed the establishment of admiralty courts in the colonies. The continental colonies were soon organized into two admiralty districts, New England, New York, and after 1702 New Jersey comprising the northern, and the rest the southern district. At a later period the districts were subdivided. In these courts there were no juries, a fact which made the admiralty courts exceedingly unpopular.

The Piracy Act.—Piracy had long existed, especially in the West Indies, and though stringent measures were taken to suppress it, the black flag still floated over many a pirate craft. Madagascar became a favorite haven, and from its harbors went forth the sea rovers to prey upon the East and West Indiamen. In many ports of the American colonies they were able to dispose of their booty, while officials closed their eyes or shared in the profits. Of the pirates of the period, the best known is Captain Kidd, about whose name has clustered much of fable and romance. The Navigation Act of 1696 made smuggling more difficult, and out and out piracy increased greatly after the passage of the act. To protect the merchant ships and make the navigation laws more effective, in 1700 an act was passed which provided that piracy and other felonies committed on the high seas might be tried in special colonial courts created by the crown.

The " Charter of Privileges " and the formation of Delaware.— Near the close of the reign of William III the government of Pennsylvania was changed. In 1701 in the hope of quieting dissension in Pennsylvania, Penn consented to the "Charter of Privileges," which was passed by the council and assembly. The proprietor continued to appoint the governor and councillors, but the assembly was henceforth composed of four representatives from each county who were elected by the freemen. The assembly was allowed to elect its own officers and to initiate legislation. Delaware was allowed to have its own assembly but remained under the jurisdiction of the proprietor.

New Jersey.—The policy of bringing all the colonies to a common type was evidenced by various attempts to send governors to the chartered and proprietary colonies, but in the end the attempts were abandoned. Various bills were introduced in parliament to make all the colonies royal, but they failed except in the case of New Jersey. The position of the proprietors in East and West New Jersey had always been precarious, and in 1702 they surrendered their rights to the crown. The two colonies were consolidated into the single colony of New Jersey, the royal type of government being established, Governor Cornbury of New York being commissioned as the first royal executive.

THE COLONIAL SYSTEM DURING THE REIGN OF ANNE

Cabinet development.—During the reign of Anne the cabinet system was gradually evolving. The privy council continued as the legal advisory body of the crown, but a small group of ministers, the forerunner of the modern cabinet, was in control.

Colonial affairs were placed definitely in the hands of the secretary of state for the southern department. The Board of Trade continued, but as the cabinet system developed, it became less important, the secretary of state for the southern department and parliament gradually encroaching upon the activities of the board. The union with Scotland in 1707 profoundly affected the commercial system, for after the union the Scots were no longer excluded from colonial commerce.

Commercial legislation.—In 1705 another important act of trade was passed which added rice, molasses, and various naval stores to the list of enumerated articles which must be shipped to England. To offset these new restrictions, bounties were to be given on naval stores produced in the colonies and shipped to England, and in 1707 colonial seamen were exempted from impressment in the royal navy. During the reign of William III the Bank of England was established and the financial system was completely renovated. No definite money system had been established in the colonies; Spanish coins were in common use, but they had no fixed value, a condition which greatly hampered commerce. In 1707 parliament passed an act which imposed penalties for taking foreign coins at a rate above the legal ratio. The colonial post-office was also reorganized. Before 1689 each colony had regulated its postal offices. In 1692 a patent for twenty-one years was issued to Thomas Neale to establish colonial post-offices; Neale's deputy, Andrew Hamilton of New Jersey, obtained the support of several of the colonial governments in establishing postal rates, but the arrangements were lacking in uniformity. In 1710 parliament passed an act reorganizing the post-office of the entire realm. In the colonies a post-office was to be established in New York and at other convenient points in each of the colonies on the continent and in each of the Leeward Isles.

Disallowance and appeals.—During the reigns of William III and Anne the crown was constantly seeking to harmonize the colonial and home governments, both in legislation and administration. The chief crown instrument for achieving harmony was the right of royal disallowance of colonial legislation. By 1692 it had been established in the royal provinces and in Pennsylvania. In 1702 it was extended to New Jersey, and at various times during the reign of Anne laws of chartered colonies were disallowed, although such action was of doubtful legality. The unity of the English court system was maintained by insistence that cases involving individuals in the colonies might be appealed to the privy council. When the colonies attempted to restrict the right, colonial legislation was disallowed.

Causes of friction.—The constitutional development in England which followed the Revolution of 1688 was reflected in the colonies, where each lower house was a miniature house of commons representing the will of the enfranchised people, while the governors and proprietors were considered as representatives of the royal will. Struggles between the governor and assembly occurred in almost every colony, the most common causes of quarrel being the control of elections and of the purse, and appointments.

Control of elections and the purse.—In several of the colonies the popular control of elections was maintained either by specific statements in the charters or by legislative enactment. In Virginia the burgesses in 1692 declared themselves the sole judges of the qualifications of their members. The Massachusetts charter provided for annual elections, and the same right was given to Pennsylvania in 1701. Legislative acts in the Carolinas secured biennial elections. The most potent factor in limiting the power of governors was the control of taxation by the lower house. That money raised by direct taxation should be disbursed by the representatives of the people was a growing idea. The assemblies frequently fixed salaries, refused to provide for fixed civil lists, specified how much should be drawn and spent, and limited grants for governors to annual appropriations. Massachusetts was the most insistent on her rights, but each of the colonies in one way or another sought to curb the executive.

Appointments.—The appointment of administrative officers by the assemblies became more and more frequent. The theory that the representatives of the people should control taxation and disbursements naturally led to the assertion of the right to appoint financial officers, and by 1715 in most of the colonies the treasurer was appointed by the assembly. The colonies also maintained agents in England who guarded their interests.

THE COLONIAL SYSTEM UNDER THE WHIGS

Whig ascendency.—The peaceful establishment of George I on the English throne marked the downfall of the Tory party. To keep England at peace and at the same time to maintain the balance of power in Europe was the difficult task which the Whig statesmen performed, in the main successfully. To build up English industry and commerce on mercantilist principles was the basis of the Whig economic system.

Establishment of the Cabinet system.—The statesmen who had placed a Hanoverian on the throne did not propose to surrender the powers of government. The king, ignorant of English speech and English politics, soon learned that a Whig-made king was also a Whig-ruled king. During the two previous reigns a small group of men within the privy council had invariably directed affairs of state. This group had gradually come to represent the majority in parliament, an arrangement which became a definitely established principle, the ministerial group forming the cabinet. From 1714 to 1721 no one man dominated, but the financial crisis, brought about by the bursting of the South Sea Bubble, gave the great financier, Robert Walpole, his opportunity. As First Lord of the Treasury and Chancellor of the Exchequer, for twenty years he maintained his leadership, the first of the prime ministers.

The Secretary of State for the Southern Department. —In the evolution of the cabinet system the machinery of colonial government also changed. Under the Whig régime the Board of Trade, which, since 1696 had been the chief instrument of colonial control, soon became of secondary importance, the Secretary of State for the Southern Department being recognized as the responsible head of the colonial system. Until 1724 no one held the office long enough to develop a colonial policy, but in that year the Duke of Newcastle was appointed to the position, which he held for twenty-four years. Newcastle is generally regarded as an inefficient administrator, a politician who found the colonial system a convenient place to reward supporters. In his hands was the power of appointment of colonial governors and other important officials; many of them proved to be excellent officials, but others were corrupt or incapable. Jealous of his authority and fearful of entrusting power to others, Newcastle attempted to attend to the mass of colonial business, with the result that it was frequently neglected.

The Board of Trade.—The Board of Trade necessarily lost in power. When the Whigs came in office, they made a clean sweep of the board. The new members were usually friends of the ministers or indigent members of the house of commons, most of whom were ignorant of colonial affairs. The board became mainly an information bureau. At a later period, when Newcastle became prime minister, it regained some of its former prestige under the able leadership of Halifax.

The privy council.—During the reign of Anne the deliberative work of the privy council had been transacted largely by a committee, the council formally approving business settled in committee. This became the uniform rule under George I. Petitions, complaints, and memorials were usually referred to the Board of Trade for investigation and report, and then considered by a committee, of which the Secretary of State for the Southern Department was invariably a member. Colonial laws were also referred to the board for examination, while appeals were usually handled by a committee of the council. The crown continued to disallow colonial legislation, but exercised the right less frequently under the first two Georges than under William and Anne.

Attitude toward colonial governments.—As compared with earlier periods, little was done to reorganize colonial governments. Though plans for doing away with the charters of Rhode Island and Connecticut were frequently discussed, no action was taken, but in the proprietary colonies changes occurred. In Maryland the Baltimore family was restored to power, and in Pennsylvania the Penn family was confirmed in its rights. In the Carolinas the colonists had grown weary of proprietary neglect in defending the colonies against the Indians, Spanish, and French. Revolutionary movements occurred which resulted in the overthrow of proprietary power and in the complete separation of North and South Carolina, a government of the royal type being established in each colony.

Trade laws.—During the Walpole period the mercantilist economic theories were still the basis of trade regulation. The colonies continued to be looked upon as a base of supply for raw material. Their industrial and commerical activities were not to interfere with those of English manufacturers and shippers. To prevent smuggling, to provide for the treasury, and at the same time foster the resources of the colonies, were the difficult tasks of Walpole and his colleagues.

Naval stores.—The wars of William and Anne had caused a great demand for naval stores, and their production in the colonies had been encouraged. During that period England had drawn her greatest supply from the Baltic countries. But the defeat of Sweden in her wars with Russia meant a decline of English influence in the Baltic, and England turned to the colonies for her ship supplies. In 1721 a new bounty act was accordingly passed to encourage the colonial supply, and the best hemp from the colonies was allowed to come into England free of duty. Eight years later the bounties on pitch, turpentine, and tar were somewhat lessened, the encouragement still being sufficient to give the producers a decided advantage over their competitors, the Carolinas being the principal gainers in the business. In 1731 the drawback on unwrought hemp exported from England to the colonies was removed, an act which also appears to have favored the colonial trade. The production of hemp, however, did not flourish in America as did that of other naval stores. In 1721 copper was placed upon the enumerated list, but every effort to include iron was defeated until 1750. In line with the policy of stimulating the production of naval stores was a provision that timber from the colonies could be imported into England duty free, the result being that New England became the source of supply for masts both in the navy and the mercantile marine.

Furs and hats.—The fur business in the Atlantic seaboard colonies had steadily declined, and the government wished to build it up. To accomplish this beaver and other peltry were placed on the enumerated list, but the duties payable in England were materially decreased. Much of the beaver was used in the colonies in the manufacture of hats. As this was an important English industry, in 1732 an act was passed which stopped the exportation of hats from the colonies and restricted their manufacture.

Rice.—The rice industry had been introduced in Carolina about 1688, and found an important market in Portugal and Spain. Rice being placed on the enumerated list in the reign of Anne, the colonies soon lost the market. To rectify this, in 1730 Carolina was allowed to send rice direct to countries south of Cape Finisterre. Five years later Georgia, and somewhat later the West Indies, were allowed the same privilege. American rice immediately regained its place in the trade of southern Europe and also found a market in Holland and Germany.

The Molasses Act.—The great staple of the West Indies was sugar. In its production the English Islands had surpassed the French colonies, a condition which was due to the restrictive measures of the French government. But in 1717 France adopted a liberal policy toward her colonies and the production of sugar increased to such an extent that the English sugar-producing islands experienced a financial depression. The thrifty colonial traders from the mainland, especially from New England, took advantage of the low price of French and Dutch sugar, molasses, and rum. To bolster up the West Indian planters and to prevent the trade with foreign colonies, in 1733 the Molasses Act was passed, imposing prohibitory duties on molasses, sugar, and rum imported into the continental colonies from other than English possessions. But in spite of the act the trade continued, and but little effort was made to enforce the law.

Constitutional principles.—During the period from 1714 to 1740 the constitutional rights of the people in the colonies were defined more clearly than before. In 1720 the principle was established that the common law applied to the colonies as well as to England, but the question of whether English statute law extended to the colonies was not satisfactorily settled. The writ of habeas corpus was usually granted under the common law. Progress was also made toward gaining the freedom of the press. After a struggle in Massachusetts in 1721 the right of the governor to censor books was abridged. In 1735 Zenger, a New York publisher, was tried for libel. The court held that it should decide the libellous nature of the statements made, and that the jury should determine the fact of publication. Zenger's lawyer argued that the jury must decide on whether or not the publication was libellous. On this ground he won his suit, thereby greatly strengthening the power of the press.

Increasing power of assemblies.—English colonial policy does not appear to have aroused serious opposition. Each colony had its political parties, but no question arose which welded together any group of colonies, or of classes in various colonies. As in the earlier period there were frequent quarrels between the assemblies and the governors, control of finance being the most usual cause of friction. The governors demanded fixed salaries, while the assemblies insisted on making temporary grants. The assemblies also ignored the necessity of the governor's warrant in drawing money, and insisted that the councils should not amend money bills. In these controversies the governors were usually bested, and by the close of the Walpole régime, the principle was well defined that the assemblies should control the purse.

Paper money.—Closely allied to the question of control of taxation and the governor's salary was that regarding the issuance of paper money. A shortage of coin was usual, and the issuance of paper money was the remedy by which the assemblies and banks attempted to provide a medium of exchange. In general the governors opposed such issues as financially unsound, but their actions were frequently misunderstood and were considered tyrannous.

Friction between colonies.—The difficulties between the executives and the assemblies might have developed into a general opposition to English control had it not been for the quarrels between colonies over boundaries and trade laws. Boundaries were based upon charters, which in many cases were conflicting and almost every colony had chronic disputes with its neighbors. The trade laws of one colony frequently discriminated against its neighbors, the natural result being retaliatory legislation. The English government was often called in as umpire, but its decisions seldom met with the approval of both parties.

READINGS

Andrews, C. M., *The Colonial Period*, 128–154; Beer, G. L., "The Commercial Policy of England toward the American Colonies," in Columbia University, *Studies in History, Economics, and Public Law*, III, No. 2;

Bingham, H., "Early History of the Scots Darien Company," in *The Scottish Historical Review*, January, April, July, 1906; Briscoe, N. A., "The Economic Policy of Robert Walpole," in Columbia University, *Studies in History, Economics, and Public Law*, XXVII, No. 1; Channing, Edward, *History of the United States*, II, 217–281; Dickerson, O. M., *American Colonial Government, 1697–1765;* Egerton, H. E., *A Short History of British Colonial Policy*, 114–152; Greene, E. B., *Provincial America*, 166–207; *The Provincial Governor in the English Colonies of North America;* Root, W. T., *The Relations of Pennsylvania with the British Government, 1696–1765;* Pitman, Frank W., *The Development of the British West Indies, 1700–1763,* pp. 127–333.

CHAPTER XX

A QUARTER-CENTURY OF CONFLICT: THE EXPULSION OF THE FRENCH

SPAIN AND THE POWERS, 1715-1739

Spanish dynastic ambitions.—From 1715 to 1739 the relations of England and Spain were frequently strained, due to the clashing of commercial and colonial interests, or to the ambitions of Spanish rulers. Philip V hoped to become the king of France. His second wife, Elizabeth Farnese, was ambitious to secure territories in Italy for her sons, the elder, Don Carlos, being destined to play an important part in Italian and Spanish history. The Spanish minister, Alberoni, devoted himself to building up Spanish influence in Italy.

The Triple and Quadruple Alliances.—Her Italian policy brought Spain into discord with the Emperor Charles VI, as the House of Austria hoped to remain the dominant factor in Italy. In 1717 Austrian acts in the Milanese provoked hostilities. Spanish forces immediately occupied Sardinia and the following year Sicily. The same year an alliance had been made between England, France, and Holland, and in 1718 Austria joined the alliance. Austrian troops were sent to Italy, a Spanish fleet was defeated by the English Admiral Byng, and in 1719 a French army crossed the Spanish frontier. Spain was brought to terms and Alberoni was dismissed. But before definite terms could be arranged, France opened negotiations with Spain and French influence was greatly strengthened. The war between Spain and France extended to their North American colonies, with important consequences, as has been set forth in an earlier chapter.

Spanish-Austrian alliance.—From 1721 to 1724 Elizabeth Farnese depended on the French alliance to attain her ends. But France made no effort to dislodge the English from Gibraltar, and Spanish merchants complained of English smugglers in the colonies. Furthermore, Don Carlos had not been established in Italy. To bring about the desired ends, in 1725 an alliance between Spain and Austria was formed. This was made possible by the ambitions of the Emperor Charles VI, who had been unable to obtain the adhesion of England, Holland, and France to the Pragmatic Sanction. He also hoped to secure a part of the Oriental trade by the formation of the Ostend East India Company, an enterprise which ran counter to English, Dutch, and French interests. Spain immediately demanded from England the cession of Gibraltar. The reply was the formation of the League of Hanover between England, France, and Prussia, the last named power, however, soon deserting its allies. Hostilities began in 1726 when an English fleet blockaded Puerto Bello and in 1727 the Spanish besieged Gibraltar. Austria was unprepared for war. Powerful parties in England and France did not favor it, and a considerable faction in Spain opposed the Austrian alliance. In consequence a peace was patched up. The operations of the Ostend Company were suspended for seven years, and the siege of Gibraltar was abandoned.

The treaty of Seville.—Abandoned by Austria, Elizabeth Farnese turned to England and Holland. A treaty was made which provided that the privileges of the Ostend Company be revoked, that England's former rights of trade in the Spanish colonies be renewed, that Spain abandon her claims to Minorca and Gibraltar, and that the succession of Don Carlos to the Italian duchies be guaranteed. The Austrian emperor was furious, but was pacified by a recognition of the Pragmatic Sanction on the part of England and Holland. In 1731 Don Carlos became Duke of Parma and Piacenza and was assured the succession to Tuscany.

French and Spanish alliance.—Walpole was not inclined to strengthen Spanish influence in Italy, so the shifty queen abandoned England and brought about an alliance with France. This was made possible by commercial difficulties in the colonies, and by the fact that French and English colonial interests were approaching a collision. The alliance of France and Spain was not disclosed, however, until 1739. In 1733 the War of the Polish Succession broke out; in the struggle England remained neutral, but France and Spain took an active part against Austria. At the end of the war Naples and Sicily were united under the rule of Don Carlos and the great ambition of Elizabeth Farnese was attained.

Commercial relations of Spain and England, 1715-1739.—By the treaty of Utrecht England had gained the right to supply the Spanish colonies with slaves and to send an annual cargo of five hundred tons to Spanish ports. English merchants were not satisfied with this paltry trade, and smuggling increased. Spanish coast guard ships seized many of the English traders, who received rough handling by the Spanish officials. During 1738 and 1739 public opinion in England became more and more inflamed against Spain. A paper presented to parliament in 1738 showed that in recent years fifty-two vessels had been plundered by the Spaniards, and that British seamen had been harshly treated. The most famous case was that of Thomas Jenkins, who declared that a coast guard captain had captured him, cut off his ears, and insolently remarked, "Carry this home to the King, your master, whom, if he were present, I would serve in like fashion." Attempts to settle difficulties by diplomacy failed, and by the summer of 1739 it became evident that war was at hand. On July 10 George II issued a proclamation authorizing reprisals and letters of marque against Spanish commerce. England declared war on October 23, and Spain on November 28.

THE WAR OF JENKINS' EAR

Puerto Bello, Cartagena, and Chagres.—As soon as war appeared inevitable, orders were despatched to Jamaica to make reprisals and Admiral Edward Vernon, in command of nine war vessels, was sent to the West Indies. Hearing that the Spanish galleons would rendezvous at Cartagena and then sail to Puerto Bello, where bullion was waiting to be exchanged for merchandise, Vernon determined to attack Puerto Bello. On November 22, 1739, the place was captured and the fortifications demolished. On March 6 and 7, 1740, Cartagena was bombarded, and a part of the fleet then attacked and captured Chagres.

The Georgia frontier.—While these events were taking place, Oglethorpe was taking measures to strengthen the Georgia frontier. Hearing that the Spanish and French were tampering with the Indians, he visited Kawita, the principal Lower Creek village, where a conference was held with chieftains of many tribes, who acknowledged the sovereignty of George II. Upon his return to Augusta, Oglethorpe was visited by Chickasaw and Cherokee chiefs, who made complaint against the traders, but he succeeded in appeasing them. By these conferences the frontier was made safe from Indian depredations in the coming war. As soon as Oglethorpe received information that a state of war existed, he recruited his forces and sent runners to the Indian villages asking for a thousand warriors to coöperate against the Spaniards. Fortifications were strengthened and vessels patrolled the coast. In November, 1739, word came that the settlement on Amelia Island had been attacked. In retaliation the Spaniards were driven from their outposts on the St. John's. On January 1, 1740, Oglethorpe proceeded against Fort Picolata on the St. John's River, surprised and captured it, and shortly afterward Fort San Francisco de Papa, only twenty-one miles from St. Augustine, was reduced but later abandoned.

Attack on St. Augustine.—Oglethorpe determined to make an attempt to capture St. Augustine. He repaired to Charleston, where he succeeded in getting the assembly to pass an act to contribute five hundred men and a schooner. The mouth of the St. John's River was to be the rendezvous for the Carolina and Georgia troops. The Indians were asked to send forces to Frederica. Oglethorpe also obtained the coöperation of nine small vessels of the British fleet. Without waiting for a complete concentration of his forces, he entered Florida in May, 1740, and soon captured the Spanish outposts. He then concentrated his forces and moved against St. Augustine. Oglethorpe expected to capture it by a combined sea and land attack, but the fleet failed to coöperate and a siege had to be instituted. The city was closely invested until June 14, when a sortie succeeded in recapturing one of the outposts. A ship of war which had been guarding the Matanzas River was withdrawn and the Spaniards took advantage of the opportunity to land reinforcements and supplies from Havana. After a consultation between the naval and military commanders, Oglethorpe decided to give up the undertaking.

Spanish and English preparations.—The Spaniards, alarmed by English activities, in July, 1740, sent out a large squadron under Admiral Don Rodrigo de Torres. France was persuaded to proclaim her close alliance with Spain and she made known her decision not to allow England to make conquests or new settlements in the West Indies, but the death of the Emperor Charles VI determined her to stay out of the war for the time being. When news of Torres' fleet reached England, twenty large vessels, several frigates and small craft, and many transports carrying nine thousand troops were sent to the West Indies, where they arrived in December. "A fleet such as had never before been assembled in the waters of the New World was now at the disposal of the British commander." Commodore George Anson was also despatched around Cape Horn to the Pacific to prey upon Spanish commerce.

English failures.—In March, 1740, the English fleet anchored before Cartagena. From March 9 to April 11 the city was besieged, but lack of harmony between the commanders of the land and sea forces, and general mismanagement coupled with sickness among the besiegers, contributed to one of the most striking failures in English naval history. After destroying the works which had been taken, the expedition sailed for Jamaica and shortly afterward eleven of the heavier vessels and five frigates were withdrawn from the West Indian station. The English ministry also hoped to conquer Cuba, but an attack on Santiago failed as dismally as that on Cartagena. In 1742 the capture of Panama by an overland expedition from Puerto Bello was planned, but after again occupying Puerto Bello the scheme was found to be impossible of attainment. The only success of the year was the occupation of Roatan Island off Honduras Bay. In October Vernon returned to England, leaving Oglethorpe in command of the West Indian station. An expedition along the Venezuelan coast failed as completely as other English ventures on the Spanish main.

The Georgia frontier, 1742–1743.—The failures of the English made it possible for the Spanish to assume the offensive, and forces estimated at about five thousand, besides a large fleet, were collected at St. Augustine for an attack upon Georgia. The Spanish attack was launched against the fortifications on

St. Simon Island, but the spirited defence disheartened the invaders and they soon withdrew to St. Augustine. In March of the following year Oglethorpe retaliated by a descent on Florida and drove the Spanish within their defences at St. Augustine, but being too weak to attack the city, withdrew again to Georgia.

THE WAR OF THE AUSTRIAN SUCCESSION

France enters the war.—The European situation had developed along lines by 1743 which brought France into an offensive alliance with Spain. In 1740 the Emperor Charles VI died and his daughter Maria Theresa became Archduchess of Austria and Queen of Hungary and Bohemia. Portions of her domains were coveted by Prussia and France. Prussia seized Silesia; this was followed by a French attack, and the War of the Austrian Succession was on. England and Holland feared that France might annex the Austrian Netherlands. France found a ready ally in Spain, and the conflict which had been waged between England and Spain since 1739, by 1743 had developed into a great European war.

French attack on Acadia.—Events in Europe and the Mediterranean were far more important in bringing the struggle to a conclusion than those in America, but it is beyond the scope of this work to deal with them. During the peace the French had fortified Louisbourg on Cape Breton Island, making it one of the strongest fortifications in America. The governor of Cape Breton decided to attempt to regain Acadia and sent out an expedition which captured Canso. After destroying the town the French proceeded to Annapolis. The place was saved, however, by the vigilance of the Massachusetts authorities, Governor Shirley and the assembly having despatched a body of volunteers, who arrived before the enemy.

Capture of Louisbourg.—Governor Shirley then proposed to the assembly the quixotic scheme of capturing Louisbourg. Nearly four thousand volunteers from Connecticut, New Hampshire, and Massachusetts were assembled and placed under the command of William Pepperel of Kittery, Maine. Each of the New England colonies furnished war vessels and transports, and Commodore Peter Warren was sent from the West Indies with several ships of war. In April, 1745, the great flotilla appeared before Louisbourg and the place was soon invested by land and sea. After one of the most remarkable sieges in American history, in which the untrained colonials acquitted themselves with bravery and efficiency, on June 28 the place surrendered.

Border warfare, 1746–1748.—The success at Louisbourg encouraged the colonists to attempt the conquest of Canada. All of the colonies as far south as Virginia furnished men, and the Duke of Newcastle promised a large force of regulars. But the English troops were diverted to Europe and the plan came to naught. The failure of the projected conquest spurred the French colonists to attack the outlying settlements; from Acadia to the New York border, bands of French and Indians harried the frontier. Grand Pré and Fort Massachusetts were captured but were soon reoccupied. Until the close of the war, the New England borders were harassed by frequent raids. The New York and Pennsylvania frontiers were protected, mainly through the influence of the Indian agent, William Johnson, who kept the Mohawks friendly, and the Pennsylvania interpreter Conrad Weiser, whose policy of favoring the Iroquois land claims in Pennsylvania at the expense of the Delawares held the powerful New York confederation on the English side.

French and English naval activity, 1745–1746.—In March, 1745, a large French fleet under DeCaylus was sent to the West Indies. As soon as the English ministry heard of this, Vice-Admiral William Rowley was sent out with large reinforcements. Though De Caylus's fleet was not engaged, on October 31 Rowley fell in with another squadron of war vessels and supply ships, and captured or destroyed thirty out of forty sail. In 1746 France made an attempt to regain Cape Breton and Acadia. Under D'Anville a fleet of eleven large war vessels, several frigates and small craft, and transports carrying thirty-five hundred troops, arrived off the Acadian coast but the fleet was shattered by a storm, and the enterprise was abandoned.

Decisive battles off Cape Finisterre.—In 1747 another French fleet was sent out to recapture Cape Breton, but an English fleet under Anson and Warren intercepted it off Cape Finisterre and nearly every French vessel was captured. Later in the year France despatched a fleet to the West Indies convoying over two hundred merchantmen, but near the scene of the former battle a second great engagement occurred in which the English were again victorious. These two great victories completed the destruction of the French fighting navy.

Knowles's attack on the Spanish, 1748.—Early in 1748 Rear-Admiral Charles Knowles attacked and captured Port Louis on the southern shore of Española. In April he bombarded Santiago de Cuba. In September an engagement with a Spanish fleet took place off Havana, but he succeeded in capturing only one vessel.

The Peace of Aix-la-Chapelle.—The long war was drawing to an end, neither side having attained unqualified success. In the Peace of Aix-la-Chapelle, signed in October, 1748, all conquests were restored. The peace was but a truce. Both England and France realized it and both put forth efforts to strengthen and extend their colonial possessions.

THE APPROACH OF ANOTHER CONFLICT

Acadia.—Acadia, the upper valley of the Ohio, and the Cherokee country were debatable territories. To insure English possession of Acadia, Lord Halifax, the president of the Board of Trade, insisted upon the strengthening of the peninsula of Nova Scotia. In 1749 twenty-five hundred emigrants were sent over and the city of Halifax was founded. Three years later the English population had increased to four thousand. Edward Cornwallis was installed as governor, and the usual form of crown colony government established. Fort Lawrence was erected on the isthmus. Since many of the Acadians had failed to be neutral in the last war, Cornwallis asked that they again take the oath of allegiance, a request which was refused, and three or four thousand emigrated rather than swear allegiance. The policy of France regarding Acadia was to restrict its boundaries to the peninsula of Nova Scotia, to incite the Indians to make depredations, and to keep the Acadians loyal to the French king. Fort Beauséjour on the isthmus was converted into a formidable fortress and Louisbourg was greatly strengthened.

English activities on the Ohio.—Victories on the sea in the recent war had made it possible for English merchants to undersell their French rivals. From Albany and Oswego officials and traders worked in unison to keep the friendship of the Iroquois. From his estate on the Mohawk, William Johnson, a nephew of Admiral Warren, exerted great influence over the neighboring tribes, an influence which was to increase as the years went by. To the southward the frontiersmen grasped the opportunity for profit, and soon the Ohio country was frequented by many traders from Virginia and Pennsylvania. They penetrated to the Indian villages as far as the Mississippi and even into the country beyond. The principal trading centers were Picka-willany in the Miami confederacy, Logstown on the Ohio, and Venango on the Alleghany. Settlers also began to cross the mountains; in 1748 Virginia frontiersmen made a settlement at Draper's Meadow on the Greenbrier River.

The Ohio Company.—In 1744, at a council held at Lancaster, Pennsylvania, the Iroquois granted to the English the control of the country north of the upper Ohio. By subsequent agree-ments title was obtained to lands south of the river. In 1749 definite action was taken to occupy the territory. The project was launched by Virginia, partly to check the western preten-sions of Pennsylvania. A charter was granted conveying a half-million acres on the upper Ohio to a group of Virginia and English gentlemen, among the stockholders being several of Washington's relatives. The grantees agreed to build a fort on the Ohio and within seven years to settle a hundred families on their lands. In the same year the Loyal Company secured a grant of 800,000 acres in the West. In 1750 Christopher Gist, a well-known fur trader, was sent by the Ohio Company to explore as far as the Falls of the Ohio, the site of modern Louis-ville. During 1750–1751 he traversed portions of what are now Ohio, Kentucky, West Virginia, Maryland, and Pennsylvania. His favorable report stimulated activity; a trading house was built at Wills' Creek where Cumberland, Maryland, now stands, and a trail was blazed to the junction of Redstone Creek and the Monongahela, the primitive beginning of the Cumberland Pike. A few Virginians immediately settled at the western terminal of the trail.

The French frontier strengthened.—In general the Iroquois had been faithful to the English, but the French continued their efforts to gain the support of the powerful confederation. An

Iroquois mission was established near Montreal, and in 1748 Father Piquet founded the mission of La Presentation at modern Ogdensburg. To divert trade from Oswego, in 1749 Fort Rouillé was built where Toronto now flourishes. A new post was established at the Niagara portage, Detroit was strengthened, and a garrison stationed at Sault Ste. Marie. The Marquis de la Galissonière, the governor of Canada, saw the danger of the English occupation of the Ohio country. In 1749 he despatched a force under Céloron de Bienville to take possession. The expedition passed from Lake Erie to Chautauqua Lake and proceeded southward to the Alleghany, where the work of taking formal possession began. The procedure was to proclaim French sovereignty, to nail to a tree a sheet of tin bearing the arms of France, and to bury at the foot of the tree a leaden plate which stated that the land along the Ohio and its tributaries belonged to the King of France. Many Indian villages in the Ohio Valley were visited and several plates buried, but wherever Céloron went he found evidences that the tribes were friendly to the English. At the Great Miami the last plate was buried, and the party proceeded to the French post on the Maumee and then returned to Canada.

French occupation of the upper Ohio.—In May, 1749, the Marquis de la Jonquiére was appointed governor general. He was instructed to get rid of Oswego by inciting the Iroquois to attack it. Jonquiére found his government permeated with dishonesty, the intendant Bigot having used his official position to fatten the purses of himself and friends. The governor was powerless to occupy the Ohio country, having neither soldiers nor money sufficient for the enterprise. When he ordered Céloron to attack Pickawillany, that officer refused because of disaffection among the neighboring Indians. But help came from an unexpected quarter. A young French trader from Green Bay named Charles Langlade gathered two hundred and fifty Ottawas and Ojibways and destroyed the Miami village. Jonquiére died in 1752; his successor, the Marquis Duquesne, proved to be of sterner stuff. In 1753 he sent an expedition of fifteen hundred men to occupy the Ohio country. Fort Presq'Isle was erected and a road was cut to French Creek, where Fort LeBoeuf was built. The French planned to build another fort at the forks of the Ohio, but sickness and the lateness of the season interrupted their operations.

Washington's mission, 1753.—Dinwiddie, the lieutenant-governor of Virginia, realized the import of the French advance. He warned the home government which authorized him to demand the departure of the enemy, and in case of refusal, to drive them out by force. He at once sent an embassy to protest. The bearer of the message was George Washington, a surveyor who had barely reached the age of twenty-one. Guided by Christopher Gist, he proceeded to the forks of the Ohio, then to Logstown where parleys were held with the Indians, and later to Venango. Washington was civilly received but was told that the French intended to keep possession of the Ohio. He then proceeded to Fort LeBoeuf, where he was told that Dinwiddie's letter would be sent to Duquesne and that in the meantime the commander would remain at his post. It was evident that force must be employed if the Ohio country was to become English territory.

The southern frontier.—The back country of the Carolinas and Georgia was the land of the hunters, cowboys, and Indian traders. The headquarters of the Georgia traders was Augusta, while those of South Carolina had a place of deposit at the residence of Peter St. Julien near Dorchester. From there the caravans followed the Congaree trail or that which led to the Chickasaw. French agents were continually working among the interior tribes and in 1753 a war broke out between the Creeks and Cherokees. Governor Glen of South Carolina called the Indians to conferences and finally succeeded in maintaining peace for the time being. The governor then visited the lower Cherokee and purchased a tract of land on which Fort Prince George was built, one hundred and seventy miles above Augusta on the Savannah River.

THE FRENCH AND INDIAN WAR

Virginia prepares to attack the French.—When Dinwiddie heard the French reply, he prepared for war. From the house of burgesses he demanded men and money, and messengers were sent to the Catawbas, Cherokees, Chickasaws, and the Iroquois of the Ohio Valley asking them to join in a war against the French.

Dinwiddie also appealed to the governors of Pennsylvania, North and South Carolina, Maryland, and New Jersey for men and he asked the governors of New York and Massachusetts to make a demonstration against Canada to distract forces from the Ohio. The replies proved disappointing. The only outside troops which immediately came were a company of regulars from South Carolina sent by royal order. Two companies of regulars from New York arrived too late to be of service.

Washington's first campaign.—Three hundred provincial troops were raised in Virginia and placed under Joshua Frye, with Washington second in command. A few backwoodsmen were sent forward in February, 1754, to build a fort at the forks of the Ohio, but were captured by a body of French and Indians. The prisoners were released and brought back the news of their mishap. The French demolished the fortification and built a stronger one which they named Fort Duquesne. Washington pushed on toward the west with a portion of the troops and by the middle of May reached the Great Meadows. Hearing that a party of French were scouting in the neighborhood, Washington, with forty men surprised them, captured twenty-two, and killed ten.

The death of Frye gave Washington the command. Realizing the imminence of an attack, he constructed a rude fortification at Great Meadows, which he called Fort Necessity, and here the rest of the Virginia troops and the regulars from South Carolina were concentrated. From Ft. Duquesne a force variously estimated at from five hundred to seven hundred men under Coulon de Villiers, was despatched to attack Washington's forces, now reduced to about three hundred and fifty effectives. The fortifications proved to be badly constructed and poorly located, and ammunition ran short. In a few hours fifty or sixty men had fallen, and when Villiers proposed terms of surrender it was evident that they must be accepted. "Not an English flag now waved beyond the Alleghanies," and the red warriors of the West and even many of the Iroquois flocked to the standards of France.

Apathy of the colonial legislatures.—Even Washington's defeat did not greatly arouse the colonial assemblies. After much delay Virginia voted twenty thousand pounds, Pennsylvania a paltry five hundred pounds for presents to the Indians, New York five thousand pounds, Maryland six thousand. In Massachusetts Governor Shirley used a rumor that the French were seizing places in the back country to obtain a large grant. He also sent eight hundred men to build two forts on the Kennebec. The southern colonies appear to have taken no action.

The Albany convention.—The encroachments of the French showed the necessity of adopting some plan of defence. In June, 1754, representatives from New York, Pennsylvania, Maryland, and the New England colonies met at Albany. The Indian chiefs stated their grievances and were sent away soothed but hardly satisfied. The representatives then took up the subject of defence. A plan of union, chiefly the work of Franklin, was proposed, but when it was submitted to the colonies they unanimously rejected it. The Board of Trade then formulated a plan of union for military purposes only, but events were occurring which made it necessary to take immediate action. The plan was laid aside, and the board suggested the appointment of a commander-in-chief over all the forces in America, a suggestion which was eventually put into effect.

Preparations for war.—In Europe, England and France were nominally at peace. At the head of the English ministry was the Duke of Newcastle, who maintained his control of a parliamentary majority by corruption rather than by statesmanship. Fortunately for England, she had a fleet which was far more numerous than that of her opponent. The strength of France lay in her army which was nearly ten times as strong as that of her rival. Major-General Edward Braddock, a former governor of Gibraltar, stubborn, irascible, and little given to taking advice, was sent to Virginia with two regiments, which embarked at Cork in January, 1755. As soon as the French heard of this, eighteen men-of-war with three thousand soldiers were sent to Canada, followed shortly by nine more war vessels. The English immediately sent twelve vessels under Admiral Boscawen in pursuit, followed shortly by seven more, but only two of the French vessels were captured.

The council of governors.—Braddock summoned the governors for a consultation and they met in April, 1755, at Alexandria in Virginia. Those who responded were the governors of Virginia,

North Carolina, Pennsylvania, Maryland, New York, and Massachusetts. William Johnson was also at Alexandria but was not in the council. A four-fold attack was planned. Braddock was to attack Fort Duquesne; Shirley was to strike at Niagara; Johnson to attack Crown Point; and Lieutenant-Colonel Monckton was to proceed against Beauséjour.

Braddock's campaign.—After great difficulty in obtaining wagons and supplies, Braddock moved toward the frontier. In May his forces, composed of about two thousand men, were gathered at Fort Cumberland. At Little Meadows, thirty miles from Fort Cumberland, Braddock left the heavy baggage and marched on, though slowly, to attack Fort Duquesne. On July 9 when the forces were about seven miles from the fort they began to march along a rough path through the forest. As the English advanced forces were crossing a ravine they were attacked by the French and Indians, who spread out on either side and fought from behind trees, while the English regulars wheeled into line and returned the fire. The bravery and discipline of the English regulars proved of little avail against the invisible enemy and they soon broke and fled. Braddock hastened up with the second division, but the troops retreating from the front threw them into hopeless confusion. Braddock realized that his force was in danger of annihilation and ordered a retreat. As he fell back he received a mortal wound. Washington, left in command, extricated the troops as best he could and once more led back the sorry remnant of a defeated force.

The harrying of the frontiers.—With the defeat of Braddock, the frontiers of Pennsylvania, Maryland, and Virginia were left almost defenceless. Washington could muster barely fifteen hundred men to protect a mountainous frontier nearly four hundred miles long. No assistance was offered by Pennsylvania, whose Quaker representatives, religiously opposed to war, quarreled with the governor over raising money for defence, in every revenue bill asserting the right to tax the lands of the proprietor, a course in which the governor was unable to acquiese. The deadlock between governor and assembly continued for months, while Indian war bands killed hundreds of settlers. The back country of Virginia was also a scene of massacre and rapine. Under Washington's supervision a plan of defence was devised.

THE
WESTERN FRONTIER
1763
+++++++ Bradstreet's Route
------- Boquet's Route
SCALE OF MILES
0   50   100   150   200

(From Thwaites, *France in America*, opposite p. 256 [Harpers])

373

Blockhouses were built at advantageous points along the frontier, the most important being Fort Ligonier near the Alleghany
River, Fort Chiswell in the Shenandoah Valley, Fort Bird on
the Holston River, and Fort Loudoun on the Little Tennessee.
Fort Cumberland protected the upper Potomac.

Operations in Acadia.—While the war was going badly on
the western frontier Nova Scotia was the scene of victory.   In
June Monckton with two thousand colonials landed at Fort
Lawrence and soon captured Fort Beauséjour.   Fort Gaspereau
and a fortification at the mouth of the St. John were also occupied.   Then followed one of those tragic dramas of war, the
removal of the Acadians.   They had constantly been in sympathy with France and many of them had broken their neutrality
in the recent conflict.   When they were again asked to take the
oath of allegiance they stubbornly refused.   Fearing their defection in case the French attempted to reconquer the peninsula,
their deportation was ordered.   Over six thousand were sent
away, many being placed in the mainland English colonies;
others went to Louisiana and the West Indies, and still others
to Canada and France.   One shipload of the unfortunates landed
in Texas and fell into the hands of the Spaniards.

The Crown Point campaign.—For the advance against Crown
Point about three thousand men from the New England colonies
and New York were brought together at Albany under William
Johnson.   It was not until August that they encamped at the
southern end of Lake George.   The slowness of Johnson's movements had given the French ample time for preparation.   Baron
Dieskau with thirty-four hundred men had been sent to Crown
Point.   He now moved southward with a part of his force to a
point almost east of the English camp.   In the first engagement
Dieskau scored a success.   He then rashly attacked the English
camp, but his forces suffered heavily, were finally routed, and the
commander captured.   After the battle Johnson, who was
wounded, decided not to attempt to capture Crown Point.

The Niagara campaign.—Governor Shirley undertook the reduction of Niagara.   With two regiments of colonials and five hundred New Jersey men he advanced to Oswego.   But there Shirley
found himself checkmated, for the French had sent fourteen
hundred men to Fort Frontenac and had brought twelve hun-

dred from Fort Duquesne to Niagara. If Shirley attacked, he would be in danger of forces from Fort Frontenac cutting his line of communications. After a summer of inactivity he left a garrison of seven hundred men at Oswego and abandoned the campaign.

The diplomatic revolution.—In 1756 the old alignment of England and Austria against Prussia, France, and Spain changed. Since the War of the Austrian Succession, Maria Theresa had bided her time, until she could recover Silesia. With the aid of her great minister, Kaunitz, she succeeded in forming new alliances, France, Russia, Austria, and some of the minor German states uniting against Frederick the Great. To protect Hanover, the hereditary possession of George II, England made an alliance with Prussia, and thus became a participant in the Seven Years' War. Although a state of war with France had existed in India and America, neither power had made a declaration of war. But there was no longer need for subterfuge; England declared war on May 18, 1756, and France on June 9.

French preparations.—Already France had despatched to America the Marquis de Montcalm to take command of the forces, with the Chevalier de Levis as second in command. Almost from the first Montcalm was beset with difficulties. Vaudreuil, who had taken Duquesne's place as governor-general, was a colonial, jealous of any official from France, a man lacking in decision, desirous of appearing as the mainspring of success, but ever ready to blame failure upon others. The Intendant Bigot was entirely venal, a man of low morality, who feathered his nest regardless of the public danger. Montcalm's command contained three thousand French regulars in Canada and eleven hundred at Louisbourg, two thousand trained colonials, and about fifteen thousand militia. The Indian allies furnished varying numbers.

English preparations.—Upon his return from Oswego Shirley planned a new offensive, which included attacks upon Ft. Duquesne, the Lake Ontario and Lake Champlain defences, and the settlements above Quebec. This was approved by a war council at Albany, but the colonies refused to embark in such an extensive scheme and the attack on Ft. Duquesne and Quebec had to be abandoned. John Winslow was commissioned to lead the troops against Ticonderoga and Crown Point, and

Shirley proposed to command against the Ontario strongholds.
But before the plan could be executed Shirley was superseded
by Colonel Daniel Webb, who in turn was followed by General
James Abercromby, with the understanding that Loudoun was
soon to take command.

The fall of Oswego.—While the colonial forces were slowly
preparing to take the offensive, Montcalm struck at Oswego.
A three days' siege made the forts untenable and the place surrendered on August 14, 1756, sixteen hundred prisoners being taken.
Montcalm then returned to Ticonderoga, where his garrison of
five thousand men defied Loudoun, who dared not attack him.
The year had been one of dismal disasters for the English: Oswego
fallen, the Ticonderoga attack abandoned, the frontiers from
Maine to South Carolina harried by Indian war, Minorca captured by the French, and Calcutta fallen to Surajah Dowlah.

Pitt becomes the moving spirit.—Newcastle's mismanagement
raised a popular outcry and in November, 1756, he resigned.
The Duke of Devonshire became Prime Minister, but Pitt was
the strong man of the new cabinet. He was not in the king's
favor, however, and, by April, 1757, was forced out of office.
In July a new ministry was formed. "To Newcastle was given
the name of Prime Minister, to Pitt the reality. With the control of foreign affairs as Principal Secretary of State he was also
to have control of the war." He saw that England's opportunity
was on the seas and in the colonies.

Louisbourg and Ft. William Henry.—At the advice of Loudoun
an attack on Louisbourg had been planned. A part of the troops
were withdrawn from the northern frontier and in June eleven
or twelve thousand men were gathered at Halifax, where they
were joined by a squadron under Vice-Admiral Holburne. The
news that Louisbourg had been heavily reinforced alarmed Loudoun and he returned to New York. Holburne cruised off
Louisbourg, hoping to attack the French, but his fleet was
shattered by a storm. Loudoun had left an insufficient force to
defend the Lake George region. Montcalm, ever on the alert to
take advantage of the blunders of the enemy, descended from
Ticonderoga and attacked Fort William Henry at the southern
end of the lake. After a three days' bombardment the English
force of about two thousand surrendered. On the continent the

British had failed dismally. An attempt to capture Rochefort
had been unsuccessful and the Duke of Cumberland had conducted an inglorious campaign in Germany. The only great
British successes of the year were in India where Calcutta and
Chandernagore were captured and the battle of Plassey was won.

Preparations and plans, 1758.—By 1758 Pitt, ably seconded
by Admiral Anson, had brought the army and navy to a high
standard. A squadron was sent to watch Brest, flying squadrons
attacked several French ports, a fleet was maintained in the
Mediterranean to prevent the fleet at Toulon from getting into
the Atlantic, and small squadrons were sent to India, to the
African coast, and the West Indies. The army was raised to a
hundred thousand. In America Loudoun was superseded by
Abercromby, Major-General Amherst was sent over, and twenty
thousand provincial troops were put in the field. A three-fold
offensive was planned. Forbes with about seven thousand men
was to attack Fort Duquesne; Abercromby and Howe with
fifteen thousand men were to clear the French from Lake Champlain, and Amherst with twelve thousand regulars aided by a
powerful fleet under Admiral Boscawen was to attack Louisbourg.

Capture of Louisbourg.—Boscawen and Amherst rendezvoused
at Halifax and on June 1, 1758, over a hundred and fifty vessels
appeared before Louisbourg. Gradually the English forces en-
compassed the fortress. The French sunk several war vessels
in the harbor mouth to prevent the entrance of the English fleet,
but in the course of the bombardment three of the remaining
French vessels caught fire and two others were destroyed by a
night attack. The defences were battered down one by one and
on July 26 Ducour, the French commander, offered to capitulate
and six thousand prisoners of war passed into English hands.

Abercromby's defeat.—While the English were besieging
Louisbourg, Abercromby led his army of fifteen thousand against
Ticonderoga. Montcalm was in command of the French fortress,
which was garrisoned by less than four thousand men. The
English army crossed Lake George on a great flotilla, and on
July 6 was within four miles of Ticonderoga. Abercromby
foolishly thought that the fortifications could be rushed with
the bayonet and on July 8 the attempt was made. The French

fire mowed down the charging ranks with frightful slaughter. A desultory fight continued, followed by a second charge which also failed, and Abercromby, after losing nearly two thousand men, decided to retreat. In October Amherst took command of the forces which were encamped at the southern end of Lake George, but the season was too far advanced to attempt another great offensive in that region until spring.

Forts Frontenac and Duquesne.—The French forces on Lake Ontario had been weakened by withdrawals. Taking advantage of this, in August Lieutenant-Colonel Bradstreet led twenty-five hundred men against Fort Frontenac. The feeble garrison of one hundred soon surrendered, and the fort and ships in the harbor were destroyed. Lake Ontario was now in the hands of the English, and French control on the upper Ohio was weakening. General Forbes gathered a force of six or seven thousand men and advanced toward Fort Duquesne. Upon the approach of the English in November, the French destroyed the fortifications and scattered to the various western posts which they still possessed.

Kerlérec and the southern Indians.—That the English did not carry the war into the Southwest was due in no small part to the Indian policy of Kerlérec, the governor of Louisiana. The Creeks and Choctaws were traditionally favorable to the French, but their loyalty was always strained by the superior quality of English goods. Kerlérec made annual visits to Mobile to distribute presents, and prevented the Choctaws from threatened defection. Through his influence, in 1755 and again in 1757 the Creeks expelled Englishmen sent to establish posts among them, and murdered English traders. In 1757 Fort Massac was built on the Ohio to prevent an English expedition descending that stream or the Cumberland. At the same time the Shawnees returned to French allegiance.

The Cherokee War.—For three years Kerlérec intrigued with the Cherokees and succeeded in winning them over. He soon incited them to attack the settlements and many depredations occurred. In October, 1759, Governor Lyttleton of South Carolina, after a show of force, patched up a truce, but shortly afterward the Cherokees surrounded Fort Prince George and killed the commander and two others. The garrison then mas-

sacred Indian hostages within the fort, and immediately the
southern frontier was ablaze with war. Hostilities assumed such
proportions that it was necessary, early in 1760, for Amherst to
send twelve hundred men to assist the colony. An expedition
under Colonel Montgomery destroyed many Cherokee villages,
but Montgomery's orders did not allow him to remain long in
the colony, and in August he departed for New York. The
Cherokees then captured Fort Loudoun. In 1761 an expedition
of twenty-six hundred Highlanders and colonials under Colonel
Grant was sent against the Indians. The heart of the Cherokee
country was penetrated and the Indians were forced to sue for
peace.

Operations in the West Indies.—Late in 1758 British reinforcements were sent to the West Indies to attempt the capture
of the French island possessions, twenty-five vessels being
gathered under Commodore John Moore. In January an attempt
was made to take Martinique, but the French force of ten thousand regulars and militia prevented the occupation. During
the following months Guadeloupe, Marie Galante, the Saintes,
La Désirade, and Petit Terre surrendered to the English.

The campaigns of 1759.—Four expeditions against the French
in North America were planned for 1759; one under Prideaux
against Niagara, a second under Stanwix against settlements on
Lake Erie, and a third under Amherst against Ticonderoga and
Crown Point. The fourth under Vice-Admiral Saunders and
Major-General Wolfe was directed against Quebec.

Niagara captured.—Prideaux arrived before Niagara in July.
In the attack the general was accidentally killed and Sir William Johnson took command. He defeated a relieving force
and the fort surrendered. The fall of Niagara made it unnecessary for Stanwix to proceed, and he devoted his energies to the
building of Fort Pitt, on the site of modern Pittsburgh.

The fall of Quebec.—While Amherst was slowly moving toward Lake Champlain, the more important operations were proceeding against Quebec. The rendezvous was at Louisbourg.
There were gathered nine thousand troops, thirty-nine men-of-
war, ten auxiliaries, twenty-six transports, and a hundred and
sixty-two other craft, manned by eighteen thousand men. In
June the vast armament sailed up the St. Lawrence to attack

the strongest fortification on the continent. For the defence of the city Montcalm was able to muster an army of seventeen thousand, four thousand of whom were French regulars. The city occupies a promontory which juts into the St. Lawrence. Behind it are the Plains of Abraham, a plateau with almost perpendicular cliffs. To the eastward flows the River St. Charles. Between the St. Charles and the Montmorency stretched the fortified French camp. The only weak place in the defence was Point Levis across the river. This Montcalm had wished to fortify but had been overruled by Vaudreuil.

On June 26 the fleet approached the city and Point Levis was immediately occupied. Then began a series of attacks upon the French positions below the city, but every assault was repulsed and frequently with heavy loss. It became evident that the French encampment could not be taken and the plan of attack was changed. The fleet, which formed a screen for land operations on the southern shore, had gradually succeeded in getting several vessels above the city, intercepting supplies and reinforcements. At a council of war an attack above the city was determined upon. Wolfe withdrew his forces from the Montmorency and they were transferred to a point above the town. This movement was covered by the movement of the ships, which continually passed up and down the river as if to make a landing. On September 12 Saunders bombarded the French camp below the city. Montcalm, completely deceived, hurried reinforcements to that quarter. Before dawn of September 13 Wolfe landed his first detachment at the foot of the cliffs two miles above the city. Up the steep side clambered a small party, who overcame the guard at the top. By sunrise forty-five hundred men had mounted to the Plains of Abraham. Montcalm made a desperate effort to regain the position but the battle went in favor of the English. Both Wolfe and Montcalm were killed. On September 17 the British troops entered Quebec, the key to the St. Lawrence.

Important naval operations.—Elsewhere the English were equally successful. In 1758 Sénégal and Gorée on the African coast had been captured, and in 1759 on the coast of India a French fleet was bested and abandoned the East Indian waters. Rodney destroyed a French fleet at Havre, Boscawen in August completely defeated the French Mediterranean fleet, and Hawke in November annihilated the channel fleet in a great battle near Quiberon Bay.

The French fail to recapture Quebec.—Although Quebec had fallen the French still had a formidable force in the field. The troops were withdrawn from Lake Champlain and new levies were raised. By April, 1760, Levis had gathered an army of eleven thousand men and he proceeded boldly to attempt the recapture of Quebec. A hard winter had greatly reduced the effectiveness of the English garrison and General Murray was able to meet the French with only three thousand men. On April 18 occurred the second battle on the Plains of Abraham. The artillery saved the English and the attack failed. An English fleet soon blocked the St. Lawrence and the possibility of aid from France was at an end.

The capture of Montreal.—The last important Canadian stronghold was Montreal, and here Vaudreuil and Levis made their final stand. Three English armies were sent against the place. Murray ascended the St. Lawrence, Haviland advanced from Lake Champlain, and Amherst with eleven thousand men proceeded from Lake Ontario down the St. Lawrence. The French, weakened by desertions and discouraged by defeats, offered little resistance; on September 8 articles of capitulation were signed and the struggle for New France was practically ended. Forts Miami, Detroit, Mackinac, and St. Joseph soon surrendered; of the mainland colonies Louisiana alone remained in the possession of France and this also she was destined to lose.

George III becomes king.—The year 1760 also saw the breaking of French power in India. Colonel Eyre Coote decisively defeated Count Lally at the battle of Wandewash and the next year Pondicherry was captured, putting an effectual end to French influence in the Carnatic. When English success was at its height George III ascended the throne of England. He opposed the war of conquest which Pitt was waging, desiring to break the power of the Whig oligarchy which long had dominated English politics. In 1761 Pitt resigned but the king was unable to bring the struggle to an immediate close, for Charles III of Spain renewed the family compact with France, and Spain entered the war.

Operations in the West Indies and the Philippines.—Against the new antagonist England's sea power was overwhelmingly superior. In 1761 Rodney was sent to take command in the West Indies. He found Dominica already in English hands. Rodney immediately ordered the blockade of Martinique and in February, 1762, the island was surrendered. Shortly afterward Granada, the Grenadines, and St. Lucia were occupied. Admiral Pocock was sent out with reinforcements, and a great fleet of fifty-three war vessels, besides transports and other craft, with an army of fifteen thousand proceeded against Havana. In June the place was invested by land and sea. On July 30 Moro Castle was carried by storm, and on August 13 the city surrendered. Nine ships of the line and loot to the value of £3,000,000 fell into English hands. The extinguishment of French power in India made it possible to turn attention to the Philippines, and a squadron under Draper was sent against Manila. The place was feebly garrisoned and quickly surrendered, the capitulation taking place on October 5.

The Peace of Paris.—France, Spain, and England were ready for peace. At the decisive moment Russia had turned to the side of Prussia, and Austria was unable to continue the war alone. France made overtures to England for peace, and on November 3, 1762, the preliminaries were signed. The definitive treaty between England, France, and Spain was signed at Paris on February 10, 1763. France surrendered to England Canada, St. John's, Cape Breton, and all that part of Louisiana which was east of the Mississippi except the Island of Orleans. France retained certain fishing rights on the Newfoundland banks and was given the islands of St. Pierre and Miquelon. She also obtained Martinique, Guadeloupe, Marie Galante, and St. Lucia. Belle Isle and Gorée were restored to France, but England kept Sénégal. Minorca was restored to England. In Asia English conquests were restored to France but no fortifications were to be erected by her in Bengal. The preliminary agreements had arranged matters with Spain. In exchange for Havana, Florida was ceded to England. Manila was eventually restored to Spain as the news of the capture did not arrive until the preliminaries had been signed. Louisiana had been an expensive province, and Louis XV gladly surrendered all the territory west of the

Mississippi and the Isle of Orleans to Spain as a compensation for the losses of his ally. France was virtually eliminated from America. England and Spain stood out as the world's great colonizing powers.

READINGS

THE WARS OF JENKINS' EAR AND THE AUSTRIAN SUCCESSION

Armstrong, E., *Elizabeth Farnese;* Clowes, W. L., *The Royal Navy,* III, 50–138, 263–289; Jones, C. C., *The History of Georgia,* I, 314–369; Mahan, A. T., *The Influence of Sea-Power upon History, 1660–1783,* pp. 254–279; McCrady, E., *The History of South Carolina under the Royal Government, 1719–1776,* pp. 187–229; Parkman, F., *A Half-Century of Conflict,* II, 33–256; Thwaites, R. G., *France in America,* 105–123; Walton, J. S., *Conrad Weiser and the Indian Policy of Colonial Pennsylvania,* 9–121; Wood, W., *The Great Fortress;* Shea, J. G., *Catholic Church in Colonial Days,* 470–479.

FRENCH AND INDIAN WAR

Beer, G. L., *British Colonial Policy, 1754-1765,* pp. 6–77; Casgrain, R. R., *Wolfe and Montcalm;* Channing, Edward, *A History of the United States,* II, 550–599; Clowes, W. L., *The Royal Navy,* III, 138–255; Kingsford, W., *The History of Canada,* III, 387–568, IV.; Lucas, C. P., *A Historical Geography of the British Colonies,* V, 216–328; McCrady, Edward, *The History of South Carolina under the Royal Government, 1719–1776,* pp. 329–352; Mahan, A. T., *The Influence of Sea-Power upon History, 1660–1783,* pp. 281–329; Parkman, Francis, *Montcalm and Wolfe;* Short, A., and Doughty, A. G., *Canada and its Provinces,* I, 231–312; Smith, P. H., *Acadia, a lost Chapter in American History,* 145–249; Stone, W. L., *The Life and Times of Sir William Johnson,* I, 327–555, II, 1–213; Thwaites, R. G., *France in America,* 143–280; Villiers du Terrage, Marc de, *Les Dernières Années de la Louisiane Française,* 48–108; Walton, J. S., *Conrad Weiser and the Indian Policy of Colonial Pennsylvania,* 121–381; Wood, W., *The Passing of New France; The Winning of Canada;* Corbett, J. S., *England in the Seven Years' War;* Wrong, G. M., *The Conquest of New France.*

CHAPTER XXI

THE RUSSIAN ADVANCE: THE OCCUPATION OF ALTA CALIFORNIA AND LOUISIANA BY SPAIN

READJUSTMENT IN SPANISH NORTH AMERICA

Effect of the Seven Years' War.—The outcome of the Seven Years' War caused several readjustments in Spanish North America. It left Spain in a position where she must restore her colonial power or sink to the rank of a third rate nation. Renewed war with England was regarded as inevitable. Florida was lost, and was poorly compensated for, it was thought, by western Louisiana. The French barrier having been removed, Spain's hold on Louisiana and the Pacific Slope was threatened by the English, advancing both through Canada and from the thirteen colonies. On the Pacific Slope the Russians seemed even more threatening than the English. Added to all this, northern New Spain was overrun by increasingly hostile tribes. Poor and unprepared though she was, therefore, Spain was forced to get ready for another war with England, occupy Louisiana and Alta California, strengthen the frontier defences of New Spain against the Indians, and explore or reëxplore the northern interior.

The Reforms of Charles III.—All these demands could be met only by the most heroic measures; and these were applied by the energetic Charles III. This king, a Bourbon, had come to the throne in 1759, after a long and forceful reign as King of Naples. By the time of his accession, Spain had already profited much by the Bourbon reforms which from time to time had been instituted since the opening of the century, but the national revenue was still small, commerce stagnant, the army and navy weak, and colonial administration corrupt. Now came the new demands entailed by the outcome of the great war. To make the program of defence possible, it was necessary to provide revenue. This could be done only by increasing commerce and reforming the fiscal administration of the colonies.

Commercial reforms.—Commercial reforms were outlined in a series of decrees enacted between 1764 and 1778.   The ends at which they aimed are indicated by the deliberations of the *junta* held in 1765.   This body condemned especially the monopoly enjoyed by Cadiz, delays due to the flota system, the export duties on Spanish goods, restrictions upon intercolonial commerce, the smuggling habit, and the English monopoly of the slave carrying trade.

Reforms of José de Gálvez.—To carry out the reforms in New Spain King Charles sent José de Gálvez, who, as *visitador general*, was entrusted with a complete overhauling of the administration. The special function of Gálvez was to increase the revenues from New Spain.   The amount collected had been limited by crude fiscal methods and by corrupt officials.   Gálvez laid a heavy hand upon "graft," and devised new sources of revenue. Conspicuous among the latter was the tobacco industry, which he made a royal monopoly.

Explorations on the Gulf coast.—One of the first steps toward readjustment of the frontier to the new situation was a series of explorations looking to the defence of the northern coast of the Gulf of Mexico against rumored dangers from the English, now in possession of Florida.   To this end, in 1766 Colonel Escandón and Colonel Parrilla explored the Nuevo Santander and Texas coasts between Tampico and Matagorda Bay.

Rubí's tour.—To inspect and report on the northern outposts of New Spain, the Marqués de Rubí was commissioned. Leaving Mexico in March, 1766, he passed through the frontier establishments from Sonora to the borders of Louisiana.   He found the whole northern frontier infested with warlike tribes, especially the Apaches and Comanches, who committed depredations all the way from the Gila to central Texas.   Rubí recommended rearranging the northern posts so as to form a cordon of fifteen, extending from Altar in Sonora to La Bahía in Texas. Regarding Texas he recommended that the Comanche harassed district of San Sabá and all of the establishments on the Louisiana border be abandoned, and that a war of extermination be made against the Eastern Apaches, relying for the purpose on the aid of their enemies.   In 1772 most of the Rubí recommendations

were adopted in the form of a "New Regulation of Presidios."
To Hugo O'Conor, as *comandante inspector*, fell the task of
arranging the line of presidios.

Expulsion of the Jesuits.—For reasons which need not be
discussed here, in 1767 the king of Spain expelled the Jesuits
from all of the Spanish dominions.   This caused a general
shifting of the missionary forces, the places of the Jesuits in the
northeastern provinces being taken by the Franciscans.   The
temporalities were at first put in the hands of soldier commissioners, but were soon turned over to the Franciscan missionaries.   To Pimería Alta were sent Franciscans from the College
of the Holy Cross of Querétaro.   To Lower California went members of the College of San Fernando of Mexico, the president
being Junípero Serra, already distinguished for work in Sierra
Gorda.

Gálvez in Lower California.—In 1768 the visitor, Gálvez, was
called to California and Sonora.   In California he restored the
temporalities to the missionaries, consolidated the Indian pueblos,
and tried to stimulate Spanish colonization and mining, but
without great success.   It was while on the Peninsula, too, that
he organized the expedition to occupy Alta California.

Gálvez in Sonora.—To end the Indian disturbance which for
many years had been menacing Sinaloa and Sonora, Gálvez sent
Colonel Domingo Elizondo at the head of eleven hundred men.
The war began in 1768.   After a year of futile campaigns, chiefly
against Cerro Prieto, the hiding place of the enemy, Gálvez
himself took command for a time, with little better results.
Elizondo was restored to the command, and for another year the
war continued.   By dint of guerrilla warfare, presents, and
coaxing, by the middle of 1771 the rebels were pacified and settled in towns.

The Provincias Internas.—Prominent among the plans of
Gálvez were the establishment of the intendant system in New
Spain, the erection of the northern provinces into an independent
commandancy general, and the establishment there of one or
more bishoprics.   The project of a separate government for
part or all of the northern provinces had often been considered.
It was felt that the viceroy was overworked, and too far from the
frontier to understand its needs.   The demand was sectional,

based on regional interests. In 1760 a separate viceroyalty had been proposed, but Gálvez favored a military commandancy general. In 1776, after he became Minister of the Indies, his ideas were put into effect. Nueva Vizcaya, Sinaloa, Sonora, the Californias, Coahuila, New Mexico, and Texas were put under the military and political government of a *comandante general* of the Interior Provinces, directly responsible to the king and practically independent of the viceroy, the Audiencia of Guadalajara retaining its judicial authority. Chihuahua became the capital, except for a short time when Arispe was the seat of government (1780–1782). The first *comandante general* (1776–1783) was Teodoro de Croix, brother of Viceroy Croix, and himself later viceroy of Peru. By writers on California history, with attention fixed on the West, he has been regarded as incompetent.

New dioceses in the North.—In 1777 the Diocese of Linares was created to embrace the northeastern provinces of Coahuila, Nuevo León, Nuevo Santander, and Texas. Two years later was formed the Diocese of Sonora, to include Sinaloa, Sonora, and the two Californias.

The intendancies.—The primary purpose of the intendancies was to provide for the fiscal administration. A French institution, the system had been established in Spain in 1749 with satisfactory results. In 1764 the intendancy of Havana was established, likewise with good results. In 1768 the system was tentatively established in Sonora. At that time Gálvez favored eleven intendancies, dependent on the viceroy as superintendent general of revenues. The plan was not put into general operation until 1786, when Gálvez was Minister of the Indies.

The captaincy-general of Havana.—Up to the middle of the eighteenth century the audiencia and captaincy-general of Santo Domingo comprised all of the West Indies and Venezuela. Though nominally within the district, Florida was a separate captaincy-general, dependent directly on the Council of the Indies for judicial and military affairs. In other respects it was subject to the Viceroy of Mexico. As a result of the English war, in 1764 Havana was made the seat of an independent captaincy-general and of an intendancy. In 1795 the Audiencia of Santo Domingo was moved to Havana.

THE RUSSIAN MENACE

The Russian advance.—Spain had long been uneasy about upper California because of the activities of the English, Dutch, and French. Now the advance of the Russians seemed more threatening, and caused the long contemplated step to be taken. In the seventeenth century the Russians had crossed Siberia and opened up trade with China. In the early eighteenth century large portions of northern Asia were conquered by Russia in the interest of the east-moving fur traders. Before he died Peter the Great set on foot the project of sending an expedition to seek the northern passage from the Pacific to the Atlantic by going east. In pursuance of this task Vitus Bering made his stupendous expeditions into the Pacific (1725–28, 1733–41), in the second of which he discovered Bering Strait, coasted the American mainland, and made known the possibilities of profit in the fur trade.

Fur trade on the Aleutian Islands.—Bering's voyage was followed by a rush of fur traders to the Aleutian Islands. Companies were formed, vessels built at the port of Okhotsk, and posts established within a few years on Bering, Unalaska, Kadiak, and other islands, for a distance of nearly a thousand miles. The principal market for furs was China. The fur trade was attended by wanton slaughter of animals and harsh treatment of natives, who sometimes rebelled, as at Unalaska in 1761.

Decision of Spain to occupy Alta California.—Though Russian activities were as yet confined largely to the Aleutian Islands, the Spanish government feared that they would be extended down the coast. Moreover, there was a growing friendship between Russia and England, Spain's chief enemy. But these dangers, like others discussed during three centuries, might have resulted in nothing but correspondence had there not been on the northern frontier of New Spain a man of action, clothed with full authority to act. This man was the visitor-general, José de Gálvez. On January 23, 1768, Grimaldi, royal minister, sent the viceroy orders to resist any aggressions of the Russians that might arise. This order, which coincided with the views of the visitor and the viceroy, reached Gálvez while on his way to California.

THE FOUNDING OF ALTA CALIFORNIA

The Portolá expedition.—While settling affairs in the Peninsula Gálvez organized the expedition. It was designed to establish garrisons at San Diego and Monterey, and to plant missions, under their protection, to convert and subdue the natives. The command was entrusted to Governor Portolá, and the missionary work to Father Junípero Serra, president of the California missions. The enterprise was carried out in 1769 by joint land and sea expeditions. The *San Carlos* under Captain Vicente Vila and the *San Antonio* under Captain Juan Pérez conducted a portion of the party, while the rest marched overland from Lower California, under Captain Rivera and Governor Portolá.

San Diego founded.—By the end of June all but one vessel had arrived at the Bay of San Diego. While Vila, Serra, and some fifty soldiers remained to found a mission and presidio there, Portolá led others to occupy the port of Monterey. Following the coast and the Salinas Valley, he reached Monterey Bay, but failed to recognize it. Continuing up the coast he discovered the present San Francisco Bay and then returned to San Diego.

Monterey founded.—At San Diego affairs had gone badly. Many persons had died, provisions were scarce, and Portolá decided to abandon the enterprise. Persuaded by Serra, he deferred the day of departure, and new supplies came. Another expedition to Monterey was successful, and the presidio and mission of San Carlos were founded there in 1770.

Plans for expansion.—At last the long talked of ports of San Diego and Monterey had been occupied. But the newly found port of San Francisco, further north, needed protection, the large Indian population called for more missions, settlers were lacking, and permanent naval and land bases were necessary. One by one these matters were considered and adjusted. To assist in the plans for expansion Serra went to Mexico in 1772 and made many recommendations. The temporary naval base at San Blas was made permanent, and thereafter played an important part in the development of California. The new foundations were assured support from the Pious Fund, and in 1771 and 1772 three new missions were founded—San Antonio,

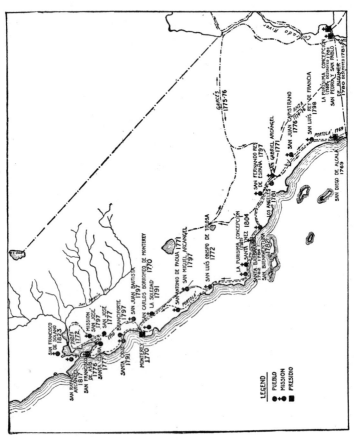

Alta California Settlements

San Gabriel, and San Luis Obispo. In 1772 California was divided, the peninsula being assigned to the Dominicans. Politically the two Californias were continued under one governor, with his residence at Loreto, Fages being replaced as commander in the north by Rivera y Moncada.

A land route to California.—The next step was the opening of a land route from Arizona to California, and was the work especially of two frontier leaders. When the Franciscans in 1768 took the place of the Jesuits in Pimería Alta, Father Francisco Garcés was sent to San Xavier del Bac, the northern outpost. He at once began to make visits to the Gila, and in 1771 alone he crossed the Yuma Desert from Sonóita, and the California Desert to the foot of the western Sierras. Encouraged by these discoveries, Captain Anza of Tubac offered to open a land route to Monterey. The plan was approved by the viceroy, and in 1774 Anza, with Garcés as guide and with twenty soldiers, made the expedition, with great hardships but with notable success.

San Francisco founded.—The opening of the land route from Sonora facilitated the occupation of the port of San Francisco. Plans for its occupation had been discussed ever since its discovery by Portolá. Meanwhile the region had been throughly explored from Monterey as a base. In December, 1774, Anza was ordered to lead a soldier colony from Sonora to occupy the port, and plans were made for a mission. Enlisting some two hundred and fifty persons, Anza assembled them at Tubac, and in October set out for California. Descending the Santa Cruz and Gila Rivers to the Colorado, thence he followed his former trail to Monterey, where he arrived in March, 1776. Aided by Father Font, he reëxplored the Bay region, selected sites for a presidio and mission, and returned to Sonora. In September the presidio and in October the mission of San Francisco were founded.

A route from New Mexico.—The Sonora base for California was not altogether satisfactory and some thought that New Mexico would serve better. Among the latter was Father Garcés, and by a most remarkable exploration he put his views to the test. He accompanied Anza's second expedition to the Gila-Colorado junction, but from there set out to explore a new route.

Ascending the Colorado to the Mojave tribe, near Needles he turned west and crossed the Mojave Desert. It was his plan to go straight to San Luis Obispo, but his guides refused, and he threaded Cajón Pass to Mission San Gabriel. From there he continued through Téjon Pass into the San Joaquin Valley, descended it to the Tulare region, emerged through an eastern pass, probably the Tehachapi, and recrossed the desert to the Mojaves. Thence he continued east to the Moquis, reaching Oraibe on July 2. Here he was given a cold reception, so he turned back to the Yumas.

Exploration by Escalante and Domínguez.—Shortly after Garcés returned, a party set out from Santa Fé to attempt reaching Monterey by a more northern route. The party consisted of Fathers Domínguez and Escalante, Captain Bernardo de Miera y Pacheco, and nine soldiers. Leaving Santa Fé on July 29, 1776, they went northward into Colorado, followed the western line across the San Juan, Dolores, Grand and Colorado Rivers, turned westward to Utah Lake and south past Sevier Lake. In October, concluding that it was too late to attempt to cross the Sierras, they returned eastward to Moqui, Zuñi, and Santa Fé. Thus had another great feat of exploration resulted from the attempt to find land connection with California.

Spanish Pueblos.—California still lacked the civil element to make it complete in outline, and this was now provided. In 1777 Governor Neve moved his capital from Loreto to Monterey, where he received orders from the viceroy to take steps toward founding colonies of settlers, as a means toward making the province self-supporting. Neve therefore proceeded to establish two Spanish pueblos.

San José.—With fourteen families from Monterey and San Francisco, in 1777 Lieutenant Moraga founded the Pueblo of San José in the Santa Clara Valley, near the head of San Francisco Bay, and near by the mission of Santa Clara was founded. The pueblo was established according to the general laws of the Indies. Five years later titles were issued to those settlers who had fulfilled their contracts.

Los Angeles.—The second pueblo was located beside Mission San Gabriel, in the southern part of the province. To procure colonists Rivera y Moncada was sent in 1779 to Sinaloa and

Sonora. Recruiting fourteen families, Rivera sent them overland by way of Loreto and the Peninsula. Rivera himself,
with forty-two soldiers, went with nearly a thousand head
of horses and mules over the Anza route by way of the Gila
junction, where he and part of his men were massacred.
The settlers reached their destination, and in September, 1781,
the Pueblo de los Angeles was founded, with eleven families
comprising forty-six persons.

Plans for a new outpost.—The old question of advancing
the Sonora frontier northward to provide missions for the Pimas
and Yumas, and a halfway station on the road to California,
had been much discussed ever since Anza's exploration in 1774.
Opinions varied as to the best location, one proposing the Gila-
Colorado junction, another the middle Gila, another the Colorado
above the Yumas, and another even the Moqui country.

Mission-Pueblos at Yuma.—But the weight of opinion was
with the Gila-Colorado junction. The chief advocate of this
location was the Yuma chief Ollyquotquiebe. In 1776 he
went with Anza to Mexico City to ask for a mission and a
presidio, made submission for his tribe, and was baptized as
Salvador Palma. In the following year the king ordered the
petition granted. Delays ensued and Palma became impatient.
In 1779 Fathers Garcés and Díaz were sent, with a small garrison,
to Palma's village. Their slender outfit of presents and supplies
was disappointing, and the Yumas were dissatisfied. In the
following year, at Croix's order, two missions were founded west
of the Colorado, at the junction, but not of the usual type.
Instead of a presidio, ten families were settled near each mission
to serve as a protection to the missionaries and an example to
the neophytes, who were to live among the settlers instead of
in an Indian pueblo.

The massacre.—Trouble soon ensued, and in July, 1781,
while Rivera y Moncada was on his way to found Los Angeles,
the Yumas, led by Palma, massacred Father Garcés, his three
companions, Rivera and his men, and most of the settlers. The
women and children were spared. The experience at the Yuma
missions is a pointed commentary on the need of soldiers to
control mission Indians, and on the wisdom of the usual Spanish
custom of separating the neophytes from the settlers. For his

part in the plan Croix has been severely critized, but it must be remembered that at the time he needed every soldier available for the Apache wars, and that the Yumas had much vaunted their friendship.

The Yumas punished.—Learning of the massacre, in September, 1781, Croix sent Pedro Fages to the scene with one hundred and ten men from Pitic and Altar. In the course of two journeys he ransomed some seventy-five captives. In the following year Captain Romeu, of Sonora, made a campaign against the Yumas, killed or captured nearly two hundred, and recovered over one thousand horses. But the massacre put an end for the time being to the long series of efforts to establish the Yuma outpost, and practically closed the Anza route to California.

The Santa Barbara Channel occupied.—From the first Father Serra had been anxious to found a group of missions among the numerous Indians along the Santa Barbara Channel, but there had been a lack of funds and soldiers. The reduction of these tribes was important also from a military standpoint, because they held a strategic position on the coast and on the road to the north. With the coming of more soldiers in 1781 the desired step was taken, and in 1782 Mission San Buenaventura and the presidio of Santa Barbara, and in 1786 Mission Santa Barbara were founded.

With the occupation of this district California was complete in outline. There were four presidios, each occupying a strategic position and protecting a group of missions. In the succeeding years new missions were planted in the interior valleys, till the total reached twenty-one. They became marvellously prosperous, converting and giving industrial training to thousands of Indians, and acquiring great wealth in farms and herds. In 1784 Father Serra, the master spirit of the missions, died.

NORTHERN EXPLORATIONS

English and Russian activities.—Continued rumors of Russian and English activities had by now led to a new series of explorations which gave Spain claim to the Pacific Coast for nearly a thousand miles beyond the points reached by Cabrillo and Vizcaino. In 1773 came rumors that an English expedition was about to attempt to pass through the Northern Strait to Cali-

fornia, and that Russia was planning an expedition from Kamt-
chatka to the American coast.

Pérez.—Accordingly, in 1774 Viceroy Bucarely sent Juan
Pérez north in the *Santiago* with orders to take formal possession
of the country as far as 60°. Sailing from San Blas, and taking
on Fathers Crespi and Peña at Monterey as diarists, Pérez sailed
to 55°, exploring Nootka Sound on the way.

Heçeta and Bodega.—Pérez having failed to reach 60°, another expedition was sent from San Blas in 1775 in two vessels,
under Heçeta and Bodega y Quadra. Heçeta reached 49°, discovering Trinidad Bay and the mouth of the Columbia River on
the way (1776). Bodega, in his thirty-six foot schooner, reached
58°, and on the way discovered Bodega Bay.

Arteaga and Bodega.—No Russians had been found, but
news had come of the preparations being made by the English
captain, James Cook, for a voyage to the northwest coast in
search of the strait. Accordingly, another expedition was ordered
by the King of Spain to explore to 70°. Through delays it was
1779 before Arteaga and Bodega, in the *Favorita* and the *Princesa*,
left San Blas. Meanwhile Cook had made his famous voyage
to Nootka Sound. Arteaga's expedition reached 60°, where it
was forced to return because of scurvy among the crews.

LOUISIANA UNDER SPAIN, 1762–1783

The cession.—On October 9, 1762, Louis XV offered western
Louisiana, with New Orleans, to Charles III, king of Spain,
both as a compensation for the loss of Florida, and to put an
end to the constant Franco-Spanish friction over contraband
trade. Charles at first rejected the gift, but reconsidered, and
the treaty of cession was signed on November 3, the day of the
signature of the preliminaries of the peace with England.

The state of the province.—With Spain's small means and
great responsibilities, the gift was not very tempting, and Spain
was not eager to take possession of it. The ceded district embraced New Orleans and the western watershed of the Mississippi
River. The principal settlements lay along the Mississippi and
Missouri, as far as the Kansas post, and along the lower Red
River, as far as the Cadadacho post. The bulk of the population
lay between Pointe Coupée and New Orleans, where there were

over 7000 persons, of whom nearly two-thirds were colored.
Other settlements in the lower district were La Balize, Attakapa,
Opelousas, Avoyelle, and Natchitoches. On the way to the Missouri district were the post opposite Natchez and the Arkansas
settlement. Near or on the Missouri were St. Charles and Ste.
Genevieve. Farther in the interior were slender trading posts,
such as St. Louis among the Cadadacho, a post on the Osage,
and Ft. Cavagnolle, near the mouth of the Kansas River. The
total population of the province ceded to Spain was estimated
at from 8250 to 11,500, over half of whom were colored.

Industries.—Rice, indigo, tobacco, and grain were cultivated in small quantities, but there was little stock raising. For
horses, mules, and cattle dependence was placed upon trade
with the Indians and the Spaniards of the West, much of which
trade was contraband. The principal industries of the province
were the fur trade and commerce with Illinois. The paper money
issued during the recent war, of which there was nearly a million
unredeemed, had depreciated to 25 per cent. of its face value.

Dissatisfaction with the transfer.—It was not till September,
1764, that the cession was known in New Orleans. The news
caused consternation and protest. Some of the inhabitants
of Illinois, left under English rule, moved across the Mississippi
River to La Clede's recently founded fur-trading post of St.
Louis. When, in 1765, the British took possession of Fort Chartres, Captain St. Ange, in charge of the latter place, moved with
his garrison to St. Louis, where he continued to rule until Spanish
possession was taken. Some French settlers from the more
southern districts moved across the Mississippi or to New
Orleans. There the feeling was intense. In January, 1765, the
inhabitants held a meeting and sent a delegate, Jean Milhet, to
France to remonstrate, but without avail, for after months of
waiting he failed even to get an audience with the king.

Ulloa expelled.—At last, in March, 1766, Don Antonio de
Ulloa arrived at La Balize as Spanish governor. The choice
was not a happy one, for although a distinguished scientist and
naval officer, Ulloa had an unpleasant and inflexible personality
which made him unpopular. In July he reached New Orleans,
with ninety soldiers. But the French militia refused to serve
him, and Aubry was left in command. Bickerings and dissatis-

faction followed. The colonists demanded the redemption of the depreciated paper money at face value; the recently arrived Acadians, who had become indentured servants, made constant complaint, until at last redeemed by Ulloa.

Ulloa did not confine his efforts to New Orleans, but established Spanish garrisons at several interior posts and issued ordinances regarding the Indian trade. In the spring of 1766, with Aubry, he visited the settlements between New Orleans and Natchitoches, and sent an officer to report on the best means of defending the upper posts against the English. In 1767 he sent Captain Francisco Rui to establish posts on the lower Missouri at St. Charles and Bellefontaine.

The prohibition of trade with France, promulgated in October, 1768, caused a veritable insurrection in New Orleans, and Ulloa was expelled from the province. His departure was followed by a removal of the Spanish garrisons from the Missouri and elsewhere in the interior, and there was an interregnum of several months, during which Aubry governed.

O'Reilly.—Charles III now sent a man made of sterner stuff. He was Alexandro O'Reilly, an officer who had served with distinction in Europe, had reorganized the defences of Havana after the recent war, and was now recalled to cope with the situation in Louisiana. With 4500 regulars he reached Balize in July, 1769. There was renewed excitement. Some talked of independence and others of joining the English colonies; but Aubry counselled against resistance and the disturbance subsided.

His coup d'état.—King Charles had demanded nothing more severe than the sending of the leaders of the opposition to France, but O'Reilly was not so mild. By a ruse he arrested a number of prominent citizens, executed five and imprisoned others. For this violent deed he has become known as "The Bloody O'Reilly." If the government of Charles III had been imbued with a full sense of its responsibility, it would never have left unpunished such a violation of the fundamental rules of justice.

The Spanish régime installed.—For thirty-four years Louisiana remained under Spanish rule, and during that time it prospered as never before. O'Reilly governed for a year or more with great vigor, not as governor, but as special commissioner to establish Spanish authority. Possession was taken of the

interior posts, and by the end of 1770 the Spanish flag had been
raised at Ste. Genevieve, the last place to haul down the French
emblem.   Having accomplished his coup d'état, O'Reilly was
conciliatory, and appointed numerous old French officers, like
Villiers and De Mézières, to important positions. After authority
had been established, the military force was reduced to 1200 men.
Spanish law was installed, although the French Black Code was
retained.   New Orleans was given a cabildo with direct appeal
to the Council of the Indies instead of to the Audiencia of Santo
Domingo.   Louisiana was put under a governor, the first incumbent being Luis de Unzaga y Amezaga.   Each of the principal
subdistricts was put under a lieutenant-governor, Pedro Piernas
going to St. Louis, Villiers to the Arkansas Post (now Fort
Carlos III), and Athanase De Mézières at Natchitoches.   Until
1771 Louisiana was an independent *gobierno* directly dependent
on the Council of the Indies.   In 1771 it was attached for military
purposes to the captaincy-general of Havana, and for judicial
matters to the Audiencia of Santo Domingo.   In 1795 it was attached to the Audiencia of Havana.   After 1783 West Florida and
Louisiana were put under one governor.   Later the province
was divided into Upper and Lower Louisiana.

Unzaga and Gálvez.—Unzaga ruled till 1776, and proved
popular, particularly since he shut his eyes to English smuggling
in the lower Mississippi River.   Unzaga's successor, Bernardo de
Gálvez, nephew of the visitor, son of the viceroy, and himself
a viceroy later, was a remarkable man.   He too, was popular; he
married a French wife, and stimulated tobacco raising by pledging
himself to buy each year eight hundred pounds of tobacco.

Encouragement of commerce.—Trade regulations, as promulgated by Ulloa in 1766, restricted all trade to Spanish vessels,
and certain specified Spanish ports.   Under these conditions
English smugglers very soon monopolized the trade of the lower
Mississippi, and made their way among the tribes of the Gulf
coast.   This contraband Unzaga tacitly permitted for the good
of the colony.   In 1776 an agreement was made with France by
which Louisiana was permitted to trade with the French West
Indies, under the supervision of two French commissioners resident in New Orleans.   Gálvez now promptly seized eleven English vessels and the commerce of the colony passed largely into

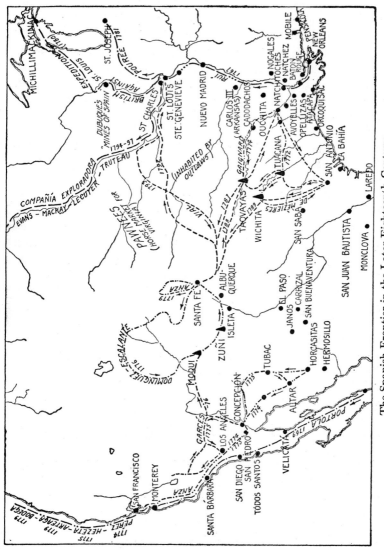

The Spanish Frontier in the Later Eighteenth Century

the hands of the French. In 1778 the produce of the colony was admitted to any of the ports of France or the United States, and to any of the ports of Spain to which the commerce of any of the colonies was admitted. The exportation of furs was encouraged by exemption from duty for a period of ten years. English trade in Louisiana was now completely ruined. Under Spanish rule population grew steadily and by 1803 had reached about 50,000. After the American Revolution efforts were made to counter-colonize against the American advance.

The English danger.—The principal military problems of the new government were to keep the English out and to keep the Indians quiet. Already English traders were entering the tribes west of the Mississippi, ascending the Missouri and the Arkansas, and reaching the borders of Texas overland, or ascending its rivers from the Gulf of Mexico. Trade in Pawnee and Spanish horses extended to the English seaboard colonies, Governor Patrick Henry being among the purchasers of thoroughbred Spanish stock. To keep out the English, defence was concentrated on the Mississippi and efforts made to control the Indian tribes.

Eastern Texas abandoned.—On the other hand, since Louisiana belonged to Spain, the defences of eastern Texas, and the weak missions which they protected, were now withdrawn. At the same time the few settlers, some five hundred in number, who lived on the border, were evicted and taken to San Antonio. But they demurred, sent their Creole leader Gil Ybarbo to Mexico to represent them, and were allowed in 1774 to settle on the Trinity River. Five years later, taking advantage of a flood and Indian raids, and led by Ybarbo, they moved to Nacogdoches (1779), and from there scattered eastward toward their former homes.

The fur trade continued.—Louisiana was Spain's first colony previously occupied by Europeans, and in it many departures were made from her traditional system. As a means of controlling the Indians of Louisiana, Spain utilized the corps of French traders already among the tribes, instead of attempting to use the mission as a means of control, as was being done at the same time in California. A regular system of licensed traders was installed, vagabonds and unlicensed persons were driven from the tribes, presents were annually distributed, and medals of merit were given to friendly chiefs. St. Louis, the Arkansas post, and Natchitoches became important centers for the fur trade and for distributing presents. To St Louis tribes went to receive presents from the Illinois country, the upper Mississippi, and the upper Missouri. To remove them from English influence, tribes were induced to cross the Mississippi to settle.

De Mézières.—One of the most difficult problems which confronted Spain was the control of the Red River tribes, which had been friendly to the French but hostile to the Spaniards. It was now necessary to win them over to Spanish allegiance. This was accomplished by Athanase de Mézières, lieutenant-governor at Natchitoches. He installed French traders, drove out vagabonds, expelled English intruders, called in the hostile Red River tribes to make treaties, and himself made a series of notable tours among them. In 1770 he held a great council at the Cadodacho post, where the Cadodacho chief Tin-hi-ou-en was mediator. Two years later he made an expedition through the Asinai, Tonkawa, and Wichita tribes, reaching the upper Brazos River, and going thence to San Antonio. His excellent report first made northern Texas well known to Spanish officials.

Croix's plans for a war on the Apaches.—It was in 1776 that the northern provinces of New Spain were put under a *comandante general* with his capital at Chihuahua. The first comandante, Teodoro de Croix, arrived at the frontier in 1777. As his first great task he set about checking Indian hostilities, particularly those of the Apaches on the Texas-Coahuila frontier. The essence of his plan was to unite the Red River and the eastern Texas tribes (the Nations of the North) and *chasseurs* from Louisiana, commanded by Gálvez, with the soldiery of the Interior Provinces, commanded by Croix, in a joint war of extermination against the eastern Apaches.

Set aside by the American Revolution.—To consider the matter Croix held a council of war at San Antonio in January, 1778. The arrangement of details with the Indians was left to De Mézières. In 1778 he made a tour of the upper Red River, and in the following year again visited the Texas tribes. Spain soon afterward entered the American war, Gálvez was unable to leave Louisiana, and the conduct of the Apache War was left for the time being to Juan de Ugalde, governor of Coahuila.

Communication with Santa Fé and the Upper Missouri.—
The explorations of De Mézières were soon followed by the opening of routes from Santa Fé to San Antonio, Natchitoches, and
St. Louis.   In this work the chief pathfinder was Pedro Vial.
Just as the American Pike in his southwestern exploration (1807)
was preceded by Vial and his associates, so Lewis and Clark, in
their ascent of the Missouri River (1804), were anticipated by
the agents of Clamorgan's fur trading and exploring company,
who operated from St. Louis to the country of the Mandans
(1794–1797).

READINGS

REFORMS OF CHARLES III AND GÁLVEZ

Addison, Joseph, *Charles the Third of Spain;* Altamira y Crevea, Rafael,
Historia de España, IV; Chapman, C. E., *The Founding of Spanish California,* ch. IV; Danvila y Collado, Manuel, *Reinado de Carlos III;* Desdevises
du Desert, Gaston, *L'Espagne de l'Ancien Régime;* Ferrer del Rio, Antonio,
Historia del Reinado de Carlos III; Hume, M. A. S., *Spain: Its Greatness and
Decay;* Priestley, H. I., *José de Gálvez, Visitor-General of New Spain;* Rousseau, François, *Règne de Charles III d'Espagne, 1759–1788;* Scelle, G., *La
Traite Négriere aux Indes de Castille;* Viollet, A., *Historie des Bourbons
d'Espagne.*

CALIFORNIA

Academy of Pacific Coast History, *Publications,* I–III; Bancroft, H. H.,
History of California, I, 110–480; Chapman, C. E., *The Founding of Spanish
California;* Eldredge, Z. S., *The Beginnings of San Francisco,* I, 31–170;
Engelhardt, Fr. Zephyrin, *Missions and Missionaries of California,* I, 289–
385; II, 3–414; Hittell, T. H., *History of California,* I, 300–429; 441–452;
509–540; Norton, H. K., *Story of California,* 1–103; Palou, Fr. Francisco,
Relación Histórica de la Vida [de] . . . *Serra;* Richman, I. B., *California
under Spain and Mexico,* 32–158.

LOUISIANA

Bolton, Herbert E., *Athanase de Mézières and the Louisiana-Texas
Frontier,* I, 66–122; Gayarré, C., *History of Louisiana,* III, 1–617; Hamilton,
P. J., *The Colonization of the South,* 423–445; 447–456; Houck, L., *The
Spanish Régime in Missouri,* I–II; Mason, E. C., "The March of the Span-
iards across Illinois," in *Magazine of American History,* XV, 457–470;
Robertson, J. A., *Louisiana under the rule of Spain, France, and the United
States;* Shepherd, W. R., "The Cession of Louisiana to Spain," in *The
Political Science Quarterly,* XIX, 439–458; Teggart, F. J., "Capture of
St. Joseph, Michigan, by the Spaniards in 1781," in *The Missouri Historical
Review,* V, 214–228; Thwaites, R. G., *France in America,* 281–295.

CHAPTER XXII

THE NEW BRITISH POSSESSIONS

PROVISIONS FOR DEFENCE, GOVERNMENT, AND THE FUR
TRADE

Amherst's plan for defence.—While the Spaniards were occupying western Louisiana the British were organizing the country ceded by France and Spain east of the Mississippi, in Canada,
and in the West Indies. In 1763 the Secretary of War asked
General Amherst, commander-in-chief in America, for a plan
of defence of the British possessions. In response he drew up a
"Plan of Forts and Garrisons prepared for the security of North
America" which reveals England's outlook upon her newly acquired territory. It provided for ten regiments of approximately
seven hundred and fifty men each. The stated purposes were:
(1) to keep the king's new subjects in Canada and Louisiana
"in due subjection," (2) to keep the old provinces "in a state of
Constitutional Dependence upon Great Britain," (3) to command
the respect of the Indians, (4) to prevent encroachments of the
French or Spaniards, (5) and to protect the colonies in case of
war. The regiments were to be distributed in posts along the
St. Lawrence, about the Great Lakes, in the Illinois country,
along the lower Mississippi, and in Nova Scotia, South Carolina,
Georgia, and the Floridas.

Purposes regarding the West.—Regarding the interior posts
the particular aims expressed were to keep open the navigation
of the St. Lawrence and the Great Lakes, maintain communication between Canada and the Gulf of Mexico, hold the western
tribes in check, and guard against French or Spanish intrusion.
A post at St. Augustine was especially desirable as a defence
against Spain, and Pensacola and Mobile would command the
commerce of the Gulf as well as the tribes of the Alabama Basin.
The lower Mississippi posts were essential to control the Chickasaws. A post at Crown Point was not only needed to maintain

a winter highway to Canada, but might also be useful to suppress disaffection in the maritime colonies, "who already begin to entertain some extraordinary Opinions, concerning their Relations to and Dependence upon the Mother Country."

The Proclamation of 1763.—In October, 1763, the king issued a proclamation creating, within the newly acquired territory, four distinct provinces, Quebec, East Florida, West Florida, and Grenada, and providing a form of government for them. Quebec comprised the Valley of the St. Lawrence from the western end of Anticosti Island to the 45th parallel and Lake Nipissing. Labrador, Anticosti, and the Magdalen Islands were attached to Newfoundland. St. Johns, Cape Breton, and the lesser adjacent islands were attached to Nova Scotia.

East Florida extended to Appalachicola River, and was bounded on the north by St. Mary's River and a line from the head of that stream to the junction of the Chattahoochee and Flint Rivers. The district between St. Mary's and Altamaha Rivers, formerly in dispute between Spain and England, was attached to Georgia. West Florida was the district south of latitude 31° and between the Appalachicola River and the Isle of Orleans. The Island of Grenada, the Grenadines, St. Vincent's, and Tobago were erected into the Government of Grenada.

Crown colonies created.—These new jurisdictions were made crown colonies. For each a governor was to be appointed, with power to call assemblies, "in such Manner and Form as is used and directed in the Colonies and Provinces in America which are under our immediate Government." Until such assemblies should meet, the governors, with their executive councils, were empowered to erect courts, having appeals to the privy council.

The Indian reservation.—For the time being all British possessions on the continent not included in the foregoing jurisdictions, or within the Territory of Hudson Bay, and all lands west or north of the streams flowing into the Atlantic Ocean, were reserved as crown lands for the use of the Indians. No colony might grant lands within this Indian reservation, and settlers were requested to move out. The considerable French settlements in the reserve were ignored.

Until 1755 the English government had managed its Indian affairs through the different colonies, but the results were far

from satisfactory. In that year the government assumed political control over the Indians, creating a southern and a northern
department, and appointing a superintendent for each. In 1761

The New British Possessions, 1763–1783

the purchase of Indian lands was taken out of the hands of the
colonies.

Regulation of Indian trade.—The acquisition of extensive
territories in 1763 called for new trade regulations. The proclamation had created an Indian reserve and opened trade to all

duly licensed subjects. In the following year Lord Hillsborough drew up a general plan for the management of Indians and the fur trade. It safeguarded the rights of the Hudson's Bay Company and provided for the continuation of the two superintendents, with three deputies for the northern and two for the southern district. In the North all trade must be conducted at regularly established posts, and in the South at the Indian towns. All traders must be licensed, must trade at schedule prices, and must have no dealings with Indians except at the prescribed places. By 1768 the plan had proved too expensive, and the management of the fur trade was restored to the individual colonies.

THE OCCUPATION OF THE FLORIDAS

The West Florida posts.—On August 6, 1763, Colonel Prevost took possession of Pensacola, which became the capital of West Florida. Shortly afterwards Mobile was occupied by Major Robert Farmar. The French troops there withdrew to New Orleans, as did some of the people, but most of the latter remained. Fort Tombecbé, renamed Fort York, was given a garrison of thirty men, for the express purpose of keeping the Choctaws hostile to the Chickasaws, but was abandoned in 1768. The French among the Choctaws moved across the Mississippi into Spanish territory, but continued to trade with the tribe.

The boundary and the river forts.—In 1764 the northern boundary of West Florida was moved north to 32° 28′ to take in the Natchez settlements, and to make room for the land speculators who were seeking land grants on the lower Mississippi. A garrison was placed at Natchez (Fort Panmure). In connection with efforts to keep the Mississippi open and to establish navigation through the Iberville River, Fort Bute was built near the latter stream in 1766. These Mississippi posts were designed also to prevent French and Spanish smuggling among the Choctaws. But there was English smuggling likewise, and to stop it Spanish posts were later built on the other bank of the river. In 1769 the troops of most of the English posts were withdrawn to St. Augustine, but there was a protest at once. Pensacola drew up a memorial, and immigrants recently arrived at the

Mississippi demanded protection. O'Reilly had just come to New Orleans, and it was feared that he might have designs on West Florida. In 1770, therefore, most of the troops were restored, and a new garrison was established at Manchac.

Indian agents and fur magnates.—The possession of West Florida proved an important asset to Great Britain in the control of the southwestern Indians, especially during the Revolution. John Stuart, Superintendent for the Southern Department, made his headquarters at Pensacola, but Mobile was the real center of control for the whole Southwest. Subagents convened at Mobile a great congress of all the tribes and effected an alliance with them, and soon afterward the Indian lands about Mobile were ceded to the English. The military authorities encouraged inter-tribal dissensions, and the Creeks and Choctaws were frequently at war, in which the Chickasaws sometimes joined. According to the general system, the fur trade of the Southwest was opened to all traders having a government license and a proper bond. The fur magnates at Mobile were the house of Swanson and McGillivray, who by 1777 had a branch house at Fort Bute, which conducted trade with the Illinois. At Pensacola Panton, Leslie, and Company, the largest business house, became an important factor in the trade and in the management of the tribes.

Politics and government.—West Florida was accorded a governor, council, and assembly. Governor George Johnstone arrived at Pensacola in October, 1764, but the first assembly was not elected until 1766. Mobile, Pensacola, and Campbell Town were electoral precincts at first, and after 1778 Natchez and Manchac were represented. The brief political experiences of the province were as interesting as those of the older colonies in early days. The governor and assembly frequently quarreled. In 1772 Governor Chester prorogued that body and for six years got along without it. More harmful than these quarrels were the factional disputes between the civil and military officials.

Development of West Florida.—When England took possession, Pensacola consisted of some forty thatched huts and small barracks, all enclosed within a palisade, but it was rebuilt, and practically dates from British rule. Mobile remained largely French, and was reduced in size by the emigration to New Orleans. British rule gave impetus to Mobile's commerce, and by 1776 the port was paying £4000 a year to the London custom house alone.

Immigration.—Efforts were made also to secure immigrants for West Florida. In 1763 the Board of Trade put an advertisement regarding land grants in the *London Gazette*, and in 1764 Governor Johnstone issued a circular to attract settlers. In 1765 or 1766 a colony from North Carolina went by sea and settled about Natchez and Baton Rouge. Speculators obtained large grants of land about Natchez as early as 1767, among them being Daniel Clark, later a great figure at New Orleans. Before the Revolution numerous settlers arrived from England, the West Indies, and most of the mainland colonies, including New England. Most of them settled on the Mississippi River between Manchac and Natchez. In 1772 three hundred persons from Virginia and the Carolinas are said to have been established on the lower Mississippi, and three or four hundred families were expected that summer. As a result, the Mississippi posts were repaired and civil government established. In 1775 a considerable immigration from New England was led by General Lyman. About the same time Colonel Putnam led a company from New England to the Yazoo district. In 1777, according to the botanist Bartram, more than half of the population of Mobile were people who had come from the northern colonies and Great Britain.

During the Revolution West Florida was a refuge for Loyalists. In November, 1776, Mathew Phelps led a colony of New Englanders to the lower Mississippi. Highland soldiers defeated in North Carolina that year took refuge in the province. Loyalists from Georgia and South Carolina settled on the Tombigbee River and Mobile Bay, and others from the same colonies settled on the Tensaws Bayou.

East Florida under British rule.—In East Florida, St. Augustine became the capital and the chief military post. St. Marks on the Gulf was occupied for military purposes and the posts of Matanzas, Picolata, and Mosquito were also maintained for a time. The military of both East and West Florida were under the general command at Pensacola. James Grant was made first governor. In East Florida there was no assembly till 1781. Difficulties between military and civil authorities prevailed as in West Florida.

At the time of the British occupation, St. Augustine was a small Spanish town with adobe houses and narrow streets. Under British rule East Florida prospered. Harbors were improved, and highways were constructed, one being built from St. Mary's River to St. Augustine. In 1766 some forty families went from the Bermudas to Mosquito Inlet to engage in shipbuilding. In the following year Dr. Turnbull brought fifteen hundred indentured colonists from the Mediterranean region and settled them at New Smyrna. In 1776 the indentures were cancelled and the settlers moved to St. Augustine, where their descendants still live. During the Revolution East Florida, like West Florida, became a Mecca for southern Loyalists.

MILITARY OCCUPATION OF THE ILLINOIS COUNTRY

Plans to occupy the Illinois country.—By the end of 1761 British troops had taken possession of all the lake posts from Niagara to Green Bay, besides Venango, Miamis, and Ouiatanon further south. In July, 1763, orders were sent by the Governor of Louisiana for the evacuation of the Illinois posts, and boats were prepared at Fort Pitt for sending four hundred English troops to relieve the French garrisons. But the conspiracy of Pontiac delayed the complete transfer of this region for nearly three years.

The conspiracy of Pontiac.—Early in the war the tribes north of the Ohio had ravaged the Virginia and Pennsylvania frontiers, but after 1758 they had been quiet, although they did not like the English. They feared eviction from their lands, English traders had proved arrogant and dishonest, and General Amherst was attempting a policy of economy in presents, in spite of the criticism of the better informed Indian agents. Pontiac, head chief of the Ottawas, organized a general revolt, embracing the Algonquins, some of the tribes of the lower Mississippi, and some of the Iroquois. By a simultaneous assault in May, 1763, all but three northwestern posts—Detroit, Fort Pitt, and Niagara—fell almost without a blow. At Presq'Isle, Le Boeuf, Venango,

Mackinac, Sandusky, St. Josephs, and Ouiatanon, there were massacres, and the garrison fled from Green Bay.

Failure of the Loftus expedition.—It being impracticable now to send troops to the Illinois country by way of the Ohio, this was attempted by an expedition up the Mississippi. Major Loftus was sent from Mobile with three hundred and fifty men to occupy Fort Massac, Kaskaskia, and Fort Chartres. In February, 1764, he left New Orleans, but when two hundred and forty miles up the river, at Rocher á Davion, he was attacked by Tunica Indians, whereupon he abandoned the expedition and returned to Mobile.

Peace.—While Colonel Bradstreet reoccupied the Lakes, General Gage, Amherst's successor, resorted to conciliation, and a series of peace embassies were sent to the Illinois country from Mobile and from the northern garrisons. The submission of the Ohio tribes, failure of hopes for aid from New Orleans, and news of the transfer of western Louisiana to Spain, led Pontiac to negotiate at Ouiatanon in 1765 with George Croghan. At Detroit Croghan secured peace with all the western tribes. Thomas Stirling then descended the Ohio with a detachment and in October occupied Fort Chartres. "Thus, after nearly three years of fighting and negotiating, British forces were in possession of the last of the French posts in the West."

Establishment of government.—In accordance with the Treaty of Paris a proclamation of General Gage guaranteed the inhabitants the free exercise of the Catholic religion. Settlers were allowed to sell their lands and emigrate, or to become British subjects on taking the oath of allegiance. The inhabitants of Kaskaskia and other places asked and received an extension of the time for decision to March, 1766. Many of them emigrated to St. Louis and Ste. Genevieve, or to New Orleans. The Proclamation of 1763 made no provision for civil government in the Indian reserve, and local administration was left to the military authorities and Indian agents. The French people were dissatisfied, and many misunderstandings arose between them and the English settlers and officers. By 1770 the complaint took the form of a demand for civil government, which was provided in 1774 by the Quebec Act.

LAND SPECULATION AND PLANS FOR WESTERN COLONIES

Western schemes.—Before the French and Indian War grants had been made by the British government of lands beyond the Alleghanies, and settlement on the back lands had been favored as a means of opposing the French and of extending British trade. During the war the frontiers of settlement were contracted, but, in anticipation of victory, new grants were sought and new schemes proposed. Not only were lands desired, but prominent men proposed new colonial governments west of the mountains. Nearly all of the proposals involved territory in the Ohio Valley. After the Albany Congress of 1754 Franklin urged the formation of two barrier colonies in the West. In 1756 Thomas Pownall, ex-governor of New Jersey, made a similar proposal. About the same time Samuel Hazard of Philadelphia promoted the formation of a Presbyterian colony to embrace most of the Ohio Valley and extending across the Mississippi. In 1757 the Greenbrier Company secured 100,000 acres of land on the western waters.

The victory over the French stimulated new speculative and colonizing schemes for the West both in England and America. In June, 1763, the Mississippi Company was formed, composed of prominent Virginians, including Colonel George Washington and Richard Henry Lee. A memorial to the king was drawn asking for 2,500,000 acres on both sides of the lower Ohio, quit rent free for twelve years, and protection by royal forts, on condition of settling two hundred families. Late in 1763 a pamphlet published in Edinborough, Scotland, proposed a colony named Charlotiana, to include the country between the Wabash, Ohio, Mississippi, and the Great Lakes. About the same time Charles Lee proposed a colony on the Illinois and another on the Ohio.

Effect of the Proclamation.—The Proclamation of 1763 closing the Trans-Alleghany country to settlement seems to have checked for a time the schemes for speculation. The Proclamation contained an implied promise that the boundary would be revised, while it was well known that influential politicians in England favored the opening of the West. New schemes for western lands, therefore, were not long suppressed. In 1766 William Franklin, governor of New Jersey, launched a plan for two colonies, one at Detroit, the other on the lower Ohio. Through the aid of Benjamin Franklin, father of the governor, the Ohio country was favored by the Board of Trade, but in 1768 the plan dropped from sight. Meanwhile many other land companies were formed.

A policy of expansion adopted.—The policy of the ministry regarding the West was vacillating, and more so, no doubt, because of the pressure of conflicting interests. But in 1768 the ministry decided on a definite plan for western settlement, the principle being that expansion should be gradual and under control of imperial agents, who should purchase land from the Indians as needed. Johnson and Stuart, Indian superintendents, had already made tentative arrangements for revising the proclamation line. In 1765 the Six Nations ceded their claims to lands between the Ohio and the Tennessee. Stuart, by a series of treaties, secured a line from the southern boundary of Virginia to the St. Mary's River, Florida, thence along the tidewater line to the Appalachicola River. West of that point the line was not completed, but important cessions were made along the Mobile coast. In 1768 the former lines were ratified, and Stuart, in two treaties with the Cherokees and Creeks (October, November, 1768), secured the extension of the line to the mouth of the Kanawha River on the north and to the Choctaw River on the south. At Fort Stanwix in 1768 the Iroquois ratified essentially their cession of 1765. The lines did not correspond, since the Iroquois cession included Western Tennessee and Kentucky, which were not within the other cessions. Meanwhile the southern line was modified by the treaty of Lochaber by running it west along the southern boundary of Virginia to the Holston River, thence direct to the mouth of the Kanawha. The purpose of the change was to take in the recently formed Watauga settlement.

Vandalia.—Having extinguished the Indian titles, it was now possible to found a new colony back of Pennsylvania and Virginia, and such a project was put on foot. Samuel Wharton of Philadelphia formed a company for the purpose of purchasing part of the lands. The company included some of the leading men in England and America, among them being Benjamin Franklin and Thomas Walpole. Official aid was enlisted by including two members of the ministry. In 1769 the purchase was made, and, in spite of Lord Hillsborough's opposition, by 1775 the project of a new and separate province named Vandalia had been approved by king and council. The outbreak of the Revolution set the plan aside. Had it been carried out it would have cut Virginia off from her back lands. The Quebec Act of 1774 operated in the same direction, by attaching the Northwest to Quebec. Virginia therefore resisted. Governor Dunmore opposed the Vandalia colony, made grants of land both within and beyond it, and joined a company which purchased Indian lands north of the Ohio.

TRANS-ALLEGHANY SETTLEMENT

Western settlements before 1763.—But it was the backwoodsmen, and not the corporations, who opened the Trans-Alleghany country. Before the war a few settlements had been made on the western waters, In 1748 Draper's Meadows, on the Greenbrier, in West Virginia, were settled. Between 1750 and 1752 a settlement was made by the Ohio Company at Redstone on the Monongahela. By 1758 several small settlements had been made on the Holston, Watauga, and Cheat Rivers. But during the war these western settlements were abandoned, and the frontier pushed eastward a hundred miles or more.

The westward movement after the war.—The French and Indian War was scarcely over when the westward movement began again, regardless of proclamations or the deliberations of the Board of Trade. In 1760 Daniel Boone, from the Yadkin in North Carolina, "cilled a bar" on the Watauga River. Between 1761 and 1765 Wallen annually led hunters to the west. In 1765 Croghan surveyed the Ohio River, and the next year James Smith and others explored the Tennessee. In 1767 Finley was in Kentucky, and Stoner, Harrod, and Lindsay were at French Lick (the site of Nashville). In 1767 and 1770 Boone was "prospecting" for Judge Richard Henderson, a land speculator of North Carolina. At the same time Mansker led a party down the Cumberland and on to Natchez. By this time others had wandered far beyond the Mississippi and were causing the Spanish officials anxiety.

The hunters, traders, and prospectors were followed by surveyors and settlers. The chief participants in the movement were from the middle region and the South:Pennsylvania, Maryland, Virginia, and North Carolina. Prominent among the pioneers on the western waters were the Scotch-Irish who had settled the back country of the older colonies and stood waiting at the western passes.

The Appalachian barrier.—To reach the Mississippi Valley the frontiersman was forced to pass the Appalachian barrier, extending from Maine to Georgia. The easiest pass through it, by way of the Hudson and Mohawk Rivers, was impeded by the Six Nations who stood between the western frontier of settlement and the vacant lands beyond. Farther south the barrier was traversed by a series of interlocking rivers, flowing in opposite directions, whose valleys afforded trails. The Susquehannah led to the Alleghany, the Potomac to the Monongahela, the James and Roanoke to the Great Kanawha, the Great Pedee, the Yadkin, and Catawba to the head waters of the Tennessee. A series of longitudinal valleys on the eastern front of the southern Appalachians gave access from Virginia and North Carolina to the upper Tennessee, from whose valley an easy pass was found to Kentucky by way of Cumberland Gap.

The Indian barrier.—The Iroquois Confederacy, though friendly, was a retarding force to the northern stream of emigration. The Algonquin tribes north of the Ohio had been friendly with the French, and after the French and Indian War they favored the French traders rather than those from the seaboard colonies. At the southern end of the Appalachians westward expansion was retarded by the strong confederacies of the Cherokees, Creeks, Choctaws, and Chickasaws. The region between the Ohio and the Tennessee was the "dark and bloody ground" between the northern and southern tribes, but permanently inhabited by neither. It was this region which was opened to settlement by the Indian cessions between 1768 and 1770. The cessions were followed immediately by a movement of settlers into the area.

THE SETTLEMENT OF EASTERN TENNESSEE

The North Carolina Regulators.—The movement across the mountains was stimulated by a popular upheaval in the back country of North Carolina. Shortly before 1740 the Scotch-Irish and German migration reached North Carolina and by 1765 the lands along the headwaters of the Yadkin, Haw, Neuse, Tar, Catawba, and Deep Rivers had been occupied. Many English and Welsh also had settled in the same region. Between the Piedmont and the coastal plain was a sparsely settled country of pine forests. "Cut off . . . from the men of the east, the men of the 'back country' felt no more sympathy for the former than they received from them." The coast country controlled the legislature and the courts. The men of the West complained that they were forced to pay excessive taxes, that the sheriffs were dishonest, and fees extortionate. An additional grievance was the scarcity of money. During 1765-1767 the frontiersmen began to organize and from 1767 to 1771 the back country was in a state of rebellion. Lawyers were seized and whipped, and the Hillsboro court was broken up. In 1771 the Regulators were defeated by Governor Tryon's troops in the battle of the Alamance and the rebellion soon subsided. During those troubled years many had sought new homes in the western valleys.

The Watauga settlement.—Permanent settlement was made in eastern Tennessee in 1769. In that year a band of pioneers moved down the valley from Virginia and settled on the Watauga River, a branch of the Tennessee, thinking that they were still in Virginia. A short time afterward they were joined by settlers from North Carolina, within whose bounds the colony proved to be. Two able leaders soon emerged. James Robertson, a backwoodsman and a "mighty hunter," went to Watauga in 1770 and took thither a colony of sixteen North Carolina families in 1771. A year later arrived John Sevier, a Virginian of Huguenot extraction. Like Robertson, he was an able Indian fighter and a leader of men.

The Watauga Association.—Finding themselves outside of Virginia and beyond the reach and protection of the North Carolina administration, the settlers, like the Pilgrim Fathers in a similar situation, reverted to the social compact—familiar to Scotch-Irish Presbyterians and to back-country North Carolinians who had "regulated" horse stealing—and formed a government for themselves. In 1772 a convention of the settlers created an independent government called the Watauga Association. It had a written constitution, vesting the administration in an executive committee of five, two of whom were Sevier and Robertson. This committee exercised most of the powers of sovereignty, making treaties, administering justice, granting lands, and making war on the Indians. In 1776 the Watauga Association, realizing the need of help, petitioned the Council of North Carolina to extend its government over the new settlements, and in 1777 they were organized as Washington County.

THE BEGINNINGS OF KENTUCKY

The surveyors and first settlers.—Settlement had also begun in what is now Kentucky. Ahead of the settlers went the prospectors and surveyors, who descended the Ohio and the Kanawha to select and survey lands. In 1770 and 1772 George Washington explored lands in what is now northeastern Kentucky. In 1773 the McAfees led a party of surveyors down the Ohio, crossed Kentucky, and returned over the Cumberland Mountains. In the following year several parties of surveyors and land hunters were sent by Virginia officials to lay out bounty lands for soldiers. Others went without official sanction. One party was led by John Floyd from Fincastle County, Virginia, who descended the Kanawha and Ohio to the Falls, crossed Kentucky, and returned by Cumberland Gap. During his expedition he surveyed lands for George Washington, Patrick Henry, and others. Attempts at settlement had already been made. In 1773 Daniel Boone led a colony from North Carolina toward Kentucky, but was driven back by Indians. The next year Harrod, of Virginia, founded a settlement in Kentucky called Harrodsburg, but it was broken up by Indians, whose hostilities drove out all settlers and land hunters.

Indian ravages.—The border war which now occurred was the culmination of a long series of troubles between the frontiersmen of Pennsylvania and Virginia, and the Indians of the Ohio Valley. The Delawares had been pushed over the Pennsylvania Mountains to the Muskingum and Tuscarawas Rivers. Among them settled the Moravian missionaries, who formed them into Christian towns and kept them peaceful when others were hostile. The Shawanee had been pushed north to the Scioto River, whence they marauded the Virginia border. Behind them were the hostile tribes who had taken part in Pontiac's War. Through 1773 an Indian uprising was threatening, and preparations were made in the westernmost settlements of Virginia. Early in 1774 many settlers fled from the Holston and Clinch Valleys. Minor outrages being committed along the Ohio, alarm spread, and in April there was a retreat across the Monongahela, which was crossed by more than a thousand refugees in a single day.

Lord Dunmore's War.—Governor Dunmore now prepared for war, which, there is some ground for thinking, he helped to bring on as a means of strengthening Virginia's claims to the Northwest. To warn the surveyors and settlers Colonel Preston, lieutenant-sheriff and surveyor of Fincastle County, Virginia, sent Boone and Stoner through Kentucky. They went as far as the Falls of the Ohio, and saved most of the men on the frontier. The governor organized a campaign, himself leading the Virginia regulars down the Ohio, while the frontier levies were led by Colonel Andrew Lewis. They were to meet at the mouth of the Great Kanawha. When Lewis reached that point he was attacked before the arrival of Dunmore by the Indians under Chief Cornstalk, whom he defeated. Thereupon the Indians sued for peace with Dunmore, who had entered their country north of the Ohio. In the following October a treaty was made at Fort Pitt which kept the northern Indians quiet during the first two years of the Revolution and made it possible to settle Kentucky.

Henderson and Transylvania.—Harrodsburg was now re-founded by Virginians (1775) who constituted the majority of the settlers. Henderson, the North Carolina land speculator, formed a land company, called the Transylvania Company. To improve his title in 1775 he made a treaty with the Over-hill Cherokees paying them £10,000 for their claims to lands along and between the Cumberland and the Kentucky. Boone, with a party of thirty men, was sent ahead to clear a road for Henderson's colony from the Holston River to the Kentucky (1775). It became the famous highway known as the Wilderness Road. Henderson followed with his colony, founded Boones-borough, built a fort, and opened a land office, naming his colony

Transylvania. He attempted to set up in the wilderness a modified proprietary régime. Having established his colony, he called
a convention; the delegates made laws which Henderson approved, and a compact was formed between the delegates and
proprietors defining the irrespective rights. The proprietors retained control by reserving to themselves the veto power.

Transylvania absorbed by Virginia.—Henderson's procedure
was regarded as illegal, and he was denounced by the governors
of both Virginia and North Carolina. When the Revolution
broke out the proprietors sent a delegate to the Continental
Congress and appealed to that body for protection, but, largely
through Virginia's influence, the delegation was rejected. The
Virginia settlers in Kentucky, led by Harrod, opposed Henderson's claim to lands, appealed to Virginia, and sent George
Rogers Clark to the assembly. Virginia asserted sovereignty
over Kentucky, and stormy times continued till 1777, when
Kentucky with her present boundaries was organized as Kentucky County, Virginia.

THE UPPER OHIO AND MIDDLE TENNESSEE

Westsylvania.—While Henderson was founding Transylvania
another region west of the mountains was being settled and was
struggling for independent statehood. Emigrants from Pennsylvania, Maryland, Virginia, and other states had crossed the
mountains and settled on the tributaries of the upper Ohio
in what are now western Pennsylvania, West Virginia, and
eastern Ohio. By the middle of 1776 there were said to be
25,000 families on the tributaries of the Ohio above the Scioto
River. But the land which they occupied was in dispute between Virginia and Pennsylvania, and the Indiana and Vandalia Companies, and the settlers took up the struggle, quarreling
over land titles and jurisdiction. The disorders prevented effective organization against the Indians. Shortly after the
Declaration of Independence the settlers memorialized Congress,
asking independent statehood as a "sister colony and fourteenth
province of the American confederacy," under the name of
Westsylvania, whose boundaries they described, but the request
was not granted.

The Cumberland settlement.—Robertson was the type of frontiersmen desirous to be ever on the move. In 1779 he prospected at French Lick, returned to Watauga, raised a colony, and in the fall led it forth. The women and children were conducted by Donelson down the Tennessee and up the Cumberland, while Robertson, guided by Mansker, led the men overland. Nashborough, now Nashville, was founded at the Cumberland Bend, and other stations were occupied along the river. In 1780 a convention formed an "Association" much like that of Watauga, but after three years of independence the district became Davidson County, North Carolina.

THE PROVINCE OF QUEBEC

The French people.—At the time of the conquest the Canadian people numbered about 65,000 living in the St. Lawrence Valley, with several thousand scattered among the western posts. The settlers were in the main a frugal, industrious, unlettered, religious people. They were of two distinct classes, the gentry and the peasant tenants. After the war there was a considerable emigration to France of the official, noble, and commercial classes, leaving chiefly cultivators of the soil and fur traders. By 1775 the population had grown to perhaps 90,000, chiefly through natural increase of the French. By 1784 the population was 113,000.

The British settlers.—The conquest left in the province and attracted to it later a small body of British settlers, but by 1775 they did not number more than five or six hundred. Most of them lived in the towns of Quebec and Montreal, and engaged in business, especially in the fur trade, many as agents for English houses, others being independent merchants. When Hillsborough restored seignorial tenure, many of them acquired seigniories, though they continued to live by trade.

Military rule.—British rule in Canada began with the capitulation of Montreal in September, 1760. General Amherst was made governor-general, with lieutenant-governors at Quebec, Montreal, and Three Rivers. From that time to the enforcement of the Proclamation of 1763 Canada was under military rule. But French law and customs were followed in the main, and there was little discontent.

Civil government established.—Civil government was established in August, 1764. The governor was assisted by an executive council composed of the lieutenant-governor, chief justice, and eight citizens. The government provided by the Proclamation of 1763 was unsuited to a population almost wholly French, professing the Catholic religion, and living under laws and customs of their own. The Proclamation provided for an assembly, but none was held in Quebec because the French people would not take the test oath, and the British settlers were too few in numbers to warrant an assembly representing them alone. Uncertainty existed regarding tithes and the future status of the Catholic Church. The Proclamation contemplated the establishment of British law, but practice was uncertain. The French inhabitants were not politically ambitious, but the British were aggressive in their demands for an assembly and the uniform establishment of English law.

The Quebec Act.—Under these circumstances a change of system was deemed necessary. It was provided by the Quebec Act of 1774, the first parliamentary legislation for Canada. The act maintained the privileges of the Catholic clergy, tithes from Catholic subjects being continued. French civil procedure was established, with some exceptions, but English criminal procedure was enforced. Provision was made for an appointive executive council with powers to make ordinances for the province, but no provision was made for a provincial assembly.

Boundaries extended.—The population of the Illinois country was similar to that of Quebec. The French *habitants* there had been demanding civil government, and it had been complained by the Montreal traders that the prosperity of Canada had been impaired by cutting off the western posts. Therefore the boundaries of Quebec were extended to include the region between the Ohio River and the Upper Mississippi. By the Proclamation of 1763 Labrador east of River St. John's, Anticosti, and the Magdalens, had been attached to Newfoundland. Labrador now began to develop commerce with the interior and the North and with Newfoundland. Opposition to the fishing admirals of Newfoundland caused these three districts to be annexed to Quebec in 1774.

Not intended as a blow at liberty.—The Quebec Act was regarded in the other colonies as a blow at popular liberties and as an encroachment upon colonies whose chartered boundaries extended into the Northwest. It was in fact an administrative act intended primarily as a means of providing for the interests of the great body of the inhabitants, the French. The attachment of the Ohio country to Quebec, however, checked the natural spread of settlement from the seaboard colonies, and the act, on the other hand, prevented the assimilation of the French people by the English in Canada.

The Loyalists in Canada.—During the American Revolution a considerable number of Loyalists crossed into Canada and settled at the border posts. Many others joined the British army against the Americans. At the close of the war some of the border counties of New York were almost depopulated. In 1783 there were in the Montreal district seventeen hundred Loyalists at seventeen posts, not counting enlisted men. Of those who migrated after the revolution the greater number at first settled in Nova Scotia. By the end of 1784 the number there exceeded 28,000 and caused the forming of the new province of New Brunswick. Over three thousand went to Cape Breton Island, and three times that number to the interior of Canada. Thirteen hundred settled at Kingston and formed the nucleus of Upper Canada, which was separated from Lower Canada in 1791. More important than this, the Revolution determined the course of Canadian history. In order not to be absorbed by the United States, Canada was forced into unswerving loyalty to the British Empire.

THE NORTHERN FUR TRADERS

Supervision of the fur trade.—The fur trade of Quebec under the new régime was supervised according to the principles of the Proclamation of 1763. The most fundamental fact was that the French monopolistic system was discontinued, except at certain "King's posts" in the lower St. Lawrence Valley. The trade was open to any duly licensed subject, superintendents were established at the posts, local courts were erected in the interior, and settlement limited to the immediate neighborhood of the posts in order not to drive away the fur bearing animals.

The French traders ruined.—The conquest had destroyed the French fur trading organization.   Under the mercantile system then in vogue, supplies and markets had now to be sought in England.   The French merchants were ruined, and the entire trade of the Great Lake region was thrown into the hands of the British traders.   The French *coureurs de bois*, however, remained in the country, and, in the employ of the British, continued to be the backbone of the fur gathering business in the interior.

The rush to the interior.—As early as 1761 British traders of Montreal began to enter the field left vacant by the French. Pontiac's War caused a suspension of their activities, and during it British traders were plundered and murdered.   By 1765, however, there was a new rush to the interior, though it was 1771 before they could safely trade in the most remote posts on the Saskatchewan.   In the meantime the Indians had learned to take their furs to the posts on Hudson Bay or down the Mississippi.

Extent of operations.—The American Revolution destroyed the western fur trade of the seaboard colonies and threw the commerce of the entire Northwest into the hands of the Quebec and Montreal traders.   By the close of the war they were conducting operations on both sides of the Great Lakes, in the Illinois country, beyond the upper Mississippi, on the Winnipeg, Saskatchewan, Churchill, and Athabasca Rivers, to the neighborhood of Great Slave Lake.   They traded on the Assiniboine, and may have reached the Missouri by that route.

Management of the trade.—During and after the Revolution the value of the furs annually sent from Montreal and Quebec to London was probably $1,000,000.   The trade centered mainly in Montreal.   In London great mercantile establishments throve by the commerce.   At Montreal other great houses were founded. Detroit and Michillimackinac were interior supply posts, where branch houses or lesser merchants conducted business.   Wintering partners and clerks went with the fleets of batteaux into the far interior, but most of the common hands or *engagés* were French and half-breed *coureurs de bois*, just as in the case of the Spanish fur trade in Louisiana.   The entire business was conducted on the credit system.

The fur magnates.—Many of the fur magnates were Scotchmen. Among the Montreal merchants of importance in this period were Alexander Henry, Benjamin and Joseph Frobisher, James Finlay, and Peter Pond. Henry was one of the earliest in the West. Finlay is said to have been among the first on the Saskatchewan River. The Frobishers were leading traders on the Saskatchewan and Churchill. Pond was probably the pioneer on the Athabasca, having wintered there in 1778–1789.

The Northwest Company formed.—The free access of all licensed traders to the interior resulted in reckless competition in regions remote from the military posts. Acts of violence were committed and Indians were involved in the contest. Besides the grave disadvantages of competition, there were obvious advantages of combination. In 1779, therefore, nine enterprises were consolidated for one year. The success caused the arrangement to be repeated, and finally in 1783-1784 the Northwest Company was organized and became permanent. This company soon monopolized the larger part of the Montreal trade, and became the great rival of the Hudson's Bay Company.

Advance of Hudson's Bay Company.—After the Peace of Utrecht the Hudson's Bay Company had returned to an era of prosperity. Urged on by French competition, by 1700 expeditions inland had been made by Kelsey (1691) and Sanford, and Henley House had been built a hundred and fifty miles inland from Fort Albany; and by 1720 other minor inland expeditions had been made by Macklish and Stewart, but in the main the Company had held to the shores of the Bay. Instead of sending employees inland, as did the French, reliance was placed on furs brought by the Indians to the posts, all of which were close to the Bay. The monopoly enjoyed was a cause of jealousy among British merchants, and critics arose, notably Arthur Dobbs, who charged that the Company had failed in its obligation to seek the northwest passage and explore the interior. Coerced by criticism, between 1719 and 1737 the Company made some explorations, but little was accomplished.

Hearne's explorations.—After 1763 criticism of the Company was reinforced by the rise of the Montreal trade, and new explorations northwestward were undertaken. After two unsuccessful attempts in 1769 and 1770 to reach the Coppermine River overland, in December, 1770, Samuel Hearne set out from Fort Prince of Wales to seek "a North-West Passage, copper-mines, or any other thing that may be serviceable to the British nation in general, or the Hudson's Bay Company in particular." Going west, then north, on July 18, 1771, Hearne reached the mouth of the Coppermine River near latitude 68°, where he took formal possession of the Arctic Ocean for the Company. Returning by way of Lake Athabasca, which he discovered and crossed, he reached his fort on June 30, 1772.

Rival posts in the interior.—Hearne's explorations were indicative of a new policy. Coerced by the aggressive Montreal traders, the Company now pushed into the interior in a struggle for the mastery. Side by side the two companies placed rival forts on all the important streams from the Hudson Bay to the Rockies and from the Red River of the North to Great Slave Lake.

READINGS

Alden, G. H., *New Governments west of the Alleghanies before 1780;* Alvord, C. W., "Virginia and the West: An Interpretation," in *The Mississippi Valley Historical Review,* III, 19–38; *The Critical Period, 1763–1765; The Mississippi Valley in British Politics;* Alvord, C. W., and Carter, C. E., editors, *The New Régime, 1765–1767;* Bassett, J. S., "The Regulators of North Carolina," in American Hist. Assoc., *Annual Report, 1894,* pp. 141–212; Bourinot, J. G., *Canada under British Rule, 1760–1905* (G. W. Wrong revision), chs. 2–3; Bryce, George, *The Remarkable History of the Hudson's Bay Company,* chs. 8–13; Carter, C. E., *Great Britain and the Illinois Country, 1763–1774;* "The Beginnings of British West Florida," in *The Mississippi Valley Historical Review,* IV, 314–341; Coffin, Victor, *The Quebec Act;* Hamilton, P. J., *Colonial Mobile,* chs. 23–31; *The Colonization of the South,* chs. 20–21; Henderson, A., "Richard Henderson and the Occupation of Kentucky, 1775," in *The Mississippi Valley Historical Review,* I, 341–363; Hinsdale, B. A., *The Old Northwest,* ch. 8; Howard, G. E., *Preliminaries of the Revolution, 1763–1775,* ch. 13; Roosevelt, Theodore, *The Winning of the West,* I–II; Siebert, W. H., "The Loyalists in West Florida and the Natchez District," in *The Mississippi Valley Historical Review,* II, 465–483; Stevens, W. E., "The Organization of the British Fur Trade, 1760–1800," in *The Mississippi Valley Historical Review,* III, 172–202; Thwaites, R. G., *Daniel Boone;* Thwaites, R. G., and Kellogg, L. P., editors, *Documentary History of Dunmore's War, 1774,* Introduction; Turner, F. J., "Western State-Making in the Revolutionary Era," in *American Historical Review,* I, 70–87, 251–269; Wallace, S., *The United Empire Loyalists;* Winsor, Justin, *The Westward Movement,* 38–100; Wood, W., *The Father of British Canada;* Davidson, G. C., *The North West Company.*

THE REVOLT OF THE ENGLISH COLONIES

CHAPTER XXIII

THE CONTROVERSY OF THE ENGLISH COLONIES WITH THE HOME GOVERNMENT

THE BACKGROUND OF THE CONTEST

Nature of the causes.—While British statesmen were working out a system of government for the newly acquired domains, in the empire forces of disintegration were at work which brought on the American Revolution. The causes of that convulsion cannot be traced to a group of events or laws. Through a long period social, political, and economic forces were at work which gradually brought thirteen of the mainland colonies into open rebellion. Because this opposition is more evident after the French and Indian War, and because the economic is the most obvious phase of the struggle, historians have sometimes concluded that the laws passed by parliament between 1763 and 1776 were the cause of the Revolution. The policy pursued by the British government no doubt hastened it, but alone does not account for it.

A mixed population.—For more than a century the colonies had been receiving new elements which were producing a society in many respects different from that of England. America had been the recipient of many of the radicals, the down-trodden, and the discontented from the mother country. The acquisition of New Netherlands had brought under British control a considerable number of Dutch, Swedes, and Finns. The Huguenot migration which followed the revocation of the Edict of Nantes had added another element. The German and Scotch-Irish influxes had brought in thousands. Welsh, Scotch, Irish, and Jews were also to be found in the colonies. America, then as now, was a melting pot of the nations.

Lack of American nationality.—Influenced largely by climatic and physiographic conditions, distinct industrial systems

had developed. In the northern colonies the small farm prevailed, in the South the plantation system. The North produced the seamen, fishermen, and merchants, while few of the
southerners were seafarers. The frontier with its foreign elements, its scattered settlements, and freedom from restraint had
produced a society which differed from the tide-water region.
The fur-trader, the cattleman, the lumberman, and the small
farmer were distinctly different in speech, dress, habits, and
point of view from the Boston merchant, the Philadelphia
Quaker, or the Virginia planter. Separatist tendencies were
stronger than those of coalescence. A Virginian was a Virginian
and not an American. There was little in common between the
New Englander and the southern planter, or between the people
of the Hudson Valley and the Quakers.

Class distinctions.—In individual colonies society was continually growing in complexity. Though the great mass of the
population continued to be rural, town life was becoming an
important factor. Members of an aristocracy, of which the
governor was usually the central social figure, were inclined to
rear their heads above their fellows. The merchants and lawyers,
ever increasing in numbers, found themselves outside the social
pale of the official aristocracy, a source of silent mortification
which was a real force in producing radicals.

Evolution of English society.—English as well as American
society had also undergone a rapid evolution. Puritan England
had passed away; the Stuarts, the Hanoverians, and foreign
conquests had transformed the viewpoint of the Englishman.
Little was there in common between John Milton and Horace
Walpole, or between a Cromwell and a Newcastle. The sudden
greatness that had come through the Seven Years' War well-
nigh turned the heads of Englishmen. To acquire wealth, to
wield power, and to live gaily seemed to be the ideals of the upper
class Englishman of the reign of George III. The colonial who
still considered the mother country as the traditional England
of Magna Carta, the Puritan Revolution, and the Bill of Rights,
had as little understanding of a Townshend as had a Townshend
a comprehension of the colonial.

The assemblies control the purse.—The governmental institutions of the colonies had gradually evolved toward a com-

mon type, whose constituent parts were the governor, council, and assembly, the governor and council, except in Connecticut and Rhode Island, representing imperial or proprietary authority, and the assembly the will of the colonial inhabitants. The power of the assemblies to control the purse had been steadily growing, until the colonies considered the principle established both by precedent and by inherent rights guaranteed by the English constitution. By controlling the budgets and the salaries of the governors, the assemblies held the whip hand over the executives.

English and colonial ideas of representation.—The meaning of the term representation differed in England and the colonies. To the Englishman parliament represented the British Empire and legislated for the whole of it, allowing the colonies to handle local matters within their chartered rights. Parliament was regarded as representing the three estates or classes of society, rather than individuals. The idea that every Englishman was represented by a man in whose selection he had had a voice had not become a part of the English political system. Members of parliament were frequently chosen in rotten boroughs. A few thousand men at most chose the entire parliamentary body. The king's ministers, selected from the party which could command a majority in the House of Commons, directed public policy and enforced their will upon a subservient commons. In America the suffrage was usually restricted by a property or church qualification, but every member of an assembly actually represented a colonial community and a known constituency. When the colonial orator declared for no taxation without representation, he was talking in the terms of a system that had grown up in America, but which England did not begin to adopt until the Reform Bill of 1832.

The causes of the development of nationalism.—French political philosophers and observant travelers had predicted that the removal of French power from America would cause the colonies to seek independence. Franklin ridiculed the idea, for he believed that colonial jealousies were too strong to allow united action, a view which was also held by Pitt. After the French and Indian War the English government, by enforcing and extending the colonial system, quickened public opinion, overthrew separatist tendencies, and brought many of the colonists to think and act together in opposition to English policy. When this was attained, a national consciousness had come into existence which gradually developed into open rebellion.

Illicit traffic during the French and Indian War.—Since the reign of Anne England had not enforced the trade laws strictly. The Molasses Act of 1733 had been practically a dead letter from the date of its passage and the other navigation acts had been frequently violated. Smuggling was winked at by governors and customs officials, who in many cases profited from the traffic. During the French and Indian War the colonies traded extensively with the French West Indies. This was especially galling to England, whose chief weapon against France was control of the seas. Though the colonies in 1756 were forbidden to trade with the French, the colonial skippers evaded the command by shipping goods to the Dutch ports of Curaçoa and St. Eustatius, or to the French West Indies. In 1757 parliament forbade the exportation of food stuffs from the colonies to foreign ports, but the colonials continued to make shipments to the French or Dutch colonies and to bring back cargoes of molasses, sugar, and rum. To stop Dutch trade with the French colonies, Dutch merchant vessels were seized. As the English navy gradually isolated or captured the French West Indies, the colonials found a new method of circumventing the regulations by shipping to Monte Cristi, a Spanish port in Española near the French boundary. A commerce of less importance but of similar nature was also maintained with Florida and Louisiana. In 1760, when the English navy had gained the upper hand, the illicit commerce diminished but did not entirely cease. When Spain entered the war a considerable increase occurred. The naval and military authorities did all in their power to end the traffic with the enemy, for they considered that its continuance meant a prolongation of the war.

Writs of assistance.—To prevent smuggling English officials resorted to the issuance of writs of assistance. These were general search warrants which enabled the holder to search any house, ship, or other property where smuggled goods might be stored. The writs naturally aroused great opposition among the merchants, who claimed that they were illegal. In 1761 when the Boston customs officers applied for the writs, the merchants objected to them. When the merchants' cause was presented before the Massachusetts Supreme Court, James Otis argued that the writs, being general, were illegal and struck at the liberty of the individual. "No acts of parliament can establish such a writ. . . . An act against the constitution is void."   The courts upheld the legality of the writs but Otis's speech did much to arouse and formulate public opinion.

The Parson's Cause.—In Virginia Patrick Henry performed a similar function in formulating public opinion. The speech which made him the leader of the Virginia radicals was delivered in connection with a suit brought by one of the Virginia clergy. Tobacco was the medium of exchange in the Old Dominion and ministers were paid annually 17,000 pounds of tobacco.   In 1755 and 1758, the burgesses passed acts which allowed debts to be redeemed at two pence for each pound of tobacco. This worked a hardship upon the ministers, who naturally desired the benefit of the high price of tobacco to compensate them for the hard years when prices were low.   The acts were disallowed by the crown in 1759, and the ministers attempted to recover their losses. In a suit brought in 1763 by Reverend James Maury, Patrick Henry appeared for the vestry. Realizing the weakness of his legal position, Henry resolved to carry the jury by an emotional attack upon the king's prerogative. He argued that the act of 1758 was a law of general utility consistent with the original compact between ruler and ruled, upon which government was based, and that the king, by disallowing this salutary act, became a tyrant and forfeited his right to the obedience of his subjects.

REFORMS OF THE GRENVILLE MINISTRY

Economy and reform.—At the end of the French and Indian War, England was burdened with a staggering debt. To build up the resources of the empire, increase the revenues, and protect the dominions were the objects of the ministers of George III. In this program the colonies were expected to play their part. The Bute Ministry planned to enforce the navigation acts, to tax the colonies directly, and to use the colonial revenue to support an army in America. The powers of the admiralty courts were immediately enlarged and commanders of war vessels were authorized to act as customs officials. Soon after Grenville came into office (April, 1763), he ordered customs collectors who were lingering in England to proceed at once to their colonial stations and he instructed the governors to enforce the trade laws rigidly.

Trade encouragement during 1764-1765.—To encourage commerce several important provisions were made during 1764 and 1765. To stimulate the fur business the old duties were abolished and an import duty of only one pence a skin and an export duty of seven pence were levied. To stimulate hemp and flax production bounties were paid on those products shipped from the colonies to England. The bounty on indigo was somewhat reduced but was still sufficient to protect the planters. The duties on whale fins were repealed to the great benefit of Massachusetts. The rice business was stimulated by allowing Georgia and the Carolinas to ship without restrictions to the southward.

The Sugar Act.—Grenville's beneficial measures were more than offset by the Sugar, Colonial Currency, Stamp, and Quartering Acts. The Sugar Act "was a comprehensive measure, whose openly expressed aim was, in the first place to raise a colonial revenue, and in the second to reform the old colonial system both in its administrative and in its economic features." The act confirmed and modified the Molasses Act of 1733. The duty on sugar shipped to the British colonies was raised but that on molasses was lowered. To injure the French island trade, the importation of foreign rum or spirits and commerce with Miquelon and St. Pierre were forbidden. Oriental and French textiles, Portuguese and Spanish wines, and coffee, if brought directly to the British colonies, were taxed heavily, but if shipped from England the duty was low. To protect South Carolina a duty was imposed upon foreign indigo shipped to the colonies. With a few exceptions no drawbacks were henceforth to be allowed, and revenues derived from the Sugar Act were to be paid into the royal exchequer. They were to be kept separate from other moneys and were to be used only for the protection of the British colonies in America.

Stringent regulations were provided for the enforcement of

the Sugar Act and other navigation laws. At the option of the informer or prosecutor, penalties for breach of the trade laws might be recovered in any court of record in the district where the offence was committed or in any admiralty court in America. The accused was required to give security for costs if he lost his suit, but if he won his case, he was not entitled to costs if the judge certified that the grounds of action seemed probable. Furthermore in the Molasses Act which was now confirmed, the burden of proof was placed upon the owner or claimant.

Every shipmaster was required to give a bond to land only enumerated goods at European ports north of Cape Finisterre and to possess a certificate from the customs collector at the point of loading. West Indian goods not properly certified were to be treated as foreign goods. Vessels cleared from British ports must contain only goods loaded in Great Britain. This, however, did not apply to salt and Irish linen. Breaches of these regulations subjected the law breaker to severe penalties.

Regulation of Colonial Currency.—Another important measure was the Colonial Currency Act. Lack of specie had compelled the issuance of colonial paper money, and though Massachusetts had retired such issues in 1749, most of the colonies were still suffering from depreciated and unstable currency. To protect the English merchant, parliament passed the Colonial Currency Act which prevented colonists from paying their debts to the home country in depreciated currency and stopped the issues of unsound money. The act caused a shortage of the medium of exchange at the time that the colonists were deprived of the West Indian commerce which had supplied them with specie to settle balances in London. The act produced embittered feeling which paved the way for greater opposition.

Colonial protests.—When it became known in the colonies that the Ministry intended to enforce a more rigid policy which included the levying of internal taxes by parliamentary enactment, vigorous protests were made. Memorials, resolutions, and addresses poured in upon the king, lords, commons, and Board of Trade, and numerous pamphlets appeared which presented the economic and constitutional viewpoint of the colonists.

The Massachusetts protest.—The Boston town meeting urged the assembly to use its influence to protect the rights of the colonies and in its instructions to the Boston representatives the principles were stated that there should be no taxation without representation and that colonials were entitled to full rights of Englishmen. It was also suggested that other injured colonies should be asked to coöperate in seeking redress. A committee of the assembly presented a memorial drafted by Otis which contained the additional principle that parliament had no right to alter the constitution. The memorial was sent to the Massachusetts agent in England with instructions to urge the repeal of the Sugar Act and to protest against the proposed Stamp Act. A committee of correspondence headed by Otis was authorized to inform the other colonies of the action of Massachusetts and to seek their coöperation. As the action had been taken by the assembly without the consent of the council, the governor was soon petitioned to call the general court. He complied and a petition was drawn which temperately protested.

The Rhode Island protest.—Before the Sugar Act was passed a remonstrance was prepared in Rhode Island, which was to be presented to the Board of Trade if three other colonial agents would coöperate. Committees of correspondence were also formed in various towns. After the passage of the act the committee of correspondence of which Governor Hopkins was a member sent out a circular letter protesting against the Sugar Act and the proposed Stamp Act. In November, 1764, the assembly sent a petition to the king in which the principle was stated that an essential privilege of Englishmen was that they should be governed by laws made by their own consent.

Connecticut protest.—In Connecticut Governor Fitch, at the suggestion of the assembly, prepared an address to parliament which protested against the proposed Stamp Act or any other bill for internal taxes. This and the governor's book of *Reasons Why the British Colonies in America should not be Charged with Internal Taxes by Authority of Parliament* were sent.

New York protest.—In March, 1764, the New York merchants presented to the council a memorial against the renewal of the Molasses Act. In October the assembly appointed a committee of correspondence and sent statements of grievances to the king and the lords, and a petition to the commons. In the petition the significant statement was made that the loss of colonial rights was likely to shake the power of Great Britain.

Pennsylvania's protest.—The Pennsylvania assembly considered that parliament had no right to tax the colony. Jackson, the colonial agent, was instructed to remonstrate against the proposed Stamp Act and to endeavor to secure the repeal or modification of the Sugar Act. Franklin was sent over to assist Jackson.

Maryland and Virginia.—In Maryland the governor prevented the meeting of the assembly, but the Virginia council and burgesses prepared an address to the king, a memorial to the lords, and a remonstrance to the commons. The Virginians claimed the rights and privileges that their ancestors had had in England and laid down the fundamental principle of no taxation without representation.

The Carolinas.—North Carolina protested strongly and in South Carolina the assembly appointed a committee which instructed the colonial agent to complain of the laws of trade. The instructions also declared that a Stamp Act would violate the inherent right of every British subject to be taxed only by his own consent or by his representatives. The governor prorogued the assembly before a vote could be taken upon the committee's action, but the instructions, nevertheless, were sent.

The Stamp Act.—In spite of colonial protests Grenville pursued his policy, the appeals of the colonies being rejected under the rule that petitions against money bills should not be received, and in March, 1765, parliament passed the Stamp Act. By its provisions stamps were to be placed on commercial and legal documents, pamphlets, newspapers, almanacs, playing cards, and dice. The enforcement of the act was placed under the management of English commissioners who were empowered to appoint persons to attend in every court or public office in the colonies to see that the law was enforced. For infringements of the law there were heavy penalties which might be collected through the admiralty courts if the informer or prosecutor so elected. Certain cases of forging and counterfeiting were punishable by death. The revenue derived from the Stamp Act was to be paid into the exchequer to be used for colonial defence.

Quartering Act.—The ministry intended to establish an army of 10,000 men in the colonies and the annual Mutiny Act of 1765 authorized the sending of such troops as might be deemed necessary. This was followed by the Quartering Act. As "*the publick houses and barracks, in his Majesty's dominions in* America, *may not be sufficient to supply quarters for such forces: and whereas it is expedient and necessary that carriages and other conveniences, upon the march of troops . . . should be supplied for that purpose,*" it was enacted that, if colonial barracks were insufficient, officers and troops were to be quartered in public hostelries. If more room were needed, vacant buildings were to be rented. Troops were to be supplied with fire, candles, vinegar, salt, bedding, cooking utensils, and small quantities of beer, cider, or rum. Persons giving houses for troops and furnishing supplies were to be reimbursed by the province. The colonies were to furnish conveyances at rates fixed by the act, but if the expense exceeded the rate, the province had to make up the deficit.

Colonial opposition.—To the colonies the Stamp Act, the Quartering Act, and the extension of admiralty jurisdiction were unconstitutional. Trials in the admiralty courts had always been looked upon with disfavor, as they violated the right of trial by jury. The new regulation allowing alleged violators of the trade laws to be taken to Halifax for trial was looked upon as a dangerous innovation. The Quartering Act was viewed as a violation of the constitutional principle that troops were not to be quartered upon the people. The provisions of the law were especially aggravating to New York which, because of the strategic position of the colony, would have to bear an undue part in the support and transportation of troops. But the Stamp Act aroused the greatest furor. All of the elements of discontent united against an act which encroached upon the right of the assemblies to control taxation. Indirect taxation was not looked upon as taxation. To the colonial economists the navigation acts were merely trade regulations and the right of parliament to regulate commerce was fully recognized. But a direct tax imposed by parliament to support an obnoxious soldiery set in motion the forces of discontent and produced a unity of opposition which surprised the ministers of George III.

The Virginia Resolutions.—Virginia took the lead in opposition. On May 29, 1765, the burgesses resolved themselves into a committee of the whole to consider the steps necessary to be taken in consequence of the Stamp Act. Patrick Henry, the "rustic and clownish youth of the terrible tongue," introduced a series of resolutions which boldly challenged the British government. The preamble stated that, as the House of Commons had raised the question of how far the general assembly had power to enact laws for laying taxes and imposing duties payable by the people of Virginia, the House of Burgesses, to settle and ascertain the same to all future time, resolved: (1) that the first adventurers and settlers of Virginia brought with them and transmitted to their posterity and to other English subjects who had come to live in the colony all the rights of the people of Great Britain; (2) that these were granted to them by two charters of James I; (3) that taxation of the people by themselves or by their representatives was a distinguishing characteristic of British freedom without which the ancient constitution could not exist; (4) that the people of Virginia had uninterruptedly enjoyed the right of being governed by their own assembly in matters of taxes and internal police, a right which had never been forfeited and had been constantly recognized by the kings and people of Great Britain. (5) Therefore it was resolved that the general assembly had the sole right and power to lay taxes and impositions upon the inhabitants of Virginia, and that every attempt to vest such power in any other person or persons had a tendency to destroy British as well as American freedom; (6) that the inhabitants of Virginia were not bound by any law or ordinance designed to impose any tax upon them other than those imposed by the general assembly; (7) and that any person who maintained that Virginians were bound to obey such laws not imposed by the assembly should be deemed an enemy of the colony.

The resolutions precipitated an acrimonious debate in which the democratic members of the western counties supported Henry against the aristocratic leaders. The committee of the whole appears to have adopted the resolutions, but on the following day the burgesses rejected the preamble and the last two resolutions, the other five being passed by a slender majority.

Henry then left the assembly and the following morning the conservatives expunged from the record the fifth resolution. The manuscript of the entire series, except the third resolution which was omitted by error, was already on its way to the other colonies and was widely published. "Beyond question the Virginia resolves mark an important crisis in the impending revolution."

Resistance and violence.—In June the Massachusetts general court, at the suggestion of Otis, sent a circular letter to the other colonial assemblies asking them to send delegates to meet at New York in the following October to consider the danger from the Stamp Act. Before the delegates met fierce opposition appeared in nearly every colony. Remonstrances came from towns, counties, and assemblies. Newspapers and pamphlets inveighed against the act, and non-importation agreements were made in many localities. Associations called "Sons of Liberty" sprang up. At first they worked secretly, but they soon announced their committees of correspondence which worked to unify the opposition.

In Boston occurred riots of greater violence than in any other place. On August 14 the stamp distributor's effigy was hung on the "Liberty Tree," and after other demonstrations, that night a mob demolished a building which it was believed the collector was erecting for an office. On August 26 the houses of two of the customs officials were sacked and the house of Chief Justice Hutchinson was pillaged and destroyed. At Newport the stamp distributor and a sympathizer found it necessary to seek safety on a British man-of-war. Scenes of violence occurred in the other colonies and the stamp distributors resigned with more haste than dignity.

REPEAL OF THE STAMP ACT

The Stamp Act Congress.—The Stamp Act Congress met at New York on October 7, 1765. Nine colonies were represented, Virginia, North Carolina, Georgia, and New Hampshire failing to send delegates. Prominent among those in attendance were John Dickinson of Pennsylvania, John Rutledge and Christopher Gadsden of South Carolina, and James Otis of Massachusetts.

On October 19 a declaration of rights and grievances, originally drafted by Dickinson, was adopted. In the declaration the argument was presented that the colonies were entitled to the inherent rights and liberties of native-born Englishmen, one of which was that no taxes were to be imposed upon them except by their own consent or by their representatives. The colonists were not and from their local circumstances could not be represented in the House of Commons, their only representatives being those in the colonies who alone had the constitutional right to impose taxes upon them. All supplies to the crown being free gifts of the people, it was unreasonable and inconsistent with the principles and spirit of the British constitution for the people of Great Britain to grant to the king the property of the colonists. Trial by jury was an inherent right of every British subject in the colonies, but the Stamp Act and other laws, by extending the jurisdiction of the admiralty courts, had a tendency to subvert the rights and liberties of the colonists. The duties imposed by recent acts of parliament would be burdensome and grievous, and from the scarcity of specie the payment of them would be impracticable. The recent restrictions would make it impossible to purchase the manufactures of Great Britain. The right to petition the king or either house of parliament was also asserted. By an address to the king and by applications to both houses of parliament, they endeavored to procure the repeal of the Stamp Act, of clauses in recent acts which increased admiralty jurisdiction, and of recent acts placing restrictions on American commerce.

Repeal of the Stamp Act.—In July, 1765, Grenville fell from power, but not because of opposition to the Stamp Act. The Marquis of Rockingham, a man of moderate ability, was selected to form the new cabinet. The question of the repeal of the Stamp Act came up in parliament early in 1766. During the debate in the commons on February 13, Franklin, then agent for Pennsylvania and Massachusetts, was questioned regarding the colonial attitude, and he made it clear that the Stamp Act could not be enforced. The American cause was strengthened by the powerful support of Pitt and by the protests of English merchants and manufacturers who were losing trade through colonial boycotts. After a momentous debate, the act was repealed.

The Declaratory Act.—Although parliament had given ground it did not surrender, for in the Declaratory Act of March 18, 1766, it asserted its right to tax the colonies. The act declared that the colonies were subordinate unto and dependent upon the crown and parliament, and that the king by and with the consent of parliament had full power and authority to make laws to bind the colonies in all cases. All resolutions, votes, orders, and proceedings in the colonies denying the power and authority of parliament to make laws imposing taxes and regulations were declared null and void.

Other legislation.—The Quartering Act was then renewed, but with certain changes to make it more effective. The imposts on textiles which had previously been collected in America were henceforth to be collected at the point of exportation. The duty on molasses was changed from three pence a gallon on the foreign product to one penny a gallon on all molasses brought to the continental colonies.

Colonial rejoicing.—The Declaratory and other acts attracted little attention in America, where there was great rejoicing over the repeal of the Stamp Act. The constitutional principles for which the colonists had contended had in no wise been conceded, but to the colonist his point seemed won. He was soon to be rudely awakened.

THE TOWNSHEND ACTS

Townshend.—In July, 1766, Rockingham fell from power and the Pitt-Grafton Ministry was formed. Unfortunately for the colonies, Pitt was in ill-health and took little part in shaping policies. The strong man of the cabinet was Charles Townshend. He was fully in sympathy with Grenville's ideas, and was responsible for a new series of irritating acts.

Suspension of the New York assembly.—Trouble had arisen in New York over the enforcement of the Quartering Act. In June, 1766, in reply to Governor Moore's request that provision be made for the expected troops, the assembly excused itself from compliance but intimated that about £4000 then in the treasury might be used. Later the assembly passed an act making provision for one year for a thousand men and one company of artillery. When a request was made for full compliance with the Quartering Act, the assembly refused. On December 19 it was prorogued, and on June 15, 1767, was suspended by act of parliament.

Colonial customs commissioners.—Another act provided for a board of commissioners of customs to be established in America. The preamble stated that, as the colonial customs officials had found it inconvenient to apply to the commissioners in England for directions when difficulties arose, and as colonial shippers were greatly delayed in carrying on business, commissioners were to be stationed in America. Five commissioners were appointed with headquarters at Boston.

Revenue acts.—A new revenue act was passed "for making a more certain and adequate provision for defraying the charge of the administration of justice and the support of civil government, in such provinces where it shall be found necessary, and toward further defraying the expenses of defending, protecting, and securing" the dominions in America. Duties were imposed upon glass, red and white lead, painter's colors, tea, and paper. Drawbacks were allowed on coffee and cocoanuts, but chinaware was no longer subject to drawback. Writs of assistance were declared legal. By another act a drawback for five years was granted on tea reëxported from England to Ireland or the colonies.

Dickinson's " Farmer's Letters."—The Townshend Acts were received with alarm throughout the colonies. "Awed by the suddenness and magnitude of the peril, the colonial leaders acted with circumspection and rare self-control." The most powerful statement of the colonial viewpoint came from John Dickinson whose "Farmer's Letters" were read throughout the colonies, were published in London, translated into French, "and were read by everybody in the two capitals of civilization who read anything more serious than a playbill." Dickinson recognized the vagueness of the constitutional relations of the colonies to the mother country. He urged that a spirit of compromise should prevail and that no abstract theory of sovereignty should be pushed to its logical conclusions. He admitted that parliament possessed legal authority to regulate the trade of the empire, but the recent attempts to raise a revenue he considered a most dangerous innovation. "Great Britain claims and exercises the right to prohibit manufactures in America. Once admit that she may lay duties upon her exportations to us, for the purpose of levying money on us only, she then will have nothing to do but to lay those duties on the articles which she prohibits us to manufacture, and the tragedy of American liberty is finished."

"I would persuade the people of these Colonies . . . to exert themselves in the most firm, but the most peaceable manner, for obtaining relief. If an inveterate resolution is formed to annihilate the liberties of the governed, English history affords examples of resistance by force."

"Let us consider ourselves as . . . freemen, . . . *firmly bound together* by the *same rights, interests,* and *dangers.* . . . What have these colonies to *ask,* while they continue free; Or what have they to *dread,* but insidious attempts to subvert their freedom? . . . They form *one* political body, of which *each colony* is a *member.*"

The Massachusetts protest.—In Massachusetts the Townshend Acts were received by a public which was already irritated by the untactful course of Governor Bernard. Soon after the repeal of the Stamp Act he had negatived the election of Otis as speaker of the assembly, and when that body retaliated by refusing to reëlect certain members of the council, the governor had refused to accept six members elected by the popular party. Difficulties had also arisen when the governor demanded compensation for those who had suffered by the Stamp Act riots and when he demanded compliance with the Quartering Act.

The first protest of Massachusetts against the Townshend Acts was on October 28, 1767, when the Boston town-meeting renewed the non-importation agreement. The General Court convened on December 30 and shortly afterward the acts were read in the assembly and referred to a committee for consideration. The committee drafted a letter to the colonial agent which reviewed the arguments against taxation and protested against the Townshend Acts. A petition to the king and letters to members of the ministry were also prepared. A circular letter to the assemblies in the other colonies, drawn by Samuel Adams, was adopted on February 11, 1768.

The circular letter stated that it seemed necessary that the representatives of the several assemblies should act in harmony "upon so delicate a point" as the recent imposition of duties and taxes.   The argument regarding taxation without representation was restated, and objection was made to the payment of the salaries of governors and judges by the crown, to the large powers of appointment given to the commissioners of the customs, and to the Quartering Act.   Denial was made that independence was in the minds of the Massachusetts representatives and the letter closed with an expression of confidence in the king.   Several of the colonies sent sympathetic replies and Virginia issued a circular letter to the other colonies calling upon them to unite with Massachusetts in her petition for redress.

Hillsborough's reply.—When the Massachusetts protests reached England, they came before a ministry which was prejudiced by letters from royal officials in America.   Lord Hillsborough, who had recently been appointed to the newly created position of colonial secretary, laid the Massachusetts protests before the cabinet.   On April 21 he sent letters to all the colonial governors, with the exception of Bernard, ordering them to ignore the Massachusetts circular letter.   If the assemblies took notice of it, they were to prorogue or dissolve them.   Bernard was commanded to require the Massachusetts assembly to rescind its action and to declare its disapprobation of its recent action.   The Massachustts assembly refused and the other assemblies commended its course.

The customs officials defied.—Acts of violence soon occurred. The warship *Romney* was anchored in Boston harbor and the captain angered the people by impressing seamen, one of whom was rescued.   On the same day the sloop *Liberty*, owned by John Hancock, arrived with a cargo of Madeira wine.   The customs collector was locked up by the crew while the cargo was landed and a false entry made.   The *Liberty* was seized and moored under the guns of the *Romney*.   A riot then occurred; the houses of two of the customs officials were damaged and a boat belonging to the controller was burned.   The officials fled to the *Romney* and later took refuge in Castle William.   The Boston town-meeting requested the removal of the war vessel, but the governor refused on the ground that such action would be beyond his jurisdiction.   At Newport a revenue cutter was burned and at Providence a coat of tar and feathers was administered to a customs official.

Action of the Boston town-meeting and the Massachusetts convention.—Before the occurrence of these riotous acts, the ministry had determined to send troops to Boston. When this became known, the town-meeting assembled in Faneuil Hall and resolved that the inhabitants defend their rights, and they were called upon to provide themselves with arms. When the governor refused to summon the assembly, the selectmen called a convention of delegates from the Massachusetts towns. Ninety-six towns responded. The governor refused to recognize the convention, but it remained in session for six days and did not adjourn until a statement of grievances had been formulated. On September 28, 1768, the day of adjournment, two regiments arrived at Boston.

Prisoners accused of treason to be tried in England.—The rebellious acts of Massachusetts were condemned by parliament which also advised the enforcement of the statute of Henry VIII which allowed the government to bring to England for trial persons accused of treason committed outside of the kingdom. This aroused a storm of protest. In Virginia the burgesses adopted resolutions which asserted that the right of taxation was vested in the House of Burgesses, that petitioning the sovereign was an undoubted privilege of the colony, and that it was lawful and expedient to procure the concurrence of other colonies "in dutiful addresses, praying the royal interposition in favour of the violated rights of America;" that trials for treason or for any felony or crime committed in the colony should be held in the courts of that colony, and that the sending of suspected persons beyond the sea for trial was derogatory of the right of trial by a jury of the vicinage and deprived the accused of summoning witnesses. The resolutions were sent to the other assemblies. When the governor dissolved the burgesses, the members met in a private house and drew up a non-importation agreement. Other assemblies approved the Virginia resolutions and non-importation agreements were signed throughout the colonies.

Departure of Bernard.—Massachusetts continued to be the center of unrest. The unpopularity of Governor Bernard increased when it became known that he was collecting evidence against Samuel Adams. The public ire grew more intense when some of the governor's letters to the Ministry were published. The council drew up charges against him and the assembly petitioned for his recall. In July, 1770, he voluntarily departed, leaving Hutchinson in charge.

The Boston " Massacre."—The troops remained in Boston where they were heartily detested. Difficulties between soldiers and townspeople became more and more frequent and in March, 1770, there was a serious collision. On the fifth a sentinel at the custom house was pelted with snow balls, and when he called for aid the guard came to his assistance. A soldier was knocked down, shots were fired by the guard, and several citizens were killed or wounded. Preston, the commanding officer of the guard, surrendered to the civil authorities, and the privates were placed under arrest. The selectmen demanded the withdrawal of the troops to Castle William and Hutchinson hesitatingly complied. When the soldiers were brought to trial, they were defended by John Adams and Josiah Quincy, who obtained acquittal for all but two who were lightly sentenced.

BEGINNING OF ORGANIZED RESISTANCE

Partial repeal of the Townshend Acts.—The Townshend Acts had proved a complete failure. Exports from England to America had dropped from £2,378,000 in 1768 to £1,634,000 in 1769. The customs were yielding little revenue while the colonial military establishment had become extremely expensive. In addition the colonies had been brought close to rebellion. Lord North, who became Prime Minister on January 31, 1770, hoped to end the commotions in America which had been so injurious to English merchants and manufacturers. He accordingly obtained a repeal of the duties on paints, glass, and paper, but at the suggestion of the king, the tea tax was retained in order to maintain the principle that parliament had the right to tax the colonies. The economic result of the repeal was immediately evident, for in 1770 the English exports to America reached nearly two million pounds sterling and during the next year more than doubled.

Arbitrary attitude of the governors.—The public, however, was kept in a state of agitation by the arbitrary acts of the governors who reflected the royal will.   In Georgia the governor vetoed the assembly's choice for speaker, provoking a controversy which ended in the dissolution of the assembly.   In South Carolina the governor was in frequent quarrels with the assembly, first over the salaries of the judges, then regarding the veto of an appropriation bill, and finally over convening the assembly at Beaufort instead of at Charleston.   Virginia was irritated by the royal instructions which forbade the governor to assent to any law which would prohibit or obstruct the importation of slaves.   In Maryland the governor by proclamation revived a law regulating fees which had expired by limitation, an action which was looked upon as an assertion of the right to levy taxes.

In Massachusetts the General Court, which was to have met at Boston in January, 1770, was called to meet at Cambridge on March 15.   The assembly objected to the change of time and place and demanded a copy of Hutchinson's instructions, but he refused to comply.   The assembly would do no business while thus constrained to hold its sessions away from Boston, and declared that the people and their representatives had a right to withstand "the abusive exercise" of the crown's prerogative.   Under protest the assembly finally proceeded to business, but another difficulty immediately arose when the colonial troops were removed from Castle William which was then garrisoned by the regulars.   In July, 1771, Hutchinson, who had recently been appointed governor, vetoed a bill which provided for the salaries of the crown officials, an action which called forth a protest from the assembly which held that royal instructions were thus given the force of law.   The following year the assembly was informed that henceforth the salaries of the governor and judges would be paid by the crown.

The Gaspee affair.—In Rhode Island an event occurred in 1772 which had far-reaching influence.   The numerous inlets and islands of Narragansett Bay made smuggling easy, and revenue vessels, though constantly on the alert, experienced great difficulty in detecting the illicit traders.   The revenue boats *St. Johns* and *Liberty* were destroyed by men from Newport and the customs officials were annoyed by suits to recover vessels and cargoes which they had seized; Admiral Montagu accordingly ordered that seized vessels be sent to Boston. To Rhode Islanders Dudington, the commander of the *Gaspee*, was especially obnoxious. According to Trevelyan, "He stopped and searched vessels without adequate pretext, seized goods illegally, and fired at the market boats as they entered Newport harbour. He treated the farmers on the islands much as the Saracens in the Middle Ages treated the coast population of Italy, cutting down their trees for fuel, and taking their sheep when his crew ran short of meat." The injured parties made their voices heard, and the case was laid before the Admiral, who approved the conduct of his subordinate officer, and announced that, " as sure as any people from Newport attempted to rescue a vessel, he would hang them as pirates." On June 9 the *Gaspee* ran aground seven miles below Providence and during the night the vessel was boarded, Dudington was wounded, he and his crew were put on shore, and the vessel was burned. The act of violence aroused the British government and orders were sent to the governor of Rhode Island, the admiralty judge at Boston, and the chief justices of Massachusetts, New Jersey, and New York to act as a commission of inquiry. The commission held sessions in January and May, 1773, but failed to obtain any evidence.

Local committees of correspondence.—The arbitrary acts of the crown officials, the extension of the royal prerogative, and the *Gaspee* affair made possible the organization of the radical elements in the colonies. In Massachusetts opposition centered in Samuel Adams, "the man of the town meeting," who put forth pamphlet after pamphlet which struck at the encroachments upon colonial rights. "While he restated the old argument against the right of parliament to tax, he closely examined the foundations of the claim of the ministers to govern by royal instructions. He had grasped the idea that the king, lords, and commons, as well as the colonies, were subject to the authority and bound by the limitations of constitutional law." In the assembly, in the town meeting, through the press, on the street, among the sailors, fishermen, and ropemakers, he advocated the necessity of union. During the contest over the salaries of the crown officials, Adams seized the opportunity to put his ideas into tangible form. On November 2, 1772, in the Boston town meeting he moved that a committee of twenty-one be appointed to state the rights of the colonists, particularly of Massachusetts, and to communicate and publish the same to the Massachusetts towns and to the world as the sense of Boston "with the infringements and violations thereof that have been or . . . may be, made; also requesting of each town a free communication of their sentiments on this subject." By January, 1773, more than eighty towns in Massachusetts had committees.

"The Boston committee of correspondence has been likened to a political party manager. It provided for regular meetings, consulted with similar bodies in the vicinity, stimulated the spread of committees in surrounding towns, kept up a correspondence with them, prepared political matter for the press, circulated it in newspapers and broadsides, matured political measures, created and guided public sentiment—in short, heated the popular temper to the boiling point of revolution and then drew from it the authority to act."

Standing committees of correspondence.—Aroused by the *Gaspee* inquiry, the Virginia burgesses on March 12, 1773, adopted resolutions which provided for a standing committee of correspondence and inquiry whose business was "to obtain the most early and authentic intelligence of all such acts and reso lutions of the British Parliament, or proceedings of Administration, as may relate to or affect the British colonies in America, and to keep up and maintain a correspondence and communication with our sister colonies, respecting these important considerations; and the result of such their proceedings, from time to time, to lay before this House." The committee was also instructed to obtain information regarding "the principles and authority on which was constituted a court of inquiry, said to have been lately held in Rhode Island, with powers to transmit persons accused of offences committed in America to places beyond the seas to be tried." The speaker was instructed to transmit to the speakers of the different assemblies of the British colonies on the continent copies of the resolutions, that they might lay them before their assemblies and request them to appoint a person or persons to communicate from time to time with the committee of the burgesses.

The Virginia suggestion was first acted upon by the Rhode Island assembly, which on May 15 informed Virginia of the appointment of a committee of correspondence.   Before the close of the month the assemblies of Connecticut, New Hampshire, and Massachusetts had appointed similar committees. The South Carolina assembly acted in July, Georgia in September, Maryland and Delaware in October, and North Carolina in December.   The New York assembly appointed its committee on January 20, 1774, and New Jersey on February 8.   The Pennsylvania assembly dissolved without taking action.

The committees did not prove to be active agents, because (1) "there was little or nothing for them to do;" (2) they "were chosen from members of the assembly, all of whom were desirous of going home when the assembly adjourned"; (3) "the assembly committees were extremely cautious about acting on their own authority."   "However, the choice of such committees was not entirely without result.   The popular assembly in each colony received preliminary testing.   Constitutional questions were raised and discussed, and arguments disseminated. . . .   More important still had been the demonstration that a body could be created which might continue to act in successful opposition to the crown when the royal governors dissolved or prorogued the assemblies."

THE TEA CONTROVERSY

Attempted relief of the East India Company.—During this period George III and his ministers took the fatal step of attempting to force tea upon the colonies.   The colonists had refrained from using tea which paid a duty and had supplied themselves with smuggled tea from France, Sweden, and Holland.   At this time the East India Company was on the verge of bankruptcy, a condition due in part to the loss of American customers.   In the company's warehouses a vast amount of tea had accumulated.   As a measure of relief the directors of the company advised the repeal of the tea duty, but "a course which went direct to the point was not of a nature to find favor with George the Third and his Ministers."   Instead they allowed the company a drawback of the entire tea duty in England, but the tea was to be subject to the three penny tax payable in the colonies.

The tea arrives.—George III was soon to learn that he could not force tea down colonial throats. Late in 1773 several tea-laden ships arrived at American ports. In Charleston the agents of the company resigned, and when the duty was not paid, the collector seized the tea and stored it in a damp cellar. In Philadelphia a public meeting resolved that the duty on tea was illegal and persons who assisted in its being landed were declared public enemies. Under pressure of public opinion the consignees resigned and the captain of the tea vessel wisely decided not to unload his cargo. "When New York learned that the tea-ships allotted to it had been driven by a gale off the coast, men scanned the horizon, like the garrison of Londonderry watching for the English fleet in Lough Foyle, in their fear lest fate should rob them of their opportunity of proving themselves not inferior in mettle to the Bostonians."

The Boston Tea Party.—The Massachusetts people had recently been greatly irritated by certain private letters of Hutchinson, Oliver, and Paxton. The letters had been obtained in England by Franklin and had been sent under the seal of secrecy to some of the Massachusetts leaders who, however, published them. Before the excitement subsided three tea-laden vessels arrived at Boston. Hutchinson refused to allow the ships to leave until regularly cleared and this could not be done until the entire cargo had been unloaded. A mass meeting held in the Old South Church resolved that the tea should not be landed, and when the governor ordered the dispersal of the meeting, the bearer of the proclamation met with insult. Neighboring towns agreed to assist Boston, with force if necessary, and a guard watched the vessels to see that none of the tea was landed. On December 17 the cargo would be seized by the collector for non-payment of duty. On the evening of December 16, fifty or sixty men disguised as Indians boarded the tea ships, rifled the chests, and threw the contents into the bay.

The course of Massachusetts.—The British government was being sorely tried by Massachusetts. On January 29, 1774, a petition of the general court for the removal of Hutchinson and Oliver came before the Privy Council Committee for Foreign Plantations. The petition was pronounced a seditious document. Franklin was summoned before the committee, was charged with intercepting letters, and was dismissed from the deputy post-master-generalship. Soon after the Boston Tea Party, the assembly voted to impeach Justice Oliver for accepting a salary from the crown. In retaliation Hutchinson dissolved the assembly and soon left the colony.

LORD NORTH'S COERCIVE POLICY

The intolerable acts.—The revolutionary acts which were taking place in America, especially those in Massachusetts, caused deep concern in England. Pitt and Burke favored conciliation as the only means of preserving the empire, but the king insisted upon repression. The ministry speedily adopted a legislative program to punish Massachusetts, and parliament legalized the ministerial policy by passing the so-called intolerable acts.

Boston Port Act.—The first of these acts closed the port of Boston from June 1, 1774, until such time as "it shall be made to appear to his Majesty, in his privy council, that peace and obedience to the laws shall be so far restored in the said town of *Boston*, that the trade of *Great Britain* may safely be carried on there, and his Majesty's customs duly collected." The king was not to open the port until the inhabitants of Boston had given full satisfaction to the East India Company and to the revenue officers and others who had suffered by the recent outbreaks.

Massachusetts Government Act.—By the "regulating act" the people of Massachusetts were deprived of most of their chartered rights. After July 1, 1774, the council was to be appointed by the king instead of by the assembly. The governor was to appoint and remove, without the consent of the council, all judges of the inferior courts, the attorney general, provosts, marshals, and other officers belonging to the council or courts of justice. Sheriffs were also appointed by the governor but could not be removed without the consent of the council. The chief justice and judges of the superior court were to be appointed by the governor, but were to hold their commissions during the king's pleasure, and they could not be removed unless by order of the crown. Grand and petit juries were to be summoned by the sheriffs instead of being chosen in town meetings. Except for elections, town meetings were to be called only by consent of the governor and discussion was to be limited to subjects stated in the leave. The people were still allowed to elect the assembly.

Administration of Justice Act.—The third act provided, "That if any inquisition or indictment shall be found, or if any appeal shall be sued or preferred against any person, for murther, or other capital offence, in the province of the *Massachusett's Bay*, and it shall appear, by information given upon oath to the governor . . , that the fact was committed by the person against whom such inquisition or indictment shall be found, or against whom such appeal shall be sued or preferred . . . , either in the execution of his duty as a magistrate, for the suppression of riots, or in the support of the laws of revenue, or in acting in his duty as an officer of revenue, or in acting under the direction and order of any magistrate, for the suppression of riots, or for the carrying into effect the laws of revenue, or in aiding and assisting in any of the cases aforesaid; and if it shall also appear, to the satisfaction of the said governor . . . that an indifferent trial cannot be had within the said province, in that case, it shall and may be lawful for the governor . . . to direct, with the advice and consent of the council, that the inquisition, indictment, or appeal, shall be tried in some other of his Majesty's colonies, or in *Great Britain.*" The act also made it possible to transport witnesses to the scene of the trial.

Quartering Act, June 2, 1774.—The fourth law was entitled "An act for the better providing suitable quarters for officers and soldiers in his Majesty's service in North America." It provided that, if any officers or soldiers should be without quarters for twenty-four hours after a proper demand had been made, the governor might order that "uninhabited houses, outhouses, barns, or other buildings" be made fit for quarters. The law was to remain in force until March 24, 1776. Though the act was general in its terms, in reality it was intended "to facilitate the establishment of a temporary military government in Massachusetts." Of ominous import was the appointment of General Gage as governor of Massachusetts.

The Quebec Act.—The Quebec Act which extended the province of Quebec to the Ohio River also aroused the anger of

Massachusetts, New York, Connecticut, and Virginia, as it deprived those colonies of large tracts of western lands which they claimed under their ancient charters. It was not intended as a coercive act, but was so considered in the colonies.

THE FIRST CONTINENTAL CONGRESS

Call for a congress.—On May 10 a copy of the Port Act was received in Boston. On the twelfth the committee of correspondence met with eight neighboring committees and recommended non-intercourse with Great Britain. The other colonies were asked to follow the same course. While this was taking place the four additional regiments which Gage had called for began to arrive and on June 1, 1774, the port was blocked by men-of-war. Boston began to receive money and supplies from other towns and colonies, and a new impetus was given to the formation of committees of correspondence. Committees in New York and Philadelphia recommended the appointment of delegates to a general congress. The Virginia burgesses resolved to set aside June 1 as a day of fasting and prayer. The governor dissolved the house, but the burgesses assembled on May 27 at the Raleigh Tavern and adopted a resolution calling for a congress. Copies of the resolution were sent to the other assemblies.

On June 17 the Massachusetts assembly resolved, "That a meeting of committees from several colonies . . . is highly expedient and necessary, to consult upon the present state of the colonies, and the miseries to which they are and must be reduced by the operation of certain acts of Parliament respecting America, and to deliberate and determine upon wise and proper measures, to be by them recommended to all the colonies, for the recovery and establishment of their just rights and liberties, civil and religious, and the restoration of union and harmony between Great Britain and the colonies, most ardently desired by all good men: Therefore, resolved, that the Hon. James Bowdoin, Esq., the Hon. Thomas Cushing, Esq., Mr. Samuel Adams and Robert Treat Paine, Esqrs., be . . . appointed a committee . . . to meet with such committees or delegates from the other colonies as have been or may be appointed, either by their respective houses of burgesses or representatives, or by convention, or by the committees of correspondence appointed by the respective houses of assembly, in the city of Philadelphia, or any other place that shall be judged most suitable by the committee, on the 1st day of September next; and that the speaker of the house be directed, in a letter to the speakers of the house of burgesses or representatives in the several colonies, to inform them of the substance of these resolves."

Meeting of the First Continental Congress.—Every colony but Georgia responded to the call. In September over fifty delegates assembled in Carpenters' Hall at Philadelphia. Among them were John and Samuel Adams of Massachusetts, John Dickinson of Pennsylvania, Richard Henry Lee, Patrick Henry and George Washington of Virginia, Roger Sherman of Connecticut, John Jay of New York, and Edward and John Rutledge of South Carolina. "The congress of 1774 was not thought of by the people as a congress in the modern legislative sense. It was rather a convention of ambassadors of subordinate, but distinct communities which had found it needful to take counsel of one another regarding a crisis in their common relations to the parent state, in order, if possible, to adopt some common plan of action. It was essentially an advisory or consultative body. In another aspect it may be regarded as the completion of the revolutionary party organization of which the basis was laid in the committees of correspondence."

The Suffolk Resolves approved.—The delegates were soon divided into well-defined groups; the radicals led by Samuel Adams wanted resistance, the conservatives headed by Joseph Galloway favored compromise. The radicals succeeded in getting Congress to approve the resolves recently drawn up in the Suffolk County convention in Massachusetts. The resolves declared that no obedience to the recent acts of parliament was due from Massachusetts, advised that no money be turned into the treasury by the tax-collectors until the restoration of the constitution, denounced as enemies the king's councillors who had not resigned, and threatened armed resistance. Congress published these resolves with its resolutions commending the course of Boston.

A plan of union.—The conservatives favored a plan of union proposed by Galloway, which provided for a crown appointed president-general and a council of deputies chosen every three years by the legislatures. The acts of the council were to be subject to parliamentary veto and acts of parliament relating to the colonies might be vetoed by the council. The plan was defeated by a narrow margin.

The Declaration and Resolves.—On September 7 a committee of two from each colony had been appointed to draw up a statement of the rights of the colonies, instances of their violation, and means of restoring them. Agreement on the committee's report was reached on October 14. The declaration of grievances thus adopted complained that parliament had imposed taxes upon them and under various pretences, but in fact for the purpose of raising revenue, had established a board of commissioners with unconstitutional powers, and had extended the jurisdiction of the admiralty courts, not only for collecting duties, but for trial of causes arising merely within the body of a county. Complaint was also made that judges had been made dependent on the crown for salaries, that standing armies had been kept in times of peace, and that the removal to distant places for trial of prisoners charged with treason and certain other crimes had been legalized. The intolerable acts were described as "impolitic, unjust, and cruel, as well as unconstitutional." Other complaints were the dissolution of assemblies when they attempted to deliberate on grievances, and treating with contempt petitions for redress.

Congress accordingly resolved that the inhabitants of the English colonies in North America were "entitled to life, liberty and property: and they had never ceded to any foreign power whatever, a right to dispose of either without their consent;" that they were entitled to the same rights as their ancestors; "that the foundation of English liberty, and of all free government, is a right in the people to participate in their legislative council: and as the English colonies are not represented . . . in the British parliament, they are entitled to a free and exclusive power of legislation in their several provincial legislatures, where their right of representation can alone be preserved, in all cases of taxation and internal policy, subject only to the negative of their sovereign." For the mutual interests of both countries they consented to parliamentary regulation of external commerce. The right of trial by their peers of the vicinage, rights confirmed by royal charters and secured by provincial codes, and the right of assembly and petition were asserted. Keeping of a standing army in time of peace without the consent of the legislature of the colony where the army was kept was declared illegal. The exercise of legislative power by a crown appointed council was declared "unconstitutional, dangerous and destructive to the freedom of American legislation."

"All and each of which the . . . deputies, in behalf of themselves, and their constituents, do claim, demand, and insist on, as their indubitable rights and liberties; which cannot be legally taken from them, altered or abridged by any power whatever, without their own consent, by their representatives in their several provincial legislatures."

The acts passed by parliament since 1763 to which they were opposed were then enumerated. "To these grievous acts and measures, Americans cannot submit, but in hopes their fellow subjects in Great-Britain will, on a revision of them, restore us to that state, in which both countries found happiness and prosperity, we have for the present, only resolved to pursue the following peaceable measures: 1. To enter into a non-importation, non-consumption, and non-exportation agreement or association. 2. To prepare an address to the people of Great-Britain, and a memorial to the inhabitants of British America: and 3. To prepare a loyal address to his majesty, agreeable to resolutions already entered into."

Non-importation, non-consumption, and non-exportation.—By commercial restrictions the delegates hoped to force the British government to change its policy. On September 22 Congress voted to request colonial merchants and others not to place orders for British goods and to delay or suspend orders already sent until Congress could make known its policy. Five days later it resolved that from December 1 there should be no importation of goods from Great Britain or Ireland, or of British or Irish make, and that such goods be neither used nor purchased. On September 30 it was resolved that exportation to Great Britain, Ireland, and the British West Indies ought to cease after September 10, 1775, unless grievances were redressed, and a committee was appointed to formulate a plan for the enforcement of non-importation, non-consumption, and non-exportation.

The Association.—On October 20 the delegates adopted the "Association" which provided that after December 1 British or Irish goods, East India tea, molasses, syrups, paneles, coffee, and pimento from the British plantations or from Dominica, wines from Madeira or the Western Islands, and foreign indigo should not be imported into British America. It was agreed that slaves should not be imported or purchased after December 1, and slave traders were not to be allowed to rent vessels or purchase goods. Non-exportation was not to be put into force until September 10, 1775, but if redress had not been obtained by that time, American goods would be cut off from Great Britain, Ireland, or the West Indies. Rice, however, might be exported to Europe. Congress agreed to encourage frugality, economy, and industry, to promote agriculture, the arts, and manufactures, especially of wool, and to discourage extravagance and dissipation. Merchants and manufacturers were not to raise prices. A committee in each county, city, and town was to observe the conduct of persons, and if violations of the Association were discovered, the truth was to be published in the newspapers. If any colony did not accede to the Association, intercourse with that colony was to be cut off.

Attempts to obtain coöperation of other Colonies.—Congress also made an effort to obtain the coöperation of neighboring colonies by an address to the people of Quebec and by letters to the inhabitants of St. Johns, Nova Scotia, Georgia, and East and West Florida. A memorial to the people of British America, an address to the people of Great Britain, and a petition to the king were also prepared. May 10, 1775, was set as the date for the assembly of another congress, and on October 26 the First Continental Congress dissolved.

North's conciliatory resolution.—In January, 1775, parliament began consideration of the petition to the king and other papers relating to America. Chatham moved the withdrawal of the troops from Boston but the motion was defeated. On February 1 he presented a plan of conciliation based upon mutual concessions, but this was also rejected. On February 20 Lord North undertook the unexpected rôle of conciliator by a resolution which was considered in committee of the whole and passed by the commons a week later. The resolution provided "that when the Governour, Council, and Assembly, or General Court, of any . . . colonies in *America*, shall propose to make provision . . . for contributing their proportion to the common defence, (such proportion to be raised under the authority of the General Court, or General Assembly, of such Province or Colony, and disposable by Parliament,) and shall engage to make provision also for the support of the Civil Government, and the Administration of Justice, in such Province or Colony, it will be proper, if such proposal shall be approved by his Majesty and . . . Parliament . . . to forbear, in respect of such Province or Colony, to levy any Duty, Tax, or Assessment, or to impose any farther Duty, Tax, or Assessment, except only such Duties as it may be expedient to continue to levy or to impose for the regulation of commerce; the nett produce of the Duties last mentioned to be carried to the account of such Province or Colony respectively."

The Restraining Act.—The effect of North's resolution was nullified by the Restraining Act, which, in spite of Burke's powerful speech on conciliation, became law on March 13. This act confined the commerce of the New England colonies to Great Britain, Ireland, and the British West Indies, and prohibited the New Englanders from fishing in the northern fisheries, until "the trade and commerce of his Majesty's subjects may be carried on without interruption." In April the act was extended to New Jersey, Pennsylvania, Delaware, Maryland, Virginia, and South Carolina. The British government thus closed the door of conciliation and made the American Revolution inevitable.

READINGS

Adams, J., *Works*, II, 337–517; Adams, S., *Writing*, II–III; Becker, C. L., *Beginnings of the American People*, 202–253; Beer, G. L., *British Colonial Policy, 1754–1765*, 72–315; Bigelow, J., *The Life of Benjamin Franklin*, II, 7–337; Channing, E., *A History of the United States*, III, 29–154; Dickinson, J., *Writings*, in Historical Society of Pennsylvania, *Memoirs*, XIV, 307–406; Doyle, J. A., "The Quarrel with Great Britain, 1761–1776," in *Cambridge Modern History*, VII, 148–208; Fisher, S. G., *The Struggle for American Independence*, I, 1–300; Frothingham, Richard, *The Rise of the Republic*, 158–455; Henry, W. W., *Patrick Henry*, I, 24–357; Howard, G. E., *Preliminaries of the Revolution;* Hutchinson, P. O., *The Diary and Letters of his Excellency Thomas Hutchinson*, I; Johnson, E. R., *History of Domestic and*

Foreign Commerce of the United States, I, 84–121; *Journals of the Continental Congress*, I (Worthington C. Ford, ed.); Lecky, W. E. H., *History of England in the Eighteenth Century*, III, 290–460; Lincoln, C. H., *The Revolutionary Movement in Pennsylvania, 1760–1776;* Macdonald, William, *Select Charters,* 272–396; Trevelyan, G. O., *The American Revolution*, Part I, 1–253; Tyler, M. C., *Literary History of the American Revolution*, I; *Patrick Henry*, 32–134; Van Tyne, C. H., *The American Revolution*, 3–24; Becker, C. L., *The Eve of the Revolution;* Eckenrode, H. J., *The Revolution in Virginia;* Schlesinger, A. M., *The Colonial Merchants and the American Revolution, 1763–1776.*

CHAPTER XXIV

FROM LEXINGTON TO INDEPENDENCE

THE OPENING OF HOSTILITIES

Enforcement of the Association.—The Association adopted by the Continental Congress was approved throughout the colonies. In county and town meetings, in assemblies, provincial congresses, or special conventions, the patriot party expressed its approval. Though the New York assembly refused to sanction the proceedings of Congress, the committee of correspondence and many counties chose inspection committees. In Georgia the patriots had a difficult time, but when the provincial congress assembled at Savannah in March, 1775, forty-five of the deputies ratified the Association and local inspection committees were formed.

Military preparations.—Throughout the colonies military preparations were in progress. In October, 1774, Charles Lee wrote from Philadelphia to an English nobleman, "Virginia, Rhode Island and Carolina are forming corps. Massachusetts Bay has long had a sufficient number instructed to become instructive of the rest. Even this Quakering province is following the example." In December the provincial convention of Maryland recommended that all males between the ages of sixteen and fifty should form themselves into military companies. Delaware made provision for the arming and drilling of militia. Connecticut ordered the towns to double their military supplies, and Rhode Islanders seized forty-four cannon from the Newport batteries.

Whigs, neutrals, and Tories.—In spite of the military ardor thus displayed, public opinion was by no means a unit. In general the people were divided into three groups, patriots, neutrals, and Loyalists. Among the patriots, or Whigs as they were called, was a small group of ultra-radicals who favored

independence. A great majority of the Whigs stood for strenuous opposition to British policy but not for independence.
The neutrals in the main presented three shades of opinion:
those with patriot sympathies but who were still wavering, those
who were indifferent or were religiously opposed to violence,
and those who had Loyalist leanings but had not made a definite
decision. The third great group was composed of Loyalists or
Tories. These were not all of like mind, one portion being openly
in favor of the king but not ready to take up arms, the rest being
openly belligerent. As the Revolution progressed shadings within
groups gradually disappeared, wavering neutrals linked themselves with patriots or Loyalists, and sections became distinctly
Whig or Tory.

Even before the adoption of the Association, ill feeling showed
itself. As Howard says, "Tarring and featherings was becoming
the order of the day. . . . Loyalists were bitterly stigmatized
as Tories and traitors, and the cause of liberty was sullied by
acts of intolerance and persecution." Channing says, "The
story of tarring and featherings, riotings and burnings becomes
monotonous, almost as much so as the reading of the papers
that poured forth from counties, towns, conventions, meetings,
congresses, and private individuals."

Revolution in Massachusetts.—The people of Massachusetts
refused to submit to the Regulating Act. The "mandamus"
councillors were threatened with violence and either declined
the appointment or resigned, and the courts were unable to sit.
On September 1, 1774, Gage sent soldiers to seize some powder
stored near Boston and a rumor spread that the war ships had
fired on Boston. The militia began to gather from neighboring
counties, and Israel Putnam summoned the Connecticut militia
to march to the assistance of Boston.

Gage refused to allow the meeting of the assembly called for
October 5, but most of the representatives met at Salem where
they declared themselves a provincial congress. A few days
later the congress moved to Concord and then to Cambridge.
It appointed a committee of safety which was empowered to call
out the militia, and other committees attended to the collecting
of stores and general defence. After the gathering of the second
provincial congress on February 1, 1775, the committee of

safety under the leadership of John Hancock and Joseph Warren
was authorized to distribute arms.

Lexington.—On April 18 the watchful patriots discovered
that British troops were preparing for an expedition, and William
Dawes and Paul Revere were sent to spread the alarm.   Soon

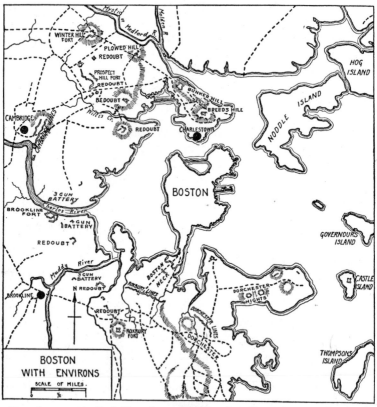

(Based on map in G. O. Trevelyan, *The American Revolution*, Part I, at end)

after dawn of April 19 the British troops approached Lexington
where they found sixty or seventy minutemen under arms.
When they did not obey the order to lay down their arms and
disperse, a shot was fired, followed by a volley which killed
eight and wounded ten of the colonials.   The regulars went on
to Concord where another encounter occurred at the old North
Bridge where the British had stationed a guard.   After destroy-

ing some stores, the troops started back toward Boston. By this time the militia had gathered, and the incensed farmers and villagers from behind trees, rocks, and fences poured in a deadly fire which did not slacken until the soldiers were relieved at Lexington by troops under Lord Percy. When the march was resumed the battle began again, nor did it cease until the weary soldiers reached Charlestown.

Boston besieged.—The news of Lexington started thousands of New England volunteers toward Boston. John Stark led the New Hampshire men; Israel Putnam left his plow in the furrow to lead the Connecticut volunteers; and Nathanael Greene headed the Rhode Islanders. The volunteer forces in a few weeks were reinforced by large bodies of colonial troops. The Massachusetts congress voted to raise thirteen thousand six hundred men, and it called upon the other New England colonies to bring the army up to thirty thousand. The Rhode Island assembly voted to raise fifteen hundred men, and Connecticut six thousand, two-thirds of whom were to be sent to the aid of Boston. Gage, who had been reinforced with troops under Howe, Clinton, and Burgoyne, found his army of six or seven thousand veterans shut up in Boston by an undisciplined and poorly organized force, which, however, outnumbered him three or four to one.

Bunker Hill.—The city was open to attack from Dorchester Heights and the Charlestown hills. To forestall the British, the colonials decided to occupy Bunker Hill. On the night of June 16 Colonel William Prescott was sent to fortify the position. For reasons which are not entirely clear, he led his men to Breed's Hill where a redoubt was constructed. When dawn disclosed the fortification, the warships and batteries opened fire. Prescott asked for reinforcements and small detachments came to his assistance. A British council of war was called. Clinton suggested the seizure of the causeway on Charlestown neck, a movement which would have cut off the colonial force from the mainland. But Gage and Howe, underestimating the fighting ability of their opponents, foolishly insisted upon a frontal attack. Twice the British were repulsed with staggering losses, but during the third charge the colonials exhausted their ammunition and were forced to retreat, first to Bunker Hill and then back to their own lines. Though the colonials technically had suffered a defeat, great was the rejoicing over the battle, for colonial troops had proven their prowess against the British regulars and had taken a toll of two for one.

Ticonderoga and Crown Point.—While the troops were gathering about Boston, it occurred to Benedict Arnold that Ticonderoga would be an easy prize. He submitted his ideas to Warren and the committee of safety, who authorized him to proceed with not over four hundred men to reduce the fort. On the way to Boston Arnold had divulged his thoughts to certain Connecticut friends who immediately organized an expedition with the same object. Ethan Allen and others from the Hampshire grants had also conceived the idea of capturing the fortress and were on the march when joined by Arnold, who had gone forward ahead of his troops. Immediately the question of rank arose and after considerable discussion Allen and Arnold agreed to command jointly for the time being.

On May 10 Ticonderoga surrendered without a struggle and this was followed by an easy conquest of Crown Point and Ft. George. By this time Allen completely ignored his colleague, but the arrival of about a hundred of Arnold's men gave him his opportunity. Having captured a British schooner Arnold decided to make a raid on St. Johns. The town was easily captured and a British sloop fell into the hands of the audacious colonial. The operations supplied the Whig army with much needed artillery and stores, and it opened the way for operations in Canada.

Rebellion in Virginia.—Virginia at the same time was in a state of rebellion. The second revolutionary convention assembled at Richmond in March, 1775, and Patrick Henry boldly sounded the call to arms. The governor, Lord Dunmore, in alarm ordered the removal of the gunpowder from the magazine at Williamsburg and soon several thousand armed men made ready to march on the capital. When some of the leaders hesitated, Henry placed himself at the head of an armed band and marched toward Williamsburg. The governor discreetly agreed to pay for the powder, but two days later (May 6, 1775) issued a proclamation charging the people "not to aid, abet, or give countenance to the said Patrick Henry, or any other persons concerned in such unwarrantable combinations." In May a legal assembly was called but the members appeared in arms, and an attempted conciliation failed when it became known that a trap was prepared to kill any one who tampered with the magazine. Fearful of the mob, the governor fled to a war vessel.

The Mecklenburg Resolves.—The news of Lexington aroused every colony. South Carolina immediately raised two regiments. In North Carolina some of the frontiersmen held a meeting at Charlotte, Mecklenburg County, and passed resolutions that crown commissions in the colonies were null and void, and that colonial constitutions were suspended. They also made governmental regulations until Congress could provide laws for them. The original resolutions were destroyed and afterward were reproduced from memory in the form of the so-called "Mecklenburg Declaration of Independence" of May 20. Reliable historians now reject the authenticity of this document, but the original resolves were undoubtedly genuine.

THE SECOND CONTINENTAL CONGRESS

The delegates.—The Second Continental Congress assembled at Philadelphia on May 10, 1775, all but Georgia and Rhode Island being represented. On May 13 Lyman Hall, representing St. John's parish, Georgia, arrived, but not until July 20 was notice received that Georgia had acceded to the Association and appointed delegates. Stephen Hopkins, the first Rhode Island delegate to appear, arrived May 18. Peyton Randolph of Virginia was elected president, but he found it necessary to leave Congress on May 24, and John Hancock was chosen president. Most of the delegates had been in the first Congress; among the new members was Benjamin Franklin, who had recently returned from England; Thomas Jefferson was elected to represent Virginia in the place of Peyton Randolph.

Nature of the work of Congress.—The conservative Whigs were still in the majority. They favored another petition to the king, but the state of war was recognized by all and Congress shouldered the responsibility of directing the Revolution as a defensive war. The early activities of Congress were devoted mainly to the raising, organizing, and equipping of the armies, to building and equipping a fleet, to perfecting the organization of the Revolution, to protecting the frontiers and obtaining alliances with the Indians, to enforcing the Association, to justifying the Revolution and seeking aid outside of the thirteen colonies, and to seeking redress from the British crown.

Military preparations.—Congress worked strenuously to raise troops and to obtain munitions and other stores. Efforts were made to stimulate recruiting, to perfect the organization of the militia, and to hasten the assembling of forces. The manufacture of cannon, guns, and gunpowder was encouraged and attempts were made to increase the supplies of lead, nitre, and salt. Congress recommended to the various assemblies and conventions that they provide sufficient stores of ammunition for their colonies and that they devise means for furnishing with arms such effective men as were too poor to buy them.

Organization of the army.—The armies already in the field were recognized by Congress. On June 14 a committee was appointed to draft rules for the army and on the following day Washington was appointed to command the continental forces. Arrangements were soon made for the appointment of four major-generals, eight brigadier-generals, and minor officers. The first major-generals were Artemus Ward, Charles Lee, Philip Schuyler, and Israel Putnam, Schuyler being placed in command of the New York department. Rules and regulations for the army were also adopted and provision was made for the establishment of a hospital.

Organization of the navy.—For the protection of the coasts Congress at first depended upon the efforts of individual colonies, recommending that they make provision, by armed vessels or otherwise, for the protection of their harbors and navigation on their coasts. Colonial vessels were utilized to capture British transports, but it soon became evident that a navy under congressional control would be more effective. During October, 1775, Congress decided to fit out four vessels and on November 28 adopted rules for the regulation of the navy. On December 13 provision was made for the building of thirteen war craft and on the twenty-second officers were appointed. Ezek Hopkins was made commander-in-chief of the fleet; the captains were Dudley Saltonstall, Abraham Whipple, Nicholas Biddle, and

John B. Hopkins. Among the first-lieutenants was John Paul Jones.

Prizes and privateers.—On November 25 Congress adopted regulations regarding prizes, and advised the legislative bodies to erect admiralty courts or to give to the local courts admiralty jurisdiction. It also provided "That in all cases an appeal shall be allowed to Congress, or such person or persons as they shall appoint for the trials of appeals." In March, 1776, Congress resolved "That the inhabitants of these colonies be permitted to fit out armed vessels to cruize on the enemies of these United Colonies." In April Congress adopted a form of commission and instructions to commanders of privateers, and decided to issue letters of marque and reprisal.

First steps in financing the Revolution.—The financing of the Revolution was one of the most difficult tasks confronting Congress. The first step in raising money was taken on June 3, 1775, when a committee was appointed to borrow £6,000 to purchase gunpowder. A committee was also appointed to bring in an estimate of money necessary to be raised. On June 22 Congress resolved to emit $2,000,000 in bills of credit and pledged the "confederated colonies" for their redemption. Once embarked upon the perilous course of paper finance, issue followed issue in rapid succession. At first the promissory notes passed readily, but they soon began to depreciate and eventually became worthless. Nevertheless they carried the Revolution through its most trying years.

Establishment of a post office.—The need of "speedy and secure conveyance of intelligence from one end of the Continent to the other" was recognized and a committee was appointed to consider the establishment of posts. On July 26 the post office was established, Benjamin Franklin being elected Postmaster General. He was authorized to establish "a line of posts . . . from Falmouth in New England to Savannah in Georgia, with as many cross posts as he shall think fit."

An Indian policy adopted.—Control of the Indians was vital for the safety of the frontier. It was felt that if the British ministry should induce the tribes to commit hostile acts, the colonies would be justified in entering into alliances with Indian nations. It was hoped that the Iroquois might be kept neutral.

"Talks" were prepared, goods to be used as presents were purchased, and money was provided. The frontier was laid off into three departments which were placed under commissioners. The Six Nations and tribes to the north of them were in the northern department; tribes between the Iroquois and the Cherokee were in the middle department; and the Cherokee and Indians south of them were in the southern department.

Enforcement of the Association.—Congress continued the policy of trade restriction. On May 17 it resolved that exports to Quebec, Nova Scotia, the Island of St. Johns, Newfoundland, Georgia except St. John's parish, and to East and West Florida, must cease, and that supplies must not be furnished to the British fisheries. After Georgia appointed delegates, the colony was admitted to the Association. On June 2 Congress resolved that no bill of exchange, draught, or order of any British officer should be honored, and that no money, provisions, or other necessaries be furnished the British army or navy.

On June 26 Congress resolved that, as attempts were being made to divide the people of North Carolina and defeat the Association, it was recommended to that colony to associate for the defence of American liberty and to organize the militia, Congress offering to provide pay for a thousand men in the colony. On July 4 a resolution was adopted that the restraining acts were "unconstitutional, oppressive, and cruel," and that commercial opposition should be made to them.

As doubts had arisen with respect to the true spirit and construction of the Association, on August 1 Congress defined it as follows: "Under the prohibition . . . to export to, or import from, the Islands of Great Britain and Ireland, this Congress intends to comprise all exportation to, and importation from, the islands of Jersey, Guernsey, Sark, Alderney, and Mann, and every European island and settlement within the British dominions: and that under the denomination of the West Indies, this Congress means to comprehend all the West India islands, British and foreign, to whatever state, power, or prince belonging, or by whomsoever governed, and also the Summer islands, Bahama Islands, Berbicia and Surinam on the Main, and every island and settlement within the latitude of the southern line of Georgia and the Equator."

The necessity of obtaining supplies forced Congress to make special provisions for the importation of munitions of war. On July 15, 1775, a resolution was adopted that "every vessel importing Gun powder, Salt petre, Sulphur, provided they bring with the sulphur four times as much salt petre, brass field pieces, or good muskets fitted with Bayonets, within nine Months from the date of this resolution, shall be permitted to load and export the produce of these colonies, to the value of such powder and stores aforesd, the non-exportation agreement notwithstanding." On November 2 Congress adopted a resolution to close the ports until March 1, but from time to time special provisions were made for the exportation and importation of goods. The delegates frequently discussed the question of opening the ports, as shown by John Adams's *Autobiography* which says: "This measure . . . labored exceedingly, because it was considered as a bold step to independence. Indeed, I urged it expressly with that view, and as connected with the institution of government in all the States, and a declaration of national independence." On April 6, 1776, the ports were opened to world commerce except trade with Great Britain and her possessions.

Letter to the people of Canada —The congressional leaders hoped to strengthen their resistance by obtaining the coöperation of the Canadians. A letter "to the oppressed inhabitants of Canada" was approved on May 29. Congress condoled with them "on the arrival of that day, in the course of which, the sun could not shine on a single freeman in all your extensive dominion. . . . By the introduction of your present form of government, or rather present form of tyranny, you and your wives and your children are made slaves. . . . We are informed you have already been called upon to waste your lives in a contest with us. Should you, by complying in this instance, assent to your new establishment [the Quebec Act], and a war break out with France, your wealth and your sons may be sent to perish in expeditions against their islands in the West Indies. We yet entertain hopes of your uniting with us in the defence of our common liberty."

Attempts to influence public opinion in the British Empire.— Congress hoped by appeals to the inhabitants of the British Isles to arouse public opinion, thereby bringing pressure to bear upon a Ministry and subservient parliament which had shown themselves to be irresponsible and tyrannous. Addresses to the people of Great Britain and Ireland were accordingly prepared. A letter to the Lord Mayor, aldermen, and liveries of London was drawn up expressing thanks "for the virtuous and unsolicited resentment you have shown to the violated rights of a free people." A letter of friendship was sent to the assembly of Jamaica and a communication regarding commerce was sent to Bermuda.

Statement to the army.—On July 6 Congress approved a declaration setting forth the causes and necessity of taking up arms, which was to be published by Washington upon his arrival at Boston. The declaration presented the usual arguments regarding constitutional rights and gave an account of the progress of events. That independence was desired was denied in the following words: "We have not raised armies with ambitious designs of separating from Great Britain, and establishing independent states. We fight not for glory or for conquest. . . . In our own native land, in defence of the freedom that is our birth right, . . . and for the protection of our property . . . we have taken up arms."

Petition to the king.—The radicals believed that a war of independence could not be avoided, but the conservatives restrained them, hoping that the force of public opinion, a bold show of resistance, and commercial restrictions would change the ministerial policy. Another direct appeal to the king was decided upon and on May 29 resolutions were adopted, "that with a sincere design of contributing by all the means in our power, not incompatible with just regard for the undoubted rights and true interests of these colonies, to the promotion of this most desirable reconciliation, an humble and dutiful petition be presented to his Majesty." The petition, signed on July 8, was couched in respectful terms as the following quotation shows: "We . . . beseech your Majesty, that your royal authority and influence may be graciously interposed to procure us relief from our afflicting fears and jealousies, occasioned by the system before mentioned, and to settle peace through every part of your dominions, with all humility submitting to your Majesty's wise consideration whether it may not be expedient for facilitating those important purposes, that your Majesty be pleased to direct some mode, by which the united applications of your faithful colonists to the throne, in pursuance of their common councils, may be improved into a happy and permanent reconciliation; and that, in the mean time, measures may be taken for preventing the further destruction of the lives of your Majesty's subjects; and that such statutes as more immediately distress any of your Majesty's colonies may be repealed."

Reply to Lord North.—As several of the colonies were desirous of knowing the congressional attitude toward Lord North's conciliatory resolution, on July 31 Congress adopted a formal report which closed with the following statement: "When the world reflects how inadequate to justice are these vaunted terms; when it attends to the rapid and bold succession of injuries, which have been aimed at these colonies, when it reviews the pacific and respectful expostulations, which . . . were the sole arms we opposed to them; when it observes that our complaints were either not heard at all, or were answered with new and accumulated injury, . . . when it considers the great armaments with which they have invaded us, and the circumstances of cruelty with which they have commenced and prosecuted hostilities; when these things we say, are laid together and attentively considered, can the world be deceived into an opinion that we are unreasonable, or can it hesitate to believe with us, that nothing but our own exertions may defeat the ministerial sentence of death or abject submission."

Stubborn attitude of the government.—George III and his ministers had gained no wisdom from the rebellious attitude in America. The petition, which had been entrusted to Richard Penn, reached London on August 14, but not until a week later did Lord Dartmouth, the secretary for the colonies, consent to look at a copy of the document and not until September was it presented to the king. On August 23 George III published a proclamation which declared the Americans rebels, and after his examination of the petition, the king saw no reason for revising it. At the next session of parliament acts were passed which prohibited trade with the thirteen colonies, ordered the seizure and confiscation of ships engaged in trade with them, and permitted British commanders to impress sailors from seized vessels.

The German mercenaries.—A reorganization of the cabinet had forced the amiable Dartmouth out of the colonial office, his successor being Lord George Germaine. Lord Rochford was made secretary of state for the southern department, and Lord Suffolk was retained in the northern department to which office fell the business with Germany. The British army was sadly in need of recruits. In Scotland the men of Argyllshire and Inverness-shire readily entered the army for colonial service, but in Ireland and England the people showed little enthusiasm for a war which was intended to subdue their freedom-loving brethren over the seas. To raise the necessary troops the king turned to the continent. An attempt to obtain the use of the Scotch troops which had long been in Dutch service failed and Catherine II refused to furnish Russian infantry, but in Germany British overtures met with better success. The Landgrave of Hesse-Cassel, the Duke of Brunswick, and some other needy princes were willing to sell the services of their subjects for British gold. During the war over thirty thousand mercenaries were hired in Germany for service in America. In the words of Lecky, "The conduct of England in hiring German mercenaries to subdue the essentially English population beyond the Atlantic, made reconciliation hopeless, and the Declaration of Independence inevitable."

PROGRESS OF THE WAR

Burning of Falmouth.—Events were also taking place in America which were convincing the public that the war for independence must be fought to the bitter end. In October, 1775, four British war vessels sailed into the harbor of Falmouth, now known as Portland, and set fire to the town. Three-fourths of the dwellings were destroyed and a thousand unoffending people were made homeless.

The Canadian campaign.—The efforts of Congress to enlist the Canadians in the colonial cause did not meet with success and the invasion of Canada was determined upon. Two forces were sent northward. One under Richard Montgomery was to proceed by the Lake Champlain route, seize Montreal, and then march to Quebec. The other under Benedict Arnold was to go up the Kennebec and down the Chaudière, and join the other force. Montgomery captured Montreal and then made a juncture with Arnold. On December 31 an attack was made on Quebec, but Montgomery was killed, Arnold was wounded, and the forces were repulsed. But in spite of terrible sufferings in his army, Arnold kept Quebec in a state of blockade the rest of the winter.

Siege of Boston.—When Washington arrived at Cambridge, he found a disorganized army which was short of food, ammunition, and uniforms, and without hospital service. Fortunately the British did not take advantage of the situation, and gradually the commander brought order out of chaos. By March, 1776, Washington was prepared to make an offensive move. Taking advantage of the fact that the British had not fortified Dorchester Heights, on the night of March 4 colonial troops seized the position which commanded Boston. On the seventeenth the British army, accompanied by about a thousand Loyalists, sailed for Halifax.

Fighting in Virginia and North Carolina.—While Washington was besieging Boston, Lord Dunmore was making reprisals along the Virginia rivers. After the defeat of some of his Loyalist supporters at Great Bridge, the governor caused the burning of Norfolk on January 1, 1776. North Carolina was also torn by civil war. Governor Martin had been driven from the colony, and from the refuge of a war vessel commissioned Donald McDonald to collect an army of Loyalists in the central and western counties. He also appealed to Sir Henry Clinton for aid. With a force of sixteen hundred men McDonald marched toward the coast, but on February 27, 1776, he was met by patriot forces at Moore's Creek and his Loyalist army was practically annihilated. When Clinton's fleet appeared off the coast, ten thousand North Carolina militia were ready to meet him. Clinton lingered for a time off Cape Fear and then sailed to Charleston where he hoped to arouse the Loyalists of the coasts and the German settlers of the interior.

Defence of Charleston.—Edward Rutledge with six thousand militia prepared to defend the city. Colonel Moultrie, with his forces back of rude fortifications on Sullivan's Island, made ready to defend the harbor. On June 28 the fleet attacked. Most of the British shot buried themselves in the palmetto logs and banks of sand from behind which Moultrie's men poured a fire which wrought havoc on the crowded decks. An attempt to make a landing proved a failure and Charleston was saved.

THE LOYALISTS

The people not united.—Up to 1774 the majority of Americans were not united in opposition to British policy, but acts of violence and retaliation, the meeting of Congress, and the organization of revolutionary committees, brought about a rapid crystallization of public opinion. Loyalty to Great Britain was the normal state. The Whigs were the nullifiers and eventually the secessionists. That they were able to perfect an organization and carry on a successful rebellion has obscured the fact that they were in reality but an active minority. The masses were indifferent or were loyal supporters of Great Britain. It is impossible to estimate accurately the number of Loyalists; they varied with localities and fluctuated with the fortunes of war. Some historians estimate them as a third of the population, others as one-half.

The Tory element in the colonies.—The great Loyalist stronghold was New York. There the moderate Tories had controlled the situation for several years. They had favored the assembling of the First Continental Congress, but when that body adopted the Association, they opposed it. After the battle of Lexington the Whigs grew in power and succeeded in setting up a provincial congress. But several counties remained Loyalist, and until the occupation of New York City by British troops a state of civil war existed in the province. After that event the British lines furnished a refuge for Tories from all the colonies.

Next to New York Pennsylvania contained the largest Tory element. There the Quakers, the proprietary interests, and a large German population combined to oppose the Whig movement. In New Jersey, Maryland, and Delaware, the Tory element was so numerous that only with the greatest difficulty did the Whigs obtain the support of those colonies for independence. In New England the Loyalists were not powerful. In Massachusetts, New Hampshire, and Rhode Island they formed an insignificant part of the population, but in the region which afterward became the state of Vermont and in Connecticut they were numerous enough to be a menace.

In the South, Virginia was dominated by the Whigs. The impolitic acts of Lord Dunmore had alienated all but a small element of the population. The Scotch merchants of Norfolk and many planters had supported the governor, but his reprisals on the coast, his proclamation offering freedom to negroes and indented servants who would enlist, and the burning of Norfolk destroyed the Tory power in the province. North Carolina which had recently been torn by the War of the Regulators was probably about equally divided, and in South Carolina and Georgia the farmers and cattlemen of the interior were usually Loyalists; but the British naval demonstrations and the defeat of Tory bands did much to win converts to the Whig cause in the three southern colonies.

A classification of the Loyalists.—The Loyalists, or Tories as they were called in derision, have been classified by Professor Van Tyne as the office holders whose incomes depended upon the existing régime; those whose friends were among the official class or who depended upon that class for preferment; the majority of the Anglican clergy; the conservative people of all classes, especially the wealthy merchants, the aristocracy of culture, of dignified professions and callings, and of hereditary wealth, and those who held office by virtue of wise selection; the king worshipers who were moved by theory of government rather than by concrete facts; the legality Tories who believed that parliament had a constitutional right to tax the colonies; the religious Tories whose dictum was fear God and honor the king; and the factional Tories who were influenced by family feuds and political animosities.

The religious division.—The religious factor was one of the most important causes of division. An Anglican bishopric for the colonies had long been contemplated and the dissenting churches believed that the ministry was about to urge its establishment. In New England where the Congregational church was in the ascendency and in those sections where the Presbyterians and Baptists were powerful, the establishment of an episcopate was especially feared. Already the Anglican church numbered three hundred parishes in America. Throughout the colonies it was the church of the official class and in the South it was the church of the aristocracy. The southern Episcopalians were divided on the paramount political questions, but in New York the religious and political parties coincided. New York politics for many years had been factional, the De Lanceys who were Episcopalians being leaders in invariable opposition to the Livingstons who were Presbyterians. Both in New York and Connecticut those of the Episcopal faith were almost invariably Loyalists.

The Tory argument.—The Tories believed in no taxation without representation, but they differed with the Whigs in their interpretation of the word representation. The Tories accepted the English meaning which was based upon the idea that a man enjoyed representation not by the fact that he had voted for a member of parliament but by his belonging to one of the three great estates of the nation, each estate being represented in parliament. They admitted that this was an imperfect type of representation, but it was the ancient constitutional type. They believed that the relationship of the colonies to the mother country should be defined more clearly, but they did not believe that the Whigs had a right to demand a fundamental change in the constitution of the British Empire.

Moses Coit Tyler has pointed out that the other Tory arguments were based upon questions of expediency. (1) Was it expedient to reject the taxing power of parliament? (2) Was separation from the empire expedient? The Whigs argued that parliamentary taxes might become confiscatory. The Tories replied that parliament recognized the principle that all parts of the empire should be taxed equitably and justly, and that a powerful minority, which counted among its members Fox and Burke, were bent upon protecting the colonies. The Tories could see no reason for separation. They pointed out that until the beginning of 1776 the Whigs had consistently disavowed the idea of independence. Why then this sudden change? The Tories believed that concessions were about to be made which would make separation unnecessary and undesirable.

Persecution of the Loyalists.—After Lexington the Loyalists became intolerable to the Whigs. They must show their all giance to the patriot cause or suffer the consequences. The favorite method of persecution was tarring and feathering, but riding the Tory on the liberty pole or ducking occurred frequently. Under the direction of the revolutionary committees freedom of speech was suppressed and the liberty of the press was destroyed. Any one who opposed the Association was considered an enemy; he must agree or be persecuted. When the Loyalists attempted to form counter associations, they were met with stern methods of repression. Whig clergymen held conferences in Loyalist communities to try to convert them, and obdurate places were visited by armed bands. When the Tories attempted to arm, their leaders were seized.

Congress attempts to control the Loyalists.—The Loyalists were lacking in organization, and when the governors were driven from the colonies, they lost their natural leaders. When calls for aid came from the deposed officials, many Tories formed bands and attempted to coöperate with the British forces. So serious was the situation that Congress, as early as October, 1775, recommended to the revolutionary governments that they arrest every person who might endanger the colonies or "the liberties of America." On December 30 a congressional committee reported that the Tories of Tryon County, New York, had collected arms and munitions, and that several Loyalists had enlisted in British service. Orders were issued to General Schuyler to seize the stores, disarm the Tories, and apprehend their leaders.

Congress extends the olive branch.—Congress hoped to win over a large part of the Loyalists and on January 2, 1776, it passed a pacific resolution which stated that as certain honest, well-meaning, but uniformed people had been deceived by ministerial agents, it recommended to the various committees and friends of American liberty to treat such persons with kindness and attention, to view their errors as proceeding from want of information, to explain to them the true nature of the controversy, and to try to convince them of the justice of the American cause. The colonial governments were instructed to frustrate the machinations of enemies and restrain wicked practices. It was the opinion of Congress that the more dangerous ones should be placed in custody, and to accomplish this the local

authorities were given the right to call to their aid the continental troops.

The Queen's County Tories.—Immediately afterward Congress learned that the Tories of Queen's County, New York, were
especially troublesome. Congress accordingly decided that they
should be put outside of the protection of the United Colonies,
that all trade and intercourse with them should cease, and that
none of them should be allowed to travel or reside outside of that
county without a certificate from the revolutionary government
of New York. Violators of this provision were to be imprisoned
for three months and lawyers were forbidden to try causes for
them. Troops were sent into the county.

Disarming of the Loyalists.—A congressional committee
which had under consideration the defence of New York, on
March 14 advised the disarming of the Loyalists on Staten
Island. Congress immediately ordered that eight thousand men
be sent to the defence of New York and recommendation was
made to all the colonies to disarm all persons "notoriously
disaffected to the cause of America," or who refused to associate
to defend, by arms, the United Colonies. The confiscated arms
were to be used in arming troops.

THE DECLARATION OF INDEPENDENCE

The colonies advised to form temporary governments.—Up
to the beginning of 1776 the Whigs disavowed the purpose or
desire for independence. But in spite of the view of the conservatives, Congress had been forced to assume the direction of
the war and had been called upon to advise several of the colonies
regarding the course to be pursued in organizing their governments. In answer to an inquiry from Massachusetts, Congress
replied that no obedience was due to the parliamentary act
altering the charter, and that the governor and lieutenant-
governor were to be considered absent and the offices vacant.
As there was no council, the provincial convention was advised
to write letters to the inhabitants of the places which were entitled to representation in the assembly, requesting them to
choose representatives; and when the assembly was chosen, it was
to elect councillors, "which assembly and council should exercise
the powers of Government, until a Governor, of his Majesty's

appointment, will consent to govern the colony according to its charter." New Hampshire was advised to call a full and free representation of the people who might establish such a form of temporary government as would "produce the happiness of the people and most effectually secure peace and good order in the province" during the dispute with Great Britain. Similar advice was given to South Carolina and Virginia.

Paine's "Common Sense."—The attitude of the British government, the events on the Canadian frontier and about Boston, and the burning of Falmouth and Norfolk, fanned the flames of rebellion to a white heat. When Tom Paine issued his pamphlet *Common Sense*, "the first open and unqualified argument in championship of the doctrine of American Independence," he found a receptive audience. The pamphlet held up to scorn the idea of kingship, argued that the security and happiness of the British people were due to their character and not to their constitution, asserted that the British colonial system was based upon English self-interest, and that only injuries and disadvantages would result from continued allegiance to Great Britain. Reconciliation, Paine argued, would result in the ruin of America, because England, ruled by self-interest, would still be the governing power, because any arrangement which might be obtained would be a temporary expedient, and because nothing but independence would keep the peace of the American continent. From every point of view, independence, he declared, was necessary. "The period of debate is closed. Arms, as the last resort, must decide the contest. . . . By referring the matter from argument to arms, a new era for politics is struck; a new method of thinking hath arisen. All plans, proposals, and so forth, prior to the nineteenth of April . . . are like the almanacs of last year." The pamphlet met with immediate success. It was read throughout the colonies and convinced thousands that independence was necessary.

The independence movement in the three southern colonies.— Early in 1776 three southern colonies took definite steps toward independence. In February a small revolutionary group in Savannah instructed delegates to agree to any measure for the general good which might be adopted by Congress. In March South Carolina gave similar instructions, and on April 12 the

provincial congress of North Carolina instructed its delegates
to concur with representatives from other colonies in declaring
independence. In spite of the action of South Carolina, the
colony was probably unconvinced of the necessity of separation
from Great Britain until the Charleston hostilities.

**Congress advises the colonies to suppress the authority of
Great Britain.**—On May 10 Congress recommended to the various assemblies and conventions that where no sufficient government had been established, such governments as would best
conduce to the happiness and safety of the people and of America
in general should be established. Five days later Congress
adopted a preamble to this resolution which contained the significant statement that the exercise of every kind of authority under
the British crown should be suppressed and all the powers of government exerted under the authority of the people of the colonies.

The German mercenaries.—On May 21 Congress received
copies of the treaties which Great Britain had made with the
Duke of Brunswick, the Landgrave of Hesse-Cassel, and the
Count of Anhalt-Zerbst, by which they agreed to furnish about
seventeen thousand troops to be used against the rebellious
colonies. These treaties were immediately published and were
a potent force in bringing some of the wavering colonies to instruct their delegates for independence.

Lee's Resolution.—In Virginia a convention was called to form
a new government, and on May 15 the Virginia delegates in
Congress were instructed to propose independence. Accordingly
on June 7 Richard Henry Lee moved in Congress "That these
United Colonies are, and of right ought to be, free and independent States, that they are absolved from all allegiance to the
British Crown, and that all political connection between them
and the State of Great Britain is, and ought to be, totally dissolved. That it is expedient forthwith to take the most effectual
measures for forming foreign alliances. That a plan of confederation be prepared and transmitted to the respective Colonies
for their consideration and approbation."

The debate on the resolution.—A declaration of independence
at that time was opposed by James Wilson, Robert R. Livingston,
John Dickinson, Edward Rutledge, and others. They declared
that they were friends of the measure but thought that it should

be postponed until the people demanded it. The middle colonies, they thought, "were not yet ripe for bidding adieu to British connection, but . . . were fast ripening." They argued that a declaration which was not unanimous would cause foreign powers either to refuse to make alliances with the colonies or to insist upon hard terms. It was believed that a successful termination of the New York campaign would make alliances possible on excellent terms.

John Adams, Lee, Wythe, and others argued for an immediate declaration. They saw no reason for waiting for every colony to express itself. They argued that a declaration of independence alone could bring about desired alliances. Without it the colonies would never know whether or not aid could be obtained from France or Spain. It was pointed out that the New York campaign might not be successful and that an alliance ought to be made while affairs bore a hopeful aspect. If an alliance were made at once with France, she might assist in cutting off British supplies and might divert enemy forces by an attack on the British West Indies. It was also pointed out that an immediate alliance would assist the people, who were in need of clothing and money.

Committees appointed.—It was decided to get the consent of the colonies before issuing the declaration, but a committee composed of Thomas Jefferson, John Adams, Benjamin Franklin, Roger Sherman, and Robert R. Livingston was appointed to prepare the document. Congress also decided to appoint committees to formulate a plan of confederation and to draft a form of treaties.

New England takes formal action.—The New England colonies had favored independence for some time. They now took formal action. In May Rhode Island instructed its delegates to agree to any acts which would hold the colonies together. In June Massachusetts, Connecticut, and New Hampshire instructed their delegates to support Lee's resolution.

The independence movement in the middle colonies.—The middle colonies still stood out and Congress made great efforts to induce them to give their support. After a hard struggle with Governor William Franklin, on June 22 the provincial congress of New Jersey authorized its delegates to agree to independence. Pennsylvania had been held back by the Quakers, Germans, and proprietary interests. When the conservative assembly refused to sanction independence, a vast crowd assembled in Philadelphia and voiced its displeasure. The Loyalists were terrorized and a patriot convention was formed which agreed to favor independence. Delaware formed a new government but failed to instruct its delegates regarding independence. In Maryland the provisional government induced Governor Eden to leave the colony and a special convention called by the council of safety gave the delegates the desired instructions. New York failed to express itself in favor of the great measure.

The Declaration of Independence.—On July 1 Lee's motion was debated in Congress, John Adams speaking for an immediate declaration of independence and Dickinson for delay. When the debate closed, nine states voted in the affirmative. Pennsylvania and South Carolina opposed immediate action; the Delaware vote was a tie, and the New York delegates were excused from voting. The final vote was postponed until the next day. The arrival of Rodney of Delaware gave the vote of that state for the Declaration. Dickinson and Morris did not appear and the other delegates from Pennsylvania voted in the affirmative. The South Carolina delegates, influenced by news that a great British fleet was off New York, took matters in their own hands and voted for independence. New York alone stood out.

The congressional committee had entrusted the preparation of the Declaration to Thomas Jefferson. After it had undergone the fire of criticism, on the evening of July 4 the document was approved by twelve states. On the following day copies signed by President Hancock and Secretary Thomson were sent to the various assemblies. The other signatures were added later. Although the New York delegates had not voted for the Declaration, on July 9 the New York provincial congress approved it, completing the long chain of states which stretched along the Atlantic seaboard from Nova Scotia to East Florida.

Contents of the Declaration.—This immortal document begins by setting forth certain "self-evident truths" concerning the rights of mankind and the nature of government. Then follow in nearly thirty paragraphs a list of charges against King George III, and a review of the efforts of the colonies to obtain redress. The last paragraph declares, in the resounding words of Lee's Resolution, "That these United Colonies are, and of right ought to be Free and Independent States; that they are absolved from all allegiance to the British Crown, and that all political connection between them and the State of Great Britain, is and ought to be totally dissolved." A new nation had been born.

READINGS

MILITARY EVENTS AND THE CONTINENTAL CONGRESS

Bolton, C. K., *The Private Soldier under Washington;* Channing, Edward, *History of the United States,* III, 155–206; Fiske, John, *The American Revolution,* I, 100–197; Greene, F. V., *The Revolutionary War,* 1–27; *Journals of the Continental Congress* (Worthington C. Ford, ed.), II–VI; Lecky, W. E. H., *History of England in the Eighteenth Century,* III, 461–500; Smith, J. H., *Our Struggle for the Fourteenth Colony,* I, 107–165; Trevelyan, G. O., *The American Revolution,* I, 254–390; Van Tyne, C. H., *The American Revolution,* 24–49; Winsor, Justin, *Narrative and Critical History,* VI, 1–274; Adams, C. F., *Studies Military and Diplomatic, 1775–1865,* pp. 1–21.

THE LOYALISTS

Flick, A. C., *Loyalism in New York* (Columbia University, *Studies in History,* etc., XIV, No. 1.); Tyler, M. C., "The Party of the Loyalists in the American Revolution," in *The American Historical Review,* I, 24–45; Van Tyne, C. H., *The Loyalists in the American Revolution;* Wallace, S., *The United Empire Loyalists.*

THE DECLARATION OF INDEPENDENCE

Friedenwald, H., *The Declaration of Independence;* Hazelton, J. H., *The Declaration of Independence;* Trevelyan, G. O., *The American Revolution,* II, 133–171; Van Tyne, C. H., *The American Revolution,* 50–101; Becker, C. L., *The Eve of the Revolution,* 200–256.

CHAPTER XXV

THE STRUGGLE FOR THE MIDDLE STATES

THE CONTEST FOR NEW YORK

Preparations to defend New York.—After the evacuation of Boston it was realized that New York would be a probable point of attack and great exertions were made to put it in a state of defence. Washington arrived on April 13, 1776; his troops, delayed by bad roads, came straggling in, and new levies began to arrive, the army being gradually augmented until it numbered about twenty thousand men. But the effective fighting force was several thousand less, for disease was ever present. Furthermore the raw recruits were poorly trained and equipped, and there were not enough artillerymen to man the batteries. The only cavalrymen who appeared were a small force from Connecticut and these, for reasons best known to himself, Washington did not retain in service. The defences were strengthened by works at Paulus Hook on the Jersey shore, and others on Governor's Island and at Red Hook on Long Island. Eleven redoubts were erected on Manhattan Island along the battery and up to a point opposite Hell Gate, and the hamlet of Brooklyn was fortified with seven redoubts. Obstructions were placed in the Hudson and a second line of defence was established at Forts Washington and Lee. Many historians point out that New York should have been abandoned, for Washington's army was too small to cope with the British, the Tories were certain to keep the enemy informed of the movements, the defences were not powerful enough to control the water approaches, and an active enemy could run by the defenses and land troops in the rear of the American army. To make the situation worse, the line of hills on Long Island, known as Brooklyn Heights, commanded New York. To occupy them it was necessary to divide the army, and in case of defeat, the defenders would be separated by a difficult channel from the main army on Manhattan Island.

As Trevelyan observes, Washington "placed, and kept, his troops in a position where they were certain to be defeated, and where, when defeated, they would most probably be surrounded and destroyed."

The British plan.—The British government hoped to annihilate the armies and cut off New England from the other colonies. By occupying New York and sending converging armies, one from the north, the other up the Hudson, the government believed that it could accomplish its purpose. Large reinforcements were sent to Quebec, and during July and August, 1776, British forces were concentrated on Staten Island and a great fleet assembled. The first forces to arrive at New York were those under General Howe which he brought from Halifax. Large reinforcements under Admiral Lord Howe and forces under Clinton and Cornwallis augmented the army until it numbered about thirty thousand men.

An attempt at conciliation.—Lord Howe hoped that peace could be made, and soon after his arrival, he addressed a letter to "George Washington, Esquire," but the epistle, which failed to recognize the position of the commander-in-chief, was returned. A personal envoy from Lord Howe also met with a rebuff. The British admiral had prepared a circular letter to several of the royal governors setting forth his authority as commissioner and stating the conciliatory terms sanctioned by the cabinet. These contained a mere promise of pardon to those who returned to allegiance and assisted in the restoration of tranquillity. In fact John Adams was marked out for a halter, but this was not divulged. The letters fell into the hands of Congress which ordered that they be published "that the good people of these United States may be informed of what nature are the commissioners, and what the terms, with the expectation of which, the insidious court of Britain has endeavoured to amuse and disarm them. . . ."

Battle of Long Island.—General Howe finally decided to attack the American position on Long Island. On the twenty-second and twenty-third of August twenty thousand troops and forty cannon were disembarked at Gravesend Bay, six or seven miles south of Brooklyn, but not until the evening of the twenty-sixth did the British advance. Washington had been misin-

formed as to the size of the landing force and had stationed only
nine thousand men on Long Island. These were under General
Nathanael Greene, but stricken by illness, he was forced to
retire from the command on August 23, and Sullivan who succeeded him was superseded by Putnam on the twenty-fifth.
Washington spent the twenty-sixth on the island and super-
intended the disposition of the forces.

The chief line of defence was the densely wooded Brooklyn
Heights which were crossed by several roads. One ran up from
Gravesend near the coast; four miles to the eastward two wagon
roads from Flatbush penetrated the heights; three miles farther
east a highway ran from the village of Jamaica. About five
thousand men were sent to defend the Gravesend and Flatbush
roads but Jamaica Pass was neglected. The British frontal
attacks met with stubborn resistance from the forces of Stirling and Sullivan, but their valor was useless for a large British
force pushed along the Jamaica road and got in the rear of the
American positions. A portion of the army succeeded in getting
back to the Brooklyn intrenchments, but Sullivan and Stirling
with about eleven hundred men were captured and several hundred were killed.

The withdrawal from Brooklyn.—Howe, who remembered
the disastrous frontal attack at Bunker Hill, decided not to
attack the Brooklyn defences until supported by the fleet, which
was held back by an adverse wind. His caution saved the
American army. Washington saw that Brooklyn was untenable
and he secretly planned to evacuate it. A brave show of force
was made by bringing over three regiments and by keeping up a
fusillade while water craft were being collected. Favored by a
subsidence of the storm and by a fog, during the night of the
twenty-ninth the entire army was successfully withdrawn.

Harlem.—After the battle of Long Island the British commissioners made overtures to Congress and a committee composed of Franklin, Edward Rutledge, and John Adams went to
Staten Island for a conference, but it failed completely. There
was nothing to do but to fight it out. That Manhattan Island
should have been abandoned immediately after the defeat at
Brooklyn Heights has been maintained by strategists, but Congress hesitated to evacuate New York City and Washington

does not appear to have insisted upon a withdrawal. As Trevelyan observes, "It is equally difficult to explain satisfactorily why Howe was so long about landing . . . , and why Washington was so slow in evacuating the city." On September 10 Hancock informed Washington that Congress did not desire to have him hold the city longer than he thought proper. Washington immediately acted. The removal of stores was hastened and most of the troops were withdrawn to Harlem Heights about halfway up the island, but Putnam was left in the city with some infantry and artillery, and five brigades were posted at points along the eastern shore. Not until September 13 did the British begin the movement for the occupation of Manhattan Island. On that day and the next several war vessels moved up into the East River and at eleven o'clock on the morning of the fifteenth British forces landed at Kip's Bay. There the American troops disgraced themselves by slight resistance followed by a confused flight. Howe neglected to follow up his initial success; had he done so he could have cut off the garrison of New York, but his procrastination allowed Putnam's force to rejoin the main army. Not until four in the afternoon did the British commence "a stately progress northward" and not until the next morning did they attack the American position. This time Washington's troops behaved well and the British were checked.

White Plains.—For four weeks the British army remained in front of the American position at Harlem. Howe finally decided upon his plan of campaign; leaving a force to protect New York City, on October 12 he moved his main army to the Westchester Peninsula with the object of getting on the flank and rear of the American army, and cutting off its supplies from the east; war ships were sent up the Hudson to cut off a retreat into New Jersey. After his landing on the peninsula Howe's movements were very slow and it was not until October 25 that he took up a position a few miles south of White Plains. The dilatory movement had given Washington the opportunity of moving his army to the mainland, and when Howe finally arrived near White Plains, he found the American army blocking his advance.

The British commander had just been heavily reinforced and his overwhelming army should have made short work of Washington's forces, but again Howe failed to win a decisive victory. On October 28 he ordered a general engagement and the first

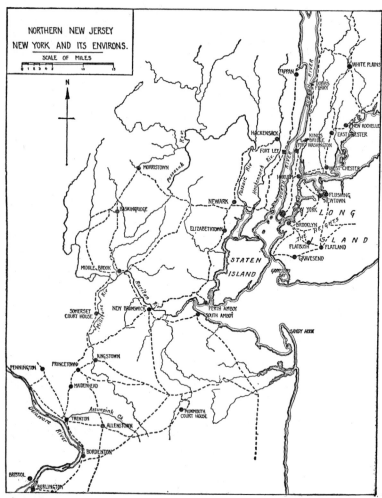

(Based on map in G. O. Trevelyan, *The American Revolution*, Part II, Vol. I, at end)

assault drove in the American outposts. A mile to the west of the main position was Chatterton's Hill which was held by fourteen hundred men. Against this hill Howe sent eight regi-

ments. Five which advanced for a frontal attack were checked
and the defenders only retired when outflanked by the other
three. A general engagement did not develop and on October
31 Washington retired to a line of heights somewhat back of
his former position.

The withdrawal from Quebec.—While Washington's army
rested at White Plains, heartening news came from the north;
and especially good news it was, for during the summer the
reports from the Canadian border had been filled with stories
of defeat and distress. Congress had made great efforts to
reinforce the army before Quebec, but on May 1 when General
Thomas arrived to take command, he had found less than two
thousand men assembled and half of them were in the hospitals.
Within a week the first British reinforcements arrived and Carleton took the offensive. Thomas was forced to fall back to Sorel
and the Americans were driven from their camp near Montreal.

The army falls back to Crown Point.—On June 5 General
John Sullivan arrived at Sorel with three thousand troops. As
Thomas had died of the smallpox Sullivan took command. He
determined to attack Three Rivers but the surprise failed and
his troops were routed. On June 14 an English fleet carrying
Carleton's army came up the river. Sullivan immediately broke
up his camp and retired to Crown Point, where for the time
being he was out of reach of the enemy, for Carleton's vessels
were of too deep draft to navigate the Sorel River. But disease
proved to be more dangerous than the British, for smallpox and
dysentery carried off the men by hundreds.

Ticonderoga becomes the base.—General Philip Schuyler was
in command of the northern department with headquarters at
Albany and General Horatio Gates was now in charge at Crown
Point. In July Gates withdrew most of the depleted force to
Ticonderoga. Large numbers of troops were sent north so that
by August the garrison numbered thirty-five hundred. Arnold
equipped a fleet of small vessels which he hoped would delay
if it would not check the British advance.

Valcour Island.—During the summer Carleton's shipyard at
St. Johns was busy building the fleet which would give him
control of Lake Champlain. On October 4 Carleton advanced
with an army of twelve thousand men. Arnold started with

his fleet manned by only five hundred men to harass the advance. He ran into the narrow channel between Valcour Island and the western shore and there on October 11 encountered the light advance craft of the British fleet. For five hours he held his own. During the night he withdrew his shattered boats to an island twelve miles to the south where he attempted to repair the damage. On October 13 when the fog lifted, it disclosed the British fleet. Arnold immediately sent off his best vessels and with his crippled ships stayed to fight. One vessel struck its colors but Arnold ran his flag ship and four gondolas into a creek and burned them. He then hastened to Ticonderoga where he displayed tremendous energy in strengthening the fortifications. The spirited fight on the lake, the strength of the American position, and the lateness of the season convinced Carleton that it was useless to continue the operations. On November 3 he evacuated Crown Point and began the withdrawal to Canada. Washington was thus relieved from the danger of an enemy from the north.

Tactical movements.—Before he was aware of Carleton's withdrawal, Howe had determined to force Washington's army into the open. He sent a force of Hessians to occupy the northern end of Manhattan Island and on November 5 moved his main army to Dobb's Ferry on the Hudson, from which vantage point he could strike at Fort Washington, advance toward Albany, or threaten Philadelphia. Washington's position was endangered and the situation was made doubly precarious by the fact that his army was being depleted by desertions and by the termination of enlistments. To counteract the British movement he sent one corps to Hackensac in New Jersey, and Heath's division was stationed at Peekskill to protect the Hudson. Charles Lee was left at White Plains with about seven thousand men subject to future orders.

Forts Washington and Lee.—The British moved next against Forts Washington and Lee, which, garrisoned by about five thousand men, were under the supervision of General Greene. They ought to have been abandoned, but Washington unfortunately left the decision to his subordinate who believed that they could be held. On November 16 overwhelming forces advanced against Fort Washington which was obliged to surrender. Cornwallis secretly sent six thousand troops across the Hudson and on November 20 advanced against Fort Lee. He all but surprised it and Greene, with the greatest difficulty, succeeded only in saving the garrison.

THE NEW JERSEY CAMPAIGN

Retreat to the Raritan.—The fall of the forts had added greatly to the difficulty of the situation, for Washington's army was in danger of being enveloped. To avert disaster he determined to retreat into New Jersey. He accordingly crossed the Passaic and moved to Newark. The forces under Lee were ordered to join the retreating army, but that vain and conceited officer, who had visions of becoming commander-in-chief as soon as Washington was eliminated, refused to obey orders. On November 28 Washington marched out of Newark and as his rear guard left the town the advanced guard of the British entered it. The American army pushed on to New Brunswick where it found a temporary haven behind the Raritan. On December 1 Cornwallis's troops reached the river, but there he was halted by an order from Howe not to advance until he arrived with reinforcements.

Expedition against Rhode Island.—A week later Howe came up with a single brigade. Instead of concentrating his troops to crush the remnant of Washington's army, the British commander decided to send two divisions to conquer Rhode Island. They easily occupied the island but it was a fruitless venture for "several thousand Royal troops were thenceforward locked up in a sea-girt strip of land no larger than the estate of many an English Lord-Lieutenant."

Retreat across the Delaware.—Washington's army was constantly reduced by desertion and sickness, and the New Jersey people failed to rally to his assistance. It has been estimated that not a hundred men enlisted during the retreat across the state. The people of New Jersey paid dearly for their indifference, for during the winter they were constantly subjected to indignities from the Hessians who were billeted upon them. Among the atrocious acts was the pillaging of Princeton College. Taking advantage of British inactivity, Washington prepared to retire beyond the Delaware, from New Brunswick having ordered the collection of boats for many miles along the river

front.   Covering his retreat with fourteen hundred of his best
troops under Stirling, the army and stores were landed on the
Pennsylvania shore.   When the British troops arrived on the
eastern bank, they were forced to halt, for not a boat was available and the short-sighted Howe had failed to provide his army
with pontoons.

To the British commander the campaign was over and he
prepared to go into winter quarters, fancying that the rebellion
was practically crushed and that the spring campaign would be
a mere parade.   The Whig cause appeared to be lost and gloomy
forebodings and grumblings of discontent took the place of declamation and heroics.   On December 10 Congress resolved to
defend Philadelphia but two days later it adjourned and hied
away to Baltimore.   Washington's lack of authority had frequently hampered his military operations, but this difficulty
was now removed, for before adjournment Congress resolved,
that until otherwise ordered, Washington was to have full power
to direct operations.

Washington's army reinforced.—The dispirited army which
crossed the Delaware was soon strongly reinforced.   After many
days of inaction, General Lee had left his camp at White Plains
with the intention, as he grandiloquently put it, of reconquering
New Jersey.   After the retreat of Carleton, Schuyler had sent
seven battalions under Sullivan to assist Washington, but Lee
succeeded in getting control of four of them.   On December 13
he was captured at a tavern at Baskingridge.   As soon as Sullivan
heard of it, he started the troops for the Delaware and on the
twentieth of December joined Washington.   Four other battalions from Schuyler's army arrived shortly afterward and General Mifflin brought in a goodly body of Pennsylvania militia.
Before Christmas the army numbered eight thousand.

Position of the Hessians.—To the east of the Delaware was
a Hessian division under Colonel Von Donop, Colonel Rall being
stationed at Trenton with three regiments.   Rall had taken no
measures to strengthen a naturally weak position; highways converged to the north of the village and artillery stationed at the
junction could sweep the streets.   Scouting parties and spies
informed Washington that Rall's troops were scattered through
the town and that the place was practically without defences.

Trenton.—Washington determined to strike. With the great-est secrecy he perfected his plans. One body of troops under Cadwalader was to attack Von Donop's position at Borden-town and Ewing with a thousand men was to strike at troops stationed on Assumpink Creek, while Washington with Greene and Sullivan in command of twenty-four hundred men and eighteen cannon were to advance against Trenton from the north. During a furious tempest on Christmas night Washington suc-ceeded in crossing the Delaware, but Ewing failed to get over and Cadwalader crossed too late to coöperate. At four in the morning Washington's troops began the weary march toward Trenton. While the valiant army was toiling over the frozen roads, the Hessians were sleeping off the effects of their Christmas wassail. At 8:15 the American forces drove in the Hessian out-posts. Aroused from his bed Rall tried to make a stand, but the streets were raked with round shot and the sharpshooters fired relentlessly into the huddled Hessians, several hundred of whom fled across the Assumpink Creek bridge and escaped to Bordentown. Rall tried to rally his men but fell mortally wounded. When Sullivan cut off the retreat to the south and Greene ordered up his reserves, resistance ended. Nine hun-dred prisoners, a thousand muskets, six field pieces, and a large quantity of stores fell into the hands of the successful commander. But not in terms of men and guns should the battle of Trenton be judged. Its importance lies in the fact that Washington had won a clean cut victory when the Whig cause was tottering and by that victory had raised the drooping spirits of a despairing nation.

Movements of the armies.—When the news of Trenton reached New York, it roused the British from their fancied security. Lord Cornwallis at the head of eight thousand men proceeded by forced marches toward the west. Washington had determined to hold a position east of the Delaware, and on December 30 he again crossed the river and by January 2, 1777, had assembled five thousand men and forty pieces of artillery just below Trenton. As Cornwallis approached the American position, he realized the costliness of a frontal attack, and decided that as soon as his forces assembled he would attempt a flanking movement from Allentown.

Princeton, January 3, 1777.—Washington saw the danger and decided on a daring plan. On the night of January 2 all was activity in the American camp. Sentinels challenged, infantry moved about in the light of the camp fires, and the sound of pick and shovel was plainly audible to the British. But in the darkness to the rear another kind of activity was in progress. Cannon, stores, and baggage were being silently moved to Bordentown and Burlington, and at one in the morning the bulk of the army began a stealthy march which at daybreak brought them out within a mile and a half of Princeton. Three of Cornwallis's regiments had remained there during the night and were now under way. Suddenly the first of these troops under Colonel Mawhood found themselves confronted by the American advance guard. The British charged bravely, scoring an initial success, but Washington's presence in front of his lines steadied the troops and they soon forced a retreat. Sullivan then led the advance against the two remaining regiments, which were driven through and beyond Princeton, leaving three hundred prisoners in Washington's hands. The roar of the guns brought the unwelcome tidings to Cornwallis that the American army had escaped, had cut across his rear, and had defeated three of his crack regiments.

Morristown.—Five miles beyond Princeton Washington turned to the north and soon established his army in a powerful position at Morristown where they remained in security the rest of the winter. Howe made no attempt to dislodge his opponent, but concentrated ten thousand troops in camps at New Brunswick and Perth Amboy. The Jersey people had been cured of their Toryism; supplies poured into the American camp, while the British experienced the greatest difficulty in securing fuel and food, and by March 1 were reduced to a ration of salt provisions and "ammunition bread." When Washington reached Morristown he had about four thousand men and during the winter his army did not increase, but he made the most of the opportunity to drill his men and perfect his organization. Throughout the country men were drilling for the spring campaign, powder mills were being built, and lead mines were being opened. The greatest shortage was in muskets, but fortunately these were obtained from France.

Middlebrook.—In May, 1777, everything was in readiness and Washington led his army to a powerful position at Middlebrook, only a few miles from the British camp at New Brunswick. On June 13 Howe transferred large forces to the southern bank of the Raritan, but he failed to draw Washington from his point of vantage and on the nineteenth he began the withdrawal of his army to Staten Island, having had the satisfaction only of a rear guard action with Stirling's division.

THE STRUGGLE WITH BURGOYNE

British plans for 1777.—Howe's plan for the campaign of 1777 called for fifteen thousand more troops. With this addition he believed that he could crush Washington and conquer Pennsylvania, New Jersey, and New York. The subjugation of the southern colonies would then be attempted, followed by operations in New England. But Lord Germaine thought otherwise. Ignoring the general in the field, he planned to send a force under St. Leger down the Mohawk Valley, a second army under Burgoyne to penetrate New York by the Lake Champlain route, while Howe was to proceed up the Hudson Valley. The three armies were to meet at Albany. The plan looked good on paper, but it failed to take into account the long distances to be traversed and the difficulties of transportation on the frontier. When Germaine planned the campaign, he should have sent precise orders to Howe, but this he failed to do, and on May 18 he even wrote acquiescing in the proposed expedition against Philadelphia and expressing the hope that the business might be concluded in season so that Howe could coöperate with Burgoyne.

Ticonderoga and Ft. Independence.—On June 15, 1777, General Schuyler learned that Burgoyne's army was in motion and that St. Leger was concentrating forces on the upper Mohawk. The American army was in a sorry plight for smallpox and dysentery were still the bane of the northern department. Congress had done much to destroy efficiency by temporarily removing Schuyler. At a time when all should have been working in harmony, Gates was intriguing with members of Congress to overthrow his superior. The advance part of the army was at Ticonderoga. Across the narrow bay Fort Independence had been erected and a bridge connected the fortifications, which were commanded by General St. Clair who had only twenty-five hundred men to man works which demanded ten thousand defenders.

Burgoyne captures the forts.—Late in June Burgoyne's flotilla carrying about eight thousand soldiers reached Crown Point.

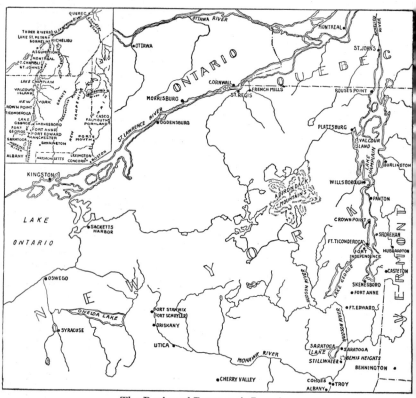

The Region of Burgoyne's Invasion

(The large map is based on E. G. Foster's *Historical Chart;* the inset is from Trevelyan, *The American Revolution*, Part II, Vol. I)

His engineers soon discovered the fundamental weaknesses of the American position. Mt. Hope dominated the passage to Lake George and Sugar Hill towered above the forts. On July 2 the former position was occupied by the British and on July 5 St. Clair saw Sugar Hill bristling with cannon. He realized that the forts were untenable and on the night of July 6 he loaded his stores and light artillery on barges and sent them under convoy to Skenesborough. The main body of troops under St. Clair attempted to reach the same place by a circuitous route which led through Hubbardtown.

The disastrous retreat.—Burgoyne's vessels broke through the impediments and pursued the American flotilla. They encountered it at anchor in South Bay and short work they made of it. The Americans destroyed the stores and buildings on the shore before they retreated. General Fraser had been sent in pursuit of St. Clair's forces and at Hubbardtown he fell in with the American rear guard and defeated it. St. Clair succeeded in getting his troops to Ft. Edward where he joined Schuyler. Only three thousand men barred the way to Albany.

The withdrawal to Stillwater.—Schuyler sent out calls for help to New England, to New York, and to Washington. While waiting for reinforcements he destroyed the standing crops, drove off the stock, and broke up the roads. Having despoiled the country, he abandoned Fort Edward and withdrew to Stillwater on the west bank of the Hudson. It was not long before reinforcements began pouring in. Although his army was inferior to that of Howe, Washington sent on Morgan's riflemen and he ordered Putnam to send two brigades. General Lincoln was sent to organize the New England militia and Benedict Arnold was called from Connecticut to help Schuyler.

Bennington.—Burgoyne reached the head of Lake Champlain on July 10, but from that point his progress was exceedingly slow, the twenty miles to Ft. Edwards being traversed in as many days. Schuyler's work of devastation had been complete and the British commissariat suffered accordingly. To replenish his depleted stores, Burgoyne embarked upon a rash enterprise. At Bennington large quantities of stores had been collected and a Tory named Philip Skene suggested that they would be an easy prize. Burgoyne followed Skene's advice and sent Colonel Baum with five or six hundred troops to make the capture. Near Bennington John Stark was in command of two brigades of New England troops and at Manchester were the remnants of regiments which had retreated from Hubbardtown. On August 15 Baum came in touch with Stark's forces, but he hesitated to attack and proceeded to intrench. The New England troops

gradually encircled the position, and when they attacked on
the afternoon of the sixteenth, they killed, wounded, or captured nearly the entire force. While the Americans were engaged
in plundering the camp, they were suddenly attacked by another force of six hundred under Breymann, sent by Burgoyne
at Baum's request. Things were going badly for Stark's men
when Seth Warner with forces from Manchester arrived. After
a sharp contest Breymann's troops were driven from the field
with a loss of a third of the rank and file. The day's fighting had
deprived the invaders of a considerable force which they could
not afford to lose in the face of an army which was increasing
daily.

Oriskany.—While Burgoyne was advancing, St. Leger was
invading the Mohawk Valley. On August 3 his army of British
regulars, Hessians, Canadians, Tories, and Indians invested Ft.
Stanwix. Colonel Herkimer gathered the Tryon County militia
and went to the relief of the fort, but at Oriskany, which was
only six miles from the fort, he was surprised. In the desperate
battle the losses were higher in proportion to men engaged than
in any other battle of the war. Herkimer was killed and so
badly cut up were the militia that the expedition was unable
to proceed.

Ft. Stanwix relieved.—Schuyler realized the danger of a flank
attack from the Mohawk Valley. St. Leger must be checked.
Schuyler called for a volunteer to lead a relief expedition. Arnold
offered his services and at the head of eight hundred men advanced up the valley. As he proceeded his force was continually
increased by recruits. As he approached Ft. Stanwix, Arnold
succeeded in creating the impression that his army was of overwhelming numbers. The Senecas were the first to desert St.
Leger and the Tories soon made off to the woods. Abandoned
by his allies, St. Leger retreated, leaving behind stores, tents,
and artillery. The battle of Bennington and the retirement
from the Mohawk Valley sealed the fate of Burgoyne.

Gates supersedes Schuyler.—By the middle of August Schuyler had the satisfaction of being in command of a force which outnumbered Burgoyne's army. But on August 19 Horatio Gates
arrived at Albany with a commission to take command. Gates
was a man of little ability, but of an unscrupulous, intriguing,

and ambitious nature. He had spent many months at the seat of government influencing members of Congress, a task made easy by the fact that the New England delegates disliked Schuyler. With victory already assured, Gates came forward to reap the honors. Burgoyne was in a sorry plight. His line of communication was in danger of being cut and his force had been reduced to about six thousand effectives. In vain he looked for despatches from Howe, but though he had sent ten messengers, an ominous silence was his only answer. Two courses were open to him; an ignominious retreat or an advance that at best was but a forlorn hope. Fortunately for the American cause he chose the latter.

First battle of Bemis's Heights, September 19.—On September 13 the British army crossed the Hudson on a bridge of boats and encamped at Saratoga. Six miles to the south was a table land called Bemis's Heights which the Americans had fortified. Between the heights and the river stretched a pasture five hundred yards in width. It was a position easily defended provided Gates extended his left wing. This he failed to do and Burgoyne, quick to see the opportunity for a turning movement, disposed his forces in such a manner that while Philips in command of the British left and Burgoyne in the center engaged the American army, General Fraser on the right could encircle the heights. Arnold saw the danger and besought Gates to let him attack the British right. Gates finally consented and Arnold immediately flung his men against Fraser's position. A confused fight occurred in the tangled underbrush, and though Morgan's riflemen got out of hand, the effect of the attack was to stop Fraser's advance. Having been reinforced, Arnold threw his troops against the British center at Freeman's Farm. A very hot engagement ensued and victory would probably have resulted had Gates engaged Philips, but the American commander failed to attack and the British left came to the assistance of the hard-pressed center. At nightfall Arnold fell back a short distance, but he had saved the American army and had inflicted such great injury that Burgoyne was unable to continue the battle the next day.

Clinton fails to coöperate.—The British commander fortified his position and there his army remained inactive for more than a fortnight. The situation was daily becoming more critical, for Lincoln had succeeded in cutting the line of communication with Canada. A belated despatch had reached Burgoyne informing him of Howe's expedition against Philadelphia. He also received information which led him to believe that Clinton expected to clear the Hudson and come to his relief. Early in October Clinton captured three forts on the lower Hudson, but instead of following up his success, he returned to New York and left the northern army to its fate.

Second battle of Bemis's Heights.—The situation in the American camp was far from harmonious. Gates had not mentioned Arnold's division in his official report of the recent battle. This slight was followed by studied insults and cowardly persecution. The protests of the regimental officers caused Arnold to postpone his resignation, but Gates deprived him of his command and elevated Lincoln. On October 7 Burgoyne again prepared to attack the American lines. His initial assault was repulsed and Fraser was mortally wounded. Soon after the fighting began Arnold put himself at the head of his old troops and broke the British center. The British right wing was also forced back, but Gates did nothing to follow up the advantage. Arnold seized the opportunity and assaulted Freeman's Farm. There he was repulsed but he turned his troops against a redoubt on the right and carried it by assault. The redoubtable general, however, was severely wounded, his thigh bone being shattered, but his generalship had won the battle which broke the British army.

Burgoyne's surrender.—The day after the battle Gates pushed forward his left wing, a movement which threatened to pen Burgoyne between the Hudson and a hostile army. The British commander should have sunk his heavy guns in the river and beaten a hasty retreat, but instead he attempted to save his stores and artillery. He fell back eight miles and took a position on the north bank of Fishkill Creek near Saratoga. Gates threw a force across the Hudson which prevented a crossing, troops were posted on the flank of the British Camp and the main army was drawn up on the south bank of Fishkill Creek. The British were trapped and Burgoyne at last realized that the game was up. On October 13 he called a council of war at which it was decided to negotiate terms. Gates demanded an unconditional surrender, but Burgoyne refused and the next day Gates, who appears neither to have been able to win a battle or to make the most of a fortunate situation created by the bravery and skill of another, agreed that Burgoyne should surrender with the honors of war and that his army should be given free passage to Great Britain upon the condition that they would not serve in North America during the war. Congress, to its shame, did not carry out the agreement and the troops were kept as prisoners in America.

THE CONTEST FOR PHILADELPHIA

Howe moves on Philadelphia.—While the northern army was struggling with Burgoyne, another great contest was taking place in Pennsylvania. Germaine had not given Howe definite orders to coöperate with Burgoyne and, in fact, had approved the proposed expedition against Philadelphia. After the retirement from before Middlebrook, Howe's movements were a mystery to Washington. In July he learned that the British fleet was being prepared for a voyage, but whether the enemy would sail up the Hudson, or strike at Boston, Philadelphia, or Charleston, he could not tell. To forestall an advance northward Washington moved his army toward the New York highlands. On July 31 he heard that the British fleet had appeared in Delaware Bay. Immediately the American army was started for Philadelphia, but before the city was reached the astonishing news came that the fleet had disappeared. Washington immediately went into camp twenty miles north of Philadelphia to await developments. Two weeks later the British fleet sailed into Chesapeake Bay and on August 25 the army, which numbered seventeen thousand, began to disembark at the Head of Elk at the northern end of the bay.

Battle of the Brandywine.—As soon as Washington heard of the British landing, he started his army southward. On August 24 eleven thousand men paraded through the spacious streets of Philadelphia and on September 9 the army was posted on the north bank of the Brandywine. The main road to Philadelphia crossed the stream at Chad's Ford and here Wayne's division was stationed. Below the ford the steep banks were

defended by a small force of militia. Above Wayne were Greene's
well-drilled brigades, and the right was held by Sullivan. On
September 10 Howe concentrated his army at the Kennet Square
meeting house, where he divided it into two columns. At four
the next morning Cornwallis in command of one column started
for the upper fords of the Brandywine; by making this wide
detour it was hoped that he could get in the rear of the American
right wing. An hour later General von Knyphausen in command
of the other column advanced toward Chad's Ford. He drove
a small group of skirmishers across the stream, arranged his
army as if for an assault, and opened with his artillery. Washington spent the morning in uncertainty, but at length Sullivan
sent word that Cornwallis's troops were getting in his rear.
Washington immediately ordered him to throw his entire force
across the path of the enemy, but the movement was not carried
out with precision and soon the wings of Sullivan's force were
routed. Stirling, who held the center, made a gallant defence,
but with both flanks exposed, he was forced to retire. When
Von Knyphausen heard the firing, he advanced across Chad's
Ford, and carried Wayne's intrenchments. Washington had
ordered Greene to go to Sullivan's assistance. His men covered
four miles in about forty minutes and then came into action
against Cornwallis's victorious troops. For an hour the battle
raged with great intensity, and as darkness set in, Greene drew
off his men. His stubborn fight had saved the army, which was
brought together at Chester.

Paoli.—Washington moved his army thirty-five miles up
the Schuylkill and the British encamped south of the river near
Valley Forge. To harass the rear of Howe's army Washington
sent Wayne's division across the Schuylkill. At 1 A. M. on
September 21 this force was surprised near the Paoli Tavern.
The British fell upon the American camp with sword and bayonet, and before the grim work was over Wayne had lost more
than three hundred men.

The British in Philadelphia.—On September 23 the British
army crossed the Schuylkill and began to advance toward Philadelphia. When the news reached the city a Whig exodus began,
probably a third of the population taking their departure.
Congress removed the prisoners, archives, and most of the

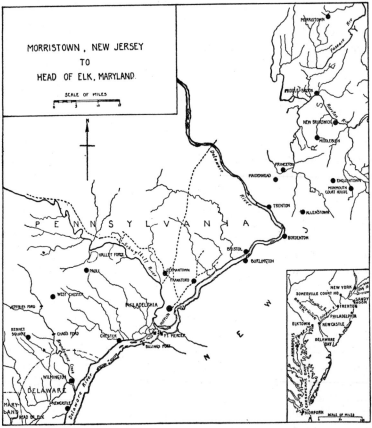

(Based on map in G. O. Trevelyan, *The American Revolution*, Part. III,
op. p. 492)

stores; upon Washington it conferred dictatorial powers for sixty days in the vicinity, and then adjourned to Lancaster and later to York. On September 25 Howe entered the capital.

Germantown.—Within a week Washington was ready to try to retake the city. The approach from the northwest lay through Germantown. In the outskirts Howe had stationed a strong force of infantry. Near the center of the village the fine brick mansion of Benjamin Chew, the Chief Justice of Pennsylvania, formed the pivot of the second line of defence which was commanded by Colonel Musgrave. A mile to the rear lay the bulk of the British army. Washington planned to advance in four columns. Armstrong with the Pennsylvania militia on the right was to get in the rear of the British left. Sullivan commanded the next column to the east and was followed by the reserve under Stirling. A third column was commanded by Greene, and the Maryland and New Jersey militia, forming the fourth column, were to strike the British right. Save for a few shots fired by Armstrong's men, the militia failed to get into the fighting.

The dawn of October 4 broke in a dense fog, which destroyed the possibility of coöperation and led to much confusion. Sullivan's men arrived first and soon drove the British from their advanced position. Then followed an attack which centered at Chew's house where Musgrave and his men had taken refuge. The sound of the firing attracted some of Greene's men who joined in the attack. The brick walls proved too strong for the American three-pounders, and most of the forces of Sullivan and Greene passed on to attack the next line where five brigades of royal troops were drawn up along a narrow lane. The American units became separated, Greene having advanced a considerable distance ahead of Sullivan's troops. Suddenly Sullivan's force broke and fled in an unaccountable panic. This placed Greene in great jeopardy, for his flank was exposed and British reinforcements were approaching, but he coolly saved his men and guns. So heavy were the British losses that no serious attempt was made to follow the retreating army which was able to get away with all its artillery.

Opening the Delaware.—Philadelphia was firmly held by the British but the Delaware was still closed. At Billingsport a fort had been built and an obstruction had been thrown across the river. Another obstruction blocked the passage below Mud Island, on which stood Fort Mifflin and opposite on the Jersey shore was Ft. Mercer. A flotilla of small craft patrolled the Delaware. On October 4 part of Lord Howe's fleet anchored in the river and two days later the obstruction at Billingsport was removed. On October 22 Colonel von Donop attempted to capture Ft. Mercer but he met with a bloody repulse. After this defeat the British proceeded with more caution in the reduction of Ft. Mifflin. Shore batteries were constructed which bombarded Mud Island for days. On November 15 two battleships navigated the difficult channel and soon battered the walls of the fort to pieces. At nightfall the garrison abandoned the fortress. Four days later Ft. Mercer was evacuated when an overwhelming force advanced against it, and on November 21 most of the American vessels were set on fire by their crews. Communication with New York was thus opened and Howe prepared to settle down in Philadelphia for the winter.

Valley Forge.—In marked contrast to the comfort of the British camp was the condition of the American army. Washington had chosen Valley Forge for his winter quarters and there a fortified camp was constructed and rude cabins erected to house the men. The camp soon became a charnel house, for Congress failed to supply the necessary food and clothing, and sickness inevitably resulted. For days the men were without meat and existed on dough baked in the embers. "Fire-cake" and water became the ration for breakfast, dinner, and supper. Blankets were lacking and the men were soon barefooted and in tatters. On Christmas day the winter broke with great severity and soon the hospitals, which were mere hovels unsupplied with beds, were crowded with the dying.

The Conway Cabal.—The anguish of Washington was intensified by an intrigue which threatened to deprive him of his command. This centered about Gates and an Irish soldier of fortune named Conway who had been sent over from France by Silas Deane. In November, 1777, Congress had vested the management of military affairs in a Board of War. Gates was made president of the board and Conway was appointed inspector general of the army. They were supported by the New England delegates in Congress and by those who opposed the Fabian policy of Washington. Fortunately the intrigues of Conway and Gates to displace Washington became known to the public and so great was the popularity of the commander-in-chief that Congress dared not remove him.

READINGS

Channing, Edward, *History of the United States*, III, 210–273; Fisher, S. G., *The Struggle for American Independence*, I, 490–574, II, 1–174; Fiske, John, *The American Revolution*, I, 198–344, II, 25–81, 110–115; Greene, F. V., *The Revolutionary War*, 28–131; Hildreth, Richard, *History of the United States of America*, III, 140–162, 186–237; Lecky, W. E. H., *History of England in the Eighteenth Century*, IV, 1–41, 55–98; Smith, J. H., *Our Struggle for the Fourteenth Colony*, I, 193–606, II; Trevelyan, G. O., *The American Revolution*, II, 172–349, III, 1–147, IV, 111–319; Van Tyne, C. H., *The American Revolution*, 102–135, 157–174, 227–247; Winsor, Justin, *Narrative and Critical History*, VI, 275–447; Adams, C. F., *Studies Military and Diplomatic, 1775–1865*, pp. 22–173.

CHAPTER XXVI

THE WAR AS AN INTERNATIONAL CONTEST

THE FRENCH ALLIANCE

The French motives.—On February 6, 1778, France entered into an alliance with the United States. That event changed the war from a struggle between England and her former colonies to an international contest in which Spain and Holland were soon engaged. The motives of France in entering the contest have been variously ascribed to revenge for the loss of her possessions and the desire to regain them, to the intellectual movement in France, to the desire to build up French commerce at the expense of England, and to the fear that Great Britain would adjust the difficulties with the colonies and unite with them in an attack upon the French West Indies. Professor Corwin, who has recently examined the question, concludes that these explanations are not adequate. He contends that the basic principle of French diplomacy was the maintenance of leadership in Europe, and that in return for this commanding position, France was willing to forego the extension of her dominion. In the Seven Years' War French prestige had been destroyed; to rebuild it was the object of her statesmen.

The policy of Vergennes.—In 1774 Louis XVI became king. No better intentioned ruler ever mounted a throne but his weak will and vacillating course led to his undoing. For two years Turgot was the reigning influence at the council board. He installed a system of economy and reform, which, had it been adhered to, would probably have saved France from the throes of her great revolution. Turgot's plans ran counter to the policy of Vergennes, the foreign minister, who desired to see his country take its place in the sun as the dictator of European politics. The attainment of Vergennes's policy was based upon three main ideas: the preservation of peace on the continent by a close alliance with Austria; a renewal of the Family Compact with Spain; and the humbling of England. The last was to be accomplished by the building up of the French navy, by secretly aiding the colonies, and when the time seemed auspicious, by entering into an alliance with them, an alliance in which Vergennes hoped that Spain would join. To win over the latter power and to overcome the aversion of Louis XVI to aiding rebellious subjects were the immediate problems of Vergennes.

Vergennes wins over the king.—A secret agent, Bonvouloir, was sent to America to ascertain the condition of the colonies. His first report, which reached Paris in March, 1776, gave a favorable statement of the military situation. Vergennes immediately attempted to convince the king that secret aid should be given the colonies. He argued that the prolongation of the struggle would be advantageous to France and Spain as it would weaken both contestants, and he pointed out that England would probably attack the French West Indies as soon as the present war was over. Aided by Beaumarchais, the author of *Le Mariage de Figaro*, Vergennes countered the advice of Turgot and won over the king to his plan.

Deane and Beaumarchais.—The secret committee on foreign correspondence of the Continental Congress in March, 1776, sent Silas Deane to Paris. His presence became known to Lord Stormont, the British ambassador, who demanded his deportation, but France refused and continually aided him in securing supplies. The French government also loaned the colonies a million livres and obtained a similar amount for them from Spain. When news of the Declaration of Independence reached Paris, Vergennes urged that France and Spain enter the war, but Washington's defeats around New York held back both countries. France continued to aid the colonies, the business being transacted by Beaumarchais through the fictitious house of Hortalez et Cie. Beaumarchais also drew heavily upon his private fortune to assist the colonies.

Franklin.—The delay of France in making an open alliance caused Congress to appoint a commission composed of Silas Deane, Arthur Lee, and Benjamin Franklin. Of all colonials Franklin was the best known in Europe. As a scientist, philosopher, wit, and statesman, his name was familiar to all classes in the French capital. His unpretentious dress, unaffected manners, and simplicity of life made him seem to Parisians the impersonation of the natural man of Rousseau's philosophy. On the street, at the theater, in the salon, Franklin was the center of interest. Artists made busts of him and jewelers exhibited his countenance on medallions, watches, and snuff-boxes. Franklin soon discovered that he could not hurry matters; he quietly bided his time, never losing an opportunity to win supporters to the American cause. Even the court became enthusiastic, and Marie Antoinette, with little understanding or prophetic vision, applauded the republicans of America.

The American proposals.—In January, 1777, the commissioners presented their views to Vergennes. They proposed that France and Spain furnish the United States eight ships of the line, twenty or thirty thousand stand of arms, and a large quantity of cannon and ammunition. Congress in return offered the two nations a commercial treaty and a guarantee of their possessions in the West Indies. Vergennes was unable to comply but he advanced two hundred and fifty thousand livres as the first instalment of a secret loan of two millions. In February the commissioners suggested that, if France and Spain became involved in war because of a treaty with the United States, the states would not conclude a separate peace. In March they proposed a triple alliance between France, Spain, and the United States. The bait for Spain was the conquest of Portugal, and the war was to continue until England was expelled from North America and the West Indies.

The attitude of Spain.—The American proposals included both France and Spain, and in the latter country the commissioners met with a stumbling block. Spain at first showed a friendly attitude. Through the firm of Josef Gardoqui and Sons supplies were secretly furnished to the United States, but when Arthur Lee attempted to go to Madrid, he was turned back by the Spanish authorities, who preferred to work in secret. In February, 1777, the Count de Florida Blanca became minister of foreign affairs. To Florida Blanca Spain's interests must take precedence over those of France in determining Spanish policy. Difficulties with Portugal had been adjusted, and Florida Blanca could see no advantage in an immediate war with Great Britain. He was willing to keep the contest in America going until both parties were exhausted. Then Spain and France might enter the war, Spain to get the Floridas and France to obtain Canada. But as to the recognition of American independence, king and minister were unalterably opposed.

Lafayette.—Of no little importance in bringing France and the United States together was the coming of the young nobleman Lafayette to America. Fired by the Declaration of Independence, he determined to enlist in the American cause. In April, 1777, Lafayette with the Baron de Kalb and several other officers sailed for America. They reached Philadelphia on July 27 but Congress gave them a chilly reception. Nothing daunted, Lafayette proudly announced that he asked nothing but the opportunity of serving as a volunteer. Congress was deeply impressed by his unselfish attitude and promptly made him a Major-General. Washington received him gladly, took him into his military family and through the long war, with the exception of a period when he was promoting American interests in France, he served as a trusted officer of the commander-in-chief.

The French alliance.—During the summer of 1777 the American question was held in abeyance at Paris but Burgoyne's surrender stirred Vergennes to action. He appears to have feared that Great Britain was about to effect a reconciliation with the United States. To prevent it he believed that France must openly espouse the American cause. One more effort was made to draw Spain into the alliance, but the reply proved unfavorable. On January 7, 1778, at a French royal council meeting the final decision was made and on February 6 treaties of commerce and alliance were signed. The latter agreement was described as a defensive alliance to maintain effectually the liberty, sovereignty, and independence of the United States, as well in matters of government as in commerce.

Lord North attempts conciliation.—When news of Burgoyne's surrender reached London, hope of subduing the rebellion by force was temporarily abandoned and Lord North was empowered to try his hand at conciliation. On February 17, 1778, the Prime Minister presented his plan to the Commons. He proposed (1) the repeal of the tea duty, (2) the passage of an act removing apprehension regarding parliamentary taxation of the colonies, (3) opening the port of Boston, (4) restoration of the Massachusetts charter, (5) opening the fisheries, (6) restoration of commerce, and (7) full pardon to those engaged in rebellion. (8) Prisoners charged with treason were not to be brought over the sea for trial, and (9) no bill for changing a colonial constitution was to be introduced in parliament except at the request of the colony involved. (10) Regulation of colonial courts was to follow colonial opinion, and (11) officials were to be elected by popular vote subject, however, to the approval of the king. (12) The royal treasury was to assist in the withdrawal of colonial currency, and (13) a promise was given that the question of colonial representation in parliament would be considered.

The Carlisle Commission.—A royal commission was to visit America to settle points in dispute. Headed by the Earl of Carlisle, the commission proceeded to Philadelphia but it was soon discovered that nothing could be accomplished. General Howe had been recalled and Clinton, who was placed in command, was under orders to evacuate Philadelphia. The alliance with France was already known in America and nothing short of a recognition of independence would satisfy the Whig leaders.

Change in British plans.—The French alliance brought about a complete change in British plans. Henceforth garrisons were to be kept in New York, Newport, Canada, and the Floridas, and hostilities on the mainland were to be devoted to the destruction of coastwise trade and coast towns, and to the harassing of the frontiers by Indian raids. Attacks in force were to be made on the French possessions in the West Indies.

Evacuation of Philadelphia and the battle of Monmouth.—In pursuance of this plan in May, 1778, the British prepared to evacuate Philadelphia. General Howe returned to England and Clinton took command. Most of the stores, some of the troops, and about three thousand Loyalists were placed on transports, and the main army on June 18 started on its march across New Jersey. Washington succeeded in getting in touch with the British army ten days later at Monmouth. Clinton's forces were stretched out to such an extent that it was difficult to bring them into action. Washington sent Lee to attack, but after a slight demonstration, the poltroon ordered a retreat. Lee's cowardice gave the British time to form and a bloody battle followed which ended only with nightfall. In the darkness the British army broke camp and when morning dawned it was beyond the reach of Washington.

The coming of D'Estaing.—On April 15 Admiral D'Estaing sailed from Toulon in command of twelve ships of the line and five frigates which carried four thousand infantry. The voyage was pursued in a leisurely fashion which gave Lord Howe time to get his transports out of the Delaware and concentrate the fleet at New York. It also made it possible for a reinforcement under Commodore Byron to arrive in American waters. Not until July 8 was D'Estaing's fleet within the Delaware capes. After landing Gérard, the French minister, the admiral proceeded to New York. Though the French fleet was superior to the British, D'Estaing failed to attack.

The failure at Newport.—Instead he entered into a plan with Washington to take Newport which was garrisoned by five or six thousand British troops. Sullivan, with about a thousand continental soldiers and several thousand militia, was to cooperate with the French fleet. The opening was auspicious. The war vessels ran by the batteries and anchored in the inner waters. The British commander to prevent capture destroyed several frigates and small craft. On August 9 Sullivan moved nine thousand troops to the island. The same day Howe's fleet appeared at the entrance of Narragansett Bay and D'Estaing, carrying his infantry with him, sailed out to meet the enemy. Before the fleets could engage a terrific storm arose which scattered the vessels. Howe finally regained New York and D'Estaing sailed to Boston for repairs, leaving Sullivan unsupported and in a precarious position. When word came that Clinton was sending large reinforcements, Sullivan abandoned the siege.

D'Estaing in the West Indies.—D'Estaing lingered at Boston ten weeks and then sailed for the West Indies. Before his arrival a French force from Martinique had captured Dominica. The English retaliated by capturing St. Lucia, and when D'Estaing attempted to relieve it, he was replused. On June 18, 1779, the French occupied St. Vincent and on July 2 Grenada. On July 6 Byron attacked the French fleet off Grenada, but D'Estaing had the better of the fighting although he failed to follow up his victory. After attempting the relief of Savannah, the French commander despatched part of his fleet to the West Indies and then sailed for Europe.

Stony Point and the evacuation of Newport.—After the Newport failure Washington drew a cordon about New York and strengthened the line of the Hudson. On May 31, 1779, Clinton seized the fortifications at Stony Point and Verplanck's Point, but on July 16 General Wayne carried the works at Stony Point. Clinton also sent raiding parties to the Chesapeake and along the Connecticut coast, but in October he ordered the evacuation of Newport and concentrated his forces at New York.

The second French expedition.—Washington still hoped for effective help from the French fleet in the West Indies, but his hopes were blasted early in 1780 by the arrival in the islands of British naval reinforcements under Admiral Rodney, who during April and May fought three indecisive actions with the French fleet. Largely through the influence of Lafayette France was induced to send a large force to America in 1780. In July a fleet of seven vessels convoying six thousand men commanded by Rochambeau arrived at Newport. The second division, however, was blockaded at Brest and was unable to sail. Washington's hopes mounted high but they were soon dashed again, for Clinton, who had just returned to New York after the capture of Charleston, was able to send a considerable armament to blockade the French at Newport, and there they remained for months to come.

Arnold's treason.—During the long contest Washington had often been disappointed by the incompetence of his subordinates, but Nathanael Greene and Benedict Arnold had seldom been found wanting. The former was soon to win fame as the conqueror of the South; the other chose a path which made his name despised. Arnold had not been justly treated by Congress, although he had the absolute confidence of Washington. Brooding over his wrongs and convinced that the country would welcome the reëstablishment of the king's authority, he determined to play the part of a General Monk. While in command of Philadelphia, he entered into a treasonable correspondence with Clinton. He then asked for the command of the great fortress

at West Point. This was readily given to him and there he
perfected his plans to deliver this key position of the Hudson to
the British. Clinton sent Major André to communicate with
Arnold, but upon his return on September 23, 1780, André was
captured and on his person were found papers which disclosed
the plot. André was condemned and hung as a spy, but Arnold
made good his escape to the British lines.

THE WAR IN THE WEST

Competition for the support of the Indians.—The westward
movement across the mountains was almost simultaneous with
the outbreak of the Revolution, and the western settlements
were soon drawn into the current. The frontiersmen held back
the Indian allies of the British, and by settlement and conquest
secured large areas of the back country. At the opening of the
war both British and Americans made great efforts to secure the
support of the Indians, but in the main the tribes favored the
British who did not encroach upon their lands and whose posts
on the frontiers were centers for the distribution of presents
and for the work of the traders. During the war British agents
were kept at work among the tribes, distributing presents and
weapons, and often leading the Indian raids.

The Cherokee War.—In the summer of 1776 the Cherokee
went on the warpath. From their villages in the southern
Alleghanies they were in a position to raid the frontier settlements of Georgia, the Carolinas, Virginia, and Tennessee. The
Cherokee towns were in three groups. The upper towns inhabited
by the Overhill Cherokee were along the mountain streams that
ran into the Tennessee. The lower towns were in the foothills
of the back country of Georgia and South Carolina. In the
mountainous region between were the middle towns. During
June and July Cherokee war parties, at times assisted by Creeks
and Tories, fell upon the Georgia and Carolina frontiers and
upon the Watauga settlements. The Georgia invaders were met
by Colonel Samuel Jack at the head of two hundred rangers
who drove them back and destroyed one or two of the lower
towns. In North Carolina the Indians came down the Catawba
and drove the settlers into the blockhouses. General Griffith
Rutherford raised the frontier levies and chased the Indians

back to their villages. In South Carolina the Cherokees from the lower and middle towns, aided by Tories and led by the British agent, Cameron, descended upon the settlements. Colonel Andrew Williamson collected eleven hundred militia, defeated the invaders, and by the middle of August destroyed the lower towns. In July seven hundred Overhill Cherokee raided the Watauga settlements. One party under Chief Dragging Canoe attacked the settlers about Eaton's Station, but the frontiersmen sallied forth and defeated the Indians at Island Flats. For three weeks Fort Watauga was invested by another band, but so stubborn was the defence conducted by Robertson and Sevier that the Indians abandoned the siege. The Carolinians and Virginians determined to carry the war into the enemy's country. In September Rutherford and Williamson completely destroyed the valley towns of the Cherokee; and in October Colonel William Christian led the Virginia troops into the Overhill country, destroyed the principal village, and brought the warriors to terms.

Indian raids in the Northwest, 1776-1778.—In the Northwest the memory of the Battle of the Kanawha kept the Indians quiet for a time while the diplomats struggled for mastery. Colonel George Morgan was made congressional agent at Fort Pitt, while Hamilton at Detroit was the most active British agent on that frontier. In the fall of 1776 Hamilton sent raiding parties along the border. During 1777 the frontiers of Pennsylvania, Virginia, and Kentucky were kept in a state of terror. Colonel Morgan urged an expedition against Detroit, and when his advice was rejected, he resigned. Governor Patrick Henry sent Virginia militia to relieve Kentucky and Congress sent General Hand to defend the upper Ohio. Hand and his successor, McIntosh, had little success, for the raids continued and by the end of 1778 Kentucky was nearly depopulated.

Willing's raids.—In 1777 James Willing, a former resident of Natchez, obtained permission from Congress to make an expedition down the Mississippi to secure the neutrality of the Tories in the Southwest. Descending the Ohio from Pittsburg, his expedition became a raid on the Loyalist plantations along the Mississippi. Far from having the desired effect, the raid drove the inhabitants into active resistance. In May Willing led a second expedition down the Mississippi but he failed to win over the inhabitants. The Chickasaw and Choctaw went over to the British side. The Southwest had thus definitely taken its stand against the United States.

Clark conquers the Northwest.—To Virginia fell the task of conquering the Northwest. The chief actor in the enterprise was George Rogers Clark, who, though only twenty-six, had already played a prominent part in Kentucky. With one hundred and seventy-five frontiersmen, mainly Virginians, in June, 1778, Clark descended the Ohio to Fort Massac, crossed Illinois, and in July took Kaskaskia, Prairie du Rocher, St. Philippe, and Cahokia, and French sympathizers secured the submission of Vincennes. Hamilton at once organized a force at Detroit to retake the lost posts. In December he occupied Vincennes without difficulty, but was unable to proceed farther. In February, 1779, after a difficult march over flooded prairies, Clark captured Hamilton and his force. In December, 1778 the Virginia legislature erected the territory north of the Ohio into the county of Illinois, John Todd being made civil and Clark military head. Clark planned the capture of Detroit, but was unable to get the necessary aid. Instead, in 1780 he founded Fort Jefferson on the Mississippi near the mouth of the Ohio and it soon became the center of a settled area.

Depredations of the Iroquois and Tories.—On the New York frontier Burgoyne's invasion had aroused the Iroquois and even after his defeat the Six Nations, except the Tuscaroras, Oneidas, and part of the Mohawks, adhered to the British. Many Tory refugees settled among the Indians and incited them to go on the warpath. In July, 1778, a force of Tories and Iroquois, mainly Senecas, descended into the Wyoming Valley and laid it waste, killing and capturing many of the inhabitants. Continental troops presently reoccupied the valley and in October the Indian town of Unadilla. The Indians and Tories retaliated by a descent on Cherry Valley. The depredations continued in 1779. Troops sent out from Ft. Stanwix destroyed the Onondaga villages. The Indians then assailed the Schoharie Valley and the western settlements in Ulster County, and spread destruction about Pittsburg.

Expeditions sent into the Iroquois country.—So extensive were the depredations that Congress decided to send an overwhelming force into the Iroquois country.   Three brigades from Washington's army were assembled at Wyoming under Sullivan. While he was waiting for a New York brigade to join him, Chief Brant and his warriors burned Minisink and ambushed the militia who went in pursuit.   Sullivan at the head of five thousand men passed up the Chemung branch of the Susquehanna, defeated a strong force of Indians and Tories on the site of modern Elmira, and then burned eighteen Indian villages and destroyed the crops.   Sullivan, however, failed to attack Niagara which was a British stronghold.   Another expedition from Pittsburg ascended the Alleghany and destroyed the Indian villages along the river.   These operations scattered the Indians and Tories but did not destroy them, and frequent depredations occurred on the New York and Pennsylvania frontiers during the remainder of the war.

SPAIN IN THE WAR [1]

Spain enters the war.—When Spain became a factor in the war in 1779, a new element entered the contest in the West. During 1778 Vergennes did not relax his efforts to induce Spain to become a belligerent.   But Carlos III and Florida Blanca had no intention of risking a war with Great Britain unless they were well paid for their assistance.   Not until they were certain that France would assist in the recovery of Gibraltar and the Floridas did they consent to make war.   On another point the king was insistent; he refused to recognize the independence of the United States.   The secret convention of Aranjuez between France and Spain was signed on April 12, 1779, and in June Spain definitely entered the war.

Gálvez on the lower Mississippi.—Orders were given at once to seize the British posts on the Mississippi.   With a hastily built fleet, Bernardo de Gálvez, the Governor of Louisiana, ascended the Mississippi at the head of fifteen hundred men. On September 7 he took Fort Bute at Manchac, and then proceeded to Baton Rouge which he captured, the capitulation including Fort Panmure at Natchez.   Meanwhile Grandpré had taken two small British outposts and a fleet had captured eight British vessels on Lake Pontchartrain.

[1] See map on page 400.

British attack on St. Louis.—As soon as war was declared, the British planned to capture New Orleans. An expedition from the north was to descend the Mississippi, attack St. Louis, reconquer the Illinois country, and meet General Campbell at Natchez with a force from Pensacola. The campaign against St. Louis was directed by Sinclair, commander at Mackinac. Emmanuel Hesse, a trader, was sent to assemble a force of Indians at the Fox-Wisconsin portage. In March, 1780, seven hundred and fifty men left Mackinac and joined Hesse at Prairie du Chien. To coöperate Charles Langlade was sent with Indians via Chicago, while Captain Bird, despatched from Detroit, was to raid Kentucky. None of the plans succeeded. Leyba, the commander at St. Louis, was forewarned and was aided by George Rogers Clark. On May 26 the British attacked St. Louis but were repulsed and forced to withdraw. Bird's expedition also miscarried, and Campbell's movement was frustrated by Gálvez.

The Spanish expedition against St. Joseph.—Sinclair at once planned a second expedition for the spring of 1781. Learning of the project, Cruzat, the new commander at St. Louis, prepared a counter stroke. He despatched parties up th Mississippi and to Peoria, and sent sixty-five men under Purée to destroy the stores at St. Joseph. On February 12 the post was taken in a surprise attack and the stores destroyed.

Capture of Mobile and Pensacola.—Meanwhile more important events had been taking place on the Gulf of Mexico. In February, 1780, Gálvez sailed from New Orleans with two thousand men to capture Fort Charlotte at Mobile, and on March 14 the place capitulated. Going to Cuba for reinforcements, after losing one fleet in a hurricane, in February, 1781, he sailed with fourteen hundred men to attack Pensacola. After a siege of nearly two months, General Campbell with more than eight hundred men surrendered. A simultaneous French and Spanish attack on Jamaica was next planned, and Gálvez sailed for Santo Domingo to command the Spanish forces, but the campaign was made unnecessary by the ending of the war. Spain had played an important part. She had defeated the British attempt to gain control of the Mississippi, had enabled Clark to maintain his hold on the Northwest, and had recovered Mobile and Pensacola.

THE WAR ON THE SEA AND THE DUTCH ALLIANCE

Washington's fleets.—From the beginning of the war American vessels were an important factor. They captured supply ships and transports, harassed commerce, captured many small war vessels, and protected trading vessels. At the opening of hostilities Washington turned to New England to supply him with vessels, and during the siege of Boston he sent out ten armed craft which made several important captures of arms and supplies. When operations were transferred to New York, he also engaged several vessels which rendered good service.

Congress provides a navy.—Largely through the influence of the Rhode Island delegates, Congress was convinced that a navy should be provided, and by January, 1776, ten vessels had been purchased and the building of thirteen others authorized. Before the end of the war over forty vessels were added to the high seas fleet in addition to minor craft on Lake Champlain.

First cruise of the fleet.—In February, 1776, Esek Hopkins, who had been appointed commander-in-chief of the navy, put to sea with a fleet of eight vessels. He cruised to the West Indies, captured New Providence, and sailed away with eighty-eight cannon, fifteen mortars, and a large quantity of stores. The fleet sailed to Long Island and off the eastern end it captured two small vessels, but on April 6 it allowed the *Glasgow* to escape.

Nature of the operations during 1776-1777.—By the end of 1776 the navy had been increased to twenty-five vessels. During the year it was constantly engaged in commerce destroying, and in capturing transports and small war craft. The operations were confined mainly to American and West Indian waters, although before the end of the year the *Reprisal*, which carried Franklin to France, had captured several vessels in European waters. During 1777 the congressional vessels, privateers, and state cruisers captured four hundred and sixty-seven vessels, many being taken near the British Isles. The depredations caused great alarm in England and the West Indies; merchants were often deterred from shipping goods, insurance rates and prices rose, and the demands for escorts became insistent.

Privateers.—The swift sailing craft of the Yankee skippers made ideal blockade runners and commerce destroyers, and hundreds of them put to sea. During the war Massachusetts commissioned nine hundred and ninety-eight. While the greater number of these vessels put out from New England, other states gave many commissions, Maryland alone commissioning two hundred and fifty. It is estimated that during the war the privateers captured or destroyed six hundred vessels with cargoes valued at $18,000,000, besides making several important captures of troops and supplies.

State navies.—With the exception of New Jersey and Delaware, the states had navies, the largest being those of Massachusetts, Connecticut, Pennsylvania, Maryland, Virginia, and South Carolina. At times these operated independently, sometimes in conjunction with privateers, and at other times as adjuncts of the regular navy. They were used chiefly to protect the trade in home waters and for coast defence.

The Penobscot expedition.—The most pretentious operation undertaken by a state navy was the attempt to capture Penobscot in 1779. The British had established a naval base near the mouth of the Penobscot River and Massachusetts determined to break it up. Fifteen hundred men were loaded on privateers and transports, and were convoyed by the *Warren*, the *Diligent*, and the *Providence*. The expedition arrived off the Penobscot late in July, but before it could take the fort, a larger British fleet appeared (August 13). The privateers and transports scattered, but the three war vessels were forced to run up the river where their crews destroyed them.

The navy during 1778-1779.—During 1778 the British navy succeeded in greatly decreasing the depredations of American vessels. By the close of the year the national navy was reduced to fourteen. But in 1779 the fleet was somewhat rehabilitated by the securing of several French vessels.

The Bonhomme Richard and the Serapis.—In 1779 the most famous sea-fight of the Revolution occurred. John Paul Jones was given command of an old French East Indiaman which was refitted with forty-two guns and renamed the *Bonhomme Richard.*

In August the French frigate *Alliance* and three small vessels accompanied the *Bonhomme Richard* on a cruise along the west coast of Ireland, northern Scotland, and the eastern coast of England, several prizes being taken.   On September 23 off Flamborough Head Jones sighted a large merchant fleet con- voyed by the forty-four gun frigate *Serapis* and the smaller *Countess of Scarborough*.   The *Bonhomme Richard* engaged the *Serapis* in one of the most thrilling of naval battles.   For three and a half hours the frigates fought at close range, much of the time being lashed together.   Although Jones's vessel was in a sinking condition, he refused to surrender.   When the English captain had lost more than a third of his crew, he pulled down his flag.   The *Pallas* captured the *Countess of Scarborough*. Jones placed his crew on board the *Serapis*, and the squadron soon after arrived at the Dutch port of Texel.

Decline of the navy.—When Charleston surrendered in 1780, four ships fell into British hands and only six vessels were left in the American navy.   At the same time parliament voted to increase the naval service.   The American coast was closely blockaded, and though cruisers occasionally got through, the navy ceased to be an important factor in the war.

The league cf armed neutrals.—As the war progressed Eng- land's exercise of the right of search on the high seas provoked the neutral powers.   At that time international law recognized a belligerent's right to seize enemy's goods, but not the vessel in which they were being carried.   England acted within the law, but her seizures worked great hardship upon neutrals. Largely through the influence of Frederick the Great, who had not forgiven England for abandoning him in the Seven Years' War, Catherine II of Russia was induced to champion the cause of the neutral states.   On February 26, 1780, she addressed a message to the neutral courts which asserted, (1) that neutral vessels should be allowed to navigate freely even upon the coasts of powers at war; (2) that, with the exception of contraband, goods belonging to the subjects of belligerents should be free in neutral ships; (3) that naval stores and provisions of neutrals should not be considered contraband; (4) that a port must be effectively guarded to constitute a blockade; and (5) that the above principles should be considered as rules in determining the legality of prizes. Denmark and Sweden promptly entered into an agreement with Russia mutually to protect their commerce, by force if necessary, the arrangement being known as the League of Armed Neutrality. The principles proclaimed by the Czarina were approved by France and Spain. The Netherlands joined the league in November, 1780; Prussia came in in May, 1781, and the Empire in October. Even Portugal, the ancient ally of England, and Turkey became parties to the league.

Attitude of the Netherlands.—At the opening of the American Revolution there were two parties in The Netherlands; the English party headed by the stadtholder, William V, and the Anti-Orange party which had strong French leanings. The strength of the Anti-Orange party lay chiefly in Holland and in the large cities, especially in Amsterdam where the great merchants were powerful. The Dutch people watched the contest between the United States and Great Britain with a filial interest, looking upon it as a counterpart of their own struggle for independence, but policy forced the government to remain neutral.

St. Eustatius.—The Dutch merchants saw an opportunity for immense profits in supplying the United States with war materials. The Dutch island of St. Eustatius in the West Indies became the center for a vast trade in contraband goods. The island became a veritable storehouse for the goods of all nations and here the American skippers brought tobacco and indigo, or gave promissory notes or continental currency in exchange for munitions of war. Great Britain complained of the trade and succeeded in getting the States General to prohibit the export of arms and munitions except by special permission from the Dutch admiralty, but nevertheless the traffic went merrily on. When British war vessels began to patrol the waters about the island and search vessels for contraband, it aroused the ire of the Dutch merchants.

The Scotch brigade and the Jones incident.—Two incidents added greatly to the ill-feeling which was growing rapidly between the two countries. The British government asked for the loan of the Scotch brigade, a body of troops which had been in Dutch service for many years. The government gave a suave answer. It was willing to loan the soldiers, but not for service outside of Europe. As George III wanted the troops for American service, the answer was practically a refusal. Another incident which increased the irritation was the sojourn of John Paul Jones at Texel. For over two months he remained on Dutch soil, while the government quibbled over its rights to order his departure.

British seizures.—During 1778 British seizures of Dutch vessels increased and the demands of the merchants for convoys became more and more insistent. France took advantage of the situation to bring The Netherlands to her side. Special commercial privileges in France had been granted to several of the Dutch cities. France now decided to force the Dutch government to take a more decided stand toward England by cutting off the special privileges to all the Dutch cities except Amsterdam. This led to a demand for an immediate adjustment with France and for convoys to protect Dutch vessels against British seizures. A climax was reached on December 31, 1779, when an encounter occurred between the convoys of a Dutch fleet and British war vessels. The result was soon evident, for The Netherlands began to build a large fleet.

The secret agreement.—The United States maintained secret agents in The Netherlands throughout the war. For several years they made unsuccessful attempts to obtain a loan, but the authorities of Amsterdam finally communicated to C. W. F. Dumas, the United States representative, that they desired to conclude a treaty provided Congress would not enter into engagements with Great Britain which might prove harmful to Dutch interests. Jean de Neufville, a prominent Amsterdam merchant, at the suggestion of Van Berckel, the pensionary of Amsterdam, visited Aix-la-Chapelle in 1778, where he met William Lee, an American representative to Germany and Austria; together they formulated the draft of a treaty which, however, was not to be considered until after the recognition of American independence by Great Britain. The agreement had no legal force, for Amsterdam could not enter into a treaty without the consent of the other provinces.

The declaration of war.—In 1780 Henry Laurens sailed for The Hague for the purpose of negotiating a loan and making a treaty with The Netherlands. On September 3 he was captured off Newfoundland. Among his papers was a copy of the secret compact drawn by Neufville and Lee. The British government demanded from the States General a disavowal of the action of Amsterdam and the punishment of Van Berckel. The States General finally disavowed the act but declared its incompetence to punish Van Berckel. On November 20, in the midst of the controversy, the States General decided to join the league of armed neutrals. When this became known at London, the British minister was ordered home, and on December 20 George III issued a manifesto which was a virtual declaration of war.

READINGS

THE FRENCH AND SPANISH ALLIANCES

Corwin, E. S., *French Policy and the American Alliance of 1778*, pp. 1–216; Hale, E. E., *Franklin in France;* Lecky, W. E. H., *History of England in the Eighteenth Century*, IV, 42–54, 99–129, 166–185; Perkins, J. B., *France in the American Revolution;* Phillips, P. C., *The West in the Diplomacy of the American Revolution;* Trescot, W. H., *Diplomacy of the American Revolution;* Trevelyan, G. O., *The American Revolution*, Part III, 387–476; Van Tyne, C. H., *The American Revolution*, 203–226; Wharton, F., *The Revolutionary Diplomatic Correspondence of the United States*, I.

THE WEST IN THE REVOLUTION

Alvord, C. W., "Virginia and the West," in *Mississippi Valley Historical Review*, III, 19–38; Alvord, C. W., ed., *Kaskaskia Records, 1778–1790*, Introduction; Gayarré, C., *History of Louisiana, the Spanish Domination*, ch. 3; Hamilton, P. J., *Colonial Mobile*, ch. 31; Hamilton, P. J., *The Colonization of the South*, ch. 23; James, J. A., ed., *George Rogers Clark Papers, 1771–1781*, Introduction; Roosevelt, Theodore, *The Winning of the West*, I, 272–327, II, 1–213; Teggart, F. J., "The Capture of St. Joseph, Michigan, by the Spaniards in 1781," in *Missouri Historical Review*, V, 214–228; Thwaites, R. G., and Kellogg, L. P., editors, *Frontier Defense on the Upper Ohio, 1778*, Introduction and maps; *The Revolution on the Upper Ohio, 1775–1777*, Introduction and maps; Van Tyne, C. H., *The American Revolution*, 269–288; Winsor, Justin, *The Westward Movement*, 101–187; Esarey, L., *A History of Indiana*, I, 47–91; McElroy, R. M., *Kentucky in the Nation's History*, 62–113.

THE NAVY, ARMED NEUTRALITY, AND DUTCH INTERVENTION

Clowes, W. L., *The Royal Navy*, III, 353–538; Edler, F., *The Dutch Republic and the American Revolution* (Johns Hopkins University, *Studies in History and Political Science*, XXIX, 187–424); Jameson, J. F., "St. Eustatius in the American Revolution," in *The American Historical Review*, VIII, 683–708; Maclay, E. S., *A History of American Privateers*, 43–222; *A History of the United States Navy*, I, 34–151; Paullin, C. O., *The Navy of the American Revolution;* Trevelyan, G. O., *George the Third and Charles Fox*, II, 36–72; Van Loon, H. W., *The Fall of the Dutch Republic*, 174–287; Van Tyne, C. H., *The American Revolution*, 309–319.

CHAPTER XXVII

THE CLOSING YEARS OF THE REVOLUTION

THE WAR IN THE SOUTH

Conquest of Georgia.—When France became the ally of the United States, British statesmen realized that the conquest of New England and the middle states was impossible, but they still hoped to conquer the South. From East Florida the British forces could strike at Georgia, and in November, 1778, the operations began. Thirty-five hundred men were sent south from New York, and General Prevost with two thousand soldiers advanced from Florida. On December 29 British forces captured Savannah and shortly afterward occupied Augusta. Within six weeks Georgia was under British control.

Reconquest fails.—General Lincoln, who had been placed in command in the South, determined to reconquer Georgia. He sent Ashe with fifteen hundred men to recapture Augusta, but the force was surprised and defeated. When Lincoln moved against Augusta, Prevost advanced against Charleston. The manœuvre succeeded and Lincoln was forced to hasten back to assist in the defence of the city. Prevost, his purpose accomplished, slowly retired to Savannah. Numerous letters were sent to the French admiral asking him to coöperate against the British. In September, 1779, D'Estaing sailed for Savannah; Lincoln advanced to assist him, and the city was besieged. On October 9 an attempt was made to carry the works by assault, but the allies were repulsed with a loss of over eight hundred men. Lincoln wished to continue the siege but D'Estaing refused. Despatching a portion of his fleet to the West Indies, with the rest he sailed for France, and Lincoln withdrew to Charleston.

Capture of Charleston.—With Georgia secure, Clinton determined to make another attempt to capture Charleston. He sailed from New York with over eight thousand men, and twelve hundred were brought from Savannah.   On February 11, 1780, the troops from New York were landed thirty miles south of Charleston and they soon advanced to the Ashley River.   Lincoln should have abandoned the city but instead he foolishly determined to defend it.   Gradually Clinton drew his lines about the city.   On April 13 Tarleton defeated the American cavalry which had kept the lines of communication open, and when British reinforcements arrived from New York the investment was completed.   Soon the garrison and inhabitants were almost starving.   On May 6 Tarleton dispersed the mounted militia at the crossing of the Santee River; on the following day Fort Moultrie surrendered, and the situation became hopeless.   On May 12 Lincoln signed articles of capitulation; over five thousand men, nearly four hundred pieces of artillery, and vast quantities of military stores fell into British hands.

Completion of the conquest of South Carolina.—After the fall of Charleston, Clinton sent out three expeditions; one northward under Tarleton against Buford's regiment which was advancing from Virginia, another toward Augusta, and a third toward Camden.   Buford started to retreat but Tarleton overtook him at the Waxhaws and almost annihilated his force.   The other expeditions met with little resistance and Clinton, believing that the conquest of South Carolina was complete, sailed for New York with a portion of the army, leaving Cornwallis in command of about eight thousand men.

Gathering of a new army.—Several weeks before the fall of Charleston, Washington had sent DeKalb southward with Maryland and Delaware regiments and these were reinforced by militia as they advanced.   South of the Virginia line they passed through a barren country, shortage of supplies and poor roads making their progress very slow.   At the Deep River they encamped and there they were joined by Gates who had been appointed by Congress to the command of the southern department.   Gates pressed on toward Camden, receiving local reinforcements as he advanced.

Camden.—A British force had collected at Camden and Cornwallis hastened from Charleston to take command.   Gates decided to attempt a surprise attack on the British force at Camden, thirteen miles away.   Cornwallis contemplated a similar move-

ment against Gates and the two armies left their encampments
about the same hour on the night of August 15. At daybreak
they met, but the militia proved to be no match for the British
soldiers and fled almost without firing a shot. The regulars

The War in the South
(Based on E. G. Foster, *Illustrative Historical Chart*)

stood firm for a time, but when DeKalb fell mortally wounded
and Tarleton's cavalry swept along their flank and rear, the
line gave way and the retreat turned into a rout. Gates fled
from the field and such was his haste that three days later he
was at Hillsborough, nearly two hundred miles away. Shortly
afterward Tarleton surprised and dispersed Sumter's band, and
resistance seemed completely broken.

Partisan warfare.—British arms had defeated the American armies, but the people of South Carolina were not conquered. The merciless raids of Tarleton's cavalry and Ferguson's Loyalists kept the spirit of resistance alive. Marion, Sumter, and Shelby gathered bands of patriots, who from swamp and forest pounced down on isolated detachments, captured the escorts of supply trains, intercepted messengers, and broke up companies of Loyalists. Between July and December, 1780, twenty-seven battles or skirmishes were fought on Carolina soil.

King's Mountain—Next to Tarleton, Major Ferguson was probably the most hated and most feared of Cornwallis's officers. His camp at Ninety-Six became a center of Loyalist recruiting, and his band of partisans grew to a thousand strong. They lived on the country, and the property of no man was safe. Ferguson boasted that if the frontiersmen from over the Alleghanies troubled him, he would cross the mountains, lay waste their valleys, and hang their leaders. On September 20, 1780, the borderers under the leadership of Colonel William Campbell, Sevier, and Shelby gathered at Sycamore Shoals on the Watauga River and started across the mountains. Ferguson heard of their coming and decided to teach the frontiersmen a lesson. He pitched his camp on the crest of King's Mountain, a position which would have been impregnable had his opponents been drilled in the tactics of European battlefields. But the Watauga men had been schooled in Indian warfare. Three times they charged up the steep mountain sides. After an hour of hot fighting the resistance began to weaken, and when Ferguson was killed, his troops threw down their arms and asked for quarter. The victory of the mountaineers is justly looked upon as the turning point in the war in the South, for it gave new life to the waning cause in the Carolinas.

Greene in command.—The difficult task of reconquering the South was assigned to General Nathanael Greene. On December 2 he arrived at Charlotte where Gates handed over to him a poorly disciplined and half-starved force of about two thousand men. With this insignificant army and aided by local militia and the partisan bands, Greene was confronted with the task of reconquering a province which was occupied by a skillful general whose veteran army outnumbered him four to one. His plan of campaign was matured with rare judgment. He proposed to use a mobile force of about two thousand men to keep Cornwallis busy, while Marion and Sumter harassed the enemy, prevented foraging, and broke up convoys.

The Cowpens.—Early in January, 1781, the main British army was at Winnsborough. Hoping to divide it, Greene sent Morgan with about a thousand men to threaten Augusta and Ninety-Six. The rest of the American army was stationed at Cheraw, sixty miles east of Winnsborough. When Cornwallis heard of Morgan's raid, he sent Tarleton in pursuit with eleven hundred men. Tarleton came in touch with Morgan at The Cowpens. The battle at first was stoutly contested, but Colonel Washington's cavalry turned the scale and Tarleton's force was almost annihilated.

Greene's retreat.—Morgan had accomplished his purpose and immediately started to rejoin the main army. When Greene heard of the victory, he realized that Cornwallis would retaliate, and a pitched battle with the larger British army meant disaster. Furthermore reinforcements were on their way from Virginia and Maryland. Greene's decision was a vital one. He determined to fall back to make a juncture with Morgan and to draw Cornwallis away from his base into a hostile and difficult country. Turning over the command of the main army to Huger with orders to march northward with all speed, Greene rode nearly a hundred and fifty miles in a pouring rain and joined Morgan in his bivouac on the Catawba. He had judged Cornwallis rightly. The British general divested his army of all unnecessary baggage and pressed forward, but in spite of his efforts, the American army escaped him. From river to river Greene retreated while Huger fell back rapidly, the two lines gradually converging until on February 8 they united at Guilford. From there the retreat was continued across the Dan into Virginia. The Fabian policy had succeeded, for Cornwallis had been drawn over two hundred miles from his base and had gotten in such a position that, even if he won a battle, a victory would be barren.

Guilford.—Cornwallis was running short of supplies and he could not with safety continue the pursuit. He decided to fall back to Hillsborough. Greene, whose army had been considerably reinforced, decided to follow the retiring British. When Cornwallis learned that the American army was advancing, he determined to risk a battle. On March 15 the armies met at Guilford. Greene posted his force of about forty-five hundred men in three lines, while the British army was stretched out in one long row without supporting reserves, a disposition made necessary by the fact that it numbered only twenty-two hundred and fifty men. When the British charged, the Carolina militia-men who occupied the front line gave way and fled from the field. The Virginia militia who held the second line stood their ground more firmly, but when their right flank was enveloped, they too retreated. The hard fighting came when the British met the con-tinental troops of the third line. Twice the British regulars were repulsed, and had Greene followed up the success, he might have won a victory. But he had no intention of risking the destruc-tion of his army. When the British advanced for a final assault, Greene decided to fall back. Covering his retreat with the first Virginia regiment, he retired from the field. He had lost the battle, but the result was as valuable as a victory.

Cornwallis retreats to Wilmington.—Cornwallis had lost nearly thirty per cent. of his fighting force; he was almost without supplies, and his foragers were being picked off by the Carolina guerrillas. His hospital service was deplorable. Leaving seventy of his most sorely wounded men to the tender mercies of General Greene, Cornwallis loaded the rest of his wounded on carts, and started on the long journey to Wilmington, the nearest base of supplies.

The reconquest of South Carolina and Georgia.—Greene fol-lowed Cornwallis only as far as the Deep River and then turned to reconquer South Carolina. In this work he was ably assisted by Marion, Sumter, Pickens, and Lee, who during April, May, and June captured several of the outlying British posts, the most important being Augusta, which evacuated on June 5. On April 25 Greene encountered Lord Rawdon's force near Camden. The British won the battle, but again they possessed a barren field, for so heavy were their losses that they retreated to Charleston. Greene next invested Ninety-Six. When he heard that Rawdon was marching to its relief, he attempted to carry it by storm. The assault failed and Greene gave up the siege. Lord Rawdon was unable to maintain his army away from his base. He accordingly ordered the evacuation of Ninety-Six and returned to Charleston. Soon afterward he sailed for England, leaving Stewart in command. The last important engagement occurred on September 8 at Eutaw Springs. The American army was again defeated, but Greene as usual gathered the fruits of victory, for Stewart, who had lost forty per cent. of his effectives, moved back to Charleston. In a campaign of eleven months Greene had lost every pitched battle, but the interior of the Carolinas and Georgia had been cleared of the enemy, who retained only Savannah, Charleston, and Wilmington.

THE YORKTOWN CAMPAIGN

Arnold and Cornwallis in Virginia.—When Benedict Arnold joined the British, he was rewarded with a brigadier-general's commission and sent to Virginia to cut off Greene's retreat if Cornwallis succeeded in driving that astute commander out of the Carolinas. Arnold marched up the James River and burned Richmond, but when the Virginia militia gathered in large numbers, he retreated to Portsmouth, where Lafayette, who had been sent to command in Virginia, held him in check. In the spring of 1781 Cornwallis transferred his forces to Petersburg, and Arnold was sent to Connecticut to conduct a campaign of rapine. Reinforcements were sent from New York and with an army of over seven thousand men Cornwallis began the conquest of Virginia, but he received no Loyalist support and he failed to crush the forces of Lafayette. After several weeks of ineffectual campaigning, he retired to Yorktown where he established himself behind strong fortifications.

Rodney and De Grasse in the West Indies.—The safety of Cornwallis's army depended upon the control of the sea. Since the beginning of the war the British had kept the sea lanes open. Time and again the fleet had enabled them to win victories or to extricate themselves from dangerous positions. Washington realized this and the burden of his letters to Franklin was the necessity of naval superiority. Vergennes made every effort to equip an overwhelming fleet and in March, 1781, a great armament under De Grasse sailed for the West Indies. And none too soon did they arrive, for Rodney was carrying all before him. In January he had been reinforced by eight ships of the line under Hood and on February 3 the British fleet captured St.

Eustatius. This was followed by the seizure of St. Martin and Saba. On April 28 De Grasse arrived at Martinique and on the following day he fought an indecisive action with Hood. An attempt on St. Lucia failed but soon afterward he captured Tobago. He then repaired to Martinique where he received despatches from Washington which determined him to sail for the Chesapeake.

Washington's plans.—When the news reached Washington that De Grasse had left France, he conferred with Rochambeau. Together they drew up a despatch to the French admiral in which they gave him his choice of coöperating with the land forces against New York or of sailing to the Chesapeake. When De Grasse received the despatch, he determined to strike at Cornwallis. On August 14 Washington received his reply and he immediately formulated a masterly plan of action. He decided to move Rochambeau's force and a portion of the continental army to Virginia, leaving General Heath with several New England regiments at West Point. Letters were written with the express intention that they should be intercepted by the British. These and the sudden activity of American engineers in constructing extensive works near Sandy Hook convinced Clinton that he had better sit tight behind his defences.

De Grasse and Graves.—On August 30 De Grasse arrived in the Chesapeake and on September 5 a fleet of nineteen British vessels under Admiral Graves appeared off Cape Henry. The fleets engaged and Graves's fleet was so badly crippled that it was forced to return to New York. Unmolested, a fleet of transports from Rhode Island carrying supplies and siege guns, and convoyed by eight war vessels, sailed into the Chesapeake. At the crucial moment the British had lost control of the seas.

The assembling of the army.—On August 20 the allied army began the passage of the Hudson, but not until they were near Philadelphia were the officers informed of their destination. At the Head of Elk Washington learned that De Grasse had arrived and that he had brought three thousand French infantry from the West Indies. After the allied army reached Williamsburg, it was reinforced by the troops under Lafayette, by the West Indian contingent, and by thirty-five hundred Virginia militia. With an army of sixteen thousand men and the greatest fleet that had ever assembled in American waters, Washington was in a position to win an overwhelming victory.

Yorktown.—The siege of Yorktown began on September 28. Earthworks were thrown up within six hundred yards of the British lines and on October 9 a terrific bombardment began. Five days later two outlying works were carried by storm and at short range the allied artillery did fearful execution. On the sixteenth a British counter-attack failed and on the following day an attempt to escape across the river was frustrated. When this failed the British commander knew that his fate was sealed. On October 19 Cornwallis surrendered and seven thousand soldiers became prisoners of war.

The last struggle in the West Indies.—Yorktown was the last important event on the mainland, but the fighting continued in the West Indies. On January 11, 1782, De Grasse captured St. Christopher and on the twentieth took Nevis. After receiving reinforcements, he planned the conquest of Jamaica, but the arrival of twelve ships from England so strengthened the British fleet that the project was not carried out. On April 12 Rodney defeated De Grasse in a final engagement off Dominica, an event which profoundly influenced the peace negotiations.

THE TREATY OF PEACE

Western Questions.—The conquests of George Rogers Clark, the entrance of Spain into the war, and the operations of Gálvez turned the attention of congressional leaders to peace terms. Would Spain be willing to grant the United States free navigation of the Mississippi? How much territory in the Southwest would Spain demand? Would France support Spanish pretensions? Such were the questions which disturbed American statesmen. To advance the interests of the United States, on October 4, 1779, Congress appointed John Adams peace commissioner and John Jay representative at Madrid.

Adams and Vergennes.—Adams arrived at Paris in February, 1780. He surprised Vergennes by disclosing powers to conclude treaties of peace and commerce with Great Britain. The protests and arguments of the French minister finally convinced Adams that he had better wait until he received new instructions from Congress, but he offended Vergennes by charging that France was purposely not exerting herself to the utmost. Vergennes distrusted Adams, for he thought that he represented the New England viewpoint which, Vergennes had been led to believe, was friendly to Great Britain. He informed Adams that in the future he would deal with Franklin.

Congressional instructions of June 15, 1781.—La Luzerne, the French representative at Philadelphia, made great efforts to have Adams curbed and to prevent a premature negotiation with Great Britain. In this he was assisted by the low state of affairs in the fall and winter of 1780. Congress finally decided to place the negotiations in the hands of a commission composed of Franklin, Jefferson, Jay, Adams, and Henry Laurens. Jefferson did not leave the United States and Laurens, who was captured by the British. did not arrive at Paris in time to take an important part in the negotiations. The instructions of the commissioners gave them considerable liberty of action, but they were to undertake nothing without the knowledge of the French ministers and were ultimately to be governed by their advice and opinion.

Jay in Spain.—In the meantime Jay had been having a difficult time in Spain. He was not officially received, and though granted occasional interviews by Florida Blanca, he was unable to make any progress toward the formulation of a treaty. When he was called to Paris in the summer of 1782 to take part in the peace negotiations, he had no illusions concerning the objects of Spain, objects which he seems to have believed were seconded by France.

The changed situation in 1782.—The commissioners were in a far stronger position than their instructions of 1781 implied. Yorktown had proved that American independence was assured, and Rodney's recent victory had weakened France at a time when her apparent support of Spain was liable to become troublesome. The situation in England had also changed. Lord North had fallen from power and at the head of the new ministry was Rockingham. Shelburne held the portfolio for the home and colonial departments and Fox was secretary of state for foreign affairs. This ministry held together from March until July, 1782, when Rockingham died. Fox, who had been unable to agree with Shelburne regarding the handling of American affairs, resigned, and Shelburne became Prime Minister.

Opening of negotiations with Great Britain.—On July 9, when Adams was at The Hague and before Jay had arrived, Franklin opened the negotiation with Oswald, the British agent, by presenting the basis of a treaty by which Great Britain was asked to acknowledge the independence of the United States, to settle boundaries and confine Canada within the bounds which maintained before the passage of the Quebec Act, and to acknowledge the right of Americans to fish on the Newfoundland banks and elsewhere.

Jay's suspicions of Vergennes.—The first hitch in the negotiations occurred when it was found that Oswald was instructed to conclude a peace or truce with the "colonies or plantations." On August 10 Jay and Franklin conferred with Vergennes about Oswald's commission. Jay contended that independence should be acknowledged by Great Britain before a treaty was negotiated, but Vergennes thought that this was of little consequence. When the question of conflicting Spanish and American claims was brought up, Vergennes became reticent, but his principal secretary, Rayneval, said that he thought the United States claimed too much. On September 7 Rayneval presented a memorial which proposed that the lands west of the mountains be divided into three Indian territories; lands north of the Ohio to be under the protection of Great Britain; south of the river the territory to be divided so that Spain would control the southwestern portion and the United States the northeastern part. On September 9 Jay learned that Rayneval had left secretly for England. Jay became thoroughly alarmed, for he believed that if the United States would not yield territory to Spain, Vergennes was ready to force his views by negotiating with England. Whether or not Jay was right in his suspicions has been a much argued question. No matter what the ultimate answer may be, the views of Jay became the determining factor in the course pursued by the American commissioners. Without consulting Franklin, Jay prevailed upon Benjamin Vaughan to visit Shelburne with the object of counteracting Rayneval's supposed mission and to let Shelburne know that the American commissioners were not to be bound by French views. A satisfactory commission was immediately issued to Oswald and negotiations proceeded with seriousness.

Proposal of October 8, 1782.—In October the American commissioners submitted proposals to Oswald. This preliminary draught provided that the independence of the United States be recognized by Great Britain and that the boundaries were to be as follows: "The said States are bounded north by a line drawn from the northwest angle of Nova Scotia, along the highlands which divide those rivers which empty themselves into the river St. Lawrence, from those which fall into the Atlantic Ocean, to the northernmost head of Connecticut River; thence down along the middle of that river to the 45th degree of north latitude, and thence due west in the latitude 45 degrees north from the equator, to the northwesternmost side of the river St. Lawrence . . . ; thence straight to the south end of the Lake Nipissing, and thence straight to the source of the river Mississippi; west by a line to be drawn along the middle of the river Mississippi, from its source to where the said line shall intersect the 31st degree of north latitude; south by a line to be drawn due east from the termination of the line last mentioned, in the latitude of 31 degrees north of the equator, to the middle of the river Apalachicola or Catahouchi; thence along the middle thereof to its junction with the Flint River; thence straight to the head of St. Mary's River; thence down along the middle of St. Mary's River to the Atlantic Ocean, and east by a line to be drawn along the middle of St. John's River from its source to its mouth in the bay of Fundy. . . ." The subjects of Great Britain and the United States were to enjoy the use of the fisheries, common commercial privileges, and the free navigation of the Mississippi. No provision was made for compensation to Loyalists, or for the collection by English merchants of debts in America.

Proposals of November 5.—The preliminary proposal was unsatisfactory to Shelburne. He accordingly sent Henry Strachey, an under official, to assist Oswald in making other arrangements. About this time Adams also arrived from The Hague. The negotiations proceeded without serious complications and in November a second draught was ready. In several important particulars it differed from the previous document. The Maine boundary on the east was to be a line drawn through the middle of the St. Croix River to its source, and thence directly north to the highlands which divide the rivers of the Atlantic from those which empty into the St. Lawrence; the line was to follow those highlands to the northwesternmost head of the Connecticut River, thence down that river to the forty-fifth parallel, and then straight west until it struck the Mississippi. British creditors were to "meet with no lawful impediment to recovering the full value or sterling amount of such *bona fide* debts as were contracted before the year 1775," but compensation to Loyalists was studiously omitted. A secret article was added to the effect, that if at the end of the war Great Britain should be, or should be put, in possession of West Florida, the boundary separating that province from the United States should be "a line drawn from the mouth of the river Yazoo, . . . due east to the river Apalachicola, and thence along the middle of that river to its junction with the Flint River, etc."

British proposal of November 25.—The failure to provide for the Loyalists caused the English government to submit other propositions which differed in two important particulars from the previous proposals. The northern boundary was changed west of the point where the Connecticut River crossed the forty-fifth parallel. From that point it was to follow the present international boundary to the Lake of the Woods, and from the northwestern point of that lake was to run due west to the Mississippi. The southern boundary was to leave the Mississippi at "the northernmost part of the 31st degree of north latitude," then "to be drawn due east . . . in the latitude of 31 degrees north of the equator to the middle of the river Apalachicola," and from there it was to follow the line of the proposal of October 8. Articles were also inserted which provided that restitution should be made of all estates, rights, and properties in America which had been confiscated during the war, that no one was to suffer in life or person, or be deprived of property on account of the part which he had taken in the war, that imprisoned Loyalists were to be set at liberty and pending prosecutions dropped. The right of Americans in the use of the fisheries were somewhat abridged.

Provisional articles of November 30. —The British proposals were satisfactory to the American commissioners except those regarding the Loyalists and the fisheries. After considerable discussion an agreement was reached and provisional articles were signed. The people of the United States were given unrestricted fishing privileges "on the Grand Bank and on all the other banks of Newfoundland," in the Gulf of St. Lawrence, and elsewhere, and the right of curing fish along the unsettled bays, harbors, and creeks of Nova Scotia, and on the shores of the Magdalen Islands and Labrador. The idea of indemnity for Loyalists was not incorporated, the articles merely pledging that Congress would make recommendations to the state legislatures that there should be no more confiscations or prosecutions, and that claimants of confiscated lands be allowed to use legal means of recovering them and might go at liberty for one year without personal risk. The articles also provided that the treaty should not be concluded until terms of peace had been agreed upon between France and Great Britain. The action of the American commissioners in arriving at an agreement without consulting the French ministers was not pleasing to Vergennes, but Franklin adroitly pacified him. It is probable that Vergennes did not have a deep feeling of resentment, for he soon obtained a loan of six million livres for the United States.

Preliminary agreements between England, France, and Spain. —Preliminary articles between England, France, and Spain were drawn in January, 1783. Spain failed to obtain Gibraltar, but received Minorca and the Floridas. France received no territory on the mainland of North America. French fishermen were granted important rights in the Newfoundland fisheries, and Great Britain gave to France Dunkirk, St. Lucia and Tobago, Senegal, and Gorée, and certain recent conquests, and guarantees of commercial privileges in India. France restored to Great Britain Grenada, the Grenadines, St. Vincent, Dominica, St. Christopher, Nevis, and Montserrat, and territory on the Gambia River.

Final agreements.—On September 3, 1783, all the definitive treaties were signed, the treaty between the United States and Great Britain being the same as the provisional articles of November 30. In the treaty the boundaries of the United States were apparently defined with exactness, but the statement of the Maine and northwestern boundaries proved to be ambiguous and became the subject of future disputes with Great Britain the southern boundary agreement led to future difficulties with Spain, as did the question of the navigation of the Mississippi. The treaty was, however, a great triumph for American diplomacy. The United States had emerged from the contest as an independent power, with a vast domain stretching from the Mississippi to the Atlantic, and from the Great Lakes to the Floridas.

The dispersion of the Loyalists.—During the war many Loyalists had fled to England, to Canada, to the West Indies, or to Florida. A still larger number had taken refuge behind the British lines, or had joined the British Army. After the treaty, as persecutions continued, the British government arranged for the transportation of all who wished to leave the United States, offered them homes in the other British colonies, granted half pay to the officers after their regiments were reduced, and appointed a commission to provide compensation for losses. Many thousands of Loyalists left the country. Of these the more influential went to England. About two hundred families went to the West Indies. The larger number migrated to Canada, where, as "United Empire Loyalists," they laid the foundation of British Canada.

READINGS

. THE WAR IN THE SOUTH AND THE YORKTOWN CAMPAIGN

Fisher, S. G., *The Struggle for American Independence*, II, 228–535; Greene, F. V., *The Revolutionary War*, 180–281; Lecky, W. E. H., *History of England in the Eighteenth Century*, IV, 130–165, 199–220; McCrady, Edward, *History of South Carolina in the Revolution*, 1780–1783; Trevelyan, G. O., *George the Third and Charles Fox*, II, 94–172.

THE TREATY OF PEACE

Channing, Edward, *History of the United States*, III, 346–373; Corwin, E. S., *French Policy and the American Alliance*, 217–377; Fiske, John, *The Critical Period*, 1–49; Lecky, W. E. H., *History of England in the Eighteenth Century*, IV, 255–322; McLaughlin, A. C., *The Confederation and the Constitution*, 3–34; Wharton, Francis, *The Revolutionary Diplomatic Correspondence of the United States*, V–VI; Winsor, Justin, *The Westward Movement*, 203–224.

CHAPTER XXVIII

GOVERNMENTAL DEVELOPMENT DURING THE REVOLUTION

The Association a step toward sovereignty.—The First Continental Congress was called to deliberate and determine upon measures to recover rights and liberties of which the colonies had been deprived and to restore harmony with Great Britain. Although the Congress was consultative in nature, it completed the revolutionary organization and made unity of action possible. The adoption of the Association was a fundamental step toward sovereignty. It could only be interpreted to mean that the colonies intended to enforce their will upon the mother country. Furthermore, Congress provided means to enforce the Association within colonies. While the petitions and addresses which were sent forth were couched in respectful terms, the tone of the declaration and resolves was distinctly revolutionary, and when considered in connection with the Association, it becomes evident that the iron hand of a sovereign power was even then visible through the mists of revolution.

THE SECOND CONTINENTAL CONGRESS

Nature of Congress.—The Second Continental Congress which convened at Philadelphia on May 10, 1775, was a purely revolutionary body, a "creature of emergency." In its inception it was in no sense a sovereign body, but was rather a great central committee, representing the revolutionary elements in the various colonies, which assumed the supreme directing power until 1781. The colonies had displayed no regularity in the method of selecting the delegates. The two New Hampshire delegates were chosen by a convention of deputies who had been appointed by various towns. The five delegates of Massachusetts were chosen by the provincial congress. The Rhode Island assembly chose two delegates, and the Connecticut house of representatives five. In New York twelve delegates were selected by a provincial convention. The five delegates from New Jersey were chosen by the assembly, as were the nine from Pennsylvania and the three from Delaware. In Maryland a meeting of deputies chose seven delegates, three or more of whom might represent the colony. In Virginia a convention of delegates selected seven. In North Carolina a convention chose three delegates who were approved by the assembly, and in South Carolina the assembly appointed five. Georgia at first was represented by a delegate from a single parish.

Original powers of the delegates.—The delegates were not empowered to perform sovereign acts, but were considered as a central revolutionary committee, which was to take such measures as would be best calculated to recover and establish American rights and liberties, restore harmony between Great Britain and her colonies, and advance the best interests of the colonies. As the revolutionary movement spread and acts of violence occurred, necessity forced Congress to perform many acts which were not contemplated in the original instructions of the delegates; but from first to last it was lacking in sovereign powers and was always the creature of the states.

Causes of the weakness of Congress.—The fundamental cause of the weakness of Congress was its lack of legal powers. When executive acts were necessary, the delegates were never certain that their joint action would be upheld by the states. Congress had no power to enforce its will, or to coerce an unruly state. Another source of weakness was the constantly changing personnel of Congress, the numbers varying from twenty-four to a hundred. Many of the strongest members were sent on foreign missions, leaving important work to be done by men who had had little experience in public affairs. Sectional jealousy frequently interfered with concerted action; the small states feared the larger ones; states holding no western lands were suspicious of those with such possessions; and theological differences made it difficult for New Englanders to work with delegates from the middle and southern states. In 1777 when Vermont was asking to be admitted as a state, New England and New York found their interests to be conflicting, as both claimed jurisdiction over the Green Mountain country. Some of the members stooped to petty acts for self-aggrandizement, breeding suspicion in the minds of many. Congress was housed at Philadelphia in the state house, which was poorly arranged for a body whose business was mainly conducted by committees. Military necessity twice forced Congress to hasten from the city, the first time in December, 1776, when it fled to Baltimore, the second time after the battle of the Brandywine, when it became an exile, first at Lancaster and later at York.

Nature of the business of Congress.—Dr. Albion W. Small has classified the business of Congress under the following heads: (1) To dispose of sundry applications in behalf of individuals; (2) to consider requests for advice and aid to individual colonies; (3) to act as the mouthpiece of the patriotic party; (4) to serve as an organ of communication between the collective colonies and other communities or individuals; (5) to devise peace plans and measures for the general good; (6) to devise offensive and defensive measures to be urged upon the individual colonies; (7) to raise, organize, and regulate a continental army, and assume general direction of military affairs.

Organization of Congress and conduct of business.—When Peyton Randolph found it necessary to leave Congress, the delegates chose John Hancock president and Charles Thomson secretary, the latter serving until 1781. Most of the work was carried on by committees. When a vote was taken in Congress, the members did not cast their ballots as individuals, but each state delegation cast a solid affirmative or negative vote. Usually committees met in the morning from 7 to 10, Congress from 10 A. M. to 4 or 5 P. M., and committees from 6 to 10 P. M. The president's duties were manifold, for in addition to acting as presiding officer, he carried on correspondence with the commander-in-chief, with state governors, and with local committees.

Early acts of Congress.—In spite of the conservatives who at first were in the majority and who desired to hold in check the revolutionary forces, circumstances forced Congress to exercise executive authority long before the Declaration of Independence. In June, 1775, Congress ordered the raising and organizing of an army, authorized a loan for the purchase of gunpowder, and issued $2,000,000 in bills of credit. In September provision was made for the fitting out of a navy, and steps were taken to open relations with foreign powers, to supervise the frontiers, and to establish a post-office. In the chaos which resulted from the overthrow of the chartered governments, several of the state revolutionary bodies appealed to Congress for advice. In answer to the Massachusetts appeal, Congress advised that, as no obedience was due to parliament and as the crown officials were absent, the provincial congress was to summon the representatives to an assembly which was to choose a council, and together the two bodies were to govern until difficulties were adjusted with the crown. Similar advice was given to New Hampshire, South Carolina, and Virginia. The various colonies were also advised to erect prize courts. In March, 1776, it advised the colonies to disarm the Loyalists, and soon afterward authorized the fitting out of privateers and opened the ports to all countries not subject to Great Britain. In May it urged all colonies which had not yet formed state governments to do so and declared that British authority should be suppressed. On July 4, 1776, it adopted the Declaration of Independence.

Judicial functions.—With the increase of privateering, prize courts became necessary, and in November, 1775, Congress advised the colonies to erect courts in which cases of capture might be tried by jury and appeals made to Congress. During 1776 the custom was followed of appointing a congressional committee to hear each appeal, but in January, 1777, a standing committee of five was appointed to hear all appeals. The increasing business and the need of legally trained men made it apparent that the committee system could not long handle the prize cases, and in January, 1780, a permanent court of appeals was established, which may be looked upon as a forerunner of the supreme court.

Military affairs.—When hostilities began, Congress acted on the theory that the colonies were loyal to the king, but were opposing Gage's ministerial army. Events soon forced it to take measures of defence, committees being appointed in May, 1775, to consider how military stores might be procured. On June 15 Washington was chosen commander-in-chief and on the following day a committee was appointed to draw up his commission and instructions. Congress also selected four major-generals, eight brigadier-generals, a quartermaster-general and commissary-general. Later a clothier-general was appointed.

At first military affairs were handled by congressional committees, but in January, 1776, a committee was appointed to consider the establishment of a war office. Five months later Congress adopted the committee's plan which provided for a Board of War and Ordnance to consist of five members of Congress and a secretary. In 1777 this congressional board was done away with and a new board, consisting of persons who were not members of Congress, was created, Gates being placed at its head. Congress also appointed an inspector-general, Thomas Conway being the first incumbent, being followed by Steuben. The system of supplying the army was found to be deficient and to rectify matters the commissary department was reorganized in 1777 and again in 1778. Congress continued to keep in touch with the army by sending special committees to examine actual conditions.

Naval affairs.—To handle maritime affairs a naval committee was appointed whose "active life lasted from October, 1775, until January, 1776, during which time it laid the foundation of the navy." On December 14, 1775, a marine committee, composed of one member from each colony, was chosen to take charge of the building and fitting out of vessels, and this committee soon assumed direction of naval affairs. Agents to superintend the work of construction were employed, and on the recommendation of the committee, Congress appointed prize agents. In November, 1776, a board of three naval experts was created to execute business under the direction of the maritime committee and a similar board was appointed in April, 1777, to handle affairs in New England alone. The marine committee continued until October, 1779. By that time it became evident that a more efficient system was needed and Congress appointed a Board of Admiralty consisting of three commissioners and two members of Congress. The board remained in charge of naval affairs until the governmental reorganization of 1781.

Foreign affairs.—To direct diplomacy was one of the difficult functions of a Congress whose members were but little versed in the intricacies of foreign courts. In the fall of 1775 a "secret committee on foreign correspondence" was chosen. In March, 1776, Silas Deane was sent to France, and in September of the same year a commission to handle American interests in

Europe, composed of Franklin, Jefferson, and Deane, was appointed. Jefferson, however, remained in America and Arthur Lee was substituted. To obtain financial aid had been the chief object up to the Declaration of Independence, but after that Congress and its agents directed their energies not only to the securing of funds, but to obtain recognition by France and Spain, and to make military and commercial alliances. In 1777 the secret committee was changed to the "committee on foreign affairs," an organization which conducted the foreign policy up to 1781.

FINANCIAL AFFAIRS

Fiscal machinery.—The most difficult problem which Congress had to solve was the raising of sufficient funds to carry on the Revolution. To handle the public moneys and devise means for raising revenue, fiscal machinery gradually came into existence. In 1775 two treasurers were appointed to receive and disburse public funds. Soon a committee of claims of thirteen members was appointed, and in February, 1776, a standing committee of five known as the Treasury Board, which supervised financial officials and attended to the emission of instruments of credit. This board, under which was an auditor-general at the head of the office of accounts, was the germ of the later treasury. In 1778 the book-keeping system was remodeled and a comptroller, auditor, treasurer, and two chambers of accounts were provided. In 1779 the old treasury board was set aside and in its place a commission of five was appointed, of which three were not congressional delegates.

Bills of credit.—Congress had three principal means of raising money: by issuance of bills of credit, by requisitions upon the states, and by domestic and foreign loans. In addition there was a considerable income from prizes and captures. The need of raising money drove Congress to the doubtful expedient of issuing large quantities of paper money unbacked by bullion or specie but based upon the credit of the states. Between June, 1775, and November, 1779, Congress authorized the issuance of $241,552,780 in denominations varying from one-sixth of a dollar to sixty-five dollars. In addition the states issued over

$200,000,000 in paper money. Such large amounts of unbacked paper could lead to but one result, a steadily increasing depreciation. At first the people took the continental money with little protest, but as issue followed issue in rapid succession, depreciation set in, and by January, 1779, the ratio of currency to specie was eight to one, by June twenty to one, and by the end of that year forty to one. In May, 1781, it ceased to pass as currency. Financiers have found it difficult to estimate the specie value of the various issues, but a careful economist has calculated that it was worth between $37,000,000 and $41,000,000.

Requisitions upon the states.—As military demands became more and more insistent, Congress found it necessary to make requisitions upon the states. The demands were met in a niggardly manner; between November, 1777, and February, 1781, the moneys received, figured in specie value, amounted to only $2,737,000. In 1780 Congress was driven to demanding specific supplies, such as corn, meat, and hay.

Domestic loans.—With the exception of a small loan for the purchase of gunpowder, Congress did not authorize a domestic loan until October, 1776, when it voted to borrow $5,000,000 at four per cent. and to establish state loan offices. Subsequent loans were at six per cent. After money from foreign loans began to come in in September, 1777, interest on the domestic debt was paid, enabling Congress to borrow more freely than before. From October, 1776, to September, 1777, only $3,787,000 was obtained from the states, and during the rest of the war $63,289,000 in paper was subscribed.

Foreign loans.—Most of the foreign financial aid came from France. In the years before France formally recognized the independence of the American states, large sums were loaned to Congress. In May, 1776, Vergennes secured a loan of a million livres from the French treasury and also obtained a small loan from Spain. Through the fictitious company of "Hortalez et Cie" in Paris organized by Beaumarchais, and the Spanish firm of Josef Gardoqui and Sons, large quantities of clothing, military stores, and considerable sums of money were placed at the disposal of the revolutionary agents. During 1777-1780 Congress borrowed from France $1,633,500.

STATE GOVERNMENTS DURING THE REVOLUTION

Organization of state governments.—As resistance to British authority intensified during 1775, the colonies took steps to organize for resistance. The colonial governors were forced to leave and the committees of safety assumed temporary executive functions. In most of the colonies revolutionary conventions were called which took over the legislative power until it became apparent that the difficulties with Great Britain could not be settled. As it grew more and more evident that the war was to be fought for independence, the conventions took steps to organize state governments. Several of them asked advice concerning such action from the Continental Congress, and that body finally advised all the colonies to proceed on the assumption that they no longer owed allegiance to the crown. The constitutional convention introduced a new principle in the theory of the state. Up to this time governmental authority had rested in England. Henceforth the powers of sovereignty were to emanate from the will of the people, the constitutional convention being the embodiment of the sovereign will.

Type of state governments.—In the formation of governments the states were guided by experience in colonial statecraft. The new constitutions disclosed the influence of the struggle with Great Britain, the framers seeking to protect the commonwealths from the possibility of encroachment of the executive at the expense of the legislative departments. The influence of the political philosophy which insisted that the separation of the departments of government was the safeguard of popular rights was also apparent in the new constitutions. Although they displayed a marked divergence on minor points, in general a common type of government prevailed. In most of the states the legislative department was in two parts, a lower and an upper house; the lower, usually elected for a year, represented the people at large, and the upper, serving for longer periods, represented the wealthier classes. In all but one state a property qualification was required for voters and representatives, and in most cases the property qualification was higher for members of the upper chamber. There was no uniformity in designation, the lower chamber being variously called the house of representatives, house of commons, or assembly; the upper house was usually called the legislative council, but in Virginia it was known as the senate, a designation afterward commonly adopted. The executive was usually weak, being vested either in a governor with limited power or in a small group. So well adapted to the needs of a state were the colonial charters of Connecticut and Rhode Island, that they continued to use their charters as constitutions for many years, merely substituting the authority of the people for that of the king.

Variations from type.—Several of the state constitutions contained unusual features. In Pennsylvania the radical convention in 1776 framed a constitution which provided for a legislature of one chamber and an executive council which could not veto an act of the assembly. Every seven years a council of censors was to be chosen by the voters to see that the constitution had not been violated. By a two-thirds vote the censors could summon a convention to amend the constitution. Georgia also set up a unicameral legislature. The Virginia constitution of 1776 contained a declaration of independence. It also provided that all bills must originate in the lower house and that money bills could not be amended by the senate. A privy council of eight members was chosen by a joint ballot of both houses. This body and the two houses selected the governor. The South Carolina constitution of 1778 provided for the election of the upper house by the people and the governor was deprived of the veto power. By the New York constitution of 1778, the governor was elected by the people, but he had neither appointive nor veto power, those functions being exercised respectively by a council of appointments chosen from the senate by the assembly, and by a council of revision composed of the governor, chancellor, and two or more judges of the supreme court. Objections raised by the council of revision could be defeated by a two-thirds vote of both houses. The first constitution of Massachusetts provided for a legislature of two houses, the upper chamber acting as a multiple executive. In 1780 a new constitution was accepted by the people. This provided that the governor be given military powers and the appointment of judges. He was to be advised by a council of nine elected from the senate by both houses.

Selection of the judiciary.—Divergences appeared in the methods of selecting judges. In Connecticut and Rhode Island they were appointed annually by the assemblies. In Georgia the chief justice was appointed by the assembly, but the people elected the county judges annually; in New Jersey, Delaware, and Pennsylvania the assemblies chose the judges for seven years; in Massachusetts, New York, and Maryland the governor and council appointed the judges who held office during good behavior; in other states the legislatures appointed them for varying terms.

The courts.—The states established superior tribunals which were authorized to review and correct decisions of inferior courts. In Georgia the county courts, when presided over by the chief-justice, acted as a final court of appeal. In New Jersey the governor and council constituted the highest appellate tribunal. In Virginia the constitution provided for a court of appeals which passed upon the constitutionality of laws and heard appeals. In Maryland and South Carolina the appellate courts were composed of the presiding officers of the district courts. In the other colonies the supreme court fulfilled the same function. The colonial system of county courts to try the smaller civil cases, and courts of session, composed of justices of the peace, for trial of petty criminal cases were retained.

English law the basis of American jurisprudence.—The English common-law forms of writs and legal process were continued with all their technicalities, a usage which has been one of the stumbling blocks in the attempts to simplify legal methods in the United States. "Either by the constitutions or by legislative enactments, English common law, and all those English statutes hitherto recognized and acted upon in the colonies respectively, were made the basis of state jurisprudence. The force of law was also continued to all existing colonial statutes until repealed or altered, except in South Carolina, where a particular enumeration and reënactment was made of the colonial statutes intended to be recognized."

The revolutionary state of Vermont.—In the Green Mountain region a new state was in the making. There New York claimed jurisdiction but her authority had never been established and in April, 1775, the inhabitants of the mountain country held a convention, eventually drew up a constitution, and asked Congress to recognize Vermont as a state. New York succeeded in defeating the movement in Congress, but the Vermonters, nothing daunted, proceeded to organize their government. The new revolutionary state soon became embroiled in disputes with New Hampshire and Massachusetts. These and the continued opposition of New York caused Congress to delay recognition, and Vermont was not formally admitted to the union until 1791, but to all intents and purposes it was a sovereign state from 1775.

Attempts at Western State-Making.—In the course of the Revolution, likewise, the settlements beyond the Alleghanies were trying experiments in state-making. The Watauga Association in eastern Tennessee, the Transylvania government in Kentucky, and the Nashborough Association are all examples. These western communities reverted to the compact theory of government, and their experiences illustrate the democratic tendencies of the frontier. As yet, however, the communities were too weak to succeed in the midst of conflicting elements and each reverted for a time to the subordinate position of a county of the older state.

THE ARTICLES OF CONFEDERATION

The confederation movement.—When danger from without threatened, a union of the colonies as a device of safety had often been suggested, but separatist tendencies had always proved too strong for the federationists. Franklin had been a friend of the idea of union, in 1754 having penned the Albany plan. In July, 1775, when it became apparent that the colonies were facing a great war, he proposed a league of friendship whose affairs should be conducted by a general congress in which each colony should have representation according to its population. Franklin's plan was not adopted, but it focused attention upon the growing need of a confederation. The Continental Congress was a revolutionary body which had no power save the sufferance of states which were themselves revolutionary. Whether or not those states were to retain sovereign powers depended entirely on the outcome of the struggle. To insure a successful issue, it was believed that a more perfect organ than the Continental Congress should be devised to conduct the Revolution.

Work of the confederation committee.—When Lee's independence resolution was introduced in the Continental Congress on June 7, 1776, it was accompanied by a motion to appoint a committee to draw up articles of confederation. On June 12 a committee composed of one delegate from each colony was chosen, among the members being John Dickinson, Samuel Adams, Roger Sherman, and Edward Rutledge. On July 12 the committee reported a plan of confederation, drawn mainly by Dickinson, which provided that each state should have a single vote in a central congress, and that an affirmative vote of nine states should be necessary to pass any measure.

Adoption of the articles.—Stress of business, military events which forced the hasty departure of Congress from Philadelphia on several occasions, and divergence of views prevented speedy action. On two ideas only was there agreement. The delegates were convinced that the English imperial system was wrong in its theory of taxation; whatever the form of the central government might be, it must not take from the states the power of taxation. They were also agreed that the executive power of the central government must be weak. The debates turned upon three main questions, taxation, representation, and congressional power to settle boundary disputes. Dickinson's plan proposed that taxation should be apportioned among the states according to population; this aroused the opposition of the Southerners, who objected to the slaves being counted as population. Franklin objected to Dickinson's proposal of one vote per state on the ground that it was an inequitable arrangement. In reply it was argued that the confederation was a league of friendship to be formed for a specific purpose and in consequence each state ought to have equal power. In regard to congressional power to settle boundary disputes, a difference arose between those states which possessed western lands and those which did not. Not until November, 1777, did Congress give the articles a favorable vote and on June 26, 1778, a form of ratification was adopted. Delegates from the New England states, New York, Pennsylvania, Virginia, and South Carolina signed the articles on July 9, North Carolina on July 21, Georgia on July 24, and New Jersey on November 26, 1778; Delaware on May 5, 1779, and Maryland not until March 1, 1781. In consequence of the tardy action of Maryland, the Continental Congress continued to conduct the war almost to its conclusion.

The more important provisions of the articles.—The preamble stated that the delegates had agreed "to certain articles of Confederation and perpetual union." Article I named the confederacy "The United States of America." Article II said, "Each State retains its sovereignty, freedom and independence, and every power, jurisdiction and right, which is not by this confederation expressly delegated to the United States, in Congress assembled." Article III stated the purpose of the entrance of the states into a league of friendship as follows: "for their common defence, the security of their liberties, and their mutual and general welfare." Article IV declared that the free inhabitants of each state should be "entitled to all privileges and immunities of free citizens in the several States" and provided for the extradition of criminals. It also stated that, "Full faith and credit shall be given in each of these States to the records, acts and judicial proceedings of the courts and magistrates of every other State."

Article V provided that delegates should "be annually appointed in such manner as the legislature of each State shall direct," and that Congress should convene annually on the first Monday in November. No state was to be represented in Congress by less than two nor more than seven members, and in determining questions, each state should have one vote.

Article VI dealt mainly with prohibitions upon the states. Without the consent of Congress, no state was to enter into treaties, confederation, or alliance with foreign courts, nor was any state to lay imposts or duties which might interfere with any stipulations in treaties entered into between the United States and foreign powers. Such naval and military forces were to be maintained by the states in time of peace as Congress might deem necessary, and no state was to engage in war without the consent of Congress unless actually invaded or in danger of Indian attack.

Article VIII provided that expenses incurred for common defence or for the general welfare, when allowed by Congress, should be defrayed out of a common treasury, to "be supplied by the several states, in proportion to the value of all land within each state, granted to or surveyed for any person, as such land and the buildings and improvements thereon shall be estimated according to such mode as the United States in Congress assembled, shall from time to time direct and appoint."

Article IX dealt with the congressional powers. Congress was given the exclusive power (1) of determining peace or war except in the cases mentioned in Article VI, (2) of sending and receiving ambassadors, (3) of entering into treaties and alliances, provided such agreements did not interfere with the rights of the states to lay such imposts and duties on foreign goods as they were subjected to by foreigners, or prohibit exportation or importation, (4) of establishing rules for deciding prize cases, (5) of granting letters of marque and reprisal in time of peace, (6) of establishing admiralty courts, and (7) of settling disputes between two or more states, an elaborate procedure in such cases being prescribed.

Congress was also given the exclusive power (8) of regulating the alloy and value of coin struck by its authority or by that of a state, (9) of fixing the standard of weights and measures, (10) of regulating affairs with Indians not members of states provided state rights were not infringed, (11) of establishing and regulating post-offices and postage, (12) of appointing military officers except regimental officers, (13) of appointing naval officers, and (14) of making rules and regulations for the army and navy.

Other powers of Congress were (15) "to appoint a committee, to sit in the recess of Congress, to be denominated 'a Committee of the States,' and to consist of one delegate from each State; and to appoint such other committees and civil officers as may be necessary for managing the general affairs of the United States under direction . . .," (16) to ascertain the necessary sums of money to be raised for the service of the United States, and to appropriate and apply the same for defraying the public expenses, (17) to borrow money or emit bills on the credit of the United States, (18) to build and equip a navy, and (19) "to agree upon the number of land forces, and to make requisition from each state for its quota, in proportion to the number of white inhabitants in each state." With the exception of a vote upon adjournment, all measures required the assent of nine states. No period of adjournment was to be longer than six months.

Article X provided that the committee of the states should be authorized to execute the delegated powers of Congress during recesses. Article XII stated that bills of credit, loans, and debts should be considered as a charge against the United States and for whose payment the United States and the public faith were pledged. Article XIII provided that every state should abide by the acts of Congress, that the union should be perpetual, and that no alteration should be made in the articles by Congress unless afterwards confirmed by the legislatures of every state.

Fundamental weaknesses of the articles.—Admirable as this document was in many respects, it contained weaknesses which were certain to make the union temporary rather than perpetual. It failed to give the central government sufficient power. The articles were distinctly the instrument of a confederation of sovereign states, and not the constitution of a federal state. Congress was not given the power to raise money or to regulate commerce. It could not compel the states to pay the national debts, to live up to treaties, or to raise armies. The articles provided for no distinct executive department, but this was remedied in part by congressional acts. With the exception of the fourth, fifth, and seventh provisions of Article IX, judicial matters were left to the states. The required vote of nine state to pass measures necessarily hindered the passage of needed regulations. The requirement that every state legislature must give its consent before an amendment could be passed made it well nigh impossible to change the instrument.

GOVERNMENTAL REORGANIZATION

Organization of executive departments.—The failure of the congressional committee system to perform executive functions had grown more apparent as the war progressed, and in the closing days of the Second Continental Congress measures were taken to concentrate the executive departmental work under individual heads. During January and February, 1781, the Continental Congress created four new offices: superintendent of finance, secretary at war, secretary of marine, and secretary of foreign affairs, a foreshadowing of the later cabinet. The policy thus inaugurated was continued under the new Congress which held its first sitting on March 2, 1781.

The work of Robert Morris.—The failure of the bills of credit, the insufficiency of state support, and the weakness of foreign credit had made it evident that the financial system must be reorganized; accordingly the treasury commission was abolished and finances were placed in the hands of Robert Morris, a suc-cessful merchant of Philadelphia who had rendered valuable assistance as a member of the Pennsylvania assembly and of Congress. Morris realized that retrenchment and economy must be his watchwords. In the words of Dewey, he endeavored "to collect the requisitions from the States, to create a national revenue and impost, and place the revenue on a specie basis. . . ." He also sought to establish foreign credit and to found a United States bank. At every turn he was handicapped by local prej-udice, petty bickerings over taxation, and the lack of power of the central government.

Foreign loans and requisitions upon states.—The adoption of the Articles of Confederation immediately strengthened foreign credit, for during 1781–1783 loans of $4,719,000 were obtained from France, $174,017 from Spain, and $1,304,000 from the bank-ers of Holland. The loans from Spain and Holland, however, probably would not have been obtained had it not been for the entry of those powers into the war. Requisitions upon states during the same period yielded $3,058,000 in specie value, but the proposals of Morris to institute a land tax, poll tax, excise, and tariff came to naught.

The Bank of North America.—In 1780 Congress had tried to establish a financial institution called the Bank of Pennsylvania, but it had been of little service. Morris planned a sounder institution to be known as the Bank of North America with a capitalization of not over $10,000,000. Only $70,000 was raised by private subscription and the government set aside $200,000 in specie which had recently arrived from France. From this bank during 1782–1783 the government borrowed on short term loans $1,272,842 As Congress repaid the bank before other creditors, a small working balance was maintained on which the government could draw for immediate needs.

War and navy departments.—Owing to factional quarrels, it was not until January, 1782, that General Benjamin Lincoln was made secretary at war. No one was appointed for the department of marine, and the work was turned over to the already overburdened superintendent of finance. The office of agent of marine was created, and this Morris held from September, 1781, until November, 1784.

Department of foreign affairs.—The first secretary of foreign affairs was Robert R. Livingston of New York, a former member of the committee which formulated the Declaration of Independence and famous later as minister to France at the time of the Louisiana purchase. He held office from August, 1781, to June, 1783, being succeeded in 1784 by John Jay. The department as conducted under Livingston consisted of the secretary, two assistant secretaries, and a clerk.

Conclusion.—Thus during the stress of war national and state governments had come into existence. Necessity had forced the people to act and though the leaders at times groped blindly and took many a false step, the political capacity of the American people had asserted itself and triumphed. They profited by their experiences and showed themselves ready to cast aside useless institutions and try new ones which gave fair promise of success. A government of the people, for the people, and by the people had come into existence which challenged the doctrine that the sovereign ruled by right divine.

READINGS

Bolles, A. S., *Financial History of the United States, 1774–1789;* Bullock, C. J., *Finances of the United States from 1775 to 1789;* Channing, Edward, *History of the United States*, III, 431–462; Dewey, D. R., *Financial History of the United States*, 33–56; Foster, J. W., *A Century of American Diplomacy*, 1–40; Guggenheim, J. C., "The Development of the Executive Departments, 1775–1789," in J. Franklin Jameson, *Essays in the Constitutional History of the United States in the Formative Period, 1775–1789;* Hatch, L. C., *Administration of the American Revolutionary Army;* Hildreth, Richard, *The History of the United States of America*, III, 374–410; Learned, H. B., *The President's Cabinet*, 47–63; McLaughlin, A. C., *The Confederation and the Constitution*, 35–70; Paullin, C. O., *The Navy of the American Revolution*, 31–251; Small, A. W., "The Beginnings of American Nationality," in Johns Hopkins University, *Studies in History and Political Science*, 8th Series, Parts I and II; Sumner, W. G., *The Financier and Finances of the American Revolution;* Van Tyne, C. H., *The American Revolution*, 175–202; Hunt, G., *The Department of State*, 1–37.

INDEX

Abenaki Indians, 257, 266; war of, 313.
Abercromby, General James, in French and Indian War, 376, 377, 378.
Acadia, colonization, 85–86; captured by England, restored to France, 86, 87; during War of Spanish Succession, English expeditions against, 271; conquest of, 272; attacked by French during War of Austrian Succession, 364, 365; French policy in, 366; during French and Indian War, 374.
Acapulco, Mexico, commercial port, 86.
Acatic, Nueva Galicia, in the Mixton War, 40.
Accau, explorer in Minnesota with Father Hennepin, 100.
Ácoma, New Mexico pueblo, 46, 72, 73.
Adams, John, defence of British soldiers, 443; in First Continental Congress, 452; argues for Declaration of Independence, 479; member of committee for drafting the Declaration, 479; diplomacy in France and Holland, 532–533; peace negotiations, 533–538.
Adams, Samuel, circular letter, 440–441; trouble with Governor Bernard, 443; the man of the town meeting, 445–446; in First Continental Congress, 451; on committee to draft Articles of Confederation, 550.
Adelantados, 54–55.
Administration of Justice Act, 450.
Admiralty, English, 182–183; courts, 349.
Africa, early ideas concerning, 1–2; Ptolemy's conception of, 1–2; trade with desired, 5; exploration of west coast, 5; Prester, John, 5; Sénégal and Gorée captured by English, 380; Sénégal given to British by Peace of Paris, 382.
African Company, formed to break Dutch monopoly, 196.

Agriculture, in Spanish colonies, 21, 75; in French Canada, 92, 93; in French West Indies, 94–95; in New England, 216–217, 330–331; in the Middle English colonies, 120, 122, 124, 128, 332; in the South, 333–335; in the British West Indies, 339–341; in Bermudas, 130, in Dutch colonies, 169, 170, 171, 173.
Aguas Calientes, 58, 59; mines of, 58.
Aguayo, Marquis of, expedition to Texas, 296–297.
Aguilar, Marcos de, governor in Mexico, 48.
Aijado Indians, 243.
Ailly, Pierre d', author of *Imago Mundi*, 2, 7.
Aix-la-Chapelle, Peace of, 366.
Alabama Indians, 251, 270.
Alabama River, 62.
Alamance, battle of the, 415.
Alarcón, Hernando de, explores Colorado River, 45.
Alarcón, Martín de, governor of Texas, and of Coahuila, 294–295.
Albany, 332.
Albany Congress, 371, 411.
Albemarle, Duke of. *See* Monk.
Albermarle district, settlement, 207; population, 211; Culpeper rebellion, 211.
Alberoni, 279, 359.
Albórnoz, royal *contador* of New Spain, 48.
Albuquerque, New Mexico, founding of, 290.
Alburquerque, Portuguese viceroy in India, 24.
Alacalá, University of, 76.
Alcaldes, 14, 34, 55.
Alcaldía Mayor, administrative district, 59.
Aleutian Islands, Russian fur trade, 388.
Alexander, Pillars of, 1.

557

INDEX

571

248. *See* New Mexico, Nuevo León, Coahuila, Texas.

Rivas, explorer of Gulf of Mexico, 249.

Rivera y Moncada, with Portolá in California, 389.

Rivera, Juan María, explores in Colorado, 291–292.

Rivera, Pedro de, inspects frontier of New Spain, 297, 298, 304.

Rich, Sir Nathaniel, interest in the Caribbean, 133.

Rich, Robert, Lord Warwick, interest in colonization, 133; land grants in New England, 140, 149; assists Reverend John White, 141.

Rising, John, governor of New Sweden, 177.

Roanoke, lost colony of, 110.

Roanoke Island, 66, 251.

Robertson, James, pioneer in Tennessee, 415, 416, 419; defense of Watauga, 513.

Roberval, French colonizer, 82; commissioned viceroy and lieutenant-general of Canada, 82.

Robinson, Rev. John, at Scrooby, 137.

Rochambeau, Comte de, 511.

Rockingham Ministry, 437–438.

Rocky Mountains, 282.

Rodney, Admiral, in the West Indies, 382, 511, 530–531; defeats de Grasse, 532.

Rodrigo del Río de Losa, expedition to open mines of Nueva Vizcaya, 56; cattle ranches of, 58.

Rodríguez, Fray Agustín, expedition to New Mexico, 72.

Roe, Sir Thomas, expedition to Guiana, 132.

Rolfe, John, 121.

Rosicrucians, 318.

Roxbury settled, 142.

Royal council, Spanish, 14; divided into three councils, justice, state, and finance, 14.

Rowley, William, English vice-admiral, 365.

Rubí, Marqués de, inspects outposts of New Spain, 385–386.

Ruí, Captain Francisco, in Missouri, 397.

Rubruquis, William de, sent to court of Great Khan, 3.

Rump Parliament, 152.

Rupert, Prince, interest in Hudson's Bay Company, 213.

Russia, 3, 375, 382, 384; expansion across Siberia, 388; expeditions of Bering on Pacific, 388; fur traders on Aleutian Islands, 388; rumors of activities of, 394.

Rutherford, Gen. Griffith, 512–513.

Rutledge, Edward, member of the First Continental Congress, 452; defense of Charleston, 471; on committee to draw up Articles of Confederation, 550.

Rutledge, John, member of the Stamp Act Congress, 436; member of the First Continental Congress, 452.

Saavedra, Alvaro de, expedition across the Pacific, 42, 46.

Saavedra, Hernando, in Honduras, 38.

Saba Island, settled by Dutch, 167; captured by English, 206, 531.

Sable Island, 81, 85.

Saco Bay, settlement, 140.

Sagres, on Cape St. Vincent, 4.

St. Augustine, Florida, founding, 62; Franciscan monastery at, 65; siege of, in War of the Spanish Succession, 269–270; attacks on, in War of Jenkins' Ear, 362, 364; under English rule, 403, 408, 409.

St. Bartholomew's, massacre of, 79.

St. Christopher Island, settled by French, 93, 94, 252; by English, 132, 133, 252; in the Leeward Isles government, 206; in wars, 261, 268; social conditions, 340; captured by De Grasse, 532; restored to Great Britain, 537.

St. Clair, Gen. Arthur, in Burgoyne campaign, 494–495.

St. Croix Island, French settlement of, 85.

St. Denis, Louis Juchereau de, founds Natchitoches, 278; expeditions to Mexico, 278, 282–283, 293; imprisonment, 283, 295; raises French expedition, 297.

St. Eustatius Island, settled by the

Tano Indians, 246.

Tápia, Cristóbal de, attempt to investigate Cortés, 34.

Tápia, Fernando de, Otomí chief in, conquest of Querétaro, 39.

Tápia, Gonzalo de, Jesuit missionary in Sinaloa, 237.

Tarahumare Indians, 242; revolt of, 246.

Tarascans, Mexican tribe, 28, 36.

Taraval, Father, Jesuit missionary in Lower California, 307.

Tarleton, Sir Banastre, 525, 526, 528.

Tartary, travelers' report of, 3.

Tea controversy, 447–449.

Tegesta, Florida, 64.

Tehuantepec, Mexico, 36.

Tehueco Indians, Sinaloa, 239.

Tejas (Texas) Indians, 245.

Tennessee, settlement of eastern, 414–416; stimulated by North Carolina troubles, 414–415; the Watauga settlement, 415; the Watauga Association, 415–416; middle, 418–419; Cumberland settlement, 419; Davidson County, North Carolina, 419.

Terán, Domingo de, governor of Texas, 251.

Terreros, Don Pedro de, gift to Apache missions, 299.

Texas, Pineda coasts, 26; Vaca crosses, 41; Moscoso in, 41; Coronado in Panhandle, 45; Espejo crosses, 72; Castaño de Sosa crosses, 72; Oñate crosses Panhandle, 73; La Salle's colony in, 98–100; Tonty in, 99; map, 99; expeditions from New Mexico to Jumanos, 243–244, 246; beginnings of El Paso, 245; the La Junta missions, 245; Azcué crosses Río Grande, 248; Cerro de la Plata, 248; Bosque-Larios expedition, 248; the Querétaro friars, 248–49; search for La-Salle's colony, 249; eastern Texas occupied (De León and Massanet), 249–251; and then abandoned, 251; map, 250; Hurtado in western Texas, 291; advance of the Coahuila frontier, 292; plans to reoccupy Texas, 292; new French intrusion, 278, 283; St. Denis in Mexico, 278, 292; eastern Texas reoccupied (Ramón, Espinosa, Margil), 293; San

Antonio founded (Olivares, Alarcón), 293–295; map, 294; French invasión (Blondel), 279, 295; the Aguayo expedition, 296–297; Texas won for Spain, 297; expansion of Texas, 297; Rivera's inspection, 297; San Antonio strengthened, 298; Apache wars, 298; Tonkawa and Apache missions, 298–299; the Gulf coast occupied (Nuevo Santander), 299; western boundary, 300; the Texas-Louisiana boundary, 300; the Lower Trinity fortified, 201; readjustment after 1763, 385; explorations of Parrilla and Escandón, 385; Rubí's tour, 385; eastern outposts abandoned, 385, 400; Gil Ybarbo, 400; De Mézières among the northern tribes, 401; Croix, Ugalde, and the Apache War, 401; communication with Louisiana and New Mexico (Vial), 402.

Thirty Years' War, 80.

Thomson, Charles, secretary of Second Continental Congress, 541.

Three Rivers, Canada, 257, 419.

Ticonderoga, captured, 462; an American base, 487; abandoned, 493–494.

Tidewater, Atlantic, settled in 16th and 17th centuries, 52-231, passim.

Tierra Firme, Las Casas' Utopian colony in, 23.

Tiguex, 45.

Tlascala, resistance to Cortés, 33.

Tlascaltecan Indians (Tlascalans), 28; 59; used as colonists, 59–66.

Tobacco industry in English colonies, 121, 122–125, 130, 183–184, 188, 228, 313, 333–334.

Tobago Island, 252; granted to the Earl of Pembroke and Montgomery, 132; captured by De Grasse, 531; given to France, 537.

Tobar, discovers Moqui pueblos, 45.

Tocobago, Florida, 64.

Toledo, victory over English at St. Kitts, 252.

Tololotlán, Río de, Mexico, 37.

Tolosa, Juan de, founder of Zacatecas, 55.

Toltecs, Nahua tribe, settle in Valley of Mexico, 27.